Philip H. Gilbert
Dover
N. J.

THE WAYS OF THE HOUR.

PREFACE.

THE object of this book is to draw the attention of the reader to some of the social evils that beset us; more particularly in connection with the administration of criminal justice. So long a time has intervened since the thought occurred, and so many interruptions have delayed the progress of the work, that it is felt the subject has been very imperfectly treated; but it is hoped that enough has been done to cause a few to reflect on a matter of vital importance; one that to them may possess the interest of novelty.

A strange indifference exists as to the composition of the juries. In our view, the institution itself, so admirable in a monarchy, is totally unsuited to a democracy. The very principle that renders it so safe where there is a great central power to resist, renders it unsafe in a state of society in which few have sufficient resolution to attempt even to resist popular impulses.

A hundred instances might be given in which the juries of this country are an evil; one or two of which we will point out. In trials between railroad companies and those who dwell along their lines, prejudice is usually so strong against the former that justice for them is nearly hopeless. In certain parts of the country, the juries are made the instruments of defeating the claim of creditors who dwell at a distance, and are believed to have interests opposed to the particular community where the debtor resides. This is a most crying evil, and has been the source of many and grievous wrongs. Whenever there is a motive for creating a simulated public opinion, by the united action of several journals, justice is next to hopeless; such combinations rarely, if ever, occurring in its behalf. In cases that are connected with the workings of political schemes, and not unfrequently in those in which political men are parties to the suits, it is often found that the general prejudices or partialities of the out-door factions enter the jury-box. This is a most serious evil too; for, even when the feeling does not produce a direct and flagrant wrong, it is very apt so far to temper the right as to deprive it of much of its virtue. In a country like this, in which party penetrates to the very bottom of society, the extent of this evil can be known only to those who are brought into close contact with the ordinary workings of the institution.

In a democracy, proper selections in the material, that are necessary to render juries safe, become nearly impossible. Then, the tendency is to the accumulation of power in bodies of men; and in a state of society like our own, the juries get to be much too independent of the opinion of the court. It is precisely in that condition of things in which the influence and authority of the judge guide the juror, and the investigation and substantial power of the juror react on the proceedings of the court, that the greatest benefits have been found to accrue from this institution. The reverse of this state of things will be very likely to produce the greatest amount of evil.

It is certain that the juries are falling into disrepute throughout the length and breadth of the land. The difficulty is to find a substitute. As they are bodies holding the lives, property and character of every member of the community, more or less, in their power, it is not to be supposed that the masses will surrender this important means of exercising their authority voluntarily, or with good will. Time alone can bring reform through the extent of the abuses.

The writer has not the vanity to suppose that anything contained in this book will produce a very serious impression on the popularity of the jury. Such is not its design. All that is anticipated is to cause a portion of his readers to reflect on the

(3)

subject; persons who probably have never yet given it a moment of thought.

There is a tendency, at the present time, to court change for its own sake. This is erroneously termed a love of reform. Something very like a revolution is going on in our midst, while there is much reason to apprehend that few real grievances are abated; the spurious too exclusively occupying the popular mind, to render easy a just distinction between them. When an American prates about aristocracy, it is pretty safe to set him down as knavish or ignorant. It is purely cant; and the declaimers would be puzzled to point to a single element of the little understood and much decried institution, the country being absolutely without any, unless the enjoyment of the ordinary rights of property can be so considered. But the demagogue must have his war-cry as well as the Indian; and it is probable he will continue to whoop as long as the country contains minds weak enough to furnish him with dupes.

COOPERSTOWN, *March* 12, 1850.

CHAPTER I.

"*Mar.*—My Lord Aumerle, is Harry Hereford
    armed?
Aum.—Yea, at all points; and longs to enter
    in."—KING RICHARD II.

IN one respect, there is a visible improvement in the goodly town of Manhattan, and that is in its architecture. Of its growth, there has never been any question, while many have disputed its pretension to improvement. A vast expansion of mediocrity, though useful and imposing, rarely satisfies either the judgment or the taste; those who possess these qualities requiring a nearer approach to what is excellent than can ever be found beneath the term just mentioned.

A town which is built of red bricks, that are faced with white marble, the whole garnished with green blinds, can never have but one outside sign—that of tawdry vulgarity. But this radical defect is slowly disappearing from the streets of Manhattan; and those who build are getting to understand that architecture, like statuary, will not admit of strong contrasts in colors. Horace Walpole tells us of a certain old Lord Pembroke, who blackened the eyes of the gods and goddesses in the celebrated gallery at Wilton, and prided himself on the achievement, as if he had been another Phidias. There have been thousands of those who have labored in the spirit of this Earl of Pembroke in the streets of all the American towns; but traveling, hints, books and example, are slowly effecting a change; and whole squares may now be seen in which the eye rests with satisfaction on blinds, facings and bricks, all brought to the same pleasing, sober, architectural tint. We regard this as the first step, in advance, that has been made in the right direction, so far as the outward aspect of the town is concerned, and look forward, with hope, to the day when Manhattan shall have banished its rag-fair finery altogether, and the place will become as remarkable for the chaste simplicity of its streets, as they have hitherto been for their marked want of taste.

With this great town, mottled as it is, in people as well as in hues, with its native population collected from all parts of this vast republic, and its European representatives amounting to scores of thousands, we shall have much to do in the succeeding pages. Our researches, however, will be bestowed more on things moral than on things physical; and we shall endeavor to carry the reader with us through scenes that, we regret to say, are far more characteristic than novel.

In one of the cross streets that communicate with Broadway and below Canal, stands a dwelling that is obnoxious to all the charges of bad taste to which there has already been allusion, as well as to certain others that have not yet been named at all. A quarter of a century since, or within the first twenty years of its own existence, the house itself would have been regarded as decidedly patrician, though it is now lost amid the thousands of similar abodes that have arisen since its own construction. There it stands, with its red bricks periodically painted redder; its marble facings, making a livery of red turned up with white; its green blinds, its high stoop, its half-buried and low basement, and all its neatness and comfort, notwithstanding its flagrant architectural sins. Into this building we now propose to enter, at the very early hour of eight in the morning.

The principal floor was divided, as usual, between a dining and a drawing-room, with large communicating doors. This was the stereotyped construction of all Manhattanese dwellings of any pretension, a quarter of a century since; and that of Mr. Thomas Dunscomb, the owner and occupant of the house in question, had been built in rigid conformity with the fashion of its day. Squire Dunscomb, as this gentleman was termed in all the adjacent country counties, where he was well known as a reliable and sound legal adviser; Mr. Thomas Dunscomb, as he was styled by various single ladies, who wondered he never married; or Tom Dunscomb, as he was familiarly called by a herd of unyoked youths, all of whom were turned of sixty, was a capital fellow in each of his many characters. As a lawyer he was as near the top of the bar as a man can be who never had any pretensions to be an orator, and whose longest effort seldom exceeded half an hour. Should the plan of placing eloquence in hobbles reach our own bar, his habit of condensing, his trick of getting *multum in parvo*, may yet bring him to the very summit; for he will have an immense advantage over those who, resembling a country buck at a town ball, need the whole field to cut their flourishes in. As a man of the world, he was well-bred, though a little cynical, very agreeable, most especially with the ladies, and quite familiar with all the better habits of the best-toned circles of the place. As a boon companion, Tom Dunscomb was an immense favorite, being particularly warm-hearted, and always ready for any extra eating or drinking. In addition to these leading qualities, Dunscomb was known be rich, having inherited a tolerable estate, as well as having added much to his means, by a large and lucrative practice. If to these circumstances we add that of a very prepossessing personal appearance, in which age was very green, the reader has all that is necessary for an introduction to one of our principal characters.

Though a bachelor, Mr. Dunscomb did not live alone. He had a nephew and a niece in his family, the orphan children of a sister who had now been dead many years. They bore the name of Wilmeter, which in the family parlance was almost always pronounced Wilmington. It was Jack Wilmington, and Sally Wilmington, at school, at home, and with all their intimates; though Mr. John Wilmeter, and Miss Sarah Wilmeter were often spoken of in their little out-door world, it being rather an affectation of the time to prove, in this manner, that one retains some knowledge of the spelling-book. We shall write the name as it is written by the parties themselves, forewarning the reader that if he desires to pronounce it by the same family standard, he must take the unauthorized spelling as a guide. We own ourselves to a strong predilection for old familiar sounds, as well as old familiar faces.

At half-past 8 A.M., of a fine morning, late in May, when the roses were beginning to show their tints amid the verdure of the leaves in Mr. Dunscomb's yard, the three individuals just mentioned were at the breakfast table of what it is the fashion of New York to term a dining-room. The windows were open, and a soft and fragrant air filled the apartment. We have said that Mr. Dunscomb was affluent, and he chose to enjoy his means, not *a la* Manhattan, in idle competition with the *nouveaux riches*, but in a more quiet and rational way. His father had occupied lots, "running through," as it is termed; building his house on one street and his stables on the other; leaving himself a space in the rear of the former that was prodigious for a town so squeezed into parallelograms of twenty-five feet by a hundred. This open space was of the usual breadth, but it actually measured a hundred and fifty feet in length, an area that would have almost justified its being termed a "park," in the nomenclature of the town. This yard Sarah had caused to be well garnished with shrubbery, and, for its dimensions, it was really a sort of oasis in that wilderness of bricks.

The family was not alone that morning. A certain Michael Millington was a guest of Jack's, and seemingly quite at home in the little circle. The business of eating and drinking was pretty well through with, though each of the four cups had its remains of tea or coffee, and Sarah sat stirring hers idly, while her soft eyes were turned with interest on the countenances of the two young men. The last had a sheet of writing paper lying between them, and their heads were close together, as both studied that which was written on it in pencil. As for Mr. Dunscomb, himself, he was fairly surrounded by documents of one sort and another. Two or three of the morning papers, glanced at but not read, lay opened on the floor; on each side of his plate was a brief, or some lease or release; while a copy of the new and much-talked-of code was in his hand. As we say in our American English, Mr. Dunscomb was "emphatically" a common-law lawyer; and, as our transatlantic brethren would remark in their sometime cockney dialect, he was not at all "agreeable" to this great innovation on "the perfection of human reason." He muttered occasionally as he read, and now and then he laid down the book and seemed to muse. All this, however, was quite lost on Sarah, whose soft blue eyes still rested on the interested countenances of the two young men. At length Jack seized the paper, and wrote a line or two hurriedly, with his pencil.

"There, Mike," he said, in a tone of self-gratulation, "I think *that* will do?"

"It has one merit of a good toast,"

answered the friend, a little doubtingly ; " it is sententious."

" As all toasts ought to be. If we are to have this dinner, and the speeches, and all the usual publications afterward, I choose that we should appear with some little credit. Pray, sir," raising his eyes to his uncle, and his voice to correspond, " what do you think of it, now ? "

" Just as I always have, Jack. It will never do at all. Justice would halt miserably under such a system of practice. Some of the forms of pleadings are infernal, if pleadings they can be called at all. I detest even the names they give their proceedings—complaints and answers ! "

" They are certainly not as formidable to the ear," returned Jack, a little saucily, " as rebutters and sur-rebutters. But I was not thinking of the code, sir ; I was asking your opinion of my new toast."

" Even a fee could not extract an opinion, unless I heard it read."

" Well, sir, here it is : ' The Constitution of the United States ; the palladium of our civil and religious liberties.' Now I do not think I can much better that, Uncle Tom."

" I am very sorry to hear you say so, Jack."

" Why so, sir ? I'm sure it is good American sentiment ; and what is more, it has a flavor of the old English principles that you so much admire, about it, too. Why do you dislike it, sir ? "

" For several reasons—it would be commonplace, which a toast should never be, were it true ; but there happens not to be a word of truth in your sentiment, sonorous as it may sound in your ears."

" Not true ! Does not the constitution guarantee to the citizen religious liberty ? "

" Not a bit of it."

" You amaze me, sir ! Why, here, just listen to its language, if you please."

Hereupon Jack opened a book, and read the clause on which he relied to confute one of the ablest constitutional lawyers and clearest heads in America. Not that Mr. Dunscomb was what is called an " expounder," great or small ; but he never made a mistake on the subject in hand, and had often caused the best of the " expounders " to retrace their steps. He was an original thinker, but of the safest and most useful sort ; one who distinguished between the *institutions* of England and America, while he submitted to the fair application of minor principles that are so common to both. As for his nephew, he knew no more of the great instrument he held in his hand than he had gleaned from ill-digested newspaper remarks, vapid speeches in

Congress, and the erroneous notions that float about the country, coming from " nobody knows whom," and leading literally to nothing. The ignorance that prevails on such subjects is really astounding, when one remembers the great number of battles that are annually fought over this much-neglected compact.

" Ay, here is the clause—just please to hear it, sir," continued Jack. " 'Congress shall make no law respecting an establishment of religion, or prohibiting the free exercise thereof ; or abridging the freedom of speech, or of the press ; or the right of the people peaceably to assemble, and to petition the government for a redress of grievances.' There, I think that will go far toward justifying the whole toast, Mike."

This was said a little triumphantly, and not a little confidently.

The only answer Mr. Dunscomb condescended to make was an expressive " Umph !" As for Michael Millington, he was a little timid about expressing an opinion, and that for two reasons ; he had often experienced Mr. Dunscomb's superior wisdom, and he knew that Sarah heard all that passed.

" I wish your uncle would lay aside the code for a minute, Jack, and let us know what he thinks of our authorities," said Michael, in an undertone.

" Come, Uncle Tom," cried the more hardy nephew—" come out of your reserve, and face the constitution of your country. Even Sarah can see that, for once, *we* are right, and that my toast is of proof."

" It is a very good proof-*sheet*, Jack, not only of your own mind, but of half the minds in the country. Ranker nonsense cannot be uttered, however, than to say that the Constitution of the United States is the palladium of anything in which civil or religious liberty is concerned."

" You do not dispute the fidelity of my quotation, sir ? "

" By no means. The clause you read is a very useless exhibition of certain facts that existed just as distinctly before it was framed, as they do to-day. Congress had no power to make an established religion, or abridge the freedom of speech, or that of the press, or the right of the people to petition, before that amendment was introduced, and consequently the clause itself is supererogatory. You take nothing by your motion, Jack."

" I do not understand you, sir. To me, it seems that I have the best of it."

" Congress has no power but what has been conceded to it directly, or by necessary connection. Now there happens to be nothing said about granting any such authority to Congress, and consequently the prohibition is not necessary. But admitting that Congress did really possess the power to establish a religion previously to the adoption of this amendment, the constitution would not prove a palladium to religious liberty, unless it prohibited everybody else from meddling with the opinions of the citizen. Any State of this Union that pleases may establish a religion, and compel its citizens to support it."

"Why, sir, but our own State constitution has a provision similar to this, to prevent it."

"Very true, but our own State constitution can be altered in this behalf, without asking permission of any one but our own people. I think that even Sarah will understand that the United States is no palladium of religious liberty, if it cannot prevent a State from establishing Mohammedanism, as soon as a few forms can be complied with."

Sarah colored, glanced timidly at Michael Millington, but made no reply. She did not understand much of what she had just heard, though rather an intelligent girl, but had hoped that Jack and his friend were nearer right than was likely to turn out to be the case. Jack, himself, being a young limb of the law, comprehended what his uncle meant, and had the grace to color, too, at the manner in which he had manifested his ignorance of the great national compact. With a view to relieve himself from his dilemma, he cried, with a ready dexterity—

"Well, since this won't do, I must try the jury. 'The trial by jury, the palladium of our liberties.' How do you like that, sir?"

"Worse than the other, boy. God protect the country that has no better shield against wrong than that which a jury can hold before it."

Jack looked at Michael, and Michael looked at Jack; while Sarah looked at both in turn.

"You surely will not deny, sir, that the trial by jury is one of the most precious of the gifts received from our ancestors?" said the first, a little categorically, Sarah brightening up at this question, as if she fancied that her brother had now got on solid ground.

"Your question cannot be answered in a breath, Jack," returned the uncle. "The trial by jury *was* undoubtedly a most precious boon bestowed on a people among whom there existed an hereditary ruling power, on the abuses of which it was often a most salutary check."

"Well, sir, is it not the same check here, assuring to the citizens independent justice?"

"Who compose the ruling power in America, Jack?"

"The people to be sure, sir."

"And who the jurors?"

"The people, too, I suppose," answered the nephew, hesitating a little before he replied.

"Well, let us suppose a citizen has a conflict of rights with the public, which is the government, who will compose the tribunal that is to decide the question?"

"A jury, to be sure, sir. The trial by jury is guaranteed by the constitution to us all."

"Ay," said Mr. Dunscomb, smiling "much as are our religious and political liberties. But according to your own admission, this is very much like making one of the parties a judge in his own case. A insists that he has a right to certain lands, for instance, which the public claims for itself. In such a case, part of the public compose the tribunal."

"But is it not true, Mr. Dunscomb," put in Millington, "that the popular prejudice is usually against government, in all cases with private citizens?"

Sarah's face looked brighter now than ever, for she felt sure that Mike, as her brother familiarly called his friend, had asked a most apposite question.

"Certainly; you are right as to particular sets of cases, but wrong as to others. In a commercial town like this, the feeling is against government in all cases connected with the collection of the revenue, I admit; and you will see that the fact makes against the trial by jury in another form, since a judge ought to be strictly impartial; above all prejudice whatever."

"But, uncle, a judge and a jury are surely very different things," cried Sarah, secretly impelled to come to Michael's rescue, though she scarce knew anything of the merits of the subject.

"Quite right, my dear," the uncle answered, nodding his head kindly, casting a glance at his niece that caused her to blush under the consciousness of being fully understood in her motives, if not in her remark. "Most profoundly right; a judge and a juror ought to be very different things. What I most complain of is the fact that the jurors are fast becoming judges. Nay, by George, they are getting to be legislators, making the law as well as interpreting it. How often does it happen, nowadays, that the court tells the jury that such is the law, and the jury comes in with a verdict which tells the court that such is *not* the law? This is an every-day occurrence, in the actual state of public opinion."

" But the court will order a new trial, if the verdict is against law and evidence," said Michael, determined that Sarah should be sustained.

"Ay, and another jury will be likely to sustain the old one. No—no—the trial by jury is no more a palladium of our liberties than the constitution of the United States."

"Who, or what is, then, sir?" demanded Jack.

"God! Yes the Deity, in his Divine Providence; if anything is to save us. It may not be his pleasure to let us perish, for it would seem that some great plan for the advancement of civilization is going on, and it may be a part of it to make us important agents. All things regarded, I am much inclined to believe such is the fact. But, did the result depend on us, miserable instruments in the almighty hands as we are, woful would be the end!"

"You do not look at things *couleur de rose*, Uncle Tom," Sarah smilingly observed.

"Because I am not a young lady of twenty, who is well satisfied with herself and her advantages. There is but one character for which I have a greater contempt than that of a senseless grumbler, who regards all things *à tort et à travers*, and who cries, there is nothing good in the world."

"And what is the exception, sir?"

" The man who is puffed up with conceit and fancies all around him perfection, when so much of it is the reverse; who ever shouts ' Liberty,' in the midst of the direst oppression."

" But direst oppression is certainly no term to be applied to anything in New York!"

" You think not? What would you say to a state of society in which the law is available to one class of citizens only, in the way of compulsion, and not at all, in the way of protection?"

" I do not understand you, sir; here, it is our boast that all are protected alike."

"Ay, so far as *boasting* goes, we are beyond reproach. But what are the facts? Here is a man that owes money. The law is appealed to, to compel payment. Verdict is rendered, and execution issued. The sheriff enters his house, and sells his very furniture, to extort the amount of the debt from him."

"That is his misfortune, sir. Such things must happen to all debtors who cannot, or will not, pay."

" If this were true, I should have noth-ing to say. Imagine this very debtor to be also a creditor; to have debts due to him of many times the sums that he owes, but which the law will *not* aid him in collecting. For him the law is all oppression—no protection."

" But surely, Uncle Tom, nothing of the sort exists here!"

" Surely, Miss Sarah Wilmeter, such things *do* exist here in practice, whatever may be the theory on the subject; what is more, they exist under the influence of facts that are directly connected with the working of the institutions. My case is not suppositious at all, but real. Several landlords have quite recently felt all the rigors of the law as debtors, when it was a dead letter to them in their character of creditors. This has actually happened, and that more than once; and it might happen a hundred times, were the landlords more in debt. In the latter case it would be an everyday occurrence."

" What, sir," exclaimed Michael Millington; " the law enforce, when it will not protect?"

" That it does, young man, in many interests that I could point out to you. But here is as flagrant a case of unmitigated tyranny as can be cited against any country in Christendom. A citizen is sold out of house and home, under process of law, for debt; and when he asks for the use of the same process of law to collect his undeniable dues, it is, in effect, denied him. And this among the people who boast that their independence is derived from a spirit that would not be taxed! A people who are hourly shouting hosannas in honor of their justice!"

" It cannot be, Uncle Tom, that this is done in terms," cried the astounded nephew.

" If, by terms, you mean professions of justice, and liberty, and equal rights, they are fair enough; in all those particulars we are irreproachable. As ' *professors*,' no people can talk more volubly or nearer to the point—I allude only to facts."

" But these facts may be explained—qualified—are not as flagrant as they seem under your statement?"

" In what manner?"

" Why, sir, this is but a *temporary* evil, perhaps."

" It has lasted not days, nor weeks, nor months, but years. What is more, it is an evil that has not occurred in a corner, where it might be overlooked; but it exists within ten miles of your capital, in plain sight of your legislators, and owes its impunity solely to their profound deference to votes. In a word, it is a part of the political system under which we live;

and that far more so than any disposition to tyranny that might happen to manifest itself in an individual king."

"Do not the tenants who refuse to pay fancy that their landlords have no right to their estates, and does not the whole difficulty arise from misapprehension?" asked Michael, a little timidly.

"What would that have to do with the service of process, if it were true? When a sheriff's officer comes among these men, they take his authority from him and send him away empty. Rights are to be determined only by the law, since they are derived from the law; and he who meets the law at the threshold, and denies it entrance, can never seriously pretend that he resists because the other party has no claims. No, no, young gentleman—this is all a fetch. The evil is of years' standing; it is of the character of the direst oppression, and of oppression of the worst sort, that of many oppressing a few; cases in which the sufferer is cut off from sympathy, as you can see by the apathy of the community, which is singing hosannas to its own perfection, while this great wrong is committed under its very nose. Had a landlord oppressed his tenants, their clamor would have made itself heard throughout the land. The worst feature in the case is that which connects the whole thing so very obviously with the ordinary working of the institutions. If it were merely human covetousness struggling against the institutions, the last might prove the strongest; but it is cupidity of the basest and most transparent nature, *using* the institutions themselves to effect its purpose."

"I am surprised that something was not done by the last convention to meet the evil!" said Jack, who was much struck with the enormity of the wrong, placed before his eyes in its simplest form, as it had been by his direct-minded and clear-headed kinsman.

"That is because you do not know what a convention has got to be. Its object is to push principles into impracticable extremes, under the silly pretension of progress, and not to abate evils. I made a suggestion myself to certain members of that convention, which, in my poor judgment, would have effectually cured this disease; but no member had the courage to propose it. Doubtless it would have been useless had it been otherwise."

"It was worth the trial, if such were likely to be the result. What was your plan, sir?"

"Simply to disfranchise any district in which the law could not be enforced by means of combinations of its people. On application to the highest court in the State, an order might be granted that no polls should be held in one or more towns or counties, in which combinations existed of a force sufficient to prevent the laws from being put in force. Nothing could be more just than to say that men who will not obey the law shall not have a voice in making it, and to me it really seems that some such provision would be the best possible expedient to check this growing evil. It would be choking the enemy with his own food."

"Why was it not done, sir?"

"Simply because our sages were speculating on votes, and not on principles. They will talk to you like so many books touching the vices of all foreign systems, but are ready to die in defense of the perfection of their own."

"Why was it necessary to make a new constitution the other day," asked Sarah, innocently, "if the old one was so very excellent?"

"Sure enough—the answer might puzzle wiser heads than yours, child. Perfection requires a great deal of tinkering in this country. We scarcely adopt one plan that shall secure everybody's rights and liberties, than another is broached to secure some newly-discovered rights and liberties. With the dire example before them, of the manner in which the elective franchise is abused, in this anti-rent movement, the sages of the land have just given to the mass the election of judges—as beautiful a scheme for making the bench coalesce with the jury-box as human ingenuity could invent!"

As all present knew that Mr. Dunscomb was bitterly opposed to the new constitution, no one was surprised at this last assertion. It did create wonder, however, in the minds of all three of the ingenuous young persons, when the fact—an undeniable and most crushing one it is, too, so far as any pretensions to true liberty is concerned—was plainly laid before them, that citizens were to be found in New York *against* whom the law was rigidly enforced, while it was powerless in their behalf. We have never known this aspect of the case presented to any mind, that it did not evidently produce a deep impression, *for the moment;* but, alas! "what is everybody's business is nobody's business," and few care for the violation of a principle when the wrong does not affect themselves. These young folk were, like all around them, unconscious even that they dwelt in a community in which so atrocious a wrong was daily done, and, for the moment, were startled when the truth was placed before their eyes.

The young men, near friends, and, by certain signs, likely to be even more closely united, were much addicted to speculating on the course of events, as they perceived them to be tending in other countries. Michael Millington, in particular, was a good deal of a general politician, having delivered several orations, in which he had laid some stress on the greater happiness of the people of this much favored land over those of all other countries, and especially on the subject of equal rights. He was too young, yet, to have learned the wholesome truth, that equality of rights, in practice, exists nowhere; the ingenuity and selfishness of man finding the means to pervert to narrow purposes the most cautious laws that have ever been adopted in furtherance of a principle that would seem to be so just. Nor did he know that the Bible contains all the wisdom and justice, transmitted as divine precepts, that are necessary to secure to every man all that it is desirable to possess here below.

The conversation was terminated by the entrance of a fourth colloquist, in the person of Edward McBrain, M. D., who was not only the family physician, but the bosom friend of the lawyer. The two liked each other on the principle of loving their opposites. One was a bachelor, the other was about to marry his third wife; one was a little of a cynic, the other much of a philanthropist; one distrustful of human nature, the other too confiding; one cautious to excess, the other absolutely impetuous, whenever anything strongly interested his feelings. They were alike in being Manhattanese by birth, somewhat a novelty in a New Yorker; in being equally graduates of Columbia, and classmates; in a real love of their fellow-creatures; in goodness of heart and in integrity. Had either been wanting in these last great essentials, the other could not have endured him.

CHAPTER II.

"O change! stupendous change!
　　There lies the soulless clod;
　　The sun eternal breaks—
　　The new immortal wakes—
　　Wakes with his God."
　　　　　　　—MRS. SOUTHEY.

As Dr. McBrain entered the room, the two young men and Sarah, after saluting him like very familiar acquaintances, passed out into what the niece called her "garden." Here she immediately set her scissors at work in clipping roses, violets, and other early flowers to make bouquets for her companions. That of Michael was much the largest and most tasteful; but this her brother did not remark, as he was in a brown study, reflecting on the singularity of the circumstance that the Constitution of the United States should not be the "palladium of his political and religious liberties." Jack saw, for the first time in his life, that a true knowledge of the constitution was not to be found floating about in society, and that "there was more in the nature of the great national compact than was dreamed of in his philosophy."

"Well, Ned," said the lawyer, holding out his hand kindly, but not rising from his chair, "what has brought you here so early? Has old Martha spoiled your tea?"

"Not at all; I have paid this visit, as it might be, professionally."

"Professionally! I never was better in my life; and set you down as a false prophet, or no doctor, if you like that better, for the gout has not even given a premonitory hint, this spring; and I hope, now I have given up Sauterne altogether, and take but four glasses of Madeira at dinner——"

"Two too many."

"I'll engage to drink nothing but sherry, Ned, if you'll consent to four, and that without any of those forbidding looks."

"Agreed; sherry has less acidity, and consequently less gout, than Madeira. But my business here this morning, though professional, does not relate to my craft, but to your own."

"To the law? Now I take another look at you, I do see trouble in your physiognomy; am I not to draw the marriage settlements, after all?"

"There are to be none. The new law gives a woman the entire control of all her property, they tell me, and I suppose she will not expect the control of mine."

"Umph! Yes, she ought to be satisfied with things as they are, for she will remain mistress of all her cups and saucers, even—ay, and of her houses and lands in the bargain. Hang me, if I would ever marry, when the contract is so one-sided."

"You never did when the contract was t'other sided. For my part, Tom, I'm disposed to leave a woman mistress of her own. The experiment is worth the trial, if it be only to see the use she will make of her money."

"You are always experimenting among the women, and are about to try a third wife. Thank Heaven, I've got on sixty years quite comfortably, without even one."

"You have only half lived your life. No old bachelor—meaning a man after forty—knows anything of real happiness. It is necessary to be married, in order to be truly happy."

"I wonder you did not add, 'two or three times.' But you may make this new contract with greater confidence than either of the others. I suppose you have seen this new divorce project that is, or has been, before the Legislature?"

"Divorce! I trust no such foolish law will pass. This calling marriage a 'contract,' too, is what I never liked. It is something far more than a 'contract,' in my view of the matter."

"Still, that is what the law considers it to be. Get out of this new scrape, Ned, if you can with any honor, and remain an independent freeman for the rest of your days. I dare say the widow could soon find some other amorous youth to place her affections on. It matters not much whom a woman loves, provided she love. Of this I'm certain, from seeing the sort of animals so many *do* love."

"Nonsense; a bachelor talking of love or matrimony usually makes a zany of himself. It is *terra incognita* to you, my boy, and the less you say about it the better. You are the only human being, Tom, I ever met with, who has not, some time or other, been in love. I really believe you never knew what the passion is."

"I fell in love, early in life, with a certain my lord Coke, and have remained true to my first attachment. Besides, I saw I had an intimate friend who would do all the marrying that was necessary for two, or even for three; so I determined, from the first, to remain single. A man has only to be firm, and he may set Cupid at defiance. It is not so with women, I do believe; it is part of their nature to love, else would no woman admire you at your time of life."

"I don't know that—I am by no means sure of that. Each time I had the misfortune to become a widower, I was just as determined to pass the remainder of my days in reflecting on the worth of her I had lost, as you can be to remain a bachelor; but somehow or other, I don't pretend to account for it, not a year passed before I have found inducements to enter into new engagements. It is a blessed thing, is matrimony; and I am resolved not to continue single an hour longer than is necessary."

Dunscomb laughed out at the earnest manner in which his friend spoke, though conversations like this we have been relating were of frequent occurrence between them.

"The same old sixpence, Ned! A Benedict as a boy, a Benedict as a man, and a Benedict as a dotard—"

"Dotard! My good fellow, let me tell you—"

"Poh! I don't desire to hear it. But as you came on business connected with the law, and that business is not a marriage settlement, what is it? Does old Kingsborough maintain his right to the Harlem lot?"

"No, he has given the claim up at last. My business, Tom, is of a very different nature. What are we coming to, and what is to be the end of it all?"

As the doctor looked far more than he expressed, Dunscomb was struck with his manner. The Siamese twins scarce understand each other's impulses and wishes better than these two men comprehended each other's feelings; and Tom saw at once that Ned was now very much in earnest.

"Coming to?" repeated Dunscomb. "Do you mean the new code, or the 'Woman-hold-the-Purse-Law,' as I call it? I don't believe you look far enough ahead to foresee all the damnable consequences of an elective judiciary."

"It is not that—this or that—I do not mean codes, constitutions, or pin money. What is the *country* coming to, Tom Dunscomb—that is the question I ask?"

"Well, and has the country nothing to do with constitutions, codes, and elective judges? I can tell you, Master Ned McBrain, M.D., that if the patient is to be saved at all, it must be by means of the judiciary, and I do not like the advice that has just been called in"

"You are a croaker. They tell me the new judges are reasonably good."

"'Reasonably' is an expressive word. The new judges are *old* judges, in part, and in so much they do pretty well, by chance. Some of the new judges are excellent—but one of the very best men on the whole bench was run against one of the worst men who could have been put in his place. At the next heat I fear the bad fellow will get the track. If you do not mean what I have mentioned, what do you mean?"

"I mean the increase of crime—the murders, arsons, robberies, and other abominations that seem to take root among us, like so many exotics transplanted to a genial soil."

"'Exotics' and 'genial' be hanged! Men are alike everywhere. No one but a fool ever supposed that a republic is to stand, or fall, by its virtue."

"Yet, the common opinion is that such must be the final test of our institutions."

"Jack has just been talking nonsense on this subject, and now *you* must come to aid him. But, what has your business with me, this morning, to do with the general depreciation in morals?"

"A great deal, as you will allow, when you come to hear my story."

Dr. McBrain then proceeded forthwith to deliver himself of the matter which weighed so heavily on his mind. He was the owner of a small place in an adjoining county, where it was his custom to pass as much time, during the pleasant months, as a very extensive practice in town would allow. This was not much, it is true, though the worthy physician so contrived matters, that his visits to Timbully, as the place was called, if not long, were tolerably numerous. A kind-hearted, as well as a reasonably-affluent man, he never denied his professional services to country neighbors, who eagerly asked his advice whenever there was need of it. This portion of the doctor's practice flourished on two accounts—one being his known skill, and the other his known generosity. In a word, Dr. McBrain never received any compensation for his advice from any in the immediate neighborhood of his country residence. This rendered him exceedingly popular; and he might have been sent to Albany, but for a little cold water that was thrown on the project by a shrewd patriot, who suggested that while the physician was attending to affairs of state he could not be administering to the ailings of his Timbully neighbors. This may have checked the doctor's advancement, but it did not impair his popularity.

Now, it happened that the bridegroom-expectant had been out to Timbully, a distance of less than fifteen miles from his house in Bleecker Street, with a view to order matters for the reception of the bride, it being the intention of the couple that were soon to be united to pass a few days there, immediately after the ceremony was performed. It was while at his place, attending to this most important duty, that an express came from the county-town, requiring his presence before the coroner, where he was expected to give his evidence as a medical man. It seems that a house had been burned, and its owners, an aged couple, had been burned in it. The remains of the bodies had been found, and an inquest was about to be held on them. This was pretty much all that the messenger could tell, though he rather thought that it was suspected the house had been set on fire, and the old people, consequently, murdered.

As a matter of course, Dr. McBrain obeyed the summons. A county town, in America, is often little more than a hamlet, though in New York they are usually places of some greater pretensions. The State has now near a dozen incorporated cities, with their mayors and aldermen, and, with one exception, we believe these are all county towns. Then come the incorporated villages, in which New York is fast getting to be rich; places containing from one to six or seven thousand souls, and which, as a rule, are steadily growing into respectable provincial towns. The largest of these usually contain " the county buildings," as it is the custom to express it. But, in the older counties, immediately around the great commercial capital of the entire republic, these large villages do not always exist; or, when they do exist, are not sufficiently central to meet the transcendental justice of democratic equality—a quality that is sometimes of as exacting pretension as of real imbecility; as witness the remarks of Mr. Dunscomb, in our opening chapter.

The county buildings of —— happen to stand in a small village, or what is considered a small village, in the lower part of the State. As the events of this tale are so recent, and the localities so familiar to many persons, we choose to call this village " Biberry," and the county "Dukes." Such was once the name of a New York county, though the appellation has been dropped, and this not from any particular distaste for the strawberry leaves; "Kings," "Queens" and "Duchess" having been wisely retained—wisely, as names should be as rarely changed as public convenience will allow.

Dr. McBrain found the village of Biberry in a high state of excitement; one, indeed, of so intense a nature as to be far from favorable to the judicial inquiry that was then going on in the court-house. The old couple who were the sufferers in this affair had been much respected by all who knew them; he as a commonplace, well-meaning man, of no particular capacity, and she as a managing, discreet, pious woman, whose greatest failing was a neatness that was carried somewhat too near to ferocity. Nevertheless, Mrs. Goodwin was, generally, even more respected than her husband, for she had the most mind, transacted most of the business of the family, and was habitually kind and attentive to every one who entered her dwelling; provided, always, that they wiped their feet on her mats, of which it was necessary to pass no less than six before the little parlor was reached, and did not spit on her carpet, or did not want any of her money. This popularity added greatly to the excitement : men, and wo-men also, commonly feeling a stronger desire to investigate wrongs done to those they esteem, than to investigate wrongs done to those concerning whom they are indifferent.

Dr. McBrain found the charred remains of this unfortunate couple laid on a table in the court-house, the coroner in attend-ance, and a jury impaneled. Much of the evidence concerning the discovery of the fire had been gone through with, and was of a very simple character. Some one who was stirring earlier than common had seen the house in a bright blaze, had given the alarm, and had preceded the crowd from the village on the road to the burn-ing dwelling. The Goodwins had resided in a neat, retired cottage, at the distance of near two miles from Biberry, though in sight from the village ; and by the time the first man from the latter reached the spot the roof had fallen in, and the mate-rials were mostly consumed. A dozen or more of the nearest neighbors were col-lected around the ruins, and some articles of household furniture had been saved ; but, on the whole, it was regarded as one of the most sudden and destructive fires ever known in that part of the country. When the engine arrived from the village it played briskly on the fire, and was the means of soon reducing all within the outer walls, which were of stone, to a pile of blackened and smoldering wood. It was owing to this circumstance that any portion of the remains of the late owners of the house had been found, as was done in the mannner thus described, in his testimony, by Peter Bacon, the person who had first given the alarm in Biberry.

"As soon as I ever seed it was Peter Goodwin's house that made the light," continued the intelligent witness, in the course of his examination—"I guv' the alarm, and started off on the run, to see what I could do. By the time I got to the top of Brudler's Hill I was fairly out of breath, I can tell you, Mr. Coroner and gentlemen of the jury, and so I was ob-liged to pull up a bit. This guv' the fire a so much better sweep, and when I reached the spot there was little chance for doing much good. We got out a chest of drawers, and the young woman who boarded with the Goodwins was helped down out of the window, and most of her clothes, I b'lieve, was saved, so far as I know."

"Stop !" interrupted the coroner ; "there was a young woman in the house, you say ?"

"Yes ; what I call a young woman, or a gal like ; though other some calls her a young woman. Waal, she was got out ; and her clothes was got out ; but nobody could get out the old folks. As soon as the ingyne come up we turned on the water, and that put out the fire about the quickest. Arter that we went to diggin', and soon found what folks call the re-mains, though to my notion there is little enough on 'em that is left."

"You dug out the remains," said the coroner, writing ; " in what state did you find them ? "

"In what I call a pretty poor state ; much as you see 'em there, on the table."

"What has become of the young *lady* you have mentioned ? " inquired the coroner, who, as a public functionary, deemed it prudent to put all of the sex into the same general category.

"I can't tell you, 'squire ; I never see'd her arter she was got out of the window."

"Do you mean that she was the hired girl of the family—or had the lady no help ? "

"I kinder think she was a boarder, like ; one that paid her keepin'," answered the witness, who was not a person to draw very nice distinctions, as the reader will have no difficulty in conceiving from his dialect. "It seems to me I hear'n tell of another help in the Goodwin family—a sorter Jarman, or Irish lady."

"Was any such woman seen about the house this morning, when the ruins were searched ? "

"Not as I'ner. We turned over the brands and sticks until we come across the old folks ; then everybody seemed to think the work was pretty much done."

"In what state or situation were these remains found ? "

"Burnt to a crisp, just as you see 'em, 'squire, as I said afore ; a pretty poor state for human beings to be in."

"But where were they lying, and were they near each other ? "

"Close together. Their heads, if a body can call them black-lookin' skulls heads, at all, almost touched, if they didn't quite touch, each other ; their feet lay further apart."

"Do you think you could place the skeletons in the same manner, as respects each other, as they were when you first saw them ? But let me first inquire if any other person is present who saw these remains before they had been re-moved ? "

Several men, and one or two women, who were in attendance to be examined, now came forward, and stated that they had seen the remains in the condition in which they had been originally found. Selecting the most intelligent of the party, after questioning them all round, the coroner desired that the skeletons might be laid, as near as might be, in the same relative positions as those in which they had been found. There was a difference of opinion among the witnesses, as to several of the minor particulars, though all admitted that the bodies, or what remained of them, had been found quite close together; their heads touching, and their feet some little distance apart. In this manner, then, were the skeletons now disposed; the arrangement being completed just as Dr. McBrain entered the court-room. The coroner immediately directed the witnesses to stand aside, while the physician made an examination of the crisp bones.

"This looks like foul play!" exclaimed the doctor, almost as soon as his examination had commenced. "The skulls of both these persons have been fractured; and, if this be anything near the positions in which the skeletons were found, as it would seem, by the same blow."

He then pointed out to the coroner and jury a small fracture in the frontal bone of each skull, and so nearly in a line as to render his conjecture highly probable. This discovery gave an entirely new coloring to the whole occurrence, and every one present began to speculate on the probability of arson and murder being connected with the unfortunate affair. The Goodwins were known to have lived at their ease, and the good woman, in particular, had the reputation of being a little miserly. As everything like order vanished temporarily from the court-room, and tongues were going in all directions, many things were related that were really of a suspicious character, especially by the women. The coroner adjourned the investigation for the convenience of irregular conversation, in order to obtain useful clews to the succeeding inquiries.

"You say that old Mrs. Goodwin had a good deal of specie?" inquired that functionary of a certain Mrs. Pope, a widow woman who had been free with her communications, and who very well might know more than the rest of the neighbors, from a very active propensity she had ever manifested to look into the affairs of all around her. "Did I understand you that you had seen this money yourself?"

"Yes, sir; often and often. She kept it in a stocking of the old gentleman's, that was nothing but darns; so darny like that nobody could wear it. Miss Goodwin wasn't a woman to put away anything that was of use. A clusser body

wasn't to be found, anywhere near Biberry."

"And some of this money was gold, I think I heard you say. A stocking pretty well filled with gold and silver."

"The foot was cramming full, when I saw it, and that wasn't three months since. I can't say there was any great matter in the leg. Yes, there was gold in it, too. She showed me the stocking the last time I saw it, on purpose to ask me what might be the valie of a piece of gold that was almost as big as half a dollar."

"Should you know that piece of gold were you to see it again?"

"That I should. I didn't know its name or its valie, for I never seed so big a piece afore; but I told Miss Goodwin I thought it must be ra'al Californy. Them's about now, they tell me, and I hope poor folks will come in for their share. Old as I am—that is, not so very old neither—but such as I am, I never had a piece of gold in my life."

"You cannot tell, then, the name of this particular coin?"

"I couldn't; if I was to have it for the telling, I couldn't. It wasn't a five dollar piece; that I know, for the old lady had a good many of them, and this was much larger, and yellower, too; better gold, I conclude."

The coroner was accustomed to garrulous, sight-seeing females, and knew how to humor them.

"Where did Mrs. Goodwin keep her specie?" he inquired. "If you ever saw her put the stocking away, you must know its usual place of deposit."

"In her chest of drawers," answered the woman eagerly. "That very chest of drawers which was got out of the house, as sound as the day it went into it, and has been brought down into the village for safe keeping."

All this was so, and measures were taken to push the investigation further, and in that direction. Three or four young men, willing volunteers in such a cause, brought the bureau into the court-room, and the coroner directed that each of the drawers should be publicly opened, in the presence of the jurors. The widow was the first sworn, however, and testified regularly to the matter of the stocking, the money, and the place of usual deposit.

"Ah! you'll not find it there," observed Mrs. Pope, as the village cabinet-maker applied a key, the wards of which happened to fit those of the locks in question. "She kept her money in the lowest drawer of all. I've seen her take the stocking out, first and last, at least a dozen times."

The lower drawer was opened accordingly. It contained female apparel, and a goodly store of such articles as were suited to the wants of a respectable woman in the fourth or fifth of the gradations into which all society so naturally and unavoidably divides itself. But there was no stocking full of darns, no silver, no gold. Mrs. Pope's busy and nimble fingers were thrust hastily into an inner corner of the drawer, and a silk dress was unceremoniously opened, that having been the precise receptacle of the treasure as she had seen it last bestowed.

"It's gone!" exclaimed the woman. "Somebody must have taken it!"

A great deal was now thought to be established. The broken skulls and the missing money went near to establish a case of murder and robbery, in addition to the high crime of arson. Men who had worn solemn and grave countenances all that morning now looked excited and earnest. The desire for a requiting justice was general and active, and the dead became doubly dear by means of their wrongs.

All this time Dr. McBrain had been attending, exclusively, to the part of the subject that most referred to his own profession. Of the fractures in the two skulls he was well assured, though the appearance of the remains was such as almost to baffle investigation. Of another important fact he was less certain. While all he heard prepared him to meet with the skeletons of a man and his wife, so far as he could judge, in the imperfect state in which they were laid before him, the bones were those of two females.

"Did you know this Mr. Goodwin, Mr. Coroner?" inquired the physician, breaking into the more regular examination with very little ceremony; "or was he well known to any here?"

The coroner had no very accurate knowledge of the deceased, though every one of the jurors had been well acquainted with him. Several had known him all their lives.

"Was he a man of ordinary size?" asked the doctor.

"Very small. Not taller than his wife, who might be set down as quite a tall old lady."

It often happens in Europe, especially in England, that the man and his wife are so nearly of a height as to leave very little sensible difference in their stature; but it is a rare occurrence in this country. In America, the female is usually delicate and of a comparatively small frame, while the average height of a man is something beyond that of the European standard.

It was a little out of the common way, therefore, to meet with a couple so nearly of a size, as these remains would make Goodwin and his wife to have been.

"These skeletons are very nearly of the same length," resumed the doctor, after measuring them for the fifth time. "The man could not have been much if any taller than his wife."

"He was not," answered a juror. "Old Peter Goodwin could not have been more than five feet five, and Dorothy was all of that, I should think. When they came to meeting together they looked much of a muchness."

Now there is nothing on which a prudent and regular physician is more cautious than in committing himself on unknown and uncertain ground. He has his theories, and his standard of opinions, usually well settled in his mind, and he is ever on the alert to protect and bolster them; seldom making any admission that may contravene either. He is apt to denounce the water cure, however surprising may have been its effects; and there is commonly but one of the "opathies" to which he is in the least disposed to defer, and that is the particular "opathy" on which he has molded his practice. As for Dr. McBrain, he belonged strictly to the allopathic school, and might be termed almost an ultra in his adherence to its laws, while the number of the new schools that were springing up around him, taught him caution, as well as great prudence, in the expression of his opinions. Give him a patient, and he went to work boldly, and with the decision and nerve of a physician accustomed to practice in an exaggerated climate; but place him before the public, as a theoretical man, and he was timid and wary. His friend Dunscomb had observed this peculiarity, thirty years before the commencement of our tale, and had quite recently told him, "You are bold in the only thing in which I am timid, Ned, and that is in making up to the women. If Mrs. Updyke were a new-fangled theory, now, instead of an old-fashioned widow, as she is, hang me if I think you would have ever had the spirit to propose."

This peculiarity of temperament, and perhaps we might add of character, rendered Dr. McBrain, now, very adverse to saying, in the face of such probability, and the statements of so many witnesses, that the mutilated and charred skeletons that lay on the court-house table were those of two females, and not those of a man and his wife. It was certainly possible he might be mistaken; for the conflagration had made sad work of these poor emblems of mortality; but science has a clear eye, and the doctor was a skillful and practiced anatomist. In his own mind, there were very few doubts on the subject.

As soon as the thoughtful physician found time to turn his attention on the countenances of those who composed the crowd in the court-room, he observed that nearly all eyes were bent on the person of one particular female, who sat apart, and was seemingly laboring under a shock of some sort or other, that materially affected her nerves. McBrain saw, at a glance, that this person belonged to a class every way superior to that of even the highest of those who pressed around the table. The face was concealed in a handkerchief, but the form was not only youthful but highly attractive. Small, delicate hands and feet could be seen; such hands and feet as we are all accustomed to see in an American girl who has been delicately brought up. Her dress was simple, and of studied modesty; but there was an air about *that* which a little surprised the kind-hearted individual, who was now so closely observing her.

The doctor had little difficulty in learning from those near him that this "young woman," so all in the crowd styled *her*, though it was their practice to term most girls, however humble their condition, "ladies," had been residing with the Goodwins for a few weeks, in the character of a boarder, as some asserted, while others affirmed it was as a *friend*. At all events, there was a mystery about her; and most of the girls of Biberry had called her proud, because she did not join in their frivolities, flirtations and visits. It was true, no one had ever thought of discharging the duties of social life by calling on *her*, or in making the advances usual to well-bred people; but this makes little difference where there is a secret consciousness of inferiority that is felt, while it is denied. Such things are of every-day occurrence, in country life in particular, while American town life is far from being exempt from the weakness. In older countries, the laws of society are better respected.

It was now plain that the blight of suspicion had fallen on this unknown and seemingly friendless girl. If the fire had been communicated intentionally, who so likely to be guilty as she?—if the money was gone, who had so many means of securing it as herself? These were questions that passed from one to another, until distrust gathered so much head, that the coroner deemed it expedient to adjourn the inquest, while the proof might be collected and offered in proper form.

Dr. McBrain was, by nature, kindhearted; then he could not easily get over that stubborn scientific fact, of both the skeletons having belonged to females. It is true that, admitting this to be the case, it threw very little light on the matter, and in no degree lessened any grounds of suspicion that might properly rest on the "young woman"; but it separated him from the throng, and placed his mind in a sort of middle condition, in which he fancied it might be prudent, as well as charitable, to doubt. Perceiving that the crowd was dispersing, though not without much animated discussion in undertones, and that the subject of all this conversation still remained in her solitary corner, apparently unconscious of what was going on, the worthy doctor approached the immovable figure and spoke.

"You have come here as a witness, I presume," he said, in a gentle tone; "if so, your attendance just now will no longer be necessary, the coroner having adjourned the inquest until to-morrow afternoon."

At the first sound of his voice, the solitary female removed a fine cambric handkerchief from her face, and permitted her new companion to look upon it. We shall say nothing, here, touching that countenance or any other personal peculiarity, as a sufficiently minute description will be given in the next chapter, through the communications made by Dr. McBrain to Dunscomb. Thanking her informant for his information, and exchanging a few brief sentences on the melancholy business which had brought both there, the young woman arose, made a slight but very graceful inclination of her body, and withdrew.

Dr. McBrain's purpose was made up on the spot. He saw very plainly that a fierce current of suspicion was setting against this pleasing, and, as it seemed to him, friendless young creature; and he determined at once to hasten back to town, and get his friend to go out to Biberry, without a moment's delay, that he might appear there that very afternoon in the character of counsel to the helpless.

CHAPTER III.

" I am informed thoroughly of the cause.
Which is the merchant here, and which the Jew ?"
—MERCHANT OF VENICE.

SUCH was the substance of the communication that Dr. McBrain now made to his friend, Tom Dunscomb. The latter had listened with an interest he did not care to betray, and when the other was done he gayly cried—

"I'll tell the Widow Updyke of you, Ned!"

"She knows the whole story already, and is very anxious lest you should have left town, to go to the Rockland circuit, where she has been told you have an important case to try."

"The case goes over on account of the opposite counsel's being in the court of appeals. Ah's me! I have no pleasure in managing a cause since this Code of Procedure has innovated on all our comfortable and *venerable modes of doing business. I believe I shall close up my affairs, and retire, as soon as I can bring all my old cases to a termination."

"If you *can* bring those old cases to a termination you will be the first lawyer who ever did."

"Yes, it is true, Ned," answered Dunscomb, coolly taking a pinch of snuff, "you doctors *have* the advantage of us, in this behalf; *your cases* certainly do not last forever."

"Enough of this, Tom—you will go to Biberry, I take it for granted?"

"You have forgotten the fee. Under the new code, compensation is a matter of previous agreement."

"You shall have a pleasant excursion, over good roads, in the month of May, in an easy carriage, and drawn by a pair of as spirited horses as ever trotted on the Third Avenue."

"The animals you have just purchased in honor of Mrs. Updyke that is—Mrs. McBrain that is to be—" touching the bell, and adding to the very respectable black who immediately answered the summons, "Tell Master Jack and Miss Sarah I wish to see them. So, Ned, you have let the widow know all about it, and she does not pout or look distrustful—that is a good symptom, at least."

"I would not marry a jealous woman, if I never had a wife."

"Then you will never marry at all. Why, Dr. McBrain, it is in the nature of woman to be distrustful—to be jealous—to fancy things that are merely figments of the brain."

"You know nothing about them, and would be wisest to be silent—but here are the young people already, to ask your pleasure."

"Sarah, my dear," resumed the uncle in a kind and affectionate tone of voice, one that the old bachelor almost universally held toward that particular relative, "I must give you a little trouble. Go into

my room, child, and put up, in my smallest traveling bag, a clean shirt, a handkerchief or two, three or four collars, and a change all round, for a short expedition into the country."

"Country! Do you quit us to-day, sir?"

"Within an hour, at latest," looking at his watch. "If we leave the door at ten, we can reach Biberry before the inquest reassembles. You told those capital beasts of yours, Ned, to come here?"

"I told Stephen to give them a hint to that effect. You may rely on their punctuality."

"Jack, you had better be of our party. I go on some legal business of importance, and it may be well for you to go along, in order to pick up an idea or two."

"And why not Michael also, sir? He has as much need of ideas as I have myself."

A pretty general laugh succeeded, though Sarah, who was just quitting the room, did not join in it. She rather looked grave, as well as a little anxiously toward the last-named neophyte of the law.

"Shall we want any books, sir?" demanded the nephew.

"Why, yes—we will take the Code of Procedure. One can no more move without *that*, just now, than he can travel in some countries without a passport. Yes, put up the code, Jack, and we'll pick it to pieces as we trot along."

"There is little need of that, sir, if what they say be true. I hear, from all quarters, that it is doing that for itself, on a gallop."

"Shame on thee, lad—I have half a mind to banish thee to Philadelphia! But put up the code; thy joke can't be worse than that joke. As for Michael, he can accompany us if he wish it; but you must both be ready by ten. At ten, precisely, we quit my door, in the chariot of Phœbus, eh, Ned?"

"Call it what you please, so you do but go. Be active, young gentlemen, for we have no time to throw away. The jury meets again at two, and we have several hours of road before us. I will run around and look at my slate, and be here by the time you are ready."

On this suggestion everybody was set in active motion. John went for his books, and to fill a small rubber bag for himself, Michael did the same, and Sarah was busy in her uncle's room. As for Dunscomb, he made the necessary disposition of some papers, wrote two or three notes, and held himself at the command of his friend. This affair was just the sort of professional business in which he liked to be engaged. Not that he had any sympathy with crime, for he was strongly averse to all communion with rogues; but it appeared to him, by the representations of the doctor, to be a mission of mercy. A solitary, young, unfriended female, accused, or suspected, of a most heinous crime, and looking around for a protector and an adviser, was an object too interesting for a man of his temperament to overlook, under the appeal that had been made. Still he was not the dupe of his feelings. All his coolness, sagacity, knowledge of human nature, and professional attainments, were just as active in him as they ever had been in his life. Two things he understood well; that we are much too often deceived by outward signs, mistaking character by means of a fair exterior and studied words, and that neither youth, beauty, sex, nor personal graces were infallible preventives of the worst offenses, on the one hand; and that, on the other, men nurture distrust and suspicion often, until it grows too large to be concealed, by means of their own propensity to feed the imagination and to exaggerate. Against these two weaknesses he was now resolved to arm himself; and when the whole party drove from the door our counselor was as clear-headed and impartial, according to his own notion of the matter, as if he were a judge.

By this time the young men had obtained a general notion of the business they were on, and the very first subject that was started, on quitting the door, was in a question put by John Wilmeter, in continuation of a discussion that had been commenced between himself and his friend.

"Mike and I have a little difference of opinion, on a point connected with this matter, which I could wish you to settle for us, as an arbiter. On the supposition that you find reason to believe that this young woman has really committed these horrible crimes, what would be your duty in the case—to continue to befriend her, and advise her, and use your experience and talents in order to shield her against the penalties of the law, or to abandon her at once?"

"In plain English, Jack, you and your brother student wish to know whether I am to act as a palladium, or as a runagate, in this affair. As neophytes in your craft, it may be well to suggest to you, in the first place, that I have not yet been feed. I never knew a lawyer's conscience trouble him about questions in casuistry until he had received something down."

"But you can suppose that something paid, in this case, sir, and then answer our question."

"This is just the case in which I can suppose nothing of the sort. Had McBrain given me to understand I was to meet a client with a well-lined purse, who was accused of arson and murder, I would have seen him married to two women at the same time before I would have budged. It's the want of a fee that takes me out of town this morning."

"And the same want, I trust, sir, will stimulate you to solve our difficulty."

The uncle laughed and nodded his head, much as if he would say, "Pretty well for *you*;" then he gave a thought to the point in professional ethics that had started up between his two students.

"This is a very old question with the profession, gentlemen," Dunscomb answered, a little more gravely. "You will find men who maintain that the lawyer has, morally, a right to do whatever his client would do; that he puts himself in the place of the man he defends, and is expected to do everything precisely as if he were the accused party himself. I rather think that some vague notion, quite as loose as this, prevails pretty generally among what one may call the minor moralists of the profession."

"I confess, sir, that I have been given to understand that some such rule *ought* to govern our conduct," said Michael Millington, who had been in Dunscomb's office only for the last six months.

"Then you have been very loosely and badly instructed in the duties of an advocate, Mr. Michael. A more pernicious doctrine was never broached, or one better suited to make men scoundrels. Let a young man practice with such notions, and two or three thieves for clients will prepare him to commit petit larceny, and a case or two of perjury would render him an exquisite at an affidavit. No, my boys, here is your rule in this matter: an advocate has a *right* to do whatever his client has a *right* to do—not what his client *would* do."

"Surely, sir, an advocate is justified in telling his client to plead not guilty, though guilty; and in aiding him to persuade a jury to acquit him, though satisfied himself he ought to be convicted!"

"You have got hold of the great point in the case, Jack, and one on which something may be said on both sides. The law is so indulgent as to permit an accused who has formally pleaded 'guilty,' thus making a distinct admission of his crime, to withdraw that plea, and put in another of 'not guilty.' Now, had the same person made a similar admission *out* of court, and under circumstances that put threats or promises out of the question, the law would have accepted *that* admission as the best possible evidence of his guilt. It is evident, therefore, that an understanding exists, to which the justice of the country is a party, that a man, though guilty, shall get himself out of the scrape if he can do so by legal means. No more importance is attached to the 'not guilty' than to the 'not at home' to a visitor; it being understood, by general convention, that neither means anything. Some persons are so squeamish as to cause their servants to say 'they are engaged,' by way of not telling a lie; but a lie consists in the intentional deception, and 'not in' and 'not guilty' mean no more, in the one case, than 'you can't see my master,' and in the other, than 'I'll run the chances of a trial.'"

"After all, sir, this is going pretty near the wind, in the way of morals."

"It certainly is. The Christian man who has committed a crime ought not to attempt to deny it to his country, as he certainly cannot to his God. Yet, nine hundred and ninety-nine out of a thousand of the most straight-laced Christians in the community would so deny their guilt if arraigned. We must not tax poor human nature too heavily, though I think the common law contains many things, originating in a jealousy of hereditary power, that it is a great folly for us to preserve. But, while we are thus settling principles we forget facts. You have told me nothing of your client, Ned."

"What would you wish to know?"

"You call her young, I remember; what may be her precise age?"

"That is more than I know; somewhere between sixteen and five-and-twenty."

"Five-and-twenty! Is she as old as that?"

"I rather think not; but I have been thinking much of her this morning, and I really do not remember to have seen another human being who is so difficult to describe."

"She has eyes, of course?"

"Two—and very expressive they are; though, sworn, I could not tell their color."

"And hair?"

"In very great profusion; so much of it, and so very fine and shining, that it was the very first thing about her person which I observed. But I have not the least notion of its color."

"Was it red?"

"No; nor yellow, nor golden, nor black, nor brown—and yet a little of all blended together, I should say."

"Ned, I'll tell the Widow Updyke of thee, thou rogue!"

"Tell her, and welcome. She has asked me all these questions herself, this very morning."

"Oh, she has, has she? Umph! Woman never changes her nature. You cannot say anything about the eyes, beyond the fact of their being very expressive?"

"And pleasing; more than that, even—engaging; winning is a better term."

"Ned, you dog, you have never told the widow one-half!"

"Every syllable. I even went further, and declared I had never beheld a countenance that, in so short an interview, made so deep an impression on me. If I were not to see this young woman again, I should never forget the expression of her face—so spirited, so sad, so gentle, so feminine, and so very intelligent. It seemed to me to be what I should call an illuminated countenance."

"Handsome?"

"Not unusually so, among our sweet American girls, except through the expression. That was really wonderful; though, you will remember, I saw her under very peculiar circumstances."

"Oh, exceedingly peculiar. Dear old soul; what a thump she has given him! How were her mouth and her teeth?—complexion, stature, figure, and smile?"

"I can tell you little of all these. Her teeth are fine; for she gave me a faint smile, such as a lady is apt to give a man in quitting him, and I saw just enough of the teeth to know that they are exceedingly fine. You smile, young gentlemen; but *you* may have a care for your hearts, in good truth; for if this strange girl interests either of you one-half as much as she has interested me, she will be either Mrs. John Wilmeter, or Mrs. Michael Millington, within a twelvemonth."

Michael looked very sure that she would never fill the last situation, which was already bespoke for Miss Sarah Wilmeter; and as for Jack, he laughed outright.

"We'll tell Mrs. Updyke of him, when we get back, and break off that affair, at least," cried the uncle, winking at the nephew, but in a way his friend should see him; "then there will be one marriage the less in the world."

"But is she a lady, doctor?" demanded John, after a short pause. "My wife must have some trifling claims in that way, I can assure you."

"As for family, education, association, and fortune, I can say nothing—I know nothing. Yet will I take upon myself to say she *is* a lady—and that, in the strict signification of the term."

"You are not serious now, Ned!" exclaimed the counselor, quickly. "Not a *bony fide*, as some of our gentlemen have it? You cannot mean *exactly* what you say."

"I do, though; and that literally."

"And she suspected of arson and murder! Where are her connections and friends—those who make her a lady? Why is she there alone, and, as you say, unfriended?"

"So it seemed to me. You might as well ask me why she is there at all. I know nothing of all this. I heard plenty of reasons in the street why she ought to be distrusted—nay, convicted; for the feeling against her had got to be intense before I left Biberry; but no one could tell me whence she came, or why she was there."

"Did you learn her name?"

"Yes; that was in every mouth, and I could not help hearing it. She was called Mary Monson by the people of Biberry— but I much doubt if that be her real name."

"So your angel in disguise will have to be tried under an 'alias.' That is not much in her favor, Ned. I shall ask no more questions, but wait patiently to see and judge for myself."

The young men put a few more interrogatories, which were civilly answered, and then the subject was dropped. Well has it been said that "God made the country; man made the town." No one feels this more than he who has been shut up between walls of brick and stone for many months, on his first escape into the open unfettered fields and winding pleasant roads. Thus was it now with Dunscomb. He had not been out of town since the previous summer, and great was his delight at smelling the fragrance of the orchards, and feasting his eyes on their beauties. All the other charms of the season came in aid of these, and when the carriage drove into the long, broad, and we might almost say single, street of Biberry, Dunscomb in particular was in a most tranquil and pleasant state of mind. He had come out to assist a friendless woman, cheerfully and without a thought of the sacrifice, either as to time or money, though in reflecting on all the circumstances he began to have his doubts of the wisdom of the step he had taken. Nevertheless, he preserved his native calmness of manner and coolness of head.

Biberry was found to be in a state of high excitement. There were at least a dozen physicians collected there, all from the county, and five or six reporters had come from town. Rumors of all sorts were afloat, and Mary Monson was a name in every person's mouth. She had not been arrested, however, it having been deemed premature for that; but she was vigilantly watched, and two large trunks of which she was the mistress, as well as an oilskin-covered box of some size, if not absolutely seized, were so placed that their owner had no access to them. This state of things, however, did not seem to give the suspected girl any uneasiness; she was content with what a carpet-bag contained, and with which she said she was comfortable. It was a question with the wiseacres whether she knew that she was suspected or not.

Had Dunscomb yielded to McBrain's solicitations, he would have gone at once to the house in which Mary Monson was now lodged, but he preferred adopting a different course. He thought it the most prudent to be a looker-on, until after the next examination, which was now close at hand. Wary by long habit, and cool by temperament, he was disposed to observe the state of things before he committed himself. The presence of the reporters annoyed him; not that he stood in any dread of the low tyranny that is so apt to characterize this class of men, for no member of the bar had held them, and the puny efforts of many among them to build up and take away professional character, in greater contempt than he had done; but he disliked to have his name mixed up with a cause of this magnitude, unless he had made up his mind to go through with it. In this temper, then, no communication was held with Mary Monson, until they met, at the hour appointed for the inquest, in the courthouse.

The room was crowded, at least twice as many having collected on this occasion as had got together on the sudden call of the previous examination. Dunscomb observed that the coroner looked grave, like a man who felt he had important business on his hands, while a stern expectation was the expression common to nearly all the others present. He was an utter stranger himself, even by sight, to every being present, his own party and two or three of the reporters excepted. These last no sooner observed him, however, than out came their little note-books, and the gold pens were at work, scribbling something. It was probably a sentence to say, "We observed among the crowd Thomas Dunscomb, Esquire, the well-known counsel *from the city*;" but Dunscomb cared very little for such vulgarisms, and continued passive.

As soon as the inquest was organized, the coroner directed a physician of the neighborhood to be put on the stand. It had gone forth that a "city doctor" had intimated that neither of the skeletons was that of Peter Goodwin, and there was a common wish to confront him with a high country authority. It was while the medical man now in request was sent for, that McBrain pointed out to Dunscomb the person of Mary Monson. She sat in a corner different from that she had occupied the day before, seemingly for the same purpose, or that of being alone. Alone she was not, strictly, however; a respectable-looking female, of middle age, being at her side. This was a Mrs. Jones, the wife of a clergyman, who had charitably offered the suspected young stranger a home under her own roof, pending the investigation. It was thought, generally, that Mary Monson had but very vague notions of the distrust that rested on her, it being a part of the plan of those who were exercising all their wits to detect the criminal that she was first to learn this fact in open court, and under circumstances likely to elicit some proofs of guilt. When Dunscomb learned this artifice, he saw how ungenerous and unmanly it was, readily imagined a dozen signs of weakness that a female might exhibit in such a strait that had no real connection with crime, and felt a strong disposition to seek an interview and put the suspected party on her guard. It was too late for this, however, just then ; and he contented himself, for the moment, with studying such signs of character and consciousness as his native sagacity and long experience enabled him to detect.

Although nothing could be more simple or unpretending than the attire of Mary Monson, it was clearly that of a lady. Everything about her denoted ·that station, or origin; though everything about her, as Dunscomb fancied, also denoted a desire to bring herself down, as nearly as possible, to the level of those around her, most probably that she might not attract particular attention. Our lawyer did not exactly like this slight proof of management, and wished it were not so apparent. He could see the hands, feet, figure, hair, and general air of the female he was so strangely called on to make the subject of his investigations, but he could not yet see her face. The last was again covered with a cambric handkerchief, the hand which held it being ungloved. It was a pretty little American hand ; white, well-proportioned, and delicate. It was clear that neither its proportions nor its color had been changed by uses unsuited to its owner's sex or years. But it had no ring, in this age of bejeweled fingers. It was the left hand, moreover, and the fourth finger, like all the rest, had no ornament, or sign of matrimony. He inferred from this that the stranger was unmarried ; one of the last things that a wife usually lays aside being her wedding-ring. The foot corresponded with the hand, and was decidedly the smallest, best-formed, and best decorated foot in Biberry. John Wilmeter thought it the prettiest he had ever seen. It was not studiously exhibited, however, but rested naturally and gracefully in its proper place. The figure generally, so far as a capacious shawl would allow of its being seen, was pleasing, graceful, and a little remarkable for accuracy of proportions, as well as of attire.

Once or twice Mrs. Jones spoke to her companion ; and it was when answering some question thus put that Dunscomb first got a glimpse of his intended client's face. The handkerchief was partly removed, and remained so long enough to enable him to make a few brief observations. It was then that he felt the perfect justice of his friend's description. It was an indescribable countenance, in all things but its effect ; which was quite as marked on the lawyer as it had been on the physician. But the arrival of Dr. Coe put an end to these observations, and drew all eyes on that individual, who was immediately sworn. The customary preliminary questions were put to this witness, respecting his profession, length of practice, residence, etc., when the examination turned more on the matter immediately under investigation.

"You see those objects on the table, doctor ?" said the coroner. "What do you say they are ?"

"*Ossa hominum :* human bones, much defaced and charred by heat."

"Do you find any proof about them of violence committed, beyond the damage done by fire ?"

"Certainly. There is the *os frontis* of each fractured by a blow ; a common blow, as I should judge."

"What do you mean, sir, by a common blow ? An accidental, or an intentional blow ?"

"By common blow, I mean that one blow did the damage to both *cranys*."

"*Crany ?*—how do you spell that word, doctor ? Common folks get put out by foreign tongues."

"Cranys, in the plural, sir. We say cran*ium* for *one* skull, and crany for two."

"I wonder what he would say for numskull ?" whispered John to Michael.

"Yes, sir; I understand you now. I trust the reporters will get it right."

"Oh! they never make any mistakes, especially in legal proceedings," quietly remarked Mr. Dunscomb to the doctor. "In matters of law and the constitution they are of proof! Talk of letters on the constitution! What are equal to those that come to us, *hibernally*, as one may say, from Washington?"

"Hibernially would be the better word," answered McBrain, in the same undertone.

"You ought to know; your grandfather was an Irishman, Ned. But listen to this examination."

"And now, Dr. Coe, have the goodness to look at these skeletons," resumed the coroner, "and tell us whether they belong to man, woman, or child. Whether they are the remains of adults, or of children."

"Of adults, certainly. On that point, sir, I conceive there can be no doubt."

"And as to sex?"

"I should think that equally clear. I have no doubt that one are the remains of Peter Goodwin, and the other those of his wife. Science can distinguish between the sexes, in ordinary cases, I allow; but this is a case in which science is at fault, for want of facts; and taking all the known circumstances into consideration, I have no hesitation in saying that, according to my best judgment, those are the remains of the missing man and woman—man and wife."

"Am I to understand that you recognize the particular skeletons by any outward, visible proofs?"

"Yes; there is the stature. Both of the deceased were well known to me; and I should say, that making the usual allowance for the absence of the *musculi*, the *pellis*, and other known substances—"

"Doctor, would it be just as agreeable to you to use the common dialect?" demanded a shrewd-looking farmer, one of the jury, who appeared equally amused and vexed at the display of learning.

"Certainly, sir—certainly, Mr. Blore; *musculi* means muscles, and *pellis* is the skin. Abstract the muscles and skin, and the other intermediate substances, from the bones, and the apparent stature would be reduced, as a matter of course. Making those allowances, I see in those skeletons the remains of Peter and Dorothy Goodwin. Of the fact I entertain no manner of doubt."

As Dr. Coe was very sincere in what he said, he expressed himself somewhat earnestly. A great many eyes were turned triumphantly toward the stranger who had presumed to intimate that the bones of both the remains were those of women, when everybody in and about Biberry knew Peter Goodwin so well, and knew that his wife, if anything, was the taller of the two. No one in all that crowd doubted as to the fact, except McBrain and his friend; and the last doubted altogether on the faith of the doctor's science. He had never known him mistaken, though often examined in court, and was aware that the bar considered him one of the safest and surest witnesses they could employ in all cases of controverted facts.

Dr. Coe's examination proceeded.

"Have you a direct knowledge of any of the circumstances connected with this fire?" demanded the coroner.

"A little, perhaps. I was called to visit a patient about midnight, and was obliged to pass directly before the door of Goodwin's house. The jury knows that it stood on a retired road, and that one would not be likely to meet with any person traveling it so early in the morning. I did pass, however, two men, who were walking very fast, and in the direction of Goodwin's. I could not see their faces, nor did I know them by their figures and movements. As I see everybody, and know almost everybody, hereabouts, I concluded they were strangers. Abot four I was on my return along the same road, and as my sulky rose to the top of Windy Hill, I got a view of Goodwin's house. The flames were just streaming out of the east end of the roof, and the little wing on that end of the building, in which the old folks slept, was in a bright blaze. The other end was not much injured; and I saw at an upper window the figure of a female—she resembled, as well as I could judge by that light, and at that distance, the young lady now present, and who is said to have occupied the chamber under the roof, in the old house, for some time past; though I can't say I have ever seen her there, unless I saw her then, under the circumstances mentioned. The old people could not have been as ailing this spring, as was common with them, as I do not remember to have been stopped by them once. They never were in the habit of sending for the doctor, but seldom let me go past the door without calling me in."

"Did you see any one besides the figure of the female at the window?"

"Yes. There were two men beneath that window, and they appeared to me to be speaking to, or holding some sort of communication with, the female. I saw gestures, and I saw one or two articles thrown out of the window. My view was only for a minute; and when I reached the house a considerable crowd had collected, and I had no opportunity to observe, particularly in a scene of such confusion."

"Was the female still at the upper window when your reached the house?"

"No. I saw the lady now present standing near the burning building, and held by a man—Peter Davidson, I think it was—who told me she wanted to rush into the house to look for the old folks."

"Did you see any efforts of that sort in her?"

"Certainly. She struggled to get away from Peter, and acted like a person who wished to rush into the burning building."

"Were the struggles natural—or might they not have beeen affected?"

"They might. If it was acting, it was *good* acting. I have seen as good, however, in my life."

The doctor had a meaning manner that said more than his words. He spoke very low—so low as not to be audible to those who sat in the further parts of the room; which will explain the perfect indifference to his testimony that was manifested by the subject of his remarks. An impression, however, was made on the jury, which was composed of men much disposed to push distrust to demonstration.

The coroner now thought it time to spring the principal mine, which had been carefully preparing during the recess in the investigation; and he ordered "Mary Monson" to be called—a witness who had been regularly summoned to attend, among the crowd of persons that had received similar notices.

CHAPTER IV.

"My deeds upon my head! I crave the law,
The penalty and forfeit of my bond."
—SHYLOCK.

THE eyes of Dunscomb were fastened intently on the female stranger, as she advanced to the place occupied by the witness. Her features denoted agitation, certainly; but he saw no traces of guilt. It seemed so improbable, moreover, that a young woman of her years and appearance should be guilty of so dark an offense, and that for money, too, that all the chances were in favor of her innocence. Still, there were suspicious circumstances, out of all question, connected with her situation, and he was too much experienced in the strange and unaccountable ways of crime not to be slow to form his conclusions.

The face of Mary Monson was now fully exposed; it being customary to cause female witnesses to remove their hats, in order that the jurors may observe their countenances. And what a countenance it was! Feminine, open, with scarce a trace of the ordinary passions about it, and illuminated from within, as we have already intimated. The girl might have been twenty, though she afterward stated her age to be a little more than twenty-one—perhaps the most interesting period of a female's existence. The features were not particularly regular, and an artist might have discovered various drawbacks on her beauty, if not positive defects; but no earthly being could have quarreled with the expression. That was a mixture of intelligence, softness, spirit, and feminine innocence that did not fail to produce an impression on a crowd which had almost settled down into a firm conviction of her guilt. Some even doubted, and most of those present thought it very strange.

The reporters began to write, casting their eyes eagerly toward this witness; and John Dunscomb, who sat near them, soon discovered that there were material discrepancies in their descriptions. These, however, were amicably settled by comparing notes; and when the accounts of that day's examination appeared in the journals of the time they were sufficiently consistent with each other; much more so, indeed, than with the truth in its severer aspects. There was no wish to mislead, probably; but the whole system has the capital defect of making a trade of news. The history of passing events comes to us sufficiently clouded and obscured by the most vulgar and least praiseworthy of all our lesser infirmities, even when left to take what may be termed its natural course; but, as soon as the money-getting principle is applied to it, facts become articles for the market, and go up and down, much as do other commodities, in the regular prices current.

Mary Monson trembled a little when sworn; but she had evidently braced her nerves for the trial. Women are very capable of self-command, even in situations as foreign to their habits as this, if they have time to compose themselves, and to come forward under the influence of resolutions deliberately formed. Such was probably the state of mind of this solitary and seemingly unfriended young woman; for, though pale as death, she was apparently composed. We say unfriended—Mrs. Jones, herself, having given all her friends to understand that she had invited the stranger to her house under a sense of general duty, and not on account of any private or particular interest she felt in her affairs. She was as much a stranger to her as to every one else in the village.

" Will you be so good as to tell us your name, place of ordinary residence, and usual occupation?" asked the coroner, in a dry, cold manner, though not until he had offered the witness a seat, in compliment to her sex.

If the face of Mary Monson was pale the instant before, it now flushed to scarlet. The tint that appears in the August evening sky, when heat-lightning illuminates the horizon, is scarcely more bright than that which chased the previous pallid hue from her cheeks. Dunscomb understood her dilemma, and interposed. She was equally unwilling to tell her real name, and to give a false one, under the solemn responsibility of an oath. There is, probably, less of deliberate, calculated false swearing than of any other offense against justice; few having the nerve, or the moral obtuseness, that is necessary to perjury. We do not mean by this, that all which legal witnesses say is true, or the half of it; for ignorance, dull imaginations working out solutions of half-comprehended propositions, and the strong propensity we all feel to see things as we have expected to find them, in a measure disqualifies fully half of those on whom the law has devolved a most important duty, to discharge it with due intelligence and impartiality.

"As a member of the bar, I interfere in behalf of the witness," said Dunscomb, rising. "She is evidently unacquainted with her true position here, and consequently with her rights. Jack, get a glass of water for the young lady;" and never did Jack obey a request of his uncle with greater alacrity. "A witness cannot, with propriety, be treated as a criminal, or one suspected, without being apprised that the law does not require of those thus circumstanced answers affecting themselves."

Dunscomb had listened more to his feelings than to his legal knowledge in offering this objection, inasmuch as no very searching question had, as yet, been put to Mary Monson. This the coroner saw, and he did not fail to let it be understood that he was aware of the weakness of the objection.

" Coroners are not governed by precisely the same rules as ordinary committing magistrates," he quietly observed, " though we equally respect the rules of evidence. No witness is obliged to answer a question before an inquest that will criminate himself, any more than at the Oyer and Terminer. If the lady will say

she does not wish to tell her real name, *because it may criminate her*, I shall not press the question myself, or allow it to be pressed by others."

" Very true, sir, but the law requires, in these preliminary proceedings, no more than such accuracy as is convenient in making out the records. I conceive that in this particular case the question might be varied by asking, ' You are known by the name of Mary Monson, I believe?' "

" What great harm can it be to this young female to give her real name, Mr. Dunscomb, as I understand you are that distinguished counselor, if she be perfectly innocent of the death of the Goodwins?"

" A perfectly innocent person may have good reasons for wishing to conceal her name. These reasons obtain additional force when we look around us, and see a committee of reporters, who stand ready to transmit all that passes to the press; but it might better serve the ends of justice to allow me to confer with the witness in private."

" With all my heart, sir. Take her into one of the jury rooms, and I will put another physician on the stand. When you are through with your consultation, Mr. Dunscomb, we shall be ready to proceed with your client."

Dunscomb offered his arm to the girl, and led her through the crowd, while a third medical man was sworn. This witness corroborated all of Dr. Coe's opinions, treating the supposition that both the skeletons were those of women with very little respect. It must be admitted that the suspected stranger lost a great deal of ground in the course of that half-hour. In the first place, the discussion about the name was received very much as an admission of guilt; for Dunscomb's argument that persons who were innocent might have many reasons for concealing their names, did not carry much weight with the good people of Biberry. Then any doubts which might have been raised by McBrain's suggestion concerning the nature of the skeletons, were effectually removed by the corroborating testimony of Dr. Short, who so fully sustained Dr. Coe. So much are the Americans accustomed to refer the decision of nearly all questions to numbers, it scarcely exaggerates the truth to say that, on the stand, the opinion of half a dozen country surveyors touching a problem in geometry would be very apt to overshadow that of a professor from West Point or old Yale. Majorities are the *primum mobile* of the common mind, and he who can get the greatest number on his side is very apt to be considered right, and to reap the benefits of being so.

A fourth and a fifth medical man were examined, and they concurred in the opinions of Dr. Coe and his neighbors. All gave it as the result of their inquiries that they believed the two skulls had been broken with the same instrument, and that the blow, if it did not cause immediate death, must have had the effect to destroy consciousness. As regards the sex, the answers were given in a tone somewhat supercilious.

"Science is a very good thing in its place," observed one of these last witnesses; "but science is subject to known facts. We all know that Peter Goodwin and his wife lived in that house; we all know that Dorothy Goodwin was a large woman, and that Peter Goodwin was a small man—that they were about of a height, in fact—and that these skeletons very accurately represent their respective statures. We also know that the house is burned, that the old couple are missing, that these bones were found in a wing in which they slept, and that no other bones have been found there. Now, to my judgment, these facts carry as much weight, ay, even more weight, than any scientific reasoning in the premises. I conclude, therefore, that these are the remains of Peter and Dorothy Goodwin—have no doubt that they are, indeed."

"Am I permitted to ask this witness a question, Mr. Coroner?" demanded Dr. McBrain.

"With all my heart, sir. The jury wishes to ascertain all they can, and our sole object is justice. Our inquests are not very rigid as to forms, and you are welcome to examine the witness as much as you please."

"You knew Goodwin?" asked McBrain, directly of the witness.

"I did, sir; quite well."

"Had he all his teeth, as you remember?"

"I think he had."

"On the supposition that his front upper teeth were all gone, and that the skeleton you suppose to be his *had* all the front upper teeth, would you still regard the facts you have mentioned as better, or even as good proof, as the evidence of science, which tells us that the man who has lost his teeth cannot possess them?"

"I scarcely call that a scientific fact, at all, sir. Any one may judge of that circumstance, as well as a physician. If it were as you say, I should consider the presence of the teeth pretty good proof that the skeleton was that of some other person, unless the teeth were the work of a dentist."

"Then why not put any other equally sure anatomical fact in opposition to what is generally supposed, in connection with the wing, the presence of the men, and all the other circumstances you have mentioned?"

"If there were any other *sure* anatomical fact, so I would. But in the condition in which those remains are, I do not think the best anatomist could say that he can distinguish whether they belonged to a man or to a woman."

"I confess that the case has its difficulties," McBrain quietly answered. "Still, I incline to my first opinion. I trust, Mr. Coroner, that the skeletons will be carefully preserved, so long as there may be any reason to continue these legal inquiries?"

"Certainly, sir. A box is made for that purpose, and they will be carefully deposited in it as soon as the inquest adjourns for the day. It is no unusual thing, gentlemen, for doctors to disagree."

This was said with a smile, and had the effect to keep the peace. McBrain, however, had all the modesty of knowledge, and was never disposed to show off his superior attainments in the faces of those who might be supposed to know less than himself. Nor was he by any means certain of his fact; though greatly inclined to believe that both the skeletons were those of females. The heat had been so powerful as to derange in some measure, if not entirely to deface, his proofs; and he was not a man to press a fact, in a case of this magnitude, without sufficient justification. All he now wanted, was to reserve a point that might have a material influence hereafter, in coming to a correct conclusion.

It was fully an hour before Dunscomb returned, bringing Mary Monson on his arm. John followed the latter closely, for, though not admitted to the room in which this long private conference had been held, he had not ceased to pace the gallery in front of its door during the whole time. Dunscomb looked very grave, and, as McBrain thought, he was very expert in interpreting the language of his friend's countenance, disappointed. The girl herself had evidently been weeping, and that violently. There was a paleness of the face, and a tremor in the frame, too, that caused the observant physician to suppose that, for the first time, she had been made to comprehend that she was the object of such dire distrust. No sooner were the two in their old seats, than the coroner prepared to renew the suspended examination.

"Witness," repeated that functionary with marked formality, "what is your name?"

The answer was given in a tremulous voice, but with sufficient readiness, as if previously prepared.

"I am known, in and around Biberry, by the name of Mary Monson."

The coroner paused, passed a hand over his brow, mused a moment, and abandoned a half-formed determination he had made, to push this particular inquiry as far as he could. To state the truth, he was a little afraid of Mr. Thomas Dunscomb, whose reputation at the bar was of too high a character to have escaped his notice. On the whole, therefore, he decided to accept the name of Mary Monson, reseving the right of the State to inquire further, hereafter.

"Where do you reside?"

"At present, in this place—lately, in the family of Peter Goodwin, whose remains are supposed to be in this room."

"How long had you resided in that family?"

"Nine weeks, to a day. I arrived in the morning, and the fire occurred at night."

"Relate all that you know concerning that fire, if you please, miss—I call you miss, supposing you to be unmarried?"

Mary Monson merely made a slight inclination of her head, as one acknowledges that a remark is heard and understood. This did not more than half satisfy the coroner, his wife, for reasons of her own, having particularly desired him to ask the "Monson girl" when she was put on the stand whether she was or was not married. But it was too late just then to ascertain this interesting fact, and the examination proceeded.

"Relate all that you know concerning the fire, if you please, ma'am."

"I know very little. I was awakened by a bright light—arose, and dressed myself as well as I could, and was about to descend the stairs, when I found I was too late. I then went to a window, and intended to throw my bed out, and let myself down on it, when two men appeared, and raised a ladder by which I got safely out."

"Were any of your effects saved?"

"All, I believe. The same two persons entered my room, and passed my trunks, box, and carpet-bag, writing-desk, and other articles, out of the room, as well as most of its furniture. It was the part of the building last on fire, and it was safe entering the room I occupied, for near half an hour after I escaped."

"How long had you known the Goodwins?"

"From the time when I first came to live in their house."

"Did you pass the evening of the night of the fire in their company?"

"I did not. Very little of my time was passed in their company, unless it was at meals."

This answer caused a little stir among the audience, of whom much the larger portion thought it contained an admission to be noted. Why should not a young woman who lived in a house so much apart from a general neighborhood, not pass most of her time in the company of those with whom she dwelt? "If they were good enough to live with, I should think they might be good enough to associate with," whispered one of the most active female talkers of Biberry, but in a tone so loud as to be heard by all near her.

This was merely yielding to a national and increasing susceptibility to personal claims; it being commonly thought aristocratic to refuse to associate with everybody, when the person subject to remark has any apparent advantages to render such association desirable. All others may do as they please.

"You did not, then, make one of the family regularly, but were there for some particular purpose of your own?" resumed the coroner.

"I think, sir, on reflection, that you will see this examination is taking a very irregular course," interposed Dunscomb. "It is more like an investigation for a commitment, than an inquest."

"The law allows the freest modes of inquiry in all such cases, Mr. Dunscomb. Recollect, sir, there have been arson and murder—two of the highest crimes known to the books."

"I do not forget it; and recognize not only all your rights, sir, but your duties. Nevertheless, this young lady has rights, too, and is to be treated distinctly in one of two characters; as a witness, or as a party accused. If in the latter, I shall at once advise her to answer no more questions in this state of the case. My duty, as her counsel, requires me to say as much."

"She has, then, regularly retained you, Mr. Dunscomb," the coroner asked, with interest.

"That, sir, is a matter between her and myself. I appear here as counsel, and shall claim the rights of one. I know that you can carry on this inquest without my interference, if you see fit; but no one can exclude the citizen from the benefit of advice. Even the new code, as extravagant and high-flying in invention as ever came from the misguided ingenuity of man, will allow of this."

"There is no wish, Mr. Dunscomb, to put any obstacles in your way. Let every man do his whole duty. Your client can certainly refuse to answer any questions she may please, on the ground that the answer may tend to criminate herself; and so may any one else."

"I beg your pardon, sir; the law is still more indulgent in these preliminary proceedings. A party who knows himself to be suspected, has a right to evade questions that may militate against his interests; else would the boasted protection which the law so far throws around every one, that he need not be his own accuser, become a mere pretense."

"I shall endeavor to put my questions in such a way as to give her the benefits of all her rights. Miss Monson, it is said that you have been seen, since the fire, to have some gold in your possession; have you any objection to let that gold be seen by the jury?"

"None in the world, sir. I have a few gold pieces—here they are, in my purse. They do not amount to much, either in numbers or value. You are at liberty to examine them as much as you please."

Dunscomb had betrayed a little uneasiness at this question; but the calm, steady manner in which the young woman answered, and the coolness with which she put her purse into the coroner's hand, reassured, or rather surprised him. He remained silent, therefore, interposing no objection to the examination.

"Here are seven half-eagles, two quarter-eagles, and a strange coin that I do not remember ever to have seen before," said the coroner. "What do you call this piece, Mr. Dunscomb?"

"I cannot tell you, sir; I do not remember ever to have seen the coin before, myself."

"It is an Italian coin, of the value of about twenty dollars, they tell me," answered Mary, quietly. "I think it is called after the reigning sovereign, whoever he may be. I got it, in exchange for some of our own money, from an emigrant from Europe, and kept it as a thing a little out of the common way."

The simplicity, distinctness, not to say nerve, with which this was said, placed Dunscomb still more at his ease, and he now freely let the inquiry take its course. All this did not prevent his being astonished that one so young, and seemingly so friendless, should manifest so much coolness and self-possession, under circumstances so very trying. Such was the fact, however; and he was fain to await further developments, in order better to comprehend the character of his client.

"Is Mrs. Pope present?" inquired the coroner. "The lady who told us yesterday she had seen the specie of the late Mrs. Goodwin, during the lifetime of the latter?"

It was superfluous to ask if any particular person were present, as nearly all Biberry were in or about the courthouse. Up started the widow, therefore, at this appeal, and coming forward with alacrity, she was immediately sworn, which she had not been the previous day, and went on the stand as a regular witness.

"Your name?" observed the coroner.

"Abigail Pope—folks write 'relict of John Pope, deceased,' in all my law papers."

"Very well, Mrs. Pope; the simple name will suffice for the present purposes. Do you reside in this neighborhood?"

"In Biberry. I was born, brought up, married, became a widow, and still dwell, all within half a mile of this spot. My maiden name was Dickson."

Absurd and forward as these answers may seem to most persons, they had an effect on the investigation that was then going on in Biberry. Most of the audience saw and felt the difference between the frank statements of the present witness, and the reserve manifested by the last.

"Now why couldn't that Mary Monson answer all these questions, just as well as Abigail Pope?" said one female talker to a knot of listeners. "She has a glib enough tongue in her head, if she only sees fit to use it! I'll engage no one can answer more readily, when she wishes to let a thing out. There's a dreadful history behind the curtain in my judgment, about that same young woman, could a body only get at it."

"Mr. Sanford *will* get at it, before he has done with her, I'll engage," answered a friend. "I have heard it said that he is the most investigating coroner in the State, when he sets about a case in good earnest. He'll be very apt to make the most of this, for we never have had anything one-half so exciting in Biberry as these murders! I have long thought we were rather out of the way of the rest of the world until now; but our time has come, and we sha'n't very soon hear the last of it!"

"It's all in the papers already!" exclaimed a third. "Biberry looks as grand as York, or Albany in the columns of every paper from town this morning! I declare it did me good to see our little place holding up its head among the great of the earth, as it might be—"

What else, in the way of local patriotism, may have escaped this individual cannot now be known, the coroner drawing off her auditors, by the question next put to the widow.

"Did you ever see any gold coins in the possession of the late Mrs. Goodwin?" asked that functionary.

"Several times—I don't know but I might say often. Five or six times at least. I used to sew for the old lady and you know how it is when a body works, in that way, in a family—it's next thing, I do suppose, to being a doctor, so far as secrets go."

"Should you know any of that coin were you to see it again, Mrs. Pope?"

"I think I might. There's one piece, in partic'lar that I suppose I should know anywhere. It's a wonderful looking piece of money, and true Californy, I conclude."

"Did any of Mrs. Goodwin's gold coins bear a resemblance to this?" showing a half-eagle.

"Yes, sir—that's a five-dollar piece—I've had one of them myself in the course of my life."

"Mrs. Goodwin had coins similar to this, I then understand you to say?"

"She had as many as fifty, I should think. Altogether she told me she had as much as four hundred dollars in that stocking! I remember the sum, for it sounded like a great deal for anybody to have who wasn't a bank like. It quite put me in mind of the *place ers*."

"Was there any coin like this?" showing the widow the Italian piece.

"That's the piece! I'd know it among a thousand! I had it in my hands as much as five minutes, trying to read the Latin on it, and make it out into English. All the rest was American gold, the old lady told me; but this piece she said was foreign."

This statement produced a great sensation in the court-room. Although Mrs. Pope was flippant, a gossip, and a little notorious for meddling with her neighbors' concerns, no one suspected her of fabricating such a story, under oath. The piece of gold passed from juror to juror; and each man among them felt satisfied that he would know the coin again, after an interval of a few weeks. Dunscomb probably put less faith in this bit of testimony than any other person present; and he was curious to note its effect on his client. To his great surprise she betrayed no uneasiness; her countenance maintaining a calm that he now began to apprehend denoted a practiced art; and he manifested a desire to examine the piece of gold for himself. It was put in his hand, and he glanced at its face a little eagerly. It was an unusual coin; but it had no defect or mark that might enable one to distinguish between it and any other piece of a similar impression. The coroner interpreted the meaning of his eye, and suspended the examination of the widow, to question Mary Monson herself.

"Your client sees the state of the question, Mr. Dunscomb," he said; "and you will look to her rights. Mine authorize me, as I understand them, to inquire of her concerning a few facts in relation to this piece of money."

"I will answer your questions, sir, without any hesitation," the accused replied, with a degree of steadiness that Dunscomb deemed astonishing.

"How long has this piece of gold been in your possession, if you please, miss?"

"About a twelvemonth. I began to collect the gold I have very nearly a year since."

"Has it been in your possession, uninterruptedly, all that time."

"So far as I know, sir, it has. A portion of the time, and a large portion of it, it has not been kept in my purse; but I should think no one could have meddled with it, when it has been elsewhere."

"Have you anything to remark on the testimony just given?"

"It is strictly true. Poor Mrs. Goodwin certainly had the store of gold mentioned by Mrs. Pope, for she once showed it to me. I rather think she was fond of such things; and had a pleasure in counting her hoards, and showing them to other persons. I looked over her coins; and finding she was fond of those that are a little uncommon, I gave her one or two of those that I happened to own. No doubt, Mrs. Pope saw the counterpart of this piece, but surely not the piece itself."

"I understand you to say, then, that Mrs. Goodwin had a gold coin similar to this, which gold coin came from yourself. What did Mrs. Goodwin allow you in the exchange?"

"Sir?"

"How much did you estimate the value of that Italian piece at, and in what money did Mrs. Goodwin pay you for it? It is necessary to be particular in these cases."

"She returned me nothing for the coin, sir. It was a present from me to her, and of course not to be paid for."

This answer met with but little favor. It did not appear to the people of Biberry at all probable that an unknown, and seemingly friendless young woman, who had been content to dwell two months in the "garret-room" of the "old Goodwin house," faring none of the best, certainly, and neglecting so many superior tenements and tables that were to be met with on every side of her, would be very likely to give away a piece of gold of that unusual size. It is true, we are living in a marvelous age, so far as this metal is concerned; but the Californian gold had not then arrived in any great quantity, and the people of the country are little accustomed to see anything but silver and paper, which causes them to attach an unwonted value to the more precious metal. Even the coroner took this view of the matter; and Dunscomb saw that the explanation just made by his client was thought to prove too much.

"Are you in the habit, miss, of giving away pieces of gold?" asked one of the jurors.

"That question is improper," interposed Mr. Dunscomb. "No one can have a right to put it."

The coroner sustained this objection, and no answer was given. As Mrs. Pope had suggested that others, besides herself, had seen Mrs. Goodwin's stockings, four more witnesses were examined to this one point. They were all females, who had been admitted by the deceased, in the indulgence of her passion, to feast their eyes with a sight of her treasure. Only one, however, of these four professed to have any recollection of the particular coin that had now become, as it might be, the pivoting point in the inquiry; and her recollections were by no means as clear as those of the widow. She *thought* she had seen such a piece of gold in Mrs. Goodwin's possession, though she admitted she was not allowed to touch any of the money, which was merely held up, piece by piece, before her admiring eyes, in the hands of its proper owner. It was in this state of the inquiry that Dunscomb remarked to the coroner, "that it was not at all surprising a woman who was so fond of exposing her treasure should be robbed and murdered!" This remark, however, failed of its intended effect, in consequence of the manner in which suspicion had become riveted, as it might be, through the testimony of Mrs. Pope, on the stranger who had so mysteriously come to lodge with the Goodwins. The general impression now appeared to be that the whole matter had been previously arranged, and that the stranger had come to dwell in the house expressly to obtain facilities for the commission of the crime.

A witness who was related to the deceased, who was absent from home, but had been told, by means of the wires, to return, and who had intimated an intention to comply, was still wanting; and the inquest was again adjourned for an hour, in order to allow of the arrival of a stage from town. During this interval, Dunscomb ascertained how strongly the current was setting against his client. A hundred little circumstances were cited, in confirmation of suspicions that had now gained a firm footing, and which were so nearly general as to include almost every person of any consequence in the place. What appeared strangest to Dunscomb was the composure of the young girl who was so likely to be formally accused of crimes so heinous. He had told her of the nature of the distrust that was attached to her situation, and she received his statement with a degree of emotion that, at first, had alarmed him. But an unaccountable calmness soon succeeded this burst of feeling, and he had found it necessary to draw confidence in the innocence of his client from that strangely illuminated countenance, to study which was almost certain to subdue a man by its power. While thus gazing at the stranger, he could not believe her guilty; but, while reflecting on all the facts of the case, he saw how difficult it might be to persuade others to entertain the same opinion. Nor were there circumstances wanting to shake his own faith in expression, sex, years, and all the other probabilities. Mary Monson had declined entering at all into any account of her previous life; evaded giving her real name even to him; carefully abstained from all allusions that might furnish any clew to her former place of abode, or to any fact that would tend to betray her secret.

At the appointed hour the stage arrived, bringing the expected witness. His testimony went merely to corroborate the accounts concerning the little hoard of gold that his kinswoman had undeniably possessed, and to the circumstance that she always kept it in a particular drawer of her bureau. The bureau had been saved, for it did not stand in the sleeping-room of the deceased, but had formed a principal embellishment of her little parlor, and the money was not in it. What was more, each drawer was carefully locked, but no keys were to be found. As these were articles not likely to be melted under any heat to which they might have been exposed, a careful but fruitless search had been made for them among the ruins. They were nowhere to be seen.

About nine o'clock in the evening, the jury brought in the result of their inquest. It was a verdict of murder in the first degree, committed, in the opinion of the jurors, by a female who was known by the name of Mary Monson. With the accusation of arson, the coroner's inquest, as a matter of course, had no connection. A writ was immediately issued, and the accused arrested.

CHAPTER V.

" It was the English," Kasper cried,
  " Who put the French to rout;
But what they killed each other for,
  I could not well make out.
But everybody said," quoth he,
" That 'twas a famous victory."
                            —SOUTHEY.

THE following day, after an early breakfast, Dunscomb and his friend the doctor were on their way back to town. The former had clients and courts, and the latter patients, who were not to be neglected, to say nothing of the claims of Sarah and Mrs. Updyke. John and Michael remained at Biberry; the first being detained there by divers commissions connected with the comforts and treatment of Mary Monson, but still more by his own inclinations; and the last remaining, somewhat against his wishes, as a companion to the brother of her who so strongly drew him back to New York.

As the commitment was for offenses so serious, crimes as grave as any known to the law, bail would not have been accepted, could any have been found. We ought not to speak with too much confidence, however, on this last point; for Dr. McBrain, a man of very handsome estate, the result of a liberal profession steadily and intelligently pursued, was more than half disposed to offer himself for one of the sureties, and to go and find a second among his friends. Nothing, indeed, prevented his doing so but Dunscomb's repeated assurances that no bondsmen would be received. Even charming young women, when they stand charged with murder and arson, must submit to be incarcerated, until their innocence is established in due form of law; or, what is the same thing, in effect, until the caprice, impulses, ignorance or corruption of a jury acquits them.

The friends did not entirely agree in their manner of viewing this affair. The doctor was firmly impressed with the conviction of Mary Monson's innocence, while Dunscomb, more experienced in the ways of crime and the infirmities of the human heart, had his misgivings. So many grounds of suspicion had occurred, or been laid open to his observation, during the hour of private communication, that it was not easy for one who had seen so much of the worst side of human nature, to cast them off under the mere influence of a graceful form, winning manner, and bright countenance. Then, the secondary facts, well established, and, in one important particular, admitted by the party accused, were not of a character to be overlooked. It often happens, and Dunscomb well knew it, that innocence appears under a repulsive exterior, while guilt conceals itself in forms and aspects so fair, as to deceive all but the wary and the experienced.

"I hope that the comfort of Miss Monson has been properly attended to, since she must be confined for a few days," said McBrain, while he took a last look at the little jail, as the carriage passed the brow of the hill. "Justice can ask no more than security."

"It is a blot on the character of the times, and on this country in particular," answered Dunscomb, coldly, "that so little attention is paid to the jails. We are crammed with false philanthropy in connection with convicted rogues, who ought to be made to feel the penalties of their offenses; while we are not even just in regard to those who are only accused, many of whom are really innocent. But for my interference, this delicate and friendless girl would, in all probability, have been immured in a common dungeon."

"What! before her guilt is established?"

"Relatively, her treatment after conviction would be far more humane than previously to that event. Comfortable, well-furnished, but secure apartments ought to be provided for the accused in every county in the State, as acts of simple justice, before another word of mawkish humanity is uttered on the subject of the treatment of recognized criminals. It is wonderful what a disposition there is among men to run into octaves, in everything they do, forgetting that your true melody is to be found only in the simpler and more natural notes. There is as much of the *falsetto* nowadays in philanthropy as in music."

"And this poor girl is thrust into a dungeon?"

"No; it is not quite as bad as that. The jail has one decent apartment, that was fitted up for the comfort of a prize-fighter, who was confined in it not long since; and as the room is sufficiently secure, I have persuaded the jailor's wife to put Mary Monson in it. Apart from loss of air and exercise, and the happiness of knowing herself respected and beloved, the girl will not be very badly off there.

I daresay, the room is quite as good as that she occupied under the roof of those unfortunate Goodwins."

"How strange that a female of her appearance should have been the inmate of such a place! She does not seem to want money, either. You saw the gold she had in her purse?"

"Ay; it were better had that gold not been there, or not seen. I sincerely wish it had been nothing but silver."

"You surely do not agree with that silly woman, the Widow Pope, as they call her, in believing that she has got the money of those persons who have been murdered?"

"On that subject, I choose to suspend my opinion—I may, or I may not, as matters shall turn up. She has money; and in sufficient quantity to buy herself out of jeopardy. At least, she offered me a fee of a hundred dollars, in good city paper."

"Which you did not take, Tom?"

"Why not? It is my trade, and I live by it. Why not take her fee, if you please, sir? Does the Widow Updyke teach you such doctrines? Will you drive about town for nothing? Why not take her fee, Master Ned?"

"Why not, sure enough! That girl has bewitched me, I believe; and that is the solution."

"I tell you what, Ned, unless there is a stop put to this folly, I'll make Mrs. Updyke acquainted with the whole matter, and put an end to nuptials number 3. Jack is head and ears in love, already; and here you are flying off at a tangent from all your engagements and professions, to fall at the feet of an unknown girl of twenty, who appears before you, on a first interview, in the amiable light of one accused of the highest crimes."

"And of which I no more believe her guilty than I believe you to be guilty of them."

"Umph! 'Time will show;' which is the English, I suppose, of the '*nous ver-rons*' that is flying about in the newspapers. Yes, she has money to buy three or four journals, to get up a 'sympathy' in her behalf, when her acquittal would be almost certain, if her trial were not a legal impossibility. I am not sure it is not her safest course, in the actual state of the facts."

"Would you think, Dunscomb, of advising any one who looked up to you for counsel, to take such a course?"

"Certainly not—and you know it well enough, McBrain; but that does not lessen, or increase, the chances of the expedient. The journals have greatly weakened their own power, by the manner in which they have abused it; but enough still remains to hoodwink, not to say to overshadow, justice. The law is very explicit and far-sighted as to the consequences of allowing any one to influence the public mind in matters of its own administration; but in a country like this, in which the virtue and intelligence of the people are said to be the *primum mobile* in everything, there is no one to enforce the ordinances that the wisdom of our ancestors has bequeathed to us.

"Any editor of a newspaper who publishes a sentence reflecting on the character or rights of a party to a pending suit, is guilty at common law of what the books call a 'libel on the courts of justice,' and can be punished for it, as for any other misdemeanor; yet, you can see for yourself, how little such a provision, healthful and most wise—nay, essential as it is to justice—is looked down by the mania which exists of putting everything into print. When one remembers that very little of what he reads is true, it is fearful to reflect that a system of which the whole merit depends on its power to extract facts, and to do justice on their warranty, should be completely overshadowed by another contrivance which, when stripped of its pretension, and regarded in its real colors, is nothing more than one of the ten thousand schemes to make money that surrounds us, with a little higher pretension than common to virtue."

"'Completely overshadowed' are strong words, Dunscomb!"

"Perhaps they are, and they may need a little qualifying. Overshadowed often —much too often, however, is not a particle stronger than I am justified in using. Every one, who thinks at all, sees and feels the truth of this; but here is the weak side of a popular government. The laws are enforced by means of public virtue, and public virtue, like private virtue, is very frail. We all are willing enough to admit the last, as regards our neighbors at least, while there seems to exist in most minds, a species of idolatrous veneration for the common sentiment, as sheer a quality of straw, as any image of a lover drawn by the most heated imagination of sixteen."

"You surely do not disregard public opinion, Tom, or set it down as unworthy of all respect!"

"By no means; if you mean that opinion which is the result of deliberate judgment, and has a direct connection with our religion, morals and manners. That is a public opinion to which we all ought to defer, when it is fairly made up, and has been distinctly and independently pronounced; most especially when it comes from high quarters, and not from low. But the country is full of simulated public opinion, in the first place, and it is not always easy to tell the false from the true. Yes, the country is full of what I shall call an artificial public opinion, that has been got up to affect a purpose, and to that no wise man will defer, if he can help it. Now look at our scheme of administering justice. Twelve men taken out of the bosom of the community, by a species of lottery, are set apart to pronounce on your fortune, or mine—nay, to utter the fearful words of 'guilty,' or 'not guilty.' All the accessories of this plan, as they exist here, make against its success. In the first place, the jurors are paid, and that just enough to induce the humblest on the list to serve, and not enough to induce the educated and intelligent. It is a day-laborer's wages, and the day-laborer will be most likely to profit by it. Men who are content to toil for seventy-five cents a day are very willing to serve on juries for a dollar; while those whose qualifications enable them to obtain enough to pay their fines, disregard the penalty, and stay away."

"Why is not an evil as flagrant as this remedied? I should think the whole bar would protest against it."

"With what result? Who cares for the bar? Legislators alone can change this system, and men very different from those who are now sent must go to the legislature, before one is found, honest enough, or bold enough, to get up and tell the people they are not all fit to be trusted. No, no; this is not the way of the hour. We have a cycle in opinion to make, and it may be that when the round is fairly made, men may come back to their senses, and perceive the necessity of fencing in justice by some of the useful provisions that we are now so liberally throwing away. To tell you the truth, Ned, the State is submitting to the influence of two of the silliest motives that can govern men—ultra conservatism, and ultra progress; the one holding back, often, to preserve that which is not worth keeping; and the other 'going ahead,' as it is termed, merely for the sake of boasting of their onward tendencies. Neither course is in the least suited to the actual wants of society, and each is pernicious in its way."

"It is thought, however, that when opinion thus struggles with opinion, a healthful compromise is made, in which society finds its advantage."

"The cant of mediocrity, depend on it, Ned. In the first place, there is no compromise about it; one side or the other gains the victory: and as success is sustained by numbers, the conquerors push their advantages to the utmost. They think of their own grosser interests, their passions and prejudices, rather than of any 'healthful compromise,' as you term it. What compromise is there in this infernal code?" Dunscomb was an ultra himself, in opposition to a system that has a good deal of that which is useful, diluted by more that is not quite so good—"or what in this matter of the election of judges by the people? As respects the last, for instance, had the tenure of office been made 'good behavior,' there would have been something like a compromise; but no—the conquerors took all; and what is worse, the conquerors were actually a minority of the voters, so easy is it to cow even numbers by political chicanery. In this respect, democracy is no more infallible than any other form of government."

"I confess, I do not see how this is shown, since the polls were free to every citizen."

"The result fairly proves it. Less than half of the known number of the electors voted for the change. Now it is absurd to suppose that men who really and affirmatively wished a new constitution would stay away from the polls."

"More so than to suppose that they who did not wish it would stay away, too?"

"More so, and for this reason. Thousands fancied it useless to stem the current of what they fancied a popular movement, and were passive in the matter. Any man, of an extensive acquaintance, may easily count a hundred such idlers. Then a good many stood on their legal rights, and refused to vote, because the manner of producing the change was a palpable violation of a previous contract; the old constitution pointing out the manner in which the instrument could be altered, which was not the mode adopted. Then tens of thousands voted for the new constitution, who did not know anything about it. They loved change, and voted for change's sake; and, possibly, with some vague notion that they were to be benefited by making the institutions as popular as possible."

"And is not this the truth? Will not the mass be all the better off by exercising as much power as they can?"

"No; and for the simple reason that masses cannot, in the nature of things, exercise more than a very limited power. You, yourself, for instance, one of the mass, cannot exercise this very power of choosing a judge, as it ought to be exercised, and of course are liable to do more harm than good."

"The deuce I cannot! Why is not my vote as good as your own? or that of any other man?"

"For the simple reason that you are ignorant of the whole matter. Ask yourself the question, and answer it like an honest man; would you—*could* you, with the knowledge you possess, lay your finger on any man in this community, and say, 'I make you a judge?'"

"Yes; my finger would be laid on you, in a minute."

"Ah, Ned, that will do, as a friend; but how would it do as a judicious selection of a judge you do not know? You are ignorant of the law, and must necessarily be ignorant of the qualifications of any particular person to be an interpreter of it. What is true of you, is equally true of a vast majority of those who are now the electors of our judges."

"I am not a little surprised, Tom, to hear you talk in this way; for you profess to be a democrat!"

"To the extent of giving the people all power, in the last resort—all power that they can intelligently and usefully use; but not to the extent of permitting them to make the laws, and to execute the laws, and to interpret the laws. All that the people want is sufficient power to secure their liberties, which is simply such a state of things as shall secure what is right between man and man. Now it is the want of this all-important security, in a practical point of view, of which I complain. Rely on it, Ned, the people gain nothing by exercising an authority that they do not know how to turn to good account. It were far better for them, and for the State, to confine themselves to the choice of general agents, of whose characters they may know something, and then confide all other powers to servants appointed by those named by these agents, holding all alike to a rigid responsibility. As for the judges, they will soon take a decided party character; and men will as blindly accuse, and as blindly defend them, as they now do their other leading partisans. What between the bench and the jury-box, we shall shortly enjoy a legal pandemonium."

"Yet there are those who think the trial by jury is the palladium of our liberties."

Dunscomb laughed outright, for he recollected his conversation with the young men, which we have already related. Then suppressing his risible propensity, he continued gravely—

"Yes, one or two papers, well feed by this young woman's spare cash, might do her more good than any service I can render her. I daresay the accounts now published, or soon to be published, will leave a strong bias against her."

"Why not fee a reporter as well as a lawyer, eh, Tom? There is no great difference, as I can see."

"Yes, you can, and will, too, as soon as you look into the matter. A lawyer is paid for a known and authorized assistance, and the public recognize in him one engaged in the interests of his client, and accepts his statements and efforts accordingly. But the conductor of a public journal sets up a claim to strict impartiality, in his very profession, and should tell nothing but what he believes to be true, neither inventing nor suppressing. In his facts he is merely the publisher of a record; in his reasoning a judge; not an advocate."

The doctor now laughed, in his turn, and well he might; few men being so ignorant as not to understand how far removed from all this are most of those who control the public journals.

"After all, it is a tremendous power to confide to irresponsible men!" he claimed.

"That it is, and there is nothing among us that so completely demonstrates how far, very far, the public mind is in the rear of the facts of the country, than the blind, reckless manner in which the press is permitted to tyrannize over the community in the midst of all our hosannas to the Goddess of Liberty. Because, forsooth, what is termed a free press is useful, and has been useful in curbing an irresponsible, hereditary power, in other hands, we are just stupid enough to think it is of equal importance here, where no such power exists, and where all that remains to be done is to strictly maintain the equal rights of all classes of citizens. Did we understand ourselves, and our real wants, not a paper should be printed in the State that did not make a deposit to meet the legal penalties it might incur by the abuse of its trust. This is or was done in France, the country of all others that best respects equality of rights in theory, if not in practice!"

"You surely would not place restrictions on the press!"

"I would though, and very severe restrictions, as salutary checks on the immense power it wields. I would, for instance, forbid the publication of any statement whatever, touching parties in the courts, whether in civil or criminal cases, pending the actions, that the public mind might not be tainted, by design.

Give the right to publish, and it will be, and is abused, and that most flagrantly, to meet the wishes of corruption. I tell you, Ned, as soon as you make a trade of news, you create a stock market that will have its rise and fall, under the impulses of fear, falsehood, and favor, just like your money transactions. It is a perversion of the nature of things, to make of news more than a simple statement of what has actually occurred."

"It is surely natural to lie?"

"That is it, and this is the very reason we should not throw extraordinary protection around a thousand tongues which speak by means of types, that we do not give to the natural member. The lie that is told by the press is ten thousand times a lie, in comparison with that which issues from the mouth of man."

"By George, Tom, if I had your views, I would see that some of this strange young woman's money should be used in sustaining her, by means of the agents you mention!"

"That would never do. This is one of the cases in which 'want of principle' has an ascendency over 'principle.' The upright man cannot consent to use improper instruments, while the dishonest fellow seizes on them with avidity. So much the greater, therefore, is the necessity of the law's watching the interests of the first with the utmost jealousy. But, unfortunately, we run away with the sound, and overlook the sense of things."

We have related this conversation at a length which a certain class of our readers will probably find tedious, but it is necessary to a right comprehension of various features in the picture we are about to draw. At the Stag's Head the friends stopped to let the horses blow, and, while the animals were cooling themselves under the care of Stephen Hoof, McBrain's coachman, the gentlemen took a short walk in the hamlet. At several points as they moved along, they overheard the subject of the murders alluded to, and saw divers newspapers, in the hands of sundry individuals, who were eagerly perusing accounts of the same events; sometimes by themselves, but oftener to groups of attentive listeners. The travelers were now so near town as to be completely within its moral, not to say physical, atmosphere—being little more than a suburb of New York. On their return to the inn, the doctor stopped under the shed to look at his horses, before Stephen checked them up again previously to a fresh start. Stephen was neither an Irishman nor a black; but a regular old-fashioned, Manhattanese coachman; a class apart, and of whom, in the confusion of tongues that pervades that modern Babel, a few still remain, like monuments of the past, scattered along the Appian Way.

"How do your horses stand the heat, Stephen?" the doctor kindly inquired, always speaking of the beasts as if they were the property of the coachman, and not of himself. "Pill looks as if he had been well warmed this morning."

"Yes, sir, he takes it somewhat hotter than Poleus, in the spring of the year, as a general thing. Pill vill vork famously, if a body vill only give him his feed in vhat I calls a genteel vay; but them 'ere country taverns has nothing nice about 'em, not even a clean manger; and a town horse that is accustomed to a sweet stable and proper company, won't stand up to the rack as he should do, in one of their holes. Now, Poleus, I calls a gineral feeder; it makes no matter vith him vhether he is at home, or out on a farm—he finishes his oats; but it isn't so vith Pill, sir—his stomach is delicate, and the horse that don't get his proper food vill sweat, summer or vinter."

"I sometimes think, Stephen, it might be better to take them both off their oats for a few days, and let blood, perhaps; they say that the fleam is as good for a horse as the lancet is for a man."

"Don't think on't, sir, I beg of you! I'm quite sure they has doctor-stuff in their names, not to crowd 'em down vith any more, jist as varm veather is a settin' in. Oats is physic enough for a horse, and vhen the creaturs vants anything more, sir, jist leave 'em to me. I knows as peculiar a drench as ever vas poured down a vheeler's throat, vithout troublin' that academy in Barclay Street, vhere so many gentlemen goes two or three times a veek, and vhere, they do say, so many goes in as never comes out whole."

"Well, Stephen, I'll not interfere with your treatment, for I confess to very little knowledge of the diseases of horses. What have you got in the paper there, that I see you have been reading?"

"Vhy, sir," answered Stephen, scratching his head, "it's all about our affair, up yonder."

"Our affair! Oh! you mean the inquest, and the murder. Well, what does the paper say about it, Hoof?"

"It says it's a most 'thrillin' account,' sir, and an 'awful tragedy,' and it vonders vhat young vomen is a-coming to next. I am pretty much of the same vay of thinking, sir, myself."

"You are in the habit of thinking very much as the newspapers do, are you not, Stephen?" asked Dunscomb.

" Vell, 'Squire Dunscomb, you've hit it! There is an onaccountable resemblance, like, in our thoughts. I hardly ever set down to read a paper, that, afore I've got half-way through it, I find it thinking just as I do! It puzzles me to know how them that writes for these papers finds out a body's thoughts so vell! "

" They have a way of doing it; but it is too long a story to go over now. So this paper has something to say about our young woman, has it, Stephen? and it mentions the Biberry business? "

" A good deal, 'Squire; and vhat I calls good sense too. Vhy, gentlemen, vhat shall we all come to, if young gals of fifteen can knock us in the head, matched, like, or in pairs, killing a whole team at one blow, and then set fire to the stables, and burn us up to our anatomies? "

" Fifteen! Does your account say that Miss Monson is only fifteen, Hoof? "

" ' She appears to be of the tender age of fifteen, and is of extr'or'nary personal attractions.' Them's the werry vords, sir; but perhaps you'd like to read it yourselves, gentlemen? "

As Stephen made this remark, he very civilly offered the journal to Dunscomb, who took it; but was not disposed to drop the conversation just then to read it, though his eye did glance at the article, as he continued the subject. This was a habit with him; his clerks often saying he could carry the chains of arguments of two subjects in his mind at the same moment. His present object was to ascertain from this man what might be the popular feeling in regard to his client, at the place they had just left, and the scene of the events themselves.

" What is thought and said, at Biberry, among those with whom you talked, Stephen, concerning this matter? "

" That it's a most awful ewent, 'Squire! One of the werry vorst that has happened in these werry vicked times, sir. I heard one gentleman go over all the murders that has taken place about York during these last ten years, and a prodigious sight on 'em there vas; so many that I began to vonder I vasn't one of the wictims myself; but he counted 'em off on his fingers, and made this out to be one of the werry vorst of 'em all, sir. He did, indeed, sir."

" Was he a reporter, Stephen? one of the persons who are sent out by the papers to collect news? "

" I believe he vas, sir. Quite a gentleman: and vith something to say to all he met. He often came out to the stables, and had a long conwersation vith as poor a feller as I be."

" Pray, what could he have to say to you, Stephen? " demanded the doctor, a little gravely.

" Oh! lots of things, sir. He began by praising the horses, and asking their names. I gave him *my* names, sir, not *yourn;* for I thought he might get it into print, somehow, that Dr. McBrain calls his coach-horses after his physic, Pill and Poleus "—" Bolus " was the real appellation that the owner had been pleased to give this beast; but as Stephen fancied the word had some connection with " polehorse," he chose to pronounce it as written. " Yes, I didn't vish *your* names to get into the papers, sir; and so I told him ' Pill ' vas called ' Marygoold,' and ' Poleus,' ' Dandelion.' He promised an article about 'em, sir; and I gave him the ages, blood, sires, and dams, of both the beauties. He told me he thought the names delightful; and I'm in hopes, sir, you'll give up *yourn,* arter all, and take to *mine* altogether."

" We shall see. And he promised an article, did he? "

" Yes, sir, quite woluntary. I know'd that the horses couldn't be outdone, and told him as much as that; for I thought, as the subject was up, it might be as vell to do 'em all the credit I could. Perhaps, vhen they gets too old for vork, you might vish to part vith 'em, sir, and then a good newspaper character could do 'em no great harm."

Stephen was a particularly honest fellow, as to things in general, but he had the infirmity which seems to be so general among men, that of a propensity to cheat in a transfer of horseflesh. Dunscomb was amused at this exhibition of character, of which he had seen so much in his day, and felt disposed to follow it up.

" I believe you had some difficulty in choosing one of the horses, Stephen "— McBrain commissioned his coachman to do all the bargaining of this sort, and had never lost a cent by his confidence— " Pill, I think it was, that didn't bring as good a character as he might have done? "

" Beg your pardon, 'Squire, 'twasn't he, but Marygoold. Vhy, the thing vas this: a gentleman of the church had bought Marygoold to go in a buggy; but soon vanted to part vith him, 'cause of his shyin' in single harness, vhich frightened his vife, *as he said.* Now all ̶ ̶ ̶ ̶ vas in this one thing—not t̶ ̶ ̶ all about the creatur's shy ̶ ̶ ̶ no great matter in double ̶ ̶ ̶ know, sir, and a body could ̶ ̶ ̶ out of the notion on it, b̶ ̶ ̶ drivin'; but the difficulty va̶ ̶ ̶ owner of a horse owned so ̶ ̶ ̶ character, there must be a great deal behind, that a feller must find out as vell as he could. I've know'd a foundered animal put off under a character for shyin'.''

"And the owner a clergyman, Stephen?''

"Perhaps not, sir. But it makes no great matter in tradin' horses; church and the world is much of a muchness.''

"Did that reporting gentleman ask any questions concerning the owner, as well as concerning the horses?''

"Vhy, yes, sir; vhen he vas done vith the animals, he did make a few observations about the doctor. He vanted to know if he vas married yet, and vhen it vas to happen; and how much I thought he might be vorth, and how much Mrs. Updyke vas counted for; and if there vas children; and vhich house the family vas to live in; and vhere he should keep the slate arter the veddin' had come off; and how much the doctor's practice vas vorth; and vhether he vas vhig or locy; and, most of all, he vanted to know vhy he and you, sir, should go to Biberry about this murder.''

"What did you tell him, Stephen, in reference to the last?''

"Vhat could I, sir? I don't know myself. I've druv' the doctor often and often to see them that has died soon arter our wisit; but I never druv' him, afore, to wisit the dead. That gentleman seemed to think he vas much mistaken about the skeletons; but it's all in the paper, sir.''

On hearing this, Dunscomb quickly turned to the columns of the journal again, and was soon reading their contents aloud to his friends; in the meantime Stephen set Marygoold and Dandelion in motion once more.

The account was much as Dunscomb expected to find it; so written as to do no possible good; while it might do a great deal of harm. The intention was to feed a morbid feeling in the vulgar for exaggerated accounts of the shocking—the motive being gain. Anything that would sell, was grist for this mill; and the more marvelous and terrible the history of the event could be made, the greater was the success likely to be. The allusions to Mary Monson were managed with a good deal of address; for, while there was a seeming respect for her rights, the reader was left to infer that her guilt was not only beyond a question, but of the darkest dye. It was while reading and commenting on these articles, that the carriage ntered Broadway, and soon set Duns- mb down at his own door. There the r left it; choosing to walk as far as

Mrs. Updyke's rather than give Stephen more materials for the reporter.

CHAPTER VI.

"Then none was for a party;
  Then all were for the state;
Then the great man help'd the poor,
  And the poor man lov'd the great:
Then lands were fairly portion'd;
  Then spoils were fairly sold;
The Romans were like brothers
  In the brave days of old.''—MACAULAY.

It has been said that John Wilmeter was left by his uncle at Biberry, to look after the welfare of their strange client. John, or Jack, as he was commonly called by his familiars, including his pretty sister, was in the main a very good fellow, though far from being free from the infirmities to which the male portion of the human family are subject, when under the age of thirty. He was frank, manly, generous, disposed to think for himself, and, what is somewhat unusual with his countrymen, of a temperament that led him to make up his mind suddenly, and was not to be easily swayed by the notions that might be momentarily floating about in the neighborhood. Perhaps a little of a spirit of opposition to the feeling that was so rapidly gaining head in Biberry inclined him to take a warmer interest in the singular female who stood charged with such enormous crimes, than he might otherwise have done.

The instructions left by Mr. Dunscomb with his nephew also gave the latter some uneasiness. In the first place, they had been very ample and thoughtful on the subject of the prisoner's comforts, which had been seen to in a way that is by no means common in a jail. Money had been used pretty freely in effecting this object, it is true; but, out of the large towns, money passes for much less on such occasions, in America, than in most other countries. The people are generally kindhearted, and considerate for the wants of others; and fair words will usually do quite as much as dollars. Dunscomb, however, had made very judicious application of both, and beyond the confinement and the fearful nature of the charges brought against her, Mary Monson had very little to complain of in her situation.

The part of his instructions which gave John Wilmeter most uneasiness, which really vexed him, related to the prisoner's innocence or guilt. The uncle distrusted; the nephew was all confidence. While the first had looked at the circumstances coolly, and was, if anything, leaning to the opinion that there might be truth in the charges, the last beheld in Mary Monson an attractive young person of the other sex, whose innocent countenance was the pledge of an innocent soul. To John, it was preposterous to entertain a charge of this nature against one so singularly gifted.

"I should as soon think of accusing Sarah of such dark offenses, as of accusing this young lady," exclaimed John to his friend Michael Millington, while the two were taking their breakfast next day. "It is preposterous—wicked—monstrous, to suppose that a young, educated female would, or could, commit such crimes. Why, Mike, she understands French and Italian, and Spanish; and I think it quite likely that she can also read German, if indeed she cannot speak it."

"How do you know this? Has she been making a display of her knowledge?"

"Not in the least—it all came out as naturally as possible. She asked for some of her own books to read, and when they were brought to her, I found that she had selected works in all four of these languages. I was quite ashamed of my own ignorance, I can assure you; which amounts to no more than a smattering of French, in the face of her Spanish, Italian and German."

"Poh! I shouldn't have minded it in the least," Michael very coolly replied, his mouth being half full of beeksteak. "The girls lead us in such things, of course. No man dreams of keeping up with a young lady who has got into the living languages. Miss Wilmeter might teach us both, and laugh at our ignorance, in the bargain."

"Sarah! Ay, she is a good enough girl, in her *way*—but no more to be compared—"

Jack Wilmeter stopped short, for Millington dropped his knife with not a little clatter, on his plate, and was gazing at his friend in a sort of fierce astonishment.

"You don't dream of comparing your sister to this unknown and suspected stranger," at length Michael got out, speaking very much like one whose head has been held under water until his breath was nearly exhausted. "You ought to recollect, John, that virtue should never be brought unnecessarily in contact with vice."

"Mike, and do you, too, believe in the guilt of Mary Monson?"

"I believe that she is committed under a verdict given by an inquest, and think it best to suspend my opinion as to the main fact, in waiting for further evidence. Remember, Jack, how often your uncle has told you that, after all, good witnesses were the *gist* of the law. Let us wait and see what a trial may bring forth."

Young Wilmeter covered his face with his hands, bowed his head to the table, and ate not another morsel that morning. His good sense admonished him of the prudence of the advice just given; while feelings, impetuous, and excited almost to fierceness, impelled him to go forth and war on all who denied the innocence of the accused. To own the truth, John Wilmeter was fast becoming entangled in the meshes of love.

And, sooth to say, notwithstanding the extreme awkwardness of her situation, the angry feeling that was so fast rising up against her in Biberry and its vicinity, and the general mystery that concealed her real name, character and history, there was that about Mary Monson, in her countenance, other personal advantages, and most of all in her manner and voice, that might well catch the fancy of a youth of warm feelings, and through his fancy, sooner or later, touch his heart. As yet, John was only under the influence of the new-born sentiment, and had he now been removed from Biberry, it is probable that the feelings and interest which had been so suddenly and powerfully awakened in him would have passed away altogether, or remained in shadow on his memory, as a melancholy and yet pleasant record of hours past, under circumstances in which men live fast, if they do not always live well. Little did the uncle think of the great danger to which he exposed his nephew, when he placed him, like a sentinel in law, on duty near the portal of his immured client. But the experienced Dunscomb was anxious to bring John into active life, and to place him in situations that might lead him to think and execute for himself; and it had been much his practice, of late, to put the young man forward, whenever circumstances would admit of it.

Although the counselor was more than at his ease in fortune, and John and Sarah each possessed very respectable means, that placed them altogether above dependence, he was exceedingly anxious that his nephew should succeed to his own business, as the surest mode of securing his happiness and respectability in a community where the number of the idle is relatively so small as to render the pursuits of a class, that is by no means without its uses where it can be made to serve the tastes and manners of a country, difficult of attainment. He had the same desire in behalf of his niece, or that she should become the wife of a man who had something to do : and the circumstance that Millington, though of highly reputable connections, was almost entirely without fortune, was no objection in his eyes to the union that Sarah was so obviously inclined to form. The two young men had been left on the ground, therefore, to take care of the interests of a client who Dunscomb was compelled to admit was one that interested him more than any other in whose services he had ever been employed, strongly as he was disposed to fear that appearances might be deceitful.

Our young men were not idle. In addition to doing all that was in their power to contribute to the personal comforts of Miss Monson, they were active and intelligent in obtaining and making notes of all the facts that had been drawn out by the coroner's inquest, or which could be gleaned in the neighborhood. These facts, or rumors, John classed into the " proved," the "reported," the "probable," and the "improbable ; " accompanying each division with such annotations as made a very useful sort of brief for any one who wished to push the inquiries further.

" There, Millington," he said when they reached the jail, on their return from a walk as far as the ruins of the house which had been burned, and after they had dined ; " there, I think we have done tolerably well for one day, and are in a fair way to give Uncle Tom a pretty full account of this miserable business. The more I see and learn of it, the more I am convinced of the perfect innocence of the accused. I trust it strikes you in the same way, Mike ? "

But Mike was by no means as sanguine as his friend. He smiled faintly at this question, and endeavored to evade a direct answer. He saw how lively were the hopes of Tom, and how deeply his feelings were getting to be interested in the matter ; while his own judgment, influenced, perhaps, by Mr. Dunscomb's example, greatly inclined him to the worst foreboding of the result. Still he had an honest satisfaction in saying anything that might contribute to the gratification of Sarah's brother, and a good opportunity now offering, he did not let it escape him.

" There is one thing, Jack, that seems to have been strangely overlooked," he said, "and out of which some advantage may come, if it be thoroughly sifted. You may remember it was stated by some of the witnesses, that there was a German woman in the family of the Goodwins, the day that preceded the fire—one employed in housework ? "

" Now you mention it, I do ! Sure enough ; what has become of that woman ? "

"While you were drawing your diagram of the ruins, and projecting your plan of the out-buildings, garden, fields, and so on, I stepped across to the nearest house, and had a chat with the ladies. You may remember I told you it was to get a drink of milk ; but I saw petticoats, and thought something might be learned from woman's propensity to talk."

" I know you left me, but I was too busy, just then, to see on what errand, or whither you went."

" It was to the old stone farm-house that stands only fifty rods from the ruins. The family in possession is named Burton, and a more talkative set I never encountered in petticoats."

" How many had you to deal with, Mike ? " John inquired, running his eyes over his notes, as he asked the question, in a way that showed how little he anticipated from this interview with the Burtons. "If more than one of the garrulous set, I pity you, for I had a specimen of them yesterday morning myself, in a passing interview."

" There were three talkers, and one silent body. As is usual, I thought that the silent member of the house knew more than the speakers, if she had been inclined to let out her knowledge."

"Ay, that is a way we have of judging of one another ; but it is as often false as true. As many persons are silent because they have nothing to say, as because they are reflecting ; and of those who *look* very wise, about one half, as near as I can judge, *look* so as a sort of apology for being very silly."

" I can't say how it was with Mrs. Burton, the silent member of the family, in this case ; but I do know that her three worthy sisters-in-law are to be classed among the foolish virgins."

" Had they no oil to trim their lamps withal ? "

" It had all been used to render their tongues limber. Never did three damsels pour out words in so full a rivulet, as I was honored with for the first five minutes. By the end of that time. I was enabled to put a question or two ; after which they were better satisfied to let me interrogate, while they were content to answer."

"Did you learn anything, Mike, to reward you for all this trouble ? " again glancing at his notes.

" I think I did. With a good deal of difficulty *eliminating* the surplusage, if I may coin a word for the occasion, I got these facts : It would seem that the German woman was a newly-arrived immigrant, who had strolled into the country, and offered to work for her food, etc. Mrs. Goodwin usually attended to all her own domestic matters; but she had an attack of rheumatism that predisposed her to receive this offer, and that so much the more willingly, because the 'help' was not to be paid. It appears that the deceased female was an odd mixture of miserly propensities with a love of display. She hoarded all she could lay her hands on, and took a somewhat uncommon pleasure in showing her hoards to her neighbors. In consequence of this last weakness, the whole neighborhood knew not only of her gold, for she turned every coin into that metal before it was consigned to her stocking, but of the amount to a dollar, and the place where she kept it. In this all agreed, even to the silent matron."

"And what has become of this German?" asked John, closing his notes with sudden interest. "Why was she not examined before the inquest? and where is she now?"

"No one knows. She has been missing ever since the fire, and a few fancy that she may, after all, be the person who has done the whole mischief. It does wear a strange look, that no trace can be heard of her!"

"This must be looked into closely, Mike. It is unaccountably strange that more was not said of her before the coroner. Yet, I fear one thing, too. Doctor McBrain is a man of the highest attainments as an anatomist, and you will remember that he inclines to the opinion that both the skeletons belonged to females. Now, it may turn out that this German woman's remains have been found; which will put her guilt out of the question."

"Surely, Jack, you would not be sorry to have it turn out that any human being should be innocent of such crimes!"

"By no means; though it really does seem to me more probable that an unknown straggler should be the guilty one in this case, than an educated young female, who has every claim in the way of attainments to be termed a lady. Besides, Michael, these German immigrants have brought more than their share of crime among us. Look at the reports of murders and robberies for the last ten years, and you will find that an undue proportion of them have been committed by this class of immigrants. To me, nothing appears more probable than this affair's being traced up to that very woman."

"I own you are right, in saying what you do of the Germans. But it should be remembered, that some of their states are said to have adopted the policy of sending their rogues to America. If *England* were to attempt that now, I fancy Jonathan would hardly stand it!"

"He ought not to stand it for an hour, from any nation on earth. If there ever was a good cause for war, this is one. Yes, yes; that German immigrant must be looked up, and examined."

Michael Millington smiled faintly at John Wilmeter's disposition to believe the worst of the High Dutch; touching the frailties of whom, however, neither of the two had exaggerated anything. Far more than their share of the grave crimes of this country have, within the period named, been certainly committed by immigrants from Germany; whether the cause be in the reason given, or in national character. This is not according to ancient opinion, but we believe it to be strictly according to fact. The Irish are clannish, turbulent, and much disposed to knock each other on the head; but it is not to rob, or to pilfer, but to quarrel. The Englishman will pick your pocket, or commit burglary, when inclined to roguery, and frequently he has a way of his own of extorting, in the way of vails. The Frenchmen may well boast of their freedom from wrongs done to persons or property in this country; no class of immigrants furnishing to the prisons, comparatively, fewer criminals. The natives, out of all proportion, are freest from crime, if the blacks be excepted, and when we compare the number of the convicted with the number of the people. Still, such results ought not to be taken as furnishing absolute rules by which to judge of large bodies of men; since unsettled lives on the one hand, and the charities of life on the other, may cause disproportions that would not otherwise exist.

"If one of these skeletons be that of the German woman, and Dr. McBrain should prove to be right," said John Wilmeter, earnestly, "what has become of the remains of Mr. Goodwin? There was a husband as well as a wife, in that family."

"Very true," answered Millington; "and I learned something concerning him, too. It seems that the old fellow drank intensely, at times, when he and his wife made the house too hot to hold them. All the Burtons agreed in giving this account of the good couple. The failing was not generally known, and had not yet gone so far as to affect the old man's general character, though it would seem to have been known to the immediate neighbors."

"And not one word of all this is to be found in any of the reports in the papers from town! Not a particle of testimony on the point before the inquest! Why, Mike, this single fact may furnish a clew to the whole catastrophe."

"In what way?" Millington very quietly inquired.

"Those bones are the bones of females; old Goodwin has robbed the house, set fire to it, murdered his wife and the German woman in a drunken frolic, and run away. Here is a history for Uncle Tom that will delight him; for if he do not feel quite certain of Mary Monson's innocence now, he would be delighted to learn its truth!"

"You make much out of a very little, Jack; and imagine far more than you can prove. Why should old Goodwin set fire to his own house—for I understand the property was his—steal his own money"—for, though married women did then hold a separate estate in a bed-quilt, or a gridiron, the law could not touch the previous accumulations of a *femme coverte*—"and murder a poor foreigner, who could neither give nor take away anything that the building contained? Then he is to burn his own house, and make himself a vagrant in his old age—and that among strangers! I learn that he was born in that very house, and has passed his days in it. Such a man would not be very likely to destroy it."

"Why not, to conceal a murder? Crime must be concealed, or it is punished."

"Sometimes," returned Michael, dryly. "This Mary Monson will be hanged, out of all question, should the case go against her, for she understands French, and Italian, and German, you say; either of which tongues would be sufficient to hang her; but had old Mrs. Goodwin murdered *her*, philanthropy would have been up and stirring, and no rope would be stretched."

"Millington, you have a way of talking at times that is quite shocking! I do wish you could correct it. What use is there in bringing a young lady like Miss Monson down to the level of a common criminal?"

"She will be brought down as low as that, depend on it, if guilty. There is no hope for one who bears about her person, in air, manner, speech, and deportment, the unequivocal signs of a lady. Our sympathies are all kept for those who are less set apart from the common herd. Sympathy goes by majorities, as well as other matters."

"You think her, at all events, a lady?" said John, quickly. "How then, can you suppose it possible that she has been guilty of the crimes of which she stands accused?"

"Simply because my old-fashioned father has given me old-fashioned notions of the meaning of terms. So thin-skinned have people become lately, that even language must be perverted to gratify their conceit. The terms 'gentleman' and 'lady' have as defined meanings as any two words we possess—signifying persons of cultivated minds, and of certain refinements in tastes and manners. Morals have nothing to do with either, necessarily, as a 'gentleman' or 'lady' may be very wicked; nay, often are. It is true there are particular acts, partaking of meanness, rather than anything decidedly criminal, that, by convention, a gentleman or lady may not commit; but there are a hundred others, that are far worse, which are not prohibited. It is unladylike to *talk* scandal; but it is not deemed always unladylike to give grounds to scandal. Here is a bishop who has lately been defining a gentleman, and, as usually happens with such men, unless they were originally on a level with their dioceses, he describes a 'Christian' rather than a 'gentleman.' This notion of making converts by means of enlisting our vanity and self-love in the cause, is but a weak one at the best."

"Certainly, Mike; I agree with you in the main. As large classes of polished people do exist, who have loose enough notions of morals, there ought to be terms to designate them, as a class, as well as to give any other name, when we have the thing. Use has applied those of 'gentlemen' and 'ladies,' and I can see no sufficient reason for changing them."

"It comes wholly from the longings of human vanity. As a certain distinction is attached to the term, everybody is covetous of obtaining it, and all sorts of reasoning is resorted to, to drag them into the categories. It would be the same, if it were a ground of distinction, to have but one ear. But this distinction will be very likely to make things go hard with our client, Jack, if the jury say 'guilty.'"

"The jury never can—never *will* render such a verdict! I do not think the grand jury will even return a bill. Why should they? The testimony wouldn't convict an old state-prison bird."

Michael Millington smiled, a little sadly, perhaps—for John Wilmeter was Sarah's only brother—but he made no reply, perceiving that an old negro, named Sip, or Scipio, who lived about the jail by a sort of sufferance, and who had now been a voluntary adherent of a place that was usually so unpleasant to men of his class for many years, was approaching, as if he were the bearer of a message. Sip was an old-school black, gray-headed, and had seen more than his three-score years and ten. No wonder, then, that his dialect partook, in a considerable degree, of the peculiarities that were once so marked in a Manhattan "nigger." Unlike his brethren of the present day, he was courtesy itself to all "gentlemen," while his respect for "common folks" was a good deal more equivocal. But chiefly did the old man despise "yaller fellers"; these he regarded as a mongrel race, who could neither aspire to the pure complexion of the Circassian stock, nor lay claim to the glistening dye of Africa.

"Mrs. Gott, she want to see masser," said Scipio, bowing to John, grinning— for a negro seldom loses his teeth—and turning civilly to Millington, with a respectful inclination of the head that was as white as snow. "Yes, sah; she want to see masser, soon as conbe'nent, and soon as he can come."

Now Mrs. Gott was the wife of the sheriff, and, alas! for the dignity of the office! the sheriff was the keeper of the county lail. This is one of the fruits born on the widespreading branches of the tree of democracy. Formerly a New York sheriff bore a strong resemblance to his English cousin. He was one of the country gentry, and executed the duties of his office with an air and a manner; appeared in court with a sword, and carried with his name a weight and an authority that now are nearly wanting. Such men would scarcely become jailers. But that universal root of all evil, the love of money, made the discovery that there was profit to be had in feeding the prisoners, and a lower class of men aspired to the offices, and obtained them; since which time, more than half the sheriffs of New York have been their own jailers.

"Do you know *why* Mrs. Gott wishes to see me, Scipio?" demanded Wilmeter.

"I b'lieve, sah, dat 'e young woman as murders old Masser Goodwin and he wife, asked her to send for masser."

This was plain enough, and it caused Jack a severe pang; for it showed how conclusively and unsparingly the popular mind had made up its opinion touching Mary Monson's guilt. There was no time to be lost, however; and the young man hastened toward the building to which the jail was attached, both standing quite near the court-house. In the door of what was her dwelling, for the time being, stood Mrs. Gott, the wife of the high sheriff of the county, and the only person in all Biberry who, as it appeared to John, entertained his own opinions of the innocence of the accused. But Mrs. Gott was, by nature, a kind-hearted woman; and, though so flagrantly out of place in her united characters, was just such a person as ought to have the charge of the female department of a prison.

Owing to the constant changes of the democratic principle of rotation in office, one of the most impudent of all the devices of a covetous envy, this woman had not many months before come out of the bosom of society, and had not seen enough of the ways of her brief and novel situation to have lost any of those qualities of her sex, such as extreme kindness, gentleness of disposition, and feminine feeling, that are anything but uncommon among the women of America. In many particulars, she would have answered the imaginative bishop's description of a "lady;" but she would have been sadly deficient in some of the requisites that the opinions of the world have attached to the character. In these last particulars, Mary Monson, as compared with this worthy matron, was like a being of another race; though, as respects the first, we shall refer the reader to the events to be hereafter related, that he may decide the question according to his own judgment.

"Mary Monson has sent for you, Mr. Wilmeter," the good Mrs. Gott commenced, in a low, confidential sort of tone, as if she imagined that she and John were the especial guardians of this unknown and seemingly ill-fated young woman's fortunes. "She is wonderfully resigned and patient—a great deal more patient than I should be, if I was obliged to live in this jail—that is, on the other side of the strong doors; but she told me, an hour ago, that she is not sure, after all, her imprisonment is not the very best thing that could happen to her!"

"That was a strange remark!" returned John. "Did she make it under a show of feeling, as if penitence, or any other strong emotion, induced her to utter it?"

"With as sweet a smile, as composed a manner, and as gentle and soft a voice as a body ever sees, or listens to! What a wonderfully soft and musical voice she has, Mr. Wilmeter!"

"She has, indeed. I was greatly struck with it, the moment I heard her speak. How much like a lady, Mrs. Gott, she uses it—and how correct and well-pronounced are her words!"

Although Mrs. Gott and John Wilmeter had very different ideas, at the bottom of the requisites to form a lady, and the pronunciation of the good woman was by no means faultless, she cordially assented to the truth of the young man's eulogy. Indeed, Mary Monson, for the hour, was her great theme; and, though still a young woman herself, and good-looking withal, she really seemed never to tire of uttering her praises.

"She has been educated, Mr. Wilmeter, far above any female hereabouts, unless it may be some of the ——s and ——s," the good woman continued. "Those families, you know, are our upper crust—not upper ten thousand, as the newspapers call it, but upper hundred, and their ladies may know as much as Mary; but, beyond *them*, no female hereabouts can hold a candle to her! Her books have been brought in, and I looked them over—there isn't more than one in three that I can read at all. What is more, they don't seem to be all in one tongue, the foreign books, but in three or four."

"She certainly has a knowledge of several of the living languages, and an accurate knowledge, too. I know a little of such things myself, but my friend Millington is quite strong in both the living and dead languages, and he says that what she knows she knows well."

"That is comforting—for a young lady that can speak so many different tongues would hardly think of robbing and murdering two old people in their beds. Well, sir, perhaps you had better go to the door and see her, though I could stay here and talk about her all day. Pray, Mr. Wilmeter, which of the languages is really dead?"

John smiled, but civilly enlightened the sheriff's lady on this point, and then, preceded by her, he went to the important door which separated the dwelling of the family from the rooms of the jail. Once opened, an imperfect communication is obtained with the interior of the last, by means of a grating in an inner door. The jail of Dukes County is a recent construction, and is built on a plan that is coming much into favor, though still wanting in the highest proof of civilization, by sufficiently separating criminals, and in treating the accused with a proper degree of consideration, until the verdict of a jury has pronounced them guilty.

The construction of this jail was very simple. A strong, low, oblong building had been erected on a foundation so filled in with stones as to render digging nearly impossible. The floors were of large, massive stones, that ran across the whole building, a distance of some thirty feet, or if there were joints, they were under the partition walls, rendering them as secure as if solid. The cells were not large,

certainly, but of sufficient size to admit of light and air. The ceilings were of the same enormous flat stones as the floors, well secured by a load of stones, and beams to brace them, and the partitions were of solid masonry. There the prisoner is incased in stone, and nothing can be more hopeless than an attempt to get out of one of these cells, provided the jailer gives even ordinary attention to their condition. Above and around them are erected the outer walls of the jail. The last comprise an ordinary stone house, with roof, windows, and the other customary appliances of a human abode. As these walls stand several feet without those of the real prison, and are somewhat higher, the latter are an *imperium in imperio;* a house within a house. The space between the walls of the two buildings forms a gallery extending around all the cells. Iron grated gates divide the several parts of this gallery into so many compartments, and in the jail of Biberry care has been had so to arrange these subdivisions that those within any one compartment may be concealed from those in all of the others but the two that immediately join it. The breezes are admitted by means of the external windows, while the height of the ceiling in the galleries, and the space above the tops of the cells, contribute largely to comfort and health in this important particular. As the doors of the cells stand opposite to the windows, the entire jail can be, and usually is, made airy and light. Stoves in the galleries preserve the temperature, and effectually remove all disagreeable moisture.

In a word, the place is as neat, convenient, and decent as the jail of convicts need ever to be; but the proper sort of distinction is not attended to between them and those who are merely accused. Our civilization in this respect is defective. While the land is filled with senseless cries against an aristocracy which, if it exists at all, exists in the singular predicament of being far less favored than the democracy, involving a contradiction in terms; against a feudality that consists in men's having bargained to pay their debts in chickens, no one complaining in behalf of those who have entered into contracts to do the same in wheat; and against *rent*, while *usury* is not only smiled on, but encouraged, and efforts are made to legalize extortion—the public mind is quiet on the subject of the treatment of those who the policy of government demands should be kept in security until their guilt or innocence be established. What reparation, under such circumstances, can be made to him to whom the gates are finally opened, for having been incarcerated on charges that are groundless? The jails of the Christian world were first constructed by an irresponsible power, and to confine the weak. We imitate the vices of the system with a cold indifference, and shout "feudality" over a bantam, or a pound of butter, that are paid under contracted covenants for rent!

CHAPTER VII.

"Sir, this is the house; please it you that I call?"
—TAMING OF THE SHREW.

THE grated window, which John Wilmeter now approached, commanded nearly an entire view of the gallery that communicated with the cell of Mary Monson. It also commanded a partial view of the cell itself. As he looked through the grates, he saw how neat and comfortable the last had been made by means of Mrs. Gott's care, aided, doubtless, by some of the prisoner's money—that gold which was, in fact, the strongest and only very material circumstance against her. Mrs. Gott had put a carpet in the cell, and divers pieces of furniture that were useful, as well as two or three that were intended to be ornamental, rendering the otherwise gloomy little apartment tolerably cheerful. The gallery, much to John's surprise, had been furnished also. Pieces of new carpeting were laid on the flags, chairs and table had been provided, and, among other articles of this nature, was a very respectable looking-glass. Everything appeared new, and as if just sent from the different shops where the various articles were sold. Wilmeter fancied that not less than a hundred dollars had been expended in furnishing that gallery. The effect was surprising; taking away from the place the chilling, jail-like air, and giving to it what it had never possessed before, one of household comfort.

Mary Monson was walking to and fro, in this gallery, with slow, thoughtful steps, her head a little bowed, and her hands hanging before her, with the fingers interlocked. So completely was she lost in thought, that John's footstep, or presence at the grate, was not observed, and he had an opportunity to watch her for near a minute, unseen himself. The occupation was not exactly excusable; but, under all the circumstances, young Wilmeter felt as if it might be permitted. It was his duty to ascertain all he fairly might, concerning his client.

It has already been said that this strange girl, extraordinary by her situation as a person accused of crimes so heinous, and perhaps still more so by her manner of bearing up against the terrors and mortifications of her condition, as well as by the mystery which so completely veiled her past life, was not a beauty, in the common acceptation of the term. Nevertheless, not one female in ten thousand would sooner ensnare the heart of a youth, by means of her personal attractions alone. It was not regularity of features, nor brilliancy of complexion, nor luster of the eyes, nor any of the more ordinary charms, that gave her this power; but an indescribable union of feminine traits, in which intellectual gifts, spirit, tenderness, and modesty, were so singularly blended as to leave it questionable which had the advantage. Her eyes were of a very gentle and mild expression, when in a state of rest; excited, they were capable of opening windows to the inmost soul. Her form was faultless; being the true medium between vigorous health and womanly delicacy; which, in this country, implies much less of the robust and solid than one meets with in the other hemisphere.

It is not easy to tell how we acquired those in-and-in habits, which get to be a sort of second nature, and almost bestow on us new instincts. It is by these secret sympathies, these tastes that pervade the moral, as the nerves form a natural telegraph through the physical system, that one *feels* rather than *sees*, when he is in the company of persons in his own class of life. Dress will not afford an infallible test on such an occasion, though the daw is instantly seen not to be the peacock; neither will *add*ress, for the distinctive qualities lie much deeper than the surface. But so it is; a gentleman can hardly be brought into the company of man or woman without his at once perceiving whether he or she belongs to his own social caste or not. What is more, if a man of the world, he detects almost instinctively the *degrees* of caste, as well as the greater subdivisions, and knows whether his strange companions have seen much, or little; whether their gentility is merely the result of the great accident, with its customary advantages, or has been smoothed over by a liberal intercourse with the better classes of a general society. Most of all, may a traveled person be known—and that more especially in a provincial country like our own —from one that has not traveled; though the company kept in other lands necessarily draws an obvious distinction between the last. Now, John Wilmeter, always mingling with the best society of his own country, had also been abroad, and had obtained that "second-sight" which so insensibly, but certainly, increases the vision of all Americans who enjoy the advantage of acquiring it.

What is more, though his years and the plans of his uncle for his future welfare had prevented his staying in Europe long enough to receive all the benefit such a tour can bestow, he had remained long enough to pass beyond the study of merely physical things; and had made certain acquisitions in other matters, more essential to taste, if not to character. When an American returns from an excursion into the Old World, with "I come back better satisfied than ever with my own country," it is an infallible sign that he did not stay long enough abroad; and when he returns only to find fault, it is equally proof that he has stayed too long. There is a happy medium which teaches something near the truth, and that would tell us that there are a thousand things to be amended and improved at home, while there are almost as many enjoyed, that the oldest and most polished people on earth might envy. John Wilmeter had not reached the point that enabled him to make the nicest distinctions, but he was sufficiently advanced to have detected what he conceived to be signs that this singular young creature, unknown, unsupported by any who appeared to take an interest in her, besides himself and the accidental acquaintances formed under the most painful circumstances, had been abroad; perhaps had been educated there. The regulated tones of one of the sweetest voices he had ever heard, the distinctness and precision of her utterance, as far as possible removed from mouthing and stiffness, but markedly quiet and even, with a total absence of all the affectations of boarding-school grammar, were so many proofs of even a European education, as he fancied; and before that week was terminated, John had fully made up his mind that Mary Monson—though an American by birth, about which there could be no dispute—had been well taught in some of the schools of the Old World.

This was a conclusion not reached immediately. He had to be favored with several interviews, and to worm himself gradually into the confidence of his uncle's client, ere he could be permitted to see enough of the subject of his studies to form an opinion so abstruse and ingenious.

When Mary Monson caught a glimpse of John Wilmeter's head at her grate— where he stood respectfully uncovered, as in a lady's presence—a slight flush passed over her face; but expecting him, as she did, she could not well be surprised.

"This bears some resemblance, Mr. Wilmeter, to an interview in a convent," she then said, with a slight smile, but with perfect composure of manner. "I am the novice—and novice am I, indeed, to scenes like this — you, the excluded friend, who is compelled to pay his visit through a grate! I must apologize for all the trouble I am giving you."

"Do not name it—I cannot be better employed than in your behalf. I am rejoiced that you sustain yourself so well against what must be a most unheard-of calamity for one like yourself, and cannot but admire the admirable equanimity with which you bear your cruel fortune."

"Equanimity!" repeated Mary, with emphasis, and a slight display of intense feeling powerfully controlled; "if it be so, Mr. Wilmeter, it must be from the sense of security that I feel. Yes; for the first time in months, I do feel myself safe—secure."

"Safe! Secure! What, in a jail?"

"Certainly; jails are intended for places of security, are they not?" answered Mary, smiling, but faintly and with a gleam of sadness on her face. "This may appear wonderful to you, but I do tell no more than sober truth, in repeating that, for the first time in months, I have now a sense of security. I am what you call in the hands of the law, and one there must be safe from everything but what the law can do to her. Of that I have no serious apprehensions, and I feel happy."

"Happy!"

"Yes; by comparison, happy. I tell you this the more willingly, for I plainly see you feel a generous interest in my welfare—an interest which exceeds that of the counsel in his client—"

"A thousands times exceeds it, Miss Monson! Nay—is not to be named with it!"

"I thank you, Mr. Wilmeter—from my heart I thank you," returned the prisoner, a slight flush passing over her features, while her eyes were cast toward the floor. "I believe you are one of strong feelings and quick impulses, and am grateful that these have been in my favor, under circumstances that might well have excused you for thinking the worst. From the hints of this kind woman, Mrs. Gott, I am afraid that the opinion of Biberry is less consoling!"

"You must know how it is in country villages, Miss Monson—every one has something to say, and every one brings all things down to the level of his own knowledge and understanding."

Mary Monson smiled again; this time more naturally, and without any painful expression to lessen the bright influence that lighting up of her features gave to a countenance so remarkable for its appearance of illumination from within.

"Is not such the case in towns, as well as in villages, Mr. Wilmeter?" she asked.

"Perhaps it is; but I mean that the circle of knowledge is more confined in a place like this than in a large town, and that the people here could not well go beyond it."

"Biberry is so near New York that I should think, taking class against class, no great difference can be found in their inhabitants. That which the good folk of Biberry think of my case, I am afraid will be thought of it by those of your own town."

"*My* own town?—and are you not really from New York, Miss Monson."

"In no manner," answered Mary, once more smiling; this time, however, because she understood how modestly and readily her companion was opening a door by which she might let a secret she had declined to reveal to his uncle, escape. "I am not what you call a Manhattanese, in either descent, birth, or residence; in no sense whatever."

"But, surely, you have never been educated in the country? You must belong to some large town—your manners show that—I mean that you—"

"Do not belong to Biberry. In that you are quite right, sir. I had never seen Biberry three months since; but, as for New York, I have not passed a month there in my whole life. The longest visit I ever paid you was one of ten days, when I landed, coming from Havre, about eighteen months since."

"From Havre! Surely you are an American, Miss Monson—our own countrywoman?"

"Your own countrywoman, Mr. Wilmeter, by birth, descent, and feelings. But an American female may visit Europe."

"Certainly; and be educated there, as I had already suspected was your case."

"In part it was, and in part it was not." Here Mary paused, looked a little arch, seemed to hesitate, and to have some doubts whether she ought to proceed or not; but finally added—"You have been abroad yourself?"

"I have. I was nearly three years in Europe; and have not been home yet quite a twelvemonth."

"You went into the East, I believe, after passing a few months in the Pyrenees?" continued the prisoner, carelessly.

"You are quite right; we traveled as far as Jerusalem. The journey has got to be so common that it is no longer dangerous. Even ladies make it now without any apprehension."

"I am aware of that, having made it myself—"

"You, Miss Monson! You have been at Jerusalem!"

"Why not, Mr. Wilmeter? You say yourself, that females constantly make the journey; why not I as well as another?"

"I scarce know, myself; but it is so strange—all about you is so very extraordinary—"

"You think it extraordinary that one of my sex, who has been partly educated in Europe, and who has traveled in the Holy Land, should be shut up in this jail in Biberry—is it not so?"

"That is one view of the matter, I will confess; but it was scarcely less strange that such a person should be dwelling in a garret-room of a cottage like that of these unfortunate Goodwins."

"That touches my secret, sir; and no more need be said. You may judge how important I consider that secret, when I know its preservation subjects me to the most cruel distrust; and that, too, in the minds of those with whom I would so gladly stand fair. Your excellent uncle, for instance, and—yourself."

"I should be much flattered could I think the last—I who have scarcely the claim of an acquaintance."

"You forget the situation in which your respectable and most worthy uncle has left you here, Mr. Wilmeter; which of itself gives you higher claims to my thanks and confidence than any that mere acquaintance could bestow. Besides, we are not"—another arch, but scarcely perceptible, smile again illumined that remarkable countenance—"the absolute strangers to each other that you seem to think us."

"Not strangers? You amaze me! If I have ever had the honor—"

"Honor!" interrupted Mary, a little bitterly. "It is truly a great honor to know one in my situation!"

"I esteem it an honor; and no one has a right to call in question my sincerity. If we have ever met before, I will frankly own that I am ignorant of both the time and place."

"This does not surprise me in the least. The time is long, for persons as young as ourselves, and the place was far away. Ah! those were happy days for me, and most gladly would I return to them! But we have talked enough on this subject. I have declined telling my tale to your most excellent and very respectable uncle; you will, therefore, the more easily excuse me if I decline telling it to yon."

"Who am not 'most excellent and very respectable,' to recommend me."

"Who are too near my own age to make you a proper confidant, were there no other objection. The character that I learned of you, when we met before, Mr. Wilmeter, was, however, one of which you have no reason to be ashamed."

This was said gently, but earnestly; was accompanied by a most winning smile, and was instantly succeeded by a slight blush. John Wilmeter rubbed his forehead, sooth to say, in a somewhat stupid manner, as if expecting to brighten his powers of recollection by friction. A sudden change was given to the conversation, however, by the fair prisoner herself, who quietly resumed:

"We will defer this part of the subject to another time. I did not presume to send for you, Mr. Wilmeter, without an object, having your uncle's authority for giving you all this trouble—"

"And my own earnest request to be permitted to serve you in any way I could."

"I have not forgotten that offer, nor shall I ever. The man who is willing to serve a woman whom all around her frown on has a fair claim to be remembered. Good Mrs. Gott and yourself are the only two friends I have in Biberry. Even your companion, Mr. Millington, is a little disposed to judge me harshly."

John started; the movement was so natural that his honest countenance would have betrayed him had he been disposed to deny the imputation.

"That Millington has fallen into the popular notion about here, I must allow, Miss Monson; but he is an excellent fellow at the bottom, and will hear reason. Prejudices that are beyond reason are detestable, and I generally avoid those whose characters manifest this weakness; but Mike will always listen to what he calls 'law and facts,' and so we get along very well together."

"It is fortunate; since you are about to be so nearly connected—"

"Connected! Is it possible that *you* know this circumstance?"

"You will find in the end, Mr. Wilmeter," returned the prisoner, smiling—this time naturally, as one manifests satisfaction without pain of any sort—"that I know more of your private affairs than you had supposed. But let me come

to business, if you please, sir. I have great occasion here for a maid-servant. Do you not think that Miss Wilmeter might send me one from town?"

"A servant! I know the very woman that will suit you. A perfect jewel, in her way!"

"That is a very housekeeper sort of a character," rejoined Mary, absolutely laughing, in spite of her prison walls and all the terrible charges that had brought her within them; "just such a character as I might have expected from Doctor McBrain's intended, Mrs. Updyke—"

"And you know it, too! Why will you not tell us more, since you tell us so much?"

"In good time I suppose all will come out. Well, I endeavor to submit to my fate, or to the will of God!" There was no longer anything merry in voice, face, or manner, but a simple, natural pathos was singularly mixed in the tones with which those few words were uttered. Then rousing herself, she gravely resumed the subject which had induced her to send for John.

"You will pardon me if I say that I would prefer a woman chosen and recommended by your sister, Mr. Wilmeter, than one chosen and recommended by yourself," said Mary. "When I shall have occasion for a footman, I shall take your advice. It is very important that I should engage a respectable, discreet woman; and I will venture to write a line myself to Miss Wilmeter, if you will be so kind as to send it. I know this is not the duty of a counsel; but you see my situation. Mrs. Gott has offered to procure a girl for me, it is true; but the prejudice is so strong against me in Biberry that I doubt if the proper sort of person could be obtained. At any rate, I should be receiving a spy into my little household, instead of a domestic in whom I could place confidence."

"Sarah would join me in recommending Marie, who has been with herself more than two years, and only left her to take care of her father in his last illness. Another, equally excellent, has been taken in her place; and now that she wishes to return to my sister's service, there is no opening for her. Mike Millington is dying to return to town, and will gladly go over this evening. By breakfast-time to-morrow the woman might be here, if—"

"She will consent to serve a mistress in my cruel situation. I feel the full weight of the objection, and know how difficult it will be to get a female, who values her character as a servant, to enter on such an engagement. You called this woman Marie ; by that I take it she is a foreigner ? ''

"A Swiss—her parents emigrated ; but I knew her in the service of an American family abroad and got her for Sarah. She is the best creature in the world—if she can be persuaded to come."

"Had she been an American I should have despaired of succeeding, unless her feelings could have been touched ; but, as she is a foreigner, perhaps money will procure her service. Should Miss Wilmeter approve of your selection, sir, I will entreat her to go as high as fifty dollars a month, rather than not get the sort of person I want. You can imagine how much importance I attach to success. To escape remarks and gossiping, the person engaged can join me as a companion, or friend, and not as a servant."

"I will get Mike off in half an hour, and Sarah will at least make an effort. Yes, Marie Moulin, or Mary Mill, as the girls call her, is just the thing ! "

"Marie Moulin ! Is that the name of the woman ? She who was in the service of the Barringers, at Paris ? Do you mean *that* person—five and thirty, slightly pockmarked, with light-blue eyes, and yellowish hair—more like a German than her French name would give reason to expect ? "

"The very same ; and you knew her, *too !* Why not bring all your friends around you at once, Miss Monson, and not remain here an hour longer than is necessary ?"

Mary was too intent on the subject of engaging the woman in question to answer this last appeal. Earnestly did she resume her instructions, therefore, and with an eagerness of manner young Wilmeter had never before observed in her.

"If Marie Moulin be the person meant," she said, " I will spare no pains to obtain her services. Her attentions to Mrs. Barringer, in her last illness, were admirable ; and we all loved her, I may say. Beg your sister to tell her, Mr. Wilmeter, that an old acquaintance, in distress, implores her assistance. That will bring Marie, sooner than money, Swiss though she be."

"If you would write her a line, inclosing your real name—for we are persuaded it is not Monson—it might have more effect than all our solicitations in behalf of one that is unknown."

The prisoner turned slowly from the grate and walked up and down her gallery for a minute or two, as if pondering on this proposal. Once she smiled, and it almost gave a luster to her remarkable countenance ; then a cloud passed over her face, and once more she appeared sad.

"No," she said, stopping near the grate again, in one of her turns. "I will not do it—it will be risking too much. I can do nothing just now that will tell more of me than your sister can state."

"Should Marie Moulin know you, she must recognize you when you meet."

"It will be wiser to proceed a little in the dark. I confide all to your powers of negotiation, and shall remain as tranquil as possible until to-morrow morning. There is still another little affair that I must trouble you with, Mr. Wilmeter. My gold is sequestered, as you know, and I am reduced to an insufficient amount of twos and threes. Might I ask the favor of you to obtain smaller notes for this, without mentioning in whose behalf it is done ? "

While speaking, Mary handed through the grate a hundred dollar note of one of the New York banks, with a manner so natural and unpretending as at once to convince John Wilmeter, ever so willing to be persuaded into anything in her favor, that she was accustomed to the use of money in considerable sums ; or, what might be considered so, for the wants and habits of a female. Luckily, he had nearly money enough in his wallet to change the note, making up a small balance that was needed, by drawing five half-eagles from his purse. The prisoner held the last in the open palm of one of the most beautiful little hands the eyes of man ever rested on.

"This metal has been my bane, in more ways than one, Mr. Wilmeter," she said, looking mournfully at the coin. "Of one of its evil influences on my fate I may not speak now, if ever ; but you will understand me when I say, that I fear that gold piece of Italian money is the principal cause of my being where I am."

"No doubt it has been considered one of the most material of the facts against you, Miss Monson, though it is by no means conclusive, as evidence, even with the most bitter and prejudiced."

"I hope not. Now, Mr. Wilmeter, I will detain you no longer, but beg you to do my commission with your sister, as you would do it for her with me. I would write, but my hand is so peculiar it were better that I did not."

Mary Monson now dismissed the young man, with the manner of one very familiar with the tone of good society—a term that it is much the fashion to ridicule just now, but which conveys a meaning that it were better the scoffers understood. This she did, however, after again apologizing for the trouble she was giving, and thanking him earnestly for the interest he took in her affairs. We believe in animal magnetism; and cannot pretend to say what is the secret cause of the powerful sympathy that is so often suddenly awakened between persons of different sexes, and in some instances between those who are of the same sex; but Mary Monson, by that species of instinct that teaches the female where she has awakened an interest livelier than common, and possibly where she has not, was certainly already aware that John Wilmeter did not regard her with the same cool indifference he would have felt toward an ordinary client of his uncle's. In thanking him, therefore, her own manner manifested a little of the reflected feeling that such a state of things is pretty certain to produce. She colored, and slightly hesitated once, as if she paused to choose her terms with more than usual care; but, in the main, acquitted herself well. The parting betrayed interest, perhaps feeling, on both sides, but nothing very manifest escaped either of our young people.

Never had John Wilmeter been at a greater loss to interpret facts than he was on quitting the grate. The prisoner was truly the most incomprehensible being he had ever met with. Notwithstanding the fearful nature of the charges against her—charges that might well have given great uneasiness to the firmest man—she actually seemed in love with her prison. It is true, that worthy Mrs. Gott had taken from the place many of its ordinary, repulsive features; but it was still a jail, and the sun could be seen only through grates, and massive walls separated her that was within from the world without. As the young man was predisposed to regard everything connected with this extraordinary young woman *couleur de rose*, however, he saw nothing but the surest signs of innocence in several circumstances that might have increased the distrust of his cooler-headed uncle; but most persons would have regarded the gentle tranquillity, that now seemed to soothe a spirit that had evidently been much troubled of late, as a sign that her hand could never have committed the atrocities with which she was charged.

"Is she not a sweet young thing, Mr. Wilmeter?" exclaimed kind Mrs. Gott, while locking the doors after John, on his retiring from the grate. "I consider it an honor to Biberry jail to have such a prisoner within its walls!"

"I believe that you and I stand alone in our favorable opinion of Miss Monson," John answered; "so far, at least, as Biberry is concerned. The excitement against her seems to be at the highest pitch; and I much doubt whether a fair trial can be had in the county."

"The newspapers won't mend the matter, sir. The papers from town this morning are full of the affair, and they all appear to lean the same way. But it's a long road that has no turning, Mr. Wilmeter."

"Very true, and nothing wheels about with a quicker step than the sort of public opinion that is got up under a cry, and runs itself out of breath at the start. I expect to see Mary Monson the most approved and most extolled woman in the county, yet!"

Mrs. Gott hoped with all her heart that it might be so, though *she* had, certainly, misgivings that the young man did not feel. Half an hour after John Wilmeter had left the jail, his friend Michael Millington was on the road to town, carrying a letter to Sarah, with a most earnest request that she would use all her influence with Marie Moulin to engage in the unusual service asked of her, for a few weeks, if for no longer a period. This letter reached its destination in due time, and greatly did the sister marvel over its warmth, as well as over the nature of the request.

"I never knew John to write so earnestly!" exclaimed Sarah, when she and Michael had talked over the matter a few moments. "Were he actually in love, I could not expect him to be more pressing."

"I will not swear that he is not," returned the friend, laughing. "He sees everything with eyes so different from mine, that I scarce know what to make of him. I have never known John so deeply interested in any human being as he is at this moment in this strange creature!"

"Creature! You men do not often call young ladies *creatures;* and my brother affirms that this Mary Monson is a lady."

"Certainly she is, so far as exterior, manner, education, and, I suppose, tastes, are concerned, Nevertheless, there is too much reason to think she is, in some way unknown to us, connected with crime."

"I have read accounts of persons of these attainments who have been leagued together, and have carried on a great system of plundering for years, with prodigious success. That, however, was in older countries, where the necessities of a crowded population drive men into extremes. We are hardly sufficiently advanced, or civilized as they call it, for such bold villainy."

"A suspicion of that nature has crossed my mind," returned Millington, looking

"This bears some resemblance, Mr. Wilmeter, to an interview in a convent. I am the novice, you the excluded friend, who is compelled to pay
his visit through a grate."—*Ways of the Hour.*

askance over his shoulder, as if he apprehended that his friend might hear him. "It will not do, however, to remotely hint to John anything of the sort. His mind is beyond the influence of testimony."

Sarah scarce knew what to make of the affair, though sisterly regard disposed her to do all she could to oblige her brother. Marie Moulin, however, was not easily persuaded into consenting to serve a mistress who was in prison. She held up her hands, turned up her eyes, uttered fifty exclamations, and declared, over and over again, *"c'est impossible"*; and wondered how a female in such a situation could suppose any respectable domestic would serve her, as it would be very sure to prevent her ever getting a good place afterward. This last objection struck Sarah as quite reasonable, and had not her brother been so very urgent with her, would of itself have induced her to abandon all attempt at persuasion. Marie, however, finally yielded to a feeling of intense curiosity when no bribe in money could have bought her. John had said the prisoner knew her—had known her in Europe—and she was soon dying with the desire to know who, of all her many acquaintances in the old world, could be the particular individual who had got herself into this formidable difficulty. It was impossible to resist this feeling, so truly feminine, which was a good deal stimulated by a secret wish in Sarah, also, to learn who this mysterious person might be; and who did not fail to urge Marie, with all her rhetoric, to consent to go and, at least, see the person who had so strong a wish to engage her services. The Swiss had not so much difficulty in complying, provided she was permitted to reserve her final decision until she had met the prisoner, when she might gratify her curiosity, and return to town prepared to enlighten Miss Wilmeter, and all her other friends, on a subject that had got to be intensely interesting.

It was not late, next morning, when Mary Moulin, attend by John Wilmeter, presented herself to Mrs. Gott, as an applicant for admission to the gallery of Mary Monson. The young man did not show himself, on this occasion; though he was near enough to hear the grating of the hinges when the prison-door opened. "C'est bien vous donc, Marie!" said the prisoner, in a quick but pleased salutation. "Mademoiselle!" exclaimed the Swiss. The kisses of women succeeded. The door closed, aud John Wilmeter learned no more, on that occasion.

CHAPTER VIII.

"And can you by no drift of conference
Get from him why he puts on this confusion."
—HAMLET.

There is something imaginative, if not very picturesque, in the manner in which the lawyers of Manhattan occupy the buildings of Nassau Street, a thoroughfare which connects Wall Street with the Tombs. There they throng, resembling the remains of so many monuments along the Appian Way, with a *"siste, viator"* of their own, to arrest the footsteps of the wayfarer. We must now transfer the scene to a building in this street, which stands about halfway between Maiden Lane and John Street, having its front plastered over with little tin signs, like a debtor marked by writs, or what are now called "complaints." Among these signs, which afforded some such pleasant reading as an almanac, was one that bore this simple and reasonably intelligent inscription:

"Thomas Dunscomb, 2d floor, in front."

It is somewhat singular that terms as simple as those of first floor, second floor, etc., should not signify the same things in the language of the mother country and that of this land of progress and liberty. Certain it is, nevertheless, that in American parlance, more especially in that of Manhattan, a first floor is never up one pair of stairs, as in London, unless indeed the flight is that by which the wearied foot-passenger climbs the high stoop to gain an entrance into the building. In other words, an English first floor corresponds with an American second; and, taking that as the point of departure, the same difference exists throughout. Tom Dunscomb's office (or offices would be the better term) occupied quite half of the second floor of a large double house, that had once been the habitation of some private family of note, but which had long been abandoned to the occupation of these ministers of the law. Into those offices it has now become our duty to accompany one who seemed a little strange in that den of the profession, at the very moment he was perfectly at home.

"Lawyer Dunscomb in?" demanded this person, who had a decided rustic mien, though his dress had a sort of legal dye on it, speaking to one of the five or six clerks who raised their heads on the stranger's entrance.

"In, but engaged in a consultation, I believe," answered one who, being paid for his services, was the working clerk of the office; most of the others being students who get no remuneration for their time, and who very rarely deserve it.

" I'll wait till he is through," returned the stranger, helping himself coolly to a vacant chair, and taking his seat in the midst of dangers that might have alarmed one less familiar with the snares, and quirks, and quiddities of the law. The several clerks, after taking a good look each at their guest, cast their eyes down on their books or foolscap, and seemed to be engrossed with their respective occupations. Most of the young men, members of respectable families in town, set the stranger down for a rustic client; but the working clerk saw at once, by a certain self-possessed and shrewd manner, that the stranger was a country practitioner.

In the course of the next half hour, Daniel Lord and George Wood came out of the sanctum, attended as far as the door by Dunscomb himself. Exchanging "good-morning" with his professional friends, the last caught a glimpse of his patient visitor, whom he immediately saluted by the somewhat brief and familiar name of Timms, inviting him instantly, and with earnestness, to come within the limits of the privileged. Mr. Timms complied, entering the sanctum with the air of one who had been there before, and appearing to be in no manner overcome by the honor he enjoyed. And now, as a faithful chronicler of events, it is here become our painful, not to say revolting duty, to record an act on the part of the man who was known throughout Dukes County as Squire Timms, which it will never do to overlook, since it has got to be perfectly distinctive and characteristic of late years, not of an individual, but of large classes, who throng the bar, the desk, the steamboats, the taverns, the streets. A thousand paragraphs have been written on the subject of American spitting, and not one line, as we can remember, on the subject of an equally common and still grosser offense against the minor morals of the country, if decency in manners may be thus termed. Our meaning will be explained more fully in the narrative of the stranger's immediate movements on entering the sanctum.

" Take a seat, Mr. Timms," said Dunscomb, motioning to a chair, while he resumed his own well-cushioned seat, and deliberately proceeded to light a cigar, not without pressing several, with a species of intelligent tenderness, between his thumb and finger. " Take a seat, sir; and take a cigar."

Here occurred the great *tour de force* in manners of Squire Timms. Consider-

ately turning his person quartering toward his host, and seizing himself by the nose, much as if he had a quarrel with that member of his face, he blowed a blast that sounded sonorously, and which fulfilled all that it promised. Now a better-mannered man than Dunscomb it would not be easy to find. He was not particularly distinguished for elegance of deportment, but he was perfectly well-bred. Nevertheless, he did not flinch before this broad hint from vulgarity, but stood it unmoved. To own the truth, so large has been the inroad from the base of society, within the last five-and-twenty years, on the habits of those who once exclusively dwelt together, that he had got hardened even to this innovation. The fact is not to be concealed, and, as we intend never to touch upon the subject again, we shall say distinctly that Mr. Timms blew his nose with his fingers, and that, in so doing, he did not innovate half as much, to-day, on the usages of the Upper Ten Thousand, as he would have done had he blown his nose with his thumb only, a quarter of a century since.

Dunscomb bore this infliction philosophically; and well he might, for there was no remedy. Waiting for Timms to use his handkerchief, which was produced somewhat tardily for such an operation, he quietly opened the subject of their interview.

"So the grand jury has actually found a bill for murder and arson, my nephew writes me," Dunscomb observed, looking inquiringly at his companion, as if really anxious for further intelligence.

" Unanimously, they tell me, Mr. Dunscomb," answered Timms. " I understand that only one man hesitated, and he was brought round before they came into court. That piece of money damns our case in old Dukes."

" Money saves more cases than it damns, Timms; and no one knows it better than yourself."

" Very true, sir. Money may defy even the new Code. Give me five hundred dollars, and change the proceedings to a civil action, and I'll carry anything in my own county that you'll put on the calendar, barring some twenty or thirty jurors I could name. There are about thirty men in the county that I can do nothing with—for that matter, whom I dare not approach."

" How the deuce is it, Timms, that you manage your causes with so much success? for I remember you have given me a good deal of trouble in suits in which law and fact were both clearly enough on my side."

"I suppose those must have been causes in which we 'horse-shedded' and 'pillowed' a good deal."

"Horse-shedded and pillowed! Those are legal terms of which I have no knowledge!"

"They are country phrases, sir, and country customs, too, for that matter. A man might practice a long life in town, and know nothing about them. The Halls of Justice are not immaculate; but they can tell us nothing of horse-shedding and pillowing. They do business in a way of which we in the country are just as ignorant as you are of our mode."

"Have the goodness, Timms, just to explain the meaning of your terms, which are quite new to me. I will not swear they are not in the Code of Practice, but they are in neither Blackstone nor Kent."

"Horse-shedding, Squire Dunscome, explains itself. In the country most of the jurors, witnesses, etc., have more or less to do with the horse-sheds, if it's only to see that their beasts are fed. Well, we keep proper talkers there, and it must be a knotty case, indeed, into which an ingenious hand cannot thrust a doubt or an argument. To be frank with you, I've known three pretty difficult suits summed up under a horse-shed in one day: and twice as many opened."

"But how is this done?—do you present your arguments directly, as in court?"

"Lord bless you, no. In court, unless the jury happen to be unusually excellent, counsel have to pay some little regard to the testimony and the law; but, in horse-shedding, one has no need of either. A skillful horse-shedder, for instance, will talk a party to pieces, and not say a word about the case. That's the perfection of the business. It's against the law, you know, Mr. Dunscomb, to talk of a case before a juror—an indictable offense—but one may make a case of a party's general character, of his means, his miserly qualities, or his aristocracy; and it will be hard to get hold of the talker for any of them qualities. Aristocracy, of late years, is a capital argument, and will suit almost any state of facts, or any action you can bring. Only persuade the jury that the plaintiff or defendant fancies himself better than they are, and the verdict is certain. I got a thousand dollars in the Springer case, solely on that ground. Aristocracy did it! It is going to do us a great deal of harm in the murder and arson indictment."

"But Mary Monson is no aristocrat—she is a stranger, and unknown. What privileges does she enjoy, to render her obnoxious to the charge of aristocracy?"

"More than will do her any good. Her aristocracy does her almost as much harm in old Dukes as the piece of gold. I always consider a cause as half lost when there is any aristocracy in it."

"Aristocracy means exclusive political privileges in the hands of a few; and it means nothing else. Now what exclusive political privilege does this unfortunate young woman enjoy? She is accused of two of the highest crimes known to the laws, is indicted, imprisoned, and will be tried."

"Yes, and by her *peers*," said Timms, taking out a very respectable-looking box, and helping himself liberally to a pinch of cut tobacco. "It's wonderful, Squire Dunscomb, how much breadth the *peerage* possesses in this country! I saw a trial, a year or two since, in which one of the highest intellects of the land was one of the parties, and in which a juror asked the judge to explain the meaning of the word 'bereaved.' *That* citizen had his rights referred to his peers, with a vengeance!"

"Yes, the venerable maxim of the common law is, occasionally, a little caricatured among us. This is owing to our adhering to antiquated opinions after the facts in which they had their origin have ceased to exist. But, by your manner of treating the subject, Timms, I infer that you give up the aristocracy."

"Not at all. Our client will have more risks to run on account of *that*, than on account of any other weak spot in her case. I think we might get along with the piece of gold, as a life is in question, but it is not quite so easy to see how we are to get along with the aristocracy."

"And this in the face of her imprisonment, solitary condition, friendless state, and utter dependence on strangers for her future fate? I see no one feature of aristocracy to reproach her with."

"But I see a great many, and so does the neighborhood. It is already getting to be the talk of half the county. In short, all are talking about it, but they who know better. You'll see, Squire Dunscomb, there are two sorts of aristocracy in the eyes of most people; *your* sort and *my* sort. *Your* sort is a state of society that gives privileges and power to a few, and keeps it there. That is what I call old-fashioned aristocracy, about which nobody cares anything in this country. We have no aristocrats, I allow, and consequently they don't signify a straw."

"Yet they are the only true aristocrats, after all. But what, or who are yours?"

"Well, now, squire, *you* are a sort of

aristocrat yourself, in a certain way. I don't know how it is—I'm admitted to the bar as well as you—have just as many rights—"

" More, Timms, if leading jurors by the nose, and horse-shedding, can be accounted rights."

" Well, more in some respects, maybe. Notwithstanding all this, there is a difference between us—a difference in our ways, in our language, in our ideas, our manner of thinking and acting, that sets you up above me in a way I should not like in any other man. As you did so much for me when a boy, sir, and carried me through to the bar on your shoulders, as it might be, I shall always look up to you ; though I must say that I do not always like even *your* superiority."

" I should be sorry, Timms, if I ever so far forget my own great defects as to parade unfeelingly any little advantages I may happen to possess over you, or over any other man, in consequence of the accidents of birth and education."

" You do not parade them unfeelingly, sir ; you do not *parade* them at all. Still, they will show themselves ; and they are just the things I do not like to look at. Now, what is true of me is true of all my neighbors. We call anything aristocracy that is a touch above us, let it be what it may. I sometimes think Squire Dunscomb is a sort of an aristocrat in the law ! Now, as for our client, she has a hundred ways with her that are not the ways of Dukes, unless you go among the tip-toppers."

" The Upper Ten—"

" Pshaw ! I know better than that myself, squire. Their Upper Ten should be upper one, or two, to be common sense. Rude and untaught as I was until you took me by the hand, sir, I can tell the difference between those who wear kids and ride in their coaches, and those who are fit for either. Our client has none of this, sir ; and that it is which surprises me. She has no Union Place, or Fifth Avenue, about her, but is the true coin. There is one thing in particular that I'm afraid may do her harm."

" It is the true coin which usually passes with the least trouble from hand to hand. But what is this particular source of uneasiness ? "

" Why, the client has a lady friend—"

A little exclamation from Dunscomb caused the speaker to pause, while the counselor removed the cigar from his mouth, knocked off its ashes, and appeared to ponder for a moment, touching the best manner of treating a somewhat delicate subject. At length, native frankness over-came all scruples, and he spoke plainly, or as the familiar instructor might be expected to address a very green pupil.

" If you love me, Timms, never repeat that diabolical phrase again," said Dunscomb, looking quite serious, however much there might have been of affectation in his aspect. " It is even worse than Hurlgate, which I have told you fifty times I cannot endure. ' Lady friend ' is infernally vulgar, and I *will* not stand it. You may blow your nose with your fingers, if it give you especial satisfaction, and you may blow out against aristocracy as much as you please ; but you shall not talk to me about ' lady friends ' or ' Hurlgate.' I am no dandy, but a respectable elderly gentleman, who professes to speak English, and who wishes to be addressed in his own language. Heaven knows what the country is coming to ! There is Webster, to begin with, cramming a Yankee dialect down our throats for good English ; then comes all the cant of the day, flourishing finical phrases, and new significations to good old homely words, and changing the very nature of mankind by means of terms. Last of all is this infernal Code, in which the ideas are as bad as possible, and the terms still worse. But whom do you mean by your ' lady friend ' ? "

" The French lady that has been with our client, now, for a fortnight. Depend on it, *she* will do us no good when we are on. She is too aristocratic altogether."

Dunscomb laughed outright. Then he passed a hand aross his brow and seemed to muse.

"All this is very serious," he at length replied, " and is really no laughing matter. A pretty pass are we coming to, if the administration of the law is to be influenced by such things as these ! The doctrine is openly held that the rich shall not, ought not to, embellish their amusements at a cost that the poor cannot compass ; and here we have a member of the bar telling us a prisoner shall not have justice because she has a foreign maid-servant ! "

"A servant ! Call her anything but that, squire, if you wish for success ! A prisoner accused of capital crimes, with a servant, would be certain to be condemned. Even the court would hardly stand *that*."

" Timms, you are a shrewd, sagacious fellow, and are apt to laugh in your sleeve at follies of this nature, as I well know from long acquaintance ; and here you insist on one of the greatest of all absurdities."

" Things are changed in Ameriky, Mr. Dunscomb. The people are beginning to govern ; and when they can't do it legally they do it without law. Don't you see what the papers say about having operas and play-houses at the people's prices, and the right to hiss? There's Constitution for you! I wonder what Kent and Blackstone would say to *that?*"

"Sure enough. They would find some novel features in a liberty which says a man shall not set the price on the seats in his own theater, and that the hissing may be done by an audience in the *streets*. The facts are, Timms, that all these abuses about O. P.'s, and controlling other persons' concerns under the pretense that the public has rights where, as a public, it has no rights at all, come from the reaction of a half-way liberty in other countries. Here, where the people are really free, having all the power, and where no political right is hereditary, the people ought, at least, to respect their own ordinances."

"Do you not consider a theater a public place, Squire Dunscomb?"

"In one sense it is, certainly; but not in the sense that bears on this pretended power over it. The very circumstance that the audience pay for their seats, makes it, in law as in fact, a matter of covenant. As for this new-fangled absurdity about its being a duty to furnish low-priced seats for the poor, where they may sit and look at pretty women because they cannot see them elsewhere, it is scarcely worth an argument. If the rich should demand that the wives and daughters of the poor should be paraded in the pits and galleries, for *their* patrician eyes to feast on, a pretty clamor there would be! If the State requires cheap theaters, and cheap women, let the State pay for them, as it does for its other wants; but, if these amusements are to be the object of private speculations, let private wisdom control them. I have no respect for one-sided liberty, let it cant as much as it may."

"Well, I don't know, sir; I have read some of these articles, and they seem to me—"

"What—convincing?"

"Perhaps not just that, squire; but very *agreeable*. I'm not rich enough to pay for a high place at an opera or a theater; and it is pleasant to fancy that a poor feller can get one of the best seats at half-price. Now in England, they tell me, the public won't stand prices they don't like."

"Individuals of the public may refuse to purchase, and there their rights cease. An opera, in particular, is a very expensive amusement; and in all countries where the rates of admission are low, the governments contribute to the expenditures. This is done from policy, to keep the people quiet, and possibly to help civilize them; but if we are not far beyond the necessity of any such expedients, institutions are nothing but a sublime mystification."

"It is wonderful, 'squire. how many persons see the loose side of democracy, who have no notion of the tight! But, all this time, our client is in jail at Biberry, and must be tried next week. Has nothing been done, 'squire, to choke off the newspapers, who have something to say about her almost every day? It's quite time the other side should be heard."

"It is very extraordinary that the persons who control these papers should be so indifferent to the rights of others as to allow such paragraphs to find a place in their columns."

"Indifferent! What do they care, so long as the journal sells? In our case, however, I rather suspect that a certain reporter has taken offense; and when men of that class get offended, look out for news of the color of their anger. Isn't it wonderful, Squire Dunscomb, that the people don't see and feel that they are sustaining low tyrants, in two-thirds of their silly clamor about the liberty of the press?"

"Many do see it; and I think this engine has lost a great deal of its influence within the last few years. As respects proceedings in the courts, there never will be any true liberty in the country, until the newspapers are bound hand and foot."

"You are right enough in one thing, squire, and that is in the ground the press has lost. It has pretty much used itself up in Dukes; and I would pillow and horse-shed a cause through against it, the best day it ever saw!"

"By the way, Timms, you have not explained the pillowing process to me."

"I should think the word itself would do that, sir. You know how it is in the country. Half a dozen beds are put in the same room, and two in a bed. Waal, imagine three or four jurors in one of these rooms, and two chaps along with 'em, with instructions how to talk. The conversation is the most innocent and nat'ral in the world; not a word too much or too little; but it sticks like a burr. The juror is a plain, simple-minded countryman, and swallows all that his room-mates say, and goes into the box next day in a beautiful frame of mind to listen to reason and evidence! No, no; give me two or three of these pillow-counselors, and I'll undo all that the journals can do, in a single conversation. You'll remember, squire, that we get the last word by this system; and if the first blow is half the battle in war, the last word is another half in the law. Oh! it's a beautiful business, is this trial by jury!"

"All this is very wrong, Timms. For a long time I have known that you have exercised an extraordinary influence over the jurors of Dukes; but this is the first occasion on which you have been frank enough to reveal the process."

"Because this is the first occasion on which we have ever had a capital case together. In the present state of public opinion, in Dukes, I much question whether we can get a jury impaneled in this trial at all."

"The Supreme Court will then send us to town, by way of mending the matter. Apropos, Timms—"

"One word, if you please, squire; what does a propos really mean? I hear it almost every day, but never yet knew the meaning."

"It has shades of difference in its signification—as I just used it, it means 'speaking of that.'"

"And is it right to say a propos to such a thing?"

"It is better to say a propos of, as the French do. In old English, it was always to; but in our later mode of speaking, we say 'of.'"

"Thank you, sir. You know how I glean my knowledge in dribblets; and out in the country not always from the highest authorities. Plain and uncouth as I know I appear to you, and to Miss Sarah, I have an ambition to be a gentleman. Now I have observation enough to see that it is these little matters, after all, and not riches and fine clothes, that make gentlemen and ladies."

"I am glad you have so much discrimination, Timms; but you must permit me to remark, that you will never make a gentleman until you learn to let your nose alone."

"Thank you, sir—I am thankful for even the smallest hints on manners. It's a pity that so handsome and so agreeable a young lady should be hanged, Mr. Dunscomb!"

"Timms, you are as shrewd a fellow in your own way, as I know. Your law does not amount to any great matter, nor do you take hold of the strong points of a case very often; but you perform wonders with the weaker. In the way of an opinion on facts, I know few men more to be relied on. Tell me, then, frankly, what do you think of the guilt or innocence of Mary Monson?"

Timms screwed up his mouth, passed a hand over his brow, and did not answer for near a minute.

"Perhaps it is right, after all, that we should understand each other on this subject," he then said. "We are associated as counsel, and I feel it a great honor to be so associated, Squire Dunscomb, I give you my word; and it is proper that we should be as free with each other as brothers. In the first place, then, I never saw such a client before, as this same lady—for lady I suppose we must call her until she is convicted—"

"Convicted! You cannot think there is much danger of that, Timms!"

"We never know, sir; we never know. I have lost cases of which I was sure, and gained them of which I had no hopes— cases which I certainly ought not to have gained—ag'in all law and the facts."

"Ay, that came of the horse-shed, and the sleeping of two in a bed."

"Perhaps it did, squire," returned Timms, laughing very freely, though without making any noise; "perhaps it did. When the small-pox is about, there is no telling who may take it. As for this case, Squire Dunscomb, it is my opinion we shall have to run for disagreements. If we can get the juries to disagree once or twice, and can get a change of venue, with a couple of charges, the deuce is in it if a man of your experience don't corner them so tightly they'll give the matter up, rather than have any more trouble about it. After all, the State can't gain much by hanging a young woman that nobody knows, even if she be a little aristocratical. We must get her to change her dress altogether, and some of her ways, too; which, in her circumstances, I call downright hanging ways; and the sooner she is rid of them the better."

"I see that you do not think us very strong on the merits, Timms, which is as much as admitting the guilt of our client. I was a good deal inclined to suspect the worst myself; but two or three more interviews, and what my nephew Jack Wilmeter tells me, have produced a change. I am now strongly inclined to believe her innocent. She has some great and secret cause of apprehension, I will allow; but I do not think these unfortunate Goodwins have anything to do with it."

"Waal, one never knows. The verdict, if 'not guilty,' will be just as good as if she was as innocent as a child a year old. I see how the work is to be done. All the law, and the summing up, will fall to your share; while the out-door work will be mine. We may carry her through—though

I'm of the opinion that, if we do, it will be more by means of bottom than by means of foot. There is one thing that is very essential, sir—the money must hold out."

"Do you want a refresher so soon, Timms? Jack tells me that she has given you two hundred and fifty dollars already!"

"I acknowledge it, sir; and a very respectable fee it is—*you* ought to have a thousand, squire."

"I have not received a cent, nor do I mean to touch any of her money. My feelings are in the case, and I am willing to work for nothing."

Timms gave his old master a quick but scrutinizing glance. Dunscomb was youthful, in all respects, for his time of life; and many a man has loved, and married, and became the parent of a flourishing family, who had seen all the days he had seen. That glance was to inquire if it were possible that the uncle and nephew were likely to be rivals, and to obtain as much knowledge as could be readily gleaned in a quick, jealous look. But the counselor was calm as usual, and no tinge of color, no sigh, no gentleness of expression, betrayed the existence of the master passion. It was reported among the bachelor's intimates that formerly, when he was about five-and-twenty, he had had an affair of the heart, which had taken such deep hold that even the lady's marriage with another man had not destroyed its impression. That marriage was said not to have been happy, and was succeeded by a second, that was still less so; though the parties were affluent, educated, and possessed all the means that are commonly supposed to produce felicity. A single child was the issue of the first marriage, and its birth had shortly preceded the separation that followed.

Three years later the father died, leaving the whole of a very ample fortune to this child, coupled with the strange request that Dunscomb, once the betrothed of her mother, should be the trustee and guardian of the daughter. This extraordinary demand had not been complied with, and Dunscomb had not seen any of the parties from the time he broke with his mistress. The heiress married young, died within the year, and left another heiress; but no further allusion to our counselor was made in any of the later wills and settlements. Once, indeed, he had been professionally consulted concerning the devises in favor of the granddaughter—a certain Mildred Millington—who was a second cousin to Michael of that name, and as rich as he was poor. For some years, a sort of

vague expectation prevailed that these two young Millingtons might marry; but a feud existed in the family, and little or no intercourse was permitted. The early removal of the young lady to a distant school prevented such a result; and Michael, in due time, fell within the influence of Sarah Wilmeter's gentleness, beauty, and affection.

Timms came to the conclusion that his old master was not in love.

"It is very convenient to be rich, squire," this singular being remarked; "and I daresay it may be very pleasant to practice for nothing, when a man has his pocket full of money. I am poor and have particular satisfaction in a good warm fee. By the way, sir, my part of the business requires plenty of money. I do not think I can even commence operations with less than five hundred dollars."

Dunscomb leaned back, stretched forth an arm, drew his check-book from its niche, and filled a check for the sum mentioned. This he quietly handed to Timms, without asking for any receipt; for, while he knew that his old student and fellow-practitioner was no more to be trusted in matters of practice than was an eel in the hand, he knew that he was scrupulously honest in matters of account. There was not a man in the State to whom Dunscomb would sooner confide the care of uncounted gold, or the administration of an estate, or the payment of a legacy, than this very individual, who, he also well knew, would not scruple to set all the provisions of the law at naught, in order to obtain a verdict, when his feelings were really in the case."

"There, Timms," said the senior counsel, glancing at his draft before he handed it to the other, in order to see that it was correct; "there is what you ask for. Five hundred for expenses, and half as much as a fee."

"Thank you, sir. I hope this is not gratuitous, as well as the services?"

"It is not. There is no want of funds, and I am put in possession of sufficient money to carry us through with credit; but it is as a trustee, and not as a fee. This, indeed, is the most extraordinary part of the whole affair; to find a delicate, educated, accomplished lady, with her pockets well lined, in such a situation!"

"Why, squire," said Timms, passing his hand down his chin, and trying to look simple and disinterested, "I am afraid clients like ours are often flush. I have been employed about the Tombs a good deal in my time, and I have gin'rally found that the richest clients were the biggest rogues."

Dunscomb gave his companion a long and contemplative look. He saw that Timms did not entertain quite as favorable an opinion of Mary Monson as he did himself, or rather that he was fast getting to entertain; for his own distrust originally was scarcely less than that of this hackneyed dealer with human vices. A long, close and stringent examination of all of Timm's facts succeeded—facts that had been gleaned by collecting statements on the spot. Then a consultation followed, from which it might be a little premature, just now, to raise the veil.

CHAPTER IX.

"——Her speech is nothing,
Yet the unshaped use of it doth move
The hearers to collection. They aim at it,
And botch the words up fit to their own thoughts."
—HAMLET.

THE reader is not to be surprised at the intimacy which existed between Thomas Dunscomb and the half-educated semi-rude being who was associated with him as counsel in the important cause that was now soon to be tried. Such intimacies are by no means uncommon in the course of events; men often overlooking great dissimilarities in principles, as well as in personal qualities, in managing their associations, so far as they are connected with the affairs of this world. The circumstance that Timms had studied in our counselor's office would, as a matter of course, produce certain relations between them in after-life; but the student had made himself useful to his former master on a great variety of occasions, and was frequently employed by him whenever there was a cause depending in the courts of Dukes, the county in which the unpolished, half-educated, but hard-working and successful county practitioner had established himself. It may be questioned if Dunscomb really knew all the agencies set in motion by his coadjutor in difficult cases; but whether he did or not, it is quite certain that many of them were of a character not to see the light.

It is very much the fashion of our good republic to turn up its nose at all other lands, a habit no doubt inherited from our great ancestors the English; and one of its standing themes of reproach are the legal corruptions and abuses known to exist in France, Spain, Italy, etc.; all over the world, in short, except among ourselves. So far as the judges are concerned, there is a surprising adherence to duty, when bribes alone are concerned, no class of men on earth being probably less obnoxious to just imputations of the character than the innumerable corps of judicial officers; underpaid, poor, hard-worked and we might almost add unhonored, as they are. That cases in which bribes are taken do occur, we make no doubt; it would be assuming too much in favor of human nature to infer the contrary; but, under the system of publicity that prevails, it would not be easy for this crime to extend very far without its being exposed. It is greatly to the credit of the vast judicial corps of the States, that bribery is an offense which does not appear to be even suspected at all; or, if there be exceptions to the rule, they exist in but few and isolated cases. Here, however, our eulogies on American justice must cease. All that Timms has intimated and Dunscomb has asserted concerning the juries is true; and the evil is one that each day increases.

The tendency of everything belonging to the government is to throw power directly into the hands of the people, who, in nearly all cases, use it as men might be supposed to do who are perfectly irresponsible, have only a remote, and half the time an invisible interest in its exercise; who do not feel or understand the consequences of their own deeds, and have a pleasure in asserting a seeming independence, and of appearing to think and act for themselves. Under such a regime it is self-apparent that principles and law must suffer; and so the result proves daily, if not hourly. The institution of the jury, one of very questionable utility in its best aspects in a country of really popular institutions, becomes nearly intolerable, unless the courts exercise a strong and salutary influence on the discharge of its duties. This influence, unhappily, has been gradually lessening among us for the last half century, until it has reached a point where nothing is more common than to find the judge charging the law one way, and the jury determining it another. In most cases, it is true, there is a remedy for this abuse of power, but it is costly, and ever attended with that delay in hope " which maketh the heart sick." Any one, of even the dullest apprehension, must, on a little reflection, perceive that a condition of things in which the *ends* of justice are defeated, or so procrastinated as to produce the results of defeat, is one of the least desirable of all those in which men can be placed under the social compact; to say nothing of its corrupting and demoralizing effects on the public mind.

All this Dunscomb saw, more vividly,

perhaps, than most others of the profession, for men gradually get to be so accustomed to abuses as not only to tolerate them, but to come to consider them as evils inseparable from human frailty. It was certain, however, that while our worthy counselor so far submitted to the force of things as frequently to close his eyes to Timms's maneuvers, a weakness of which nearly every one is guilty who has much to do with the management of men and things, he was never known to do aught himself that was unworthy of his high standing and well-merited reputation at the bar. There is nothing unusual in this convenient compromise between direct and indirect relations with that which is wrong.

It had early been found necessary to employ local counsel in Mary Monson's case, and Timms was recommended by his old master, as one every way suited to the particular offices needed. Most of the duties to be performed were strictly legal; though it is not to be concealed that some soon presented themselves that would not bear the light. John Wilmeter communicated to Timms the particular state of the testimony, as he and Michael Millington had been enabled to get at it; and among other things he stated his conviction that the occupants of the farm nearest to the late dwelling of the Goodwins were likely to prove some of the most dangerous of the witnesses against their client. This family consisted of a sister-in-law, the Mrs. Burton already mentioned, three unmarried sisters, and a brother, who was the husband of the person first named. On this hint Timms immediately put himself in communication with these neighbors, concealing from them, as well as from all others but good Mrs. Gott, that he was retained in the case at all.

Timms was soon struck with the hints and half-revealed statements of this household; more especially with those of the female portion of it. The man appeared to him to have observed less than his wife and sisters; but even he had much to relate, though, as Timms fancied, more that he had gleaned from those around him, than from his own observations. The sisters, however, had a good deal to say; while the wife, though silent and guarded, seemed to this observer, as well as to young Millington, to know the most. When pressed to tell all, Mrs. Burton looked melancholy and reluctant, frequently returning to the subject of her own accord when it had been casually dropped, but never speaking explicitly, though often invited so to do. It was not the cue of the counsel for the defense to drag out unfavorable evidence; and Timms employed certain confidential agents, whom he often used in the management of his causes, to sift this testimony as well as it could be done without the constraining power of the law. The result was not very satisfactory, in any sense, more appearing to be suppressed than was related. It was feared that the legal officers of the State would meet with better success.

The investigations of the junior counsel did not end here. He saw that the public sentiment was setting in a current so strongly against Mary Monson, that he soon determined to counteract it, as well as might be, by producing a reaction. This is a very common, not to say a very powerful agent, in the management of all interests that are subject to popular opinion, in a democracy. Even the applicant for public favor is none the worse for beginning his advances by "a little aversion," provided he can contrive to make the premeditated change in his favor take the aspect of a reaction. It may not be so easy to account for this caprice of the common mind, as it is certain that it exists. Perhaps we like to yield to a seeming generosity, have a pleasure in appearing to pardon, find a consolation for our own secret consciousness of errors, in thus extending favor to the errors of others, and have more satisfaction in preferring those who are fallible, than in exalting the truly upright and immaculate; if indeed, any such there be. Let the cause be what it may, we think the facts to be beyond dispute; and so thought Timms also, for he no sooner resolved to counteract one public opinion by means of another, than he set about the task with coolness and intelligence—in short, with a mixture of all the good and bad qualities of the man.

The first of his measures was to counteract, as much as he could, the effects of certain paragraphs that had appeared in some of the New York journals. A man of Timm's native shrewdness had no difficulty in comprehending the more vulgar moral machinery of a daily press. Notwithstanding its "we's," and its pretension to represent public opinion, and to protect the common interests, he thoroughly understood it was merely one mode of advancing the particular views, sustaining the personal schemes, and not unfrequently of gratifying the low malignity of a single individual; the press in America differing from that of nearly all other countries in the fact that it is not controlled by associations, and does not reflect the decisions of many minds, or contend for principles that, by their very character, have a tendency to elevate the thoughts. There are some immaterial exceptions as relates to the latter characteristic, perhaps, principally growing out of the great extra-constitutional question of slavery, that has quite unnecessarily been drawn into the discussions of the times through the excited warmth of zealots; but, as a rule, the exciting political questions that elsewhere compose the great theme of the newspapers, enlarging their views, and elevating their articles, may be regarded as settled among ourselves. In the particular case with which Timms was now required to deal, there was neither favor nor malice to counteract. The injustice, and a most cruel injustice it was, was merely in catering to a morbid desire for the marvelous in the vulgar, which might thus be turned to profit.

Among the reporters there exists the same diversity of qualities as among other men, beyond a question; but the tendency of the use of all power is to abuse; and Timms was perfectly aware that these men had far more pride in the influence they wielded, than conscience in its exercise. A ten or twenty dollar note, judiciously applied, would do a great deal with this " Palladium of our Liberties," there being at least a dozen of these important safeguards interested in the coming trial—our associate counsel very well knew; and Dunscomb suspected that some such application of the great persuader had been made, in consequence of one or two judicious and well-turned paragraphs that appeared soon after the consultation. But Timms's management of the press was mainly directed to that of the county newspapers. There were three of these; and as they had better characters than most of the Manhattanese journals, so were they more confided in. It is true, that the Whig readers never heeded in the least anything that was said in " The Dukes County Democrat;" but the friends of the last took their revenge in discrediting all that appeared in the columns of the " Biberry Whig." In this respect, the two great parties of the country were on a par; each manifesting a faith, that, in a better cause, might suffice to move mountains; and, on the other hand, an unbelief that drove them into the dangerous folly of disregarding their foes. As Mary Monson had nothing to do with politics, it was not difficult to get suitable paragraphs inserted in the hostile columns, which was also done within eight-and-forty hours after the return of the junior counsel to his own abode.

Timms, however, was far from trusting to the newspapers alone. He felt that it might be well enough to set " fire to fight fire"; but his main reliance was on the services that could be rendered by a timely and judicious use of " the little member." *Talkers* was what he wanted; and well did he know where to find them, and how to get them at work. A few he paid in a direct, business-like way; taking no vouchers for the sum bestowed, the reader may be assured, but entering each item carefully in a little memorandum-book kept for his own private information. These strictly confidential agents went to work with experienced discretion but great industry, and soon had some ten or fifteen fluent female friends actively engaged in circulating "They says," in their respective neighborhoods.

Timms had reflected a great deal on the character of the defense it might be most prudent to get up and enlarge on. Insanity had been worn out by too much use of late; and he scarce gave that plea a second thought. This particular means of defense had been discussed between him and Dunscomb, it is true; but each of the counsel felt a strong repugnance against resorting to it; the one on account of his indisposition to rely on anything but the truth; the other, to use his own mode of expressing himself on the occasion in question, because he " believed that jurors could no longer be humbugged with that plea. There have been all sorts of madmen and mad-women—"

" Gentlemen and lady murderers"—put in Dunscomb, dryly.

" I ask your pardon, squire; but, since you give me the use of my nose, I will offend as little as possible with the tongue —though I rather conclude "—a form of expression much in favor with Timms— " that should our verdict be 'guilty,' you will be disposed to allow there may be one lady criminal in the world."

"She is a most extraordinary creature, Timms; bothers me more than any client I ever had!"

"Indeed! Waal, I had set her down as just the contrary—for to me she seems to be as unconcerned as if the wise four-and-twenty had not presented her to justice in the name of the people."

" It is not in that sense that I am bothered—no client ever gave counsel less trouble than Mary Monson in that respect. To me, Timms, she does not appear to have any concern in reference to the result."

" Supreme innocence, or a well-practiced experience. I have defended many a person whom I knew to be guilty, and two or three whom I believed to be innocent; but never before had as cool a client as this!"

And very true was this. Even the announcement of the presentment by the grand jury appeared to give Mary Monson no great alarm. Perhaps she anticipated it from the first, and had prepared herself for the event, by an exercise of a firmness little common to her sex until the moments of extreme trial, when their courage would seem to rise with the occasion. On her companion, whom Timms had so elegantly styled her 'Lady Friend,' certainly as thoroughly vulgar an expression as was ever drawn into the service of the heroics in gentility, warm-hearted and faithful Marie Moulin, the intelligence produced far more effect.

It will be remembered that Wilmeter overheard the single cry of "Mademoiselle" when this Swiss was first admitted to the jail; after which an impenetrable veil closed around their proceedings. The utmost good feeling and confidence were apparent in the intercourse between the young mistress and her maid; if, indeed, Marie might thus be termed, after the manner in which she was treated. So far from being kept at the distance which it is usual to observe toward an attendant, the Swiss was admitted to Mary Monson's table; and to the eyes of indifferent observers she might very well pass for what Timms had so elegantly called a "lady friend." But Jack Wilmeter knew too much of the world to be so easily misled. It is true, that when he paid his short visits to the jail, Marie Moulin sat sewing at the prisoner's side, and occasionally she even hummed low, national airs while he was present; but knowing the original condition of the maid-servant, our young man was not to be persuaded that his uncle's client was her peer, any more than were the jurors who, agreeably to that profound mystification of the common law, are thus considered and termed.

Had not Jack Wilmeter known the real position of Marie Moulin, her "mademoiselle" would have let him deeper into the secrets of the two than it is probable either ever imagined. This word, in common with those of "monsieur" and "madame," are used, by French servants, differently from what they are used in general society. Unaccompanied by the names, the domestics of France commonly and exclusively apply them to the heads of families, or those they more immediately serve. Thus, it was far more probable that Marie Moulin, meeting a mere general acquaintance in the prisoner, would have called her "Mademoiselle Marie," or "Mademoiselle Monson," or whatever might be the name by which she had known the young lady, than by the general and still more respectful appellation of "mademoiselle." On this peculiarity of deportment Jack Wilmeter speculated profoundly; for a young man who is just beginning to submit to the passion of love is very apt to fancy a thousand things that he would never dream of seeing in his cooler moments. Still, John had fancied himself bound in the spells of another, until this extraordinary client of his uncle's so unexpectedly crossed his path. Such is the human heart.

Good and kind-hearted Mrs. Gott allowed the prisoner most of the privileges that at all comported with her duty. Increased precautions were taken for the security of the accused, as soon as the presentment of the grand jury was made, by a direct order from the court; but, these attended to, it was in the power of her whom Timms might have called the "lady sheriff," to grant a great many indulgences, which were quite cheerfully accorded, and, to all appearances, as gratefully accepted.

John Wilmeter was permitted to pay two regular visits at the grate each day, and as many more as his ingenuity could invent plausible excuses for making. On all occasions Mrs. Gott opened the outer door with the greatest good will; and, like a true woman as she is, she had the tact to keep as far aloof from the barred window where the parties met, as the dimensions of the outer room would allow. Marie Moulin was equally considerate, generally plying her needle at such times, in the depth of the cell, with twice the industry manifested on other occasions. Nevertheless, nothing passed between the young people that called for this delicate reserve. The conversation, it is true, turned as little as possible on the strange and awkward predicament of one of the colloquists, or the employment that kept the young man at Biberry. Nor did it turn at all on love. There is a premonitory state in these attacks of the heart, during which skillful observers may discover the symptoms of approaching disease, but which do not yet betray the actual existence of the epidemic. On the part of Jack himself, it is true that these symptoms were getting to be not only somewhat apparent, but they were evidently fast becoming more and more distinct; while, on the part of the lady, any one disposed to be critical might have seen that her color deepened, and there were signs of daily increasing interest in them, as the hours for these interviews approached. She was interested in her young legal adviser; and interest, with women, is the usual precursor of the master-passion. Wo betide the man who cannot interest, but who only amuses!

Although so little to the point was said in the short dialogues between Wilmeter and Mary Monson, there were dialogues held with the good Mrs. Gott, by each of the parties respectively, in which less reserve was observed; and the heart was permitted to have more influence over the movements of the tongue. The first of these conversations that we deem it necessary to relate, that took place after the presentment, was one that immediately succeeded an interview at the barred window, and which occurred three days subsequently to the consultation in town; and two after Timm's machinery was actively at work in the county.

"Well, how do you find her spirits to-day, Mr. Wilmington?" asked Mrs. Gott, kindly, and catching the conventional sound of the young man's name, from having heard it so often in the mouth of Michael Millington. "It is an awful state for any human being to be in, and she a young, delicate woman; to be tried for murder, and for setting fire to a house, and all so soon!"

"The most extraordinary part of this very extraordinary business, Mrs. Gott," Jack replied, "is the perfect indifference of Miss Monson to her fearful jeopardy! To me, she seems much more anxious to be closely immured in jail, than to escape from a trial than one would think, of itself, might prove more than so delicate a young lady could bear up against."

"Very true, Mr. Wilmington; and she never seems to think of it all! You see what she has done, sir?"

"Done! Nothing in particular, I hope?"

"I don't know what *you* call particular; but to me it does seem to be remarkably particular. Didn't you hear a piano, and another musical instrument, as you approached the jail?"

"I did, certainly, and wondered who could produce such admirable music in Biberry."

"Biberry has a great many musical ladies, I can tell you, Mr. Wilmington," returned Mrs. Gott, a little coldly, though her good nature instantly returned, and shone out in one of her most friendly smiles; "and those, too, that have been to town and heard all the great performers from Europe, of whom there have been so many of late years. I have heard good judges say that Dukes County is not much behind the island of Manhattan, with the piano in particular."

"I remember when at Rome to have heard an Englishman say that some young ladies from Lincolnshire were astonishing the Romans with their Italian accent, in singing Italian operas," answered Jack, smiling. "There is no end, my dear Mrs. Gott, to provincial perfection in all parts of the world."

"I believe I understand you, but I am not at all offended at your meaning. We are not very sensitive about the jails. One thing I will admit, however; Mary Monson's harp is the first, I rather think, that was ever heard in Biberry. Gott tells me"—this was the familiar manner in which the good woman spoke of the *high* sheriff of Dukes, as the journals affectedly call that functionary—"that he once met some German girls strolling about the country, playing and singing for money, and who had just such an instrument, but not one-half as elegant; and it has brought to my mind a suspicion that Mary Monson may be one of these traveling musicians."

"What? to stroll about the country, and play and sing in the streets of villages!"

"No, not that; I see well enough she cannot be of *that* sort. But there are all descriptions of musicians, as well as all descriptions of doctors and lawyers, Mr. Wilmington. Why may not Mary Monson be one of those foreigners who get so rich by singing and playing? She has just as much money as she wants, and spends it freely, too. This I know, from seeing the manner in which she uses it. For my part, I wish she had less music and less money just now; for they are doing her no great good in Biberry!"

"Why not? Can any human being find fault with melody and a liberal spirit?"

"Folks will find fault with anything, Mr. Wilmington, when they have nothing better to do. You know how it is with our villagers here as well as I do. Most people think Mary Monson guilty, and a few do not. Those that think her guilty say it is insolent in her to be singing and playing in the very jail in which she is confined; and talk loud against her for that very reason."

"Would they deprive her of a consolation as innocent as that she obtains from her harp and her piano, in addition to her other sufferings? Your Biberry folks must be particularly hard-hearted, Mrs. Gott."

"Biberry people are like New York people, and American people, and English people, and all other people, I fancy, if the truth was known, Mr. Wilmington. What they don't like they disapprove of, that's all. Now, was I one of them that believe Mary Monson did actually murder the Goodwins, and plunder their drawers, and set fire to their house, it would go ag'in *my* feelings too, to hear her music, well as she plays, and sweet as she draws out the sounds from those wires. Some of our folks take the introduction of the harp into the jail particularly hard!"

"Why that instrument more than another? It was the one on which David played."

"They say it *was* David's favorite, and ought only to be struck to religious words and sounds."

"It is a little surprising that your excessively conscientious people so often forget that charity is the chiefest of all the Christian graces."

"They think that the love of God comes first, and that they ought never to lose sight of his honor and glory. But I agree with you, Mr. Wilmington; 'feel for your fellow-creatures' is my rule; and I'm certain I am then feeling for my Maker. Yes; many of the neighbors insist that a harp is unsuited to a jail, and they tell me that the instrument on which Mary Monson plays is a real antique."

"Antique! What, a harp made in remote ages?"

"No, I don't mean that exactly," returned Mrs. Gott, coloring a little; "but a harp made so much like those used by the Psalmist, that one could not tell them apart."

"I daresay David had many varieties of stringed instruments, from the lute up; but harps are very common, Mrs. Gott— so common that we hear them now in the streets, and on board the steamboats even. There is nothing new in them, even in this country."

"Yes, sir, in the streets and on board the boats; but the public will tolerate things done for *them*, that they won't tolerate in individuals. I suppose you know *that*, Mr. Wilmington?"

"We soon learn as much in this country —but the jails are made for the public, and the harps ought to be privileged in them, as well as in other public places."

"I don't know how it is—I'm not very good at reasoning—but, somehow or another, the neighbors don't like that Mary Monson should play on the harp or even on the piano, situated as she is. I do wish, Mr. Wilmington, you could give her a hint on the subject."

"Shall I tell her that the music is unpleasant to *you*?"

"As far from that as possible! I delight in it; but the neighbors do not. Then she never shows herself at the grate to folks outside, like all the other prisoners. The public wants to see and converse with her."

"You surely could not expect a young and educated female to be making a spectacle of herself, for the gratification of the eyes of all the vulgar and curious in and about Biberry?"

"Hush—Mr. Wilmington, you are most too young to take care of such a cause. Squire Timms, now, is a man who understands Dukes County, and he would tell you it is not wise to talk of the vulgar hereabouts; at least, not until the verdict is in. Besides, most people would think that folks have a right to look at a prisoner in the common jail. I know they act as if they thought so."

"It is hard enough to be accused and confined, without subjecting the party to any additional degradation. No man has a right to ask to look at Miss Monson but those she sees fit to receive, and the officials of the law. It would be an outrage to tolerate mere idle curiosity."

"Well, if you think so, Mr. Wilmington, do not let everybody know it. Several of the clergy have either been here, or have sent to offer their visits, if acceptable."

"And what has been the answer?" demanded Jack, a little eagerly.

"Mary Monson has received all these offers as if she had been a queen—politely, but coldly; once or twice, or when the Methodist and the Baptist came, and they commonly come first, I thought she seemed hurt. Her color went and came like lightning. Now, she was pale as death—next, as bright as a rose—what a color she has at times, Mr. Wilmington! Dukes is rather celebrated for rosy faces; but it would be hard to find her equal when she is not thinking."

"Of what, my good Mrs. Gott?"

"Why, most of the neighbors say, of the Goodwins. For my part, as I do not believe she ever hurt a hair of the head of the old man and old woman, I can imagine she has disagreeable things to think of that are in nowise connected with *them*."

"She certainly has disagreeable things to make her cheeks pale that *are* connected with that unfortunate couple. But, I ought to know all. To what else do the neighbors object?"

"To the foreign tongues—they think when a grand jury has found a bill, the accused ought to talk nothing but plain English, so that all near her can understand what she says."

"In a word, it is not thought sufficient to be accused of such a crime as murder, but all other visitations must follow to render the charge as horrible as may be!"

"That is not the way they look at it. The public fancies that in a public matter they might have a right to know all about a thing."

"And when there is a failure in the proof, they imagine, invent, and assert."

"'Tis the ways of the land. I suppose all nations have their ways, and follow them."

"One thing surprises me a little in this matter," Jack rejoined, after musing a moment; "it is this. In most cases in which women have any connection with the law, the leaning in this country, and more particularly of late, has been in their favor."

"Well," Mrs. Gott quietly but quickly interrupted, "and ought it not to be so?"

"It ought not, unless the merits are with them. Justice is intended to do that which is equitable; and it is not fair to assume that women are always right, and men always wrong. I know my uncle thinks that not only the decisions of late years, but the laws, have lost sight of the wisdom of the past, and are gradually placing the women above the men, making *her* instead of *him* the head of the family."

"Well, Mr. Wilmington, and isn't that quite right?" demanded Mrs. Gott, with a good-natured nod.

"My uncle thinks it very wrong, and that by a mistaken gallantry the peace of families is undermined, and their discipline destroyed; as, in punishment, by a false philanthropy, rogues are petted at the expense of honest folks. Such are the opinions of Mr. Thomas Dunscomb, at least."

"Ay, Mr. Thomas Dunscomb is an old bachelor; and bachelor's wives, and bachelor's children, as we well know, are always admirably managed. It is a pity they are not more numerous," retorted the indomitably good-humored wife of the sheriff. "But, you see that, in this case of Mary Monson, the feeling is against, rather than in favor, of a woman. That may be owing to the fact that one of the persons murdered was a lady also."

"Doctor McBrain says that both were females—or lady-murdered—as I suppose we must call them; as doubtless you have heard, Mrs. Gott. Perhaps he is believed, and the fact may make doubly against the accused."

"He is *not* believed. Everybody hereabouts *knows* that one of the skeletons was that of Peter Goodwin. They say

that the district attorney means to show *that*, beyond all dispute. They tell me that it is a law, in a case of this sort, first to show there has been a murder; second, to show who did it."

"This is something like the course of proceeding, I believe; though I never sat on a trial for this offense. It is of no great moment what the district attorney does, so that he do not prove that Miss Monson is guilty; and this, my kind-hearted Mrs. Gott, you and I no not believe he *can* do."

"In that we are agreed, sir. I no more think that Mary Monson did these things, than I think I did them myself."

Jack expressed his thanks in a most grateful look, and there the interview terminated.

CHAPTER X.

"In peace, Love tunes the shepherd's reed;
In war he mounts the warrior's steed;
In halls, in gay attire is seen;
In hamlets, dances on the green.
Love rules the court, the camp, the grove,
And men below, and saints above;
For love is heaven, and heaven is love."
—SCOTT.

"IT is the ways of the land," said good Mrs. Gott, in one of her remarks in the conversation just related. Other usages prevail, in connection with other interests; and the time is come when we must refer to one of them. In a word, Dr. McBrain and Mrs. Updyke were about to be united in the bonds of matrimony. As yet we have said very little of the intended bride; but the incidents of our tale render it now necessary to bring her more prominently on the stage, and to give some account of herself and family.

Anna Wade was the only child of very respectable and somewhat affluent parents. At nineteen she married a lawyer of suitable years, and became Mrs. Updyke. This union lasted but eight years, when the wife was left a widow with two children; a son and a daughter. In the course of time these children grew up, the mother devoting herself to their care, education, and well-being. In all this there was nothing remarkable, widowed mothers doing as much daily, with a self-devotion that allies them to the angels. Frank Updyke, the son, had finished his education, and was daily expected to arrive from a tour of three years in Europe. Anna, her mother's namesake, was at the sweet age of nineteen, and the very counterpart of what the elder Anna had been at the same period in life. The intended bride was far from being unattractive, though fully five-and-forty. In the eyes of Dr. McBrain, she was even charming; although she did not exactly answer those celebrated conditions of female influence that have been handed down to us in the familiar toast of a voluptuous English prince. Though forty, Mrs. Updyke was neither "fat" nor "fair"; being a brunette of a well preserved and still agreeable person.

It was perhaps a little singular, after having escaped the temptations of a widowhood of twenty years, that this lady should think of marrying at a time of life when most females abandon the expectation of changing their condition. But Mrs. Updyke was a person of a very warm heart; and she foresaw the day when she was to be left alone in the world. Her son was much inclined to be a rover and, in his letters, he talked of still longer journeys, and of more protracted absences from home. He inherited an independency from his father, and had now been his own master for several years. Anna was much courted by the circle to which she belonged; and young, affluent, pretty to the very verge of beauty, gentle, quiet and singularly warm-hearted, it was scarcely within the bounds of possibility that she could escape an early marriage in a state of society like that of Manhattan. These were the reasons Mrs. Updyke gave to her female confidantes, when she deemed it well to explain the motives of her present purpose. Without intending to deceive, there was not a word of truth in these explanations. In point of fact, Mrs. Updyke, well as she had loved the husband of her youth, preserved *les beaux restes* of a very warm and affectionate heart; and McBrain, a well-preserved, good-looking man, about a dozen years older than herself, had found the means to awaken its sympathies to such a degree, as once more to place the comely widow completely within the category of Cupid.

It is very possible for a woman of forty to love, and to love with all her heart; though the world seldom takes as much interest in her weakness, if weakness it is, as in those of younger and fairer subjects of the passion. To own the truth, Mrs. Updyke was profoundly in love, while her betrothed met her inclination with an answering sympathy that, to say the least, was fully equal to any tender sentiment he had succeeded in awakening.

All this was to Tom Dunscomb what he called "nuts." Three times had he seen his old friend in this pleasant state of feeling, and three times was he chosen to be an attendant at the altar; once in the recognized character of a groomsman, and on the other two occasions in that of a chosen friend. Whether the lawyer had himself completely escaped the darts of the little god, no one could say, so completely had he succeeded in veiling this portion of his life from observation; but, whether he had or not, he made those who did submit to the passion the theme of his untiring merriment.

Children usually regard these tardy inclinations of their parents with surprise, if not with downright distaste. Some little surprise the pretty Anna Updyke may have felt, when she was told by a venerable great-aunt that her mother was about to be married; but of distaste there was none. She had a strong regard for her new step-father, that was to be; and thought it the most natural thing in the world to love. Sooth, to say, Anna Updyke had not been out two years—the American girls are brought out so young! —without having sundry suitors. Manhattan is the easiest place in the world for a pretty girl, with a good fortune, to get offers. Pretty girls with good fortunes are usually in request everywhere; but it requires the precise state of society that exists in the "Great *Commercial* Emporium," to give a young woman the highest chance in the old lottery. There where one-half of the world came from other worlds some half a dozen years since; where a good old Manhattan name is regarded as upstart among a crowd that scarcely knows whence it was itself derived, and whither it is destined, and where few have any real position in society, and fewer still know what the true meaning of the term is, money and beauty are the constant objects of pursuit. Anna Updyke formed no exception. She had declined, in the gentlest manner possible, no less than six direct offers, coming from those who were determined to lose nothing by diffidence; had thrown cold water on more than twice that number of little flames that were just beginning to burn; and had thrown into the fire some fifteen or sixteen anonymous effusions, in prose and verse, that came from adventurers who could admire from a distance, at the opera and in the streets, but who had no present means of getting any nearer than these indirect attempts at communication. We say "thrown into the fire;" for Anna was too prudent, and had too much self-respect, to retain such documents, coming as they did, from so many "Little Unknowns."

The anonymous effusions were consequently burnt—with one exception. The exception was in the case of a sonnet, in which her hair—and very beautiful it was —was the theme. From some of the little freemasonry of the intercourse of the sexes, Anna fancied these lines had been written by Jack Wilmeter, one of the most constant of her visitors, as well as one of her admitted favorites. Between Jack and Anna there had been divers passages of gallantry, which had been very kindly viewed by McBrain and the mother. The parties themselves did not understand their own feelings; for matters had not gone far, when Mary Monson so strangely appeared on the stage, and drew Jack off, on the trail of wonder and mystery, if not on that of real passion. As Sarah Wilmeter was the most intimate friend of Anna Updyke, it is not extraordinary that this singular fancy of the brother's should be the subject of conversation between the two young women, each of whom probably felt more interest in his movements than any other person on earth. The dialogue we are about to relate took place in Anna's own room, the morning of the day which preceded that of the wedding, and followed naturally enough, as the sequence of certain remarks which had been made on the approaching event.

"If *my* mother were living, and *must* be married," said Sarah Wilmeter, "I should be very well content to have *such* a man as Dr. McBrain for a step-father. I have known him all my life, and he is, and ever has been, so intimate with Uncle Tom, that I almost think him a near relation."

"And I have known him as long as I can remember," Anna steadily rejoined, "and have not only a great respect, but a warm regard for him. Should I ever marry myself, I do not believe I shall have one-half the attachment for my father-in law as I am sure I shall feel for my step-father."

"How do you know there will be any father-in-law in the case? I am sure John has no parent."

"John!" returned Anna, faintly— "What is John to me?"

"Thank you, my dear—he is something, at least to *me*."

"To be sure—a brother naturally is— but Jack is no brother of mine, you will please to remember."

Sarah cast a quick, inquiring look at her friend; but the eyes of Anna were thrown downward on the carpet, while the bloom on her cheeks spread to her temples. Her friend saw that, in truth, Jack was no *brother* of *hers*.

"What I mean is this"—continued Sarah, following a thread that ran through her own mind, rather than anything that had been already expressed—"Jack is making himself a very silly fellow just now."

Anna now raised her eyes; her lip quivered a little, and the bloom deserted even her cheek. Still, she made no reply. Women can listen acutely at such moments; but it commonly exceeds their powers to speak. The friends understood each other, as Sarah well knew, and she continued her remarks precisely as if the other had answered them.

"Michael Millington brings strange accounts of Jack's behavior at Biberry. He says that he seems to do nothing, think of nothing, talk of nothing, but of the hardship of this Mary Monson's case."

"I'm sure it *is* cruel enough to awaken the pity of a rock," said Anna Updyke, in a low tone; "a woman, and she a lady, accused of such terrible crimes—murder and arson!"

"What is arson, child?—and how do *you* know anything about it?"

Again Anna colored, her feelings being all sensitiveness on this subject, which had caused her far more pain than she had experienced from any other event in her brief life. It was, however, necessary to answer.

"Arson is setting fire to an inhabited house," she said, after a moment's reflection; "and I know it from having been told its signification by Mr. Dunscomb."

"Did Uncle Tom say anything of this Mary Monson, and of Jack's singular behavior?"

"He spoke of his client as a very extraordinary person, and of her accomplishments, and readiness, and beauty. Altogether, he does not seem to know what to make of her."

"And what did he say about Jack? You need have no reserve with me, Anna; I am his sister."

"I know that very well, dear Sarah— but Jack's name was not mentioned, I believe—certainly not at the particular time, and in the conversation to which I now refer."

"But at some *other* time, my dear, and in some *other* conversation."

"He did once say something about your brother's being very attentive to the interests of the person he calls his Dukes County client—nothing more, I do assure you. It is the duty of young lawyers to be very attentive to the interests of their clients, I should think."

"Assuredly—and that most especially when the client is a young lady with a pocket full of money. But Jack is above want, and can afford to act right at all times and on all occasions. I wish he had never seen the strange creature."

Anna Updyke sat silent for some little time, playing with the hem of her pocket-handkerchief. Then she said timidly, speaking as if she wished an answer, even while she dreaded it—

"Does not Marie Moulin know something about her?"

"A great deal, if she would only tell it. But Marie, too, has gone over to the enemy. Not a word can I get out of her, though I have written three letters, beyond the fact that she knows *Mademoiselle*, and that she cannot believe her guilty."

"The last, surely, is very important. If really innocent, how hard has been the treatment she has received! It is not surprising that your brother feels so deep an interest in her. He is very warm-hearted and generous, Sarah; and it is just like him to devote his time and talents to the service of the oppressed."

It was Sarah's turn to be silent and thoughtful. She made no answer, for she well understood that an impulse very different from that mentioned by her friend was, just then, influencing her brother's conduct.

We have related this conversation as the briefest mode of making the reader acquainted with the true state of things, in and about the neat dwelling of Mrs. Updyke in Eighth street. Much, however, remains to be told; as the morning of the very day which succeeded that on which the foregoing dialogue was held was the one named for the wedding of the mistress of the house.

At the very early hour of six, the party met at the church door, one of the most Gothic structures in the new quarter of the town; and five minutes sufficed to make the two one. Anna sobbed as she saw her mother passing away from her, as it then appeared to her, and the bride herself was a little overcome. As for Mc-Brain, as his friend Dunscomb expressed it, in a description given to a brother bachelor, who met him at dinner:

"He stood the fire like a .veteran! You're not going to frighten a fellow who has held forth the ring three times. You will remember that Ned has previously killed two wives, besides all the other folk he has slain; and I make no doubt the fellow's confidence was a good deal increased by the knowledge he possesses that none of us are immortal—as husbands and wives, at least."

But Tom Dunscomb's pleasantries had no influence on his friend's happiness.

Odd as it may appear to some, this connection was one of a warm and very sincere attachment. Neither of the parties had reached the period of life when nature begins to yield to the pressure of time, and there was the reasonable prospect before them of their contributing largely to each other's future happiness. The bride was dressed with great simplicity, but with a proper care; and she really justified the passion that McBrain insisted, in his conversation with Dunscomb, that he felt for her. Youthful, for her time of life, modest in demeanor and aspect, still attractive in person, the "Widow Updyke" became Mrs. McBrain, with as charming an air of womanly feeling as might have been exhibited by one of less than half her age. Covered with blushes, she was handed by the bridegroom into his own carriage, which stood at the church door, and the two proceeded to Timbully.

As for Anna Updyke, she went to pass a week in the country with Sarah Dunscomb; even a daughter being a little *de trop*, in a honey-moon. Rattletrap was the singular name Tom Dunscomb had given to his country-house. It was a small villa-like residence, on the banks of the Hudson, and within the Island of Manhattan. Concealed in a wood, it was a famous place for a bachelor to hide his oddities in. Here Dunscomb concentrated all his out-of-the-way purchases, including plows that were never used, all sorts of farming utensils that were condemned to the same idleness, and such contrivances in the arts of fishing and shooting as struck his fancy; though the lawyer never handled a rod or leveled a fowling-piece. But Tom Dunscomb, though he professed to despise love, had fancies of his own. It gave him a certain degree of pleasure to *seem* to have these several tastes; and he threw away a good deal of money in purchasing these characteristic ornaments for Rattletrap. When Jack Wilmeter ventured one day to ask his uncle what pleasure he could find in collecting so many costly and perfectly useless articles, implements that had not the smallest apparent connection with his ordinary pursuits and profession, he got the following answer:

"You are wrong, Jack, in supposing that these traps are useless. A lawyer has occasion for a vast deal of knowledge that he will never get out of his books. One should have the elements of all the sciences, and of most of the arts, in his mind, to make a thoroughly good advocate; for their application will become necessary on a thousand occasions, when

Blackstone and Kent can be of no service. No, no; I prize my profession highly, and look upon Rattletrap as my Inn of Court."

Jack Wilmeter had come over from Biberry to attend the wedding, and had now accompanied the party into the country, as it was called; though the place of Dunscomb was so near town that it was not difficult, when the wind was at the southward, to hear the fire-bell on the City Hall. The meeting between John Wilmeter and Anna Updyke had been fortunately a little relieved by the peculiar circumstance in which the latter was placed. The feeling she betrayed, the pallor of her cheek, and the nervousness of her deportment, might all, naturally enough, be imputed to the emotions of a daughter, who saw her own mother standing at the altar, by the side of one who was not her natural father. Let this be as it might, Anna had the advantage of the inferences which those around her made on these facts. The young people met first in the church, where there was no opportunity for any exchange of language or looks. Sarah took her friend away with her alone, on the road to Rattletrap, immediately after the ceremony, in order to allow Anna's spirits and manner to become composed, without being subjected to unpleasant observation. Dunscomb and his nephew drove out in a light vehicle of the latter's; and Michael Millington appeared later at the villa, bringing with him to dinner, Timms, who came on business connected with the approaching trial.

There never had been any love-making, in the direct meaning of the term, between John Wilmeter and Anna Updyke. They had known each other so long and so intimately, that both regarded the feeling of kindness that each knew subsisted, as a mere fraternal sort of affection. "Jack is Sarah's brother,," thought Anna, when she permitted herself to reason on the subject at all; "and it is natural that I should have more friendship for him than for any other young man." "Anna is Sarah's most intimate friend," thought Jack, "and that is the long and short of my attention for *her*. Take away Sarah, and Anna would be nothing to me; though she is so pretty and clever, and gentle and lady-like. I must like those Sarah likes, or it might make us both unhappy." This was the reasoning of nineteen, and when Anna Updyke was just budding into young womanhood; at a later day, habit had got to be so much in the ascendant, that neither of the young people *thought* much

on the subject at all. The preference was strong in each—so strong, indeed, as to hover over the confines of passion, and quite near to its vortex; though the long-accustomed feeling prevented either from entering into its analysis.

The attachments that grow up with our daily associations, and get to be so interwoven with our most familiar thoughts, seldom carry away those who submit to them in the whirlwind of passion; which are much more apt to attend sudden and impulsive love. Cases do certainly occur in which the parties have long known each other, and have lived on for years in a dull appreciation of mutual merit—sometimes with prejudices and alienation active between them; when suddenly all is changed, and the scene that was lately so tranquil and tame becomes tumultuous and glowing, and life assumes a new charm, as the profound emotions of passion chase away its dullness; substituting hope, and fears, and lively wishes, and soul-felt impressions in its stead. This is not usual in the course of the most wayward of all our impulses; but it does occasionally happen, brightening existence with a glow that might well be termed divine, were the colors bestowed derived from a love of the Creator, in lieu of that of one of his creatures. In these sudden awakenings of dormant feelings, some chord of mutual sympathy, some deep-rooted affinity is aroused, carrying away their possessors in a torrent of the feelings. Occasionally, wherever the affinity is active, the impulse natural and strongly sympathetic, these sudden and seemingly wayward attachments are the most indelible, coloring the whole of the remainder of life; but oftener do they take the character of mere impulse, rather than that of deeper sentiment, and disappear as they were first seen, in some sudden glow of the horizon of the affections.

In this brief analysis of some of the workings of the heart, we may find a clew to the actual frame of mind in which John Wilmeter returned from Biberry, where he had now been, like a sentinel on post, for several weeks, in vigilant watchfulness over the interests of Mary Monson. During all that time, however, he had not once been admitted within the legal limits of the prison; holding his brief, but rather numerous conferences with his client, at the little grate in the massive door that separated the jail from the dwelling of the sheriff. Kind-hearted Mrs. Gott would have admitted him to the gallery, whenever he chose to ask that favor; but this act of courtesy had been forbidden by

Mary Monson herself. Timms she did receive, and she conferred with him in private on more than one occasion, manifesting great earnestness in the consultations that preceded the approaching trial. But John Wilmeter she would receive only at the grate, like a nun in a well-regulated convent. Even this coyness contributed to feed the fire that had been so suddenly lighted in the young man's heart, on which the strangeness of the prisoner's situation, her personal attractions, her manners, and all the other known peculiarities of person, history, education and deportment, had united to produce a most lively impression, however fleeting it was to prove in the end.

Had there been any direct communications on the subject of the attachment that had so long, so slowly, but so surely been taking roots in the hearts of John and Anna, any reciprocity in open confidence, this unlooked-for impulse in a new direction could not have overtaken the young man. He did not know how profound was the interest that Anna took in him ; nor, for that matter, was she aware of it herself, until Michael Millington brought the unpleasant tidings of the manner in which his friend seemed to be entranced with his uncle's client at Biberry. Then, indeed, Anna was made to feel that surest attendant of the liveliest love, a pang of jealousy ; and for the first time in her young and innocent life she became aware of the real nature of her sentiments in behalf of John Wilmeter. On the other hand, drawn aside from the ordinary course of his affections by sudden, impulsive and exciting novelties, John was fast submitting to the influence of the charms of the fair stranger, as more than once intimated in our opening pages, as the newly-fallen snow melts under the rays of a noonday sun.

Such, then, was the state of matters, in this little circle when the wedding took place, and John Wilmeter joined the family party. Although Dunscomb did all he could to make the dinner gay, Rattletrap has seldom entertained a more silent company than that which sat down at its little round table on this occasion. John thought of Biberry and Mary Monson ; Sarah's imagination was quite busy in wondering why Michael Millington stayed away so long ; and Anna was on the point of bursting into tears half a dozen times, under the depression produced by the joint events of her mother's marriage, and John Wilmeter's obvious change of deportment toward her.

"What the deuce has kept Michael Millington and that fellow Timms from joining us at dinner?" said the master of the house, as the fruit was placed upon the table ; and, closing one eye, he looked with the other through the ruby rays of a glass of well-cooled Madeira—his favorite wine. "Both promised to be punctual ; yet here are they both sadly out of time. They knew the dinner was to come off at four."

"As is one, so are both," answered John. "You will remember they were to come together?"

"True—and Millington is rather a punctual man—especially in visiting at Rattletrap"—here Sarah blushed a little ; but the engagement in her case being announced, there was no occasion for any particular confusion. "We shall have to take Michael with us into Dukes next week, Miss Wilmeter ; the case being too grave to neglect bringing up all our forces."

"Is Jack, too, to take a part in the trial, Uncle Tom ?" demanded the niece, with a little interest in the answer.

"Jack, too—everybody in short. When the life of a fine young woman is concerned, it behooves her counsel to be active and diligent. I have never before had a cause into which my feelings have so completely entered—no, never."

"Do not counsel always enter, heart and hand, into their clients' interests, and make themselves, as it might be, as you gentlemen of the bar sometimes term these things, a ' part and parcel ' of their concerns ? "

The question was put by Sarah, but it caused Anna to raise her eyes from the fruit she was pretending to eat, and to listen intently to the reply. Perhaps she fancied that the answer might explain the absorbed manner in which John had engaged in the service of the accused.

"As far from it as possible, in many cases," returned the uncle ; "though there are certainly others in which one engages with all his feelings. But every day lessens my interest in the law, and all that belongs to it."

"Why should that be so, sir ? I have heard you called a devotee of the profession."

"That's because I have no wife. Let man live a bachelor, and ten to one he gets some nickname or other. On the other hand, let him marry two or three times, like Ned McBrain—beg your pardon, Nanny, for speaking disrespectfully of your papa—but let a fellow just get his third wife, and they tack ' family ' to his appellation at once. He's an excellent *family* lawyer, or a capital *family* physician, or a supremely pious—no, I don't know that they've got so far as the parsons, for *they* are all *family* fellows."

"You have a spite against matrimony, Uncle Tom."

"Well, if I have, it stops with me, as a *family* complaint. *You* are free from it, my dear; and I'm half inclined to think Jack will marry before he is a year older. But here are the tardies at last."

Although the uncle made no allusion to the person his nephew was to marry, everybody but himself thought of Mary Monson at once. Anna turned pale as death; Sarah looked thoughtful, and even sad; and John became as red as scarlet. But the entrance of Michael Millington and Timms caused the conversation to turn on another subject, as a matter of course.

"We expected you to dinner, gentlemen," Dunscomb dryly remarked, as he pushed the bottle to his guests.

"Business before eating is my maxim, Squire Dunscomb," Timms replied. "Mr. Millington and I have been very busy in the office, from the moment Doctor McBrain and his lady—"

"Wife—say 'wife,' Timms, if you please. Or 'Mrs. McBrain,' if you like that better."

"Well, sir, I used the word I did out of compliment to the other ladies present. They love to be honored and signalized in our language, when we speak of them, sir, I believe."

"Poh! poh! Timms; take my advice, and let all these small matters alone. It takes a life to master them, and one must begin from the cradle. When all is ended, they are scarce worth the trouble they give. Speak good, plain, direct and manly English, I have always told you, and you'll get along well enough, but make no attempts to be fine. 'Doctor McBrain and *lady*' is next thing to 'going through Hurlgate' or meeting a 'lady friend.' You'll never get the right sort of a wife until you drop all such absurdities."

"I'll tell you how it is, squire; so far as law goes, or even morals, and I don't know but I may say general government politics, I look upon you as the best adviser I can consult. But when it comes to matrimony, I can't see how you should know any more about it than I do myself. I *do* intend to get married one of these days, which is more, I fancy, than you ever had in view."

"No; my great concern has been to escape matrimony; but a man may get a very tolerable notion of the sex while maneuvering among them, with that intention. I am not certain that he who has had two or three handsomely man-aged escapes, doesn't learn as much as he who has had two or three wives—I mean of useful information. What do you think of all this, Millington?"

"That I wish for no escapes, when my choice has been free and fortunate."

"And you, Jack?"

"Sir!" answered the nephew, starting as if aroused from a brown study. "Did you speak to me, Uncle Tom?"

"*He*'ll not be of much use to us next week, Timms," said the counselor, coolly, filling his own and his neighbor's glass, as he spoke, with iced Madeira—"These capital cases demand the utmost vigilance; more especially when popular prejudice sets in against them."

"Should the jury find Mary Monson to be guilty, what would be the sentence of the court?" demanded Sarah, smiling, even while she seemed much interested—"I believe that is right, Mike—the court 'sentences,' and the jury 'convicts.' If there be any mistake, you must answer for it."

"I am afraid to speak of laws or constitutions in the presence of your uncle, since the rebuke Jack and I got in that affair of the toast," returned Sarah's betrothed, arching his eyebrows.

"By the way, Jack, did that dinner ever come off?" demanded the uncle, suddenly; "I looked for your toasts in the journals, but do not remember ever to have seen them."

"You could not have seen any of mine, sir; for I went to Biberry that very morning, and only left there last evening"—Anna's countenance resembled a lily, just as it begins to droop—"I believe, however, the whole affair fell through, as no one seems to know, just now, who are and who are not the friends of liberty. It is the people to-day; some prince to-morrow; the Pope next day; and by the end of the week, we may have a Masaniello or a Robespierre uppermost. The times seem sadly out of joint just now, and the world is fast getting to be upside down."

"It's all owing to this infernal Code, Timms, which is enough to revolutionize human nature itself!" cried Dunscomb, with an animation that produced a laugh in the young folk (Anna excepted), and a simper in the person addressed. "Ever since this thing has come into operation among us, I never know when a case is to be heard, the decision had, or the principles that are to come uppermost. Well, we must try and get some good out of it, if we can, in this capital case."

"Which is drawing very near, squire; and I have some facts to communicate in that affair which it may be well to compare with the law, without much more delay."

"Let us finish this bottle—if the boys help us, it will not be much more than a glass apiece."

"I don't think the squire will ever be up*held* at the polls by the temperance people," said Timms, filling his glass to the brim ; for, to own the truth, it was seldom that he got such wine.

"As *you* are expecting to be held *up* by them, my fine fellow. I've heard of your management, Master Timms, and am told you aspire as high as the State Senate. Well ; there is room for better, but much worse men have been sent there. Now let us go to what I call the ' Rattletrap office.' "

CHAPTER XI.

" The strawberry grows underneath the nettle,
And wholesome berries thrive and ripen best,
Neighbor'd by fruit of baser quality."
—KING HENRY V.

THERE stood a very pretty pavilion in one of the groves of Rattletrap, over-hanging the water, with the rock of the river-shore for its foundation. It had two small apartments, in one of which Dunscomb had caused a bookcase, a table, a rocking-chair, and a lounge to be placed. The other was furnished more like an or-dinary summer-house, and was at all times accessible to the inmates of the family. The sanctum, or office, was kept locked ; and here its owner often brought his pa-pers, and passed whole days, during the warm months, when it is the usage to be out of town, in preparing his cases. To this spot, then, the counselor now held his way, attended by Timms, having or-dered a servant to bring a light and some cigars ; smoking being one of the regular occupations of the office. In a few min-utes, each of the two men of the law had a cigar in his mouth, and was seated at a little window that commanded a fine view of the Hudson, its fleet of sloops, steamers, tow-boats, and colliers, and its high, rocky western shore, which has obtained the not inappropriate name of the Palisades.

The cigars, the glass, and the pleasant scenery, teeming as was the last with movement and life, appeared, for the moment, to drive from the minds of the two men of the law the business on which they had met. It was a proof of the effect of habit that a person like Duns-comb, who was really a good man, and one who loved his fellow-creatures, could just then forget that a human life was in some measure dependent on the decis-ions of this very interview, and permit his thoughts to wander from so impor-tant an interest. So it was, however ; and the first topic that arose in this con-sultation had no reference whatever to Mary Monson or her approaching trial, though it soon led the colloquists round to her situation, as it might be, without their intending it.

"This is a charming retreat, Squire Dunscomb," commenced Timms, settling himself with some method in a very com-modious arm-chair ; "and one that I should often frequent, did I own it."

"I hope you will live to be a master of one quite as pleasant, Timms, some time or other. They tell me your practice now is one of the best in Dukes ; some two or three thousand a year, I daresay, if the truth were known."

"It's as good as anybody's on our cir-cuit, unless you count the bigwigs from New York. I won't name the sum, even to as old a friend as yourself, squire ; for the man who lets the world peep into his purse, will soon find it footing him up, like a sum in arithmetic. You've gentle-men in town, however, who sometimes get more for a single case, that I can 'arn in a twelvemonth."

"Still, considering your beginning, and late appearance at the bar, Timms, you are doing pretty well. Do you lead in many trials at the circuit ? "

"That depends pretty much on age, you know, squire. Gen'rally older law-yers are put into all my causes ; but I have carried one or two through on my own shoulders, and that by main strength too."

"It must have been by your facts, rather than by your law. The verdicts turned altogether on testimony, did they not ? "

" Pretty much—and *that's* the sort of a case *I* like. A man can prepare his evi-dence beforehand, and make some calcula-tions where it will land him ; but, as for the law, I do not see that studying it as hard as I will, makes me much the wiser. A case is no sooner settled one way by a judge in New York, than it is settled in another, in Pennsylvany or Virginny."

"And that, too, when courts were identical and had a character ? Now, we have eight Supreme Courts, and they are beginning to settle the law in eight differ-ent ways. Have you studied the Code pretty closely, Timms ? "

"Not I, sir. They tell me things will come round under it in time, and I try to be patient. There's one thing about it that I *do* like. It has taken all the Latin out of the law, which is a great help to us poor scholars."

"It has that advantage, I confess; and before it is done, it will take all the law out of the Latin. They tell me it was proposed to call the old process of '*ne exeat*' a writ of 'no go.'"

"Well, to my mind, the last would be the best term of the two."

"Ay, to *your* mind, it might, Timms. How do you like the fee-bills, and the new mode of obtaining your compensation?"

"Capital! The more they change them matters, the deeper we'll dig into 'em, squire! I never knew reform help the great body of the community—all it favors is individuals."

"There is more truth in that, Timms, than you are probably aware of yourself. Reform, fully half the time, does no more than shift the pack-saddle from one set of shoulders to another. Nor do I believe much is gained by endeavoring to make law cheap. It were better for the community that it should be dear; though cases do occur in which its charges might amount to a denial of justice. It is to be regretted that the world oftener decides under the influence of exceptions, rather than under that of the rule. Besides, it is no easy matter to check the gains of a thousand or two hungry attorneys."

"There you're right, squire, if you never hit the nail on the head before. But the new scheme is working well for *us*, and, in one sense, it may work well for the people. The compensation is the first thing thought of now; and when that is the case, the client stops to think. It isn't every person that holds as large and as open a purse as our lady at Biberry!"

"Ay, she continues to fee you, does she, Timms? Pray, how much has she given you, altogether?"

"Not enough to build a new wing to the Astor Library, nor to set up a person in a Gothic temple; still, enough to engage me, heart and hand, in her service. First and last, my receipts have been a thousand dollars, besides money for the outlays."

"Which have amounted to—"

"More than as much more. This is a matter of life and death, you know, sir; and prices are accordingly. All I have received have been handed to me either in gold or in good current paper. The first troubled me a good deal, for I was not certain some more pieces might not be recognized, though they were all eagles and half-eagles."

"Has any such recognition occurred?" demanded Dunscomb, with interest.

"To be frank with you, Squire Dunscomb, I sent the money to town at once, and set it afloat in the great current in Wall Street, where it could do neither good nor harm on the trial. It would have been very green in me to pay out the precise coin among the people of Dukes. No one could say what might have been the consequences."

"It is not very easy for me to foretell the consequences of the substitutes which, it seems, you *did* use. A fee to a counsel I can understand; but what the deuce you have done, legally, with a thousand dollars out-of-doors, exceeds my penetration. I trust you have not been attempting to purchase jurors, Timms?"

"Not I, sir. I know the penalties too well, to venture on such a defense. Besides, it is too soon to attempt that game. Jurors may be bought; sometimes *are* bought, I have heard say"—here Timms screwed up his face into a most significant mimicry of disapprobation—"but *I* have done nothing of the sort in the 'State *vs.* Mary Monson.' It is too soon to operate, even should the testimony drive us to *that*, in the long run."

"I forbid all illegal measures, Timms. You know my rule of trying causes is never to overstep the limits of the law."

"Yes, sir; I understand your principle, which will answer, provided both sides stick to it. But, let a man act as close to what is called honesty as he please, what certainty has he that his adversary will observe the same rule? This is the great difficulty I find in getting along in the world, squire; opposition upsets all man's best intentions. Now, in politics, sir, there is no man in the country better disposed to uphold respectable candidates and just principles than I am myself; but the other side squeezes us up so tight, that before the election comes off I'm ready to vote for the devil, rather than get the worst of it."

"Ay, that's the wicked man's excuse all the world over, Timms. In voting for the gentleman you have just mentioned, you will remember you are sustaining the enemy of your race, whatever may be his particular relation to his party. But in this affair at Biberry, you will please to remember it is not an election, nor is the devil a candidate. What success have you had with the testimony?"

"There's an abstract of it, sir; and a pretty mess it is! So far as I can see, we shall have to rest entirely on the witnesses of the State; for I can get nothing out of the accused."

"Does she still insist on her silence, in respect of the past?"

"As close as if she had been born dumb. I have told her in the strongest language, that her life depends on her appearing before the jury with a plain tale and a good character ; but she will help me to neither. I never had such a client before—"

"Open-handed you mean, I suppose, Timms ?"

"In that partic'lar, Squire Dunscomb, she is just what the profession likes— liberal, and pays down. Of course, I am so much the more anxious to do all I can in her case; but she will not let me serve her."

"There must be some strong reason for all this reserve, Timms. Have you questioned the Swiss maid that my niece sent to her ? We know *her,* and it would seem that she knows Mary Monson. Here is so obvious a way of coming at the past, I trust you have spoken to her ?"

"She will not let me say a word to the maid. There they live together, chatter with one another from morning to night, in French that nobody understands ; but will see no one but me, and me only in public, as it might be."

"In public ! You have not asked for *private* interviews, eh, Timms ? Remember your views upon the county, and the great danger there is of the electors finding you out."

"I well know, Squire Dunscomb, that your opinion of me is not very flattering in some partic'lars ; while in others I think you place me pretty well up the ladder. As for old Dukes, I believe I stand as well in that county as any man in it, now the Revolutionary patriots are nearly gone. So long as any of *them* lasted, we modern fellows had no chance ; and the way in which relics were brought to light was wonderful ! If Washington only had an army one-tenth as strong as these patriots make it out to be, he would have driven the British from the country years sooner than it was actually done. Luckily, my grandfather *did* serve a short tour of duty in that war ; and my own father was a captain of militia in 1814, lying out on Harlem Heights and Harlem Common, most of the fall ; when and where he caught the rheumatism. This was no bad capital to start upon : and, though you treat it lightly, squire, I'm a favorite in the county—I *am !*"

"Nobody doubts it, Timms ; or can doubt it, if he knew the history of these matters. Let me see—I believe I first heard of you as a temperance lecturer ?"

"Excuse me, I began with the Common Schools, on which I lectured with some success, one whole season. *Then* came the temperance cause, out of which, I will own, not a little capital was made."

"And do you stop there, Timms ; or do you ride some other hobby into power ?"

"It's my way, Mr. Dunscomb, to try all sorts of medicines. Some folks that won't touch rhubarb will swallow salts; and all palates must be satisfied. Free Sile and Emancipation Doctrines are coming greatly into favor ; but they are ticklish things, that cut like a two edged sword, and I do not fancy meddling with them. There are about as many opposed to meddling with slavery in the free States, as there are in favor of it. I wish I knew your sentiments, Squire Dunscomb, on this subject. I've always found your doctrines touching the constitution to be sound, and such as would stand examination."

"The constitutional part of the question is very simple, and presents no difficulties whatever," returned the counselor, squinting through the ruby of his glass, with an old-bachelor sort of delight, "except for those who have special ends to obtain."

"Has, or has not, Congress a legal right to enact laws preventing the admission of slaves into California ?"

"Congress has the legal right to govern any of its territories despotically ; of course, to admit or to receive what it may please within their limits. The resident of a territory is not a citizen, and has no *legal* claim to be so considered. California, as a conquered territory, may be thus governed by the laws of nations, unless the treaty of cession places some restrictions on the authority of the conqueror. A great deal of absurdity is afloat among those who should kuow better, touching the powers of government in this country. You, yourself, are one of those fellows, who get things upside-down, and fancy the constitution is to be looked into for everything."

"And is it not, squire ?—that is, in the way of theory—in practice, I know it is a very different matter. Are we not to look into the constitution for all the powers of the government ?"

"Of the *government,* perhaps, in one sense—but not for those of the *nation.* Whence come the powers to make war and peace, to form treaties and alliances, maintain armies and navies, coin money, etc ?"

"You'll find them all in the constitution, as I read it, sir."

"There is just your mistake ; and connected with it are most of the errors that are floating about in our political world. The *country* gets its legal right to do all these things from the laws of nations ; the constitution merely saying *who* shall be its agents in the exercise of these powers. Thus *war* is rendered legal by the custom of nations ; and the constitution says Congress shall declare war. It also says Congress shall pass all laws that become necessary to carry out this power.

It follows, Congress may pass any law that has a legitimate aim to secure a conquest. Nor is this all the functionaries of the government can do, on general principles, in the absence of any special provisions by a direct law. The latter merely supersedes or directs the power of the former. The constitution guarantees nothing to the territories. They are strictly subject, and may be governed absolutely. The only protection of their people is in the sympathy and habits of the people of the States. We give them political liberty, not as of legal necessity, but as a boon to which they are entitled in good fellowship—or as the father provides for his children."

"Then you think Congress has power to exclude slavery from California?"

"I can't imagine a greater legal absurdity than to deny it. I see no use in any legislation on the subject, as a matter of practice, since California will shortly decide on this interest for herself; but, as a right in theory, it strikes me to be madness to deny that the government of the United States has full power over all its territories, both on general principles and under the constitution."

"And in the Deestrict—you hold to the same power in the Deestrict?"

"Beyond a question. Congress can abolish domestic servitude or slavery in the District of Columbia whenever it shall see fit. The *right* is as clear as the sun at noonday."

"If these are your opinions, Squire, I'll go for Free Sile and Abolition in the Deestrict. They have a popular cry, and take wonderfully well in Dukes, and will build me up considerable. I like to be right; but, most of all, I like to be strong."

"If you'll adopt such a course, you will espouse trouble without any dower, and that will be worse than McBrain's three wives; and what is more, in the instance of the District, you will be guilty of an act of oppression. You will remember that the possession of a legal power to do a particular thing, does not infer a moral right to exercise it. As respects your Free Soil, it may be well to put down a foot; and so far as votes legally used can be thrown, to prevent the further extension of slavery. In this respect you are right enough, and will be sustained by an overwhelming majority of the nation; but, when it comes to the District, the question has several sides to it."

"You said yourself, Squire, that Con-

gress has all power to legislate for the Deestrict?"

"No doubt it has—but the possession of a power does not necessarily imply its use. We have power, as a nation, to make war on little Portugal, and crush her: but it would be very wicked to do so. When a member of Congress votes on any question that strictly applies to the District, he should reason precisely as if his constituents all lived in the District itself. You will understand, Timms, that liberty is closely connected with practice, and is not a mere creature of phrases and professions. What more intolerable tyranny could exist than to have a man elected by New Yorkers legislating for the District on strictly New York policy; or, if you will, on New York prejudices? If the people of the District wish to get rid of the institution of domestic slavery, there are ways for ascertaining the fact; and once assured of that, Congress ought to give the required relief. But in framing such a law, great care should be taken not to violate the comity of the Union. The comity of nations is, in practice, a portion of their laws, and is respected as such; how much more, then, ought we to respect this comity in managing the relations between the several States of this Union!"

"Yes, the *sovereign* States of the Union," laying emphasis on the word we have italicized.

"Pshaw—they are no more sovereign than you and I are sovereign."

"Not sovereign, sir!" exclaimed Timms, actually jumping to his feet in astonishment; "why, this is against the National Faith—contrary to all the theories."

"Something so, I must confess; yet very good common sense. If there be any sovereignty left in the States, it is the very minimum, and a thing of show, rather than of substance. If you will look at the constitution, you will find that the equal representation of the States in the Senate is the only right of a sovereign character that is left to the members of the Union separate and apart from their confederated communities."

Timms rubbed his brows, and seemed to be in some mental trouble. The doctrine of the "Sovereign States" is so very common, so familiar in men's mouths, that no one dreams of disputing it. Nevertheless, Dunscomb had a great reputation in his set as a constitutional lawyer, and the "expounders" were very apt to steal his demonstrations, without giving him credit for them. As before the nation, a school-boy would have carried equal weight; but the direct, vigorous, common-sense arguments that he brought to the discussions, as well as the originality of his views, ever commanded the profound respect of the intelligent. Timms had cut out for himself a path by which he intended to ascend in the scale of society; and had industriously, if not very profoundly, considered all the agitating questions of the day, in the relations they might be supposed to bear to his especial interests. He had almost determined to come out an abolitionist; for he saw that the prejudices of the hour were daily inclining the electors of the Northern States, more and more, to oppose the further extension of domestic slavery, so far as surface was concerned, which was in effect preparing the way for the final destruction of the institution altogether. For Mr. Dunscomb, however, this wily limb of the law, and skillful manager of men, had the most profound respect; and he was very glad to draw him out still further on a subject that was getting to be of such intense interest to himself, as well as to the nation at large; for, out of all doubt, it is *the* question, not only of the "Hour," but for years to come.

"Well, sir, this surprises me more and more. The States not sovereign! Why, they *gave* all the power it possesses to the Federal Government!"

"Very true; and it is precisely for *that* reason they are not sovereign—that which is given away is no longer possessed. All the great powers of sovereignty are directly bestowed on the Union, which alone possesses them."

"I will grant you that, squire; but enough is retained to hang either of us. The deuce is in it if that be not a sovereign power."

"It does not follow from the instance cited. Send a squadron abroad, and its officers can hang; but they are not sovereign, for the simple reason that there is a recognized authority over them, which can increase, sustain or take away altogether any such and all other power. Thus is it with the States. By a particular clause, the constitution can be amended, including all the interests involved, with a single exception. This is an instance in which the exception does strictly prove the rule. All interests but the one excepted can be dealt with, by a species of legislation that is higher than common. The Union can constitutionally abolish domestic slavery altogether—"

"It can! It would be the making of any political man's fortune to be able to show *that!*"

"Nothing is easier than to show it, in the way of theory, Timms; though nothing would be harder to achieve, in the way of practice. The constitution can be legally amended so as to effect this end, provided majorities in three-fourths of the States can be obtained, though every living soul in the remaining States were opposed to it. That this is the just construction of the great fundamental law, as it has been solemnly adopted, no discreet man can doubt; though, on the other hand, no discreet person would think of attempting such a measure, as the vote necessary to success cannot be obtained. To talk of the sovereignty of a community over this particular interest, for instance, when all the authority on the subject can be taken from it in direct opposition to the wishes of every man, woman and child it contains, is an absurdity. The sovereignty, as respects slavery, is in the Union, and not in the several States; and therein you can see the fallacy of contending that Congress has nothing to do with the interest, when Congress can take the initiative in altering this or any other clause of the great natural compact."

"But, the Deestrict—the Deestrict, Squire Dunscomb—what can and ought to be done there?"

"I believe in my soul, Timms, you have an aim on a seat in Congress! Why stop short of the Presidency? Men as little likely as yourself to be elevated to that high office have been placed in the executive chair: and why not you as well as another?"

"It is an office 'neither to be sought nor declined,' said an eminent statesman," answered Timms, with a seriousness that amused his companion, who saw, by his manner, that his old pupil held himself in reserve for accidents of political life. "But, sir, I am very anxious to get right on the subject of the Deestrict"—Timms pronounced this word as we have spelt it—"and I know that if any man can set me right, it is yourself."

"As respects the District, Mr. Timms, here is my faith. It is a territory provided for in the constitution for a national purpose, and must be regarded as strictly national property, held exclusively for objects that call all classes of citizens within its borders. Now, two great principles, in my view, should control all legislation for this little community. As I have said already, it would be tyranny to make the notions and policy of New York or Vermont bear on the legislation of the District; but every member is bound to act strictly as a representative of the people of the spot for whom the law is intended. If I were in Congress, I would at any time, on a respectable application, vote to refer the question of abolition to the people of the District; if they said ay, I would say ay; if no, no. Beyond this I would never go; nor do I think the man who wishes to push matters beyond this sufficiently respects the general principles of representative government, or knows how to respect the spirit of the national compact.

"On the supposition that the District ask relief from the institution of slavery, great care should be observed in granting the necessary legislation. Although the man in South Carolina has no more right to insist that the District should maintain the 'peculiar institution,' because his particular State maintains it, than the Vermontese to insist on carrying his Green Mountain notions into the District laws; yet has the Carolinian rights in this territory that must ever be respected, let the general policy adopted be what it may. Every American has an implied right to visit the District on terms of equality. Now there would be no equality if a law were passed excluding the domestics from any portion of the country. In the slave States, slaves exclusively perform the functions of domestics; and sweeping abolition might very easily introduce regulations that would be unjust toward the slave-holders. As respects the Northern man, the existence of slavery in or out of the District is purely a speculative question; but it is not so with the Southern. This should never be forgotten; and I always feel disgust when I hear a Northern man swagger and make a parade of his morality on this subject."

"But the Southern men swagger and make a parade of their chivalry, squire, on the other hand!"

"Quite true; but, with them, there is a strong provocation. It is a matter of life and death to the South; and the comity of which I spoke requires great moderation on our part. As for the threats of dissolution, of which we have had so many, like the cry of 'Wolf,' they have worn themselves out and are treated with indifference."

"The threat is still used, Mr. Dunscomb!"

"Beyond a doubt, Timms; but of one thing you may rest well assured—if ever there be a separation between the free and the slave States of this Union, the wedge will be driven home by Northern hands; not by indirection, but coolly, steadily, and with a thorough Northern determination to open the seam. There will be no fuss about chivalry, but the thing will be done. I regard the measure as very unlikely to happen, the Mississippi and its tributaries binding the States together, to say nothing of ancestry, history, and moral ties, in a way to render a rupture very difficult to effect; but, should it come at all, rely on it, it will come directly from the North. I am sorry to say there is an impatience of the threats and expedients that have so much disfigured Southern policy that have set many at the North 'to calculating the value'; and thousands may now be found, where ten years since it would not have been easy to meet with one, who deem separation better than union with slavery. Still, the general feeling of the North is passive; and I trust it will so continue."

"Look at the laws for the recovery of fugitives, squire, and the manner in which they are administered."

"Bad enough, I grant you, and full of a want of good faith. Go to the bottom of this subject, Timms, or let it alone altogether. Some men will tell you that slavery is a sin, and contrary to revealed religion. This I hold to be quite untrue. At all events, if it be a sin it is a sin to give the son the rich inheritance of the father, instead of dividing it among the poor; to eat a dinner while a hungrier man than yourself is within sound of your voice; or, indeed, to do anything that is necessary and agreeable, when the act may be still more necessary to, or confer greater pleasure on, another. I believe in a Providence, and make little doubt that African slavery is an important feature in God's laws, instead of being disobedience to them. But enough of this, Timms—you will court popularity, which is your Archimedean lever, and forget all I tell you. Is Mary Monson in greater favor now than when I last saw you?"

"The question is not easily answered, sir. She pays well, and money is a powerful screw!"

"I do not inquire what you do with her money," said Dunscomb, with the evasion of a man who knew that it would not do to probe every weak spot in morals, any more than it would do to inflame the diseases of the body; "but, I own, I should like to know if our client has any suspicions of its uses?"

Timms now cast a furtive glance behind him, and edged his chair nearer to his companion, in a confidential way, as if he would trust him with a private opinion that he should keep religiously from all others.

"Not only does she know all about it," he answered with a knowing inclination of the head, "but she enters into the affair, heart and hand. To my great surprise, she has even made two or three suggestions that were capital in their way! Capital! yes, sir; quite capital! If you were not so stiff in your practice, squire, I should delight to tell you all about it. She's sharp, you may depend on it! She's wonderfully sharp!"

"What! That refined, lady-like, accomplished young woman!"

"She has an accomplishment or two you've never dreamed of, squire. I'd pit her ag'in the sharpest practitioner in Dukes, and she'd come out ahead. I thought I knew something of preparing a cause; but she has given hints that will be worth more to me than all her fees!"

"You do not mean that she shows *experience* in such practices?"

"Perhaps not. It seems more like mother-wit, I acknowledge; but it's mother-wit of the brightest sort. She understands them reporters by instinct, as it might be. What is more, she backs all her suggestions with gold, or current bank-notes."

"And where can she get so much money?"

"That is more than I can tell you," returned Timms, opening some papers belonging to the case, and laying them a little formally before the senior counsel, to invite his particular attention. "I've never thought it advisable to ask the question."

"Timms, you do not, *cannot* think Mary Monson guilty?"

"I never go beyond the necessary facts of a case; and my opinion is of no consequence whatever. We are employed to defend her; and the counsel for the State are not about to get a verdict without working some for it. That's my conscience in these matters, Squire Dunscomb."

Dunscomb asked no more questions. He turned gloomily to the papers, shoved his glass aside, as if it gave him pleasure no longer, and began to read. For near four hours he and Timms were earnestly engaged in preparing a brief, and in otherwise getting the cause ready for trial.

CHAPTER XII.

"*Hel.*—Oh, that my prayers could such affection move.
   Her.—The more I hate, the more he follows me.
  Hel.—The more I love, the more he hateth me.
  Her.—His folly, Helena, is no fault of mine."
        —MIDSUMMER NIGHT'S DREAM.

WHILE Dunscomb and Timms were thus employed, the younger members of the party very naturally sought modes of entertainment that were more in conformity with their tastes and years. John Wilmeter had been invited to be present at the consultation; but his old feelings were revived, and he found a pleasure in being with Anna that induced him to disregard the request. His sister and his friend were now betrothed, and they had glided off along one of the pretty paths of the Rattletrap woods, in a way that is so very common to persons in their situation. This left Jack alone with Anna. The latter was timid, shy even; while the former was thoughtful. Still, it was not easy to separate; and they, too, almost unconsciously to themselves, were soon walking in that pleasant wood, following one of its broadest and most frequented paths, however.

John, naturally enough, imputed the thoughtfulness of his companion to the event of the morning; and he spoke kindly to her, and with a gentle delicacy on the subject, that more than once compelled the warm-hearted girl to struggle against her tears. After he had said enough on this topic, the young man followed the current of his own thoughts, and spoke of her he had left in the jail of Biberry.

"Her case is most extraordinary," continued John, "and it has excited our liveliest sympathy. By ours, I mean the disinterested and intelligent; for the vulgar prejudice is strong against her. Sarah, or even yourself, Anna,"— his companion looked more like herself, at this implied compliment, than she had done before that day—"could not seem less likely to be guilty of anything wrong, than this Miss Monson; yet she stands indicted, and is to be tried for murder and arson! To me, it seems monstrous to suspect such a person of crimes so heinous."

Anna remained silent half a minute; for she had sufficient good sense to know that appearances, unless connected with facts, ought to have no great weight in forming an opinion of guilt or innocence. As Jack evidently expected an answer, however, his companion made an effort to speak.

"Does she say nothing of her friends, nor express a wish to have them informed of her situation?" Anna succeeded in asking.

"Not a syllable. I could not speak to her on the subject, you know—"

"Why not?" demanded Anna quickly.

"Why not? You've no notion, Anna, of the kind of person this Miss Monson is. You cannot talk to *her* as you would to an every-day sort of young lady; and, now she is in such distress, one is natu-

rally more cautious about saying anything to add to her sorrow."

"Yes, I can understand *that*," returned
the generous-minded girl; "and I think
you are very right to remember all this,
on every occasion. Still, it is so natural
for a female to lean on her friends, in
every great emergency, I cannot but wonder that your client—"

"Don't call her my *client*, Anna, I beg
of you. I hate the word as applied to this
lady. If I serve her in any degree, it is
solely as a friend. The same feeling prevails with Uncle Tom; for I understand
he has not received a cent of Miss Monson's money, though she is liberal of it to
profuseness. Timms is actually getting
rich on it."

"Is it usual for you gentlemen of the
bar to give your services gratuitously to
those who can pay for them?"

"As far from it as possible," returned
Jack, laughing. "We look to the main
chance like so many merchants or brokers,
and seldom open our mouths without shut-
ting our hearts. But this is a case altogether out of the common rule; and Mr.
Dunscomb works for love, and not for
money."

Had Anna cared less for John Wilmeter,
she might have said something clever
about the nephew's being in the same category as the uncle; but her feelings were
too deeply interested to suffer her even to
think what would seem to her profane.
After a moment's pause, therefore, she
quietly said:

"I believe you have intimated that Mr.
Timms is not quite so disinterested?"

"Not he—Miss Monson has given him
fees amounting to a thousand dollars, by
his own admission; and the fellow has
had the conscience to take the money. I
have remonstrated about his fleecing a
friendless woman in this extravagant
manner; but he laughs in my face for my
pains. Timms has good points, but honesty is not one of them. He says no
woman can be friendless who has a pretty
face, and a pocket full of money."

"You can hardly call a person unfriended who has so much money at command, John," Anna answered with timidity; but not without manifest interest in
the subject. "A thousand dollars sounds
like a large sum to me!"

"It is a good deal of money for a fee;
though much more is sometimes given. I
daresay Miss Monson would have gladly
given the same to Uncle Tom, if he would
have taken it. Timms told me that she
proposed offering as much to him; but he
persuaded her to wait until the trial was
over."

"And where does all this money come
from, John?"

"I'm sure I do not know—I am not at
all in Miss Monson's confidence; on her
pecuniary affairs, at least. She *does*
honor me so much as to consult me about
her trial occasionally, it is true; but to
me she has never alluded to money, except
to ask me to obtain change for large
notes. I do not see anything so very
wonderful in a lady's having money.
You, who are a sort of heiress yourself,
ought to know that."

"I do not get money in thousands, I
can assure you, Jack; nor do I think that
I have got it to get. I believe my whole
income would not much more than meet
the expenditure of this strange woman—"

"Do not call her *woman*, Anna; it
pains me to hear you speak of her in such
terms."

"I beg her pardon and yours, Jack;
but I meant no disrespect. We are all
women."

"I know it is foolish to feel nervous on
such a subject; but I cannot help it. One
connects so many ideas of vulgarity and
crime with prisons, and indictments, and
trials, that we are apt to suppose all who
are accused to belong to the commoner
classes. Such is not the fact with Miss
Monson, I can assure you. Not even
Sarah—nay, not even *yourself*, my dear
Anna, can pretend to more decided marks
of refinement and education. I do not
know a more distinguished young woman—"

"There, Jack; now *you* call her a woman yourself," interrupted Anna, a little
archly; secretly delighted at the compliment she had just heard.

"*Young* woman—anybody can say that,
you know, without implying anything
common or vulgar, and *woman*, too,
sometimes. I do not know how it was;
but I did not exactly like the word as
you happened to use it. I believe close
and long watching is making me nervous;
and I am not quite as much myself as
usual."

Anna gave a very soft sigh, and that
seemed to afford her relief, though it was
scarcely audible; then she continued the
subject.

"How old is this extraordinary young
lady?" she demanded, scarcely speaking
loud enough to be heard.

"Old! How can I tell? She is very
youthful in appearance; but, from the
circumstance of her having so much
money at command, I take it for granted
she is of age. The law now gives to every
woman the full command of all her prop-

erty, even though married, after she become of age.''

"Which I trust you find a very proper attention to the rights of our sex ? "

"I care very little about it ; though Uncle Tom says it is of a piece with all our late New York legislation."

"Mr. Dunscomb, like most elderly persons, has little taste for change."

"It is not that. He thinks that minds of an ordinary stamp are running away with the conceit that they are on the road of progress ; and that most of our recent improvements, as they are called, are marked by empiricism. This ' tea-cup law,' as he terms it, will set the women above their husbands, and create two sets of interests where there ought to be but one."

"Yes ; I am aware such is his opinion. He remarked, the day he brought home my mother's settlement for the signatures, that it was the most ticklish part of his profession to prepare such papers. I remember one of his observations, which struck me as being very just."

"Which you mean to repeat to me, Anna ? "

"Certainly, John, if you wish to hear it," returned a gentle voice, coming from one unaccustomed to refuse any of the reasonable requests of this particular applicant. "The remark of Mr. Dunscomb was this : He said that most family misunderstandings grew out of money ; and he thought it unwise to set it up as a bone of contention between man and wife. Where there was so close a union in all other matters, he thought there might safely be a community of interests in this respect. He saw no sufficient reason for altering the old law, which had the great merit of having been tried."

"He could hardly persuade rich fathers and vigilant guardians, who have the interests of heiresses to look after, to subscribe to all his notions. They say that it is better to make a provision against imprudence and misfortune, by settling a woman's fortune on herself, in a country where speculation tempts so many to their ruin."

"I do not object to anything that may have an eye to an evil day, provided it be done openly and honestly. But the income should be common property, and like all that belongs to a family, should pass under the control of its head."

"It is very liberal in you to say and think this, Anna ! "

"It is what every woman, who has a true woman's heart, could wish, and would do. For myself, I would marry no man whom I did not respect and look up to in most things ; and surely, if I gave him my heart and my hand, I could wish to give him as much control over my means as circumstances would at all allow. It might be prudent to provide against misfortune by means of settlements ; but this much done, I feel certain it would afford me the greatest delight to commit all that I could to a husband's keeping."

"Suppose that husband were a spendthrift, and wasted your estate ? "

"He could waste but the income, were there a settlement ; and I would rather share the consequences of his imprudence with him, than sit aloof in selfish enjoyment of that in which he did not partake."

All this sounded very well in John's ears ; and he knew Anna Updyke too well to suppose she did not fully mean all that she said. He wondered what might be Mary Monson's views on this subject.

"It is possible for the husband to partake of the wife's wealth, even when he does not command it," the young man resumed, anxious to hear what more Anna might have to say.

"What ! as a dependent on her bounty ? No woman who respects herself could wish to see her husband so degraded ; nay, no female, who has a true woman's heart, would ever consent to place the man to whom she has given her hand in so false a position. It is for the woman to be dependent on the man, and not the man on the woman. I agree fully with Mr. Dunscomb, when he says that ' silken knots are too delicate to be rudely undone by dollars.' The family in which the head has to ask the wife for the money that is to support it must soon go wrong ; as it is placing the weaker vessel uppermost."

"You would make a capital wife, Anna, if these are really your opinions ! "

Anna blushed, and almost repented of her generous warmth ; but, being perfectly sincere, she would not deny her sentiments.

"They ought to be the opinion of every wife," she answered. "I could not endure to see the man to whom I could wish on all occasions to look up, soliciting the means on which we both subsisted. It would be my delight, if I had money and he had none, to pour all into his lap, and then come and ask of him as much as was necessary to my comfort."

"If he had the soul of a man he would not wait to be asked, but would endeavor to anticipate your smallest wants. I believe you are right, and that happiness is best secured by confidence."

"And in not reversing the laws of nature. Why do women vow to obey and honor their husbands, if they are to retain them as dependents? I declare, John Wilmeter, I should almost despise the man who could consent to live with me on any terms but those in which nature, the Church, and reason, unite in telling us he ought to be the superior."

"Well, Anna, this is good, old-fashioned, womanly sentiment; and I will confess it delights me to hear it from *you*. I am the better pleased, because, as Uncle Tom is always complaining, the weakness of the hour is to place your sex above ours, and to reverse all the ancient rules in this respect. Let a woman, now-adays, run away from her husband, and carry off the children; it is ten to one but some crotchety judge, who thinks more of a character built up on gossip than of deferring properly to that which the laws of God and the wisdom of man have decreed, refuse to issue a writ of *habeas corpus* to restore the issue to the father."

"I do not know, John,"—Anna hesitatingly rejoined, with a true woman's instinct—"it *would* be so hard to rob a mother of her children!"

"It might be *hard*, but in such a case it would be *just*. I like that word 'rob,' for it suits both parties. To me it seems that the father is the party robbed, when the wife not only steals away from her duty to her husband, but deprives him of his children too."

"It is wrong, and I have heard Mr. Dunscomb express great indignation at what he called the 'soft-soapiness' of certain judges in cases of this nature. Still, John, the world is apt to think a woman would not abandon the most sacred of her duties without a cause. That feeling must be at the bottom of what you call the decision, I believe, of these judges."

"If there be such a cause as would justify a woman in deserting her husband, and in stealing his children—for it is robbery after all, and robbery of the worst sort, since it involves breaches of faith of the most heinous nature—let that cause be shown, that justice may pronounce between the parties. Besides, it is not true that women will not sometimes forget their duties without sufficient cause. There are capricious, and uncertain, and egotistical women, who follow their own wayward inclinations, as well as selfish men. Some women love power intensely, and are never satisfied with simply filling the place that was intended for them by nature. It is hard for such to submit to their husbands, or, indeed, to submit to any one."

"It must be a strange female," an-

swered Anna, gently, "who cannot suffer the control of the man of her choice, after quitting father and mother for his sake."

"Different women have different sources of pride that make their husbands very uncomfortable, even when they remain with them and affect to discharge their duties. One will pride herself on family, and take every occasion to let her beloved partner know how much better she is connected than he may happen to be; another is conceited, and fancies herself cleverer than her lord and master, and would fain have him take *her* advice on all occasions; while a third may have the most money, and delight in letting it be known that it is *her* pocket that sustains the household."

"I did not know, John, that you thought so much of these things," said Anna, laughing; "though I think you are very right in your opinions. Pray, which of the three evils that you have mentioned would you conceive the greatest?"

"The second. I might stand family pride; though it is disgusting when it is not ridiculous. Then the money might be got along with for its own sake, provided the purse were in my hand; but I really do not think I could live with a woman who fancied she knew the most."

"But, in many things, women ought to, and *do*, know the most."

"Oh! as to accomplishments, and small talk, and making preserves, and dancing, and even poetry and religion—yes, I will throw in religion—I could wish my wife to be clever—very clever—as clever as you are yourself, Anna?"—the fair listener colored, though her eyes brightened at this unintended but very direct compliment—"yes, yes; all that would do well enough. But when it came to the affairs of men, out-of-door concerns, or politics, or law, or anything, indeed, that called for a masculine education and understanding, I could not endure a woman who fancied she knew the most."

"I should think few wives would dream of troubling their husbands with their opinions touching the law!"

"I don't know that. You've no notion, Anna, to what a pass conceit can carry a person; you, who are so diffident and shy, and always so ready to yield to those who ought to know best. I've met with women who, not content with arraying their own charms in their own ways, must fancy they can teach us how to put on our clothes, tell us how to turn over a wristband, or settle a shirt-collar!"

"This is not conceit, John, but good taste," cried Anna, now laughing outright, and appearing herself again. "It is merely female tact teaching male awkwardness how to adorn itself. But surely no woman, John, would bother herself about law, let her love of domination be as strong as it might."

"I am not so sure of that. The only really complaisant thing I ever saw about this Mary Monson"—a cloud again passed athwart the bright countenance of Anna— "was a sort of strange predilection for law. Even Timms has remarked it, and commented on it, too."

"The poor woman—"

"Do not use that word in speaking of her, if you please, Anna."

"Well, lady—if you like that better—"

"No—say young lady—or Miss Monson—or Mary, which has the most agreeable sound of all."

"Yet, I think I have been told that none of you believe she has been indicted by her real name."

"Very true; but it makes no difference. Call her by that she has assumed; but do not call her by an *alias* as wretched as that of 'poor woman.' "

"I meant no slight, I do assure you, John; for I feel almost as much interest in Miss Monson as you do yourself. It is not surprising, however, that one in her situation should feel an interest in the law."

"It is not this sort of interest that I mean. It has seemed to me, once or twice, that she dealt with the difficulties of her own case as if she took a pleasure in meeting them—had a species of professional pleasure in conquering them. Timms will not let me into his secrets, and I am glad of it, for I fancy all of them would not bear the light; but he tells me, honestly, that some of Miss Monson's suggestions have been quite admirable !"

"Perhaps she has been" — Anna checked herself with the consciousness that what she was about to utter might appear to be, and what was of still greater importance in her own eyes, might really be, ungenerous.

"Perhaps what? Finish the sentence, I beg of you." Anna shook her head.

"You intended to say that perhaps Miss Monson had some *experience* in the law, and that it gave her a certain satisfaction to contend with its difficulties, in consequence of previous training. Am I not right ?"

Anna would not answer in terms; but she gave a little nod of assent, coloring scarlet.

"I knew it; and I will be frank enough to own that Timms thinks the same thing. He has hinted as much as that; but the thing is impossible. You have only to look at her to see that such a thing is impossible."

Anna Updyke thought that almost anything of the sort might be possible to a female who was in the circumstances of the accused; this, however, she would not say, lest it might wound John's feelings, for which she had all the tenderness of warm affection, and a woman's self-denial. Had the case been reversed, it is by no means probable that her impulsive companion would have manifested the same forbearance on her account. John would have contended for victory, and pressed his adversary with all the arguments, facts and reasons he could muster, on such an occasion. Not so with the gentler and more thoughtful young woman who was now walking quietly, and a little sadly, at his side, instinct with all the gentleness, self-denial, and warm-hearted affection of her sex.

"No, it is worse than an absurdity"— resumed John—"it is cruel to imagine anything of the sort of Miss—— By the way, Anna, do you know that a very singular thing occurred last evening, before I drove over to town, to be present at the wedding. You know Marie Mill ?"

"Certainly—Marie Moulin, you should say."

"Well, in answering one of her mistress's questions she said ' *oui, madame.*'"

"What would you have her say ?— ' *non,* madame ? ' "

"But why madame at all ? Why not mademoiselle ? "

"It would be very vulgar to say ' Yes, miss,' in English."

"To be sure it would; but it is very different in French. One *can* say—*must* say mademoiselle to a young unmarried female in that language; though it be vulgar to say miss, without the name, in English. French, you know, Anna, is a much more precise language than our own; and those who speak it do not take the liberties with it t hat we take with the English. *Madame* always infers a married woman; unless, indeed, it be with a woman a hundred years old."

"No French woman is ever *that,* John —but it *is* odd that Marie Moulin, who so well understands the usages of her own little world, should have said *madame* to a *demoiselle.* Have I not heard, nevertheless, that Marie's first salutation, when she was admitted to the jail, was a simple exclamation of ' mademoiselle' ? "

"That is very true; for I heard it myself. What is more, that exclamation was almost as remarkable as this; French servants always adding the name under such circumstances, unless they are addressing their own particular mistresses. Madame and mademoiselle are appropriated to those they serve; while it is mademoiselle this, or madame that, to every one else."

"And now she calls her *mademoiselle* or *madame!* It only proves that too much importance is not to be attached to Marie Moulin's sayings and doings."

"I'm not so sure of that. Marie has been three years in this country, as we all know. Now the young person that she left a *mademoiselle* might very well have become a *madame* in that interval of time. When they met, the domestic may have used the old and familiar term in her surprise; or she may not have known of the lady's marriage. Afterward, when there had been leisure for explanations between them, she gave her mistress her proper appellation."

"Does she habitually say madame now, in speaking to this singular being?"

"Habitually she is silent. Usually she remains in the cell when any one is with Miss—or Mrs. Monson, perhaps I ought to say "—John used this last term with a strong expression of spite, which gave his companion a suppressed but infinite delight—"but when any one is with the mistress, call her what you will, the maid commonly remains in the dungeon or cell. Owing to this, I have never been in the way of hearing the last address the first, except on the two occasions named. I confess I begin to think—"

"What, John?"

"Why, that our *Miss* Monson may turn out to be a married woman, after all."

"She is very young, is she not? Almost too young to be a wife?"

"Not at all! What do you call too young? She is between twenty and twenty-two or three. She may even be twenty-five or six."

Anna sighed, though almost imperceptibly to herself; for these were ages that well suited her companion, though the youngest exceeded her own by a twelvemonth. Little more, however, was said on the subject at that interview.

It is one of the singular effects of the passion of love, more especially with the generous-minded and just of the female sex, that a lively interest is often awakened in behalf of a successful or favored rival. Such was now the fact as regards the feeling that Anna Updyke began to entertain toward Mary Monson. The critical condition of the lady would of itself excite interest where it failed to produce distrust; but the circumstance that John Wilmeter saw so much to admire in this unknown female, if he did not actually love her, gave her an importance in the eyes of Anna that at once elevated her into an object of the highest interest. She was seized with the liveliest desire to see the accused, and began seriously to reflect on the possibility of effecting such an end. No vulgar curiosity was mingled with this new-born purpose; but, in addition to the motives that were connected with John's state of mind, these was a benevolent and truly feminine wish, on the part of Anna, to be of service to one of her own sex, so cruelly placed, and cut off, as it would seem, from all communication with those who should be her natural protectors and advisers.

Anna Updyke gathered, through that which had fallen from Wilmeter and his sister, that the intercourse between the former and his interesting client had been of the most reserved character; therein showing a discretion and self-respect on the part of the prisoner that spoke well for her education and delicacy. How such a woman came to be in the extraordinary position in which she was placed was of course as much a mystery to her as to all others; though, like every one else who knew aught of the case, she indulged in conjectures of her own on the subject. Being of a particularly natural and frank disposition, without a particle of any ungenerous or detracting quality, and filled with woman's kindness in her very soul, this noble-minded young woman began now to feel far more than an idle curiosity in behalf of her who had so lately caused herself so much pain, not to say bitterness of anguish. All was forgotten in pity for the miserable condition of the unconscious offender; unconscious, for Anna was sufficiently clear-sighted and just to see and to admit that, if John had been led astray by the charms and sufferings of this stranger, the fact could not rightfully be imputed to the last, as a fault. Every statement of John's went to confirm this act of justice to the stranger.

Then, the unaccountable silence of Marie Moulin doubled the mystery and greatly increased the interest of the whole affair. This woman had gone to Biberry pledged to communicate to Sarah all she knew or might learn, touching the accused; and well did Anna know that her friend would make her the repository of her own information, on this as well as on other subjects; but a most unaccountable silence governed the course of the domestic, as well as that of her strange mistress. It really seemed that, in passing the principal door of the jail, Marie Moulin had buried herself in a convent, where all communication with the outer world was forbidden. Three several letters from Sarah had John handed in at the grate, certain that they must have reached the hands of the Swiss; but no answer had been received. All attempts to speak to Marie were quietly but most ingeniously evaded by the tact and readiness of the prisoner; and the hope of obtaining information from that source was abandoned by Sarah, who was too proud to solicit a servant for that which the last was reluctant to communicate. With Anna the feeling was different. She had no curiosity on the subject, separated from a most generous and womanly concern in the prisoner's forlorn state; and she thought far less of Marie Moulin's disrespect and forgetfulness of her word than of Mary Monson's desolation and approaching trial.

CHAPTER XIII.

"Was it for this we sent out
Liberty's cry from our shore?
Was it for this that her shout
Thrill'd to the world's very core?"
—MOORE'S NATIONAL AIRS.

THE third day after the interviews just related, the whole party left Rattletrap for Timbully, where their arrival was expected by the bride and bridegroom, if such terms can be applied to a woman of forty-five and a man of sixty. The Dukes County circuit and Oyer and Terminer were about to be held, and it was believed that Mary Monson was to be tried. By this time so lively an interest prevailed among the ladies of the McBrain and Dunscomb connections in behalf of the accused, that they had all come to a determination to be present in court. Curiosity was not so much at the bottom of this movement as womanly kindness and sympathy. There seemed a bitterness of misery in the condition of Mary Monson, that appealed directly to the heart; and that silent but eloquent appeal was answered, as has just been stated, generously and with warmth by the whole party from town. With Anna Updyke the feeling went materially further than with any of her friends. Strange as it may seem, her interest in John increased that which she felt for his mysterious client; and her feelings became enlisted in the stranger's behalf so much the more in consequence of this triangular sort of passion.

The morning of the day on which the party crossed the country from Rattletrap to Timbully, Timms arrived at the latter place. He was expected, and was soon after closeted with the senior counsel in the pending and most important cause.

"Does the district attorney intend to move for the trial?" demanded Dunscomb, the instant the two were alone.

"He tells me he does, sir; and that early in the week, too. It is my opinion we should go for postponement. We are hardly ready, while the State is too much so."

"I do not comprehend this, Timms. The law officers of the public would hardly undertake to run down a victim, and she a solitary and unprotected woman!"

"That's not it. The law officers of the State don't care a straw whether Mary Monson is found guilty or is acquitted. That is, they care nothing about it *at present*. The case may be different when they are warmed up by a trial and opposition. Our danger comes from Jesse Davis, who is a nephew of Peter Goodwin, his next of kin and heir, and who thinks a great deal of money was hoarded by the old people; much more than the stocking ever held or could hold, and who has taken it into his wise head that the prisoner has laid hands on this treasure, and is carrying on her defense with his cash. This has roused him completely, and he has retained two of the sharpest counsel on our circuit, who are beginning to work as if the bargain has been clinched in the hard metal. Williams has given me a great deal of trouble already. I know him; he will not work without pay; but pay him liberally, and he is up to anything."

"Ay, you are diamond cut diamond, Timms—outsiders in the profession. You understand that I work only in the open court, and will know nothing of this outdoor management."

"We do not mean to let you know anything about it, squire," returned Timms, dryly. "Each man to his own manner of getting along. I ought to tell you, however, it has gone out that you are working without a fee, while I am paid in the most liberal manner."

"I am sorry for that. There is no great harm in the thing itself; but I dislike the parade of seeming to be unusually generous. I do not remember to have spoken of this circumstance where it would be likely to be repeated; and I beg you will be equally discreet."

"The fact has not come from me, I can assure you, sir. It puts me in too awkward a position to delight me; and I make it a point to say as little as possible of what is disagreeable. I do not relish the idea of being thought selfish by my future constituents. Giniros'ty is my cue before *them*. But they say you work for love, sir."

"Love!" answered Dunscomb, quickly. "Love of what?' or of *whom?*"

"Of your client—that's the story now. It is said that you admire Miss Monson; that she is young, and handsome, and rich; and she is to marry you, if acquitted. If found guilty and hanged, the bargain is off, of course. You may look displeased, squire; but I give you my word such is the rumor."

Dunscomb was extremely vexed; but he was too proud to make any answer. He knew that he had done that which, among the mass of this nation, is a very capital mistake, in not placing before its observation an intelligible *motive*—one on the level of the popular mind—to prevent these freaks of the fancy dealing with his affairs. It is true, that the natural supposition would be that he worked for his fee, as did Timms, had not the contrary got out; when he became subject to all the crude conjectures of those who ever look for the worst motives for everything. Had he been what is termed a favorite public servant, the very reverse would have been the case, and there was little that he might not have done with impunity; but, having no such claims on the minds of the mass, he came under the common law which somewhat distinguishes their control. Too much disgusted, however, to continue this branch of the subject, the worthy counselor at once adverted to another.

"Have you looked over the list of the jurors, Timms?" he demanded, continuing to sort his papers.

"That I never fail to do, sir, the first thing. It's my brief, you know, Squire Dunscomb. All *safe* York law, nowadays, is to be found in that learned body; especially in criminal cases. There is but one sort of suit in which the jury counts for nothing, and might as well be dispensed with."

"Which is—?"

"An ejectment cause. It's not one time in ten that they understand anything about the matter, or care anything about it; and the court usually leads in those actions—but our Dukes County juries are beginning to understand their powers in all others."

"What do you make of the list?"

"It's what I call reasonable, squire. There are two men on it who would not hang Cain, were he indicted for the murder of Abel."

"Quakers, of course?"

"Not they. The time was when we were reduced to the 'thee's,' and the 'thou's,' for this sort of support; but philanthropy is abroad, sir, covering the land. Talk of the schoolmaster! Why, squire, a new philanthropical idee will go two feet to the schoolmaster's one. Pro-nigger, anti-gallows, eternal peace, woman's rights, the people's power, and anything of that sort sweeps like a tornado through the land. Get a juror who has just come into the anti-gallows notion, and I would defy the State to hang a body-snatcher who lived by murdering his subjects."

"And you count on two of these partisans for our case!"

"Lord, no, sir. The district attorney himself knows them both; and Davis's counsel have been studying that list for the last week, as if it were Blackstone in the hands of a new beginner. I can tell you, Squire Dunscomb, that the jury-list is a most important part of a case out here in the country!"

"I am much afraid it is, Timms; though I never examined one in my life."

"I can believe you, sir, from what I have seen of your practice. But principles and facts won't answer in an age of the world when men are ruled by talk and prejudice. There is not a case of any magnitude tried, nowadays, without paying proper attention to the jury. We are pretty well off, on the whole; and I am tolerably sanguine of a disagreement, though I fear an acquittal is quite out of the question."

"You rely on one or two particularly intelligent and disinterested men, ha! Timms?"

"I rely on five or six particularly ignorant and heated partisans, on the contrary; men who have been reading about the abolishing of capital punishments, and who, in gin'ral, because they've got hold of some notions that have been worn out as far back as the times of the Cæsars, fancy themselves philosophers and the children of progress. The country is getting to be full of what I call donkeys and racers; the donkey is obstinate, and backs going up-hill; while the racers will not only break their own necks, but those of their riders, too, unless they hold up long before they reach their goal."

"I did not know, Timms, that you think so much on such subjects. To me, you have always appeared to be a purely working man—no theorist."

"It is precisely because I am a man of action, and live in the world, and see things as they were meant to be seen, that I laugh at your theories. Why, sir, this country, in my judgment, for the time being, could much better get along without preaching, than without hanging. I don't say always; for there is no telling yet what is to be the upshot of preaching. It may turn out as many think; in which case human natur' will undergo a change that will pretty much destroy our business. Such a state of things would be worse for the bar, squire, than the Code or the last fee-bill."

"I'm not so sure of that, Timms; there are few things worse than this infernal Code."

"Well, to my taste, the fee-bill is the most disagreeable of the two. A man can stand any sort of law, and any sort of practice; but he can't stand any sort of pay. I hear the circuit is to be held by one of the new judges—a people's man, altogether."

"You mean by that, I suppose, Timms, one of those who did not hold office under the old system! It is said that the new broom sweeps clean—it is fortunate ours has not brushed away all the old incumbents."

"No, that is to come; and come it will, as sure as the sun rises. We must have rotation on the bench, as well as in all other matters. You see, squire, rotation is a sort of *claim* with many men, who have no other. They fancy the earth to have been created on a sort of Jim Crow principle, because it turns round."

"That is it; and it explains the clamor that is made about it. But to return to this jury, Timms; on the whole, you like it, I should infer?"

"Not too well, by any means. There are six or eight names on the list that I'm always glad to see; for they belong to men who are friendly to me—"

"Good God, man—it cannot be possible that you count on such assistants in a trial for a human life!"

"Not count on it, Squire Dunscomb! I count on it from an action of trespass on the case, to this indictment—count on it, quite as much, and a good deal more rationally, than you count on your law and evidence. Didn't I carry that heavy case *for* the railroad company on that principle altogether? The law was dead against us, they say, and the facts were against us; but the verdict was in our favor. That's what I call practicing law!"

"Yes; I remember to have heard of that case, and it was always a wonder with the bar how you got along with it. Had it been a verdict *against* a corporation, no one would have thought anything of it—but to carry a bad case *for* a com-

pany, nowadays, is almost an unheard-of thing."

"You are quite right, sir. I can beat any railroad in the State, with a jury of a neighborhood, let the question or facts be what they may; but, in this instance, I beat the neighborhood, and all through the faith the jury had in *me*. It's a blessed institution, this of the jury, Squire Dunscomb! no doubt it makes us the great, glorious, and free people that we are!"

"If the bench continues to lose its influence as it has done, the next twenty years will see it a curse of the worst character. It is now little more than a popular cabal in all cases in the least calculated to awaken popular feeling or prejudice."

"There's the rub in this capital case of ours. Mary Monson has neglected popularity altogether; and she is likely to suffer for it."

"Popularity!" exclaimed Dunscomb, in a tone of horror—"and this in a matter of life and death! What are we coming to in the law, as well as in politics! No public man is to be found of sufficient moral courage, or intellectual force, to stem this torrent; which is sweeping away everything before it. But in what has our client failed, Timms?"

"In almost everything connected with this one great point; and what vexes me is her wonderful power of pleasing, which is completely thrown away. Squire Dunscomb, I would carry this county for Free Sile or ag'in it, with that lady to back me, as a wife."

"What if she should refuse to resort to popular airs and graces?"

"I mean, of course, she aiding and abetting. I would give the world, now, could we get the judge into her company for half an hour. It would make a friend of him; and it is still something to have a friend in the judge in a criminal case."

"You may well say '*still*,' Timms; how much longer it will be so, is another matter. Under the old system it would be hopeless to expect so much complaisance in a judge; but I will not take it on myself to say what a people's judge will not do."

"If I thought the thing could be managed, by George, I would attempt it! The grand jurors visit the jails, and why not the judges? What do you think, sir, of an anonymous letter hinting to his honor that a visit to Mrs. Gott—who is an excellent creature in her way—might serve the ends of justice!"

"As I think of all underhanded movements and trickery. No, no, Timms; you had better let our client remain unpopular, than undertake anything of this nature."

"Perhaps you are right, sir. Unpopular she is, and will be as long as she pursues her present course; whereas she might carry all classes of men with her. For my part, Squire Dunscomb, I've found this young lady"—here Timms paused, hemmed, and concluded by looking a little foolish—a character of countenance by no means common with one of his shrewdness and sagacity.

"So, so, Master Timms," said the senior counsel, regarding the junior with a sort of sneer—"you are as great a fool as my nephew, Jack Wilmeter; and have fallen in love with a pretty face, in spite of the grand jury and the gallows?"

Timms gave a gulp, seemed to catch his breath, and regained enough of his self-command to be able to answer.

"I'm in hopes that Mr. Wilmeter will think better of this, sir," he said, "and turn his views to a quarter where they will be particularly acceptable. It would hardly do for a young gentleman of his expectations to take a wife out of a jail."

"Enough of this foolery, Timms, and come to the point. Your remarks about popularity may have some sense in them, if matters have been pushed too far in a contrary direction. Of what do you complain?"

"In the first place, she will not show herself at the windows; and that offends a great many persons who think it proud and aristocratic in her not to act as other criminals act. Then, she has made a capital mistake with a leading reporter, who sent in his name and desired an interview; which she declined granting. She will hear from that man, depend on it, sir."

"I shall look to him, then—for, though this class of men is fast putting the law under foot, it may be made to turn on them, by one who understands it, and has the courage to use it. I shall not allow the rights of Mary Monson to be invaded by such a fungus of letters."

"Fungus of letters! Ahem—if it was anybody but yourself, squire, that I was talking to, I might remind you that these funguses flourish on the dung-hill of the common mind."

"No matter; the law *can* be made to touch them, when in good hands; and mine have now some experience. Has this reporter resented the refusal of the prisoner to see him?"

"He is squinting that way, and has got himself sent to Biberry by two or three journals, to report the progress of the trial. I know the man; he is vindictive, impudent, and always uses his craft to indulge his resentments."

"Ay, many of those gentry are up to that. Is it not surprising, Timms, that in a country forever boasting of its freedom, men do not see how much abuse there is of a very important interest, in suffering these irresponsible tyrants to ride rough-shod over the community?"

"Lord, squire, it is not with the reporters only that abuses are to be found. I was present, the other day, at a conversation between a judge and a great town lawyer, when the last deplored the state of the juries! 'What would you have?' says his honor; 'angels sent down from heaven to fill the jury-boxes?' Waal"—Timms never could get over the defects of his early associations—"Waal, squire," he continued, with a shrewd leer of the eyes, "I thought a few saints might be squeezed in between the lowest angel in heaven and the average of our Dukes County panels. This is a great fashion of talking that is growing up among us to meet an objection by crying out, 'Men are not angels;' as if some men are not better than others."

"The institutions clearly maintain that some men are better than others, Timms!"

"That's news to me, I will own. I thought the institutions declared all men alike—that is, all white men; I know that the niggers are nonsuited."

"They are unsuited, at least, according to the spirit of the institutions. If all men are supposed to be alike, what use is there in the elections? Why not draw lots for office, as we draw lots for juries? Choice infers inequalities, or the practice is an absurdity. But here comes McBrain, with a face so full of meaning, he must have something to tell us."

Sure enough, the bridegroom-physician came into the room at that instant; and without circumlocution he entered at once on the topic that was then uppermost in his mind. It was the custom of the neighborhood to profit by the visits of this able practitioner to his country-place, by calling on him for advice in such difficult cases as existed anywhere in the vicinity of Timbully. Even his recent marriage did not entirely protect him from these appeals, which brought so little pecuniary advantage as to be gratuitous; and he had passed much of the last two days in making professional visits in a circle around his residence that included Biberry. Such was the means by which he had obtained the information that now escaped from him, as it might be, involuntarily.

"I have never known so excited a state

of the public mind," he cried, "as now exists all around Biberry, on the subject of your client, Tom, and this approaching trial. Go where I may, see whom I will, let the disease be as serious as possible, all, patients, parents, friends and nurses, commence business with asking me what I think of Mary Monson, and of her guilt or innocence."

"That's because you are married, Ned" —Dunscomb coolly answered. "Now no one thinks of putting such a question to *me*. I see lots of people, as well as yourself; but not a soul has asked me whether I thought Mary Monson guilty or innocent."

"Poh! you are her counsel, and no one could take the liberty. I daresay that even Mr. Timms, here, your associate, has never compared notes with you on that particular point."

Timms was clearly not quite himself; and he did not look as shrewd as he once would have done at such a remark. He kept in the background, and was content to listen.

"I do suppose association with a brother in the law, and in a case of life and death, is something like matrimony, Dr. McBrain. A good deal must be taken for granted, and not a little on credit. As a man is bound to believe his wife the most excellent, virtuous, most amiable and best creature on earth, so is a counsel bound to consider his client innocent. The relation, in each case, is confidential, however; and I shall not pry into your secrets, any more than I shall betray one of my own."

"I asked for none, and wish none; but one may express surprise at the intense degree of excitement that prevails all through Dukes, and even the adjacent counties."

"The murder of a man and his wife in cold blood, accompanied by robbery and arson, are enough to arouse the community. In this particular case the feeling of interest is increased, I make no doubt, by the extraordinary character, as well as by the singular mystery, of the party accused. I have had many clients, Ned, but never one like this before; as you have had many wives, but no one so remarkable as the present Mrs. McBrain."

"Your time will come yet, Master Dunscomb—recollect I have always prognosticated that."

"You forget that I am approaching sixty. A man's heart is as hard and dry as a bill in chancery at that age—but, I beg your pardon, Ned; *you* are an exception."

"I certainly believe that a man can have affections, even at four score—and what is more, I believe that when the reason and judgment come in aid of the passions—"

Dunscomb laughed outright; nay, he even gave a little shout, his bachelor habits having rendered him more exuberant in manner than might otherwise have been the case.

"Passions!" he cried, rubbing his hands, and looking round for Timms, that he might have some one to share in what he regarded as a capital joke. "The passions of a fellow of three-score! Ned, you do not flatter yourself that you have been marrying the Widow Updyke in consequence of any *passion* you feel for her?"

"I do, indeed," returned the doctor, with spirit; mustering resolution to carry the war into the enemy's country. "Let me tell you, Tom Dunscomb, that a warm-hearted fellow can love a woman dearly, long after the age you have mentioned—that is, provided he has not let all feeling die within him, for want of watering a plant that is the most precious boon of a most gracious Providence."

"Ay, if he begin at twenty, and keep even pace with his beloved down the descent of time."

"That may all be true: but, if it has been his misfortune to lose one partner, a second—"

"And a third, Ned, a third—why not foot the bill at once, as they say in the market?"

"Well, a third, too, if circumstances make that demand on him. Anything is better than leaving the affections to stagnate for want of cultivation."

"Adam in Paradise, by Jove! But I'll not reproach you again, since you have got so gentle and kind a creature, and one who is twenty years your junior—"

"Only eighteen, if you please, Mr. Dunscomb."

"Now I should be glad to know whether you have added those two years to the bride's age, or substracted them from that of the bridegroom! I suppose the last, however, as a matter of course."

"I do not well see how you can suppose any such thing, knowing my age as well as you do. Mrs. McBrain is forty-two, an age when a woman can be as lovable as at nineteen—more so, if her admirer happens to be a man of sense."

"And sixty-two. Well, Ned, you are incorrigible; and, for the sake of the excellent woman who has consented to have you, I only hope this will be the last exhibition of your weakness. So they talk a good deal of Mary Monson, up and down the country, do they ? ''

" Of little else, I can assure you. I am sorry to say, the tide seems to be setting strongly against her."

"That is bad news ; as few jurors, now-adays, are superior to such an influence. What is said, in particular, Dr. McBrain ? In the way of facts, I mean ? ''

" One report is that the accused is full of money ; and that a good deal of that which she is scattering broadcast has been seen by different persons, at different times, in the possession of the deceased Mrs. Goodwin.''

" Let them retail the lie, far and near, squire, and we'll turn it to good account,'' said Timms, taking out his notebook, and writing down what he had just heard. "I have reason to think that every dollar Mary Monson has uttered since her confinement—''

" Imprisonment would be a better word, Mr. Timms,'' interrupted the doctor.

"I see no great difference,'' replied the literal attorney—"but imprisonment if you prefer it. I have reason to think that every dollar Mary Monson has put in circulation since she entered the jail at Biberry, has come from either young Mr. Wilmeter or myself, in exchange for hundred-dollar notes—and, in one instance, for a note of five hundred dollars. She is well off, I can tell you, gentlemen ; and if she is to be executed, her executor will have something to do when all is over.''

" You do not intend to allow her to be hanged, Timms ?'' demanded McBrain, aghast.

" Not if I can help it, doctor ; and this lie about the money, when clearly disproved, will be of capital service to her. Let them circulate it as much as they please, the rebound will be in proportion to the blow. The more they circulate that foolish rumor, the better it will be for our client when we come to trial.''

"I suppose you are right, Timms ; though I could prefer plainer dealings. A cause in which you are employed, however, must have more or less of management.''

" Which is better, squire, than your law and evidence. But what else has Dr. McBrain to tell us ?''

" I hear that Peter Goodwin's nephew, who it seems had some expectations from the old people, is particularly savage, and leaves no stone unturned to get up a popular feeling against the accused.''

" He had best beware,'' said Dunscomb, his usually colorless but handsome face flushing as he spoke. "I shall not trifle in a matter of this sort—ha ! Timms ?''

" Lord bless you, squire, Dukes County folks wouldn't understand a denial of the privilege to say what they please in a case of this sort. They fancy this is liberty ; and ' touch my honor, take your poker,' is not more sensitive than the feelin' of liberty in these parts. I'm afraid that not only this Joe Davis, but the reporters, will say just what they please ; and Mary Monson's rights will whistle for it. You will remember that our judge is not only a brand new one, but he drew the two years' term into the bargain. No, 1 think it will be wisest to let the law, and old principles, and the right, and *true* liberty, quite alone ; and to bow the knee to things as they are. A good deal is said about our fathers, and their wisdom, and patriotism, and sacrifices ; but nobody dreams of doing as they *did*, or of reasoning as they *reasoned*. Life is made up, in reality, of these little matters in a corner ; while the great principles strut about in buckram, for men to admire them and talk about them. I do take considerable delight, Squire Dunscomb, in hearing them enlarge on a principle, whether it be in law, morals, or politics ; but I should no more think of practysing on 'em, than I should think of refusing a thousand dollar fee.''

" Is that your price ?'' demanded McBrain, with curiosity. " Do you work for as large a sum as that, in this case, Timms ?''

" I'm paid, doctor ; just as you was ''— the attorney never stuck at grammar— " just as you was for that great operation on the Wall Street Millenary'ian—''

" Millionaire, you mean, Timms,'' said Dunscomb, coolly—" it means one worth a million.''

" I never attempt a foreign tongue but I stumble,'' said the attorney, simply ; for he knew that both his friends were familiar with his origin, education, and advancement in life, and that it was wisest to deny nothing to *them ;* " but since I have been so much with Mary Monson and her woman, I do own a desire to speak the language they use.''

Again Dunscomb regarded his associate intently ; something comical gleaming in his eye.

" Timms, you have fallen in love with your handsome client,'' he quietly remarked.

" No, sir ; not quite as bad as that, *yet ;* though I will acknowledge that the lady is very interesting. Should she be acquitted, and could we only get some knowledge of her early history—why, that *might* put a new face on matters.''

" I must drive over to Biberry in the

morning, and have another interview with the lady myself. And now, Ned, I will join your wife, and read an epithalamium prepared for this great occasion. You need not trouble yourself to follow, the song being no novelty; for I have read it twice before on your account."

A hearty laugh at his own wit concluded the discourse on the part of the great York counselor; though Timms remained some time longer with the doctor, questioning the latter touching opinions and facts gleaned by the physician in the course of his circuit.

CHAPTER XIV.

"From his brimstone bed at break of day,
    A-walking the devil is gone,
To visit his little snug farm of the earth,
    And see how his stock went on."—COLERIDGE.

DUNSCOMB was as good as his word. Next morning he was on the way to Biberry. He was thoughtful; had laid a bundle of papers on the front seat of the carriage, and went his way musing and silent. Singularly enough, his only companion was Anna Updyke, who had asked a seat in the carriage timidly, but with an earnestness that prevailed. Had Jack Wilmeter been at Biberry, this request would not have been made; but she knew he was in town, and that she might make the little excursion without the imputation of indelicacy, so far as he was concerned. Her object will appear in the course of the narrative.

The "best tavern" in Biberry was kept by Daniel Horton. The wife of this good man had a native propensity to talk that had been essentially cultivated in the course of five-and-twenty years' practice in the inn where she had commenced her career as maid; and was now finishing it as mistress. As is common with persons of her class, she knew hundreds of those who frequented her house; calling each readily by name, and treating every one with a certain degree of professional familiarity that is far from uncommon in country inns.

"Mr. Dunscomb, I declare!" cried this woman, as she entered the room and found the counselor and his companion in possession of her best parlor. "This is a pleasure I did not expect until the circuit. It's quite twenty years, squire, since I had the pleasure of first waiting on you in this house. And a pleasure it has always been; for I've not forgotten the ejectment suit that you carried for Horton when we was only new beginners. I am glad to see you, sir; welcome to Biberry, as is this young lady, who is your daughter, I presume, Mr. Dunscomb."

"You forget that I am a bachelor, Mrs. Horton—no marrying man, in any sense of the word."

"I might have known that, had I reflected a moment; for they say Mary Monson employs none but bachelors and widowers in her case; and you are her counsel, I know."

"This is a peculiarity of which I was not aware. Timms is a bachelor, certainly, as well as myself; but to whom else can you allude? Jack Wilmeter, my nephew, can hardly be said to be employed at all; nor, for that matter, Michael Millington; though neither is married."

"Yes, sir; we know both of the last well, they having lodged with us. If young Mr. Wilmeter is single, I fancy it is not his own fault"—here Mrs. Horton looked very wise, but continued talking— "Young gentlemen of a good appearance and handsome fortunes commonly have not much difficulty in getting wives—not as much as young ladies; for you men make the law, and you give your own sex the best chance, almost as a matter of course—"

"Pardon me, Mrs. Horton," interrupted Dunscomb, a little formally, like one who felt great interest in the subject— "you were remarking that we have the best chance of getting married; and here have I been a bachelor all my life, trying in vain to enter into the happy state of matrimony—if, indeed, it deserves to be so termed."

"It could not be very difficult for *you* to find a companion," said the landlady, shaking her head; "and for the reason I have just given."

"Which was—?"

"That you men have made the laws, and profit by them. *You* can *ask* whom you please; but a woman is obliged to wait to be asked."

"You never were in a greater mistake in your life, I do assure you, my good Mrs. Horton. There is no such law on the subject. Any woman may put the question, as well as any man. This *was* the law, and I don't think the Code has changed it."

"Yes, I know that well enough—and get laughed at, and pointed at, for her pains. I know that a good deal is said about leap-year; but who ever heard of a woman's putting the question? I fancy that even Mary Monson would think twice before she took so bold a step once."

"Mary Monson!" exclaimed Dunscomb, suddenly turning toward his hostess —"Has she a reputation for being attentive to gentlemen?"

"Not that I know of; but—"

"Then allow me to say, my good Mrs. Horton," interrupted the celebrated counselor, with a manner that was almost austere, "that you have been greatly to blame in hazarding the sort of remark you did. If you *know* nothing of the character you certainly insinuated, you should have said nothing. It is very extraordinary that women, alive as they must be to the consequences to one of their own sex, are ever more ready than men to throw out careless, and frequently malicious hints, that take away a reputation, and do a melancholy amount of harm in the world. Slander is the least respectable, the most unchristian-like, and the most unlady-like vice, of all the secondary sins of your sex. One would think the danger you are all exposed to in common would teach you greater caution."

"Yes, sir, that is true; but this Mary Monson is in such a pickle already that it is not easy to make *her* case much worse," answered Mrs. Horton, a good deal frightened at the austerity of Dunscomb's rebuke; for his reputation was too high to render his good or bad opinion a matter of indifference to her. "If you only knew the half that is said of her in Dukes, you wouldn't mind a careless word or so about her. Everybody thinks her guilty; and a crime more or less can be of no great matter to the likes of *her*."

"Ah, Mrs. Horton, these careless words do a vast deal of harm. They insinuate away a reputation in a breath; and my experience has taught me that they who are the most apt to use them are persons whose own conduct will least bear the light. Women with a whole log-heap of beams in their own eyes, are remarkable for discovering motes. Give me the female who floats along quietly in her sphere, unoffending and charitable, wishing for the best, and as difficult to be brought to *think* as to *do* evil. But they talk a good deal against my client, do they?"

"More than I have ever known folks talk against any indicted person, man or woman. The prize-fighters, who were in for murder, had a pretty hard time of it; but nothing to Mary Monson's. In short, until Squire Timms came out in her favor, she had no chance at all."

"This is not very encouraging, certainly—but what is said, Mrs. Horton, if you will suffer me to put the question?"

"Why, Squire Dunscomb," answered the woman, pursing up a very pretty American mouth of her own, "a body is never sure that you won't call what she says slander—"

"Poh—poh—you know me better than that. I never meddle with that vile class of suits. I am employed to defend Mary Monson, you know—"

"Yes, and are well paid for it, too, Squire Dunscomb, if all that a body hears is true," interrupted Mrs. Horton, a little spitefully. "Five thousand dollars, they say, to a cent!"

Dunscomb, who was working literally without other reward than the consciousness of doing his duty, smiled, while he frowned at this fresh instance of the absurdities into which rumor can lead its votaries. Bowing a little apology, he coolly lighted a cigar, and proceeded.

"Where is it supposed that Mary Monson can find such large sums to bestow, Mrs. Horton?" he quietly asked, when his cigar was properly lighted. "It is not usual for young and friendless women to have pockets so well lined."

"Nor is it usual for young women to rob and murder old ones, squire."

"Was Mrs. Goodwin's stocking thought to be large enough to hold sums like that you have mentioned?"

"Nobody knows. Gold takes but little room, as witness Californy. There was General Wilton—every one thought him rich as Cæsar—"

"Do you not mean Crœsus, Mrs. Horton?"

"Well, Cæsar or Crœsus; both were rich, I do suppose, and General Wilton was thought the equal of either; but when he died, his estate wouldn't pay his debts. On the other hand, old Davy Davidson was set down by nobody at more than twenty thousand, and he left ten times that much money. So I say nobody knows. Mrs. Goodwin was always a saving woman, though Peter would make the dollars fly, if he could get at them. There was certainly a weak spot in Peter, though known to but very few."

Dunscomb now listened attentively. Every fact of this nature was of importance just then; and nothing could be said of the murdered couple that would not influence all engaged in the cause to prick up their ears.

"I have always understood that Peter Goodwin was a very respectable sort of a man," observed Dunscomb, with a profound knowledge of human nature, which was far more likely to induce the woman to be communicative, in the way of opposition, than by any other process—"as respectable a man as any about here."

"So he might be, but he had his weak

points as well as other respectable men; though, as I have said already, his'n wasn't generally known. Everybody is respectable, I suppose, until they're found out. But Peter is dead and gone, and I have no wish to disturb his grave, which I believe to be a sinful act."

This sounded still more ominously, and it greatly increased Dunscomb's desire to learn more. Still he saw that great caution must be used, Mrs. Horton choosing to affect much tenderness for her deceased neighbor's character. The counselor knew human nature well enough to be aware that indifference was sometimes as good a stimulant as opposition; and he now thought it expedient to try the virtue of that quality. Without making any immediate answer, therefore, he desired the attentive and anxious Anna Updyke to perform some little office for him; thus managing to get her out of the room, while the hostess stayed behind. Then his cigar did not quite suit him, and he tried another, making divers little delays that set the landlady on the tenter-hooks of impatience.

"Yes, Peter is gone—dead and buried —and I hope the sod lies lightly on his remains!" she said, sighing ostentatiously.

"Therein you are mistaken, Mrs. Horton," the counselor coolly remarked— "the remains of neither of those found in the ruins of the house are under ground yet; but are kept for the trial."

"What a time we shall have of it !— so exciting and full of mystery !"

"And you might add 'custom,' Mrs. Horton. The reporters alone, who will certainly come from town like an inroad of Cossacks, will fill your house."

"Yes, and themselves, too. To be honest with you, Squire Dunscomb, too many of those gentry wish to be kept for nothing to make them pleasant boarders. I daresay, however, we shall be full enough next week. I sometimes wish there was no such thing as justice, after a hard-working Oyer and Terminer court."

"You shall be under no concern, my good Mrs. Horton, on that subject. There is really so little of the thing you have mentioned that no reasonable woman need make herself unhappy about it. So Peter Goodwin was a faultless man, was he?"

"As far from it as possible, if the truth was said of him; and seeing the man is not absolutely under ground, I do not know why it may not be told. I can respect the grave, as well as another; but, as he is not buried, one may tell the truth. Peter Goodwin was, by no means, the man he seemed to be."

"In what particular did he fail, my good Mrs. Horton?"

To be *good* in Dunscomb's eyes, the landlady well knew, was a great honor; and she was flattered as much by the manner in which the words were uttered, as by their import. Woman-like, Mrs. Horton was overcome by this little bit of homage; and she felt disposed to give up a secret which, to do her justice, had been religiously kept now for some ten or twelve years between herself and her husband. As she and the counsel were alone, dropping her voice a little, more for the sake of appearances than for any sufficient reason, the landlady proceeded.

"Why, you must know, Squire Dunscomb, that Peter Goodwin was a member of meetin', and a professing Christian, which I suppose was all the better for him, seeing that he was to be murdered."

"And do you consider his being a 'professing Christian,' as you call it, a circumstance to be concealed?"

"Not at all, sir; but I consider it a good reason why the facts I am about to tell you ought not to be generally known. Scoffers abound; and I take it that the feelings of a believer ought to be treated more tenderly than those of an unbeliever, for the church's sake."

"That is the fashion of the times, too— one of the ways of the hour, whether it is to last or not. But proceed if you please, my good Mrs. Horton; I am quite curious to know by what particular sin Satan managed to overcome this 'professing Christian?'"

"He drank, Squire Dunscomb—no, he *guzzled*, for that is the best word. You must know that Dolly was avarice itself —that's the reason she took this Mary Monson in to board, though her house was no ways suited for boarders, standing out of the way, with only one small spare bed-room, and that under the roof. Had she let this stranger woman come to one of the regular houses, as she might have done, and been far better accommodated than it was possible for her to be in a garret, it is not likely she would have been murdered. She lost her life, as I tell Horton, for meddling with other people's business."

"If such were the regular and inevitable punishment of that particular offense, my good landlady, there would be a great dearth of ladies," said Tom Dunscomb, a little dryly—"but you were remarking that Peter Goodwin, the member of meeting, and Mary Monson's supposed victim, had a weakness in favor of strong liquor?"

"Juleps were his choice—I've heard of a part of the country, somewhere about Virginny I believe it is, where teetotalers make an exception in favor of juleps—it may do *there*, Squire Dunscomb, but it won't do *here*. No liquor undoes a body, in this part of the country, sooner than mint juleps. I will find you ten constitutions that can hold out ag'in brandy, or plain grog, or even grog, beer, and cider, all three together, where you can find me one that will hold out ag'in juleps. I always set down a reg'lar julep fancier as a case—that is, in this part of the country."

"Very true, my good landlady, and very sensible and just. I consider you a sensible and just woman, whose mind has been enlarged by an extensive acquaintance with human nature—"

"A body does pick up a good deal in and around a bar, Squire Dunscomb!"

"Pick up, indeed—I've known 'em picked up by the dozen myself. And Peter *would* take the juleps?"

"Awfully fond of them! He no more dared to take one at home, however, than he dared to go and ask Minister Watch to make him one. No, he know'd better where the right sort of article was to be had, and always came down to our house when he was dry. Horton mixes stiff, or we should have been a good deal better off in the world than we are—not that we're mis'rable, as it is. But Horton takes it strong himself, and he mixes strong for others. Peter soon found this out, and he fancied his juleps more, as he has often told me himself, than the juleps of the great Bowery-man, who has a name for 'em, far and near. Horton *can* mix a julep, if he can do nothing else."

"And Peter Goodwin was in the habit of frequenting your house privately, to indulge this propensity?"

"I'm almost ashamed to own that he did—perhaps it was sinful in us to let him; but a body must carry out the idee of trade—our trade is tavern-keeping, and it's our business to mix liquors, though Minister Watch says, almost every Sabbath, that professors should do nothing out of sight that they wouldn't do before the whole congregation. I don't hold to that, however, for it would soon break up tavern-keeping altogether. Yes, Peter did drink awfully, in a corner."

"To intoxication, do you mean, Mrs. Horton?"

"To delirrum tremus, sir—yes, full up to that. His way was to come down to the village on the pretense of business, and to come right to our house, where I've known him to take three juleps in the first half-hour. Sometimes he'd pretend to go to town to see his sister, when he would stay two or three days upstairs in a room that Horton keeps for what he calls his *cases*—he has given the room the name of his *ward*—hospital-ward he means."

"Is the worthy Mr. Horton a member of the meeting also, my good landlady?"

Mrs. Horton had the grace to color; but she answered without stammering, habit fortifying us in moral discrepancies much more serious than even this.

"He was, and I don't know but I may say he is yet; though he hasn't attended, now, for more than two years. The question got to be between meetin' and the bar; and the bar carried the day, so far as Horton is concerned. I've held out better, I hope, and expect to gain a victory. It's quite enough to have one backslider in a family, I tell my husband, squire."

"A sufficient supply, ma'am—quite a sufficiency. So Peter Goodwin lay in your house drunk, days at a time?"

"I'm sorry to say he did. He was here a week once, with delirrum tremus on him; but Horton carried him through by the use of juleps; for *that's* the time to take 'em, everybody says; and we got him home without old Dolly's knowing that he hadn't been with his sister that whole time. The turn satisfied Peter for three good months."

"Did Peter pay as he went, or did you keep a score?"

"Ready money, sir. Catch us keeping an account with a man when his wife ruled the roast! No, Peter paid like a king for every mouthful he swallowed."

"I am far from certain that the comparison is a good one, kings being in no degree remarkable for paying their debts. But is it not possible that Peter may have set his own house on fire, and thus have caused all this calamity, for which my client is held responsible?"

"I've thought that over a good deal since the murder, squire, but don't well see how it can be made out. Setting the building on fire is simple enough; but who killed the old couple, and who robbed the house, unless this Mary Monson did both?"

"The case has its difficulties, no doubt; but I have known the day to dawn after a darker night than this. I believe that Mrs. Goodwin and her husband were very nearly of the same height?"

"Exactly; I've see them measure, back to back. He was a very short man, and she a very tall woman!"

"Do you know anything of a German female who is said to have lived with this unfortunate couple?"

"There has been some talk of such a person since the fire; but Dolly Goodwin kept no help. She was too stingy for that; then she had no need of it, being very strong and stirring for her time of life."

"Might not a boarder, like Miss Monson, have induced her to take this foreigner into her family for a few weeks? The nearest neighbors, those who would be most likely to know all about it, say that no wages were given, the woman working for her food and lodging."

"Squire Dunscomb, you'll never make it out that any German killed Peter and his wife."

"Perhaps not; though even that is possible. Such, however, is not the object of my present inquiries—but, here comes my associate counsel, and I will take another occasion to continue this conversation, my good Mrs. Horton."

Timms entered with a hurried air. For the first time in his life he appeared to his associate and old master to be agitated. Cold, calculating, and cunning, this man seldom permitted himself to be so much thrown off his guard as to betray emotion; but now he actually did. There was a tremor in his form which extended to his voice; and he seemed afraid to trust the latter even in the customary salutations. Nodding his head, he drew a chair and took his seat.

"You have been to the jail?" asked Dunscomb.

A nod was the answer.

"You were admitted, and had an interview with our client?"

Nod the third was the only reply.

"Did you put the question to her, as I desired?"

"I did, sir; but I would sooner cross-examine all Dukes, than undertake to get anything she does not wish to tell, out of that one young lady."

"I fancy most young ladies have a faculty for keeping such matters to themselves as they do not wish to reveal. Am I to understand that you got no answers?"

"I really do not know, squire. She was polite, and obliging, and smiling—but, somehow or other, I do not recollect her replies."

"You must be falling in love, Timms, to return with such an account," retorted Dunscomb, a cold but very sarcastic smile passing over his face. "Have a care, sir; 'tis a passion that makes a fool of a man sooner than any other. I do not think there is much danger of the lady's returning your flame; unless, indeed, you can manage to make her acquittal a condition of the match."

"I am afraid—dreadfully afraid, her acquittal will be a very desperate affair," answered Timms, passing his hands down his face, as if to wipe away his weakness. "The deeper I get into the matter, the worse it appears!"

"Have you given our client any intimation to this effect?"

"I hadn't the heart to do it. She is just as composed, and calm, and tranquil, and judicious—yes, and ingenious, as if *she* were only the counsel in this affair of life and death! I couldn't distrust so much tranquillity. I wish I knew her history!"

"My interrogatories pointed out the absolute necessity of her furnishing us with the means of enlightening the court and jury on that most material point, should the worst come to the worst."

"I know they did, sir; but they no more got at the truth than my own pressing questions. I should like to see that lady on the stand, above all things! I think she would bother saucy Williams, and fairly put him out of countenance. By the way, sir, I hear he is employed against us by the nephew, who is quite furious about the loss of the money, which he pretends was a much larger sum than the neighborhood had commonly supposed."

"I have always thought the relations would employ some one to assist the public prosecutor in a case of this magnitude. The theory of our government is that the public virtue will see the laws executed, but in my experience, Timms, the public virtue is a very acquiescent and indifferent quality, seldom troubling itself even to abate a nuisance, until its own nose is offended, or its own pocket damaged."

"Roguery is always more active than honesty—I found that out long since, squire. But it is nat'ral for a public prosecutor not to press one on trial for life, and the accused a woman, closer than circumstances seem to demand. It is true that popular feeling is strong ag'in Mary Monson; but it was well in the nephew to fee such a bull-dog as Williams, if he wishes to make a clean sweep of it."

"Does our client know this?"

"Certainly; she seems to know all about her case, and has a strange pleasure in entering into the mode and manner of her defense. It would do your heart good, sir, to see the manner in which she listens, and advises, and consults. She's wonderful handsome at such times!"

"You are in love, Timms; and I shall have to engage some other assistant. First Jack, and then you! Umph! This is a strange world, of a verity."

"I don't think it's quite as bad with

me as that," said Timms, this time rubbing his shaggy eyebrows, as if to ascertain whether or not he were dreaming, "though I must own I do not feel precisely as I did a month since. I wish you would see our client yourself, sir, and make her understand how important it is to her interest that we should know something of her past history."

"Do you think her name is rightly set forth in the indictment?"

"By no means—but, as she has called herself Mary Monson, she cannot avail herself of her own acts."

"Certainly not—I asked merely as a matter of information. She must be made to feel the necessity of fortifying us on that particular point, else it would go far toward convicting her. Jurors do not like aliases."

"She knows this already; for I have laid the matter before her, again and again. Nothing seems to move her, however; and as to apprehensions, she appears to be above all fear."

"This is most extraordinary! Have you interrogated the maid?"

"How can I? She speaks no English; and I can't utter a syllable in any foreign tongue."

"Ha! Does she pretend to that much ignorance? Marie Moulin speaks very intelligible English, as I know from having conversed with her often. She is a clever prudent Swiss, from one of the French cantons, and is known for her fidelity and trustworthiness. With me she will hardly venture to practice this deception. If she has feigned ignorance of English, it was in order to keep her secrets."

Timms admitted the probability of its being so; then he entered into a longer and more minute detail of the state of the case. In the first place, he admitted that in spite of all its own efforts to the contrary, the popular feeling was setting strong against their client. "Frank Williams," as he called the saucy person who bore that name, had entered into the struggle might and main, and was making his customary impressions.

"His fees must be liberal," continued Timms, "and I should think are in some way dependent on the result; for I never saw the fellow more engaged in my life."

"This precious Code does allow such a bargain to be made between the counsel and his client, or any other bargain that is not downright conspiracy," returned Dunscomb; "but I do not see what is to be shared, even should Mary Monson be hanged.

"Do not speak in that manner of so agreeable a person," cried Timms, actually manifesting emotion—"it is unpleasant to think of. It is true, a conviction will not bring money to the prosecution, unless it should bring to light some of Mrs. Goodwin's hoards."

Dunscomb shrugged his shoulders, and his associate proceeded with his narrative. Two of the reporters were offended, and their allusions to the cause, which were almost daily in their respective journals, were ill-natured, and calculated to do great harm, though so far covered as to wear an air of seeming candor. The natural effect of this "constant dropping," in a community accustomed to refer everything to the common mind, had been "to wear away the stone." Many of those who, at first had been disposed to sustain the accused, unwilling to believe that one so young, so educated, so modest in deportment, so engaging in manners, and of the gentler sex, could possibly be guilty of the crimes imputed, were now changing their opinions, under the control of this potent and sinister mode of working on the public sentiment. The agents employed by Timms to counteract this malign influence had failed of their object; they working merely for money, while those of the other side were resenting what they regarded as an affront.

The family of the Burtons, the nearest neighbors of the Goodwins, no longer received Timms with the frank cordiality that they had manifested in the earlier period of his intercourse with them. Then, they had been communicative, eager to tell all that they knew, and, as the lawyer fancied, even a little more; while they were now reserved, uneasy, and indisposed to let one half of the real facts within their knowledge be known. Timms thought they had been worked upon, and that they might expect some hostile and important testimony from that quarter. The consultation ended by an exclamation from Dunscomb on the subject of the abuses that were so fast creeping into the administration of justice, rendering the boasted freemen of America, though in a different mode, little more likely to receive its benefit from an unpolluted stream, than they who live under the wornout and confessedly corrupt systems of the old world. Such is the tendency of things, and such one of the ways of the hour.

CHAPTER XV.

"Are those *her* ribs through which the sun
  Did peer, as through a gate?
And is that woman all her crew?
Is that a Death, and are they two?
Is Death that woman's mate?"
  —THE PHANTOM SHIP.

AFTER a short preparatory interview
with Anna Updyke, Dunscomb repaired
to the jail, whither he had already dispatched a note to announce his intended
visit. Good Mrs. Gott received him with
earnest attention; for as the day of trial
approached, this kind-hearted woman
manifested a warmer and warmer interest
in the fate of her prisoner.

"You are welcome, Mr. Dunscomb,"
said this well-disposed and gentle turnkey, as she led the way to the door that
opened on the gallery of the jail; "and
welcome, again and again. I do wish this
business may fall into good hands; and
I'm afraid that Timms is not getting on
with it as well as he might."

"My associate has the reputation of
being a skillful attorney and a good manager, Mrs. Gott."

"So he has, Mr. Dunscomb; but somehow—I scarce know how myself—but
somehow he doesn't get along with *this*
cause, as well as I have known him to get
along with others. The excitement in the
county is terrible; and Gott has had seven
anonymous letters to let him know that
if Mary Monson escape, his hopes from
the public are gone forever. I tell him
not to mind such contemptible things;
but he is frightened half out of his wits.
It takes good courage, squire, to treat
an anonymous letter with the contempt it
merits."

"It sometimes does, indeed. Then you
think we shall have up-hill work with the
defense?"

"Dreadful! I've never known a cause
so generally tried out of doors as this.
What makes the matter more provoking,
Mary Monson might have had it all her
own way, if she had been so minded; for,
at first, she was popularity itself with all
the neighbors. Folks nat'rally like
beauty, and elegance, and youth; and
Mary has enough of each to make friends
anywhere."

"What! with the ladies?" said Dunscomb, smiling. "Surely not with your
sex, Mrs. Gott?"

"Yes, with the women, as well as with
the men, if she would only use her means
—but she stands in her own light. Crowds
have been round the outer windows to
hear her play on the harp—they tell me
she uses the real Jew's-harp, Squire Dunscomb; such as Royal David used to play

on; and that she has great skill. There
is a German in the village who knows all
about music, and he says Mary Monson
has been excellently taught—by the very
best masters."

"It is extraordinary; yet it would seem
to be so. Will you have the goodness to
open the door, Mrs. Gott?"

"With all my heart," answered this,
in one sense, very singular turnkey,
though in another, a very every-day
character, jingling her keys, but not taking a forward step to comply; "Mary
Monson expects you. I suppose, sir, you
know that saucy Frank Williams is retained by the friends of the Goodwins?"

"Mr. Timms has told me as much as
that. I cannot say, however, that I have
any particular apprehension of encountering Mr. Williams."

"No, sir; not *you* I'll engage, not in
open court; but out of doors he's very
formidable."

"I trust this cause, one involving the
life and reputation of a very interesting
female, will not be tried out of doors, Mrs.
Gott. The issue is too serious for such a
tribunal."

"So a body would think; but a great
deal of law business is settled, they tell
me, under the sheds, and in the streets,
and in the taverns; most especially in the
juror's bedrooms; and settled in a way it
ought not to be."

"I am afraid you are nearer right than
every just-minded person could wish. But
we will talk of this another time—the
door, if you please, now."

"Yes, sir, in one minute. It would be
so easy for Mary Monson to be just as
popular with everybody in Biberry as she
is with me. Let her come to one of the
side windows of the gallery this evening,
and show herself to the folks, and play on
that harp of hers, and Royal David himself could not have been better liked by
the Jews of old than she would soon be by
our people hereabouts."

"It is probably now too late. The
court sits in a few days; and the mischief, if any there be, must be done."

"No such thing, begging your pardon,
squire. There's that in Mary Monson that
can carry anything she pleases. Folks now
think her proud and consequential, because she will not just stand at one of the
grates and let them look at her a little."

"I am afraid, Mrs. Gott, your husband
has taught you a greater respect for
those you call 'the people,' than they
deserve to receive at your hands."

"Gott is deadfully afraid of them—"

"And he is set apart by the laws to
see them executed on these very people,"

interrupted Dunscomb, with a sneer ; "to levy on their possessions, keep the peace, enforce the laws ; in short, to make them *feel*, whenever it is necessary, that they are *governed!*"

"Gott says 'that the people *will* rule.' That's *his* great saying."

"Will *seem* to rule is true enough ; but the most that the mass of any nation *can* do, is occasionally to check the proceedings of their governors. The every day work is most effectually done by a favored few here, just as it is done by a favored few everywhere else. The door, now, if you please, my good Mrs. Gott."

"Yes, sir, in one minute. Dear me ! how odd that you should think so. Why, I thought that you were a Democrat, Mr. Dunscomb ?"

"So I am, as between forms of government ; but I never was fool enough to think that the people can really rule, further than by occasional checks and rebukes."

"What would Gott say to this ? Why, he is so much afraid of the people that he tells me he never does anything, without fancying some one is looking over his shoulders."

"Ay, that is a very good rule for a man who wishes to be chosen *sheriff*. To be a *bishop*, it would be better to remember the omniscient eye."

"I do declare—oh ! Gott never thinks of *that*, more's the pity," applying the key to the lock. "When you wish to come out, squire, just call at this grate "—then dropping her voice to a whisper—"try and persuade Mary Monson to show herself at one of the side grates."

But Dunscomb entered the gallery with no such intention. As he was expected, his reception was natural and easy. The prisoner was carefully though simply dressed, and she appeared all the better, most probably, from some of the practiced arts of her woman. Marie Moulin, herself, kept modestly within the cell, where, indeed, she passed most of her time, leaving the now quite handsomely furnished gallery to the uses of her mistress.

After the first few words of salutation, Dunscomb took the chair he was invited to occupy, a good deal at a loss how to address a woman of his companion's mien and general air as a culprit about to be tried for her life. He first attempted words of course.

"I see you have had a proper regard to your comforts in this miserable place," he remarked.

"Do not call it by so forbidding a name, Mr. Dunscomb," was the answer, given with a sorrowful, but exceedingly winning smile—" it is *my* place of *refuge*."

"Do you still persist in refusing to tell me against *what*, Miss Monson ?"

"I persist in nothing that ought not to be done, I hope. At another time I may be more communicative. But, if what Mrs. Gott tells me is correct, I need these walls to prevent my being torn to pieces by those she calls the people outside."

Dunscomb looked with amazement at the being who quietly made this remark on her own situation. Of beautiful form, with all the signs of a gentle origin and refined education, young, handsome, delicate, nay, dainty of speech and acts, there she sat, indicted for arson and murder, and about to be tried for her life, with the composure of a lady in her drawing-room ! The illuminated expression that, at times, rendered her countenance so very remarkable, had now given place to one of sobered sadness ; though apprehension did not appear to be in the least predominant.

"The sheriff has instilled into his wife a very healthful respect for those she calls the people—healthful, for one who looks to their voices for his support. This is very American."

"I suppose it to be much the same everywhere. I have been a good deal abroad, Mr. Dunscomb, and cannot say I perceive any great difference in men."

"Nor is there any, though circumstances cause different modes of betraying their weaknesses, as well as what there is in them that is good. But the people in this country, Miss Monson, possess a power that, in your case, is not to be despised. As Mrs. Gott would intimate, it may be prudent for you to remember *that*."

"Surely *you* would not have me make an exhibition of myself, Mr. Dunscomb, at the window of a jail !"

"As far from that as possible. I would have you do nothing that is unbecoming one of your habits and opinions—nothing, in short, that would be improper, as a means of defense, by one accused and tried by the State. Nevertheless, it is always wiser to make friends than to make enemies."

Mary Monson lowered her eyes to the carpet, and Dunscomb perceived that her thoughts wandered. They were not on her critical situation. It was indispensably necessary, however, that he should be explicit, and he did not shrink from his duty. Gently, but distinctly, and with a clearness that a far less gifted mind than that of the accused could comprehend, he now opened the subject of the approaching trial. A few words were first ventured on its grave character, and on the vast importance it was in all respects to his client; to which the latter listened attentively, but without the slightest visible alarm. Next, he alluded to the stories that were in circulation, the impression they were producing, and the danger there was that her rights might be affected by these sinister opinions.

"But I am to be tried by a judge and a jury, they tell me," said Mary Monson, when Dunscomb ceased speaking—"they will come from a distance, and will not be prejudiced against me by all this idle gossip."

"Judges and jurors are only men, and nothing goes further with less effort than your 'idle gossip.' Nothing is repeated accurately, or it is very rare to find it so; and those who only half comprehend a subject are certain to relate with exaggerations and false colorings."

"How, then, can the electors discover the real characters of those for whom they are required to vote?" demanded Mary Monson, smiling; "or get just ideas of the measures they are to support or to oppose?"

"Half the time they do neither. It exceeds all our present means, at least, to diffuse sufficient information for *that*. The consequence is that appearances and assertions are made to take the place of facts. The mental food of the bulk of this nation is an opinion simulated by the artful to answer their own purposes. But the power of the masses is getting to be very formidable—more formidable in a way never contemplated by those who formed the institutions, than in any way that was foreseen. Among other things, they begin to hold the administration of justice in the hollow of their hands."

"I am not to be tried by the masses, I trust. If so, my fate would be very hard, I fear, judging from what I hear in my little excursions in the neighborhood."

"Excursions, Miss Monson!" repeated the astonished Dunscomb.

"Excursions, sir; I make one for the benefit of air and exercise, every favorable night, at this fine season of the year. Surely you would not have me cooped up here in a jail, without the relief of a little fresh air?"

"With the knowledge and concurrence of the sheriff, or that of his wife?"

"Perhaps not strictly with those of either; though I suspect good Mrs. Gott has an inkling of my movements. It would be too hard to deny myself air and exercise, both of which are very necessary to my health, because I am charged with these horrid crimes."

Dunscomb passed a hand over his brow, as if he desired to clear his mental vision by friction of the physical, and, for a moment, sat absolutely lost in wonder. He scarce knew whether he was or was not dreaming.

"And you have actually been outside of these walls, Miss Monson!" he exclaimed, at length.

"Twenty times, at least. Why should I stay within them, when the means of quitting them are always in my power?"

As Mary Monson said this, she showed her counsel a set of keys that corresponded closely with those which good Mrs. Gott was in the habit of using whenever she came to open the door of that particular gallery. A quiet smile betrayed how little the prisoner fancied there was anything remarkable in all this.

"Are you aware, Miss Monson, it is felony to assist a prisoner to escape?"

"So they tell me, Mr. Dunscomb; but as I have not escaped, or made any attempt to escape, and have returned regularly and in good season to my jail, no one can be harmed for what I have done. Such, at least, is the opinion of Mr. Timms."

Dunscomb did not like the expression of face that accompanied this speech. It might be too much to say it was absolutely cunning; but there was so much of the maneuvering of one accustomed to manage in it, that it awakened the unpleasant distrust that existed in the earlier days of his intercourse with this singular young woman, and which had now been dormant for several weeks. There was, however, so much of the cold polish of the upper classes in his client's manner, that the offending expression was thrown off from the surface of her looks, as light is reflected from the ground and silvered mirror. At the very instant which succeeded this seeming gleam of cunning, all was calm, quiet, refined, gentle, and without apparent emotion in the countenance of the accused.

"Timms!" repeated Dunscomb, slowly. "So *he* has known of this, and I daresay has had an agency in bringing it about!"

"As you say it is felony to aid a prisoner to escape, I can say neither yes nor no to this, Mr. Dunscomb, lest I betray an accomplice. I should rather think, however, that Mr. Timms is not a person to be easily caught in the meshes of the law."

Again the counselor disliked the expression; though Mary Monson looked unusually pretty at that particular moment. He did not pause to analyze his feelings notwithstanding, but rather sought to relieve his own curiosity, which had been a good deal aroused by the information just received.

"As you have not hesitated to tell me of what you call your 'excursions,' Miss Monson," he continued, "perhaps you will so far extend your confidence as to let me know where you go?"

"I can have no objection to that. Mr. Timms tells me the law cannot compel a counsel to betray his client's secrets; and of course I am safe with you. Stop—I have a duty to perform that has been too long delayed. Gentlemen of your profession are entitled to their fees; and, as yet, I have been very remiss in this respect. Will you do me the favor, Mr. Dunscomb, to accept that which you will see has been some time in readiness to be offered?"

Dunscomb was too much of a professional man to feel any embarrassment at this act of justice; but he took the letter, broke the seal, even before his client's eyes, and held up for examination a note for a thousand dollars. Prepared as he was by Timm's account for a liberal reward, this large sum took him a good deal by surprise.

"This is an unusual fee, Miss Monson!" he exclaimed; "one much more considerable than I should expect from you, were I working for remuneration, as in your case I certainly am not."

"Gentlemen of the law look for their reward, I believe, as much as others. We do not live in the times of chivalry, when gallant men assisted distressed damsels as a matter of honor; but in what has well been termed a 'bank-note world.'"

"I have no wish to set myself up above the fair practices of my profession, and am as ready to accept a fee as any man in Nassau Street. Nevertheless, I took your case in hand with a very different motive. It would pain me to be obliged to work for a fee, on the present unhappy occasion."

Mary Monson looked grateful, and for a minute she seemed to be reflecting on some scheme by which she could devise a substitute for the old-fashioned mode of proceeding in a case of this sort.

"You have a niece, Mr. Dunscomb," she at length exclaimed—"as Marie Moulin informs me? A charming girl, and who is about to be married?"

The lawyer assented by an inclination of the head, fastening his penetrating black eyes on the full, expressive, grayish-blue ones of his companion.

"You intend to return to town this evening?" said Mary Monson, in continuation.

"Such is my intention. I came here to-day to confer with you and Mr. Timms, on the subject of the trial, to see how matters stand on the spot, by personal observation, and to introduce to you one who feels the deepest interest in your welfare, and desires most earnestly to seek your acquaintance."

The prisoner was now silent, interrogating with her singularly expressive eyes.

"It is Anna Updyke, the step-daughter of my nearest friend, Doctor McBrain; and a very sincere, warm-hearted, and excellent girl."

"I have heard of her, too," returned Mary Monson, with a smile so strange, that her counsel wished she had not given this demonstration of a feeling that seemed out of place, under all the circumstances. "They tell me she is a most charming girl, and that she is a very great favorite with your nephew, the young gentleman whom I have styled my legal vedette."

"Vedette! That is a singular term to be used by *you!*"

"Oh! you will remember that I have been much in countries where such persons abound. I must have caught the word from some of the young soldiers of Europe. But, Mr. John Wilmeter is an admirer of the young lady you have named?"

"I hope he is. I know of no one with whom I think he would be more likely to be happy."

Dunscomb spoke earnestly, and at such times his manner was singularly sincere and impressive. It was this appearance of feeling and nature that gave him the power he possessed over juries; and it may be said to have made no small part of his fortune. Mary Monson seemed to be surprised; and she fastened her remarkable eyes on the uncle, in a way that might have admitted of different interpretations. Her lips moved as if she spoke to herself; and the smile that succeeded was both mild and sad.

"To be sure," added the prisoner, slowly, "my information is not on the very best authority, coming, as it does, from a servant—but Marie Moulin is both discreet and observant."

"She is tolerably well qualified to speak of Anna Updyke, having seen her almost daily for the last two years. But we are surprised that *you* should know anything of this young woman."

"know her precisely as she is known [...] Miss Updyke—in other [...] much esteemed [...] apparently [...] we are forgetting the purpose of your visit, all this time, Mr. Dunscomb. Do me the favor to write your address in town, and that of Dr. McBrain on this card, and we will proceed to business."

Dunscomb did as desired, when he opened on the details that were the object of his little journey. As had been the case in all his previous interviews with her, Mary Monson surprised him with the coolness with which she spoke of an issue that involved her own fate, for life or for death. While she carefully abstained from making any allusion to circumstances that might betray her previous history, she shrank from no inquiry that bore on the acts of which she had been accused. Every question put by Dunscomb that related to the murders and the arson, was answered frankly and freely, there being no wish apparent to conceal the minutest circumstances. She made several exceedingly shrewd and useful suggestions on the subject of the approaching trial, pointing out defects in the testimony against her, and reasoning with singular acuteness on particular facts that were known to be much relied on by the prosecution. We shall not reveal these details any further in this stage of our narrative, for they will necessarily appear at length in our subsequent pages; but shall confine ourselves to a few of those remarks that may be better given at present.

"I do not know, Mr. Dunscomb," Mary Monson suddenly said, while the subject of her trial was yet under discussion, "that I have ever mentioned to you the fact that Mr. and Mrs. Goodwin were not happy together. One would think, from what was said at the time of the inquest, that they were a very affectionate and contented couple; but my own observation, during the short time I was under their roof, taught me better. The husband drank, and the wife was avaricious and very quarrelsome. I am afraid, sir, there are few really happy couples to be found on earth!"

"If you knew McBrain better, you would not say that, my dear Miss Monson," answered the counselor with a sort of glee—"there's a husband for you!— a fellow who is not only happy with *one* wife, but who is happy with *three*, as he will tell you himself."

"Not all at the same time, I hope"

Dunscomb did justice to his character, by relating how matters really stood; after ...... mission to intr.............. Monson, ... and ...., which induced her counsel to surmise that she was fear-

ful of being recognized. Nor was Dunscomb pleased with all the expedients adopted by his client in order to extract information from him. He thought they slightly indicated cunning, a quality that he might be said to abhor. Accustomed as he was to all the efforts of ingenuity in illustrating a principle or maintaining a proposition, he had always avoided everything like sophistry and falsehood. This weakness on the part of Mary Monson, however, was soon forgotten in the graceful manner in which she acquiesced in the wish of the stranger to be admitted. The permission was finally accorded, as if an honor were received, with the tact of a female and the easy dignity of a gentlewoman.

Anna Updyke possessed a certain ardor of character that had more than once given her prudent and sagacious mother uneasiness, and which sometimes led her into the commission of acts, always innocent in themselves, and perfectly under the restraint of principles, which the world would have been apt to regard as imprudent. Such, however, was far from being her reputation; her modesty, and the diffidence with which she regarded herself, being amply sufficient to protect her from the common observation, even while most beset by the weakness named. Her love for John Wilmeter was so disinterested, or to herself so seemed to be, that she fancied she could even assist in bringing about his union with another woman, were that necessary to his happiness. She believed that this mysterious stranger was, to say the least, an object of intense interest with John, which soon made her an object of intense interest with herself; and each hour increased her desire to become acquainted with one so situated, friendless, accused, and seemingly suspended by a thread over an abyss, as she was. When she first made her proposal to Dunscomb to be permitted to visit his client, the wary and experienced counselor strongly objected to the step.

It was imprudent, could lead to no good, and might leave an impression unfavorable to Anna's own character. But this advice was unheeded by a girl of Anna Updyke's generous temperament. Quiet and gentle as she ordinarily appeared to be, there was a deep undercurrent of feeling and enthusiasm in her moral constitution, that bore her onward in any course which she considered to be right, with a total abnegation of self. This was a quality to lead to good or evil, as it might receive a direction; and happily nothing had yet occurred in her brief existence to carry her away toward the latter goal.

Surprised at the steadiness and warmth with which his young friend persevered in her request, Dunscomb, after obtaining the permission of her mother and promising to take good care of his charge, was permitted to convey Anna to Biberry, in the manner related.

Now that her wish was about to be gratified, Anna Updyke, like thousands of others who have been more impelled by impulses than governed by reason, shrunk from the execution of her own purposes. But the generous ardor revived in her in time to save appearances; and she was admitted by well-meaning Mrs. Gott to the gallery of the prison, leaning on Dunscomb's arm, much as she might have entered a drawing-room, in a regular morning call.

The meeting between these two charming young women was frank and cordial, though slightly qualified by the forms of the world. A watchful and critical observer might have detected less of nature in Mary Monson's manner than in that of her guest, even while the welcome she gave her visitor was not without cordiality and feeling. It is true that her courtesy was more elaborate and European, if one may use the expression, than it is usual to see in an American female, and her air was less ardent than that of Anna; but the last was highly struck with her countenance and general appearance, and, on the whole, not dissatisfied with her own reception.

The power of sympathy and the force of affinities soon made themselves felt, as between these two youthful females. Anna regarded Mary as a stranger most grievously wronged; and forgetting all that there was which was questionable or mysterious in her situation, or remembering it only to feel the influence of its interest, while she submitted to a species of community of feeling with John Wilmeter, as she fancied, and soon got to be as much entranced with the stranger as seemed to be the fate of all who approached the circle of her acquaintance. On the other hand, Mary Monson felt a consolation and gratification in this visit to which she had long been a stranger. Good Mrs. Gott was kind-hearted and a woman, but she had no claim to the refinement and peculiar sensibilities of a lady; while Marie Moulin, discreet, respectful, even wise as she was in her own way, was, after all, nothing but an upper servant. The chasm between the cultivated and the uncultivated, the polished and the unpolished, is wide; and the accused fully appreciated the change, when one of her own class in life, habits, associations, and if the reader

will, prejudices, so unexpectedly appeared to sympathize with, and to console her. Under such circumstances, three or four hours made the two fast and deeply-interested friends, on their own accounts, to say nothing of the effect produced by the generous advances of one, and the perilous condition of the other.

Dunscomb returned to town that evening, leaving Anna Updyke behind him, ostensibly under the care of Mrs. Gott. Democracy has been carried so far on the high road of ultraism in New York, as in very many interests to become the victim of its own expedients. Perhaps the people are never so far from exercising a healthful, or, indeed, any authority at all, as when made to seem, by the expedients of demagogues, to possess an absolute control. It is necessary merely to bestow a power which it is impossible for the masses to wield with intelligence, in order to effect this little piece of legerdemain in politics; the quasi-people in all such cases becoming the passive instruments in the hands of their leaders, who strengthen their own authority by this seeming support of the majority. In all cases, however, in which the agency of numbers can be felt, its force is made to prevail; the tendency necessarily being to bring down all representation to the level of the majority. The effect of the change has been pretty equally divided between good and evil. In many cases benefits have accrued to the community by the exercise of this direct popular control, while in probably quite as many the result has been exactly the reverse of that which was anticipated. In no one instance, we believe it will be generally admitted, has the departure from the old practice been less advantageous than in rendering the office of sheriff elective. Instead of being a leading and independent man, who has a pride in his position, and regards the character of his county as he does his own, this functionary has got to be, nine times in ten, a mere political maneuverer, who seeks the place as a reward for party labors, and fills it very much for his personal benefit, conferring no dignity on it by his own position and character, lessening its authority by his want of the qualities calculated to increase it, and, in a good many instances, making it quite as difficult to wrest money from *his* hand, as from those of the original debtor.

It is a consequence of this state of things that the sheriff has quite lost all, or nearly all, the personal consideration that was once connected with his office; and has sunk, in most of the strictly rural coun ties, into a jailer, and the head of the active bailiffs. His object is altogether money; and the profit connected with the keeping of the prisoners, now reduced almost entirely to felons, the accused, and persons committed for misdemeanors, is one of the inducements for aspiring to an office once so honorable.

In this state of things, it is not at all surprising that Dunscomb was enabled to make such an arrangement with Mrs. Gott as would place Anna Updyke in a private room in the house attached to the jail, and which formed the sheriff's dwelling. The counselor preferred leaving her with Mrs. Horton; but to this Anna herself objected, both because she had taken a strong dislike to the garrulous but shrewd landlady, and because it would have separated her too much from the person she had come especially to console and sympathize with.

The arrangement made, Dunscomb, as has already been mentioned, took his departure for town, with the understanding that he was to return the succeeding week; the Circuit and Oyer and Terminer sitting on Monday, and the district attorney, Mr. Garth, having given notice to her counsel that the indictment against Mary Monson would be certainly traversed the second day of the sitting, which would be on Tuesday.

CHAPTER XVI.

"Let her locks be the reddest that ever were seen,
And her eyes may be e'en any color but green;
Be they light, gray, or black, their luster and hue,
I swear I've no choice, only let her have two."
—THE DUENNA.

TWO days after this, Dunscomb was in his library late at night, holding a brief discourse with McBrain's coachman, who has been already introduced to the reader. Some orders had been given to the last, in relation to another trip to Biberry, whither the master and our lawer were to proceed next day. The man was an old and indulged servant, and often took great liberties in these conferences. In this respect the Americans of his class differ very little from the rest of their fellow-creatures, notwithstanding all that has been said and written to the contrary. They obey the impulses of their characters much as the rest of mankind, though not absolutely without some difference in manner.

"I s'poses, Squire Dunscomb, that this is like to be the last journey that I and the doctor will have to take soon ag'in, in *that* quarter," coolly observed Stephen, when his master's friend had told him the hour to be at the door, with the other preparations that would be necessary; "unless we should happen to be called in at the *post mortal.*"

"*Post mortem*, you must mean, Hoof," a slight smile flashing on the lawyer's countenance, and as quickly disappearing. "So you consider it a settled thing that my client is to be found guilty?"

"That's what they say, sir; and things turn out, in this country, pretty much the same as they say aforehand. For my part, sir, I never quite liked the criminal's looks."

"Her *looks!* I do not know where you would go to find a more lovely young woman, Stephen!"

This was said with a vivacity and suddenness that startled the coachman a little. Even Dunscomb seemed surprised at his own animation, and had the grace to change color. The fact was that he too was feeling the influence of woman, youthful, lovely, spirited, refined, and surrounded with difficulties. This was the third of Mary Monson's conquests since her arrest, if John Wilmeter's wavering admiration could be placed in this category, viz.: Timms, the nephew, and the counselor himself. Neither was absolutely in love; but each and all submitted to an interest of an unusual degree in the person, character, and fortunes of this unknown female. Timms, alone, had got so far as to contemplate a marriage; the idea having crossed his mind that it might be almost as useful as popularity, to become the husband of one possessed of so much money.

"I'll not deny her *good* looks, squire," returned Stephen Hoof—or Stephen Huff, as he called himself—"but it's her *bad* looks that isn't so much to my fancy. Vhy, sir, once the doctor had a horse that was agreeable enough to the eye, having a good color and most of the p'ints, but who wasn't no traveler, not a bit on't. One that know'd the animal could see where the fault lay; the fetlock j'int being oncommon longish; and that's what I call *good* looks and *bad* looks."

"You mean, Stephen," said Dunscomb, who had regained all his *sang froid*, "that Mary Monson has a bad-looking ankle, I suppose, wherein I think you miserably mistaken. No matter; she will not have to travel under your lash very far. But, how is it with the reporters? Do you see any more of your friend that asks so many questions?"

"They be an axing set, squire, if anybody can be so called," returned Stephen, grinning. "Would you think it, sir? one day when I was comin' in from Timbully empty, one on 'em axed me for a ride! a chap as hadn't his foot in a reg'lar private coach since he was born, a wantin' to drive about in a vehicle as well known as Doctor McBrain's best carriage! Them's the sort of chaps that spreads all the reports that's going up and down the land, they tell me."

"They do their share of it, Stephen; though there are enough to help them who do not openly belong to their corps. Well, what does your acquaintance want to know now?"

"Oncommon curious, squire, about the bones. He axed me more than forty questions; what we thought of them; and about there being' male or female bones; and how we know'd; and a great many more sich matters. I answered him accordin' to my abilities; and so he made an article on the subject, and has sent me the papers."

"An article! Concerning Mary Monson, and on your information?"

"Sartain, sir; and the bones. Vhy, they cut articles out of much narrower cloth, I can tell you, squire. There's the cooks, and chambermaids, and vaiters about town, none of vich can hold up their heads with a reg'lar, long-established physician's coachman, who goes far ahead of even an omnibus driver in public estimation, as you must know, squire—but such sort of folks furnish many an article for the papers nowadays—yes, and articles that ladies and gentlemen read."

"That is certainly a singular source of useful knowledge—one must hope they are well-grounded, or they will soon cease to be ladies and gentlemen at all. Have you the paper about you, Stephen?"

Hoof handed the lawyer a journal folded with a paragraph in view, that was so much thumbed and dirtied it was not very easy to read it.

"We understand that the trial of Mary Monson, for the murder of Peter and Dorothy Goodwin," said the "article," "will come off in the adjoining County of Dukes, at a very early day. Strong attempts have been made to make it appear that the skeletons found in the ruins of Goodwin's dwelling, which our readers will remember was burned at the time of the murders, are not human bones; but we have been at great pains to investigate this very material point, and have no hesitation in giving it as our profound conviction that it will be made to appear that these melancholy memorials are all that remain of the excellent couple who were so suddenly taken out of existence. We do not speak lightly on this subject, having gone to the fountain-head for our facts, as well as for our science."

"Hoof on McBrain!' muttered Dunscomb, arching his brows—"this is much of a piece with quite one-half of the knowledge that is poured into the popular mind nowadays. Thank you, Stephen; I will keep this paper, which may be of use at the trial."

"I thought our opinions was worth something more than nothing, sir," answered the gratified coachman; "a body doesn't ride at all hours, day and night, year after year, and come out where he started. I vishes you to keep that 'ere paper, squire, a little carefully, for it may be wanted in the college, where they reads all sorts of things, one of these days."

"It shall be cared for, my friend—I hear some one at the street-door bell. It is late for a call, and I fear Peter has gone to bed. See who is there, and good-night."

Stephen withdrew, the ringing being repeated a little impatiently, and was soon at the street door. The fellow admitted the visitors, and went ruminating homeward. Dunscomb maintaining a very respectable reputation, in a bachelor point of view, for morals. As for the lawyer himself, he was in the act of reading a second time the precious opinion expressed in the journals, when the door of his library opened, a little hesitatingly it must be confessed, and two females stood on its threshold. Although his entirely unexpected visitors were so much muffled in shawls and veils it was not possible to distinguish even the outlines of their persons, Dunscomb fancied each was youthful and handsome, the instant he cast his eyes on them. The result showed how well he guessed.

Throwing aside the garments that concealed their forms and faces, Mary Monson and Anna Updyke advanced into the room. The first was perfectly self-possessed and brilliantly handsome; while her companion, flushed with excitement and exercise, was not much behind her in this important particular. Dunscomb started, and fancied there was felony even in his hospitality.

"You know how difficult it is for me to travel by daylight," commenced Mary Monson, in the most natural manner in the world; "that, and the distance we had to drive, must explain the unseasonableness of this visit. You told me once, yourself, that you are both a late and an early man, which encouraged me to venture. Mr. Timms has written me a letter, which I have thought it might be well to show you. There it is; and when you have cast an eye over it, we will speak of its contents."

"Why, this is very much like a conditional proposal of marriage!" cried Dunscomb, dropping the hand that held the letter, as soon as he had read the first paragraph. "Conditional, so far as the result of your trial is concerned."

"I forgot the opening of the epistle, giving very little thought to its purport; though Mr. Timms has not written me a line lately that has not touched on this interesting subject. A marriage between him and me is so entirely out of the way of all the possibilities, that I look upon his advances as mere embellishment. I have answered him directly in the negative once, and that ought to satisfy any prudent person. They tell me no woman should marry a man she has once refused; and I shall plead this as a reason for continued obduracy."

This was said pleasantly, and without the least appearance of resentment; but in a way to show she regarded her attorney's proposal as very much out of the beaten track. As for Dunscomb, he passed his hand over his brows, and read the rest of a pretty long letter with grave attention. The purely business part of this communication was much to the point; important, clearly put, and every way creditable to the writer. The lawyer read it attentively a second time, ere he once opened his mouth in comments.

"And why is this shown to me?" he asked, a little vexed, as was seen in his manner. "I have told you it is felony to assist a prisoner in an attempt to escape."

"I have shown it to you, because I have not the remotest intention, Mr. Dunscomb, to attempt anything of the sort. I shall not quit my asylum so easily."

"Then why are you here, at this hour, with the certainty that most of the night must be passed on the road, if you mean to return to your prison ere the sun reappears?"

"For air, exercise, and to show you this letter. I am often in town, but am compelled, for more reasons than you are acquainted with, to travel by night."

"May I ask where you obtain a vehicle to make these journeys in?"

"I use my own carriage, and trust to a very long-tried and most faithful domestic. I think Miss Updyke will say he drove us not only carefully, but with great speed. On that score, we have no grounds of complaint. But I am very much fatigued, and must ask permission to sleep for an hour. You have a drawing-room, I take it for granted, Mr. Dunscomb?"

"My niece fancies she has two. Shall I put lights in one of them?"

"By no means. Anna knows the house as well as she does her mother's, and will do the honors. On no account let Miss Wilmeter be disturbed. I am a little afraid of meeting *her*, since we have practiced a piece of treachery touching Marie Moulin. But, no matter; one hour on a sofa, in a dark room, is all I ask. That will bring us to midnight, when the carriage will again be at the door. You wish to see your mother, my dear, and here is a safe and very suitable attendant to accompany you to the house and back again."

All this was said pleasantly, but with a singular air of authority, as if this mysterious being were accustomed to plan out and direct the movements of others. She had her way. In a minute or two she was stretched on a sofa, covered with a shawl, the door was closed on her, and Dunscomb was on his way to Mrs. McBrain's residence, which was at some distance from his own, with Anna leaning on his arm.

"Of course, my dear, said the lawyer, as he and his beautiful companion left his own door at that late hour of the night, "we shall see no more of Mary Monson?"

"Not see her again! I should be very, very sorry to think that, sir!"

"She is no simpleton, and means to take Timms's advice. That fellow has written a strong letter, in no expectation of its being seen, I fancy, in which he points out a new source of danger; and plainly advises his client to abscond. I can see the infatuation of love in this; for the letter, if produced, would bring him into great trouble."

"And you suppose, sir, that Mary Monson intends to follow this advice?"

"Beyond a question. She is not only a very clever, but she is a very cunning woman. This last quality is one that I admire in her the least. I should be half in love with her myself"—this was exactly the state of the counselor's feelings toward his client, in spite of his bravado and affected discernment; a woman's charms often overshadowing a philosophy that is deeper even than his—"but for this very trait, which I find little to my taste. I take it for granted you are sent home to be put under your mother's care, where you properly belong; and I am got out of the way to save me from the pains and penalties of an indictment for felony."

"I think you do not understand Mary Monson, Uncle Tom"—so Anna had long called her friend's relative, as it might be in anticipation of the time when the appellation would be correct. "She is not the sort of person to do as you suggest; but would rather make it a point of honor to remain, and face any accusation whatever."

"She must have nerves of steel to confront justice in a case like hers, and in the present state of public feeling in Dukes. Justice is a very pretty thing to talk about, my dear; but we old practitioners know that it is little more, in human hands, than the manipulations of human passions. Of late years, the outsiders —outside barbarians they might very properly be termed—have almost as much to do with the result of any warmly-contested suit as the law and evidence. 'Who is on the jury?' is the first question asked nowadays; not what are the facts. I have told all this very plainly to Mary Monson—"

"To induce her to fly?" asked Anna, prettily, and a little smartly.

"Not so much that, as to induce her to consent to an application for delay. The judges of this country are so much overworked, so little paid, and usually are so necessitous, that almost any application for delay is granted. Business at chambers is sadly neglected; for that is done in a corner, and does not address itself to the public eye, or seek public eulogiums; but he is thought the cleverest fellow who will soonest sweep out a crowded calendar. Causes are tried by tallow candles until midnight, with half the jurors asleep; and hard-working men, accustomed to be asleep by eight each night, are expected to keep their thoughts and minds active in the face of all these obstacles."

"Do you tell me this, Uncle Tom, in the expectation that I am to understand it?"

"I beg your pardon, child; but my heart is full of the failing justice of the land. We shout hosannas in praise of the institutions, while we shut our eyes to the gravest consequences that are fast undermining us in the most important of all our interests. But here we are already; I had no notion we had walked so fast. Yes, there is Papa McBrain's one-horse vehicle, well emptied of its contents, I hope, by a hard day's work."

"A doctor's life must be so laborious!" exclaimed the pretty Anna. "I think nothing could tempt me to marry a physician."

"It is well a certain lady of our acquaintance was not of your way of thinking," returned Dunscomb, laughing; for his good humor always returned when he could give his friend a rub on his matrimonial propensities, "else would McBrain have been troubled to get his last and best. Never mind, my dear, he is a good-natured fellow, and will make a very kind papa."

Anna made no reply, but rang the bell a little pettishly; for no child likes to have a mother married a second time, there being much greater toleration for fathers, and asked her companion in. As the wife of a physician in full practice, the bride had already changed many of her long-cherished habits. In this respect, however, she did no more than follow the fortunes of woman, who so cheerfully makes any sacrifice in behalf of him she loves. If men were only one-half as disinterested, as self-denying, and as true as the other sex, in all that relates to the affections, what a blessed state would that of matrimony be! Still, there are erring, and selfish, and domineering, and capricious, vain, heartless, and self-willed females, whom nature never intended for married life, and who are guilty of a species of profanation, when they stand up and vow to love, honor and obey their husbands. Many of these disregard their solemn pledges, made at the altar, and under the immediate invocation of the Deity, as they would disregard a promise made in jest, and think no more of the duties and offices that are so peculiarly the province of their sex, than of the passing and idle promises of vanity. But, if such women exist, and that they do our daily experience proves, they are as exceptions to the great law of female faith, which is tenderness and truth. They are not women in character, whatever they may be in apperance, but creatures in the guise of a sex that they discredit and caricature.

Mrs. McBrain was not a person of the disposition just described. She was gentle and good, and bid fair to make the evening of her second husband's days very happy. Sooth to say, she was a good deal in love, notwithstanding her time of life, and the still more mature years of the bridegroom; and had been so much occupied with the duties and cares that belonged to her recent change of condition as to be a little forgetful of her daughter. At no other period of their joint lives would she have permitted this beloved child to be absent from her, under such circumstances, without greater care for her safety and comforts; but there is a honey-week, as well as a honey-moon; and the intenseness of its feelings might very well disturb the ordinary round of even maternal duties. Glad enough, however, was she now to see her daughter, when Anna, blooming, and smiling, and blushing, flew into her mother's arms.

"There she is, widow—Mrs. Updyke—I beg pardon—married woman, and Mrs. McBrain," cried Dunscomb. "Ned is such an uneasy fellow, he keeps all his friends in a fever with his emotions, and love and matrimony; and that just suits him, as he has only to admidister a pill and set all right again. But there she is, safe and *unmarried,* thank Heaven; which is always a sort of consolation to me. She's back again, and you will do well to keep her until my nephew, Jack, comes to ask permission to carry her off for good and all."

Anna blushed more deeply than ever, while the mother smiled and embraced her child. Then succeeded questions and answers, until Mrs. McBrain had heard the whole story of her daughter's intercourse with Mary Monson, so far as it has been made known to the reader. Beyond that, Anna did not think herself authorized to go; or, if she made any revelation, it would be premature for us to repeat it.

"Here we are, all liable to be indicted for felony," cried Dunscomb, as soon as the young lady had told her tale. "Timms will be hanged, in place of his client; and we three will have cells at Sing Sing, as accessories before the act. Yes, my dear bride, you are what the law terms a 'particeps criminis,' and may look out for the sheriff before you are a week older."

"And why all this, Mr. Dunscomb?" demanded the half-amused, half-frightened Mrs. McBrain.

"For aiding and abetting a prisoner in breaking jail. Mary Monson is off, beyond a question. She lay down in Sarah's drawing-room, pretending to be wearied, ten minutes since, and has, no doubt, got through with her nap already, and is on her way to Canada, or Texas, or California, or some other out-of-the-way country—Cuba, for aught I know."

"Is this so, think you, Anna?"

"I do not, mamma. So far from believing Mary Monson to be flying to any out-of-the-way place, I have no doubt that we shall find her fast asleep on Mr. Dunscomb's sofa."

"*Uncle* Dunscomb's sofa, if you please, young lady."

"No, sir; I shall call you uncle no longer," answered Anna, blushing scarlet —"until—until—"

"You have a legal claim to the use of the word. Well, that will come in due time, I trust; if not, it shall be my care to see you have a title to a still dearer appellation. There, widow—Mrs. McBrain, I mean—I think you will do. But, seriously, child, you cannot imagine that Mary Monson means ever to return to her prison, there to be tried for life?"

"If there is faith in woman, she does, sir; else would I not have exposed myself to the risk of accompanying her."

"In what manner did you come to town, Anna?" asked the anxious mother. "Are you now at the mercy of some driver of a hackney-coach, or of some public cabman?"

"I understand that the carriage which was in waiting for us, half a mile from Biberry, is Mrs. Monson's—"

"Mrs.!" interrupted Dunscomb. "Is she, then, a married woman?"

Anna looked down, trembled, and was conscious of having betrayed a secret. So very precious to herself had been the communication of Marie Moulin on this point, that it was ever uppermost in her thoughts; and it had now escaped her under an impulse she could not control. It was too late, however, to retreat; and a moment's reflection told her it would every way be better to tell all she knew on this one point at least.

This was soon done, for even Marie Moulin's means of information were somewhat limited. This Swiss had formerly known the prisoner by another name, though what name she would not reveal. This was in Europe, where Marie had actually passed three years in this mysterious person's employment. Marie had even come to America, in consequence of this connection, at the death of her own mother; but, unable to find her former mistress, had taken service with Sarah Wilmeter. Mary Monson was single and unbetrothed when she left Europe. Such was Marie Moulin's statement. But it was understood she was now married; though to whom, she could not say. If Anna Updyke knew more than this, she did not reveal it at that interview.

"Ah! Here is another case of a wife's elopement from her husband," interrupted Dunscomb, as soon as Anna reached this point in her narration; "and I daresay something or other will be found in this wretched Code to uphold her in her disobedience. You have done well to marry, Mrs. McBrain; for, according to the modern opinions in these matters, instead of providing yourself with a lord and master, you have only engaged an upper servant."

"No true-hearted woman can look upon her husband in so degrading a light," answered the bride, with spirit.

"That will do for three days, but wait to the end of three years. There are runaway wives enough, at this moment, roaming up and down the land, setting the laws of God and man at defiance, and jingling their purses, when they happen to have money, under their lawful husbands' noses; ay, enough to set up a three-tailed pacha! But this damnable Code will uphold them, in some shape or other, my life for it. One can't endure her husband because he smokes; another finds fault with his not going to church but once a day; another quarrels with him for going three times; another says he has too much dinner company; and another protests she can't get a male friend inside of her house. All these ladies, forgetful as they are of their highest earthly duties, forgetful as they are of woman's very nature, are the models of divine virtues, and lay claim to the sympathies of mankind. They get those of fools, but prudent and reflecting men shake their heads at such wandering deesses."

"You are severe on us women, Mr. Dunscomb," said the bride.

"Not on you, my dear Mrs. McBrain—never a syllable on you. But, go on, child; I have had the case of one of these vagrant wives in my hands, and know how mistaken has been the disposition to pity her. Men lean to the woman's side; but the frequency of the abuse is beginning to open the eyes of the public. Go on, Anna dear, and let us hear it all—or all you have to tell us."

Very little remained to be related. Marie Moulin, herself, knew very little of that which had occurred since her separation from her present mistress in France. She did make one statement, however, that Anna had deemed very important; but which she felt bound to keep as a secret, in consequence of the injunctions received from the Swiss.

"I should have a good deal to say about this affair," observed Dunscomb, when his beautiful companion was done, "did I believe that we shall find Mary Monson on our return to my house. In that case, I should say to you, my dear widow—Mrs. McBrain, I mean—the devil take that fellow Ned, he'll have half the women in town bearing his name before he is done. Well, Heaven be praised! he can neither marry *me*, nor give me a step-father, let him do his very best. There's comfort in that consideration, at any rate."

"You were about to tell us what you would do," put in the bride, slightly vexed, yet too well assured of the counselor's attachment to her husband to feel angry; "you must know how much value we give to your advice."

"I was about to say that Anna should not return to this mysterious convict—no, she is not *yet* convicted, but she is in-dicted, and that is something—but return she should not, were there the least chance of our finding her on our return home. Let her go then, and satisfy her curiosity, and pass the night with Sarah, who must be through with her first nap by this time."

Anna urged her mother to consent to this arrangement, putting forward her engagement with Mary Monson, not to desert her; McBrain driving to the door, from paying his last visit that night, his wife gave her assent to the proposition; the tenderest mother occasionally permitting another and more powerful feeling to usurp the place of maternal care. Mrs. McBrain, it must be admitted, thought more of the bridegroom, sixty as he was, than of her charming daughter, nor was she quite free from the awkwardness that ever accompanies a new connection of this nature when there are grown-up children, more especially on the part of the female. Then Anna had communicated to her mother a most material circumstance, which it does not suit our present purpose to reveal.

"Now for a dozen pair of gloves that we do not find Mary Monson," said the lawyer, as he walked smartly toward his own residence, with Anna Updyke under his arm.

"Done!" cried the young lady—"and you shall *pay* if you lose."

"As bound in honor. Peter"—the gray-headed black who answered the summons to the door—"will be glad enough to see us, for the old fellow is not accustomed to let his young rogue of a master in at midnight, with a charming young woman under his arm."

Anna Updyke was right. Mary Monson was in a deep sleep on the sofa. So profound was her rest, there was a hesitation about disturbing her; though twelve, the hour set for the return of the carriage to Biberry, was near. For a few minutes Dunscomb conversed with his agreeable companion in his own library.

"If Jack knew of your being in the house, he would never forgive my not having him called."

"I shall have plenty of occasions for seeing Jack," returned the young lady, coloring. "You know how assiduous he is in this cause, and how devoted he is to the prisoner."

"Do not run away with any such notion, child; Jack is yours, heart and soul."

"Hist—there is the carriage; Mary must be called."

Away went Anna, laughing, blushing, but with tears in her eyes. In a minute

Mary Monson made her appearance somewhat refreshed and calmed by her short nap.

"Make no excuse for waking me," said this unaccountable woman. "We can both sleep on the road. The carriage is as easy as a cradle; and, luckily, the roads are quite good."

"Still they lead to a prison, Mrs. Monson."

The prisoner smiled, and seemed to be lost in thought. It was the first time any of her new acquaintances had ever addressed her as a married woman; though Marie Moulin, with the exception of her first exclamation at their recent meeting, had invariably used the appellation of Madame. All this, however, was soon forgotten in the leave-taking. Dunscomb thought he had seldom seen a female of higher tone of manners, or greater personal charms, than this singular and mysterious young woman appeared to be, as she courtesied her adieu.

CHAPTER XVII.

" What then avail impeachments, or the law's
Severest condemnation, while the queen
May snatch him from the uplifted hand of justice?"
—EARL OF ESSEX.

PERHAPS the most certain proof that any people can give of a high moral condition, is in the administration of justice. Absolute infallibility is unattainable to men; but there are wide chasms in right and wrong, between the legal justice of one state of society and that of another. As the descendants of Englishmen, we in this country are apt to ascribe a higher tone of purity to the courts of the mother country, than to those of any other European nation. In this we may be right, without inferring the necessity of believing that the ermine of England is spotless; for it can never be forgotten that Bacon and Jeffries once filled her highest judicial seats, to say nothing of many others, whose abuses of their trusts have doubtless been lost in their comparative obscurity. Passing from the parent to its offspring, the condition of American justice, so far as it is dependent on the bench, is a profound moral anomaly. It would seem that every known expedient of man has been restored to, to render it corrupt, feeble, and ignorant; yet he would be a hardy, not to say an audacious commentator, who should presume to affirm that it is not entitled to stand in the very foremost ranks of human integrity.

Ill paid, without retiring pensions, with nothing to expect in the way of family and hereditary honors and dignities; with little, in short, either in possession or in prospect, to give any particular inducement to be honest, it is certain that, as a whole, the judges of this great Republic may lay claim to be classed among the most upright of which history furnishes any accounts. Unhappily, popular caprice, and popular ignorance, have been brought to bear on the selection of the magistrates, of late; and it is easy to predict the result, which, like that on the militia, is soon to pull down even this all-important machinery of society to the level of the common mind.

Not only have the obvious and well-earned inducements to keep men honest—competence, honors, and security in office—been recklessly thrown away by the open hand of popular delusion, but all the minor expedients, by which those who cannot think might be made to feel, have been laid aside, leaving the machinery of justice as naked as the hand. Although the colonial system was never elaborated in these last particulars, there were some of its useful and respectable remains, down as late as the commencement of the present century. The sheriff appeared with his sword, the judge was escorted to and from the court-house to his private dwelling with some show of attention and respect, leaving a salutary impression of authority on the ordinary observer. All this has disappeared. The judge slips into the county-town almost unknown; lives at an inn amid a crowd of lawyers, witnesses, suitors, jurors, and horse-shedders, as Timms calls them; find his way to the bench as best he may; and seems to think that the more work he can do in the shortest time is the one great purpose of his appointment.

Nevertheless, these men, *as yet*, are surprisingly incorrupt and intelligent. How long it will remain so, no one can predict; if it be for a human life, however, the working of the problem will demonstrate the fallibility of every appreciation of human motives. One bad consequence of the depreciation of the office of a magistrate, however, has long been apparent, in the lessening of the influence of the judge on the juries: the power that alone renders the latter institution even tolerable. This is putting an irresponsible, usually an ignorant, and often corrupt arbiter, in the judgment seat, in lieu of the man of high qualities, for which it was alone intended. The Circuit and Oyer and Terminer for Dukes presented nothing novel, in its bench, its bar, its jurors, and, we might add, its witnesses. The first was a cool-headed, dispassionate man, with a very respectable amount of legal learning and experience, and a perfectly fair character. No one suspected him of acting wrong from evil motives; and when he did err, it was ordinarily from the pressure of business; though, occasionally, he was mistaken, because the books could not foresee every possible phase of a case. The bar was composed of plain, hard-working men, materially above the level of Timms, except in connection with mother-wit; better educated, better mannered, and, as a whole, of materially higher origin; though, as a body, neither profoundly learned nor of refined deportment. Nevertheless, these persons had a very fair portion of all the better qualities of the Northern professional men. They were shrewd, quick in the application of their acquired knowledge, ready in their natural resources, and had that general aptitude for affairs that is the fruit of a practice that includes all the different branches of the profession.

Here and there was a usurer and extortioner among them; a fellow who disgraced his calling by running up unnecessary bills of cost, by evading the penal statutes passed to prevent abuses of this nature, and by cunning attempts to obtain more for the use of his money than the law sanctioned. But such was not the general character of the Dukes County bar, which was rather to be censured for winking at irregular proceedings out of doors, for brow-beating witnesses, and for regarding the end so intensely as not always to be particular in reference to the means, than for such gross and positively illegal and oppressive measures as those just mentioned. As for the jurors, they were just what that ancient institution might be supposed to be, in a country where so many of the body of the people are liable to be summoned. An unusually large proportion of these men, when all the circumstances are considered, were perhaps as fit to be thus employed as could be obtained from the body of the community of any country on earth; but a very serious number were altogether unsuited to perform the delicate duties of their station. Fortunately the ignorant are very apt to be influenced by the more intelligent, in cases of this nature; and by this exercise of a very natural power, less injustice is committed than might otherwise occur. Here, however, is the opening for the "horse-shedding" and "pillowing," of which Timms has spoken, and of which so much use is made around every country court-house

in the State. This is the crying evil of the times; and, taken in connection with the enormous abuse which is rendering a competition in news a regular money-getting occupation, one that threatens to set at defiance all laws, principles, and facts.

A word remains to be said of the witnesses. Perhaps the rarest thing connected with the administration of justice all over the world is an intelligent, perfectly impartial, clear-headed, discriminating witness; one who distinctly knows all he says, fully appreciates the effect of his words on the jury, and who has the disposition to submit what he knows solely to the law and the evidence. Men of experience are of opinion that an oath usually extracts the truth. We think so, too, but it is truth as the witness understands it; facts as he has seen them; and opinions that, unconsciously to himself, have been warped by reports, sneers, and malice. In a country of popular sway like this, there is not one man in a thousand, probably, who has sufficient independence of mind, or sufficient moral courage, to fancy he has seen even a fact, if it be of importance, differently from what the body of the community has seen it; and nothing is more common than to find witnesses coloring their testimony, lessening its force by feeble statements, or altogether abandoning the truth, under this pressure from without, in cases of a nature and magnitude to awake a strong popular feeling. It is by no means uncommon, indeed, to persuade one class of men, by means of this influence, that they did not see that which actually occurred before their eyes, or that they did see that which never had an existence.

Under no circumstances do men congregate with less meritorious motives than in and around a court of justice. The object is victory, and the means of obtaining it will not always bear the light. The approaching Circuit and Oyer and Terminer of Dukes was no exception to the rule; a crowd of evil passions, of sinister practices, and of plausible pretenses, being arrayed against justice and the law in two-thirds of the causes on the calendar. Then it was that Timms and Saucy Williams, or Dick Williams, as he was familiarly termed by his associates, came out in their strength, playing off against each other the out-door practices of the profession. The first indication that the former now got of the very serious character of the struggle that was about to take place between them was in the extraordinary civility of saucy Williams when they met in the bar-room of the inn they each frequented, and which had long been the arena of their antagonistical wit and practices.

"I never saw you look better, Timms," said Williams, in the most cordial manner imaginable; "on the whole, I do not remember to have ever seen you looking so well. You grow younger instead of older every day of your life. By the way, do you intend to move on Butterfield against Town this circuit?"

"I should be glad to do it, if you are ready. Cross-notices have been given, you know."

Williams knew this very well; and he also knew that it had been done to entitle the respective parties to costs, in the event of anything occurring to give either side an advantage; the cause being one of those nuts out of which practitioners are very apt to extract the whole of the kernel before they are done with it.

"Yes, I am aware of that, and I believe we are quite ready. I see that Mr. Town is here, and I observe several of his witnesses; but I have so much business, I have no wish to try a long slander cause; words spoken in heat, and never thought of again, but to make a profit of them."

"You are employed against us in the murder case, I hear?"

"I rather think the friends of the deceased so regard it; but I have scarcely had time to look at the testimony before the coroner." This was a deliberate mystification, and Timms perfectly understood it as such, well knowing that the other had given the outdoor work of the case nearly all of his time for the last fortnight—"and I don't like to move in one of these big matters without knowing what I am about. Your senior counsel has not yet arrived from town, I believe?"

"He cannot be here until Wednesday, having to argue a great insurance case before the Superior Court to-day and to-morrow."

This conversation occurred after the grand jury had been charged, the petit jurors sworn, and the judge had several motions for correcting the calender, laying causes over, etc. Two hours later, the district attorney being absent in his room, engaged with the grand jury, Williams arose and addressed the court, which had just called the first civil cause on the calender.

"May it please the court," he said, coolly, but with the grave aspect of a man who felt he was dealing with a very serious matter—"there is a capital indictment depending, a case of arson and murder, which it is the intention of the State to call on at once."

The judge looked still more grave than the counsel, and it was easy to see that he deeply regretted it should fall to his lot to try such an issue. He leaned forward, with an elbow on the very primitive sort of desk with which he was furnished by the public, indented it with the point of his knife, and appeared to be passing in review such of the circumstances of this important case as he had become acquainted with, judicially. We say "judicially;" for it is not an easy thing for either judge, counsel, or jurors, in the state of society that now exists, to keep distinctly in their minds that which has been obtained under legal evidence, from that which floats about the community on the thousand tongues of rumor—fact from fiction. Nevertheless, the respectable magistrate whose misfortune it was to preside on this very serious occasion was a man to perform all his duty to the point where public opinion or popular clamor is encountered. The last is a bugbear that few have moral courage to face; and the evil consequences are visible, hourly, daily, almost incessantly, in most of the interests of life. This popular feeling is the great moving lever of the republic; the wronged being placed beneath the fulcrum, while the outer arm of the engine is loaded with numbers. Thus it is that we see the oldest families among us quietly robbed of their estates, after generations of possession; the honest man proscribed; the knave and demagogue defied; mediocrity advanced to high places; and talents and capacity held in abeyance, if not actually trampled under foot. Let the truth be said: these are evils to which each year gives additional force, until the tyranny of the majority has taken a form and combination which, unchecked, must speedily place every personal right at the mercy of plausible, but wrong-doing, popular combinations.

"Has the prisoner been arraigned?" asked the judge. "I remember nothing of the sort."

"No, your honor," answered Timms, now rising for the first time in the discussion, and looking about him as if to scan the crowd for witnesses. "The prosecution does not yet know the plea we shall put in."

"You are retained for the prisoner, Mr. Timms?"

"Yes, sir; I appear in her behalf. But Mr. Dunscomb is also retained, and will be engaged in the New York Superior Court until Wednesday, in an insurance case of great magnitude."

"No insurance case can be of the magnitude of a trial for life," returned Williams. "The justice of the State must be vindicated, and the person of the citizen protected."

This sounded well, and it caused many a head in the crowd, which contained both witnesses and jurors, to nod with approbation. It is true that every thoughtful and observant man must have had many occasions to observe how fallacious such a declaration is in truth ; but it sounded well, and the ears of the multitude are always open to flattery.

"We have no wish to interfere with the justice of the State, or with the protection of the citizen," answered Timms, looking around to note the effect of his words— "our object is to defend the innocent ; and the great and powerful community of New York will find more pleasure in seeing an accused acquitted than in seeing fifty criminals condemned."

This sentiment sounded quite as well as that of Williams's, and heads were again noded in approbation. It told particularly well in a paragraph of a newspaper that Timms had engaged to publish what he considered his best remarks.

"It seems to me, gentlemen," interposed the judge, who understood the meaning of these *ad captandum* remarks perfectly well, "that your conversation is premature at least, if not altogether improper. Nothing of this nature should be said until the prisoner has been arraigned."

"I submit, your honor, and acknowledge the justice of the reproof," answered Williams. "I now move the court, on behalf of the district attorney, that Mary Monson, who stands indicted for murder and arson, *be* arraigned, and her pleas entered—"

"I could wish this step might be delayed until I can hear from the leading counsel for the defense," objected Timms, "which must now occur in the course of a very few hours."

"I perceive that the prisoner is a female," said the judge, in a tone of regret.

"Yes, your honor, she is, and young and handsome, they tell me," answered Williams; "for I have never been able to get a sight of her. She is too much of a great lady to be seen at a grate, by all I can learn of her and her proceedings. Plays on the harp, sir ; has a French *valet de chambre*, or something of that sort—"

"This is all wrong, Mr. Williams, and must be checked," again interposed the judge, though very mildly ; for, while his experience taught him that the object of such remarks was to create prejudice, and his conscience prompted him to put an end to a proceeding so unrighteous, he stood in so much awe of this particular counsel, who had half a dozen presses at his command, that it required a strong inducement to bring him out, as he ought to be, in opposition to any of his more decided movements. As for the community, with the best intentions as a whole, it stood passive under this gross wrong. What is "everybody's business" is literally "nobody's business," when the public virtue is the great moving power ; the upright preferring their ease to everything else, and the ill-disposed manifesting the ceaseless activity of the wicked. All the ancient barriers to this species of injustice, which have been erected by the gathered wisdom of our fathers and the experience of ages, have been thrown down by the illusions of a seeming liberty, and the whole machinery of justice is left very much at the mercy of an outside public opinion, which, in itself, is wielded by a few of the worst men in the country. These are sober truths, as a close examination will show to any one who may choose to enter into the investigation of the ungrateful subject. It is not what is *said*, we very well know ; but it is what is *done*.

Williams received the mild rebuke of the judge like one who felt his position ; paying very little respect to its spirit or its letter. He knew his own power, and understood perfectly well that this particular magistrate was soon to run for a new term of office, and might be dealt with more freely on that account.

"I know it is very wrong, your honor— very wrong "—rejoined the wily counsel to what had been said—" so wrong, that I regard it as an insult to the State. When a person is capitally indicted, man or woman, it is his or her bounden duty to put all overboard, that there may be no secrets. The harp was once a sacred instrument, and it is highly improper to introduce it into our jails and criminals' cells—"

"There is no criminal as yet—no crime can be established without proof, and the verdict of twelve good men and true," interrupted Timms—" I object, therefore, to the learned counsel's remarks, and—"

"Gentlemen, gentlemen," put in the judge, a little more pointedly than in his former rebuke—" this is all wrong, I repeat."

"You perceive, my brother Timms," rejoined the indomitable Williams, " the court is altogether against you. This is not a country of lords and ladies, fiddles and harps, but of the *people;* and when the people find a bill for a capital offense, capital care should be taken not to give more offense."

Williams had provided himself with a set of supporters that are common enough in the courts, whose business it was to grin, and sneer, and smile, and look knowing at particular hits of the counsel, and otherwise to back up his wit, and humor, and logic, by the agency of sympathy. This expedient is getting to be quite common, and is constantly practiced in suits that relate in any manner to politics or political men. It is not so common, certainly, in trials for life; though it may be, and has been, used with effect even on such serious occasions. The influence of these wily demonstrations, which are made to have the appearance of public opinion, is very great on the credulous and ignorant; men thus narrowly gifted invariably looking around them to find support in the common mind.

The hits of Williams told, to Timm's great annoyance; nor did he know exactly how to parry them. Had he been the assailant himself, he could have wielded the weapons of his antagonist with equal skill; but his dexterity was very much confined to the offensive in cases of this nature; for he perfectly comprehended all the prejudices on which it was necessary to act, while he possessed but a very narrow knowledge of the means of correcting them. Nevertheless, it would not do to let the prosecution close the business of the day with so much of the air of triumph, and the indomitable attorney made another effort to place his client more favorably before the public eye.

"The harp is a most religious instrument," he coolly observed, "and it has no relation to the violin, or any light and frivolous piece of music. David used it as the instrument of praise, and why should not a person who stands charged—"

"I have told you, gentlemen, that all this is irregular, and cannot be permitted," cried the judge, with a little more of the appearance of firmness than he had yet exhibited.

The truth was, that he stood less in fear of Timms than of Williams; the connection of the last with the reporters being known to be much the more extensive. But Timms knew his man, and understood very well what the committal of counsel had got to be, under the loose notions of liberty that have grown up in the country within the last twenty years. Time was, and that no remote period, when the lawyer who had been thus treated for indecorum at the bar would have been a disgraced man, and would have appealed in vain to the community for sympathy; little

or none would he have received. Men then understood that the law was their master, established by themselves, and was to be respected accordingly.

But that feeling is in a great measure extinct. Liberty is every hour getting to be more and more personal; its concentration consisting in rendering every man his own legislator, his own judge, and his own juror. It is monarchical and aristocratic, and all that is vile and dangerous, to see power exercised by any but the people; and those whom the constitution and the laws have set apart expressly to discharge a delegated authority being obliged, by clamors sustained by all the arts of cupidity and fraud, to defer to the passing opinions of the hour. No one knew this better than Timms, who had just as lively a recollection as his opponent that this very judge was to come before the people in the next autumn, as a candidate for re-election. The great strain of American foresight was consequently applied to this man's conscience, who, overworked and under-paid, was expected to rise above the weaknesses of humanity, as a sort of sublimated political theory that is getting to be much in fashion, and which, *if true*, would supersede the necessity of any court or any government at all. Timms knew this well, and was not to be restrained by one who was thus stretched, as it might be, on the tenterhooks of political uncertainty.

"Yes, your honor," returned this indomitable individual, "I am fully aware of its impropriety, and was just as much so when the counsel for the prosecution was carrying it on to the injury of my client; I might say almost unchecked, if not encouraged."

"The court did its best to stop Mr. Williams, sir; and must do the same to keep you within the proper limits of practice. Unless these improprieties are restrained I shall confine the counsel for the State to the regular officer, and assign new counsel to the accused, as from the court."

Both Williams and Timms looked amused at this menace, neither having the smallest notion the judge dare put such a threat in execution. What! presume to curb licentiousness when it chose to assume the aspect of human rights? This was an act behind the age, more especially in a country in which liberty is so fast getting to be all means, with so very little regard to the end.

A desultory conversation ensued, when it was finally settled that the trial must be postponed until the arrival of the counsel expected from town. From the beginning of the discussion, Williams knew that such must be the termination of that day's work; but he had accomplished two great objects by his motion. In the first place, by conceding delay to the accused it placed the prosecution on ground where a similar favor might be asked, should it be deemed expedient. This resisting motions for delay is a common *ruse* of the bar, since it places the party whose rights are seemingly postponed in a situation to demand a similar concession. Williams knew that his case was ready as related to his brief, the testimony, and all that could properly be produced in court, but he thought it might be strengthened out of doors, among the jurors and witnesses. We say the witnesses, because even this class of men get their impressions, quite frequently, as much from what they subsequently hear, as from what they have seen and known. A good reliable witness, who relates no more than he actually knows, conceals nothing, colors nothing, and leaves a perfectly fair impression of the truth, is perhaps the rarest of all the parties concerned in the administration of justice. No one understood this better than Williams; and his agents were, at that very moment, actually employed in endeavoring to persuade certain individuals that they knew a great deal more of the facts connected with the murders than the truth would justify. This was not done openly or directly; not in a way to alarm the consciences or pride of those who were to be duped, but by the agency of hints, and suggestions, and plausible reasonings, and all the other obvious devices, by means of which the artful and unprincipled are enabled to act on the opinions of the credulous and inexperienced.

While all these secret engines were at work in the streets of Biberry the external machinery of justice was set in motion with the usual forms. Naked, but business-like, the blind goddess was invoked with what is termed " republican simplicity," one of the great principles of which, in some men's estimation, is to get the maximum of work at the minimum of cost. We are no advocates for the senseless parade and ruthless expenditure— ruthless, because extracted from the means of the poor—with which the governments of the old world have invested their dignity; and we believe that the reason of men may be confided in, in managing these matters, to a certain extent; though not to the extent that it would seem to be the fashion of the American theories, to be desirable. Wigs of all kinds, even when there is a deficiency of hair, we hold in utter detestation; and

we shall maintain that no more absurd scheme of clothing the human countenance with terror was ever devised than to clothe it with flax. Nevertheless, as comfort, decency, and taste unite in recommending clothing of some sort or other, we do not see why the judicial functionary should not have his appropriate attire as well as the soldier, the sailor, or the priest. It does not necessarily follow that extravagances are to be imitated if we submit to this practice; though we incline to the opinion that a great deal of the nakedness of "republican simplicity," which has got to be a sort of political idol in the land, has its origin in a spirit that denounces the past as a species of moral sacrifice to the present time.

Let all this be as it may, it is quite certain that "republican simplicity "—the slang lever by means of which the artful move the government—has left the administration of justice among us, so far as externals are concerned, as naked as may be. Indeed, so much have the judges become exposed to sinister influences, by means of the intimacies with which they are invested by means of "republican simplicity," that it has been found expedient to make a special provision against undue modes of approaching their ears, all of which would have been far more efficiently secured by doubling their salaries, making a respectable provision for old age in the way of pensions, and surrounding them with such forms as would keep the evil disposed at reasonable distance. Neither Timms nor "saucy Williams," however, reasoned in this fashion. They were, in a high degree, practical men, and saw things as they are; not as they ought to be. Little was either troubled with theories, regrets, or principles. It was enough for each that he was familiar with the workings of the system under which he lived; and which he knew how to pervert in a way the most likely to effect his own purposes.

The reader may be surprised at the active pertinacity with which Williams pursued one on trial for her life; a class of persons with whom the bar usually professes to deal tenderly and in mercy. But the fact was that he had been specially retained by the next of kin, who had large expectations from the extracted hoards of his aunt; and that the fashion of the day had enabled him to achieve such a *cent per cent* bargain with his client as caused his own compensation altogether to depend on the measure of his success. Should Mary Monson be sentenced to the gallows it was highly probable her revelations would put the wronged in the way of being righted, when this limb of the law would, in all probability, come in for a full share of the recovered gold. How different all this was from the motives and conduct of Dunscomb, the reader will readily perceive; for, while the profession in this country abounds with Williamses and Timmses, men of the highest tone of feeling, the fairest practice, and the clearest perceptions of what is right, are by no means strangers to the bar.

CHAPTER XVIII.

"Thou hast already racked me with thy stay;
Therefore require me not to ask thee twice:
Reply at once to all. What is concluded?"
—MORNING BRIDE.

DURING the interval between the occurrence of the scene in court that has just been related, and the appearance of Dunscomb at Biberry, the community was rapidly taking sides on the subject of the guilt or innocence of Mary Monson. The windows of the jail were crowded all day; throngs collecting there to catch glimpses of the extraordinary female, who was rightly enough reported to be living in a species of luxury in so unusual a place, and who was known to play on an instrument that the popular mind was a good deal disposed to regard as sacred. As a matter of course, a hundred stories were in circulation, touching the character, history, sayings, and doings of this remarkable person, that had no foundation whatever in truth; for it is an infirmity of human nature to circulate and place its belief in falsehoods of this sort; and more especially of human nature as it is exhibited in a country where care has been taken to stimulate the curiosity of the vulgar, without exactly placing them in a condition to appease its longings, either intelligently or in a very good taste.

This interest would have been manifested, in such a case, had there been no particular moving cause; but the secret practices of Williams and Timms greatly increased its intensity, and was bringing the population of Dukes to a state of excitement that was very little favorable to an impartial administration of justice. Discussions had taken place at every corner, and in all the bar-rooms; and many were the alleged facts connected with the murders which had their sole existence in rumor, that was adduced in the heat of argument, or to make out a suppositious case. All this time, Williams was either in court, attending closely to his different causes, or was seen passing between the court-house and the tavern, with bundles of papers under his arms, like a man absorbed in business. Timms played a very similar part, though *he* found leisure to hold divers conferences with several of his confidential agents. Testimony was his aim; and, half a dozen times, when he fancied himself on the point of establishing something new and important, the whole of the ingenious fabric he had reared came tumbling about his ears, in consequence of some radical defect in the foundation.

Such was the state of things on the evening of Wednesday, the day preceding that which had been set down for the trial, when the stage arrived bringing "Squire Dunscomb," his carpet-bags, his trunk, and his books. McBrain shortly after drove up in his own carriage, and Anna was soon in her mother's arms. The excitement, so general in the place, had naturally enough extended to these females; and Mrs. McBrain and her daughter were soon closeted, talking over the affair of Mary Monson.

About eight that evening, Dunscomb and Timms were busy looking over minutes of testimony, briefs, and other written documents that were connected with the approaching trial. Mrs. Horton had reserved the best room in her house for this distinguished counsel; an apartment in a wing that was a good deal removed from the noise and bustle of a leading inn, during a circuit. Here Dunscomb had been duly installed, and here he early set up "his traps," as he termed his flesh-brushes, sponges, briefs, and calf-skin-covered volumes. Two tallow candles threw a dim, lawyer-like light on the scene; while unrolled paper-curtains shut out as much of night as such an imperfect screen could exclude. The odor of cigars —excellent Havanas, by the way—was fragrant in the place; and one of the little fountains of smoke was stuck knowingly in the corner of the eminent counsel's mouth, while Timms had garnished his skinny lips with the short stump of a pipe. Neither said anything; one of the parties presenting documents that the other read in silence. Such was the state of matters, when a slight tap at the door was succeeded by the unexpected appearance of "saucy Williams." Timms started, gathered together all his papers with the utmost care, and awaited the explanation of this unlooked-for visit with the most lively curiosity. Dunscomb, on the other hand, received his guest with urbanity, and like one who felt that the wrangling of the bar, in which, by the way, he had too much self-respect and good temper to indulge, had no necessary connection with the courtesies of private life.

Williams had scarcely a claim superior to those of Timms, to be considered a gentleman; though he had the advantage of having been what is termed liberally educated—a phrase of very doubtful import, when put to the test of old-fashioned notions on such subjects. In manners, he had the defects, and we may add the merits, of the school in which he had been educated. All that had been said of Timms on this subject, in the way of censure, was equally applicable to Williams; but the last possessed self-command, an admirable reliance on his own qualities, which would have fitted him, as regards this one quality, to be an emperor. Foreigners wonder at the self-possession of Americans in the presence of the great; and it is really one of the merits of the institution that it causes every person to feel that he is a man, and entitled to receive the treatment due to a being so high in the scale of earthly creations. It is true that this feeling often degenerates into a vulgar and oversensitive jealousy, frequently rendering its possessor exacting and ridiculous; but on the whole, the effect is manly, not to say ennobling.

Now Williams was self-possessed by nature, as well as by association and education. Though keenly alive to the differences and chances of fortune, he never succumbed to mere rank and wealth. Intriguing by disposition, not to say by education, he could affect a deference he did not feel; but, apart from the positive consequences of power, he was not to be daunted by the presence of the most magnificent sovereign who ever reigned. No wonder, then, that he felt quite at home in the company of his present host, though fully aware that he was one of the leading members of the New York bar. As a proof of this independence may be cited the fact that he had no sooner paid his salutations and been invited to be seated, than he deliberately selected a cigar from the open box of Dunscomb, lighted it, took a chair, raised one leg coolly on the corner of a table, and began to smoke.

" The calendar is a little crowded," observed this free-and-easy visitor, " and is likely to carry us over into the middle of next week. Are you retained in Daniels against Fireman's Insurance ? "

" I am not—a brief was offered by the plaintiffs, but I declined taking it."

" A little conscientious, I suppose. Well, I leave all the sin of my suits on the shoulders of my clients. It is bad enough to *listen* to their griefs, without being called on to *smart* for them. I have heard you are in Cogswell against Davidson ? "

" In that cause I have been retained. I may as well say, at once, we intend to move it on."

" It's of no great moment—if you beat us at the circuit, our turn will come on execution."

" I believe, Mr. Williams, your clients have a knack at gaining the day in that mode. It is of no great interest to me, however, as I rarely take the management of a cause after it quits the courts."

" How do you like the Code, Brother Dunscomb."

" Damnable, sir. I am too old, in the first place, to like change. Then change from bad to worse is adding folly to imbecility. The Common Law practice had its faults, I allow; but this new system has no merits."

" I do not go as far as that; and I rather begin to like the new plan of remuneration. We are nothing out of pocket, and sometimes are a handsome sum in. You defend Mary Monson ? "

Timms felt assured that his old antagonist had now reached the case that had really brought him to the room. He fidgeted, looked eagerly round to see that no stray paper could fall beneath the hawkeye of the party, and then sat in comparative composure, waiting the result.

" I do," Dunscomb quietly replied; " and I shall do it *con amore*—I suppose you know what that means, Mr. Williams ? "

A sarcastic smile passed over the steeled countenance of the other, his appearance being literally sardonic for an instant.

" I presume I do. We know enough Latin in Dukes to get along with such a quotation; though our friend Timms here despises the classics. ' Con amore ' means, in this instance, ' a lover's zeal,' I suppose; for they tell me that all who approach the criminal submit to her power to charm."

" The *accused*, if you please," put in the opposing attorney; " but no *criminal*, until the word ' *guilty* ' has been pronounced."

" I am convicted. They say you are to be the happy man, Timms, in the event of an acquittal. It is reported all over the county that you are to become Mr. Monson as a reward for your services ; and if half that I hear be true, you will deserve her, with a good estate in the bargain."

Here Williams laughed heartily at his own wit; but Dunscomb looked grave, while his associate counsel looked angry.

In point of fact the nail had been hit on the head ; and consciousness lighted the spirit within, with its calm, mild glow. The senior counsel was too proud and too dignified to make any reply ; but Timms was troubled with no such feeling.

"If there are any such rumors in old Dukes," retorted the last, "it will not need mesmerism to discover their author. In my opinion, the people ought to carry on their suits in a spirit of liberality and justice ; and not in a vindictive, malicious temper."

"We are all of the same way of thinking," answered Williams with a sneer. "I consider it liberal to give you a handsome young woman with a full purse ; though no one can say how, or by whom, it has been filled. By the way, Mr. Dunscomb, I am instructed to make a proposal to you ; and as Timms is in the court, this may be as good a moment as another to present it for consideration. My offer is from the nephew, next of kin, and sole heir of the late Peter Goodwin ; by whom, as you probably know, I am retained. This gentleman is well assured that his deceased relatives had a large sum in gold by them, at the time of the murders—"

"No verdict has yet shown that there have been any murders at all," interrupted Timms.

"We have the verdict of the inquest, begging your pardon, brother Timms— that is something, surely ; though not enough, quite likely, to convince your mind. But, to proceed with my proposition :—My client is well assured that such a secret fund existed. He also knows that *your* client, gentlemen, is flush of money, and money in gold coins that correspond with many pieces that have been seen by different individuals in the possession of our aunt—"

"Ay, eagles, and half-eagles," interrupted Timms—"a resemblance that comes from the stamp of the mint."

"Go on with your proposition, Mr. Williams," said Dunscomb.

"We offer to withdraw all our extra counsel, myself included, and to leave the case altogether with the State, which is very much the same thing as an acquittal ; provided you will *return* to us five thousand dollars in this gold coin. Not *pay*, for that might be compounding a felony ; but *return*."

"There could be no compounding a felony, if the indictment be not quashed, but traversed," said the senior counsel for the defense.

"Very true ; but we prefer the word 'return.' That leaves everything clear, and will enable us to face the county. Our object is to get our *rights*—let the State take care of its justice for itself."

"You can hardly expect that such a proposition should be accepted, Williams ?"

"I am not so sure of that, Timms ; life is sweeter than money even. I should like to hear the answer of your associate, however. You, I can see, have no intention of lessening the marriage portion, if it can be helped."

Such side-hits were so common in court, as between these worthies, that neither thought much of them out of court. But Williams gave a signal proof of the acuteness of his observation when he expressed a wish to know in what light his proposal was viewed by Dunscomb. That learned gentleman evidently paid more respect to the offer than had been manifested by his associate, and now sat silently ruminating on its nature. Thus directly appealed to, he felt the necessity of giving some sort of an answer.

"You have come expressly to make this proposition to us, Mr. Williams ?" Dunscomb demanded.

"To be frank with you, sir, such is the main object of my visit."

"Of course it is sanctioned by your client, and you speak by authority ?"

"It is fully sanctioned by my client, who would greatly prefer the plan ; and I act directly by his written instructions. Nothing short of these would induce me to make the proposition."

"Very well, sir. Will an answer by ten o'clock this evening meet your views ?"

"Perfectly so. An answer at any time between this and the sitting of the court to-morrow morning will fully meet our views. The terms, however, cannot be diminished. Owing to the shortness of the time, it may be well to understand *that*."

"Then, Mr. Williams, I ask a little time for reflection and consultation. We may meet again to-night."

The other assented, rose, coolly helped himself to another cigar, and got as far as the door, when an expressive gesture from Timms induced him to pause.

"Let us understand each other," said the last, with emphasis. "Is this a truce, with a complete cessation of hostilities ; or is it only a negotiation to be carried on in the midst of war ?"

"I hardly comprehend your meaning, Mr. Timms. The question is simply one of taking certain forces—allied forces, they may be called—from the field, and leaving you to contend only with the main enemy. There need be nothing said of a truce, since nothing further can be done until the court opens."

"That may do very well, Williams, for those that haven't practiced in Dukes as long as myself; but it will not do for me. There is an army of reporters here, at this moment; and I am afraid that the allies of whom you speak have whole corps of skirmishers."

Williams maintained a countenance so unmoved that even the judicious Timms was a little shaken; while Dunscomb, who had all the reluctance of a gentleman to believe in an act of meanness, felt outraged by his associate's suspicions.

"Come, come, Mr. Timms," the last exclaimed. "I beg we may have no more of this. Mr. Williams has come with a proposition worthy of our consideration; let us meet it in the spirit in which it is offered."

"Yes," repeated Williams, with a look that might well have explained his *sobriquet* of "saucy"; "yes, in the spirit in which it is offered. What do you say to that, Timms?"

"That I shall manage the defense precisely as if no such proposition had been made, or any negotiation accepted. You can do the same for the prosecution."

"Agreed!" Williams rejoined, making a sweeping gesture with his hand, and immediately quitting the room.

Dunscomb was silent for a minute. A thread of smoke arose from the end of his cigar; but the volume no longer poured from between his lips. He was ruminating too intensely even to smoke. Rising suddenly, he took his hat, and motioned toward the door.

"Timms, we must go to the jail," he said; "Mary Monson must be spoken to at once."

"If Williams had made his proposition ten days ago, there might be some use in listening to it," returned the junior, following the senior counsel from the room, carrying all the papers in the cause under an arm; "but, now that all the mischief is done, it would be throwing away five thousand dollars to listen to his proposition."

"We will see—we will see," answered the other, hurrying downstairs—"what means the rumpus in that room, Timms? Mrs. Horton has not treated me well, to place a troublesome neighbor so near me. I shall stop and tell her as much, as we go through the hall."

"You had better not, squire. We want all our friends just now; and a sharp word might cause us to lose this woman, who has a devil of a tongue. She tells me that a crazy man was brought here privately; and, being well paid for it, she has consented to give him what she calls her 'drunkard's parlor,' until the court has settled his affairs. His room, like your own, is so much out of the way, that the poor fellow gives very little trouble to the great body of the boarders."

"Ay, very little trouble to *you*, and the rest of you, in the main building; but a great deal to me. I shall speak to Mrs. Horton on the subject, as we pass out."

"Better not, squire. The woman is our friend now, I know; but a warm word may turn her to the right-about."

It is probable Dunscomb was influenced by his companion; for he left the house without putting his threat into execution. In a few minutes he and Timms were at the jail. As counsel could not well be refused admission to their client on the eve of trial, the two lawyers were admitted to the gallery within the outer door that has been so often mentioned. Of course, Mary Monson was notified of the visit; and she received them with Anna Updyke, the good, gentle, considerate Anna, who was ever disposed to help the weak and to console the unhappy, at her side. Dunscomb had no notion that the intimacy had grown to this head; but when he came to reflect that one of the parties was to be tried for her life next day, he was disposed to overlook the manifest indiscretion of his old favorite in being in such a place. Mrs. McBrain's presence released him from all responsibility; and he returned the warm pressure of Anna's hand in kindness, if not with positive approbation. As for the girl herself, the very sight of "Uncle Tom," as she had so long been accustomed to call the counselor, cheered her heart, and raised new hopes in behalf of her friend.

In a few clear, pointed words, Dunscomb let the motive of his visit be known. There was little time to throw away, and he went directly at his object, stating everything succinctly, but in the most intelligible manner. Nothing could have been more calm than the manner in which Mary Monson listened to his statement; her deportment being as steady as that of one sitting in judgment herself, rather than that of a person whose own fate was involved in the issue.

"It is a large sum to raise in so short a time," continued the kind-hearted Dunscomb; "but I deem the proposition so important to your interest, that, rather than lose this advantage, I would not hesitate about advancing the money myself, should you be unprepared for so heavy a demand."

"As respects the money, Mr. Dunscomb," returned the fair prisoner, in the most easy and natural manner, "*that* need give us no concern. By sending a confidential messenger to town— Mr. John Wilmeter, for instance—" here Anna pressed less closely to her friend's side—"it would be very easy to have five hundred eagles or a thousand half eagles here, by breakfast time to-morrow. It is not on account of any such difficulty that I hesitate a moment. What I dislike is the injustice of the thing. I have never touched a cent of poor Mrs. Goodwin's hoard; and it would be false to admit that I am *returning* that which I never received."

"We must not be particular, ma'am, on immaterial points, when there is so much at stake."

"It may be immaterial whether I pay money under one form or another, Mr. Dunscomb; but it cannot be immaterial to my future standing, whether I am acquitted in the teeth of this Mr. Williams's opposition, or under favor of his purchase."

"Acquitted! Our case is not absolutely clear, Miss Monson—it is my duty to tell you as much!"

"I understand such to be the opinion of both Mr. Timms and yourself, sir; I like the candor of your conduct, but am not converted to your way of thinking. I shall be acquitted, gentlemen—yes, honorably, triumphantly acquitted; and I cannot consent to lessen the impression of such a termination to my affair, by putting myself in the way of being even suspected of a collusion with a man like this saucy Williams. It is far better to meet him openly, and to defy him to do his worst. Perhaps some such trial, followed by complete success, will be necessary to my future happiness."

Anna now pressed nearer to the side of her friend; passing an arm, unconsciously to herself, around her waist. As for Dunscomb, he gazed at the handsome prisoner in a sort of stupefied wonder. The place, the hour, the business of the succeeding day, and all the accessories of the scene, had an effect to increase the confusion of his mind, and, for the moment, to call in question the fidelity of his senses. As he gazed at the prison-like aspect of the gallery, his eye fell on the countenance of Marie Moulin, and rested there in surprise for half a minute. The Swiss maid was looking earnestly at her mistress, with an expression of concern and of care so intense, that it caused the counselor to search for their cause. For the first time it flashed on his mind that Mary Monson might be a lunatic, and that the defense so often set up in capital cases as to weary the common mind, might be rendered justly available in this particular instance. The whole conduct of this serving-woman had been so singular; the deportment of Mary Monson herself was so much out of the ordinary rules; and the adhesion of Anna Updyke, a girl of singular prudence of conduct, notwithstanding her disposition to enthusiasm, so marked, that the inference was far from unnatural. Nevertheless, Mary Monson had never looked more calm, more intellectual; never manifested more of a mien of high intelligence, than at that very instant. The singular illumination of the countenance to which we have had occasion already to allude, was conspicuous, but it was benignant and quiet; and the flush of the cheeks added luster to her eyes. Then the sentiments expressed were just and noble, free from the cunning and mendacity of a maniac; and such as any man might be proud to have the wife of his bosom entertain. All these considerations quickly chased the rising distrust from Dunscomb's mind, and his thoughts reverted to the business that had brought him there.

"You are the best judge, ma'am, of what will most contribute to your happiness," rejoined the counselor, after a brief pause. "In the ignorance in which we are kept of the past, I might well add, the *only* judge; though it is possible that your female companions know more, in this respect, than your legal advisers. It is proper I should say, once more, and probably for the last time, that your case will be greatly prejudiced unless you enable us to dwell on your past life freely and truly."

"I am accused of murdering an unoffending female and her husband; of setting fire to the dwelling, and of robbing them of their gold. These are accusations that can properly be answered only by a complete acquittal, after a solemn investigation. No half-way measures will do. I must be found not guilty, or a blot rests on my character for life. My position is singular—I had almost said cruel—in some respects owing to my own willfulness—"

Here Anna Updyke pressed closer to her friend's side, as if she would defend her against these self-accusations; while Marie Moulin dropped her needle, and listened with the liveliest curiosity.

"In *many* respects, perhaps," continued Mary, after a short pause, "and I must take the consequences. Willfulness has ever been my greatest enemy. It has been fed by perfect independence and too much money. I doubt if it be good for woman to be thus tried. We were created for dependence, Mr. Dunscomb; dependence on our fathers, on our brothers, and perhaps on our husbands—" here there was another pause; and the cheeks of the fair speaker flushed, while her eyes became brilliant to light.

"*Perhaps!*" repeated the counselor, with solemn emphasis.

"I know that men think differently from us on this subject—"

"From *us*—do you desire me to believe that most women wish to be independent of their husbands! Ask the young woman at your side, if *that* be her feeling of the duties of her sex."

Anna dropped her head on her bosom, and blushed scarlet. In all her day-dreams of happiness with John Wilmeter, the very reverse of the feeling now alluded to, had been uppermost in her mind; and to her nothing had ever seemed half as sweet as the picture of leaning on him for support, guidance, authority and advice. The thought of independence would have been painful to her; for a principle of nature, the instinct of her sex, taught her that the part of woman was "to love, honor, and obey." As for Mary Monson, she quailed a little before the severe eye of Dunscomb; but education, the accidents of life, and possibly a secret principle of her peculiar temperament, united to stimulate her to maintain her original ground.

"I know not what may be the particular notions of Miss Updyke," returned this singular being, "but I can feel my own longings. They are all for independence. Men have not dealt fairly by women. Possessing the power, they have made all the laws, fashioned all the opinions of the world, in their own favor. Let a woman err, and she can never rise from her fall; while men live with impunity in the midst of their guilt. If a woman think differently from those around her, she is expected to conceal her opinions, in order to receive those of her masters. Even in the worship of God, the highest and most precious of all our duties, she is expected to play a secondary part, and act as if the Christian faith favored the sentiment of another, which teaches that women have no souls."

"All this is as old as the repinings of a very treacherous nature, young lady," answered Dunscomb, coolly; "and I have often heard it before. It is not surprising, however, that a young, handsome, highly-educated, and I presume rich, person of your sex, should be seduced by notions seemingly so attractive, and long for what she will be apt to term the emancipation of her sex. This is an age of emancipation; prudent gray-headed men become deluded, and exhibit their folly by succumbing to wild and exceedingly silly philanthropical hurrah! Even religion is emancipated! There are churches it is true, but they exist as appendages of society, instead of being divine institutions, established for the secret purposes of unerring wisdom; and we hear men openly commending this or that ecclesiastical organization, because it has more or less of the savor of republicanism. But one new dogma remains to be advanced—that the government of the universe is democratical—in which the 'music of the spheres' is a popular song; and the disappearance of a world a matter to be referred to the people in their primary capacity. Among other absurdities of the hour is a new law, giving to married women the control of their property, and drawing a line of covetousness across the bolster of every marriage bed in the State!"

"Surely, Mr. Dunscomb, a man of your integrity, character, manliness and principles, would defend the weaker sex in the maintenance of its rights against prodigality, tyranny, and neglect?"

"These are so many words, my dear ma'am, and are totally without meaning, when thoroughly sifted. God created woman to be a helpmeet to man—to comfort, solace, and aid him in his pursuit after worldly happiness; but always in a dependent relation. The marriage condition, viewed in its every-day aspect, has sufficient causes of disagreement, without drawing in this of property. One of the dearest and nearest of its ties, indeed, that of a perfect identification of interests, is at once cut off by this foolish, not to say wicked, attempt to light the torch of contention in every houshold. It were better to teach our women not to throw themselves away on men who can not be trusted; to inculcate the necessity of not marrying in haste to repent at leisure, than to tinker the old, venerable and long-tried usages of our fathers, by crochets that come far more from the feverish audacity of ignorance, than from philosophy or wisdom. Why, unless the courts interpose their prudence to rectify the blunders of the legislature, as they have already done a hundred times, the laborer's wife may have her action against her husband for the earthen bowl he has broken; and the man may be sued by the wife for rent! The happiness of every home is hourly put in jeopardy, in order that, now and then, a wife may be saved from the courses of a speculator or a spendthrift."

"Might not this have been done before, Uncle Tom, by means of settlements?" asked Anna, with interest.

"Certainly; and that it is which renders all this silly quackery so much the worse. In those cases in which the magnitude of the stake might seem to demand extraordinary care, the means already existed for providing all useful safeguards; and any new legislation was quite unnecessary. This very law will produce twenty-fold more unhappiness in families, than it will prevent of misery, by setting up distinct, and often conflicting interests, among those who ought to live as 'bone of their bone, and flesh of their flesh.'"

"You do not give to woman her proper place in society, Mr. Dunscomb," returned Mary Monson, haughtily; "your comments are those of a bachelor. I have heard of a certain Miss Millington, who once had an interest with you, and who, if living, would have taught you juster sentiments on this subject."

Dunscomb turned as white as a sheet; his hand and lip quivered; and all desire to continue the discourse suddenly left him. The gentle Anna, ever attentive to his wishes and ailings, stole to his side, silently offering a glass of water. She had seen this agitation before, and knew there was a leaf in "Uncle Tom's" history that he did not wish every vulgar eye to read.

As for Mary Monson, she went into her cell, like one who declined any further communication with her counsel. Timms was struck with her lofty and decided manner; but stood too much in awe of her, to interpose a remonstrance. After a few minutes taken by Dunscomb to regain his self-command, and a brief consultation together, the two lawyers quitted the prison. All this time, the accused remained in her cell, in resentful silence, closely and anxiously watched by the searching eye of her senior attendant.

CHAPTER XIX.

"Methinks, if, as I guess, the fault's but small,
It might be pardoned."—THE ORPHAN.

PERHAPS no surer test of high principles, as it is certain no more accurate test of high breeding can be found, than a distaste for injurious gossip. In woman, subject as she is unquestionably by her education, habits, and active curiosity, to the influence of this vice, its existence is deplorable, leading to a thousand wrongs, among the chief of which is a false appreciation of ourselves; but, when men submit to so vile a propensity, they become contemptible, as well as wicked. As a result of long observation, we should say that those who are most obnoxious to the just condemnation of the world, are the most addicted to finding faults in others; and it is only the comparatively good, who are so because they are humble, that abstain from meddling and dealing in scandal.

When one reflects on the great amount of injustice that is thus inflicted, without even the most remote hope of reparation, how far a loose, ill-considered and ignorant remark will float on the tongues of the idle, how much unmerited misery is oftentimes entailed by such unweighed assertions and opinions, and how small is the return of benefit in any form whatever, it would almost appear a necessary moral consequence that the world, by general consent, would determine to eradicate so pernicious an evil, in the common interest of mankind. That it does not, is probably owing to the power that is still left in the hands of the Father of Sin, by the Infinite Wisdom that has seen fit to place us in this condition of trial. The parent of all lies, gossip, is one of the most familiar of the means he employs to put his falsehoods in circulation.

This vice is heartless and dangerous when confined to its natural limits, the circles of society; but, when it invades the outer walks of life, and, most of all, when it gets mixed up with the administration of justice, it becomes a tyrant as ruthless and injurious in its way, as he who fiddled while Rome was in flames. We have no desire to exaggerate the evils of the state of society in which we live; but an honest regard to truth will, we think, induce every observant man to lament the manner in which this power, under the guise of popular opinion, penetrates into all the avenues of the courts, corrupting, perverting, and often destroying the healthful action of their systems.

Biberry furnished a clear example of the truth of these remarks on the morning of the day on which Mary Monson was to be tried.

The jail-window had its crowd, of course; and though the disposition of curtains, and other similar means of concealment completely baffled vulgar curiosity, they could not cloak the resentful feelings to which this reserve gave birth. Most of those who were drawn thither belonged to a class who fancied it was not affliction enough to be accused of two of the highest crimes known to the laws; but that to this grievous misfortune should be added a submission to the stare of the multitude. It was the people's laws the accused was supposed to have disregarded; and it was their privilege to anticipate punishment by insult.

"Why don't she show herself, and let the public look on her?" demanded one curious old man, whose head had whitened under a steadily increasing misconception of what the rights of this public were. "I've seen murderers afore now, and ain't a bit afeard on 'em, if they be well ironed and look'd a'ter."

This sally produced a heartless laugh; for, sooth to say, where *one* feels, under such circumstances, as reason, and justice, and revelation would tell them to feel, ten feel as the demons prompt.

"You cannot expect that a lady of fashion, who plays on the harp and talks French, will show her pretty face to be gazed at by common folks," rejoined a shabby genteel sort of personage, out of whose waistcoat pocket obtruded the leaves of a small note-book, and the end of a gold pen. This man was a reporter, rendered malignant by meeting with opposition to his views of imagining that the universe was created to furnish paragraphs for newspapers. He was a half-educated European, who pronounced all of his words in a sort of boarding-school dialect, as if abbreviation offended a taste "sickened by over learning."

Another laugh succeeded this supercilious sneer; and three or four lads, half-grown and clamorous, called aloud the name of "Mary Monson," demanding that she should show herself. At that moment the accused was on her knees, with Anna Updyke at her side, praying for that support which, as the crisis arrived, she found to be more and more necessary.

Changing from this scene to the open street, we find a pettifogger, one secretly prompted by Williams, spreading a report that had its origin no one knew where, but which was gradually finding its way to the ears of half the population of Dukes, exciting prejudice and inflicting wrong.

"It's the curi'stest story I ever heard," said Sam Tongue, as the pettifogger was usually styled, though his real name was Hubbs; "and one so hard to believe, that, though I tell it, I call on no man to believe it. You see, gentlemen"—the little group around him was composed of suitors, witnesses, jurors, grand-jurors, and others of a stamp that usually mark these several classes of men—"that the account now is, that this Mary Monson was sent abroad for her schoolin' when only ten years old; and that she stayed in the old countries long enough to l'arn to play the harp, and other deviltries of the same natur'. It's a misfortin', as I say, for any young woman to be sent out of Ameriky for an edication. Edication, as everybody knows, is the great glory of *our* country; and a body would think that what can't be l'arnt *here*, isn't worth knowin'."

This sentiment was well received, as would be any opinion that asserted American superiority, with that particular class of listeners. Eye turned to eye, nod answered nod, and a murmur expressive of approbation passed through the little crowd.

"But there was no great harm in that," put in a person named Hicks, who was accustomed to connect consequences with their causes, and to trace causes down to their consequences. "Anybody might have been edicated in France as well as Mary Monson. *That* will hardly tell ag'in her on the trial."

"I didn't say it would," answered Sam Tongue; "though it's gin'rally conceded that France is no country for religion or true freedom. Give me religion and freedom, say I; a body can get along with bad crops, or disappointments in gin'ral, so long as he has plenty of religion and plenty of freedom."

Another murmur, another movement in the group, and other nods denoted the spirit in which this was received, too.

"All this don't make ag'in Mary Monson; 'specially as you say she was sent abroad so young. It wasn't her fault if her parents—"

"She had no parents—there's the great mystery of her case. Never had, so far as can be discovered. A gal without parents, without fri'nds of any sort, is edicated in a foreign land, l'arns to speak foreign tongues, plays on foreign music, and comes home a'ter she's grown up, with her pockets as full as if she'd been to Californy and met a vein; and no one can tell where it all come from!"

"Well, *that* won't tell ag'in her, ne'ther," rejoined Hicks, who had now defended the accused so much that he began to take an interest in her acquittal. "Evidence must be direct, and have a p'int, to tell ag'in man or woman. As for Californy, it's made lawful by treaty, if Congress will only let it alone."

"I know that as well as the best lawyer in Dukes; but *character* can tell ag'in an accused, as is very likely to be shown in the Oyer and Terminer of this day. Character counts, let me tell you, when the facts get a little confused; and this is just what I was about to say. Mary Mon-

son has money; where does it come
from?"

"Those that think her guilty say that
it comes from poor Mrs. Goodwin's stockin'," returned Hicks, with a laugh; "but,
for my part, I've *seen* that stockin', and
am satisfied it didn't hold five hundred
dollars, if it did four."

Here the reporter out with his notes,
scribbling away for some time. That evening a paragraph, a little altered to give it
point and interest, appeared in an evening
paper, in which the conflicting statements
of Tongue and Hicks were so presented
that neither of these worthies could have
recognized his own child. That paper was
in Biberry next morning, and had no inconsiderable influence, ultimately, on the
fortunes of the accused.

In the barroom of Mrs. Horton, the discussion was also lively and wily on this
same subject. As this was a place much
frequented by jurors, the agents of Timms
and Williams were very numerous in and
around that house. The reader is not to
suppose that these men admitted directly
to themselves even, the true character of
the rascally business in which they were
engaged; for their employers were much
too shrewd not to cover, to a certain degree, the deformity of their own acts.
One set had been told that they were favoring justice, bringing down aristocratic
pride to the level of the rights of the mass,
demonstrating that this was a free country, by one of the very vilest procedures
that ever polluted the fountains of justice
at their very source. On the other hand,
the agents of Timms had been persuaded
that they were working in behalf of a persecuted and injured woman, who was
pressed upon by the well-known avarice
of the nephew of the Goodwins, and who
was in danger of becoming the victim of
a chain of extraordinary occurrences that
had thrown her into the meshes of the
law. It is true, this reasoning was backed
by liberal gifts; which, however, were
made to assume the aspect of compensation fairly earned, for the biggest villain
going derives a certain degree of satisfaction in persuading himself that he is acting under the influence of motives to
which he is, in truth, a stranger. The
homage which vice pays to virtue is on a
much more extended scale than is commonly supposed.

Williams's men had much the best of it
with the mass. They addressed themselves to prejudices as wide as the dominion of man; and a certain personal zeal
was mingled with their cupidity. Then
they had, by far, the easiest task. He
who merely aids the evil principles of our
nature, provided he conceal the cloven
foot, is much more sure of finding willing
listeners than he who looks for support in
the good. A very unusual sort of story
was circulated in this bar-room at the expense of the accused, and which carried
with it more credit than common, in consequence of its being so much out of the
beaten track of events as to seem to set
invention at defiance.

Mary Monson was said to be an heiress,
well connected, and well educated—or, as
these three very material circumstances
were stated by the Williams men—"well
to do herself, of friends well to do, and of
excellent schooling." She had been married to a person of equal position in society,
wealth, and character, but many years
her senior—too many, the story went,
considering her own time of life; for a
great difference, when one of the parties
is youthful, is apt to tax the tastes too
severely—and that connection had not
proved happy. It had been formed
abroad, and more on foreign than on
American principles; the bridegroom being a Frenchman. It was what is called
a *mariage de raison*, made through the
agency of friends and executors, rather
than through the sympathies and feelings
that should alone bring man and woman
together in this, the closest union known
to human beings.

After a year of married life abroad, the
unmatched couple had come to America,
where the wife possessed a very ample
fortune. This estate the recently enacted
laws gave solely and absolutely to herself; and it soon became a source of dis-
sension between man and wife. The husband, quite naturally, considered himself
entitled to advise and direct, and, in some
measure, to control, while the affluent,
youthful, and pretty wife was indisposed
to yield any of the independence she so
much prized, but which, in sooth, was asserted in the very teeth of one of the most
salutary laws of nature. In consequence
of this very different manner of viewing
the marriage relations, a coolness ensued,
which was shortly followed by the disappearance of the wife. This wife was
Mary Monson, who had secreted herself
in the retired dwelling of the Goodwins,
while the hired agents of her husband
were running up and down the land in
search of the fugitive in places of resort.
To this account, so strange, and yet in
many respects so natural, it was added
that a vein of occult madness existed in
the lady's family; and it was suggested
that, as so much of her conduct as was
out of the ordinary course might be traced
to this malady, so was it also possible

that the terrible incidents of the fire and the deaths were to be imputed to the same deep affliction.

We are far from saying that any rumor expressed in the terms we have used was circulating in Mrs. Horton's bar-room; but one that contained all their essentials was. It is one of the curious effects of the upward tendency of truth that almost every effort to conceal it altogether fails; and this at the very time when idle and heartless gossip is filling the world with lies. The tongue does a thousand times more evil than the sword; destroys more happiness, inflicts more incurable wounds, leaves deeper and more indelible scars. Truth is rarely met with unalloyed by falsehood.

"This or that unmix'd, no mortal e'er shall find"—

was the judgment of Pope a century since; nor has all the boasted progress of these later times induced a change. It is remarkable that a country which seems honestly devoted to improvement of every sort, that has a feverish desire to take the lead in the warfare against all sorts and species of falsehood, gives not the slightest heed to the necessity of keeping the channels of intelligence *pure*, as well as *open!* Such is the fact; and it is a melancholy but a just admission to acknowledge that with all the means of publicity preserved by America, there is no country in which it is more difficult to get unadulterated truth impressed on the common mind. The same wire that transmits a true account of the price of cotton from Halifax to New Orleans, carries a spark that imparts one that is false. The two arrive together; and it is not until each has done its work that the real fact is ascertained.

Notwithstanding these undoubted obstacles to the circulation of unalloyed truth, that upward tendency to which we have alluded occasionally brings out clear and strong rays of the divine quality, that illuminate the moral darkness on which they shine, as the sun touches the verge of the thunder-cloud. It is in this way that an occasional report is heard, coming from no one knows where; originating with no one knows whom; circulating in a sort of under-current beneath the torrents of falsehood that is singularly if it be not absolutely correct.

Of this character was the strange rumor that found its way into Biberry on the morning of Mary Monson's trial, touching the history of that mysterious young woman's past life. Wilmeter heard it first, with a pang of disappointment, though Anna had nearly regained her power in his heart; and this pang was immediately succeeded by unbounded surprise. He told the tale to Millington; and together they endeavored to trace the report to something like its source. All efforts of this nature were in vain. One had heard the story from another; but no one could say whence it came originally. The young men gave the pursuit up as useless, and proceeded together toward the room of Timms, where they knew Dunscomb was to be found, just at that time.

"It is remarkable that a story of this nature should be in such general circulation," said John, "and no one be able to tell who brought it to Biberry. Parts of it seem extravagant. Do they not strike you so, sir?"

"There is nothing too extravagant for some women to do," answered Millington, thoughtfully. "Now, on such a person as Sarah, or even on Anna Updyke, some calculations might be made—certain calculations, I might say; but they are women, Jack, on whom one can no more depend, than on the constancy of the winds."

"I admire your—'even on Anna Updyke!'"

"Do you not agree with me?" returned the unobservant Millington. "I have always considered Sarah's friend as a particularly reliable sort of a person."

"Even on Anna Updyke!—and a particularly reliable and safe sort of person! You have thought this, Mike, because she is Sarah's bosom friend?"

"That *may* have prejudiced me in her favor, I will allow; for I like most things that Sarah likes."

John looked at his friend and future brother-in-law with an amused surprise; the idea of liking Anna Updyke on any account but her own, striking him as particularly absurd. But they were soon at Timms's door, and the conversation dropped as a matter of course.

No one who has ever traveled much in the interior of America, can easily mistake the character of one of the small edifices, with the gable to the street, ornamented with what are erroneously termed Venetian blinds, painted white, and with an air of tobacco-smoke and the shabby-genteel about it, notwithstanding its architectural pretensions. This is a lawyer's office, thus brought edgeways to the street, as if the owner felt the necessity of approaching the thoroughfare of the world a little less directly than the rest of mankind. It often happens that these buildings, small as they usually are, contain two, or even three rooms; and that the occupants, if single men, sleep in them as well as transact their business. Such was the case with Timms, his "office," as the structure was termed, containing his bedroom, in addition to an inner and an outer department devoted to the purposes of the law. Dunscomb was in the sanctum, while a single clerk and three or four clients, countrymen of decent exterior and very expecting countenances, occupied the outer room. John and Millington went into the presence with little or no hesitation.

Wilmeter was not accustomed to much circumlocution; and he at once communicated the substance of the strange rumor that was in circulation, touching their interesting client. The uncle listened with intense attention, turning pale as the nephew proceeded. Instead of answering or making any comment, he sunk upon a chair, leaned his hands on a table and his head on his hands, for fully a minute. All were struck with these signs of agitation; but no one dared to interfere. At length, this awful pause came to a close, and Dunscomb raised his head, the face still pale and agitated. His eye immediately sought that of Millington.

"You had heard this story, Michael?" demanded the counselor.

"I had, sir. John and I went together to try and trace it to some authority."

"With what success?"

"None whatever. It is in every one's mouth, but no one can say whence it came. Most rumors have a clew, but this seems to have none."

"Do you trace the connection which has struck—which has *oppressed* me?"

"I do, sir, and was so struck the moment I heard the rumor; for the facts are in singular conformity with what you communicated to me some months since."

"They are, indeed, and create a strong probability that there is more truth in this rumor than is commonly to be found in such reports. What has become of Timms?"

"On the ground, squire," answered that worthy from the outer room—"just dispatching my clerk"—this word he pronounced "clurk" instead of "clark,"—by way of showing he knew how to spell —"with a message to one of my men. He will find him and be with us in a minute."

In the meantime, Timms had a word to say to each client in succession; getting rid of them all by merely telling each man, in his turn, there was not the shadow of doubt that he would get the better of his opponent in the trial that was so near at hand. It may be said here, as a proof how much a legal prophet may be mistaken, Timms was subsequently

beaten in each of these three suits, to the great disappointment of as many anxious husbandmen, each of whom fondly counted on success, from the oily promises he had received.

In a very few minutes the agent expected by Timms appeared in the office. He was plain-looking, rather rough and honest in appearance, with a most wily, villainous leer of the eye. His employer introduced him as Mr. Johnson.

"Well, Johnson, what news?" commenced Timms. "These are friends to Mary Monson, and you can speak out, always avoiding partic'lar partic'lars."

Johnson leered, helped himself to a chew of tobacco with great deliberation, a trick he had when he needed a moment of thought before he made his revelations; bowed respectfully to the great York lawyer; took a good look at each of the young men, as if to measure their means of doing good or harm; and then condescended to reply.

"Not very good," was the answer. "That foreign instrument, which they say is just such a one as David used when he played before Saul, has done a good deal of harm. It won't do, Squire Timms, to fiddle off an indictment for murder! Mankind gets engaged in such causes; and if they desire music on the trial, it's the music of law and evidence that they want."

"Have you heard any reports concerning Mary Monson's past life?—if so, can you tell where they come from?"

Johnson knew perfectly well whence a portion of the rumors came; those which told in favor of the accused; but these he easily comprehended were not the reports to which Timms alluded.

"Biberry is full of all sorts of rumors," returned Johnson, cautiously, "as it commonly is in court-time. Parties like to make the most of their causes."

"You know my meaning—we have no time to lose; answer at once."

"I suppose I do know what you mean, Squire Timms; and I have heard the report. In my judgment, the person who set it afloat is no friend of Mary Monson's."

"You think, then, it will do her damage?"

"To the extent of her neck. Eve, before she touched the apple, could not have been acquitted in the face of such a rumor. I look upon your client as a lost woman, Squire Timms."

"Does that seem to be the common sentiment—that is, so far as you can judge?"

"Among the jurors it does."

"The jurors!" exclaimed Dunscomb—"what can you possibly know of the opinions of the jurors, Mr. Johnson?"

A cold smile passed over the man's face, and he looked steadily at Timms, as if to catch a clew that might conduct him safely through the difficulties of his case. A frown that was plain enough to the agent, though admirably concealed from all others in the room, told him to be cautious.

"I only know what I see and hear. Jurors are men, and other men can sometimes get an insight into their feelings, without running counter to law. I heard the rumor related myself, in the presence of seven of the panel. It's true, nothing was said of the murder, or the arson; but such a history of the previous life of the accused was given as Lady Washington couldn't have stood up ag'in, had she been livin', and on trial for her life."

"Was anything said of insanity?" asked Dunscomb.

"Ah, that plea will do no good, nowadays; it's worn out. They'd hang a murderer from Bedlam. Insanity has been overdone, and can't be depended on any longer."

"Was anything said on the subject?" repeated the counselor.

"Why, to own the truth, there was; but, as that told *for* Mary Monson, and not *ag'in* her, it was not pressed."

"You think, then, that the story has been circulated by persons in favor of the prosecution?"

"I know it. One of the other side said to me, not ten minutes ago—'Johnson,' said he, 'we are old friends'—he always speaks to me in that familiar way—'Johnson,' said he, 'you'd a done better to have gi'n up. What's five thousand dollars to the likes of her? and them, you know, is the figures.'"

"That is a pretty exhibition of the manner of administering justice!" exclaimed the indignant Dunscomb. "Long as I have been at the bar, I had no conception that such practices prevailed. At all events, this illegality will give a fair occasion to demand a new trial."

"Ay, the sharpest lawyer that ever crossed Harlem Bridge can l'arn something in old Dukes," said Johnson, nodding. "Squire Timms will stand to *that.* As for new trials, I only wonder the lawyers don't get one each time they are beaten; for the law would bear them out."

"I should like to know how, Master Johnson," put in Timms. "That would be a secret worth knowing."

"A five-dollar note will buy it."

"There's one of ten—now, tell me your secret."

"Well, squire, you *be* a gentleman, whatever folks may say or think of you. I'd rather do business with you, by one-half, than do business with Williams; notwithstanding he has such a name up and down the country. Stick to it, and you'll get the nomination to the Sinat'; and the nomination secured, you're sure of the seat. Nomination is the government of Ameriky; and that's secured by a wonderful few!"

"I believe you are more than half right, Johnson."

Here Dunscomb, his nephew, and Millington left the office, quite unnoticed by the two worthies, who had entered on a subject as engrossing as that of Timms's elevation to the Senate. And, by the way, as this book is very likely to be introduced to the world, it may be well enough to explain that we have two sorts of "Senates" in this country; wheels within wheels. There is the Senate of each State, without an exception now, we believe; and there is the Senate of the United States; the last being, in every sense, much the more dignified and important body. It being unfortunately true that "nominations" are the real people of America, unless in cases which arouse the nation, the State Senates very often contain members altogether unsuited to their trusts; men who have obtained their seats by party legerdemain, and who had much better, on their own account, as well as on that of the public, be at home attending to their own private affairs. This much may be freely said by any citizen, of a State Senate, a collection of political partisans that commands no particular respect; but it is very different with that of the United States; and we shall confine ourselves to saying, in reference to that body, which it is the fashion of the times to reverence as the most illustrious political body on earth, that it is not quite as obnoxious to this judgment as the best of its sisterhood of the several States; though very far from being immaculate, or what, with a little more honesty in political leaders, it might be.

"I believe you are half right, Johnson," answered Timms. "Nomination is the government in this country; liberty, people, and all! Let a man get a nomination on the *right* side, and he's as good as elected. But now for this mode of getting new trials, Johnson?"

"Why, squire, I'm amazed a man of your experience should ask the question! The law is sharp enough in keeping jurors, and constables, and door-keepers, in their places; but the jurors, and constables, and door-keepers, don't like to be kept in their places; and there isn't one cause in ten, if they be of any length, in which the jurors don't stray, or the constables don't get into the jury rooms. You can't pound free-born American citizens like cattle!"

"I understand you, Johnson, and will take the hint. I knew there was a screw loose in this part of our jurisprudence, but did not think it as important as I now see it is. The fact is, Johnson, we have been telling the people so long that they are perfect, and every man that he, in his own person, is one of these people, that our citizens don't like to submit to restraints that are disagreeable. Still, we are a law-abiding people, as every one says."

"That may be so, squire; but we are not jury-room-abiding, nor be the constables outside-of-the-door-abiding, take my word for it. As you say, sir, every man is beginning to think he is a part of the people, and a great part, too; and he soon gets the notion that he can do as he has a mind to do."

"Where is Mr. Dunscomb?"

"He stepped out with the young gentlemen, a few moments since. I daresay, Squire Timms, he's gone to engage men to talk down this rumor about Mary Monson. That job should have been mine, by rights!"

"Not he, Johnson—not he. Your grand lawyers don't meddle with such matters; or, when they do, they pretend not to. No, he has gone to the jail, and I must follow him."

At the jail was Dunscomb, sure enough. Mary Monson, Anna and Sarah, with Marie Moulin, all dressed for the court; the former with beautiful simplicity, but still more beautiful care; the three last plainly, but in attire well suited to their respective stations in life. There was a common air of concern and anxiety; though Mary Monson still maintained her self-command. Indeed, the quiet of her manner was truly wonderful, for the circumstances.

"Providence has placed me in a most trying situation," she said; "but I see my course. Were I to shrink from this trial, evade it in any manner, a blot would rest on my name as long as I am remembered. It is indispensable that I should be *acquitted*. This, by God's blessing on the innocent, must come to pass, and I may go forth and face my friends with a quiet mind."

"These friends ought to be known," answered Dunscomb, "and should be here to countenance you with their presence."

"They! He! Never—while I live, never!"

"You see this young man, Mary Monson—I believe he is known to you, by name?"

Mary Monson turned her face toward Millington, smiled coldly, and seemed undisturbed.

"What is he to me? Here is the woman of his heart—let him turn to *her*, with all his care."

"You understand me, Mary Monson—it is important that I should be assured of *that*."

"Perhaps I do, Mr. Dunscomb, and perhaps I do *not*. You are enigmatical this morning; I cannot be certain."

"In one short half-hour the bell of yonder court-house will ring, when you are to be tried for your life."

The cheek of the accused blanched a little; but its color soon returned, while her eye assumed a look even prouder than common.

"Let it come"—was her quiet answer —"the innocent need not tremble. These two pure beings have promised to accompany me to the place of trial, and to give me *their* countenance. Why, then, should I hesitate?"

"I shall go, too"—said Millington steadily, like one whose mind was made up.

"You! Well, for the sake of this dear one, you may go, too."

"For no other reason, Mary?"

"For no other reason, sir. I am aware of the interest you and Mr. Wilmeter have taken in my case; and I thank you both from the bottom of my heart. Ah! kindness was never lost on me—"

A flood of tears, for the first time since her imprisonment, so far as any one knew, burst from this extraordinary being; and, for a few minutes, she became woman in the fullest meaning of the term.

During this interval, Dunscomb retired, perceiving that it was useless to urge anything on his client while weeping almost convulsively; and aware that he had several things to do before the court met. Besides, he left the place quite satisfied on an all-important point; and he and Millington walked by themselves toward the court-house, their heads close together, and their voices reduced nearly to whispers.

CHAPTER XX.

"I blush, and am confounded to appear
  Before thy presence, Cato."
"What's thy crime?"
"I am a Numidian."   —CATO.

WITHIN the half-hour mentioned by Dunscomb, the court-house bell rang, and there was a rush toward that building, in order to secure seats for the approaching trial. All that has been related in the preceding chapter occurred between the hours of six and nine that morning, it being one of the "ways of the hour" in the march of improvement, to drive the administration of justice with as near an approach to railroad speed as is practicable. Many of the modern judges go to work as early as eight in the morning—perhaps most do in the country circuits—and continue to call causes until nine and ten at night, illustrating the justice of the land by means of agents who are half asleep, and stupid from fatigue.

We have said that everything like dignity, except as it is to be found in the high character of its duties, and the manner in which they are performed, has been banished from the courts of New York. Even on this solemn occasion, when a human being was to be put on trial for her life, and she a woman, there was no departure from the naked simplicity that has been set up on the pedestal of reason, in open opposition to the ancient accessories by which the law asserted its power. It remains to be seen whether human nature has not been as much overestimated under the new arrangement as it was underrated by the old. There is a medium, in truth, that is ever safe to respect; and there is reason to apprehend that in throwing away the useless vestments of idle parade, those necessary to decency were cast aside with them.

Quite a fourth of the audience assembled in Dukes County court-house, on this occasion, were females. The curiosity, which is said to be so natural to the sex, was, on this occasion, quickened by the peculiar circumstances of the case, a woman having been murdered, and a woman accused of having committed the offense. It was said, however, that many were summoned as witnesses, it being generally understood that the State had subpœnaed the country far and near.

At length a general and expecting silence succeeded the bustle of the crowds entering and obtaining seats, and the eyes of the spectators were very generally turned toward the door, in the wish to get a glimpse of the principal personage in the approaching scene. We know not why it is that the spectacle of others' woes has so great a charm for most persons. Nature has given us sympathy and compassion, and a desire to alleviate misery; yet most of us like to look upon it, as a mere spectacle, when we have neither the wish nor the power to be more than useless spectators. Thousands will assemble to see a man hanged, when all know that the law has a grasp too tight to be unloosed, and that the circle of the gallows is no place for feelings of commiseration. But so it is; and many a female that day, who would have gladly alleviated any distress that it was in her power to lessen, sat there, a curious and interested observer of all that passed; to note the workings of the countenance, the writhings of the inner soul, if any such there should be, or the gleams of hope that might, at intervals, lighten the gloom of despair.

The court was occupied for half an hour with hearing motions, and in granting orders, nothing seeming to impede its utilitarian progress. Then the movement within the bar ceased, and an expectation that was even solemn fell on the whole mass of human beings that were collected in that narrow space.

"This is the day for which the trial of Mary Monson was, by arrangement, set down," observed the judge. "Mr. District Attorney, are you ready?"

"We are, sir—entirely so, I believe. If the court please, Mr. Williams and Mr. Wright will be associated with me in this case. It is one of importance, and I do not like the responsibility of trying it alone."

"The court has so understood it—who is for the accused?"

"I am retained to defend Mary Monson," answered Dunscomb, rising with dignity, and speaking with the self-possession of one long accustomed to the courts. "Mr. Timms will assist me."

"Are you ready, gentlemen?"

"I believe we are, your honor; though the prisoner has not yet been arraigned."

"Mr. District Attorney, we will proceed."

As the sheriff now left the room in person, rather an unusual thing in bringing a prisoner into court, expectation was at its height. In the midst of a breathing silence the door swung round—court-room doors are now made to swing like turnpikes, in order to prevent noise—and Mr. Gott entered, followed by Mary Monson, Anna, Sarah, Marie Moulin, and the two young men. The kind-hearted wife of the sheriff was already in the room, and, by means of a constable, had managed to keep seats reserved for those who might attend the prisoner. To these seats the party now retired, with the exception of Marie Moulin, who attended her mistress within the bar.

Every observer was struck with the unexpected air, manner, and attire of the prisoner. Dunscomb saw, at a glance, that her appearance had made a most favorable impression. This was something, and he hoped it might counteract much of the maneuvering of Davis and Williams. The judge, in particular, a kind-hearted and very well-meaning man, was taken altogether by surprise. There is nothing in which there is more freemasonry than in the secret symptoms of social castes. Each individual is more or less of a judge of these matters, up to the level of his own associations, while all beyond is mystery. It happened that the judge now about to try Mary Monson, belonged to an old, historical New York family, a thing of rather rare occurrence in the great movements of the times, and he possessed an hereditary tact in discerning persons of his own habits of life. Almost at a glance he perceived that the prisoner had the air, manners, countenance and finesse of one accustomed, from infancy, to good company. The reader may smile at this, but he must pardon us if we say the smile will betray ignorance, rather than denote the philosophy that he may fancy controls his opinions. Dunscomb was much gratified when the judge rather earnestly interposed against the act of the sheriff, who was about to place the prisoner at the bar in the little barricaded place allotted to the use of ordinary criminals, directing him to—

"Give the prisoner a chair *within* the bar, Mr. Sheriff. Gentlemen, be so good as to make room, that the accused may sit near her counsel. Mr. Attorney, let the prisoner be arraigned as soon as she has rested from the fatigue and agitation of appearing here."

This ceremony, now little more than a blank form, was soon ended, and the plea of "not guilty" was entered. The next step was to impanel the jury, a task of infinite difficulty, and one that has got to be so much an outwork, in the proceedings in criminal cases, as almost to baffle the powers of the law. It is no unusual thing for the time of the court to be occupied a week or two in this preliminary proceeding, until the evil has got to be so crying as to induce the executive to recommend that the legislature may devise some mode of relief. One of the most besetting vices of all American legislation in those cases in which abuses are not the offspring of party, is a false philanthropy, in which the wicked and evil-doer has been protected at the expense of the upright and obedient. The abuse just mentioned is one of those in which the bottom has been reached somewhat sooner than common; but it is hazarding little to predict that more than half which has

been done within the last few years, under the guise of liberty and philanthropy, will have to be undone, ere the citizen will be left to the quiet enjoyment of his rights, or can receive the just protection of the laws.

One of the common-sense and real improvements of the day is to swear the jurors, in all the causes that are to be tried, by one process. This is a saving of time; and though the ceremony might be, and ought to be made, much more solemn and impressive than it is, as by causing all other business to cease, and to make every one present rise, and stand in reverential silence, while the name of the God of heaven and earth is invoked, still it is a great improvement on the ancient mode, and has reason to sustain it. It gives us pleasure to note such circumstances in the "ways of the hour," whenever a sense of right can induce one who loathes the flattery of the people quite as much as he loathes that of princes, and flattery of all sorts, to say aught in favor of what has been done, or is yet doing around him.

The clerk called the name of Jonas Wattles, the first juror drawn. This man was a respectable mechanic, of no great force in the way of mind, but meaning well, and reputed honest. Timms gave the senior counsel a look, which the other understood to mean, "he may do." No objection being made on account of the State, Jonas Wattles took his seat in the jury-box, which was thought great good luck for a capital case.

"Ira Trueman," cried the clerk.

A meaning pause succeeded the announcement of this name. Trueman was a person of considerable local influence, and would probably carry great weight in a body composed principally of men even less instructed than he was himself. What was more, both Timms and Williams knew that their respective agents had been hard at work to gain his ear, though neither knew exactly with what degree of success. It was consequently equally hazardous to accept or to oppose, and the two legal gladiators stood at bay, each waiting for the other to betray his opinion of the man. The judge soon became wearied, and inquired if the juror was accepted. It was a somewhat amusing sight, now, to observe the manner in which Timms proceeded with Williams, and Williams met Timms.

"I should like to hear the gentleman's objections to this juror," observed Timms, "as I do not see that his challenge is peremptory."

"I have not challenged the juror at all,"

answered Williams, " but have understood the challenge comes from the defence."

" This is extr'or'nary ! The gentleman looks defiance at the juror, and now declares he does not challenge ! "

" Looks ! If looks made a challenge, the State might at once suffer these foul murders to go unpunished, for I am sure the gentleman's countenance is a perfect thunder-cloud—"

" I trust that counsel will recollect the gravity of this cause, and suffer it to be conducted with the decorum that ought never to be wanting in a court of justice," interposed the judge. " Unless there is a direct challenge, from one side or the other, the juror must take his seat, of course."

" I should like to ask the juror a question or two," Timms replied, speaking very cautiously, and like one who was afraid of hurting the feelings of the party under examination ; and in truth wary, lest on investigation he might discover that Trueman was likely to be the sort of person he wanted. " You have been at Biberry, juror, since the opening of the court ? "

Trueman nodded his head.

" Of course, you have been round among your friends and neighbors, that you have met with here ! "

Another nod from Trueman, with a sort of affirmative grunt.

" You have probably heard more or less said concerning Mary Monson—I mean in a legal and proper way ? "

A third nod of assent.

" Can you speak anything, in particular, that has been said in your presence ? "

Trueman seemed to tax his memory, then he raised his head, and answered deliberately and with great clearness. " I was going from the tavern to the court-house, when I met David Johnson—"

" Never mind those particulars, Mr. Trueman," interrupted Timms, who saw that the juror had been talking with one of his own most confidential agents— " what the court wishes to know is, if any one has been reporting circumstances *unfavorable* to Mary Monson in your presence ? "

" Or in her *favor*," put in Williams, with a sneer.

" Juror," interposed the judge—" tell us if any one has spoken to you on the merits of this case—for or against ? "

" *Merits* "—repeated Trueman, seeming to. reflect again. " No, your honor ; I can't say that there has."

Now, this was as bold a falsehood as was ever uttered ; but Trueman reconciled the answer to his conscience by choosing to consider that the conversation he had heard had been on the *demerits* of the accused.

" I do not see, gentlemen, that you can challenge for cause," observed his honor —" unless you have further facts."

" Perhaps we have, sir," answered Williams. " You were saying, Mr. Trueman, that you met David Johnson as you were going from the inn to the court-house. Did I understand you correctly ? "

" Just so, squire. I had been having a long talk with Peter Titus"—one of Williams's most active and confidential agents—" when Johnson came up. Johnson says, says he, ' A pleasant day, gentlemen—I'm glad to see you both out ; for the faces of old friends is getting scarce—' "

" I see no objection to the juror's being received," Williams carelessly remarked ; satisfied that Titus had not neglected his duty in that long talk.

" Yes. he is as good a juror as Dukes can furnish," observed Timms, perfectly sure Johnson had turned to account the advantage of having the last word. Trueman was accordingly admitted to the box, as the second man of the twelve. The two managers of this cause were both right. Titus *had* crammed his old acquaintance Trueman with all that was circulating to the prejudice of the prisoner ; expressing surprise when he had said all he had to say, at hearing that his friend was on the panel, " Well," said Titus, as Johnson approached, " if questioned, you'll remember I said I didn't dream of your being a juryman—but, just as like as not, you'll not be drawn for the case at all." On the other hand, Johnson was quite eloquent and pathetic in giving his old acquaintance the history of Mary Monson's case, whom he pronounced " a most injured and parsecuted woman." Trueman, a shrewd, managing fellow in general, fancied himself just as impartial, and fit to try the cause, after he had heard the stories of the two men, as he had ever been ; but in this he was mistaken. It requires an unusually clear head, exceedingly high principles, and a great knowledge of men, to maintain perfect impartiality in these cases ; and certainly Truman was not the man to boast of all these rare qualities. In general, the last word tells ; but it sometimes happens that first impressions become difficult to eradicate. Such was the fact in the present instance ; Trueman taking his seat in the jury box with an exceedingly strong bias against the accused.

We are aware that these are not the colors in which it is the fashion to delineate the venerable and much vaunted institution of the jury, certainly a most efficient agent in curtailing the power of a prince; but just as certainly a most irresponsible, vague, and quite often an unprincipled means of administering the law, when men are not urged to the desire of doing right by political pressure from without, and are left to the perverse and free workings of a very evil nature. We represent things as we believe them to exist, knowing that scarce a case of magnitude occurs in which the ministers of corruption are not at work among the jurors or a verdict rendered in which the fingers of the Father of Lies might not be traced, were the veil removed, and the facts exposed to the light of day. It is true, that in trials for life, the persecution of the prisoner rarely takes so direct a form as has been represented in the case of Mary Monson; but the press and the tongue do an incalculable amount of evil, even in such cases; all the ancient safeguards of the law having been either directly removed by ill-considered legislation, or rendered dead-letters by the "ways of the hour."

It was regarded as exceedingly good progress to get two jurors into the box, in a capital case, in the first half-hour. His honor had evidently resigned himself to a twenty-four hours' job; and great was his satisfaction when he saw Wattles and Trueman safely seated on their hard and uncomfortable seats; for it would almost seem that discomfort has been brought into the court-houses as a sort of auxiliary to the old practice of starving a jury into a verdict.

Whether it was owing to a suspicion, on the part of Timms, of the truth in regard to his being overreached in the case of Trueman, or to some other cause, he raised no objections to either of the six jurors next called. His moderation was imitated by Williams. Then followed two peremptory challenges; one in behalf of the prisoner, and one in behalf of the people, as it is termed. This was getting on so much better than everybody expected, that all were in good humor, and, it is not exceeding the truth, if we add, in a slight degree more disposed to view the prisoner and her case with favor. On such trifles do human decisions often depend.

All this time, fully an hour, did Mary Monson sit in resigned submission to her fate, composed, attentive, and singularly ladylike. The spectators were greatly divided in their speculations on her guilt or innocence. Some saw in her quiet manner, curious interest in the proceedings, and unchanging color, proofs not only of a hardened conscience, but of an experience in scenes similar to that in which she was now engaged; overlooking all the probabilities, to indulge in conjectures so severe against one so young.

"Well, gentlemen," cried the judge, "time is precious. Let us proceed."

The ninth juror was drawn, and it proved to be a country trader of the name of Hatfield. This person was known to be a man of considerable influence among persons of his own class, and to have a reputation for judgment, if not for principles. "They might as well send the other eleven home, and let Hatfield pronounce the verdict," whispered one lawyer to another; "there is no material in that box to withstand his logic."

"Then he will hold this young woman's life in his hand," was the reply.

"It will be pretty much so. The glorious institution of the jury is admirably devised to bring about such results."

"You forget the judge; he has the last word, you will remember."

"Thank God it is so; else would our condition be terrible. Lynch law is preferable to laws administered by jurors who fancy themselves so many legislators."

"It cannot be concealed that the spirit of the times has invaded the jury-box; and the court has not one-half its ancient influence. I should not like to have this Hatfield against me."

It would seem that Williams was of the same way of thinking; for he muttered to himself, desired the juror not to enter the box, and seemed to be pondering on the course he ought to pursue. The truth was that he himself had recently sued Hatfield for debt, and the proceedings had been a little vindictive. One of the dangers that your really skillful lawyer has to guard against is the personal animosity that is engendered by his own professional practice. Many men have minds so constituted that their opinions are affected by prejudices thus created; and they do not scruple to transfer their hostility from the counsel to the cause he is employed to defend. It is consequently incumbent on the prudent lawyer to make his estimate of character with judgment, and be as sure, as the nature of the case will allow, that his client is not to suffer for his own acts. As hostility to the counsel is not a legal objection to a juror, Williams was under the necessity of presenting such as would command the attention of the court.

"I wish the juror may be sworn to make true answers," said Williams.

Timms now pricked up his ears; for, if it were important for Williams to *oppose* the reception of this particular individual it was probably of importance to Mary Monson to have him received. On this principle, therefore, he was ready to resist the attack on the juror, who was at once sworn.

"You reside in the adjoining town of Blackstone, I believe, Mr. Hatfield," asked Williams.

A simple assent was the reply.

"In practice there, in one of the learned professions?"

Hatfield was certain his interrogator knew better, for Williams had been in his store fifty times, but he answered with the same innocent manner as that with which the question was put.

"I'm in trade."

"In trade! Keep a store, I daresay, Mr. Hatfield?"

"I do—and one in which I have sold you hundreds myself."

A general smile succeeded this sally; and Timms looked round at the audience, with his nose pointed upward, as if he scented his game.

"I dare say—I pay as I go," returned Williams, "and my memory is not loaded with such transactions—"

"Mr. Williams," interrupted the judge, a little impatiently, "the time of the court is very precious."

"So is the dignity of the outraged laws of the State, your honor. We shall soon be through, sir. — Many people in the habit of frequenting your store, Mr. Hatfield?"

"As much so as is usual in the country."

"Ten or fifteen at a time, on some occasions?"

"I dare say there may be."

"Has the murder of Peter Goodwin ever been discussed by your customers in your presence?"

"I don't know but it has—such a thing is very likely; but one hears so much, I can't say."

"Did you ever join in such a discussion yourself?"

"I may, or I may not."

"I ask you, now, distinctly, if you had no such discussion on the 26th of May last, between the hours of eleven and twelve in the forenoon?"

The sharpness of the manner in which this question was put, the minuteness of the details, and the particularity of the interrogatories, quite confounded the juror, who answered accordingly.

"Such a thing *might* have taken place, and it might *not*, I do not remember."

"Is Jonas White" (a regular country loafer) "in the habit of being in your store?"

"He is—it is a considerable lounge for laboring men."

"And Stephen Hook?"

"Yes; he is there a good deal of his time."

"Now, I beg you to remember—did not such a conversation take place, in which you bore a part, between the hours of eleven and twelve in the forenoon; White and Hook being present?"

Hatfield seemed perplexed. He very conscientiously desired to tell the truth, having nothing to gain by an opposite course; but he really had no recollection of any such discussion, as well might be the case; no such conversation ever having taken place. Williams knew the habits of the loafers in question, had selected the time at random, and adopted the particularity merely as a means of confounding the juror, of whom he was seriously afraid.

"Such a thing *may* have happened," answered Hatfield, after a pause—"I don't remember."

"It *may* have happened. Now, sir, allow me to ask you, if, in that conversation you did not express an opinion that you did not, and *could* not believe that a lady educated and delicate, like the prisoner at the bar, did, or would, under any circumstances, commit the offense with which Mary Monson is charged?"

Hatfield grew more and more confounded; for Williams's manner was more and more confident and cool. In this state of feeling he suffered the reply to escape him—

"I *may* have said as much—it seems quite natural."

"I presume, after this," observed Williams, carelessly, "your honor will order the juror not to enter the box?"

"Not so fast—not so fast, brother Williams," put in Timms, who felt it was now his turn to say a word, and who was thumbing a small pocket-almanac very diligently the while.

"This discussion, I understand the learned gentleman, took place in the juror's store."

"It did, sir," was the answer—"a place where such discussions are very apt to occur. Hook and White loaf half their time away in that store."

"All quite likely—very likely to happen —Mr. Hatfield, do you open your store on the Sabbath?"

"Certainly not—I am very particular to do nothing of the sort."

"A church-member, I suppose, sir?"

"An undeserving one, sir."

"Never, on any account, in the practice of opening your store of a Sabbath, I understand you to say?"

"Never, except in cases of sickness. We must all respect the wants of the sick."

"Are Hook and White in the habit of loafing about on your premises of a Sunday?"

"Never—I wouldn't tolerate it. The store is a public place on a week-day, and they can come in if they please; but I wouldn't tolerate such visits on the Sabbath."

"Yet, if the court please, the 26th of last May happened to fall on the Sabbath day! My brother Williams forgot to look into the almanac before he made up his brief."

Here Timms sat down, cocking his nose still higher, quite certain of having made a capital hit toward his views on the Senate, though he actually gained nothing for the cause. There was a general simper in the audience; and Williams felt that he had lost quite as much as his opponent had gained. "Well, gentlemen, time is precious—let us go on," interposed the judge. "Is the juror to enter the box or not?"

"I trust a trifling mistake as to the day of the month is not about to defeat the ends of justice," answered Williams, raising himself higher on his stilts, as he found himself sinking lower in his facts. "I put it on the 26th by a miscalculation, I can now see. It was probably on the 25th—Saturday is the loafer's holiday; yes, it must have been on Saturday the 25th that the conversation took place."

"Do you remember this fact, juror?"

"I remember, now so much has been said on the subject," answered Hatfield, firmly, "that I was not at home at all between the 20th and the 27th of May last. I could have held no such conversation on the 25th or 26th of May; nor do I know that I think Mary Monson either innocent or guilty."

As all this was true, and was uttered with the confidence of truth, it made an impression on the audience. Williams doubted; for so fine was his skill in managing men, that he often succeeded in gaining jurors by letting them understand he suspected them of being prejudiced against his case. With the weak and vain, this mode of proceeding has frequently more success than a contrary course; the party suspected being doubly anxious to illustrate his impartiality in his verdict. This was what Williams, and indeed the bar, very generally calls "standing so erect as to lean backward."

"Mr. Williams," said the judge, "you must challenge peremptorily, or the juror will be received."

"No, your honor, the State will accept the juror; I now see that my information has been wrong."

"We challenge for the defense," said Timms, deciding on the instant, on the ground that if Williams was so ready to change his course of proceeding, there must be a good reason for it. "Stand aside, juror."

"Peter Bailey," called the clerk.

No objection being made, Peter Bailey took his seat. The two next jurors were also received unquestioned; and it only remained to draw the twelfth man. This was so much better luck than commonly happens in capital cases, that everybody seemed more and more pleased, as if all were anxious to come to the testimony. The judge evidently felicitated himself, rubbing his hands with very great satisfaction. The bar, generally, entered into his feelings, for it helped along its business.

"On the whole," observed one of the lawyers, who was in extensive practice, speaking to another at his side, "I would as soon try one of these murder cases as to go through with a good water-cause."

"Oh! *they* are excruciating! Get into a good water-cause, with about thirty witnesses on a side, and you are in for a week. I was three days at one, only last circuit."

"Are there many witnesses in this case?"

"About forty, I hear," glancing toward the benches where most of the females sat. "They tell me there will be a very formidable array as to character. Ladies from York by the dozen!"

"They will be wanted, if all they say is true."

"If all you hear is true, we have reached a new epoch in the history of mankind. I have never seen the day when half of that I hear is more than half true. I set the rest down as ' leather and prunella.' "

"Robert Robinson," cried the clerk.

A respectable-looking man of fifty presented himself, and was about to enter the box without stopping to ascertain whether or not he would be welcome there. This person had much more the air of the world than either of the other jurors; and with those who are not very particular, or very discriminating in such matters, might readily enough pass for a gentleman. He was neatly dressed, wore gloves, and had certain chains, an eyeglass, and other appliances of the sort that it is not usual to see at a country circuit. Neither Williams nor Timms seemed to know the juror; but each looked surprised and undecided how he ought to act. The peremptory challenges were not exhausted; and there was a common impulse in the two lawyers, first to accept one so respectable in mien, and attire, and general air; and then, by a sudden revolution of feeling, to reject one of whom they knew nothing.

"I suppose the summons is all right," Williams carelessly remarked. "The juror resides in Dukes?"

"I do," was the answer.

"Is a freeholder, and entitled to serve?"

A somewhat supercilious smile came over the countenance of the juror; and he looked round at the person who could presume to make such a remark, with something very like an air of contempt.

"I am *Doctor* Robinson," he then observed, laying emphasis on his learned appellation.

Williams seemed at a loss; for, to say the truth, he had never heard of any such physician in the county. Timms was quite as much mystified; when a member of the bar leaned across a table, and whispered to Dunscomb that the juror was a celebrated quack, who made pills that would cure all diseases; and who, having made a fortune, had bought a place in the county, and was to all legal purposes entitled to serve.

"The juror can stand aside," said Dunscomb, rising in his slow dignified manner. "If it please the court, we challenge peremptorily."

Timms looked still more surprised; and when told the reason for the course taken by his associate, he was even sorry.

"The man is a *quack*," said Dunscomb, "and there is quackery enough in this system of a jury, without calling in assistance from the more open practitioners."

"I'm afraid, squire, he is just the sort of a man we want. I can work on such spirits, when I fail altogether with more every-day kind of men. A little quackery does no harm to some causes."

"Ira Kingsland," called out the clerk.

Ira Kingsland appeared, a staid, solid, respectable husbandman—one of those it is a mistaken usage of the country to term yeomen; and of a class that contains more useful information, practical good sense and judgment, than might be imagined, under all the circumstances.

As no objection was raised, this juror was received, and the panel was complete. After cautioning the jurors about listening and talking, in the usual way, the judge adjourned the court for dinner.

CHAPTER XXI.

"I know it is dreadful! I feel the
    Anguish of thy generous soul—but I was born
To murder all who love me."
                        —GEORGE BARNWELL.

DUNSCOMB was followed to his room by Millington, between whom and himself, John Wilmeter had occasion to remark, a sudden intimacy had sprung up. The counselor had always liked his student, or he would never have consented to give him his niece; but it was not usual for him to hold as long, or seemingly as confidential conversations with the young man, as now proved to be the case. When the interview was over, Millington mounted a horse and galloped off, in the direction of town, in that almost exploded manner of moving. Time was, and that within the memory of man, when the gentlemen of New York were in their saddles hours each day; but all this is changing with the times. We live in an age of buggies, the gig, phaeton, and curricle having disappeared, and the utilitarian vehicle just named having taken their places. Were it not for the women, who still have occasion for closer carriages, the whole nation would soon be riding about in buggies! Beresford is made, by one of his annotators, to complain that everything like individuality is becoming lost in England, and that the progress of great improvements must be checked, or independent thinkers will shortly be out of the question.

If this be true of England, what might not be said on the same subject of America? Here, where there is so much community as to have completely ingulfed everything like individual thought and action, we take it the most imitative people on earth are to be found. This truth is manifested in a thousand things. Every town is getting its Broadway, thus defeating the very object of names; to-day the country is dotted with Grecian temples, to-morrow with Gothic villages, all the purposes of domestic architecture being sadly forgotten in each; and, as one of the Spensers is said to have introduced the article of dress which bears his name, by betting he could set the fashion of cutting off the skirts of the coat, so might one who is looked up to, in this country, almost set the fashion of cutting off the nose.

Dunscomb, however, was a perfectly original thinker. This he manifested in his private life, as well as in his public profession. His opinions were formed in his own way, and his acts were as much those of the individual as circumstances would at all allow. His motives in dispatching Millington so suddenly to town were known to himself, and will probably be shown to the reader, as the narrative proceeds.

"Well, sir, how are we getting on?" asked John Wilmeter, throwing himself into a chair, in his uncle's room, with a heated and excited air. "I hope things are going to your mind?"

"We have got a jury, Jack, and that is all that can be said in the matter," returned the uncle, looking over some papers as the conversation proceeded. "It is good progress, in a capital case, to get a jury impaneled in the first forenoon."

"You'll have the verdict in by this time to-morrow, sir, I'm afraid!"

"Why, afraid, boy? The sooner the poor woman is acquitted, the better it will be for *her*."

"Ay, if she be acquitted; but I fear everything is looking dark in the case."

"And this from *you*, who fancied the accused an angel of light, only a week since!"

"She is certainly a most fascinating creature, *when she chooses to be*," said John, with emphasis; "but she does not always choose to appear in that character."

"She is most certainly a fascinating creature, *when she chooses to be!*" returned the uncle, with very much the same sort of emphasis.

But Dunscomb's manner was very different from that of his nephew. John was excited, petulant, irritable, and in a state to feel and say disagreeable things; dissatisfied with himself, and consequently not very well pleased with others. A great change had come over his feelings, truly, within the last week, and the image of the gentle Anna Updyke was fast taking the place of that of Mary Monson. As the latter seldom saw the young man, and then only at the gate, the former had got to be the means of communication between the youthful advocate and his client, throwing them constantly in each other's way. On such occasions Anna was always so truthful, so gentle, so earnest, so natural, and so sweetly feminine, that John must have been made of stone to remain insensible of her excellent qualities. If women did but know how much their power, not to say charms, are increased by gentleness, by tenderness in lieu of coldness of manner, by keeping within the natural circle of their sex's feelings, instead of aping an independence and spirit more suited to men than to their own condition, we should see less of discord in domestic life, happier wives, better mothers, and more reasonable mistresses. No one knew this better than Dunscomb, who had not been an indifferent spectator of his nephew's course, and who fancied this a favorable moment to say a word to him, on a subject that he felt to be important.

"This *choosing* to be is a very material item in the female character," continued the counselor, after a moment of silent and profound thought. "Whatever else you may do, my boy, in the way of matrimony, marry a gentle and feminine woman. Take my word for it, there is no true happiness with any other."

"Women have their tastes and caprices, and like to indulge them, sir, as well as ourselves."

"All that may be true; but avoid what is termed a woman of independent spirit. They are usually so many devils incarnate. If they happen to unite moneyed independence with moral independence, I am not quite certain that their tyranny is not worse than that of Nero. A tyrannical woman is worse than a tyrannical man, because she is apt to be capricious. At one time she will blow hot, at the next cold; at one time she will give, at the next clutch back her gifts; to-day she is the devoted and •obedient wife, to-morrow the domineering partner. No, no, Jack, marry a *woman;* which means a kind, gentle, affectionate, thoughtful creature, whose heart is so full of *you*, there is no room in it for herself. Marry just such a girl as Anna Updyke, if you can get her."

"I thank you, sir," answered John, coloring. "I daresay the advice is good, and I shall bear it in mind. What would you think of a woman like Mary Monson for a wife?"

Dunscomb turned a vacant look at his nephew, as if his thoughts were far away, and his chin dropped on his bosom. This abstraction lasted but a minute, however, when the young man got his answer.

"Mary Monson is a wife, and I fear a bad one," returned the counselor. "If she be the woman I suppose her to be, her history, brief as it is, is a very lamentable one. John, you are my sister's son, and my heir. You are nearer to me than any other human being, in one sense, though I certainly love Sarah quite as well as I do you, if not a little better. These ties of feeling are strange links in our nature! At one time I loved your mother with a tenderness such as a father might feel for a child; in short, with a brother's love— a brother's love for a young, and pretty, and good girl, and I thought I could never love another as I loved Elizabeth. She returned my affection, and there was a period of many years when it was supposed that we were to pass down the vale of life in company, as brother and sister—old bachelor and old maid. Your father deranged all this, and at thirty-four my sister left me. It was like pulling my heart-strings out of me, and so much the worse, boy, because they were already sore."

John started. His uncle spoke hoarsely, and a shudder, that was so violent as to be perceptible to his companion, passed through his frame. The cheeks of the counselor were usually colorless; now they appeared absolutely pallid.

"This, then," thought John Wilmeter, "is the insensible old bacheler, who was thought to live altogether for himself. How little does the world really know of what is passing within it! Well may it be said,' 'There is a skeleton in every house.'"

Dunscomb soon recovered his self-command. Reaching forth an arm, he took his nephew's hand, and said affectionately—

"I am not often thus, Jack, as you must know. A vivid recollection of days that have long been past came freshly over me, and I believe I have been a little unmanned. To you, my early history is a blank; but a very few words will serve to tell you all you need ever know. I was about your time of life, Jack, when I loved, courted, and became engaged to Mary Millington—Michael's great-aunt. Is this news to you?"

"Not entirely, sir; Sarah has told me something of the same sort—you know the girls get hold of family anecdotes sooner than we men."

"She then probably told you that I was cruelly, heartlessly jilted for a richer man. Mary married, and left one daughter; who also married early, her own cousin, Frank Millington, the cousin of Michael's father. You may now see why I have ever felt so much interest in your future brother-in-law."

"*He* is a good fellow, and quite free from all jilting blood. I'll answer for it. But, what has become of this Mrs. Frank Millington? I remember no such person."

"Like her mother, she died young, leaving an only daughter to inherit her name and very ample fortune. The reason you never knew Mr. Frank Millington is probably because he went to Paris early, where he educated his daughter, in a great degree—there, and in England—and when he died, Mildred Millington, the heiress of both parents, is said to have had quite twenty theusand a year. Certain officious friends made a match for her, I

have heard, with a Frenchman of some family, but small means, and the recent revolution had driven them to this country, where, as I have been told, she took the reins of domestic government into her own hands, until some sort of a separation has been the consequence."

"Why this account is surprisingly like the report we have concerning Mary Monson, this morning!" cried Jack, springing to his feet with excitement.

"I believe her to be the same person. Many things unite to create this opinion. In the first place, there is certainly a marked family resemblance to her grandmother and mother; then the education, manners, languages, money, Marie Moulin, and the initials of the assumed name, each and all have their solution in this belief. The 'madamoiselle' and the 'madame' of the Swiss maid are explained; in short, if we can believe this Mary Monson to be Madame de Larochefort, we can find an explanation of everything that is puzzling in her antecedents."

"But why should a woman of twenty thousand a year be living in a cottage of Peter Goodwin?"

"Because she *is* a woman of twenty thousand a year. Monsieur de Larocheforte found her money was altogether at her own command, by this new law, and naturally enough, he desired to play something more than a puppet's part in his own abode and family. The lady clings to her dollars, which she loves more than her husband; a quarrel ensues, and she chooses to retire from her protection, and conceals herself, for a time, under Peter Goodwin's roof, to evade pursuit. Capricious and wrong-headed women do a thousand strange things, and thoughtless gabblers often sustain them in what they do."

"This is rendering the marriage tie very slight!"

"It is treating it with contempt; setting at naught the laws of God and man—one's duties and the highest obligations of woman. Still, many of the sex fancy if they abstain from one great and distinct offense, the whole catalogue of the remaining misdeeds is at their mercy."

"Not to the extent of murder and arson, surely! Why should such a woman commit these crimes?"

"One never knows. We are fearfully constituted, John: morally and physically. The fairest form often conceals the blackest heart, and *vice versa*. But I am now satisfied that there is a vein of insanity in this branch of the Millingtons; and it is possible Madame de Larocheforte is more to be pitied than to be censured."

" You surely do not think her guilty, Uncle Tom ? "

The counsellor looked intently at his nephew, shaded his brow a moment, gazed upward, and answered—

" I do. There is such a chain of proof against her as will scarce admit of explanation. I am afraid, Jack—I am afraid that she has done these deeds, terrible as they are ! Such has been my opinion, now, for some time ; though my mind has vacillated, as I make no doubt will prove to be the case with those of most of the jurors. It is a sad alternative ; but I see no safety for her except in the plea of insanity. I am in hopes that something may be made out in that respect."

" We are quite without witnesses to the point ; are we not, sir ? "

" Certainly ; but Michael Millington has gone to town to send by telegraph for the nearest connections of Madame de Larocheforte, who are in the neighborhood of Philadelphia. The husband himself is somewhere on the Hudson. He must be hunted up too. Michael will see to all this. I shall get the judge to adjourn early this evening ; and we must spin out the trial for the next day or two, in order to collect our forces. The judge is young and indulgent. He has certain ridiculous notions about saving the time of the public ; but does not feel secure enough in his seat to be very positive."

At this instant Timms burst into the room, in a high state of excitement, exclaiming, the moment he was sure that his words would not reach any hostile ears—

" Our case is desperate ! All the Burtons are coming out dead against us ; and neither ' the new philanthropy,' nor ' Friends,' nor ' anti-gallows,' can save us. I never knew excitement get up so fast. It is the infernal aristocracy that kills us ! Williams makes great use of it ; and our people will not stand aristocracy. See what a magnanimous report to the legislature the learned attorney-general has just made on the subject of aristocracy. How admirably he touches up the kings and countesses ! "

" Pshaw ! " exclaimed Dunscomb, with a contemptuous curl of the lip—" not one in a thousand knows the meaning of the word and he among the rest. The report you mention is that of a refined gentleman, to be sure, and is addressed to his equals. What exclusive political privilege does Mary Monson possess ? or what does the patroon, unless it be the privilege of having more stolen from him, by political frauds, than any other man in the State ? This cant about social aristocracy, even

in a state of society in which the servant deserts his master with impunity in the midst of a dinner, is very miserable stuff ! Aristocracy, forsooth ! If there be aristocracy in America, the blackguard is the aristocrat. Away, then, with all this trash, and speak common-sense in future."

" You amaze me, sir ! Why I regard *you* as a sort of aristocrat, Mr. Dunscomb."

" Me ! And what do you see aristocratic about me, pray ? "

" Why, sir, you don't *look* like the rest of us. Your very *walk* is different— your language, manners, dress, habits and opinions, all differ from those of the Dukes County bar. Now, to my notion, that is being exclusive and peculiar ; and whatever is peculiar is aristocratic, is it not ? "

Here Dunscomb and his nephew burst out in a laugh ; and, for a few minutes, Mary Monson was forgotten. Timms was quite in earnest ; for he had fallen into the every-day notions in this respect, and it was not easy to get him out of them.

" Perhaps the Dukes County bar contains the aristocrats, and I am the serf ! " said the counselor.

" That cannot be—you *must* be the aristocrat, if any there be among us. I don't know *why* it is so, but so it is ; yes, *you* are the aristocrat, if there be one at our bar."

Jack smiled, and looked funny, but he had the discretion to hold his tongue. He had heard that a Duke of Norfolk, the top of the English aristocracy, was so remarkable for his personal habits as actually to be offensive ; a man who, according to Timms's notions, would have been a long way down the social ladder ; but who, nevertheless, was a top peer, if not a top sawyer. It was easy to see that Timms confounded a gentleman with an aristocrat ; a confusion in ideas that is very common, and which is far from being unnatural, when it is remembered how few formerly acquired any of the graces of deportment who had not previously attained positive, exclusive, political rights. As for the attorney-general and his report, Jack had sufficient sagacity to see it was a document that said one thing and meant another ; professing deference for a people that it did not stop to compliment with the possession of either common honesty or good manners.

" I hope *my* aristocracy is not likely to affect the interests of my client."

" No ; there is little danger of that. It is the democracy of the Burtons which will do that. I learn from Johnson that they are coming out stronger and stronger; and I feel certain Williams is sure of their testimony. By the way, sir, I had a hint from him, as we left the court-house, that the five thousand dollars might *yet* take him from the field."

"This Mr. Williams, as well as yourself, Timms, must be more cautious, or the law will yet assert its power. It is very much humbled, I am aware, under the majesty of the people and a feeble administration of its authority; but its arm is long, and its gripe potent, when it chooses to exert its force. Take my advice, and have no more to do with such arrangements."

The dinner-bell put an end to the discussion. Timms vanished like a ghost; but Dunscomb, whose habits were gentleman-like, and who knew that Mrs. Horton had assigned a particular seat to him, moved more deliberately; following his nephew about the time Timms was half through the meal.

An American tavern-dinner, during the sitting of the circuit, is every way worthy of a minute and graphic description; but our limits will hardly admit of our assuming the task. If "misery makes a man acquainted with strange bed-fellows," so does the law. Judges, advocates, witnesses, sheriffs, clerks, constables, and not unfrequently the accused, dine in common, with railroad speed. The rattling of knives, forks and spoons, the clatter of plates, the rushing of waiters, landlord, landlady, chambermaids, hostler and bar-keeper included, produce a confusion that would do honor to the most profound "republican simplicity." Everything approaches a state of nature but the eatables; and they are invariably overdone. On an evil day some Yankee invented an article termed a "cooking-stove;" and since its appearance, everything like good cookery has vanished from the common American table. There is plenty spoiled, abundance abused. Of made dishes, with the exception of two or three of very simple characters, there never were any; and these have been burned to cinders by the baking processes of the "cook-stoves."

It matters little, however, to the *convives* of a circuit-court dinner, what the dishes are called, or of what they are composed. "Haste" forbids "taste;" and it actually occurred that day, as it occurs almost invariably on such occasions, that a very clever country practitioner was asked the *matériel* of the dish he had been eating, and he could not tell it! Talk of the mysteries of French cookery! The "cook-stove" produces more mystery than all the art of all the culinary artists of Paris; and this, too, on a principle that tallies admirably with that of the purest "republican simplicity"; since it causes all things to taste alike.

To a dinner of this stamp Dunscomb now sat down, just ten minutes after the first clatter of a plate was heard, and just as the only remove was seen, in the form of slices of pie, pudding, and cake. With his habits, railroad speed, or lightning-like eating could find no favor; and he and Jack got their dinner, as best they might, amid the confusion and remnant of the close of such a repast. Nine-tenths of those who had so lately been at work as trenchermen were now picking their teeth, smoking cigars, or preparing fresh quids for the afternoon. A few clients were already holding their lawyers by the button; and here and there one of the latter led the way to his room to "settle" some slander cause in which the plaintiff had got frightened.

It is a bad sign when eating is carried on without conversation. To converse, however, at such a table, is, morally if not physically, impossible. Morally, because each man's mind is so intent on getting as much as he wants that it is almost impossible to bring his thoughts to bear on any other subject; physically, on account of the clatter, a movement in which an eclipse of a plate by the body of a waiter is no unusual thing, and universal activity of the teeth. Conversation under such circumstances would be truly a sort of ventriloquism; the portion of the human frame included in the term being all in all just at that moment.

Notwithstanding those embarrassments and unpleasant accompaniments, Dunscomb and his nephew got their dinners, and were about to quit the table as McBrain entered. The doctor would not expose his bride to the confusion of the common table, where there was so much that is revolting to all trained in the usages of good company, singularly blended with a decency of deportment, and a consideration for the rights of each, that serve to form bright spots in American character; but he had obtained a more private room for the females of his party.

"We should do pretty well," observed McBrain, in explaining his accommodations, "were it not for a troublesome neighbor in an adjoining room, who is either insane or intoxicated. Mrs. Horton has put us in your wing, and I should think you must occasionally hear from him too?"

"The man is constantly drunk, they tell me, and is a little troublesome at times.

On the whole, however, he does not annoy me much. I shall take the liberty of dining with you to-morrow, Ned; this eating against time does not agree with my constitution."

"To-morrow! I was thinking that my examination would be ended this afternoon, and that we might return to town in the morning. You will remember I have patients to attend to."

"You will have more reason for *patience*. If you get through in a week, you will be lucky."

"It is a curious case! I find all the local faculty ready to swear through thick and thin against her. My own opinion is fixed—but what is the opinion of one man against those of several in the same profession?"

"We will put that question to Mrs. Horton, who is coming to ask how we have dined. Thank'ee, my good Mrs. Horton, we have done *remarkably* well, considering all the circumstances."

The landlady was pleased, and smirked, and expressed her gratification. The *sous entendu* of Dunscomb was lost upon her; and human vanity is very apt to accept the flattering, and to overlook the disagreeable. She was pleased that the great York lawyer was satisfied.

Mrs. Horton was an American landlady, in the strictest sense of the word. This implies many features distinct from her European counterpart; some of which tell greatly in her favor, and others not so much so. Decency of exterior, and a feminine deportment, are so characteristic of the sex in this country, that they need scarcely be adverted to. There were no sly jokes, no *double entendres* with Mrs. Horton; who maintained too grave a countenance to admit of such liberties. Then, she was entirely free from the little expedients of a desire to gain that are naturally enough adopted in older communities, where the pressure of numbers drives the poor to their wits' end in order to live. American abundance had generated American liberality in Mrs. Horton; and if one of her guests asked for bread, she would give him the loaf. She was, moreover, what the country round termed "accommodating"; meaning that she was obliging and good-natured. Her faults were a fierce love of gossip, concealed under a veil of great indifference and modesty, a prying curiosity, and a determination to know everything touching everybody who ever came under her roof. This last propensity had got her into difficulties, several injurious reports having been traced to her tongue, which was indebted to her imagination for fully one-half of what she had circulated. It is scarcely necessary to add that, among the right set, Mrs. Horton was a great talker. As Dunscomb was a favorite, he was not likely to escape on the present occasion; the room being clear of all the guests but those of his own party.

"I am glad to get a little quiet talk with you, Squire Dunscomb," the landlady commenced; "for a body can depend on what is heard from such authority. Do they mean to hang Mary Monson?"

"It is rather premature to ask that question, Mrs. Horton. The jury is impaneled, and there we stand at present."

"Is it a good jury? Some of our Dukes County juries are none too good, they tell me."

"The whole institution is a miserable contrivance for the administration of justice. Could a higher class of citizens compose the juries, the system might still do, with a few improvements."

"Why not elect them?" demanded the landlady, who was, *ex officio*, a politician, much as women are usually politicians in this country. In other words, she *felt* her opinion, without knowing their reasons.

"God forbid, my good Mrs. Horton—we have elective judges; that will do for the present. Too much of a good thing is as injurious as the positively bad. I prefer the present mode of drawing lots."

"Have you got a Quaker in the box? If you have, you are safe enough."

"I doubt if the district attorney would suffer that; although he appears to be kind and considerate. The man who goes into that box must be prepared to hang if necessary."

"For my part, I wish all hanging was done away with. I can see no good that hanging can do a man."

"You mistake the object, my dear Mrs. Horton, though your argument is quite as good as many that are openly advanced on the same side of the question."

"Just hear me, squire," rejoined the woman; for she loved dearly to get into a discussion on any question that she was accustomed to hear debated among her guests. "The country hangs a body to reform a body; and what good can that do when a body is dead?"

"Very ingeniously put," returned the counselor, politely offering his box to the landlady, who took a few grains; and then deliberately helping himself to a pinch of snuff—"quite as ingeniously as much of the argument that appears in public. The objection lies to the premises, and not to the deduction, which is absolutely logical and just. A hanged body is certainly an unreformed body; and, as you say, it is quite useless to hang in order to reform."

"There!" exclaimed the woman in triumph—"I told Squire Timms that a gentleman who knows as much as you do must be on our side. Depend on one thing, Lawyer Dunscomb, and you too, gentlemen—depend on it, that Mary Monson will never be hanged."

This was said with a meaning so peculiar, that it struck Dunscomb, who watched the woman's earnest countenance while she was speaking, with undeviating interest and intensity.

"It is my duty and my wish, Mrs. Horton, to believe as much, and to make others believe it also, if I can," he answered, now anxious to prolong a discourse that a moment before he had found tiresome.

"You can, if you will only try. I believe in dreams—and I dreamt a week ago that Mary Monson would be acquitted. It would be ag'in all our new notions to hang so nice a lady."

"Our *tastes* might take offense at it; and taste is of *some* influence yet, I am bound to agree with you."

"But you do agree with me in the uselessness of hanging, when the object is to reform?"

"Unfortunately for the force of that argument, my dear landlady, society does not punish for the purposes of reformation—that is a very common blunder of superficial philanthropists."

"Not for the purpose of reformation, squire! You astonish me! Why, for what else should it punish?"

"For its own protection. To prevent others from committing murder. Have you no other reason than your dream, my good Mrs. Horton, for thinking Mary Monson will be acquitted?"

The woman put on a knowing look, and nodded her head significantly. At the same time she glanced toward the counselor's companions, as much as to say that their presence prevented her being more explicit.

"Ned, do me the favor to go to your wife, and tell her I shall stop in, and say a kind word as I pass her door;—and, Jack, go and bid Sarah be in Mrs. McBrain's parlor, ready to give me my morning's kiss."

The doctor and John complied, leaving Dunscomb alone with the woman.

"May I repeat the question, my good landlady? Why do you think Mary Monson is to be acquitted?" asked Dunscomb, in one of his softest tones.

Mrs. Horton mused, seemed anxious to speak, but struggling with some power

that withheld her. One of her hands was in a pocket where the jingling of keys and pence made its presence known. Drawing forth this hand mechanically, Dunscomb saw that it contained several eagles. The woman cast her eyes on the gold, returned it hastily to her pocket, rubbed her forehead, and seemed the wary, prudent landlady once more.

"I hope you like your room, squire?" she cried in a thoroughly inn-keeping spirit. "It's the very best in this house; though I'm obliged to tell Mrs. McBrain the same story as to her apartment. But you have the best. You have a troublesome neighbor between you, I'm afraid; but he'll not be there many days, and I do all I can to keep him quiet."

"Is that man crazy?" asked the counselor rising, perceiving that he had no more to expect from the woman just then; "or is he only drunk? I hear him groan, and then I hear him swear; though I cannot understand what he says."

"He's sent here by his friends; and your wing is the only place we have to keep him in. When a body is well paid, squire, I suppose you know that the fee must not be forgotten? Now, inn-keepers have fees, as well as you gentlemen of the bar. How wonderfully Timms is getting along, Mr. Dunscomb!"

"I believe his practice increases; and they tell me he stands next to Mr. Williams in Dukes."

"He does, indeed; and a 'bright particular star,' as the poet says, has he got to be!"

"If he be a star at all," answered the counselor, curling his lips, "it must be a very particular one, indeed. I am sorry to leave you, Mrs. Horton; but the intermission is nearly up."

Dunscomb gave a little friendly nod, which the landlady returned; the former went his way with a singular coolness of manner, when it is remembered that on him rested the responsibility of defending a fellow-creature from the gallows. What rendered this deliberation more remarkable, was the fact that he had no faith in the virtue of Mrs. Horton's dream.

CHAPTER XXII.

"Wilt thou behold me sinking in my woes,
    And wilt thou not reach out a friendly arm,
To raise me from amidst this plunge of sorrow?"
                                —ADDISON.

"CALL the names of the jurors, Mr. Clerk," said the judge. "Mr. Sheriff, I do not see the prisoner in her place."

This produced a stir. The jurors were called, and answered to their names; and shortly after Mary Monson appeared. The last was accompanied by the ladies, who might now be said to belong to her party, though no one but herself and Marie Moulin came within the bar.

There was profound stillness in the hall, for it was felt that now the issue of life or death was actually approaching. Mary Monson gazed, not with disquietude, but interest, at the twelve men who were to decide on her innocence or guilt—men of habits and opinions so different from her own—men so obnoxious to prejudices against those whom the accidents of life had made objects of envy or hatred—men too much occupied with the cares of existence to penetrate the arena of thought, and who consequently held their opinions at the mercy of others—men unskilled, because without practice, in the very solemn and important office now imposed on them by the law—men who might indeed be trusted, so long as they would defer to the court and reason, but who were terrible and dangerous, when they listened, as is too apt to be the case, to the suggestions of their own impulses, ignorance and prejudice. Yet these men were Mary Monson's peers, in the eyes of the law—would have been so viewed and accepted in a case involving the feelings and practices of social caste, about which they knew absolutely nothing, or, what is worse than nothing, a very little through the medium of misrepresentation and mistaken conclusions.

It is the fashion to extol the institution of the jury. Our own experience, by no means trifling, as foreman, as suitor, and as a disinterested spectator, does not lead us to coincide in this opinion. A narrative of the corrupt, misguided, partial, prejudiced, or ignorant conduct that we have ourselves witnessed in these bodies, would make a legend of its own. The power that most misleads such men is one unseen by themselves, half the time, and is consequently so much the more dangerous. The feelings of neighborhood, political hostility, or party animosities, are among the commonest evils that justice has to encounter, when brought in contact with tribunals thus composed. Then come the feelings engendered by social castes, an inexhaustible source of evil passions. Mary Monson had been told of the risks she ran from that source; though she had also been told, and with great truth, that so much of the spirit of God still remains in the hearts and minds of men, as to render a majority of those who were to be the arbiters of her fate conscientious and careful in a capital case. Perhaps, as a rule, the singularity of his situation, with a man who finds himself, for the first time, sitting as a juror in a trial for a human life, is one of the most available correctives of his native tendencies to do evil.

"Mr. District Attorney, are you ready to proceed?" inquired the judge.

This functionary rose, bowed to the court and jury, and commenced his opening. His manner was unpretending, natural, and solemn. Although high talent and original thought are very rare in this country, as they are everywhere else there is a vast fund of intellect of a secondary order ever at the command of the public. The district attorney of Dukes was a living witness of this truth. He saw all within his reach clearly, and, possessing great experience, he did his duty, on this occasion, in a very creditable manner. No attempt was made to awaken prejudice of any sort against the accused. She was presented by the grand inquest, and it was his and their painful duty, including his honor on the bench, to investigate this matter, and make a solemn decision, on their oaths. Mary Monson was entitled to a fair hearing, to all the advantages that the lenity of the criminal law of a very humane state of society could afford, and for "God's sake let her be acquitted should the State fail to establish her guilt!"

Mr. District Attorney then proceeded to give a narrative of the events as he supposed them to have occurred. He spoke of the Goodwins as "*poor*, but *honest*" people, a sort of illustration that is in much favor, and deservedly so, when true. "It seems, gentlemen," the district attorney continued, "that the wife had a propensity, or a fancy, to collect gold pieces, no doubt as a store against the wants of age. This money was kept in a stocking, according to the practice of country ladies, and was often exhibited to the neighbors. We may have occasion, gentlemen, to show you that some fifteen or twenty persons, at different times, have seen and handled this gold. You need not be told what natural curiosity is, but must all know how closely persons little accustomed to see money of this sort would be apt to examine the more rare pieces in particular. There happened to be several of these pieces among the gold of Mrs. Goodwin; and one of them was an Italian or Dutch coin, of the value of four dollars, which commonly goes by the name of the king whose likeness is on the piece. This Dutch or Italian coin, no matter which, or William, was seen, and handled, and examined, by several persons, as we shall show you.

"Now, gentlemen, the stocking that contained the gold coins was kept in a bureau, which bureau was saved from the fire, with all its contents; but the stocking and the gold were missing! These facts will be shown to you by proof that puts them beyond a peradventure. We shall next show to you, gentlemen, that on a public examination of the prisoner at the bar, the contents of her purse were laid open, and the Dutch or Italian coin I have mentioned was found, along with more than a hundred dollars of other pieces, which, being in American coin, cannot so readily be identified.

"The prosecution relies, in a great degree, on the proof that will be offered in connection with this piece of money, to establish the guilt of the prisoner. We are aware that, when this piece of money was found on her person, she affirmed it was hers; that she had been possessed of *two* such pieces, and that the one seen in Mrs. Goodwin's stocking had been a present from herself to that unfortunate woman.

"Gentlemen, if persons accused of crimes would vindicate themselves by their own naked statements, there would be very few convictions. Reason tells us that proof must be met by proof. Assertions will not be received as against the accused, nor will they be taken in her favor. Your own good sense will tell you, gentlemen, that if it be shown that Dorothy Goodwin possessed this particular piece of gold, valued it highly, and was in the practice of hoarding all the gold she could lay her hands on lawfully; that the said Dorothy Goodwin's residence was burned, she herself murdered by a savage and cruel blow or blows on the occiput or head; that Mary Monson, the prisoner at the bar, knew of the existence of this little stock of gold coins, had seen it, handled it, and doubtless *coveted* it; residing in the same house, with easy access to the bedside of the unhappy couple, with easy access to the bureau, to the keys which opened that bureau, for its drawers were found locked, just as Mrs. Goodwin was in the habit of leaving them; but, gentlemen, if all this be shown to you, and we then trace the aforesaid piece of coin to the pocket of Mary Monson, we make out a *prima facie* case of guilt, as I conceive; a case that will throw on her the *onus* of showing that she came in possession of the said piece of coin lawfully, and by no improper means. Failing of this, your duty will be plain.

"It is incumbent on the prosecution to make out its case, either by direct proof, on the oaths of credible witnesses, or by such circumstances as shall leave no doubt in your minds of the guilt of the accused. It is also incumbent that we show that the crimes of which the prisoner is accused have been committed, and committed by her.

"Gentlemen, we shall offer you this proof. We shall show you that the skeletons of which I have spoken, and which lie under that pall, sad remains of a most ruthless scene, are beyond all question the skeletons of Peter and Dorothy Goodwin. This will be shown to you by proof; though all who know the parties can almost see the likeness in these sad relics of mortality. Peter Goodwin, as will be shown to you, was a very short but sturdy man, while Dorothy, his wife, was a woman of large size. The skeletons meet this description exactly. They were found on the charred wood of the bedstead the unhappy couple habitually used, and on the very spot where they had passed so many previous nights in security and peace. Everything goes to corroborate the identity of the persons whose remains have been found, and I regret it should be my duty to add that everything goes to fasten the guilt of these murders on the prisoner at the bar. Gentlemen, although we rely mainly on the possession of the Dutch or Italian coin, no matter which, to establish the case for the State, we shall offer you a great deal of sustaining and secondary proof. In the first place, the fact that a female, young, handsome, well, nay expensively educated, coming from nobody knows whence, to go nobody knows whither, should suddenly appear in a place as retired as the house of Peter Goodwin, why no one can say, is in itself very suspicious. Gentlemen, 'all is not gold that glitters.' Many a man, and many a woman, in places large as New York, are not what they seem to be. They dress, and laugh, and sing, and appear to be among the gayest of the gay, when they do not know where to lay their heads at night. Large towns are moral blotches, they say, on the face of the community, and they conceal many things that will not bear the light. From one of these large towns, it is to be presumed from her dress, manners, education, amusements, and all belonging to her, came Mary Monson, to ask an asylum in the dwelling of the Goodwins. Gentlemen, why did she come? Had she heard of the hoard of Mrs. Goodwin, and did she crave the possession of the gold? These questions it will be your duty to answer in your verdict. Should the reply be in the affirmative, you obtain, at once, a direct clew to the motives of the murder.

"Among the collateral proof that will be offered are the following circumstances, to which I now ask your particular attention, in order that you may give to the testimony its proper value: It will be shown that Mary Monson had a large sum in gold in her possession, *after* the arson and murders, and consequently *after* the robbery, but no one knew of her having any *before*. It will be shown that she has money in abundance, scattering it right and left, as we suppose, to procure her acquittal, and this money, we believe, she took from the bureau of Mrs. Goodwin— how much is not known. It is thought that the sum was very large; the gold alone amounted to near a thousand dollars, and two witnesses will testify to a still larger amount in bank-notes. The Goodwins talked of purchasing a farm, valued at five thousand dollars; and as they were known never to run in debt, the fair inference is that they must have had at least that sum by them. A legacy was left Dorothy Goodwin within the last six months, which we hear was very considerable, and we hope to be able to put a witness on the stand who will tell you all about it.

"But, gentlemen, a circumstance worthy of all attention in an investigation like this, is connected with an answer to this question: Who is Mary Monson? What are her parentage, birthplace, occupation, and place of residence? Why did she come to Biberry at all? In a word, what is her past history? Let this be satisfactorily explained, and a great step is taken toward her vindication from these most grave charges. Shall we have witnesses to character? No one will be happier to listen to them than myself. My duty is far from pleasant. I sincerely hope the prisoner will find lawful means to convince you of her innocence. There is not one within the walls of this building who will hear such a verdict, if sustained by law and evidence, with greater pleasure than it will be heard by me."

After pursuing this vein some time longer, the worthy functionary of the State showed a little of that cloven foot which seems to grow on all, even to the cleanest heels, who look to the popular voice for preferment. No matter who the man is, rich or poor, young or old, foolish or wise, he bows down before the idol of Numbers, and there worships. Votes being the one thing wanted, must be bought by sacrifices on the altar of conscience. Now, it is by wild, and, half the time, impracticable schemes of philanthropy, that, while they seem to work good to the majority, are quite likely to disregard the rights of the minority; now they are flourishes against negro slavery, or a revolution in favor of the oppressed inhabitants of Crim-Tartary, of the real state of which country we are all as ignorant as its inhabitants are ignorant of us; now it's an exemption law, to enable a man to escape from the payment of his just debts, directly in the teeth of the sound policy, not to say morality, that if a man owe he should be made to pay as long as he has anything to do it with; now it is a hymn in praise of liberty, that the poet neither comprehends nor cares to look into further than may suit his own selfish patriotism; and now it is some other of the thousand modes adopted by the designing to delude the masses and advance themselves.

On this occasion the district attorney was very cautious, but he showed the cloven foot. He paid a passing tribute to the god of Numbers, worshiped before the hierarchy of votes. "Gentlemen," he continued, "like myself, you are plain, unpretending citizens. Neither you, nor your wives and daughters, speak in foreign tongues, or play on foreign instruments of music. We have been brought up in republican simplicity [God bless it! say we, could we ever meet with it], and lay no claims to superiority of any sort. Our place is in the body of the nation, and there we are content to remain. We shall pay no respect to dress, accomplishments, foreign languages, or foreign music; but the evidence sustaining us will show the world that the law frowns as well on the great as on the little: on the pretending as well as on the unpretending."

As these grandiose sentiments were uttered, several of the jurors half rose from their seats, in the eagerness to hear, and looks of approbation passed from eye to eye. This was accepted as good republican doctrine: no one there seeing, or feeling, as taste and truth would have shown, that the real pretension was on the side of an exaggerated self-esteem, that prompted to resistance ere resistance was necessary, under the influence of, perhaps, the lowest passion of human nature—we allude to envy. With a little more in the same vein, the district attorney concluded his opening.

The great coolness, not to say indifference, with which Mary Monson listened to this speech, was the subject of general comment among the members of the bar. At times she had been attentive, occasionally betraying surprise; then indignation would just gleam in her remarkable eye; but, on the whole, an uncommon calmness reigned in her demeanor. She had prepared tablets for notes; and twice she wrote in them as the district attorney proceeded. This was when he adverted to her past life, and when he commented on the Dutch coin. While he was speaking of castes, flattering one set under the veil of pretending humility, and undermining their opposites, a look of quiet contempt was apparent in every feature of her very expressive face.

"If it please the court," said Dunscomb, rising in his deliberate way, "before the prosecution proceeds with its witnesses, I could wish to appeal to the courtesy of the gentlemen on the other side for a list of their names."

"I believe we are not bound to furnish any such list," answered Williams quickly.

"Perhaps not bound exactly in law; but, it strikes me, bound in justice. This is a trial for life; the proceedings are instituted by the State. The object is justice, not vengeance—the protection of society through the agency of an impartial, though stern justice. The State cannot wish to effect anything by surprise. We are accused of murder and arson, with no other notice of what is to be shown, or *how* anything is to be shown, than what is contained in the bill or complaint. Any one can see how important it may be to us, to be apprised of the names of the witnesses a little in advance, that we may inquire into character and note probabilities. I do not insist on any *right*; but I ask a favor that humanity sanctions."

"If it please the court," said Williams, "we have an important trust. I will here say that I impute nothing improper to either of the prisoner's counsel; but it is my duty to suggest the necessity of our being cautious. A great deal of money has been expended already in this case, and there is always danger of witnesses being bought off. On behalf of my client, I protest against the demands being complied with."

"The court has no objection to the course asked by the prisoner's counsel," observed the judge, "but cannot direct it. The State can never wish its officers to be harsh or exacting; but it is their duty to be prudent. Mr. District Attorney, are you ready with your evidence? Time is precious, sir."

The testimony for the prosecution is now offered. We shall merely advert to most of it, reserving our details for those witnesses on whom the cause might be said to turn. Two very decent-looking and well-behaved men, farmers who re-

sided in the vicinity of Biberry, were put on the stand to establish the leading heads of the case. They had known Peter and Dorothy Goodwin; had often stopped at the house; and were familiarly acquainted with the old couple, as neighbors. Remembered the fire—was present at it, toward its close. Saw the prisoner there; saw her descend, by a ladder; and assisted in saving her effects. Several trunks, carpet-bags, band-boxes, writing-desks, musicial instruments, etc., etc. All were saved. "*It seemed to them that they had been placed near the windows, in a way to be handy.*" "After the fire, had never seen or heard anything of the old man and his wife, unless two skeletons that had been found were their skeletons. Supposed them to be the skeletons of Peter Goodwin and his wife." Here the remains were for the first time on that trial exposed to view. "Those are the same skeletons, should say—had no doubt of it; they are about the size of the old couple. The husband was short; the wife tall. Little or no difference in their height. Had never seen the stocking or the gold; but had heard a good deal of talk of them, having lived near neighbors to the Goodwins five-and-twenty years."

Dunscomb conducted the cross-examination. He was close, discriminating, and judicious. Separating the hear-say and gossip from the facts known, he at once threw the former to the winds, as matter not to be received by the jury. We shall give a few of his questions and their answers that have a bearing on the more material points of the trial.

"I understand you to say, witness, that you knew both Peter Goodwin and his wife."

"I did—I knew them well—saw them almost every day of my life."

"For how long a time?"

"This many a day. For five-and-twenty years, or a little more."

"Will you say that you have been in the habit of seeing Peter Goodwin and his wife daily, or almost daily, for five-and-twenty years?"

"If not right down daily, quite often; as often as once or twice a week, certainly."

"Is this material, Mr. Dunscomb?" inquired the judge. "The time of the court is very precious."

"It *is* material, your honor, as showing the looseness with which witnesses testify; and as serving to caution the jury how they receive their evidence. The opening of the prosecution shows us that if the charge is to be made out at all against the prisoner, it is to be made out on purely circumstantial evidence. It is not pretended that any one *saw* Mary Monson kill the Goodwins; but the crime is to be *inferred* from a series of collateral facts, that will be laid before the court and jury. I think your honor will see how important it is, under the circumstances, to analyze the testimony, even on points that may not seem to bear directly on the imputed crimes. If a witness testify loosely, the jury ought to be made to see it. I have a life to defend, your honor will remember."

"Proceed, sir; the court will grant you the widest latitude."

"You now say, as often as once or twice a week, witness; on reflection, will you swear to even *that?*"

"Well, if not twice, I am sure I can say *once.*"

Dunscomb was satisfied with this answer, which went to show that the witness could reply a little at random, and was not always certain of his facts when pressed.

"Are you certain that Dorothy Goodwin is dead?"

"I suppose I am as certain as any of the neighbors."

"That is not an answer to my question. Will you, and do you swear on your oath, that Peter Goodwin, the person named in the indictment, is actually dead?"

"I'll swear that I *think* so."

"That is not what I want. You see those skeletons—will you say, on your oath, that you *know* them to be the skeletons of Peter and Dorothy Goodwin?"

"I'll swear that I believe it."

"That does not meet the question. Do you *know* it?"

"How can I know it? I'm not a doctor or a surgeon. No, I do not absolutely *know* it. Still, I believe that one is the skeleton of Peter Goodwin, and the other the skeleton of his wife."

"Which do you suppose to be the skeleton of Peter Goodwin?"

This question puzzled the witness not a little. To the ordinary eye, there was scarcely any difference in the appearance of these sad remains; though one skeleton had been ascertained by actual measurement to be about an inch and a half longer than the other. This fact was known to all in Biberry; but it was not easy to say which was which, at a glance. The witness took the safe course, therefore, of putting his opinion altogether on a different ground.

"I do not pretend to tell one from the other," was the answer. "What I know of my own knowledge is this, and this only. I knew Peter and Dorothy Goodwin; knew the house they lived in; know that the house has been burnt down, and that the old folks are not about their old ha'nts. The skeletons I never saw until they were moved from the place where they tell me they were found; for I was busy helping to get the articles saved under cover."

"Then you do not pretend to know which skeleton is that of a man, or which that of a woman?"

This question was ingeniously put, and had the effect to make all the succeeding witnesses shy on this point; for it created a belief that there was a difference that might be recognized by those who are skilled in such matters. The witness assented to the view of Dunscomb; and having been so far sifted as to show he knew no more than all the rest of the neighbors, he was suffered to quit the stand. The result was that very little was actually established by means of this testimony. It was evident that the jury was now on the alert, and not disposed to receive all that was said as gospel.

The next point was to make out all the known facts of the fire, and of the finding of the skeletons. The two witnesses just examined had seen the close of the fire, had *heard* of the skeletons, but had said very little more to the purpose. Dunscomb thought it might be well to throw in a hint to this effect in the present state of the case, as he now did by remarking—

"I trust that the district attorney will see precisely where he stands. All that has yet been shown by legal proof are the facts that there were such persons as Peter and Dorothy Goodwin; facts we are not at all disposed to deny—"

"And that they have not appeared in the flesh since the night of the fire?" put in Williams.

"Not to the witnesses; but, to how many others, does not appear."

"Does the learned counsel mean to set up the defense that Goodwin and his wife are not dead?"

"It is for the prosecution to show the contrary affirmatively. If it be so, it is fair to presume they can do it. All I now contend for is the fact that we have no proof as yet that either is dead. We have proof that the house was burned; but we are now traversing an indictment for murder, and not that for arson. As yet, it strikes me, therefore, nothing material has been shown."

"It is certainly material, Mr. Dunscomb, that there should have been such persons as the Goodwins, and that they have disappeared since the night of the fire ; and this much is proved, unless you impeach the witnesses,'' observed the judge.

"Well, sir, that much we are not disposed to deny. There *were* such persons as the Goodwins, and they have disappeared from the neighborhood. We believe that much ourselves.''

"Crier, call Peter Bacon.''

Bacon came forward, dressed in an entire new suit of clothes, and appearing much more respectable than was his wont. This man's testimony was almost word for word as it has already been given in the coroner's inquest. He established the facts of the fire, about which there could be no prudent contention indeed, and of the finding of the skeletons ; for he had been one of those who aided in first searching the ruins for the remains. This man told his story in an extremely vulgar dialect, as we have had already occasion to show ; but in a very clear, distinct manner. He meant to tell the truth, and succeeded reasonably well ; for it does not occur to all who have the same upright intentions to effect their purposes as well as he did himself. Dunscomb's cross-examination was very brief ; for he perceived it was useless to attempt to deny what had been thus proved.

"Jane Pope,'' called out the district attorney. "Is Mrs. Jane Pope in court ?''

The Widow Pope was on the spot, and ready and willing to answer. She removed her bonnet, took the oath, and was shown to the seat with which it is usual to accommodate persons of her sex.

"Your name,'' said Dunscomb, holding his pen over the paper.

"Pope—Jane Pope since my marriage ; but Jane Anderson from my parents.''

Dunscomb listened politely, but recorded no more than the appellation of the widow. Mrs. Pope now proceeded to tell her story, which she did reasonably well, though not without a good deal of unnecessary amplitude, and some slight contradictions. It was *her* intention, also, to tell nothing but the truth ; but persons whose tongues move as nimbly as that of this woman's do not always know exactly what they do say. Dunscomb detected the contradictions ; but he had the tact to see their cause, saw that they were not material, and wisely abstained from confounding whatever of justice there was in the defense with points that the jury had probably sufficient sagacity to see were of no great moment. He made no note, therefore, of these little oversights, and allowed the woman to tell her whole story uninterrupted. When it came to his turn

to cross-examine, however, the duty of so doing was not neglected.

"You say, Mrs. Pope, that you had often seen the stocking in which Mrs. Goodwin kept her gold. Of what material was that stocking ?''

"Wool—yes, of blue woolen yarn. A stocking knit by hand, and very darny.''

"Should you know the stocking, Mrs. Pope, were you to see it again ?''

"I think I might. Dolly Goodwin and I looked over the gold together more than once ; and the stocking got to be a sort of acquaintance.''

"Was this it ?'' continued Dunscomb, taking a stocking of the sort described from Timms, who sat ready to produce the article at the proper moment.

"If it please the court,'' cried Williams, rising in haste, and preparing eagerly to interrupt the examination.

"Your pardon, sir,'' put in Dunscomb, with great self-command, but very firmly —"words must not be put into the witness's mouth, nor ideas into her head. She has sworn, may it please your honor, to a certain stocking, which stocking she described in her examination in chief ; and we now ask her if this is that stocking. All this is regular, I believe ; and I trust we are not to be interrupted.''

"Go on, sir,'' said the judge ; "the prosecution will not interrupt the defense. But time is very precious.''

"Is this the stocking ?'' repeated Dunscomb.

The woman examined the stocking, looking inside and out, turning it over and over, and casting many a curious glance at the places that had been mended.

"It's dreadful darny, isn't it ?'' she said, looking inquiringly at the counselor.

"It is as you see, ma'am. I have made no alteration in it.''

"I declare I believe this *is* the very stocking.''

"At the proper time, your honor, we shall show that this is *not* the stocking, if, indeed, there ever was such a stocking at all,'' said Timms, rolling up the article in qustion, and handing it to the clerk to keep.

"You saw a certain piece of gold, you say,'' resumed Dunscomb, "which piece of gold I understand you to say was afterward found in the pocket of Mary Monson. Will you have the goodness to say whether the piece of gold which you saw in Mrs. Goodwin's possession is among these ''— showing a dozen coins ; "or whether one resembling it is here ?

The woman was greatly puzzled. She meant to be honest ; had told no more than was true, with the exception of the little embellishments that her propensity to imagine and talk rendered almost unavoidable; but, for the life of her, she could not distinguish the piece of money, or its counterpart. After examining the coins for several minutes she frankly admitted her ignorance.

"It is scarcely necessary to continue this cross-examination," said Dunscomb, looking at his watch. "I shall ask the court to adjourn, and to adjourn over until morning. We have reached the hour for lighting candles; but we have agents out in quest of most important witnesses; and we ask the loss of this evening as a favor. It can make no great difference as to the length of the trial; and the jurors will be all the fresher for a good night's rest."

The court acquiesced, and allowed of the adjournment, giving the jury the usual charge about conversing or making up their opinions until they had heard the whole testimony; a charge that both Williams and Timms took very good care to render of no use in several instances, or as regarded particular individuals.

A decided impression was made in favor of the prisoner by Mrs. Pope's failure to distinguish the piece of money. In her examination in chief she saw no difficulty in recognizing the single piece then shown to her, and which was the Dutch coin actually found in Mary Monson's purse; but, when it was put among a dozen others resembling it, more or less, she lost all confidence in herself, and, to a certain point, completely broke down as a witness. But Dunscomb saw that the battle had not yet in truth begun. What had passed was merely the skirmishing of light troops, feeling the way for the advance of the heavy columns and the artillery that were to decide the fortunes of the day.

CHAPTER XXIII.

"'Tis the wisest way, upon all tender topics, to be silent; for he who takes upon himself to defend a lady's reputation, only publishes her favors to the world."—CUMBERLAND.

THE wing of Horton's Inn, that contained the room of Dunscomb, was of considerable extent, having quite a dozen rooms in it, though mostly of the diminutive size of an American tavern bedroom. The best apartment in it, one with two windows, and of some dimensions, was that appropriated to the counselor. The doctor and his party had a parlor, with two bedrooms; while, between these and the room occupied by Dunscomb, was that of the troublesome guest—the individual who was said to be insane. Most of the remainder of the wing, which was much the most quiet and retired portion of the house, was used for a better class of bedrooms. There were two rooms, however, that the providence of Horton and his wife had set apart for a very different purpose. These were small parlors, in which the initiated smoked, drank, and played.

Nothing sooner indicates the school in which a man has been educated than his modes of seeking amusement. One who has been accustomed to see innocent relaxation innocently indulged, from childhood up, is rarely tempted to abuse those habits which have never been associated, in his mind, with notions of guilt, and which, in themselves, necessarily imply no moral delinquency. Among the liberal, cards, dancing, music, all games of skill and chance that can interest the cultivated, and drinking, in moderation and of suitable liquors, convey no ideas of wrong-doing. As they have been accustomed to them from early life, and have seen them practiced with decorum and a due regard to the habits of refined society, there is no reason for concealment or consciousness. On the other hand, an exaggerated morality, which has the temerity to enlarge the circle of sin beyond the bounds for which it can find any other warranty than its own metaphysical inferences, is very apt to create a factitious conscience, that almost invariably takes refuge in that vilest of all delinquency—direct hypocrisy. This, we take it, is the reason that the reaction of ultra godliness so generally leaves its subjects in the mire and slough of deception and degradation. The very same acts assume different characters, in the hands of these two classes of persons; and that which is perfectly innocent with the first, affording a pleasant, and in that respect a useful relaxation, becomes low, vicious, and dangerous with the other, because tainted with the corrupting and most dangerous practices of deception. The private wing of Horton's Inn, to which there has been allusion, furnished an example in point of what we mean, within two hours of the adjournment of the court.

In the parlor of Mrs. McBrain, late Dunscomb's Widow Updyke, as he used to call her, a little table was set in the middle of the room, at which Dunscomb himself, the doctor, his new wife and Sarah were seated, at a game of whist. The door was not locked, no countenance manifested either a secret consciousness of wrong, or an overweening desire to transfer another's money to its owner's pocket, although a sober sadness might be said to reign in the party, the consequence of the interest all took in the progress of the trial.

Within twenty feet of the spot just mentioned, and in the two little parlors already named, was a very different set collected. It consisted of the rowdies of the bar, perhaps two-thirds of the reporters in attendance on Mary Monson's trial, several suitors, four or five country doctors, who had been summoned as witnesses, and such other equivocal gentry as might aspire to belong to a set as polished and exclusive as that we are describing. We will first give a moment's attention to the party around the whist-table in the parlor first described.

"I do not think the prosecution has made out as well to-day, all things considered, as it was generally supposed it would," observed McBrain. "There is the ace of trumps, Miss Sarah, and if you can follow it with the king, we shall get the odd trick."

"I do not think I shall follow it with anything," answered Sarah, throwing down her cards. "It really seems heartless to be playing whist, with a fellow-creature of our acquaintance on trial for her life."

"I have not half liked the game," said the quiet Mrs. McBrain; "but Mr. Dunscomb seemed so much bent on a rubber, I scarce knew how to refuse him."

"Why, true enough, Tom," put in the doctor, "this is all your doings, and if there be anything wrong about it, you will have to bear the blame."

"Play anything but a trump, Miss Sarah, and *we* get the game. You are quite right, Ned"—throwing down the pack—"the prosecution has not done as well as I feared they might. That Mrs. Pope as a witness I dreaded, but her testimony amounts to very little in itself; and what she said has been pretty well shaken by her ignorance of the coin."

"I really begin to hope the unfortunate lady may be innocent," said the doctor.

"Innocent!" exclaimed Sarah—"surely, Uncle Ned, you can never have doubted it!"

McBrain and Dunscomb exchanged significant glances, and the latter was about to answer, when, raising his eyes, he saw a strange form glide stealthily into the room, and place itself in a dark corner. It was a short, sturdy figure of a man, with all those signs of squalid misery in his countenance and dress that usually denote mental imbecility. He seemed anxious to conceal himself, and did succeed in getting more than half of his person beneath a shawl of Sarah's ere he was seen by any of the party but the counselor. It at once occurred to the latter that this was the being who had more than once disturbed him by his noise, and who Mrs. Horton had pretty plainly intimated was out of his mind; though she had maintained a singularly discreet silence, for her, touching his history and future prospects. She believed " he had been brought to court by his friends, to get some order, or judgment— maybe his visit had something to do with the new Code, about which Squire Dunscomb said so many hard things.''

A little scream from Sarah soon apprised all in the room of the presence of this disgusting-looking object. She snatched away her shawl, leaving the idiot, or madman, or whatever he might be, fully exposed to view, and retreated herself behind her uncle's chair.

"I fancy you have mistaken your room, my friend," said Dunscomb, mildly. "This, as you see, is engaged by a card-party—I take it you do not play."

A look of cunning left very little doubt of the nature of the malady with which this unfortunate being was afflicted. He made a clutch at the cards, laughed, then drew back, and began to mutter.

"She won't let me play," mumbled the idiot—"she never *would*."

"Whom do you mean by she?" asked Dunscomb. "Is it any one in this house— Mrs. Horton, for instance?"

Another cunning look, with a shake of the head for an answer in the negative.

"Be you Squire Dunscomb, the great York lawyer?" asked the stranger, with interest.

"Dunscomb is certainly my name— though I have not the pleasure of knowing yours."

"I haven't got any name. They may ask me from morning to night, and I won't tell. She won't let me."

"By *she* you again mean Mrs. Horton, I suppose?"

"No, I don't. Mrs. Horton's a *good* woman; she gives me victuals and drink."

"Tell us whom you do mean, then?"

"Won't you tell?"

"Not unless it be improper to keep the secret. Who is this *she?*"

"Why, *she.*"

"Ay, but who?"

"Mary Monson. If you're the great lawyer from York, and they say you be, you must know all about Mary Monson."

"This is very extraordinary!" said Dunscomb, regarding his companion in surprise. "I *do* know something about Mary Monson, but not *all* about her. Can you tell me anything?"

Here the stranger advanced a little from his corner, listened, as if fearful of being surprised, then laid a finger on his lip, and made the familiar sign for "hush."

"Don't let her hear you: if you do you may be sorry for it. She's a witch!"

"Poor fellow! she seems, in truth, to have bewitched you, as I daresay she may have done many another man."

"That has she! I wish you'd tell me what I want to know, if you really be the great lawyer from York."

"Put your questions, my friend; I'll endeavor to answer them."

"Who set fire to the house? Can you tell me *that?*"

"That is a secret yet to be discovered —do you happen to know anything about it?"

"Do I? I think I do. Ask Mary Monson; *she* can tell you."

All this was so strange that the whole party now gazed at each other in mute astonishment; McBrain bending his looks more intently on the stranger, in order to ascertain the true nature of the mental malady with which he was obviously afflicted. In some respects the disease wore the appearance of idiocy; then again there were gleams of the countenance that savored of absolute madness.

"You are of opinion, then, that Mary Monson knows who set fire to the house?"

"Sartain, she does. I know, too, but I won't tell. They might want to hang me, as well as Mary Monson, if I told. I know too much to do anything so foolish. Mary has said they would hang *me* if I tell. I don't want to be hanged a bit."

A shudder from Sarah betrayed the effect of these words on the listeners, and Mrs. McBrain actually rose with the intention of sending for her daughter, who was then in the jail, consoling the much-injured prisoner, as Anna Updyke firmly believed her to be, by her gentle but firm friendship. A word from the doctor, however, induced her to resume her seat, and to await the result with a greater degree of patience.

"Mary Monson would seem to be a very prudent counselor," rejoined Dunscomb.

"Yes; but she isn't the great counselor from York—you be that gentleman, they tell me."

"May I ask who told you anything about me?"

"Nancy Horton—and so did Mary Monson. Nancy said if I made so much noise

I should disturb the great counselor from York, and he might get me hanged for it. I was only singing hymns, and they say it is good for folks in trouble to sing hymns. If you be the great counselor from York I wish you would tell me one thing. Who got the gold that was in the stocking?"

"Do you happen to know anything of that stocking, or of the gold?"

"Do I—" loooking first over one shoulder, then over the other, but hesitating to proceed. "Will they hang me if I tell?"

"I should think not, though I can only give you an opinion. Do not answer, unless it be agreeable to you."

"I want to tell—I want to tell *all*, but I'm afeard. I don't want to be hanged."

"Well, then, speak out boldly, and I will promise that you shall not be hanged. Who got the gold that was in the stocking?"

"Mary Monson. That's the way she has got so much money."

"I cannot consent to leave Anna another instant in such company!" exclaimed the anxious mother. "Go, McBrain, and bring her hither at once."

"You are a little premature," coolly remarked Dunscomb. "This is but a person of weak mind, and too much importance should not be attached to his words. Let us hear what further he may have to say."

It was too late. The footstep of Mrs. Horton was heard in the passage, and the extraordinary being vanished as suddenly and as stealthily as he had entered.

"What can be made of this?" McBrain demanded, when a moment had been taken to reflect.

"Nothing, Ned; I care not if Williams knew it all. The testimony of such a man cannot be listened to for an instant. It is wrong in us to give it a second thought, though I perceive that you do. Half the mischief in the world is caused by misconceptions, arising from a very numerous family of causes, one of which is a disposition to fancy a great deal from a little. Do you pronounce the man an idiot—or is he a madman?"

"He does not strike me as absolutely either. There is something peculiar in his case; and I shall ask permission to look into it. I suppose we are done with the cards—shall I go for Anna?"

The anxious mother gave a ready assent, and McBrain went one way, while Dunscomb retired to his room, not without stopping before his neighbor's door, whom he heard muttering and menacing within.

All this time the two little parlors mentioned were receiving their company. The law is doubtless a very elevated profession, when its practice is on a scale commensurate with its true objects. It becomes a very different pursuit, however, when its higher walks are abandoned, to choose a path amid its thickets and quagmires. Perhaps no human pursuit causes a wider range of character among its votaries than the practice of this profession.

In the first place, the difference, in an intellectual point of view, between the man who sees only precedents, and the man who sees the principles on which they are founded, is as marked as the difference between black and white. To this great distinction in mind is to be added another that opens a still wider chasm, the results of practice, and which depends on morals. While one set of lawyers turn to the higher objects of their calling, declining fees in cases of obviously questionable right, and struggle to maintain their honesty in direct collision with the world and its temptations, another, and much the largest, falls readily into the practices of their craft—the word seems admirably suited to the subject—and live on, encumbered and endangered not only by their own natural vices, but greatly damaged by those that in a manner they adopt, as it might be *ex officio*. This latter course is unfortunately that taken by a vast number of the members of the bar all over the world, rendering them loose in their social morality, ready to lend themselves and their talents to the highest bidder, and causing them to be at first indifferent, and in the end blind, to the great features of right and wrong. These are the moralists who advance the doctrine that "the advocate has a right to act as his client would act"; while the class first named allow that "the advocate has a right to do what his client *has a right* to do," and no more.

Perhaps there was not a single member of the profession present that night in the two little parlors of Mrs. Horton, who recognized the latter of these rules; or who did not, at need, practice on the former. As has been already said, these were the rowdies of the Dukes County bar. They chewed, smoked, drank, and played, each and all coarsely. To things that were innocent in themselves they gave the aspect of guilt by their own manners. The doors were kept locked; even amid their coarsest jokes, their ribaldry, their oaths, that were often revolting and painfully frequent, there was an uneasy watchfulness, as if they feared detection. There was nothing frank and manly in the deportment of these men. Chicanery, management, double-dealing, mixed up with the outbreakings of a coarse standard of manners, were visible in all they said or did, except, perhaps, at those moments when hypocrisy was paying its homage to virtue. This hypocrisy, however, had little, or at most a very indirect connection with anything religious. The offensive offshoots of the exaggerations that were so abounding among us half a century since, are giving place to hypocrisy of another school. The homage that was then paid to principles, however erroneous and forbidding, is now paid to the ballot-boxes. There was scarcely an individual around those card-tables, at which the play was so obviously for the stakes as to render the whole scene revolting, who would not have shrunk from having his amusements known. It would seem as if conscience consulted taste. Everything was coarse and offensive; the attitudes, oaths, conversation, liquors, and even the manner of drinking them. Apart from the dialogue, little was absolutely done that might not have been made to lose most of its repulsiveness, by adopting a higher school of manners; but of this these scions of a noble stock knew no more than they did of the parent stem.

It is scarcely necessary to say that both Williams and Timms were of this party. The relaxation was, in fact, in conformity with their tastes and practices; and each of these excrescences of a rich and beneficent soil counted on the meetings in Mrs. Horton's private rooms, as the more refined seek pleasure in the exercise of their tastes and habits.

"I say, Timms," bawled out an attorney of the name of Crooks, "you play'd a trump, sir—all right—go ahead—first rate —good play, that—ours dead. I say, Timms, you're going to save Mary Monson's neck. When I came here, I thought she was a case; but the prosecution is making out miserably."

"What do you say to that, Williams?" put in Crooks's partner, who was smoking, playing, and drinking, with occasional "asides" of swearing, all, as might be, at the same time. "I trump that, sir, by your leave—what do you say to that, Williams?"

"I say that this is not the court; and trying such a cause once ought to satisfy a reasonable man."

"He's afraid of showing his hand, which I am not," put in another, exposing his cards as he spoke. "Williams always has some spare trumps, however, to get him out of all his difficulties."

"Yes, Williams has a spare trump, and there it is, giving me the trick," answered the saucy lawyer, as coolly as if he had been engaged in an inferior slander-suit. "I shall be at Timms pretty much by the same process to-morrow."

"Then you will do more than you have done to-day, Master Williams. This Mrs. Jane Pope *may be* a trump, but she is not the ace. I never knew a witness break down more completely."

"We'll find the means to set her up again—*I think* that knave is yours, Green—yes, I now see my game, which is to take it with the queen—very much, Timms, as we shall beat you to-morrow. I keep my trump card always for the last play, you know."

"Come, come, Williams," put in the oldest member of the bar, a man whose passions were cooled by time, and who had more gravity than most of his companions. "Come, come, Williams, this is a trial for a life, and joking is a little out of place."

"I believe there is no juror present, Mr. Marvin, which is all the reserve the law exacts."

"Although the law may tolerate this levity, feeling will not. The prisoner is a fine young woman; and for my part, though I wish to say nothing that may influence any one's opinion, I have heard nothing yet to justify an indictment, much less a conviction."

Williams laid down his cards, rose, stretched his arms, gaped, and taking Timms by the arm, he led the latter from the room. Not content with this, the wary limb of the law continued to move forward, until he and his companion were in the open air.

"It is always better to talk secrets outside than inside of a house," observed Williams, as soon as they were at a safe distance from the inn-door. "It is not too late yet, Timms—you must see how weak we are, and how bunglingly the district attorney has led off. Half those jurors will sleep to-night with a feeling that Mary Monson has been hardly dealt by."

"They may do the same to-morrow night, and every night in the month," answered Timms.

"Not unless the arrangement is made. We have testimony enough to hang the governor."

"Show us your list of witnesses, then, that we may judge of this for ourselves."

"That would never do. They might be bought off for half the money that is necessary to take us out of the field. Five thousand dollars can be no great matter for such a woman and her friends."

"Whom do you suppose to be her friends, Williams? If you know them you are better informed than her own counsel."

"Yes, and a pretty point *that* will make when pressed against you. No, no, Timms; your client has been ill-advised, or she is unaccountably obstinate. She has friends, although you may not know who they are; and friends who can, and who *would* very promptly help her, if she would consent to ask their assistance. Indeed, I suspect she has cash enough on hand to buy us off."

"Five thousand dollars is a large sum, Williams, and is not often to be found in Biberry jail. But if Mary Monson has these friends, name them, that we may apply for their assistance."

"Harkee, Timms; you are not a man so ignorant of what is going on in the world as to require to be told the letters of the alphabet. You know that there are extensive associations of rogues in this young country, as well as in most that are older."

"What has that to do with Mary Monson and our case?"

"Everything. This Mary Monson has been sent here to get at the gold of the poor old dolt, who has not been able to conceal her treasure after it was hoarded. She made a sub-treasury of her stocking, and exhibited the coin, like any other sub-treasurer. Many persons like to look at it, just to feast their eyes."

"More to finger it, and you are of the number, Williams!"

"I admit it. The weakness is general in the profession, I believe. But this is idle talk, and we are losing very precious time. Will you, or will you not, apply again to your client for the money?"

"Answer me, candidly, a question or two, and I will do as you desire. You know, Williams, that we are old friends, and never had any serious difficulty since we have been called to the bar."

"Oh, assuredly," answered Williams, with an ironical smile, that it might have been fortunate for the negotiation the obscurity concealed from his companion; "excellent friends from the beginning, Timms, and likely to continue so, I trust, to the last. Men who *know* each other as well as you and I ought to be on the best of terms. For my part, I never harbored a wrangle at the bar in my mind five minutes after I left the court. Now for your question."

"You surely do not set down Mary Monson as the stool-pigeon of a set of York thieves!"

"Who, or what else can she be, Mr. Timms? Better educated, and belonging to an 'upper ten' in villainy, but of a company of rogues. Now, these knaves stand by each other much more faithfully than the body of the citizens stand by the law; and the five thousand will be forthcoming for the asking."

"Are you serious in wishing me to believe you think my client guilty?"

• Here Williams made no bones of laughing outright. It is true that he suppressed the noise immediately, lest it should attract attention; but laugh he did, and with right good will.

"Come, Timms, you have asked your question, and I leave you to answer it yourself. One thing I will say, however, in the way of admonition, which is this—we shall make out such a case against her to-morrow as would hang a governor, as I have already told you."

"I believe you've done your worst already—why not let me know the names of your witnesses?"

"You know the reason. We wish the whole sum ourselves, and have no fancy to its being scattered all over Dukes. I give you my honor, Timms—and you know what *that* is—I give you my honor that we hold this testimony in reserve."

"In which case the district attorney will bring the witnesses on the stand; and we shall gain nothing, after all, by your withdrawal."

"The district attorney has left the case very much to me. I have prepared his brief, and have taken care to keep to myself enough to turn the scales. If I quit, Mary Monson will be acquitted—if I stay, she will be hanged: A pardon for *her* will be out of the question—she is too high among the 'upper ten' to expect *that*—besides, she is not an anti-renter."

"I wonder the thieves do not combine, as well as other folks, and control votes!"

"They do—these anti-renters belong to the gangs, and have already got their representatives in high places. They are 'land pirates,' while your *client* goes for old stockings. The difference in principle is by no means important, as any clear-headed man may see. It is getting late, Timms."

"I cannot believe that Mary Monson is the sort of person you take her for! Williams, I've always looked upon you, and treated you, as a friend. You may remember how I stood by you in the Middlebury case?"

"Certainly—you did your duty by me in that matter, and I have not forgot it."

The cause alluded to was an action for a "breach of promise," which, at one time, threatened all of Williams's "future usefulness," as it is termed; but which was put to sleep in the end by means of Timms's dexterity in managing the "outdoor" points of a difficult case.

"Well, then, be *my* friend in this matter. I will be honest with you, and acknowledge that, as regards my client, I have had—that is provided she is acquitted, and her character comes out fair—that I have had—and *still* have, for that matter—what—"

"Are called 'ulterior views.' I understand you, Timms, and have suspected as much these ten days. A great deal depends on what you consider a fair character. Taking the best view of her situation, Mary Monson will have been tried for murder and arson."

"Not if acquitted of the first. I have the district attorney's promise to consent to a *nolle prosequi* on the last indictment, if we traverse the first successfully."

"In which case Mary Monson will have been tried for murder only," returned Williams, smiling. "Do you really think, Timms, that your heart is soft enough to receive and retain an impression as deep as that made by the seal of the court?"

"If I thought, as you do, that my client is or has been connected with thieves, and burglars, and counterfeiters, I would not think of her for a moment as a wife. But there is a vast difference between a person overtaken by sudden temptation and one who sins on calculation, and by regular habit. Now, in my own case, I sometimes act wrong—yes, I admit as much as that—"

"It is quite unnecessary," said Williams, dryly.

"It is not according to Christian doctrine to visit old offenses on a sinner's head, when repentance has washed away the crime."

"Which means, Timms, that you will marry Mary Monson, although she may be guilty; provided always that two very important contingencies are favorably disposed of."

"What contingencies do you allude to, Williams? I know of none."

"One is, provided she will have you; the other is, provided she is not hanged."

"As to the first, I have no great apprehension; women that have been once before a court, on a trial for a capital offense, are not very particular. On my side, it will be easy enough to persuade the public that, as counsel in a most interesting case, I became intimately acquainted with her virtues, touched by her misfortunes, captivated by her beauty and accomplishments, and finally overcome by her charms. I don't think, Williams, that such an explanation would fail of its effect, before a caucus even. Men are always favorably disposed to those they think worse off than they are themselves. A good deal of capital is made on that principle."

"I do not know that it would. Nowadays the elections generally turn more on public principles than on private conduct. The Americans are a most forgiving people, unless you tell them the *truth*. *That* they will not pardon."

"Nor any other nation, I fancy. Human natur' revolts at it. But *that*"—snapping his fingers—"for your elections; it is the caucuses that I lay myself out to meet. Give me the *nomination*, and I am as certain of my seat as, in the old countries, a first-born is to his father's throne."

"It is pretty safe, as a rule, I allow; but nominations sometimes fail."

"Not when regular, and made on proper principles. A nomination is almost as good as popularity."

"Often better; for men are just asses enough to work in the collar of party, even when overloaded. But all this time the night is wearing away. If I go into court in the morning it will be too late. This thing must be settled at once, and that in a very explicit manner."

"I wish I knew what you have picked up concerning Mary Monson's early life!" said Timms, like a man struggling with doubt.

"You have heard the rumor as well as myself. Some say she is a wife already; while others think her a rich widow. My opinion you know; I believe her to be the stool-pigeon of a York gang, and no better than she should be."

This was plain language to be addressed to a lover; and Williams meant it to be so. He had that sort of regard for Timms which proceeds from a community in practices, and was disposed to regret that a man with whom he had been so long connected, either as an associate or an antagonist, should marry a woman of the pursuits that he firmly believed marked the career of Mary Monson.

The gentlemen of the bar are no more to be judged by appearances than the rest of mankind. They will wrangle, and seem to be at swords' points with each other, at one moment; when the next may find them pulling together in harmony in the next case on the calendar. It was under this sort of feeling that Williams had a species of friendship for his companion.

"I will try, Williams," said the last, turning toward the jail, "Yes, I will make one more trial."

"Do, my good fellow—and, Timms—remember one thing; you can never marry a woman that has been hanged."

CHAPTER XXIV.

"The time is precious; I'll about it straight."
—EARL OF ESSEX.

THE jail presented a very different scene. A solemn stillness reigned in its gallery; and even good Mrs. Gott had become weary with the excitement of the day, and had retired to rest. A single lamp was burning in the cell; and dark forms were dimly visible in the passage, without the direct influence of its rays. Two were seated, while a third paced the stone but carpeted pavement, with a slow and quiet step. The first were the shadowy forms of Anna Updyke and Marie Moulin; the last, that of Mary Monson. For half an hour the prisoner had been on her knees, praying for strength to endure a burden that surpassed her expectations; and, as is usual with those who look above for aid, more especially women, she was reaping the benefit of her petition. Not a syllable had she uttered, however, since quitting the cell. Her voice, soft, melodious, and lady-like, was now heard for the first time.

"My situation is most extraordinary, Anna," she said; "it proves almost too much for my strength! This has been a terrible day, calm as I may have appeared; and I fear that the morrow will be still harder to be borne. There is an expression about the eyes of that man, Williams, that both alarms and disgusts me. I am to expect in him a most fiery foe."

"Why, then, do you not escape from scenes for which you are so unsuited, and leave this saucy Williams to himself, and his schemes of plunder?"

"That would not do. Several sufficient reasons exist for remaining. Were I to avail myself of the use of the keys I possess, and quit the jail not to return, good Mrs. Gott and her husband would probably both be ruined. Although they are ignorant of what money and ingenuity have done for me, it would be difficult to induce the world to believe them innocent. But a still higher reason for remaining is the vindication of my own character."

"No one will think of confounding *you* with Mary Monson; and by going abroad, as you say it is your intention to do, you would effectually escape from even suspicion."

"You little know the world, my dear,

I see that all the useful lessons I gave you, as your school-mamma, are already forgotten. The six years between us in age have given me an experience that tells me to do nothing of the sort. Nothing is so certain to follow us as a bad name; though the good one is easily enough forgotten. As Mary Monson, I am indicted for these grievous crimes; as Mary Monson will I be acquitted of them. I feel an affection for the character, and shall not degrade it by any act as base as that of flight."

"Why not, then, resort to the other means you possess, and gain a speedy triumph in open court?"

As Anna put this question, Mary Monson came beneath the light and stopped. Her handsome face was in full view, and her friend saw an expression on it that gave her pain. It lasted only a moment; but that moment was long enough to induce Anna to wish she had not seen it. On several previous occasions this same expression had rendered her uneasy; but the evil look was soon forgotten in the quiet elegance of manners that borrowed charms from a countenance usually as soft as the evening sky in September. Ere she resumed her walk, Mary Monson shook her head in dissent from the proposition of her friend, and passed on, a shadowy but graceful form, as she went down the gallery.

"It would be premature," she said, "and I should fail of my object. I will not rob that excellent Mr. Dunscomb of his honest triumph. How calm and gentlemanlike he was to-day; yet how firm and prompt, when it became necessary to show these qualities."

"Uncle Tom is all that is good; and we love him as we would love a parent."

A pause succeeded, during which Mary Monson walked along the gallery once, in profound thought.

"Yours promises to be a happy future, my dear," she said. "Of suitable ages, tempers, stations, country—yes, country; for an American woman should never marry a foreigner!"

Anna Updyke did not reply; and a silence succeeded that was interrupted by the rattling of a key in the outer door.

"It is your new father, Anna; come to see you home. Thank you, kind-hearted and most generous-minded girl. I feel the sacrifices that you and your friend are making in my behalf, and shall carry the recollection of them to the grave. On her, I had no claims at all; and on you, but those that are very slight. You have been to me, indeed, most excellent friends, and a great support when both were most needed. Of my own sex, and of the same social level, I do not now see how I should have got on without you. Mrs. Gott is kindness and good-nature themselves; but she is so different from us in a thousand things, that I have often been pained by it. In our intercourse with you, how different! Knowing so much, you pry into nothing. Not a question, not a look to embarrass me, and with a perfect and saint-like reliance on my innocence; were I a sister, your support could not be more warm-hearted or firm."

After a short pause, in which this singular young woman smiled, and appeared to be talking to herself, she continued, after kissing her companion most affectionately for good-night, and walking with her as far as the door of the gallery, where it had been announced that the doctor was waiting for his step-daughter:

"I wish I knew whether the same faith goes through the connection—Mr. John Wilmeter?"

"Oh! He is persuaded of your entire innocence. It was he who excited so much interest in me, on your behalf, before I had the least idea of our having ever met before."

"He is a noble-hearted young man, and has many excellent qualities—a little romantic, but none the worse for that, my dear, as you will find in the end. Alas! alas! Those marriages that are made over a rent-roll, or an inventory, need a great deal of something very different from what they possess to render them happy! Mr. Wilmeter has told me that *no evidence* could make him believe in my guilt. There is a confidence that might touch a woman's heart, Anna, did circumstances admit of such a thing. I like that Michael Millington, too; the *name* is dear to me, as is the race of which he comes. No matter; the world *va son train*, let us regret and repine as we may. And uncle Tom, Anna—what do you think of his real opinion? Is it in my favor or not?"

Anna Updyke had detected in Dunscomb a disposition to doubt, and was naturally averse to communicating a fact so unpleasant to her friend. Kissing the latter affectionately, she hurried away to meet McBrain, already waiting for her without. In quitting the dwelling of the building annexed to the jail, the doctor and Anna met Timms hurrying forward to seek an interview with his client before she retired to rest. An application at once obtained permission for the limb of the law to enter.

"I have come, Miss Mary," as Timms now called his client, "on what I fear will prove a useless errand ; but which I have thought it my duty to see performed, as your best friend, and one of your legal advisers. You have already heard what I had to say on the subject of a certain proposal of the next of kin to withdraw from the prosecution, which will carry with him this Williams, with whom I should think you would, by this time, be heartily disgusted. I come now to say that this offer is repeated with a good deal of emphasis, and that you have still an opportunity of lessening the force that is pressing on your interests by at least one-half. Williams may well count for more than half of the vigor and shrewdness of what is doing for the State in your case."

"The proposal must be more distinctly made, and you must let me have a clear view of what is expected from me, Mr. Timms, before I can give any reply," said Mary Monson. "But you may wish to be alone with me before you are more explicit. I will order my woman to go into the cell."

"It might be more prudent were we to go into the cell ourselves, and leave your domestic outside. These galleries carry sounds like ear-trumpets, and we never know who may be our next neighbor in a jail."

Mary Monson quietly assented to the proposal, calling to her woman in French to remain outside, in the dark, while she profited by the light of the lamp in the cell. Timms followed and closed the door.

In size, form, and materials, the cell of Mary Monson was necessarily like that of every other inmate of the jail. Its sides, top, and bottom, were of massive stones ; the two last being flags of great dimensions. But taste and money had converted even this place into an apartment that was comfortable in all respects but that of size. Two cells opening on the section of gallery that the consideration of Mrs. Gott had caused to be screened off, and appropriated to the exclusive use of the fair prisoner, one had been furnished as a sleeping apartment, while that in which Timms was now received had more the air of a sort of *boudoir*. It was well carpeted, like all the rest of what might be termed the suite ; and had a variety of those little elegancies that women of cultivated tastes and ample means are almost certain to gather about them.

The harp which had occasioned so much scandal, as well as a guitar, stood near by, and chairs of different forms and various degrees of comfort crowded the room, perhaps to superfluity. As this was the first time Timms had been admitted to the cell, he was all eyes, gazing about him at the numerous signs of wealth it contained with inward satisfaction. It was a minute after he was desired to be seated before he could comply, so lively was the curiosity to be appeased. It was during this minute that Marie Moulin lighted four candles that were already arranged in bronzed candle-sticks, making a blaze of light for that small room. These candles were of spermaceti, the ordinary American substitute for wax. Nothing that he then saw, or had ever seen in his intercourse with his client, so profoundly impressed Timms as this luxury of light. Accustomed himself to read and write by a couple of small inferior articles in tallow, when he did not use a lamp, there seemed to be something regal to his unsophisticated imagination in this display of brilliancy.

Whether Mary Monson had a purpose to answer in giving Timms so unusual a reception, we shall leave the reader to discover by means of his own sagacity ; but circumstances might well lead one to the conclusion that she had. There was a satisfied look, as she glanced around the cell and surveyed its arrangements, that possibly led fairly enough to such an inference. Nevertheless, her demeanor was perfectly quiet, betraying none of the fidgeting uneasiness of an underbred person, lest all might not be right. Every arrangement was left to the servant ; and when Marie Moulin finally quitted the cell and closed the door behind her, every thought of the apartment and what it contained seemed to vanish from the mind of her extraordinary mistress.

"Before you proceed to communicate the purpose of your visit, Mr. Timms," Mary Monson said, "I shall ask permission to put a few questions of my own, touching the state of our cause. Have we gained or lost by this day's proceedings ?"

"Most clearly gained, as every man at the bar will confirm by his opinion."

"That has been my own way of thinking ; and I am glad to hear it corroborated by such competent judges. I confess the prosecution does not seem to me to show the strength it really possesses. This Jane Pope made a miserable blunder about the piece of coin."

"She has done the other side no great good, certainly."

"How stands the jury, Mr. Timms ?"

Although this question was put so directly, Timms heard it with uneasiness. Nor did he like the expression of Mary Monson's eyes, which seemed to regard him with a keenness that might possibly imply distrust. But it was necessary to answer, though he did so with caution, and with a due regard to his own safety.

"It is pretty well," he said, "though not quite as much opposed to capital punishment as I had hoped for. We challenged off one of the sharpest chaps in the county, and have got in his place a man who is pretty much under my thumb."

"And the stories — the reports — have they been well circulated?"

"A little too well, I'm afraid. That concerning your having married a Frenchman, and having run away from him, has gone through all the lower towns of Dukes like wildfire. It has even reached the ears of Squire Dunscomb, and will be in the York papers to-morrow."

A little start betrayed the surprise of the prisoner; and a look accompanied it which would seem to denote dissatisfaction that a tale put in circulation by herself, as it would now appear, had gone quite so far.

"Mr. Dunscomb!" she repeated musingly. "Anna Uydyke's uncle Tom; and one whom such a story may very well set thinking. I wish it had not reached *him*, of all men, Mr. Timms."

"If I may judge of his opinions by some little acts and expressions that have escaped him, I am inclined to think he believes the story to be, in the main, true."

Mary Monson smiled; and, as was much her wont when thinking intensely, her lips moved; even a low muttering became audible to a person as near as her companion then was.

"It is now time, Mr. Timms, to set the other story in motion," she said quickly. "Let one account follow the other; that will distract people's belief. We must be active in this matter."

"There is less necessity for our moving in the affair, as Williams has got a clew to it, by some means or other; and his men will spread it far and near, long before the cause goes to the jury."

"That is fortunate!" exclaimed the prisoner, actually clapping her pretty gloved hands together in delight. "A story as terrible as *that* must react powerfully, when its falsehood comes to be shown. I regard that tale as the cleverest of all our schemes, Mr. Timms."

"Why—yes—that is—I think, Miss Mary, it may be set down as the *boldest*."

"And this saucy Williams, as you call him, has got hold of it already, and believes it true?"

"It is not surprising; there are so many small and probable facts accompanying it."

"I suppose you know what Shakespeare calls such an invention, Mr. Timms?" said Mary Monson, smiling.

"I am not particularly acquainted with that author, ma'am; I know there was such a writer, and that he was thought a good deal of, in his day; but I can't say I have ever read him."

The beautiful prisoner turned her large, expressive blue eyes on her companion with a gaze of wonder; but her breeding prevented her from uttering what she certainly thought and felt.

"Shakespeare is a writer very generally esteemed," she answered, after one moment of muttering, and one moment to control herself; "I believe he is commonly placed at the head of our English literature, if not at the head of that of all times and nations—Homer, perhaps, excepted."

"What! higher, do you think, Miss Mary, than Blackstone and Kent?"

"Those are authors of whom I know nothing, Mr. Timms; but now, sir, I will listen to your errand here to-night."

"It is the old matter. Williams has been talking to me again, touching the five thousand dollars."

"Mr. Williams has my answer. If five thousand *cents* would buy him off, he should not receive them from me."

This was said with a frown; and then it was that the observer had an opportunity of tracing, in a face otherwise so lovely, the lines that indicate self-will, and a spirit not easily controlled. Alas! that women should ever so mistake their natural means to influence and guide, as to have recourse to the exercise of agents that they rarely wield with effect, and ever with a sacrifice of womanly character and womanly grace. The person who would draw the sex from the quiet scenes that they so much embellish, to mingle in the strifes of the world; who would place them in stations that nature has obviously intended men should occupy, is not their real friend, any more than the weak adviser who resorts to reputed specifics when the knife alone can effect a cure. The Creator intended woman for a "help-meet," and not for the head of the family circle; and most fatally ill-judging are the laws that would fain disturb the order of a domestic government, which is directly derived from divine wisdom as from divine benevolence.

"I told him as much, Miss Mary," answered Timms; "but he does not seem disposed to take 'no' for an answer. Williams has the true scent for a dollar."

"I am quite certain of an acquittal, Mr. Timms; and having endured so much, and hazarded so much, I do not like to throw away the triumph of my approaching victory. There is a powerful excitement in my situation; and I like excitement to weakness, perhaps. No, no; my success must not be tarnished by any such covert bargain. I will not listen to the proposal for an instant!"

"I understand that the raising of the sum required would form no particular obstacle to the arrangement?" asked Timms, in a careless sort of way, that was intended to conceal the real interest he took in the reply.

"None at all. The money might be in his hands before the court sits in the morning, but it never shall be as coming from me. Let Mr. Williams know this definitely; and tell him to do his worst."

Timms was a little surprised, and a good deal uneasy at this manifestation of a spirit of defiance, which could produce no good, and which might be productive of evil. While he was delighted to hear, for the fourth or fifth time, how easy it would be for his fair client to command a sum as large as that demanded, he secretly determined not to let the man who had sent him on his present errand know the temper in which it had been received. Williams was sufficiently dangerous as it was; and he saw all the hazard of giving him fresh incentives to increase his exertions.

"And now, as this matter is finally disposed of, Mr. Timms—for I desire that it may not be again mentioned to me," resumed the accused, "let us say a word more on the subject of our new report. Your agent has set on foot a story that I belong to a gang of wretches who are combined to prey on society; and that, in this character, I came into Dukes to carry out one of its nefarious schemes?"

"That is the substance of the rumor we have started at your own desire; though I could wish it were not quite so strong, and that there were more time for the reaction."

"The strength of the rumor is its great merit; and, as for time, we have abundance for our purposes. Reaction is the great power of popularity, as I have heard again and again. It is always the most effective, too, at the turn of the tide. Let the public once get possessed with the notion that a rumor so injurious has been in circulation at the expense of one in my cruel condition, and the current of feeling will set the other way in a torrent that nothing can arrest!"

"I take the idea, Miss Mary, which is well enough for certain cases, but a little too hazardous for this. Suppose it should be ascertained that this report came from us?"

"It never can be, if the caution I directed was observed. You have not neglected my advice, Mr. Timms?"

The attorney had not; and great had been his surprise at the ingenuity and *finesse* manifested by this singular woman, in setting afloat a report that would certainly act to her injury, unless arrested and disproved at a moment most critical in her future fate. Nevertheless, in obedience to Mary Monson's positive commands, this very bold measure had been undertaken; and Timms was waiting with impatience for the information by means of which he was to counteract these self-inflicted injuries, and make them the instruments of good on the reaction.

If that portion of society which takes delight in gossip could be made to understand the real characters of those to whom they commit the control of their opinions, not to say principles, there would be far more of reserve and self-respect observed in the submission to this social evil than there is at present. Malice, the inward impulses of the propagators of a lie, and cupidity, are at the bottom of half the tales that reach our ears; and in those cases in which the world in its ignorance fancies it has some authority for what it says, it as often happens that some hidden motive is at the bottom of the exhibition as the one which seems so apparent. There are a set of vulgar vices that may be termed the "stereotyped," they lie so near the surface of human infirmities. They who are most subject to their influence always drag these vices first into the arena of talk; and fully one-half of that of this nature which we hear has its origin as much in the reflective nature of the gossip's own character, as in any facts truly connected with the acts of the subjects of his or her stories.

But Mary Monson was taking a far higher flight than the circulation of an injurious rumor. She believed herself to be putting on foot a master-stroke of policy. In her intercourse with Timms so much was said of the power of opinion, that she had passed hours, nay days, in the study of the means to control and counteract it. Whence she obtained her notion of the virtue of reaction it might not be easy to say, but her theory was not without its truth, and it is certain that her means of producing it were of remarkable simplicity and ingenuity.

Having settled the two preliminaries of the rumor and of Williams's proposition, Timms thought the moment favorable to making a demonstration in his own affairs. Love he did not yet dare to propose openly, though he had now been for some time making covert demonstrations toward the tender passion. In addition to the motive of cupidity, one of great influence with such a man, Timms's heart, such as it was, had really yielded to the influence of a beauty, manners, accomplishments, and information, all of a class so much higher than he had been accustomed to meet with, as to be subjects of wonder with him, not to say of adoration. This man had his affections as well as another; and, while John Wilmeter had submitted to a merely passing inclination, as much produced by the interest he took in an unknown female's situation as by any other cause, poor Timms had been hourly falling more and more in love. It is a tribute to nature that this passion can be, and is, felt by all. Although a purifying sentiment, the corrupt and impure can feel its power, and, in a greater or less degree, submit to its influence, though their homage may be tainted by the grosser elements that are so largely mixed up with the compound of their characters. We may have occasion to show hereafter how far the uncouth attorney of Mary Monson succeeded in his suit with his fair client.

CHAPTER XXV.

"I challenge envy,
  Malice, and all the practices of hell,
  To censure all the actions of my past
Unhappy life, and taint me if they can."
  —THE ORPHAN.

IT is to be presumed that Timms found the means to communicate to Williams the rejection of the latter's offer, before the court met next morning. It is certain that the counsel associated with the district-attorney manifested unusual zeal in the performance of duties that most men would have found unpleasant, if not painful, and that he was captious, short, and ill-natured. Just as Mary Monson came within the bar, a letter was put into the hands of Dunscomb, who quietly broke the zeal, and read it twice, as the observant Timms fancied; then put it in his pocket, with a mien so undisturbed that no mere looker-on would have suspected its importance. The letter was from Millington, and it announced a general want of success in his mission. The whereabouts of M. de Larocheforte could not be ascertained; and those who knew anything about his movements were of opinion that he was traveling in the West, accompanied by his fair, accomplished, and affluent young consort. None

of those who would naturally have heard of such an event, had it occurred, could say there had ever been a separation between the French husband and the American wife. Millington himself had never seen his kinswoman, there being a coolness of long standing between the two branches of the family, and could give little or no information on the subject. In a word, he could discover nothing to enable him to carry out the clew obtained in the rumor; while, on the other hand, he found a certain set, who occupied themselves a good deal with intelligence of that sort, were greatly disposed to believe the report, set on foot by herself, that Mary Monson was a stool-pigeon of a gang of marauders, and doubtless guilty of everything of which she had been accused. Millington would remain in town, however, another day, and endeavor to push his inquiries to some useful result. Cool, clearheaded, and totally without romance, Dunscomb knew that a better agent than his young friend could not be employed, and was fain to wait patiently for the discoveries he might eventually succeed in making. In the meantime the trial proceeded.

"Mr. Clerk," said his honor, "let the jury be called."

This was done, and Mary Monson's lips moved, while a lurking smile lighted her countenance, as her eyes met the sympathy that was expressed in the countenances of several of the grave men who had been drawn as arbiters, in her case, between life and death. To her it was apparent that her sex, her youth, perhaps her air and beauty, stood her friends, and that she might largely count on the compassion of that small but important body of men. One of her calculations had succeeded to the letter. The tale of her being a stool-pigeon had been very actively circulated, with certain additions and embellishments that it was very easy to disprove; and another set of agents had been hard at work, all the morning, in brushing away such of the collateral circumstances as had, at first, been produced to confirm the main story, and which, in now being pulled to pieces as of no account, did not fail to cast a shade of the darkest doubt over the whole rumor. All this Mary Monson probably understood, and understanding, enjoyed; a vein of wild willfulness certainly running through her character, leading in more directions than one.

"I hope there will be no delay on account of witnesses," observed the judge. "Time is very precious."

"We are armed at all points, your honor, and intend to bring the matter to an early conclusion," answered Williams, casting one of those glances at the prisoner which had obtained for him the merited *sobriquet* of "saucy." "Crier, call Samuel Burton."

Timms fairly started. This was breaking ground in a new spot, and was producing testimony from a source that he much dreaded. The Burtons had been the nearest neighbors of the Goodwins, and were so nearly on a social level with them, as to live in close and constant communication. These Burtons consisted of the man, his wife, and three maiden sisters. At one time, the last had conversed much on the subject of the murders ; but, to Timms's great discontent, they had been quite dumb of late. This had prevented his putting in practice a method of anticipating testimony, that is much in vogue, and which he had deliberately attempted with these sometime voluble females. As the reader may not be fully initiated in the mysteries of that sacred and all-important master of the social relations, the law, we shall set forth the manner in which justice is often bolstered, when its interests are cared for by practitioners of the Timms and Williams school.

No sooner is it ascertained that a particular individual has a knowledge of an awkward fact, than these worthies of the bar set to work to extract the dangerous information from him. This is commonly attempted, and often effected, by inducing the witness to relate what he knows, and by leading him on to make statements that, on being sworn to in court, will either altogether invalidate his testimony, or throw so much doubt on it as to leave it of very little value. As the agents employed to attain this end are not very scrupulous, there is great danger that their imaginations may supply the defects in the statements, and substitute words and thoughts that the party never uttered. It is so easy to mistake another's meaning, with even the best intentions, that we are not to be surprised if this should seriously happen when the disposition is to mislead. With the parties to suits, this artifice is often quite successful, admissions being obtained or supposed to be obtained, that they never, for an instant, intended to make. In the States where speculation has cornered men, and left them loaded with debt, these devices of the eaves-droppers and suckers are so common as to render their testimony no immaterial feature in nearly every cause of magnitude that is tried. In such a state of society it is, indeed, unsafe for a suitor to open his lips on his affairs, lest some one near him be employed to catch up his words and carry them into court with shades of meaning gathered from his own imagination.

At first, Timms was under the impression that the Burtons were going to sustain the defense, and he was placing himself on the most amiable footing with the females, three of whom might very reasonably be placed within the category of matrimony with this rising lawyer ; but it was not long ere he ascertained that Williams was getting to be intimate, and had proved to be a successful rival. Davis, the nephew and heir of the Goodwins, was a single man, too, and it is probable that his frequent visits to the dwelling of the Burtons had a beneficial influence on his own interests. Let the cause be what it might, the effect was clearly to seal the lips of the whole family, not a member of which could be induced by any art practiced by the agents of Timms to utter a syllable on a subject that now really seemed to be forbidden. When, therefore, Burton appeared on the stand, and was sworn, the two counsel for the defense waited for him to open his lips, with a profound and common interest.

Burton knew the deceased, had lived all his life near them, was at home the night of the fire, went to assist the old people, saw the two skeletons, had no doubt they were the remains of Peter Goodwin and his wife; observed the effects of a heavy blow across the foreheads of each, the same that was still to be seen ; inferred that this blow had destroyed them, or so far stunned them as to leave them incapable of escaping from the fire.

This witness was then questioned on the subject of the stocking, and Mrs. Goodwin's hoard of money. He had seen the stocking but once, had often heard it mentioned by his sisters ; did not think his wife had ever alluded to it ; did not know the amount of gold, but supposed it might be very considerable ; saw the bureau examined, and knew that the stocking could not be found. In a word, his testimony in chief went generally to sustain the impression that prevailed relative to the murders, though it is unnecessary to repeat it in this form, as the cross-examination will better explain his statements and opinions.

"Mr. Burton," said Dunscomb, "you knew the Goodwins well ?"

"Very well, sir. As well as near neighbors generally know each other."

"Can you swear that these are the skeletons of Peter and Dorothy Goodwin?"

"I can swear that I *believe* them to be such—have no doubt of the fact."

"Point out that which you suppose to be the skeleton of Peter Goodwin."

This request embarrassed the witness. In common with all around him, he had no other clew to his facts than the circumstances under which these vestiges of mortality had been found, and he did not know what ought to be his reply.

"I suppose the shortest of the skeletons to be Peter Goodwin's, and the longest that of his wife," he at length answered. "Peter was not as tall as Dorothy."

"Which is the shortest of these remains?"

"That I could not say, without measuring. I know that Goodwin was not as tall as his wife by half an inch, for I have seen them measured."

"Then you would say that, in your opinion, the longest of these two skeletons is that of Dorothy Goodwin, and the shortest that of her husband?"

"Yes, sir; that is my opinion—formed to the best of my knowledge. I have seen them measured."

"Was this measurement accurate?"

"Very much so. They used to dispute about their height, and they measured several times, when I was by; generally in their stocking feet, and once barefoot."

"The difference being half an inch in favor of the wife?"

"Yes, sir, as near as could be; for I was umpire more than once."

"Did Peter Goodwin and his wife live happily together?"

"Tolerable—much as other married folks get along."

"Explain what you mean by that."

"Why, there's ups and downs, I suppose, in all families. Dorothy was high-tempered, and Peter was sometimes cross-grained."

"Do you mean that they quarreled?"

"They got r'iled with each other, now and then."

"Was Peter Goodwin a sober man?"

The witness now appeared to be bothered. He looked around him, and meeting everywhere with countenances which evidently reflected "yes," he had not the moral courage to run counter to public opinion, and say "no." It is amazing what a tyrant this concentration of minds gets to be over those who are not very clear-headed themselves, and who are not constituted, morally, to resist its influence. It almost possesses a power to persuade these persons not to put faith in their own senses, and disposes them to believe what they hear rather than what they have seen. Indeed, one effect is to cause them to see with the eyes of others. As the "neighbors," those inquisitors who know so much of persons of their association and intimacy, and so little of all others, very generally fancied Peter a sober man, Burton scarce knew what to answer. Circumstances had made him acquainted with the delinquency of the old man, but his allegations would not be sustained were he to speak the whole truth, since Peter had succeeded in keeping his infirmity from being generally known. To a man like the witness, it was easier to sacrifice the truth than to face a neighborhood.

"I suppose he was much as others," answered Burton, after a delay that caused some surprise. "He was human, and had a human natur'. Independence days, and other rejoicings, I've known him give in more than the temperance people think is quite right; but I shouldn't say he was downright intemperate."

"He drank to excess, then, on occasions?"

"Peter had a very weak head, which was his greatest difficulty."

"Did you ever count the money in Mrs. Goodwin's stocking?"

"I never did. There was gold and paper; but how much I do not know."

"Did you see any strangers in or about the house of the Goodwins, the morning of the fire?"

"Yes; two strange men were there, and were active in helping the prisoner out of the window, and afterward in getting out the furniture. They were very particular in saving Mary Monson's property."

"Were those strangers near the bureau?"

"Not that I know. I helped carry the bureau out myself; and I was present afterward in court when it was examined for the money. We found none."

"What became of those strangers?"

"I cannot tell you. They were lost to me in the confusion."

"Had you ever seen them before?"

"Never."

"Nor since?"

"No, sir."

"Will you have the goodness to take that rod and tell me what is the difference in length between the two skeletons?"

"I trust, your honor, that this is testimony which will not be received," put in Williams. "The fact is before the jury, and they can take cognizance of it for themselves."

Dunscomb smiled as he answered—

"The zeal of the learned gentleman runs ahead of his knowledge of the rules of evidence. Does he expect a jury to measure the remains; or are we to show the fact by means of witnesses?"

"This is a cross-examination; and the question is one in chief. The witness belongs to the defense, if the question is to be put at all."

"I think not, your honor. The witness has testified, in chief, that he believes these remains to be those of Peter and Dorothy Goodwin; he has further said, on his cross-examination, that Dorothy was half an inch taller than Peter; we now wish to put to the test the accuracy of the first opinion, by comparing the two facts—his knowledge of the difference by the former measurement as compared with the present. It has been said that these two skeletons are very nearly of a length. We wish the truth to be seen."

"The witness will answer the question," said the judge.

"I doubt the power of the court to compel a witness to obtain facts in this irregular mode," observed the pertinacious Williams.

"You can note your exceptions, brother Williams," returned the judge, smiling; "although it is not easy to see with what useful consequences. If the prisoner be acquitted, you can hardly expect to try her again; and, if convicted, the prosecution will scarcely wish to press any objection."

Williams, who was as much influenced by a bull-dog tenacity as by any other motive, now sumbitted; and Burton took the rod and measured the skeletons, an office he might have declined, most probably, had he seen fit. The spectators observed surprise in his countenance; and he was seen to repeat the measurement, seemingly with more care.

"Well, sir, what is the difference in the length of those skeletons?" inquired Dunscomb.

"I make it about an inch and a half, if these marks are to be relied on," was the slow, cautious, well-considered reply.

"Do you now say that you believe these skeletons to be the remains of Peter and Dorothy Goodwin?"

"Whose else can they be? They were found on the spot where the old couple used to sleep."

"I ask you to answer *my* question; I am not here to answer *yours*. Do you still say that you believe these to be the skeletons of Peter and Dorothy Goodwin?"

"I am a good deal nonplussed by this measurement—though the flesh, and skin, and muscles may have made a considerable difference in life."

"Certainly," said Williams, with one of his withering sneers—sneers that had carried many a cause purely by their impudence and sarcasm—"Every one knows how much more muscle a man has than a woman. It causes the great difference in their strength. A bunch of muscles, more or less, in the heel, would explain all this, and a great deal more."

"How many persons dwelt in the house of Goodwin at the time of the fire?" demanded Dunscomb.

"They tell me Mary Monson was there, and I saw her there during the fire; but I never saw her there before."

"Do you know of any other inmate besides the old couple and the prisoner?"

"I did see a strange woman about the house for a week or two before the fire, but I never spoke to her. They tell me she was High Dutch."

"Never mind what they *tell* you, Mr. Burton"—observed the judge—"testify only to what you *know*."

"Did you see this strange woman at the fire, or after the fire?" continued Dunscomb.

"I can't say that I did. I remember to have looked round for her, too; but I did not find her."

"Was her absence spoken of in the crowd at the time?"

"Something was said about it; but we were too much taken up with the old couple to think a great deal of this stranger."

This is an outline of Burton's testimony; though the cross-examination was continued for more than an hour, and Williams had him again examined in chief. That intrepid practitioner contended that the defense had made Burton its own witness in all that related to the measurement of the skeletons; and that he had a right to a cross-examination. After all this contest, the only fact of any moment elicited from the witness related to the difference in stature between Goodwin and his wife, as has been stated already.

In the meantime, Timms ascertained that the last report set on foot by his own agents, at the suggestion of Mary Monson herself, was circulating freely; and, though it was directly opposed to the preceding rumor, which had found great favor with the gossips, this extravagant tale was most greedily swallowed. We conceive that those persons who are so constituted, morally, as to find pleasure in listening to the idle rumors that float about society, are objects of pity; their morbid desire to talk of the affairs of others being a disease that presses them down beneath the level they might otherwise occupy. With such persons, the probabilities go for nothing; and they are more inclined to give credit to a report that excites their interest, by running counter to all the known laws of human actions, than to give faith to its contradiction, when sustained by every reason that experience sustains. Thus was it on the present occasion.

There was something so audacious in the rumor that Mary Monson belonged to a gang of rogues in town, and had been sent especially to rob the Goodwins, that vulgar curiosity found great delight in it; the individual who heard the report usually sending it on with additions of his own, that had their authority purely in the workings of a dull imagination. It is in that way that this great faculty of the mind is made to perform a double duty; which in the one case is as pure and ennobling as in the other it is debasing and ignoble. The man of a rich imagination, he who is capable of throwing the charms of poetical feeling around the world in which we dwell, is commonly a man of truth. The high faculty which he possesses seems in such cases to be employed in ferreting out facts which, on proper occasions, he produces distinctly, manfully, and logically. On the other hand, there is a species of subordinate imagination that is utterly incapable of embellishing life with charms of any sort, and which delights in the false. This last is the imagination of the gossip. It obtains some modicum of facts, mixes it with large quantities of stupid fiction, delights in the idol it has thus fashioned out of its own head, and sends it abroad to find worshipers as dull, as vulgar-minded, and as uncharitable, as itself.

Timms grew frightened at the success of his client's scheme, and felt the necessity of commencing the reaction at once, if the last were to have time in which to produce its effect. He had been warmly opposed to the project in the commencement, and had strenuously resisted its adoption; but Mary Monson would not listen to his objections. She even threatened to employ another, should he fail her. The conceit seemed to have taken a strong hold on her fancy, and all the willfulness of her character had come in aid of this strange scheme. The thing was done; and it now remained to prevent its effecting the mischief it was so well adapted to produce.

All this time the fair prisoner sat in perfectly composed silence, listening attentively to everything that was said, and occasionally taking a note. Timms ventured to suggest that it might be better were she to abstain from doing the last, as it gave her the air of knowing too much, and helped to deprive her of the interesting character of an unprotected female; but she turned a perfectly deaf ear to his admonitions, hints, and counsel. He was a safe adviser, nevertheless, in matters of this sort; but Mary Monson was not accustomed so much to follow the leadings of others as to submit to her own impulses.

The sisters of Burton were next examined. They proved all the admitted facts; testified as to the stocking and its contents, and two of them recognized the piece of gold which was said to have been found in Mary Monson's purse as that which had once been the property of Dorothy Goodwin. On this head the testimony of each was full, direct, and explicit. Each had often seen the piece of gold, and they had noted a very small notch or scratch near the edge, which notch or scratch was visible on the piece now presented in court. The cross-examination failed to shake this testimony, and well it might, for every word these young women stated was strictly true. The experiment of placing the piece of coin among other similar coin failed with them. They easily recognized the true piece by the notch. Timms was confounded; Dunscomb looked very grave; Williams raised his nose higher than ever, and Mary Monson was perfectly surprised. When the notch was first mentioned she arose, advanced far enough to examine the coin, and laid her hand on her forehead as if she pondered painfully on the circumstance. The testimony that this was the identical piece found in her purse was very ample, the coin having been sealed up and kept by the coroner, who had brought it into court; while it must now be admitted that a very strong case was made out to show that this foreign coin had once been among the hoards of Dorothy Goodwin. A very deep impression was made by this testimony on all who heard it, including the court, the bar, the jury, and the audience. Every person present, but those who were in the immediate confidence of the accused, was firmly convinced of Mary Monson's guilt. Perhaps the only other exceptions to this mode of thinking were a few experienced practitioners, who, from long habit, knew the vast importance of hearing both sides before they made up their minds in a matter of so much moment.

We shall not follow Dunscomb through his long and arduous cross-examination of the sisters of Burton, but confine ourselves to a few of the more pertinent of the interrogatories that he put to the eldest, and which were duly repeated when the other two were placed on the stand.

"Will you name the persons dwelling in the house of the Goodwins at the time of the fire?" asked Dunscomb.

"There were the two old folks, this Mary Monson, and a German woman named Yetty (Jette) that aunt Dorothy took in to wait on her boarders."

"Was Mrs. Goodwin your aunt, then?"

"No; we wasn't related no how; but, being such near neighbors, and she so old, we just called her aunt by way of a compliment."

"I understand that," said Dunscomb, arching his brows—"I am called uncle, and by very charming young persons, on the same principle. Did you know much of this German?"

"I saw her almost every day for the time she was there, and talked with her as well as I could; but she spoke very little English. Mary Monson was the only person who could talk with her freely; she spoke her language."

"Had you much acquaintance with the prisoner at the bar?"

"I was some acquainted, as a body always is when they live such near neighbors."

"Were your conversations with the prisoner frequent, or at all confidential?"

"To own the truth, I never spoke to her in my life. Mary Monson was much too grand for me."

Dunscomb smiled; he understood how common it was for persons in this country to say they are "well acquainted" with this or that individual when their whole knowledge is derived from the common tongue. An infinity of mischief is done by this practice; but the ordinary American who will admit that he lives near any one without having an acquaintance with him, if acquaintance is supposed to confer credit, is an extraordinary exception to a very general rule. The idea of being "too grand" was of a nature to injure the prisoner and to impair her rights, and Dunscomb deemed it best to push the witness a little on this point.

"Why did you think Mary Monson was 'too grand' for you?" he demanded.

"Because she *looked* so."

"*How* did she look? In what way does or did her looks indicate that she was or thought herself 'too grand' for your association?"

"Is this necessary, Mr. Dunscomb?" demanded the judge.

"I beg your honor will suffer the gentleman to proceed," put in Williams, cocking his nose higher than ever, and looking round the court-room with an air of intelligence that the great York counselor did not like. "It is an interesting subject; and we, poor ignorant Dukes County folks, may get useful ideas, to teach us how to look 'too grand!'"

Dunscomb felt that he had made a false step, and he had the self-command to stop.

"Had you any conversation with the German woman?" he continued, bowing slightly to the judge to denote submission to *his* pleasure.

"She couldn't talk English. Mary Monson talked with her, I didn't, to any account."

"Were you at the fire?"

"I was."

"Did you see anything of this German during the fire or afterward?"

"I didn't. She disappeared, unaccountable!"

"Did you visit the Goodwins as often after Mary Monson came to live with them as you had done previously?"

"I didn't—grand looks and grand language isn't agreeable to me."

"Did Mary Monson ever speak to you?"

"I think, your honor," objected Williams, who did not like the question, "that this is traveling out of the record."

"Let the gentleman proceed—time is precious, and a discussion would lose us more of it than to let him proceed—go on, Mr. Dunscomb."

"Did Mary Monson ever speak to you?"

"She never did, to my knowledge."

"What then do you mean by 'grand language?'"

"Why, when she spoke to Aunt Dorothy she didn't speak as I was used to hear folks speak."

"In what respect was the difference?"

"She was grander in her speech, and more pretending like."

"Do you mean louder?"

"No—perhaps she wasn't as loud as common—but 'twas more like a book, and uncommon."

Dunscomb understood all this perfectly, as well as the feeling which lay at its bottom, but he saw that the jury did not; and he was forced to abandon the inquiry, as often happens on such occasions, on account of the ignorance of those to whom the testimony was addressed. He soon after abandoned the cross-examination of the sister of Burton; when his wife was brought upon the stand by the prosecution.

This woman, coming from a different stock, had none of the family characteristics of the sisters. As they were garrulous, forward, and willing enough to testify, she was silent, reserved in manner, thoughtful, and seemingly so diffident that she trembled all over, as she laid her hand on the sacred volume. Mrs. Burton passed for a very good woman among all who dwelt in or near Biberry; and there was much more confidence felt in her revelations than in those of her sisters-in-law. Great modesty, not to say timidity of manner, an air of singular candor, a low, gentle voice, and an anxious expression of countenance, as if she weighed the import of every syllable she uttered, soon won for this witness the sympathy of all present, as well as perfect credence. Every word she uttered had a direct influence on the case; and this so much the more since she testified reluctantly, and would gladly have been permitted to say nothing.

The account given by Mrs. Burton, in her examination in chief, did not materially differ from that previously stated by her sisters-in-law. She knew more, in some respects, than those who had preceded her, while, in others, she knew less. She had been more in the confidence of Dorothy Goodwin than any other member of her family, had seen her oftener, and knew more of her private affairs. With the stocking and its contents she admitted that she was familiarly acquainted. The gold exceeded twelve hundred dollars in amount; she had counted it, in her own hands. There was paper, also, but she did not know how much, exactly, as Dorothy kept *that* very much to herself. She knew, however, that her neighbors talked of purchasing a farm, the price of which was quite five thousand dollars, a sum that Dorothy often talked of paying down. She thought the deceased must have had money to that amount, in some form or other.

On the subject of the piece of gold found in Mary Monson's purse, Mrs. Burton gave her testimony with the most amiable discretion. Every one compared the reserve and reluctance of her manner most favorably with the pert readiness of Mrs. Pope and the sisters. This witness appeared to appreciate the effect of all she said, and uttered the facts she knew with a gentleness of manner that gave great weight to her testimony. Dunscomb soon saw that this was the witness the defense had most reason to dread, and he used the greatest care in having every word she said written out with precision.

Mrs. Burton swore point blank to the piece of notched gold, although she fairly trembled as she gave her testimony. She knew it was the very piece that she had often seen in Dorothy Goodwin's possession; she had examined it, at least a dozen times, and could have selected it among a thousand similar coins, by means of its private marks. Besides the notch, there was a slight defect in the impression of the date. This had been pointed out to her by Dorothy Goodwin herself, who had said it was a good mark by which to know the piece, should it be stolen. On this head, the witness's testimony was firm, clear and full. As it was corroborated by so much other evidence, the result was a deep and very general impression of the prisoner's guilt.

It was late when the examination in chief of Mrs. Burton terminated. She stated that she was much fatigued, and was suffering under a severe headache; and Williams asked, in her behalf, that the court would adjourn over, until next day, ere the cross-examination was gone into. This suited Dunscomb's views altogether, for he knew he might lose an essential advantage by allowing the witness a night to arrange her thoughts, pending so searching a process. There being no resistance on the part of the prisoner to the request of the prosecution, the judge so far waived his regard for the precious time of the court, as to consent to adjourn at eight o'clock in the evening, instead of pushing the case to ten or eleven. As a consequence the jurors took their rest in bed, instead of sleeping in the jury-box.

Dunscomb left the court-house, that night, dejected, and with no great expectation of the acquittal of his client. Timms had a better feeling, and thought nothing had yet appeared that might not be successfully resisted.

CHAPTER XXVI.

"I've not wronged her."
"Far be it from my fears."
"Then why this argument?"
"My lord, my nature's jealous, and
　　you'll bear it."　　—OTWAY.

So great was the confidence of Sarah Wilmeter and Anna Updyke in the innocence of their friend, that almost every step that the trial advanced appeared to them as so much progress toward an eventual acquittal. It was perhaps a little singular that the party most interested, she who knew her own guilt or innocence, became dejected, and for the first half hour after they had left the court-room she was silent and thoughtful. Good Mrs. Gott was quite in despair, and detained Anna Updyke, with whom she had established a sort of intimacy, as she opened the door of the gallery for the admission of the party, in order to say a word on the subject that lay nearest to her heart.

"Oh! Miss Anna," said the sheriff's wife, "it goes from bad to worse! It was bad enough last evening, and it is worse to-night."

"Who tells you this, Mrs. Gott? So far from thinking as you do, I regard it as appearing particularly favorable."

"You must have heard what Burton said, and what his wife said, too. They are the witnesses I dread."

"Yes, but who will mind what such persons say! I am sure if fifty Mr. and Mrs. Burtons were to testify that Mary Monson had taken money that did not belong to her, I should not believe them."

"You are not a Dukes County jury! Why, Miss Anna, these men will believe almost anything you tell them. Only swear to it, and there's no accounting for their credulity. No; I no more believe in Mary Monson's guilt than I do in my own, but law is law, they say, and rich and poor must abide by it."

"You view the matter under a false light, my kind-hearted Mrs. Gott, and after a night's rest will see the case differently. Sarah and I have been delighted with the course of things. You must have remarked no one said that Mary Monson had been seen to set fire to the house, or to harm the Goodwins, or to touch their property, or to do anything that was wrong; and of course she must be acquitted."

"I wish that piece of gold had not been found in her pocket! It's that which makes all the trouble."

"I think nothing of that, my good friend. There is nothing remarkable in two pieces of money having the same marks on them; I have seen that often, myself. Besides, Mary Monson explains all that, and her declaration is as good as that of Mrs. Burton's, any day."

"Not in law, Miss Anna; no, not in law. Out of doors it might be much better, and probably is; but not in court, by what they tell me. Gott says it is beginning to look very dark, and that we, in the jail, here, must prepare for the very worst. I tell him, if I was he, I'd resign before I'd execute such a beautiful creature!"

"You make me shudder with such horrid thoughts, Mrs. Gott, and I will thank you to open the door. Take courage; we shall never have to lament such a catastrophe, or your husband to perform so revolting a duty."

"I hope not—I'm sure I hope not, with all my heart. I would prefer that Gott should give up all hopes of ever rising any higher, than have him do this office. One never knows, Miss Anna, what is to happen in life, though I was as happy as a child when he was made sheriff. If my words have any weight with him, and he often says they have, I shall never let him execute Mary Monson. You are young, Miss Anna; but you've heard the tongue of flattery, I make no doubt, and know how sweet it is to woman's ear."

Mrs. Gott had been wiping her eyes with one hand, and putting the key into the lock with the other, while talking, and she now stood regarding her young companion with a sort of motherly interest, as she made this appeal to her experience. Anna blushed "rosy red," and raised her gloved hand to turn the key, as if desirous of getting away from the earnest look of the matron.

"That's just the way with all of us, Miss Anna!" continued Mrs. Gott. "We listen, and listen, and listen; and believe, and believe, and believe, until we are no longer the gay, light-hearted creatures that we were, but become mopy, and sightful, and anxious, to a degree that makes us forget father and mother, and fly from the paternal roof."

"Will you have the kindness, now, to let me into the jail?" said Anna, in the gentlest voice imaginable.

"In a minute, my dear—I call you my dear, because I like you; for I never use what Gott calls 'high-flown.' There is Mr. John Wilmeter, now, as handsome and agreeable a youth as ever came to Biberry. He comes here two or three times a day, and sits and talks with me in the most agreeable way, until I've got to like him better than any young man of my acquaintance. He talks of you, quite half the time; and when he is not *talking* of you, he is *thinking* of you, as I know by the way he gazes at this very door."

"Perhaps his thoughts are on Mary Monson," answered Anna, blushing scarlet. "You know she is a sort of client of his, and he has been here in her service for a good while."

"She hardly ever saw him; scarcely ever, except at this grate. His foot never crossed this threshold, until his uncle came; and since, I believe, he has gone in but once. Mary Monson is not the being he worships."

"I trust he worships the Being we all worship, Mrs. Gott," struggling gently to turn the key and succeeding. "It is not for us poor frail beings to talk of being worshiped."

"Or of worshiping, as I tell Gott," said the sheriff's wife, permitting her companion to depart.

Anna found Mary Monson and Sarah

walking together in the gallery, conversing earnestly.

"It is singular that nothing reaches us from Michael Millington!" exclaimed the last, as Anna interlocked arms with her, and joined the party. "It is now near eight-and-forty hours since my uncle sent him to town."

"On my business?" demanded Mary Monson, quickly.

"Certainly; on no other—though what it was that took him away so suddenly I have not been told. I trust you will be able to overturn all that these Burtons have said, and to repair the mischief they have done?"

"Fear nothing for me, Miss Wilmeter," answered the prisoner, with singular steadiness of manner—"I tell you, as I have often told your friend, *I must be acquitted*. Let justice take its course, say I, and the guilty be punished. I have a clew to the whole story, as I believe, and must make provision for to-morrow. Do you two, dear warm-hearted friends as you are, now leave me; and when you reach the inn, send Mr. Dunscomb hither, as soon as possible. Not that Timms; but noble, honest, and upright Mr. Dunscomb. Kiss me, each of you, and so good night. Think of me in your prayers. I am a great sinner, and have need of your prayers."

The wishes of Mary Monson were obeyed, and the young ladies left the jail for the night. Ten minutes later Dunscomb reached the place, and was admitted. His conference with his client was long, intensely interesting, and it quite unsettled the notions he had now, for some time, entertained of her guilt. She did not communicate anything concerning her past life, nor did she make any promises on that subject; but she did communicate facts of great importance, as connected with the result of her trial. Dunscomb left her, at a late hour, with views entirely changed, hopes revived, and his resolution stimulated. He made ample entries in his brief; nor did he lay his head on his pillow until it was very late.

The little court-house bell rang as usual, next morning, and judge, jurors, witnesses, lawyers, and the curious in general, collected as before, without any ceremony, though in decent quiet. The case was now getting to be so serious, that all approached it as truly a matter of life and death; even the reporters submitting to an impulse of humanity, and viewing the whole affair less in a business point of view, than as one which might carry a singularly gifted woman into the other world. The first act of the day opened by putting Mrs. Burton on the stand, for her cross-examination. As every intelligent person present understood that on her testimony depended the main result, the fall of a pin might almost have been heard, so profound was the general wish to catch what was going on. The witness, however, appeared to be calm, while the advocate was pale and anxious. He had the air of one who had slept little the past night. He arranged his papers with studied care, made each movement deliberately, compressed his lips, and seemed to be bringing his thoughts into such a state of order and distinctness that each might be resorted to as it was needful. In point of fact, Dunscomb foresaw that a human life depended very much on the result of this cross-examination, and, like a conscientious man, he was disposed to do his whole duty. No wonder, then, that he paused to reflect, was deliberate in his acts, and concentrated in feeling.

"We will first give our attention to this piece of gold, Mrs. Burton," the counsel for the prisoner mildly commenced, motioning to the coroner, who was in court to show the witness the piece of money so often examined. "Are you quite certain that it is the very coin that you saw in the possession of Mrs. Goodwin?"

"Absolutely certain, sir. As certain as I am of anything in the world."

"Mrs. Burton, I wish you to remember that the life of the prisoner at the bar will, most probably, be affected by your testimony. Be kind enough, then, to be very guarded and close in your answers. Do you still say that this is the precise coin that you once saw in Mrs. Goodwin's stocking?"

The witness seemed suddenly struck with the manner of the advocate. She trembled from head to foot. Still, Dunscomb spoke mildly, kindly even; and the idea conveyed in the present was but a repetition of that conveyed in the former question. Nevertheless those secret agencies, by means of which thought meets thought, unknown to all but their possessors; that set in motion, as it might be, all the covert currents of the mind, causing them to flow toward similar streams in the mind of another, were now at work, and Dunscomb and the witness had a clew to each other's meaning that entirely escaped the observation of all around them. There is nothing novel in this state of secret intelligence. It doubtless depends on a mutual consciousness, and a common knowledge of certain material facts, the latter being applied by the former, with promptitude and tact. Notwithstanding her sudden alarm, and the change it brought over her entire manner, Mrs. Burton answered the question as before; what was more, she answered it truly. The piece of gold found in Mary Monson's purse, and now in possession of the coroner, who had kept it carefully, in order to identify it, had been in Dorothy Goodwin's stocking.

"Quite certain, sir. I know that to be the same piece of money that I saw at different times, in Mrs. Goodwin's stocking."

"Did you ever have that gold coin in your own hand, Mrs. Burton, previously to this trial?"

This was a very natural and simple interrogatory; one that might be, and probably was, anticipated; yet it gave the witness uneasiness, more from the manner of Dunscomb, perhaps, than from anything in the nature of the inquiry itself. The answer, however, was given promptly, and, as before, with perfect truth.

"On several occasions, sir. I saw that notch, and talked with Mr. Goodwin about it more than once."

"What was the substance of Mrs. Goodwin's remarks in relation to that notch?"

"She asked me, one time, if I thought it lessened the weight of the coin; and if so, how much I thought it might take away from its value?"

"What was your answer?"

"I believe I said I did not think it could make any great difference."

"Did Mrs. Goodwin ever tell you how, or where, she got that piece of money?"

"Yes, sir, she did. She told me it came from Mary Monson."

"In pay for board; or, for what purpose did it pass from one to the other?"

This, too, was a very simple question, but the witness no longer answered promptly. The reader will remember that Mary Monson had said before the coroner that she had two of these coins, and that she had given one of them to the poor unfortunate deceased, and had left the other in her own purse. This answer had injured the cause of the accused, inasmuch as it was very easy to tell such a tale, while few in Biberry were disposed to believe that gold passed thus freely, and without any consideration, from hand to hand. Mrs. Burton remembered all this, and, for a reason best known to herself, she shrank a little from making the required reply. Still she did answer this question also and answered it truly.

"I understood Aunt Dolly to say that

Mary Monson made her a present of that piece of money."

Here Timms elevated his nose and looked around him in a meaning manner, that appealed to the audience to know if his client was not a person of veracity. Sooth to say, this answer made a strong impression in favor of the accused, and Dunscomb saw with satisfaction that, in so much, he had materially gained ground. He was not a man to gain it, however, by dramatic airs; he merely paused for a few moments, in order to give full effect to this advantage.

"Mrs. Goodwin, then, owned to you that she had the coin from Mary Monson, and that it was a present?" was the next question.

"She did, sir."

"Did she say anything about Mary Monson's having another piece of money, like the one before you, and which was given by her to Dorothy Goodwin?"

A long pause succeeded. The witness raised a hand to her brow, and appeared to meditate. Her reputation for taciturnity and gravity of deportment was such, that most of those in court believed she was endeavoring to recollect the past, in order to say neither more nor less than the truth. In point of fact, she was weighing well the effect of her words, for she was a person of extreme caution, and of great reputed probity of character. The reply came at length—

"She did speak on the subject," she said, "and did state something of the kind."

"Can you recollect her words—if so, give them to the jury—if not her very words, their substance."

"Aunt Dolly had a way of her own in talking, which makes it very difficult to repeat her precise words; but she said, in substance, that Mary Monson had two of these pieces of money, one of which was given to *her*."

"Mary Monson, then, kept the other?"

"So I understood it, sir."

"Have you any knowledge yourself on this subject? If so, state it to the jury."

Another pause, one even longer than before, and again the hand was raised to the brow. The witness now spoke with extreme caution, seeming to feel her way among the facts as a cat steals on its prey.

"I believe I have—a little—some—I have seen Mary Monson's purse, and I *believe* I saw a piece of money in it which resembled this."

"Are you not *certain* of the fact?"

"Perhaps I am."

Here Dunscomb's face was lighted with a smile; he evidently was encouraged.

" Were you present, Mrs. Burton, when Mary Monson's purse was examined, in presence of the inquest ? "

" I was."

" Did you then see the contents ? "

" I did "—after the longest pause of all.

" Had you that purse in your hand, ma'am ? "

The brow was once more shaded, and the recollection seemingly taxed.

" I think I had. It was passed round among us, and I believe that I touched it, as well as others."

" Are you not certain that you did so ? "

" Yes, sir. Now, I reflect, I know that I did. The piece of money found in Mary Monson's purse was passed from one to another, and to me, among the rest."

" This was very wrong," observed his honor.

" It was wrong, sir ; but not half as wrong as the murders and arson," coolly remarked Williams.

" Go on, gentlemen—time is precious."

" Now, Mrs. Burton, I wish to ask you a very particular question, and I beg that your answer may be distinct and guarded —did you ever have access to the piece of gold found, or said to be found, in Mary Monson's purse, except on the occasion of the inquest ? "

The longest pause of all, and the deepest shading of the brow. So long was the self-deliberation this time, as to excite a little remark among the spectators. Still, it was no more than prudent, to be cautious in a cause of so much importance.

" I certainly have, sir," was the reply that came at last. " I saw it in Dorothy Goodwin's stocking, several times ; had it in my hand, and examined it. This is the way I came to discover the notch. Aunt Dolly and I talked about that notch, as I have already told the court."

" Quite true, ma'am, we remember that, all your answers are carefully written out—"

" I'm sure nothing that I have said can be written out, which is not true, sir."

" We are to suppose that. And now, ma'am, permit me to ask if you ever saw that piece of money at any other time than at those you have mentioned. Be particular in the answer."

" I may," after a long pause.

" Do you not *know ?* "

" I do not, sir."

" Will you say, on your oath, that you cannot recollect any one occasion, other than those you have mentioned, on which you have seen and handled that piece of money ? "

" When Aunt Dolly showed it to me, before the coroner, and here in court. I recollect no other time."

" Let me put this question to you again, Mrs. Burton—recalling the solemnity of the oath you have taken—have you, or have you not, seen that piece of money on any other occasion than those you have just mentioned ? "

" I do not remember ever to have seen it at any other time," answered the woman, firmly.

Mary Monson gave a little start, and Dunscomb appeared disappointed. Timms bit his lip, and looked anxiously at the jury, while Williams once more cocked *his* nose, and looked around him in triumph. If the witness spoke the truth, she was now likely to adhere to it ; if, on the other hand, there were really any ground for Dunscomb's question, the witness had passed the Rubicon, and would adhere to her falsehood even more tenaciously than she would adhere to the truth. The remainder of this cross-examination was of very little importance. Nothing further was obtained from the witness that went to shake her testimony.

Our limits will not permit a detailed account of all the evidence that was given in behalf of the prosecution. All that appeared before the inquest was now introduced, methodized and arranged by Williams ; processes that rendered it much more respectable than it had originally appeared to be. At length it came to the turn of the defense to open. This was a task that Dunscomb took on himself, Timms, in his judgment, being unequal to it. His opening was very effective, in the way of argument, though necessarily not conclusive, the case not making in favor of his client.

The public expected important revelations as to the past history of the prisoner, and of this Timms had apprised Dunscomb. The latter, however, was not prepared to make them. Mary Monson maintained all her reserve, and Millington did not return. The cause was now so far advanced as to render it improbable that any facts, of this nature, could be obtained in sufficient season to be used, and the counsel saw the necessity of giving a new turn to this particular point in the case. He consequently complained that the prosecution had neglected to show anything in the past life of the accused to render it probable she had been guilty of the offenses with which she was charged. " Mary Monson appears here," he went on to say, " with a character as fair as that of any other female in the community. This is the presumption of law, and you will truly regard her, gentlemen, as one that is inno-

THE WAYS OF THE HOUR.

cent until she is proved to be guilty."
The inference drawn from the silence of
the prosecution was not strictly logical,
perhaps; but Dunscomb managed at least
to mystify the matter in such a way as to
prepare the jury to hear a defense that
would be silent on this head, and to leave
a doubt whether this silence were not
solely the fault of the counsel for the
prosecution. While he was commenting
on this branch of the subject, Williams
took notes furiously, and Timms foresaw
that he meant to turn the tables on them,
at the proper moment.

Pretty much as a matter of course,
Dunscomb was compelled to tell the court
and jury that the defense relied principally on the insufficiency of the evidence
of the other side. This was altogether
circumstantial; and the circumstances,
as he hoped to be able to convince the
jury, were of a nature that admitted of
more than one construction. Whenever
this was the case, it was the duty of the
jury to give the accused the full benefit of
these doubts. The rest of the opening
had the usual character of appeals to the
sympathy and justice of the jury, very
prudently and properly put.

Dr. McBrain was now placed upon the
stand, when the customary questions
were asked, to show that he was a witness entitled to the respect of the court.
He was then further interrogated, as follows:

"Have you seen the two skeletons that
are now in court, and which are said to
have been taken from the ruins of the
house of the Goodwins?"

"I have. I saw them before the inquest;
and I have again examined them here, in
court."

"What do you say, as to their sex?"

"I believe them both to be the skeletons
of females."

"Do you feel certain of this fact?"

"Reasonably so, but not absolutely.
No one can pronounce with perfect certainty in such a case; more especially
when the remains are in the state in
which these have been found. We are
guided principally by the comparative
size of the bones; and, as these are affected by the age of the subject, it is
hazardous to be positive. I can only say
that I think both of these skeletons belonged to female subjects; particularly
the shortest."

"Have you measured the skeletons?"

"I have, and find one rather more than
an inch and a half shorter than the other.
The longest measures quite five feet seven
and a half, in the state in which it is;
while the shortest measures a trifle less

than five feet six. If women, both were
of unusual stature; particularly the first.
I think that the bones of both indicate
that they belonged to females; and I
should have thought the same had I known
nothing of the reports which have reached
my ears touching the persons whose remains these are said to be."

"When you first formed your opinion
of the sex of those to whom these remains
belonged, had you heard that there was
a German woman staying in the house of
the Goodwins at the time of the fire?"

"I think not; though I have taken so
little heed of these rumors as to be uncertain when I first heard this circumstance.
I do remember, however, that I was under the impression the remains were,
beyond a doubt, those of Peter Goodwin
and his wife, when I *commenced* the examination of them; and I very distinctly
recollect the surprise I felt when the conviction crossed my mind that both were
the skeletons of women. From the nature
of this feeling, I rather think I could not
have heard anything of the German female at that time."

The cross-examination of Dr. McBrain
was very long and searching, but it did
not materially affect the substance of his
testimony. On the contrary, it rather
strengthened it; since he had it in his
power to explain himself more fully under
the interrogatories of Williams, than he
could do in an examination in chief. Still,
he could go no further than give his strong
belief; declining to pronounce positively
on the sex of either individual, in the state
in which the remains were found.

Although nothing positive was obtained
from this testimony, the minds of the
jurors were pointedly directed to the circumstance of the sudden and unexplained
disappearance of the German woman;
thus making an opening for the admission
of a serious doubt connected with the fate
of that person.

It was a sad thing to reflect that, beyond this testimony of McBrain, there
was little other direct evidence to offer in
behalf of the accused. It is true, the insufficiency of that which had been produced by the prosecution might avail her
much; and on this Dunscomb saw that
his hopes of an acquittal must depend;
but he could not refrain from regretting,
and that bitterly, that the unmoved resolution of his client not to let her past life
be known, must so much weaken his case,
were she innocent, and so much fortify
that of the prosecution, under the contrary supposition. Another physician or
two were examined to sustain McBrain;
but, after all, the condition of the remains

were such as to render any testimony questionable. One witness went so far as to say, it is true, that he thought he could distinguish certain unerring signs of the sex in the length of the lower limbs, and in other similar proof; but even McBrain was forced to admit that such distinctions were very vague and unsatisfactory. His own opinion was formed more from the size of the bones, generally, than from any other proof. In general, there was little difficulty in speaking of the sex of the subject, when the skeleton was entire and well preserved, and particularly when the teeth furnished some clew to the age; but, in this particular case, as has already been stated, there could be no such thing as absolute certainty.

It was with a heavy heart, and with an anxious glance cast toward the door, in the hope of seeing Michael Millington enter, that Dunscomb admitted the prisoner had no further testimony to offer. He had spun out the little he did possess, in order to give it an appearance of importance which it did not actually bring with it, and to divert the minds of the jurors from the impression they had probably obtained, of the remains necessarily being those of Goodwin and his wife.

The summing up on both sides was a grave and solemn scene. Here Williams was thrown out, the district attorney choosing to perform his own duty on an occasion so serious. Dunscomb made a noble appeal to the justice of the court and jury; admonishing both of the danger of yielding too easily to circumstantial evidence. It was the best possible proof, he admitted, when the circumstances were sufficiently clear and sufficiently shown to be themselves beyond controversy. That Mary Monson dwelt with the Goodwins, was in the house at the time of the arson and murder, if such crimes were ever committed at all; that she escaped and all her property was saved, would of themselves amount to nothing. The testimony, indeed, on several of these heads, rather told in her favor than the reverse. The witnesses for the prosecution proved that she was in her room, beneath the roof, when the flames broke out, and was saved with difficulty. This was a most material fact, and Dunscomb turned it to good account.

Would an incendiary be apt to place herself in a situation in which her own life was in danger: and this, too, under circumstances that rendered no such measure necessary? Then, all the facts connected with Mary Monson's residence and habits told in her favor. Why should she remain so long at the cottage if robbery was her only purpose? The idea of her belonging to a gang that had sent her to make discoveries and to execute its plans was preposterous; for what hindered any of the men of that gang from committing the crimes in the most direct manner, and with the least loss of time? No; if Mary Monson were guilty, she was undoubtedly guilty on her own account; and had been acting with the uncertain aim and hand of a woman. The jury must discard all notions of accomplices, and consider the testimony solely in connection with the acts of the accused. Accomplices, and those of the nature supposed, would have greatly simplified the whole of the wretched transaction. They would have rendered both the murders and arson unnecessary. The bold and strong do not commit these crimes, except in those cases in which resistance renders them necessary. Here was clearly no resistance, as was shown by the quiet positions in which the skeletons had been found. If a murder was directly committed, it must have been by the blow on the heads; and the jury was asked to consider whether a delicate female like Mary Monson had even the physical force necessary to strike such a blow. With what instrument was it done? Nothing of the sort was found near the bodies; and no proof of any such blow was before the jury.

One witness had said that the iron-work of a plow lay quite near the remains; and it had been shown that Peter Goodwin kept such articles in a loft over his bedroom. He would suggest the possibility of the fire's having commenced in that loft, through which the pipe of a cooking-stove led; of its having consumed the beams of the floor; letting down this plow and share upon the heads of the sleeping couple below, stunning, if not killing them; thus leaving them unresisting subjects to the action of the element. McBrain had been examined on this point, which we omitted to state in its place, to prevent repetition. He, and the two other doctors brought forward for the defense, had tried to place the plowshare on the skulls, and were of opinion that the injuries might have been inflicted by that piece of iron. But Mary Monson could not use such an instrument. This was beyond all dispute. If the plowshare inflicted the blow—and the testimony on this point was at least entitled to respect—then was Mary Monson innocent of any murder committed by *direct* means. It is true, she was responsible for all her acts; and if she set fire to the building, she was probably guilty of murder as well as of arson. But would she have done this, and made no provision for her own escape? The evidence was clear that she was rescued by means of a ladder, and through a window; and that there were no other means of escape.

Dunscomb reasoned on these several points with great force and ingenuity. So clear was his statements, so logical his inferences, and so candid his mode of arguing, that he had produced a great effect ere he closed this branch of his subject. It is true, that one far more difficult remained to be met; to answer which he now set about with fear and trembling.

We allude to the piece of money alleged to have been found in Mary Monson's purse. Dunscomb had very little difficulty in disposing of the flippant Widow Pope; but the Burton family gave him more trouble. Nevertheless, it was his duty to endeavor to get rid of them, or at least so far to weaken their testimony as to give his client the benefit of the doubt. There was, in truth, but one mode of doing this. It was to impress on the jury the probability that the coin had been changed in passing from hand to hand. It is true, it was not easy to suggest any plausible reason why such an act of treachery should have been committed; but it was a good legal point to show that this piece of money had not, at all times, been absolutely under the eye or within the control of the coroner. If there were a possibility of a change, the fact should and ought to tell in favor of his client. Mrs. Burton had made admission on this point which entitled the prisoner to press the facts on the minds of the jurors; and her counsel did not fail so to do, with clearness and energy. After all, this was much the most difficult point of the case; and it would not admit of a perfectly satisfactory solution.

The conclusion of Dunscomb's summing up was manly, touching, even eloquent. He spoke of a lone and defenseless female, surrounded by strangers, being dragged to the bar on charges of such gravity; pointed to his client, where she sat enthralled by his language, with all the signs of polished refinement on her dress, person, and manners; delicate, feminine, and beautiful; and asked if any one, who had the soul and feelings of a man, could believe that such a being had committed the crimes imputed to Mary Monson.

The appeal was powerful, and was dwelt on just long enough to give it full and fair effect. It left the bench, the bar, the jury-box, the whole audience, in fact, in tears. The prisoner alone kept an unmoistened eye; but it was in a face flushed with feeling. Her self-command was almost supernatural.

CHAPTER XXVII.

"I'll brave her to her face:
I'll give my anger its free course against her.
Thou shalt see, Phœnix, how I'll break her pride."
—THE DISTRESSED MOTHER.

THE district attorney was fully impressed with the importance of the duty that had now devolved on him. Although we have daily proofs on all sides of us, of the truth of that remark of Bacon's, "that no man rises to eminence in the State without a mixture of great and mean qualities," this favorite of the people had his good points as well as another. He was a humane man; and, contrary to the expectations, and greatly to the disappointment of Williams, he now took on himself the office of summing-up.

The public functionary commenced in a mild, quiet manner, manifesting by the key on which he pitched his voice a natural reluctance to his painful duty; but he was steady and collected. He opened with a brief summary of the facts. A strange female, of high personal pretensions, had taken lodgings in an humble dwelling. That dwelling contained a considerable sum of money. Some counted it by thousands; all by hundreds. In either case, it was a temptation to the covetous and ill-disposed. The lodgings were unsuited to the habits of the guest; but she endured them for several weeks. A fire occurred, and the house was consumed. The remains of the husband and wife were found, as the jury saw them, with marks of violence on their skulls. A deadly blow had been struck by some one. The bureau containing the money was found locked, but the money itself was missing. One piece of that money was known, and it was traced to the purse of the female lodger. This stranger was arrested; and, in her mode of living in the jail, in her expenditures of every sort, she exhibited the habits and profusion of one possessed of considerable sums. Doubtless many of the reports in circulation were false; exaggerations ever accompanied each statement of any unusual occurrence; but enough was proved to show that Mary Monson had a considerable amount of money at command. Whence came these funds? That which was lightly obtained went lightly. The jury were exhorted to reject every influence but that which was sustained by the evidence. All that had been here stated rested on uncontradicted, unresisted testimony.

There was no desire to weaken the force of the defense. This defense had been ingeniously and powerfully presented; and to what did it amount? The direct, unequivocal evidence of Mrs. Burton, as to her knowledge of the piece of money, and all that related to it, and this evidence sustained by so much that was known to others, the coroner included, was met by a *conjecture*. This conjecture was accompanied by an insinuation that some might suppose reflected on the principal witness; but it was only an insinuation. There were two legal modes of attacking the credibility of a witness. One was by showing habitual mendacity; the other by demonstrating from the evidence itself that the testimony could not be true. Had either been done in the present instance? The district attorney thought not. One, and this the most common course, had not even been attempted. Insinuations, rather than just deductions, he was compelled to say, notwithstanding his high respect for the learned counsel opposed to him, had been the course adopted. That counsel had contended that the circumstances were not sufficient to justify a verdict of guilty. Of this, the jury were the sole judges. If they believed Mrs. Burton, sustained as she was by so much other testimony, they must admit that Dorothy Goodwin's money was found in Mary Monson's purse. This was the turning point of the case. All depended on the construction of this one fact. He left it to the jury, to their good sense, to their consciences.

On the part of the defense, great stress had been laid on the circumstance that Mary Monson was herself rescued from the flames with some difficulty. But for assistance, she would most probably have perished. The district attorney desired to deny nothing that could justly go to prove the prisoner's innocence. The fact was unquestionably as stated. But for assistance, Mary Monson *might* have perished. But assistance was *not* wanting; for strangers were most *opportunely* at hand, and they did this piece of good service. They remained until all was over, and vanished. No one knew them; whence they came, or whither they went. Important agents in saving a life, they had gone without their reward, and were not even named in the newspaper accounts of the occurrence. Reporters generally tell more than happens; in this instance, they were mute.

As for the danger of the prisoner, it might have happened in a variety of ways that affected neither her guilt nor her innocence. After committing the murders, she may have gone into her room and been unexpectedly inclosed by the flames; or the whole may have been previously planned in order to give her the plea of this very dangerous situation, as a proof of innocence. Such immaterial circumstances were not to overshadow the very material facts on which the prosecution rested.

Another important question was to be asked by the jury—If Mary Monson did not commit those crimes, who did? It had been suggested that the house might have taken fire by accident, and that the plowshare was the real cause of the death of its owners. If this were so, did the plowshare remove the money? did the plowshare put the notched piece in Mary Monson's purse?

Such is an outline of the manner in which the district attorney reasoned on the facts. His summing-up made a deep impression; the moderation of the manner in which he pressed the guilt of the accused, telling strongly against her. Nothing was said of aristocracy, or harps, or manners, or of anything else that did not fairly belong to the subject. A great deal more was said, of course; but we do not conceive it necessary to advert to it.

The charge was exceedingly impartial. The judge made a full exposition of all the testimony, pointed out its legitimate bearing, and dissected its weak points. As for the opinion of McBrain and his associates, the court conceived it entitled to a great deal of consideration. Here were several highly respectable professional men testifying that, in their judgment, both the skeletons were those of females. The German woman was missing. What had become of her? In any case, the disappearance of that woman was very important. She may have committed the crimes, and absconded; or one of the skeletons may have been hers. It was in evidence that Peter Goodwin and his wife did not always live in the most happy mood; and he may have laid hands on the money, which was probably his in the eyes of the law, and left the place. He had not been seen since the fire. The jury must take all the facts into consideration, and decide according to their consciences.

This charge was deemed rather favorable to the accused than otherwise. The humanity of the judge was conspicuous throughout; and he leaned quite obviously to Dunscomb's manner of treating the danger of Mary Monson from the flames, and dwelt on the fact that the piece of money was not sufficiently watched to make out an absolute case of identity. When he had done, the impression was very general that the prisoner would be acquitted.

As it was reasonably supposed that a

case of this importance would detain the jury a considerable time, the court permitted the prisoner to withdraw. She left the place, attended by her two friends; the latter in tears, while Mary herself was still seemingly unmoved. The thoughtful Mrs. Gott had prepared refreshments for her; and for the first time since her trial commenced, the fair prisoner ate heartily.

"I shall owe my triumph, not to money, my dear girls," she said, while at table, "not to friends, nor to a great array of counsel; but to truth. I did not commit these crimes; and on the testimony of the State alone, with scarcely any of my own, the jury will have to say as much. No stain will rest on my character, and I can meet my friends with the unclouded brow of innocence. This is a very precious moment to me; I would not part with it for all the honors that riches and rank can bestow."

"How strange that you, of all women, my dear mamma," said Anna, kissing her cheek, "should be accused of crimes so horrible to obtain a little money; for this poor Mrs. Goodwin could have had no great sum after all, and you are so rich!"

"More is the pity that I have not made a better use of my money. You are to be envied, girls, in having the fortunes of gentlewomen, and in having no more. I do believe it is better for our sex barely to be independent in their respective stations, and not to be rendered rich. Man or woman, money is a dangerous thing, when we come to consider it as a part of our natural existence; for it tempts us to fancy that money's worth gives rights that nature and reason both deny. I believe I should have been much happier, were I much poorer than I am."

"But those who are rich are not very likely to rob!"

"Certainly not, in the sense that you mean, my dear. Send Marie Moulin on some errand, Anna; I wish to tell you and Sarah what I think of this fire, and of the deaths for which I am now on trial."

Anna complied; and the handsome prisoner, first looking cautiously around to make certain she was not overheard, proceeded with her opinion.

"In the first place, I make no doubt Doctor McBrain is right, and that both the skeletons are those of women. The German woman got to be very intimate with Mrs. Goodwin; and as the latter and her husband quarreled daily, and fiercely, I think it probable that she took this woman into her bed, where they perished together. I should think the fire purely accidental, were it not for the missing stocking."

"That is just what the district attorney said," cried Anna, innocently. "Who, then, *can* have set the house on fire?"

Mary Monson muttered to herself; and she smiled as if some queer fancies crowded her brain; but no one was the wiser for her ruminations. These she kept to herself, and continued:

"Yes, that missing stocking renders the arson probable. The question is, who did the deed; I or Mrs. Burton?"

"Mrs. Burton!" exclaimed both the girls, in a breath. "Why, her character is excellent—no one has ever suspected her! You cannot suppose that she is the guilty person!"

"It is she, or it is I; which, I will leave you to judge. I was aware that the notch was in the coin; for I was about to give the other piece to Mrs. Goodwin, but preferred to keep the perfect specimen myself. The notched piece must have been in the stocking until *after* the fire; and it was changed by some one while my purse was under examination."

"And you suppose that Mrs. Burton did it?"

"I confess to a suspicion to that effect. Who else could or *would* have done it? I have mentioned this distrust to Mr. Dunscomb, and he cross-examined in reference to this fact; though nothing very satisfactory was extracted. After my acquittal, steps will be taken to push the inquiry further."

Mary Monson continued discussing this subject for quite an hour; her wondering companions putting questions. At the end of that time Mr. Gott appeared to say that the jury had come into court; and that it was his duty to take the prisoner there to meet them.

Perhaps Mary Monson never looked more lovely than at that moment. She had dressed herself with great simplicity, but with exceeding care; excitement gave her the richest color; hope, even delight, was glowing in her eyes; and her whole form was expanded with the sentiment of triumph. There is no feeling more general than sympathy with success. After the judge's charge, few doubted of the result; and on every side, as she walked with a light firm step to her chair, the prisoner read kindness, sympathy, and exultation. After all that had been said, and all the prejudices that had been awakened, Mary Monson was about to be acquitted! Even the reporters became a little humanized; had juster perceptions than common of the rights of their fellow-creatures; and a more smiling, benignant assembly was never collected in that hall. In a few minutes silence was obtained, and the jurors were called. Every man answered to his name, when the profound stillness of expectation pervaded the place.

"Stand up, Mary Monson, and listen to the verdict," said the clerk, not without a little tremor in his voice. "Gentlemen, what do you say—is the prisoner guilty or not guilty?"

The foreman arose, stroked down a few scattering gray hairs, then, in a voice barely audible, he pronounced the portentous word "Guilty." Had a bomb suddenly exploded in the room, it could not have produced greater astonishment, and scarcely more consternation. Anna Updyke darted forward, and, as with a single bound, Mary Monson was folded in her arms.

"No, no!" cried this warm-hearted girl, totally unconscious of the impropriety of her acts; "she is *not* guilty. You do not know her. I *do*. She was my school-mamma. She is a lady, incapable of being guilty of such crimes. No, no, gentlemen, you will think better of this, and alter your verdict—perhaps it was a mistake, and you meant to say 'Not guilty!'"

"Who is this young lady?" asked the judge, in a tremulous voice—"a relative of the prisoner's?"

"No, sir," answered the excited girl, "no relative, but a very close friend. She was my 'school-mamma' once, and I know she is not a person to rob, and murder, and set fire to houses. Her birth, education, character, all place her above it. You will think better of this, gentlemen, and change your verdict. Now, go at once and do it or you may distress her!"

"Does any one know who this young lady is?" demanded his honor, his voice growing more and more tremulous.

"I am Anna Updyke—Doctor McBrain's daughter now, and uncle Tom's niece," answered Anna, scarce knowing what she said. "But never mind *me*— it is Mary Monson, here, who has been tried, and who has so wrongfully been found guilty. She never committed these crimes, I tell you, sir—is incapable of committing them—had no motive for committing them; and I beg you will put a stop to these proceedings, before they get so far as to make it difficult to recede. Just tell the jury to alter their verdict. No, no, Mary Monson is no murderess! She would no more hurt the Goodwins, or touch a particle of their gold, than either of us all. You do not know her, sir. If you did, you would smile at this mistake of the jury, for it is all a cruel mistake. Now do, my dear sir,

send them away again, and tell them to be more reasonable."

"The young lady had better be removed," interposed the judge, wiping his eyes. "Such scenes may be natural, and the court looks on them leniently; but time is precious, and my duty renders it necessary to interpose my authority to maintain the order of our proceedings. Let some of the ladies remove the young lady; she is too delicate for the touch of a constable—but time is precious."

The judge was not precisely conscious, himself, of what he was saying, though he knew the general drift of his remarks. The process of blowing his nose interrupted his speech more than once, and Anna was removed by the assistance of Marie Moulin, Sarah Wilmeter, and good Mrs. Gott; the latter sobbing like a child, while the other two scarce realized the consequences of the momentous word that had just been pronounced. Dunscomb took care that the whole group should quit the building and be removed to the tavern.

If the bar, and the spectators in general, had been surprised at the calmness of exterior maintained by the prisoner, previously to the verdict, their wonder was sensibly increased by the manner which succeeded it. Mary Monson's beauty shone with increasing radiance as the justice of her country seemed to threaten her existence more and more; and at the particular moment when she was left alone, by the withdrawal of her female companions, many present fancied that she had increased in stature. Certainly, it was a rare sight to observe the illuminated countenance, the erect mien, and the offended air with which one of the weaker sex, and one so youthful and charming, met a doom so terrible. Of the jury she took no notice. Her eye was on the judge, who was endeavoring to muster sufficient fortitude to pronounce the final decision of the law.

"Before the court pronounces sentence, Mr. Dunscomb," observed that functionary, "it will cheerfully hear anything you may have to offer in behalf of the prisoner, or it will hear the prisoner herself. It is better, on every account, that all my painful duties be discharged at once, in order that the prisoner may turn her attention to the only two sources of mercy that now remain open to her—the earthly and the heavenly. My duty, as you well know, cannot now be avoided; and the sooner it is performed, perhaps, the better for all concerned. It shall be my care to see that the condemned has time to make all her appeals, let them be to the authorities here, or to the more dreaded Power above."

"I am taken so much by surprise, your honor, at a verdict that, to say the least, is given on very doubtful testimony, that I hardly know what to urge. As the court, however, is disposed to indulgence, and there will be time to look at the law of the case, as well as to address our petitions and affidavits to the authority at Albany, I shall interpose no objection; and, as your honor well remarks, since the painful duty *must* be discharged, it were better, perhaps, that it were discharged now."

"Prisoner at the bar," resumed the judge. "you have heard the finding of the jury, in your case. A verdict of 'guilty' has been rendered, and it has become my painful duty to pronounce the awful sentence of the law. If you have anything to say previously to this, the last and most painful of all my duties, the court will give your words a kind and lenient hearing."

In the midst of a stillness that seemed supernatural, the sweet melodious voice of Mary Monson was heard, "first gentle, almost inaudible," but gathering strength as she proceeded, until it became clear, distinct and silvery. There are few things that impart a higher charm than the voice; and the extraordinary prisoner possessed an organ which, while it was feminine and sweet, had a depth and richness that at once denoted her power in song. On the present occasion it was not even tremulous.

"I believe I understand you, sir," Mary Monson commenced. "I have been tried and found guilty of having murdered Peter and Dorothy Goodwin, after having robbed them, and then of setting fire to the house."

"You have been tried for the murder of Peter Goodwin, only, the indictments for the second murder, and for the arson, not having yet been tried. The court has been obliged to separate the cases, lest the law be defeated on mere technicalities. This verdict renders further proceedings unnecessary, and the two remaining indictments will probably never be traversed."

"I believe I still understand you, sir; and I thank you sincerely for the kind manner in which you have communicated these facts, as well as for the consideration and gentleness you have manifested throughout these proceedings. It has been very kind in you, sir; and whatever may come of this, God will remember and reward you for it."

"The court will hear you, Mary Mon-

son, if you have anything to say, before sentence be passed."

"Perhaps I might say and do much to affect your decision, sir," returned the prisoner, leaning her fair brow, for a moment, on her hand, "but there would be little satisfaction in it. It was my wish to be acquitted on the testimony of the State. I did hope that this jury would not have seen the proofs of guilt, in the evidence that has been brought against me; and I confess there would be very little satisfaction to me in any other acquittal. As I understand the case, should I be acquitted as respects Peter Goodwin, I must still be tried as respects his wife; and lastly for setting fire to his house."

"You are not acquitted of the murder of Peter Goodwin," mildly interposed the judge; "the finding of the court has been just to the contrary."

"I am aware of this, sir. America has many enemies. I have lived in foreign lands, and know this from near and long observation. There are those, and those, too, who are in power, that would gladly see the great example in prosperity, peace, and order, that this country has hitherto given to the world, beaten down by our own vices, and the mistaken uses to which the people put the blessings of Divine Providence. I do not reverence the justice of my country, as I did; it is impossible that I should do so. I now see plainly that its agents are not all of the character they should be; and that, so far from Justice's being blind through her impartiality alone, she is also blind through her ignorance. Why am I found guilty of this act? On what evidence—or even on what probability? The whole of the proof is connected with that piece of money. Mrs. Burton has testified that Mrs. Goodwin, herself, admitted that I had given her that coin—just what I told the coroner, and which I then saw was not believed, for it has been my misfortune to be tried by strangers. Will these gentlemen ask themselves why I have committed the crime of which they have found me guilty? it could not be for money; as of that I have, of my own, more than I want, more, perhaps, than it is good for me to be mistress of."

"Why have not these facts been shown to the jury, at the proper time and in the proper manner, if true?" demanded the judge, kindly. "They are material, and might have influenced the verdict."

The jury was discharged, but not one of them all had left the box. One or two of them now arose, and looks of doubt and indecision began to flicker over their countenances. They had been influenced by one man, a friend and political confident of Williams, who had led the undecided to his own opinions. We do not mean to say that this man was perjured, or that he was himself conscious of the extent of the wrong he was doing; but his mind had been perverted by the serpent-like report, and he tried the cause under the influence of rumors, which had no foundation in truth. The case was one of honest doubt, as no one will deny; but instead of giving the accused the benefit of this doubt, as by law and in reason he was bound to do, he had taken a bias altogether from outside influences, and that bias he communicated to others, until by the sheer force of numbers, the few who wavered were driven into a corner, and soon capitulated. Then, there was a morbid satisfaction in the minds of several of the jurors, in running counter to the charge of the judge. This was a species of independence that is grateful to some men, and they are guided by their vanity, when they fancy they are only led by conscience. These malign influences were unknown to themselves; for not one of the twelve was absolutely corrupt, but neither of them all was qualified by nature, or education, to be a judge, freed from the influence of the bench, in a case affecting a human life.

Any one in the least observant of what is going on around him, must have had many opportunities of perceiving how strangely juries render their verdicts, and how much the last appear to be opposed to the inferences of the looker-on, as well as to the expressed opinions of the courts. The falling off in the power of the judges over the minds of the jurors, we suppose to be derived from a combination of causes. The tendency of the times is to make men confident in their own judgments, and to defer less than formerly to knowledge and experience. Seeing this very general trait, the judges themselves defer to the tendency, manifest less confidence in their station and knowledge and perhaps really feel it; while the unceasing cry of the infallibility of the common mind, induces the vulgar, or average intellect, to shrink from any collision with that which wears the semblance, even though simulated, of the popular will. In this way is the institution of the jury gradually getting to be perverted, rendering that which is safe as an human tribunal can well be, when under the guidance of the court, as dangerous as ignorance, party, self-will and obstinacy can well make it.

"I do not know," resumed Mary Monson, "that one is yet obliged, in America, to lay open her account-books, and show her rent-roll, or her bonds and mortgages, in order to avoid the gallows. I have been told that crime must be brought home by unanswerable proof, in order to convict. Who can say that such has been adduced in my case? It has not even been made certain that a man was killed, at all. Most respectable witnesses have testified that they believe those revolting remains of poor humanity, belonged once to women. Nor has it been shown that any one has been murdered. The fire may have been accidental, the deaths a simple consequence of the fire, and no one guilty."

"You forget, Mary Monson," interposed the judge, mildly, "that the robbery, and the piece of money found in your purse, give a color to the supposition of crime. The jury have doubtless been influenced by these facts, and important facts they are. No one can deny this; and I think you overlook that feature of your case. If, however, your counsel has any good reason to offer why sentence should not now be pronounced, the court will hear it. There is no impatience on the part of justice, which would much rather draw in than stretch forth its arm. Perhaps, Mary Monson, you might do well to leave to your counsel the objections you wish to urge, and let them be presented to us in a form that we can recognize."

"I see no great use in deferring the sentence," Dunscomb remarked, quietly enough for the circumstances. "It must be pronounced; and any question of law, should one occur to my mind, though I confess none does at present, can as well be raised after this ceremony as before."

"I am disposed to wait, if a good reason can be urged for the delay. I will acknowledge that the case is one involved in a great deal of doubt and uncertainty, and am much inclined to do all the law will sanction. Still, I leave you to decide on your own course."

"In my judgment, may it please your honor, we shall have to go to the executive, and it were, perhaps, better to get all the most revolting parts of the case over, while the accused—"

"Convicted, Mr. Dunscomb—it is a distinction painful to make, but one that cannot now be avoided."

"I beg pardon of the court—convicted."

"Yes," said Mary Monson, solemnly, "I am convicted, and of the revolting crime of murder. All my hopes of a triumphant acquittal are blasted; and, whatever may be the termination of this extraordinary affair, a dark spot will always rest on my name. Sir, I am as innocent of this crime as the youngest child in your county. I may have been willful, perverse, ill-judging, unwise, and have a hundred other failings; but neither Peter nor Dorothy Goodwin did I ever harm. I had not been long in the house before I discovered that the old couple were not happy together. They quarreled often, and bitterly. The wife was managing, dictatorial, and sordidly covetous, while he used every shilling he could obtain for the purchase of liquors. His mind was affected by his debauches, and he driveled. In this state, he came to me for sympathy and advice. There were passages in my own past life, short as it has been, which disposed me to feel for one who was not happy in the married state.

"It is no matter what my own experience has been; I had sympathy for that poor man. So far from wishing to do him harm, I desired to do him good. I advised him to quit the house, and live apart from his wife, for a time, at least; and this he consented to do, if I would furnish him with the means. Those means I promised; and, that he might not suffer, being of only feeble intellect, and in order to keep him from liquor, I had directed two of my agents to come to the house early in the morning of the very day that the fire happened, that they might convey Peter Goodwin to another residence, where he would be secret and safe, until his wife might repent of her treatment of him. It was fortunate for me that I had done this. Those two men, servants of my own, in the dress of countrymen, were the instruments of saving my life; without their aid, I should have perished in the flames. What they did, and how they did it, it would be premature now to say. Alas! alas! I have not been acquitted as I desired to be, and a dark shadow will forever rest on my name!"

For the first time, a doubt of the sanity of the prisoner crossed the mind of the judge. It was not so much the incoherence of her language, as her eye, the flushed cheek, and a certain air of stealthy cunning, that awakened this distrust. Nevertheless, Mary Monson's manner was sincere, her language chosen and perfectly proper, and her explanations not without force. There was something so strange, however, in a portion of her statements; so irreconcilable with a sound discretion, that, taken with the little which had come to light concerning this singular woman's past life, the doubt arose.

"Perhaps it were better, Mr. District Attorney," the judge observed, "if we delay the sentence."

"As you honor may think fit. The State is not overanxious for life."

"What say you, Mr. Dunscomb—shall there be delay, or shall I sentence?"

"As the sentence *must* come, the sooner it is over the better. We have no ground on which to carry up the case, the jury being judges of the facts. Our principal hope must be in the discretion of the governor."

"Mary Monson," continued the judge, evidently treating the affair as purely a matter of form, "you have been tried for feloniously depriving Peter Goodwin of his life—"

"I never did it," interrupted the prisoner, in a voice so low as to be melodious, yet so clear as to be audible as the sound of a clarion. "These men have been influenced by the rumors they have heard, and were not fit to act as my judges. Men should have minds superior to mere reports to sit in that box."

"My duty is to pronounce the sentence of the law. After a fair trial, and, so far as it appears to us, by an impartial jury, you have been found guilty. For reasons that are of sufficient weight to my mind, I shall not dwell on the character of the awful change you will have to undergo, should this decree be put in force, but confine myself simply to the duty of pronouncing the sentence of the law, which is this: that you be carried back to the jail, and there be guarded until Friday, the sixth day of September next, when, between the hours of twelve and two P.M., you be carried to the place of execution, and hanged by the neck, until you are dead—and God have mercy on your soul!"

A shudder passed through the audience, at hearing language like this applied to a person of Mary Monson's appearance, education and sex. This feeling might have manifested itself more strongly, had not Mrs. Horton attracted attention to herself, by forcing her way through the crowd, until she stood within the bar. Here the good woman, accustomed to bandy words with her guests, did not scruple to make her presence known to the court, by calling out—

"They tell me, your honor, that Mary Monson has just been found guilty of the murder of Peter Goodwin?"

"It is so, my good woman—but that case is ended. Mr. Sheriff, remove the prisoner—time is precious—"

"Yes, your honor, and so is eternity. Mary Monson is no more guilty of taking the life of Peter Goodwin than I am guilty. I've always said some great disgrace would befall our juries, one of these days, and now my prophecy will come true. Dukes is disgraced. Constable, let that poor man come within the bar."

The driveling creature who entered the room of McBrain tottered forward, when twenty voices cried aloud the name of *"Peter Goodwin."* Every word that Mary Monson had stated was true!

CHAPTER XXVIII.

"Now Marcia, now call up to thy assistance,
Thy wonted strength and constancy of mind;
Thou canst not put it to a greater trial."
—ADDISON.

BENCH, bar, jury, witnesses, and audience were all astounded. The trial had been carried on in the most perfect good faith; and not a human being but the few who had felt the force of McBrain's testimony doubted of the death of the individual who now appeared alive, if not well, in open court. The reader can better imagine than we can describe the effects of a resurrection so entirely unexpected.

When the confusion naturally produced by such a scene had a little subsided; when all had actually seen, and many had actually felt, the supposed murdered man, as if to assure themselves of his being really in the flesh, order was restored; and the court and bar began to reflect on the course next to be pursued.

"I suppose, Mr. District Attorney," observed his honor, "there is no mistake in the person of this individual; but it were better if we had an affidavit or two. Will you walk this way, sir?"

A long, private conference now took place between the public prosecutor and the judge. Each expressed his astonishment at the result, as well as some indignation at the deception which had been practiced on the court. This indignation was a little mollified by the impression, now common to both, that Mary Monson was a person not exactly in her right mind. There was so much deception practiced among persons accused of crimes, however, and in connection with this natural infirmity, that public functionaries like themselves were necessarily very cautious in admitting the plea. The most offensive part of the whole affair was the discredit brought on the justice of Dukes! It was not in nature for these individuals to be insensible to the sort of disgrace the reappearance of Peter Goodwin entailed on the county and circuit; and there was a very natural desire to wipe off the stain. The conference lasted until the affidavits to establish the facts connected with Goodwin's case were ready.

"Had these affidavits been presented earlier," said his honor, as soon as the papers were read, "sentence would not have been pronounced. The case is novel, and I shall want a little time to reflect on the course I am to take. The sentence must be gotten rid of by some means or other; and it shall be my care to see it done. I hope, brother Dunscomb, the counsel for the accused have not been parties to this deception?"

"I am as much taken by surprise as your honor can possibly be," returned the party addressed, with earnestness, "not having had the most remote suspicion of the existence of the man said to have been murdered; else would all the late proceedings have been spared. As to the course to be taken next, I would respectfully suggest that the Code be examined. It is an *omnium gatherum;* and must contain something to tell us how to undo all we have done."

"It were better for all parties had there so been. There are still two indictments pending over Mary Monson: one for the arson, and the other for the murder of Dorothy Goodwin. Mr. District Attorney feels the necessity of trying these cases, or one of them at least, in vindication of the justice of the State and county; and I am inclined to think that, under all the circumstances, this course should be taken. I trust we shall have no more surprises, and that Dorothy Goodwin will be brought forward at once, if still living —time is precious."

"Dorothy Goodwin is dead," said Mary Monson, solemnly, "Poor woman! she was called away suddenly, and in her sins. Little fear of her ever coming here to flout your justice."

"It may be well to caution your client, Mr. Dunscomb, against hasty and indiscreet admissions. Let the accused be arraigned, and a jury be impaneled. Which case do you choose to move on, Mr. District Attorney?"

Dunscomb saw that his honor was offended, and much in earnest. He was offended himself, and half disposed to throw up his brief; but he felt for the situation of a lovely and defenseless woman. Then his doubts touching his client's sanity began to take the character of certainty; and he saw how odious it would be to abandon one so afflicted in her emergeny. He hinted his suspicion to the court; but was told that the fact, under all the circumstances of the case, was one properly for the jury. After reflection, the advocate determined not to desert his trust.

We pass over the preliminary proceedings. A jury was impaneled with very little difficulty; not a challenge having been made. It was composed, in part, of those who had been in the box on the late occasion; and in part of new men. There was an air of earnestness and business about them all that Timms did not like, but it was too late to raise objections. To own the truth, the senior counsel cared much less than before for the result; feeling satisfied that his contemplated application at Albany would meet with consideration. It is true, Mary Monson was no anti-renter. She could not come forward with her demand for mercy with hands dyed in the blood of an officer of that public which lives under the deception of fancying it rules the land; murderers who added to their crimes the hateful and pestilent fraud of attempting to cloak robbery in the garb of righteous liberty; nor could she come sustained by numbers around the ballot-box, and bully the executive into acts which the reason and conscience of every honest man condemn; but Dunscomb believed that she might come with the plea of a being visited by the power of her Creator, in constituting her as she was, a woman not morally accountable for her acts.

All the leading facts, as shown on the former trial, were shown on this. When the country practitioners were called on to give their opinions concerning the effect of the blow, they necessarily became subject to the cross-examination of the counsel for the prisoner, who did not spare them.

"Were you examined, sir, in the late trial of Mary Monson, for the murder of Peter Goodwin?" demanded Dunscomb of the first of these modern Galens who was put on the stand.

"I was, sir."

"What did you say on that occasion"—looking at his notes of the other trial—"touching the sex of the persons to whom those skeletons were thought to have belonged?"

"I said *believed*—not *knew*, but *believed*, they were the remains of Peter and Dorothy Goodwin."

"Did you not use stronger language than that?"

"Not that I remember. I may have done so; but I do not remember it."

"Did you not say you had '*no doubt*' that those were the remains of Peter and Dorothy Goodwin?"

"I may have said as much as that. Now you mention the words, I believe I did."

"Do you think so now?"

"Certainly not. I cannot think so, after what I have seen."

"Do you know Peter Goodwin, personally?"

"Very well. I have practiced many years in this neighborhood."

"Whom then do you say that this unfortunate man here, whom we see alive, though a driveler, really is?"

"Peter Goodwin—he who was thought to have been murdered. We are all liable to mistakes."

"You have testified in chief that, in your judgment, the two persons, of whom we have the remains here in court, were stunned at least, if not absolutely killed, by the blow that you think fractured each of their skulls. Now I would ask if you think the prisoner at the bar possesses the physical force necessary to enable her to strike such a blow?"

"That would depend on the instrument she used. A human skull may be fractured easily enough by a moderate blow struck by a heavy instrument."

"What sort of instrument, for instance?"

"A sword—a bar of iron—or anything that has weight and force."

"Do you believe those fractures were given by the same blow?"

"I do. By one and the same blow."

"Do you think that Mary Monson possesses the strength necessary to cause those two fractures at a single blow?"

Witness had no opinion on the subject.

"Are the fractures material?"

"Certainly—and must have required a heavy blow to produce them."

This was all that could be got from either of the witnesses on that material point. As respected McBrain, he was subsequently examined in reference to the same facts. Dunscomb made good use of this witness, who now commanded the respect of all present. In the first place he was adroitly offered to the jury, as the professional man who had, from the first, given it as his opinion that both the skeletons were those of females; and this in the face of all the collected wisdom of Dukes County; an opinion that was now rendered so probable as almost to amount to certainty. He (Dunscomb) believed most firmly that the remains were those of Dorothy Goodwin and the German woman who was missing.

"Have you examined these skeletons, Dr. McBrain?" Dunscomb asked.

"I have, sir; and carefully, since the late trial."

"How do you think the persons to whom they belonged came to their deaths?"

"I find fractures in the skulls of both. If they lie now as they did when the remains were found (a fact that had been proved by several witnesses), I am of the opinion that a single blow inflicted the injuries on both; it may be that blow was not sufficient to produce death; but it must have produced a stupor, or insensibility, which would prevent the parties from seeking refuge against the effects of the flames—"

"Is the learned witness brought to sum up the cause?" demanded Williams, with one of those demoniacal sneers of his, by means of which he sometimes carried off a verdict. "I wish to know, that I may take notes of the course of this argument."

McBrain drew back, shocked and offended. He was naturally diffident, as his friend used to admit, in everything but wives; and as regarded them "he had the impudence of the devil. Ned would never give up the trade until he had married a dozen, if the law would see him out in it. He ought to have been a follower of the great Mohammed, who made it a point to take a new wife at almost every new moon!" The judge did not like this sneer of Williams; and this so much the less, because, in common with all around him, he had imbibed a profound respect for the knowledge of the witness. It is true, he was very much afraid of the man, and dreaded his influence at the polls; but he really had too much conscience to submit to everything. A judge may yet have a conscience—if the Code will let him.

"This is very irregular, Mr. Williams, not to say improper," his honor mildly remarked. "The witness has said no more than he has a right to say; and the court must see him protected. Proceed with your testimony, sir."

"I have little more to say, if it please the court," resumed McBrain, too much dashed to regain his self-possession in a moment. As this was all Williams wanted, he permitted him to proceed in his own way; and all the doctor had to say was soon told to the jury. The counsel for the prosecution manifested great tact in not cross-examining the witness at all. In a subsequent stage of the trial, Williams had the impudence to insinuate to the jury that they did not attach sufficient importance to his testimony to subject him to this very customary ordeal.

But the turning point of this trial, as it had been that of the case which preceded it, was the evidence connected with the piece of money. As the existence of the notch was now generally known, it was easy enough to recognize the coin that had been found in Mary Monson's purse; thus depriving the accused of one of her simplest and best means of demonstrating the ignorance of the witnesses. The notch, however, was Mrs. Burton's great mark, under favor of which her very material testimony was now given as it had been before.

Dunscomb was on the point of commencing the cross-examination, when the clear melodious voice of Mary Monson herself was heard for the first time since the commencement of the trial.

"Is it permitted to *me* to question this witness?" demanded the prisoner.

"Certainly," answered the judge. "It is the right of every one who is arraigned by the country. Ask *any* question that you please."

This was a somewhat liberal decision as to the right of cross-examining, and the accused put on it a construction almost as broad as the privilege. As for the witness, it was very apparent she had little taste for the scrutiny that she probably foresaw she was about to undergo; and her countenance, attitude and answers each and all betrayed how much distaste she had for the whole procedure. As permission was obtained, however, the prisoner did not hesitate to proceed.

"Mrs. Burton," said Mary Monson, adopting, as well as she knew how, the manner of the gentlemen of the bar, "I wish you to tell the court and jury *when* you first saw the notched piece of money?"

"When I first saw it? I saw it first when Aunt Dolly first showed it to me," answered the witness.

Most persons would have been dissatisfied with this answer, and would probably have caused the question to be repeated in some other form; but Mary Monson seemed content, and went on putting her questions, just as if she had obtained answers to meet her views.

"Did you examine it well?"

"As well as I desired to. There was nothing to prevent it."

"Did you know it immediately, on seeing it in my purse?"

"Certainly—as soon as I saw the notch."

"Did Mrs. Goodwin point out the notch to you, or did you point out the notch to her?"

"She pointed it out to me; she feared that the notch might lessen the value of the coin."

"All this I have heard before; but I now ask you, Mrs. Burton, in the name of that Being whose eye is everywhere, did you not yourself put that piece of money in my purse, when it was passing from hand to hand, and take out of it the piece without a notch? Answer me, as you have a regard for your soul?"

Such a question was altogether out of the rules regulating the queries that may be put to witnesses, an answer in the affirmative going directly to criminate the respondent; but the earnest manner, solemn tones, and, we may add, illuminated countenance of Mary Monson, so far imposed on the woman, that she quite lost sight of her rights, if she ever knew them. What is much more remarkable, neither of the counsel for the prosecution interposed an objection. The district attorney was willing that justice should have its way; and Williams began to think it might be prudent to manifest less anxiety for a conviction than he had done in the case in which the party murdered had been resuscitated. The judge was entranced by the prisoner's manner.

"I believe I have as much regard for my soul as any of the neighbors have for theirs," answered Mrs. Burton, sullenly.

"Let us learn that in your reply. Did you, or did you not, change those pieces of gold?"

"Perhaps I might, It's hard to say, when so much was said and done."

"How came you with the other piece, with which to make the exchange? Answer, Sarah Burton, as you fear God?"

The witness trembled like an aspen-leaf. So remarkable was the scene, that no one thought of interfering; but the judge, the bar, and the jury, seemed equally willing to leave the two females to themselves, as the most efficient means of extorting the truth. Mary Monson's color heightened; her mien and countenance grew, as it were, with the occasion; while Sarah Burton's became paler and paler, as each question was put, and the reply pressed.

"I can have money, I hope, as well as other folks," answered the witness.

"That is no reply. How came you with the piece of gold that is notched, that you could exchange it for the piece which was not notched, and which was the one really found in my purse? Answer me that, Sarah Burton; here, where we both stand in the presence of our great Creator?"

"There's no need of your pressing a body so awfully—I don't believe it's law."

"I repeat the question—or I will answer it for you. When you fired the house—"

The woman screamed, and raised her hands in natural horror.

"I never set the house on fire," she cried. "It took from the stove-pipe in the garret, where it had taken twice before."

"How can you know *that*, unless you saw it? How see it, unless present?"

"I was *not* there, and did not see it; but I know the garret had caught twice before from that cook-stove pipe. Aunt Dolly was very wrong to neglect it as she did."

"And the blows on the head—who struck those blows, Sarah Burton?"

"How can I tell? I wasn't there—no one but a fool could believe *you* have strength to do it."

"How, then, *was* it done? Speak—I see it in your mind?"

"I saw the plowshare lying on the heads of the skeletons; and I saw Moses Steen throw it off, in the confusion of first raking the embers. Moses will be likely to remember it, if sent for, and questioned."

Here was a most important fact elicited under the impulse of self-justification; and a corresponding expression of surprise passed, in a murmur, through the audience. The eye of Mary Monson kindled with triumph; and she continued with renewed powers of command over the will and conscience of the witness.

"This is well, Sarah Burton—it is right, and what you ought to say. You think that the fire was accidental, and that the fractured skulls came from the fall of the plow?"

"I do. I know that the plow stood in the garret, directly over the bed, and the stove-pipe passed quite near it. There was an elbow in that pipe, and the danger was at that elbow."

"This is well; and the eye above looks on you with less displeasure, Sarah Burton"—as this was said, the witness turned her eyes timidly upward, as if to assure herself of the fact. "Speak holy truth, and it will soon become benignant and forgiving. Now tell me how you came by the stocking and its contents?"

"The stocking!" said the witness, starting, and turning white as a sheet. "Who says I took the stocking?"

"I do. I know it by that secret intelligence which has been given me to discover truth. Speak, then, Sarah, and tell the court and jury the truth, the whole truth, and nothing but the truth."

"Nobody saw me take it; and nobody can say I took it."

"Therein you are mistaken. You *were* seen to take it. I saw it, for one; but there was another who saw it, with its motive, whose eye is ever on us. Speak, then, Sarah, and keep nothing back."

"I meant no harm, if I did take it. There was so many folks about. I was afraid that some stranger might lay hands on it. That's all."

"You were seen to unlock the drawers, as you stood alone near the bureau, in the confusion and excitement of the finding of the skeletons. You did it stealthily, Sarah Burton."

"I was afraid some one might snatch the stocking from me. I always meant to give it up, as soon as the law said to whom it belongs. Davis wants it, but I'm not sure it is his."

"What key did you use? Keep nothing back."

"One of my own. My keys unlocked many of Aunt Dolly's drawers. She knew it, and never found any fault with it. Why should she? Her keys unlocked *mine!*"

"Another word—where is that stocking, and where are its contents?"

"Both are safe in the third drawer of my own bureau, and here is the key," taking one from her bosom. "I put them there for security, as no one opens that drawer but myself."

Timms took the key from the unresisting hand of the woman, and followed by Williams, Davis, and one or two more, he left the court-house. At that instant, Sarah Burton fainted. In the confusion of removing her into another room, Mary Monson resumed her seat.

"Mr. District Attorney, it can hardly be your intention to press this indictment any further?" observed the judge, wiping his eyes, and much delighted with the unexpected termination of the affair.

The functionary addressed was glad enough to be rid of his unwelcome office, and at once signified his willingness to enter a *nolle prosequi,* by an application to the bench, in the case of the arson, and to submit to an acquittal in that now being traversed. After a brief charge from the judge, the jury gave a verdict of acquittal without leaving the box; and just as this was done, Timms and his companions returned, bring with them the much-talked-of stocking.

It required months completely to elucidate the whole affair; but so much is already known, and this part of our subject being virtually disposed of, we may as well make a short summary of the facts, as they were already in proof, or as they have since come to light.

The fire was accidental, as has been recently ascertained by circumstances it is unnecessary to relate. Goodwin had left his wife, the night before the accident, and she had taken the German woman to sleep with her. As the garret floor above this pair was consumed, the plow fell, its share inflicting the blow which stunned them, if it did not inflict a greater injury. That part of the house was first consumed, and the skeletons were found, as has been related, side by side. In the confusion of the scene, Sarah Burton had little difficulty in opening the drawer and removing the stocking. She fancied herself unseen; but Mary Monson observed the movement, though she had then no idea what was abstracted. The unfortunate delinquent maintains that her intention, at the time, was good; or, that her sole object was to secure the gold; but is obliged to confess that the possession of the treasure gradually excited her cupidity, until she began to hope that this hoard might eventually become her own. The guilty soonest suspect guilt. As to "the pure, all things are pure," so it is with the innocent, who are the least inclined to suspect others of wicked actions. Thus was it with Mrs. Burton. In the commission of a great wrong herself, she had little difficulty in supposing that Mary Monson was the sort of person that rumor made her out to be. She saw no great harm, then, in giving a shove to the descending culprit. When looking into the stocking, she had seen, and put in her own pocket, the notched piece, as a curiosity, there being nothing more unusual in the guilty thus incurring unnecessary risks, than there is in the moth's temerity in fluttering around the candle.

When the purse of Mary Monson was examined, as usually happens on such occasions, we had almost said as *always* happens, in the management of cases that are subsequently to form a part of the justice of the land, much less attention was paid to the care of that purse than ought to have been bestowed on it. Profiting by the neglect, Sarah Burton exchanged the notched coin for the perfect piece, unobserved, as she again fancied; but once more the watchful eye of Mary Monson was on her. The first time the woman was observed by the last, it was accidentally; but suspicion once aroused, it was natural enough to keep a lookout on the suspected party. The act was seen, and at the moment that the accused thought happy, the circumstance was brought to bear on the trial. Sarah Burton maintains that, at first, her sole intention was to exchange the imperfect for the perfect coin; and that she was induced to swear to the piece subsequently produced, as that found on Mary Monson's person, as a literal fact, ignorant of what might be its consequences. Though the devil doubtless leads us on, step by step, deeper and deeper, into crime and sin, it is probable that, in this particular, the guilty woman applied a flattering unction to her conscience that the truth would have destroyed.

Great was the wonder, and numberless were the paragraphs that this unexpected issue of the "great Biberry murders" produced. As respects the last, anything that will fill a column is a god-send, and the falsehood has even a value that is not to be found in the truth, as its contradiction will help along quite as much as the original statements. If the public could only be brought to see what a different thing publicity becomes in the hands of those who turn it to *profit,* from what it is thought to be by those who fancy it is merely a mode of circulating facts, a great step toward a much-needed reformation would be taken, by confining the last within their natural limits.

Mary Monson's name passed from one end of the Union to the other, and thousands heard and read of this extraordinary woman, who never had the smallest clew to her real character or subsequent history. How few reflected on the defects of the system that condemned her to the gallows on insufficient testimony; or, under another phase of prejudice, might have acquitted her when guilty! The random decisions of the juries, usually well-meaning, but so rarely discriminating or as intelligent as they ought to be, attract very little attention beyond the bar; and even the members of that often strike a balance in error, with which they learn to be content; gaining in one cause as much as they lose in another.

There was a strong disposition in the people assembled at Biberry, on the occasion of the trial, to make a public spectacle of Mary Monson. The right to do this, with all things in heaven and earth, seems to belong to "republican simplicity," which is beginning to rule the land with a rod of iron. Unfortunately for this feeling, the subject of momentary sympathy was not a person likely to allow such a license. She did not believe, because she had endured one set of atrocious wrongs, that she was bound to submit to as many more as gaping vulgarity might see fit to inflict. She sought the protection of good Mrs. Gott and her jail, some forms being necessary before the sentence of death could be legally gotten rid of. In vain were the windows again crowded, with the virtuous wish of seeing how Mary Monson *looked,* now she was acquitted, just as they had been previously thronged in order to ascertain how she looked when there was a chance of her being condemned to the gallows. The most extraordinary part of the affair was the circumstance that the harp became popular; the very sentiment, act, or thing that, in one condition of the common mind, is about to be "cut down and cast into the fire," becoming, in another, all that is noble, commendable, or desirable. The crowd about the windows of the jail, for the first few hours after the acquittal, was dying to hear the prisoner sing and play, and would gladly have tolerated the harp and a "foreign tongue" to be thus gratified.

But Mary Monson was safe from all intrusion, under the locks of the delighted Mrs. Gott. This kind-hearted person kissed her prisoner, over and over again, when she admitted her within the gallery, and then she went outside, and assured several of the more respectable persons in the crowd how thoroughly she had been persuaded from the first of the innocence of her friend. The circumstances of this important trial rendered Mrs. Gott a very distinguished person herself, in that crowd, and never was a woman happier than she while delivering her sentiments on the recent events.

"It's altogether the most foolish trial we have ever had in Dukes, though they tell me foolish trials are getting to be only too common," said the kind-hearted wife of the sheriff, addressing half a dozen of the more respectable of the crowd. "It gave me a big fright, I will own. When Gott was elected sheriff, I did hope he would escape all executions but debt executions. The more he has of *them* the better. It's bad enough to escort thieves to Sing Sing; but the gallows is a poor trade for a decent man to meddle with. Then, to have the very first sentence one against Mary Monson, who is as much above such a punishment as virtue is above vice. When I heard those dreadful words, I felt as if a cord was round my own neck. But I had faith to the last. Mary has always told me that she should be acquitted, and here it has all come true, at last."

"Do you know, Mrs. Gott," said one of her friends, "it is reported that this woman—or lady, I suppose one must *now* call her—has been in the habit of quitting the jail whenever she saw fit?"

"Hu-s-h, neighbor Brookes; there is no need of alarming the county! I believe you are right; though it was all done without my knowledge, or it never would have been permitted. It only shows the power of money. The locks are as good as any in the State; yet Mary certainly did find means, unbeknown to me, to open them. It can't be called breaking jail, since she always came back! I had a good fright the first time I heard of it, but use reconciles us to all things. I never let Gott into the secret, though he's responsible, as he calls it, for all his prisoners."

"Well, when a matter turns out happily, it does no good to be harping on it always."

Mrs. Gott assented, and in this case, as in a hundred others, the end was made to justify the means. But Mary Monson was felt to be an exception to all rules, and there was no longer any disposition to cavil at any of her proceedings. Her innocence had been established so very triumphantly, that every person regarded her vagaries and strange conduct with indulgence.

At that very moment, when Mrs. Gott was haranguing her neighbors at the door of the jail, Dunscomb was closeted with Michael Millington at the inn; the young man having returned at hot-speed only as the court adjourned. He had been successful, notwithstanding his original disappointment, and had ascertained all about the hitherto mysterious prisoner of the Biberry jail. Mary Monson was, as Dunscomb suspected, Mildred Millington by birth—Mme. de Larocheforte by marriage — and she was the granddaughter of the very woman to whom he had been betrothed in youth. Her insanity was not distinctly recognized, perhaps could not have been legally established, though it was strongly suspected by many who knew her intimately, and was a source of great uneasiness with all who felt an interest in her welfare. Her marriage was unhappy, and it was supposed she had taken up her abode in the cottage of the Goodwins to avoid her husband. The command of money gave her a power to do very much as she pleased, and, though the breath of calumny had never yet blown its withering blast on her name, she erred in many things that are duties as grave as that of being chaste. The laws came in aid of her whims and caprices. There is no mode by which an errant wife can be made to perform her duties in boldly experimenting New York, though she can claim a support and protection from her husband. The "cup-and-saucer" law comes in aid of this power, and the men who cannot keep their wives in the chains of Hymen in virtue of the affections. may just as well submit, with a grace, to be the victims of an ill-judging and most treacherous regard for the rights of what are called the weaker sex.

CHAPTER XXIX.

"Why wilt thou add to all the griefs I suffer,
Imaginary ills, and fancied tortures?"—CATO.

THE scene must now be shifted to Rattletrap. Biberry was deserted. Even the rumors with which its streets had been so lately filled were already forgotten. None have memories as frail as the gossip. Not only does this class of persons—and a numerous class it is, including nearly all whose minds are not fitted to receive more elevated materials —not only, we say, does this class of persons overlook the contradictions and absurdities of the stories they repeat, but they forget the stories themselves almost as soon as heard. Such was now the case at Biberry. Scarce an individual could be found in the place who would acknowledge that he or she had ever heard that Mary Monson was connected with robbers, or who could recollect that he once fancied the accused guilty.

We may as well say here, that nothing has ever been done with Sarah Burton. She is clearly guilty; but the law, in these times of progress, disdains to pursue the guilty. Their crimes are known; and of what use can it be to expose those whom every one can see are offenders? No, it is the innocent who have most reason to dread the law. *They* can be put to trouble, cost, vexation and loss, if they cannot be exactly condemned. We see how thousands regard the law in a recent movement in the Legislature, by which suits have been ordered to try the titles of most of the large landed proprietors, with the very honest and modest proposal annexed, that their cases shall be prejudged, and the landlords deprived of the means of defending themselves, by sequestering their rents! Everybody says this is the freest country on earth; the only country that is truly free; but we must be permitted to say, that such a law, like twenty more that have been passed in the same interest within the last ten years, savors a good deal of the character of a ukase.

Our characters, with the exception of Mr. and Mrs. McBrain, were now assembled at Rattletrap. Dunscomb had ascertained all it was necessary to know concerning Mildred, and had taken the steps necessary to protect her. Of her qualified insanity he did not entertain a doubt; though it was a madness so concealed by the blandishments of education and the graces of a refined woman that few saw it, and fewer still wished to believe it true. On most subjects this unhappy lady was clear-minded and intelligent enough, more especially on that of money; for, while her expenditures were generous, and her largesses most liberal, she manifested wonderful sagacity in taking care of her property. It was this circumstance that rendered it so difficult to take any steps to deprive her of its control; though

Dunscomb had seen enough, in the course of the recent trial, to satisfy him that such a measure ought to be resorted to in the interest of her own character.

It was in cunning, and in all the low propensities connected with that miserable quality, that Mildred Millington, as she now insisted on calling herself, most betrayed her infirmity. Many instances of it have been incidentally related in the course of our narrative, however unpleasant such an exhibition has been. There is nothing more repugnant to the principles or tases of the right thinking and right feeling, than the practices which cunning engenders. Timms, however, was a most willing agent in all the schemes of his client; though some of her projects had puzzled him by their elaborate duplicity, as much as they had astounded him by their boldness.

These were the schemes that had their origin in obliquity of mind. Still they were not without merit in the eyes of Timms, who was cunning without being mad.

Before quitting Biberry, Timms was liberally paid and dismissed. Dunscomb explained to him the situation of his handsome client, without adverting to the state of her mind, when the attorney at once caught at the chances of a divorce. Among the other "ways of the hour," that of dissolving the marriage tie has got to be a sort of fashionable mania. Neither time, nor duties, nor children, seem to interpose any material obstacle; and, if our own laws do not afford the required facilities, those of some of our more liberal neighbors do. Timms keeps this principle in his mind, and is at this moment ruminating on the means by which he can liberate his late client from her present chains, and bind her anew in some of his own forging. It is scarcely necessary to add, that Mildred troubles herself very little in the premises, so far as this covert lover is concerned.

The ridicule of Williams was at first the sorest portion of Timms's disappointment. Bachelors alike, and rivals for popular favor, these two worthies had long been looking out for advantageous marriages. Each had the sagacity to see that his chances of making a more eligible connection were increasing slowly, and that it was a great thing for a rising man to ascend without dragging after him a wife chosen from among those that prop the base of the great social ladder. It was nuts to one of these competitors for the smiles of the ladies to discover that his rival was in love with a married woman; and this so much the more, because the prospects of Timms's success arising from his seeming intimacy with the fair occupant of the jail had given Williams a very serious fright. Place two men in competition, no matter in what, and all their energies become concentrated in rivalry. Again and again had these two individuals betrayed their mutual jealousy; and now that one of them had placed himself in a position so false, not to say ridiculous, the other did not fail to enjoy his disappointment to the top of his bent. It was in this manner that Saucy Williams took his revenge for the defeat in the trial.

Mrs. Gott was also at Rattletrap. Dunscomb retained much of his original tenderness for Mildred, the grandmother of his guest of that name, and he granted her descendant every indulgence she could ask. Among other things, one of the requests of the liberated prisoner was to be permitted to manifest this sense of her gratitude for the many acts of kindness received from the wife of the sheriff. Gott, accordingly, was left to take care of himself, while his nice little companion was transported to a scene that she found altogether novel, of a temporary residence in a gentleman's dwelling. Sarah's housekeeping, Sarah's good nature, attentions, neatness, attire and attractions, would have been themes to monopolize all of the good little woman's admiration, had not Anna Updyke, then on a visit at Rattletrap, quite fairly come in for her full share. She might almost be said to be in love with both.

It was just after breakfast that Mildred locked an arm in that of Anna, and led her young friend by one of the wooded paths that run along the shores of the Hudson, terminating in a summer-house, with a most glorious view. In this there was nothing remarkable; the eye rarely resting on any of the "bits" that adorn the banks of that noble stream, without taking in beauties to enchant it. But to all these our two lovely young women were momentarily as insensible as they were to the fact that their own charming forms, floating among shrubbery as fragrant as themselves, added in no slight degree to the beauty of the scene. In manner, Mildred was earnest, if not ardent, and a little excited; on the other hand, Anna was placid, though sensitive, changing color without ceasing, as her thoughts were drawn nearer and nearer to that theme which now included the great object of her existence.

"Your uncle brought me letters from town last evening, Anna, dear," commenced the liberated lady; "one of them is from Monsieur de Larocheforte. Is that not strange?"

"What is there so strange in a husband writing to a wife? To me it seems the most natural thing in the world."

"It does? I am surprised to hear you say so—you, Anna, whom I regarded as so truly my friend. I have discarded Monsieur de Larocheforte, and he ought to respect my pleasure."

"It would have been better, my dear mamma, had you discarded him before marriage, instead of after."

"Ah—your dear mamma, indeed! I was your school mamma, Anna, and well had it been for me had I been left to finish my education in my own country. Then I should have escaped this most unfortunate marriage! Do not marry, Anna—take my advice and never marry. Matrimony is unsuited to ladies."

"How long have you been of this opinion, dear mamma?" asked the young girl, smiling.

"Just as long as I have been made to feel how it crushes a woman's independence, and how completely it gives her a master, and how very, very humiliating and depressing is the bondage it inflicts. Do you not feel the force of my reasons?"

"I confess I do not," answered Anna, in a subdued, yet clear and distinct voice. "I see nothing humiliating or depressing in a woman's submission to her husband. It is the law of nature, and why should we wish to alter it? My mother has ever inculcated such opinions, and you will excuse me if I say I think the Bible does, also."

"The Bible! Yes, that is a good book, though I am afraid it is very little read in France. I ought, perhaps, to say, 'read very little by strangers resident in France.' The Frenchwomen themselves are not one-half as negligent of their duties, in this respect, as are the strangers who go to reside among them. When the roots, that have grown to any size in their native soil, are violently transplanted to another, it is not often that the tree obtains its proper dimensions and grace. I wish I had never seen France, Anna, in which case I should never have been Madame de Larocheforte—*vicomtesse*, by the old law, and I am afraid it was that idle appellation that entrapped me. How much more truly respectable I should have been as Mrs. John Smith, or Mrs. John Brown, or Mrs. David Smith, the wife of a countryman, if I must be a wife at all!"

"Choose at least some name of higher pretension," said Anna, laughing. "Why not a Mrs. Van Rensselaer, or a Mrs. Van Cortlandt, or a Mrs. Livingston, or a Mrs. Somebody else, of one of our good old families?"

"Families! Do you know, child, it is treason to talk of families in this age of anti-rentism. They tell me that the man who makes an estate may enjoy it, should he happen to know how, and this, though he may have cheated all he ever dealt with, in order to become rich; but, that he who inherits an estate has no claim. It is his tenants who have the high moral claim to his father's property."

"I know nothing of all this, and would rather talk of things I understand."

"By which you mean wedlock and its cares! No, my dear, you little understand what matrimony is, or how much humiliation is required of us women to become wives, or you would never think of marrying."

"I have never told you that I *do* think of marrying—that is, not much."

"There spoke your honest nature, which will not permit even an unintended deception. This it was that so much attached me to you as a child; for though I am not very ingenuous myself, I can admire the quality in another."

"This admission does not exactly prove the truth of your words, mamma!" said Anna, smiling.

"No matter—let us talk of matrimony. Has John Wilmeter proposed to you, Anna?"

This was a home question; no wonder the young lady started. After a short, musing pause, however, the native candor of Anna Updyke prevailed, and she admitted that he had.

"Thank you for this confidence; but you must go further. Remember, I am your mamma. Is the gentleman accepted?"

A rosy blush, succeeded by a nod of the head, was the answer.

"I am sorry I was not consulted before all this happened; though I have managed my own matters so ill, as to have very few claims to your confidence. You scarce know what you undertake, my child."

"I undertake to become Jack Wilmeter's wife," answered the betrothed, in a very low but a very firm voice; "and I hope I shall make him a good one. Most of all, do I pray to be obedient and submissive."

"To no man that breathes, Anna!—no, to no man breathing! It is *their* business to submit to *us*; not we to them!"

"This is not my reading of the great rule of woman's conduct. In my view of our duties it is the part of woman to be affectionate, mild, patient, and sympathizing—if necessary, forgiving. I firmly believe that, in the end, such a woman cannot fail to be as happy as is permitted to us to be, here on earth."

"Forgiving!" repeated Mildred, her eyes flashing, "yes, that is a word often used, yet how few truly practice its teachings? Why should I forgive any one that has wronged me? Our nature tells us to resent, to punish, if necessary, as you say —to revenge."

A slight shudder passed through the frame of Anna, and she unconsciously moved further from her companion, though their arms still continued locked.

"There must be a great difference between France and America, if revenge is ever taught to a woman as a part of her duty," returned the younger female, now speaking with an earnestness she had not before betrayed; "here, we are told that Christianity forbids the very thought of it, and that to forgive is among the very first of our duties. My great instructor in such things has told me that one of the surest evidences of a hopeful state of the feelings is the banishment of everything like resentment, and a desire to be at peace with all around us—to have a perception that we love the race as beings of our wants and hopes."

"Is this the sort of love, then, with which you give your hand to young Wilmeter?"

Scarlet is not brighter than was the color that now glowed in the cheeks of Anna, stole into her temples, and even diffused itself over her neck and chest. To herself it seemed as if her very hands blushed. Then the power of innocence came to sustain her, and she became calm and steady.

"It is *not* the feeling with which I shall marry John," she said. "Nature has given us another sentiment, and I shall not endeavor to be superior to all of my sex and class. I love John Wilmeter, I own; and I hope to make him happy."

"To be a dutiful, obedient wife, forever studying his tastes and caprices!"

"I trust I shall not be *forever* studying the indulgence of my own. I see nothing degrading to a woman, in her filling the place nature and Christianity have assigned to her, and in her doing her duty as a wife."

"These are not *my* feelings, receiving your terms as you wish them to be understood. But several have told me I ought never to have married; I myself know that I should have been an American, and not a French wife."

"I have ever heard that greater latitude is given to our sex, in France, than in this country."

"That is true in part only. Nothing can exceed the *retenue* of a French girl, or anything that is decent exceed the want of it that is manifested by many Americans. On the other hand, a married woman here has no privileges at all, not even in society; while in France, under an air of great seeming propriety, she does very much as she sees fit. It is a mistake, however, to suppose that faithful wives and devoted mothers, most especially the last, are not to be found all over Europe—in France, in particular."

"I am glad to hear it," cried Anna, with a really gratified air; "it gives me pleasure when I hear of any of our sex behaving as they should behave."

"Should behave! I fear, Anna, a little covert reproach is intended, in that remark. Our estimate of the conduct of our friends must depend on our notions of our own duties. Now, hearken to my manner of reasoning on this subject. In a physical sense, man is strong, woman is weak; while, in a moral sense, woman is strong and man is weak. You admit my premises?"

"The first part of them, certainly," said Anna, laughing, "while I pretend to no knowledge of the last."

"You surely do not believe that John Wilmeter is as pure, ingenuous, good, as you are yourself?"

"I see no reason why he should not be. I am far from certain Jack is not even better."

"It is useless to discuss such a subject with you. The principle of pride is wanting, without which you can never enter into my feelings."

"I am glad it is so. I fancy John will be all the happier for it. Ah! my dear mamma, I never knew any good come of what you call this ' principle of pride.' We are told to be humble and not to be proud. It may be all the better for us females that rulers are given to us here, in the persons of our husbands."

"Anna Updyke, do you marry John Wilmeter with the feeling that he is to rule? You overlook the signs of the times, the ways of the hour, child, if you do aught so weak! Look around you, and see how everybody, almost everything, is becoming independent, our sex included. Formerly, as I have heard elderly persons say, if a woman suffered in her domestic relations, she was compelled to suffer all. The quarrel lasted for a life. Now, no one thinks of being so unreasonably wretched. No, the wronged wife, or even the offended wife—Monsieur de Larocheforte snuffs abominably—abominably—yes, abominably—but no wife is obliged, in these times of independence and reason, to endure a snuffy husband—"

"No," broke in Dunscomb, appearing from an adjoining path, "she has only to pack up her spoons and be off. The Code can never catch her. If it could on one page, my life for it there is a hole for her to get out of its grasp on the next. Your servant, ladies; I have been obliged to overhear more of your conversation than was intended for my ears, perhaps; these paths running so close to each other, and you being so animated—and now, I mean to take an old man's privilege and speak my mind. In the first place, I shall deal with the agreeable. Anna, my love, Jack is a lucky fellow—far luckier than he deserves to be. You carry the right sentiment into wedlock. It is the right of the husband to be the head of his family; and the wife who resists his authority is neither prudent nor a Christian. He may abuse it, it is true; but, even then, so long as criminality is escaped, it were better to submit. I approve of every word you have uttered, dear, and thank you for it all in my nephew's name. And now, Mildred, as one who has a right to advise you, by his avowed love for your grandmother, and recent close connection with yourself, let me tell you what I think of those principles that you avow, and also of the state of things that is so fast growing up in this country. In the first place, he is no true friend of your sex who teaches it this doctrine of independence. I should think —it is true, I am only a bachelor, and have no experience to back me—but, I should think that a woman who truly loves her husband, would find a delight in her dependence—"

"Oh! certainly!" exclaimed Anna— biting her tongue at the next instant, and blushing scarlet at her own temerity.

"I understand you, child, and approve again—but there comes Jack, and I shall have to turn you over to him, that you may receive a good scolding from headquarters, for this abject servitude feeling that you have betrayed. Go—go—his arm is held out already—and harkee, young folk, remember that a new maxim in morals has come in with the Code— 'Principles depend on Circumstances.' That is the rule of conduct nowadays— that, and anti-rentism, and 'republican simplicity,' and the 'cup-and-saucer law,' and — and — yes — and the ever-blessed Code!"

Dunscomb was obliged to stop for breath, which gave the young couple an opportunity to walk away. As for Mildred, she stood collected, extremely ladylike in mien, but with a slight degree of hauteur expressed in her countenance.

"And now, sir, that we are alone," she said, "permit me to inquire what *my* part of the lecture is to be. I trust you will remember, however, that, while I am Mildred Millington by birth, the law which you so much reverence and admire makes me Madame de Larocheforte."

"You mean to say that I have the honor of conversing with a married woman."

"Exactly so, Mr. Dunscomb."

"I comprehend you, ma'am, and shall respect your position. You are not about to become my niece, and I can claim no right to exceed the bounds of friendship—"

"Nay, my dear sir, I do not wish to say this. You have every right to advise. To me you have been a steady and well-judging friend, and this in the most trying circumstances. I am ready to hear you, sir, in deference, if not in your beloved humility."

"That which I have to say refers solely to your own happiness, Mildred. Your return to America has, I fear, been most inopportune. Among other innovations that are making on every side of us, even to the verge of dissolution of civilized society, comes the liberty of women. Need I tell you what will be the next step in this downward career?"

"You needs must, Mr. Dunscomb—I do not comprehend you. What will that step be?"

"Her licentiousness. No woman can throw off the most sacred of all her earthly duties, in this reckless manner, and hope to escape from the doom of her sex. After making a proper allowance for the increase of population, the increase in separated married people is getting to be out of all proportion. Scarce a month passes that one does not hear of some wife who has left her husband, secreted herself with a child, perhaps as you did, in some farm house, passing by a different name, and struggling for her rights, as she imagines. Trust me, Mildred, all this is as much opposed to nature, as it is to prescribed duties. That young woman spoke merely what an inward impulse, that is incorporated with her very being, prompted her to utter. A most excellent mother—oh! what a blessing is that to one of your sex—how necessary, how heavenly, how holy!—an excellent mother has left her in ignorance of no one duty, and her character has been formed in what I shall term harmony with her sex. I must be plain, Mildred—you have not enjoyed this advantage. Deprived of your parent young, known to be rich, and transplanted to another soil, your education has necessarily been intrusted to hirelings, flatterers, or persons indifferent to your real well-being; those who have consulted most the reputation of their instruction, and have paid the most attention to those arts which soonest strike the eye, and most readily attract admiration. In this their success has been complete.''

'' While you think it has not been so much so, sir, in more material things?'' said the lady, haughtily.

'' Let me be sincere. It is due to my relation to you—to your grandmother— to the past—to the present time. I know the blood that runs in your veins, Mildred. You are self-willed by descent, rich by inheritance, independent by the folly of our legislators. Accident has brought you home, at the very moment when our ill-considered laws are unhinging society in many of its most sacred interests; and, consulting only an innate propensity, you have ventured to separate from your husband, to conceal yourself in a cottage, a measure, I daresay, that comported well with your love of the romantic—''

'' Not so—I was oppressed, annoyed, unhappy at home, and sought refuge in that cottage. Monsieur de Larocheforte has such a passion for snuff! He uses it night and day.''

''Then followed the serious consequences which involved you in so many fearful dangers—''

''True,'' interrupted the lady, laying her small, gloved hand hastily on his arm —'' very true, dear Mr. Dunscomb; but how cleverly I contrived to escape them all!—how well I managed your Mr. Timms, good Mrs. Gott, the puffy, pompous sheriff, that wily Williams too, whose palm felt the influence of my gold —oh! the excitement of the last two months has been a gift of paradise to me, and, for the first time since my marriage, have I known what true happiness was!''

Dunscomb turned, astonished, to his companion, and stared her in the face. Never was the countenance more lovely to the cursory glance, the eye brighter, the cheek with a richer glow on it, or the whole air, mien and attitude more replete with womanly loveliness, and womanly graces; but the observant eye of the lawyer penetrated beyond all these, and detected the unhappy spirit which had gained possession of a tenement so lovely. The expression of the countenance denoted

the very triumph of cunning. We pretend not to a knowledge of the arcana of nature, to be able to detect the manner in which the moving principles prompt to good or evil, but we must reject all sacred history, and no small portion of profane, not to believe that agencies exist that are not visible to our ordinary senses; and that our boasted reason, when abandoned to its own support, becomes the victim of those that are malign. We care not by what names these agents are called, imps, demons, evil spirits, or evil passions; but this we do know, let him beware who submits to their control. Better, far better, were it that such an one had never been born!

Three days later Mildred Millington was in a state that left no doubt of her infirmity. The lucid intervals were long, however, and at such times her mind seemed clear enough on all subjects but one. Divorce was her ''ruling passion,'' and, in order to effect her purpose, all the extraordinary ingenuity of a most fertile mind was put in requisition. Although means were promptly, but cautiously, taken to see that she did not squander her large pecuniary resources, Dunscomb early saw that they were uncalled for. Few persons were better qualified to look after their money than was this unfortunate lady, in the midst of the dire visitation that intellectually reduced her below the level of most around her. On this head her sagacity was of proof; though her hand was not closed with the grip of a miser. Accustomed from childhood to a liberal expenditure, she was willing still to use the means that an inscrutable Providence had so liberally placed in her way, her largesses and her charities continuing the same as ever. Down to the present moment, the fundholder, the owner of town property, the mortgagee, and the trader is allowed to enjoy his own, without any direct interference of the demagogue with his rights; but how much longer this exception is to last is known only to the Being who directs the destinies of nations; or, at least, not to any who are now on earth, surrounded equally by the infirmities and ignorance of the present state.

But Mildred was, and is yet, permitted to exercise her rights over her own property, though care is had to see that no undue advantage is taken of her sex, years, and ignorance. Beyond this her control was not disputed, and she was suffered to manage her own affairs. She set about the matter of a divorce with the whole energy of her nature, and the cunning of her malady. Timms was again summoned to her service, unknown to Dunscomb, who would never have winked at the measures that were taken, though so much in accordance with "the ways of the hour."

Provided with proper credentials, this managing agent sought an interview with M. de Larocheforte, a worn-out debauchee of some rank, who, sooth to say, had faults even graver than that of taking snuff. Notwithstanding the great personal attractions of Mildred, the motive for marrying her had been money, as is usually the case in a very great proportion of the connections of the old world, among persons of condition. Love is to succeed, and not to precede, matrimony. Mildred had been taught that lesson, and grievously had she been disappointed. The snuff got into her eyes. M. de Larocheforte—M. le Vicomte as he had been, and was still determined to be, and in all probability will be, in spite of all the French "republican simplicity" that was ever summoned to a nation's rescue—M. le Vicomte was directly approached by Timms, and a proposal made that he should put himself in a condition to be divorced, for a stipulated price. Notwithstanding the opinion of the learned attorney-general of this great State, of the European aristocracy, and who is so every way qualified to give such an opinion, *ex-officio* as it might be, M. de Larocheforte declined lending himself to so vile a proposition, Frenchman and noble as he was. Nor did the husband believe that the discreditable proposal came from his wife. He compelled Timms to admit as much, under a menace of losing his case. That worthy was puzzled at this result, for he had made the proposal on his "own hook," as he afterward explained the matter to Williams, in the fullest confidence of "republican simplicity," and was astonished at meeting with the self-respect of a gentleman, if with no very elevated principles in a nobleman! It was accordingly necessary to have recourse to some other mode of proceeding.

Luckily for the views of Timms and his fair client, one can scarcely go amiss in this country, when a divorce is desired. Although a few of the older States remain reasonably inflexible on this subject, in some respects *unreasonably* so, indeed, they are generally surrounded by communities that are more indulgent. By means of some *hocus pocus* of the law, that we pretend not to explain, the names of Gabriel Jules Vincent Jean Baptiste de Larocheforte ads. Mildred de Larocheforte were just beginning to steal on the dawn of the newspapers, in a case that, ere long, might blaze in the meridian of gossip.

Dunscomb frowned, and reproached, but it was too late to recede. He has told Mildred, and he has told Timms, that nuptial knots tied in one community cannot be so readily unloosed in another as many imagine; and that there must, at least, be good faith—the *animus revertendi*—in the change of residence that usually precedes the application. But money is very powerful, and smooths a thousand difficulties. No one could predict the termination; and, as the vicomte, though only to be approached in a more delicate way than that adopted by Timms, was as tired of the connection as his wife, and was very anxious to obtain a larger share of the fortune than the "cup and saucer" law will give him, it was by no means improbable that the end of the affair would be a quasi-divorce, that would at least enable each party to take his or her own course, without fear of molestation from the other.

In the meantime, Millington was married very shortly after the trial. The engagement had not been long, but the parties had known each other intimately for years. The bridegroom, in one sense, was the head of his family, though by no means possessed of its largest fortune. In this character, it devolved on him to care for the interests of his fair relative. Although as much opposed as Dunscomb to the course she was taking, he did not shrink from his duties as a relative; and it is understood that his house is Mildred's home when in town. Rattletrap opened its hospitable doors to the unfortunate woman, whenever she chose to visit the place; and Timbully has also claims on her time and presence.

Dunscomb announced his intention to retire from practice at the end of a twelve-month, the morning that Michael and Sarah were married. In the intervening time, John Wilmeter and his new nephew were received as partners, and the worthy bachelor is now sedulously but silently transferring as respectable and profitable a list of clients as any man in the courts can claim. His own advice is promised, at all times, to his old friends; and, as not a soul has objected, and the young men bid fair, there is every reason to hope that useful and profitable labor will keep both out of mischief.

CHAPTER XXX.

"Some curate has penn'd this invective,
And you have studied it."—MASSINGER.

THE day set apart for the nuptials of John Wilmeter and Anna Updyke finally arrived. The ceremony was to take place in a little church that had stood, time out of mind, in the immediate neighborhood of Timbully. This church was colonial in its origin, and, while so much around it had undergone vital changes, there stands that little temple, reared in honor of God, in its simplicity, unpretending yet solid and durable architecture, resembling, in all these particulars, the faith it was erected to sustain. Among the other ways of the hour that are worthy of our notice, the Church itself has sustained many rude shocks of late—shocks from within as well as from without. The Father of Lies has been roving through its flocks with renewed malice, damaging the shepherds, perhaps, quite as much as the sheep, and doing things hitherto unheard of in the brief annals of American Ecclesiastical History. Although we deeply regret this state of things, we feel no alarm. The hand which first reared this moral fabric will be certain to protect it as far as that protection shall be for its good. It has already effected a great reform. The trumpet is no longer blown in Zion in our own honor; to boast of the effects of a particular discipline; to announce the consequences of order, and of the orders; or, in short, to proclaim a superiority that belongs only to the Head of all the Churches, let them be further from, or nearer to, what are considered distinctive principles. What the Church is now enduring the country itself most sadly wants—a lesson in humility; a distrust of self, a greater dependence on that wisdom which comes, not from the voices of the people, not from the ballot-boxes, not from the halls of senates, from heroes, god-likes, or stereotyped opinions, but from above, the throne of the Most High.

In one of those little temples reared by our fathers in the days of the monarchy, when, in truth, greater republican simplicity really reigned among us, in a thousand things, than reigns to-day, the bridal party from Timbully was assembled at an early hour of the morning. The company was not large, though it necessarily included most of the nearest relatives of the bride and groom. Dunscomb was there, as were Millington and his wife; Dr. and Mrs. McBrain, of course, and two or three other relations on the side of the bride's father, besides Mildred. It was to be a private wedding, a thing that is fast getting to be forgotten. Extravagance and parade have taken such deep root among us that young people scarce consider themselves legally united unless there are six bridesmaids, one, in particular, to "pull off the glove"; as many attendants of the other sex, and some three or four hundred friends in the evening, to bow and courtesy before the young couple, utter a few words of nonsense, and go their way to bow and courtesy somewhere else.

There was nothing of this at Timbully, on that wedding day. Dunscomb and his nephew drove over from Rattletrap, early in the morning, even while the dew was glittering on the meadows, and Millington and his wife met them at a cross-road, less than a mile from McBrain's country-house. The place of rendezvous was at the church itself, and thither the several vehicles directed their way. Dunscomb was just in time to hand Mildred from her very complete traveling-carriage, of which the horses were in a foam, having been driven hard all the way from town. Last of all, appeared Stephen Hoof, driving the very respectable-looking rockaway of Mrs. McBrain—we were on the point of writing "his master," but there are no longer any "masters" in New York. Stephen himself, who had not a spark of pride except in his horses, and who was really much attached to the person he served, always spoke of the doctor as his "boss." Jack Wilmeter, somewhat of a wag, had perplexed the honest coachman, on a certain occasion, by telling him that "boss" was the Latin for "ox," and that it was beneath his dignity to be using Pill and Poleus (Bolus) to drag about "oxen." But Stephen recovered from this shock in due time, and has gone on ever since calling his master "boss." We suppose this touch of "republican simplicity" will maintain its ground along with the other sacred principles that certain persons hold on to so tightly that they suffer others, of real importance, to slip through their fingers.

Stephen was proud of his office that day. He liked his new mistress—there are no bossesses—and he particularly liked Miss Anna. His horses were used a good deal more than formerly, it is true; but this he rather liked too, having lived under the *régimes* of the two first Mrs. McBrain. He was doubly satisfied because his team came in fresh, without having a hair turned, while that of *Madame*, as all the domestics now called Mildred, were white with foam. Stephen took no account of the difference in the distance, as he conceived that a careful coachman would have had his "boss" up early enough to get over the ground in due season, without all this haste. Little did he understand the bossess that his brother-whip had to humor. She paid high, and had things her own way.

Anna thought Stephen had never driven

so fast as he did that morning. The doctor handed her from the carriage, leading her and his wife directly up to the altar. Here the party was met by John and his uncle, the latter of whom facetiously styled himself the "groomsman." It is a ceremony much more easily done than undone—great as the facilities for the last are getting to be. In about five minutes, John Wilmeter and Anna Updyke were pronounced to be "one flesh." In five minutes more, Jack had his sweet, smiling, happy, tearful bride in his own light vehicle, and was trotting away toward a pretty little place in Westchester, that he owns, and which was all ready to receive the young couple. The ponies seemed to understand their duty, and soon carried the bride and bridegroom out of sight.

"Them's awful trotters, them nags of Mr. Jack Wilmington's," said Stephen, as the double phaeton whirled away from the church door, "and if Miss Anny doesn't disapprove on 'em, afore long, I'm no judge of a team. I'm glad, however, the young gentleman has married into our family, for he does like a hoss, and the gentleman that likes a hoss commonly likes his vife."

His remark was overheard by Dunscomb, though intended only for the ears of the counselor's coachman. It drew an answer, as might have been foreseen.

"I am glad you approve of the connection, Stephen," said the counselor in his good-natured way. "It is a great satisfaction to know that my nephew goes among friends."

"Fri'nds, sir! Admirers is a better tarm. I'm a downright admirer of Mr. Jack, he's sich tastes; always with his dog, or his gun, or his hoss, in the country; and I dares to say, with his books in town."

"Not just all that, Stephen; I wish it were so; but truth compels me to own that the young rogue thinks quite as much of balls, and suppers, and tailors, and the opera, as he does of Coke upon Lyttleton, or Blackstone and Kent."

"Vell, that's wrong," answered Stephen, "and I'll uphold no man in vot's wrong, so long as I can do better. I know'd both them racers, having heard tell on 'em at the time they vos run, and I've heard good judges say, that timed the hosses, that Kent came in neck and neck, if justice had been done. Mr. Jack will rectify, and come to see the truth afore long—mattermony will do that much for him. It's a great help to the seekers arter truth, is mattermony, sir!"

"That is the reason you have so much of it at Timbully, I suppose," returned Dunscomb, nodding familiarly toward his friend the doctor, who had heard all that was said. "If matrimony rectifies in this way you must be three times right at home, Stephen."

"Yes, sir," answered the coachman, nodding his head in reply; "and when a body does better and better, as often as he tries, there's no great harm in trying. Mr. Jack vill come round, in time."

"I daresay he will, Stephen, when he has sown all his wild oats; though the dog pretends to like the Code, and what is more, has the impudence to say he understands it."

"Yes, sir, all wrong, I dares to say. But Miss Anna will set him right, as a righter young lady never sat on the back seat of a coach. I vish, now ve're on the subject, Squire Dunscomb, to hear your ra'al opinion about them vild oats; vether they be a true thing, or merely a fancy consarning some vegetable that looks like the true feed. I've often heard of sich things, but never seed any."

"Nor will you, Stephen, until the doctor turns short round, and renews his youth. Then, indeed, you may see some of the grain growing beneath your feet. It is doctor's food."

"Meshy, and good for the grinders of old hosess, I dares to say."

"Something of the sort. It's the harvest that age reaps from the broadcast of youth. But we are keeping Mrs. McBrain waiting. Stephen will take one less back with him than he brought, my dear lady."

"I trust not. Mr. McBrain has given me reason to hope for the pleasure of your company. Your nephew has carried off my daughter; the least you can do is to come and console me."

"What is then to become of that dear, but unfortunate young lady?" glancing toward Mildred.

"She goes with her relatives, the Millingtons. Next week we are all to meet at Rattletrap, you know."

The next week the meeting took place, as appointed.

"Here I am," cried Dunscomb, "truly and finally a bachelor again. Now for the reign of misrule, negligence, and bad housekeeping. Sarah has left me; and John has left me; and Rattletrap will soon become the chosen seat of discomfort and cynicism."

"Never the last, I should think," answered Mme. de Larocheforte, gayly, "as long as you are its master. But why should you dwell alone here, in your declining years—why may I not come and be your housekeeper?"

"The offer is tempting, coming, as it

THE WAYS OF THE HOUR.

does, from one who cannot keep house for herself. But you think of returning to Europe, I believe?"

"Never—or not so long as my own country is so indulgent to us women!"

"Why, yes—you are right enough in that, Mildred. This is woman's paradise, in a certain sense, truly; though much less attention is paid to their weaknesses and wants, by the affluent, than in other lands. In every Christian country but this, I believe, a wife may be compelled to do her duty. Here she is free as the air she breathes, so long as she has a care not to offend in one essential. No, you are right to remain at home, in your circumstances; that is to say, if you still insist on your mistaken independence; a condition in which nature never intended your sex to exist."

"And yourself, sir! Did not nature as much intend that you should marry as another?"

"It did," answered Dunscomb, solemnly; "and I would have discharged the obligation, had it been in my power. You well know why I have never been a husband—the happy parent of a happy family."

Mildred's eyes swam with tears. She had heard the history of her grandmother's caprice, and had justly appreciated the wrongs of Dunscomb. This it was not difficult for her to do, in the case of third parties, even while so obtuse on the subject of her own duties. She took the hand of her companion, by a stealthy and unexpected movement, and raised it still more unexpectedly to her lips. Dunscomb started; turned his quick glance on her face, where he read all her contrition and regrets. It was by these sudden exhibitions of right feeling and correct judgment, that Mme. de Larocheforte was able to maintain her position. The proofs of insanity were so limited in the range of its influence, occurred so rarely, now she was surrounded by those who really took an interest in her, and this not for the sake of her money, but for her own sake, that her feelings had become softened, and she no longer regarded men and women as being placed near her to prey on her means, and to persecute her. By thus giving her affections scope her mind was gradually getting to be easier, and her physical existence improved. McBrain was of opinion that, with care, and with due attention to avoid excitement and distasteful subjects, her reason might again be seated on its throne, and bring all the faculties of her mind in subjection to it.

At length the time for the visit of the young people arrived. Anxious to see happy faces assembled around him, Dunscomb had got Mildred, the McBrains, and the Millingtons, at Rattletrap, to do honor to the bride and groom. Good Mrs. Gott had not been overlooked, and by an accident Timms drove in at the gate just as the whole party, including Jack and his blooming wife, were sitting down to a late breakfast. The counselor welcomed his man-of-all-work, for habit renders us less fastidious in our associations than most of us imagine.

Timms was very complimentary to both of the young couples, and in a slight degree witty, agreeably to his own mode of regarding the offspring of that effort of the imagination.

"What do you think of Williams's getting married, Squire Dunscomb?" the attorney asked. "There's a man for matrimony! He regards women and niggers as inferior beings."

"Pray, how do *you* regard them, Timms? The women only, I suppose?"

"Oh! dear, no, squire; as far as possible from that! I reverence the ladies, without whom our state in this life would be—"

"Single—I suppose you wish to say. Yes, that is a very sensible remark of yours—without women we should certainly all get to be old bachelors in time. But, Timms, it is proper that I should be frank with you. Mildred de Larocheforte may manage to get a divorce, by means of some of the quirks of the law; but were she to be proclaimed single, by sound of trumpet, she would never marry *you*."

"You are sharp on me this morning, sir; no one but the lady herself can say *that*."

"There you are mistaken. I *know* it, and am ready to give my reasons for what I say."

"I should be pleased to hear them, sir —always respect your reasoning powers, though I think no man can say who a lady will or will not marry."

"In the first place, she does not like you. That is one sufficient reason, Timms—"

"Her dislike may be overcome, sir."

"Her tastes are very refined. She dislikes her present husband principally because he takes snuff."

"I should have thought she might have discovered her feelings on that subject before she went so far."

"Not as they manage matters in Europe. There, the suitor is not permitted to kiss his intended, as so often happens among ourselves, I fancy; and she had no opportunity of ascertaining how unpleasant snuff is. You chew and smoke, and she will endure neither."

"I'll forswear both, rather than not be agreeable to dear Mary Monson."

"Ah, my poor Timms, I see you are deeper in this affair than I had supposed. But I shall turn you over to Mrs. Gott, who has promised to have an explanation with you, and who, I believe, will speak by authority."

Timms was not a little surprised to see his old master very unceremoniously leave him, and the sheriff's wife occupy his place.

"Squire Timms," the latter commenced, without a moment's hesitation, "we live in a very strange world, it must be admitted. Gott says as much as this, and Gott is commonly right. He always maintained he never should be called on to hang Mary Monson."

"Mr. Gott is a very prudent man, but he would do well to take more care of his keys."

"I have not been able to find out how that was done! Mary laughs when I ask her, and says it was witchcraft; I sometimes think it *must* have been something of the sort."

"It was money, Mrs. Gott, which kept Goodwin concealed to the last moment, and brought about half of all that happened."

"You knew that Peter Goodwin was alive, and hid up at Mrs. Horton's?"

"I was as much surprised, when he entered the court, as any one there. My client managed it all for herself. She, and her gold."

"Well, you have the credit of it, let me tell you, and many in the county think it was very well done. I am your friend, and ever have been. You stood by Gott like a man, at his election, and I honor you for it. So I am about to give you a great proof of my friendship. Give up all thoughts of Mary Monson; she'll never have you."

"What reasons have you for saying this?"

"In the first place she is married already."

"She may get a divorce. Besides, her present husband is not a citizen. If I go to the senate, I intend to introduce a bill to prevent any but citizens getting married. If foreigners want wives, let them be naturalized!"

"You talk like a simpleton! Another reason why you should not think of Mary Monson is that you are unsuited to be her husband?"

"In what particular, I beg leave to ask?"

"Oh! in several. You are both too sharp, and would quarrel about your wit, in the very first month," returned Mrs. Gott, laughing. "Take my advice, Timms, and cast your eyes on some Dukes County young woman, who has a natur' more like your own."

Timms growled out a dissent to this very rational proposition, but the discussion was carried on for some time longer. The woman made an impression at last, and when the attorney left the house it was with greatly lessened hopes for the future, and with greatly lessened zeal on the subject of the divorce.

It was singular, perhaps, that Mrs. Gott had not detected the great secret of Mary Monson's insanity. So many persons are going up and down the country, who are mad on particular subjects, and sane on most others, that it is not surprising the intelligence and blandishments of a woman like Mildred should throw dust into the eyes of one as simple-minded as Mrs. Gott. With the world at large, indeed, the *equivoque* was kept up, and while many thought the lady very queer, only a few suspected the truth. It may be fortunate for most of us that writs of lunacy are not taken out against us; few men or women being under the control of a good, healthful reason at all times, and on all subjects.

In one particular, Mme. de Larocheforte was singularly situated. She was surrounded, in her ordinary associations, with newly married persons, who were each and all strenuously resolved to regard the relation in the most favorable point of view. Perhaps there is nothing on earth that so nearly resembles the pure happiness of the blessed, as the felicity that succeeds the entire union of two hearts that are wrapped up in each other. Such persons live principally for themselves, regarding the world at large as little more than their abiding-place. The affinity of feelings, the community of thought, the steadily increasing confidence which, in the end, almost incorporates the moral existence of two into one, are so many new and precious ties, that it is not wonderful the novices believe they are transplanted to a new and ethereal state of being. Such was, in a measure, the condition of those with whom Mildred was now called on to associate most intimately. It is true, that the state of the doctor and his wife might be characterized as only happy, while those of the young people amounted to absolute felicity. Mildred had experienced none of the last, and very little of the first, on the occasion of her own marriage, which had been entered into more as a contract of reason than a union of love. She saw how much she had missed, and profound was the grief it occasioned her.

"You seem very happy," she remarked one day to Anna, as they were again treading the pretty little wood at Rattletrap—"more than that—delighted would be a better word."

"Jack is very kind to me, and the only complaint I have to make of him is, that he is more fond of me than I deserve. I tell him I tremble lest our happiness may not last!"

"Enjoy it while you may. It is so rare to find married persons who are so completely devoted to each other, that it is a pleasant sight to look upon. I never knew any of this, Anna."

"I regret to hear it, dear mamma—it must be that you began wrong. There should be a strong attachment before the nuptial benediction is pronounced; then, with good hearts, and good principles, I should think almost any woman might be content with her fate."

"It may be so," returned Mildred, with a profound sigh; "I suppose it *must* be so. We are created by God, to fulfill these kind offices to each other, and to love our husbands; and there must be something very wrong when different results follow. For myself, I ought never to have married at all. My spirit is too independent for matrimony."

Anna was silent; for, possibly, she might have read "headstrong" for "independent." The most truly independent thinkers are those who are willing to regard all sides of a subject, and are not particularly wedded to one. Mildred was acute enough to see that the beautiful young bride did not exactly like the allusion she had made to her new character.

"You do not agree with me?" she demanded quickly, bending forward to look into her companion's eyes.

"How can I, mamma Mildred! As I think no one, man or woman, should have a spirit that disqualifies her for the duties imposed by nature, which is merely the law of our great Creator, how can I agree to your notion of so much independence. We are not intended for all this independence, but have been placed here to do honor to God, and to try to render each other happy. I wish—but I am too bold, for one so young and inexperienced."

"Speak freely, dear. I listen with pleasure—not to say with curiosity."

"I am afraid, dear mamma, that the great guide of human conduct is not as much studied in France as it should be. That teaches us the great lesson of humility. Without humility we are nothing—cannot be Christians—cannot love our neighbors as ourselves—cannot even love God, as it is our duty, as we ought to do."

"This is very strange, Anna, coming from one of your age! Is it common for American girls to reason and feel in this way?"

"Perhaps not, though I hope more so than is commonly supposed. You will remember what a mother it is my good fortune to possess. But, since you really wish me to be frank with you, let me finish what I have to say. I suppose you know, Mildred, how much more you have to contend with than most of your sex?"

"Monsieur de Larocheforte, you mean?"

"Not at all," returned Mrs. John Wilmeter, slightly smiling. "I put all thought of contention with a husband out of the question. You know I have not been married long enough for that, and I could almost hope that the first day of such a scene might be the last of my life! John would cease to love me, if I quarreled with him."

"You will be an extraordinary pair, my dear, if scenes, as you call them, do not occasionally occur between you."

"I do not expect faultlessness in Jack; and, as for myself, I know that I have very many motes to get rid of, and which I trust may, in a measure, be done. But let us return to the case of a woman, young, well-educated, handsome, rich to superfluity, and intellectual."

"All of which are very good things, my child," observed Mme. de Larocheforte, with a smile so covert as to be scarcely seen, though it betrayed to her companion the consciousness of her making the application intended—"what next?"

"Willful, a lover of power, and what she called independent."

"Good and bad together. The two first, very bad, I acknowledge; the last, very good."

"What do you understand by independence? If it mean a certain disposition to examine and decide for ourselves, under all the obligations of duty, then it is a good thing, a *very* good thing, as you say; but if it merely mean a disposition to do as one pleases, to say what one likes, and to behave as one may at the moment fancy, then it strikes me as a very bad thing. This independence, half the time, is only pride and obstinacy, dear mamma!"

"Well, what if it is? Men are proud and obstinate, too; and they must be fought with their own weapons."

"It is easy to make smart speeches, but, by the difficulties I meet with in endeavoring to conquer my own heart, I know it is very hard to do right. I know I am a very young monitress—"

"Never mind that. Your youth gives piquancy to your instructions. I like to hear you."

"Well, I will finish what I had to say. I have ever found that the best assistant, or it might be more reverent to say, the best mode of subduing error, was to comport ourselves with humility. Ah! my dear mamma, if you could understand how very strong the humble get to be in time, you would throw aside your cherished independence, and rely on other means to secure happiness!"

Perhaps Mildred was as much struck with the circumstances under which this rebuke or admonition was given as with the advice itself. It had an effect, however, and Dunscomb coming in aid of his niece, this singular woman was gradually drawn from the exaggerated notions she had ever entertained of herself and her rights to the contemplation of her duties, as they are exercised in humility.

If there were no other evidence of the divine origin of the rules of conduct taught by the Redeemer than the profound knowledge of the human heart, that is so closely connected with the great lessons in humility everywhere given in his teachings, we conceive it would be sufficient in itself to establish their claim to our reverence. If men could be made to feel how strong they become in admitting their weaknesses; how clearly they perceive truth, when conscious of gazing at its form amid the fogs of error; and how wise we may become by the consciousness of ignorance, more than half of the great battle in morals would be gained.

Humility was, indeed, a hard lesson for Milfred Millington to study. Her whole life had been in direct opposition to its precepts, and the great failing of her mind had a strong leaning to a love of power. Nevertheless, there is a still, searching process of correcting, so interwoven with the law of the New Testament, as to be irresistible when brought to aid us, in the manner prescribed by its own theory. No one knew this better than Dunscomb; and he so directed the reading, thoughts, and feelings of his interesting charge, as to produce an early and a very sensible change on her character. The tendency to insanity is still there, and probably will ever remain; for it is not so much the consequence of any physical derangement as of organization; but it already promises to be so far controlled as to leave its unhappy subject generally rational, and, for most of her time, reasonably satisfied.

Dunscomb had several interviews with the *vicomte*—no-vicomte—whom he found a much more agreeable person than he had been prepared to meet, though certainly addicted to snuff. He was made acquainted with the mental hallucinations of his wife as well as with the fact of their being hereditary, when a great change came over the spirit of his dream! He had married to perpetuate the family De Larocheforte, but he had no fancy for a race of madmen. Dunscomb found him very reasonable, in consequence, and an arrangement was soon made, under the advice of this able counselor, by means of which Mildred virtually became her own mistress. M. de Larocheforte accepted an ample provision from the estate, and willingly returned to Europe, a part of the world that is much more agreeable, usually, to men of his class than our own "happy country." His absence has proved a great assistance to those who have assumed the care of Mildred's mental state. As all the schemes for a divorce have been discontinued—schemes that could have led to no strictly legal consequence—and her husband has left the country, the mind of Mildred has become calmer, and the means have been found to bring her almost completely within the control of her reason.

We have very little to say of the other characters. Timms is still himself. He boasts of the fees he got in the great Mary Monson case. His prospects for the State Senate are far from bad, and should he succeed, we shall expect to see him whining about "republican simplicity," abusing "aristocracy," which, in his secret heart, means a clean shirt, clean nails, anti-tobacco chewing and anti-blowing-the-nose-with-the-fingers, and aiding anti-rentism. He is scamp enough for anything.

Williams is actually married, and, in reply to Timms's accounts of the fees, he intimates that Peter Goodwin's ghost would not have appeared, had *he* not "been choked off." It ought to be strange that these two men like to boast of their rascality; but it is in obedience to a law of our nature. Their tongues merely echo their thoughts.

The McBrains seem very happy. If the wife be an "old man's darling," it is not as a young woman. Dunscomb still calls her "widow," on occasions, but nothing can interrupt the harmony of the friends. It is founded on mutual esteem and respect.

Michael and Sarah promise well. In

that family, there is already a boy, to its great-uncle's delight. The parents exult in this gift, and both are grateful.

We care little for Jack Wilmeter, though a very good fellow, in the main. Anna loves him, however, and that gives him an interest in our eyes he might not otherwise enjoy. His charming wife is losing her superfluous enthusiasm in the realities of life, but she seems to gain in womanly tenderness and warmth of healthful feeling, precisely in the degree in which she loses the useless tenant of her imagination.

END OF "THE WAYS OF THE HOUR."

WING AND WING.

CHAPTER I.

THE charms of the Tyrrhenian Sea have been sung since the days of Homer. That the Mediterranean generally, and its beautiful boundaries of Alps and Apennines, with its deeply indented and irregular shores, forms the most delightful region of the known earth, in all that relates to climate, productions, and physical formation, will be readily enough conceded by the traveler. The countries that border on this midland water, with their promontories buttressing a mimic ocean —their mountain-sides teeming with the picturesque of human life—their heights crowned with watch-towers—their rocky shelves consecrated by hermitages, and their unrivaled sheet dotted with sails, rigged, as it might be, expressly to produce effect in a picture, form a sort of world apart, that is replete with charms which not only fascinate the beholder, but which linger in the memories of the absent like visions of a glorious past.

Our present business is with this fragment of a creation that is so eminently beautiful, even in its worst aspects, but which is so often marred by the passions of man, in its best. While all admit how much nature has done for the Mediterranean, none will deny that, until quite recently, it has been the scene of more ruthless violence, and of deeper personal wrongs, perhaps, than any other portion of the globe. With different races, more widely separated by destinies than even by origin, habits, and religion, occupying its northern and southern shores, the outwork, as it might be, of Christianity and Mohammedanism, and of an antiquity that defies history, the bosom of this blue expanse has mirrored more violence, has witnessed more scenes of slaughter, and heard more shouts of victory, between the days of Agamemnon and Nelson, than all the rest of the dominions of Neptune together. Nature and the passions have united to render it like the human countenance, which conceals, by its smiles and godlike expression, the furnace that so often glows within the heart, and the volcano that consumes our happiness. For centuries the Turk and the Moor rendered it unsafe for the European to navigate these smiling coasts; and when the barbarian's power temporarily ceased, it was merely to give place to the struggles of those who drove him from the arena.

The circumstances which rendered the period that occurred between the years of 1790 and 1815 the most eventful of modern times are familiar to all; though the incidents which checkered that memorable quarter of a century have already passed into history. All the elements of strife that then agitated the world appear now to have subsided as completely as if they owed their existence to a remote age; and living men recall the events of their youth as they regard the recorded incidents of other centuries. Then, each month brought its defeat or its victory; its account of a government overturned, or of a province conquered. The world was agitated like men in a tumult. On that epoch the timid look back with wonder; the young, with doubt; and the restless, with envy.

The years 1798 and 1799 were two of

the most memorable of this ever memorable period; and to that stirring and teeming season we must carry the mind of the reader, in order to place it in the midst of the scenes it is our object to portray.

Toward the close of a fine day in the month of August, a light, fairy-like craft was fanning her way before a gentle westerly air, into what is called the canal of Piombino, steering easterly. The rigs of the Mediterranean are proverbial for their picturesque beauty and quaintness, embracing the xebec, the felucca, the polacre, and the bombarda, or ketch; all unknown, or nearly so, to our own seas; and occasionally the lugger. The latter, a species of craft, however, much less common in the waters of Italy than in the Bay of Biscay and the British Channel, was the construction of the vessel in question; a circumstance that the mariners who eyed her from the shores of Elba deemed indicative of mischief. A three-masted lugger, that spread a wide breadth of canvas, with a low, dark hull, relieved by a single and almost imperceptible line of red beneath her channels, and a waist so deep that nothing was visible above it but the hat of some mariner taller than common, was considered a suspicious vessel; and not even a fisherman would have ventured out within reach of a shot, so long as her character was unknown. Privateers, or corsairs, as it was the fashion to call them (and the name with even its English signification was often merited by their acts), not unfrequently glided down that coast; and it was sometimes dangerous for those who belonged to friendly nations to meet them, in moments when the plunder, that a relic of barbarism still legalizes, had failed.

The lugger was actually of about one hundred and eighty tons admeasurement, but her dark paint and low hull gave her an appearance of being much smaller than she really was; still, the spread of her canvas, as she came down before the wind, wing-and-wing, as seamen term it, or with a sail fanning like the heavy pinions of a sea-fowl, on each side, betrayed her pursuits; and, as has been intimated, the mariners on the shore, who watched her movements, shook their heads in distrust as they communed among themselves, in very indifferent Italian, concerning her destination and object. This observation, with its accompanying discourse, occurred on the rocky bluff above the town of Porto Ferrajo, in the island of Elba, a spot that has since become so renowned as the capital of the mimic Dominion of Napoleon. Indeed, the very dwelling which was subsequently used by the fallen emperor as a palace stood within a hundred yards of the speakers, looking out toward the entrance of the canal and the mountains of Tuscany; or rather of the little principality of Piombino, the system of merging the smaller in the larger states of Europe not having yet been brought into extensive operation. This house, a building of the size of a better sort of country residence of our own, was then, as now, occupied by the Florentine governor of the Tuscan portion of the island. It stands on the extremity of a low, rocky promontory that forms the western ramparts of the deep, extensive bay, on the side of which, ensconced behind a very convenient curvature of the rocks, which here incline westward in the form of a hook, lies the small port, completely concealed from the sea, as if in dread of visits like those which might be expected from craft resembling the suspicious stranger. This little port, not as large in itself as a modern dock in places like London or Liverpool, was sufficiently protected against any probable dangers, by suitable batteries; and as for the elements, a vessel laid upon a shelf in a closet would be scarcely more secure. In this domestic little basin, which, with the exception of a narrow entrance, was completely surrounded by buildings, lay a few feluccas, that traded between the island and the adjacent main, and a solitary Austrian ship, which had come from the head of the Adriatic, in quest of iron.

At the moment of which we are writing, however, but a dozen living beings were visible in or about all these craft. The intelligence that a strange lugger, resembling the one described, was in the offing, had drawn nearly all the mariners ashore; and most of the habitues of the port had followed them up the broad steps of the crooked streets which led to the heights behind the town; or to the rocky elevation that overlooks the sea from northeast to west. The approach of the lugger produced some such effect on the mariners of this unsophisticated and little frequented port, as that of the hawk is known to excite among the timid tenants of the barnyard. The rig of the stranger had been noted two hours before by one or two old coasters, who habitually passed their idle moments on the heights, examining the signs of the weather, and indulging in gossip; and their conjectures had drawn to the Porto Ferrajo mall some twenty men, who fancied themselves, or who actually were, *cognoscenti* in matters of the sea. When, however, the low, long, dark hull, which upheld such wide sheets of canvas, became fairly visible,

WING AND WING. 195

the omens thickened, rumors spread, and hundreds collected on the spot, which, in Manhattanese parlance, would probably have been called a battery. Nor would the name have been altogether inappropriate, as a small battery was established there, and that, too, in a position which would easily throw a shot two-thirds of a league into the offing; or about the distance that the stranger was from the shore.

Tommaso Tonti was the oldest mariner of Elba, and luckily, being a sober, and usually a discreet man, he was the oracle of the island in most things that related to the sea. As each citizen, wine-dealer, grocer, innkeeper, or worker in iron, came up on the height, he incontinently inquired for Tonti, or 'Maso, as he was usually called; and getting the bearings and distance of the gray-headed old seaman, he invariably made his way to his side, until a group of some two hundred men, women and children had clustered near the person of the *pilota*, as the faithful gather about a favorite expounder of the law, in moments of religious excitement. It was worthy of remark, too, with how much consideration this little crowd of gentle Italians treated their aged seaman, on this occasion; none bawling out their questions, and all using the greatest care not to get in front of his person, lest they might intercept his means of observation. Five or six old sailors, like himself, were close at his side: these, it is true, did not hesitate to speak as became their experience. But Tonti had obtained no small part of his reputation by exercising great moderation in delivering his oracles, and perhaps by seeming to know more than he actually revealed. He was reserved, therefore; and while his brethren of the sea ventured on sundry conflicting opinions concerning the stranger, and a hundred idle conjectures had flown from mouth to mouth, among the landsmen and females, not a syllable that could commit the old man escaped his lips. He let the others talk at will; as for himself, it suited his habits, and possibly his doubts, to maintain a grave and portentous silence.

We have spoken of females; as a matter of course, an event like this, in a town of some three or four thousand souls, would be likely to draw a due proportion of the gentler sex to the heights. Most of them contrived to get as near as possible to the aged seaman, in order to obtain the first intelligence, that it might be the sooner circulated; but it would seem that among the younger of these there was also a sort of oracle of their own, about whose person gathered a dozen of the prettiest girls; either anxious to hear what Ghita might have to say in the premises, or, perhaps influenced by the pride and modesty of their sex and condition, which taught them to maintain a little more reserve than was necessary to the less refined portions of their companions. In speaking of condition, however, the word must be understood with an exceedingly limited meaning. Porto Ferrajo had but two classes of society, the tradespeople and the laborers; although there were, perhaps, a dozen exceptions in the persons of a few humble functionaries of the government, an avvocato, a medico, and a few priests The governor of the island was a Tuscan of rank, but he seldom honored the place with his presence; and his deputy was a professional man, a native of the town, whose original position was too well-known to allow him to give himself airs on the spot where he was born.

Ghita's companions, then, were daughters of shop-keepers, and persons of that class who, having been taught to read, and occasionally going to Leghorn, besides being admitted by the deputy to the presence of his housekeeper, had got to regard themselves as a little elevated above the more vulgar curiosity of the less cultivated girls of the port. Ghita herself, however, owed her ascendency to her qualities, rather than to the adventitious advantage of being a grocer's or an innkeeper's daughter, her origin being unknown to most of those around her, as, indeed, was her family name. She had been landed six weeks before, and left, by one who passed as her father, at the inn of Christoforo Dovi, as a boarder, and had acquired all her influence, as so many reach notoriety in our own simple society, by the distinction of having traveled; aided, somewhat, by her strong sense, great decision of character, perfect modesty and propriety of deportment, with a form which was singularly graceful and feminine, and a face that, while it could scarcely be called beautiful, was in the highest degree winning and attractive. No one thought of asking her family name, and she never appeared to deem it necessary to mention it. Ghita was sufficient; it was familiar to every one, and, although there were two or three others of the same appellation in Porto Ferrajo, this, by common consent, got to be *the* Ghita within a week after she had landed.

Ghita, it was known, had traveled, for

she had publicly reached Elba in a felucca, coming, as was said, from the Neapolitan States. If this were true, probably she was the only person of her sex in the town who had ever seen Vesuvius, or planted her eyes on the wonders of a part of Italy that has a reputation second only to that of Rome. Of course, if any girl in Porto Ferrajo could imagine the character of the stranger, it must be Ghita; and it was on this supposition that she had unwittingly, and, if the truth must be owned, unwillingly, collected around her a *clientelle* of at least a dozen girls of her own age, and apparently of her own class. The latter, however, felt no necessity for the reserve maintained by the curious who pressed near 'Maso; for while they respected their guest and friend, and would rather listen to her surmises than those of any other person, they had such a prompting desire to hear their own voices, that not a minute escaped without a question, or a conjecture, both volubly and quite audibly expressed. The interjections, too, were somewhat numerous, as the guesses were crude and absurd. One said it was a vessel with dispatches from Livorno, possibly with "His Eccellenza" on board; but she was reminded that Leghorn lay to the north, and not to the west. Another thought it was a cargo of priests, going from Corsica to Rome; but she was told that priests were not in sufficient favor just then in France to get a vessel so obviously superior to the ordinary craft of the Mediterranean to carry them about. While a third, more imaginative than either, ventured to doubt whether it was a vessel at all; deceptive appearances of this sort not being of rare occurrence, and usually taking the aspect of something out of the ordinary way.

"*Si*," said Annina, "but that would be a miracle, Maria; and why should we have a miracle, now that Lent and most of the holidays are past? *I* believe it is a real vessel."

The others laughed, and, after a good deal of eager chattering on the subject, it was quite generally admitted that the stranger was a *bona fide* craft of some species or another, though all agreed she was not a felucca, a bombarda, or a sparanara. All this time Ghita was thoughtful and silent; quite as much so, indeed, as Tommaso himself, though from a very different motive. Notwithstanding all the gossip, and the many ludicrous opinions of her companions, her eyes scarcely turned an instant from the lugger, on which they seemed to be riveted by a sort of fascination. Had there been

one there sufficiently unoccupied to observe this interesting girl, he might have been struck with the varying expression of a countenance that was teeming with sensibility, and which too often reflected the passing emotions of its mistress's mind. Now an expression of anxiety and even of alarm would have been detected by such an observer, if acute enough to separate these emotions, in the liveliness of sentiment, from the more vulgar feelings of her companions; and now, something like gleamings of delight and happiness flashed across her eloquent countenance. The color came and went often, and there was an instant, during which the lugger varied in her course, hauling to the wind and then falling off again, like a dolphin at its sports, when the radiance of the pleasure that glowed about her soft blue eyes rendered the girl perfectly beautiful; but none of these passing expressions were noticed by the garrulous group around the stranger female, who was left very much to the indulgence of the influences which gave them birth, unquestioned and altogether unsuspected.

Although the cluster of girls had, with feminine sensitiveness, gathered a little apart from the general crowd, there were but a few yards between the spot where it stood and that occupied by 'Maso; so that when the latter spoke, an attentive listener among the former might hear his words. This was an office that Tonti did not choose to undertake, however, until he was questioned by the podesta, Vito Viti, who now appeared on the hill in person, puffing like a whale that rises to breathe, from the vigor of his ascent.

"What dost thou make of her, good 'Maso?" demanded the magistrate, after he had examined the stranger himself some time in silence, feeling authorized, in virtue of his office, to question whom he pleased.

"Signore, it is a lugger," was the brief, and certainly the accurate reply.

"Aye, a lugger; we all understood that, neighbor Tonti; but what sort of a lugger? There are felucca-luggers, and polacre-luggers, and bombarda-luggers, and all sorts of luggers; which sort of lugger is this?"

"Signor Podesta, this is not the language of the port. We call a felucca, a felucca; a bombarda, a bombarda; a polacre, a polacre; and a lugger, a lugger. This is therefore a lugger."

'Maso spoke authoritatively, for he felt that he was now not out of his depth, and it was grateful to him to let the public know how much better he understood all these matters than a magistrate. On the other hand, the podesta was nettled, and disappointed into the bargain, for he really imagined he was drawing nice distinctions, much as it was his wont to do in legal proceedings; and it was his ambition to be thought to know something of everything.

"Well, Tonti," answered Signor Viti, in a protecting manner, and with an affable smile, "as this is not an affair that is likely to go to the higher courts at Florence, your explanations may be taken as sufficient, and I have no wish to disturb them—a lugger is a lugger."

"Si, signore; that is just what we say in the port. A lugger is a lugger."

"And yonder strange craft you maintain, and at need are ready to swear, is a lugger?"

Now 'Maso seeing no necessity for any oath in the affair, and being always somewhat conscientious in such matters, whenever the custom-house officers did not hold the book, was a little startled at this suggestion, and he took another and a long look at the stranger before he answered.

"Si, signore," he replied, after satisfying his mind once more, through his eyes, "I will swear that the stranger yonder is a lugger."

"And canst thou add, honest Tonti, of what nation? The nation is of as much moment, in these troubled times, as the rig."

"You say truly, Signor Podesta; for if an Algerine, or a Moor, or even a Frenchman, he will be an unwelcome visitor in the Canal of Elba. There are many different signs about him, that sometimes make me think that he belongs to one people, and then to another; and I crave your pardon if I ask a little leisure to let him draw nearer, before I give a positive opinion."

As this request was reasonable, no objection was raised. The podesta turned aside, and observing Ghita, who had visited his niece, and of whose intelligence he entertained a favorable opinion, he drew nearer to the girl, determined to lose a moment in dignified trifling.

"Honest 'Maso, poor fellow, is sadly puzzled," he observed, smiling benevolently, as if in pity for the pilot's embarrassment; "he wishes to persuade us that the strange craft yonder is a lugger, though he cannot himself say to what country she belongs!"

"It is a lugger, signore," returned the girl, drawing a long breath, as if relieved by hearing the sound of her own voice.

"How! dost thou pretend to be so skilled in vessels as to distinguish these particulars at the distance of a league?"

"I do not think it a league, signore— not more than half a league; and the distance lessens fast, though the wind is so light. As for knowing a lugger from a felucca, it is as easy as to know a house from a church, or one of the reverend padri, in the streets, from a mariner."

"Aye, so I would have told 'Maso on the spot, had the obstinate old fellow been inclined to hear me. The distance is just about what you say; and nothing is easier than to see that the stranger is a lugger. As to nation?"

"That may not be so easily told, signore, unless the vessel shows us her flag."

"By San Antonio! thou art right, child; and it is fitting she should show us her flag. Nothing has a right to approach so near the port of his imperial and royal highness that does not show its flag, thereby declaring its honest purpose and its nation. My friends, are the guns in the battery loaded as usual?"

The answer being in the affirmative, there was a hurried consultation among some of the principle men in the crowd, and then the podesta walked toward the government-house with an important air. In five minutes, soldiers were seen in the batteries, and preparations were made for leveling an eighteen-pounder in the direction of the stranger. Most of the females turned aside, and stopped their ears, the battery being within a hundred yards of the spot where they stood; but Ghita, with a face that was pale certainly, though with an eye that was steady, and without the least indications of fear, as respected herself, intensely watched every movement. When it was evident the artillerists were about to fire, anxiety induced her to break silence.

"They surely will not aim *at* the lugger!" she exclaimed. "That cannot be necessary, Signor Podesta, to make the stranger hoist his flag. Never have I seen that done in the south."

"You are unacquainted with our Tuscan bombardiers, signorina," answered the magistrate, with a bland smile, and an exulting gesture. "It is well for Europe that the grand duchy is so small, since such troops might prove even more troublesome than the French!"

Ghita, however, paid no attention to this touch of provincial pride, but pressing her hands on her heart, she stood like a statue of suspense while the men in the battery executed their duty. In a minute the match was applied, and the gun was discharged. Though all her companions uttered invocations to the saints, and other exclamations, and some even crouched to the earth in terror, Ghita, the most delicate of any in appearance, and with more real sensibility than all united expressed in her face, stood firm and erect. The flash and the explosion evidently had no effect on her; not an artillerist among them was less unmoved in frame, at the report, than this slight girl. She even imitated the manner of the soldiers, by turning to watch the flight of the shot, though she clasped her hands as she did so, and appeared to await the result with trembling. The few seconds of suspense were soon passed, when the ball was seen to strike the water fully a quarter of a mile astern the lugger, and to skip along the placid sea for twice that distance further, when it sank to the bottom by its own gravity.

"Santa Maria be praised!" murmured the girl, a smile half pleasure, half irony, lighting her face, as unconsciously to herself she spoke, "these Tuscan artillerists are no fatal marksmen!"

"That was most dexterously done, belle Ghita!" exclaimed the magistrate, removing his two hands from his ears; "that was amazingly well aimed! Another such shot as far ahead, with a third fairly between the two, and the stranger will learn to respect the rights of Tuscany. What say'st thou now, honest 'Maso; will this lugger tell us her country, or will she further brave our power?"

"If wise, she will hoist her ensign; and yet I see no signs of preparation for such an act."

Sure enough, the stranger, though quite within effective range of shot from the height, showed no disposition to gratify the curiosity, or to appease the apprehensions of those in the town. Two or three of her people were visible in her rigging, but even these did not hasten their work, or in any manner seem deranged at the salutation they had just received. After a few minutes, however, the lugger jibbed her mainsail, and then hauled up a little, so as to look more toward the headland, as if disposed to steer for the bay, by doubling the promontory. This movement caused the artillerists to suspend their own, and the lugger had fairly come within a mile of the cliffs, ere she lazily turned aside again, and shaped her course once more in the direction of the entrance of the canal. This drew another shot which effectually justified the magistrate's eulogy, for it certainly flew as much ahead of the stranger, as the first had flown astern.

"There, signore," cried Ghita eagerly, as she turned to the magistrate, "they are about to hoist their ensign, for now they know your wishes. The soldiers surely will not fire again!"

"That would be in the teeth of the law of nations, signorina, and a blot on Tuscan civilization. Ah! you perceive the artillerists are aware of what you say, and are putting aside their tools. Cospetto! 'tis a thousand pities, too, they couldn't fire the third shot, that you might see it strike the lugger; as yet you have only beheld their preparations."

"It is enough, Signor Podesta," returned Ghita, smiling, for she could smile now that she saw the soldiers intended no further mischief; "we have all heard of your Elba gunners, and what I have seen convinces me of what they can do, when there is occasion. Look, signore! the lugger is about to satisfy our curiosity."

Sure enough, the stranger saw fit to comply with the usages of nations. It has been said already that the lugger was coming down before the wind wing-and-wing, or with a sail expanded to the air on each side of her hull, a disposition of the canvas that gives to the felucca, and to the lugger in particular, the most picturesque of all their graceful attitudes. Unlike the narrow-headed sails that a want of hands has introduced among ourselves, these foreign, we might almost say classical mariners, send forth their long-pointed yards aloft, confining the width below by the necessary limits of the sheet-making up for the difference in elevation by the greater breadth of their canvas. The idea of the felucca's sails, in particular, would seem to have been literally taken from the wing of the large sea-fowl, the shape so nearly corresponding that, with the canvas spread in the manner just mentioned, one of those light craft has a very close resemblance to the gull or the hawk, as it poises itself in the air or is sweeping down upon its prey. The lugger has less of the beauty that adorns a picture, perhaps, than the strictly lateen rig; but it approaches so near it as to be always pleasing to the eye, and, in the particular evolution described, is scarcely less attractive. To the seaman, however, it brings with it an air of greater service, being a mode of carrying canvas that will buffet with the heaviest gale or the roughest seas, while it appears so pleasant to the eye in the blandest airs and smoothest water.

The lugger that was now beneath the heights of Elba had three masts, though sails were spread only on the two that were forward. The third mast was stepped on the taffrail; it was small, and carried a little sail, that, in English, is termed a jigger, its principal use being to press the bows of the craft up to the wind, when close-hauled, and render her what is termed weatherly. On the present occasion, there could scarcely be said to be anything deserving the name of wind, though Ghita felt her cheek, which was warmed with the rich blood of her country, fanned by an air so gentle that occasionally it blew aside tresses that seemed to vie with the floss silk of her native land. Had the natural ringlets been less light, however, so gentle a respiration of the sea air could scarcely have disturbed them. But the lugger had her lightest duck spread, reserving the heavier canvas for the storms, and it opened like the folds of a balloon, even before these gentle impulses; occasionally collapsing, it is true, as the ground-swell swung the yards to and fro, but, on the whole, standing out and receiving the air, as if guided more by volition than any mechanical power. The effect on the hull was almost magical; for, notwithstanding the nearly imperceptible power, owing to the lightness and exquisite mold of the craft, it served to urge her through the water at the rate of some three or four knots in the hour; or quite as fast as an ordinary active man is apt to walk.

Her motion was nearly unobservable to all on board, and might rather be termed gliding than sailing, the ripple under her cut-water not much exceeding that which is made by the finger as it is moved swiftly through the element; still the slightest variation of the helm changed her course, and this so easily and gracefully as to render her deviations and inclinations like those of a duck. In her present situation, too, the jigger, which was brailed, and hung festooned from its light yard, ready for use, should occasion suddenly demand it, added singularly to the smart air which everything wore about this craft, giving her, in the seaman's eyes, that particularly knowing and suspicious look which had awakened 'Maso's distrust.

The preparations to show the ensign, which caught the quick and understanding glance of Ghita, and which had not escaped even the duller vision of the artillerists, were made at the outer end of this jigger-yard. A boy appeared on the taffrail, and he was evidently clearing the ensign-halyards for that purpose. In half a minute, however, he disappeared; then a flag rose steadily, and by a continued pull, to its station. At first, the bunting hung suspended in a line, so as to evade all examination; but, as if anything on board this light craft were on a scale as airy and buoyant as herself,

the folds soon expanded, showing a white field, traversed at right angles with a red cross, and having a union of the same tint in its upper and inner corner.

"*Inglese!*" exclaimed 'Maso, infinitely aided in this conjecture by the sight of the stranger's ensign; "Si, signore, it is an Englishman; I thought so from the first, but as the lugger is not a common rig for vessels of that nation, I did not like to risk anything by saying it."

"Well, honest Tommaso, it is a happiness to have a mariner as skillful as yourself, in these troublesome times, at one's elbow! I do not know how else we should ever have found out a stranger's country. An Inglese! Corpo di Bacco! Who would have thought a nation so maritime, and which lies so far off, would send so small a craft this vast distance! Why, Ghita, it is a voyage from Elba to Livorno, and yet, I daresay, England is twenty times further."

"Signore, I know little of England, but I have heard that it lies beyond our own sea. This is the flag of the country, however; for that have I often beheld. Many ships of that nation come upon the coast further south."

"Yes, and it is a great country for mariners; though they tell me it has neither wine nor oil. They are allies of the emperor, too; and the deadly enemies of the French, who have done so much harm in upper Italy. That is something, Ghita, and every Italian should honor the flag. I fear the stranger does not intend to enter our harbor!"

"He steers as if he did not, Signor Podesta," said Ghita, sighing so gently that the respiration was audible only to herself. "Perhaps he is in search of some of the French, of which they say so many were seen, last year, going east."

"Aye, that was truly an enterprise!" answered the magistrate, gesticulating on a large scale, and opening his eyes by way of accompaniments. "General Bonaparte, he who had been playing the devil in the Milanese and the States of the Pope for the last two years, sailed, they sent us word, with two or three hundred ships, the saints, at first, knew whither. Some said it was to destroy the Holy Sepulcher; some to overturn the Grand Turk; and some thought to seize the islands. There was a craft in here, the same week, which said he had got possession of the Island of Malta; in which case we might look out for trouble in Elba. I had my suspicions from the first!"

"All this I heard at the time, signore, and my uncle probably could tell you more —how we all felt at the tidings!"

"Well, that is all over now, and the French are in Egypt. Your uncle, Ghita, has gone upon the main, I hear?" This was said inquiringly, and it was intended to be said carelessly; but the podesta could not prevent a glance of suspicion from accompanying the question.

"Signore, I believe he has; but I know little of his affairs. The time has come when I ought to expect him. See, eccellenza," a title that never failed to mollify the magistrate, and turn his attention from others entirely to himself, "the lugger really appears disposed to look into your bay, if not actually to enter it!"

This sufficed to change the discourse. Nor was it said altogether without reason; the lugger, which by this time had passed the western promontory, actually appearing disposed to do as Ghita conjectured. She jibbed her mainsail, brought both sheets of canvas on her larboard side, and luffed a little, so as to cause her head to look toward the opposite side of the bay, instead of standing on, as before, in the direction of the canal. This change in the lugger's course produced a general movement in the crowd, which began to quit the heights, hastening to descend the terraced streets in order to reach the haven. 'Maso and the podesta led the van, in this descent; and the girls, with Ghita in their midst, followed with equal curiosity, but with eager steps. By the time the throng was assembled on the quays, in the streets, on the decks of feluccas, or at other points that commanded the view, the stranger was seen gliding past, in the center of the wide and deep bay, with his jigger hauled out, and his sheets aft, looking up nearly into the wind's eye, if that could be called wind which was still little more than the sighing of the classical zephyr. His motion was necessarily slow, but it continued light, easy, and graceful. After passing the entrance of the port a mile or more, he tacked and looked up toward the haven. By this time, however, he had got so near in to the western cliffs that their lee deprived him of all air; and, after keeping his canvas open half an hour in the little roads, it was all suddenly drawn to the yards and the lugger anchored.

CHAPTER II.

It was now nearly dark, and the crowd, having satisfied its idle curiosity, began slowly to disperse. The Signor Viti remained to the last, conceiving it to be his duty to be on the alert, in such troubled times; but with all his bustling activity, it escapes his vigilance and means of observation to detect the circumstance that the stranger, while he steered into the bay with so much confidence, had contrived to bring up at a point where not a single gun from the batteries could be brought to bear on him; while his own shot, had he been disposed to hostilities, would have completely raked the little haven. But Vito Viti, though so enthusiastic an admirer of the art, was no gunner himself, and little liked to dwell on the effect of shot, except as it applied to others, and not at all to himself.

Of all the suspicious, apprehensive and curious, who had been collected in and about the port, since it was known the lugger intended to come into the bay, Ghita and 'Maso alone remained on watch, after the vessel was anchored. A loud hail had been given by those intrusted with the execution of the quarantine laws, the great physical bugbear and moral mystification of the Mediterranean; and the questions put had been answered in a way to satisfy all scruples for the moment. The "From whence came ye?" asked, however, in an Italian idiom, had been answered by "Inghilterra, touching at Lisbon and Gibraltar," all regions beyond distrust, as to the plague, and all happening at that moment to give clean bills of health. But the name of the craft herself had been given in a way to puzzle all the proficients in Saxon English that Porto Ferrajo could produce. It had been distinctly enough pronounced by some one on board, and, at the request of the quarantine department, had been three times slowly repeated, very much after the following form, namely:

"*Come chiamate il vostro boastimento?*"

"The Wing-and-Wing."

"Come?"

"The Wing-and-Wing."

A long pause, during which the officials put their heads together, first to compare the sounds of each with those of his companions' ears, and then to inquire of one who professed to understand English, but whose knowledge was such as is generally met with in a linguist of a little frequented port, the meaning of the term.

"Ving-y-Ving!" growled this functionary, not a little puzzled. "What ze devil sort of name is zat? Ask zem again."

"*Come si chiana la vostra barca, Signori Inglesi?*" repeated he who hailed.

"*Diable!*" growled one back, in French, "she is called ze Wing-and-Wing—'*Ala-e-Ala,*'" giving a very literal translation of the name, in Italian.

" *Ala-e-Ala!* " repeated they of the quarantine, first looking at each other in surprise, and then laughing, though in a perplexed and doubtful manner ; " Ving-y-Ving ! "

This passed just as the lugger anchored and the crowd began to disperse. It caused some merriment, and it was soon spread in the little town that a craft had just arrived from Inghilterra, whose name, in the dialect of that island, was " Ving-y-Ving," which meant " *Ala-e-Ala* " in Italian ; a cognomen that struck the listeners as sufficiently absurd. In confirmation of the fact, however, the lugger hoisted a small square flag, at the end of her main-yard, on which were painted, or wrought, two large wings, as they are sometimes delineated in heraldry, with the beak of a galley between them ; giving the whole conceit something very like the appearance that the human imagination has assigned to those heavenly beings, cherubs. This emblem seemed to satisfy the minds of the observers, who were too much accustomed to the images of art not to obtain some tolerably distinct notions, in the end, of what " *Ala-e-Ala* " meant.

But 'Maso, as has been said, remained after the rest had departed to their homes and their suppers, as did Ghita. The pilot, for such was Tonti's usual appellation, in consequence of his familiarity with the coast, and his being principally employed to direct the navigation of the different crafts in which he served, kept his station on board a felucca to which he belonged, watching the movements of the lugger ; while the girl had taken her stand on the quay, in a position that better became her sex, since it removed her from immediate contact with the rough spirits of the port, while it enabled her to see what occurred about the *Wing-and-Wing*. More than half an hour elapsed, however, before there were any signs of an intention to land ; but, by the time it was dark, a boat was ready, and it was seen making its way to the common stairs, where one or two of the regular officials were ready to receive it.

It is unnecessary to dwell on the forms of the pratique officers. These troublesome persons had their lanterns, and were vigilant in examining papers, as is customary ; but it would seem the mariner in the boat had everything *en regle*, for he was soon suffered to land. At this instant Ghita passed near the group and took a close and keen survey of the stranger's form and face, her own person being so enveloped in a mantle as to render a recognition of it difficult, if not impossible. The girl seemed satisfied with this scrutiny, for she immediately disappeared. Not so with 'Maso, who by this time had hurried round from the felucca, and was at the stairs in season to say a word to the stranger.

"Signore," said the pilot, " his eccellenza, the podesta, has bidden me say to you that he expects the honor of your company at his house, which stands so near us, hard by here, in the principal street, as will make it only a pleasure to go there. I know he would be disappointed if he failed of the happiness of seeing you."

" His eccellenza is a man not to be disappointed," returned the stranger, in very good Italian, " and five minutes shall prove to him how eager I am to salute him." Then, turning to the crew of his boat, he ordered them to return on board the lugger, and not to fail to look out for the signal by which he might call them ashore.

'Maso, as he led the way to the dwelling of Vito Viti, would fain ask a few questions, in the hope of appeasing certain doubts that beset him.

" Since when, Signore Capitano," he inquired, " have you English taken to sailing luggers ? It is a novel rig for one of your craft."

" Corpo di Bacco ! " answered the other, laughing, " friend of mine, if you can tell me the precise day when brandy and laces were first smuggled from France into my country, I will answer your question. I think you have never navigated as far north as the Bay of Biscay and our English Channel, or you would know that a Guernseyman is better acquainted with the rig of a lugger than with that of a ship."

" Guernsey is a country I never heard of," answered 'Maso, simply. " Is it like Holland—or more like Lisbon ? "

" Very little of either. Guernsey is a country that was once French, and where many of the people still speak the French language, but of which the English have been masters this many an age. It is an island subject to King George, but which is still half Gallic in names and usages. This is the reason why we like the lugger better than the cutter, which is a more English rig."

'Maso was silent, for if true, the answer at once removed many misgivings. He had seen so much about the strange craft which struck him as French, that doubts of her character obtruded ; but, if her captain's account could only be substantiated, there was end of distrust. What could be more natural than the circumstance that a vessel fitted out in an island of French origin should betray some of the peculiarities of the people who built her?

The podesta was at home, in expectation of this visit, and 'Maso was first admitted to a private conference, leaving the stranger in an outer room. During this brief conference, the pilot communicated all he had to say, both his suspicions and the seeming resolution of the difficulties; and then he took his leave, after receiving the boon of a paul. Vito Viti now joined his guest, but it was so dark, lights not having yet been introduced, that neither could distinguish the other's countenance.

"Signor Capitano," observed the magistrate, "the deputy-governor is at his residence, on the hill, and he will expect me to do him the favor to bring you thither, that he may do you the honors of the port."

This was said so civilly, and was, in itself, both so reasonable and so much in conformity with usage, that the other had not a word to say against it. Together, then, they left the house, and proceeded toward the government-dwelling, a building which has since become celebrated as having been the residence of a soldier who came so near subjugating Europe. Vito Viti was a short pursy man, and he took his time to ascend the stairs-resembling street; but his companion stepped from terrace to terrace with an ease and activity that, of themselves, would have declared him to be young, had not this been apparent by his general bearing and his mien, as seen through the obscurity.

Andrea Barrofaldi, the vice-governatore, was a very different sort of person from his friend the podesta. Although little more acquainted with the world, by practice, the vice-governatore was deeply read in books: owing his situation, in short, to the circumstance of his having written several clever works, of no great reputation, certainly, for genius, but which were useful in their way, and manifested scholarship. It is very seldom that a man of mere letters is qualified for public life; and yet there is an affectation, in all governments, most especially in those which care little for literature in general, of considering some professions of respect for it necessary to their own characters. Andrea Barrofaldi had been inducted into his present office without even the sentimental profession of never having asked for it. The situation had been given to him by the Fossombrone of his day, without a word having been said in the journals of Tuscany of his doubts about accepting it, and everything passed, as

things are apt to pass when there are true simplicity and good faith at the bottom, without pretension or comment. He had now been ten years in office, and had got to be exceedingly expert in discharging all the ordinary functions of his post, which he certainly did with zeal and fidelity. Still, he did not desert his beloved books, and, quite apropos of the matter about to come before him, the Signor Barrofaldi had just finished a severe, profound, and extensive course of study in geography.

The stranger was left in the ante-chamber, while Vito Viti entered an inner room and had a short communication with his friend, the vice-governatore. As soon as this was ended, the former returned, and ushered his companion into the presence of the substitute for the grand duke. As this was the sailor's first appearance within the influence of a light sufficiently strong to enable the podesta to examine his person, both he and Andrea Barrofaldi turned their eyes on him with lively curiosity, the instant the rays of a strong lamp enabled them to scrutinize his appearance. Neither was disappointed, in one sense at least; the countenance, figure and mien of the mariner much more than equaling his expectations.

The stranger was a man of six-and-twenty, who stood five feet ten in his stockings, and whose frame was the very figure of activity, united to a muscle that gave very fair indications of strength. He was attired in an undress naval uniform, which he wore with a smart air, that one who understood these matters more by means of experience, and less by means of books, than Andrea Barrofaldi, would at once have detected did not belong to the manly simplicity of the English wardrobe. Nor were his features in the slightest degree those of one of the islanders, the outline being beautifully classical, more especially about the mouth and chin, while the cheeks were colorless, and the skin swarthy. His eye, too, was black as jet, and his cheek was half covered in whiskers of a hue dark as the raven's wing. His face, as a whole, was singularly beautiful; for handsome is a word not strong enough to express all the character that was conveyed by a conformation that might be supposed to have been copied from some antique medal,. more especially when illuminated by a smile that, at times, rendered the whole countenance almost as bewitching as that of a lovely woman. There was nothing effeminate in the appearance of the young stranger, notwithstanding; his manly, though sweet voice, well-knit frame, and firm look, affording every pledge of resolution and spirit.

Both the vice-governatore and the podesta were struck with the unusual personal advantages and smart air of the stranger, and each stood looking at him half a minute in silence, after the usual salutations had passed, and before the party were seated. Then, as the three took chairs, on a motion from Signor Barrofaldi, the latter opened the discourse.

"They tell me that we have the honor to receive into our little haven a vessel of Inghilterra, Signor Capitano," observed the vice-governatore, earnestly regarding the other through his spectacles as he spoke, and that, too, in a manner not altogether free from distrust.

"Signor Vice-governatore, such is the flag under which I have the honor to serve," returned the mariner.

"You are an Inglese, yourself, I trust, Signor Capitano; what name shall I enter in my book, here?"

"Jaques Smeet," answered the other, betraying what might have proved two very fatal shibboleths, in the ears of those who were practiced in the finesse of our very unmusical language, by attempting to say "Jack Smith."

"Jaques Smeet," replied the vice-governatore; "that is, Giacomo, in our Italian—"

"No—no, signore," hastily interrupted Captain Smeet, "not Jaqueomo, but Jaques—Giovanni turned into Jaques by the aid of a little salt water."

"Ah! I begin to understand you, signore; you English have this usage in your language, though you have softened the word a little, in mercy to our ears. But we Italians are not afraid of such sounds: and I know the name—' Giac Smeet '—Il Capitano Giac Smeet; I have long suspected my English master of ignorance, for he was merely one of our Leghorn pilots, who has sailed in a bastimento de guerra of your country; he called your honorable name ' Smees,' signore."

"He was very wrong, Signor Vice-governatore," answered the other, clearing his throat by a slight effort; "we always call our family ' Smeet.'"

"And the name of your lugger, Signor Capitano Smeet?" suspending the pen over the paper in expectation of the answer.

"Ze *Ving-and-Ving;*" pronouncing the w's in a very different way from what they had been sounded in answering the hails.

"Ze *Ving-y-Ving,*" repeated Signor Barrofaldi, writing the name in a manner to show it was not the first time he had heard it; "ze *Ving-y-Ving:* that is a poetical appellation, Signor Capitano; may I presume to ask what it signifies?"

"*Ala-e-Ala,* in your Italian, Mister Vice-governatore. When a craft like mine has a sail spread on each side, resembling a bird, we say, in English, that she marches 'Ving-and-Ving.'"

Andrea Barrofaldi mused, in silence, near a minute. During this interval, he was thinking of the improbability of any but a *bona fide* Englishman's dreaming of giving a vessel an appellation so thoroughly idiomatic, and was fast mystifying himself as so often happens by tyros in any particular branch of knowledge, by his own critical acumen. Then he half whispered a conjecture on the subject to Vito Viti, influenced quite as much by a desire to show his own readiness in such matters, as by any other feeling. The podesta was less struck by the distinction than his superior; but, as became one of his limited means, he did not venture an objection.

"Signor Capitano," resumed Andrea Barrofaldi, "since when have you English adopted the rig of the lugger? It is an unusual craft for so great a naval nation, they tell me."

"Bah! I see how it is, Signor Vice-governatore—you suspect me of being a Frenchman, or a Spaniard, or something else than I claim to be. On this head, however, you may set your heart at rest, and put full faith in what I tell you. My name is Capitaine Jaques Smeet; my vessel is ze *Ving-and-Ving;* and my service that of the king of England."

"Is your craft, then, a king's vessel; or does she sail with the commission of a corsair?"

"Do I look like a corsair, signore?" demanded le Capitaine Smeet, with an offended air. "I have reason to feel myself injured by so unworthy an imputation!"

"Your pardon, Signor Capitano Smees; but our duty is a very delicate one, on this unprotected island, in times as troubled as these in which we live. It has been stated to me, as coming from the most experienced pilot of our haven, that your lugger has not altogether the appearance of a vessel of the Inglese, while she has many that belong to the corsairs of France; and a prudent caution imposes on me the office of making certain of your nation. Once assured of that, it will be the delight of the Elbans to prove how much we honor and esteem our illustrious allies."

"This is so reasonable, and so much according to what I do myself, when I meet a stranger at sea," cried the captain, stretching forth both arms in a frank and inviting manner, "that none but a knave would object to it. Pursue your own course, Signor Vice-governatore, and satisfy all your scruples, in your own manner. How shall this be done? will you go on board ze *Ving-and-Ving*, and look for yourself, send this honorable magistrate, or shall I show you my commission? Here is the last, altogether at your service, and that of his imperial highness, the grand duke."

"I flatter myself with having sufficient knowledge of Inghilterra, Signor Capitano, though it be by means of books, to discover an impostor, could I believe you capable of appearing in so unworthy a character; and that, too, in a very brief conversation. We book-worms," added Andrea Barrofaldi, with a glance of triumph at his neighbor, for he now expected to give the podesta an illustration of the practical benefits of general learning, a subject that had often been discussed between them, "we book-worms can manage these trifles in our own way; and if you will consent to enter into a short dialogue on the subject of England, her habits, language, and laws, this question will be speedily put at rest."

"You have me at command; and nothing would delight me more than to chat for a few minutes about that little island. It is not large, signore, and is doubtless of little worth; but as my country, it is much in my eyes."

"This is natural. And now, Signor Capitano," added Andrea, glancing at the podesta, to make sure that he was listening, "will you have the goodness to explain to me what sort of a government this Inghilterra possesses—whether monarchy, aristocracy, or democracy?"

"Peste! that is not so easily answered. There is a king, and yet there are powerful lords; and a democracy, too, that sometimes gives trouble enough. Your question might puzzle a philosopher, Signor Vice-governatore."

"This may be true enough, neighbor Vito Viti, for the constitution of Inghilterra is an instrument of many strings. Your answer convinces me you have thought on the subject of your government, capitano, and I honor a reflecting man in all situations in life. What is the religion of the country?"

"Corpo di Bacco! that is harder to answer than all the rest! We have as many religions in England as we have people. It is true the law says one thing on this head, but then the men, women, and children say another. Nothing has

troubled me more than this same matter of religion!"

"Ah! you sailors do not disquiet your souls with such thoughts, if the truth must be said. Well, we will be indulgent on this subject; though, out of doubt, you and all your people are Luterani."

"Set us down as what you please," answered the captain, with an ironical smile. "Our fathers, at any rate, were all good Catholics once. But seamanship and the altar are the best of friends, living quite independent of each other."

"That I will answer for. It is much the same here, caro Vito Viti, though our mariners do burn so many lamps and offer up so many aves."

"Your pardon, Signor Vice-governatore," interrupted the Signor Smeet, with a little earnestness; "this is the great mistake of your seamen in general. Did they pray less, and look to their duties more, their voyages would be shorter, and the profits more certain."

"Scandalous!" exclaimed the podesta, in hotter zeal than it was usual for him to betray.

"Nay, worthy Vito Viti, it is even so," interrupted the deputy, with a wave of the hand that was as authoritative as the concession was liberal, and indicative of a spirit enlightened by study; "the fact must be conceded. There is the fable of Hercules and the wagoner to confirm it. Did our men first strive, and then pray, more would be done than by first praying and then striving; and now, Signor Capitano, a word on your language, of which I have some small knowledge, and which, doubtless, you speak like a native."

"Sairtain*lee*," answered the captain, with perfect self-composure, changing the form of speech from the Italian to the English with a readiness that proved how strong he felt himself on this point; "one cannot fail to speak ze tongue of his own muzzair."

This was said without any confusion of manner, and with an accent that might very well mislead a foreigner, and it sounded imposing to the vice-governatore, who felt a secret consciousness that he could not have uttered such a sentence to save his own life, without venturing out of his depth; therefore he pursued the discourse in Italian.

"Your language, signore," observed Andrea Barrofaldi, with warmth, "is no doubt a very noble one, for the language in which Shakespeare and Milton wrote cannot be else; but you will permit me to say that it has a uniformity of sound, with words of different letters, that I find as unreasonable as it is embarrassing to a foreigner."

"I have heard such complaints before," answered the captain, not at all sorry to find the examination, which had proved so awkward to himself, likely to be transferred to a language about which he cared not at all, "and have little to say in its defense. But as an example of what you mean—"

"Why, signore, here are several words that I have written on this bit of paper, which sound nearly alike, though as you perceive they are quite differently spelled. Bix, bax, box, bux, and bocks," continued Andrea, endeavoring to pronounce "big," "bag," "bug," "bog," and "box," all of which, it seemed to him, had a very close family resemblance in sound, though certainly spelled with different letters, "these are words, signore, that are enough to drive a foreigner to abandon your tongue in despair."

"Indeed they are; and I often told the person who taught me the language—"

"How! did you not learn your own tongue as we all get our native forms of speech, by ear, when a child?" demanded the vice-governatore, his suspicions suddenly revived.

"Without question, signore; but I speak of books, and of learning to read. When 'big,' 'bag,' 'bug,' 'bog,' and 'box,'" reading from the paper in a steady voice, and a very tolerable pronunciation, "first came before me I felt all the embarrassment of which you speak."

"And did you only pronounce these words when first taught to read them?"

This question was awkward to answer; but Vito Viti began to weary of a discourse in which he could take no part, and most opportunely he interposed an objection of his own.

"Signor Barrofaldi," he said, "stick to the lugger. All our motives of suspicion came from Tommaso Tonti, and all of his from the rig of Signor Smees' vessel. If the lugger can be explained, what do we care about bixy, buxy, boxy!"

The vice-governatore was not sorry to get creditably out of the difficulties of the language, and smiling on his friend, he made a gentle bow of compliance. Then he reflected a moment, in order to plan another mode of proceeding, and pursued the inquiry.

"My neighbor Vito Viti is right," he said, "and we will stick to the lugger. Tommaso Tonti is a mariner of experience, and the oldest pilot of Elba. He tells us that the lugger is a craft much in use among the French, and not at all among

the English, so far as he has ever witnessed."

"In that Tommaso Tonti is no seaman. Many luggers are to be found among the English; though, certainly more among the French. But I have already given the Signor Viti to understand that there is such an island as Guernsey, which was once French, but which is now English, and that accounts for the appearance he has observed. We are Guernsey-men, the lugger is from Guernsey, and, no doubt, we have a Guernsey look. This is being half French, I allow."

"That alters the matter altogether. Neighbor Viti, this is all true about the island, and about its habits and its origin; and if one could be as certain about the names, why nothing more need to be said. Are Giac Smees, and Ving-y-Ving, Guernsey names?"

"'They are not particularly so," returned the sailor, with difficulty refraining from laughing in the vice-governatore's face; "Jaques Smeet being so English that we are the largest family, perhaps, in all Inghilterra. Half the nobles of the island are called Smeet, and not a few are named Jaques. But little Guernsey was conquered; and our ancestors, who performed that office, brought their names with them, signore. As for Ving-and-Ving, it is capital English."

"I do not see, Vito, but this is reasonable. If the capitano, now, only had his commission with him, you and I might go to bed in peace, and sleep till morning."

"Here, then, signore, are your sleeping potions," continued the laughing sailor, drawing from his pocket several papers. "These are my orders from the admiral; and, as they are not secret, you can cast your eyes over them. This is my commission, Signore Vice-governatore; this is the signature of the English minister of marine, and here is my own, 'Jaques Smeet,' as you see, and here is the order to me, as a lieutenant, to take command of the *Ving-and-Ving.*"

All the orders and names were there, certainly, written in a clear, fair hand, and in perfectly good English. The only thing that one who understood the language would have been apt to advert to, was the circumstance that the words which the sailor pronounced "Jaques Smeet," were written plainly enough, "Jack Smith," an innovation on the common practice which, to own the truth, had proceeded from his own obstinacy, and had been done in the very teeth of the objections of the scribe who forged the papers. But Andrea was still too little of an English scholar to understand the blunder, and the Jack passed, with him, quite as currently as would "John," "Edward," or any other appellation. As to the Wing-and-Wing, all was right; though, as the words were pointed out and pronounced by both parties, one pertinaciously insisted on calling them "Ving-and-Ving," and the other "Ving-y-Ving." All this evidence had a great tendency toward smoothing down every difficulty, and 'Maso Tonti's objections were pretty nearly forgotten by both of the Italians, when the papers were returned to their proper owner.

"It was an improbable thing that an enemy or a corsair would venture into this haven of ours, Vito Viti," said the vice-governatore, in a self-approving manner; "we have a reputation for being vigilant, and for knowing our business, as well as the authorities of Livorno, or Genova, or Napoli."

"And that too, signore, with nothing in the world to gain but hard knocks and a prison," added the Captain Smeet, with one of his most winning smiles, a smile that even softened the heart of the podesta, while it so far warmed that of his superior as to induce him to invite the stranger to share his own frugal supper. The invitation was accepted as frankly as it had been given, and, the table being in an adjoining room, in a few minutes Il Capitano Smees and Vito Viti were sharing the vice-governatore's evening meal.

From this moment, if distrust existed any longer in the breasts of the two functionaries of Porto Ferrajo, it was so effectually smothered as to be known only to themselves. The light fare of an Italian kitchen, and the light wines of Tuscany, just served to strengthen the system and enliven the spirits; the conversation becoming general and lively as the business of the moment proceeded. At that day tea was known throughout southern Europe as an ingredient only for the apothecary's keeping: nor was it often to be found among his stores; and the convives used, as a substitute, large draughts of the pleasant mountain liquors of the adjacent main, which produced an excitement scarcely greater, while it may be questioned if it did as much injury to the health. The stranger, however, both ate and drank sparingly, for, while he affected to join cordially in the discourse and the business of restoration, he greatly desired to be at liberty to pursue his own designs.

Andrea Barrofaldi did not let so excellent an opportunity to show his acquirements to the podesta go by neglected. He talked much of England, its history, its religion, government, laws, climate and industry; making frequent appeals to the Capitano Smees for the truth of his opinions. In most cases the parties agreed surprisingly, for the stranger started with a deliberate intention to assent to everything; but even this compliant temper had its embarrassments, since the vice-governatore so put his interrogatories as occasionally to give to acquiescence the appearance of dissent. The other floundered through his difficulties tolerably well, notwithstanding; and so successful was he, in particular, in flattering Andrea's self-love by expressions of astonishment that a foreigner should understand his own country so well—better, indeed, in many respects than he understood it himself—and that he should be so familiar with its habits, institutions and geography, that by the time the flask was emptied, the superior functionary whispered to his inferior that the stranger manifested so much information and good sense, he should not be surprised if he turned out, in the long run, to be some secret agent of the British government, employed to make philosophical inquiries as to the trade and navigation of Italy, with a view to improve the business relations between the countries.

"You are an admirer of nobility, and a devotee of aristocracy," added Andrea Barrofaldi, in pursuit of the subject then in hand; "if the truth were known, a scion of some noble house yourself."

"I? Peste! I hate an aristocrat, Signor Vice-governatore, as I do the devil!"

This was said just after the freest draught the stranger had taken, and with an unguarded warmth that he himself immediataly regretted.

"This is extraordinary in an Inglese! Ah, I see how it is; you are in the *opposizione*, and find it necessary to say this. It is most extraordinary, good Vito Viti, that these Inglese are divided into two political castes, that contradict each other in everything. If one maintains that object is white, the other side swears it is black; and so *vice versa*. Both parties profess to love their country better than anything else; but the one that is out of power abuses even power itself until it falls into its own hands."

"This is so much like Giorgio Grondi's course toward me, signore, that I could almost swear he was one of these very *opposizione*. I never approve of a thing that he does not condemn, or condemn that he does not approve. Do you confess this much, Signor Capitano?"

"Il vice-governatore knows us better than we know ourselves, I fear. There is too much truth in his account of our politics ; but, signori," rising from his chair, " I now crave your permission to look at your town, and to return to my vessel. The darkness has come, and discipline must be observed."

As Andrea Barrofaldi had pretty well exhausted his stores of knowledge, no opposition was made ; and, returning his thanks, the stranger took his departure, leaving the two functionaries to discuss his appearance and character over the remainder of the flask.

CHAPTER III.

IL CAPITANO SMEET was not sorry to get out of the government house—palazzo, as some of the simple people of Elba called the unambitious dwelling. He had been well badgered by the persevering erudition of the vice-governatore ; and, stored as he was with nautical anecdotes, and a tolerable personal acquaintance with sundry seaports, for any expected occasion of this sort, he had never anticipated a conversation which would aspire as high as the institutions, religion, and laws of his adopted country. Had the worthy Andrea heard the numberless maledictions that the stranger muttered between his teeth, as he left the house, it would have shocked all his sensibilities, if it did not revive his suspicions.

It was now night ; but a starry, calm, voluptuous evening, such as is familiar to those who are acquainted with the Mediterranean and its shores. There was scarcely a breath of wind, though the cool air, that appeared to be a gentle respiration of the sea, induced a few idlers still to linger on the heights, where there was a considerable extent of land, that might serve for a promenade. Along this walk the mariner proceeded, undetermined, for the moment, what to do next. He had scarcely got into the open space, however, before a female, with her form closely enveloped in a mantle, brushed near him, anxiously gazing into his face. Her motions were too quick and sudden for him to obtain a look in return ; but, perceiving that she held her way along the heights beyond the spot most frequented by the idlers, he followed until she stopped.

"Ghita !" said the young man, in a tone of delight, when he had got near enough to the female to recognize a face and form she no longer attempted to conceal ; "this is being fortunate, indeed, and saves a vast deal of trouble. A thousand, thousand thanks, dearest Ghita,

for this one act of kindness. I might have brought trouble on you, as well as on myself, in striving to find your residence."

"It is for that reason, Raoul, that I have ventured so much more than is becoming in my sex, to meet you. A thousand eyes, in this gossiping little town, are on your lugger, at this moment, and be certain they will also be on its captain, as soon as it is known he has landed. I fear you do not know for what you and your people are suspected, at this very instant ! "

"For nothing discreditable, I hope, dear Ghita, if it be only not to dishonor your friend ! "

"Many think and say you are Frenchmen, and that the English flag is only a disguise."

"If that be all, we must bear the infamy," answered Raoul Yvard, laughing. "Why, this is just what we are to a man, a single American excepted, who is an excellent fellow to make out British commissions, and help us to a little English when harder pushed than common ; and why should we be offended, if the good inhabitants of Porto Ferrajo take us for what we are ? "

"Not offended, Raoul, but endangered. If the vice-governatore gets this notion, he will order the batteries to fire upon you, and will destroy you as an enemy."

"Not he, Ghita. He is too fond of le Capitaine Smeet, to do so cruel a thing ; and then he must shift all his guns before they will hurt *Le Feu-Follet* where she lies. I never leave my little Jack-o'-Lantern * within reach of an enemy's hand. Look here, Ghita ; you can see her through this opening in the houses—that dark spot on the bay, there ; and you will perceive no gun from any battery in Porto Ferrajo can as much as frighten, much less harm her."

"I know her position, Raoul, and understood why you anchored in that spot. I knew, or thought I knew you, from the first moment you came in plain sight ; and so long as you remained outside, I was not sorry to look on so old a friend ; nay, I will go further, and say I rejoiced, for it seemed to me you passed so near the island, just to let some whom you knew to be on it understand you had not forgotten them ; but when you came into the bay, I thought you mad ! "

"Mad I should have been, dearest Ghita, had I lived longer without seeing you. What are these miserables of Elbans, that I should fear them ! They have no cruiser

---

* The English of Feu-Follet.

—only a few feluccas—all of which are not worth the trouble of burning. Let them but point a finger at us, and we will tow their Austrian polacre out into the bay, and burn her before their eyes. *Le Feu-Follet* deserves her name; she is here, there, and everywhere, before her enemies suspect her."

"But her enemies suspect her now, and you cannot be too cautious. My heart was in my throat a dozen times, while the batteries were firing at you this evening."

"And what harm did they? they cost the grand duke two cartridges, and two shot, without even changing the lugger's course! You have seen too much of these things, Ghita, to be alarmed by smoke and noise."

"I have seen enough of these things, Raoul, to know that a heavy shot, fired from these heights, would have gone through your little *Feu-Follet,* and coming out under water would have sunk you to the bottom of the Mediterranean."

"We should have had our boats then," answered Raoul Yvard, with an indifference that was not affected, for reckless daring was his vice rather than his virtue; "besides, a shot must first hit before it can harm, as the fish must be taken before it can be cooked. But enough of this, Ghita; I get quite enough of shot, and ships, and sinking, in every-day life, and, now I have at last found this blessed moment, we will not throw away the opportunity by talking of such matters—"

"Nay, Raoul, I can think of nothing else, and therefore can talk of nothing else. Suppose the vice-governatore should suddenly take it into his head to send a party of soldiers to *Le Feu-Follet,* with orders to seize her; what would then be your situation?"

"Let him; and I would send a boat's crew to his palazzo, here," the conversation was in French, which Ghita spoke fluently, though with an Italian accent, "and take him on a cruise after the English and his beloved Austrians! Bah! the idea will not cross his constitutional brain, and there is little use in talking about it. In the morning, I will send my prime minister, mon Barras, mon Carnot, mon Cambaceres, mon Ithuel Bolt, to converse with him on politics and religion."

"Religion," repeated Ghita, in a saddened tone; "the less you say on that holy subject, Raoul, the better I shall like it, and the better it will be for yourself, in the end. The state of your country makes your want of religion matter of regret, rather than of accusation, but it is none the less a dreadful evil."

"Well, then," resumed the sailor, who felt he had touched a dangerous ground, "we will talk of other things. Even supposing we are taken, what great evil have we to apprehend? We are honest corsairs, duly commissioned, and acting under the protection of the French Republic, one and undivided, and can but be made prisoners of war. That is a fortune which has once befallen me, and no greater calamity followed than my having to call myself le Capitaine Smeet, and finding out the means of mystifying le vice-governatore."

Ghita laughed, in spite of the fears she entertained, for it was one of the most powerful of the agencies the sailor employed in making other converts to his opinions, to cause them to sympathize with his light-hearted gayety, whether it suited their natural temperaments or not. She knew that Raoul had already been a prisoner in England two years, where, as he often said himself, he stayed just long enough to acquire a very respectable acquaintance with the language, if not with the institutions, manners, and religion, when he made his escape, aided by the American called Ithuel Bolt, an impressed seaman of our own Republic, who, fully entering into all the plans imagined by his more enterprising friend and fellow-sufferer, had cheerfully enlisted in the execution of his future schemes of revenge. States, like powerful individuals in private life, usually feel themselves too strong to allow any considerations of the direct consequences of departures from the right to influence their policy; and a nation is apt to fancy its power of such a character as to despise all worldly amends, while its moral responsibility is divided among too many to make it a matter of much concern to its particular citizens. Nevertheless, the truth will show that none are so low but they may become dangerous to the highest; and even powerful communities seldom fail to meet with their punishment for every departure from justice. It would seem, indeed, that a principle pervades nature, which renders it impossible for man to escape the consequences of his own evil deeds, even in this life; as if God had decreed the universal predominance of truth, and the never-failing downfall of falsehood from the beginning; the success of wrong being ever temporary, while the triumph of the right is eternal.

To apply these consoling considerations to the matter more immediately before us: The practice of impressment, in its day, raised a feeling among the seamen of other nations, as well as, in fact, among those of Great Britain herself, that probably has had as much effect in

Ghita, however, paid no attention to this touch of provincial pride, but pressing her hands on her heart, she stood like a statue of suspense, while the men in the battery executed their duty.—*Wing and Wing.*

destroying the prestige of her nautical invincibility, supported as was that prestige by a vast existing force, as any other one cause whatever. It was necessary to witness the feeling of hatred and resentment that was raised by the practice of this despotic power, more especially among those who felt that their foreign birth ought at least to have insured them impunity from the abuse, in order fully to appreciate what might so readily become its consequences. Ithuel Bolt, the seaman just mentioned, was a proof, in a small way, of the harm that even an insignificant individual can effect, when his mind is fully and wholly bent on revenge. Ghita knew him well; and, although she little liked either his character or his appearance, she had often been obliged to smile at the narrative of the deceptions he practiced on the English, and of the thousand low inventions he had devised to do them injury. She was not slow, now, to imagine that his agency had not been trifling in carrying on the present fraud.

"You do not openly call your lugger *Le Feu-Follet*, Raoul," she answered, after a minute's pause; "that would be a dangerous name to utter, even in Porto Ferrajo It is not a week since I heard a mariner dwelling on her misdeeds, and the reason that all good Italians have to detest her. It is fortunate the man is away, or he could not fail to know you."

"Of that I am not so certain, Ghita. We alter our paint often, and, at need, can alter our rig. You may be certain, however, that we hide our Jack-o'-Lantern, and sail under another name. The lugger, now she is in the English service, is called the *Ving-and-Ving.*"

"I heard the answer given to the hail from the shore, but it sounded different from this."

"Non—*Ving-and-Ving*, Ithuel answered for us, and you may be sure he can speak his own tongue. Ving-and-Ving is the word, and he pronounces it as I do."

"*Ving-y-Ving!*" repeated Ghita, in her pretty Italian tones, dropping naturally into the vice-governatore's fault of pronunciation; "it is an odd name, and I like it less than *Feu-Follet.*"

"I wish, dearest Ghita, I could persuade you to like the name of Yvard," rejoined the young man, in a half-reproachful, half-tender manner, "and I should care nothing for any other. You accuse me of disrespect for priests; but no son could ever kneel to a father for his blessing half so readily, or half so devoutly, as I could kneel with thee, before any friar in Italy, to receive that nuptial benediction which I have asked at your hand, but which you have so constantly and cruelly refused."

"I am afraid the name would not then be Feu-Follet, but Ghita-Folie," said the girl, laughing, though she felt a bitter pang at the heart, that cost her an effort to control; "no more of this, now, Raoul; we may be observed and watched; it is necessary that we separate."

A hurried conversation of more interest to the young couple themselves than it would prove to the reader, though it might not have been wholly without the latter, but which it would be premature to relate, now followed, when Ghita left Raoul on the hill, insisting that she knew the town too well to have any apprehensions about threading its narrow and steep streets, at any hour, by herself. This much, in sooth, must be said in favor of Andrea Barrofaldi's administration of justice, he had made it safe for the gentle, the feeble, and the poor, equally to move about the island by day or by night; it seldom happening that so great an enemy to peace and tranquillity appeared among his simple dependents as was the fact at this precise moment.

In the meantime, there was not quite as much tranquillity in Porto Ferrajo as the profound silence which reigned in the place might have induced a stranger to imagine. Tommaso Tonti was a man of influence, within his sphere, as well as the vice-governatore; and having parted from Vito Viti, as has been related, he sought the little *clientelle* of padroni and piloti, who were in the habit of listening to his opinions as if they were oracles. The usual place of resort of this set, after dark, was a certain house kept by a widow of the name of Benedetta Galopo, the uses of which were plainly enough indicated by a small bush that hung dangling from a short pole, fastened above the door. If Benedetta knew anything of the proverb, that "Good wine needs no bush," she had not sufficient faith in the contents of her own casks to trust to their reputation; for this bush of hers was as regularly renewed as its withering leaves required. Indeed, it was a common remark among her customers, that her bush was always as fresh as her face, and that the latter was one of the most comely that was to be met with on the island; a circumstance that aided much indifferent wine in finding a market. Benedetta bore a reasonably good name, nevertheless, though it was oftener felt, perhaps, than said, that she was a confirmed coquette. She tolerated 'Maso principally on two accounts; because, if he were old and unattractive in his own person, many of his followers were among the smartest seamen of the port, and because he not only drank his full proportion, but paid with punctuality. These inducements rendered the pilot always a welcome guest at La Santa Maria degli Venti, as the house was called, though it had no other sign than the often-renewed bush, already mentioned.

At the very moment, then, when Raoul Yvard and Ghita parted on the hill, 'Maso was seated in his usual place at the table in Benedetta's upper room, the windows of which commanded as full a view of the lugger as the hour permitted; that craft being anchored about a cable's length distant, and, as a sailor might have expressed it, just abeam. On this occasion he had selected the upper room, and but three companions, because it was his wish that as few should enter into his counsels as at all comported with the love of homage to his own experience. The party had been assembled a quarter of an hour, and there had been time to cause the tide to ebb materially in the flask, which, it may be well to tell the reader at once, contained very little less than half a gallon of liquor, such as it was.

"I have told it all to the podesta," said 'Maso, with an important manner, as he put down his glass, after potation the second; which quite equaled potation the first in quantity. "Yes, I have told it all to Vito Viti, and no doubt he has told it to Il Signor Vice-governatore, who now knows as much about the whole affair as either of us four. Cospetto! to think such a thing dare happen in a haven like Porto Ferrajo! Had it come to pass over on the other side of the island, at Porto Longone, one wouldn't think so much of it, for they are never much on the lookout; but to take place here, in the very capital of Elba! I should as soon have expected it at Livorno!"

"But, 'Maso," put in Daniele Bruno, in the manner of one who was a little skeptical, "I have often seen the pavilion of the Inglese, and this is as much like that which all their frigates and corvettes wear as one of our feluccas is like another. The flag, at least, is all right."

"What signifies a flag, Daniele, when a French hand can hoist an English ensign as easily as the king of Inghilterra himself? If that lugger was not built by the Francese, you were not built by an Italian father and mother. But I should not think so much of the hull, for that may have been captured, as the English take many of their enemies on

the high seas; but look at the rigging and sails—Santa Maria! I could go to the shop of the very sailmaker, in Marseilles, who made that foresail! His name is Pierre Benoit, and a very good workman he is, as all will allow who have had occasion to employ him."

This particularity greatly aided the argument, common minds being seldom above yielding to the circumstances which are so often made to corroborate imaginary facts. Tommaso Tonti, though so near the truth as to his main point—the character of the visitor—was singularly out as to the sail, notwithstanding; *Le Feu-Follet* having been built, equipped, and manned at Nantes, and Pierre Benoit never having seen her or her foresail either; but it mattered not in the way of discussion and assertion. one sailmaker being as good as another, provided he was French.

"And have you mentioned this to the podesta?" inquired Benedetta, who stood with the empty flask in her hand, listening to the discourse. "I should think that sail would open his eyes."

"I cannot say I have; but then I told him so many other things more to the point, that he cannot do less than believe this when he hears it. Signor Viti promised to meet me here, after he has had a conversation with the vice-governatore; and we may now expect him every minute."

"Il Signor Podesta will be welcome," said Benedetta, wiping off a spare table, and bustling round the room to make things look a little smarter than they ordinarily did; "he may frequent grander wine-houses than this, but he will hardly find better liquor."

"Poverina! Don't think that the podesta comes here on any such errand; he comes to meet me," answered 'Maso, with an indulgent smile; "he takes his wine too often on the heights, to wish to come as low as this after a glass. Friends of mine (*amigi mii*), there is wine up at that house that, when the oil is once out of the neck of the flask,[*] goes down a man's throat as smoothly as if it were all oil itself! I could drink a flask of it without once stopping to take breath. It is that liquor which makes the nobles so light and airy."

"I know the washy stuff," put in Benedetta, with more warmth than she was used to betray to her customers; "well may you call it smooth, a good spring running near each of the wine-presses that

---

[*] It is a practice in Tuscany to put a few drops of oil in the neck of each flask of the more delicate wines, to exclude the air.

have made it. I have seen some of it that even oil would not float on!"

This assertion was a fair counterpoise to that of the sail, being about as true. But Benedetta had too much experience in the inconstancy of men not to be aware that if the three or four customers who were present should seriously take up the notion that the island contained any better liquor than that she habitually placed before them, her value might be sensibly diminished in their eyes. As became a woman who had to struggle singly with the world, too, her native shrewdness taught her, that the best moment to refute a calumny was to stop it as soon as it began to circulate, and her answer was as warm in manner as it was positive in terms. This was an excellent opening for an animated discussion, and one would have been very likely to occur, had there not fortunately been steps heard without that induced 'Maso to expect the podesta. Sure enough, the door opened, and Vito Viti appeared, followed, to the astonishment of all the guests, and to the absolute awe of Benedetta, by the vice-governatore himself.

The solution of this unexpected visit is very easily given. After the departure of the Capitano Smees, Vito Viti returned to the subject of 'Maso's suspicions, and by suggesting certain little circumstances in the mariner's manner, that he had noted during the interview, he so far succeeded in making an impression on himself, that, in the end, his own distrust revived, and with it that of the deputy-governor. Neither, however, could be said to be more than uneasy, and the podesta happening to mention his appointment with the pilot, Andrea determined to accompany him, in order to reconnoitre the strange craft in person. Both the functionaries wore their cloaks, by no means an unusual thing in the cool night air of the coast, even in midsummer, which served them for all the disguise that circumstances required.

"Il Signor Vice-governatore!" almost gasped Benedetta, dusting a chair, and then the table, and disposing the former near the latter by a sort of mechanical process, as if only one errand could ever bring a guest within her doors; "your eccellenza is most welcome; and it is an honor I could oftener ask. We are humble people down here at the water side, but I hope we are just as good Christians as if we lived upon the hill."

"Doubt it not, worthy Bettina—"

"My name is Benedetta, at your eccellenza's command—Benedettina, if it please the vice-governatore; but not Bettina. We think much of our names, down here at the water side, eccellenza."

"Let it be so, then, good Benedetta, and I make no doubt you are excellent Christians. A flask of your wine, if it be convenient."

The woman dropped a courtesy that was full of gratitude; and the glance of triumph that she cast at her other guests, may be said to have terminated the discussion that was about to commence, as the dignitaries appeared. It disposed of the question of the wine at once, and forever silenced caviling. If the vice-governatore could drink her liquor, what mariner would henceforth dare calumniate it !

"Eccellenza, with a thousand welcomes," Benedetta continued, as she placed the flask on the table, after having carefully removed the cotton and the oil with her own plump hand; this being one of half a dozen flasks of really sound, well-flavored Tuscan liquor that she kept for special occasions; as she well might, the cost being only a paul, or ten cents for nearly half a gallon. "Eccellenza, a million times welcome. This is an honor that don't befall the Santa Maria degli Venti more than once in a century; and you, too, Signor Podesta, once before, only, have you ever had leisure to darken my poor door."

"We bachelors"—the podesta, as well as the vice-governatore, belonged to that fraternity—"we bachelors are afraid to trust ourselves too often in the company of a sprightly widow like yourself, whose beauty has rather improved than lessened by a few years."

This brought a coquettish answer, during which time Andrea Barrofaldi, having first satisfied himself that the wine might be swallowed with impunity, was occupied in surveying the party of silent and humble mariners who were seated at the other table. His object was to ascertain how far he might have committed himself by appearing in such a place, when his visit could not well be attributed to more than one motive. 'Maso he knew, as the oldest pilot of the place, and he had also some knowledge of Daniele Bruno; but the three other seamen were strangers to him.

"Inquire if we are not among friends, here, and worthy subjects of the grand duke all," observed Andrea to Vito Viti, in a low voice.

"Thou hearest, 'Maso," observed the podesta; "canst thou answer for all of thy companions?"

"Every one of them, signore; this is Daniele Bruno, whose father was killed in a battle with the Algerines, and whose mother was the daughter of a mariner, as well known in Elba as—"

"Never mind the particulars, Tommaso Tonti," interrupted the vice-governatore; "it is sufficient that thou knowest all thy companions to be honest men, and faithful servants of the *sovrano*. You all know, most probably, the errand which has brought the Signor Viti and myself to this house, to-night?"

The men looked at each other, as the ill-instructed are apt to do when it becomes necessary to answer a question that concerns many; assisting the workings of their minds, as it might be, with the aid of their senses; and then Daniele Bruno took on himself the office of spokesman.

"Signore, vostro eccellenza, we think we do," answered the man. "Our fellow, 'Maso here, has given us to understand that he suspects the Inglese that is anchored in the bay to be no Inglese at all, but either a pirate or a Frenchman—the blessed Maria preserve us! but in these troubled times it does not make much difference which."

"I will not say as much as that, friend; for one would be an outcast among all people, while the other would have the rights which shield the servants of civilized nations," returned the scrupulous and just-minded functionary. "The time was when his imperial majesty, the emperor, and his illustrious brother, our sovereign, the grand duke, did not allow that the republican government of France was a lawful government; but the fortune of war removed his scruples, and a treaty of peace has allowed the contrary. Since the late alliance, it is our duty to consider all Frenchmen as enemies, though it by no means follows that we are to consider them as pirates."

"But their corsairs seize all our craft, signore, and treat their people as if they were no better than dogs; then, they tell me that they are not Christians; no, not even Luterani or heretics!"

"That religion does not flourish among them is true," answered Andrea, who loved so well to discourse on such subjects that he would have stopped to reason on religion or manners with the beggar to whom he gave a pittance, did he only meet with encouragement; "but it is not as bad in France, on this important head, as it has been; and we hope that there will be further improvement in due time."

"But, Signor Vice-governatore," put in 'Maso, "these people have treated the Holy Father and his States in a way that one would not treat an infidel or a Turk!"

"Aye, that is it, signori," observed Benedetta; "a poor woman cannot go to mass without having her mind disturbed by the thoughts of the wrongs done the head of the Church. Had these things come from Luterani, it might have been borne; but they say the Francese were once all good Catholics!"

"So were the Luterani, bella Benedetta, to their chief schismatic and leader, the German monk himself."

This piece of information caused great surprise, even the podesta himself turning an inquiring glance at his superior, as much as to acknowledge his own wonder that a Protestant should ever have been anything but a Protestant—or rather a Lutheran anything but a Lutheran—the word Protestant being too insignificant to be in favor among those who deny there were any just grounds for a protest at all. That Luther had ever been a Romanist was perfectly wonderful, even in the eyes of Vito Viti.

"Signore, you would hardly mislead these honest people, in a matter as grave as this?" exclaimed the podesta.

"I do but tell you the truth; and one of these days you shall hear the whole story, neighbor Viti. 'Tis worth an hour of leisure to any man, and is very consoling and useful to a Christian. But whom have you below, Benedetta? I hear steps on the stairs, and wish not to be seen."

The widow stepped promptly forward to meet her new guests, and to show them into a commoner room below stairs, when her movement was anticipated by the door opening, and a man standing on the threshold. It was now too late to prevent the intrusion, and a little surprise at the appearance of the new-comer held all mute and observant for a minute.

The person who had followed his ears, and thus reached the sanctum sanctorum of Benedetta, was no other than Ithuel Bolt, the American seaman, already named in the earlier part of this chapter. He was backed by a Genoese, who had come in the double capacity of interpreter and boon companion. That the reader may the better understand the character he has to deal with, however, it may be necessary to digress, by giving a short account of the history, appearance, and peculiarities of the former individual.

Ithuel Bolt was a native of what, in this great Union, is called the Granite State. Notwithstanding he was not absolutely made of the stone in question, there was an absence of the ordinary symptoms of natural feeling about him, that had induced many of his French acquaintances in particular to affirm that there was a good deal more of marble in his moral temperament, at least, than usually fell to the lot of human beings. He had the outline of a good frame, but it was miserably deficient in the filling up. The bone predominated; the sinews came next in consideration; nor was the man without a proper share of muscle; but this last was so disposed of as to present nothing but angles, whichever way he was viewed. Even his thumbs and fingers were nearer square than round; and his very neck which was bare, though a black silk kerchief was tied loosely round the throat, had a sort of pentagon look about it, that defied all symmetry or grace. His stature was just six feet and an inch, when he straightened himself; as he did from time to time, seemingly with a desire to relieve a very inveterate stoop in his shoulders; although it was an inch or two less, in the position he most affected. His hair was dark, and his skin had got several coats of confirmed brown on it, by exposure, though originally rather fair; while the features were good, the forehead being broad and full, and the mouth positively handsome. This singular countenance was illuminated by two keen, restless, whitish eyes, that resembled, not spots on the sun, but rather suns on a spot.

Ithuel had gone through all the ordinary vicissitudes of American life, beneath those pursuits which are commonly thought to be confined to the class of gentleman. He had been farmer's boy, printer's devil, schoolmaster, stage-driver, and tin-peddler, before he ever saw the sea. In the way of what he called "chores," too, he had practiced all the known devices of rustic domestic economy; having assisted even in the washing and house-cleaning, besides having passed the evenings of an entire winter in making brooms. Ithuel had reached his thirtieth year before he dreamed of going to sea. An accident then put preferment in this form before his eyes, and he engaged as the mate of a small coaster, on his very first voyage. Fortunately, the master never found out his deficiencies, for Ithuel had a self-possessed, confident way with him, that prevented discovery, until they were outside of the port from which they sailed, when the former was knocked overboard by the main boom, and drowned. Most men, so circumstanced, would have returned, but Bolt never laid his hand to the plow and looked back. Besides, one course was quite as easy to him as another. Whatever he undertook he usually completed, in some fashion or other, though it were often much better had it never been attempted.

Fortunately it was summer, the wind was fair, and the crew wanted little ordering; and as it was quite a matter of course to steer in the right direction, until the schooner was carried safely into her proper port, she arrived safely; her people swearing that the new mate was the easiest and cleverest officer they had ever sailed with. And well they might, for Ithuel took care not to issue an order, until he had heard it suggested in terms by one of the hands; and then he never failed to repeat it, word for word, as if it were a suggestion of his own. As for the reputation of "cleverest" officer, which he so easily obtained, it will be understood, of course, that the term was used in the provincial signification that is so common in the part of the world from which Ithuel came. He was "clever" in this sense precisely in proportion as he was ignorant. His success, on this occasion, gained him friends, and he was immediately sent out again as the regular master of the craft, in which he had so unexpectedly received his promotion. He now threw all the duty on the mate; but so ready was he in acquiring, that, by the end of six months, he was a much better sailor than most Europeans would have made in three years. As the pitcher that goes too often to the well is finally broken, so did Ithuel meet with shipwreck, at last, in consequence of gross ignorance on the subject of navigation. This induced him to try a long voyage, in a more subordinate situation, until in the course of time he was impressed by the commander of an English frigate, who had lost so many of his men by the yellow fever, that he seized upon all he could lay his hands on, to supply their places, even Ithuel being acceptable in such a strait.

CHAPTER IV.

THE glance which Ithuel cast around him was brief, but comprehensive. He saw that two of the party in the room were much more superior to the other four, and that the last were common Mediterranean mariners. The position which Benedetta occupied in the household could not be mistaken, for she proclaimed herself its mistress by her very air; whether it were in the upper or in the lower room.

"Vino," said Ithuel, with a flourish of the hand, to help along his Italian, this and one or two more being the only words of the language he ventured to use directly, or without calling in the assistance of his interpreter; "vino—vino, vino signora."

"Si, si, si, signore," answered Benedetta, laughing, and this with her meaning eyes so keenly riveted on the person of her new guest as if to make it very questionable whether she were amused by anything but his appearance; "your eccellenza shall be served; but whether at a paul, or a half-paul the flask, depends on your own pleasure. We keep wine at both prices, and," glancing toward the table of Andrea Barrofaldi, "usually serve the first to signori of rank and distinction."

"What does the woman say?" growled Ithuel to his interpreter, a Genoese, who, from having served several years in the British navy, spoke English with a very tolerable facility; "you know what we want, and just tell her to hand it over, and I will fork out her St. Paul without more words. What a desperate liking your folks have for saints, Philip-o," for so Ithuel pronounced Filippo, the name of his companion—"what a desperate liking your folks have for saints, Philip-o, that they must even call their money after them."

"It not so in America, Signor Bolto?" asked the Genoese, after he had explained his wishes to Benedetta, in Italian; "it no ze fashion in your country to honor ze saints?"

"Honor the saints!" repeated Ithuel, looking curiously around him, as he took a seat at a third table, shoving aside the glasses at the same time, and otherwise disposing of everything within reach of his hand, so as to suit his own notions of order, and then leaning back on his chair until the two ends of the uprights dug into the plaster behind him, while the legs on which the fabric was poised cracked with his weight; "honor the saints! we should be much more like to dishonor them! What does any one want to honor a saint for? A saint is but a human, a man like you and me, after all the fuss you make about 'em. Saints abound in my country, if you'd believe people's account of themselves."

"Not quite so, Signor Bolto. You and me no great saint; Italian honor saint because he holy and good."

By this time Ithuel had got his two feet on the round of his seat, his knees spread so as to occupy as much space as unusual length of leg would permit, and his arms extended on the tops of two chairs, one on each side of him, in a way to resemble what is termed a spread eagle.

Andrea Barrofaldi regarded all this with wonder. It is true, he expected to meet

with no great refinement in a wine-house like that of Benedetta; but he was unaccustomed to see such nonchalance of manner in a man of the stranger's class, or, indeed of any class; the Italian mariners present occupying their chairs in simple and respectful attitudes, as if each one had the wish to be as little obtrusive as possible. Still he let no signs of his surprise escape him, noting all that passed in a grave but attentive silence. Perhaps he saw traces of national peculiarities, if not of national history, in the circumstances.

"Honor saint because he holy and good!" said Ithuel, with a very ill-concealed disdain, "why, that is the very reason we don't honor 'em. When you honor a holy man, mankind may consait you do it on that very account, and so fall into the notion you worship him, which would be idolatry, the awfulest of all sins, and the one to which every ra'al Christian gives the widest bairth. I would rayther worship this flask of wine any day, than worship the best saint on your parsons' books."

As Filippo was no casuist, but merely a believer, and Ithuel applied the end of the flask to his mouth at that moment, from an old habit of drinking out of jugs and bottles, the Genoese made no answer; keeping his eye on the flask, which, by the length of time it remained at the other's mouth, appeared to be in great danger of being exhausted; a matter of some moment to one of his own relish for liquor.

"Do you call this wine!" exclaimed Ithuel, when he stopped literally to take breath; "there isn't as much true granite in a gallon on't as in a pint of our cider. I could swallow a butt, and then walk a plank as narrow as your religion, Philip-o!"

This was said, nevertheless, with a look of happiness which proved how much the inward man was consoled by what it had received, and a richness of expression about the handsome mouth that denoted a sort of consciousness that it had been the channel of a most agreeable communication to the stomach. Sooth to say, Benedetta had brought up a flask at a paul, or at about four cents a bottle; a flask of the very quality which she had put before the vice-governatore; and this was a liquor that flowed so smoothly over the palate, and of a quality so really delicate, that Ithuel was by no means aware of the potency of the guest which he had admitted to his interior.

All this time the vice-governatore was making up his mind concerning the nation, and character of the stranger. That he should mistake Bolt for an Englishman was natural enough, and the fact had an influence in again unsettling his opinion as to the real flag under which the lugger sailed. Like most Italians of that day, he regarded all the families of the northern hordes as a species of barbarians, an opinion that the air and deportment of Ithuel had no direct agency in changing; for, while this singular being was not brawlingly rude and vulgar, like the coarser set of his own countrymen, with whom he had occasionally been brought in contact, he was so manifestly uncivilized in many material points, as to put his claim to gentility much beyond a cavil, and that in a negative way.

"You are a Genoese?" said Andrea to Filippo, speaking with the authority of one who had a right to question.

"Signore, I am, at your eccellenza's orders, though in foreign service at this present moment."

"In what service, friend? I am in authority, here in Elba, and ask no more than is my duty."

"Eccellenza, I can well believe this," answered Filippo, rising and making a respectful salutation, and one, too, that was without any of the awkwardness of the same act in a more northern man, "as it is to be seen in your appearance. I am now in the service of the king of England."

Filippo said this steadily, though his eyes dropped to the floor, under the searching scrutiny they endured. The answer of the vice-governatore was delivered coolly, though it was much to the point.

"You are happy," he said, "in getting so honorable masters: more especially as your own country has again fallen into the hands of the French. Every Italian heart must yearn for a government that has its existence and its motives on this side of the Alps."

"Signore, we are a republic to-day, and ever have been, you know."

"Aye—such as it is. But your companion speaks no Italian; he is an Inglese?"

"No, signore; an Americano; a sort of an Inglese, and yet not Inglese, after all. He loves England very little, if I can judge by his discourse."

"Un' Americano!" repeated Andrea Barrofaldi; "Americano!" exclaimed Vito Viti; "Americano!" said each of the mariners in succession, every eye turning with lively curiosity toward the subject of the discourse, who bore it all with appropriate steadiness and dignity. The reader is not to be surprised that an American

was then regarded with curiosity, in a country like Italy; for two years later, when an American ship of war was anchored suddenly before the town of Constantinople, and announced her nation, the authorities of the Sublime Porte were ignorant that such a country existed. It is true, Leghorn was beginning to be much frequented by American ships, in the year 1799; but even with these evidences before their eyes, the people of the very ports into which these traders entered, were accustomed to consider their crews a species of Englishmen, who managed to sail the vessel for the negroes at home.* In a word, two centuries and a half of national existence, and more than half a century of national independence, have not yet sufficed to teach all the inhabitants of the Old World that the great modern republic is peopled by men of a European origin, and possessing white skins. Even of those who are aware of the fact, the larger proportion, perhaps, have obtained this information through works of a light character, similar to this of our own, rather than by the more legitimate course of regular study, and a knowledge of history.

"Si," repeated Ithuel, with emphasis, as soon as he heard his nationality thus alluded to, and found all eyes on himself; " si, oon Americano : I'm not ashamed of my country, and if you're any way partic'lar in such matters, I come from New Hampshire, or what we call the Granite State. Tell 'em this, Philip-o, and let me know their idees, in answer."

Filippo translated this speech as well as he could, as he did the reply; and it may as well be stated here, once for all, that in the dialogue which succeeded, the instrumentality of this interpreter was necessary that the parties might understand each other. The reader will, therefore, give Filippo credit for this arrangement, although we shall furnish the different speeches very much as if the parties fully comprehended what was said.

"*Uno stato di granito!*" repeated the vice-governatore, looking at the podesta with some doubt in the expression of his countenance; "it must be a painful existence which these poor people endure, to toil for their food in such a region. Ask him, good Filippo, if they have any wine in his part of the world."

"Wine!" echoed Ithuel; "tell the sig-

---

* As recently as 1828, the author of this book was at Leghorn. The *Delaware*, 80, had just left there ; and speaking of her appearance to a native of the place, who supposed the writer to be an Englishman, the latter observed, "Of course, her people were all blacks?" "I thought so, too, signore, until I went on board the ship," was the answer; "but they are as white as you and I are."

nore that we shouldn't call this stuff wine at all. Nothing goes down our throats that doesn't rasp like a file, and burn like a chip out of Vesuvius. I wish, now, we had a drink of New England rum here, in order to show him the difference. I despise the man who thinks all his own things the best, just because they're his'n; but taste is taste, a'ter all, and there's no denying it."

"Perhaps the Signor Americano can give us an insight into the religion of his country; or are the Americani pagans? I do not remember, Vito, to have read anything of the religion of that quarter of the world."

"Religion, too! well, a question like this, now, would make a stir among our folks in New Hampshire! Look here, signore; we don't call your ceremonies, and images, and robes, and ringing of bells, and bowing and scraping, a religion at all; any more than we should call this smooth liquor, wine."

Ithuel was more under the influence of this "smooth liquor" than he was aware of, or he would not have been so loud in the expression of his dissent; as experience had taught him the necessity of reserve on such subjects, in most Catholic communities. But of all this Signor Barrofaldi was ignorant, and he made his answer with the severity of a good Catholic, though it was with the temper of a gentleman.

"What the Americano calls our ceremonies, and images, and ringing of bells, are probably not understood by him," he said; "since a country as little civilized as his own cannot very well comprehend the mysteries of a profound and ancient religion."

"Civilized! I calculate that it would stump this part of the world to produce such a civilization as our very youngest children are brought up on. But it's of no use talking, and so we will drink."

Andrea perceiving, indeed, that there was not much use in talking, more especially as Filippo had been a good deal mystified by the word "stump," was now disposed to abandon the idea of a dissertation on "religion, manners, and laws," to come at once to the matter that brought him into the present company.

"This American is also a servant of the English king, it would seem," he carelessly remarked; "I remember to have heard that there was a war between his country and that of the Inglesi, in which the French assisted the Americani to obtain a sort of national independence. What that independence is, I do not know; but it is probable that the people of the New World are still obliged to find mariners to serve in the navy of their former masters."

Ithuel's muscles twitched, and an expression of intense bitterness darkened his countenance. Then he smiled in a sort of derision, and gave vent to his feelings in words.

"Perhaps you're right, signore; perhaps this is the raal truth of the matter; for the British do take our people just the same as if they had the best right in the world to 'em. After all, we may be serving our masters; and all we say and think at home, about independence, is just a flash in the pan! Notwithstanding, some on us contrive, by hook or by crook, to take our revenge when occasion offers; and if I don't sarve master John Bull an ill turn, whenever luck throws a chance in my way may I never see a bit of the old State again—granite or rotten wood."

This speech was not very closely translated, but enough was said to awaken curiosity in the Vice-governatore, who thought it odd one who served among the English should entertain such feelings toward them. As for Ithuel himself, he had not observed his usual caution; but, unknown to himself, the oily wine had more "granite" in it than he imagined, and then he seldom spoke of the abuse of impressment without losing more or less of his ordinary self-command.

"Ask the Americano when he first entered into the service of the king of Inghilterra," said Andrea, "and why he stays in it, if it is unpleasant to him, when so many opportunities of quitting it offer."

"I never entered," returned Ithuel, taking the word in its technical meaning; "they pressed me, as if I had been a dog they wanted to turn a spit, and kept me seven long years fighting their accursed battles, and otherwise sarving their eends. I was over here, last year, at the mouth of the Nile, and in that pretty bit of work —and off Cape St. Vincent, too—and in a dozen more of their battles, and sorely against my will, on every account. This was hard to be borne, but the hardest of it has not yet been said; nor do I know that I shall tell on't at all."

"Anything that the Americano may think proper to relate will be listened to with pleasure."

Ithuel was a good deal undecided whether to go on or not; but taking a fresh pull at the flask, it warmed his feelings to the sticking point.

"Why, it was adding insult to injury. It's bad enough to injure a man, but when it comes to insulting him into the bargain, there must be but little grit in his natur' if it don't strike fire."

"And yet few are wronged who are not calumniated," observed the philosophical vice-governatore. "This is only too much the case with our Italy, worthy neighbor Vito Viti."

"I calculate the English treat all mankind alike, whether it's in Italy or Ameriky," for so Ithuel would pronounce this word, notwithstanding he had now been cruising in and near the Mediterranean several years; "but what I found hardest to be borne, was their running their rigs on me about my language and ways, which they were all the time laughing at as Yankee conversation and usages, while they pretended that the body out of which all on it come was an English body, and so they set it up to be shot at by any of their inimies that might happen to be jogging along our road. Then, squire, it is generally consaited among us in Ameriky that we speak much the best English a-going; and sure am I that none on us call a 'hog' an 'og,' an 'anchor' a 'hancor,' or a 'horse' an 'orse.' What is thought of that matter in this part of the world, Signor Squire?"

"We are not critics in your language, but it is reasonable to suppose that the English speak their own tongue better than any other people. That much must be conceded to them, at least, Signor Bolto."

"I shall acknowledge no such advantage as belonging to them. I have not been to school for nothing; not I. The English call c-l-e-r-k, clark; and c-u-c-u-m-b-e-r, cowcumber; and a-n-g-e-l, aingel; and no reasoning can convince me that's right. I've got a string of words of this sort that they pronounce out of all reason that's as long as a pair of leading-lines, or a ship's tiller-rope. You must know, Signor Squire, I kept school in the early part of my life."

"*Non e possibile!*" exclaimed the vice-governatore, astonishment actually getting the better of his habitual good breeding; "you must mean, Signor Americano, that you gave lessons in the art of rigging and sailing luggers."

"You never was more mistaken, signore. I taught, on the general system, all sorts of things in the edication way; and had one of my scholars made such a blunder as to say 'clark,' or 'aingel,' or 'harth,' or 'cowcumber,' he wouldn't have heard the last of it, for that week, at least. But I despise an Englishman from the very bottom of my soul; for heart isn't deep enough for my feelings."

Absurd as Ithuel's critical dissertations must appear to all who have any familiarity with real English, they were not greatly below many criticisms on the same subject that often illustrate the ephemeral literature of the country; and, in his last speech, he had made a provincial use of the word "despise," that is getting to be so common as almost to supplant the true signification. By "despising," Ithuel meant that he "hated;" the passion, perhaps, of all others, the most removed from the feeling described by the word he had used, inasmuch as it is not easy to elevate those for whom we have a contempt to the level necessary to be hated.

"Notwithstanding, the Inglese are not a despicable people," answered Andrea, who was obliged to take the stranger literally, since he knew nothing of his provincial use of terms; "for a nation of the north, they have done marvelous things of late years, especially on the ocean."

This was more than Ithuel could bear. All his personal wrongs, and sooth to say they had been of a most grievous nature, arose before his mind, incited and inflamed by national dislike; and he broke out into such an incoherent tirade of abuse as completely set all Filippo's knowledge of English at fault, rendering a translation impossible. By this time, Ithuel had swallowed so much of the wine, a liquor which had far more body than he supposed, that he was ripe for mischief, and it was only his extreme violence that prevented him from betraying more than, just at the moment, would have been prudent. The vice-governatore listened with attention, in the hope of catching something useful; but it all came to his ears a confused mass of incoherent vituperation, from which he could extract nothing. The scene, consequently, soon became unpleasant, and Andrea Barrofaldi took measures to put an end to it. Watching a favorable occasion to speak, he put in a word as the excited Bolt paused a moment to take breath.

"Signore," observed the vice-governatore, "all this may be very true: but as coming from one who serves the Inglese, to one who is the servant of their ally, the grand duke of Tuscany, it is quite as extraordinary as it is uncalled for; and we will talk of other things. This lugger, on board of which you sail, is out of all question English, notwithstanding what you tell us of the nation."

"Aye, *she* is English," answered Ithuel, with a grim smile, "and a pretty boat she is. But then it is no fault of hers, and what can't be cured must be endured.

A Guernsey craft, and a desperate goer, when she wakes up and puts on her traveling boots."

"These mariners have a language of their own," remarked Andrea to Vito Viti, smiling as in consideration of Ithuel's nautical habits; "to you and me, the idea of a vessel's using boots, neighbor, seems ridiculous; but the seamen, in their imaginations, bestow all sorts of objects on them. It is curious to hear them converse, good Vito; and now I am dwelling here on our island, I have often thought of collecting a number of their images, in order to aid in illustrating the sort of literature that belongs to their calling. The idea of a lugger's putting on her boots is quite heroic."

Now Vito Viti, though an Italian with so musical a name, was no poet, but a man so very literal, withal, as to render him exceedingly matter of fact in most of his notions. Accordingly, he saw no particular beauty in the idea of a vessel's wearing boots; and, though much accustomed to defer to the vice-governatore's superior knowledge and more extensive reading, he had the courage, on this occasion, to put in an objection to the probability of the circumstance mentioned.

"Signor Vice-governatore," he replied, "all is not gold that glitters. Fine words sometimes cover poor thoughts, and, I take it, this is an instance of what I mean. Long as I have lived in Porto Ferrajo, and that is now quite fifty years, seeing that I was born here, and have been off the island but four times in my life—and long, therefore, as I have lived here, I never saw a vessel in the harbor that wore boots or even shoes."

"This is metaphorical, good Vito, and must be looked at in a poetical point of view. Homer speaks of goddesses holding shields before their favorite warriors; while Ariosto makes rats and asses hold discourse together, as if they were members of an academy. All this is merely the effect of imagination, signore; and he who has the most is the aptest at inventing circumstances, which, though not strictly true, are vastly agreeable."

"As for Homer and Ariosto, Signor Vice-governatore, I doubt if either ever saw a vessel with a boot on, or if either ever knew as much about craft in general as we who live in Porto Ferrajo. Harkee, friend Filippo, just ask this Americano if, in his country, he ever saw vessels wear boots. Put the question plainly, and without any of your accursed poetry."

Filippo did as desired, leaving Ithuel to put his own construction on the object of the inquiry; all that had just passed being sealed to him, in consequence of its having been uttered in good Tuscan.

"Boots!" repeated the native of the Granite State, looking round him drolly; "perhaps not exactly the foot-part, and the soles, for they ought, in reason, to be under water; but every vessel that isn't coppered shows her boot-top; of them, I'll swear I've seen ten thousand more or less."

This answer mystified the vice-governatore, and completely puzzled Vito Viti. The grave mariners at the other table, too, thought it odd, for in no other tongue is the language of the sea as poetical or figurative, as in the English; and the term of boot-top as applied to a vessel, was Greek to them, as well as to the other listeners. They conversed among themselves on the subject, while their two superiors were holding a secret conference on the other side of the room, giving the American time to rally his recollection, and remember the precise circumstances in which not only he himself, but all his shipmates, were placed. No one could be more wily and ingenious than this man, when on his guard, though the inextinguishable hatred with which he regarded England and Englishmen, had come so near causing him to betray a secret which it was extremely important, at that moment, to conceal. At length a general silence prevailed, the different groups of speakers ceased to converse, and all looking toward the vice-governatore, as if in expectation that he was about to suggest something that might give a turn to the discourse. Nor was this a mistake, for, after inquiring of Benedetta if she had a private room, he invited Ithuel and the interpreter to follow him into it, leading the way, attended by the podesta. As soon as these four were thus separated from the others, the door was closed, and the two Tuscans came at once to the point.

"Signore Americano," commenced the vice-governatore, "between those who understand each other, there is little need of many words. This is a language which is comprehended all over the world, and I put it before you in the plainest manner, that we may have no mistake."

"It is tolerable plain, sartain!" exclaimed Ithuel; "two—four—six—eight—ten; all good-looking gold pieces, that in this part of the world you call *zecchini*, or sequins, as we name 'em in English. What have I done, Signor Squire, or what am I to do for these twenty dollars? Name your tarms; this working in the dark is agin the grain of my natur'!"

"You are to tell the truth; we suspect

the lugger of being French; and by putting the proof in our hands, you will make us your friends, and serve yourself."

Andrea Barrofaldi knew little of America and Americans, but he had imbibed the common European notion that money was the great deity worshiped in this hemisphere, and that all he had to do was to offer a bribe, in order to purchase a man of Ithuel's deportment and appearance. In his own island ten sequins would buy almost any mariner of the port to do any act short of positive legal criminality; and the idea that a barbarian of the West would refuse such a sum, in preference to selling his shipmates, never crossed his mind. Little, however, did the Italian understand the American. A greater knave than Ithuel, in his own way, it was not easy to find; but it shocked all notions of personal dignity, self-respect, and republican virtue, to be thus unequivocally offered a bribe; and had the lugger not been so awkwardly circumstanced, he would have been apt to bring matters to a crisis at once by throwing the gold into the vice-governatore's face; although, knowing where it was to be found, he might have set about devising some means of cheating the owner out of it at the very next instant. Boon or bribe, directly or unequivocally offered in the shape of money, as coming from the superior to the inferior, or from the corrupter to the corrupted, had he never taken, and it would have appeared in his eyes a species of degradation to receive the first, and of treason to his nationality to accept the last; though he would lie, invent, manage, and contrive from morning till night, in order to transfer even copper from the pocket of his neighbor to his own, under the forms of opinion and usage.

In a word, Ithuel, as relates to such things, was what is commonly called law-honest, with certain broad salvos, in favor of smuggling of all sorts, in foreign countries (at home he never dreamed of such a thing), custom-house oaths, and legal trickery; and this is just the class of men apt to declaim the loudest against the roguery of the rest of mankind. Had there been a law giving half to the informer, he might not have hesitated to betray the lugger, and all she contained. more especially in the way of regular business; but he had long before determined that every Italian was a treacherous rogue, and not at all to be trusted like an English rogue; and then his indomitable dislike of England would have kept him true in a case of much less complicated risk than this. Commanding himself, however, and regarding the sequins with natural longing, he answered with a simplicity of manner that both surprised and imposed on the vice-governatore.

"No—no—Signor Squire," he said; "in the first place, I've no secret to tell; and it would be a trickish thing to touch your money and not give you its worth in return; and then the lugger is Guernsey built, and carries a good King George's commission. In my part of the world we never take gold unless we sell something of equal value. Gifts and begging we look upon as mean and unbecoming, and the next thing to going on the town as a pauper; though if I can sarve you lawfully, like, I'm just as willing to work for your money as for that of any other man. I've no preference for kings in that particular."

All this time Ithuel held out the sequins with a show of returning them, though in a very reluctant manner, leaving Andrea, who comprehended his actions much better than his words, to understand that he declined selling his secret.

"You can keep the money, friend," observed the vice-governatore, "for when we give, in Italy, it is not our practice to take the gift back again. In the morning, perhaps, you will remember something that it may be useful for me to know."

"I've no occasion for gifts, nor is it exactly accordin' to the Granite rule to accept 'em," answered Ithuel, a little sharply. "Handsome conduct is handsome conduct; and I call the fellow-creetur' that would oppress and overcome another with a gift, little better than an English aristocrat. Hand out the dollars in the way of trade, in as large amounts as you will, and I will find the man, and that, too, in the lugger, who will see you out in't to your heart's content. Harkee, Philip-o; tell the gentleman, in an undertone, like, about the three kegs of tobacco we got out of the Virginy ship the day we made the north end of Corsica, and perhaps that will satisfy him we are not his enemies. There is no use in bawling it out so that the woman can hear what you say, or the men who are drinking in the other room."

"Signor Ithuello," answered the Genoese in English, "it will not do to let these gentlemen know anything of them kegs— one being the deputy-governor and the other a magistrate. The lugger will be seized for a smuggler, which will be the next thing to being seized for an enemy."

"Yet I've a longing for them 'ere sequins, to tell you the truth, Philip-o? I see no other means of getting at 'em, except it be through them three kegs of tobacco."

"Why you don't take 'em, when the signore put 'em into your very hand? All you do is put him in your pocket, and say, 'Eccellenza, what you please to wish?'"

"That isn't Granite, man, but more in the natur' of you Italians. The most disgraceful thing on 'airth is a paupe"— so Ithuel pronounced "pauper"—" the next is a street-beggar; after him comes your chaps who take sixpences and shillin's, in the way of small gifts; and last of all an Englishman. All these I despise; but let this signore say but the word, in the way of trade, and he'll find me as ready and expair't as he can wish. I'd defy the devil in a trade!"

Filippo shook his head, positively declining to do so foolish a thing as to mention a contraband article to those whose duty it would be to punish a violation of the revenue laws. In the meanwhile the sequins remained in the hands of Andrea Barrofaldi, who seemed greatly at a loss to understand the character of the strange being whom chance had thus thrown in his way. The money was returned to his purse, but his distrust and doubts were by no means removed.

"Answer me one thing, Signor Bolto," asked the vice-governatore, after a minute of thought; "if you hate the English so much, why do you serve in their ships? why not quit them on the first good occasion? The land is as wide as the sea, and you must be often on it."

"I calculate, Signor Squire, you don't often study charts, or you wouldn't fall into such a consait. There's twice as much water as solid ground, on this airth, to begin with; as in reason there ought to be, seeing that an acre of good productive land is worth five or six of ocean; and then you have little knowledge of my character and prospects to ask such a question. I sarve the king of England to make him pay well for it. If you want to take an advantage of a man, first get him in debt; then you can work your will on him, in the most profitable and safe manner!"

All this was unintelligible to the vice-governatore, who, after a few more questions and answers, took a civil leave of the strangers, intimating to Benedetta that they were not to follow him back into the room he had just quitted.

As for Ithuel, the disappearance of the two gentlemen gave him no concern; but as he felt that it might be unsafe to drink any more wine, he threw down his reckoning, and strolled into the street, followed by his companion. Within an hour from that moment, the three kegs of tobacco were in the possession of a shopkeeper of the place, that brief interval sufficing to enable the man to make his bargain, and to deliver the articles, which was his real object on shore. This little smuggling transaction was carried on altogether without the knowledge of Raoul Yvard, who was to all intents and purposes the captain of his own lugger, and in whose character there were many traits of chivalrous honor, mixed up with habits and pursuits that would not seem to promise qualities so elevated. But this want of a propensity to turn a penny in his own way, was not the only distinguishing characteristic between the commander of the little craft, and the being he occasionally used as a mask to his true purposes.

CHAPTER V.

WHATEVER may have been the result of the vice-governatore's farther inquiries and speculations that night, they were not known. After consuming an hour in the lower part of the town, in and around the port, he and the podesta sought their homes and their pillows, leaving the lugger riding quietly at her anchor in the spot where she was last presented to the reader's attention. If Raoul Yvard and Ghita had another interview, too, it was so secretly managed as to escape all observation, and can form no part of this narrative.

A Mediterranean morning, at midsummer, is one of those balmy and soothing periods of the day, that affect the mind as well as the body. Everywhere we have the mellow and advancing light that precedes the appearance of the sun, the shifting hues of the sky, that pearly softness that seems to have been invented to make us love the works of God's hand, and the warm glow of the brilliant sun; but it is not everywhere that these fascinating changes occur, on a sea whose blue vies with the darkest depths of the void of space, beneath a climate that is as winning as the scenes it adorns, and amid mountains whose faces reflect every varying shade of light, with the truth and the poetry of nature.

Such a morning as this last, was that which succeeded the night with which our tale opened, bringing with it the reviving movements of the port and town. Italy, as a whole, is remarkable for an appearance of quiet and repose, that are little known in the more bustling scenes of the greedier commerce of our own quarter of the world, or, indeed, in those of most of the northern nations of Europe. There is in her aspect, modes of living, and even in her habits of business, an air of decayed gentility, that is wanting to the ports, shops and marts of the more vulgar parts of the world; as if conscious of having so long been the focus of a human refinement, it was unbecoming in these later days to throw aside all traces of her history and power. Man, and the climate, too, seem in unison; one meeting the cares of life with a *far niente* manner that is singularly in accordance with the dreamy and soothing atmosphere he respires.

Just as the day dawned, the fall of a billet of wood on the deck of the *Feu-Follet* gave the first intimation that any one was stirring in or near the haven. If there had been a watch on board that craft throughout the night—and doubtless such had been the case—it had been kept in so quiet and unobtrusive a manner as to render it questionable to the jealous eyes which had been riveted on her from the shore until long past midnight. Now, however, everything was in motion, and in less than five minutes after that billet of wood had fallen from the hands of the cook, as he was about to light his galley fire, the tops of the hats and caps of some fifty or sixty sailors were seen moving to and fro, just above the upper edge of the bulwarks. Three minutes later, and two men appeared near the knightheads, each with his arms folded, looking at the vessel's hawse, and taking a survey of the state of the harbor and of objects on the surrounding shore.

The two individuals who were standing in the conspicuous position named were Raoul Yvard himself and Ithuel Bolt. Their conversation was in French, the part borne by the last being most execrably pronounced, and paying little or no attention to grammar; but it is necessary that we should render what was said by both into the vernacular, with the peculiarities that belonged to the men.

"I can see only the Austrian that is worth the trouble of a movement," quietly observed Raoul, whose eye was scanning the inner harbor, his own vessel lying two hundred yards without it, it will be remembered, "and she is light, and would scarce pay for sending her to Toulon. These feluccas would embarrass us, without affording much reward; and then their loss would ruin the poor devils of owners, and bring misery into many a family."

"Well, that's a new idea for a privateer?" said Ithuel, sneeringly. "Luck's luck, in these matters, and every man must count on what war turns up. I wish you'd read the history of our revolution, and then you'd ha' seen that liberty and equality are not to be had without some ups and downs in fortin's and chances."

"The Austrian might do," added Raoul, who paid little attention to his companion's remarks, "if he were a streak or two lower in the water; but, after all, E-too-*ell*," for so he pronounced the other's name, "I do not like a capture that is made without any *éclat*, or spirit, in the attack and defense."

"Well"—this word Ithuel invariably pronounced "wa-a-l"—"well, to my notion, the most profitable and the most agreeable battles are the shortest, and the pleasantest victories are them in which there's the most prize money. Howsever, as that brig is only an Austrian, I care little what you may determine to do with her. Was she English, I'd head a boat myself to go in and tow her out here, expressly to have the satisfaction of burning her. English ships make a cheerful fire!"

"And that would be a useless waste of property, and perhaps of blood, and would do no one any good, Etoo*ell*."

"But it would do the accursed English harm, and that counts for a something, in my reckoning. Nelson wasn't so over-scrupulous at the Nile about burning your ships, Mr. Rule—"

"*Tonnerre!* why do you always bring in that *malheureux* Nile? Is it not enough that we were beaten—disgraced—destroyed, that a friend must tell us of it so often?"

"You forget, Mr. Rule, that I was an inimy then," returned Ithuel, with a grin and a grim smile. "If you'll take the trouble to examine my back, you'll find on it the marks of the lashes I got for just telling my captain that it was agin the grain for me, a republican as I was by idee and natur', to fight other republicans. He told me he would first try the grain of my skin, and see how that would agree with what he called my duty; and I must own he got the best on't; I fit like a tiger agin you rather than be flogged twice the same day. Flogging on a sore back is an awful argument!"

"And now has come the hour of revenge, *pauvre Etooell;* this time you are on the right side, and may fight with heart and mind those you so much hate."

A long and gloomy silence followed, during which Raoul turned his face aft, and stood looking at the movements of the men as they washed the decks, while Ithuel seated himself on a knighthead, and his chin resting on his hand, he sat ruminating, in bitterness of spirit, like Milton's devil in some of his dire cogitations, on the atrocious wrong of which he had really been the subject. Bodies of men are proverbially heartless. They commit injustice without reflection, and vindicate their abuses without remorse. And yet it may be doubtful if either a nation or an individual ever tolerated or was an accessory in a wrong, that the act, sooner or later, did not recoil on the offending party, through that mysterious principle of right which is implanted in the nature of things, bringing forth its own results as the seed produces its grain, and the tree its fruits; a supervision of holiness that it is usual to term (and rightly enough, when we remember who created principles) the providence of God. Let that people dread the future, who, in their collective capacity, systematically encourage injustice of any sort; since their own eventual demoralization will follow as a necessary consequence, even though they escape punishment in a more direct form.

We shall not stop to relate the moody musings of the New Hampshire man. Unnurtured, and, in many respects, unprincipled, as he was, he had his clear conceptions of the injustice of which he had been one among thousands of other victims; and at that moment he would have held life itself as a cheap sacrifice could he have had his fill of revenge. Time and again, while a captive on board the English ship in which he had been immured for years, had he meditated the desperate expedient of blowing up the vessel; and had not the means been wanting, mercenary and selfish as he ordinarily seemed, he was every way equal to executing so dire a scheme, in order to put an end to the lives of those who were the agents in wronging him and his own sufferings, together. The subject never recurred to his mind without momentarily changing the current of its thoughts, and tinging all his feelings with an intensity of bitterness that it was painful to bear. At length, sighing heavily, he rose from the knight-head, and turned toward the mouth of the bay, as if to conceal from Raoul the expression of his countenance. This act, however, was scarcely done, ere he started, and an exclamation escaped him, that induced his companion to turn quickly on his heel, and face the sea. There, indeed, the growing light enabled both to discover an object that could scarcely be other than one of interest to men in their situation.

It has been said already that the deep bay, on the side of which stands the town of Porto Ferrajo, opens to the north, looking in the direction of the headland of Piombino. On the right of the bay the land, high and broken, stretches several miles ere it forms what is called the canal, while, on the left, it terminates with the low bluff on which stands the residence then occupied by Andrea Barrofaldi; and which has since become so celebrated as the abode of one far greater than the worthy vice-governatore. The haven lying under these heights, on the left of the bay, and by the side of the town, it followed as a matter of course, that the anchorage of the lugger was also in this quarter of the bay, commanding a clear view to the north, in the direction of the mainland, as far as the eye could reach. The width of the canal, or the passage between Elba and the Point of Piombino, may be some six or seven miles; and at the distance of less than one mile from the northern end of the former, stands a small rocky islet, which has since become known to the world as the spot on which Napoleon stationed a corporal's guard, by way of taking possession, when he found his noble empire dwindled to the sea-girt mountains in its vicinity. With the existence and position of this island both Raoul and Ithuel were necessarily acquainted, for they had seen it and noted its situation the previous night, though it had escaped their notice that, from the place where the *Feu-Follet* had brought up, it was not visible. In their first look to seaward, that morning, which was ere the light had grown sufficiently strong to render the houses on the opposite side of the bay distinct, an object had been seen in this quarter, which had then been mistaken for the rock; but, by this time, the light was strong enough to show that it was a very different thing. In a word, that which both Raoul and Ithuel had fancied an islet, was neither more nor less than a ship.

The stranger's head was to the northward, and his motion, before a light, southerly air, could not have exceeded a knot an hour. He had no other canvas spread than his three topsails and jib; though his courses were hanging in the brails. His black hull was just beginning to show its details; and along the line of light yellow that enlivened his side were visible the dark intervals of thirteen ports; a real gun frowning in each. Although the hammocks were not stowed, and the hammock-cloths had that empty and undressed look which is so common to a man-of-war in the night, it was apparent that the ship had an upper-deck, with quarter-deck and forecastle batteries; or, in other words, that she was a frigate. As she had opened the town of Porto

Ferrajo several minutes before she was herself seen from the *Feu-Follet*, an ensign was hanging from the end of her gaff, though there was not sufficient air to open its folds in a way to let the national character of the stranger be known.

"Peste!" exclaimed Raoul Yvard, as soon as he had gazed a minute at the stranger, in silence; "a pretty *cul-de-sac* are we in, if that gentleman should happen to be an Englishman! What say you, Etooell; can you make out anything of that ensign? your eyes are the best in the lugger."

"It is too much for my sight to determine at this distance, and that before the sun is risen; but by having a glass ready, we shall soon know. Five minutes will bring us the great luminary, as our minister used to call him."

Ithuel had descended from the bulwark, while speaking; and he now went aft in quest of a glass, returning to his old station, bringing two of the instruments; one of which he handed to his commander, while he kept the other himself. In another minute both had leveled their glasses at the stranger, whom each surveyed attentively, for some time, in profound silence.

"*Pardie!*" exclaimed Raoul, "that ensign is the tricolor, or my eyes are untrue to my own country. Let me see, Etooell; what ship of forty-two, or forty-four, has the republic on this coast?"

"Not that, Monsieur Yvard," answered Ithuel, with a manner so changed, and an emphasis so marked, as at once to draw his companion's attention from the frigate to his own countenance; "not that, Monsieur Capitaing. It is not easy for a bird to forget the cage in which he was shut up for years: if that is not the accursed *Proserpine*, I have forgotten the cut of my own jib!"

"*La Proserpine?*" repeated Raoul, who was familiar with his shipmate's adventures, and did not require to be told his meaning; "if you are not mistaken, Etooell, *Le Feu-Follet* needs put her lantern under a shade. This is only a forty, if I can count her ports."

"I care nothing for ports or guns; it is the *Proserpine;* and the only harm I wish her is, that she were at the bottom of the ocean. The *Proserpine*, thirty-six, Captain Cuffe, though Captain Flog would have been a better name for him. Yes, the *Proserpine*, thirty-six, Captain Cuffe, Heaven bless her!"

"Bah! this vessel has forty-four guns —now I can see to count them; I make twenty-two of a side."

"Ay, that's just her measure, a thirty-six on the list and by rate, and forty-four by count; twenty-six long eighteens below; twelve thirty-twos, carronades, on her quarter-deck; and four more carronades, with two barkers, for'ard. She'd just extinguish your Jack-o'-Lantern, Monsieur Rule, at one broadside; for what are ten twelve-pound carronades, and seventy men, to such a frigate?"

"I am not madman enough, Etooell, to dream of fighting a frigate, or even a heavy sloop-of-war, with the force you have just mentioned; but I have followed the sea too long to be alarmed before I am certain of my danger. *La Railleuse* is just such a ship as that."

"Hearken to reason, Monsieur Rule," answered Ithuel, earnestly; "*La Railleuse*, nor no other French frigate, would show her colors to an enemy's port; for it would be useless telling her errand. Now an English ship might show a French ensign, for she always has it in her power to change it; and then *she* might be benefited by the cheat. The *Proserpine* is French built, and has French legs, too, boots or no boots,"—here Ithuel laughed a little, involuntarily, but his face instantly became serious again,—"and I have heard she was a sister vessel of the other. So much for size and appearance; but every shroud, and port, and sail, about yonder craft, is registered on my back in a way that no sponge will ever wash out."

"Sa-a-c-r-r-r-e," muttered Raoul between his teeth; "Etooell, if an Englishman, he may very well take it into his head to come in here, and perhaps anchor within half-a-cable's length of us! What think you of that, *mon brave Americain?*"

"That it may very well come to pass; though one hardly sees, either, what is to bring a cruiser into such a place as this. Every one hasn't the curiosity of a Jack o' Lantern."

"*Mais que diable allait-il faire dans cette galere! Bien!* we must take the weather as it comes; sometimes a gale, and sometimes a calm. As he shows his own ensign so loyally, let us return the compliment, and show ours. Hoist the ensign there, aft."

"Which one, monsieur!" demanded an old demure-looking quartermaster, who was charged with that duty, and who was never known to laugh: "The captain will remember that we came into port under the *drapeau* of Monsieur Jean Bull."

"*Bien!* Hoist the drapeau of Monsieur Jean Bull again. We must brazen it out, now we have put on the mask. Monsieur Lieutenant, clap on the hawser, and run the lugger ahead, over her anchor, and see everything clear for spreading our pocket-handkerchiefs. No one knows when *Le Feu-Follet* may have occasion to wipe her face. Ah! now Etooell, we can make out his broadside fairly; he is heading more to the westward."

The two seamen leveled their glasses, and renewed their examinations. Ithuel had a peculiarity that not only characterized the man, but which is so common among Americans of his class, as in a sense to be national. On ordinary occasions he was talkative, and disposed to gossip; but, whenever action and decision became necessary, he was thoughtful, silent, and, though in a way of his own, even dignified. This last fit was on him, and he waited for Raoul to lead the conversation. The other, however, was disposed to be as reserved as himself, for he quitted the knighthead, and took refuge from the splashing of the water, used in washing the decks, in his own cabin.

Two hours, though they brought the sun, with the activity and hum of the morning, had made no great change in the relative positions of things within and without the bay. The people of *Le Feu-Follet* had breakfasted, had got everything on board their little craft in its proper place, and were moody, observant, and silent. One of the lessons that Ithuel had succeeded in teaching his shipmates, was to impress on them the necessity of commanding their voluble propensities, if they would wish to pass for Englishmen. It is certain more words would have been uttered, in this little lugger, in one hour, had her crew been indulged to the top of their bent, than would have been uttered in an English first-rate, in two: but the danger of using their own language, and the English peculiarity of grumness, had been so thoroughly taught them, that her people rather caricatured, than otherwise, *ce grand talent pour le silence* that was thought to distinguish their enemies. Ithuel, who had a waggery of his own, smiled as he saw the seamen folding their arms, throwing discontent and surliness into their countenances, and pacing the deck singly, as if misanthropical and disdaining to converse, whenever a boat came alongside from the shore. Several of these visitors arrived, in the course of the two hours mentioned; but the sentinel at the gangway, who had his orders, repulsed every attempt to come on board, pretending not to understand French, when permission was asked in that language.

Raoul had a boat's crew of four, all of whom had acquired the English, like himself, in a prison-ship, and with these men he now prepared to land; for, as yet, he had made little progress in the business which brought him into his present awkward predicament, and he was not a man to abandon an object so dear to him, lightly. Finding himself in a dilemma, he was resolved to make an effort to reap, if possible, some advantage from his critical situation. Accordingly, after he had taken his coffee, and given his orders, the boat's crew was called, and he left the lugger's side. All this was done tranquilly, as if the appearance of the stranger in the offing gave no trouble to any in *Le Feu-Foltet*.

On this occasion the boat pulled boldly into the little harbor, its officer touching the shore at the common landing. Nor were the men in any haste to return. They lounged about the quay, in waiting for their captain, cheapening fruits, chatting with the women in such Italian as they could muster, and affecting to understand the French of the old sea dogs that drew near them, all of whom knew more or less of that universal language, with difficulty. That they were the objects of suspicion their captain had sufficiently warned them, and practice rendered them all good actors. The time they remained in waiting for Raoul was consequently spent in eluding attempts to betray themselves, and caricaturing Englishmen. Two of the four folded their arms, endeavored to look surly, and paced the quay in silence, refusing even to unbend to the blandishments of the gentler sex, three or four of whom endeavored to insinuate themselves into their confidence, by offerings of fruit and flowers.

"Amico," said Annunziate, one of the prettiest girls of her class in Porto Ferrajo, and who had been expressly employed by Vito Viti to perform this office, "here are figs from the main land. Will you please to eat a few, that when you go back to Inghilterra, you may tell your countrymen how we poor Elbans live?"

"Bad fig," sputtered Jacques, Raoul's cockswain, to whom this offering was made, and speaking in broken English; "better at 'ome. Pick up better in ze street of Portsmout'!"

"But, signore, you need not look as if they would hurt you or bite you; you can eat them, and take my word for it, you will find them as pleasant as the melons of Napoli!"

"No melon good but English melon. English melon plenty as pomme de terres —bah!"

"Yes, signore, as the melons of Napoli," continued Annunziate, who did not understand a syllable of the ungracious answers she received; "Signore Vito Viti, our prodesta, ordered me to offer those figs to the forestieri—the Inglesi, who are in the bay—"

"God-dam!" returned Jacques, in a quick, sententious manner, that was intended to get rid of the fair tormentor, and which, temporarily at least, was not without effect.

But leaving the boat's crew to be badgered in this manner, until relief came, as will be hereafter related, we must follow our hero in his way through the streets of the town. Raoul, guided by an instinct, or having some special object before his eye, walked swiftly up the heights, ascending to the promontory so often mentioned. As he passed every eye was turned on him, for, by this time, the distrust in the place was general; and the sudden appearance of a frigate, wearing a French ensign, before the port, had given rise to apprehensions of a much more serious nature than any which could possibly attend the arrival of a craft as light as the lugger, by herself. Vito Viti had long before gone up the street, to see the vice-governatore; and eight or ten of the principal men of the place had been summoned to a council, including the two senior military dignitaries of the island. The batteries, it was known, were manned; and although it would have puzzled the acutest mind of Elba to give a reason why the French should risk so unprofitable an attack as one on their principal port, long ere Raoul was seen among them such a result was not only dreaded, but in a measure anticipated with confidence. As a matter of course, then, every eye followed his movements as he went with bounding steps up the narrow terraces of the steep street, and the least of his actions was subjected to the narrowest and most jealous scrutiny.

The heights were again thronged with spectators of all ages and classes, and of both sexes. The mantles and flowing dresses of females prevailed as usual; for whatever is connected with curiosity, is certain to collect an undue proportion of a sex whose imaginations are so apt to get the start of their judgments. On a terrace in front of the palace, as it was the custom to designate the dwelling of the governor, was the group of magnates, all of them paying the gravest attention to the smallest change in the direction of the ship, which had now become an object of general solicitude and apprehension. So intent, indeed, were they in gazing at this apprehended enemy that Raoul stood in front of Andrea Barrofaldi, cap in hand, and bowing his salutation before his approach was even anticipated. This sudden and unannounced arrival created great surprise and some little confusion; one or two of the group turning away instinctively, as it might be to conceal the flushes that mounted to their cheeks at being so unexpectedly confronted by the very man whom the minute before they had been strongly denouncing.

"'Bon giorno,' Signor Vice-governatore," commenced Raoul, in his gay, easy, and courteous manner, and certainly with an air that betrayed any feeling but those of apprehension and guilt; "we have a fine morning on the land, here; and apparently a fine frigate of the French Republic in the offing yonder."

"We were conversing of that vessel, Signor Smees," answered Andrea, "as you approached. What, in your judgment, can induce a Frenchman to appear before our town in so menacing a manner?"

"'Cospetto!' you might as well ask me, signore, what induces these republicans to do a thousand other out-of-the-way things. What has made them behead Louis XVI.? What has made them overrun half of your Italy, conquer Egypt, and drive the Austrians back upon their Danube?"

"To say nothing of their letting Nelsoni destroy them at Aboukir," added Vito Viti, with a grunt.

"True, signore, or letting Nelson, my gallant countryman, annihilate them near the mouth of the Nile. I did not consider it proper to boast of English glory, though that case, too, may very well be included. We have several men in ze Ving-and-Ving who were in that glorious battle, particularly our sailing-master, Etooell Bolt, who was on board Nelson's own ship, having accidentally been sent on service from the frigate to which he properly belonged, and carried off expressly to share, as it might be, in the glory of this famous battle."

"I have seen the signore," dryly remarked Andrea Barrofaldi; "e uno Americano!"

"An American!" exclaimed Raoul, starting a little in spite of his assumed indifference of manner; "why, yes, I believe Bolt was born in America—English America, you know, signori, and that is much the same thing as having been born in England herself. We look upon 'ze Yankees' as but a part of our own people, and take them into our service most cheerfully."

"So the Signor Ituello has given us reason to believe; he is seemingly a great lover of the English nation."

Raoul was uneasy; for he was entirely ignorant of all that had passed in the wine-house, and thought he detected irony in the manner of the vice-governatore.

"Certainly, signore," he answered, however, with unmoved steadiness; "certainly, signore, the Americani adore Inghilterra; and well they may, considering all that great nation has done for them. But, Signore Vice-governatore, I have come to offer you the services of my lugger, should this Frenchman really intend mischief. We are small, it is true, and our guns are but light; nevertheless, we may break the frigate's cabin windows, while you are doing him still greater injury from these heights. I trust you will assign ze *Ving-and-Ving* some honorable station, should you come to blows with the republicans."

"And what particular service would it be most agreeable to you to undertake, signore?" inquired the vice-governatore, with considerable courtesy; "we are no mariners, and must leave the choice to yourself. The colonello, here, expects some firing, and has his artillerists already at their guns."

"The preparation of Porto Ferrajo is celebrated among the mariners of the Mediterranean, and, should the Frenchman venture within the reach of your shot, I expect to see him unrigged faster than if he were in a dock-yard. As for ze leetl' *Ving-and-Ving*, in my opinion, while the frigate is busy with these batteries, it might be well for us to steer along the shore on the east side of the bay until we can get outside of her, when we shall have the beggars between two fires. That was just what Nelson did at Aboukir, Signor Podesta, a battle you seem so much to admire."

"That would be a maneuver worthy of a follower of Nelsoni, signore," observed the colonel, "if the metal of your guns were heavier. With short pieces of twelve, however, you would hardly venture within reach of long pieces of eighteen; although the first should be manned by Inglese, and the last by Francese?"

"One never knows. At the Nile one of our fifties laid the *Orient*, a three-decker, athwart-hawse, and did her lots of injury. The vaisseau, in fact, was blown up. Naval combats are decided on principles altogether different from engagements on the land, Signor Colonello."

"It must be so, truly," answered the soldier; "but what means this movement? you, as a seaman, may be able to tell us, capitano."

This drew all eyes to the frigate again, where, indeed, were movements that indicated some important changes. As these movements have an intimate connection with the incidents of the tale, it will be necessary to relate them in a manner to render them more intelligible to the reader.

The distance of the frigate from the town might now have been five English miles. Of current there was none; and there being no tides in the Mediterranean, the ship would have lain perfectly stationary all the morning, but for a very slight air from the southward. Before this air, however, she had moved to the westward about a couple of miles, until she had got the government-house nearly abeam. At the same time she had been obliquely drawing nearer, which was the circumstance that produced the alarm. With the sun had risen the wind, and a few moments before the colonel interrupted himself in the manner related, the topsails of the stranger had swelled, and he began to move through the water at the rate of some four or five knots an hour. The moment her people felt that they had complete command of their vessel, as if waiting only for that assurance, they altered her course, and made sail. Putting her helm a-starboard, the ship came close by the wind, with her head looking directly in for the promontory, while her tacks were hauled on board, and her light canvas aloft was loosened and spread to the breeze. Almost at the same instant, for everything seemed to be done at once, and as by instinct, the French flag was lowered, another went up in its place, and a gun was fired to leeward—a signal of amity. As this second emblem of nationality blew out and opened to the breeze, the glasses showed the white field and St. George's cross of the noble old ensign of England.

An exclamation of surprise and delight escaped the spectators on the promontory, as their doubts and apprehensions were thus dramatically relieved. No one thought of Raoul at that happy moment, though to him there was nothing of new interest in the affair, with the exception of the apparent intention of the stranger to enter the bay. As *Le Feu-Follet* lay in plain view from the offing, he had his doubts, indeed, whether the warlike appearance of that craft was not the true reason of this sudden change in the frigate's course. Still, lying as he did in a port hostile to France, there was a probability that he might yet escape without a very critical or close examination.

"Signor Smees, I felicitate you on this visit of a countryman," cried Andrea Barrofaldi, a pacific man by nature, and certainly no warrior, and who felt too happy at the prospects of passing a quiet day, to feel distrust at such a moment; "I shall do you honor in my communications with Florence, for the spirit and willingness which you have shown in the wish to aid us on this trying occasion."

"Signor Vice-governatore, do not trouble yourself to dwell on my poor services," answered Raoul, scarce caring to conceal the smile that struggled about his handsome mouth; "think rather of these gallant signori, who greatly regret that an opportunity for gaining distinction has been lost. But here are signals that must be meant for us; I hope my stupid fellows will be able to answer them in my absence."

It was fortunate for *Le Feu-Follet*, perhaps, that her commander was not on board, when the stranger, the *Proserpine*, the very ship that Ithuel so well knew, made her number. The mystification that was to follow was in much better hands, while conducted by the New Hampshire man, than it could possibly be in his own. Ithuel answered promptly, though what, he did not know himself; but he took good care that the flags he showed should become so entangled as not to be read by those in the frigate, while they had every appearance of being hoisted fearlessly and in good faith.

CHAPTER VI.

WHAT success attended the artifice of Ithuel it was impossible to tell, so far as the frigate was concerned ; though the appearance of mutual intelligence between the two vessels had a very favorable tendency toward removing suspicion from the lugger among those on shore. It seemed so utterly improbable that a French corsair could answer the signals of an English frigate, that even Vito Viti felt compelled to acknowledge to the vice-governatore in a whisper, that, so far, the circumstance was much in favor of the lugger's loyalty. Then the calm exterior of Raoul counted for something, more especially as he remained apparently an unconcerned observer of the rapid approach of the ship.

"We shall not have occasion to use your gallant offer, Signor Smees," said Andrea, kindly, as he was about to retire into the house with one or two of his counselors; "but we thank you none the less. It is a happiness to be honored with the visit of two cruisers of your great nation on the same day, and I hope you will so far favor me as to accompany

your brother commander, when he shall do me the honor to pay the customary visit, since it would seem to be his serious intention to pay Porto Ferrajo the compliment of a call. Can you not guess at the name of the frigate ? "

"Now I see she is a countryman, I think I can, signore," answered Raoul carelessly; "I take her to be *La Proserpine*, a French-built ship, a circumstance that first deceived me as to her character."

"And the noble cavalier, her commander—you doubtless know his name and rank ? "

"O! perfectly; he is the son of an old admiral, under whom I was educated, though we happen ourselves never to have met. Sir Brown is the name and title of the gentleman."

"Ah! that is a truly English rank and name, too, as one might say. Often have I met that honorable appellation in Shakespeare and other of your eminent authors. Miltoni has a Sir Brown, if I am not mistaken, signore ? "

"Several of them, Signor Vice-governatore," answered Raoul, without a moment's hesitation or the smallest remorse ; though he had no idea whatever who Milton was. "Milton, Shakespeare, Cicero, and all our great writers often mention signori of this family."

"Cicero ! " repeated Andrea, in astonishment, "he was a Roman and an ancient, capitano, and died before Inghilterra was known to the civilized world."

Raoul perceived that he had reached too far, though he was not in absolute danger of losing his balance. Smiling, as in consideration of the other's provincial view of things, he rejoined, with an *aplomb* that would have done credit to a politician, in an explanatory and half-apologetic tone :

"Quite true, Signor Vice-governatore, as respects him you mention," he said, "but not true as respects Sir Cicero, my illustrious compatriot. Let me see—I do not think it is yet a century since our Cicero died. He was born in Devonshire" —this was the county in which Raoul had been imprisoned—"and must have died in Dublin. Si—now I remember, it *was* in Dublin that this virtuous and distinguished author yielded up his breath."

To all this Andrea had nothing to say, for, half a century since, so great was the ignorance of civilized nations, as related to such things, that one might have engrafted a Homer on the literature of England, in particular, without much risk of having the imposition detected. Signor Barrofaldi was not pleased to find that the barbarians were seizing on the

Italian names, it is true; but he was fain to set the circumstance down to those very traces of barbarism which were the unavoidable fruits of their origin. As for supposing it possible that one who spoke with the ease and innocence of Raoul, was inventing as he went along, it was an idea he was himself much too unpracticed to entertain; and the very first thing he did, on entering the palace, was to make a memorandum which might lead him, at a leisure moment, to inquire into the nature of the writings, and the general merits of Sir Cicero, the illustrious namesake of him of Rome. As soon as this little digression terminated he entered the palace, after again expressing the hope that "Sir Smees" would not fail to accompany "Sir Brown" in the visit which the functionary fully expected to receive from the latter in the course of the next hour or two. The company now began to disperse, and Raoul was soon left to his own meditations; which just at that moment were anything but agreeable.

The town of Porto Ferrajo is so shut in from the sea by the rock against which it is built, its fortifications, and the construction of its own little port, as to render the approach of a vessel invisible to its inhabitants, unless they choose to ascend to the heights, and the narrow promenade already mentioned. This circumstance had drawn a large crowd upon the hill again; among which Raoul Yvard now threaded his way, wearing his sea cap, and his assumed naval uniform, in a smart, affected manner, for he was fully sensible of all the advantages he possessed on the score of personal appearance. His unsettled eye, however, wandered from one pretty face to another, in quest of Ghita, who alone was the object of his search, and the true cause of the awkward predicament into which he had brought not only himself, but *Le Feu-Follet*. In this manner, now thinking of her he sought, and then reverting to his situation in an enemy's port, he walked along the whole line of the cliff, scarce knowing whether to return or to seek his boat, by doubling on the town, when he heard his own name pronounced in a sweet voice, which went directly to his heart. Turning on his heel, Ghita was within a few feet of him.

"Salute me distantly, and as a stranger," said the girl, in almost breathless haste, "and point to the different streets, as if inquiring your way through the town. This is the place where we met last evening; but, remember, it is no longer dark."

As Raoul complied with her desire, any distant spectator might well have fancied the meeting accidental, though he poured forth a flood of expressions of love and admiration.

"Enough, Raoul," said the girl, blushing and dropping her eyes, though no displeasure was visible on her serene and placid face; "another time I might indulge you. How much worse is your situation now than it was last night! Then you had only the port to fear; now you have both the people of the port and this strange ship—an Inglese, as they tell me."

"No doubt; *La Proserpine*, Etooell says, and he knows. You remember Etooell, dearest Ghita, the American who was with me at the tower? Well, he has served in this very ship, and knows her to be *La Proserpine*, of forty-four." Raoul paused a moment; then he added, laughing in a way to surprise his companion, "Oui, *La Proserpine*, le Capitaine Sir Brown?"

"What you can find to amuse you in all this, Raoul, is more than I can discover. Sir Brown, or Sir anybody else, will send you again to those evil English prison-ships, of which you have so often told me; and there is surely nothing pleasant in that idea."

"Bah! My sweet Ghita, Sir Brown, or Sir White, or Sir Black has not yet got me. I am not a child, to tumble into the fire because the leading-strings are off; and *Le Feu-Follet* shines or goes out exactly as it suits her purposes. The frigate, ten to one, will just run close in and take a near look, and then square away and go to Livorno, where there is much more to amuse her officers than here in Porto Ferrajo. This Sir Brown has his Ghita, as well as Raoul Yvard."

"Not a Ghita, I fear, Raoul," answered the girl, smiling in spite of herself, while her color almost insensibly deepened. "Livorno has few ignorant country girls like me, who have been educated in a lone watch-tower on the coast."

"Ghita," answered Raoul, with feeling, "that poor lone watch-tower of thine might well be envied by many a noble dame at Roma and at Napoli. It has left thee innocent and pure—a gem that gay capitals seldom contain; or, if found there, not in its native beauty, which they sully by use."

"What know'st thou, Raoul, of Roma and Napoli, and of noble dames and rich gems?" asked the girl, smiling, the tenderness which had filled her heart at that moment betraying itself in her eyes.

"What do I know of such things, truly! Why, I have been at both places, and have seen what I describe. I went to Roma on purpose to see the Holy Father, in order to make certain whether our French opinions of his character and infallibility were true or not, before I set up in religion for myself."

"And thou *didst* find him holy and venerable, Raoul," interposed the girl, with earnestness and energy, for this was the great point of separation between them—"I *know* thou found'st him thus, and worthy to be the head of an ancient and true Church. My eyes never beheld him, but this do I know to be true."

Raoul was aware that the laxity of his religious opinions, opinions that he may be said to have inherited from his country, as it then existed morally, alone prevented Ghita from casting aside all other ties, and following his fortunes, in weal and in woe. Still he was too frank and generous to deceive, while he had ever been too considerate to strive to unsettle her confiding and consoling faith. Her infirmity even, for so he deemed her notions to be, had a charm in his eyes; few men, however loose or skeptical in their own opinions on such matters, finding any pleasure in the contemplation of a female infidel, and he had never looked more fondly into her anxious but lovely face, than he did at this very instant, making his reply with a truth that bordered on magnanimity.

"*Thou* art my religion, Ghita!" he said; "in thee I worship purity, and holiness, and—"

"Nay, nay, Raoul, *do* not! refrain, if thou really lov'st me; utter not this frightful blasphemy; tell me rather, if thou didst not find the Holy Father as I describe him?"

"I found him a peaceable, venerable, and, I firmly believe, a good old man, Ghita; but only a man. No infallibility could I see about him; but a set of roguish cardinals, and other plotters of mischief, who were much better calculated to set Christians by the ears than to lead them to heaven, surrounded his chair."

"Say no more, Raoul; I will listen to no more of this. Thou knowest not these sainted men, and thy tongue is thine own enemy, without—hark! what means that?"

"It is a gun from the frigate, and must be looked to; say, when and where do we meet again?"

"I know not, now. We have been too long, much too long together, as it is; and must separate. Trust to me to provide the means of another meeting; at all events, we shall shortly be in our tower again."

Ghita glided away as she ceased speaking, and soon disappeared in the town.

As for Raoul, he was at a loss for a moment whether to follow or not; then he hastened to the terrace in front of the government house again, in order to ascertain the meaning of the gun. The report had drawn others to the same place, and on reaching it the young man found himself in another crowd.

By this time the *Proserpine*, for Ithuel was right as to the name of the stranger, had got within a league of the entrance of the bay, and had gone about, stretching over to its eastern shore, apparently with the intention to fetch fairly into it on the next tack. The smoke of her gun was sailing off to leeward, in a little cloud, and signals were again flying at her main-royal-mast-head. All this was very intelligible to Raoul, it being evident at a glance that the frigate had reached in nearer both to look at the warlike lugger that she saw in the bay, and to communicate more clearly with her by signals. Ithuel's expedient had not sufficed; the vigilant Captain Cuffe, alias Sir Brown, who commanded the *Proserpine*, not being a man likely to be mystified by so stale a trick. Raoul scarcely breathed, as he watched the lugger, in anticipation of her course.

Ithuel certainly seemed in no hurry to commit himself, for the signal had now been flying on board the frigate several minutes, and yet no symptoms of any preparations for an answer could be discovered. At length the halyards moved, and then three fair, handsome flags rose to the end of *Le Feu-Follet's* jigger-yard, a spar that was always kept aloft in moderate weather. What the signal meant Raoul did not know, for though he was provided with signals by means of which to communicate with the vessels of war of his own nation, the Directory had not been able to supply him with those necessary to communicate with the enemy. Ithuel's ingenuity, however, had supplied the deficiency.

While serving on board the *Proserpine*, the very ship that was now menacing the lugger, he had seen a meeting between her and a privateer English lugger, one of the two or three of that rig which sailed out of England, and his observant eye had noted the flags she had shown on the occasion. Now, as privateersmen are not expected to be expert, or even very accurate, in the use of signals, he had ventured to show these very numbers, let it be for better or worse. Had he been on the quarter-deck of the frigate, he would have ascertained, through the benedictions bestowed by Captain Cuffe, that his ruse had so far succeeded as to cause that officer to attribute his unintelligible answer to ignorance, rather than to design. Nevertheless, the frigate did not seem to alter her course; for, either influenced by a desire to anchor, or by a determination to take a still closer look at the lugger, she stood on, nearing the eastern side of the bay, at the rate of some six miles to the hour.

Raoul Yvard now thought it time to look to the safety of *Le Feu-Follet* in person. Previously to landing he had given instructions as to what was to be done in the event of the frigate's coming in; but matters now seemed so very serious, that he hurried down the hill, overtaking Vito Viti in his way, who was repairing to the harbor to give instructions to certain boatmen concerning the manner in which the quarantine laws were to be regarded, in an intercourse with a British frigate.

"You ought to be infinitely happy at the prospect of meeting an honorable countryman in this Sir Brown," observed the short-winded podesta, who usually put himself out of breath both in ascending and descending the steep street, "for he really seems determined to anchor in our bay, Signor Smees."

"To tell you the truth, Signor Podesta, I wish I was half as well persuaded that it is Sir Brown, and *La Proserpine*, as I was an hour ago. I see symptoms of its being a republican, after all, and must have a care for ze *Ving-and-Ving*."

"The devil carry away all republicans, is my humble prayer, Signor Capitano; but I can hardly believe that so graceful and gracious-looking a frigate can possibly belong to such wretches."

"Ah! signore, if that were all, I fear we should have to yield the palm to the French," answered Raoul, laughing; "for the best-looking craft in his majesty's service are republican prizes. Even should this frigate turn out to be the *Proserpine* herself, she can claim no better origin. But I think the vice-governatore has not done well in deserting the batteries, since the stranger does not answer our signals as she should. The last communication has proved quite unintelligible to him."

Raoul was nearer to the truth than he imagined, perhaps, for certainly Ithuel's number had made nonsense, according to the signal book of the *Proserpine*; but his confident manner had an effect on Vito Viti, who was duped by his seeming earnestness, as well as by a countenance which, rightly considered, told as much against, as it did in favor of his companion.

"And what is to be done, signore?" demanded the podesta, stopping short in the street.

"We must do as well as we can, under the circumstances. My duty is to look out for ze *Ving-and-Ving*, and yours to look out for the town. Should the stranger actually enter the bay and bring his broadside to bear on this steep hill, there is not a chamber window that will not open on the muzzles of his guns. You will grant me permission to haul into the inner harbor, where we shall be sheltered by the buildings from his shot, and then, perhaps, it will be well enough to send my people into the nearest battery. I look for bloodshed and confusion ere long."

All this was said with so much apparent sincerity, that it added to the podesta's mystification. Calling a neighbor to him, he sent the latter up the hill, with a message to Andrea Barrofaldi, and then he hurried down toward the port, it being much easier for him, just at that moment, to descend than to ascend. Raoul kept at his side, and together they reached the water's edge.

The podesta was greatly addicted to giving utterance to any predominant opinion of the moment, being one of those persons who feel quite as much as they think. On the present occasion he did not spare the frigate, for, having caught at the bait that his companion had so artfully thrown out to him, he was loud in the expression of his distrust. All the signaling and showing of colors, he now believed to be a republican trick; and precisely in proportion as he became resentful of the ship, he was disposed to confide blindly in the honesty of the lugger. This was a change of sentiment in the magistrate; and, as in the case of sudden but late conversions, he was in a humor to compensate for his tardiness by the excess of his zeal.

In consequence of this disposition, and the character and loquacity of the man, all aided by a few timely suggestions on the part of Raoul, in five minutes it came to be generally understood that the frigate was greatly to be distrusted, while the lugger rose in public favor exactly in the degree in which the other fell. This interposition of Vito Viti's was exceedingly apropos, so far as *Le Feu-Follet* and her people were concerned, inasmuch as the examination of, and intercourse with the boat's crew, had rather left the impression of their want of nationality in a legal sense, than otherwise. In a word, had not the podesta so loudly and so actively proclaimed the contrary, Tommaso and his fellows were about to report their conviction that these men were all *bona fide* wolves in sheep's clothing—alias Frenchmen.

"No, no, amici mici," said Vito Viti, bustling about on the narrow little quay, "all is not gold that glitters, of a certainty; and this frigate is probably no ally, but an enemy. A very different matter is it with the *Ving-y-Ving* and Il Signor Smees; we may be said to know him—have seen his papers, and the Vice-governatore and myself have examined him, as it might be, on the history and laws of his island; for England is an island, neighbors, as well as Elba; another reason for respect and amity; but we have gone over much of the literature and history of Inghilterra together, and find everything satisfactory and right; therefore we are bound to show the lugger protection and love."

"Most true, Signor Podesta," answered Raoul, from his boat; "and such being the case, I hasten to haul my vessel into the mouth of your basin, which I will defend against boats, or any attempt of these rascally republicans to land."

Waving his hand, the young sailor pulled quickly out of the crowded little port, followed by a hundred vivas. Raoul now saw that his orders had not been neglected. A small line had been run out from the lugger, and fastened to a ring in the inner end of the eastern side of the narrow haven, apparently with the intention of hauling the vessel into the harbor itself. He also perceived that the light anchor, or large kedge, by which *Le Feu-Follet* rode, was under foot, as seamen term it; or, that the cable was nearly "up and down." With a wave of the hand he communicated a new order, and then he saw that the men were raising the kedge from the bottom. By the time his foot touched the deck, indeed, the anchor was up and stowed, and nothing held the vessel but the line that had been run to the quay. Fifty pairs of hands were applied to this line, and the lugger advanced rapidly toward her place of shelter. But an artifice was practiced to prevent her heading into the harbor's mouth, the line having been brought inboard abaft her larboard cathead, a circumstance which necessarily gave her a sheer in the contrary direction, or to the eastward of the entrance. When the reader remembers that the scale on which the port had been constructed was small, the entrance scarce exceeding a hundred feet in width, he will better understand the situation of things. Seemingly to aid the movement, too, the jigger was set, and the wind being south, or directly aft, the lugger's motion was soon light and rapid.

As the vessel drew nearer to the entrance, her people made a run with the line, and gave her a movement of some three or four knots to the hour, actually threatening to dash her bows against the pierhead.

But Raoul Yvard contemplated no such blunder. At the proper moment, the line was cut, the helm was put aport, the lugger's head sheered to starboard, and just as Vito Viti, who witnessed all without comprehending more than half that passed, was shouting his vivas, and animating all near him with his cries, the lugger glided past the end of the harbor, on its outside, however, instead of entering it. So completely was every one taken by surprise by this evolution, that the first impression was of some mistake, accident, or blunder of the helmsman, and cries of regret followed, lest the frigate might have it in her power to profit by the mishap. The flapping of canvas, notwithstanding, showed that no time was lost, and presently *Le Feu-Follet* shot by an opening between the warehouses, under all sail. At this critical instant, the frigate, which saw what passed, but which had been deceived like all the rest, and supposed the lugger was hauling into the haven, tacked and came round with her head to the westward. But intending to fetch well into the bay, she had stretched so far over toward the eastern shore, as, by this time, to be quite two miles distant; and as the lugger rounded the promontory close under its rocks, to avoid the shot of the batteries above, she left, in less than five minutes, her enemy that space directly astern. Nor was this all. It would have been dangerous to fire as well as useless, on account of the range, since the lugger lay directly in a line between her enemy's chase guns and the residence of the vice-governatore. It only remained, therefore, for the frigate to commence what is proverbially "a long chase," namely, "a stern chase."

All that has just been related may have occupied ten minutes; but the news reached Andrea Barrofaldi and his counselors soon enough to allow them to appear on the promontory in time to see the *Ving-y-Ving* pass close under the cliffs underneath them, still keeping her English colors flying. Raoul was visible, trumpet in hand; but as the wind was light, his powerful voice sufficed to tell his story.

"Signori," he shouted, "I will lead the rascally republican away from your port, in chase; that will be the most effectual mode of doing you a service."

These words were heard and understood, and a murmur of applause followed from some, while others thought the whole affair mysterious and questionable. There was no time to interpose by acts, had such a course been contemplated, the lugger keeping too close in to be exposed to shot, and there being, as yet, no new preparations in the batteries to meet an enemy. Then there were the doubts as to the proper party to assail, and all passed too rapidly to admit of consultation or preconcert.

The movement of *Le Feu-Follet* was so easy, as to partake of the character of instinct. Her light sails were fully distended, though the breeze was far from fresh; and as she rose and fell on the long ground-swells, her wedgelike bows caused the water to ripple before them like a swift current meeting a sharp obstacle in the stream. It was only as she sank into the water, in stemming a swell, that anything like foam could be seen under her fore-foot. A long line of swift receding bubbles, however, marked her track, and she no sooner came abreast of any given group of spectators, than she was past it, resembling the progress of a porpoise as he sports along a harbor.

Ten minutes after passing the palace, or the pitch of the promontory, the lugger opened another bay, one wider and almost as deep as that on which Porto Ferrajo stands, and here she took the breeze without the intervention of any neighboring rocks, and her speed was essentially increased. Hitherto, her close proximity to the shore had partially becalmed her, though the air had drawn round the promontory, making nearly a fair wind of it; but now the currents came fully on her beam, and with much more power. She hauled down her tacks, flattened in her sheets, luffed, and was soon out of sight: breasting up to windward of a point that formed the eastern extremity of the bay last mentioned.

All this time the *Proserpine* had not been idle. As soon as she discovered that the lugger was endeavoring to escape, her rigging was alive with men. Sail after sail was set, one white cloud succeeding another, until she was a sheet of canvas from her trucks to her bulwarks. Her lofty sails taking the breeze above the adjacent coast, her progress was swift, for this particular frigate had the reputation of being one of the fastest vessels in the English marine.

It was just twenty minutes, by Andrea Barrofaldi's watch, after *Le Feu-Follet* passed the spot where he stood, when the *Proserpine* came abreast of it. Her greater draught of water induced her to keep half a mile from the promontory, but she was so near as to allow a very good opportunity to examine her general construction and appearance, as she went by. The batteries were now manned, and a consultation was held on the propriety of punishing a republican for daring to come so near a Tuscan port. But there flew the respected and dreaded English ensign; and it was still a matter of doubt whether the stranger were friend or enemy. Nothing about the ship showed apprehension, and yet she was clearly chasing a craft which, coming from a Tuscan harbor, an Englishman would be bound to consider entitled to his protection rather than to his hostility.

In a word, opinions were divided, and when that is the case, in matters of this nature, decision is obviously difficult. Then, if a Frenchman, she clearly attempted no injury to any one on the island, and those who possessed the power to commence a fire were fully aware how much the town lay exposed, and how little benefit might be expected from even a single broadside. The consequence was, that the few who were disposed to open on the frigate, like the two or three who had felt the same disposition toward the lugger, were restrained in their wishes, not only by the voice of superior authority, but by that of numbers.

In the meanwhile the *Proserpine* pressed on, and in ten minutes more she was not only out of the range, but beyond the reach of shot. As she opened the bay west of the town, *Le Feu-Follet* was seen from her decks, fully a league ahead, close on a wind, the breeze hauling round the western end of the island, glancing through the water at a rate that rendered pursuit more than doubtful. Still the ship persevered, and in a little more than an hour from the time she had crowded sail, she was up with the western extremity of the hills, though more than a mile to leeward.

Here she met the fair southern breeze, uninfluenced by the land, as it came through the pass between Corsica and Elba, and got a clear view of the work before her. The studding-sails and royals had been taken in, twenty minutes earlier; the bowlines were now all hauled and the frigate was brought close upon the wind. Still the chase was evidently hopeless, the little *Feu-Follet* having everything as much in her mind as if she had ordered the weather expressly to show her powers. With her sheets flattened in until her canvas stood like boards, her head looked fully a point to windward of that of the ship, and, what was of equal importance, she even went to windward of the point she looked at, while the *Proserpine*, if anything, fell off a little, though but a very little, from her own course. Under these differences, the lugger went through the water six feet to the frigate's five, beating her in speed almost as much as she did in her weatherly qualities.

The vessel to windward was not the first lugger, by fifty, that Captain Cuffe had assisted in chasing, and he knew the hopelessness of following such a craft, under circumstances so directly adapted to its qualities. Then he was far from certain that he was pursuing an enemy at all, whatever distrust the signals may have excited, since she had clearly come out of a friendly port. Bastia, too, lay within a few hours' run, and there was the whole of the east coast of Corsica, abounding with small bays and havens, in which a vessel of that size might take refuge, if pressed. After convincing himself, therefore, by half-an-hour's further trial in open sailing under the full force of the breeze, of the fruitlessness of his effort, that experienced officer ordered the *Proserpine's* helm put up, the yards squared, and he stood to the northward, apparently shaping his course for Leghorn, or the Gulf of Genoa. When the frigate made this change in her course, the lugger, which had tacked some time previously, was just becoming shut in by the western end of Elba, and she was soon lost to view entirely, with every prospect of her weathering the island altogether, without being obliged to go about again.

It was no more than natural that such a chase should occasion some animation in a place as retired, and ordinarily as dull, as Porto Ferrajo. Several of the young idlers of the garrison obtained horses, and galloped up among the hills, to watch the result; the mountains being pretty well intersected with bridle-paths, though totally without regular roads. They who remained in the town, as a matter of course, were not disposed to let so favorable a subject for discourse die away immediately, for want of a disposition to gossip on it. Little else was talked of, that day, than the menaced attack of the republican frigate, and the escape of the lugger. Some, indeed, still doubted, for every question has its two sides, and there was just enough dissent to render the discussion lively, and the arguments ingenious. Among the disputants, Vito Viti acted a prominent part. Having committed himself so openly by his "vivas," and his public remarks in the port, he felt it due to his own character to justify all

he had said, and Raoul Yvard could not have desired a warmer advocate than he had in the podesta. The worthy magistrate exaggerated the vice-governatore's knowledge of English, by way of leaving no deficiency in the necessary proofs of the lugger's national character. Nay, he even went so far as to affirm that he had comprehended a portion of the documents exhibited by the "Signor Smees," himself; and as to "ze *Ving-y-Ving*," any one acquainted in the least with the geography of the British Channel would understand that she was precisely the sort of craft that the semi-Gallic inhabitants of Guernsey and Jersey would be apt to send forth to cruise against the out-and-out Gallic inhabitants of the adjacent main.

During all these discussions, there was one heart in Porto Ferrajo that was swelling with the conflicting emotions of gratitude, pleasure, disappointment, joy and fear, though the tongue of its owner was silent. Of all her sex in the place, Ghita had nothing to conjecture, no speculation to advance, no opinion to maintain, nor any wish to express. Still she listened eagerly, and it was not the least of her causes of satisfaction to find that her own hurried interviews with the handsome privateersman had apparently escaped observation. At length her mind was fully lightened of its apprehensions, leaving nothing but tender regrets, by the return of the horsemen from the mountains. These persons reported that the upper sails of the frigate were just visible in the northern board, so far as they could judge, even more distant than the island of Capraya, while the lugger had beaten almost as far to windward as Pianosa, and then seemed disposed to stand over toward the coast of Corsica, doubtless with an intention to molest the commerce of that hostile island.

CHAPTER VII.

Such was the state of things at Porto Ferrajo, at noon, or about the hour when its inhabitants bethought them of their midday meal. With most, the siesta followed, though the sea air, with its invigorating coolness, rendered that indulgence less necessary to these islanders, than to most of their neighbors on the main. Then succeeded the reviving animation of the afternoon, and the return of the zephyr, or the western breeze. So regular, indeed, are these changes in the currents of the air during the summer months, that the mariner can rely with safety on meeting a light breeze from southward throughout the morning, a calm at noon,—the siesta of the Mediterranean—and the delightfully cool wind from the west, after three or four o'clock; this last is again succeeded, at night, by a breeze directly from the land. Weeks at a time have we known this order of things to be uninterrupted; and when the changes did occasionally occur, it was only in the slight episodes of showers and thunderstorms, of which, however, Italy has far fewer than our own coast.

Such, then, was the state of Porto Ferrajo, toward the evening that succeeded this day of bustle and excitement. The zephyr again prevailed; the idle once more issued forth for their sunset walk; and the gossips were collecting to renew their conjectures, and to start some new point in their already exhausted discussions, when a rumor spread through the place, like fire communicated to a train, that "ze Ving-y-Ving" was once more coming down on the weather side of the island, precisely as she had approached on the previous evening, with the confidence of a friend, and the celerity of a bird. Years had passed since such a tumult was awakened in the capital of Elba. Men, women, and children poured from the houses, and were seen climbing the streets, all hastening to the promenade, as if to satisfy themselves with their own eyes of the existence of some miracle. In vain did the infirm and aged call on the vigorous and more youthful for the customary assistance; they were avoided like the cases of plague, and left to hobble up the terraced street as best they might. Even mothers, after dragging them at their own sides till fearful of being too late, abandoned their young in the highway, certain of finding them rolled to the foot of the declivity, should they fail of scrambling to its summit. In short, it was a scene of confusion in which there was much to laugh at, something to awaken wonder, and not a little that was natural.

Ten minutes had not certainly elapsed, after the rumor reached the lower part of the town, ere two thousand persons were on the hill, including nearly all the principal personages of the place, 'Maso Tonti, Ghita, and the different characters known to the reader. So nearly did the scene of this evening resemble that of the past, the numbers of the throng on the hill and the greater interest excepted, that one who had been present at the former, might readily have fancied the latter merely its continuation. There, indeed, was the lugger, under her foresail and mainsail, with the jigger brailed, coming down wing-and-wing, and glancing along the sea like the duck sailing toward her nest. This time, however, the English ensign was flying at the end of the jigger yard, as if in triumph; and the little craft held her way nearer to the rocks, like one acquainted with the coast, and fearing no danger. There was a manner of established confidence in the way in which she trusted herself under the muzzles of guns that might have destroyed her in a very few minutes, and no one who saw her approach could very well believe that she was anything but a known, as well as a confirmed friend.

"Would any of the republican rascals, think you, Signor Andrea," asked Vito Viti, in triumph, "dare to come into Porto Ferrajo in this style; knowing, too, as does this 'Sir Smees,' the sort of people he will have to deal with? Remember, vice-governatore, that the man has actually been ashore among us, and would not be likely to run his head into the lion's mouth."

"Thou hast changed thine opinion greatly, neighbor Vito," answered the vice-governatore, somewhat dryly, for he was far from being satisfied on the subject of Sir Cicero, and on those of certain other circumstances in English history and politics; "it better becomes magistrates to be cautious and wary."

"Well, if there be a more cautious and circumspect man in Elba than the poor podesta of the Porto Ferrajo, let him stand forth, o' God's name, and prove his deeds! I do not esteem myself, Signor Vice-governatore, as the idlest or as the most ignorant man in the grand duke's territories. There may be wiser, among whom I place your excellenza; but there is not a more loyal subject, or a more zealous friend of truth."

"I believe it, good Vito," returned Andrea, smiling kindly on his old associate, "and have ever so considered thy advice and services. Still, I wish I knew something of this Sir Cicero; for, to be frank with thee, I have even foregone my siesta in searching the books in quest of such a man."

"And do they not confirm every syllable the Signor Smees has said?"

"So far from it, that I do not even find the name. It is true, several distinguished orators of that nation are English Ciceros; but then all people do this by way of commendation."

"I do not know that, signor—I do not know that; it may happen in our Italy;

but would it come to pass, think you, among remote and so lately barbarous nations as England, Germany, and France?"

"Thou forgettest, friend Vito," returned the vice-governatore, smiling now in pity of his companion's ignorance and prejudices, as just before he had smiled in kindness, "that we Italians took the pains to civilize these people a thousand years ago, and that they have not gone backward all this time. But there can be no doubt that 'ze *Ving-y-Ving*' means to enter our bay again, and there stands the 'Signor Smees' examining us with a glass, as if he, too, contemplated another interview."

"It strikes me, vice-governatore, that it would be a sin next to heresy to doubt the character of those who so loyally put their trust in us. No republican would dare to anchor in the bay of Porto Ferrajo a second time. *Once*, it might possibly be done. But *twice!*—no, never, never!"

"I do not know but you are right, Vito, and I am sure I hope so. Will you descend to the port, and see that the forms are complied with? Then glean such useful circumstances as you can."

The crowd was now in motion toward the lower part of the town, to meet the lugger; and at this suggestion the podesta hurried down in the throng to be in readiness to meet the "Signor Smees" as soon as he should land. It was more dignified and proper for the vice-governatore to remain and await to hear the report of the supposed English officer where he was. Ghita was one of the few, also, who remained on the heights, her heart now beating with renewed apprehensions of the danger that her lover had again braved on her account, and now nearly overflowing with tenderness, as she admitted the agreeable conviction that, had she not been in Porto Ferrajo, Raoul Yvard would never have incurred such risks.

Ghita delle Torri, or Ghita of the Towers, as the girl was ordinarily termed by those who knew her, from a circumstance in her situation that will appear as we advance in the tale, or Ghita Caraccioli, as was her real name, had been an orphan from infancy. She had imbibed a strength of character and a self-reliance from her condition that might otherwise have been wanting in one so young and of a native disposition so truly gentle. An aunt had impressed on her mind the lessons of female decorum; and her uncle, who had abandoned the world on account of a strong religious sentiment, had aided in making her deeply devout and keenly conscientious. The truth of her character rendered her indisposed to the deception which Raoul was practicing, while feminine weakness inclined her to forgive the offense in the motive. She had shuddered again and again, as she remembered how deeply the young sailor was becoming involved in frauds, and frauds, too, that might so easily terminate in violence and bloodshed; and then she had trembled under the influence of a gentler emotion, as she remembered that all these risks were run for her. Her reason had long since admonished her that Raoul Yvard and Ghita Caraccioli ought· to be strangers to each other; but her heart told a different story. The present was an occasion suited to keeping these conflicting feelings keenly alive, and, as has been said, when most of the others hastened down toward the port to be present when the *Wing-and-Wing* came in, she remained on the hill, brooding over her own thoughts, much of the time bathed in tears.

But Raoul had no intention of trusting his Jack-o'-Lantern where it might be so readily extinguished by the hand of man. Instead of taking shelter against any new roving republican who might come along behind the buildings of the port, as had been expected, he shot past the end of the quay, and anchored within a few fathoms of the very spot he had quitted that morning, merely dropping his kedge under foot as before. Then he stepped confidently into his boat, and pulled for the landing.

"Eh, Signor Capitano," cried Vito Viti, as he met his new protégé with an air of cordiality as soon as the foot of the latter touched the shore, "we looked for the pleasure of receiving you into our bosom, as it were, here in the haven. How ingeniously you led off that *sans culotte* this morning! Ah, the Inglese are the great nation of the ocean, Columbo notwithstanding! The vice-governatore told me all about your illustrious female admiral, Elisabetta, and the Spanish armada; and there was Nelsoni; and now we have Smees!"

Raoul accepted these compliments, both national and personal, in a very gracious manner, squeezing the hand of the podesta with suitable cordiality and condescension, acting the great man as if accustomed to this sort of incense from infancy. As became his public situation, as well as his character, he proposed paying his duty immediately to the superior authorities of the island.

"King George, my master," continued Raoul, as he and Vito Viti walked from the quay toward the residence of Andrea Barrofaldi, "is particularly pointed on this subject, with us all, in his personal orders. 'Never enter a port of one of my allies, Smeet,' he said, the very last time I took leave of him, 'without immediately hastening with your duty to the commandant of the place. You never lose anything by being liberal of politeness, and England is too polished a country to be outdone in these things, by even the Italians, the parents of modern civilization.'"

"You are happy in having such a sovrano, and still more so in being allowed to approach his sacred person."

"O! as to the last, the navy is his pet; he considers us captains, in particular, as his children. 'Never enter London, my dear Smeet,' he said to me, 'without coming to the palace, where you will always find a father;' you know he has one son among us who was lately a captain, as well as myself."

"San Stefano! and he the child of a great king! I did not know that, I confess, signore."

"Why, it is a law in England that the king shall give at least one son to the marine. 'Yes,' said his majesty, 'always be prompt in calling on the superior authorities, and remember me benevolently and affectionately to them, one and all, even down to the subordinate magistrates, who live in their intimacy.'"

Raoul delighted in playing the part he was now performing. But he was a little addicted to overacting it. Like all exceedingly bold and decided geniuses, he was constantly striding across that step which separates the sublime from the ridiculous, and consequently ran no small hazard in the way of discovery. But with Vito Viti he incurred little risk on this score, provincial credulity and a love of the marvelous coming in aid of his general ignorance, to render him a safe depository of anything of this sort that the other might choose to advance. Vito Viti felt it to be an honor to converse with a man who, in his turn, had conversed with a king; and as he puffed his way up the steep ascent again, he did not fail to express some of the feelings which were glowing in his breast.

"Is it not a happiness to serve such a prince?" he exclaimed; "nay, to die for him!"

"The latter is a service I have not yet performed," answered Raoul, innocently, "but which may one day well happen. Do you not think, podesta, that he who lays down his life for his prince merits canonization?"

"That would fill the calendar too soon in these wars, Signor Smees; but I will concede you the generals and admirals, and other great personages. Si—a general or an admiral who dies for his sovereign does deserve to be made a saint; this would leave these miserable French republicans, signore, without hope or honor."

"They are *canaille,* from the highest to the lowest, and can really expect nothing better. If they wish to be canonized, let them restore the Bourbons, and put themselves lawfully in the way of such a blessing. The chase of this morning, Signor Vito Viti, must at least have amused the town?"

The podesta wanted but this opening to pour out a history of his own emotions, sensations, and raptures. He expatiated in glowing terms on the service the lugger had rendered the place by leading off the rascally republicans, showing that he considered the maneuver of passing the port, instead of entering it, as one of the most remarkable of which he had ever heard or even read.

"I defied the vice-governatore to produce an example of a finer professional inspiration in the whole range of history, beginning with his Tacitus and ending with your new English work on Roma. I doubt if the elder Pliny, or Marc Antony, or even Cæsar, ever did a finer thing, signore; and I am not a man addicted to extravagance in compliments. Had it been a fleet of vessels of three decks, instead of a little lugger, Christendom would have rung with the glory of the achievement!"

"Had it been but a frigate, my excellent friend, the maneuver would have been unnecessary. Peste! it is not a single republican ship that can make a stout English ship skulk along the rocks, and fly like a thief at night."

"Ah, there is the vice-governatore walking on his terrace, Sir Smees, and dying with impatience to greet you. We will drop the subject for another occasion, and a bottle of good Florence liquor."

The reception which Andrea Barrofaldi gave Raoul was far less warm than he received from the podesta, though it was polite, and without any visible signs of distrust.

"I have come, Signor Vice-governatore," said the privateersman, "in compliance with positive orders from my master, to pay you my respects again, and to report my arrival once more in your bay, though the cruise made since my last departure has not been so long as an East India voyage."

"Short as it has been, we should have reason to regret your absence, signore, were it not for the admirable proofs it has afforded us of your resources and seamanship," returned Andrea, with due complaisance. "To own the truth, when I saw you depart, it was with the apprehension that we should never enjoy this satisfaction again. But, like your English Sir Cicero, the second coming may prove even more agreeable than the first."

Raoul laughed, and he even had the grace to blush a little; after which he appeared to reflect intensely on some matter of moment. Smiles struggled round his handsome mouth, and then he suddenly assumed an air of sailor-like frankness, and disclosed his passing sensations in words.

"Signor Vice-governatore, I ask the favor of one moment's private conference; Signor Vito Viti, give us leave a single moment, if you please. I perceive, signore," continued Raoul, as he and Andrea walked a little aside, "that you have not easily forgotten my little fanfaronade about our English Cicero. But what will you have?—we sailors are sent to sea children, and we know little of books. My excellent father, Milord Smeet, had me put in a frigate when I was only twelve, an age at which one knows very little of Ciceros, or Dantes, or Corneilles, even, as you will confess. Thus, when I found myself in the presence of a gentleman whose reputation for learning has reached far beyond the island he so admirably governs, a silly ambition has led me into a folly that he finds it hard to forgive. If I had talked of names of which I know nothing, it may be a weakness such as young men will fall into; but surely it is no heinous crime."

"You allow, signore, that there has been no English Sir Cicero?"

"The truth compels me to say, I know nothing about it. But it is hard for a very young man, and one, too, that feels his deficiencies of education, to admit all this to a philosopher on first acquaintance. It becomes a different thing, when natural modesty is encouraged by a familiar goodness of heart; and a day's acquaintance with the Signor Barrofaldi is as much as a year with an ordinary man."

"If this be the case, Sir Smees, I can readily understand, and as willingly overlook what has passed," returned the vice-governatore, with a self-complacency that in nothing fell short of that which Vito Viti had so recently exhibited. "It must be painful to a sensitive mind to feel the deficiencies which unavoidably accompany the want of opportunities for study; and I, at least, can now say how delightful it is to witness the ingenuousness which admits it. Then, if England has never possessed a Cicero in name, doubtless she has had many in qualifications, after allowing for the halo which time ever throws around a reputation. Should your duty often call you this way, signore, during the summer, it will add to the pleasure I experience in enjoying the advantage of your acquaintance, to be permitted, in some slight degree, to direct your reading to such works, as, with a mind like yours, will be certain to lead to profit and pleasure."

Raoul made a suitable acknowledgment for this offer, and from that moment the best understanding existed between the parties. The privateersman, who had received a much better education than he pretended to, and who was a consummate actor, as well as, on certain occasions, a practiced flatterer, determined to be more cautious in future, sparing his literary conjectures, whatever liberties he might take with other subjects. And yet this reckless and daring mariner never flattered nor deceived Ghita in anything! With her he had been all sincerity, the influence he had obtained over the feelings of that pure-minded girl being as much the result of the nature and real feelings he had manifested, as of his manly appearance and general powers of pleasing. It would have been, indeed, matter of interesting observation, for one curious in the study of human nature, to note how completely the girl's innocence and simplicity of character had extended itself over every act of the young man, that was any way connected with her; preventing his even feigning that religion which he certainly did not feel, and the want of which was the sole obstacle to the union he had now solicited for near a twelvemonth, and which, of all others, was the object by far the closest to his heart. With Andrea Barrofaldi and Vito Viti, and most especially with the hated English, it was a very different thing, however; and seldom was Raoul happier than when he was employed in precisely such a scene of mystification as that in which he was at that moment engaged.

The vice-governatore having established relations so completely amicable with the "Signor Smees," could do no less than invite his guest to enter the palazzo, along with himself and the podesta. As it was yet too light for the sailor to seek an interview with Ghita, he cheerfully accepted the offer; making a careful examination of the whole of the northern margin of the sea, from his elevated position, however, before he crossed the threshold. This little delay on Raoul's part enabled the podesta to have a passing word with his friend unobserved.

"You have found 'Sir Smees,'" said Vito Viti, with earnestness, "all that your wisdom and prudence could desire, I trust? For my part, I consider him a most interesting youth; one destined, at some future time, to lead fleets and dispose of the fortunes of nations."

"He is more amiable and even better informed than I had thought, neighbor Vito Viti. He gives up his Sir Cicero with a grace that causes one to regret it was necessary; and, like yourself, I make no doubt of his becoming an illustrious admiral in time. It is true his father, 'Milordo Smees,' has not done justice to his education; but it is not too late for you to repair that evil. Go, desire him to enter; for I am impatient to draw his attention to certain works that may be useful to one in his line of life."

At this suggestion the podesta returned to the door, in order to usher the imaginary Guernsey-man into the residence. He found Raoul still standing on the entrance, examining the sea. There were two or three coasters, feluccas, as usual, stealing along the coast, in the Italian fashion, equally afraid of the barbarians of the south shore, and of the French of the north. All these would have been good prizes; but, to do the privateersman justice, he was little in the habit of molesting mariners of so low a class. There was one felucca, however, that was just rounding the promontory, coming in from the north; and with the people of this ♦ craft he determined to have some communication as soon as he returned to the port, with a view to ascertain whether she had fallen in with the frigate. Just as he had come to this resolution, the podesta joined him, and he was ushered into the house.

It is unnecessary to give the discourse which succeeded. It related more to literature and matters in general, than to anything connected with our tale, the worthy vice-governatore being disposed to reward the ingenuousness of the young sailor, by furnishing him as much instruction as the time and circumstances would allow. Raoul bore this very well, waiting patiently for the light to disappear, when he felt a perfect confidence of again meeting Ghita on the promenade. As he had discovered how much more safety there was in diffidence than in pretension, he found his task of deception comparatively easy; and by letting the vice-governatore

have his own way, he not only succeeded in gaining that functionary over to a full belief in his assumed nationality, but in persuading him to believe the "Signor Smees" a young man of even more erudition than he had at first supposed. By means as simple and natural as these, Raoul made more progress in the good graces of Andrea Barrofaldi in the next two hours, than he could have done in a year by setting up his own knowledge and reading as authority.

There is little doubt the vice-governatore found this interview agreeable, from the time he was disposed to waste on it; and it is certain Raoul thought it some of the hardest duty in which he had ever been engaged. As for Vito Viti, he was edified, and he did not care to conceal it, giving frequent manifestations of his satisfaction, by expressions of delight; occasionally venturing a remark as if expressly to betray his own ignorance.

"I have often known you great, vice-governatore," he cried, when Andrea had closed a dissertation on the earlier history of all the northern nations, which lasted fully half an hour, "but never so great as you are to-night! Signore, you have been most illustrious this evening? Is it not so, Signor Smees? Could any professor of Pisa, or even of Padua, do more justice to a subject than we have seen done to this to which we have been listening?"

"Signor Podesta," added Raoul, "but one feeling has prevailed in my mind while attending to what has been said; and that has been deep regret that my profession has cut me off from all these rich stores of profound thought. But it is permitted us to admire that even which we cannot imitate."

"Quite true, Signori," answered Andrea, with gentle benevolence, "but with dispositions like yours, Sir Smees, it is not so very difficult to imitate what we admire. I will write out a list of works, which I would recommend to your perusal; and, by touching at Livorno or Napoli, you will obtain all the books at reasonable prices. You may expect to see the list on your breakfast-table to-morrow morning, as I shall not sleep until it is completed."

Raoul gladly seized upon this promise as a hint to depart, and he took his leave with suitable acknowledgments of gratitude and delight. When he got out of the palazzo, however, he gave a long, low whistle, like a man who felt he had escaped from a scene in which persecution had been a little lightened by the ridiculous, and uttered a few curses on the nations of the north, for being so inconsiderate as to have histories so much longer and more elaborate than he conceived to be at all necessary. All this passed as he hastened along the promenade, which he found deserted, every human being having apparently left it. At length he thought he perceived a female form some distance ahead of him, and in a part of the walk that was never much frequented. Hastening toward it, his quick eye discerned the person of her he sought, evidently waiting for his approach.

"Raoul," exclaimed Ghita, reproachfully, "in what will these often repeated risks finally end? When so fairly and cleverly out of the harbor of Porto Ferrajo, why did you not possess the prudence to remain there?"

"Thou know'st the reason, Ghita, and why ask this question? San Nettuno! was it not handsomely done; and is not this brave vice-governatore rarely mystified! I sometimes think, Ghita, I have mistaken my vocation, which should have been that of a diplomat."

"And why a diplomat in particular, Raoul? Thou art too honest to deceive long, whatever thou mayst do on an occasion like this, and in a pressing emergency."

"Why? but no matter. This Andrea Barrofaldi, and this Vito Viti, will one day know why. And now to our business, Ghita, since *Le Feu Follet* cannot always decorate the bay of Porto Ferrajo."

"True," interrupted the girl, "and I have come for no other purpose than to say as much myself. My dear uncle has arrived, and he intends to sail for the Torri with the first felucca."

"There! this has done more to make me believe in a Providence than all the preaching of all the padri of Italy! Here is the lugger to take the place of the felucca, and we can sail this very night. My cabin shall be yours entirely, and with your uncle for a protector, no one can raise an evil tongue against the step."

Ghita, to own the truth, expected this very offer, which, agreeable as it was, her sense of propriety would certainly have prevented her from accepting but for one consideration. It might be made the means of getting Raoul out of an enemy's port, and, in so much, out of harm's way. This, with one of her affectionate heart, was an object to which she would have sacrificed appearances of even a graver character. We do not wish the reader, however, to get a false impression of this girl's habits and education. Although the latter, in many particulars, was superior to that received by most young

women of her class in life, the former were simple and suited to her station, as well as to the usages of her country. She had not been brought up with that severe restraint which regulates the deportment of the young Italian females of condition, perhaps in a degree just as much too severely as it leaves the young American too little restrained; but she had been taught all that decorum and delicacy required, either for the beautiful or the safe; and her notions inculcated the inexpediency, if not the impropriety, of one in her situation taking a passage in a privateer at all, and particularly so one commanded by an avowed lover. But, on the other hand, the distance between Porto Ferrajo and the Towers was only about fifty miles, and a few hours would suffice to place her in safety beneath her own roof; and, what was of more importance in her view just then, Raoul in safety along with her. On all this had she pondered, and she was consequently prepared with an answer to the proposal that had just been made.

"If my uncle and myself could accept this generous offer, when would it be convenient for you to sail, Raoul!" the girl demanded. "We have now been absent longer than we intended, and longer than we ought."

"Within an hour, if there were any wind. But you see how it is, Ghita; the zephyr has done blowing, and it now seems as if every fan of Italy had gone to sleep. You can depend on our sailing the instant it shall be in our power. At need, we will use the sweeps."

"I will then see my uncle, and mention to him that there is a vessel about to sail, in which we had better embark. Is it not odd, Raoul, that he is profoundly ignorant of your being in the bay? He gets more and more lost to things around him every day, and I do believe he does not recollect that you command an enemy's vessel half the time."

"Let him trust to me; he shall never have occasion to know it, Ghita."

"We are assured of that, Raoul. The generous manner in which you interposed to save us from the corsair of the Algerines, which began our acquaintance, and for which we shall always have occasion to bless you, has made peace between you and us forever. But for your timely succor last summer, my uncle and myself would now have been slaves with barbarians."

"That is another thing that inclines me to believe in a Providence, Ghita. Little did I know, when rescuing you and your good kinsman from the boat of the Algerine, whom I was saving. And yet you see how all has come to pass, and that in serving you I have merely been serving myself.''

"Would thou could'st learn to serve that God who disposes of us all at His holy pleasure!" murmured Ghita, tears forcing themselves to her eyes, and a convulsive effort alone suppressing the deep emotion with which she uttered the words; "but we thank thee again and again, Raoul, as the instrument of His mercy in the affair of the Algerine, and are willing to trust to thee now and always. It will be easy to induce my uncle to embark; but, as he knows thy real character when he chooses to recollect it, I hardly think it will do to say with whom. We must arrange an hour and a place to meet, when I will see to his being there, and in readiness.''

Raoul and Ghita next discussed the little details; a place of rendezvous without the town, a short distance below the wine-house of Benedetta, being selected in preference to choosing one that would necessarily subject them to observation. This portion of the arrangements was soon settled, and then Ghita thought it prudent to separate. In this proposal her companion acquiesced with a better grace than he might have done, had he not the girl's assurance of meeting him within an hour, in order that everything might be ready for a start with the first appearance of wind.

When left alone, Raoul bethought him that Ithuel and Filippo were on shore as usual, the New Hampshire man consenting to serve only on condition of being allowed to land; a privilege he always abused by driving a contraband trade on occasions like the present. So great was the fellow's dexterity in such matters, that Raoul—who disdained smuggling, while he thought himself compelled to wink at it in others—had less apprehensions of his committing the lugger than he might have felt in the case of one less cunning. But it was now necessary to get these two men off or abandon them; and fortunately remembering the name of the wine-house where they had taken their potations the previous night, he repaired to it without delay, luckily finding Ithuel and his interpreter deep in the discussion of another flask of the favorite Tuscan beverage.

'Maso and his usual companions were present also, and there being nothing unusual in the commander of an English ship of war's liking good liquor, Raoul, to prevent suspicion, drew a chair and asked for his glass. By the conversation that followed, the young privateersman felt

satisfied that, though he might have succeeded in throwing dust into the eyes of the vice-governatore and the podesta, these experienced old seamen still distrusted his character. It was so unusual a thing for a French frigate, while it was so usual for an English frigate to be standing along the coast, near in, that these mariners—who were familiar with all such matters, had joined this circumstance to the suspicious signs about the lugger, and were strongly disposed to believe the truth concerning both vessels. To all this, however, Raoul was more indifferent than he might have been but for the arrangement to sail so soon. He took his wine, therefore, with apparent indifference, and in proper season withdrew, carrying with him Ithuel and the Genoese.

CHAPTER VIII.

It was dark when Raoul quitted the government-house, leaving Andrea Barrofaldi and Vito Viti in the library of the former. No sooner was the young seaman's back turned, than the vice-governatore, who was in a humor to display his acquirements, resumed a discussion that he had found so agreeable to his self-esteem.

"It is easy to see, good Vito Viti, that this young Inglese is a gentleman of noble birth, though not of a liberal education," he said; "doubtless his father, Milordo Smees, has a large family, and the usages of England are different from those of Italy, in respect to birthright. There, the eldest son alone inherits the honors of the family, while the cadets are put into the army and navy to earn new distinctions. Nelsoni is the son of a priest, I hear—"

"Cospetto! of a padre! Signor Vice-governatore," interrupted the podesta, "it is most indecent to own it. A priest must be possessed of the devil, himself, to own his issue; though issue he may certainly have.''

"There, again, good Vito, it is different with the Luterani and us Catholics. The priests of England, you will please remember, marry, while ours do not.''

"I should not like to be shrived by such a padre! The man would be certain to tell his wife all I confessed; and the saints could only say what would be the end on't. Porto Ferrajo would soon be too hot to hold an honest man, ay, or even an honest woman in the bargain.''

"But the Luterani do not confess, and are never shrived at all, you will remember.''

"San Stefano! How do they expect, then, ever to get to heaven?"

"I will not answer that they do, friend Vito; and we are certain, that if they have such expectations, they must be most treacherous to them. But, talking of this Sir Smees, you perceive in his air and manner the finesse of the Anglo-Saxon race; which is a people altogether distinct from the ancient Gauls, both in history and character. Pietro Giannone, in his 'Storia Civile del Regno di Napoli,' speaks of the Normans, who were a branch of these adventurers, with great interest and particularity; and I think I can trace, in this youth, some of the very peculiarities that are so admirably delineated in his well-told, but too free writings. Well, Pietro; I was not speaking of thee, but of a namesake of the family of Giannona, an historian of Naples, of note and merit; what is thy will?"

This question was put to a servant, who entered at that moment, holding in his hand a piece of paper, which he desired to lay before his master.

"A cavaliere is without, Signor Andrea, who asks the honor of an audience, and who sends in his name, as your eccellenza will find it on this paper."

The vice-governatore took the slip of paper, and read aloud: "Edward Griffin, tenente della marina Inglesa."

"Ah! here is an officer sent from 'ze *Ving-y-Ving*' with some communication, friend Vito; it is fortunate you are still here, to hear what he has to say. Show the lieutenant in, Pietro."

One who understood Englishmen better than Andrea Barrofaldi would have been satisfied, at a glance, that he who now entered was really a native of that country. He was a young man of some two or three and twenty, of a ruddy, round, good-natured face, wearing an undress coat of the service to which he professed to belong, and whose whole air and manner betrayed his profession, quite as much as his country. The salutations he uttered were in very respectable Italian, familiarity with the language being the precise reason why he had been selected for the errand on which he had come. After these salutations, he put a piece of parchment into Andrea's hand, remarking.

"If you read English, signore, you will perceive by that commission I am the person I represent myself to be."

"Doubtless, Signor Tenente, you belong to ze *Ving-y-Ving*, and are a subordinate of Sir Smees?"

The young man looked surprised, and, at the same time, half disposed to laugh;

though a sense of decorum suppressed the latter inclination.

"I belong to His Britannic Majesty's ship, *Proserpine*, signore," he dryly answered, "and know not what you mean by the *Ving-y-Ving*, Captain Cuffe, of that ship, the frigate you saw off your harbor this morning, has sent me down in the felucca that got in this evening, to communicate intelligence concerning the lugger, which we chased to the southward about nine o'clock, but which, I see, is again snug at her anchor in this bay. Our ship was lying behind Capraya, when I left her, but will be here to take me off, and to hear the news, before daylight, should the wind ever blow again."

Andrea Barrofaldi and Vito Viti stared, and that, too, as if a messenger had come from the lower regions to summon them away for their misdeeds. Lieutenant Griffin spoke unusually good Italian, for a foreigner; and his manner of proceeding was so straightforward and direct as to carry with it every appearance of truth.

"You do not know what I mean by ze *Ving-y-Ving?*" demanded the vice-governatore, with emphasis.

"To be frank with you, I do not, signore. *Ving-y-Ving* is not English; nor do I know that it is Italian."

Mr. Griffin lost a good deal of ground by this assertion, which implied a doubt of Andrea's knowledge of foreign tongues.

"You say, Signor Tenente, if I comprehend your meaning, that Ving-y-Ving is not English?"

"Indeed I do, sir; at least no English that I have ever heard spoken, at sea or ashore; and we seamen have a language of our own."

"Will you, then, permit me to ask you what is the translation of *Ala-e-Ala* word for word."

The lieutenant paused a moment, and pondered. Then he laughed involuntarily, checking himself almost immediately, with an air of respect and gravity.

"I believe I now understand you, Signor Vice-governatore," he said: "we have a sea-phrase something like this to describe a fore-and-aft vessel with her sails swinging off on both sides; but we call it wing-and-wing."

"Si, signore—ving-y-ving. Such is the name of the lugger of your king that now lies in our bay."

"Ah! we thought as much, signori; the scoundrel has deceived you, as he has done a hundred before you, and will do a hundred again, unless we catch him tonight. The lugger is a celebrated French privateer, that we have six cruisers in chase of at this moment, our own ship included. She is called *Le Feu-Follet*, which is not Wing-and-Wing, but Will-o'-the-Wisp, or Jack-o'-Lantern, in English; and which you, in Italian, would call Il Fuoco Fatuo. Her commander is Raoul Yvard, than whom there is not a greater desperado sailing out of France, though it is admitted that the fellow has some good—nay, some noble qualities."

At every word uttered by the lieutenant a page of history was blotted out from the memory of his listener. The vice-governatore had heard the name of Raoul Yvard, and even that of *Le Feu-Follet*, which the malignancy of a bitter war had blackened nearly to the hues of piracy. The thought that he had been the dupe of this corsair —nay, that he had actually been entertaining him with honors and hospitality, within an hour, was almost too much for his philosophy. Men do not often submit to such humiliating sensations without a struggle; and before he would, or could, accord full credence to what was now told him, it was natural to oppose the objections that first offered.

"All this must be a mistake," observed the vice-governatore; "there are English as well as French luggers; and this is one of the former. Her commander is a noble English gentleman, a son of Milordo Smees; and though his education had been in a trifling degree neglected, he shows his origin and national character in all he says and does. Ze *Ving-y-Ving* is commanded by Sir Smees, a young officer of merit, as you must have seen yourself, signore, by his evolutions this very morning. Surely you have heard of Il Capitano Sir Smees, the son of Milordo Smees!"

"We do not deny that his escape this morning was a clever thing, vice-governatore, for the fellow is a seaman, every inch of him; and he is as brave as a lion; but, then, he is as impudent as a beggar's dog. There is no Sir Smees, nor sir anybody else, in command of any of our luggers anywhere. In the Meriterranean we have no cruiser of this rig at all; and the two or three we have elsewhere are commanded by old sea-dogs, who have been brought up in that sort of craft. As for sirs, they are scarce out here, though the battle of the Nile has made a few of them for the navy. Then you'll not meet with a nobleman's son in a clipper like this, for that sort of gentry generally go from a frigate's quarter-deck into a good sloop, as commander, and after a twelvemonth's work, or so, in the small one, into a fast frigate again, as a post-captain."

Much of this was gibberish to Andrea Barrofaldi, but Griffin being exclusively naval, he fancied every one ought to take the same interest as he did himself in all these matters. But, while the vice-governatore did not understand more than half of the other's meaning, that half sufficed to render him exceedingly uneasy. The natural manner of the lieutenant, too, carried conviction with it, while all the original impressions against the lugger were revived by his statements.

"What say you, Signor Vito Viti?" demanded Andrea; "you have been present at the interviews with Sir Smees."

"That we have been deceived by one of the most oily-tongued rogues that ever took in honest men, if we have been deceived at all, vice - governatore. Last evening, I would have believed this; but since the escape and return of the lugger I could have sworn that we had an excellent friend and ally in our bay."

"You had your signals, Signor Tenente; and that is proof of amity and understanding."

"We made our number when we saw the lugger with an English ensign set, for we did not suppose a Frenchman would be quietly lying in a Tuscan port; but the answer we got was nonsense; and then we remembered to have heard that this Raoul Yvard was in the habit of playing such tricks all along the Italian coast. Once on the scent, we were not the men to be easily thrown off it. You saw the chase, and know the result."

"There must be some mistake in all this! Would it not be well, signore, to see the commander of the lugger—or to go on board of her and satisfy yourself, with your own eyes, of the truth or falsehood of your surmises? Ten minutes might clear up everything."

"Your pardon, Signor Vice-governatore; were I to trust myself on board *Le Feu-Follet*, I might remain a prisoner until a peace was made; and I have yet two steps to gain before I can afford that risk. Then as to letting Yvard know of my presence here, it would just give him the alarm, and cause us to lose the bird before we can spring the net. My orders are positive not to let any one but the authorities of the island know of my visit or its object. All we ask of you is to detain the lugger until morning; then we will see to it that she will never trouble the Italian coast again."

"Nay, signore, we have guns of our own, and could easily dispose of so small a vessel, once assured of her being an enemy," returned the vice-governatore, with a little pride and loftiness of manner; "convince us of that fact, and we'll sink the lugger at her anchors."

"That is just what we do not wish you to do, signore," answered the lieutenant with interest. "From what passed this morning, Captain Cuffe has thought it probable that Monsieur Yvard, for some reason best known to himself, would come back here as soon as he was rid of us ; or that finding himself on the south side of the island, he might put into Porto Longone ; and, had I not met him here, I was to get a horse and ride across to the latter place, and make my arrangements there. We wish by all means to get possession of the lugger, which, in smooth water, is the fastest craft in all the Mediterranean, and would be of infinite service to us. We think the *Proserpine* would prove too much for her, blowing fresh ; but, in moderate weather, she will go six feet to our five. Now if you open on her, she will either escape or be sunk ; for Raoul Yvard is not a man to strike to a town. All I ask is to be permitted to make night signals, for which I am prepared, as soon as the frigate approaches, and that you will throw all the delays, by means of forms and permits, in the way of the Frenchman's sailing until to-morrow morning. We will answer for the rest."

"I should think there would be but little danger of the lugger's departing in the night, Signor Tenente, her commander rather expressing an intention of passing several days with us ; and it is this ease and confidence of his which cause me to think that he cannot be the person you take him for. Why should Raoul Yvard and *Le Feu-Follet* come into Porto Ferrajo at all ?"

"No one knows ; it is the man's habit ; and doubtless he has reasons for it. 'Tis said he has even been in Gibraltar ; and it is certain he has cut several valuable store-ships out of our convoys. There is an Austrian loading with iron, I perceive, in the harbor ; probably he is waiting for her to fill up, and finds it easier to watch her at an anchor than by lying outside."

"You naval gentlemen have ways known only to yourselves ; all this may be so, but it seems an enigma to me. Have you any other proofs of your own character, Signor Tenente, than the commission you have shown me ? for Sir Smees, as I have been taught to call the commander of the lugger, has one too that has an air of as much authenticity as this you have shown ; and he wears quite as English-looking a uniform ; how am I to judge between you ?"

"That difficulty has been foreseen, Signor Vice-governatore, and I come well provided with the necessary proofs. I handed you my commission, as that is a document, which, if wanting, might throw a distrust on all other proofs. But here is a communication from your superior at Florence, recommending us to the kindness of the authorities of all the Tuscan ports, which you will readily understand. Captain Cuffe has furnished me with other proofs, which you can look over at your leisure."

Andrea Barrofaldi now set about a cautious and deliberate examination of the papers shown him. They proved to be of a nature to remove every doubt ; and it was not possible to distrust the party that presented them. This was a great deal toward convicting the Signor Smees of imposition, though both the vice-governatore and the podesta were of opinion that Captain Cuffe might yet be mistaken as to the identity of the lugger.

"It is impossible, signori," answered the lieutenant ; "we know every English cruiser in these seas, by name and description at least, and most of them by sight. This is none ; and everything about her, particularly her sailing, betrays her real name. We hear there is a man in her who once belonged to our own ship, a certain Ithuel Bolt—"

"Cospetto !" exclaimed the podesta ; "then we must set down this Sir Smees, after all, as an arrant rogue ; for this is the very man we met at Benedetta's the past night. An Americano, Signor Tenente, is he not ?"

"Why the fellow pretends some such thing," answered the young man, coloring, for he was loth to confess the wrong that had been done the deserter ; "but half the British seamen one falls in with nowadays call themselves Americans, in order to escape serving his majesty. I rather think this rascal is a Cornish or Devonshire man ! he has the twang and natural sing-song of that part of the island. If an American, however, we have a better right to him than the French ; speaking our language, and being descended from a common ancestry, and having a common character, it is quite unnatural for an American to serve any but the English."

"I did not know that, vice-governatore ! I thought the Americani a very inferior sort of people to us Europeans, generally ; and that they could scarcely claim to be our equals in any sense."

"You are quite right, Signor Podesta," said the lieutenant, briskly ; "they are all you think them ; and any one can see that at a glance. Degenerate Englishmen, we call them in the service."

"And yet you take them occasionally,

Signor Tenente; and, as I understand from this Ithuello, frequently contrary to their wishes, and by force," dryly observed Andrea Barrofaldi.

"How can we help it? the king has a right to and he has need of the services of all his own seamen; and in the hurry of impressing we sometimes make a mistake. Then, these Yankees are so like our own people that I defy the devil himself to tell them apart."

The vice-governatore thought there was something contradictory in all this, and he subsequently said as much to his friend the podesta; but the matter went no farther at the moment, most probably because he ascertained that the young lieutenant was only using what might be termed a national argument; the English government constantly protesting that it was impossible to distinguish one people from the other, *quoad* this particular practice; while nothing was more offensive, in their eyes, in the abstract, than to maintain any affinity in appearance and characteristics.

The result of this discussion, notwithstanding, was to make the two Italians reluctant converts to the opinion of the Englishman that the lugger was the dreaded and obnoxious *Feu-Follet*. Once convinced, however, shame, revenge, and mortification, united with duty to quicken their exertions, and to render them willing assistants in executing the schemes of Captain Cuffe. It was, perhaps, fortunate for Raoul and his associates that the English officers had so strong a desire, as Griffin expressed it, "to take the lugger alive;" else she might have been destroyed where she lay, by removing a gun or two from its embrasure, and planting them behind some natural ramparts among the rocks. The night was dark, it is true, but not so much so as to render a vessel indistinct at the short distance at which *Le Feu-Follet* lay; and a cannonade would have been abundantly certain.

When all parties were of a mind as to the true character of the little craft in the bay, a consultation was had on the details of the course proper to be pursued. A window of the government-house that looked toward the direction of the Capraya, or that in which the *Proserpine* was expected to arrive, was assigned to Griffin. The young man took his station at it about midnight, in readiness to burn the blue lights with which he was provided, the instant he should discern the signals of his ship. The position of this window was well adapted to the desired object, inasmuch as the lights could not be seen from the town, while they were plainly open to the sea. The same was essentially true as to the frigate, the heights interposing between her and the houses; and there being a still greater physical impossibility that anything lying in the bay should discover an object at sea on the northern side of the promontory.

In this manner, then, did hour after hour pass away, a light land-breeze blowing, but coming so directly into the bay as to induce Raoul not to lift his kedge. Ghita, and her uncle, Carlo Giuntotardi, had come off about ten; but there were still no signs of movement on board the lugger. To own the truth, Raoul was in no hurry to sail, for the longer his departure was protracted, the longer would he have the happiness of retaining the lovely girl on board; and the zephyr of the succeeding day would be almost certain to carry *Le Feu-Follet* up to the island-like promontory of Monte Argentaro, the point where stood the watch-towers of which Carlo was the keeper, and in one of which he resided. Under these circumstances, therefore, it is not surprising that the rising of the land-breeze was overlooked, or at least disregarded; and that Raoul sat conversing with Ghita on deck until long past midnight, ere he allowed her to seek her little cabin, where everything had been properly arranged for her reception. To own the truth, Raoul was so confident of having completely mystified all on shore, that he felt no apprehensions from that quarter, and, desirous of prolonging his present happiness as much as possible, he had very coolly determined not to sail until the southerly air of the morning should come; which, as usual, would just suffice to carry him well into the canal, when the zephyr would do the rest. Little did this hardy adventurer suspect what had occurred on shore since he quitted it, nor was he at all aware that Tommaso Tonti was at watch in the harbor, ready to report the slightest indication on the part of the lugger of a wish to quit the bay.

But, while Raoul was so indifferent to the danger he ran, the feeling was quite the reverse with Ithuel Bolt. The *Proserpine* was the bane of this man's life; and he had not only hated every stick and every timber in her, but every officer and man who was attached to her, the king whose colors she wore, and the nation whose interest she served. An active hatred is the most restless of all passions; and this feeling made Ithuel keenly alive to every chance which might still render the frigate dangerous to the lugger. He thought it probable the former would return in quest of her enemy; and expressly with a view to this object, when he turned in at nine, he left orders to be called at two, that he might be on the alert in season.

Ithuel was no sooner awaked than he called two trusty men, whom he had prepared for the purpose, entered a light boat that was lying in readiness, on the off side of the lugger, and pulled with muffled oars to the eastern part of the bay. When sufficiently distant from the town to escape observation, he changed his course, and proceeded directly out to sea. Half an hour sufficed to carry the boat as far as Ithuel deemed necessary, leaving him about a mile from the promontory, and so far to the westward as to give him a fair view of the window at which Griffin had taken post.

The first occurrence out of the ordinary course of things that struck the American was the strong light of a lamp shining through an upper window of the government-house—not that at which the lieutenant was posted, but one above it—and which had been placed there expressly as an indication to the frigate that Griffin had arrived, and was actively on duty. It was now two o'clock, or an hour or two before the appearance of light, and the breeze off the adjoining continent was sufficiently strong to force a good sailing vessel, whose canvas had been thickened by the damps of night, some four knots through the water; and as Capraya was less than thirty miles from Porto Ferrajo, abundant time had been given to the *Proserpine* to gain her offing, that ship having come from behind her cover as soon as the sun had set and the haze of evening settled upon the sea.

Ithuel, usually so loquacious and gossiping in moments of leisure, was silent and observant when he had anything serious on hand. His eye was still on the window in which the lamp was visible, the pure olive oil that was burning in it throwing out a clear strong flame; when suddenly a blue light flashed beneath the place, and he got a momentary glimpse of the body of the man who held it as he leaned forward from another window. The motion which now turned his head seaward was instinctive; it was just in time to let him detect a light descending apparently into the water like a falling star; but which, in fact, was merely a signal lantern of the *Proserpine* coming rapidly down from the end of her gaff.

"Ah! d—n you," said Ithuel, grating his teeth, and shaking his fist in the direction of the spot where this transient gleam

of brightness had disappeared, "I know you and your old tricks, with your lanterns and night-signals. Here goes the answer."

As he said this he touched a rocket, of which he had several in the boat, with the lighted end of a cigar he had been smoking, and it went hissing up into the air, ascending so high as to be plainly visible from the deck of *Le Feu-Follet* before it exploded. Griffin saw this signal with wonder; the frigate noticed it with embarrassment, for it was far to seaward of the lamp; and even 'Maso conceived it necessary to quit his station, in order to report the circumstance to the colonel, whom he was to call in the event of any unusual occurrence. The common impression, however, among all these parties was that a second cruiser had come through the canal from the southward, in the course of the night, and that she wished to notify the *Proserpine* of her position, probably expecting to meet that ship off the island.

On board *Le Feu-Follet* the effect was different. The land-breeze of Italy is a side-wind to vessels quitting the bay of Porto Ferrajo, and two minutes after the rocket exploded the lugger was gliding almost imperceptibly, and yet at the rate of a knot or two, under her jigger and jib, toward the outer side of the port, or along the very buildings past which she had brushed the previous day. This movement was made at the critical instant when 'Maso was off his watch, and the ordinary sentinels of the works had other duties to attend to. So light was this little vessel that a breath of air set her in motion; and nothing was easier than to get three or four knots out of her in smooth water, especially when she opened the comparatively last folds of her two principal lugs. This she did when close under the citadel, or out of sight of the town, the sentinels above hearing the flaps of her canvas without exactly understanding whence they came. At this instant Ithuel let off a second rocket, and the lugger showed a light on her starboard bow, so concealed, however, on all sides but one, as to be visible only in the direction of the boat. As this was done, she put her helm hard down, and hauled her foresheet over flat to windward. Five minutes later Ithuel had reached her deck, and the boat was hauled in as if it had been inflated silk.

Deceived by the second rocket, the *Proserpine* now made her number with regular signal lanterns, with the intention of obtaining that of the stranger, trusting that the promontory would conceal it from the vessels in the bay. This told Raoul the precise position of his enemy, and he was not sorry to see that he was already to the westward of her, a fact that permitted him to slip round the island again, so near in as to be completely concealed by the background of cliffs. By the aid of an excellent night-glass, too, he was enabled to see the frigate, distant about a league, under everything that would draw, from her royals down, standing toward the mouth of the bay on the larboard tack; having made her calculations so accurately as to drop into windward of her port, with the customary breeze off the land. At this sight Raoul laughed, and ordered the mainsail taken in. Half an hour later he directed the foresail to be brailed, brought his jigger-sheet in flat, put his helm hard down, and hauled the jib sheet to windward.

As this last order was executed, day was just breaking over the mountains of Radicofani and Aquapendente. By this time *Le Feu-Follet* lay about a league to the westward of the promontory, and abreast of the deep bay that has been already mentioned as being in that direction from the town. Of course she was far beyond the danger of missiles from the land. The night wind, however, had not failed, and there was every appearance that the morning would be calm. In this there was nothing extraordinary, at that season; the winds which prevailed from the south being usually short and light, unless accompanied by a gust. Just as the sun appeared, the south air came, it is true, but so lightly as to render it barely possible to keep the little lugger in command by heaving to, with her head to the southwest.

The *Proserpine* stood in until the day had advanced far enough to enable her lookouts to detect *Le Feu-Follet* braving her, as it might be, in the western board, at the distance of about a league and a half, under her jib and jigger, as described. This sight produced a great commotion in the ship, even the watch below "tumbling up," to get another sight of a craft so renowned for evading the pursuit of all the English cruisers of those seas. A few minutes later Griffin came off, chopfallen and disappointed. His first glance at the countenance of his superior announced a coming storm; for the commander of a vessel of war is no more apt to be reasonable under disappointment than any other potentate. Captain Cuffe had not seen fit to wait for his subordinate on deck; but as soon as it was ascertained that he was coming off in a shore-boat, he retired to his cabin, leaving orders with the first

lieutenant, whose name was Winchester, to send Mr. Griffin below the instant he reported himself.

"Well, sir," commenced Cuffe, as soon as his lieutenant came into the after-cabin, without offering him a seat, "here we are; and out yonder, two or three leagues at sea, is the d——d *Few-Folly!*" for so most of the seamen of the English service pronounced *Feu-Follet*.

"I beg your pardon, Captain Cuffe," answered Griffin, who found himself compelled to appear a delinquent, whatever might be the injustice of the situation; "it could not be helped. We got in, in proper time; and I went to work with the deputy-governor, and an old chap of a magistrate who was with him, as soon as I could get up to the house of the first. Yvard had been beforehand with me; and I had to under-run about a hundred of his lying yarns before I could even enter the end of an idea of my own—"

"You speak Italian, sir, like a Neapolitan born; and I depended on your doing everything as it should have been."

"Not so much like a Neapolitan, I hope, Captain Cuffee, as like a Tuscan or a Roman," returned Griffin, biting his lip. "After an hour of pretty hard and lawyer-like work, and overhauling all the documents, I did succeed in convincing the two Elban gentry of my own character, and of that of the lugger!"

"And while you were playing advocate, Master Raoul Yvard coolly lifted his anchor, and walked out of the bay, as if he were just stepping into his garden to pick a nosegay for his sweetheart!"

"No, sir, nothing of the sort happened. As soon as I had satisfied the Signor Barrofaldi, the vice-governatore—"

"Veechy govern-the-tory! D—n all veechys and d—n all the governatorys, too; do speak English, Griffin, on board an English ship, if you please, even should your Italian happen to be Tuscan. Call the fellow vice-governor at once, if that be his rank."

"Well, sir, as soon as I had satisfied the vice-governor that the lugger was an enemy, and that we were friends, everything went smoothly enough. He wanted to sink the lugger, as she lay at her anchor."

"And why the devil didn't he do it? Two or three heavy shot would have given her a stronger dose than she could bear."

"You know, Captain Cuffe, it has all along been your wish to take her alive. I thought it would tell so well for the ship, to have it to say she had caught *Le Feu-Follet*, that I opposed the project. I know

Mr. Winchester hopes to get her, as a reward for carrying her, himself."

"Ay, and that would make you first. Well, sir, even if you didn't. sink her, it was no reason for letting her escape."

"We could not prevent it, Captain Cuffe. I had a lookout set upon her—one of the very best in Porto Ferrajo, as everybody will tell you, sir; and I made the signals of the lamp and the blue-lights, as agreed upon; and the ship answering, I naturally thought all was as it should be, until—"

"And who burned the rockets off here, where we are at this moment? They deceived me, for I took them to be signals of their presence from the *Weasel* or the *Sparrow.* When I saw those rockets, Griffin, I was just as certain of the *Few-Folly* as I am now of having my own ship!"

"Yes, sir, those rockets did all the mischief; for I have since learned that as soon as the first one was thrown, Master Yvard tripped his kedge, and went out of the bay as quietly as one goes out of a dining-room when he don't wish to disturb the company."

"Ay, he took French leave, the *b—y sans culotte,*" returned the captain, putting himself into a better humor, with his own pun. "But did you see nothing of all this?"

"The first I knew of the matter, sir, was seeing the lugger gliding along under the rocks, so close in that you might have jumped aboard her; and it was too late to stop her. Before those lazy *far nientes* could have pricked and primed, she was out of gun-shot."

"Lazy what?" demanded the captain.

"*Far nientes,* sir; which is a nickname we give these siesta-gentry, you know, Captain Cuffe."

"I know nothing about it, sir; and I'll thank you always to speak to me in English, Mr. Griffin. That is a language which I flatter myself I understand; and it's quite good enough for all my wants."

"Yes, sir, and for any man's wants. I'm sure I am sorry I can speak Italian, since it has led to this mistake."

"Poh—poh—Griffin, you mustn't lay everything to heart that comes wrong end foremost. Dine with me to-day, and we'll talk the matter over at leisure."

CHAPTER IX.

THUS terminated the setting-down, like many others that Captain Cuffe had resolved to give, but which usually ended in a return to good-nature and reason. The steward was told to set a plate for Mr. Griffin among the other guests, and then the commander of the frigate followed the lieutenant on deck. Here he found every officer in the ship, all looking at *Le Feu-Follet* with longing eyes, and most of them admiring her appearance, as she lay on the mirror-like Mediterranean, with the two light sails mentioned, just holding her stationary.

"A regular-built snake-in-the-grass!" growled the boatswain, Mr. Strand, who was taking a look at the lugger over the hammock-cloths of the waist, as he stood on the heel of a spare topmast to do so; "I never fell in with a scamp that had a more d——n-my-eyes look!"

This was said in a sort of soliloquy, for Strand was not exactly privileged to address a quarter-deck officer on such an occasion, though several stood within hearing, and was far too great a man to enlighten his subordinates with his cogitations. It was overheard by Cuffe, however, who just at that instant stepped into the gangway to make an examination for himself.

"It is a snake-out-of-the-grass, rather, Strand," observed the captain, for he could speak to whom he pleased, without presumption or degradation. "Had she stayed in port, now, she would have been in the grass, and we might have scotched her."

"Well, your honor, we can *English* her, as it is; and that'll be quite as natural, and quite as much to the purpose, as *Scotching* her, any day," answered Strand, who, being a native of London, had a magnificent sort of feeling toward all the dependencies of the empire, and to whom the word Scotch, in that sense, was Greek, though he well understood what it meant "to clap a Scotchman on a rope;" "we are likely to have a flat calm all the morning, and our boats are in capital order; and, then, nothing will be more agreeable to our gentlemen than a row."

Strand was a gray-headed seaman, and he had served with Captain Cuffe when the latter was a midshipman, and had even commanded the top, of which the present boatswain had been the captain. He knew the "cut of the captain's jib" better than any other man in the *Proserpine,* and often succeeded with his suggestions when Winchester and the other lieutenants failed. His superior now turned round and looked him intently in the face, as if struck with the notion the other thus indirectly laid before him. This movement was noted; and, at a sign secretly given by Winchester, the whole crew gave three hearty cheers; Strand leading off, as soon as he caught the idea. This is the only manner in which the crew of a man-of-war can express their wishes to their commander; it being always tolerated, in a navy, to hurrah, by way of showing the courage of a ship's company. Cuffe walked aft, in a thoughtful manner, and descended to his cabin again; but a servant soon came up, to say that the captain desired to see the first lieutenant.

"I do not half like this boat-service in open daylight, Winchester," observed the senior, beckoning to the other to take a chair. "The least bungling may spoil it all; and then it's ten to one but your ship goes half manned for a twelvemonth, until you are driven to pressing for colliers and neutrals."

"But we hope, sir, there'll be no bungling in anything that the *Proserpine* undertakes. Nine times in ten, an English man-of-war succeeds, when she makes a bold dash in boats against one of these picaroons. The lugger is so low in the water, too, that it will be like stepping from one cutter into another to get upon her decks; and then, sir, I suppose you don't doubt what Englishmen will do?"

"Ay, Winchester, once on her deck, I make no doubt you'd carry her; but it may not be so easy as you imagine to get on her deck. Of all duty to a captain, this of sending off boats is the most unpleasant. He cannot go in person, and if anything unfortunate turns up, he never forgives himself. Now it's a very different thing with a fight in which all share alike; and the good or evil comes equally on all hands."

"Quite true, Captain Cuffe; and yet this is the only chance that the lieutenants have for getting ahead a little out of the regular course. I have heard, sir, that you were made commander for cutting out some coasters in the beginning of the war."

"You have not been misinformed; and a devil of a risk we all ran. Luck saved us, and that was all. One more fire from a cursed carronade would have given a Flemish account of the whole party; for, once to get a little under, and you suffer like game in a *batteau*." Captain Cuffe wished to say *battue;* but, despising foreign languages, he generally made sad work with them, whenever he did condescend to resort to their terms, however familiar. "This Raoul Yvard is a devil incarnate, himself, at this boarding work; and is said to have taken off the head of a master's mate of the *Theseus* with one clip of his sword, when he retook that ship's prize, in the affair of last winter—that which happened off Alicant!"

"I'll warrant you, sir, the master's mate was some slender-necked chap, that might better have been at home, craning at the girls, as they came out at the church-door. I should like to see Raoul Yvard, or any Frenchman who was ever born, take off *my* head at a single clip!"

"Well, Winchester, to be frank with you, I should not. You are a good first; and that is an office in which a man usually wants all the head he has; and I'm not at all certain you have any to spare. I wonder if one could not hire a felucca, or something larger than a boat, in this place, by means of which we could play a trick upon this fellow, and effect our purpose quite as well as by going up to him in our open boats, bull-dog fashion?"

"No question of it at all, sir; Griffin says there are a dozen feluccas in port here, all afraid to budge an inch, in consequence of this chap's being in the offing. Now one of these trying to slip along shore might just serve for a bait for him, and then he would be famously hooked."

"I think I have it, Winchester. You understand; we have not yet been seen to communicate with the town; and luckily, our French colors have been flying all the morning. Our head, too, is in shore; and we shall drift so far to the eastward, in a few minutes, as will shut in our hull, if not our upper sails, from the lugger where she now lies. As soon as this is done, you shall be off, with forty picked men, for the shore. Engage a felucca, and come out, stealing along the rocks, as close as you can, as if distrusting *us*. In due time, we will chase you in the boats; and then you must make for the lugger for protection, as fast as you can, when, betwixt the two, I'll answer for it, you get this Master Yvard, by fair means or foul."

Winchester was delighted with the scheme; and in less than five minutes orders were issued for the men to be detailed and armed. Then a conference was held, as to all the minor arrangements; when, the ship having become shut in from the lugger by the promontory, as expected, the boats departed. Half an hour later, or just as the *Proserpine*, after wearing, had got near the point where the lugger would be again open, the boats returned and were run up. Presently the two vessels were again in sight of each other, everything on board of each remaining apparently *in statu quo*. Thus far, certainly, the stratagem had been adroitly managed. To add to it, the batteries now fired ten or twelve guns at the frigate, taking very good care not to hit her; which the *Proserpine* returned, under the French ensign, having used the still greater precaution of drawing the shot. All this was done by an arrangement between Winchester and Andrea Barrofaldi, and with the sole view to induce Raoul Yvard to fancy that he was still believed to be an Englishman by the worthy vice-governatore, while the ship in the offing was taken for an enemy. A light air from the southward, which lasted from eight to nine o'clock, allowed the frigate to get somewhat more of an offing the while, placing her seemingly beyond the reach of danger.

During the prevalence of the light air mentioned Raoul Yvard did not see fit to stir tack or sheet, as it is termed among seamen. *Le Feu-Follet* remained so stationary that, had she been set by compass from any station on the shore, her direction would not have varied a degree the whole time. But this hour of comparative breeze sufficed to enable Winchester to get out of the harbor with *La Divina Providenza*, the felucca he had hired, and to round the promontory, under the seeming protection of the guns by which it was crowned; coming in view of the lugger precisely as the latter relieved her man at the helm for ten o'clock. There were eight or nine men visible on the felucca's deck, all dressed in the guise of Italians, with caps and striped shirts of cotton. Thirty-five men were concealed in the hold.

Thus far everything was favorable to the wishes of Captain Cuffe and his followers. The frigate was about a league from the lugger, and half that distance from *La Divina Providenza;* the latter had got fairly to sea, and was slowly coming to a situation from which it might seem reasonable, and a matter of course, for the *Proserpine* to send boats in chase; while the manner in which she gradually drew nearer to the lugger was not such as to excite distrust, or to appear in the least designed. The wind, too, had got to be so light as to favor the whole scheme.

It is not to be supposed that Raoul Yvard and his followers were unobservant of what was passing. It is true, that the latter willfully protracted his departure, under the pretense that it was safer to have his enemy in sight during the day, knowing how easy it would be to elude him in the dark; but, in reality, that he might prolong the pleasure of having Ghita on board; and it is also true, that he had passed a delightful hour, that morning, in the cabin; but, then, his understanding

eye noted the minutest fact that occurred, and his orders were always ready to meet any emergency that might arise. Very different was the case with Ithuel. The *Proserpine* was his bane; and, even while eating his breakfast, which he took on the heel of the bowsprit, expressly with that intent, his eye was seldom a minute off the frigate, unless it was for the short period she was shut in by the land. It was impossible for any one in the lugger to say whether her character was or was not known in Porto Ferrajo; but the circumstance of the blue lights burned in the government-house itself, and witnessed by Ithuel, rendered the latter, to say the least, probable, and induced more caution than might otherwise have been shown. Still, there was no reason to suspect the character of the felucca; and the confident manner in which she came down toward the lugger, though considerably in-shore of her, gave reason to believe that she, at least, was ignorant that *Le Feu-Follet* was an enemy.

"That felucca is the craft which lay near the landing," quietly observed Raoul, who had now come on the forecastle with a view to converse with Ithuel; "her name is *La Divina Providenza;* she is given to smuggling between Leghorn and Corsica, and is probably bound to the latter at this moment. It is a bold step, too, to stand directly for her port under such circumstances!"

"Leghorn is a free port," returned Ithuel; "and smuggling is not needed."

"Ay, free as to friends, but not free to come and go, between enemies. No port is free, in that sense; it being treason for a craft to communicate with the foe, unless she happen to be *Le Feu-Follet*," observed Raoul, laughing; "we are privileged, *mon brave!*"

"Corsica or Capraya, she'll reach neither to-day, unless she finds more wind. I do not understand why the man has sailed, with no more air than will serve to blow out a pocket-handkerchief."

"These little feluccas, like our little lugger, slip along even when there seems to be no wind at all. Then he may be bound to Bastia; in which case he is wise in getting an offing before the zephyr sets in for the afternoon. Let him get a league, or two out here, more to the northwest, and he can make a straight wake to Bastia, after his siesta is over."

"Ay, there go those greedy Englishmen a'ter him!" said Ithuel; "it's as I expected; let 'em see the chance of making a guinea, and they'll strive for it, though it be ag'in law or ag'in natur'. Now what have they to do with a Neapolitan felucca, England being a sworn friend of Naples?''

Raoul made no reply to this, but stood watching the movement in silence, The reader will readily enough understand that Ithuel's remark was elicited by the appearance of the boats which, five in number, at that instant pulled off from the frigate's side and proceeded steadily toward the felucca.

It may be necessary now to mention the relative positions of the parties, the hour, and the precise state of the weather, with a view to give the reader clear ideas of the events that succeeded. *Le Feu-Follet* had not materially changed her place since her jib-sheet was first hauled over. She still lay about a league, a little north-of-west, from the residence of Andrea Barrofaldi, and in plain view of it; a deep bay being south of her, and a-beam. No alterations had been made in her canvas or her helm; most of the first being still in her brails, and the latter down. As the head of the frigate had been kept to the westward for the last hour, she had forged some distance in that direction, and was now quite as near the lugger as was the promontory, though near two miles off the land. Her courses were hauled up, on account of the lightness of the air; but all her upper-sails stood, and were carefully watched and trimmed in order to make the most of the cats'-paws, or rather of the breathings of the atmosphere, which occasionally caused the royals to swell outward. On the whole she might be drawing nearer to the lugger at the rate of about a knot in an hour. *La Divina Providenza* was just out of gun-shot from the frigate, and about a mile from the lugger, when the boats shoved off from the former, though quite near the land, just opening the bay so often named. The boats, of course, were pulling in a straight line from the vessel they had just left toward that of which they were in pursuit.

As to the time, the day had advanced as far as eleven, which is a portion of the twenty-four hours when the Mediterranean, in the summer months, is apt to be as smooth as a mirror, and as calm as if it never knew a tempest. Throughout the morning, there had been some irregularity in the currents of air; the southerly breeze, generally light, and frequently fickle, having been even more light and baffling than common. Still, as has been seen, there was sufficient air to force a vessel through the water; and, had Raoul been as diligent as the people of the two other craft, he might at that moment have been off the western end of the island, and far out of harm's way.

As it was, he had continued watching the result, but permitting all the other parties gradually to approach him.

It must be allowed that the ruse of the felucca was well planned; and it now seemed about to be admirably executed. Had it not been for Ithuel's very positive knowledge of the ship, his entire certainty of her being his old prison, as he bitterly called her, it is not improbable that the lugger's crew might have been the dupe of so much well acted ingenuity; and as it was, opinions were greatly divided, Raoul himself being more than half disposed to fancy that his American ally, for once, was wrong, and that the ship in sight was actually what she professed to be, a cruiser of the republic.

Both Winchester, who was in *La Divina Providenza*, and Griffin, who commanded the boats, played their parts in perfection. They understood too well the character of the wily and practiced foe with whom they had to deal to neglect the smallest of the details of their well concerted plan. Instead of heading toward the lugger, as soon as the chase commenced, the felucca appeared disposed to enter the bay, and to find an anchorage under the protection of a small battery that had been planted, for this express purpose, near its head. But the distance was so great as obviously to render such an experiment bootless; and, after looking in that direction a few minutes, the head of *La Divina Providenza* was laid off shore, and she made every possible effort to put herself under the cover of the lugger. All this was done in plain view of Raoul, whose glass was constantly at his eye, and who studied the smallest movement with jealous distrust. Winchester, fortunately for his purpose, was a dark complexioned man, of moderate stature, and with bushy whiskers, such as a man-of-war's-man is apt to cultivate on a long cruise; and, in his red Phrygian cap, striped shirt, and white cotton trousers, he looked the Italian as well as could have been desired. The men in sight, too, had been selected for their appearance, several of them being actually foreigners, born on the shores of the Mediterranean; it being seldom, indeed, that the crew of an English, or an American vessel of war, does not afford a representation of half the maritime nations of the earth. These men exhibited a proper degree of confusion and alarm, too; running to and fro as soon as the chase became lively; exerting themselves, but doing it without order and concert. At length, the wind failing almost entirely, they got out two sweeps, and began to pull lustily; the real, as well as the apparent desire being to get as near as possible to the lugger.

"Peste!" exclaimed Raoul; "all this seems right—what if the frigate should be French, after all? These men in the boats look like my brave compatriotes!"

"They are regular John Bulls," answered Ithuel, positively, "and the ship is the spiteful *Proserpyne*," for so the New Hampshire man always called his old prison. "As for them French hats, and the way they have of rowing, they act it all for a take-in. Just let a six-pound shot in among 'em, and see how they'll throw off their French airs, and take to their English schooling."

"I'll not do that; for we might injure a friend. What are those fellows in the felucca about, now?"

"Why, they've got a small gun—yes, it's a twelve-pound carronade, under the tarpaulin, for'ard of their foremast, and they're clearing it away for sarvice. We shall have something doin' fore the end of the week!"

"Bien—it is as you say—and, voila, they train the piece on the boats!"

As this was said, the felucca was half concealed in smoke. Then came the discharge of the gun. The shot was seen skipping along the water, at a safe distance from the leading boat, certainly, and yet sufficiently near to make it pass for indifferent gunnery. This leading boat was the *Proserpine's* launch, which carried a similar carronade on its grating, forward, and not half a minute was suffered to pass before the fire was returned. So steady were the men, and so nicely were all parts of this plot calculated, that the shot came whistling through the air in a direct line for the felucca, striking its main-yard about half-way between the mast and the peak of the sail, letting the former down by the run.

"Human natur'!" ejaculated Ithuel; "this is acting up to the contract, dollars and cents! Captain Rule, they shoot better in sport than when they're in downright airnest."

"This looks like real work," answered Raoul. "A man does not often shoot away the main-yard of his friend on purpose."

As soon as the crews of the boats saw the end of the yard come down, they ceased rowing, and gave three hearty cheers, taking the signal from Griffin, who stood erect in the stern of the launch to give it.

"Bah!" cried Raoul, "these are English John Bulls, without a shadow of doubt. Who ever knew the men of the republic shout like so many Italian fan-

toccini pulled by wires! Ah! Messieurs les Anglais, you have betrayed your secret by your infernal throats; now look to hear us tell the remainder of the story."

Ithuel rubbed his hands with delight, perfectly satisfied that Raoul could no longer be deceived, though the fire between the felucca and the launch was kept up with spirit, the shooting being such as might have done credit to a *bona fide* conflict. All this time the sweeps of the felucca were plied, the boats advancing at least two feet to the chase's one. *La Divina Providenza* might now have been three hundred yards from the lugger; and the launch, the nearest of the pursuers, about the same distance astern of the felucca. Ten minutes more would certainly bring the seeming combatants alongside of each other.

Raoul ordered the sweeps of *Le Feu-Follet* to be run out and manned. At the same time her guns, twelve-pound carronades, were cast loose and primed. Of these she had four of a side, while the two sixes on her forecastle were prepared for similar service. When everything was ready, the twelve sweeps dropped into the water, as by a common instinct, and a powerful effort started the lugger ahead. Her jib and jigger were both brailed at the same instant. A single minute sufficed to teach Winchester how hopeless pursuit would be in the felucca, if not in the boats themselves, should the lugger attempt to escape in this manner; it being quite practicable for her strong crew to force her through the water, by means of the sweeps alone, from three to three and a half knots an hour. But flight did not appear to be her object; for her head was laid toward *La Divina Providenza*, as if, deceived by the artifice of the English, she intended to prevent the capture of the felucca, and to cover a friend.

Raoul, however, understood himself far better than this supposition would give reason to suppose. He swept the lugger up in a line with *La Divina Providenza* and the boats, in the first place, as the position in which she would be the least likely to suffer from the fire of the latter; well knowing that whatever shot were thrown were purposely sent so high as to do no mischief; and in the second place, that he might bring his enemies in a single range from his own guns. In the meanwhile, the felucca and the boats not only continued to use their carronades, but they commenced on both sides a brisk fire of musketry; the former being now distant only a hundred yards from *Le Feu-*

Follet, exceedingly hard pressed by her adversaries, so far as appearances were concerned. There being no wind at all, at this juncture, the little there had been having been entirely killed by the concussion of the guns, the sea was getting to be fast covered with smoke; the felucca, in particular, showing more than common of the wreathy canopy over her decks and about her spars; for, in truth, powder was burned in considerable quantities, in different parts of the vessel, with this express object. Ithuel observed, too, that in the midst of this confusion and cloud the crew of *La Divina Providenza* was increasing in numbers, instead of diminishing by the combat, four sweeps next being out, each manned by three men, while near twenty more were shortly visible, running to and fro, and shouting to each other in a language that was intended to be Italian, but which sounded much more, in his practiced ear, like bastard English. The felucca was not fifty yards distant, when this clamor became the loudest; and the crisis was near. The cheers of the boats on the other side of her proclaimed the quick approach of Griffin and his party; the bows of *La Divina Providenza* having been laid in a species of blind haste directly in a line which would carry her athwart-hawse of *Le Feu-Follet*.

" *Mes enfans,*" shouted Raoul, " *soyez calmes—fire!*"

The whole of the five guns loaded heavily with canister were discharged into the smoke of *La Divina Providenza*. The shrieks that succeeded sufficiently proclaimed with what effect. A pause of wondering silence followed on the part of the English; and then arose a manly shout, as if prepared for every contingency, they were resolved to brave the worst. The boats were next seen coming round the bows and stern of the felucca, dashing earnestly at their real enemy, while their two carronades returned the fire, this time loaded and aimed with deadly intent. But it was too late for success. As Griffin in the launch came out of *La Divina Providenza's* smoke he saw the lugger's sails all open, and filled with the dying effort of the southerly air. So light, however, was *Le Feu-Follet*, that a duck could hardly have sailed away more readily from the fowler than this little craft shot ahead, clearing the smoke, and leaving her pursuers an additional hundred yards behind her. As the air seemed likely to stand long enough to place his party in extreme jeopardy, under the fire of the French, Winchester promptly ordered the boats to relinquish the pursuit, and to rally them round the felucca. This command was reluctantly obeyed, when a moment was given to both sides for deliberation.

Le Feu-Follet had sustained no injury worth mentioning; but the English had not less than a dozen men slain or hurt. Among the latter was Winchester himself; and as he saw that any success which followed would fall principally to the share of his subordinate, his wound greatly indisposed him to pursue any further a struggle that was nearly hopeless as it was. Not so with Raoul Yvard, however. Perceiving that the frigate had taken the breeze as well as himself, and that she was stealing along in the direction of the combatants, he determined to take an ample revenge for the audacity of the attempt, and then proceed on his voyage.

The lugger accordingly tacked, and passed to windward of the felucca, delivering a close and brisk fire as she approached. At first the fire was returned, but the opposition soon ceased; and when *Le Feu-Follet* ranged up against her adversary, a few yards to windward, it was seen that the English had deserted her to a man, carrying off their wounded. The boats were pulling through the smoke, toward the bay, taking a direction opposite to that in which the lugger's head was laid. It would have been easy for the French to wear, and probably to have overtaken the fugitives, sinking or capturing them to a man; but there was a touch of high chivalry in the character of Raoul Yvard, and he declared that as the artifice had been ingeniously planned, and daringly attempted, he would follow up his success no further. Perhaps the appearance of Ghita on deck, imploring him to be merciful, had its influence; it is certain that not another shot did he allow to be fired at the enemy. Instead of pursuing her advantage in this manner, the lugger took in her after-sails, wore short round on her heel, came to the wind to leeward of the felucca, shivered all forward, set her jigger again, and luffed up so near what may be called the prize that the two vessels came together so gently as not to break an egg, as it is termed. A single rope secured the felucca to the lugger, and Raoul, Ithuel, and a few more stepped on board the former.

The decks of *La Divina Providenza* were reeking with blood; and grape and canister were sticking in handfuls, in different parts of the vessel. Three dead bodies were found in her hold, but nothing having life was met with on board. There was a tar bucket filled at hand, and this was placed beneath the hatch, covered with all the combustible materials that could be laid hold of, and set on fire. So active were the flames, at that dry season, that Raoul regretted he had not taken the precaution to awaken them after he had removed his own vessel; but the southerly air continuing, he was enabled to get to a safe distance before they actually ascended the felucca's rigging, and seized upon her sails.

Ten minutes were thus lost, and they had sufficed to carry the boats out of gun-shot, in shore, and to bring the frigate very nearly down within gun-shot from the southeast. But, hauling aft all his sheets, Raoul soon took the lugger clear of her flaming prize; and then she stood toward the west end of Elba, going, as usual, in so light an air, three feet to the frigate's two. The hour, however, was not favorable to the continuance of the breeze, and in ten more minutes it would have puzzled the keenest senses to have detected the slightest current of air over the surface of the sea. Such flickerings of the lamp before it burned entirely out were common, and Raoul felt certain that there would be no more wind that day, until they got the zephyr. Accordingly, he directed all the sails to be hauled up, an awning to be spread over the quarter-deck, and permission was given to the people to attend to their own affairs. The frigate, too, seemed to be aware that it was the moment for the siesta of vessels as well as of men; for she clewed up her royals and top-gallant-sails, brailed her jib and spanker, hauled up her courses, and lay on the water as motionless as if sticking on a shoal. The two vessels were barely long gun-shot apart, and, under ordinary circumstances, the larger might have seen fit to attack the smaller in boats, but the lesson just given was a sufficient pledge to the French against the renewal of any such attempt, and they scarcely paid their neighbor's prowess the compliment to watch him. Half an hour later, when Winchester got back to the ship, limping with a hurt in his leg, and with his people exhausted and mortified, it was found that the undertaking had cost the lives of seven good men, besides the temporary suspension of the services of fifteen more.

Captain Cuffe was aware that his enterprise had failed, as soon as he perceived the lugger under her canvas, playing around the felucca, and the boats held in perfect command. But, when he discovered the latter pulling for the shore, he was certain that they must have suffered, and he was prepared to learn a serious loss, though not one that bore so large a proportion to the whole numbers of the party sent on the expedition. Winchester he considerately declined questioning while his wound was being dressed; but Griffin was summoned to his cabin, as soon as the boats were hoisted in and stowed.

"Well, Mr. Griffin, a d——d pretty scrape is this into which you have led me, among you, with your wish to go boating about after luggers and Raoul Yvards! What will the admiral say, when he comes to hear of twenty-two men being laid on the shelf, and a felucca to be paid for, as a morning's amusement?"

"Really, Captain Cuffe, we did our best; but a man might as well have attempted to put out Vesuvius with snow-balls as to stand the canister of that infernal lugger! I don't think there was a square yard in the felucca that was not peppered. The men never behaved better; and down to the moment when we last cheered, I was as sure of *Le Feu-Folett* as I ever was of my own promotion."

"Ay, they needn't call her *Few-Folly* any longer, the *Great-Folly* being a better name. What the devil did you cheer for at all, sir? did you ever know a Frenchman to cheer in your life? That very cheering was the cause of your being found out before you had time to close. You should have shouted *Vive la republique!* as all their craft do when we engage them. A regular English hurrah would split a Frenchman's throat."

"I believe we did make a mistake there, sir; but I never was in an action in which we did not cheer; and when it got to be warm—or to seem warm—I forgot myself a little. But we should have had her, sir, for all that, had it not been for one thing."

"And what was that, pray? You know, Griffin, I must have something plausible to tell the admiral; it will never do to have it published in the gazette that we were thrashed by our own hallooing."

"I was about to say, Captain Cuffe, that had not the lugger fired her first broadside just as she did, and had she given us time to get out of the range of her shot, we should have come in upon her before she could have loaded again, and carried her in spite of the breeze that so much favored her. Our having three men hurt in the launch made some difference, too, and set as many oars catching crabs at a most critical instant. Everything depends on chance in these matters, you know, sir, and that was our bad luck."

"Umph! It will never do to tell Nelson that. 'Everything was going well, my lord, until three of the launch's people went to work catching crabs with their oars, which threw the boat astern.' No, no, that will never do for a gazette. Let me see, Griffin ; after all, the lugger made off from you ; you would have had her had she not made sail, and stood to the southward and westward on a bowline."

"Yes, sir, she certainly did that. Had she not made sail as you say, nothing could have prevented our getting alongside."

"Well, then, she ran. Wind sprung up, enemy made sail ; every attempt to get alongside unsuccessful. Brave fellows, cheering and doing their utmost. Not so bad an account, after all ; but, how about that d——d felucca ? You see, she is burned to the water's edge, and will go down in a few minutes."

"Very true, Captain Cuffe, but not a Frenchman entered her while we were there—"

"Yes, I now see how it was ; threw all hands into the boats, in chase, the felucca being too unwieldy, and every effort to get alongside unsuccessful. He's a devil of a fellow, that Nelson and Bronte ; and I had rather hear the thunder of ten thousand tempests, than get one of his tempestuous letters. Well, I think I understand the affair now, and shall speak of you as you deserve. 'Twas a gallant thing, though it failed. You deserved success, whatever may have caused you to lose it."

In this Captain Cuffe was nearer right than in anything else he uttered on the occasion.

CHAPTER X.

THE situation of Ghita Caraccioli, on board the lugger, was of the most unpleasant nature, during the fierce struggle we have related. Fortunately for her, this struggle was very short, Raoul having kept her in profound ignorance of the approach of any danger, until the instant *Le Feu-Follet* commenced her fire. It is true she heard the guns between the felucca and the boats, but this she had been told was an affair in which the privateer had no participation ; and the reports sounding distant to one in the cabin, she had been easily deceived. While the actual conflict was going on, she was on her knees, at the side of her uncle ; and the moment it ceased, she appeared on deck, and interposed to save the fugitives in the manner related.

Now, however, the scene was entirely changed. The lugger had escaped all damage worthy of notice ; her decks had not been stained with blood ; and her suc-

cess had been as complete as could be desired. In addition to these advantages, the result removed all apprehension from the only source of danger that Raoul thought could exist as between his own vessel and the frigate, of a boat attack in a calm ; for men who had just been so roughly handled in an enterprise so well concealed, would not be likely to renew the attempt while they still smarted under the influence of the late repulse. Affairs of this sort exact all the discipline and resolution that a well-regulated service can afford ; and are not to be thought of under the temporary demoralization of defeat. All in the lugger, therefore, considered this collision with the *Proserpine* at an end, for the moment at least.

Ghita had dined, for the day had now turned some time, and the girl had come on deck, to escape the confinement of a very small cabin, leaving her uncle to enjoy his customary siesta. She was seated under the awning of the quarter-deck, using her needle, as was her wont, at that hour on the heights of Argentaro. Raoul had placed himself on a gun-slide, near her, and Ithuel was busy within a few feet of them, dissecting a spy-glass, with a view to clean its lenses.

"I suppose the most excellent Andrea Barrofaldi will sing a Te Deum for his escape from our fangs," suddenly exclaimed Raoul, laughing. "Pardie ! he is a great historian, and every way fit to write an account of this glorious victory, which Monsieur l'Anglais, la bas, is about to send to his government ! "

"And you, Raoul, have you no occasion for a Te Deum after your escape ? " demanded Ghita, gently, and yet with emphasis. "Is there no God for you to thank, as well as for the vice-governatore ? "

"Peste ! Our French deity is little thought of just now, Ghita. Republics, as you know, have no great faith in religion—is it not so, mon brave Americain ? Tell us, Etooell ; have you any religion in America ? "

As Ithuel had often heard Raoul's opinion on this subject, and knew the prevailing state of France in this particular, he neither felt nor expressed any surprise at the question. Still, the idea ran counter to all his own notions and prejudices, he having been early taught to respect religion, even when he was most serving the devil. In a word, Ithuel was one of those descendants of Puritanism who, "Godward," as it is termed, was quite unexceptionable, so far as his theory extended, but who, "manward," was "as the Scribes and Pharisees." Nevertheless, as he expressed it himself, "he always stood up for religion," a fact that his English companions had commented on in jokes; maintaining that he even "stood up" when the rest of the ship's company were on their knees.

"I'm a little afraid, Monsieur Rule," he answered, "that in France you have entered the rope of republicanism at the wrong end. In Ameriky, we even put religion before dollars, and if that isn't convincing, I'll give it up. Now, I do wish you could see a Sunday once in the Granite State, Signorina Ghita, that you might get some notion what our western religion raaly is."

"All real religion, and real devotion to God, is, or ought to be, the same, Signor Ithuello, whether in the East or in the West. A Christian is a Christian, let him live or die where he may."

"That's not exactly platform, I fancy. Why, Lord bless ye, young lady, your religion, now, is no more like mine than my religion is like that of the archbishop of Canterbury's, or Monsieur Rule's here!"

"La mienne!" exclaimed Raoul, "I pretend to none, mon brave; there can be no likeness to nothing."

Ghita's glance was kind, rather than reproachful; but it was profoundly sorrowful.

"In what can our religion differ," she asked, "if we are both Christians? Americans or Italians, it is all the same."

"That comes of knowing nothing about Ameriky," said Ithuel, filled with the conceit of his own opinion of himself, and of the part of the world from which he came. "In the first place, you have a Pope, and cardinals, and bishops, and all such things in your religion, while we have none."

"Certainly, there is the Holy Father, and there are cardinals; but they are not my religion," answered Ghita, looking surprised. "Bishops, it is true, are appointed of God, and form part of His Church; and the bishop of Rome is the head of the Church on earth, but nothing more!"

"Nothing more! Don't you worship images, and take off and put on garments at your prayers, and kneel down in a make-believe, profane way; and don't you turn everything into vain ceremonies?"

Had Ithuel been engaged, body and soul, in maintaining one of the propositions of the Oxford Tracts' controversy, he could not have uttered these words with greater zeal, or with a more self-righteous emotion. His mind was stored with the most vulgar accusations of an exceedingly vulgar set of sectarian distinctions; and he fancied it a high proof of Protestant perfection to hold all the discarded usages in abhorrence. On the other hand, Ghita listened with surprise; for, to her, the estimation in which the rites of the Roman Church are held by the great bulk of Protestants was a profound secret. The idea of worshiping an image never crossed her innocent mind; and although she often knelt before her own little ivory crucifix, she had never supposed any could be so ignorant as to confound the mere material representation of the sacrifice it was meant to portray with the divine expiation itself.

"It is decent to use proper vestments at the altar," she replied; "and its servants ought not to be clad like other men. We know it is the heart, the soul, that must be touched, to find favor with God; but this does not make the outward semblance of respect that we show even to each other the less necessary. As to worshiping images, that would be idolatry; and as bad as the poor heathens themselves."

Ithuel looked mystified; for he never doubted in the least that the worshiping of images was a material part of Catholic devotion; and as for the Pope and the cardinals, he deemed them all as indispensable to the creed of this Church, as he fancied it important in his own that the priests should not wear gowns, and that the edifices in which they worshiped should have square-topped windows. Absurd as all this may seem to-day, and wicked as it will probably appear a century hence, it formed, and forms, no small part of sectarian belief; and entered into the animosities and jealousies of those who seem to think it necessary to quarrel for the love of God. Could we but look back at our own changes of opinion, it would render us less confident of the justice of our sentiments; and most of all, one would think that the American who has lived long enough to witness the somersaults that have been thrown in the more modern sects of his own country, within the last quarter of a century, would come to have something like a suitable respect for the more stable and venerable divisions of the Christian world.

"Proper vestments!" replied Ithuel, with contempt; "what vestments are wanting in the eyes of the Supreme Being? No; if I must have religion—and I know it's necessary and hullsom'—let it be a pure, naked religion that will stand to reason. Is not that your way of thinking, Monsieur Rule?"

"Ma foi, oui. Reason before all things, Ghita; and, most of all, reason in religion."

"Ah, Raoul! this it is which misleads and betrays you," returned the girl, earnestly. "Faith, and a meek dependence, is what makes a proper state of feeling ; and yet you demand a reason of Him who created the universe, and breathed into you the breath of life ! "

"Are we not reasoning creatures, Ghita ? " returned Raoul, gently, and yet with a sincerity and truth, for the circumstances, that rendered even his skepticism piquant and respectable ; "and is it unreasonable to expect us to act up to our natures ? Can I worship a God I do not understand ? "

"Couldst thou worship one thou didst ? He would cease to be a deity, and would become one of ourselves, were his nature and attributes brought down to the level of our comprehensions. Did one of thy followers come on this quarter-deck, and insist on hearing all thine own motives for the orders given in this little felucca, how readily wouldst thou drive him back as mutinous and insolent ; and yet thou wouldst question the God of the universe, and pry into his mysteries ! "

Raoul was mute, while Ithuel stared. It was so seldom that Ghita lost her exceeding gentleness of manner, that the flush of her cheek, the severe earnestness of her eyes, the impassioned modulations of her voice, and the emphasis with which she spoke on this occasion, produced a sort of awe, that prevented the discourse from proceeding farther.

The girl herself was so much excited that, after sitting for a minute with her hands before her face, the tears were seen forcing their way through her fingers. She then arose, and darted into the cabin. Raoul was too observant of the rules of propriety to think of following ; but he sat moody and lost in thought, until Ithuel drew his attention to himself.

"Gals will be gals," said that refined and philosophical observer of the human family, "and nothing touches their naturs sooner than a little religious excitement. I daresay, if it wasn't for images, and cardinals, and bishops, and such creatur's, the Italians (Ithuel always pronounced this *Eye*talians) would make a very good sort of Christians."

But Raoul was in no humor to converse ; and as the hour now arrived when the zephyr was to be expected, he rose, ordered the awning to be taken in, and prepared to make himself master of the state of things around him. There lay the frigate, taking her siesta, like all near ; her three topsails standing, but every other sail that was loose, hanging in festoons, waiting for the breeze. Notwithstanding her careless appearance, so closely had she been tended, for the last few hours, however, and so sedulously had even the smallest breath of air been improved, that Raoul started with surprise, when he found how much nearer she was than when he had last looked at her. The whole trick was apparent to him at a glance ; and he was compelled to acknowledge his own remissness, when he perceived that he lay within the reach of the shot of his powerful foe ; though still so distant as to render her aim a little uncertain, more especially should a sea get up. The felucca had burnt to the water's edge ; but, owing to the smoothness of the water, her wreck still floated, and was slowly setting into the bay, there being a slight current in that direction, where she now lay. The town was basking in the afternoon's sun, though hid from view, and the whole island of Elba had the appearance of being asleep.

"What a siesta ! " said Raoul to Ithuel, as both stood on the heel of the bowsprit, looking curiously at the scene ; "sea, land, mountains, bourgeois and mariners all dozing. Bien ; there is life yonder at the west, and we must get further from votre *Proserpine*. Call the hands, Monsieur Lieutenant. Let us get our sweeps, and put the head of *Le Feu-Follet* the other way. Peste ! the lugger is so sharp, and has such a trick of going exactly where she looks, that I am afraid she has been crawling up toward her enemy, as the child creeps into the fire that burns its fingers."

All hands were soon in motion on board *Le Feu-Follet*, the sweeps were on the point of being handled, when the jigger fluttered, and the first puff of the expected western breeze swept along the surface of the waters. To the seamen, it was like inhaling oxygen gas. Every appearance of drowsiness deserted the people of both vessels, and every one was instantly busy in making sail. Raoul had a proof into what dangerous proximity to the frigate he had got, by the sound of the calls on board her ; and the stillness of the sea was yet so great, that the creaking of her foreyard was actually audible to him, as the English rounded in their braces briskly, while laying their fore-topsail aback.

At that moment a second respiration of the atmosphere gave birth to the breeze, Raoul whistled for the wind, and the lugger moved ahead, gliding toward the frigate. But, in half a minute, she had gathered sufficient way, her helm was put down, and she came round as easily and as gracefully as the bird turns on his wing. Not so with the heavier frigate. She had hauled in her starboard head-braces, and had to get the fore-topsail aback, and to pay well off with her head leeward, in order to swing her yards and fill her sails, while *Le Feu-Follet* was slipping through the water, going seemingly into the wind's eye. By this single evolution the lugger gained more than a cable's length on her enemy, and five minutes more would have put her beyond all immediate danger. But Captain Cuffe knew this as well as his competitor, and had made his preparations accordingly. Keeping head-yards aback, he knocked his ship round off, until her broadside bore on the lugger, when he let fly every gun of his starboard batteries, the utmost care having been taken to make the shot tell. Twenty-two heavy round-shot coming in at once upon a little craft like *Le Feu-Follet* was a fearful visitation ; and, the "boldest held their breath for a time," as the iron whirlwind whistled past them. Fortunately, the lugger was not hulled ; but a grave amount of mischief was done aloft.

The jigger-mast was cut in two, and flew upward like a pipe-stem. A serious wound was given to the mainmast below the hounds, and the yard itself was shivered in the slings. No less than six shot plunged through both lugs, leaving holes in the canvas that made it resemble a beggar's shirt, and the jib-stay was cut in two, half-way between the mast-head and the end of the bowsprit. No one was hurt ; and yet, for a moment, every one looked as if destruction had suddenly lighted on the lugger. Then it was that Raoul came out in his true colors. He knew he could not spare a stitch of canvas just at that moment, but that on the next ten minutes depended everything. Nothing was taken in, therefore, to secure spars and sails, but all was left to stand, trusting to the lightness of the breeze, which usually commenced very moderately. Hands were immediately set to work to get up a new stay ; a new main-yard and sail were got along, and everything was prepared for hoisting both, as soon as it could be ascertained that the mast would bear them. Nearly similar preparations were made forward, as the shortest way of getting rid of the torn foresail ; for that, it was the intention to unbend and bend, the yard being sound.

Luckily, Captain Cuffe determined to lose no more time with his guns, but swinging his head-yards, the frigate came sweeping up to the wind, and in three minutes everything was trimmed for the utmost. All this time *Le Feu-Follet* had not stood still. Her canvas fluttered, but it held on, and even the spars kept their places, though so much injured. In a word, the wind was not yet strong enough to tear the one, or to carry away the other. It was an advantage, too, that these casualties, particularly the loss of her jigger, rendered *Le Feu-Follet* less weatherly than she would otherwise have been, since by keeping the frigate directly in her wake, she was less exposed to the chase-guns than she would have been a little on either bow. Of this truth Raoul was soon persuaded, the *Proserpine* beginning to work both her bow-guns, as soon as she came to the wind, though neither exactly bore ; the shot of one ranging a little to windward, and the other about as much on the other side. By these shot, too, the young Frenchman soon had the satisfaction of seeing that, notwithstanding her injuries, the lugger was drawing ahead, a fact of which the English became so sensible themselves, that they soon ceased firing.

So far things went better than Raoul had reason, at first, to hope, though he well knew that the crisis was yet to come. The westerly wind often blew fresh at that period of the day, and should it now increase he would require all his canvas to get clear of a ship with the known qualities of the vessel in chase. How much longer his mast or his main-yard would stand he did not know, but as he was fast gaining, he determined to make hay while the sun shone, and get far enough ahead, if possible, before the breeze grew fresh, to enable him to shift his sails and fish his spars, without being again brought within the reach of visitors as rude as those who had so lately come hurtling into his thin hamper. The proper precautions were not neglected in the meantime. Men were sent aloft to do what they could, under the circumstances, with the two spars ; and the strain was a little relieved by keeping the lugger as much away, as might be done without enabling the frigate to set her studding-sails.

There is always something so exciting in a chase that seamen never fail to wish for more wind ; forgetful that the power which increases their own speed, may also increase the speed of the other party, and that too in an undue proportion. It would have been more favorable to *Le Feu-Follet* to have had less wind than even now blew, since her relative rate of sailing was greater in light than in strong breezes. Raoul knew, from Ithuel's statements, that the *Proserpine* was an exceedingly fast ship, more especially when it blew fresh ; and yet it did not appear to him that his lugger got along with sufficient speed, though his enemy would be certain to follow at a rate of sailing in a just proportion to his own, did there come more wind.

The wish of the young privateersman, however, was soon gratified. The wind freshened materially, and by the time the two vessels opened the canal of Corsica, as the passage between that island and Elba is called, the frigate was obliged to take in her royals, and two or three of those light and lofty staysails, which it was then the custom for ships to carry. At first, Raoul had thought he might fetch into Bastia, which lies due-west of the southern end of Elba; but though the wind drew a little down through the canal, it soon blew too fresh to allow any formation of the land materially to alter its current. The zephyr, as the afternoon's summer breeze of southern Italy, in particular, was termed by the ancients, is seldom a due-west wind, there generally being a little northing in it, as seamen say; and, as one gets further up the coast, this same wind ordinarily comes round the head of Corsica, blowing from nearly west-north-west. This would have enabled the lugger to lay her course for a deep bay on which lies the town of Biguglia, could she have been jammed up on a wind, as might usually have been done; but a few minutes of experiment convinced Raoul that he must be more tender on his wounded spars, and keep off for the mouth of the Golo. This was a river of some size into which it was possible for a vessel of a light draught to enter; and, as there stood a small battery near the anchorage, he determined to seek shelter in that haven, in order to repair his damages. His calculations were made accordingly, and, taking the snow-clad peaks in the neighborhood of Corte as his landmarks, he ordered the lugger to be steered in the proper direction.

On board the *Proserpine*, there was scarcely less interest felt in the result than on board *Le Feu-Follet*. If the people of the frigate had nothing to apprehend, they had something to revenge; in addition to the anticipated credit of having captured the boldest privateer that sailed out of France. For a short time, as the ship came up with the west end of Elba, it was a serious question whether she would be able to weather it, the lugger having gone past, within a cable's length of the cliffs, on the very verge of the breakers, and much closer in than the frigate would dare to follow. But the last had taken the breeze further off the land than the first, and might possibly fetch past the promontory on the tack

she was then steering. To have gone about, would have been to have abandoned the chase, as it would have carried the ship off due north, while *Le Feu-Follet* was gliding down to the southward and westward at the rate of seven knots. The distance across the canal is only about thirty miles, and there would not have been time to recover the lost ground.

This uncertainty made a most feverish moment on board the *Proserpine*, as she came up fast toward the headland. All depended on getting by without tacking. The appearances were favorable for deep water, close in; but there is always the danger of rocks to be dreaded, near mountainous coasts. The promontory, too, was comparatively low; and this was rather an indication that it ought not to be approached too closely. Winchester was in his berth, just beginning to feel the smart of his wound; but Griffin was at the captain's elbow, both he and the third lieutenant entering keenly into all their commander's wishes and anxieties.

"There she goes, into the very breakers!" exclaimed Cuffe, as they watched *Le Feu-Follet* in her attempt to pass the promontory; "Monsieur Yvard must be determined to cast away his craft rather than be taken. It will be touch and go with him."

"I think not, Captain Cuffe," answered Griffin; "the coast is bold hereabouts, and even the *Proserpine* would find sufficient water there, where the lugger now is. I hope we shall not be obliged to tack, sir."

"Ay, this is very well for an irresponsible; but, when it got to a court, and punishment, I fear that all the last would fall on my shoulders, should his majesty's ship happen to lay her bones along-shore here. No, no, Griffin; we must go clear a cable's length to windward of that, or I go about, though Raoul Yvard were never taken."

"There, he fetches up, by George!" cried Yelverton, the youngest lieutenant; and, for a moment, it was in truth believed in the frigate that *Le Feu-Follet*, as a breaker actually curled directly under her lee, was aground. But this notion lasted a moment only, the little lugger continuing her course as swiftly as before; and, a minute or two later, keeping a little away, to ease her spars, having been jammed up as close as possible previously, in order to weather the extreme end of what was thought to be the dangerous point. The frigate was fully two miles astern; and, instead of losing anything of her vantage-ground, she was kept so near the wind as to be occasionally touching. This was the more safe, inasmuch as the sea was perfectly smooth, and the vessel made no leeway. Still the frigate looked, as it is termed, barely up to the point it was deemed indispensable to weather; and as ships rarely "do" better than they "look," it became a question of serious doubt on board the *Proserpine*, as she came up with the headland, whether she could clear it.

"I am afraid, Captain Cuffe, we shall never clear it with a good enough berth, sir," observed the fidgeting Griffin; "it seems to me the ship sets unaccountably to leeward to-day."

"She never behaved better, Griffin. I am really in hopes there is a slight current off-shore here; if anything, we actually open the highlands of Corsica by this promontory. You see that the wreck of *La Divina Providenza* is sweeping round the bay, and coming out to windward again."

"That may serve us, indeed! All ready in the chains, sir! Shall we make a cast of the lead?"

Cuffe assented, and the lead was hove. At this moment the ship was going eight knots, and the man reported no bottom, with fifteen fathoms of line out. This was well; and two or three subsequent casts confirmed it. Orders were now given to drag every bowline, swing-off on every brace, and flatten-in all the sheets. Even the halyards were touched, in order that the sails might stand like boards. The trying moment was near; five minutes must decide the matter.

"Let her shake a little, Mr. Yelverton, and eat into the wind," said Cuffe, addressing the officer of the watch; "we must do all we can here; for, when abreast of the breakers, everything must be a rap-full, to keep the ship under quick command. There—meet her with the helm, and give her a good full."

This experiment was repeated twice, and each time the frigate gained her length to windward, though she necessarily lost more than three times the distance in her velocity. At length the trial came, and a profound silence, one in which nervousness and anxiety were blended with hope, reigned in the vessel. The eyes of all turned from the sails to the breakers; from the breakers to the sails; and from both to the wake of the ship.

At such moments the voice of the lead's-man prevails over all other sounds. His warning cry is listened to with breathless attention when the songs of a siren would be unheard. Cast after cast was made, as the ship drove on, and the answer to Cuffe's questions invariably was, "no

bottom, sir, with fifteen fathoms out;" but just at this moment arose the regular song from the weather main-chains of "by the mark seven!" This came so suddenly on the captain's ear, that he sprang upon the taffrail, where he could command a good view of all he wanted to see; and then he called out, in a stentorian voice:

"Heave again, sir? be brisk, my lad! be brisk!"

"Be-e-e-ther-r-r-dee-e-e-eep six!" followed almost as soon as the captain's voice had ceased.

"Ready about!" shouted Cuffe. "See all clear, gentlemen. Move lively, men; move lively!"

"And-a-a-eh half-ef-four!"

"Stand by! What the devil are you at, sir, on that forecastle? Are you ready, forward?"

"All ready, sir!"

"Down with your helm—hard down at once?"

"Be-e-e-ther-r-r-dee-e-e-p nine!"

"Meet her! up with your helm. Haul down your sheets, forward — brail the spanker—let go all the bowlines aft. So —well, there, well. She flew round like a top, but, by Jove, we've caught her, gentlemen. Drag your bowlines again. What's the news from the chains?"

"No bottom, sir, with fifteen fathoms out; and as good a cast, too, sir, as we've had to-day."

"So—you're rap-full—don't fall off— very well dyce" (*Anglice*, thus); "keep her as you are. Well, by the Lord, Griffin, that *was* a shave; half-four was getting to be squally, in a quarter of the world where a rock makes nothing of pouting its lips fifteen or twenty times at a mariner. We are past it all, however, and here is the land, tending away to the southward, like a man in a consumption, fairly under our lee. A dozen Raoul Yvards wouldn't lead me into such a d—d scrape again."

"The danger that is over, is no danger at all," sir," answered Griffin, laughing. "Don't you think, Captain Cuffe, that we might ease her about half a point? that would be just her play; and the lugger keeps off just a little, I rather suspect to ease her mainmast. I'm certain I saw chips fly from it when we dosed her with those two-and-twenty pills."

"Perhaps you're right, Griffin. Ease her with the helm a little, Mr. Yelverton. If Master Yvard stands on his present course an hour longer, Biguglia would be too far to windward for him; and as for Bastia, that has been out of the question from the first. There is a river called

Golo, into which he might run; and that, I rather think, is his aim. Four hours, however, will let us into his secret.''

And four intensely interesting hours were those which succeeded. The wind was a cap-full; a good, fresh, westerly breeze, which seemed to have started out of the ovenlike heat of a week of intensely hot weather that had preceded it, and to have collected the force of two or three zephyrs into one. It was not a gale at all, nor did it induce either party to think of reefing, no trifle would have done that, under the circumstances; but it caused the *Proserpine* to furl her fore and mizzen top-gallant sails, and put Raoul in better humor with the loss of his jigger. When fairly round the headland, and at a moment when he fancied the frigate would be compelled to tack, the latter had seized an opportunity to get in his foresail, to unbend it, and to bend and set a new one; an operation that took just four minutes by the watch. He would have tried the same experiment with the other lug, but the mast was scarce worth the risk, and he thought the holes might act as reefs, and thus diminish the strain. In these four hours, owing to the disadvantage under which *Le Feu-Follet* labored, there was not a difference of half a knot in the distance run by the two vessels, though each passed over more than thirty miles of water.

During this time they had been drawing rapidly nearer to the coast of Corsica, the mountains of which, ragged and crowned with nearly eternal snows, had been glittering in the afternoon's sun before them, though they lay many a long league inland. But the formation of the coast itself had now become plain, and Raoul, an hour before the sun disappeared, noted his landmarks, by which to make for the river he intended to enter. The eastern coast of Corsica is as deficient in bays and harbors as its western is affluent with them; and this Golo, for which the lugger was shaping her course, would never have been thought of as a place of shelter under ordinary circumstances. But Raoul had once anchored in its mouth, and he deemed it the very spot in which to elude his enemy. It had shoals off its embouchure; and these, he rightly enough fancied, would induce Captain Cuffe to be wary.

As the evening approached, the wind began to decrease in force, and then the people of the lugger lost all their apprehensions. The spars had all stood, and Raoul no longer hesitated about trusting his wounded mainmast with a new yard and sail. Both were got up, and the repairs were immediately commenced. The superiority of the lugger, in sailing, was now so great as to put it out of all question that she was not to be overtaken in the chase; and Raoul at one time actually thought of turning up along the land, and going into Bastia, where he might even provide himself with a new mainmast at need. But this idea, on reflection, he abandoned as too hazardous; and he continued on in the direction of the mouth of the Golo.

Throughout the day the *Proserpine* had shown no colors, except for the short period when her boats were engaged, and while she herself was firing at the lugger. The same was the fact with *Le Feu-Follet*, though Raoul had run up the tricolor as he opened on the felucca, and he kept it flying as long as there was any appearance of hostilities. As the two vessels drew in near to the land, several coasters were seen beating up against the westerly wind, or running down before it, all of which, however, seemed so much to distrust the appearance of the lugger as to avoid her as far as was possible. This was a matter of indifference to our hero, who knew that they were all probably countrymen; or, at least, smugglers, who would scarcely reward him for the trouble, had he time to bring them to and capture them. Corsica was then again in the hands of the French, the temporary and imperfect possession of the English having terminated three or four years earlier; and Raoul felt certain of a welcome anywhere in the island, and of protection wherever it could be offered. Such was the state of things when, just as the lugger was preparing to enter among the shoals, the *Proserpine* unexpectedly tacked, and seemed to bestow all her attention on the coasters, of which three or four were so near that two fell into her hands almost without an effort to escape.

It appeared to Raoul, and those with him in his little craft, that the English seized these insignificant vessels solely with a wish for vengeance, since it was not usual for ships of the force of the *Proserpine* to turn aside to molest the poor fishermen and coasters. A few execrations followed, quite as a matter of course, but the intricacy of the channel, and the necessity of having all his eyes about him, soon drove every other thought from the mind of the dashing privateersman but such as were connected with the care and safety of his own vessel.

Just as the sun set *Le Feu-Follet* anchored. She had chosen a berth sufficiently within the shallow water to be safe from the guns of the frigate, though scarcely within the river. The latter the depth of the stream scarcely permitted, though there was all the shelter that the season and weather required. The *Proserpine* manifested no intention to give up her pursuit; for she, too, came off the outlet, and brought up with one of her bowers about two miles to seaward of the lugger. She seemed to have changed her mind as to the coasters, having let both proceed after a short detention; though, it falling calm, neither was enabled to get any material distance from her until the land-breeze should rise. In these positions the belligerents prepared to pass the night, each party taking the customary precautions as to his ground tackle, and each clearing up the decks and going through the common routine of duty as regularly as if he lay in a friendly port.

CHAPTER XI.

It is unnecessary to dwell on the glories of the Mediterranean. They are familiar to every traveler, and books have, again and again, laid them before the imaginations of readers of all countries and ages. Still, there are lights and shades peculiar to every picture, and this of ours has some of its own that merit a passing notice. A sunset in midsummer can add to the graces of almost any scene. Such was the hour when Raoul anchored; and Ghita, who had come on deck, now that the chase was over, and the danger was thought to be passed, fancied she had never seen her own Italy, or the blue Mediterranean, more lovely.

The shadows of the mountains were cast far upon the sea, long ere the sun had actually gone down, throwing the witchery of eventide over the whole of the eastern coast, some time before it came to grace its western. Corsica and Sardinia resemble vast fragments of the Alps, which have fallen into the sea by some accident of nature, where they stand in sight of their native beds, resembling, as it might be, outposts of those great walls of Europe. Their mountains have the same formations, the same white peaks, for no small portion of the year at least, and their sides the same mysterious and riven aspect. In addition, however, to their own charms, they have one that is wanting in most of Switzerland, though traces of it are to be found in Savoy and on the southern side of the Alps; they have that strange admixture of the soft and the severe, of the sublime and the beautiful, that so peculiarly characterize the witchery of Italian nature.

Such was now the aspect of all visible from the deck of *Le Feu-Follet.* The sea, with its dark blue tint, was losing every trace of the western wind, and was becoming glassy and tranquil; the mountains on the other side were solemn and grand, just showing their ragged outlines along a sky glowing with "the pomp that shuts the day;" while the nearer valleys and narrow plains were mysterious, yet soft, under the deep shadows they cast. Pianosa lay nearly opposite, distant some twenty miles, rising out of the water, like a beacon; Elba was visible to the northeast, a gloomy, confused pile of mountains at that hour; and Ghita once or twice thought she could trace on the coast of the main, the dim outline of her own hill, Monte Argentaro; though the distance, some sixty or seventy miles, rendered this improbable. Outside, too, lay the frigate, riding on the glassy surface of the sea, her sails furled, her yards squared, everything about her cared for and in its place, until she formed a faultless picture of nautical symmetry and naval propriety. There are all sorts of men in a marine, as well as in civil life; these taking things as they come, content to perform their duties in the most quiet manner, while others again have some such liking for their vessels as the dandy has for his own person, and are never happy unless embellishing them.

The truth in this, as in most other matters, lies in a medium; the officer who thinks too much of the appearance of his vessel, seldom having mind enough to bestow due attention on the great objects for which she was constructed, and is sailed; while, on the other hand, he who is altogether indifferent to these appearances is usually thinking of things foreign to his duty and his profession; if, indeed, he thinks at all. Cuffe was near the just medium, inclining a little too much, perhaps, to the naval dandy. The *Proserpine*, thanks to the builders of Toulon, was thought to be the handsomest model then afloat in the Mediterranean, and, like an established beauty, all who belonged to her were fond of decorating her, and of showing her fine proportions to advantage. As she now lay at single anchor, just out of gunshot from his own berth, Raoul could not avoid gazing at her with envy, and a bitter feeling passed through his mind, when he recalled the chances of fortune and birth, which deprived him of the hope of ever rising to the command of such a frigate, but which doomed him, seemingly, to the fate of a privateersman for life.

Nature had intended Raoul Yvard for a much higher destiny than that which apparently awaited his career. He had come into active life with none of the advantages that accompany the accidents of birth, and at a moment in the history of his great nation, when its morals and its religious sentiments had become unsettled by the violent reaction which was throwing off the abuses of centuries. They who imagine, however, that France, as a whole, was guilty of the gross excesses that disfigured her struggles for liberty, know little of the great mass of moral feeling that endured through the abominations of the times; and mistake the crimes of a few desperate leaders, and the exaggerations of misguided impulses, for a radical and universal depravity. The France of the Reign of Terror, even, has little more to answer for than the compliance which makes bodies of men the instruments of the enthusiastic, the designing, and the active; our own country often tolerating error, that differs only in the degree, under the same blind submission to combinations and impulses; this very degree, too, depending more on the accidents of history and natural causes, than any agencies, which are to be imputed to the one party, as a fault, or to the other, as a merit.

It was with Raoul, as it had been with his country; each was the creature of circumstances; and if the man had some of the faults, he had also most of the merits of his nation and his age. The looseness on the subject of religion, which was his principal defect in the eyes of Ghita, but which could scarcely fail to be a material one, with a girl educated and disposed as was the case with our heroine, was the error of the day, and with Raoul it was at least sincere; a circumstance that rendered him, with one so truly pious as the gentle being he loved, the subject of a holy interest, which, in itself, almost rivaled the natural tenderness of her sex, in behalf of the object of her affections.

While the short engagement with the boats lasted, and during the few minutes he was under the fire of the frigate, Raoul had been himself; the excitement of actual war always nerving him to deeds worthy of his command, and the high name he had acquired; but, throughout the remainder of the day, he had felt little disposed to strife. The chase, once assured that his spars were likely to stand, gave him little concern; and now that he was at anchor within the shallow water he felt much as the traveler who has found a comfortable inn, after the fatigue of a hard day's ride. When Ithuel suggested the possibility of a night attack in boats, he laughingly reminded the American that "the burnt child dreads the fire," and gave himself no great concern in the matter. Still no proper precaution was neglected. Raoul was in the habit of exacting much of his men, in moments of necessity; but, at all other times, he was as indulgent as a kind father among obedient and respectful children. This quality, and the never-varying constancy and coolness that he displayed in danger, was the secret of his great influence with them; every seaman under his orders feeling that no severe duty was required at his hands, without a corresponding necessity for it.

On the present occasion, when the people of *Le Feu-Follet* had supped, they were indulged in their customary dance; and the romantic songs of Provence were heard on the forecastle. A light-hearted gayety prevailed, that wanted only the presence of women, to make the scene resemble the evening amusement of some hamlet on the coast. Nor was the sex absent in the sentiment of the hour, or wholly in person. The songs were full of chivalrous gallantry, and Ghita listened, equally touched and amused. She sat on the taffrail, with her uncle standing at her side, while Raoul paced the quarter-deck, stopping, in his turn, to utter some thought or wish, to ears that were always attentive. At length the song and dance were ended, and all but the few who were ordered to remain on watch, descended to their hammocks. The change was as sudden as it was striking. The solemn, breathing stillness of a star-lit night succeeded to the light laugh, melodious song, and spirited merriment of a set of men, whose constitutional gayety seemed to be restrained by a species of native refinement that is unknown to the mariners of other regions, and who, unnurtured as they might be deemed in some respects, seldom or never offended against the proprieties, as is so common with the mariners of the boasted Anglo-Saxon race.

By this time the cool air from the mountains began to descend, and floating over the heated sea, it formed a light land-breeze that blew in an exactly contrary direction to that which, about the same hour, came off from the adjacent continent. There was no moon, but the night could not be called dark. Myriads of stars gleamed out from the fathomless firmament, filling the atmosphere with a light that served to render objects sufficiently distinct; while it left them clad in a semi-obscurity that suited the witchery of the scene and the hour. Raoul felt the influence all of these circumstances in an unusual degree. It disposed him to more sobriety of thought than always attended his leisure moments, and he took a seat on the taffrail, near Ghita, while her uncle went below, to his knees and his prayers.

Every footfall in the lugger had now ceased. Ithuel was posted on a knight-head, where he sat watching his old enemy, the *Proserpine;* the proximity of that ship not allowing him to sleep. Two experienced seamen, who alone formed the regular anchor-watch, as it is termed, were stationed apart, in order to prevent conversation; one on the starboard cat-head, and the other in the main rigging; both keeping vigilant ward over the tranquil sea, and the different objects that floated on its placid bosom. In that retired spot, these objects were necessarily few, embracing the frigate, the lugger, and three coasters; the latter of which had all been boarded before the night set in, by the *Proserpine,* and, after short detentions, dismissed. One of these coasters lay about half-way between the two hostile vessels, at anchor, having come-to, after making some fruitless efforts to get to the northward, by means of the expiring west wind. Although the light land-breeze would now have sufficed to carry her a knot or two through the water, she preferred maintaining her position, and giving her people a good night's rest, to getting under way. The situation of this felucca, and the circumstance that she had been boarded by the frigate, rendered her an object of some distrust with Raoul, through the early part of the evening, and he had ordered a vigilant eye to be kept on her; but nothing had been discovered to confirm these suspicions. The movements of her people, the manner in which she brought up, the quiet that prevailed on board her, and even the lubberly disposition of her spars and rigging, went to satisfy Raoul that she had no man-of-war's men on board her.

Still, as she lay less than a mile outside of the lugger, though now dead to leeward all that distance, she was to be watched; and one of the seamen, he in the rigging, rarely had his eyes off her a minute at a time. The second coaster was a little to the southward of the frigate, under her canvas, hauling in for the land; doubtless with a view to get as much as possible of the breeze from the mountains; and standing slowly to the south. She had been set by compass, an hour before, and all that time had altered her bearings but half a point, though not a league off; a proof how light she had the wind. The third coaster, a small felucca, too, was to the northward; but, ever since the land-breeze, if breeze it could be called, had come, she had been busy turning slowly up to windward; and seemed disposed either to cross the shoals closer in than the spot where the lugger lay, or to enter the Golo. Her shadowy outline was visible, though drawn against the land, moving slowly athwart the lugger's hawse, perhaps half-a-mile in-shore of her. As there was a current setting out of the river, and all the vessels rode with their heads to the island, Ithuel occasionally turned his head to watch her progress; which was so slow, however, as to produce very little change.

After looking around him several minutes in silence, Raoul turned his face upward and gazed at the stars.

"You probably do not know, Ghita," he said, "the use those stars may be, and are, to us mariners. By their aid, we are enabled to tell where we are, in the midst of the broadest oceans—to know the points of the compass, and to feel at home even when furthest removed from it. The seaman must go far south of the equator, at least, ere he can reach a spot where he does not see the same stars that he beheld from the door of his father's house."

"That is a new thought to me," answered Ghita, quickly, her tender nature at once struck with the feeling and poetry of such an idea; "that is a new thought to me, Raoul; and I wonder you never mentioned it before. It is a great thing to be able to carry home any familiar objects with you, when so distant from those you love."

"Did you never hear that lovers have chosen an hour and a star, by gazing at which they might commune together, though separated by oceans and countries?"

"That is a question you might put to yourself, Raoul; all I have ever heard of lovers and love having come from your own lips."

"Well, then, I tell it you; and hope that we shall not part again, without selecting our star and our hour—if, indeed, we ever part more. Though I have forgotten to tell you this, Ghita, it is because you are never absent from my thoughts; no stars is necessary to recall Monte Argentaro and the towers."

If we should say Ghita was not pleased with this, it would be to raise her above an amiable and natural weakness. Raoul's protestations never fell dead on her heart; and few things were sweeter, to her ear, than his words, as they declared his devotedness and passion. The frankness with which he admitted his delinquencies, and most especially the want of that very religious sentiment which was of so much value in the eyes of his mistress, gave an additional weight to his language, when he affirmed his love. Notwithstanding Ghita blushed, as she now listened, she did not smile ; she rather appeared sad. For near a minute she made no reply ; and when she did answer, it was in a low voice, like one who felt and thought intensely.

"Those stars may well have a higher office," she said. "Look at them, Raoul ; count them we cannot, for they seem to start out of the very depths of heaven, one after another, as the eye rests upon the space, until they mock our efforts at calculation. We see they are there in thousands, and may well believe they are in myriads. Now, thou hast been taught, else couldst thou never be a navigator, that those stars are worlds, like our own, or suns, with worlds sailing around them ; how is it possible to see and know this, without believing in a God, and feeling the insignificance of our being ? "

"I do not deny that there is a power to govern all this, Ghita, but I maintain that it is a principle ; not a being, in our shape and form ; and that it is the reason of things, rather than a deity."

"Who has said that God is a being in our shape and form, Raoul ? None know that, none can know it ; none say it, who reverence and worship him as they ought ! "

"Do not your priests say that man has been created in his image ? and is not this creating him in his form and likeness ? "

"Nay, not so, dear Raoul, but in the image of his spirit ; that man has a soul which partakes, though in a small degree, of the imperishable essence of God ; and thus far doth he exist in his image. More than this none have presumed to say. But what a being, to be the master of all those bright worlds ! "

"Ghita, thou know'st my way of thinking on these matters ; and thou also know'st that I would not wound thy gentle spirit by a single word that could grieve thee."

"Nay, Raoul, it is not thy way of thinking, but thy fashion of talking, that makes the difference between us. No one who thinks, can ever doubt the existence of a being superior to all of earth, and of the universe ; and who is Creator and Master of all."

"Of a principle, thou wilt, Ghita ; but of a being, I ask for proof. That a mighty principle exists, to set all these planets in motion, to create all these stars, and to plant all these suns in space, I never doubted ; it would be to question a fact which stands, day and night, before my eyes ; but to suppose a being capable of producing all these things, is to believe in beings I never saw."

"And why not as well suppose it is a being who does all this, Raoul, as suppose it what you call a principle ? "

"Because I see principles, beyond my understanding, at work all around me ; in yonder heavy frigate, groaning under her load of artillery, which floats on this thin water ; in the trees of the land that lies so near us ; in the animals, which are born, and die ; the fishes, the birds, and the human beings. But I see no being, know no being, that is able to do all this."

"That is because thou know'st not God ! He is the creator of the principles of which thou speak'st, and is greater than thy principles themselves."

"It is easy to say this, Ghita, but hard to prove. I take the acorn, and put it in the ground ; in due time it comes up a plant ; in the course of years, it becomes a tree. Now all this depends on a certain mysterious principle, which is unknown to me, but which I am sure exists, for I can cause it myself to produce its fruits, by merely opening the earth and laying the seed in its bosom. Nay, I can do more ; so well do I understand this principle, to a certain extent, that by choosing the season and the soil, I can hasten or retard the growth of the plant, and, in a manner, fashion the tree."

"True, Raoul, to a certain extent thou canst ; and it is precisely because thou hast been created after the image of God. The little resemblance thou enjoyest to that mighty being enables thee to do this much more than the beasts of the field ; wert thou his equal, thou couldst create this principle of which thou speakest, and which, in thy blindness, thou mistakest for his master."

This was said with more feeling than Ghita had ever before manifested in their frequent discourses on this subject, and with a solemnity of tone that startled her listener. Ghita had no philosophy, in the common acceptation of the term, while Raoul fancied he had much, under the limitations of a deficient education ; and yet the strong religious sentiment of the girl so quickened her faculties, that he had often been made to wonder why she had seemingly the best of the argument, on a subject in which he flattered himself with being so strong.

"I rather think, Ghita, we scarcely understand each other," answered Raoul. "I pretend not to see any more than is permitted to man; or, rather, more than his powers can comprehend; but this proves nothing, as the elephant understands more than the horse, and the horse more than the fish. There is a principle which pervades everything, which we call Nature; and this it is which has produced these whirling worlds, and all the mysteries of creation. One of its own laws is, that nothing it produces shall comprehend its secrets."

"You have only to fancy your principle a spirit, a being with mind, Raoul, to have the Christian's God. Why not believe in Him as easily as you believe in your unknown principle, as you call it? You know that you exist—that you can build a lugger—can reason on the sun and stars, so as to find your way across the widest ocean, by means of your mind; and why not suppose that some superior being exists, who can do even more than this? Your principles can be thwarted, even by yourself; the seed can be deprived of its power to grow—the tree destroyed; and, if principles can thus be destroyed, some accident may one day destroy creation, by destroying its principle. I fear to speak to you of revelation, Raoul, for I know you mock it!"

"Not when it comes from thy lips, dearest. I may not believe, but I never mock at what thou utterest and reverencest."

"I could thank you for this, Raoul, but I feel it would be taking to myself a homage that ought to be paid elsewhere. But, here is my guitar, and I am sorry to say that the hymn to the Virgin has not been sung on board this lugger to-night; thou canst not think how sweet is a hymn sung upon the waters. I heard the crew that is anchored toward the frigate singing that hymn, while thy men were at their light Provencal songs in praise of woman's beauty, instead of joining in praise of their Creator."

"Thou mean'st to sing thy hymn, Ghita, else the guitar would not have been mentioned?"

"Raoul, I do. I have ever found thy soul softest, after holy music. Who knows, but the mercy of God may some day touch it, through the notes of this very hymn!"

Ghita paused for a moment, and then her light fingers passed over the strings of her guitar, in a solemn symphony; after which came the sweet strains of "Ave Maria," in a voice and melody that might, in sooth, have touched a heart of stone. Ghita, a Neapolitan by birth, had all her country's love for music; and she had caught some of the science that seems to pervade nations in that part of the world. Nature had endowed her with one of the most touching voices of her sex; one less powerful than mellow and sweet; and she never used it in a religious office without its becoming tremulous and eloquent with feeling. While she was singing this well-known hymn, a holy hope pervaded her moral system, that, in some miraculous manner, she might become the agent of turning Raoul to the love and worship of God; and the feeling communicated itself to her execution. Never before had she sung so well; as a proof of which Ithuel left his knighthead, and came aft, to listen, while the two French mariners on watch temporarily forgot their duty in entranced attention.

"If anything could make me a believer, Ghita," murmured Raoul, when the last strain had died on the lips of his beloved, "it would be to listen to thy melody! What now, Monsieur Etooell! are you, too, a lover of holy music?"

"This is rare singing, Captain Rule; but we have different business on hand. If you will step to the other end of the lugger, you can take a look at the craft that has been crawling along, in-shore of us, for the last three hours; there is something about her that is unnat'ral; she seems to be dropping down nearer to us, while she has no motion through the water. The last circumstance I hold to be unnat'ral with a vessel that has all sail set, and in this breeze."

Raoul pressed the hand of Ghita, and whispered her to go below, as he was fearful the air of the night might injure her. He then went forward, where he could command as good a view of the felucca inshore as the obscurity of the hour permitted; and he felt a little uneasiness when he found how near she had got to the lugger. When he last noted her position, this boat was quite half-a-mile distant, and seemed to be crossing the bows of Le Feu-Follet, with sufficient wind to have carried her a mile ahead in the interval; yet could he not perceive that she had advanced as far, in that direction, as she had drifted down upon the lugger the while.

"Have you been examining her long?" he demanded of the New Hampshire man.

"Ever since she has seemed to stand still; which is now some twenty minutes. She is dull, I suppose, for she has been several hours getting along a league; and there is air enough for such a craft to go three knots to the hour. Her coming down upon us is easily accounted for, there being a considerable current out of this river, as you may see by the ripple at our own cut-water; but I find nothing to keep her from going ahead at the same time. I set her by the light you see, here, in the wake of the nearest mountain, at least a quarter of an hour since, and she has not advanced five times her own length since."

"'Tis nothing but a Corsican coaster, Etooell; I hardly think the English would risk our canister again, for the pleasure of being beaten off in another attempt to board!"

"They're a spiteful set, aboard the frigate; and the Lord only knows! See, here is a good heavy night air, and that felucca is not a cable's length from us; set her by the jib stay, and judge for yourself how slowly she goes ahead! _That_ it is, which non-plushes _me!_"

Raoul did as the other desired, and, after a short trial, he found that the coaster had no perceptible motion ahead, while it was certain she was drifting down with the current directly athwart the lugger's hawse. This satisfied him that she must have drags astern; a circumstance that at once denoted a hostile intention. The enemy was probably on board the felucca, in force; and it was incumbent on him to make immediate preparations for defense.

Still, Raoul was reluctant to disturb his people. Like all firm and cool men, he was averse to the parade of a false alarm; and it seemed so improbable that the lesson of the morning was so soon forgotten, that he could hardly persuade himself to believe his senses. Then the men had been very hard at work throughout the day; the most of them were sleeping the sleep of the weary. On the other hand, every minute brought the coaster nearer, and increased the danger, should the enemy be really in possession of her. Under all the circumstances, he determined, first, to hail; knowing that his crew could be got up in a minute, and that they slept with arms at their sides, under an apprehension that a boat attack might possibly be attempted in the course of the night.

"Felucca, ahoy!" called out the captain of _Le Feu-Follet_, the other craft being too near to render any great effort of the voice necessary; "what felucca is that? and why have you got so great a drift?"

"_La Bella Corsienne!_" was the answer, in a patois, half French, half Italian, as Raoul expected, if all were right. "We are bound into La Padululla, and wish to keep in with the land to hold the breeze longer. We are no great sailer at the best, and have a drift, because we are just now in the strength of the current."

"At this rate you will come athwart my hawse. You know I am well armed, and cannot suffer that!"

"Ah, signore, we are friends of the republic, and would not harm you if we could. We hope you will not injure poor mariners like us. We will keep away, if you please, and pass under your stern."

This proposition was made so suddenly and so unexpectedly, that Raoul had not time to object; and had he been disposed to do so, the execution was too prompt to allow him the means. The felucca fell broad off, and came down almost in a direct line for the lugger's bows, before the wind and current; moving fast enough now to satisfy all Ithuel's scruples.

"Call all hands to repel boarders!" cried Raoul, springing aft to the capstan, and seizing his own arms; "come up lively, _mes enfans!_ here is treachery!"

These words were hardly uttered before Raoul was back on the heel of the bowsprit, and the most active of his men—some five or six at most—began to show themselves on deck. In that brief space, the felucca had got within eighty yards, when, to the surprise of all in the lugger, she luffed into the wind again, and drifted down, until it was apparent that she was foul of the lugger's cable, her stern swinging round directly on the latter's starboard bow. At that instant, or just as the two vessels came in actual contact, and Raoul's men were thronging around him to meet the expected attack, the sounds of oars, pulled for life or death, were heard, and flames burst upward from the open hatch of the coaster. Then the boat was dimly seen gliding away in a line with the hull, by the glowing light.

"Un brulot!—un brulot!—a fire-ship!" exclaimed twenty voices together, the horror that mingled in the cries proclaiming the extent of a danger which is, perhaps, the most terrific that seamen can encounter.

But the voice of Raoul Yvard was not among them. The moment his eye caught the first glimpse of the flames, he disappeared from the bowsprit. He might have been absent about twenty seconds. Then he was seen on the taffrail of the felucca, with a spare shank-painter, which had been lying on the forecastle, on his shoulder.

"Antoine!—Francois!—Gregoire!" he called out, in a voice of thunder, "follow me! the rest clear away the cable, and bend the hawser to the better end!"

The people of *Le Feu-Follet* were trained to order and implicit obedience. By this time, too, the lieutenants were among them ; and the men set about doing as they had been directed. Raoul himself passed into the felucca, followed by the three men he had selected by name. The adventurers had no difficulty, as yet, in escaping the flames, though, by this time, they were pouring upward from the hatch in a torrent. As Raoul suspected, his cable had been grappled ; and, seizing the rope, he tightened it to a severe strain, securing the inboard part. Then he passed down to the cable himself, directing his companions to hand him the rope-end of the shank-painter, which he fastened to the cable by a jamming hitch. This took half a minute ; in half a minute more he was on the felucca's forecastle again. Here the chain was easily passed through a hawse-hole ; and a knot tied, with a manlinspike passed through its center. To pass the fire, on the return, was now a serious matter ; but it was done without injury, Raoul driving his companions before him. No sooner did his foot reach the bows of *Le Feu-Follet* again, than he shouted—

"Veer away !—pay out cable, men, if you would save our beautiful lugger from destruction ! "

Nor was there a moment to spare. The lugger took the cable that was given her, fast enough, under the pressure of the current and helped by the breeze ; but at first, the fire-vessel, already a sheet of flame, her decks having been saturated with tar, seemed disposed to accompany her. To the delight of all in the lugger, however, the stern of the felucca was presently seen to separate from their own bows ; and a sheer having been given to *Le Feu-Follet*, by means of the helm, in a few seconds even her bowsprit and jib had cleared the danger. The felucca rode stationary, while the lugger dropped astern, fathom after fathom, until she lay more than a hundred yards distant from the fiery mass. As a matter of course, while the cable was paid out, the portion to which the lanyard, or rope part of the shank-painter was fastened, dropped into the water, while the felucca rode by the chain. These events occupied less than five minutes, and all had been done with a steadiness and promptitude that seemed more like instinct than reason. Raoul's voice was not heard except in the few orders mentioned ; and when, by the glaring light which illuminated all in the lugger and the adjacent water to some distance, nearly to the brightness of noon-day, he saw Ghita gazing at the

spectacle in awed admiration and terror, he went to her, and spoke as if the whole were merely a brilliant spectacle, devised for their amusement.

"Our girandola is second only to that of St. Peter," he said, smiling. " 'Twas a narrow escape, love ; but thanks to thy God, if thou wilt it shall be so, we have received no harm."

"And you have been the agent of His goodness, Raoul; I have witnessed all from this spot. The call to the men brought me on deck ; and, O! how I trembled as I saw you on the flaming mass ! "

"It has been cunningly planned, on the part of Messieurs les Anglais ; but it has signally failed. That coaster has a cargo of tar and naval stores on board ; and, capturing her this evening, they have thought to extinguish our lantern by the brighter and fiercer flame of their own. But *Le Feu-Follet* will shine again, when their fire is dead ! "

"Is there, then, no danger that the brulot will yet come down upon us—she is fearfully near ! "

"Not sufficiently to do us harm ; more especially as our sails are damp with dew. Here she cannot come, so long as our cable stands ; and, as that is under water where she lies, it cannot burn. In half an hour there will be little of her left ; and we will enjoy the bonfire while it lasts."

And, now the fear of danger was past, it was a sight truly to be enjoyed. Every anxious and curious face in the lugger was to be seen, under that brilliant light, turned toward the glowing mass, as the sun-flower follows the great source of heat, in its track athwart the heavens ; while the spars, sails, guns, and even the smallest object on board the lugger started out of the obscurity of night into the brightness of such an illumination, as if composing parts of some brilliant scenic display. But so fierce a flame soon exhausted itself. Ere long, the felucca's masts fell, and with them a pyramid of fire. Then the glowing deck tumbled in ; and, finally, timber after timber, and plank after plank fell, until the conflagration, in a great measure, extinguished itself in the water on which it floated. An hour after the flames appeared, little remained but the embers which were glowing in the hold of the wreck.

CHAPTER XII.

RAOUL was not mistaken as to the manner in which they were obtained, and the means employed by his enemies. The frigate had found one of the feluccas loaded with naval stores, including some ten or fifteen barrels of tar; and it instantly struck Griffin, who was burning to revenge the defeat of the morning, that the prize might be converted into a fire-vessel. As the second lieutenant volunteered to carry her in, always a desperate service, Cuffe gave his consent. Nothing could have been better managed than the whole duty connected with this exploit, including the manner in which our hero saved his vessel from destruction. The frigate kept between her prize and the lugger, to conceal the fact that a boat remained on board the former; and when all was ready, the felucca was apparently permitted to proceed on her voyage. The other two prizes were allowed to go free, also, as cloaks to the whole affair. Griffin, as has been seen, kept standing in for the land; his object being to get up stream from the lugger, and as near her as possible. When he found himself almost as far ahead as was desirable, drags were used, to keep the craft stationary; and, in this manner, she drifted down on her intended victim, as has been already described. But for the sagacity and uneasiness of Ithuel, the plan would altogether have escaped detection, and, but for the coolness, courage and resources of Raoul, it would infallibly have succeeded, notwithstanding the suspicions that had been excited.

Cuffe, and the people on deck, watched the whole affair with the deepest interest. They were barely able to see the sails of the felucca, by means of a night-glass, as she was dropping down on the lugger; and Yelverton had just exclaimed that the two vessels were foul of each other, when the flames broke out. As a matter of course, at that distance, both craft seemed on fire; and when Le Feu-Follet had dropped a hundred yards nearer to the frigate, leaving the felucca blazing, the two were so exactly in a line, as to bring them together, as seen from the former's deck. The English expected every moment to hear the explosion of the lugger's magazine; but, as this did not happen, they came to the conclusion that it had been drowned. As for Griffin, he pulled in shore, both to avoid the fire of Le Feu-Follet, in passing her broadside, and in the hope of intercepting Raoul, while endeavoring to escape in a boat. He even went to a landing in the river, quite a league from the anchorage, and waited there until long past midnight, when, finding the night beginning to cloud over, and the obscurity to increase,

he returned to the frigate, giving the smoldering wreck a wide berth, for fear of accidents.

Such, then, was the state of things, when Captain Cuffe appeared on deck, just as the day began to dawn, on the following morning. He had given orders to be called at that hour, and was now all impatience to get a view of the sea, more particularly in-shore. At length the curtain began slowly to rise, and his view extended farther and farther toward the river, until all was visible, even to the very land. Not a craft of any sort was in sight. Even the wreck had disappeared, though this was subsequently discovered in the surf; having drifted out with the current, until it struck an eddy, which carried it in again, when it was finally stranded. No vestige of Le Feu-Follet, however, was to be seen. Not even a tent on the shore, a wandering boat, a drifting spar, or a rag of a sail! All had disappeared, no doubt, in the conflagration. As Cuffe went down below, he walked with a more erect mien than he had done since the affair of the previous morning; and, as he opened his writing-desk, it was with the manner of one entirely satisfied with himself, and his own exertions. Still, a generous regret mingled with his triumph. It was a great thing to have destroyed the most pernicious privateer that ever sailed out of France; and yet it was a melancholy fate to befall seventy or eighty human beings, to perish like so many curling caterpillars, destroyed by fire. Nevertheless, the thing was done; and it must be reported to the authorities above him. The following letter was subsequently written to the commanding officer in that sea, namely:

HIS MAJESTY'S SHIP PROSERPINE,
OFF THE MOUTH OF THE GOLO,
ISLAND OF CORSICA, July 24, 1799.

MY LORD: I have the satisfaction of reporting, for the information of my Lords Commissioners of the Admiralty, the destruction of the republican privateer, the Le Few-Folly, commanded by the notorious Raoul Yvard, on the night of the 22d inst. The circumstances attending this important success are as follows: Understanding that the celebrated picaroon had been on the Neapolitan and Roman coasts, doing much mischief, I took his Majesty's ship close in, following up the peninsula, with the land in sight, until we got through the canal of Elba, early on the morning of the 21st. On opening Porto Ferrajo bay, we saw a lugger lying at anchor off the town, with English colors flying. As this was a friendly port, we could not suppose the craft to be the Le Few-Folly; but, determined to make sure, we beat in, signaling the stranger, until he took advantage of our stretching well over to the eastward, to slip round the rocks, and get to the windward. We followed, for a short distance, and then ran over under the lee of Capraya, where we remained until the morning of the 22d, when we again went off the town.

We found the lugger in the offing; and being now well satisfied of her character, and it falling calm, I sent the boats after her, under Messrs. Winchester and Griffin, the first and second of this ship. After a sharp skirmish, in which we sustained some loss, though that of the republicans was evidently much greater, Monsieur Yvard succeeded in effecting his escape in consequence of a breeze suddenly springing up. Sail was now made on the ship, and we chased the lugger into the mouth of the Golo. Having fortunately captured a felucca, with a quantity of tar and other combustible material on board, as we drew in with the land, I determined to make a fire-ship of her, and to destroy the enemy by that mode; he having anchored within the shoals, beyond the reach of shot. Mr. Winchester, the first, having been wounded in the boat affair, I intrusted the execution of this duty to Mr. Griffin, who handsomely volunteered, and by whom it was effectually discharged, about ten last evening, in the coolest and most officer-like manner. I inclose this gentleman's report, and beg leave to recommend him to the favor of my lords commissioners. With Mr. Winchester's good conduct, under a sharp fire, in the morning, the service has also every reason to be satisfied. I hope this valuable officer will soon be able to return to duty.

Permit me to congratulate you, my lord, on the complete destruction of this most pernicious cruiser of the enemy. So effectual has it been, that not a spar or a fragment of wreck remains. We have reason to think every soul on board perished; and though this fearful loss of human life is to be deeply deplored, it has been made in the service of good government and religion. The lugger was filled with loose women; our people hearing them singing their philosophical and irreligious songs, as they approached with the fire-vessel. I shall search the coast for any rafts that may be drifting about, and then proceed to Leghorn for fresh provisions.

I have the honor to be, my lord,

Your lordship's most obedient servant,
RICHARD CUFFE.

To Rear Admiral the Right Hon. Lord Nelson, Duke of Bronte, etc., etc.

Cuffe read this report over twice; then he sent for Griffin, to whom he read it aloud, glancing his eye meaningly at his subordinate, when he came to the part where he spoke of the young man's good conduct.

"So much for that d——d Jack-o'-Lantern, Griffin! I fancy it will lead no one else on a wild-goose chase."

"I trust not, sir. Will you allow me to suggest a slight alteration in the spelling of the lugger's name, Captain Cuffe, the clerk can make it, when he writes out the letter fairly."

"Ay; I daresay it is different from what *we* would have it, French spelling being no great matter, in general. Put it as you please; though Nelson has as great a contempt for their boasted philosophy and learning as I have myself. I fancy you will find all the English spelled right. How do *you* write their confounded gibberish?"

"*Feu-Follet*, sir, pronouncing the last part of it fol-*lay;* not fol-*ly*. I was thinking of asking leave, Captain Cuffe, to take one of the cutters, and pull up to the lugger's anchorage, and see if anything can be found of her wreck. The ship will hardly get under way until the westerly wind comes."

"No; probably not. I will order my gig manned, and we'll go together. Poor Winchester must keep house awhile; so there is no use asking him. I saw no necessity for putting Nelson into a passion by saying anything about the exact amount of our loss in that boat scrape, Grffin."

"I agree with you, sir, that it is best as it is. 'Some loss' covers everything; it means 'more or less.'"

"That was just my notion. I daresay there may have been twenty women in the lugger."

"I can't answer for the number, sir; but I heard female singing as we got near, in the fire-ship; and think it likely there may have been that number. The lugger was full-manned; for they were like bees swarming on her forecastle, when we were dropping foul. I saw Raoul Yvard by the light of the fire as plainly as I now see you, and might have picked him off with a musket; but that would hardly have been honorable."

To this Cuffe assented, and then he led the way on deck, having previously ordered the boats manned. The two officers proceeded to the spot where they supposed the *Feu-Follet* had been anchored, and rowed round for an hour, endeavoring to find some traces of her wreck on the bottom. Griffin suggested that when the magazine was drowned, in the hurry and confusion of the moment, the cock may have been left open, a circumstance that might very well have carried down the bottom of so small a vessel, in two or three hours; more, especially after her hull had burned to the water's edge. The next thing was to find this bottom, by no means a hopeless task, as the waters of the Mediterranean are usually so clear that the eye can penetrate several fathoms, even off the mouth of the Golo, a stream that brought more or less debris from the mountains.

It is scarcely necessary to say that the search was not rewarded with success, the *Feu-Follet* being, just at that time, snug at anchor at Bastia, where her people had already taken out her wounded mainmast, with a view to step a new one in its place. At that very moment, Carlo Giuntotardi, his niece, and Raoul Yvard, were walking up the principal street of the town, the place standing on a hill, like Porto Ferrajo, perfectly at their ease, as regards fire-ships, English frigates, and the dangers of the seas. But all this was a profound mystery to Cuffe and his companions, who had long been in the habit of putting the most favorable constructions on the results of their professional undertakings, and certainly not altogether without reason; and who nothing doubted that *Le Feu-Follet* had, to use their own language, "laid her bones somewhere along shore, here."

After two or three hours passed in fruitless search, Cuffe determined to return to his ship. He was a keen sportsman, and had brought a fowling-piece with him in his gig, with a half-formed design of landing, and whiling away the time, until the westerly wind came, among some marshes that he saw near the shore; but had been persuaded by Griffin not to venture.

"There must be woodcock in that wet ground, Griffin," he said, as he reluctantly yielded a little in his intention; "and Winchester would fancy a bird exceedingly in a day or two. I never was hit in my life that I did not feel a desire for game, after the fever was gone. Snipe, too, must live on the banks of that stream. Snipe are coming in season now, Griffin?"

"It's more likely, sir, that some of the privateersmen have got ashore on planks and empty casks, and are prowling about in the weeds, watching our boats. Three or four of them would be too much for you, Captain Cuffe, as the scoundrels all carry knives as long as ship's cutlasses."

"I suppose your notion may be true; and I shall have to give it up. Pull back to the frigate, Davy, and we'll be off after some more of these French ragamuffins."

This settled the matter. In half an hour the boats were swinging at the *Proserpine's* quarters; and three hours later the ship was under her canvas, standing slowly off the land. That day, however, the zephyr was exceedingly light, and the sun set just as the ship got the small island of Pianosa abeam, when the air came from the northward, and the ship's head was laid in to the eastward; the course lying between the land just mentioned and that of Elba. All night the *Proserpine* was slowly fanning her way along the south side of the latter island, when, getting the southerly air again in the morning, she re-appeared in the Canal of Piombino, as the day advanced, precisely as she had done the day before, when first introduced to the acquaintance of the reader. Cuffe had given orders to be called, as usual, when the light was about to return; it being a practice with him, in that active and pregnant war, to be on deck at such moments, in order to ascertain with his own eyes what the fortunes of the night had brought within his reach.

"Well, Mr. Griffin," he said, as soon as he had received the salutation of the officer of the watch, "you have had a still night of it. Yonder is the Point of Piombino, I see; and here we have got Elba, and this little rocky island again, on our larboard hand. One day is surprisingly like another about these times, for us mariners in particular."

"Do you really think so, Captain Cuffe? Now, to my notion, this day hasn't had its equal on the *Proserpine's* log since we got hold of *L'Eperrier* and her convoy. You forget, sir, that we destroyed *Le Feu-Follet* last night!"

"Ay—that is something—especially for *you*, Griffin. Well, Nelson will hear of it by mail, as soon as we can get into Leghorn, which will be immediately after I have had an opportunity of communicating with these people in Porto Ferrajo. After all that has passed, the least we can do is to let your veech-govern-the-tories know of our success."

"Sail, ho!" shouted the lookout, on the fore-topsail-yard.

The two officers turned and gazed round them in every direction, when the captain made the customary demand of "Whereaway?"

"Here, sir, close aboard of us on our larboard hand, and on our weather quarter."

"On our weather quarter! D——n me if that can be true, Griffin. There is nothing but the island there. The fellow cannot have mistaken this little island for the hull of a ship?"

"If he has, sir," answered Griffin, laughing, "it must be for a twenty-decker. That is Ben Brown aloft; and he is as good a lookout as we have in the ship."

"Do you see her, sir?" demanded Ben Brown, looking over his shoulder.

"Not a bit of her," cried Cuffe. "You must be dreaming, fellow. What does she look like?"

"There, this small island shuts her in from the deck, sir. She is a lugger; and looks as much like the one we burned last night, sir, as one of our catheads is like t'other."

"A lugger!" exclaimed Cuffe. "What, another of the blackguards! By Jove! I'll go aloft, and take a look for myself. It's ten to one that I see her from the main-top."

In three minutes more, Captain Cuffe was in the top in question; having passed through the lubber-hole, as every sensible man does, in a frigate, more especially when she stands up for want of wind. That was an age in which promotion was rapid, there being few gray-bearded lieutenants, then, in the English marine; and even admirals were not wanting who had not cut all their wisdom teeth. Cuffe, consequently, was still a young man; and it cost him no great effort to get up his ship's ratlines in the manner named. Once in the top, he had all his eyes about him. For quite a moment he stood motionless, gazing in the direction that had been pointed out by Ben Brown. All this time, Griffin stood on the quarter-deck, looking quite as intently at his superior as the latter gazed at the strange sail. Then Cuffe deigned to cast a glance literally beneath him, in order to appease the curiosity, which, he well understood, it was so natural for the officer of the watch to feel. Griffin did not dare to ask his captain what he saw; but he looked a volume of questions on the interesting subject.

"A sister corsair, by Jupiter Ammon!" cried Cuffe; "a twin sister, too; for they are as much alike as one cathead is like another. More, too, by Jove, if I am any judge."

"What would you have us do, Captain Cuffe?" inquired the lieutenant. "We are now going to leeward all the while. I don't know, sir, that there is positively a current here, but—"

"Very well, sir—very well; haul up on the larboard tack as soon as possible, and get the larboard batteries clear. We may have to cripple the chap in order to get hold of him."

As this was said Cuffe descended through the same lubber-hole, and soon reappeared on deck. The ship now became a scene of activity and bustle. All hands were called, and the guns were cleared away by some, while others braced the yards according to the new line of sailing.

The reader would be greatly aided, in understanding what is to follow, could he, perchance, cast a look at a map of the coast of Italy. He will there see that the eastern side of the Island of Elba runs in a nearly north and south direction, Piombino lying off about north-northeast from its northern extremity. Near this northern extremity lies the little rocky islet, so often mentioned, or the spot which Napoleon, fifteen years later, selected as the advanced redoubt of his insular empire. Of course, the *Proserpine* was on one side of this islet, and the strange lugger on the other. The first had got so far through the canal as to be able to haul close upon the wind, on the larboard tack, and yet to clear the islet; while the last was just far enough to windward, or sufficiently to the southward, to be shut out from view from the frigate's decks, by the intervening rocks. As the distance from the islet to the island did not much exceed a hundred or two yards, Captain Cuffe, hoped to inclose his chase between himself and the land, never dreaming that the stranger would think of standing through so narrow and rocky a pass. He did not know his man, however, who was Raoul Yvard; and who had come this way, from Bastia, in the hope of escaping any further collision with his formidable foe. He had seen the frigate's lofty sails, above the rock, as soon as it was light; and being under no hallucination on the subject of her existence, he knew her at a glance. His first order was to haul everything as flat as possible; and his great desire was to get from under the lee of the mountains of Elba into this very pass, through which the wind drew with more force than it blew anywhere near by.

As the *Proserpine* was quite a league off, in the canal, *Le Feu-Follet*, which sailed so much the fastest in light winds, had abundance of time to effect her object. Instead of avoiding the narrow pass between the two islands, Raoul glided boldly into it; and, by keeping vigilant eyes on his fore-yard, to apprise him of danger, he succeeded in making two stretches in the strait itself, coming out to the southward on the starboard tack, handsomely clearing the end of the islet at the very instant the frigate appeared on the other side of the pass. The lugger had now an easy task of it; for she had only to watch her enemy, and tack in season, to keep the islet between them; since the English did not dare to carry so large a ship through so narrow an opening. This advantage Raoul did not overlook, and Cuffe had gone about twice, closing, each time, nearer and nearer to the islet, before he was satisfied that his guns would be of no service, until he could at least weather the intervening object; after which they would most probably be useless, in so light a wind, by the distance between them and their enemy.

"Never mind, Mr. Griffin; let this scamp go," said the captain, when he made this material discovery; "it is pretty well to have cleared the seas of one of them. Besides, we do not know that this is an enemy at all. He showed no colors, and seems to have just come out of Porto Ferrajo, a friendly haven."

"Raoul Yvard did that, sir, not once, but twice," muttered Yelverton, who, from the circumstance that he had not been employed in the different attempts on *Le Feu-Follet*, was one of the very few dissentients in the ship touching her fate. "These twins are exceedingly alike, especially Pomp, as the American negro said of his twin children."

This remark passed unheeded; for so deep was the delusion in the ship touching the destruction of the privateer, it would have been as hopeless an attempt to try to persuade her officers, and people generally, that *Le Feu-Follet* was not burned, as it would be to induce a "great nation" to believe it had any of the weaknesses and foibles that confessedly beset smaller communities. The *Proserpine* was put about again, and, setting her ensign, she stood into the bay of Porto Ferrajo; anchoring quite near the place that Raoul had selected for the same purpose, on two previous occasions. The gig was lowered, and Cuffe, accompanied by Griffin as an interpreter, landed, to pay the usual visit of ceremony to the authorities.

The wind being so light, several hours were necessary to effect all these changes; and, by the time the two officers were ascending the terraced street, the day had advanced sufficiently to render the visit suitable as to time. Cuffe appearing in full uniform, with epaulettes and sword, his approach attracted notice; and Vito Viti hurried off to apprise his friend of the honor he was about to receive. The vice-governatore was not taken by surprise, therefore, but had some little time to prepare his excuses for being the dupe of a fraud as impudent as that which Raoul Yvard had so successfully practiced on him. The reception was dignified, though courteous; and it had none the less of ceremony from the circumstance that all that was said by the respective colloquists had to be translated before it could be understood. This circumstance rendered the few first minutes of the interview a little constrained; but each party having something on his mind, of which it was his desire to be relieved, natural feelings soon got the better of forms.

"I ought to explain to you, Sir Cuffe, the manner in which a recent event occurred in our bay, here," observed the vice-governatore; "since, without such explanation, you might be apt to consider us neglectful of our duties, and unworthy of the trust which the grand duke reposes in us. I allude, as you will at once understand, to the circumstance that *Le Feu-Follet* has twice been lying peaceably under the guns of our batteries, while her commander, and indeed some of her crew, have been hospitably entertained on shore."

"Such things must occur in times like these, Mr. Veechy-governatory; and we seamen set them down to the luck of war," Cuffe answered graciously, being much too magnanimous, under his own success, to think of judging others too harshly. "It might not be so easy to deceive a man-of-war's-man like myself; but I dare say, veechy-governatory, had it been anything relating to the administration of your little island here, even Monsieur Yvard would have found you too much for him!"

The reader will perceive that Cuffe had got a new way of pronouncing the appellation of the Elban functionary; a circumstance that was owing to the desire we all have, when addressing foreigners, to speak in their own language rather than in our own. The worthy captain had no more precise ideas of what a vice-governor means, than the American people, just now, seem to possess of the significance of vice-president; but, as he had discovered that the word was pronounced "veechy," in Italian, he was quite willing to give it its true sound; albeit a smile struggled round the mouth of Griffin while he listened.

"You do me no more than justice, Signor Kooffe, or Sir Kooffe, as, I presume, I ought to address you," answered the functionary; "for, in matters touching our duties on shore here, we are by no means as ignorant as on matters touching your honorable calling. This Raoul Yvard presented himself to me in the character of a British officer, one I esteem and respect; having audaciously assumed the name of a family of high condition, and of great power, I believe, among your people—"

"Ah, the barone!" exclaimed Cuffe, who, having discovered by his intercourse with the southern Italians that this word meant a "rascal," as well as a "baron," was fond of using it on suitable occasions. "Pray, Veechy-governatory, what name did he assume? Ca'endish, or Howard, or Seymour, or some of those great nobs. Griffin, I'll engage! I wonder that he spared Nelson!"

"No, signore, he took the family appellation of another illustrious race. The republican corsair presented himself before me as a Sir Smees—the son of a certain Milordo Smees."

"Smees—Smees—Smees! I've no recollection of any such name in the peerage. It can't be Seymour that the veechy means! This is a great name, certainly; and some of them have been in the service; it is possible this barone may have the impudence to hail for a Seymour!"

"I rather think not, Captain Cuffe. 'Smees,' is very much as an Italian would pronounce 'Smith,' as, you know, the French call it 'Smeet.' It will turn out that this Mr. Raoul has seized upon the first English name he fell in with, as a man overboard clutches at a spar adrift, or a life-buoy; and that happened to be 'Smith.'"

"Who the devil ever heard of a my lord Smith! A pretty sort of aristocracy we should have, Griffin, if it were made up of such fellows?"

"Why, sir, the name can make no great difference; the deeds and the antiquity forming the essentials."

"And he assumed a title too—Sir Smees! I daresay he was ready to swear his majesty made him a knight banneret, under the royal ensign, and on the deck of his own ship; as was done with some of the old admirals. The veechy, however, has forgotten a part of the story, as it must have been Sir John or Sir Thomas Smees, at least."

"No, sir; that is the way with the French and Italians, who do not understand our manner of using Christian names with titles; as in our Sir Edwards, and Lord Harrys, and Lady Bettys."

"Blast the French! I can believe anything of them, though I should have thought that these Italians knew better. However, it may be well to give the veechy a hint of what we have been saying, or it may seem rude; and, harkye, Griffin, while you are about it, rub him down a little touching books, and that sort of thing; for the surgeon tells me he has heard of him, in Leghorn, as a regular leaf-cutter."

The lieutenant did as ordered, throwing in an allusion to Andrea's reputation for learning, that, under the circumstances, was not ill-timed; and which, as it was well enough expressed, was exceedingly grateful to his listener just at that awkward moment.

"My claims to literature are but small, signore," answered Andrea, with humility, "as I beg you will inform Sir Kooffe; but they were sufficient to detect certain assumptions of this corsair; a circumstance that came very near bringing about an exposure at a most critical moment. He had the audacity, signore, to wish to persuade me that there was a certain English orator of the same name, and of equal merit of him of Roma and Pompeii—one Sir Cicero!"

"The barone!" again exclaimed Cuffe, when this new offense of Raoul's was explained to him. "I believe the rascal was up to anything. But there is an end of him, now, with all his Sir Smees and Sir Ciceros in the bargain. Just let the veechy into the secret of the fellow's fate, Griffin."

Griffin then related to the vice-governatore the manner in which it was supposed that *Le Feu-Follet*, Raoul Yvard, and all his associates, had been consumed, like caterpillars on a tree. Andrea Barrofaldi listened, with a proper degree of horror expressed in his countenance; but Vito Viti heard the tale with signs of indifference and incredulity he did not care to conceal. Nevertheless, Griffin persevered, until he had even given an account of the manner in which he and Cuffe examined the lugger's anchorage, in the bootless attempt to discover the wreck.

To all this the two functionaries listened with profound attention, and a lively surprise. After looking at each other several times, and exchanging significant gestures, Andrea assumed the office of explaining.

"There is some extraordinary mistake in this, Signor Tenente," he said; "for Raoul Yvard still lives. He passed this promontory just as day dawned in his lugger, this very morning!"

"Ay, he has got that notion from having seen the fellow we fell in with off the harbor here," answered Cuffe, when this speech was translated to him; "and I don't wonder at it, for the two vessels were surprisingly alike. But the barone that we saw burned with our own eyes, Griffin, can never float again. I say barone; for, in my opinion, the *Few-Folly* was just as much of a rascal as her commander, and all who sailed in her."

Griffin explained this; but it met with no favor from the Italians.

"Not so, Signor Tenente—not so," returned the vice-governatore; "the lugger that passed this morning we know to be *Le Feu-Follet*, inasmuch as she took one of our own feluccas, in the course of the night, coming from Livorno, and Raoul Yvard permitted her to come in, as he said to her padrone, on account of the civil treatment he had received while lying in our port. Nay, he even carried his presumption so far as to send me, by means of the same man, the compliments of 'Sir Smees,' and his hopes of being able, some day, to make his acknowledgments in person."

The English captain received this intelligence as might be expected; and unpleasant as it was, after putting various questions to the vice-governatore, and receiving the answers, he was obliged, unwillingly enough, to believe it all. He had brought his official report in his pocket; and, as the conversation proceeded, he covertly tore it into fragments so small that even a Mohammedan would reject them, as not large enough to write the word "Allah" on.

"It's d——h lucky, Griffin, that the letter didn't get to Leghorn, this morning," he said, after a long pause, "Nelson would have Bronted me famously, had he got it! Yes, I never believed half as devoutly in the twenty-nine articles—"

"I believe there are thirty-nine of them, Captain Cuffe," modestly put in Griffin.

"Well, thirty-nine, if you will; what signifies ten more or less in such matters? A man is ordered to believe them all, if there were a hundred. But I never believed in them as devoutly as I believed in the destruction of that infernal picaroon. My faith is unsettled for life!"

Griffin offered a few words of condolence, but he was also too much mortified to be very able to administer consolation. Andrea Barrofaldi understanding the state of the case, now interposed with his courtesies, and the two officers were invited to share his bachelor's breakfast. What followed, in consequence of this visit, and the communications to which it gave rise, will appear in the course of the narrative.

CHAPTER XIII.

It is now necessary to advance the time, and to transfer the scene of our tale to another, but not a distant part of the same sea. Let the reader fancy himself standing at the mouth of a large bay of some sixteen or eighteen miles in diameter in nearly every direction; though the shores must be indented with advancing promontories and receding curvatures, while the depth of the whole might a little exceed the greatest width. He will then occupy the spot of which we wish to present to him one of the fairest panoramas of earth. On his right stands a high, rocky island of dark tufa, rendered gay, amid all its magnificent formations, by smiling vineyards and teeming villages, and interesting by ruins that commemorate events as remote as the Cæsars. A narrow passage of the blue Mediterranean separates this island from a bold cape on the main, whence follows a succession of picturesque, village-clad heights and valleys, relieved by scenery equally bold and soft, and adorned by the monkish habitations called in the language of the country Camaldolis, until we reach a small city that stands on a plain that rises above the water between one and two hundred feet, on a base of tufa, and the houses of which extend to the very verge of the dizzy cliffs that limit its extent on the north.

The plain itself is like a hive, with its dwellings and scenes of life, while the heights behind it teem with cottages and the signs of human labor. Quitting this smiling part of the coast, we reach a point, always following the circuit of the bay, where the hills or heights tower into ragged mountains, which stretch their pointed peaks upwards to some six or seven thousand feet toward the clouds, having sides now wide with precipices and ravines, now picturesque with shooting-towers, hamlets, monasteries, and bridle-paths; and bases dotted, or rather lined, with towns and villages. Here the mountain formation quits the margin of the bay, following the coast southward, or running into the interior of the country; and the shore sweeping round to the north and west, offers a glimpse into a background of broad plain, ere it meets a high, insulated, conical mountain, which properly forms the head of the coast indentation. The human eye never beheld a more affluent scene of houses, cities, villages, vineyards, and country residences, than was presented by the broad breast of this isolated mountain; passing which a wider view is obtained of the rich plain that seems to lie behind it, bounded as it is by a wall of a distant and mysterious-looking yet bold range of the Apennines.

Returning to the shore, which now begins to incline more westwardly, we come to another swell of tufa, which has all the characteristic fertility and abruptness of that peculiar formation, a vast and populous town of near half a million of souls being seated, in nearly equal parts, on the limits of the plain, and along the margin of the water, or on the hillsides, climbing to their summits. From this point the northern side of the bay is a confused mass of villages, villas, ruins, palaces, and vines, until we reach its extremity ; a low promontory, like its opposite neighbor. A small island comes next, a sort of natural sentinel ; then the coast sweeps northward into another and smaller bay, rich to satiety with relics of the past, terminating at a point some miles farther seaward, with a high, reddish, sandy bluff, which almost claims to be a mountain.

After this we see two more islands, lying westward, one of which is flat, fertile, and more populous, as is said, than any other part of Europe of the same extent ; while the other is a glorious combination of pointed mountains, thronged towns, fertile valleys, castles, country houses, and the wrecks of the long dormant volcanoes, thrown together in a grand, yet winning confusion. If the reader will, to this description, add a shore that has scarce a foot that is not interesting with some lore of the past, extending from yesterday into the darkest recesses of history, give life to the water-view with a fleet of little lateen-rigged craft, rendered more picturesque by an occasional ship, dot the bay with countless host of fishermen, and send up a wreath of smoke from the summit of the cone-like mountain that forms the head of the bay, he will get an outline of all that strikes the eye, as the stranger approaches Naples from the sea.

The zephyr was again blowing, and the daily fleet of sparanaras, or undecked feluccas, that pass every morning, at this season, from the south shore to the capital, and returns at this hour, was stretching out from under Vesuvius ; some looking up as high as Massa ; others heading toward Sorrento or Nico or Persano, and many keeping more before the wind toward Castel-a-Mare, or the landings in the neighborhood. The breeze was getting to be so fresh that the fishermen were beginning to pour in toward the land, breaking up their lines, which, in some places, had extended nearly a league, and this, too, with the boats lying within speaking distance of each other. The head of the bay, indeed, was alive with craft moving in different directions, while a large fleet of English, Russians, Neapolitans and Turks composed of two-deckers, frigates and sloops, lay at their anchors in front of the town. On board of one of the largest of the former was flying the flag of a rear-admiral at the mizzen, the symbol of the commander's rank. A corvette, alone, was under way. She had left the anchorage an hour before, and with studding-sails on her starboard side, was stretching diagonally across the glorious bay, apparently heading toward the passage between Capri and the point of Campanella, bound to Sicily. This ship might easily have weathered the island ; but her commander, an easy sort of person, chose to make a fair wind of it from the start, and he thought, by hugging the coast, he might possibly benefit by the land breeze, during the night, trusting to the zephyr that was then blowing, to carry him across the Gulf of Salerno.

A frigate, too, shot out of the fleet, under her stay-sails, as soon as the westerly wind made ; but she had dropped an anchor under-foot, and seemed to wait some preparation, or orders, before taking her departure ; her captain being at that moment on board the flag-ship, on duty with the rear admiral. This was the *Proserpine*, thirty-six, Captain Cuffe, a vessel and an officer that are already both acquaintances of the reader. About an hour before the present scene opens, Captain Cuffe, in fact, had been called on board the *Foudroyant* by signal, where he had found a small, sallow-looking, slightly-built man, with his right arm wanting, pacing the deck of the forecabin, impatient for his appearance.

"Well, Cuffe," said the uninviting-looking personage, twitching the stump of the maimed arm, "I see you are out of the flock ; are you all ready for sailing ? "

" We have one boat ashore after letters, my lord ; as soon as she comes off, we shall lift our anchor, which is only under-foot."

"Very well ; I have sent the *Ringdove* to the southward, on the same errand, and I see she is half-a-league from the anchorage, on her way, already. This Mr. Griffin appears to be a fine young man ; I like his account of the way he handled his fire-ship, though the French scoundrel did contrive to escape ! After all, this Rowl E—— E——, how do you pronounce the fellow's name, Cuffe ? I never can make anything out of their gibberish."

" Why, to own the truth, Sir Horatio —I beg pardon : my lord—there is something in the English grain of my feelings that would prevent my ever learning French, had I been born and brought up in Paris. There is too much Saxon in me to swallow words that half the time have no meaning."

"I like you all the better for that, Cuffe," answered the admiral, smiling, a change that converted a countenance that was almost ugly, in a state of rest, into one that was almost handsome; a peculiarity that is by no means of rare occurrence when a strong will gives expression to the features, and the heart, at bottom, is really sound. "An Englishman has no business with any Gallic tendencies. This young Mr. Griffin seems to have spirit; and I look upon it always as a good sign, when a young man volunteers for a desperate thing of this sort; but he tells me he is only second; where was your first, all the while?"

"Why, my lord, he got a little hurt in the brush of the morning; and I would not let him go, as a matter of course. His name is Winchester; I think you must remember him, as junior of the captain, at the affair off St. Vincent. Miller * had a good opinion of him; and, when I went from the *Arrow* to the *Proserpine*, he got him sent as my second. The death of poor Drury made him first, in the natural way."

"I have some recollection of him, Cuffe. That was a brilliant day, and all its events should be impressed on my mind. You tell me, Mr. Griffin fairly grappled the lugger's cable?"

"Of that there can be no manner of doubt. I saw the two vessels foul of each other, with my night-glass—and, seemingly, both were on fire—as plainly as I ever saw Vesuvius, in a dark night."

"And yet this *Few-Folly* has escaped! Poor Griffin has run a desperate risk for little purpose."

"He has, indeed, my lord."

Here Nelson, who had been pacing the cabin with quick steps, while Cuffe stood, respectfully declining the gesture to be seated, at the table in its center, suddenly stopped, and looked the captain steadily in the face. The expression of his countenance was now mild and earnest, and the pause which preceded his words gave the latter solemnity and weight.

"The day will come, Cuffe," he said, "when this young man will rejoice that his design on these picaroons, Frenchmen

as they are, failed. Yes, from the bottom of his heart will he be glad."

"My lord!"

"I know you think this strange, Captain Cuffe; but no man sleeps the sounder for having burned or blown up a hundred of his fellow-creatures, like so many widows at a suttee. But we are not the less to commend those who did what was certainly their duty."

"Am I to understand, Lord Nelson, that the *Proserpine* is not to destroy the *Few-Folly* at every hazard, should we again have the luck to fall in with her?"

"By no means, sir. Our orders are to burn, sink, and destroy. Such is England's policy, in this desperate war; and it must be carried out. You know what we are contending for as well as I do; and it is a struggle that is not to be carried on with courtesies; still, one would not wish to see a glorious and sacred cause tarnished by inhumanity. Men that fall in fair, manly combat, are to be envied rather than pitied, since it is only paying the great debt of nature a little sooner than might otherwise have happened; but there is something revolting to humanity in burning up our fellow creatures as one would burn rags after the plague. Nevertheless, this lugger must be had at any price, for English commerce and English power are not to be cut up and braved, in this audacious manner, with impunity. The career of these French tigers must be stopped at any sacrifice, Captain Cuffe."

"I know that, my lord; and I like a republican as little as you can do; or his majesty himself, for that matter; and I take it, he has as little relish for the animal as flesh and blood can give."

"I know you do, Cuffe—I'm sure you do; and I esteem you all the more for it. It is part of an Englishman's religion, in times like these, to hate a Frenchman. I went across the channel, after the peace of '83, to learn their language, but had so little sympathy with them, even in peaceable times, as never to be able to make out to write a letter in it, or even to ask intelligibly for the necessaries of life."

"If you can ask for anything, it far surpasses my efforts; I never can tell head from stern in their dialect."

"It is an infernal jargon, Cuffe, and has got to be so confused by their academies, and false philosophy, and infidelity, that they will shortly be at a loss to understand it themselves. What sort of names they give their ships, for instance, now they have beheaded their king, and denounced their God! Who ever heard of christening a craft, as you tell me this

---

* Ralph Willet Miller, the officer who commanded the ship to which Nelson shifted his pennant, at the battle of Cape St. Vincent. This gentleman was an American, and a native Manhattanese; his near relatives of the same name still residing in New York. It is believed that he got the name of *Willet* from the first English Mayor, a gentleman from whom are descended many of the old families of the lower part of the State; more particular those on Long Island.

lugger is named, the *Few-Folly?* I believe I've got the picaroon's title right?"

"Quite right; Griffin pronounces it so, though he has got to be a little queerish in his own English, by using so much French and Italian. The young man's father was a consul; and he has half a dozen foreign lingoes stowed away in his brain. He pronounces Folly broadish—like Fol*lay*, I believe; but it means all the same thing. Folly is folly, pronounce it as you will."

Nelson continued to pace his cabin, working the stump of his arm, and smiling half bitterly; half in a sort of irony that inclined him to be in a good humor with himself.

"Do you remember the ship, Cuffe, we had the sharp brush with off Toulon, in old *Agamemnon?*" he said, after making a turn or two in silence. "I mean the dismasted eighty four, that was in tow of the frigate, and which we peppered until their gallic soup had some taste to it! Now do you happen to know her real name, in good, honest English?"

"I do not, my lord. I remember they said she was called the *Ca Ira;* and I always supposed that it was the name of some old Greek or Roman, or, perhaps, of one of their new-fangled republican saints."

"They! D——n 'em, they've got no saints to name, my good fellow, since they cashiered all the old ones! There is something respectable in the names of a Spanish fleet; and one feels that he is flogging gentlemen, at least, while he is at work on them. No, sir, *Ca Ira* means neither more nor less than 'That'll Do'; and I fancy, Cuffe, they thought of their own name more than once while the old Greek was hanging on their quarter, smashing their cabin windows for them! A pretty sound it would have been, had we got her and put her into our own service—his majesty's ship 'That'll Do,' eighty-four, Captain Cuffe!"

"I certainly should have petitioned my lords commissioners to change her name."

"You would have done quite right. A man might as well sail in a man-of-war called the *Enough.* Then, there was the three-decker that helped her out of the scrape, the *Sans-Culottes*, as the French called her; I suppose you know what that means?"

"Not I, my lord; to own the truth, I'm no scholar; and am entirely without ambition in that way. 'Sans,' I suppose, is the French for 'saint,' but who 'Culottes' was, I've not the least notion."

Nelson smiled, and the turn the conversation had taken appeared to give him secret satisfaction. If the truth were known, something lay heavily on his mind; and, with one of his strong impulses, his feelings disposed him to rush from one extreme to the other, as is often the case with men who are controlled by such masters; more especially if their general disposition is to the right.

"You're wrong this time, my dear Cuffe," he said; "for 'sans' means 'without' in French, and 'culottes' means 'breeches.' Think of naming a three-decker the *Without Breeches!* I do not see how any respectable flag-officer can mention such names in his dispatches without a feeling of awkwardness that must come near to capsizing all his philosophy. The line was formed by the republic's ship, the *That'll Do*, leading, supported by the *Without Breeches* as her second astern! Ha! Cuffe; d——e, sir, if I'd serve in a marine that had such names to the ships! It's a thousand times worse than all those saints the Spaniards tack on their vessels; like a line of boats towing her ship up to her moorings!"

Here the conversation was interrupted by the appearance of a midshipman, who came down to say that a man and a woman from the shore wished to see the rear-admiral on pressing business.

"Let them come down, sir," answered Nelson; "I've a hard life of it, Cuffe; there is not a washerwoman or a shopkeeper in Naples who does not treat me exactly as if I were a podesta, and it were my duty to hear all the contentions about lost clothes and mislaid goods. His majesty must appoint a lord chief justice of the steerage, to administer the law for the benefit of the young gentlemen, or he'll soon get no officer to serve with a flag at his masthead."

"Surely, my lord, the captains can take this weight off your shoulders!"

"Ay, there are men in the fleet that can, and there are men who do; but there are men who do not. But here comes the plaintiff, I suppose; you shall hear the case, and act as a puisne judge in the matter."

This was said as the cabin door opened, and the expected guests entered. They were, a man turned of fifty, and a girl of nineteen. The former was a person of plain exterior, abstracted air, and downcast look; but the latter had all the expression, beauty, nature and grace of mien that so singularly marked the deportment and countenance of Ghita Caraccioli.* In

---

* It may aid the reader, who is ignorant of Italian, to tell him this name is pronounced Ca-rach-cho-li. The same is true of Gwe-cho-li—or Guiccioli—Byron's mistress.

a word the two visitors were Carlo Giuntotardi and his gentle niece. Nelson was
struck with the modesty of mien and loveliness of the latter, and he courteously invited her to be seated, though he and
Cuffe both continued standing. A few
efforts at making himself understood,
however, soon satisfied this renowned admiral that he had need of an interpreter,
his guests speaking no English, and his
own Italian being too imperfect to carry on
anything like a connected conversation.
He hesitated an instant, and then went to
the door of the inner-cabin, an apartment
in which voices had occasionally been
heard the whole time, one of the speakers
being a female. Here he stood leaning
against the bulkhead, as if in doubt; and
then he uttered his wishes.

"I must ask a service of you, which I
would not think of doing in any ordinary
case," he said, with a gentleness of voice
and manner that showed he addressed one
who had habitual influence over him. "I
want an interpreter between myself and
the second handsomest woman in the
kingdom of Naples: I know no one so fit
for the office as the first."

"With all my heart, dear Nelson," answered a full rich female voice from within.
"Sir William is busied in his antiquities;
and I was really getting to be ennuied for
want of an occupation. I suppose you
have the wrongs of some injured lady to
redress, in your capacity of lord high
chancellor of the fleet."

"I am yet ignorant of the nature of
the complaint; but it is not unlikely it
will turn out to be something like that
which you suspect. Even in such a case,
no better intercessor can be required than
one who is so much superior to the frailties and weaknesses of her sex in general."

The lady who now made her appearance
from the inner cabin, though strikingly
handsome, had not that in her appearance
which would justify the implied eulogium
of the British admiral's last speech. There
was an appearance of art and worldliness
in the expression of her countenance that
was only so much the more striking, when
placed in obvious contrast to the ingenuous
nature and calm purity that shone in every
lineament of the face of Ghita. One might
very well have passed for the image of the
goddess Circe; while the other would have
made no bad model for a vestal, could the
latter have borne the moral impression of
the sublime and heart-searching truths
that are inculcated by the real oracles of
God. Then the lady was a woman in the
meridian of her charms, aided by all the
cunning of the toilet, and a taste that was
piquant and peculiar, if not pure; while

the other stood, in her simple, dark Neapolitan bodice, and a head that had no
other ornament than its own silken tresses;
a style of dress, however, that set off her
faultless form and winning countenance
more than could have been done by any of
the devices of the mantua-maker or the
milliner. The lady betrayed a little surprise, and, perhaps, a shade of uneasiness,
as her first glance fell on Ghita; but, much
too good an actress to be disconcerted
easily, she smiled, and immediately recovered her ease.

"Is this the being, Nelson, who comes
with such a petition?" she demanded, with
a touch of natural, womanly sensibility in
her voice; "and that poor old man, I dare
say, is the heart-stricken father."

"As to the errand, you will remember,
I know nothing as yet; and pledge myself
to nothing."

"Captain Cuffe, I hope I have the
pleasure to see you well. Sir William
joins the admiral in hoping you will make
one of our little family party to-day, at
dinner, and—"

"And what says the mistress, not of
the house, but of the ship?" put in Nelson, whose eyes had scarce turned an
instant from the face of the siren since she
entered the forecabin.

"That she—always disclaiming the
title—honorable though it be—that she
unites with all the rest in inviting Captain Cuffe to honor us with his company.
Nelson tells me you were one of his old
Agamemnons, as he calls you all, aged
and young, men and boys, little and big;
and I love even the sound of the name.
What a glorious title for a ship—*Agamemnon!* A Greek, led on by a true English
heart!"

"Ay, it is somewhat better than
'That'll Do,' and the other affair, ha!
Cuffe?" returned the admiral, smiling,
and glancing at his subordinate; "but
all this time we are ignorant of the errand
of this honest-looking Italian, and his exceedingly innocent-looking companion."

"Well then, in this matter, gentlemen,
I am only to be regarded as a mere mouth-
piece," put in the lady; "an echo, to
repeat what reaches mine ear, though it
be an Irish echo, which repeats in a different tongue from that in which the sounds
first reach it. Put your questions, my
lord; they shall be faithfully rendered,
with all the answers that may be given.
I only hope Captain Cuffe may come out
of this affair as innocent as he now looks."

The two gentlemen smiled; but the
trifling could not disturb its subject, as
he was profoundly ignorant of the existence of the two strangers, five minutes

before; while the boldness of the allusion rather suited the freedom of a ship, and the habits of the part of the world in which they happened to be.

"We will first inquire the name of this worthy man, if you will condescend to ask it," observed Nelson, to his fair friend.

"Carlo Giuntotardi, noble lady; once a poor scholar, in Napoli, here, and now a keeper of the prince's watch-towers on the heights of Argentaro," was the quiet, but respectful answer of the man, who, like his niece, had declined taking a seat, a circumstance that left the whole party standing; "Carlo Giuntotardi, illustrious lady."

"A very good name, signore, and one of which you have no need to be ashamed. And thine?" turning to the girl.

"Ghita Caraccioli, eccellenza; the sister's daughter of this honest tower-keeper of the prince."

Had a bomb exploded over the *Foudroyant*, Nelson certainly would not have been as much startled; while the lady's beautiful face assumed a look of dark resentment, not unmingled with fear. Even Cuffe understood enough of the sounds to catch the name, and he advanced a step, with lively curiosity, and an anxious concern expressed on his ruddy face. But these emotions soon subsided, the lady first regaining her self-possession, though Nelson paced the cabin five or six times, working the stump of his arm, before he even looked up again.

"I was about to ask if there never is to be an end to these annoyances," observed the lady, in English; "but there must be some mistake in this. The house of Caraccioli is one of the most illustrious of Italy, and can scarcely have any of this class who feel an interest in him of whom we are thinking. I will, therefore, inquire further into this matter. Signorina,"—changing the language to Italian, and speaking with severity, like one who questioned what she heard—"Caraccioli is a noble name; and is not often borne by the daughter of any prince's tower-keepers!"

Ghita trembled, and she looked abashed. But she was sustained by too high a principle, and was too innocent, herself, to stand long rebuked in the presence of guilt; and, as the flush which resembled that which so often passes over her native skies at even, left her countenance, she raised her eyes to the dark-looking face of the lady, and gave her answer.

"I know what your eccellenza means," she said, "and feel its justice. Still it is cruel to the child, not to bear the name of her parent. My father was called Carac-cioli; and he left me his name as my sole inheritance. What may have been his right to it, let my uncle say."

"Speak, then, Signor Giuntotardi. First, give us the history of this name; then tell us what has brought you here."

"Noble lady, my sister, as pious and innocent a woman as ever lived in Italy, and now blessed in heaven, married Don Francesco Caraccioli, the son of Don Francesco of that illustrious family, who now stands condemned to death for having led the fleet against the king; and Ghita, here, is the only fruit of the union. It is true, that the Church did not authorize the connection which brought my niece's father into being; but the noble admiral never hesitated to acknowledge his son, and he gave him his name, until love bound him in wedlock with a poor scholar's sister. Then, indeed, his father turned his face from him; and death soon removed both husband and wife from the reach of all earthly displeasure. This is our simple story, noble and illustrious signora; and the reason why my poor niece, here, bears the name as great as that of Caraccioli."

"You mean us to understand, Signor Giuntotardi, that your niece is the grand-daughter of Don Francesco Caraccioli, through a natural son of that unfortunate admiral?"

"Such is the fact, signora. As my sister was honestly married, I could do no less than bring up her daughter to bear a name that her father was permitted to bear before her."

"Such things are common, and require no apology. One question more, before I explain to the English admiral what you have said. Does Prince Caraccioli know of the existence of this grand-daughter?"

"Eccellenza, I fear not. Her parents died so soon—I loved the child so well—and there was so little hope that one illustrious as he would wish to acknowledge a connection through the Holy Church with persons humble as we, that I have never done more to make my niece known than to let her bear the same name as her father."

The lady seemed relieved by this; and she now briefly explained to Nelson the substance of what the other had said.

"It may be," she added, "they are here on that errand, concerning which we have already heard so much and so uselessly; but I rather think not, from this account; for what interest can they feel in one who is absolutely a stranger to them? It may be some idle conceit, however, connected with this same affair.

What is your wish, Ghita? This is Don Horatio Nelsoni, the illustrious English admiral, of whom you have heard so much."

"Eccellenza, I am sure of it;" answered Ghita, earnestly; "my good uncle, here, has told you who we are; and you may well guess our business. We came from St. Agata, on the other side of the bay, only this morning and heard, from a relation in the town, that Don Francesco had been seized that very hour. Since, we are told that he has been condemned to die, for treason against the king; and that, by officers who met in this very ship. Some even say, signora, that he is to meet his fate ere the sun set!"

"If this should be so, what reason is it that thou shouldst give thyself concern?"

"Eccellenza, he was my father's father; and though I never saw him, I know that the same blood runs in our veins. When this is so, there should be the same feelings in our hearts."

"This is well, Ghita, in appearance, at least; but thou canst hardly feel much for one thou never saw'st and who has even refused to own thee for a child. Thou art young, too, and of a sex that should be cautious; it is unwise for men, even, to meddle with politics in these troubled times."

"Signora, it is not politics that brings me here, but nature, and duty, and pious love for my father's father."

"What wouldst thou say, then?" answered the lady impatiently, "remember thou occupiest one whose time is precious, and of high importance to entire nations."

"Eccellenza, I believe it; and will try to be brief. I wish to beg my grandfather's life of this illustrious stranger. They tell me the king will refuse him nothing; and he has only to ask it of Don Ferdinando to obtain it."

Many would have thought the matured charms of the lady superior to the innocent-looking beauty of the girl: but no one could have come to such an opinion who saw them both at that moment. While Ghita's face was radiant with a holy hope, and the pious earnestness which urged her on, a dark expression lowered about the countenance of the English beauty, that deprived it of one of its greatest attractions by depriving it of the softness and gentleness of her sex. Had there not been observers of what passed, it is probable the girl would have been abruptly repulsed; but management formed no small part of the character of this woman, and she controlled her feelings, in order to effect her purpose.

"This admiral is not a Neapolitan, but an Englishman," she answered; "and can have no concern with the justice of your king. He would scarcely think it decent to interfere with the execution of the laws of Naples."

"Signora, it is always decent to interfere to save life; nay, it is more; it is merciful, in the eyes of God."

"What canst thou know of this? A conceit that thou hast the blood of the Caraccioli has made thee forget thy sex and condition, and placed a romantic notion of duty before thine eyes."

"No, signora, it is not so. For eighteen years I have been taught that the unfortunate admiral was my grandfather; but, as it has been his pleasure to wish not to see me, never have I felt the desire to intrude on his time. Before this morning, never has the thought that I have the blood of the Caraccioli crossed my mind, unless it was to mourn for the sin of my grandmother; and even now, it has come to cause me to mourn for the cruel fate that threatens the days of her partner in guilt."

"Thou art bold, to speak thus of thy parents, girl; and they, too, of the noble and great!"

This was said with a flushed brow, and still more lowering look; for, happily, there were incidents in the past life of that lady which made the simple language of a severe morality alike offensive to her ears and her recollections.

"It is not I, eccellenza, but God, that speaketh thus. The crime, too, is another reason why this great admiral should use his influence to save a sinner from so hurried an end. Death is terrible to all but to those who trust, with heart and soul, to the mediation of the Son of God; but it is doubly so when it comes suddenly and unlooked for. It is true, Don Francesco is aged; but have you not remarked, signora, that it is these very aged who become hardened to their state, and live on, as if never to die? I mean those aged, who suffer youth to pass, as if the pleasures of life are never to have an end."

"Thou art too young to set up for a reformer of the world, girl; and forgettest that this is the ship of one of the greatest officers in Europe, and that he has many demands on his time. Thou canst now go; I will repeat what thou hast said."

"I have another request to ask, eccellenza—permission to see Don Francesco; that I may at least receive his blessing."

"He is not in this ship. Thou wilt find him on board the *Minerva* frigate; no doubt, he will not be denied. Stop—these few lines will aid thy request. Addio, signorina."

"And may I carry hope with me, eccellenza? Think how sweet life is to those who have passed their days so long in affluence and honor. It would be like a messenger from Heaven for a grandchild to bring but a ray of hope."

"I authorize none. The matter is in the hands of the Neapolitan authorities; and we English cannot meddle. Go, now, both of you; the illustrious admiral has business of importance that presses."

Ghita turned, and slowly and sorrowfully she left the cabin. At the very door, she met the English lieutenant, who was in charge of the unhappy prisoner, coming with a last request that he might not be suspended like a thief, but might at least die the death of a soldier. It would exceed the limits set to our tale, were we to dwell on the conversation which ensued; but every intelligent reader knows that the application failed.

CHAPTER XIV.

IT is probable that Nelson never knew precisely what passed between Ghita and the lady mentioned in the last chapter. At all events, like every other application that was made to the English admiral, in connection with this sad affair, that of Ghita produced no results. Even the mode of execution was unchanged; an indecent haste accompanying the whole transaction, as in the equally celebrated trial and death of the unfortunate Duc d'Enghien. Cuffe remained to dine with the commander-in-chief, while Carlo Giuntotardi and his niece got into their boat, and took their way through the crowded roadstead toward the Neapolitan frigate that now formed the prison of the unfortunate Caraccioli.

A request, at the gangway, was all that was necessary to procure an admission on board the ship. As soon as the Signor Giuntotardi reached the quarter-deck, he let his errand be known, and a messenger was sent below to ascertain if the prisoner would see two visitors, the name of the uncle being alone given. Francesco Caraccioli, of the Princes Caraccioli, or, as he was more commonly called in English, Prince Caraccioli, was now a man approaching seventy; and being a member of one of the most illustrious houses of Lower Italy, he had long been trusted in employments of high dignity and command. On his offense—its apology—the indecent haste of his trial and execution, and the irregularity of the whole proceedings, it is now unnecessary to dwell; they have all passed into history, and are fa-

miliarly known to the world. That very morning had he been seized, and sent on board the *Foudroyant;* in the cabin of that vessel had a court of his own countrymen convened; and there had he been hastily condemned to death. The hour of doom was near; and he was already in the ship where the execution was to take place.

The messenger of Carlo Giuntotardi found this unfortunate man with his confessor, by whom he had just been shrived. He heard the request with cold indifference, but granted it on the instant, under the impression that it came from some dependent of his family or estates, who had a last favor to ask, or an act of justice to see performed.

"Remain here, father, I beseech you," said the prisoner, perceiving that the priest was about to retire; "it is some contadino, or some tradesman, whose claims have been overlooked. I am happy that he has come; one would wish to stand acquitted of injustice before he dies. Let them come in, my friend."

A sign was given with these words, the door of the cabin was opened, and Ghita, with her uncle, entered. A pause of quite a minute followed, during which the parties regarded each other in silence; the prisoner endeavoring in vain to recall the countenances of his guests and the girl trembling, equally with grief and apprehension. Then the last advanced to the feet of the condemned man, kneeled, bowed her head, and said—

"Grandfather, your blessing on the child of your only son."

"Grandfather! son! and his child!" repeated Don Francesco. "I had a son, to my shame and contrition be it now confessed; but he has long been dead. I never knew that he left a child!"

"This is his daughter, signore," replied Carlo Giuntottardi; "her mother was my sister. You thought us then too humble to be received into so illustrious a connection, and we have never wished to bring ourselves before your eyes until we thought our presence might be welcome."

"And thou comest now, good man, to claim affinity with a condemned criminal!"

"Not so, grandfather," answered a meek voice at his feet, "it is your son's daughter that craves a blessing from her dying parent. The boon will be well requited in prayers for your soul!"

"Holy Father! I deserve not this! Here has this tender plant lived, neglected in the shade, until it raises its timid head to offer its fragrance in the hour of death! I deserve not this!"

"Son, if Heaven offered no mercies until they are merited, hopeless, truly, would be the lot of man. But we must not admit illusions at such a moment. Thou art not a husband, Don Francesco; hadst thou ever a son?"

"That, among other sins, have I long since confessed; and, as it has been deeply repented of, I trust it is forgiven. I had a son—a youth who bore my name, even; though he never dwelt in my palace; until a hasty and indiscreet marriage banished him from my presence. I ever intended to pardon him, and to make provision for his wants; but death came too soon to both husband and wife to grant the time. This much I did know, and it grieved me that it was so; but of his child, never, before this instant, have I heard! 'Tis a sweet countenance, father; it seems the very abode of truth!'"

"Why should we deceive you, grandfather?" rejoined Ghita, stretching her arms upward, as if yearning for an embrace; "most of all at a time like this. We come not for honors, or riches, or your great name; we come simply to crave a blessing, and to let you know that a child of your own blood will be left on earth, to say aves in behalf of your soul."

"Holy priest, there can be no deception here! This dear child even looks like her wronged grandmother! and my heart tells me she is mine. I know not whether to consider this discovery a good or an evil, at this late hour, coming, as it does, to a dying man!"

"Grandfather, your blessing. Bless Ghita once, that I may hear the sound of a parent's benediction."

"Bless thee! bless thee, daughter!" exclaimed the admiral, bending over the weeping girl, to do the act she solicited, and then raising her to his arms, and embracing her tenderly; "this must be my child—I feel that she is no other."

"Eccellenza" said Carlo, "she is the daughter of your son, Don Francesco, and of my sister, Ghita Giuntotardi, born in lawful wedlock. I would not deceive any; least of all a dying man."

"I have no estate to bequeath, no honors to transmit, no name to boast of. Better the offspring of the lazzaroni than a child of Francesco Caraccioli at this moment."

"Grandfather, we think not of this—care not for this. I have come only to ask the blessing you have bestowed, and to offer the prayers of believers, though we are so lowly. More than this we ask not—wish not—seek not. Our poverty is familiar to us, and we heed it not. Riches would but distress us, and we care not for them."

"I remember, holy father, that one great reason of displeasure at my son's marriage was distrust of the motive of the family which received him; yet here have these honest people suffered me to live on unmolested in prosperity, while they now first claim the affinity in my disgrace and ignominy! I have not been accustomed to meet with wishes and hearts like these!"

"You did not know us, grandfather," said Ghita simply, her face nearly buried in the old man's bosom. "We have long prayed for you, and reverenced you, and thought of you as a parent, whose face was turned from us in anger; but we never sought your gold and honors."

"Gold and honors!" repeated the admiral, gently placing his granddaughter in a chair. "These are things of the past for me. My estates are sequestered—my name disgraced; and, an hour hence, I shall have suffered an ignominious death. No selfish views can have brought these good people, father, to claim affinity with me at a moment like this."

"It comes from the goodness of God, son. By letting you feel the consolation of this filial love, and by awakening in your own bosom the spark of parental affection, he foreshadows the fruits of his own mercy and tenderness to the erring but penitent. Acknowledge his bounty in your soul; it may bring a blessing on your last moment."

"Holy priest I hope I do. But what says this?"

Don Francesco took a note from the hand of a servant and read its contents eagerly; the world, and its feelings, having too much hold on his heart to be plucked out in an instant. Indeed so sudden had been his arrest, trial, and conviction, that it was not surprising the priest found in him a divided spirit, even at an instant like that. His countenance fell; and he passed a hand before his eyes, as if to conceal a weakness that was unbecoming.

"They have all denied my request, father," he said; "and I must die like a felon!"

"The Son of God suffered on the cross, suspended between thieves."

"I believe there is far less in these opinions than we are accustomed to think; yet it is cruel for one who has filled so high employments, a prince, a Caraccioli, to die like a lazzarone!"

"Grandfather—"

"Did you speak, child? I wonder not that this indignity should fill thee with horror."

"It is not that, grandfather," resumed

Ghita, shaking off her doubts, and looking up with flushed cheeks, and a face radiant with holy feelings. "O, it is not that. If my life could save thine, gladly would I give it up for such a purpose; but, do not—do not; at this awful moment, mistake the shadow for the substance. What matters it how death is met, when it opens the gates of heaven? Pain, I am sure, you cannot fear; even I, weak and feeble girl that I am, can despise that: what other honor can there be in the hour of death than to be thought worthy of the mercy and care of God? Caraccioli or lazzarone, prince or beggar, it will matter not, two hours hence; and let me reverently beg of you to humble your thoughts to the level which becomes all sinners."

"Thou say'st thou art my grandchild, Ghita, the daughter of my son Francesco?"

"Signore, I am, as all tell me; as my heart tells me, and as I believe."

"And thou lookest upon these opinions as unworthy, unsuited, if thou lik'st that better, to this solemn moment, and considerest the manner of a death matter of indifference, even to a soldier?"

"When placed in comparison with his hopes of heaven; when viewed through his own demerits, and the merits of his Saviour, grandfather?"

"And wilt thou, then, just entering on the stage of life, with the world before thee, and all that its future can offer, accompany me to the scaffold; let it be known to the mocking crowd that thou derivest thy being through the felon, and art not ashamed to own him as a parent?"

"I will, grandfather; this have I come to do," answered Ghita, steadily. "But do not ask me to look upon thy sufferings! All that can be done to lessen, by sharing thy disgrace, if disgrace it be, will I most gladly do, though I dread to see thy aged form in pain!"

"And this wilt thou do for one thou never beheld'st until this hour? one thou canst hardly have been taught to consider just to thyself?"

"If I have never seen thee before this visit, grandfather, I have loved thee and prayed for thee from infancy. My excellent uncle early taught me this duty; but he never taught me to hate thee or any one. My own father is taken away; and that which he would have been to thee this day, will I endeavor to be for him. The world is naught to me; and it will console thee to think that one is near whose heart weeps for thee, and whose soul is lost in prayers for thy eternal pardon."

"And this being, father, is made known to me an hour before I die! God punishes me sufficiently for the wrong I have done her, in letting me thus know her worth when it is too late to profit by it. No, Ghita, blessed child, such a sacrifice shall not be asked of thee. Take this cross; it was my mother's, worn on her bosom, and has long been worn on mine; keep it as a memorial of thy unhappy parent, and pray for me; but quit this terrible ship, and do not grieve thy gentle spirit with a scene that is so unfit for thy sex and years. Bless thee—bless thee, my child! Would to Heaven I had earlier known thee! but even this glimpse of thy worth has lightened my heart. Thou find'st me here a poor condemned criminal, unable to provide for thy future wants—nay, I can yet do a little for thee too. This bag contains gold. It has been sent to me by a relative, thinking it might be of service in averting the punishment that awaits me. For that purpose it is now useless; with thy simple habits, however, it will render thy life easy and above care."

Ghita, with streaming eyes, steadily put aside the gold, though she pressed the cross to her bosom, kissing it fervently again and again.

"Not that—not that, grandfather," she said; "I want it not—wish it not. This is enough; and this will I keep to my own last moment. I will quit the ship too; but not the place. I see many boats collecting, and mine shall be among them; my prayers shall go up to God for thee, now thou art living; and daily, after thou art dead. There needs no gold, grandfather, to purchase a daughter's prayers."

Don Francesco regarded the zealous and lovely girl with intense feeling; then he folded her to his heart once more, blessing her audibly, again and again. While thus employed, the *Foudroyant's* bell struck once, and then those of all the surrounding ships, English and Neapolitan, repeated the stroke. This, Caraccioli, a seaman himself, well knew denoted that the time was half-past four; five being the hour named for his execution. He felt it necessary, therefore, to dismiss his new-found relative, that he might pass a few more minutes alone with his confessor. The parting was solemn, but tender; and as Ghita left the cabin, her condemned grandfather felt as he would had he taken leave forever of one whom he had long loved, and whose virtues had been a solace to him from the hour of his birth.

The deck of the *Minerva* presented a sorrowful scene. Although the prisoner had been condemned by a court of Neapolitan officers, the trial was held under the

British ensign; and the feeling of the public was with the prisoner. There existed no necessity for the hurry in which everything had been done; no immediate danger pressed, and an example would have been more impressive had there been less of the appearance of a desire for personal vengeance, and more of the calm deliberation of justice in the affair. Ghita's connection with the prisoner could not even be suspected; but as it was known she had been in the cabin, and believed that she felt an interest in the condemned, the officers manifested an interest in her wishes and too evident emotions. An immense throng of boats had assembled around the ship; for hasty as had been the proceedings, the tidings that Francesco Caraccioli was to be hanged for treason, spread like wild-fire; and scarce a craft of proper size was left within the mole, so eager was the desire to witness that which was to occur. Either in the confusion, or bribed by money, the man who had brought off Carlo Giuntotardi and his niece, was no longer to be found; and the means of quitting the ship seemed, momentarily, to be lost.

"Here is a boat, close to our gangway," said the officer of the deck, who had kindly interested himself in behalf of so interesting a girl, "with a single man in it; a few grani would induce him to put you ashore."

The fellow in the boat was of the class of the lazzaroni, wearing a clean cotton shirt, a Phrygian cap, and cotton trousers, that terminated at the knees, leaving his muscular arms and legs entirely bare; models of the statuary in their neatness, vigor, and proportions. The feet, alone, formed an exception to the ordinary attire, for they were cased in a pair of quaint canvas shoes, that were ornamented a little like the moccasins of the American Indian. Carlo caught the eye of this man, who appeared to be eagerly watching the frigate's gangway for a fare, and holding up a small piece of silver, in a moment the light boat was at the foot of the accommodation ladder. Ghita now descended; and as soon as her uncle and she were seated, the skiff, for it was little more, whirled away from the ship's side, though two or three more, who had also been left by recreant boatmen for better fares, called out to him to receive them also.

"We had better go alone, even though it cost us a heavier price," quietly observed Carlo to his niece, as he noted this occurrence. "Pull us a short distance from the ship, friend—here, where there are fewer boats; and thou shall meet with a fair reward. We have an interest in this solemn scene, and could wish not to be observed."

"I know that well, Signor Carlo," answered the boatman; "and will see that you are not molested."

Ghita uttered a faint exclamation, and, looking up, first saw that the feigned lazzarone was no other than Raoul Yvard. As her uncle was too unobservant, in general, to detect his disguise, he made a sign for her to command herself, and continued rowing as if nothing had occurred.

"Be at ease, Ghita," said Carlo; "it is not yet the time, and we have twenty good minutes for our aves."

Ghita, however, was far from being at ease. She felt all the risks that the young man now ran, and she felt that it was solely on her account that he incurred them. Even the solemn feeling of the hour, and the occasion, was disturbed by his presence; and she wished he were away, on more accounts than one. Here he was, nevertheless, and in the midst of enemies; and it would not have been in nature, for one of her tender years and sex, and most of all, of her feelings, not to indulge in a sentiment of tender gratitude toward him, who had, as it were, thrust his head into the very lion's mouth, to do her a service. Between Raoul and Ghita there had been no reserves on the subject of parentage; and the former understood why his mistress was here, as well as the motive that brought her. As for the last, she glanced timidly around her, fearful that the lugger, too, had been brought into the throng of ships that crowded the anchorage. For this, however, Raoul was much too wary, nothing resembling his little craft being visible.

The reader will have understood that many vessels of war, English, Russian, Turkish, and Neapolitan, were now anchored in the bay. As the French still held the castle of St. Elmo, or the citadel that crowns the heights, that, in their turn, crown the town, the shipping did not lie quite as close to the mole as usual, lest a shot from the enemy above might do them injury; but they were sufficiently near to permit all the idle and curious of Naples, who had the hearts and the means, to pull off and become spectators of the sad scene that was about to occur. As the hour drew near, boat after boat arrived, until the *Minerva* was surrounded with spectators, many of whom belonged even to the higher classes of society.

The distance between the Neapolitan

frigate and the ship of the English rear-admiral was not great; and everything that occurred on board the former, and which was not actually hidden by the sides and bulwarks of the vessel itself, was easily to be seen from the deck of the latter. Still the *Foudroyant* lay a little without the circle of boats; and in that direction Raoul had pulled to avoid the throng, resting on his oars when about a third of a cable's length from the British admiral's stern. Here it was determined to wait for the awful signal and its fatal consequences. The brief interval was passed, by Ghita, in telling her beads, while Carlo joined in the prayers with the devotion of a zealot. It is scarcely necessary to say, that all this Raoul witnessed without faith, though it would be doing injustice to his nature, as well as to his love for Ghita, to say he did so without sympathy.

A solemn and expecting silence reigned in all the neighboring ships. The afternoon was calm and sultry, the zephyr ceasing to blow earlier than common, as if unwilling to disturb the melancholy scene with its murmurs. On board the *Minerva* no sign of life—scarcely of death—was seen; though a single whip was visible, rigged to the fore-yard-arm, one end being led in-board, while the other ran along the yard, passed through a leading block, in its quarter, and descended to the deck. There was a platform fitted on two of the guns beneath this expressive but simple arrangement; but, as it was in-board it was necessarily concealed from all but those who were on the *Minerva's* decks. With these preparations Raoul was familiar, and his understanding eye saw the particular rope that was so soon to deprive Ghita of her grandfather, though it was lost to her and her uncle among the maze of rigging by which it was surrounded.

There might have been ten minutes passed in this solemn stillness, during which the crowd of boats continued to collect: and the crews of different ships were permitted to take such positions as enabled them to become spectators of a scene that it was hoped might prove admonitory. It is part of the etiquette of a vessel of war to make her people keep close; it being deemed one sign of a well ordered ship to let as few men be seen as possible, except on those occasions when duty requires them to show themselves. This rigid rule, however, was momentarily lost sight of, and the teeming masses that floated around *La Minerva* gave up their thousands like bees clustering about their hives. It was in the midst of such

signs of expectation that the call of the boatswain was heard piping the side on board the *Foudroyant*, and four side-boys lay over on the accommodation-ladder, a mark of honor never paid to one of a rank less than that of a captain.

Raoul's boat was within fifty yards of that very gangway, and he turned his head in idle curiosity to see who might descend into the gig that was lying at the foot of the long flight of steps. An officer with one epaulette came first, showing the way to two civilians, and a captain followed. All descended in a line, and entered the boat. The next instant the oars fell, and the gig whirled around under the *Foudroyant's* stern, and came glancing up toward his own skiff. Four or five of the strong man-of-war jerks sufficed to send the long, narrow boat as far as was desired when the men ceased rowing, their little craft losing her way within ten feet of the skiff occupied by our party. Then it was that Raoul, to his surprise, discovered that the two civilians were no other than Andrea Barrofaldi and Vito Viti, who had accompanied Cuffe and Griffin, their companions in the gig, on a cruise, of which the express object was to capture himself and his vessel.

Another man would have been alarmed at finding himself in such close vicinity to his enemies; but Raoul Yvard was amused, rather than rendered uneasy, by the circumstance. He had faith in his disguise; and he was much too familiar with incidents of this sort not to retain his self-command and composure. Of course he knew nothing of the persons of the two Englishmen; but perfectly aware of the presence of the *Proserpine*, he guessed at their identity, and very correctly imagined the circumstances that brought companions so ill-assorted together. He had taken no precautions to disguise his face; and the red Phrygian cap which he wore, in common with thousands on that bay, left every feature and lineament fully expressed. With Ghita, however, the case was different. She was far better known to the two Elbans, as indeed was the person of her uncle, than he was himself; but both had veiled their faces in prayer.

"I do not half like this business, Griffin," observed the captain, as his gig entirely lost its way; "and wish with all my heart we had nothing to do with it. I knew this old Caraccioli, and a very good sort of man he was; and as to treason, it is not easy to say who is and who is not a traitor in times like these, in such a nation as this. Ha! I believe in my soul this is the same old man, and the same pretty girl, that came to see Nelson half an hour ago about this very execution!"

"What could they have to do with Prince Caraccioli, or his treason, sir? The old chap looks bookish; but he is not a priest; and, as to the girl, she is trim-built enough; I fancy the face is no great matter, however, or she would not take so much pains to hide it."

Raoul muttered a "sacr-r-re," between his teeth, but he succeeded in suppressing all outward expression of feeling. Cuffe, on the contrary, saw no other motive for unusual discretion beyond the presence of his boat's crew, before whom, however, he was accustómed to less reserve than with his people in general.

"If she be the same as the one we had in the cabin," he answered, "there is no necessity for a veil; for a prettier or more modest-looking girl is not often fallen in with. What she wanted exactly is more than I can tell you, as she spoke Italian altogether; and 'miladi' had the interview pretty much to herself. But her good looks seem to have taken with this old bachelor, the justice of the peace, who eyes her as if he had an inclination to open his mind to the beauty. Ask him in Italian, Griffin, what mare's nest he has run foul of now."

"You seem to have found something to look at besides the *Minerva*, Signor Podesta," observed Griffin, in an undertone. "I hope it is not Venus."

"Cospetto!" grunted Vito Viti, nudging his neighbor, the vice-governatore, and nodding toward the other boat; "if that be not little Ghita, who came to our island like a comet, and went out of it—to what shall I liken her sudden and extraordinary disappearance, Signor Andrea?"

"That of *Le Feu-Follet*, or ze *Ving-y-Ving*," put in Griffin, who, now he had got the two functionaries fairly afloat, spares none of the jokes that come so easy to a man-of-war's man. "She went out, too, in an 'extraordinary disappearance,' and perhaps the lady and the lugger went out together."

Vito Viti muttered an answer; for by this time he had discovered he was a very different personage on board the *Proserpine* from what the other had appeared to consider him while in his native land. He might have expressed himself aloud, indeed; but, at that instant, a column of smoke glanced out of the port bow of the *Minerva*, a yellow flag was shown aloft, and then came the report of the signal gun.

It has been said that vessels of war of four different nations were at that time lying in the Bay of Naples. Nelson had come in but a short time previously, with seventeen ships of the line; and he found several more of his countrymen lying there. This large force had been assembled to repel an expected attack on the island of Minorca, and it was still kept together in an uncertainty of the future movements of the enemy. A Russian force had come out of the Black Sea, to act against the French, bringing with it a squadron of the grand signior; thus presenting to the world the singular spectacle of the followers of Luther, devotees of the Greek Church, and disciples of Mohammed, uniting in defense of "our rights, our firesides, and our altars!" To these vessels must be added a small squadron of ships of the country; making a mixed force of four different ensigns that was to witness the melancholy scene we are about to relate.

The yellow flag and the signal-gun brought everything to a stand-still in all the fleets. The hoarse commands ceased, the boatswains and their mates laid aside their calls, and echoing midshipmen no longer found orders to repeat. The seamen gathered to the sides of their respective vessels; every port glistened with expectant eyes; the booms resembled clusters of bees suspended from the boughs of a forest; and the knightheads, taffrails, gangways and stretchers of the rigging were garnished with those whom bright buttons, glazed hats, epaulettes and dark-blue dresses denoted to belong to the privileged classes of a ship. Notwithstanding all this curiosity, nothing like the feeling which is apt to be manifested at an exhibition of merited punishment was visible in a single countenance. An expression resembling a somber gloom appeared to have settled on all those grim warriors of the deep; English, Russian, Neapolitan or Turk, apparently reserving all his sympathies for the sufferer, rather than for the majesty of justice. Still, no murmur arose, no sign of resistance was made, no look of remonstrance given.

The unseen mantle of authority covered all; and these masses of discontented men submitted; as we bow to what is believed to be the fiat of fate. The deep-seated and unresisting habit of discipline suppressed complaint; but there was a general conviction that some act was about to be committed that it were better for humanity and justice should not be done; or, if done at all, that it needed more of form, greater deliberation, and a fairer trial, to be so done as to obtain the commendation of men. The Turks alone showed apathy, though all showed submission. These subjects of destiny looked on coldly, though even among them a low rumor had passed that a malign influence prevailed in the fleet, and that a great and proud spirit had got to be mastered by the passion that so often deprives heroes of their self-command and independence.

Ghita ceased her prayers, as the report of the gun broke rudely on her ears, and with streaming eyes, she even dared to look toward the frigate. Raoul and all the rest bent their gaze in the same direction. The sailors among them saw the rope at the fore-yard-arm move, and then heads rose slowly above the hammock-cloths, when the prisoner and his attendant priest were visible even to their feet. The unfortunate Caraccioli, as has been said, had nearly numbered his threescore and ten years, in the regular course of nature; and his bare head now showed the traces of time. He wore no coat; and his arms were bound behind his back at the elbows, leaving just motion enough to the hands to aid him in the slighter offices about his own person. His neck was bare, and the fatal cord was tightened sufficiently around it to prevent accidents, constantly admonishing its victim of its revolting office.

A low murmur arose among the people in the boats as this spectacle presented itself to their eyes; and many bowed their faces in prayer. The condemned man caught a ray of consolation from this expression of sympathy; and he looked around him an instant with something like a return of those feelings of the world, which it had been his effort and his desire totally to eradicate, since he had taken leave of Ghita, and learned that his last request—that of changing his mode of punishment—had been denied. That was a fearful moment for one like Don Francesco Caraccioli, who had passed a long life in the midst of the scene that surrounded him; illustrious by birth, affluent, honored for his services, and accustomed to respect and deference. Never had the glorious panorama of the bay appeared more lovely than it did at that instant, when he was about to quit it forever, by a violent and disgraceful death. From the purple mountains—the cerulean void above him—the blue waters over which he seemed already to be suspended—and the basking shores, rich in their towns, villas and vines, his eye turned toward the world of ships, each alive with its masses of living men.

A glance of melancholy reproach was cast upon the little flag that was just waving at the mizzen mast-head of the *Foudroyant;* and then it fell on the carpet of faces beneath, that seemed fairly to change the surface of the smooth sea into an arena of human countenances. His look was steady, though his soul was in a tumult. Ghita was recognized by her companion, and by her dress. He moved toward the edge of his narrow scaffolding, endeavored to stretch forth his arms, and blessed her again aloud. The poor girl dropped on her knees in the bottom of the boat, bowed her head, and in that humble attitude did she remain until all was over; not daring once to look upward again.

"Son," said the priest, "this is a moment when the beautiful earth, and its feelings, must be forgotten."

"I know it, father," answered the old man, his voice trembling with emotion, for his sensations were too powerful, too sublime, even, for the degrading passion of fear; "but never before did this fair piece of the creation seem so lovely in my eyes as now, when I am about to quit it for the last time."

"Look beyond this scene, into the long vista of eternity, son; there thou wilt behold that which mocks at all human, all earthly means. I fear that our time is but short; hast thou aught yet to say, in the flesh?"

"Let it be known, holy priest, that in my dying moment I prayed for Nelson, and for all who have been active in bringing me to this end. It is easy for the fortunate, and the untempted, to condemn; but he is wiser, as he is safer, who puts more reliance on the goodness of God than on his own merits."

A ray of satisfaction gleamed athwart the pale countenance of the priest—a sincerely pious man, or fear of personal consequences might have kept him aloof from such a scene—and he closed his eyes, while he expressed his gratitude to God, in the secret recesses of his own spirit. Then he turned to the prince, and spoke cheeringly.

"Son," he said, "if thou quittest life with a due dependence on the Son of God, and in this temper toward thy fellow-creatures, of all this living throng, thou art he who is most to be envied! Address thy soul in prayer once more to Him who thou feelest can alone serve thee."

Caraccioli, aided by the priest, knelt on the scaffold; for the rope hung loose enough to permit that act of humiliation, and the other bent at his side.

"I wish to God Nelson had nothing to do with this!" muttered Cuffe, as he turned away his face, inadvertently bending his eyes on the *Foudroyant*, nearly under the stern of which ship his gig lay. There, in the stern-walk, stood the lady, already mentioned in this chapter, a keen spectator of the awful scene. No one but a maid was near her, however; the men of her companionship not being of moods stern enough to be at her side. Cuffe turned away from this sight, in still stronger disgust; and just at that moment a common cry arose from the boats. Looking round, he was just in time to see the unfortunate Caraccioli dragged from his knees by the neck, until he rose by a steady man-of-war pull to the end of the yard; leaving his companion alone on the scaffold, lost in prayer. There was a horrible minute, of the struggles between life and death, when the body, so late the tenement of an immortal spirit, hung, like one of the jewel-blocks of the ship, dangling passively at the end of the spar, as insensible as the wood which sustained it.

CHAPTER XV.

A LONG summer's evening did the body of Francesco Caraccioli hang suspended at the yardarm of the *Minerva;* a revolting spectacle to his countrymen, and to most of the strangers who had been the witnesses of his end. Then was it lowered into a boat, its feet loaded with a double-headed shot, and it was carried out a league or more into the bay, and cast into the sea. The revolting manner in which it rose to the surface and confronted its destroyers, a fortnight later, has passed into history; and to this day, forms one of the marvels related by the ignorant and wonder-loving of that region.[*] As for Ghita, she disappeared, no one knew how; Vito Viti and his companions being too much absorbed with the scene to note the tender and considerate manner in which Raoul rowed her off from a spectacle that could but be replete with horrors to one so situated. Cuffe, himself, stood but a few minutes longer; but he directed the boat's crew to pull alongside

of the *Proserpine*. In half-an-hour after the execution took place, this frigate was aweigh; and then she was seen standing out of the bay, before a light air, covered with canvas from her truck to the hammock-cloths. Leaving her for the moment, we will return to the party in the skiff.

Neither Carlo Giuntotardi nor Ghita Caraccioli—for so we must continue to call the girl, albeit the name is much too illustrious to be borne by one of her humble condition in life—but, neither of these two had any other design, in thus seeking out the unfortunate admiral, than to perform what each believed to be a duty. As soon as the fate of Caraccioli was decided, both were willing to return to their old position in life; not that they felt ashamed to avow their connection with the dead, but because they were quite devoid of any of that worldly ambition which renders rank and fortune necessary to happiness.

When he left the crowd of boats, Raoul pulled toward the rocks which bound the shores of the bay, near the gardens of Portici. This was a point sufficiently removed from the common anchorage to be safe from observation; and yet so near as to be reached in considerably less than an hour. As the light boat proceeded, Ghita gradually regained her composure. She dried her eyes and looked around her inquiringly, as if wondering whither their companion was taking them.

"I will not ask you, Raoul, why you are here, at a moment like this, and whence you have come," she said; "but I may ask whither you are now carrying us? Our home is at St. Agata, on the heights above Sorrento, and on the other side of the bay. We come there, annually, to pass a month with my mother's sister, who asks this much of our love."

"If I did not know all this, Ghita, I would not, and could not be here. I have visited the cottage of your aunt this day; followed you to Naples, heard of the admiral's trial and sentence, understood how it would affect your feelings, traced you on board the admiral's ship, and was in waiting as you found me; having first contrived to send away the man who took you off. All this has come about as naturally as the feeling which has induced me to venture again into the lion's mouth."

"The pitcher that goes often to the well, Raoul, gets broken at last," said Ghita, a little reproachfully, though it surpassed her power to prevent the tones of tenderness from mingling with her words.

---

[*] Singular as was this occurrence, and painful as it must have proved to the parties to the execution, it is one of the simplest consequences of natural causes. All animal matter swells in water previous to turning corrupt. A body that has become twice its natural size in this manner, as a matter of course, displaces twice the usual quantity of water: the weight of the mass remaining the same. Most human frames floating, in their natural state, so long as the lungs are inflated with air, it follows that one in this condition would bring up with it as much weight in iron as made the difference between its own gravity and that of the water it displaced. The upright attitude of Caraccioli was owing to the shot attached to his feet; of which, it is also probable, one or two had become loosened.

He moved towards the edge of his narrow scaffolding, endeavored to stretch forth his arms, and blessed her, again, aloud. The poor girl dropped on her knees, in the bottom of the boat, bowed her head, and in that humble attitude did she remain until all was over.—*Wing and Wing.*

"You know all, Ghita. After months of perseverance, and a love such as a man seldom felt before, you deliberately and coldly refused to be my wife; nay, you have deserted Monte Argentaro, purposely to get rid of my importunities; for there I could go with the lugger at any moment; and have come here, upon this bay, crowded with the English and other enemies of France, fancying that I would not dare to venture hither. Well, you see with what success; for neither Nelson nor his two-deckers can keep Raoul Yvard from the woman he loves, let him be as victorious and skillful as he may!"

The sailor had ceased rowing, to give vent to his feelings in this speech, neither of the two colloquists regarding the presence of Giuntotardi any more than if he had been a part of themselves. This indifference to the fact that a third person was a listener, proceeded from habit, the worthy scholar and religionist being usually too abstracted to attend to concerns as light as love and the youthful affections. Ghita was not surprised either at the reproaches of her suitor or at his perseverance; and her conscience told her he uttered but the truth, in attributing to her the motives he had, in urging her uncle to make their recent change of residence; for, while a sense of duty had induced her to quit the towers, her art was not sufficient to suggest the expediency of going to any other abode than that which she was accustomed to inhabit periodically, and about which Raoul knew, from her own innocent narrations, nearly as much as she knew herself.

"I can say no more than I have said already," the thoughtful girl answered, after Raoul had begun again to row. "It is better, on every account, that we should part. I cannot change my country; nor can you desert that glorious republic, of which you feel so proud. I am an Italian, and you are French; while, more than all, I worship my God, while you believe in the new opinions of your own nation. Here are causes enough for separation, surely, however favorably and kindly we may happen to think of each other in general."

"Tell me not any more of the heart of an Italian girl, and of her readiness to fly to the world's end with the man of her choice!" exclaimed Raoul, bitterly. "I can find a thousand girls in Languedoc who would make the circuit of the earth yearly, rather than be separated a day from the seamen they have chosen for their husbands."

"Then look among the girls of Languedoc for a wife," answered Ghita, with a smile so melancholy that it contradicted her words. "Better to take one of your own nation and opinions, Raoul, than risk your happiness with a stranger, who might not answer all your hopes, when you come to know her better."

"We will not talk further of this, now, dearest Ghita; my first care must be to carry you back to the cottage of your aunt; unless, indeed, you will at once embark in *Le Fou-Follet*, and return to the tower?"

"*Le Feu-Follet!* She is hardly here, in the midst of a fleet of her enemies! Remember, Raoul, your men will begin to complain, if you place them too often in such risks to gratify your own wishes."

"Peste! I keep them in good humor by rich prizes. They have been successful; and that which makes yonder Nelson popular, and a great man, makes Raoul Yvard popular, and a great man also, in his little way. My crew is like its captain; it loves adventures and it loves success."

"I do not see the lugger; among a hundred ships, there is no sign of yours?"

"The Bay of Napoli is large, Ghita" returned Raoul, laughing; "and *Le Feu-Follet* takes but little room. See, yonder vaisseaux-de-ligne appear trifling among these noble mountains, and on this wide gulf; you cannot expect my little lugger to make much show. We are small, Ghita mia, if not insignificant!"

"Still, where there are so many vigilant eyes, there is always danger, Raoul! Besides, a lugger is an unusual rig, as you have owned to me yourself."

"Not here, among all these Eastern craft. I have always found, if I wished to be unnoticed, it was best to get into a crowd; whereas, he who lives in a village, lives in open daylight. But we will talk of these things when alone, Ghita; yonder fisherman is getting ready to receive us."

By this time the skiff was near the shore, where a little yawl was anchored, containing a solitary fisherman. This man was examining them as they approached; and recognizing Raoul, he was gathering in his lines, and preparing to raise his grapnel. In a few minutes the two craft lay side by side; and then, though not without difficulty. owing to a very elaborate disguise, Ghita recognized Ithuel Bolt. A very few words sufficed to let the American into all that was necessary he should know, when the whole party made its arrangements to depart. The skiff which Raoul, having found it lying on the beach, had made free with without leave, he anchored, in the full expectation that its right owner might find it some day or other; while its cargo was transferred to the yawl, which was one of the lugger's own attendants. The latter was a light, swift-pulling little boat, admirably constructed, and fit to live in a seaway; requiring, moreover, but two good oars, one of which Raoul undertook to pull himself, while Ithuel managed the other. In five minutes after the junction was made the party was moving again from the land, in a straight line across the bay, steering in the direction of its southern cape, and proceeding with the steady, swift movement of men accustomed to the toil.

There are few portions of the sea in which a single ship or boat is an object of so little notice as the Bay of Naples. This is true of all times and seasons; the magnificent scale on which nature has created her panorama rendering ordinary objects of comparative insignificance; while the constant movement, the fruit of a million souls thronging around its teeming shores, covers it in all directions with boats, almost as the streets of a town are crowded with pedestrians. The present occasion, too, was one likely to set everything in motion; and Raoul judged rightly when he thought himself less likely to be observed in such a scene, than on a smaller and less frequented water. As a matter of course, while near the mole, or the common anchorage, it was necessary to pass amid a floating throng; but, once beyond the limits of this crowd, the size of the bay rendered it quite easy to avoid unpleasant collisions, without any apparent effort; while the passage of a boat, in any direction, was an occurrence too common to awaken distrust. One would think no more of questioning a craft that was encountered, even in the center of that spacious bay, than he would think of inquiring about the stranger met in the market-place. All this both Raoul and Ithuel knew and felt; and once in motion, in their yawl, they experienced a sense of security, that, for the four or five previous hours, had not always existed.

By this time, the sun was low, though it was possible, as Raoul perceived, to detect the speck that was still swinging at the *Minerva's* fore-yardarm; a circumstance to which the young man, with considerate feeling, refrained from adverting. The *Proserpine* had been some time in motion, standing out of the fleet under a cloud of canvas, but with an air so light as to permit the yawl to gain on her, though the heads of both were turned in the same direction. In this manner, mile after mile was passed, until darkness came. Then the moon arose, rendering the bay less distinct, it is true,

but scarcely more mysterious or more lovely than in the hours of stronger light. The gulf, indeed, forms an exception in this particular to the general rule, by the extent of its shores, the elevation of its mountains, the beauty of its water —which has the deep tint of the ocean off soundings—and the softness of the atmosphere; lending to it, by day, all the mellowed and dreamy charms that other scenes borrow from the illusions of night, and the milder brilliance of the secondary planets. Raoul did not exert himself at the oar; and, as he sat aft, his companion was obliged to take the stroke from his movement. It was so pleasant to have Ghita with him, on his own element, that he never hurried himself while in the enjoyment of her society. The conversation, it will readily be imagined, was not lively; but the saddened melancholy of Ghita's voice, as she occasionally hazarded a remark of her own, or answered one of his questions, sounded sweeter, in his ears, than the music of the ship's bands that was now wafted to them across the water.

As the evening advanced, the land-breeze increased, and the *Proserpine* gradually gained upon the boat. When the latter was about two-thirds of the distance across the bay, the frigate caught the stronger current that came down athwart the campagna, between Vesuvius and the mountains behind Castel-a-Mare, when she drove ahead fast. Her sails, as seamen express it, were all asleep; or swelled outward, without collapsing; and her rate of sailing was between five and six miles in the hour. This brought them up with the boat, hand-over-hand, as it is called; and Ghita, at Raoul's request, put the helm aside, in order that they might get out of the way of the huge body that was approaching. It would seem that there was some design, on the part of the ship, in coming so near, for she made a sheer toward the yawl, in a way to frighten the timid helmswoman, and to induce her to relinquish her hold of the tiller.

"Fear nothing," cried out Griffin, in Italian, "we intend to offer you a tow. Stand by, and catch the line. Heave!"

A small rope was thrown; and, falling directly across Ithuel's head, that person could do no less than seize it. With all his detestation of the English in general, and of this vessel in particular, the man-of-all-work had the labor-saving propensity of his countrymen; and it struck him as a good thing to make a "king's ship" aid an enemy's privateer, by accepting the offer. As he used the line with proper dexterity, the yawl was soon towing on the quarter of the frigate; Raoul taking the helm, and giving the boat the sheer necessary to prevent her dragging in alongside. This was a change so sudden, and so unexpected, that Ghita murmured her disapprobation, lest it should lead to a discovery of the true character of her companions.

"Fear nothing, dearest," answered Raoul, "they cannot suspect us; and we may learn something useful by being here. At all events, *Le Feu-Follet* is safe from their designs, just at this moment."

"Are you boatmen of Capri?" called out Griffin, who stood on the taffrail of the ship, with Cuffe and the two Italians near by; the first dictating the questions his lieutenant put.

"S'nore, si," answered Raoul, adopting the patois of the country, as well as he could, and disguising his deep mellow voice, by speaking in a high shrill key. "Boatmen of Capri, that have been to Napoli with wine, and have been kept out later than we intended by the spectacle at the yardarm of the *Minerva*. Cospetto! them signori make no more of a prince than we do of a quail, in the season, on our little island. (Pardon me, dearest Ghita; but we must throw dust into their eyes.)"

"Has any strange sail been seen about your island within the last twenty-four hours?"

"The bay is full of strange sail, s'nore; even the Turks coming to see us, since the last trouble with the French."

"Ay; but the Turks are now your allies, like us English. Have you seen any other strangers?"

"They tell me there are ships from the north, too, s'nore, off the town. Russians, I believe, they call them."

"They, too, are allies; but I mean enemies. Has there not been a lugger seen off your island, within the last day or two—a lugger of the French."

"Si—si—I know what you mean, now, s'nore; there has been a vessel like that you mention, off the island; for I saw her with my own eyes—si—si. It was about the twenty-third hour, last evening—a lugger, and we all said she must be French, by her wicked looks."

"Raoul!" said Ghita, as if reproaching him.

"This is the true way to befog them," answered the young man; "they have certainly heard of us; and by seeming to tell a little truth frankly, it will give me an opportunity of telling more untruth."

"Ah, Raoul, it is a sad life that renders untruths necessary!"

"It is the art of war, dearest; without it, we should soon be outwitted by these knaves of England. Si—si, s'nori; we all said just that, concerning her looks and rig."

"Will you sheer your boat alongside, friend," inquired Griffin, "and come on board of us? We have a ducat here that wants an owner; I fancy it will fit your pocket as well as another's. We will haul you ahead abreast of the gangway."

"Oh! Raoul, do not think of this rash act," whispered Ghita; "the vice-governatore, or the podesta, will recollect you; then all will be lost!"

"Fear nothing, Ghita! a good cause and keen wit will carry me through; while the least hesitation might, indeed, ruin us. These English first ask, and then take without asking, if you tell them no. Corpo di Bacco! who ever heard, either, of a lazzarone's refusing a ducat!"

Raoul then whispered a few words to Ithuel, when, the boat being by this time far enough ahead, he gave it a sheer alongside of the ship, seized a man-rope, and went up the cleats as actively as a cat. It is certain, not a soul on board that fine frigate had the least suspicion of the true character of the individual who now confidently trod her quarter-deck. The young man, himself, loved the excitement of such an adventure, and he felt the greater confidence in his impunity from the circumstance that there was no other light than that of the moon. The sails, too, cast their shadows upon deck; and then, neither of the two Italians was a wizard at detecting impostors, as he knew by experience.

The watch was set for the night, and Winchester, who had returned to duty, held the trumpet, while Griffin had no other immediate office but to interpret. Two or three midshipmen were lounging about the quarter-deck; here and there a seaman was on the lookout, at the halyards, or on a cathead; some twenty or thirty old sea-dogs were pacing the gangways or the forecastle, with their arms crossed, and their hands stuck in their jackets; and a quick-eyed, active quartermaster stood near the man at the wheel, conning the ship. The remainder of the watch had stowed themselves between the guns, or among the booms, in readiness to act, but in truth dozing. Cuffe, Griffin, and the two Italians descended from the taffrail, and awaited the approach of the supposed lazzerone, or boatman of Capri, as he was now believed to be, near the stern of the vessel. By an arrangement among themselves, Vito Viti became the spokesman; Griffin translating to the captain all that passed in an undertone as soon as it was uttered.

"Come hither, friend," commenced the podesta, in a patronizing, but somewhat lofty manner, "this generous and noble English captain, Sir Kooffe, desires me to present you with a ducat, by way of showing that he asks no more of you than he is willing to pay for. A ducat* is a great deal of money, as you know; and good pay merits good services."

"S'nore, si; your eccellenza says the truth; a good ducat certainly deserves good services."

"Bene. Now tell these signori all you know about that said lugger; where you saw her; when you saw her; and what she was about. Keep your mind clear, and tell us one thing at a time."

"S'nore, si. I will keep my mind clear, and tell you no more than one thing at a time. I believe, eccellenza, I am to begin with where I saw her; then I'm to tell you when I saw her; after which, you wish to know what she was about. I believe this is the way you put it, s'nore?"

"Excellently well; answer in that order, and you will make yourself understood. But first, tell me—do all the natives of Capri speak the same sort of Italian as you do, yourself, friend?"

"S'nore, si—though my mother having been a French woman, they tell me that I have caught a little from her. We all get something from our mothers, eccellenza; and it's a pity we could not keep more of it."

"True, friend; but now for the lugger. Remember that honorable signori will hear what you say; therefore, for your own credit, speak to the point; and speak nothing but truth, for the love of God."

"Then, s'nore, first as to where I saw her—does your eccellenza mean where I was at the time, or where the lugger was?"

"Where the lugger was, fellow. Dost think Sir Kooffe cares where thou spent thy day!"

"Well, then, eccellenza, the lugger was near the Island of Capri, on the side next the Mediterranean, which, you know, s'nore, is on the side opposite to the bay, and near, as might be, abreast of the house of Giacomo Alberti; does your eccellenza know anything of the house I mean?"

"Not I; but tell your story as if I knew all about it. It is these particulars which

give value to a tale. How far from the nearest land? Mention that fact by all means, if you happen to remember."

"Well, eccellenza, could the distance be measured, now, I think it would prove to be about as far—not quite, s'nore, but I say, about—about as far from the said Giacomo's large fig tree, to the Vines of Giovanni, his wife's cousin. Si—I think, just about that distance."

"And how far might that be, friend? Be precise as much may depend on your answers."

"S'nore, that may be a trifle farther than it is from the church to the top of the stairs that lead to Anna Capri."

"Cospetto! Thou wilt earn thy ducat speedily, at this rate! Tell us at once, in miles: was the lugger one, two, six, or twenty miles from your island at the time thou speak'st of?"

"Eccellenza, you bid me speak of the *time*, in the second place; after I had told you *where*, in the first place. I wish to do whatever will give you pleasure, s'nore."

"Neighbor Vito Viti," put in the vice-governatore, "it may be well to remember that this matter is not to be recorded as you would put on file the confession of a thief; it may be better to let the honest boatman tell his story in his own way."

"Aye, now the veechy has set to work, I hope we shall get the worth of our ducat," observed Cuffe in English.

"S'nori," rejoined Raoul, "it shall be just as your eccellenzi say. The lugger you speak of was off the island last evening, sterring toward Ischia; which place she must have reached in the course of the night, as there was a good land wind from the twenty-third to the fifth hour."

"This agrees with our account as to the time and place," said Griffin; "but not at all as to the direction the corsair was steering. We hear she was rather rounding the southern cape for the Gulf of Salerno."

Raoul started, and gave thanks, mentally, that he had come on board, as this statement showed that his enemies had received only too accurate information of his recent movements. He had hopes, however, of being able yet to change their intentions, and of putting them on the wrong scent.

"S'nori," he said, "I should like to know who it is that mistakes southeast for southwest. None of our pilots or boatmen, I should think, could ever make so great a blunder. S'nore, you are an officer, and understand such things; and I will just ask you, if Ischia does not lie northwest of Capri?"

* The silver ducat of Naples is worth 80 grani, or rather less than 80 cents; the golden ducat, or sequin, of Italy, Holland, Turkey, etc., is worth a trifle more than two American dollars. Raoul was offered the former.

"Of that fact there can be no manner of doubt," returned Griffin; "it is equally true that the Gulf of Salerno lies southeast of both—"

"There, now!" interrupted Raoul, with a well-acted assumption of vulgar triumph; "I knew your eccellenza, when you came to look into it, would see the folly of saying that a vessel which was standing from Capri toward Ischia, was going on any other course than northwest!"

"But this not the question, amico. We all understand the bearings of these islands, which are the bearings of the whole coast, down heraway; but the question is which way the lugger was steering?"

"I thought I had said, eccellenza, that she was heading across toward Ischia," answered Raoul, with an air of obtuse innocence.

"If you do, you give an account exactly different from that which has been sent to the admiral by the good bishop of your own island. May I never eat another of his own quails, if I think *he* would deceive us; and it is not easy to suppose a man like him does not know north from south."

Raoul inwardly muttered a malediction on all priests; a class of men which, rightly enough, he believed to be united in their hostility to France. But it would not do to express this, in his assumed character; and he affected to listen, as one of his class ought to give ear to a fact that came from his spiritual father.

"North from south, eccellenza! Monsignore knows a great deal more than that, if the truth were said; though, I suppose, these noble signori are acquainted with the right reverend father's great infirmity?"

"Not we—none of us, I fancy, ever had the honor to be in his company. Surely, fellow, your bishop is a man of truth?"

"Truth! Yes, eccellenza, so true is he that if he were to tell me that the thing I saw myself, had not, and could not happen, I should rather believe monsignore than believe my own eyes. Still, signori, eyes are something; and as the right reverend father has none, or what are as bad as none, for any use they can be in looking at a vessel half a mile off, he may not always see what he thinks he sees. When monsignore tells us that so and so is gospel, we all believe it, for we know the time has been when he could read; but we never think of going to his door to ask which way a ship is steering, having the use of our own senses."

"Can this fellow tell us the truth, Griffin?" asked Cuffe, a good deal mystified by Raoul's artifice, and his assumed simplicity. "If so, we shall be going exactly on the wrong scent, by hauling round Campanella, and running into the Gulf of Salerno. The French hold Gaeta yet, and it is quite likely that Master Yvard may wish to keep a friendly port open under his lee!"

"You forget, Captain Cuffe, that his lordship has sent a light cruiser already up that way; and *Le Feu-Follet* would hardly dare to show herself near one of our regular fellows—"

"Umph! I don't know that, Mr. Griffin; I don't exactly know that. The *Proserpine* is a 'regular fellow,' after a fashion, at least; and the *Few-Folly* has dared to show herself to her. Jack-o'-Lantern? D—n me, Griffin, but I think she is well named now. I'd rather chase a jack-'o-lantern in the Island of Sicily, than be hunting after such a chap; first he's here; then he's there; and presently he's nowhere. As for the sloop, she's gone south, at my suggestion, to look into the bays along the Calabrian coast. I told Nelson I wanted another ship; for, just so certain as this Rule—Raw-owl—what the d—l do you call the pirate, Griffin?"

"Raoul, Captain Cuffe; Raoul Yvard is his name. 'Tis thoroughly French. Raoul means Rodolph."

"Well, I told Nelson if this lad should get to dodging round one of the islands, we might as well set about playing 'puss in the corner,' by the week, as to think of driving him off the land, for a fair chase. He works his boat like a stage-coach turning into an inn-yard!"

"I wonder my lord did not think of this, and give us a sloop or two to help us."

"Catch Nell at that! He might send one Englishman to look after two Frenchmen; but he'd never dream of sending two Englishmen to look after one Frenchman."

"But this is not a fighting matter, sir, only a chase; and one Frenchman will run faster than two Englishmen, any day of the week."

"Sa-c-r-r-e!" muttered Raoul, in a tone that he endeavored to suppress, and which was inaudible to all ears but those of Andrea Barrofaldi; the vice-governatore happening to stand nearer his person just at that moment than any other of the party.

"Very true," answered Cuffe; "but so it is. We are sent alone; and if this *Few-Folly* get in between Ischia and Procida, it will be easier to unearth the fox than to drive her out single-handed.

As for any more boat service against her, I suppose you've all had enough of that?"

"Why, sir, I rather think the people would be shy," answered Griffin, with a little hesitation of manner, and yet with the directness and simplicity of a truly great man. "We must let them get over the last brush before they are depended on much for any new set-to of that sort."

"Bon!" muttered Raoul, quite unconscious he was overheard.

"Nevertheless, we must catch this fellow, if we wear out our shoes in the chase."

All this time Andrea Barrofaldi and Vito Viti were profoundly ignorant of what was passing between the two officers, though Raoul listened eagerly, and so well understood every syllable they uttered. Until this moment the vice-governatore had been rather indifferent and inattentive as to what occurred; but the two exclamations of Raoul awakened a vague distrust in his mind, which, while it had no direct object, was certainly pregnant with serious consequences to the Frenchman himself. Deep mortification at the manner in which they had been duped by this celebrated privateersman, with a desire to absent themselves from the island until the edge was a little taken off the ridicule they both felt they merited, blended with certain longings to redeem their characters, by assisting in capturing the corsair, were the reasons why these two worthies, the deputy-governor and the podesta, were now on board the *Proserpine.*

Cuffe had offered them cots in his cabin, and seats at his table, in a moment of confidence; and the offer was gladly accepted. Andrea had not been on board the ship a day, however, before he became thoroughly convinced of his utter uselessness; a circumstance that added materially to the awkwardness of his situation. Like all well-meaning and simple-minded men he had a strong wish to be doing; and day and night he ruminated on the means by himself, or discussed them in private dialogues with his friend the podesta. Vito Viti frankly admonished him to put his faith in Heaven, affirming that something worth while would yet turn up in the cruise, to render the enterprise memorable; it being the habit of the magistrate to say an ave or two on all trying occasions, and then trust to God.

"You never knew a miracle, vice-governatore," said Vito Viti one day, when they were discussing the matter by themselves; "you never knew a miracle come to pass that another was not close on its heels; the first being a mere prepa-

ration for the last, and the last always proving to be the most remarkable. Now, when Annina Gotti fell off the cliffs, it was a miracle she didn't break her neck; but, when she rolled over into the sea, it was a much greater she wasn't drowned!"

"It is better to leave these things to the Church, neighbor Vito," was the vice-governatore's answer; "nor do I see that there has been any miracle in the affair to start with."

"How! Do you not call it a miracle, Signor Andrea, that two such men as you and I should be deceived, as we were beyond all doubt, by this knave of a French corsair? I look upon it as so great a miracle, myself, that it ought to follow, instead of going before its companion."

To this Andrea made an answer, suitable to his greater information, and the discourse took its usual direction toward the means of doing something to relieve the two functionaries from the stigma that they mutually felt now rested on their sagacity, and that, too, as this sagacity might be considered conjointly or individually.

It was probably owing to this fever of the mind that the vice-governatore, a man usually so simple and confiding, was now so suspicious and keen-sighted. The presence of Carlo Giuntotardi and Ghita had at first struck him as a little out of the common way; and though he could not distinguish their faces by the light of the moon, and at the distance at which they were placed in the yawl, he fancied from the first that his old acquaintances were in the boat the ship was towing. Now Andrea Barrofaldi certainly had never before that day connected Ghita or her uncle in any manner with Raoul Yvard; but it was beyond dispute that the mysterious manner in which they disappeared from the island had excited some remark; and in his present state of mind, it was not an extraordinary circumstance that he had some distant and vague glimmerings of the truth. But for Raoul's indiscreet exclamations, however, nothing probably would have come of these indistinct fancies; and we are to refer all that followed to those unguarded outbreakings of the Frenchman's humor, rather than to any very clear process of ratiocination on the part of the vice-governatore.

Just as Cuffe made the declaration last recorded, Andrea stepped up to the spot where he and Griffin were conversing apart, and whispered a few words in the ear of the latter.

"The d——l!" exclaimed the lieutenant, in English. "If what the vice-governatore tells me be true, Captain Cuffe, the work is half done to our hands!"

"Ay, the veechy is a good fellow at the bottom, Griffin; though he'll never burn the bay of Naples. What has he to say now?"

Griffin led his captain a little aside, and conferred a moment with him alone. Orders were then passed to the officer of the watch, when Cuffe and his companion went below, like men in a hurry.

CHAPTER XVI.

DURING the momentous five minutes occupied in these private movements, Raoul affected to be gaping about in vulgar astonishment, examining the guns, rigging, ornaments of the quarter-deck, etc.; though, in truth, nothing that passed among those near him escaped his attention. He was uneasy at the signs of the times, and now regretted his own temerity; but still he thought his incognito must be impenetrable. Like most persons who fancy they speak a foreign language well, he was ignorant, too, in how many things he betrayed himself; the Englishman, *cœteris paribus*, usually pronouncing the Italian better than the Frenchman, on account of the greater affinity between his native language and that of Italy, in what relates to emphasis and sounds. Such was the state of mind of our hero then, as he got an intimation that the captain of the ship wished to see him below. Raoul observed, as he descended the ladder to comply with what sounded very much like an order, that he was followed by the two Elban functionaries.

The cabin-lamp was trimmed, and the privateersman found himself under a strong light, as soon as he had crossed the threshold of the apartment. Cuffe and Griffin were standing near the table, where the vice-governatore and the podesta took their stations also; giving the arrangement a most uncomfortable air of investigation and justice. For an instant, Raoul wished that it was a portion of the Holy Inquisition, rather than the tribunal before which he now found himself so unexpectedly arraigned.

"You must be cool," said Griffin, as the other moved slowly up to the table, maintaining the outward signs of steadiness, but cursing in his heart the severe ordeal which he felt he was undergoing; "do me the favor to put this silk handkerchief about your neck."

"S'nore, your eccellenza is pleased to joke; we men of Capri think little of the nights at this season of the year; still, as it seems to be your wish I will honor myself so much."

In that age, a black silk handkerchief was the certain mark of a military man. The old-fashioned stock had gone out, with all but old-fashioned people, and the new-fashioned substitute did not make its appearance until many years later; the present usage, indeed, having come in from a military mania which pervaded Christendom at the close of the last general war. Black around the neck, properly relieved by the white of the linen, was then deemed properly military; and even in the ordinary dress, such a peculiarity was as certain a sign as the cockade that the owner bore arms. Raoul knew this, and he felt he was aiding in unmasking himself, by complying; but he thought there might be greater danger should he refuse to assume the kerchief.

"Your eccellenza is making a prince of a very humble boatman," he said, when his neck was fairly enveloped; "and my wife will think some great general is coming, when I enter the door."

"To help the delusion, friend, wear this also," continued Griffin, throwing the other one of his own undress uniform coats, his stature and that of Raoul being very nearly the same.

The true state of the case was now getting to be somewhat unequivocal; nevertheless, as steadiness and compliance were his only hopes, Raoul did as desired, and stood with all his upper man decorated in an English naval undress uniform, while his nether remained a la lazzarone.

"What say you now, vice-governatore," resumed Griffin; "here are lights, and the dress!"

"I say that this gentleman has done me the honor of several visits in my poor residence at Porto Ferrajo," returned Andrea; "and that never has he been more welcome than he is at this moment. Signor Smees, you are a great lover of masquerades, and make a carnival of the whole year. I trust your distinguished countryman, Sir Cicero, will have it in his power to convince these brave Inglese that all is done in pure pleasantry, and without a crime."

"Messieurs," said Raoul, stripping himself of his borrowed plumes, "it is too late to feign any longer. If I am Raoul Yvard, as you say, I am certainly not *Le Feu-Follet.*"

"Of course, you are aware, monsieur," observed Griffin, in French, "that you are a prisoner to his Britannic Majesty?"

"Sa Majeste Britannique has not made a conquest equal to his success at the Nile," returned Raoul, ironically; "but he has me in his hands. It is not the first time that I have had the honor to be a prisoner of war, and that, too, in one of his own ships."

"You are not to suppose that such will be your situation now, Monsieur Yvard. We arrest you in a totally different character."

"Not as a friend, I trust, monsieur; for, I protest, I have not the smallest claim to the character; as witness a short interview off Porte Ferrajo, and an interesting incident at the mouth of the Golo."

"Your taunts may be spared, sir; fortune favored you then, we allow; but now we arrest you as a spy."

"Espion!" repeated Raoul, starting; "that is an office I never contemplated, monsieur, on coming on board your ship. You will do me the justice to acknowledge that it was only at your own invitation that I came on deck. 'Twould be an infamy to pretend differently."

"We will endure the infamy of our acts, Monsieur Yvard. No one accuses you of having come on board the *Proserpine* as a spy; but, when an enemy is found rowing about our fleet, which is anchored in a hostile bay, and this in a disguise like yours, it must be a very scrupulous conscience that hesitates to pronounce him a spy, and liable to the punishment of one."

This was so true that the unfortunate young man now felt the exceeding delicacy of his situation. In coming into the bay, he had certainly been led by no other intention than to find Ghita; and yet he could not but confess to himself that he should not have hesitated about profiting, in his public character, by any information incidentally obtained. He had subjected himself to the severest penalties of military law, by yielding to his passion for Ghita; and he could not discover a single available excuse to plead in mitigation.

"What does the poor fellow say, Griffin?" asked Cuffe, who felt regret that so brave an enemy should be reduced to so desperate a strait, notwithstanding his determined hostility to all Frenchmen; "do not bear too hard upon him, at his first go off. Has he any excuse for his disguise?"

"The usual apology, no doubt, sir—a desire to serve his one and undivided republic! If we should believe all chaps tell us, Captain Cuffe, we might go home and send deputies to the National Convention; if, indeed, they would do us the favor to admit them to seats."

"Gentlemen," said Raoul, in English, "there is no longer any occasion for an interpreter between us; I speak your language sufficiently well to make myself understood."

"I am sorry for your situation, Mr. Yvard," said Cuffe, "and wish, with all my heart, you had fallen into our hands in open battle instead of in this irregular way."

"In which case, Monsieur le Capitaine, *Le Feu-Follet* would have been in your power also!" returned Raoul, smiling ironically; "but, messieurs, words are idle now; I am your prisoner, and must take my chance with you. There is no necessity, however, for causing others to suffer for my indiscretion. I shall esteem it a favor, messieurs, if you will let the good people in the boat alongside pull ashore without molestation. It is getting late, and we must now be nearly or quite abeam of the place where they wish to land; which is the Maria Grande of Sorrento."

"Do you wish us to understand that your companions are not French, Monsieur Yvard?"

"Oui, Monsieur le Capitaine; there is not a Frenchman among them, I give you my parole d'honneur."

"Of that fact it may be well to satisfy ourselves by an examination, Captain Cuffe," put in Griffin, dryly.

"I have sent up to beg Mr. Winchester would get these people on board—"

"There is a young woman in the boat who is unaccustomed to entering ships," interrupted Raoul, hastily, "and I implore your tenderness in her behalf. Let the men come on board, if you think it necessary; but the signorina can never climb this frigate's sides!"

"We will see to that, more especially, Monsieur Yvard, as you appear to be so much interested in the lady's comfort. At present it will be my duty to put you under a sentry's charge, and that it may be done in a way the least offensive to yourself, your prison, for the night at least, shall be this cabin. Mr. Griffin, give orders to the marine officer accordingly."

In a few minutes a soldier was introduced into the forward cabin, and Raoul was regularly placed under his charge. Not till then did the officers return to the quarter-deck. All this time Ithuel and his companions in the yawl were left to their own reflections, which were anything but agreeable. Matters had been conducted so quietly in-board, however, that they possessed no clew to what had actually occurred; though Ghita, in particular, was full of forebodings and apprehensions. The frigate towed them quite abreast of their landing, and within a league of it ; and yet she showed no signs of an intention to abate her speed, nor did any one appear at the gangway to speak to them. At length a hoarse call was heard on deck, and the ship began to shorten sail. Her forecourse was hauled up, and the spanker was brailed ; then the royals were clewed up and furled ; the topgallant-sails followed and presently the *Proserpine* was reduced to her three topsails and jib. All this, finished just as Cuffe reappeared on deck, was done by the watch, and in about five minutes. As soon as sail was thus taken in the helm was put to port, the ship came up to the wind on the starboard tack, and the main topsail was laid to the mast, bringing the yawl under her lee, and close alongside of the ship.

The maneuver was no sooner executed than a seaman ran lightly down the vessel's side, and entered the yawl. After examining forward and aft he called out, "All right sir,"and shoved the boat off to a little distance from the frigate. The yard and stay-tackles fell, at the next instant were overhauled down, and hooked by the man in the boat. The boatswain's mate, in the gangway, piped "Haul taut!" and the slack of the tackle was pulled in ; then followed a long, steady blow of the call, piping "Sway away!" and the boat, with all in her, rose from the water, and ascended as high as the hammock-cloths in the waist, when the stay-tackles took the strain, the yard-tackles "eased off," and the boat was landed in the waist of the ship as gingerly as if it were made of glass, and as steadily as if it had no more weight than a seaman's hammock. Ghita uttered a faint scream when she found herself rising into the air, and then she hid her face, awaiting the result with dread. As for Carlo Giuntotardi, the movement aroused him a little from his customary apathy, and that was all ; whereas, Ithuel bethought him seriously of leaping into the water, and striking out for the land. He could swim a league, he thought ; but there was the certainty of being followed by boats, and overtaken ; a consideration that effectually curbed his impatience.

It is not easy to describe the sensation with which this man found himself once more standing on the deck of his old prison, with the additional danger of being detected and treated as a deserter. It may sound revolting, at the present day, to suppose a case in which a foreigner was thrown by violence into the military service of a nation, and then was put in jeopardy of his life, because he used a privilege of nature to fly from such persecution as soon as circumstances placed the means in his power. The last age, however, witnessed many scenes of similar wrongs ; and, it is to be feared, in spite of all the mawkish philanthropy and unmeaning professions of eternal peace that it is now the fashion to array against the experience of mankind, that the next age will present their parallels, unless the good sense of this nation infuse into the federal legislative bodies juster notions of policy, more extended views of their own duties, and more accurate opinions of the conditions of the several communities of Christendom, than has marked their laws and reasoning for the past few months.* In a word, the subject of all these tribulations felt an intimate conviction that his rights, legal and moral, would avail him but little on the present occasion. Then a man never does wrong, even in the defense of that which is inherently his due, without the secret consciousness that "Evil may not be done, that good may come of it ; " and Ithuel had a certain inward monitor to remind him that, much as he had in the way of justifiable complaint, he had carried the war into the enemy's country.

The boat had no sooner touched the deck, than its cargo was handed out by the boatswain, who, keeping no watch, had not yet turned in : and who was almost as important a functionary on board the *Proserpine* as was Vito Viti in the town of Porto Ferrajo. He examined each individual, as he or she landed, as he called it : Ghita attracting so much of his attention as completely to eclipse her companions. The soft air and manner of the girl appeared so winning, indeed, by the light of the moon, which now fell clear upon the decks, that all near her, including the officers, submitted to very much the same influence.

"So, so, Master Yvard," said Cuffe, in English, "if you do come into an enemy's camp incognito, it is in reasonably good company. That girl is Italian, Winchester; and she even seems modest!"

"Little Ghita!" exclaimed Vito Viti, "as I hope one day to lie in the bosom of Father Abraham! Bellissima Ghita, what has brought thee here, and in such evil company?"

Ghita was in tears ; but, uncertain how far Raoul was committed, she struggled

---

* The question of impressment is now settled forever. The United States have now a mortgage on the Canadas to secure the good behavior of Great Britain.

for self-command, and did succeed in suppressing emotions that might otherwise have rendered his situation more dangerous. Drying her eyes, she courtesied to the vice-governatore and the podesta, and then answered the question.

"Signori," she said, "it is a relief to meet countrymen and old acquaintances on board this strange ship; and I look to you for protection. I do not call it strange, or evil company, for an orphan niece to be on the water with her uncle, and one that has ever been a father to her."

"Ah! sure enough, vice-governatore, this is Carlo Giuntotardi, the uncle; and the man who dwells so much with the saints, even on earth, that he seldom speaks to a sinner. But thou knowest, little Ghita, that one of thy watermen is no less a person than Raoul Yvard, the wickedest corsair that sails out of France, and the pest and persecution of the whole Italian coast? Did the Church condescend to notice such an unbelieving republican, it would be to command all its faithful to unite in their prayers for his destruction."

" Raoul Yvard!" repeated Ghita, with sufficient astonishment in her manner to satisfy any reasonable amount of wonder, on the part of the other. "Are you certain, Signor Podesta, of the truth of what you say?"

"As certain as the confession of the party himself can make us."

"Confession, signore!"

"Si, bella Ghita, confession; your boatman—your man of Capri—your lazarone, confesses himself to be neither more nor less than the commander of that worker of iniquity, *Le Feu-Follet*."

"Does *Le Feu-Follet* do more than other cruisers of the enemy?" but Ghita felt she was getting to be indiscreet, and she ceased.

"I do believe, Winchester," said Cuffe, "that this is the very girl, and yonder is the very old man, who came into Nelson's cabin to-day, with something to say about the poor prince who was executed this afternoon!"

"What could such people have in common with the unfortunate Caraccioli?"

"Sure enough; yet these are the people. The Queen of the Fleet, our Lady Admiraless, had it all to herself; and what passed between them in Italian, I know no more than if it had been in Greek. She never told me, you may rest assured; and, from the look of her eye, I question a good deal if she ever told Nelson."

"I wish to heaven his lordship would cut adrift from his moorings alongside that craft, Captain Cuffe. I do assure you, sir, the fleet begins to talk loudly on the subject; was it any other man, there'd be the devil to pay about it—but we can all stand a good deal from Nelson and Bronte."

"Well—well; let every man father his own children; you ought to be quiet, Winchester, for he asked very kindly about your hurt to-day, and would have sent you aboard some knick-knack or other for the stomach, but I told him you were all ataunto again, and at duty. What between his head, and his arm, and his eye, he's got to be such a hulk himself that he thinks every wounded man a sort of a relation. I should not complain, however, if the small-pox could lay hold of that beauty."

"This has been a bad day's work for England, depend on it, Captain Cuffe!"

"Well, if it has, St. Vincent and the Nile were good days' works; and we'll let one balance the other. Inquire of this young woman, Mr. Griffin, if I had not the pleasure of seeing her to-day on board the *Foudroyant?*"

The question was put, as desired, and Ghita quietly, but unhesitatingly, answered in the affirmative.

"Then ask her to explain how she happened to fall into the company of Raoul Yvard?"

"Signori," said Ghita, naturally, for she had nothing to conceal on this point, "we live on Monte Argentaro, where my uncle is the keeper of the prince's towers. You know, we have much to fear from the barbarians along all that coast; and last season, when the peace with France kept the Inglesi at a distance—I know not how it is, signori, but they say the barbarians are always hardest on the enemies of Inghilterra—but, the past season, a boat from a rover had seized upon my uncle and myself, and were carrying us off into captivity, when a Frenchman, and his lugger, rescued us. From that time we became friends; and our friend has often stopped near our towers to visit us. To-day, we found him in a boat, by the side of the English admiral's ship; and as an old acquaintance, he undertook to bring us to the Sorrentine shore, where we are at present staying with my mother's sister."

This was told so naturally, as to carry with it the conviction of its truth; and when Griffin had translated it, he did not fail to assure his superior that he would pledge himself for the accuracy of the statement.

"Ay, you young luffs, Griffin, are never backward with your vows for or to pretty girls," answered Cuffe. "The girl does seem honest, however; and, what is more extraordinary, for the company she is in, she seems modest, too. Tell her she shall not be harmed, though we cannot deprive ourselves of the pleasure of her company immediately. She shall have the larboard stateroom in my cabin until morning, where she and her uncle may live a great deal more comfortably than in one of their out-of-door Neapolitan rookeries. Monte Argentaro, ha! That's a bluff just beyond the Roman coast, and it is famously besprinkled with towers, half a dozen of them at least within as many miles, and who knows but this Jack-o'-Lantern may be extinguished some fine morning, should we fail of laying our hands on it now?"

"We can hardly fail of the last, Captain Cuffe, having her commander in our possession."

Orders were then given to dispose of the prisoners, leaving the boat on deck. Raoul was sent below, and put in a canvas state-room, the arms having been removed, even to the razors, and a sentinel placed at the door. Escape from such a situation was impossible; and as for self-violence, when that point was considered, Cuffe had coolly remarked, "Poor devil! hanged he must be, and if he should be his own executioner, it will save us the discomfort of having a scene on board. I suppose Nelson will order him to our fore-yard-arm as a jewel-block. I don't see why he cannot use a Neapolitan frigate for this job, too; they are good for nothing else."

"I rather think, Captain Cuffe, he will swing on board his own lugger, should we succeed in catching her," answered the lieutenant.

"By George, you're right, Griffin; and that's another inducement for looking out sharp for the *Few-Folly*. How much better it would have been had we burnt them all in a bunch off the Golo!"

Then followed the arrangement by which the prisoner was put into the gun-room, as mentioned. Ghita and her uncle were shown into the empty cabin state-room, and mattresses were provided on which they might repose. Then the captain and his two guests retired to the after-cabin, whither Griffin was invited to accompany them. Here the captain recollected that there had been a fourth individual in the boat, and he sent an order on deck for him to come down for examination. Ithuel, observing the attention of the officers occupied by Ghita and her uncle, had stolen back toward his own yawl, of which he had taken posession, stretching himself out at length, with the

apparent design to sleep, but in reality to keep himself "out of mind" by remaining "out of sight;" receiving, *in petto*, an intention to jump overboard, should the ship go near enough to the land to give him a chance for his life, after the moon set. In this situation he was found, aroused from his lair, and led into the cabin.

It has been mentioned that Ithuel would not consent to trust himself near the *Proserpine* without disguising his person. Raoul being well provided with all the materials for a masquerade, this had been effected by putting a black curling wig over his own lank, sandy hair, coloring his whiskers and eyebrows, and trusting the remainder to the transformation which might be produced by the dress, or rather undress of a Neapolitan waterman. The greatest obstacle to this arrangement had been a certain queue, which Ithuel habitually wore in a cured eel-skin that he had brought with him from America, eight years before, and both of which, "queue and eel-skin," he cherished as relics of better days. Once a week this queue was unbound and combed, but all the remainder of the time it continued in a solid mass quite a foot in length, being as hard and about as thick as a rope an inch in diameter. Now the queue had undergone its hebdomadal combing just an hour before Raoul announced his intention to proceed to Naples in a yawl, and it would have been innovating on the only thing that Ithuel treated with reverence to undo the work until another week had completed its round. The queue, therefore, was disposed of under the wig, in the best manner that its shape and solidity would allow.

Ithuel was left in the forecabin, and his presence was announced to Cuffe.

"It's no doubt some poor devil belonging to the *Few-Folly's* crew," observed the English captain in a rather compassionate manner, "and we can hardly think of stringing him up most probably for obeying an order. That would never do, Griffin; so we'll just step out and overhaul his log, in French, and send him off to England to a prisonship, by the first return vessel."

As this was said, the four in the after-cabin left it together and stood before this new prisoner. Of course Ithuel understood all that was said in English, while the very idea of being catechized in French threw him into a cold sweat. In this strait, the idea suddenly crossed his mind that his greatest security would be in feigning dumbness.

"Ecoutez, mon ami," commenced Griffin, in very respectable English-French, "you are to tell me nothing but the truth, and it may be all the better for you. You belong to the *Feu-Follet*, of course?"

Ithuel shook his head in strong disgust, and endeavored to make a sound that he intended to represent a dumb man struggling to utter the word "Napoli."

"What is the fellow after, Griffin?" said Cuffe. "Can it be he doesn't understand French! Try him a touch in Italian, and let us see what he will say to that."

Griffin repeated very much what he had said before, merely changing the language, and received the same gagging sounds for an answer. The gentlemen looked at each other, as much as to express their surprise. But, unluckily for Ithuel's plan, he had brought with him from the Granite State a certain propensity to pass all the modulations of his voice through his nose; and the effort to make a suppressed sound brought that member more than usually into requisition, thereby producing a certain disagreeable combination that destroyed everything like music that commonly characterizes the Italian words. Now Andrea had been struck with this peculiarity about the tones of the American's voice, in the interview at Benedetta's wine-house; and the whole connection between Raoul and this singular person being associated in his mind, the truth flashed on him, as it might be, at a glance. His previous success that night emboldened the worthy vice-governatore, and, without any remark, he walked steadily up to Ithuel, removed the wig, and permitted the eel-skin queue to resume its natural position on the back of its owner.

"Ha! What, Veechy," exclaimed Cuffe, laughing, "you unearth them like so many foxes to-night. Now, Griffin, hang me if I do not think I've seen that chap before! Isn't he the very man we found at the wheel of *La Voltiguese*, when we boarded her?"

"Lord bless me, Captain Cuffe—no, sir. This fellow is as long as two of that chap; and yet I know the face too. I wish you'd let me send for one of the young gentlemen, sir; they're worth all the rest of the ship at remembering faces."

The permission was given, and the cabin-steward was sent on deck to desire Mr. Roller, one of the oldest midshipmen, and who was known to have the watch, to come below.

"Look at this fellow, Mr. Roller," said Griffin, as soon as the youngster had taken his place in the group, "and tell if you can make anything of him."

"It's the lazy-rony, sir, we hoisted in, a bit ago, when we struck the boat on deck."

"Ay, no doubt of that; but we think we have seen his face before; can you make that out?"

Roller now walked round the immovable subject of all these remarks; and he, too, began to think the singular-looking object was no stranger to him. As soon, however, as he got a sight of the queue, he struck Ithuel a smart slap on the shoulder and exclaimed—

"You're welcome back, my lad! I hope you'll find your berth aloft as much to your mind as it used to be. This is Bolt, Captain Cuffe, the foretop-man, who ran from us when last in England, was caught and put in a guard-ship, from which they sent us word he stole a boat, and got off with two or three French prisoners who happened to be there at the moment on some inquiry or other. Don't you remember it all, Mr. Griffin? you may remember the fellow pretended to be an American."

Ithuel was now completely exposed, and he at once perceived that his wisest way was to submit. Cuffe's countenance darkened, for he regarded a deserter with a species of professional horror, and the impressed deserter, to whose services England had no other right than that of might, with an additional degree of resentment that was very fairly proportioned to the inward consciousness he felt that a great wrong was done in detaining the man at all. There is nothing extraordinary in these feelings; a very common resource, under such circumstances, being to imagine delinquencies that justify us to ourselves by endeavoring to believe that the subject of any act of our oppression at least merits the infliction.

"Do you dare to deny what this young gentleman has just said, sirrah?" demanded the captain. "1 now remember you, too; you are Bolt, the foretop-man, that ran at Plymouth."

"You'd 'a' run, too, Captain Cuffe, had you been in my place, had the ship been at Jericho."

"Enough! no impudence, sir; send for the master-at-arms, Mr. Griffin, and have the fellow ironed: to-morrow we'll look into the affair."

These orders were obeyed. and Ithuel was removed to the place where the master-at-arms usually reigns on board ship. Cuffe now gave the lieutenant his conge, and then withdrew to the inner-cabin to prepare a dispatch for the rear admiral. He was near an hour writing a letter to his mind, but finally succeeded.

Its purport was as follows: He reported the capture of Raoul, explaining the mode and the circumstances under which that celebrated privateersman had fallen into their hands. He then asked for instructions as to the manner in which he was to dispose of his prisoner. Having communicated this important fact, he ventured some suggestions as to the probable vicinity of the lugger, and the hopes he entertained of being able to find out her precise situation, through the agency of Bolt, whose condition he also explained, hinting at the same time the expediency of bringing both delinquents to as speedy trials as possible, as the most certain manner of using their apprehensions in seizing *Le Feu-Follet*. The letter concluded with an earnest request that another frigate, which was mentioned, her captain being junior to Cuffe, and a fast-sailing sloop that was lying off Naples, might be sent down to assist him in "heading off" the lugger, as he feared the latter was too swift to be overtaken by the *Proserpine* alone, more especially in the light winds which prevailed.

When this letter was written, addressed, and sealed, Cuffe went on deck again. It was nine o'clock, or two bells, and Winchester had the quarter-deck nearly to himself. All was as tranquil and calm on the deck of that fine frigate as a moonlight night, a drowsy watch, a light wind, and smooth water, could render things in a bay like that of Naples. Gleamings of fire were occasionally seen over Vesuvius, but things in that direction looked misty and mysterious, though Capri loomed up dark and grand, a few miles to leeward, and Ischia was visible, a confused but distant pile on the lee-bow. An order from Cuffe, however, set everybody in motion. Yard and stay-tackles were overhauled and hooked on, the boatswain's mate piped the orders, and the first cutter was hoisted over the waist cloths, and lowered into the water. "Away, there, you first cutters!" had been harshly called on the berth-deck, and the crew were ready to enter the boat by the time the latter was lowered. The masts were stepped, Roller appeared, in a pea-jacket, to guard against the night air, and Cuffe gave him his instructions.

"Set your sails, and stretch over under the north shore, Mr. Roller," said the captain, who stood in the lee gang-way to give a last word. "You will fetch in about Queen Joan's Palace. There, you had better take to your oars and pull up along the land. Remember, sir, to join us by the first ship that comes out; and, if none is sent, to come down with the morning breeze in the boat."

Roller gave the customary "Ay, ay, sir;" the boat shoved off; as soon as from under the lee of the ship, the lugs were set, and half an hour later the night had swallowed up her form. Cuffe remained an hour longer, walking the deck with his first lieutenant; and then, satisfied that the night would prove propitious, he went below, leaving orders to keep the ship lying to until morning.

As for Roller, he pulled alongside of the *Foudroyant* just as the bells of the fleet were striking eight, or at midnight. Nelson was still up, writing in his cabin. The dispatch was delivered, and then the secretary of the admiral, and a clerk or two were called from their berths, for nothing lagged that this active-minded man had in charge. Orders were written, copied, signed, and sent to different ships, by two o'clock, that the morning breeze might not be lost; and not till then did the employes think of rest.

Roller left the flag-ship at two, having eaten a hearty supper in Nelson's own cabin, and repaired on board the *Terpsichore*, a smart little frigate of thirty-two guns, twelve-pounders, with instructions to her captain to receive him. Two hours later, this ship, in company with another still smaller, the *Ringdove*, eighteen, left her anchorage, under a cloud of canvas, and stood down the bay, carrying studding-sails on both sides, with a light wind at northwest, heading toward Capri.

CHAPTER XVII.

WHEN the idlers of the *Proserpine* appeared on deck the following morning, the ship was about a league to windward of Capri, having forged well over toward the noth side of the bay, during the night, wore round, and got thus far back on the other tack. From the moment light returned, lookouts had been aloft with glasses, examining every nook and corner of the bay, in order to ascertain whether any signs of the lugger were to be seen, under its bold and picturesque shore. So great is the extent of this beautiful basin, so grand the natural objects which surround it, and so clear the atmosphere, that even the largest ships loom less than usual on its waters; and it would have been a very possible thing for *Le Feu-Follet* to anchor near some of the landings, and lie there unnoticed for a week, by the fleet above, unless tidings were carried to the latter by observers on the shore.

Cuffe was the last to come on deck, six

bells, or seven o'clock striking, as the group on the quarter-deck first lifted their hats to him. He glanced around him, and then turned toward Griffin, who was now officer of the watch.

"I see two ships coming down the bay, Mr. Griffin," he said; "no signal yet, I suppose, sir?"

"Certainly not. sir, or they would have been reported. We make out the frigate to be the *Terpsichore,* and the sloop, I know by her new royals, is the *Ringdove.* The first ship, Captain Cuffe, brags of being able to travel faster than anything within the Straits!"

"I'll bet a month's pay the *Few-Folly* walks away from her, on a bowline, ten knots to her nine. If she can do that with the *Proserpine,* she'll at least do that with *Mistress Terpsichore.* Well, quartermaster, what do you make it out to be?"

"It's the *Terpsichore's* number, sir; and the other ship has just made the *Ringdove's.*"

"Show ours, and keep a sharp lookout; there'll be something else to tell us presently."

In a few minutes the *Terpsichore* expressed a wish to speak the *Proserpine,* when Cuffe filled his main-topsail and hauled close upon a wind. An hour later, the three ships passed within hail of each other, when both the junior commanders lowered their gigs and came on board the *Proserpine* to report.

Roller followed in the first cutter, which had been towed down by the *Terpsichore.*

The *Terpsichore* was commanded by Captain Sir Frederick Dashwood, a lively young baronet, who preferred the active life of a sailor to indolence and six thousand a year on shore; and who had been rewarded for his enterprise by promotion and a fast frigate, at the early age of two-and-twenty. The *Ringdove* was under a master-commandant of the name of Lyon, who was just sixty years old, having worked his way up to the present rank by dint of long and arduous services, owing his last commission and his command to the accident of having been a first lieutenant at the battle of Cape St. Vincent. Both these gentlemen appeared simultaneously on the quarter-deck of the *Proserpine,* where they were duly received by the captain and all the assembled officers.

"Good-morrow to you, Cuffe," said Dashwood, giving the other the tip of his fingers, as soon as the ceremonious part of the reception was over; and casting a glance half admiring, half critical, at the appearance of things on deck. "What has Nelson sent us down here about, this fine morning, and—ha! how long have you had those brass ornaments on your capstan?"

"They were only put there yesterday, Sir Frederick; a little slush money did it all."

"Has Nelson seen them? I rather fancy not; they tell me he's as savage as an Arab about knick-knackery nowadays. What an awkward job that was yesterday afternoon, by the way, Cuffe!"

"It has been a bad business, and, as an old Agamemnon, I would give a year's rank that it never had taken place."

"A year's rank! that's a great deal; a year would set me back, hard aground alongside of old Lyon, here. I was a lieutenant less than three years since, and couldn't afford half a year. But all you old Agamemnons think as much of your little Nel. as if he were a pretty girl; isn't that true, Lyon?"

"I daresay it may be, Sir Frederick," answered Lyon; "and if you had been the first lieutenant of a two-decker, off Cape St. Vincent, on the 14th February, 1797, you would have thought as much of him, too. Here we were, only fifteen sail in all—that is, of vessels of the line—with the wind at—"

"O, hang your battle, Lyon; I've heard all that at least seventeen times!"

"Well, if ye have, Sir Frederick," returned Lyon, who was a Scotchman, "it'll be just once a year since ye war' born, leaving out the time ye war' in the nursery. But we've not come here to enlighten Captain Cuffe in these particulars so much as in obedience to an order of the rear-admiral's—little Nel., as ye'll be calling him, I suppose, Sir Frederick Dashwood?"

"Nay, it's you old Agamemnons, or old fellows, who gave him that name—"

"Ye'll please excuse me, sir," interrupted Lyon, a little dogmatically, "ye've never heard me call him anything but my lord, since his majesty, God bless him! was graciously pleased to elevate him to the peerage—nothing but 'my lord,' and 'the rear-admiral'; naval rank being entitled to its privileges even on the throne. Many a king has been a colonel, and I see no disparagement in one's being an admiral. Won't ye be thinking, Captain Cuffe, that since my lord is made duke of Bronte, he is entitled to be called 'your grace?' all the Scottish dukes are so designated, and I see no reason why the rear-admiral should not have his just dues as well as the best of them."

"Let him alone for that," said Cuffe, laughing; "Nel. will look out for himself, as well as for the king. But, gentlemen, I suppose you have not come down here merely for a morning walk; have I any reports to hear?"

"I beg your pardon, Captain Cuffe, but I was really forgetting my errand," answered Dashwood. "Here are your orders, and we are both directed to report to you. The lieutenant who brought the package aboard me said there would be a spy to try, and a lugger to catch. Did they tell you anything of this matter, Lyon?"

"No, Sir Frederick; not being inquisitive, I hear but little of what is going on in the fleet. My orders are to report myself and ship to Captain Cuffe, for service, which I have the honor now to do."

"Well, gentlemen, here are further instructions for you. This is an order to hold a court, composed of Captain Richard Cuffe, of the *Proserpine*, president; Captain Sir Frederick Dashwood, Bart., of the *Terpsichore*, etc., etc.; and Lyon, Winchester and Spriggs, your first lieutenant, Sir Frederick, for the trial of Raoul Yvard, a French citizen, on the charge of being a spy, and Ithuel Bolt, seaman, etc., on the charge of being a deserter. Here is everything in rule, and here are your respective orders, gentlemen."

"Bless me! I'd no notion of this," exclaimed Lyon, who was greatly averse to this part of an officer's duty. "I thought it altogether a trial of speed after a Frenchman, for which purpose, the rear-admiral, or my lord, or his grace, whichever it may be right to call him, had seen fit to bring three of his fastest ships together."

"I wish it was nothing but the last, Captain Lyon; but we have the disagreeable duty of trying a spy and a deserter before us. You will return to your ships, gentlemen, and follow us to an anchorage. I intend to bring up, at a single anchor, under the shore at Capri, where we can lie during the calm and get through with our courts. The cases will be clear and not detain us long, and we can send lookouts up on the heights to examine the sea and the coast outside. You will attend to the signal for the court."

At this order the two visitors got into their boats, and the *Proserpine* again filled. The three vessels now made the best of their way toward the point of destination, anchoring off the town, or village, in the island of Capri, just as two bells struck. Ten minutes later, the *Proserpine* fired a gun, and ran up the flag which denotes the sitting of a court-martial.

Although it has not been deemed necessary to relate them, the reader will understand that all the details required by the law had been observed, as regards these trials; the promptitude of the proceedings being partly characteristic of the decision of the admiral, but more in consequence of a wish to use the charges against the delinquents as a means of seizing the true hero of our tale, the little *Feu-Follet*. While a mistaken, not to say a mawkish, philanthropy is unsettling so many of the ancient landmarks of society, and, among other heresies, in preaching the doctrine that "The object of punishment is the reformation of the criminal," it is a truth which all experience confirms that nothing renders justice so terrible, and consequently so efficient, as its promptitude and certainty.

When all its requirements are observed, the speediest exercise of its functions is the most conducive to the protection of society, the real motive for the existence of all human regulations of this nature; and it is a great merit of the much abused English ordinances, that the laws are rarely made stalking-horses for the benefit of the murderer or the forger; but that once fairly tried and convicted, the expiation of their crimes awaits the offenders with a certainty and energy that leave the impression on the community that punishments were intended to produce. That this people has done well in liberating itself from many of their inherited usages and laws is as certain as that one age has interests different from another; one set of circumstances governing principles at variance with those which precede them; but, it would be well also to remember, that, while moral changes are as necessary as physical exercise, there are truths that are eternal, and rules of right and prudence which can never be departed from with impunity.

When the members of the court mentioned assembled in the cabin of the *Prosperine*, it was with all the forms and exterior observances that were necessary to command respect. The officer to whom had been assigned the duty of provost-marshal was directed to produce his prisoners.

Raoul Yvard and Ithuel Bolt were brought into the cabin at the same moment, though they came from different parts of the ship, and were allowed to hold no communication with each other. When both were present, they were arraigned, and the accusations were read to them. Raoul having admitted his knowledge of English, no interpreter was sworn, but the proceedings were had in the usual manner. As it was intended to try the Frenchman first, and Ithuel might be wanted as a witness, the latter was taken out of the cabin again, courts-martial never permitting one witness to hear what another has testified, although an ingenious substitute for ears has been adopted of late, by publishing in the journals, from day to day, whatever passes, when the length of the proceedings will admit of such a device.

"We will now swear the Signor Andrea Barrofaldi," commenced the judge advocate, as soon as the preliminaries were served. "This is a Catholic Bible, sir, and I will put the oaths in Italian, if you will have the goodness first to swear me in as interpreter."

This was done, when the oath was duly administered to the vice-governatore. Then came a few questions as to the station, country, etc., of the witness, after which more material matter was inquired into.

"Signor vice-governatore, do you know the prisoner by sight?" demanded the judge advocate.

"Sir, I have had the honor to receive him in my residence in the island of Elba,"

"Under what name and circumstances was he known to you, signor?"

"Eh—he called himself Signor Smees, a capitano in the service of the English king."

"What vessel did he pretend to command?"

"Ze *Ving-y-Ving*—a lugger, which I have since had reason to think is *Le Feu-Follet*, a corsair under the French flag. Monsieur did me the favor to make two visits to Porto Ferrajo, in the character of Sir Smees."

"And you know now that this is Raoul Yvard, the French privateersman you have mentioned?"

"Eh—know? I know they say this is the Signor Yvard, and that ze *Ving-y-Ving* is *Le Feu-Follet.*"

"They say, will not do, Signor Barrofaldi. Can you not say thus much of your own knowledge?"

"Non, signore."

The court was now cleared; when it reopened Vito Viti was sent for, and properly sworn, his attention being particularly directed to the cross on the back of the book.

"Did you ever see the prisoner before this occasion, Signor Viti?" demanded the judge advocate, after the preliminary questions had been put.

"Signore, oftener than it is agreeable to remember. I do not think that two grave magistrates were ever more mystified than were the vice-governatore and myself! Eh-h-h — signori, the wisest

sometimes become like sucking children, when there passes a mist before the understanding."

"Relate the circumstances under which this occurred, to the court, Signor Podesta."

"Why, signori, the facts were just these: Andrea Barrofaldi, as you know, is the vice-governatore of Porto Ferrajo, and I am its unworthy podesta. Of course it is our duty to look into all matters affecting the public weal, and more especially into the business and occupations of strangers who come into our island. Well, it is now three weeks or more since the lugger or felucca was seen—"

"Which was it, a felucca or a lugger?" demanded the judge advocate, holding his pen ready to write the answer.

"Both, signore; a felucca and a lugger."

"Ah, there were two; a felucca and a lugger?"

"No, signore; but this felucca was a lugger. Tommaso Tonti wished to mystify me about that, too; but I have not been podesta in a sea-port so many years for nothing. No, signori, there are all sorts of feluccas: ship-feluccas, brig-feluccas, and lugger-feluccas."

When this answer was translated, the members of the court smiled, while Raoul Yvard laughed out honestly.

"Well, Signor Podesta," resumed the judge advocate, "the prisoner came into Porto Ferrajo in a lugger?"

"So it was said, signori. I did not see him actually on board of her, but he professed to be the commander of a certain vessel, in the service of the king of Inghilterra, called ze *Ving-y-Ving*, and said that his own name was Smees—si—il capitano, or Sir Smees."

"Professed? Do you know that this lugger was the notorious French privateer, *Le Feu-Follet?*"

"I know they say so, now, signori; but the vice-governatore and I supposed her to be ze *Ving-y-Ving.*"

"And do you not know that the prisoner is actually Raoul Yvard; of your own knowledge, I mean?"

"Corpo di Bacco! how should I know any such thing, Signor Guideca-Avvocato," exclaimed Vito Viti, who literally translated what he understood to be the title of his interrogator, thereby converting him into a sort of ship-felucca—"how should I know any such thing? I do not keep company with corsairs, except when they come upon our island and call themselves 'Sir Smees.'"

The judge advocate and the members

of the court looked gravely at each other. No one in the least doubted that the prisoner was Raoul Yvard, but it was necessary legally to prove it, before he could be condemned. Cuffe was now asked if the prisoner had not confessed his own identity, but no one could say he had done so in terms, although his conversation would seem to imply as much. In a word, justice was like to be in what is by no means an unusual dilemma for that upright functionary, namely, unable to show a fact that no one doubted. At length Cuffe recollected Ghita and Ithuel, and he wrote their names on a piece of paper, and passed them down the table to the judge advocate. The latter nodded his head, as much as to say he understood the president's meaning; and then he told the prisoner he might cross-examine the witness, if he saw fit.

Raoul fully understood his situation. Although he certainly had not entered the Bay of Naples with any of the ordinary views of a spy, he was aware how far he had committed himself, and foresaw the readiness with which his enemies would destroy him, could they find the legal means of so doing. He also comprehended the dilemma in which his accusers were placed for the want of testimony, and at once resolved to turn the circumstance as much as possible to his advantage. Until that moment, the idea of denying his own identity had never crossed his mind; but perceiving what he fancied an opening for escape, it was but natural to avail himself of its protection. Turning, then, to the podesta, he put his questions in English, that they might go fairly through the same process of interpretation as the rest of the examination.

"You say, Signor Podesta," he commenced, "that you saw me in the town of Porto Ferrajo, and in the island of Elba?"

"Si; in which town I have the honor to be one of the authorities."

"You say I professed to command a vessel in the service of the king of England; a felucca, called *Ving-and-Ving?*"

"Si—ze *Ving-y-Ving*—the commander of that felucca."

"I understood you to say, Mr. Podesta," put in Lyon, "that the craft was a lugger?"

"A felucca-lugger, Signor Capitano; nothing more nor less than that, on my honor."

"And all these honorable officers well know," observed Raoul, ironically, "that a felucca-lugger, and a lugger, such as *Le Feu-Follet* is understood to be, are very different things. Now, signore, you have never heard me say that I am a Frenchman?"

"Non; you have not been so weak as to confess that to one who hates the name of the Francese. Cospetto! If all the grand duke's subjects detested his enemies as I do, he would be the most powerful prince in Italy!"

"No doubt, signore; and now suffer me to inquire if you heard any other name for that felucca than ze *Ving-and-Ving*. Did I ever call her *Le Feu Follet?*"

"Non; always ze *Ving-y-Ving;* never anything else; bu—"

"Your pardon, signore; have the goodness to answer my questions. I called the felucca ze *Ving-and-Ving;* and I called myself Le Capitaine Smeet; is it not true?"

"Si; *Ving-y-Ving*, and Il Capitano Smees—Sir Smees, a signore of an illustrious English family of that name, if I remember right."

Raoul smiled, for he was confident this notion proceeded principally from the self-illusion of the two Italians themselves; the little he had said on the subject having been drawn out more by their suggestions than by any design on his part. Still he did not deem it prudent to contradict the podesta, who, as yet, had testified to nothing that could possibly criminate him.

"If a young man has the vanity to wish to be thought noble," answered Raoul, calmly, "it may prove his folly, but it does not prove him a spy. You did not hear me confess myself a Frenchman, you say; now did you not hear me say I was born in Guernsey?"

"Si; the signore did say that the family of Smees came from that island, as the vice-governatore calls it, though I acknowledge I never heard of such an island. There are Sicilia, Sardegna, Elba, Caprea, Ischia, Irlanda, Inghilterra, Scozia, Malta, Capraya, Pianosa, Gorgona, and America, with several more in the east; but I never heard of such an island as Guernsey. Si, signore; we are humble people, and I hope modest people, in the island of Elba, but we do know something of the rest of the world, notwithstanding. If you wish to hear these matters touched on ingeniously, however, you will do well to call in the vice-governatore for half an hour, and invite him to open his stores of knowledge. San Antonio! I doubt if Italy has his equal—at islands, in particular."

"Good!" continued Raoul; "and now tell these officers, Signor Podesta, if you can say on your oath that I had anything to do with that felucca, ze *Ving-and-Ving*, at all."

"I cannot, signore, except from your own words. You were dressed like one of the officers, here, in an English uniform, and said you commanded ze *Ving-y-Ving*. While speaking of islands, signori, I forgot Palmavola and Ponza, both of which we passed in this ship on our voyage from Elba."

"Good! it is always well to be particular under oath. Now, Signor Podesta, the result of all your evidence is, that you do not know that the felucca you mention was *Le Feu-Follet*, that I am a Frenchman even, much less that I am Raoul Yvard, and that I told you that I was from Guernsey, and that my name was Jaques Smeet; is it not so?"

"Si; you did say your name was Giac Smees, and you did not say you were Raoul Yvard. But, signore, I saw you firing your cannon at the boats of this frigate, with French colors flying, and that is some signs of an enemy, as we understand these matters in Porto Ferrajo."

Raoul felt that this was a direct blow; still, it wanted the connecting link to make it testimony.

"But you did not see me doing this? You mean you saw ze *Ving-and-Ving* in a combat with the frigate's boats."

"Si—that was it; but you told me you were commander of ze *Ving-y-Ving*."

"Let me understand you," put in the judge advocate; "is it the intention of the prisoner to deny his being a Frenchman and an enemy?"

"It is my intention, sir, to deny everything that is not proved."

"But your accent—your English—nay, your appearance, show that you are a Frenchman."

"Your pardon, sir. There are many nations that speak French, which are not French to-day. All along the north frontier of France, is French spoken by foreigners—Savoy, and Geneva, and Vaud; also the English have French subjects in the Canadas, besides Guernsey and Jersey. You will not hang a man because his accent is not from London?"

"We shall do you justice, prisoner," observed Cuffe, "and you shall have the benefit of every doubt that makes in your favor. Still, it may be well to inform you that the impression of your being a Frenchman and Raoul Yvard is very strong; and if you can show to the contrary you would do well to prove it by direct testimony."

"How will this honorable court expect that to be done? I was taken in a boat last night, and am tried this morning, at a notice as short as that which was given to Caraccioli. Give me time to send for witnesses, and I will prove who and what I am."

This was said coolly, and with the air of a man assured of his own innocence, and it produced a slight effect on his judges; for an appeal to the unvarying principles of right seldom falls unheeded on the ear. Nevertheless, there could be no doubt in the minds of the officers of the *Proserpine*, in particular, either as to the character of the lugger or as to that of the prisoner; and men, under such circumstances, were not likely to allow an enemy who had done them so much injury to escape. The appeal only rendered them more cautious, and more determined to protect themselves against charges of unfair proceedings.

"Have you any further questions to put to the witness, prisoner?" inquired the president of the court.

"None, at present, sir—we will go on, if you please, gentlemen."

"Call Ithuel Bolt," said the judge advocate, reading the new witness's name from a list before him.

Raoul started, for the idea of the American's being brought forward in this capacity had never occurred to him. In a minute Ithuel appeared, was sworn, and took his place at the foot of the table.

"Your name is Ithuel Bolt?" observed the judge advocate, holding his pen in readiness to record the answer.

"So they say aboard here," answered the witness, coolly; "though for my part, I've no answer to give to such a question."

"Do you deny your name, sir?"

"I deny nothing—want to say nothing, or to have anything to do with this trial or this ship."

Raoul breathed easier: for to own the truth, he had not much confidence in Ithuel's constancy or disinterestedness; and he apprehended that he had been purchased with the promise of a pardon for himself.

"You will remember that you are under oath, and may be punished for contumacy, on refusing to answer."

"I've some gineral idees of law," answered Ithuel, passing his hand over his queue to make sure it was right, "for we all do a little at that in Ameriky. I practiced some myself, when a young man, though it was only afore a justice-peace. We used to hold that a witness needn't answer agin himself."

"Is it, then, on account of criminating yourself that you answer thus vaguely?"

"I decline answering that question," answered Ithuel, with an air of dignity.

"Witness, have you any personal knowledge of the prisoner?"

"I decline to answer that question, too."

"Do you know anything of such a person as Raoul Yvard?"

"What if I do? I'm a native American, and have a right to form acquaintances, in foreign lands, if I see it's to my interest or it's agreeable to my feelin's."

"Have you never served on board his majesty's ships?"

"What majesty? There's no majesty in Ameriky, as I know, but the majesty of Heaven."

"Remember that your answers are all recorded, and may tell against you on some other occasion."

"Not lawfully; a witness can't be made to give answers that tell against himself."

"Certainly not made to do it; still he may do it of his own accord."

"Then it's the duty of the court to put him on his guard. I've heard that, again and again, in Ameriky."

"Did you ever see a vessel called *Le Feu Follet?*"

"How, in natur', is a mariner to tell all the vessels he may happen to see on the wide ocean!"

"Did you ever serve under the French flag?"

"I decline entering at all into my private affairs. Being free, I am free to sarve where I please."

"It is useless to ask this witness any further questions," Cuffe quietly observed. "The man is well known in this ship, and his own trial will most probably take place as soon as this is ended."

The judge advocate assented, and Ithuel was permitted to withdraw, his contumacy being treated with the indifference that power is apt to exhibit toward weakness. Still there was no legal proof on which to convict the prisoner. No one doubted his guilt, and there were the strongest reasons, short of a downright certainty, for supposing that he commanded the lugger which had so recently fought the boats of the very ship in which the court was sitting; but notwithstanding, supposition was not the evidence the laws required; and the recent execution of Caraccioli had made so much conversation, that few would condemn without seeing their justification before them. Things were really getting to be seriously awkward, and the court was again cleared for the purpose of consultation. In the private discourse that followed, Cuffe stated all that had occurred, the manner in which Raoul had been identified, and the probabilities—nay, moral certainties of the case.

At the same time, he was forced to allow that he possessed no direct evidence that the lugger he had chased was a Frenchman at all, and least of all *Le Feu-Follet*. It is true, she had worn the French flag, but she had also worn the English, and the *Proserpine* had done the same thing. To be sure the lugger had fought under the *drapeau tricolor*, which might be taken as a strong circumstance against her; but it was not absolutely conclusive, for the circumstances might possibly justify deception to the last moment; and he admitted that the frigate herself had appeared to fire at the batteries, under the same ensign. The case was allowed to be embarrassing; and, while no one really doubted the identity of Raoul, those who were behind the curtains greatly feared they might be compelled to adjourn the trial for want of evidence, instead of making an immediate sentence the means of getting possession of the lugger, as had been hoped. When all these points had been sufficiently discussed, and Cuffe had let his brethren into his view of the real state of the case, he pointed out a course that he still trusted would prove effectual. After a few minutes of further deliberation on this information, the doors were opened, and the court resumed its public sitting, as before.

"Let a young woman who is known by the name of Ghita be brought in next," said the judge advocate, consulting his notes.

Raoul started, and a shade of manly concern passed over his face; but he soon recovered, and seemed unmoved. Ghita and her uncle had been taken from the cabin state-room and placed below, in order that the private consultation might be perfectly secret, and it was necessary to wait a few minutes, until she could be summoned. These past, the door opened and the girl entered the room. She cast a glance of tender concern at Raoul; but the novelty of her situation, and the awful character of an oath to one of her sensitive conscience and utter inexperience, soon drew her attention entirely to the scene more immediately before her. The judge advocate explained the nature of the oath she was required to take; and then he administered it. Had Ghita been taken less by surprise, or had she in the least foreseen the consequences, no human power could have induced her to be sworn; but, ignorant of all this, she submitted passively, kissing the cross with reverence, and even offering to kneel as she made the solemn protestation. All this was painful to the prisoner, who distinctly foresaw the consequences. Still, so profound was his reverence for Ghita's single-ness of heart and mind, that he would not, by look or gesture, in any manner endeavor to undermine that sacred love of truth which he knew formed the very foundations of her character. She was accordingly sworn, without anything occurring to alarm her affections, or to apprise her of what might be the sad result of the act.

CHAPTER XVIII.

"Your name is Ghita," continued the judge advocate, examining his memoranda; "Ghita what?"

"Ghita Caraccioli, signore," answered the girl, in a voice so gentle and sweet as to make a friend of every listener.

The name, however, was not heard without producing a general start, and looks of surprise were exchanged among all in the room; most of the officers of the ship who were not on duty being present as spectators.

"Caraccioli!" repeated the judge advocate, with emphasis. "That is a great name in Italy. Do you assume to belong to the illustrious house that bears this appellation?"

"Signore, I assume to own nothing that is illustrious, being merely an humble girl who lives with her uncle, in the prince's towers on Monte Argentaro."

"How happens it, then, that you bear the distinguished name of Caraccioli, signorina?"

"I dare say, Mr. Medford," observed Cuffe, in English, of course, "that the young woman doesn't know herself whence she got the name. These matters are always managed very loosely in Italy."

"Signore," resumed Ghita, earnestly, after waiting respectfully for the captain to get through, "I bear the name of my father, as it is usual with children, but it is a name on which a heavy disgrace has fallen, so lately as yesterday; his father having been a sight for the thousands of Naples to gaze on, as his aged body hung at the yard of one of your ships."

"And do you claim to be the grand-daughter of that unfortunate admiral?"

"So I have been taught to consider myself; may his soul rest in a peace that his foes would not grant to his body! That criminal, as you doubtless believe him, was my father's father, though few knew it, when he was honored as a prince and a high officer of the king's."

A deep silence followed; the singularity of the circumstance, and the air of truth which pervaded the manner of the girl, uniting to produce a profound sensation.

"The admiral had the reputation of being childless," observed Cuffe, in an undertone. "Doubtless this girl's father has been the consequence of some irregular connection."

"If there had been a promise, or any words of recognition uttered before witnesses," muttered Lyon, "accordin' to the laws of Scotland, issue, and a few pairtenant expressions, will splice a couple as strongly as ye'll be doing it in England, before either of the archbishops."

"As this is Italy, it is not probable that the same law rules here. Proceed, Mr. Judge Advocate."

"Well, Ghita Caraccioli—if that be your name—I wish to know if you have any acquaintance with a certain Raoul Yvard; a Frenchman, and the commander of a private lugger-of-war, called *Le Feu-Follet?* Remember you are sworn to tell the truth, the whole truth, and nothing but the truth."

Ghita's heart beat violently, and the color came into her face with the impetuosity of sensitive alarm. She had no knowledge of courts, and the object of inquiry was unknown to her. Then followed the triumph of innocence; the purity of her mind and the quiet of her conscience re-assuring her, by bringing the strong conviction that she had no reason to blush for any sentiment she might happen to entertain.

"Signore," she said, dropping her eyes to the floor, for the gaze of all the court was fastened on her face, "I am acquainted with Raoul Yvard, the person you mention; that is he who sits between those two cannon. He is a Frenchman, and he does command the lugger called the *Feu-Follet.*"

"I knew we should get it all by this witness!" exclaimed Cuffe, unable to suppress the relief he felt at obtaining the required testimony.

"You say that you know this of your own knowledge," resumed the judge advocate—

"Messieurs," said Raoul, rising, "will you grant me leave to speak? This is a cruel scene, and rather than endure it—rather than give this dear girl the cause for future pain that I know her answers will bring, I ask that you permit her to retire, when I promise to admit all that you can possibly prove by her means."

A short consultation followed, when Ghita was told to withdraw. But the girl had taken the alarm from the countenance of Raoul, although she did not understand what passed in English; and she was reluctant to quit the place in ignorance.

"Have I said aught to injure thee, Raoul?" she anxiously asked; "I was sworn on the Word of God, and by the sacred cross; had I foreseen any harm to thee, the power of England would not have made me take so solemn an oath, and then I might have been silent."

"It matters not, dearest; the fact must come out in some way or other, and, in due time, you shall know all. And now, messieurs," the door closing on Ghita, "there need be no further concealment between us. I am Raoul Yvard, the person you take me for, and the person that some of you must well know me to be. I fought your boats, Monsieur Cuffe, avoided your brulot, and led you a merry chase round Elba. I deceived the Signor Barrofaldi, and his friend the podesta, and all for the love of this beautiful and modest girl who has just left the cabin; no other motive having carried me into Porto Ferrajo, or into this Bay of Naples, on the honor of a Frenchman."

"Umph!" muttered Lyon, "it must be admitted, Sir Frederick, that the prisoner appeals to a most eligible standard!"

On another occasion national antipathy and national prejudices might have caused the rest of the court to smile at this sally; but there was an earnestness and sincerity in the manner and countenance of Raoul which, if they did not command entire belief, at least commanded respect. It was impossible to deride such a man; and long cherished antipathies were rebuked by his manly and spirited declarations.

"There will be no farther occasion for witnesses, Mr. Judge Advocate, if the prisoner be disposed to acknowledge the whole truth," observed Cuffe. "It is proper, however, Monsieur Yvard, to apprise you of the possible consequences. You are on trial for your life; the charge being that of coming on board an English ship in disguise, or rather, into the center of an English fleet, you being an alien enemy, engaged in carrying on open warfare against his majesty."

"I am a Frenchman, monsieur, and I serve my country," answered Raoul, with dignity.

"Your right to serve your country no one will dispute; but you must know it is against the laws of civilized warfare to act the part of a spy. You are now on your guard, and will decide for yourself. If you have anything to say, we will hear it."

"Messieurs, there is little more to be said," answered Raoul. "That I am your enemy, as I am of all those who seek the downfall of France, I do not deny. You know who I am, and what I am, and I have no excuses for being either. As a brave Englishman, you will know how to allow for the love a Frenchman bears his country. As for coming on board this ship, you cannot bring that as a charge against me, since it was at your own invitation I did it. The rites of hospitality are as sacred as they are general."

The members of the court exchanged significant glances with each other, and there was a pause of more than a minute. Then the judge advocate resumed his duties, by saying,

"I wish you to understand, prisoner, the precise legal effect of your admissions; then I wish them to be made formally and deliberately; else we must proceed to the examination of other witnesses. You are said to be Raoul Yvard, an alien enemy, in arms against the king."

"Monsieur, this I have already admitted; it cannot honorably be denied."

"You are accused of coming on board of his majesty's ship *Proserpine* disguised, and of calling yourself a boatman of Capri, when you were Raoul Yvard, an alien enemy bearing arms against the king."

"This is all true; but I was invited on board the ship, as I have just stated."

"You are furthermore accused of rowing in among the ships of his majesty, now lying in the Bay of Naples, and which ships are under the orders of Rear-Admiral Lord Nelson, Duke of Bronte, in Sicily, you being in the same disguise, though an alien enemy, with the intent to make your observations as a spy, and, doubtless, to avail yourself of information thus obtained to the injury of his majesty's subjects, and to your own advantage, and that of the nation you serve."

"Monsieur, this is not so; parole d'honneur, I went into the bay in search of Ghita Caraccioli, who has my whole heart, and whom I would persuade to become my wife. Nothing else carried me into the bay; and I wore this dress, because I might otherwise have been known and arrested."

"This is an important fact, if you can prove it; for, though it might not technically acquit you, it would have its effect on the commander-in-chief, when he comes to decide on the sentence of this court."

Raoul hesitated. He did not doubt that Ghita, she whose testimony had just proved so serious a matter against him, would testify that she believed such was alone his motive; and this, too, in a way, and with corroborative circumstances, that would carry weight with them, more particularly as she could testify that he had done the same thing before, in the island of Elba, and was even in the practice of paying her flying visits at Monte Argentaro. Nevertheless, Raoul felt a strong reluctance to have Ghita again brought before the court. With the jealous sensitiveness of true love, he was averse to subjecting its object to the gaze and comments of the rude of his own sex; then he knew his power over the feelings of the girl, and had too much sensibility not to enter into all the considerations that might influence a man on a point so delicate; and he could not relish the idea of publicly laying bare feelings that he wished to be as sacred to others as they were to himself.

"Can you prove what you have just averred, Raoul Yvard?" demanded the judge advocate.

"Monsieur, I fear it will not be in my power. There is one—but—I much fear it will not be in my power—unless, indeed, I am permitted to examine my companion; he who has already been before you."

"You mean Ithuel Bolt, I presume. He has not yet been regularly before us, but you can produce him, or any other witness; the court reserving to itself the right to decide, afterward, on the merits of the testimony."

"Then, monsieur, I could wish to have Etoo-ell here."

The necessary directions were given, and Ithuel soon stood in the presence of his judges. The oath was tendered, and Ithuel took it like a man who had done such things before.

"Your name is Ithuel Bolt," commenced the judge advocate.

"So they tell me on board this ship; but if I am to be a witness, let me swear freely; I don't wish to have words put into my mouth, or idees chained to me with iron."

As this was said, Ithuel raised his arm, and exhibited his handcuffs, which the master-at-arms had refuse to remove, and the officers of the court had overlooked. A reproachful glance from Cuffe, and a whisper from Yelverton, disposed of the difficulty; Ithuel was released.

"Now I can answer more conscientiously," continued the witnesss, grinning sardonically; "when iron is eating into the flesh, a man is apt to swear to what he thinks will be most agreeable to his masters. Go on, 'squire, if you have anything to say."

"You appear to be an Englishman."

"Do I? Then I appear to be what I am not. I'm a native of the Granite State, in North America. My fathers went to that region, in times long gone by, to uphold their religious idees. The whole country thereabouts sets onaccountable store by their religious privileges."

"Do you know the prisoner, Ithuel Bolt—the person who is called Raoul Yvard?"

Ithuel was a little at a loss exactly how to answer this question. Notwithstanding the high motives which had led his fathers into the wilderness, and his own peculiar estimate of his religious advantages, an oath had got to be a sort of convertible obligation with him ever since the day he had his first connection with a custom-house. A man who had sworn to so many false invoices was not likely to stick at a trifle in order to serve a friend; still, by denying the acquaintance he might bring discredit to himself, and put it out of his power to be of use to Raoul on some more material point. As between himself and the Frenchman, there existed a remarkable moral discrepancy; for, while he who prided himself on his religious ancestry and pious education had a singularly pliable conscience, Raoul, almost an atheist in opinions, would have scorned a simple lie, when placed in a situation that touched his honor. In the way of warlike artifices, few men were more subtle, or loved to practice them oftener, than Raoul Yvard; but, the mask aside, or when he fell back on his native dignity of mind, death itself could not have extorted an equivocation from him. On the other hand, Ithuel had an affection for a lie—more especially if it served himself, or injured his enemy; finding a mode of reconciling all this to his spirituality, that is somewhat peculiar to fanaticism, as it begins to grow threadbare. On the present occasion, he was ready to say whatever he thought would most conform to his shipmate's wishes, and luckily he construed the expression of the other's countenance aright.

"I *do* know the prisoner, as you call him, 'squire," Ithuel answered, after the pause that was necessary to come to his conclusion. "I *do* know him *well*, and a a master critter he is, when he fairly gets into a current of your English trade. Had there been a Rule Yvard on board each of the Frenchmen at the Nile, over here in Egypt, Nelson would have found that his letter stood in need of some postcripts, I guess."

"Confine your answers, witness, to the purport of the question," put in Cuffe, with dignity.

Ithuel stood too much in habitual awe of the captain of his old ship to venture on an answer; but if looks could have done harm, that functionary would not have escaped altogether uninjured. As he said nothing, the examination proceeded.

"You know him to be Raoul Yvard, the commander of the French privateer lugger, *Le Feu-Follet?*" continued the judge advocate, deeming it prudent to fortify his record of the prisoner's confession of identity, with a little collateral evidence.

"Why, I some think"—answered Ithuel, with a peculiar provincialism, that had a good deal of granite in it—"that is, I kind o' conclude"—catching an assent from Raoul's eye—"O, yes, of that there isn't the smallest mite of doubt in the world. He's the captain of the lugger, and a right down good one he is!"

"You were with him in disguise, when he came into the Bay of Naples yesterday?"

"I in disguise, 'squire! What have I got to disguise? I am an American of different callings, all of which I practyse, as convenience demands; being a neutral, I've no need of disguises to go anywhere. I am never disguised, except when my jib is a little bowsed out; and that, you know, is a come-over that befalls most seafaring men, at times."

"You need answer nothing concerning yourself that will tend to criminate you. Do you know with what inducement, or on what business, Raoul Yvard came into the Bay of Naples yesterday?"

"To own to you the candid truth,'squire, I do not," answered Ithuel, simply; for the nature of the tie which bound the young Frenchman so closely to Ghita was a profound mystery, in all that related to its more sacred feelings, to a being generally so obtuse on matters of pure sentiment. "Captain Rule is a good deal given to prying about on the coast; and what particular end he had in view, in this expedition, I cannot tell you. His arr'nds in shore, I must own, be sometimes onaccountable! Witness the island of Elby, gentlemen!"

Ithuel indulged in a small laugh, as he made this allusion; for, in his own way, he had a humor in which he occasionally indulged, after a manner that belonged to the class of which he was a conspicuous member.

"Never mind what occurred at Elba. Prisoner, do you wish to question the witness?"

"Etuelle," said Raoul, "do you not know that I love Ghita Caraccioli?"

"Why, Captain Rule, I know you think so, and say so; but I set down all these matters as somewhat various and onaccountable."

"Have I not often landed on the enemy's coast solely to see her and to be near her?"

By this time, Ithuel, who was a little puzzled at first to understand what it all meant, had got his cue, and no witness could have acquitted himself better than he did from that moment.

"That you have," he answered, "a hundred times, at least; and right in the teeth of my advice."

"Was not my sole object in coming into the bay yesterday, to find Ghita, and Ghita only?"

"Just so. Of that, gentlemen, there can be no more question than there is about Vesuvius standing up at the head of the bay, smoking like a brick-kiln. That was Captain Rule's sole arr'nd."

"I jest understood ye to say, witness," put in Lyon, "and that only a bit since, that ye did not know the prisoner's motive in coming into the Bay of Naples. Ye called his behavior unaccountable?"

"Very true, sir, and so it is to me. I know'd all along that love was at the bottom of it; but I don't call love a motive, while I do call it onaccountable. Love's a feelin', and not a nature. That's the explanation on't. Yes, I know'd it was love for Miss Gyty, but then that's not a motive in law."

"Answer to the facts. The court will judge of the motive itself. How do you know that love for the young woman you mention was Raoul Yuard's only object in coming into the bay?"

"One finds out such things by keeping company with a man. Captain Rule went first to look for the young woman up on the mountain yonder, where her aunt lives, and I went with him to talk English, if it got to be necessary; and, not finding Gyty at home, we got a boat and followed her over to Naples. Thus, you see, sir, that I have reason to know what craft he was in chase of the whole time."

As all this was strictly true, Ithuel related it naturally, and in a way to gain some credit.

"You say you accompanied Raoul Yvard, witness, in a visit to the aunt of the young woman called Ghita Caraccioli," observed Cuffe, in a careless way, that was intended to entrap Ithuel into an unwary answer; "where did you go from, when you set out on your journey?"

"That would depend on the place one kept his reckoning from, and the time of starting. Now I might say I started from

Ameriky, which part of the world I left some years since; or I might say from Nantes, the port which we fitted for sea. As for Captain Rule, he would probably say Nantes."

"In what manner did you come from Nantes?" continued Cuffe, without betraying resentment at an answer that might be deemed impertinent; or surprise, as if he found it difficult to comprehend. "You did not make the journey on horseback, I should think?"

"O, I begin to understand you, Captain Cuffe. Why, if the truth must be said, we came in the lugger, the *Few-Folly.*"

"I supposed as much. And when you went to visit this aunt, where did you leave the lugger?"

"We didn't leave her at all, sir; being under her canvas, our feet were no sooner in the boat, and the line cast off, than she left us as if we had been stuck up like a tree on dry ground."

"Where did this happen?"

"Afloat, of course, Captain Cuffe; such a thing would hardly come to pass ashore."

"All that I understand; but you say the prisoner left his vessel in order to visit an aunt of the young woman's; thence he went into the bay, for the sole purpose of finding the young woman herself. Now this is an important fact, as it concerns the prisoner's motives, and may affect his life. The court must act with all the facts before it; as a commencement, tell us where Raoul Yvard left his lugger to go on yonder headland."

"I do not think, Captain Cuffe, you've got the story exactly right. Captain Rule didn't go on the mountain, a'ter all, so much to see the aunt as to see the niece at the aunt's dwelling; if one would end right in a story, he must begin right."

"I left *Le Feu-Follet,* Monsieur le Capitaine," Raoul calmly observed, "not two cables' length from the very spot where your own ship is now lying; but it was at an hour of the night when the good people of Capri were asleep, and they knew nothing of our visit. You see the lugger is no longer here."

"And do you confirm this story under the solemnity of your oath?" demanded Cuffe of Ithuel, little imagining how easy it was to the witness to confirm anything he saw fit, in the way he mentioned.

"Sartin; every word is true, gentlemen," answered Ithuel. "It was not more than a cable's length from this very spot, according to my judgment."

"And where is the lugger now?" asked Cuffe, betraying the drift of all

his questions, in his eagerness to learn more.

Ithuel was not to be led on so hurriedly, or so blindly. Affecting a girlish sort of coyness, he answered, simpering:

"Why, Captain Cuffe, I cannot think of answering a question like that, under the solemnity of an oath, as you call it. No one can know where the little *Folly* is but them that's in her."

Cuffe was a little disconcerted at the answer, while Lyon smiled ironically; the latter then took upon himself the office of cross-examining, with an opinion of his own penetration and shrewdness that at least ought to have made him quite equal to encountering one of Ithuel's readiness in subterfuges.

"We do not expect you to tell us of your own knowledge, witness," he said, "precisely the position by latitude and longitude, or by the points of the compass, at this identical instant, of the craft called by some the *Le Few-Folly,* by others the *Feu-Follay,* and, as it would now seem, by yourself, the *Little Folly;* for that, as ye've well obsairved, can be known only to those who are actually on board her; but ye'll be remembering, perhaps, the place it was agreed on between you, where ye were to find the lugger at your return from this hazardous expedition, that ye've been making amang ye, into the Bay of Naples?"

"I object to that question as contrary to law," put in Ithuel, with a spirit and promptitude that caused the judge advocate to start, and the members of the court to look at each other in surprise.

"Nay, if ye object to the question on the ground that a true ainswer will be criminating yoursel', ye'll be justified in so doing, by reason and propriety; but then ye'll consider well the consequences it may have on your own case when that comes to be investigated."

"I object on gin'ral principles," said Ithuel. "Whatever Captain Rule may have said on the subject, admitting that he said anything, just to bear out the argument (by the way, Ithuel called this argooment, a pronunciation against which we enter solemn protest)—admitting, I say, that he said anything on the subject, it cannot be testimony, as hearsay evidence is agin law all the world over."

The members of the court looked at the judge advocate, who returned the glance with an air of suitable gravity; then, on a motion of Sir Frederick's, the court was cleared to discuss the point in private.

"How's this, Mr. Judge Advocate," demanded Cuffe, as soon as the coast was clear; "it is of the last importance to find where that lugger is; do you hold that the question is contrary to law?"

"Its importance makes it pertinent, I think, sir; as for the legality, I do not see how it can be affected by the circumstance that the fact came up in discourse."

"D'ye think so?" observed Sir Frederick, looking much more profound than was his wont. "Legality is the boast of English law, and I should dislike excessively to fail in that great essential. What is said, must be heard, to be repeated; and this seems very like hearsay testimony. I believe it's admitted all round we must reject that."

"What is your opinion, Captain Lyon?" demanded the president.

"The case is somewhat knotty, but it may be untied," returned the Scot, with a sneer on his hard features. "No need of Alexander and his sword to cut the rope, I'm thinking, when we bring common sense to bear on the point. What is the matter to be ascertained? Why, the place which was agreed on as the point of rendezvous between this Rawl Eevart and his people. Now this arrangement must have been made orally, or in writing; if orally, testimony to the words uttered will not be hearsay, further than testimony to what a man has seen will be eyesight."

"Quite true, Mr. President and gentlemen!" exclaimed the judge advocate, who was not a little relieved at finding a clew to lead him out of the difficulty. "If the agreement had been made in writing, then that writing would have to be produced, if possible, as the best evidence the case affords; but being made in words, those words can be sworn to."

Cuffe was much relieved by this opinion, and, as Sir Frederick did not feel disposed to push his dissent very far, the matter would have been determined on the spot, but for a love of disputation that formed part and parcel, to speak legally on a legal subject, of Lyon's moral temperament.

"I'm agreeing with the judge advocate as to his distinction about the admissibility of the testimony on the ground of its not being technically what is called hearsay evidence," he observed; "but a difficulty suggests itself to my mind touching the pairtenency. A witness is sworn to speak to the point before the court, but he is not sworn to discuss all things in Heaven and airth. Now is it pairtenent to the fact of Rawl Eevart's being a spy, that he made sairtain agreements to meet this or that fellow-creature, in this or that place? Now, as I comprehend the law, it divides all questions into two great classes—the pairtenent and the impairtenent, of which the first are legal and the second illegal."

"I think it would be a great piece of audacity," said Sir Frederick, disdainfully, "for such a fellow as this Bolt to pretend to call any question we can put to him impertinent!"

"That's no just the p'int, Sir Frederick; this being altogether a matter of law, while ye'll be thinking of station and etiquette. Then, there's two classes of the pairtement, and two of the impairtement; one being legal and logical, as it might, and the other conventional and civil, as one may say. There's a nice distinction latent between the two."

"I believe the court is of the opinion that the question may be put," observed Cuffe, who was impatient of the Scotchman's subtleties, bowing to Sir Frederick, to ask an acquiescence which he immediately received. "We will reopen the doors, and proceed in the examination."

"The court is of the opinion, witness," resumed the judge advocate, when every one was in his place again, "that you must answer the question. In order that you may understand it, I will now repeat it. Where was it agreed between Raoul Yvard and his people that they should meet again?"

"I do not think the people of the lugger had anything to say in the matter," answered Ithuel, in the most unmoved manner. "If they had, I knew nothing on't."

The court felt embarrassed, but it would never do to be thwarted in this manner; a look of determination was exchanged between the members, and the examination proceeded.

"If not the people, the officers, then. Where was it agreed between the prisoner and his officers that the former should find the lugger, when he returned from his expedition into the bay?"

"Well, now, gentlemen," answered Ithuel, turning his quid from one cheek to the other, "I some conclude you've no great acquaintance with Captain Rule, a'ter all. He is not apt to enter into any agreements, at all. What he wants done, he orders; and what he orders, must be done."

"What did he order, then, as respects the place where the lugger was to wait for his return?"

"I am sorry to be troublesome, please the court," returned the witness, with admirable self-possession; "but law is law, all over the world, and I rather guess this question is ag'in it. In the Granite State, it is always held, when a thing can be proved by the person who said any particular words, that the question must be put to him, and not to a bystander."

"Not if that person is a prisoner, and on his trial," answered the judge advocate, staring to hear such a distinction from such a source; "though the remark is a good one, in the cases of witnesses purely. You must answer, therefore."

"It is unnecessary," again interposed Raoul. "I left my vessel here, where I have told you, and had I made a certain signal, the last night, from the heights of St. Agata, *Le Feu-Follet* would have stood in, near to the rocks of the Sirens, and taken me off again. As the hour is past, and the signal is not likely to be made, it is probable my lieutenant is gone to another rendezvous, of which the witness knows nothing, and which, certainly, I shall never betray."

There was so much manliness and quiet dignity in Raoul's deportment that whatever he said made an impression. His answer disposed of the matter; for the moment at least. The judge advocate, accordingly, turned to other inquiries. Little remained, however, to be done. The prisoner had admitted his identity; his capture, with all the attendant circumstances, was in proof; and his defense came next.

When Raoul rose to speak, he felt a choking emotion; but it soon left him, and he commenced in a steady, calm tone, his accent giving point and interest to many of his expressions.

"Messieurs," said he, "I will not deny my name, my character, or my manner of life. I am a Frenchman, and the enemy of your country. I am also the enemy of the King of Naples, in whose territories you found me. I have destroyed his and your ships. Put me on board my lugger, and I should do both again. Whoever is the enemy of La France is the enemy of Raoul Yvard. Honorable seamen, like yourselves, messieurs, can understand this. I am young. My heart is not made of rock; evil as it may be, it can love beauty, and modesty, and virtue, in the other sex. Such has been my fate—I love Ghita Caraccioli; have endeavored to make her my wife for more than a year. She has not authorized me to say that my suit was favored—this I must acknowledge; but she is not the less admirable for that. We differ in our opinions of religion, and I fear she left Monte Argentaro, because, refusing my hand, she thought it better, perhaps, that we should not meet again. It is so with maidens, as you must know, messieurs.

"But it is not usual for us, who are less refined, to submit to such self-denial. I learned whither Ghita had come, and followed; my heart was a magnet, that her beauty drew after it, as our needles are drawn toward the pole. It was necessary to go into the Bay of Naples, among the vessels of enemies, to find her I loved; and this is a very different thing from engaging in the pitiful attempts of a spy. Which of you would not have done the same, messieurs? You are brave Anglais, and I know you would not hesitate. Two of you are still youthful, like myself, and must still feel the power of beauty: even the monsieur that is no longer a young man, has had his moments of passion, like all that are born of woman. Messieurs, I have no more to say; you know the rest. If you condemn me, let it be as an unfortunate Frenchman, whose heart had its weaknesses—not as an ignominious and treacherous spy."

The earnestness and nature with which Raoul spoke, were not without effect. Could Sir Frederick have had his way, the prisoner would have been acquitted on the spot. But Lyon was skeptical as to the story of love, a sentiment about which he knew very little; and there was a spirit of opposition in him, too, that generally induced him to take the converse of most propositions that were started. The prisoner was dismissed, and the court closed its doors, to make up its decision by itself, in the usual form.

We should do injustice to Cuffe, if we did not say that he had some feeling in favor of the gallant foe who had so often foiled him. Could he have had his will at that moment he would have given Raoul his lugger, allowed the latter a sufficient start, and then gladly have commenced a chase round the Mediterranean, to settle all questions between them. But it was too much to give up the lugger as well as the prisoner. Then his oath as a judge had its obligations also, and he felt himself bound to yield to the arguments of the judge advocate, who was a man of technicalities, and thought no more of sentiment than Lyon himself.

The result of the deliberation, which lasted an hour, was a finding against the prisoner. The court was opened, and the record made up and read, the offender introduced, and the judgment delivered. The finding was, "that Raoul Yvard had been caught in disguise, in the midst of the allied fleets, and that he was guilty as a spy." The sentence was, to suffer death the succeeding day, by hanging at the yardarm of such ship as the commander-in-chief might select, on approving the sentence.

As Raoul expected little else, he heard his doom with steadiness, bowing with dignity and courtesy to the court, as he was led away to be placed in irons, as befitted one condemned.

CHAPTER XIX.

BOLT had not been tried. His case had several serious difficulties, and the orders allowed of a discretion. The punishment could scarcely be less than death, and, in addition to the loss of a stout, sinewy man, it involved questions of natural right, that were not always pleasant to be considered. Although the impressment of American seamen into the British ships of war was probably one of the most serious moral as well as political wrongs that one independent nation ever received at the hands of another, viewed as a practice of a generation's continuance, it was not wholly without some relieving points. There was a portion of the British marine that disdained to practice it at all; leaving it to the coarser spirits of the profession to discharge a duty that they themselves found repugnant to their feelings and their habits. Thus we remember to have heard an American seaman say, one who had been present on many occasions when his countrymen were torn from under their flag, that in no instance he ever witnessed, was the officer who committed the wrong of an air and manner that he should describe as belonging to the class of gentlemen on shore. Whenever one of the latter boarded his vessel, the crew was permitted to pass unquestioned.

Let this be as it might, there is no question that a strong and generous feeling existed in the breasts of hundreds in the British navy, concerning the nature of the wrong that was done a foreign people, by the practice of impressing men from under their flag. Although Cuffe was too much of a martinet to carry his notions on the subject to a very refined point, he was too much of a man not to be reluctant to punish another for doing what he felt he would have done himself, under similar circumstances, and what he could not but know he would have had a perfect right to do. It was impossible to mistake one like Ithuel, who had so many of the Granite peculiarities about him, for anything but what he was; and so well was his national character established in the ship, that the *sobriquet* of The Yankee had been applied to him, by his shipmates, from the very first. The fact, therefore, stood him so far in hand, that Cuffe, after a consultation with Winchester, determined not to put the alleged deserter on trial; but, after letting him remain a short time in irons, to turn him to duty again, under a pretense that was often used on such occasions, namely, to give the man an opportunity of proving his American birth, if he really were what he so strenu-ously professed to be. Poor Ithuel was not the only one who was condemned to this equivocal servitude, hundreds passing weary years of probation, with the same dim ray of hope, forever deferred, gleaming in the distance. It was determined, however, not to put Ithuel on his trial until the captain had conversed with the admiral on the subject, at least; and Nelson, removed from the influence of the siren by whom he was enthralled, was a man inclined to leniency, and of even chivalrous notions of justice. To such contradictions is even a great mind subject, when it loses sight of the polar star of its duties!

When the sentence on Raoul was pronounced, therefore, and the prisoner was removed, the court adjourned; a boat being immediately dispatched to the *Fourdroyant* with a copy of the proceedings, for the rear-admiral's approbation. Then followed a discussion on much the most interesting topic for them all; the probable position of, and the means of capturing, the lugger. That *Le Fue-Follet* was near, all were convinced; but where she was to be found, it was hard to tell. Officers had been sent on the heights of Caprice, one of which towers more than a thousand feet above the sea; but they returned from a bootless errand. Nothing resembling the lugger was visible in the offing, among the islands, or in the bays. A cutter had been sent to look round Campaneila, and another crossed the mouth of the bay, to take a look to the northward of Ischia, in order to make certain that the treacherous craft had not gone behind the mountains of that island for a refuge. In short, no expedient likely to discover the fugitive was neglected. All failed, however; boat after boat came back without success, and officer after officer returned, worried and disappointed.

Much of the day was passed in this manner, for it was a calm, and moving either of the ships was out of the question. In the full expectation of discovering the lugger somewhere in striking distance, Cuffe had even gone so far as to detail a party from each vessel, with a view to attack her in boats again, feeling no doubt of success, now that he had the disposal force of three vessels to send against his enemy. Winchester was to have commanded as a right purchased by his blood; nor was the hope of succeeding in this way abandoned, until the last boat, that which had been sent round Ischia, returned, reporting its total want of success.

"I have heard it said," observed Cuffe, as he and his brother captains stood conversing together on the quarter-deck of the *Proserpine*, just after this last report had been made, "I have heard it said, that this Raoul Yvard has actually gone boldly into several of our ports, under English or neutral colors, and lain there a day or two at a time, unsuspected until it had suited him to go out again. Can it be possible he is up, off the town? There is such a fleet of craft in and about the mole, that a little lugger with her paint and marks altered might be among them. What think you, Lyon?"

"It is sartainly a law of nature, Captain Cuffe, that smaller objects should be overlooked in the presence of greater; and such a thing might happen, therefore; though I should place it among the impossibles. 'Twould be far safer, nevertheless, to run in, in the manner you designate, among the hundred or two of ships, than to venture alone into a haven or a roadstead. If you wish for retirement, Sir Frederick, plunge at once into the Strand, or take lodgings on Ludgate Hill; but if you wish to be noticed, and chased, go into a Highland village, and just conceal your name for a bit! Ah, he knows the difference well who has tried both modes of life?"

"This is true, Cuffe," observed the baronet, "yet I hardly think a Frenchman, big or little, would be apt to come and anchor under Nelson's nose."

"'Twould be something like the lion's lying down with the lamb, certainly, and ought not to be counted on as very likely. Mr. Winchester, is not that our boat coming round the sloop's quarter?"

"Yes, sir; she has got back from Naples—quartermaster—"

"Ay, quartermaster!" interrupted Cuffe, sternly, "A pretty lookout is this! Here is our own boat close in upon us, and not a word from your lips on the interesting subject, sir!"

This word, *sir*, is much used on board a man-of-war, and in all its convertible significations. From the inferior to the superior, it comes as natural as if it were a gift from above; from equal to equal it has a ceremonious and be-on-guard air that sometimes means respect, sometimes disrespect; while from a captain to a quartermaster, it always means reproof, if it does not mean menace. In discussions of this sort, it is wisest for the weaker party to be silent; and nowhere is this truth sooner learned than on shipboard. The quartermaster, consequently made no answer, and the gig came alongside, bringing back the officer who had carried the proceedings of the court up to Naples.

"Here we have it," said Cuffe, opening the important document, as soon as he and his brother captains were again in the cabin. "Approved: ordered that the sentence be carried into execution on board his majesty's ship, the *Proserpine*, Captain Cuffe, to-morrow, berween the ohurs of sunrise and sunset."

Then followed the date, and the well-known signature of "Nelson and Bronte." All this was what Cuffe both wished and expected, though he would have preferred a little more grace in carrying out the orders. The reader is not to suppose from this that our captain was either vengeful or bloody-minded; or that he really desired to inflict on Raoul any penalty for the manner in which he had baffled his own designs and caused his crew to suffer. So far from this, his intention was to use the sentence to extort from the prisoner a confession of the orders he had given to those left in the lugger, and then to use this confession as a means of obtaining his pardon, with a transfer to a prison-ship. Cuffe had no great veneration for privateersmen, nor was his estimate of their morality at all unreasonable, when he inferred that one who served with gain for his principal object, would not long hesitate about purchasing his own life by the betrayal of a secret like that he now asked. Had Raoul belonged even to a republican navy, the English man-of-war's man might have hesitated about carrying out his plans; but, with the master of a corsair, it appeared to be the most natural thing imaginable to attempt its execution. Both Sir Frederick and Lyon viewed the matter in the same light; and, now that everything was legally done that was necessary to the design, the capture of the lugger was deemed more than half accomplished.

"It is somewhat afflicting, too, Cuffe," observed Sir Frederick, in his drawling. indolent way; "it is somewhat afflicting, too, Cuffe, to be compelled to betray one's friends, or to be hanged! In Parliament, now, we say we'll be hanged if we do, and here you say you'll be hanged if you don't."

"Poh, poh! Dashwood; no one expects this Raoul Yvard will come to that fate, for no one thinks he will hold out. We shall get the lugger, and that will be the end of it. I'd give a thousand pounds to see that d——d *Few-Folly* at anchor within pistol-shot of my stern, at this blessed moment. My feelings are in the matter."

"Five hundred would be a high price," observed Lyon dryly. "I much doubt if the shares of us three come to as much as a hundred apiece, even should the craft fall into our hands."

"By the way, gents," put in Sir Frederick, gaping, "suppose we toss up or throw the dice, to see which shall have all, on supposition we get her within the next twenty-four hours, timing the affair by this ship's chronometers. You've dice on board, I daresay, Cuffe, and we can make a regular time of it, here, for half-an-hour, and no one the wiser."

"Your pardon, Captain Dashwood; I can suffer no such amusement. It is unmilitary, and contrary to regulations; and, then, hundreds are not as plenty with Lyon and myself as they are with you. I like to pocket my prize-money first, and sport on it afterward."

"You're right, Captain Cuffe," said Lyon; "though there can be no great innovation in sporting on Sir Frederick's portion, if he sees fit to indulge us. Money is an agreeable acquisition beyond a doubt, and life is sweet to saint and sinner alike; but I much question your facility in persuading this Monshure Rawl to tell you his secret consairning the lugger, in the manner ye anticipate."

This opinion met with no favor; and after discussing the point among themselves a little longer, the three captains were on the point of separating, when Griffin burst into the cabin, without even knocking, and altogether regardless of the usual observances.

"One would think it blew a typhoon, Mr. Griffin," said Cuffe, coldly, "by the rate at which you run before it."

"It's an ill wind that blows no luck, sir," answered the lieutenant, actually panting for breath, so great had been his haste to communicate what he had to say. "Our lookout, on the heights above Campanella, has just signaled us that he sees the lugger to the southward and eastward, somewhere near the point of Piane, I suppose, sir; and what is better, the wind is coming off shore earlier than common this evening."

"That is news!" exclaimed Cuffe, rubbing his hands with delight. "Go on deck, Griffin, and tell Winchester to unmoor; and then make a signal to the other ships to do the same. Now, gentlemen, we have the game in our own hands, and let us see and play it skillfully. In a couple of hours it will be dark, and our movements can all be made without being seen. As the *Proserpine* is, perhaps, the fastest ship"—at this remark Sir Frederick smiled ironically, while Lyon raised his eyebrows like one who saw a marvel—"as the *Proserpine* is, perhaps, the fastest ship, she ought to go the the furthest to leeward; and I will get under way, and stand off at sea, keeping

well to the northward and eastward, as if I were running for the Straits of Bonifacio, for instance, until it gets to be dark, when I will haul up south for a couple of hours or so; then come up as high as southeast until we are to the southward of the Gulf of Salerno. This will be before daylight, if the wind stand. At daylight, then, you may look out for me, off Piane, say two leagues, and to seaward, I hope, of the lugger. You shall follow, Sir Frederick, just as the sun sets, and keep in my wake, as near as possible; heaving-to, however, at midnight. This will bring you fairly abreast of the gulf, and about midway between the two capes, a little west of south from Campanella. Lyon, you can lie here until the night has fairly set in, when you can pass between Capri and the cape, and run down south two hours, and heave-to. This will place you in a position to watch the passage to and from the gulf, under the northern shore."

"And this arrangement completed to your satisfaction, Captain Cuffe," asked Lyon, deliberately helping himself to an enormous pinch of snuff, "what will be your pleasure in the posterior evolutions?"

"Each ship must keep her station until the day has fairly dawned. Should it turn out, as I trust it may, that we've got *Le Few-Folly* in-shore of us, all we'll have to do will be to close in upon her, and drive her up higher and higher into the bay. She will naturally run into shallow water; when we must anchor off, man the boats, send them north and south of her, and let them board her, under cover of our fire. If we find the lugger embayed, we'll have her as sure as fate."

"Very prettily conceived, Captain Cuffe; and in a way to be handsomely executed. But if we should happen to find the heathen outside of us?"

"Then make sail in chase to seaward, each ship acting for the best. Come, gentlemen, I do not wish to be inhospitable, but the *Proserpine* must be off. She has a long road before her; and the winds of this season of the year can barely be counted on for an hour at a time."

Cuffe being in such a hurry, his guests departed without further ceremony. As for Sir Frederick, the first thing he did was to order dinner an hour earlier than he had intended, and then to invite his surgeon and marine officer, two capital pairs of knives and forks, to come and share it with him, after which he sat down to play somewhat villainously on a flute. Two hours later, he gave the necessary orders to his first lieutenant; after which he troubled himself very little about the frigate he commanded. Lyon, on the other hand, sat down to a very frugal meal alone, as soon as he found himself again in his sloop; first ordering certain old sails to be got on deck, and to be mended for the eighth or ninth time.

With the *Proserpine* it was different. Her capstan-bars flew around, and one anchor was actually catted by the time her captain appeared on deck. The other soon followed, and three topsails fell, were sheeted home and hoisted, and sail was set until the ship went steadily past the low promontory of Ana Capri a cloud of canvas. Her head was to the westward, inclining a little north; and had there been any one to the southward to watch her movements, as there was not, so far as the eye could see, it would have been supposed that she was standing over toward the coast of Sardinia, most probably with an intention of passing by the Straits of Bonifacio, between that island and Corsica. The wine being nearly east, and it blowing a good breeze, the progress of the ship was such as promised to fulfill all the expectations of her commander.

As the sun set, and darkness diffused itself over the Mediterranean, the lighter steering-sails were taken in, and the *Proserpine* brought the wind a-beam, standing south. One of the last things visible from the decks, besides the mountains of the island and of the main, the curling smoke of Vesuvius, the blue void above and the bluer sea below, was the speck of the *Terpsichore*, as that ship followed, as near as might be, in her wake; Sir Frederick and his friends still at table, but with a vigilant and industrious first lieutenant on deck, who was sufficient in himself for all that was required of the vessel in any emergency. The latter had his orders, and he executed them with a precision and attention that promised to leave nothing to be wished for. On the other hand, the people of the *Ringdove* were kept at work mending old sails until the hour to " knock off work " arrived; then the ship unmoored. At the proper time the remaining anchor was lifted, and the sloop went through the pass between Capri and Campanella, as directed, when Lyon sent for the first lieutenant to join him in the cabin.

" Look you here, McBean," said Lyon, pointing to the chart which lay on the table. " Captain Cuffe has just run down off Piane, and will find himself well to leeward when the west wind comes to-morrow; Sir Frederick has followed, famously clear of the land, and won't be in a much better box. Now this lugger must be

pretty picking, if all they say of her be true. Ten to one but she has gold in her. These corsairs are desperate rogues after the siller, and, taking hull, sails, armament, head money, and the scrapings of the lockers together, I shouldn't marvel if she come to something as good as £8,000 or £10,000. This would be fair dividing for a sloop, but would amount to a painfully small trifle, as between the officers of three ships, and deducting the admiral's share. What are you thinking of, Airchy?"

" Of just that, Captain Lyon. It would be dividing every lieutenant's share by three, as well as every captain's."

" That's it, Airchy, and so ye'll have a shairp lookout on deck. There'll be no occasion to run down quite as far as Captain Cuffe suggested, ye'll obsairve; for, if in the bay, the lugger will work her way up toward this headland, and we'll be all the more likely to fall in with her, by keeping near it ourselves. Ye'll take the idea?"

" It's plain enou', Captain Lyon; and I'll be obsairving it. How is the law understood as respects dairkness? I understand that none share but such as are in sight; but is dairkness deemed a legal impediment?"

" To be sure it is; the idea being that all who can see may act. Now if we catch the lugger before Captain Cuffe and Sir Frederick even know where she is, on what principle can they aid and sustain us in the capture?"

" And you wish a shairp lookout, the night, Captain Lyon?"

" That just it, Airchy. Ye'll all be doing your best in the way of eyes, and we may get the lugger alone. 'Twould be such a pity, Mr. McBean, to divide by three, when the sums might be kept entire!"

Such was the state of feeling with which each of these three officers entered his present duty. Cuffe was earnest in the wish to catch his enemy, and this principally for the credit of the thing, though a little out of a desire to revenge his own losses; Sir Frederick Dashwood, indifferent to all but his own pleasures; and Lyon, closely attentive to the main chance. An hour or two later, or just before Cuffe turned in, he sent a message to request the presence of his first lieutenant if the latter were still up. Winchester was writing up his private journal; closing the book, he obeyed the order, in that quiet, submissive manner, which a first lieutenant is more apt to use toward his captain than toward any one else.

"Good evening, Winchester,"said Cuffe,

in a familiar, friendly way, which satisfied the subordinate that he was not sent for to be "rattled down"; "draw a chair and try a glass of this Capri wine, with some water. It's not carrying sail hard to drink a gallon of it; yet I rather think it fills up the chinks better than nothing."

"Thank'ee, Captain Cuffe, we like it in the gun-room, and got off a fresh cask or two this morning, while the court was sitting. So they tell me, sir, his lordship has put his name to it, and that this Frenchman is to swing from our fore-yardarm sometime to-morrow?"

"It stands so on the paper, Winchester; but if he confess where his lugger lies, all will go smoothly enough with him. However, as things look now, we'll have her, and thanks only to ourselves."

"Well, sir, that will be best, on the whole. I do not like to see a man selling his own people."

"There you are right enough, Winchester, and I trust we shall get along without it; though the lugger must be ours. I sent for you, by the way, about this Bolt; something must be done with that fellow."

"It's a clear case of desertion, Captain Cuffe; and, as it would now seem, of treason in the bargain. I would rather hang ten such chaps than one man like the Frenchman."

"Well, it's clear, Mr. Winchester, you do not bear malice! Have you forgotten Porto Ferrajo, and the boats, already? or do you love them that despitefully use you?"

"'Twas all fair service, sir, and one never thinks anything of that. I owe this Monsieur Yvard no grudge for what he did; but now it's all fairly over, I rather like him the better for it. But it's a very different matter as to this Bolt; a skulking scoundrel, who would let other men fight his country's battles, while he goes a privateering against British commerce."

"Aye, there's the rub, Winchester. Are they his country's battles?"

"Why, we took him for an Englishman, sir, and we must act up to our own professions, in order to be consistent."

"And so hang an innocent man for a treason that he could not commit?"

"Why, Captain Cuffe, do you believe the fellow's whining story about his being a Yankee? If that be true, we have done him so much injustice already as to make his case a very hard one. For my part, I look upon all these fellows as only so many disaffected Englishmen, and treat them accordingly."

"That is a sure way to quiet one's feelings, Winchester; but it's most too serious when it comes to hanging. If Bolt deserves any punishment, he deserves death; and that is a matter about which one ought to be tolerably certain before he pushes things too far. I've sometimes had my doubts about three or four of our people's being Englishmen, after all."

"There can be no certainty in these matters unless one could carry a parish register for the whole kingdom in his ship, Captain Cuffe. If they are not Englishmen, why do they not produce satisfactory proofs to show it? This is but reasonable, you must allow, sir."

"I don't know, Winchester; there are two sides to that question too. Suppose the king of Naples should seize you here, ashore, and call on you to prove that you are not one of his subjects. How would you go to work to make it out, no parish register being at hand?"

"Well, then, Captain Cuffe, if we are so very wrong, we had better give all these men up at once, though one of them is the very best hand in the ship; I think it right to tell you that, sir."

"There is a wide difference, sir, between giving a man up and hanging him. We are short-handed as it is, and cannot spare a single man. I've been looking over your station bills, and they never appeared so feeble before. We want eighteen or nineteen good seamen to make them respectable again; and though this Bolt is no great matter as a seaman, he can turn his hand to so many things, that he was as useful as the boatswain. In a word, we cannot spare him; either to let him go, or to hang him; even were the latter just."

"I'm sure, sir, I desire to do nothing that is unjust or inconvenient, and so act your pleasure in the affair."

"My pleasure is just this, then, Winchester. We must turn Bolt to duty. If the fellow is really an American, it would be a wretched business even to flog him for desertion; and as to treason, you know, there can be none without allegiance. Nelson gives me a discretion, and so we'll act on the safe side, and just turn him over to duty again. When there comes an opportunity, I'll inquire into the facts of the case, and if he can make out that he is not an Englishman, why, he must be discharged. The ship will be going home in a year or two, when everything will be settled fairly and deliberately. I dare say Bolt will not object to the terms."

"Perhaps not, sir. Then there's the crew, Captain Cuffe. They may think it strange treason and desertion go unpunished. These fellows talk and reason more than is always known aft."

"I've thought of all that, Winchester. I dare say you have heard of such a thing as a king's evidence? Well, here has Raoul Yvard been tried and found guilty as a spy; Bolt having been a witness. A few remarks judiciously made may throw everything off on that tack; and appearances may be preserved, so far as discipline is concerned."

"Yes, sir, that might be done, it's true; but an uneasy berth will the poor devil have of it, if the people fancy he has been a king's evidence. Men of that class hate a traitor worse than they do crime, Captain Cuffe, and they'll ride Bolt down like the main tack."

"Perhaps not; and if they do 'twill not be as bad as hanging. The fellow must think himself luckily out of a bad scrape, and thank God for all his mercies. You can see he suffers nothing unreasonable, or greatly out of the way. So send an order to the master-at-arms to knock the irons off the chap, and send him to duty, before you turn in, Winchester."

This settled the matter as to Ithuel, for the moment, at least. Cuffe was one of those men who was indisposed to push things too far, while he found it difficult to do his whole duty. There was not an officer in the *Proserpine* who had any serious doubts about the true country of Bolt, though there was not one officer among them all who would openly avow it. There was too much "granite" about Ithuel to permit Englishmen long to be deceived, and that very language on which the impressed man so much prided himself would have betrayed his origin, had other evidence been wanting. Still there was a tenacity about an English ship of war, in that day, that did not easily permit an athletic hand to escape its grasp, when it had once closed upon him. In a great and enterprising service like that of Great Britain, an *esprit de corps* existed in the respective ships, which made them the rivals of each other, and men being the great essentials of efficiency, a single seaman was relinquished with a reluctance that must have been witnessed, fully to be understood. Cuffe consequently could not make up his mind to do full justice to Ithuel, while he could not make up his mind to push injustice so far as trial and punishment. Nelson had left him a discretion, as has been said, and this he chose to use in the manner just mentioned.

Had the case of the New Hampshire man been fairly brought before the British admiral, his discharge would have been ordered without hesitation. Nelson was too far removed from the competition of the separate ships, and ordinarily under the control of too high motives, to be accessory to the injustice of forcibly detaining a foreigner in his country's service; for it was only while under the malign influence to which there has already been allusion, that he ceased to be high-minded and just. Prejudiced he was, and in some cases exceedingly so; America standing but a little better in his eyes than France herself. For the first of these antipathies he had some apology; since in addition to the aversion that was naturally produced by the history of the Cisatlantic republic, accident had thrown him in the way, in the West Indies, of ascertaining the frauds, deceptions, and cupidities of a class of men that never exhibit national character in its brightest and most alluring colors. Still, he was too upright of mind, willingly to countenance injustice, and too chivalrous to oppress. But Ithuel had fallen into the hands of one who fell far short of the high qualities of the admiral, while at the same time he kept clear of his more prominent weaknesses, and who was brought within the sphere of the competition between the respective ships and their crews.

Winchester, of course, obeyed his orders. He roused the master-at-arms from his hammock, and directed him to bring Bolt to the quarter-deck.

"In consequence of what took place this morning," said the first lieutenant, in a voice loud enough to be heard by all near him, "Captain Cuffe has seen fit to order you to be released, Bolt, and turned to duty again. You will know how to appreciate this leniency, and will serve with greater zeal than ever, I make no doubt. Never forget that you have been with a yard-rope, as it might be, round your neck. In the morning you will be stationed and berthed anew."

Ithuel was too shrewd to answer. He fully understood the reason why he escaped punishment, and it increased his hopes of eventually escaping from the service itself. Still he gagged a little at the idea of passing for one who peached, or for a "State's evidence," as he called it; that character involving more sin, in vulgar eyes, than the commission of a thousand legal crimes. This gave Winchester no concern. After dismissing his man, he gossiped a minute or two with Yelverton, who had the watch, gaped once or twice somewhat provokingly, and going below, was in a deep sleep in ten minutes.

CHAPTER XX.

THE dawning of day, on the morning which succeeded, was a morning of great interest on board the different English ships which then lay off the Gulf of Salerno. Cuffe and Lyon were called, according to especial orders left by themselves, while even Sir Frederick Dashwood allowed himself to be awakened, to hear the report of the officer of the watch. The first was up quite half-an-hour before the light appeared. He even went into the maintop again, in order to get as early and as wide a survey of the horizon as he wished. Griffin went aloft with him, and together they stood leaning against the topmast rigging, watching the slow approach of those rays which gradually diffused themselves over the whole of a panorama that was as bewitching as the hour and the lovely accessories of an Italian landscape could render it.

"I see nothing in-shore," exclaimed Cuffe, in a tone of disappointment, when the light permitted a tolerable view of the coast. "If she should be outside of us, our work will be only half done!"

"There is a white speck close in with the land, sir," returned Griffin; "here, in the direction of those ruins, of which our gentlemen that have been round in the boats to look at, tell such marvels; I believe, however, it is only a felucca or a sparanara. There is a peak to the sail that does not look lugger-fashion."

"What is this, off here at the north-west, Griffin? Is it too large for the *Le Few-Folly?*"

"That must be the *Terpsichore*, sir. It's just where she ought to be, as I understand the orders; and I suppose Sir Frederick has carried her there. But yonder's a sail, in the northern board, which may turn out to be the lugger; she is fairly within Campanella, and is not far from the north shore of the bay."

"By George! that must be she; Monsieur Yvard has kept her skulking round and about Amalfi all this time! Let us go down, and set everything that will draw, at once, sir."

In two minutes Griffin was on deck, hauling the yards, and clearing away to make sail. As usual, the wind was light at the southward again, and the course would be nearly before it. Studding-sail booms were to be run out, the sails set, and the ship's head laid to the northward, keeping a little to seaward of the chase. At this moment the *Proserpine* had the Point of Piane and the little village of Abate nearly a-beam. The ship might have been going four knots through the water, and the distance across the mouth of the bay was something like thirty miles. Of course, eight hours would be necessary to carry the frigate over the intervening space, should the wind stand, as it probably would not, at that season of the year. A week later, and strong southerly winds might be expected, but that week was as interminable as an age, for any present purpose.

Half-an-hour's trial satisfied all on the deck of the *Proserpine*, that the chase was keeping off, like themselves, and that she was standing towards the mountains of Amalfi. Her progress, too, was about equal to that of the frigate, for, dead before the wind, the latter ship was merely a good sailer; her great superiority commencing only when she brought the breeze forward of the beam. It had been supposed that the stranger, when first seen, was about fifteen miles distant, his canvas appearing both small and shapeless; but some doubts now began to be entertained, equally as to his rig, his size, and his distance. If a large or a lofty vessel, of course he must be materially farther off, and if a large or lofty vessel it could not be *Le Feu-Follet*.

The other frigate took her cue from the *Proserpine*, and stood across from the northern side of the gulf; a certain proof that nothing was visible, from her mastheads, to lead her in any other direction. Two hours, however, satisfied all on board the latter ship that they were on the wrong scent, and that the vessel to leeward was their own consort, the sloop; Lyon having, in his eagerness to get the prize before she could be seen from the other ships, carried the *Ringdove* quite within the bay, and thus misled Cuffe and Sir Frederick.

"There can no longer be any doubt!" exclaimed the captain of the *Proserpine*, dropping his glass, with vexation too strongly painted in his manner to be mistaken; "that is a ship; and, as you say, Winchester, it must be the *Ringdove;* though what the devil Lyon is doing away in there with her, unless he sees something close under the land, is more than I can tell. As there is clearly nothing in this quarter, we will stand on, and take a look for ourselves."

This nearly destroyed the hopes of success. The officers began to suspect that their lookout on Campanella had been deceived, and that what he had supposed to be a lugger, was, in truth, a felucca, or perhaps a xebec, a craft which might well be mistaken for a lugger, at the distance of a few leagues. The error, however, was with those in the ship. The officer sent upon the heights was a shrewd, practiced master's mate, who knew everything about his profession that properly came within his line, and knew little else. But for a habit of drinking, he would long since have been a lieutenant, being, in truth, an older sailor than Winchester; but, satisfied of his own infirmity, and coming from a class in life in which preferment was viewed as a God-send rather than as a right, he had long settled down into the belief that he was to live and die in his present station, thereby losing most of the desire to rise.

The name of this man was Clinch. In consequence of his long experience, within the circle of his duties, his opinion was greatly respected by his superiors, when he was sober; and, as he had the precaution not to be otherwise when engaged on service, his weakness seldom brought him into any serious difficulties. Cuffe, as a last hope, had sent him up on the heights of Campanella, with a perfect conviction that, if anything was really in sight, he would not fail to see it. All this confidence, however, had now ended in disappointment; and, half an hour later, when it was announced to Cuffe, that "the cutter, with Mr. Clinch, was coming down the bay towards them," the former even heard the name of his drunken favorite with disgust. As was usual with him when out of humor, he went below as the boat drew near, leaving orders for her officer to be sent down to him, the instant the latter got on board. Five minutes later, Clinch thrust his hard-looking, weather-beaten, but handsome red countenance in at the cabin door.

"Well, sir," commenced the captain, on a tolerably high key, "a d——d pretty wild-goose chase you've sent us all on, down here, into this bay! The southerly wind is failing already, and in half an hour the ships will be frying the pitch off their decks, without a breath of air; when the wind does come, it will come out at west, and bring us all four or five leagues dead to leeward!"

Clinch's experience had taught him the useful man-of-war lesson, and to bow to the tempest, and not to attempt to brave it. Whenever he was "rattled down," as he called it, he had the habit of throwing an expression of surprise, comically blended with contrition, into his countenance, that seemed to say, "What have I done now?" or, "If I have done anything amiss, you see how sorry I am for it." He met his irritated commander, on the present occasion, with this expression, and

it produced the usual effect of mollifying him a little.

"Well, sir; explain this matter, if you please," continued Cuffe, after a moment's hesitation.

"Will you please tell me, sir, what you wish explained?" inquired Clinch, throwing more surprise than common, even, into his countenance.

"That is an extraordinary question, Mr. Clinch! I wish the signal you made from yonder headland explained, sir. Did you not signal the ship to say that you saw the Le Few-Folly down here, at the southward?"

"Well, sir, I'm glad there was no mistake in the matter," answered Clinch, in a confident and relieved manner. "I was afraid at first, Captain Cuffe, my signal had not been understood."

"Understood! How could it be mistaken? You showed a black ball for 'The lugger's in sight.' You'll not deny that, I trust?"

"No, sir; one black ball for 'The lugger's in sight.' That's just what I did show, Captain Cuffe."

"And three black balls together for 'She bears due south from Capri.' What do you say to that?"

"All right, sir. Three black balls together for 'She bears due south from Capri.' I didn't tell the distance, Captain Cuffe, because Mr. Winchester gave me no signals for that."

"And these signals you kept showing every half hour, as long as it was light; even until the Proserpine was off."

"All according to orders, Captain Cuffe, as Mr. Winchester will tell you. I was to repeat every half hour, as long as the lugger was in sight and the day lasted."

"Ay, sir; but you were not ordered to send us after some jack-o'-lantern, or to mistake some xebec or other from one of the Greek islands for a light, handy French lugger."

"Nor did I, Captain Cuffe, begging your pardon, sir. I signaled the Few-Folly, and nothing else, I give you my word for it."

Cuffe looked hard at the master's mate for half a minute, and his ire insensibly lessened as he gazed.

"You are too old a seaman, Clinch, not to know what you are about! If you saw the privateer, be good enough to tell us what has become of her."

"That is more than I can say, Captain Cuffe, though see her I did; and that so plainly, as to be able to make out her jigger, even. You know, sir, we shot away her jigger-mast in the chase off Elba, and she got a new one, that steves for'ard uncommonly. I noticed that when we fell in with her in the Canal of Piombino; and seeing it again, could not but know it. But there's no mistaking the saucy *Folly*, for them that has ever seen her; and I am certain we made her out, about four leagues to the southward of the cape, at the time I first signaled."

"Four leagues! I had thought she must be at least eight or ten, and kept off that distance, to get her in the net. Why did you not let us know her distance?"

"Had no signals for that, Captain Cuffe."

"Well, then, why not send a boat to tell us the fact?"

"Had no orders, sir. Was told by Mr. Winchester just to signal the lugger and her bearings; and this, you must own, Captain Cuffe, we did plain enough. Besides, sir—"

"Well; besides what?" demanded the captain, observing that the master's-mate hesitated.

"Why, sir, how was I to know that any one in the ship would think a lugger could be seen eight or ten leagues? That's a long bit of water, sir; and it would take a heavy ship's spars to rise high enough for such a sight."

"The land you were on, Clinch, was much loftier than any vessel's spars."

"Quite true, sir; but not lofty enough for that, Captain Cuffe. That I saw the *Folly*, I'm as certain as I am of being in this cabin."

"What has become of her, then? You perceive she is not in the bay now."

"I suppose, Captain Cuffe, that she stood in until near enough for her purpose, and that she must have hauled off the land after the night set in. There was plenty of room for her to pass out to sea again, between the two frigates, and not be seen in the dark."

This conjecture was so plausible as to satisfy Cuffe; yet it was not the fact. Clinch had made *Le Feu-Follet*, from his elevated post, to the southward, as his signal had said; and he was right in all his statements about her, until darkness concealed her movements. Instead of passing out of the bay, as he imagined, however, she had hauled up within a quarter of a league of Campanella, doubled that point, brushed along the coast to the northward of it, fairly within the bay of Naples, and pushed out to sea between Capri and Ischia, going directly athwart the anchorage the men-of-war had so recently quitted, in order to do so.

When Raoul quitted his vessel, he ordered her to stand directly off the land, just keeping Ischia and Capri in view, lying-to under her jigger. As this was low sail, and a lugger shows so little aloft, it was a common expedient of cruisers of that rig, when they wished to escape observation. Monsieur Pintard, Raoul's first lieutenant, had expected a signal from his commander, at the very spot where Clinch had taken his station; but seeing none, he had swept along the coast after dark, in the hope of discovering his position by the burning of a blue light. Failing in this, however, he went off the land again, in time to get an offing before the return of day, and to save the wind. It was the boldness of the maneuver that saved the lugger; Lyon going out through the pass between Capri and Campanella, about twenty minutes before Pintard brushed close round the rocks, under his jigger and jib only, anxiously looking out for a signal from his captain. The Frenchmen saw the sloop-of-war quite plainly, and by the aid of their night-glasses ascertained her character, mistaking her, however, for another ship, bound to Sicily or Malta; while their own vessel escaped observation, owing to the little sail she carried, the want of hamper, and her situation so near the land, which gave her a background of rocks. Clinch had not seen the movements of the lugger after dark, in consequence of his retiring to the village of St. Agata, to seek lodgings, as soon as he perceived that his own ship had gone to sea, and left him and his boat's crew behind. The following morning, when he made the ship to the southward, he pushed off, and pulled toward his proper vessel, as related.

"Where did you pass the night, Clinch?" demanded the captain, after they had discussed the probability of the lugger's escape. "Not on the heights, under the canopy of heaven?"

"On the heights, and under the great canopy that has covered us both so often, Captain Cuffe; but with a good Neapolitan mud-roof between it and my head. As soon as it was dark, and I saw that the ship was off, I found a village, named St. Agata, that stands on the heights, just a-beam of those rocks they call the Sirens, and there we were well berthed until morning."

"You are lucky in bringing back all the boat's crew, Clinch. You know it's low water with us as to men just now, and our fellows are not at all to be trusted ashore, in a country that is full of stone walls, good wine, and pretty girls."

"I always take a set of regular steady ones with me, Captain Cuffe; I haven't lost a man from a boat these five years."

"You must have some secret, then,

worth knowing; for even the admirals sometimes lose their bargemen. I daresay, now, yours are all married chaps, that hold on to their wives as to so many sheet anchors; they say that it is often a good expedient.''

"Not at all, sir. I did that, till I found that half the fellows would run to get rid of their wives. The Portsmouth and Plymouth marriages don't always bring large estates with them, sir, and the bridegrooms like to cut adrift at the end of the honeymoon. Don't you remember when we were in the *Blenheim* together, sir, we lost eleven of the launch's crew at one time; and nine of them turned out to be vagabonds, sir, that deserted their weeping wives and suffering families at home!''

"Now you mention it, I do remember something of the sort; draw a chair, Clinch, and take a glass of grog. Tim, put a bottle of Jamaica before Mr. Clinch. I have heard it said that you are married yourself, my gallant master's mate?''

"Lord, Captain Cuffe, that's one of the young gentlemen's stories! If a body believed all they say, the Christian religion would soon get athwart-hawse, and mankind be all adrift in their morals,'' said Clinch, smacking his lips after a very grateful draught. "We've a regular set of high-flyers aboard this ship, at this blessed minute, Captain Cuffe, sir, and Mr. Winchester has his hands full of them. I often wonder at his patience, sir.''

"We were young once ourselves, Clinch, and ought to be indulgent to the follies of youth. But what sort of a berth did you find last night upon the rocks yonder?''

"Why, sir, as good as one can expect out of old England. I fell in with an elderly woman calling herself Giuntotardi—which is regular built Italian, isn't it, sir?''

"That it is; but, you speak the language, I believe, Clinch?''

"Why, sir, I have been drifting about the world so long, that I speak a little of everything, finding it convenient when I stand in need of victuals and drink. The old lady on the hill and I overhauled a famous yarn between us, sir. It seems she has a niece and brother at Naples, who ought to have been back night before last; and she was in lots of tribulation about them, wanting to know if our ship had seen anything of the rovers.''

"By George, Clinch, you were on the soundings there, had you but known it! Our prisoner has been in that part of the world, and we might get some clew to his maneuvers, by questioning the old woman closely; I hope you parted good friends?''

"The best in the world. No one that feeds and lodges me well need dread me as an enemy!''

"I'll warrant it! That's the reason you are so loyal, Clinch?''

The hard, red face of the master's mate worked a little, and though he could not well look all sorts of colors, he looked all ways but in his captain's eye. It was now ten years since he ought to have been a lieutenant, having once actually outranked Cuffe, in the way of date of service at least; and his conscience told him two things quite distinctly; first, the fact of his long and weary probation; second, that it was, in a great degree, his own fault.

"I love his majesty, sir,'' Clinch observed, after giving a gulp, "and I never lay anything that goes hard with myself to his account. Still memory will be memory, and spite of all I can do, sir, I sometimes remember what I might have been as well as what I am. If his majesty does feed me, it is with the spoon of the master's mate, and if he does lodge me, it is in the cock-pit.''

"I have been your shipmate often, and for years at a time, answered Cuffe, good-naturedly, though a little in the manner of a superior; "and no one knows your history better. It is not your friends who have failed you at need, so much as a certain enemy, with whom you will insist on associating, though he harms them most who love him best.''

"Ay, ay, sir; that can't be denied, Captain Cuffe; yet it's a hard life that passes altogether without hope.''

This was uttered with an expression of melancholy that said more for Clinch's character than Cuffe had witnessed in the man for years, and it revived many early impressions in his favor. Clinch and he had once been messmates, even; and though years of a decided disparity in rank had since interposed their barrier of etiquette and feeling, Cuffe never could entirely forget the circumstance.

"It is hard, indeed, to live as you say, without hope,'' returned the captain; "but hope ought to be the last thing to die. You should make one more rally, Clinch, before you throw up in despair.''

"It is not so much for myself, Captain Cuffe, that I mind it, as for some that live ashore. My father was as reputable a tradesman as there was in Plymouth, and when he got me on the quarter-deck he thought he was about to make a gentleman of me, instead of leaving me to pass a life in a situation that may be said to be even beneath what his own was."

"Now you undervalue your station, Clinch. The berth of a master's-mate in one of his majesty's finest frigates, is something to be proud of ; I was once a master's mate—nay, Nelson has doubtless filled the same station. For that matter, one of his majesty's own sons may have gone through the rank."

"Ay, gone through it, as you say, sir," returned Clinch, with a husky voice. "It does well enough for them that go through it, but it's death to them that stick. It's a feather in a midshipman's cap to be rated a mate ; but it's no honor to be a mate at my time of life, Captain Cuffe."

"What's your age, Clinch? You are not much my senior ? "

"Your senior, sir ! The difference in our years is not as great as in our rank, certainly, though I never shall see thirty-two again. But it's not so much that, after all, as the thoughts of my poor mother, who set her heart on seeing me with his majesty's commission in my pocket ; and of another, who set her heart on one that I'm afraid was never worthy of her affection."

"This is new to me, Clinch," returned the captain, with interest. "One so seldom thinks of a master's-mate marrying, that the idea of your being in that way has never crossed my mind, except in the manner of a joke."

"Master's-mates have married, Captain Cuffe, and they have ended in being very miserable. But Jane, as well as myself, has made up her mind to live single, unless we can see brighter prospects before us than what my present hopes afford."

"Is it quite right, Jack, to keep a poor young woman towing along in this uncertainty, during the period of life when her chances for making a good connection are the best ? "

Clinch stared at his commander until his eyes filled with tears. The glass had not touched his lips since the conversation took its present direction ; and the usual hard settled character of his face was becoming expressive once more, with human emotions.

"It's not my fault, Captain Cuffe," he answered, in a low voice ; "it's now quite six years since I insisted on her giving me up ; but she wouldn't hear of the thing. A very respectable attorney wished to have her, and I even prayed her to accept his offer ; and the only unkind glance I ever got from her eye was when she heard me make a request that she told me

sounded impiously almost to her ears. She would be a sailor's wife or die a maid."

"The girl has unfortunately got some romantic notions concerning the profession, Clinch, and they are ever the hardest to be convinced of what is for their own good."

"Jane Weston! Not she, sir. There is not as much romance about her as in the fly-leaves of a prayer-book. She is all heart, poor Jane ; and how I came to get such a hold of it, Captain Cuffe, is a great mystery to myself. I certainly do not deserve half her affection, and now I begin to despair of ever being able to repay her for it."

Clinch was still a handsome man, though exposure and his habits had made some inroads on a countenance that by nature was frank, open, and prepossessing. It now expressed the anguish that occasionally came over his heart, as the helplessness of his situation presented itself fully to his mind. Cuffe's feelings were touched, for he remembered the time when they were messmates, with a futute before them that promised no more to the one than to the other, the difference in the chances which birth afforded the captain, alone excepted.

Clinch was a prime seaman, and as brave as a lion, too ; qualities that secured to him a degree of respect that his occasional self-forgetfulness had never entirely forfeited. Some persons thought him the most skillful mariner the *Proserpine* contained ; and, perhaps, this was true, if the professional skill were confined strictly to the handling of a ship, or to taking care of her on critical occasions. All these circumstances induced Cuffe to enter more closely into the master's-mate's present distress than he might otherwise have done. Instead of shoving the bottle to him, however, as if conscious how much disappointed hope had already driven the other to its indiscreet use, he pushed it gently aside, and taking his old messmate's hand with a momentary forgetfulness of the difference in rank, he said in a tone of kindness and confidence that had long been strangers to Clinch's ears—

"Jack, my honest fellow, there is good stuff in you yet, if you will only give it fair play. Make a manly rally, respect yourself for a few months, and something will turn up that will yet give you your Jane, and gladden your poor old mother's heart."

There are periods in the lives of men when a few kind words, backed by a friendly act or two, might save thousands of human beings from destruction. Such was the crisis in the fate of Clinch. He had almost given up hope, though it did occasionally revive in him whenever he got a cheering letter from the constant Jane, who pertinaciously refused to believe anything to his prejudice, and religiously abstained from all reproaches. But it is necessary to understand the influence of rank on board a man-of-war fully to comprehend the effect which was now produced on the master's mate by the captain's language and manner. Tears streamed out of the eyes of Clinch, and he grasped the hand of his commander, almost convulsively.

"What can I do, sir? Captain Cuffe, what can I do?" he exclaimed. "My duty is never neglected; but there are moments of despair, when I find the burden too hard to be borne, without calling upon the bottle for support."

"Whenever a man drinks with such a motive, Clinch, I would advise him to abstain altogether. He cannot trust himself; and that which he terms his friend is, in truth, his direst enemy. Refuse your rations, even; determine to be free. One week, nay, one day, may give a strength that will enable you to conquer by leaving your reason unimpaired. Absence from the ship has accidentally befriended you; for the little you have taken here has not been sufficient to do any harm. We are now engaged on a most interesting duty, and I will throw service into your way that may be of importance to you. Get your name once fairly in a dispatch, and your commission is safe. Nelson loves to prefer old tars; and nothing would make him happier than to be able to serve you. Put it in my power to ask it of him, and I'll answer for the result. Something may yet come out of your visit to the cottage of this woman, and do you be mindful to keep yourself in fortune's way."

"God bless you, Captain Cuffe; God bless you, sir," answered Clinch, nearly choked; "I'll endeavor to do as you wish."

"Remember Jane and your mother. With such a woman dependent for her happiness on his existence, a man must be a brute not to struggle hard."

Clinch groaned—for Cuffe probed his wound deep; though it was done with an honest desire to cure. After wiping the perspiration from his face, and writhing on his chair, however, he recovered a little of his self-command, and became comparatively composed.

"If a friend could only point out the way by which I might recover some of the lost ground," he said, "my gratitude to him would last as long as life, Captain Cuffe."

"Here is an opening then, Clinch. Nelson attaches as much importance to our catching this lugger as he ever did to falling in with the fleet. The officer who is serviceable on this occasion may be sure of being remembered, and I will give you every chance in my power. Go, dress yourself in your best; make yourself look as you know you can; then be ready for boat service. I have some duty for you now, which will be but the beginning of good luck, if you only remain true to your mother, to Jane, and to yourself."

A new life was infused into Clinch. For years he had been overlooked—apparently forgotten, except when thorough seamanship was required; and even his experiment of getting transferred to a vessel commanded by an old messmate had seemingly failed. Here was a change, however, and a ray, brighter than common, shone across the darkness of his future. Even Cuffe was struck with the cheerfulness of his countenance, and the alacrity of the master's-mate's movements and he reproached himself with having so long been indifferent to the best interests of one who certainly had some claims on his friendship. Still, there was nothing unusual in the present relations between these old messmates. Favored by family and friends, Cuffe had never been permitted to fall into despondency, and had pursued his career successfully and with spirit; while the other, unsupported, and failing of any immediate opportunity for getting ahead, had fallen into evil ways, and come to be, by slow degrees, the man he was. Such instances as the latter are of not unfrequent occurrence, even in a marine in which promotion is as regular as our own, though it is rare indeed that a man recovers his lost ground, when placed in circumstances so trying.

In half an hour Clinch was ready dressed in his best. The gentlemen of the quarter-deck saw all these preparations with surprise; for, of late, the master's mate had seldom been seen in that part of the ship at all. But in a man-of-war, discipline is a matter of faith, and no one presumed to ask questions. Clinch was closeted with the captain for a few minutes, received his orders, and went over the ship's side with a cheerful countenance, actually entering the captain's gig, the fastest rowing-boat of the ship. As soon as seated, he shoved off, and held his way toward the point of Campanella, then distant about three leagues. No one knew whither he was bound, though all believed it was on duty that related to the lugger, and duty that required a seaman's judgment. As for Cuffe, his manner, which had begun to be uneasy and wandering, became more composed when he saw his old messmate fairly off, and that, too, at a rate which would carry him even to Naples in the course of a few hours, should his voyage happen to be so long.

CHAPTER XXI.

It was now certain that *Le Feu-Follet* was not in the Bay of Salerno. By means of the lofty spars of the ship, and the aid of glasses, the whole coast had been effectually surveyed, and no signs of such a craft were visible. Even Lyon had given it up, had wore round, and was standing along the land again, toward Campanella, a disappointed man. As Cuffe expected the next wind from the westward, he continued on to the northward, however, intending to go off Amalfi and question any fisherman he might fall in with. Leaving the ship slowly pursuing her course in that direction, then, we will turn our attention to the state of the prisoners.

Ghita and her uncle had been properly cared for all this time. The gunner's wife lived on board, and, being a respectable woman, Cuffe had the delicacy to send the poor girl forward to the stateroom and mess of this woman. Her uncle was provided for near by, and, as neither was considered in any degree criminal, it was the intention to put them ashore as soon as it was certain that no information concerning the lugger was to be obtained from them. Ithuel was at duty again, having passed half the morning in the fore-top. The shore-boat, which was in the way on deck, was now struck into the water, and was towing astern, in waiting for the moment when Carlo Giuntotardi and his niece were to be put in possession of it again, and permitted to depart. This moment was delayed, however, until the ship should again double Campanella, and be once more in the Bay of Naples, as it would have been cruel to send two such persons as the uncle and niece adrift at any material distance from their proper place of landing.

It was very different with Raoul Yvard, however. He was under the charge of a sentry on the berth-deck, in waiting for the fearful moment when he should be brought forth for execution. His sentence was generally known in the ship, and with a few he was an object of interest; though punishment, deaths in battle, and all the other casualties of nautical life, were much too familiar in such a war to awaken anything like a sensation in an active cruising frigate. Still, some had a thought for the prisoner's situation. Winchester was a humane man, and, to his credit, he bore no malice for his own defeat and sufferings; while in his capacity of first lieutenant it was in his power to do much toward adding to the comfort of the condemned. He had placed the prisoner between two open ports, where the air circulated freely, no trifling consideration in so warm a climate, and had ordered a canvas bulkhead to be placed around him, giving Raoul the benefit of a state-room for his meditations at so awful a moment. His irons, too, had been removed as useless; though care had been had to take away from the prisoner everything by which he might attempt his own life. The probability of his jumping through a port had been discussed between the first and second lieutenants; but the sentry was admonished to be on his guard against any such attempt, and little apprehension was felt, Raoul being so composed and so unlikely to do anything precipitately. Then it would be easy to pick him up, while the vessel moved so slowly. To own the truth, too, many would prefer his drowning himself, to see him swinging at a yard-arm.

In this narrow prison, then, Raoul passed the night and morning. It would be representing him as more stoical than the truth, if we said he was unmoved. So far from this, his moments were bitter, and his anguish would have been extreme, were it not for a high resolution which prompted him to die, as he fancied it, like *un Francais*. The numerous executions by the guillotine had brought fortitude under such circumstances into a sort of fashion, and there were few who did not meet death with decorum. With our prisoner, however, it was still different; for, sustained by a dauntless spirit, he would have faced the great tyrant of the race, even in his most ruthless mood, with firmness, if not with disdain. But, to a young man and a lover, the last great change could not well approach without bringing with it a feeling of hopelessness, that, in the case of Raoul, was unrelieved by any cheering expectations of the future. He fully believed his doom to be sealed, and that, less on account of his imaginary offense as a spy, than on account of the known and extensive injuries he had done to the English commerce.

Raoul was a good hater; and according to the fashion of past times, which we apprehend, in spite of the vast deal of equivocal philanthropy that now circulates freely from mouth to mouth and from pen to pen, will continue to be the fashion of times to come, he heartily disliked the people with whom he was at war, and consequently was ready to believe anything to their prejudice that political rivalry might invent; a frame of mind that led him to think his life would be viewed as a trifle when put in the scales against English ascendency or English profit. He was accustomed to think of the people of Great Britain as a "nation of shopkeepers," and, while engaged himself in a calling that bears the brand of rapacity on its very brow, he looked upon his own pursuit as comparatively martial and honorable; qualities, in sooth, it was far from being without, as he himself had exercised its functions. In a word, Raoul understood Cuffe, as little as Cuffe understood him; facts that will sufficiently appear in the interview which it has now become our office to relate.

The prisoner received one or two friendly visits in the course of the morning; Griffin, in particular, conceiving it to be his duty to try to cheer the condemned man, on account of his own knowledge of foreign tongues. On these occasions the conversation was prevented from falling into anything like the somber, by the firmness of the prisoner's manner. With a view to do the thing handsomely, Winchester had caused the canvas bulk-head to include the guns on each side, which, of course, gave more air and light within the narrow apartment, as it brought both ports into the little room. Raoul adverted to this circumstance, as, seated on one stool, he invited Griffin, in the last of his visits, to take another.

"You find me here, supported by a piece of eighteen on each side," observed the prisoner, smiling, "as becomes a seaman who is about to die. Were my death to come from the mouths of your cannon, Monsieur Lieutenant, it would only meet me a few months, or perhaps a few days sooner that it might happen by the same mode in the ordinary course of events."

"We know how to feel for a brave man in your situation," answered Griffin, with emotion; "and nothing would make us all happier than to have it as you say; you in a good warm frigate, on our broadside, and we in this of our own, contending fairly for the honor of our respective countries."

"Monsieur, the fortune of war has ordered it otherwise but, you are not seated, Monsieur Lieutenant."

"Mon pardon—Captain Cuffe has sent me to request you will favor him with your company, in his cabin, as soon as it may be agreeable to yourself, Monsieur Yvard."

There is something in the polished expressions of the French language that would have rendered it difficult for Griffin to have been other than delicate in his communications with the prisoner, had he been so disposed; but such was not his inclination; for, now that their gallant adversary was at their mercy, all the brave men in the *Proserpine* felt a disposition to deal tenderly with him. Raoul was touched with these indications of generosity, and, as he had witnessed Griffin's spirit in the different attempts made on his lugger, it inclined him to think better of his foes. Rising, he professed his readiness to attend the captain at that very moment.

Cuffe was waiting in the after-cabin. When Griffin and the prisoner entered, he courteously requested both to be seated, the former being invited to remain, not only as a witness of what might occur, but to act as interpreter in case of need. A short pause succeeded, and then the captain opened the dialogue, which was carried on in English, with occasional assistance from Griffin, whenever it became necessary.

"I greatly regret, Monsieur Yvard, to see a brave man in your situation," commenced Cuffe, who, sooth to say, apart from the particular object he had in view, uttered no more than the truth. "We have done full justice to your spirit and judgment, while we have tried the hardest to get you into our power. But the laws of war are severe, necessarily, and we English have a commander-in-chief who is not disposed to trifle in matters of duty."

This was said, partly in policy and partly from a habit of standing in awe of the character of Nelson. Raoul received it, however, in the most favorable light; though the politic portion of the motive was altogether thrown away, as will be seen in the sequel.

"Monsieur, un Francais knows how to die in the cause of liberty and his country," answered Raoul, courteously, yet with emphasis.

"I do not doubt it, monsieur; still I see no necessity of pushing things to that extremity. England is as liberal of her rewards as she is powerful to resent injuries. Perhaps some plan may be adopted which will avert the necessity of sacrificing the life of a brave man in so cruel a mode."

"I shall not affect to play the hero, Monsieur le Capitaine. If any proper mode of relieving me, in my present crisis, can be discovered, my gratitude will be in proportion to the service rendered."

"This is talking sensibly and to the purpose; I make no doubt, when we come to a right understanding, everything will be amicably arranged between us. Griffin, do me the favor to help yourself to a glass of wine and water, which you will find refreshing, this warm day. Monsieur Yvard will join us; the wine coming from Capri, and being far from bad; though some do prefer the Lachrymæ Christi that grows about the foot of Vesuvius, I believe."

Griffin did as desired, though his own countenance was far from expressing all the satisfaction that was obvious in the face of Cuffe. Raoul declined the offer; waiting for the forthcoming explanation with an interest he did not affect to conceal. Cuffe seemed disappointed and reluctant to proceed; but, finding his two companions silent, he was obliged to make his proposal.

"Oui, monsieur," he added, "England is powerful to resent, but ready to forgive. You are very fortunate in having it in your power, at so serious a moment, to secure her pardon for an offense that is always visited in war with a punishment graver than any other."

"In what way can this be done, Monsieur le Capitaine? I am not one who despises life; more especially when it is in danger of being lost by a disgraceful death."

"I am rejoiced, Monsieur Yvard, to find you in this frame of mind; it will relieve me from the discharge of a most painful duty, and be the means of smoothing over many difficulties. Without doubt, you have heard of the character of our celebrated Admiral Nelson?"

"His name is known to every seaman, monsieur," answered Raoul, stiffly; his natural antipathies being far from cured by the extremity of his situation. "He has written it on the waters of the Nile, in letters of blood!"

"Ay, his deeds, there or elsewhere, will not soon be forgotten. He is a man of an iron will; when his heart is set on a thing, he sticks at no risk to obtain it, especially if the means be lawful, and the end glory. To be frank, monsieur, he wishes much for your lugger, the *Le Feu-Folly.*"

"Ah!" exclaimed Raoul, smiling ironically, "Nelson is not the only English admiral who has had the same desire. *Le Feu-Follet*, Monsieur le Capitaine, is so charming that she has many admirers!"

"Among whom Nelson is one of the warmest. Now this makes your case so much the easier to be disposed of. You have nothing to do but put the lugger into our hands, when you will be pardoned and treated as a prisoner of war."

"Does Monsieur Nelson authorize you to make this proposal to me?" asked Raoul, gravely.

"He does. Intrusted with the care of his country's interests, he is willing to overlook the offense against her, under the law of nations, to deprive the enemy of doing so much harm. Put the lugger into our hands and you shall be sent to an ordinary prison-ship. Nay, merely let us into the secret of her position and we will see to her capture."

"Monsieur Nelson doubtless does no more than his duty," answered Raoul, quietly, but with an air of severe self-respect. "It is his business to have a care for English commerce, and he has every right to make this bargain. But the treaty will not be conducted on equal terms; while he is doing no more than his duty, I have no powers."

"How? You have the power of speech; that will suffice to let us into the secret of the orders you have given the lugger, and where she is probably to be found at this moment."

"Non, Monsieur; I have not even that in my power. I can do nothing that must cover me with so much infamy. My tongue is under laws that I never made, when treachery is in question."

Had Raoul assumed a theatrical tone and manner, as might have been expected, probably it would have made very little impression on Cuffe; but his quiet simplicity and steadiness carried conviction with them. To say the truth, the captain was disappointed. He would have hesitated about making his proposition to an officer of the regular French marine, low as even these stood, at that day, in the estimation of Nelson's fleet in particular; but from a privateersman he expected a greedy acquiescence in a plan that offered life as a reward in exchange for a treachery like that he proposed. At first he felt disposed to taunt Raoul with the contradiction between what he, Cuffe, conceived to be his general pursuits, and his present assumption of principles, but the unpretending calmness of the other's manner, and the truth of his feelings, prevented it. Then, to do Cuffe himself justice, he was too generous to abuse the power he had over his prisoner.

"You may do well to think of this, Monsieur Yvard," observed the captain, after a pause of quite a minute. "The interest at stake is so heavy that reflection may yet induce you to change your mind."

"Monsieur Cuffe, I pardon you, if you can pardon yourself," answered Raoul, with severe dignity in his manner, rising as he spoke, as if disdaining civilities which came from his tempter. "I know what you think of us corsairs; but an officer in an honorable service should hesitate long before he tempts a man to do an act like this. The fact that the life of your prisoner is at stake, ought to make a brave seaman still more delicate how he tries to work on his terrors or his principles. But, I repeat, I forgive you, monsieur, if you can forgive yourself."

Cuffe stood confounded. The blood rushed to his heart; after which, it appeared as if about to gush through the pores of his face. A feeling of fierce resentment almost consumed him; then he became himself again, and began to see things as was his wont in cooler moments. Still he could not speak, pacing the cabin to recover his self-command.

"Monsieur Yvard," he at length said, "I ask your forgiveness sincerely, and from the bottom of my heart. I did not know you, or such a proposal would never have insulted you, or disgraced a British officer, in my person. Nelson, too, is the last man living to wound the feelings of an honorable enemy; but we did not know you. All privateersmen are not of your way of thinking, and it was there we fell into our mistake."

"Touchez-la," said Raoul, frankly extending his hand. "Monsieur le capitaine, you and I ought to meet in two fine frigates, each for his country's honor; let what would be the result, it would lay the foundations of an eternal friendship. I have lived long enough in votre Angleterre to understand how little you know notre France; mais n'importe. Brave men can understand one another all over the world; for the little time which is left me, we shall be friends."

Cuffe seized Raoul's hand, and even a tear escaped him, as he squeezed it warmly.

"This has been a d—d miserable business, Griffin," said the captain, as soon as he could speak without betraying weakness, "and one no man will ever find me employed in again, though a fleet as large as that up in the bay yonder were the price."

"I never thought it would succeed, sir; and, to say the truth, I never hoped it would. You'll excuse me, Captain Cuffe, but we English don't give the continentals exactly the credit they deserve; and particularly the French. I thought it wouldn't do, from the first."

Cuffe now repeated his apologies; and after a few expressions of friendly esteem on both sides, Raoul returned to his little room, declining the captain's offer to occupy one of the cabin staterooms. Griffin was soon back again; then the conversation was resumed between the two officers.

"This is altogether a most painful business, Griffin," observed Cuffe. "There is no doubt that Monsieur Yvard is technically a spy, and guilty, according to the forms of law; but I entertain not the smallest doubt of the truth of his whole story. This Ghita Caraccioli, as the girl calls herself, is the very picture of truth; and was actually in Nelson's cabin the day before yesterday, under circumstances that leave no doubt of the simplicity and truth of her character, while every part of the tale corresponds with the other. Even the veechy, and this pursy old podesta, confirm the account; for they have seen Ghita in Porto Ferrajo, and begin to think that the Frenchman came in there solely on her account."

"I make no doubt, Captain Cuffe, that Lord Nelson will give a respite, or even a pardon, were the facts fairly laid before him," observed Griffin, who felt a generous interest in preserving the life of Raoul, the very man he had endeavored to destroy by fire only a few weeks before; but such is the waywardness of man, and such are the mixed feelings generated by war.

"This is the most serious part of the affair, Griffin. The sentence is approved; with an order that it shall be carried into effect this very day, between the hours of sunrise and sunset; while here it is already noon, and we are to the southward of Campanella, and so distant from the flag-ship as to put signals out of the question."

Griffin started; all the grave difficulties of the case glancing upon his mind in a moment. An order, according to the habits of the service, and more especially an order of this serious character, was not to be questioned; yet here was a dilemma in which there appeared no means of relief.

"Good God, Captain Cuffe, how unlucky! Cannot an express be sent across by land, so as yet to reach the flag-ship in time?"

"I have thought of that, Griffin, and Clinch has gone precisely on that errand."

"Clinch! Pardon, me, sir; but such a duty requires a very active and sober officer!"

"Clinch is active enough, and I know his besetting weakness will have no power over him to-day. I have opened the way for a commission to him, and no one in the ship can go to Naples in a boat sooner than Clinch, if he really try. He will make the most of the afternoon's breeze, should there be any, and I have arranged a signal with him, by which he may let us know the result even at the distance of eight or ten miles."

"Has Lord Nelson left no discretion in the orders, sir?"

"None; unless Raoul Yvard distinctly consents to give up the lugger. In that case, I have a letter, which authorizes me to delay the execution, until I can communicate directly with the commander-in-chief."

"How very unlucky it has been, all round! There is no possibility, sir, of making up a case that might render this discretion available?"

"That might do among your irresponsibles, Mr. Griffin," answered Cuffe, a little sharply, "but I would rather hang forty Frenchmen than be Bronted by Nelson for neglect of duty."

Cuffe spoke more strongly than he intended, perhaps; but the commander of a ship of war does not always stop to weigh his words, when he condescends to discuss a point with an inferior. The reply put a check upon Griffin's zeal, however, though the discourse did not the less proceed.

"Well, sir," the lieutenant answered, "I'm sure we are all as anxious as you can be to avert this affair from our ship. 'Twas but the other day we were boasting in the gun-room, to some of the *Lapwing's* officers that were on a visit here, that the *Proserpine* never had an execution or a court-martial flogging on board her, though she had now been under the British ensign near four years, and had been seven times under fire!"

"God send, Griffin, that Clinch find the admiral, and get back in time!"

"How would it do, sir, to send the vice-governatore to try the prisoner; perhaps he might persuade him to seem to consent, or some such thing, you know, sir, as might justify a delay. They say the Corsicans are the keenest-witted fellows in all these seas; and Elba is so near to Corsica, that one cannot fancy there is much difference between their people."

"Ay, your veechy is a regular witch! He made out so well in his first interview with Yvard, that no one can doubt his ability to overlay him in another!"

"One never knows, Captain Cuffe. The Italian has more resources than most men; and the Signor Barrofaldi is a discreet, sensible man, when he acts with his eyes open. *Le Feu-Follet* has cheated others beside the vice-governatore and podesta."

"Ay, these d——d Jack-o'-Lanterns are never to be trusted. It would hardly surprise me to see the *Folly* coming down wing-and-wing from under the land, and passing out to sea, with a six-knot breeze, while we lay as still as a cathedral, with not air enough to turn the smoke of the galley fire from the perpendicular."

"She's not inside of us, Captain Cuffe; of that we may be certain. I have been on the main-top-gallant yard, with the best glass in the ship, and have swept the whole coast, from the ruins over against us, here to the eastward, up to the town of Salerno; there is nothing to be seen as large as a sparanara."

"One would think, too, this Monsieur Yvard might give up, to save his own life, after all!"

"*We* should hardly do it, I hope, Captain Cuffe?"

"I believe you are right, Griffin; one feels forced to respect the privateersman, in spite of his trade. Who knows but something might be got out of that Bolt. He must know as much about the lugger as Yvard himself?"

"Quite true, sir; I was thinking of proposing something of the sort, not a minute since. Now that's a fellow one may take pleasure in riding down, as one would ride down the main tack. Shall I have him sent for, Captain Cuffe?"

The captain hesitated; for the previous experiments on Ithuel's selfishness had failed. Still the preservation of Raoul's life, and the capture of the lugger, were now objects of nearly equal interest with Cuffe, and he felt disposed to neglect no plausible means of effecting either. A sign of approbation was all the lieutenant needed; and, in a few minutes, Ithuel stood again in the presence of his captain.

"Here is an opportunity for you to fetch up a good deal of leeway, Master Bolt," commenced the captain; "and I am willing to give you a chance to help yourself. You know where you last left the *Few-Folly*, I suppose?"

"I don't know but I might, sir," answered Ithuel rolling his eyes around him, curious to ascertain what the other would be at. "I don't know but I might remember, on a pinch, sir; though, to own the truth, my memory is none of the most desperate best."

"Well, then, where was it! Recollect that the life of your late friend Raoul Yvard, may depend on your answer."

"I want to know! Well, this Europe *is* a curious part of the world, as all must admit that come from Ameriky. What has Captain Rule done now, sir, that he stands in such jeopardy?"

"You know that he is convicted as a spy; and my orders are to have him executed, unless we can get his lugger. Then, indeed, we may possibly show him a little favor, as we do not make war so much on individuals as on nations."

Cuffe would probably have been puzzled to explain the application of his own sentiment to the case before him; but, presuming on his having to deal with one who was neither very philosophical nor logical himself, he was somewhat indifferent to his own mode of proceeding, so that it effected the object. Ithuel, however, was not understood. Love for Raoul or the lugger, or, indeed, for anything else, himself excepted, formed no part of his character; while hatred of England had got to be incorporated with the whole of his moral system; if such a man could be said to have a moral system at all. He saw nothing to be gained by serving Raoul in particular; though this he might have done did nothing interfere to prevent it; while he had so strong an aversion to suffering the English to get Le Feu-Follet, as to be willing even to risk his own life to prevent it. His care, therefore, was to accomplish his purpose with the least hazard to himself.

"And, if the lugger can be had, sir, you intend to let Captain Rule go?" he asked, with an air of interest.

"Ay, we may do that; though it will depend on the admiral. Can you tell us where you left her, and where she probably now is?"

"Captain Rule has said the first already, sir. He told the truth about that before the court. But, as to telling where the lugger is now, I'll defy any man to do it! Why, sir, I've turned in at eight bells, and left her, say ten to fifteen leagues dead to leeward of an island or a lighthouse, perhaps; and on turning out at eight bells in the morning, found her just as far to windward of the same object. She's as oncalculating a craft as I ever put my foot aboard of."

"Indeed!" said Cuffe, ironically; "I do not wonder that her captain's in a scrape."

"Scrape, sir! The Folly is nothing but a scrape. I've tried my hand at keeping her reck'nin'."

"You!"

"Yes, sir. I—Ithuel Bolt; that's my name at hum or abroad; and I've tried to keep the Folly's reck'nin', with all the advantage of thermometer, and lead-lines, and logarithms, and such necessaries, you know, Captain Cuffe, and I never yet could place her within a hundred miles of the spot where she was actually seen to be."

"I am not at all surprised to hear this, Bolt; but what I want at present is to know what you think may be the precise position of the lugger, without the aid of the thermometer and of logarithms; I've a notion you would make out better by letting such things alone."

"Well, who knows but I might, sir! My idea of the Folly, just now, sir, is that she is somewhere off the Capri, under short canvas, waiting for Captain Rule and I to join her, and keeping a sharp lookout after the inimies' cruisers."

Now this was not only precisely the position of the lugger at that very moment, but it was what Ithuel actually believed to be her position. Still nothing was farther from this man's intention than to betray his former messmates. He was so very cunning as to have detected how little Cuffe was disposed to believe; and he told the truth as the most certain means of averting mischief from the lugger. Nor did his ruse fail of its object. His whole manner had so much deceit and low cunning about it, that neither Cuffe nor Griffin believed a word he said; and after a little more pumping, the fellow was dismissed in disgust, with a sharp intimation that it would be singularly for his interest to look out how he discharged his general duties in the ship.

"This will never do, Griffin," exclaimed the captain, vexed and disappointed. "Should anything occur to Clinch, or should the admiral happen to be off with the king, on one of his shooting excursions, we shall be in a most serious dilemma. Would to God we had not left the anchorage at Capri! Then one might communicate with the flag with some certainty. I shall never forgive myself if anything fatal actually takes place!"

"When one does all for the best, Captain Cuffe, his mind ought to be at ease, and you could not possibly foresee what has happened. Might not—one wouldn't like either—but necessity is a hard master—"

"Out with it, Griffin; anything is better than suspense."

"Well, sir, I was just thinking that possibly this young Italian girl might know something about the lugger, and, as she clearly loves the Frenchman, we should get a strong purchase on her tongue by means of her heart."

Cuffe looked intently at his lieutenant for half-a-minute; then he shook his head in disapprobation.

"No, Griffin, no," he said, "to this I never can consent. As for this quibbling, equivocating Yankee, if Yankee he be, one wouldn't feel many scruples of delicacy; but to probe the affections of a poor, innocent girl in this way, would be going too far. The heart of a young girl should be sacred under every circumstance."

Griffin colored and he bit his lip. No one likes to be outdone, in the appearance of generosity, at least; and he felt vexed that he should have ventured on a proposition that his superior treated as unbecoming.

"Nevertheless, sir, she might think the lugger cheaply sold," he said, with emphasis, "provided her lover's life was what she got in exchange. It would be a very different thing were we to ask her to sell her admirer, instead of a mere privateer."

"No matter, Griffin. We will not meddle with the private feelings of a young female that chance has thrown into our hands. As soon as we get near enough in with the land, I intend to let the old man take his boat, and carry his niece ashore. That will be getting rid of them, at least, honorably and fairly. God knows what is to become of the Frenchman."

This terminated the conference. Griffin went on deck, where duty now called him, and Cuffe sat down to reperuse, for the ninth or tenth time, the instructions of the admiral.

CHAPTER XXII.

By this time the day had materially advanced, and there were grave grounds for the uneasiness which Cuffe began so seriously to feel. All three of the ships were still in the Bay of Salerno, gathering in toward its northern shore, however; the *Proserpine*, the deepest embayed, the *Terpsichore*, and the *Ringdove*, having hauled out toward Campanella, as soon as satisfied nothing was to be seen in shore of them. The heights which line the coast, from the immediate vicinity of the town of Salerno, to the headland that ends near Capri, have long been celebrated, not only for their beauty and grandeur, but in connection with the lore of the middle ages. As the *Proserpine* had never been in this bay before, or never so near its head, her officers found some temporary relief from the very general uneasiness that was felt on account of their prisoner, in viewing scenery that is remarkable even in that remarkable section of the globe. The ship had gone up abreast of Amalfi, and so close in, as to be less than a mile from the shore. The object was to communicate with some fishermen, which had been done; the information received going to establish the fact, that no craft resembling the lugger had been in that part of the bay.

The vessel's head was now laid to the southward and westward, in waiting for the zephyr, which might soon be expected. The gallant frigate, seen from the impending rocks, looked like a light merchantman, in all but her symmetry and warlike guise; nature being molded on so grand a scale all along the coast as to render objects of human art unusually diminutive to the eye. On the other hand, the country-houses, churches, hermitages, convents, and villages clustered all along the mountain sides, presented equally delusive forms, though they gave an affluence to the views, that left the spectators in a strange doubt which most to admire, their wildness, or their picturesque beauty. The little air that remained, was still at the southward, and as the ship moved slowly along this scene of singular attraction, each ravine seemed to give up a town, each shelf of rock, a human habitation, and each natural terrace, a villa and a garden.

Of all men, the sailors get to be the most *blasé* in the way of sensations produced by novelties and fine scenery. It appears to be a part of their calling to suppress the emotions of a greenhorn; and, generally, they look upon anything that is a little out of the ordinary track, with the coolness of those who feel it is an admission of inferiority to betray surprise. It seldom happens with them, that anything occurs, or anything is seen, to which the last cruise, or, if the vessel be engaged in trade, the last voyage, did not at least furnish a parallel; usually the past event, or the more distant object has the advantage. He who has a sufficient store of this reserved knowledge and experience, it will at once be seen, enjoys a great superiority over him who has not, and is placed above the necessity of avowing a sensation as humiliating as wonder. On the present occasion, however, but few held out against the novelty of the actual situation of the ship; most on board being willing enough to allow that they had never before been beneath cliffs that had such a union of the magnificent, the picturesque, and the soft; though a few continued firm, acting up to the old characters, with the consistency of settled obstinacy.

Strand, the boatswain, was one of those who, on all such occasions, "die hard." He was the last man in the ship who ever gave up a prejudice; and this for three several reasons: he was a cockney, and believed himself born in the center of human knowledge; he was a seaman, and understood the world; he was a boatswain, and stood upon his dignity.

As the *Proserpine* fanned slowly along the land, this personage took a position between the knightheads, on the bowsprit, where he could overlook the scene, and at the same time hear the dialogue of the forecastle; and both with suitable decorum. Strand was as much of a monarch forward, as Cuffe was aft; though the appearance of a lieutenant, or of the master, now and then, a little dimmed the luster of his reign. Still, Strand succumbed completely to only two of the officers—the captain and the first lieutenant; and not always to these, in what he conceived to be purely matters of sentiment. In the way of duty, he understood himself too well ever to hesitate about obeying an order; but when it came to opinions, he was a man who could maintain his own, even in the presence of Nelson.

The first captain of the forecastle was an old seaman of the name of Catfall. At the precise moment when Strand occupied the position named, between the knightheads, this personage was holding a discourse with three or four of the forecastle-men, who stood on the heel of the bowsprit, inboard—the etiquette of the ship not permitting these worthies to show their heads above the nettings. Each of the party had his arms folded; each chewed tobacco; each had his hair in a queue; and each occasionally hitched up his trousers, in a way to prove that he did not require the aid of suspenders in keeping his nether garments in their proper place. It may be mentioned, indeed, that the point of division between the jacket and the trousers was marked in each by a bellying line of a clean white shirt, that served to relieve the blue of the dress, as a species of marine facing. As was due to his greater experience and his rank, Catfall was the principal speaker among those who lined the heel of the bowsprit.

"This here coast is moun*tain*ous, as one may own," observed the captain of the forecastle; "but what I say is, that it's not as moun*tain*ous as some I've seen. Now when I went round the 'arth with Captain Cook, we fell in with islands that were so topped off with rocks, and the like o' that, that these here affairs alongside on 'em wouldn't pass for anything more than a sort of jury mountains."

"There you're right, Catfall," said Strand, in a patronizing way; "as anybody knows as has been round the Horn. I didn't sail with Captain Cook, seeing

that I was then the boatswain of the *Hussar*, and she couldn't have made one of Cook's squadron, being a post-ship, and commanded by a full-built captain; but I was in them seas when a younker, and can back Catfall's account of the matter by my largest anchor, in the way of history. D——e, if I think these hillocks would be called even jury mountains, in that quarter of the world. They tell me there's several noblemen's and gentlemen's parks near Lunnun, where they make mountains just to look at; that must be much of a muchness with these here chaps. I never drift afar from Wappin', when I'm at home, and so I can't say I've see these artifice hills, as they calls them, myself; but there's one Joseph Shirk, that lives near St. Catherine's Lane, that makes trips regularly into the neighborhood, who gives quite a particular account of the matter."

"I dare to say it's all true, Mr. Strand," answered the captain of the forecastle, "for I've knowed some of them traveling chaps who have seen stranger sights than that. No, sir, I calls these mountains no great matter; and as to the houses and villages on 'em, where you see one here, you might say you could see two on some of the desert islands—"

A very marvelous account of Cook's discoveries was suddenly checked by the appearance of Cuffe on the forecastle. It was not often the captain visited that part of the ship; but he was considered a privileged person, let him go where he would. At his appearance, all the "old salts" quitted the heel of the spar, tarpaulins came fairly down to a level with the bag-reefs of the shirts, and even Strand stepped into the nettings, leaving the place between the knightheads clear. To this spot Cuffe ascended with a light, steady step, for he was but six-and-twenty, just touching his hat in return to the boatswain's bow.

A boatswain on board an English man-of-war is a more important person than he is apt to be on board an American. Neither the captain nor the first lieutenant disdains conversing with him on occasions; and he is sometimes seen promenading the starboard side of the quarter-deck in deep discourse with one or the other of those high functionaries. It has been said that Cuffe and Strand were old shipmates, the latter having actually been boatswain of the ship in which the former first sailed. This circumstance was constantly borne in mind by both parties, the captain seldom coming near his inferior, in moments of relaxation, without having something to say to him.

"Rather a remarkable coast this, Strand," he commenced, on the present occasion, as soon as fairly placed between the knightheads; "something one might look for a week, in England, without finding it."

"I beg your pardon, sir, but I'm not of the same way of thinking. I was just telling the forecastle lads, down there, that there's many a nobleman and gentleman at home as has finer hills than these, made by hand, in his parks and gardens, just to look at."

"The d——l you have! And what did the forecastle lads down there say to you?"

"What could they, sir? It just showed the superiority of an Englishman to an Italian, and that ended the matter. Don't you remember the Injees, sir?"

"The Indies! Why, the coast between Bombay and Calcutta is as flat as a pancake most of the distance."

"Not them Injees, sir, but t'other—the West, I mean. The islands and mountains we passed and went into in the *Rattler*; your honor was only a young gentleman then, but was too much aloft to miss the sight of anything — and all along America too."

As Strand was speaking he glanced complacently around, as if to intimate to the listeners what an old friend of the captain's they enjoyed in the person of their boatswain.

"O! the West Indies—you're nearer right there, Strand: and yet they have nothing to compare with this. Why, here are mountains, alive with habitations, that fairly come up to the sea."

"Well, sir, as to habitations, what's these to a street in Lunnun? Begin on the starboard side, for instance, as you walk down Cheapside, and count as you go; my life for it, you'll reel off more houses in half an hour's walk than are to be found in all that there village yonder. Then you'll remember, sir, that the starboard side only has one half, every Jack having his Jenny. I look upon Lunnon as the finest sight in nature, Captain Cuffe, after all I have seen in many cruises."

"I don't know, Mr. Strand. In the way of coast, one may very well be satisfied with this. Yonder town, now, is called Amalfi; it was once a place of great commerce, they say."

"Of commerce, sir!—why, it's nothing but a bit of a village, or, at most, of a borough built in a hollow. No haven, no docks, no comfortable place even for setting up the frame of a ship on the beach. The commerce of such a town must have been mainly carried on by means of mules and jackasses, as one reads of in the trade of the Bible."

"Carried on as it might be, trade it once had. There does not seem to be any hiding-place along this shore for a lugger like the *Folly*, after all, Strand."

The boatswain smiled, with a knowing look, while, at the same time, the expression of his countenance was like that of a man who did not choose to let others into all his secrets.

"The *Folly* is a craft we are not likely to see again, Captain Cuffe," he then answered, as if it were only out of respect for his superior.

"Why so? The *Proserpine* generally takes a good look at everything she chases."

"Ay, ay, sir; that may be true, as a rule, but I never knew a craft found after a third look for her. Everything seems to go by thirds in this world, sir; and I always look upon a third chase as final. Now, sir, there are three classes of admirals, and three sets of flags; a ship has three masts; the biggest ships are three deckers; then there are three planets—"

"The d——l there are! How do you make that out, Strand?"

"Why, sir, there's the sun, moon, and stars; that makes just three by count."

"Ay, but what do you say to Jupiter, Saturn, Venus, and all the rest of them, the earth included?"

"Why, sir, they're all the rest of the stars, and not planets at all. Then, sir, look around you, and you'll find everything going by threes. There are three topsails, three jibs, and three top-gallant-sails—"

"And two courses," said the captain, to whom this theory of the threes was new.

"Quite true, sir, in name; but your honor will recollect that the spanker is nothing but a fore-and-aft course, rigged to a mast, instead of to a jack-yard, as it used to be."

"There are neither three captains nor three boatswains to a ship, Master Strand."

"Certainly not, sir; that would be oppressive, and they would stand in each other's way; still, Captain Cuffe, the thirds hold out wonderfully, even in all these little matters. There's the three lieutenants; and there's the boatswain, gunner and carpenter; and—"

"Sailmaker, armorer, and captain of the mast," interrupted Cuffe, laughing.

"Well, sir, you may make anything seem doubtful, by bringing forward a plenty of reasons; but all my experience says, a third chase never comes to anything, unless it turns out successful ; but that after a third chase, all may as well be given up.''

"I fancy Lord Nelson holds a different doctrine, Strand. He tells us to follow a Frenchman round the earth, rather than let him escape.''

"No doubt, sir. Follow him round three earths, if you can keep in sight ; but not round four. That is all I contend for, Captain Cuffe. Even women, they tell me, take what is called their thirds, in a fellow's fortin'.''

"Well, well, Strand, I suppose there must be some truth in your doctrine, or you wouldn't hold out for it so strenuously ; and, as for this coast, I must give it up, for I never expect to see another like it ; much less a third.''

"It's my duty to give up to your honor ; but I ask permission to think a third chase should always be the last one. That's a melancholy sight to a man of feelin', Captain Cuffe, the object between the two midship-guns, on the starboard side of the main-deck, sir.''

"You mean the prisoner ? I wish with all my heart he was not there, Strand. I think I would rather he were in his lugger again, to run the chances of that fourth chase of which you seem to think so lightly.''

"Your hanging ships are not often lucky ships, Captain Cuffe. In my judgment, asking your pardon, sir, there ought to be a floating jail in every fleet, where all the courts and all the executions should be held.''

"It would be robbing the boatswains of no small part of their duty, were the punishments to be sent out of the different vessels,'' answered Cuffe, smiling.

"Ay, ay, sir ; the punishments, I grant your honor ; but hanging is an execution, and not a punishment, God forbid that, at my time of life, I should be ordered to sail in a ship that has no punishment on board ; but I am really getting to be too old to look at executions with any sort of pleasure. Duty that isn't done with pleasure is but poor duty, at the best, sir.''

"There are many disagreeable, and some painful duties to be performed, Strand ; this of executing a man, let the offense be what it may, is among the most painful.''

"For my part, Captain Cuffe, I do not mind hanging a mutineer so very much, for he is a being that the world ought not to harbor ; but it is a different thing with an enemy and a spy. It's our duty to spy as much as we can for our king and country, and one ought never to bear too hard on such as does their duty. With a fellow that can't obey orders, and who puts his own will above the pleasure of his superiors, I have no patience ; but I do not so much understand why the gentlemen of the courts are so hard on such as do a little more reconn'iterin' than common.''

"That is because ships are less exposed to the attempts of spies than armies. A soldier hates a spy as much as you do a mutineer. The reason is, that he may be surprised by an enemy through his means, and butchered in his sleep. Nothing is so unpleasant to a soldier as a surprise ; and the law against spies, though a general law of war, originated with soldiers, rather than with us sailors, I should think.''

"Yes, sir, I daresay your honor is right. He's a rum 'un, a soldier, at the best ; and this opinion proves it. Now, sir, Captain Cuffe, just suppose a Frenchman of about our own metal took it into his head to surprise the *Proserpine*, some dark night ; what would come of it, after all ? There's the guns, and it's only to turn the hands up, to set 'em at work, just the same as if there wasn't a spy in the world. And should they prefer to come on board us, and to try their luck at close quarters, I rather think, sir, the surprise would meet 'em face to face. No, no, sir ; spies is nothing to us—though it might teach 'em manners to keel-haul one, once-and-awhile.''

Cuffe now became thoughtful and silent, and even Strand did not presume to speak, when the captain was in this humor. The latter descended to the forecastle, and walked aft, his hands behind his back, and his head inclining downward. Every one he met made way for him, as a matter of course. In that mood he moved among the throng of a ship-of-war as a man tabooed. Even Winchester respected his commander's abstraction, although he had a serious request to make, which it is time to explain.

Andrea Barrofaldi and Vito Viti remained on board the frigate, inmates of the cabin, and gradually becoming more accustomed to their novel situation. They did not escape the jokes of a man-of-war, but, on the whole, they were well treated, and were tolerably satisfied ; more especially as the hope of capturing *Le Feu-Follet* began to revive. As a matter of course, they were apprised of the condition of Raoul ; and, both kind and benevolent men in the main, they were desirous of conversing with the prisoner, and of proving to him that they bore no malice. Winchester was spoken to on the subject ; but before he granted the permission, he thought it safest to consult the captain in the matter. At length an opportunity offered, Cuffe suddenly rousing himself, and giving an order in relation to the canvas the ship was under.

"Here are the two Italian gentlemen, Captain Cuffe," observed Winchester, "desirous of speaking to the prisoner. I did not think it right, sir, to let him have communication with any one, without first ascertaining your pleasure."

"Poor fellow! His time is getting very short, unless we hear from Clinch; and there can be no harm in granting him every indulgence. I have been thinking of this matter, and do not possibly see how I can escape ordering the execution, unless it be countermanded from Nelson himself."

"Certainly not, sir. But Mr. Clinch is an active and experienced seaman, when he is in earnest; we may still have something from him. What is to be done with the Italians, sir?"

"Let them, or any one else that poor Yvard is willing to see, go below."

"Do you mean to include old Giuntotardi and his niece, Captain Cuffe? and this deserter of our own, Bolt—he, too, has had something to say of a wish to take leave of his late shipmate."

"We might be justified in denying the request of the last, Mr. Winchester, but hardly of the others. Still, if Raoul Yvard wishes to see even him, his desire may as well be granted."

Thus authorized, Winchester no longer hesitated about granting the several permissions. An order was sent to the sentinel, through the corporal of the guard, to allow any one to enter the prisoner's room whom the latter might wish to receive. A ship was not like a prison on shore, escape being next to impossible, more especially from a vessel at sea. The parties accordingly received intimation that they might visit the condemned man, should the latter be disposed to receive them.

By this time, something like a general gloom had settled on the ship. The actual state of things was known to all on board, and few believed it possible that Clinch could reach the *Foudroyant*, receive his orders, and be back in time to prevent the execution. It wanted now but three hours of sunset, and the minutes appeared to fly, instead of dragging. The human mind is so constituted that uncertainty increases most of its sensations; the apprehension of death even, very usually exciting a livelier emotion than its positive approach.

Thus it was with the officers and people of the *Proserpine;* had there been no hope of escaping the execution, they would have made up their minds to submit to the evil, as unavoidable; but the slight chance which did actually exist, created a feverish excitement that soon extended to all hands; and this as completely as if a chase were in sight, and each individual was bent on overtaking her. As minute after minute flew by, the feeling increased, until it would not much exceed the bounds of truth to say, that, under none of the vicissitudes of war did there ever exist so feverish an hour, on board his Britannic majesty's ship, the *Proserpine*, as the very period of which we are now writing. Eyes were constantly turned toward the sun, and several of the young gentlemen collected on the forecastle, with no other view than to be as near as possible to the headland around which the boat of Clinch was expected to make her reappearance, as behind it she had last been seen.

The zephyr had come at the usual hour, but it was light, and the ship was so close to the mountains as to feel very little of its force. It was different with the two other vessels. Lyon had gone about in time to get clear of the highest mountains, and his lofty sails took enough of the breeze to carry him out to sea three or four hours before; while the *Terpsichore*, under Sir Frederick Dashwood, had never got near enough in with the land to be becalmed at all. Her head had been laid to the southwest at the first appearance of the afternoon wind; and that frigate was now hull-down to seaward—actually making a free wind of it, as she shaped her course up between Ischia and Capri. As for the *Proserpine*, when the bell struck three in the first dog-watch, she was just abeam of the celebrated little islets of the Sirens, the western breeze now beginning to die away, though getting more of it the ship was drawing ahead faster than she had been since the turn of the day.

Three bells in the first dog-watch indicate the hour of half-past five. At that season of the year the sun sets a few minutes past six. Of course there remained but little more than half an hour in which to execute the sentence of the law. Cuffe had never quitted the deck, and he actually started, when he heard the first sound of the clapper. Winchester turned toward him, with an inquiring look; for everything had been previously arranged between them; he received merely a significant gesture in return. This, however, was sufficient. Certain orders were privately issued. Then there appeared a stir among the foretop-men, and on the forecastle, where a rope was rove at the fore-yardarm, and a grating was rigged for a platform—unerring signs of the approaching execution.

Accustomed as these hardy mariners were to brave dangers of all sorts, and to witness human suffering of nearly every degree, a singular humanity had come over the whole crew. Raoul was their enemy, it is true, and he had been sincerely detested by all hands, eight-and-forty hours before; but circumstances had entirely changed the ancient animosity into a more generous and manly sentiment. In the first place, a successful and a triumphant enemy was an object very different from a man in their own power, and who lay entirely at their mercy. Then, the personal appearance of the young privateersman was unusually attractive, and altogether different from what it had been previously represented, and that too by an active rivalry that was not altogether free from bitterness. But chiefly was the generous sentiment awakened by the conviction that the master-passion, and none of the usual inducements of a spy, had brought their enemy into this strait; and though clearly guilty in a technical point of view, that he was influenced by no pitiful wages, even allowing that he blended with the pursuit of his love some of the motives of his ordinary warfare. All these considerations, coupled with the reluctance that seamen ever feel to having an execution in their ship, had entirely turned the tables; and there, where Raoul would have found so lately between two and three hundred active and formidable enemies, he might almost be said now to have as many sympathizing friends.

No wonder, then, that the preparations of the fore-topmen were regarded with unfavorable eyes. The unseen hand of authority, nevertheless, held all in restraint. Cuffe himself did not dare to hesitate any longer. The necessary orders were given, though with deep reluctance, and then the captain went below, as if to hide himself from human eyes.

The ten minutes that succeeded were minutes of intense concern. All hands were called, the preparations had been completed, and Winchester waited only for the reappearance of Cuffe, to issue the order to have the prisoner placed on the grating. A midshipman was sent into the cabin, after which the commanding officer came slowly and with a lingering step, upon the quarter-deck.

The crew was assembled on the forecastle and in the waists; the marine guard was under arms; the officers clustered around the capstan; and a solemn, uneasy expectation pervaded the whole ship. The lightest footfall was audible. Andrea and his friend stood apart, near the taffrail, but no one saw Carlo Giuntotardi or his niece.

"There is yet some five-and-twenty minutes of sun, I should think, Mr. Winchester," observed Cuffe, feverishly glancing his eye at the western margin of the sea, toward which the orb of day was slowly settling, gilding all that side of the vault of heaven with the mellow luster of the hour and the latitude.

"Not more than twenty, I fear, sir," was the reluctant answer.

"I should think five might suffice, at the worst; especially if the men make a swift run." This was said in a half whisper, and thick, husky tones, the captain looking anxiously at the lieutenant the while.

Winchester shrugged his shoulders, and turned away, unwilling to reply.

Cuffe now had a short consultation with the surgeon, the object of which was to ascertain the minimum of time a man might live suspended by the neck at the yardarm of a frigate. The result was not favorable; for a sign followed to bring forth the prisoner.

Raoul came on deck, in charge of the master-at-arms, and the officer who had acted as provost-marshal. He was clad in his clean white lazzarone garb, wearing the red Phrygian cap already mentioned, Though his face was pale, no man could detect any tremor in the well turned muscles that his loose attire exposed to view. He raised his cap courteously to the group of officers, and threw an understanding glance forward at the fearful arrangement on the fore-yard. That he was shocked when the grating and rope met his eye, is unquestionable; but, rallying in an instant, he smiled, bowed to Cuffe, and moved toward the scene of his contemplated execution, firmly, but without the smallest signs of bravado in his manner.

A deathlike stillness prevailed, while subordinates adjusted the rope, and placed the condemned man on the grating. Then the slack of the rope was drawn in by hand, and the men were ordered to lay hold of the instrument of death, and to stretch it along the deck.

"Stand by, my lads, to make a swift run and a strong jerk, at your first pull," said Winchester, in a low voice, as he passed down the line. "Rapidity is mercy, at such a moment."

"Good God!" muttered Cuffe, "can the man die in this manner, without a prayer; without even a glance toward Heaven, as if asking for mercy?"

"He is an unbeliever, I hear, sir," returned Griffin. "We have offered him all the religious consolation we could; but he seems to wish for none."

"Hail the top-gallant yards once more, Mr. Winchester," said Cuffe, huskily.

"Fore-top-gallant yard, there!"

"Sir?"

"Any signs of the boat—look well into the Bay of Naples—we are opening Campanella now sufficiently to give you a good look up toward the head."

A pause of a minute succeeded. Then the lookout aloft shook his head in the negative, as if unwilling to speak. Winchester glanced at Cuffe, who turned anxiously, mounted a gun, and strained his eyes in a gaze to the northward,

"All ready, sir," said the first lieutenant, when another minute elapsed.

Cuffe was in the act of raising his hand, which would have been the signal of death, when the dull, heavy report of a distant gun came booming down from the direction of the town of Naples.

"Stand fast!" shouted Cuffe, fearful the men might get the start of him. "Make your mates take their calls from their mouths, sir. Two more guns, Winchester, and I am the happiest man in Nelson's fleet!"

A second gun did come, just as those words were uttered; then followed a breathless pause of half a minute, when a third smothered but uneqivocal report succeeded.

"It must be a salute, sir," Griffin uttered, inquiringly.

"The interval is too long. Listen! I hope to God we have had the last!"

Every ear in the ship listened intently, Cuffe holding his watch in his hand. Two entire minutes passed and no fourth gun was heard. As second after second went by, the expression of the captain's countenance changed, and then he waved his hand in triumph.

"It's as it should be, gentlemen," he said. "Take the prisoner below, Mr. Winchester. Unreeve the rope, and send that d——d grating off the gun. Mr. Strand, pipe down."

Raoul was immediately led below. As he passed through the after-hatch, all the officers on the quarter-deck bowed to him; and not a man was there in the ship who did not feel the happier for the reprieve.

CHAPTER XXIII.

RAOUL YVARD was indebted to a piece of forethought in Clinch for his life. But for the three guns fired so opportunely from the *Foudroyant*, the execution could not have been stayed; and but for a prudent care on the part of the master's mate, the guns would never have been fired. The explanation is this: When Cuffe was giving his subordinate instructions how to proceed, the possibility of detention struck the latter, and he bethought him of some expedient by which such an evil might be remedied. At his suggestion, then, the signal of the guns was mentioned by the captain in his letter to the commander-in-chief, and its importance pointed out. When Clinch reached the fleet, Nelson was at Castel-a-Mare, and it became necessary to follow him to that place by land. Here Clinch found him in the palace of Qui-Si-Sane, in attendance on the court, and delivered his dispatches. Nothing gave the British admiral greater pleasure than to be able to show mercy, the instance to the contrary already introduced existing as an exception in his private character and his public career; and it is possible that an occurrence so recent, and so opposed to his habits, may have induced him the more willingly now to submit to his ordinary impulses, and to grant the respite asked with the greater promptitude.

"Your captain tells me here, sir," observed Nelson, after he had read Cuffe's letter a second time, "little doubt exists that Yvard was in the bay on a love affair, and that his purposes were not those of a spy, after all?"

"Such is the opinion aboard us, my lord," answered the master's-mate. "There are an old man and a very charming woman in his company, who Captain Cuffe says were in the cabin of this ship, on a visit to your lordship, only a few days since."

Nelson started, his face flushed. Then he seized a pen, and, with the only hand he had, scratched a letter, directing a reprieve until further orders. This he signed and handed to Clinch, saying, as he did so—

"Get into your boat, sir, and pull back to the frigate as fast as possible; God forbid that any man suffer wrongfully!"

"I beg your pardon, my lord—but there is not time, now, for me to reach the ship before sunset. I have a signal prepared in the boat, it is true; but the frigate may not come around Campanella before the last moment, and then all these pains will be lost. Does not Captain Cuffe speak of some guns to be fired from the flag-ship, my lord?"

"He does, sir; and this may be the safest mode of communicating, after all.

With this light westerly air, a gun will be heard a long distance at sea. Take the pen and write as I dictate, sir.''

Clinch seized the pen, which the admiral, who had lost his right arm only a few years before, really felt unable to use, and wrote as follows:

SIR : Immediately on the receipt of this you will fire three heavy guns, at intervals of half a minute, as a signal to the *Proserpine* to suspend an execution.

To the Commanding Officer of His Majesty's ship *Foudroyant*.

As soon as the magical words of " Nelson and Bronte " were affixed to this order, with a date, Clinch rose to depart. After he had made his bows he stood with his hand on the lock of the door, as if uncertain whether to prefer a request or not.

"This is a matter of moment, sir, and no time is to be lost," added Nelson. "I feel great anxiety about it, and wish you to desire Captain Cuffe to send you back with a report of all that has passed, as soon as convenient.''

"I will report your wishes, my lord," answered Clinch, brightening up; for he only wanted an opportunity to speak of his own promotion, and this was now offered in perspective. "May I tell the commanding officer of the flag-ship to use the lower-deck guns, my lord ? ''

"He will do that of his own accord, after reading those orders; heavy guns mean the heaviest. Good afternoon, sir ; for God's sake lose no time.''

Clinch obeyed this injunction to the letter. He reached the *Foudroyant* some time before sunset, and placed the order in her captain's hands. A few words of explanation set everything in motion, and the three guns were fired on the side of the ship toward Capri, most opportunely for our hero.

The half hour that succeeded on board the *Proserpine* was one of gayety and merriment. Every person was glad that the ship had escaped an execution; and then it was the hour for piping down the hammocks, and for shifting the dogwatches. Cuffe recovered all his animation, and conversed cheerfully, having Griffin for an interpreter with his two Italian guests. These last had been prevented from paying their visit to the prisoner, on account of the latter's wish to be alone ; but the intention was now renewed ; and sending below, to ascertain if it would be agreeable, they proceeded together on their friendly mission. As the two worthies, who had not altogether

got their sea-legs, slowly descended the ladder, and threaded their way among the throng of a ship, the discourse did not flag between them.

" Cospetto ! '' exclaimed the podesta; " Signor Andrea, we live in a world of wonders ! A man can hardly say whether he is actually alive, or not. To think how near this false Sir Smees was to death, half an hour since ; and now, doubtless, he is as much alive, and as merry as any of us.''

"It would be more useful, friend Vito Viti,'' answered the philosophical vice-governatore, "to remember how near those who live are always to Death, who has only to open his gates, to cause the strongest and fairest to pass at once into the tomb.''

" By San Stephano, but you have a way with you, vice-governatore, that would become a cardinal ! It's a thousand pities the Church was robbed of such a support ; though I do think, Signor Andrea, if your mind would dwell less on another state of being it would be more cheerful ; and I may say, more cheering to those with whom you discourse. There are evils enough in this life, without thinking so much of death.''

" There are philosophers who pretend, good Vito, that nothing that we see around us actually has an existence ; that we fancy everything ; fancy that this is a sea, called the Mediterranean ; fancy this is a ship—yonder is the land ; fancy that we live ; and even fancy death.''

" Corpo di Bacco ! Signor Andrea,'' exclaimed the other, stopping short at the ladder, and seizing his companion by a button, afraid he would desert him in the midst of a strange delusion, "you would not trifle in such a matter with an old friend ; one who has known you from childhood ? Fancy that I am alive ! ''

" Si ; I have told you only the truth. The imagination is very strong, and may easily give the semblance of reality to unreal things.''

"And that I am not a podesta in fact, but one only in fancy ! ''

" Just so, friend Vito ; and that I am only a vice-governatore, too, in the imagination.''

"And that Elba is not a real island, or Porto Ferraja a real town ; and that even all our iron, of which we seem to send so much about the world, in good wholesome ships, is only a sort of ghost of solid substantial metal ! ''

"Si, si ; that everything which appears to be material, is, in fact, imaginary : iron, gold, or flesh.''

"And then I am not Vito Viti, but an

impostor? What a rascally philosophy is this! Why, both of us are as bad as Sir Smees, if what you say be true, vice-governatore—or make-believe vice-governatore."

"Not an impostor, friend Vito; for there is no real being of thy name, if thou art not he."

"Diavolo! A pretty theory this, which would teach the young people of Elba that there is no actual podesta in the island, but only a poor, miserable, sham one; no Vito Viti on earth. If they get to think this, God help the place, as to order and sobriety."

"I do not think, neighbor, that you fully understand the matter, which may be owing to a want of clearness on my part, but, as we are now on our way to visit an unfortunate prisoner, we may as well postpone the discussion to another time. There are many leisure moments on board a ship, to the language of which one is a stranger, that might be usefully and agreeably relieved by going into the subject more at large."

"Your pardon, Signor Andrea; but there is no time like the present. Then, if the theory be true, there is no prisoner at all—or, at the most, an imaginary one —and it can do Sir Smees no harm to wait; while, on the other hand, I shall not have a moment's peace until I learn whether there is such a man as Vito Viti or not, and whether I am he."

"Brother Vito, you are impatient; these things are not learned in a moment; moreover every system has a beginning and an end, like a book; and who would ever become learned that should attempt to read a treatise backward?"

"I know what is due to you, Signor Andrea, both on account of your higher rank, and on account of your greater wisdom, and will say no more at present; though to keep from thinking on a philosophy that teaches I am not a podesta, or you a vice-governatore, is more than flesh and blood can bear."

Andrea Barrofaldi, glad that his companion was momentarily appeased, now proceeded toward Raoul's little prison, and was immediately admitted by the sentry, who had his orders to that effect. The prisoner received his guests courteously and cheerfully; for we are far from wishing to represent him as so heroic as not to rejoice exceedingly at having escaped death by hanging, even though it might prove to be a respite, rather than a pardon. At such a moment, the young man could have excused a much more offensive intrusion, and the sudden change in his prospects disposed him a little to be jocular; for truth compels us to add that gratitude to God entered but little into his emotions. The escape from death, like his capture and the other incidents of his cruise, was viewed simply as the result of the fortune of war.

Winchester had directed that Raoul's state-room should be supplied with every little convenience that his situation required, and, among other things, it had two common ship's stools. One of these was given to each of the Italians, while the prisoner took a seat on the gun-tackle of one of the two guns that formed the sides of his apartment. It was now night, and a mist had gathered over the arch above, which hid the stars, and rendered it quite dark. Still, Raoul had neither lamp nor candles; and, though they had been offered him, he declined their use, as he had found stranger eyes occasionally peeping through the openings in the canvas, with the idle curiosity of the vulgar, to ascertain the appearance and employments of one condemned to die. He had experienced a good deal of annoyance from this feeling the previous night; and the same desire existing to see how a criminal could bear a respite, he had determined to pass his evening in obscurity. There was a lantern or two, however, on the gun-deck, which threw a dim light even beyond the limits of the canvas bulk-heads. As has been said already, these bulk-heads extended from gun to gun, so as to admit light and air from the ports. This brought the tackles, on one side, into the room; and on one of these Raoul now took his seat.

Andrea Barrofaldi, from his superior condition in life, as well as from his better education and nicer natural tact, far surpassed his companion in courtesy of demeanor. The latter would have plunged *in medias res* at once, but the vice-governatore commenced a conversation on general matters, intending to offer his congratulations for the recent respite when he conceived that a suitable occasion should arise. This was an unfortunate delay in one respect; for Vito Viti no sooner found that the main object of the visit was to be postponed, than he turned with eagerness to the subject in discussion, which had been interrupted in order to enter the stateroom.

"Here has the vice-governatore come forward with a theory, Sir Smees," he commenced, the moment a pause in the discourse left him an opening—"here has the vice-governatore come forward with a theory that I insist the Church would call damnable, and at which human nature revolts—"

"Nay, good Vito, thou dost not state the case fairly," interrupted Andrea, whose spirit was a little aroused at so abrupt an assault. "The theory is not mine; it is that of a certain English philosopher, in particular, who, let it be said, too, was a bishop."

"A Lutheran! was it not so, Signor Andrea? a bishop so called?"

"Why, to confess the truth, he was a heretic, and not to be considered as an apostle of the true Church."

"Ay; I would have sworn to that. No true son of the Church would ever broach such a doctrine. Only fancy, signori, the number of imaginary fires, tongues, and other instruments of torture that would become necessary to carry on punishment under such a system! To be consistent, even the devils ought to be imaginary."

"Comment, signori!" exclaimed Raoul, smiling, and arousing to a sudden interest in the discourse; "did any English bishop broach such a doctrine? Imaginary devils and imaginary places of punishment are coming near to our revolutionary France! After this, I hope our much abused philosophy will meet with more respect."

"My neighbor has not understood the theory of which he speaks," answered Andrea, too good a churchman not to feel uneasiness at the direction things were taking; and so, worthy Vito Viti, I feel the necessity of explaining the whole matter at some length. Sir Smees"—so the Italians called Raoul, out of courtesy still, it being awkward for them, after all that had passed, to address him by his real name—"Sir Smees will excuse us for a few minutes; perhaps it may serve to amuse him to hear to what a flight the imagination of a subtle-minded man can soar."

Raoul civilly expressed the satisfaction it would give him to listen, and stretching himself on the gun-tackle, in order to be more at ease, he leaned back, with his head fairly within the port, while his feet were braced against the inner truck of the gun-carriage. This threw him into a somewhat recumbent attitude, but it being understood as intended to render what was but an inconvenient seat at the best, tolerably comfortable, no one thought it improper.

It is unnecessary for us to repeat here all that Andrea Barrofaldi thought proper to say in his own justification, and in explanation of the celebrated theory of Bishop Berkeley. Such a task was not performed in a minute; and, in truth, prolixity, whenever he got upon a favorite theme, was apt to be one of the vice-governatore's weaknesses. He was far from acquiescing in the doctrine, though he annoyed his old neighbor exceedingly by presenting the subject in such a way as to render it respectable in appearance, if not conclusive in argument. To the latter it was peculiarly unpleasant to imagine, even for the sake of argument, that there was no such island as Elba, and that he was not its podesta; and all his personal and egotistical propensities came in aid of his official reluctance, to disgust him thoroughly with a theory that he did not hesitate to say "was an outrage on every honest man's nature."

"There are fellows in the world, Signor Andrea," the straightforward podesta urged, in continuation of his objections, "who might be glad enough to find everything imaginary, as you say—chaps that cannot sleep of nights for bad consciences, and to whom it would be a great blessing if the earth would throw them overboard, as they say in this ship, and let them fall into the great ocean of oblivion. But they are baroni in grain, and ought not to pass for anything material among honest people. I've known several of those rogues at Livorno, and I daresay Napoli is not altogether without them; but that is a very different matter from telling a handsome and virtuous young maiden that her beauty and modesty are both seeming; and respectable magistrates, that they are as great impostors as the very rogues they send to the prisons; perhaps, to the galleys."

To speeches like these, Andrea opposed his explanations and his philosophy, until the discussion became animated, and the dialogue loud. It is rather a peculiarity of Italy that one of the softest languages of Christendom is frequently rendered harsh and unpleasant by the mode of using it. On this occasion, certainly, the animation of the disputants did not mitigate the evil. Griffin happened to pass the spot, on the outside of the canvas, just at this moment, and, catching some of the words, he stopped to listen. His smiles and translations soon collected a group of officers, and the sentry respectfully dropping a little on one side, the deck around the stateroom of the prisoner became a sort of parquet to a very amusing representation. Several of the young gentlemen understood a little Italian, and Griffin translating rapidly, though in an undertone, the whole affair was deemed to be particularly diverting.

"This is a rum way of consoling a man who is condemned to die," muttered the master; "I wonder the Frenchman stands all their nonsense."

"O!" rejoined the marine officer, "drill will do anything. These revolutionists are so drilled into hyprocrisy, that, I daresay, the fellow is grinning the whole time, as if perfectly delighted."

Raoul, in fact, listened with no little amusement. At first, his voice was occasionally heard in the discussion, evidently aiming at exciting the disputants; but the warmth of the latter soon silenced him, and he was fain to do nothing but listen. Shortly after the discussion got to be warm, and just as Griffin was collecting his group, the prisoner stretched himself still further into the port, to enjoy the coolness of the evening breeze, when, to his surprise, a hand was laid gently on his forehead.

"Hush!" whispered a voice close to his ear, "it is the American—Ithuel—be cool; now is the moment to pull for life."

Raoul had too much self-command to betray his astonishment, but, in an instant, every faculty he possessed was on the alert. Ithuel he knew was a man for exigencies. Experience had taught him a profound respect for his enterprise and daring, when it became necessary to act. Something must certainly be in the wind, worthy of his attention, or this cautious person would not have exposed himself in a situation which would be sure to lead to punishment if detected. Ithuel was seated astride of one of the chains, beneath the main-channel of the ship, a position which might be maintained without detection, possibly, so long as it continued dark; but which, in itself, if seen, would have been taken as a proof of an evil intention.

"What would you have, Etooelle?" whisperered Raoul, who perceived that his companions were too much occupied to observe his movements or to hear his words.

"The *Eye*talian, and his niece, are about to go ashore. Everything is ready and understood. I've consaited you might pass out of the port, in the dark, and escape in the boat. Keep quiet; we shall see."

Raoul understood his respite to be a thing of doubtful termination. Under the most favorable results, an English prison remained in prospective, and then the other side of the picture offered the image of Ghita to his eye! He was in a tumult of feeling, but, accustomed to self-command, no exclamation escaped him.

"When, cher Etooelle?" he asked, his whisper being tremulous, in spite of every effort to command himself.

"Now; too-der-sweet (tout-de-suite); the boat is at the gangway, and old Giun-totardi is in her; they are rigging a chair for the gal. Ay, there she swings off! don't you hear the call?"

Raoul did hear the whistle of the boatswain, which was piping the "lower away" at that very moment. He listened intently, as he lay stretched upon the gun-tackles; and then he heard the splash in the water, as the boat was hauled closer to, in order to be brought beneath the chair. The rattling of oars, too, was audible, as Ghita left the seat, and moved aft. "Round in," called out the officer of the deck; after which Carlo Giuntotardi was left in quiet possession of his own boat.

The moment was exceedingly critical. Some one, in all probability, was watching the boat from the deck; and, though the night was dark, it required the utmost caution to proceed with any hopes of success. At this instant, Ithuel again whispered—

"The time's near. Old Carlo has his orders, and little Ghita is alive to see them obeyed. All now depends on silence and activity. In less than five minutes the boat will be under the port."

Raoul understood the plan, but it struck him as hopeless. It seemed impossible that Ghita could be permitted to quit the ship without a hundred eyes watching her movements; and though it was dark, it was far from being sufficiently so to suppose it practicable for any one to join her and not be seen. Yet this risk must be taken, or escape was out of the question. An order given through the trumpet was encouraging; it announced that the officer of the watch was employed at some duty that must draw his attention another way. This was a great deal; few presuming to look aside while this functionary was inviting their attention in another direction. Raoul's brain was in a whirl.

The two Italians were at the height of their discussion; and fortunately, the clamor they made was at the loudest. Even the suppressed laughter of the officers on the outside of the canvas was audible to him; though the disputants could hear nothing but their own voices. Every knock of the boat against the ship's side, every sound of the oars, as Carlo's foot rattled them about, and the wash of the water was audible. It seemed as if all the interests of life—the future, the past, and the present, together with the emotions of his whole heart, were compressed into that single instant. Ignorant of what was expected, he asked Ithuel, in French, the course he ought to take.

"Am I to fall head-foremost into the water? What would you have of me?" he whispered.

"Lie quiet, till I tell you to move. I'll make the signal, Captain Rule; let the Eyetalians blaze away."

Raoul could not see the water, as he lay with his head fairly in the port; and he had to trust entirely to the single sense of hearing. Knock, knock, knock; the boat dropped slowly along the ship's side, as if preparing to shove off. All this Carlo Giuntotardi managed exceedingly well. When he lay immediately beneath the main channels, it would not have been an easy thing to see his boat, even had there been any one on the lookout. Here he held on, for he was not so lost to external things as not fully to understand what was expected of him. Perhaps he was less attended to by those on deck, from the circumstance that no one believed him capable of so much worldly care.

"Is everything safe for a movement, inboard?" whispered Ithuel.

Raoul raised his head and looked about him. That a group was collected around the stateroom he understood by the movements, the low conversation, and the suppressed laughter; still, no one seemed to be paying any attention to himself. As he had not spoken for some time, however, he thought it might be well to let his voice be heard; and taking care that it should sound well within the port, he made one of the light objections to the vice-governatore's theory that he had urged at the commencement of the controversy. This was little heeded, as he expected; but it served to make those without know that he was in his prison, and might prevent an untimely discovery. Everything else seemed propitious; and lying down again at his length, his face came within a few inches of Ithuel's.

"All safe," he whispered; "what would you have me do?"

"Nothing but shove yourself ahead, carefully, by means of your feet."

This Raoul did; at first, as it might be, inch by inch, until Ithuel put the end of a rope into his hands, telling him it was well fast to the channel above. The rope rendered the rest easy; the only danger now being of too much precipitation. Nothing would have been easier than for Raoul to drag his body out at the port, and to drop into the boat, but, to escape, it was still necessary to avoid observation. The ship was quite half-a-league from the point of Campanella, and directly abreast of it; and there was no security to the fugitives, unless they got some distance the start of any pursuers. This consideration induced the utmost caution on the part of Ithuel; nor was it entirely lost on his friend. By this time, however, Raoul found he was so completely master of his movements, as to be able to swing his legs out of the port, by a very trifling effort; then the descent into the boat would be the easiest thing imaginable. But a pressure from the hand of Ithuel checked him.

"Wait a little," whispered the latter, "till the Eyetalians are at it, cat and dog fashion."

The discussion was now so loud and warm, that it was not necessary to lose much time. Ithuel gave the signal, and Raoul dragged his head and shoulders up by his arms, while he placed his feet against the gun; the next moment he was hanging perpendicularly beneath the main-chains. To drop lightly and noiselessly into the boat, took but a second. When his feet struck athwart he found that the American was there before him. The latter dragged him down to his side, and the two lay concealed in the bottom of the yawl, with a cloak of Ghita's thrown over their persons. Carlo Guintotardi was accustomed to the management of a craft like that in which he now found himself, and simply releasing his boat-hook from one of the chains, the ship passed slowly ahead, leaving him, in about a minute, fairly in her wake, a hundred feet astern.

So far, everything had succeeded surprisingly. The night was so dark as to embolden the two fugitives now to rise, and to take their seats on the thwarts; though all this was done with exceeding caution, and without the least noise. The oars were soon out, Carlo took the tiller, and a feeling of exultation glowed at the heart of Raoul, as he bent his ashen implement, and felt the boat quiver with the impulse.

"Take it coolly, Captain Rule," said Ithuel in a low voice; "it's a long pull, and we are still within ear-shot of the frigate. In five minutes more we shall be dropped so far as to be beyond sight; then we may pull directly out to sea if we wish."

Just then the bell of the *Proserpine* struck four; the signal it was eight o'clock. Immediately after, the watch was called, and a stir succeeded in the ship.

"They only turn the hands up," said Raoul, who perceived that his companion paused, like one uneasy.

"That is an uncommon movement for shifting the watch! What is *that!*"

It was clearly the overhauling of

tackles ; the plash of a boat, as it struck the water, followed.

CHAPTER XXIV.

IT has been seen that a generous sympathy had taken place of hostile feeling, as respects Raoul, in the minds of most on board the *Proserpine*. Under the influence of this sentiment, an order had been passed through the sentries, not to molest their prisoner by too frequent or unnecessary an examination of the anteroom. With a view to a proper regard to both delicacy and watchfulness, however, Winchester had directed that the angle of the canvas nearest the cabin door lantern should be opened a few inches, and that the sentinel should look in every half hour; or as often as the ship's bell told the progress of time.

The object was simply to be certain that the prisoner was in his room, and that he was making no attempt on his own life; a step that had been particularly apprehended previously to the respite. Now the whole of the dispute between the two Italians, and that which had passed beneath the ship's channels, did not occupy more than six or seven minutes; and the little cluster of officers was still gaining recruits, when Raoul was fairly in the yawl of his own lugger. At this moment the ship's bell struck the hour of eight. The marine advanced, with the respect of a subordinate, but with the steadiness of a man on post, to examine the state-room. Although the gentlemen believed this caution unnecessary, the loud voices of Andrea and Vito Viti being of themselves a sort of guaranty that the prisoner was in his cage, they gave way to a man, fully understanding that a sentinel was never to be resisted. The canvas was opened a few inches, the light of the lantern at the cabin door shut in, and there sat the vice-governatore and the podesta, gesticulating and staring into each other's faces, still in hot dispute; but the place of Raoul Yvard was empty!

Yelverton happened to look into the room with the sentinel. He was a young man of strong power of perception, with all the phrenological bumps that are necessary to the character, and he saw at a glance that the bird had flown. The first impression was that the prisoner had thrown himself into the sea, and he rushed on deck without speaking to those around him, made a hurried statement to the officer of the watch, and had a quar-

ter-boat in the water in a surprisingly short time. His astonished companions below were less precipitate, though the material fact was soon known to them—Griffin gave a hasty order, and the can. vas bulk-head came down, as it might be at a single jerk, leaving the two dispu, tants in full view, utterly unconscious of the escape of their late companion, sputtering and gesticulating furiously.

"Hallo! vice-governatore," cried Griffin, abruptly, for he saw that the moment was not one for ceremony; "what have you done with the Frenchman? where is Raoul Yvard?"

"Il Signor Smees? Monsieur Yvard, if you will? Neighbor Vito, what, indeed, has become of the man who lately sat *there?*"

"Cospetto!—according to your doctrine, Signor Andrea, there never was a man there at all—only the imagination of one; it is not surprising that such a being should be missed. But I protest against any inferences being drawn from this accident. All Frenchmen are flighty and easily carried away, and now that they are no longer ballasted by religion, they are so many moral feathers. No, no; let a man of respectable information, of sound principles, and a love for the saints with a good, substantial body, like myself, vanish only once, and then I may confess it will tell in favor of your logic, vice-governatore."

"An obstinate man, neighbor Vito, is a type of the imperfections that a—"

"Your pardon, Signor Barrofaldi," interrupted Griffin, "this is not a moment for philosophical theories, but for us seamen to do our duty. What has become of Raoul Yvard—your Sir Smees?"

"Signor Tenente, as I hope to be saved, I have not the smallest idea! There he was, a minute or two since, seated by that cannon, apparently an attentive and much edified auditor of a discussion we were holding on the celebrated theory of a certain bishop of your own country; which theory, rightly considered—mind I say rightly considered, neighbor Vito; for the view you have taken of this matter is—"

"Enough of this for the present, signori," added Griffin. "The Frenchman was in this place when you came here?"

"He was, Signor Tenente, and seemed greatly to enjoy the discussion in which—"

"And you have not seen him quit you through the canvas, or the port?"

"Not I, on my honor; I did suppose him too much entertained to leave us."

"Ah! Sir Smees has just vanished into the imagination," growled the podesta, "which is going home to the great logical family of which he is an ideal member! There being no lugger, no corsair, no sea, and no frigate, it seems to me that we are all making a stir about nothing."

Griffin did not stop to question farther. He was quickly on deck, where he found Cuffe, who had just been brought out of his cabin by a hurried report.

"What the d——l is the meaning of all this, gentlemen?" demanded the latter, in that tone which a commander so naturally assumes when things go wrong. "Whoever has suffered the prisoner to escape may expect to hear from the admiral directly, on the subject."

"He is not in his stateroom, sir," answered Griffin, "and I directed the boatswain to pipe away all the boats' crews, as I came up the ladder."

As this was said, boat after boat was falling, and, in two or three minutes, no less than five were in the water, including that in which Yelverton was already rowing round the ship, to catch the presumed swimmer, or drowning man.

"The Frenchman is gone, sir," said Winchester, "and he must have passed out of the port. I have sent one of the gentleman to examine if he is not stowed away about the chains."

"Where is the boat of the old Italian and his niece?"

A pause succeeded this question, and the light broke in upon all at the same instant.

"The yawl was alongside," cried Griffin; "no one was in her, however, but Giuntotardi and the girl."

"Beg your pardon, sir," said the young foretop-man, who had just descended the rigging, "I saw the boat from aloft, sir, and it hung some time, sir, under the starboard main-chains. It was so dark, I couldn't fairly make it out; but summat seemed to be passed into it, from a port. I didn't like the look of the thing, and so our captain just told me to come on deck, and report it, sir."

"Send Ithuel Bolt here, Mr. Winchester; bear a hand, sir, and let us have a look at that gentleman."

It is needless to say that the call was unanswered; and then all on board began to understand the mode of escape. Officers rushed into the several boats, and no less than five different parties commenced the pursuit. At the same time the ship hoisted a lantern, as a signal for the boats to rally to.

It has been said that the *Proserpine*, when this incident occurred, was off the point of the Campanella, distant about half a marine league. The wind was light at east, or was what is called the land breeze, and the vessel had about three knots way on her. The headland was nearly a-beam, and she was looking up through the pass which separates Capri from the main, hauling round into the Bay of Naples, intending to anchor in the berth she had landed in the previous day. The night was too dark to permit an object as small as a boat to be seen at any distance, but the black mass of Capri was plainly visible in its outlines, towering into the air near two thousand feet; while the formation of the coast on the other side might be traced with tolerable certainty and distinctness. Such was the state of things when the five boats mentioned quitted the ship.

Yelverton had acted as if a man were overboard; or, he had not waited for orders. While pulling round the ship alone, he caught sight, though very dimly, of the yawl, as it moved in toward the land; and, without communicating with any on board, the truth flashed on his mind also, and he gave chase. When the other boats were ready, the two that were on the outside of the ship pulled off to seaward a short distance, to look about them in that direction; while the two others, hearing the oars of the light gig in which Yelverton was glancing ahead, followed the sound, under the impression that they were in pursuit of the yawl. Such was the state of things at the commencement of an exceedingly vigorous and hot pursuit.

As Raoul and Ithuel had been at work, while time was lost in doubt in and around the ship, they had got about three hundred yards the start of even Yelverton. The boat pulled unusually well; and being intended for only two oars, it might be deemed fully manned, with two as vigorous hands in it as those it had. Still, it was not a match for the second gig, and the four chosen men who composed its crew, which was the boat taken by Yelverton, in the hurry of the moment. In a pull of a mile and a half, the yawl was certain to be overtaken; and the practical ears of Raoul soon assured him of the fact. His own oars were muffled. He determined to profit by the circumstance, and turn aside, in the hope that his fleet pursuers would pass him unseen.

A sheer was accordingly given to the boat, and instead of pulling directly toward the land, the fugitives inclined to the westward; the sea appearing the most obscure in that direction, on account of the proximity of Capri. This artifice was completely successful. Yelverton was so eager in the chase, that he kept his eyes riveted before him, fancying from time to time that he saw the boat ahead, and he passed within a hundred and fifty yards of the yawl, without in the least suspecting her vicinity. Raoul and Ithuel ceased rowing, to permit this exchange of position, and the former had a few sarcastic remarks on the stupidity of his enemies, as some relief to the feelings of the moment. None of the English had muffled oars. On the contrary, the sounds of the regular man-of-war jerks were quite audible in every direction; but so familiar were they to the ears of the Proserpines, that the crews of the two boats that came next after Yelverton actually followed the sounds of his oars, under the belief that they were in the wake of the fugitives. In this manner, then, Raoul suffered three of the five boats to pass ahead of him. The remaining two were so distant as not to be heard; and when those in advance were sufficiently distant, he and Ithuel followed them, with a leisurely stroke, reserving themselves for any emergency that might occur.

It was a fair race between the gig and the two cutters that pursued her. The last had the sounds of the former's oars in the ears of their crews to urge them to exertion, it being supposed they came from the strokes of the pursued; while Yelverton was burning with the desire to outstrip those who followed, and to secure the prize for himself. This made easy work for those in the yawl, which was soon left more than a cable's length astern.

"One would think, Ghita," said Raoul, laughing, though he had the precaution to speak in an undertone, " one would think that your old friends, the vice-governatore and the podesta, commanded the boats in-shore of us, were it not known that they are at this very moment quarreling about the fact whether there is such a place as Elba on this great planet of ours or not."

" Ah ! Raoul, remember the last dreadful eight-and-forty hours ! do not stop to trifle until we are once more fairly beyond the power of your enemies."

" Peste ! I shall be obliged to own hereafter that there is some generosity in an Englishman. I cannot deny their treatment, and yet I had rather it had been more ferocious."

"This is an unkind feeling; you should strive to tear it from your heart."

" It's a great deal to allow to an Englishman, Captain Rule, to allow him gineros'ty," interrupted Ithuel. "They're a fierce race, and fatten on mortal misery."

" Mais, bon Etooelle, your back has escaped this time; you ought to be thankful."

"They're short-handed, and didn't like to cripple a top-man," answered he of the Granite State, unwilling to concede anything to liberal or just sentiments. "Had the ship's complement been full, they wouldn't have left as much skin on my back as would cover the smallest size pin-cushion. I owe them no thanks, therefore."

"Bien; quant a moi, I shall speak well of the bridge which carries me over," said Raoul. "Monsieur Cuffe has given me good food, good wine, good words, a good state-room, a good bed, and a most timely reprieve."

" Is not your heart grateful to God for the last, dear Raoul ? " asked Ghita, in a voice so gentle and tender the young man could have bowed down and worshiped her.

After a pause, however, he answered, as if intentionally to avoid the question by levity.

" I forgot the philosophy, too," he said. "That was no small part of the good cheer. Ciel ! it was worth some risk to have the advantage of attending such a school. Did you understand the matter in dispute between the two Italians, brave Etoolle ? "

" I heerd their *Eye*talian jabber," answered Ithuel; "but supposed it was all about saints' days and eating fish. No reasonable man makes so much noise when he is talking sense."

"Pardie—it was philosophy ! They laugh at us French for living by the rules of reason rather than those of prejudice; and then to hear what they call philosophy ! You would scarce think it, Ghita," continued Raoul, who was now light of heart, and full of the scene he had so lately witnessed, " you would hardly think it, Ghita, but Signor Andrea, sensible and learned as he is, maintained that it was not folly to believe in a philosophy which teaches that nothing we see or do actually exists, but that everything was mere seeming. In short, that we live in an imaginary world, with imaginary people in it; float on an imaginary sea, and cruise in imaginary ships."

"And was all that noise about an idee, Captain Rule ? "

" Si; but men will quarrel about an idea, an imaginary thing, Etooelle, as stoutly as about substantials. Hist ! they will chase imaginary things, too, as are the boats ahead of us at this moment."

"There are others following us," observed Carlo Giuntotardi, who was more alive to surrounding objects than common; and who, from his habitual silence, often heard that which escaped the senses of others. "I have noticed the sound of their oars some time."

This produced a pause, and even a cessation in the rowing, in order that the two seamen might listen. Sure enough, the sound of oars was audible outside, as well as in shore, leaving no doubt that some pursuers were still behind them. This was bringing the fugitives between two fires, as it might be; and Ithuel proposed pulling off at right angles to the course again, in order to get into the rear of the whole party. But to this Raoul objected. He thought the boats astern were still so distant as to enable them to reach the shore in time to escape. Once on the rocks, there could be little danger of being overtaken in the darkness. Still, as it was a first object with Raoul to rejoin his lugger as soon as possible, after landing Ghita, he did not wish to place his boat in any situation of much risk. This induced some deliberation; and it was finally determined to take a middle course, by steering into the pass between Capri and Campanella, in the expectation that when the leading English boats reached the point of the latter, they would abandon the suit as hopeless, and return to the ship.

"We can land you, dearest Ghita, at the Marina Grande of Sorrento; then your walk to St. Agata will be neither long nor painful."

"Do not mind me, Raoul; put me on the land at the nearest place, and go to your vessel. God has relieved you from this great jeopardy, and your duty is to strive to act as it is evident he intends you to do. As for me, leagues will be light, if I can only be satisfied that thou art in safety."

"Angel! Thou never thinkest of self! But not a foot this side of Sorrento will I quit thee. We can pull thither in an hour or two; then I shall feel that I have done a duty. Once ashore, Etooelle and I can set our little sail, and will run to sea between the two islands. No fear but what we can do that, with this land breeze; after which, a few rockets burned will tell us where to find *Le Feu-Follet*."

Ghita again remonstrated, but in vain. Raoul persisted, and she was obliged to submit. The conversation now ceased; the two men plying the oars diligently, and to good effect. Occasionally they ceased, and listened to the sounds of the oars in the frigate's boats, all which were evidently collecting in the vicinity of the point or cape. By this time the yawl had the extremity of the land a-beam,

and it soon passed so far into the bay as to bring most if not all of the pursuers astern. In the darkness, with no other guide than the sounds mentioned, and with so many pursuers, there was some uncertainty, of course, as to the position of all the boats, but there was little doubt that most of them were now somewhere in the immediate vicinity of Campanella. As Raoul gave this point a good berth, and his own progress was noiseless, this was bringing himself and companions, after their recent dangers, into comparative security.

More than an hour of steady rowing followed, during which time the yawl was making swift way toward the Marina Grande of Sorrento. After passing Massa, Raoul felt no further uneasiness, and he requested Carlo Giuntotardi to sheer in toward the land, where less resistance from the breeze was met with, and where it was also easier to know the precise position. Apprehension of the boats now ceased, though Ithuel fancied, from time to time, that he heard smothered sounds, like those of oars imperfectly muffled. Raoul laughed at his conceits and apprehensions, and, to confess the truth, he became negligent of his duty, again, in the soothing delight of finding himself, once more free, in all but heart, in the company of Ghita. In this manner the yawl moved ahead, though with materially diminished speed, until, by the formation of the heights, and the appearance of the lamps and candles on the piano, Ghita knew that they were drawing quite near to the indentation of the coast on which is situate the town of Sorrento.

"As soon as my uncle and myself have landed at the Marina Grande, Raoul," said Ghita, "thou and the American will be certain to seek thy lugger; then thou promisest to quit the coast?"

"Why ask promises of one that thou dost not sufficiently respect to think he will keep them?"

"I do not deserve this, Raoul; between thee and me, no promise has ever been broken."

"It is easy to break vows with one who will neither give nor accept them. I cannot boast of keeping such idle faith as this! Go with me before some priest, Ghita, ask all that man ever has or can swear to, and then thou shalt see how a sailor can be true to his vow."

"And why before a priest? Thou know'st, Raoul, that in thine eyes, all the offices of the Church are mummery; that nothing is more sacred with thee for being sworn to at the altar of God, and with one of his holy ministers for a witness!"

"Every oath or promise made to thee, Ghita, is sacred in my eyes. It wanteth not any witness, or any consecrated place, to make it more binding than thy truth and tenderness can insure. Thou art my priest—my altar—my—"

"Forbear!" exclaimed Ghita, in alarm, lest he should utter the name of that holy Being toward whom her heart was even at that moment swelling with gratitude for his own recent escape from death. "Thou know'st not the meaning of thine own words, and might'st add that which would give me more pain than I can express."

"Boat, ahoy!" cried a deep nautical voice, within twenty yards of them, and in shore; the hail coming in the sudden, quick demand that distinguishes the call of a man-of-war's-man.

A pause of half a minute succeeded, for they in the yawl were completely taken by surprise.

At length, Ithuel, who felt the necessity of saying something, if he would not bring the stranger close alongside of them, answered in the customary manner of the Italians.

Clinch, for it was he, scouring the shore in quest of the lugger, on his way back to the *Proserpine*, gave a growl when he found that he must speak in a foreign tongue, if he would continue the discourse; then he mustered all the Italian of which he was master for the occasion. Having cruised long on the station, this was sufficient, however, for his present purpose.

"Is that a boat from Massa or from Capri?" he inquired.

"Neither, s'nore," answered Raoul, afraid to trust Carlo's conscience with the management of such a dialogue. "We came round the cape, from St. Agata, and carry figs to Napoli."

"St. Agata, ay, that is the village on the heights; I passed a night there myself, in the house of one Maria Giuntotardi—"

"Who can this be?" murmured Ghita; "my aunt knows no forestieri!"

"An Inglese, by his thick speech and accent. I hope he will not ask for figs for his supper!"

Clinch was thinking of other things at that moment; and when he continued, it was to follow the train of his own thoughts.

"Have you seen anything of a barone-looking lugger?" he asked; "French-rigged and French-manned, skulking anywhere about this coast?"

"Si; she went north, in the Gulf of Gaeta, just as the sun was setting, and is, no doubt, gone to anchor under the cannon of her countrymen."

"If she has, she'll find herself in hot water," answered Clinch, in English. "We've craft enough up there to hoist her in and dub her down to a jolly-boat's size, in a single watch. Did you see anything of a frigate this evening, near the Point of the Campanella?—an Inglese, I mean; a tight six-and-thirty, with three new topsails."

"Si, the light you see here, just in a range with Capri, is at her gaff; we have seen her the whole afternoon and evening. In fact she towed us kindly round the cape, until we got fairly into this bay."

"Then you are the people for me! Was there a man hanged on board her or not about sunset?"

This question was put with so much interest, that Raoul cursed his interrogator in his heart, imagining that he was burning with the wish to learn his exection. He was also now aware that this was the boat which had left the *Proserpine* about noon.

"I can tell you there was not, s'nore, if that will gladden your heart. A man was all ready to be hanged when Captain Cuffe was pleased to order him taken down."

"Just as three heavy guns were fired up at town; was it not so?" Clinch eagerly inquired.

"Diable; this man may have been my preserver after all! You say true, s'nore; it *was* just as three guns were fired up at Naples, though I did not know those guns had anything to do with the intended execution. Can you tell me if they had?"

"If they had! Why, I touched them off with my own hands; they were signals made by the admiral to spare poor Raoul Yvard, for a few days, at least. I am rejoiced to hear that all my great efforts to reach the fleet were not in vain. I don't like this hanging, Mr. Italian."

"S'nore, you showed a kind heart, and will one day reap the reward of such generous feelings. I wish I knew the name of so humane a gentleman, that I might mention him in my prayers."

"They'll never fancy that Captain Rule said *that*," muttered Ithuel, grinning.

"As for my name, friend, it's no great matter. They call me Clinch, which is a good fast word to sail under too, but it has no handle to it, other than of a poor devil of a master's mate; and that, too, at an age when some men carry broad pennants."

This was said bitterly, and in English; when uttered, the supposed Italian was wished a "Bonna sera," and the gig proceeded.

"That is un brave," said Raoul, with emphasis, as they departed. "If ever I meet with Monsieur Cleench, he will learn that I do not forget his good wishes. Peste! if there were a hundred such men in the British marine, Etooelle, we might love it."

"They're fiery sarpents, Captain Rule, and not to be trusted, any on 'em. As for fine words, I might have fancied myself a cousin of the king's, if I'd only put my name in their shipping articles. This Mr. Clinch is well enough in the main; being his own worst inimy, in the way of the grog pitcher."

"Boat, ahoy!" shouted Clinch again, now about a hundred yards distant, having passed toward the cape. Raoul and Ithuel mechanically ceased rowing, under the impression that the master's mate had still something to communicate.

"Boat, ahoy! Answer at once, or you'll hear from me," repeated Clinch.

"Ay, ay," answered another voice, which, in fact, was Yelverton's; "Clinch, is that you?"

"Ay, ay, sir; Mr. Yelverton, is it not? I think I know the voice, sir."

"You are quite right, but make less noise; who was that you hailed a moment or two since?"

Clinch began to answer; but as the two gigs were approaching each other all the time, they were soon so near as to render it unnecessary to speak loud enough to be heard at any distance. All this time, Raoul and Ithuel lay on their oars, almost afraid to stir the water, and listening with an attention that was nearly breathless. They were satisfied that the oars of the English were now muffled; a sign that they were in earnest in the pursuit, and bent on making a thorough search. The two gigs could not be more than a hundred yards from the yawl, and Ithuel knew that they were the two fastest rowing boats of the English fleet; so fast, indeed that Cuffe and his lieutenants had made several successful matches with them, against the officers of different vessels.

"Hist!" said Ghita, whose heart was in her mouth. "O! Raoul, they come!"

Coming, indeed, were they; and that with vast velocity. So careful, however, was the stroke, that they were within two hundred feet of the yawl before Raoul and his companions took the alarm, and plunged their oars again into the water. Then, indeed, the gigs might be dimly seen; though the shadows of the land deepened the obscurity of night so far as to render objects at even a less distance quite indistinct. The suddenness and imminence of the danger appeared to arouse all there was of life in Carlo Giuntotardi. He steered, and steered well, being accustomed to the office, by living so long on the coast; and he sheered in for the rocks, with the double view of landing, if necessary, and of getting still deeper within the shadows. It was soon evident that the English gained. Four oars against two were fearful odds; and it was plainly apparent the yawl must be overtaken.

"O, uncle! toward the arch and water-cavern of the point," whispered Ghita, whose hands were clasped on her breast, as if to keep down her emotions. "That may yet save him!"

The yawl was in the act of whirling round the rocks which form the deep cove on which the Marina Grande of Sorrento lies. Carlo caught his niece's idea, and he kept his tiller hard a-port, telling Raoul and Ithuel at the same time to take in their oars as soon as possible. The men obeyed, supposing it was the intention to land them and take to the heights for shelter. But just as they supposed the boat was about to strike against some perpendicular rock, and Raoul was muttering his surprise that such a spot should be chosen to land at, it glided through a low, natural arch, and entered a little basin as noiselessly as a bubble floating in a current.

The next minute the two gigs came whirling round the rocks; one following the shore close in, to prevent the fugitives from landing, and the other steering more obliquely athwart the bay. In still another minute they had passed a hundred yards ahead, and the sound of their movements was lost.

CHAPTER XXV.

THE spot in which Carlo Giuntotardi had taken refuge is well known on the Sorrentine shore, as the water-cavern at the ruins of Queen Joan's country-house. Cavern it is not, though the entrance is beneath a low, natural arch, the basin within being open to the heavens, and the place resembling an artificial excavation made to shelter boats. Let the origin of this little haven be what it may, art could not have devised a more convenient or a more perfect refuge than it afforded to our fugitives. Once through the arch, they would have been effectually concealed from their pursuers under a noon-day sun; nor would any who were unacquainted with the peculiarities of the entrance, dream of a boat's lying, as it might be, buried in the rocks of the little promontory. Neither Ghita nor her uncle any longer felt any concern; but the former announced her intention to land here, assuring Raoul that that she could easily find her way into the bridle-path which leads to St. Agata.

The desperate character of the recent chase, aided by his late almost miraculous escape from death, joined to the necessity of parting from his mistress, rendered our hero melancholy, if not moody. He could not ask Ghita to share his dangers any longer; yet he felt, if he permitted her now to quit him, the separation might be forever. Still he made no objection; but leaving Ithuel in charge of the boat, he assisted Ghita up the funnel-like sides of the basin, and prepared to accompany her on her way to the road. Carlo preceded the pair, telling his niece that she would find him at a cottage on the way that was well known to both.

The obscurity was not so great as to render the walking very difficult, and Raoul and Ghita pursued their course slowly along the walks, each oppressed with the same sensation of regret at parting, though influenced by nearly opposite views for the future. The girl took the young man's arm without hesitation, and there was a tenderness in the tones of her voice, as well as in her general manner, that betrayed how nearly her heart was interested in what was passing. Still, principle was ever uppermost in her thoughts, and she determined now to speak plainly and to the purpose.

"Raoul," she said, after listening to some of those fervent declarations of love that were peculiarly agreeable to one of her affectionate and sincere nature, even when she most felt the necessity of repelling the insinuating suit, "there must be an end of this. I can never go through again the scenes I have lately witnessed, nor allow you to run such fearful risks. The sooner we understand each other, and, I may say, the sooner we part, it will be the wiser, and the better for the interests of both. I blame myself for suffering the intimacy to last so long, and for proceeding so far."

"And this is said by a fervent-souled Italian girl! One of eighteen years; who comes of a region in which it is the boast that the heart is even warmer than the sun: of a race, among which it is hard to find one—oui, even a poor *one*—who is not ready to sacrifice home, country, hopes, fortune, nay, life itself, to give happiness to the man who has chosen her from all the rest of her sex."

"It would seem easy to me to do all this, Raoul. Si, I think I could sacrifice everything you have named to make you happy! Home, I have not, unless the prince's towers can thus be called; country, since the sad event of this last week, I feel as if I had altogether lost. Of hopes, I have few in this world with which your image has not been connected; but those which were once so, so precious to me, are now, I fear, lost; you know I have no fortune to tempt me to stay, or you to follow; as for my life, I fear it will soon be very valueless—am sure it will be miserable."

"Then why not decide at once, dearest Ghita, to throw the weight of your sorrows on the shoulders of one strong enough to bear them? You care not for dress or gay appearances, and can take a bridegroom even with the miserable aspect of a lazzarone, when you know the heart is right. You will not despise me because I am not decked as I might be for the bridal. Nothing is easier than to find an altar and a priest among these monasteries; and the hour for saying mass is not very distant. Give me a right to claim you, and I will appoint a place of rendezvous, bring in the lugger to-morrow night, and carry you off in triumph to our gay Provence; where you will find hearts gentle as your own, to welcome you with joy, and call you sister."

Raoul was earnest in his manner, and it was not possible to doubt his sincerity; though an air of self-satisfaction gleamed in his face when he alluded to his present personal appearance, for he well knew all his advantages in that way, in spite of the dress of a lazzarone.

"Urge me not, dear Raoul," Ghita answered, though, unconsciously to herself, she pressed closer to his side, and both sadness and love were in the very tones of her voice; "urge me not, dear Raoul; this can never be. I have already told you the gulf that lies between us; you will not cross it to join me, and I cannot cross it to join you. Nothing but that could separate us; but that, to my eyes, grows broader and deeper every hour."

"Ah, Ghita, thou deceivest me, and thyself. Were thy feelings as thou fanciest, no human inducement could lead thee to reject me."

"It is no human inducement, Raoul; it is one above earth, and all it holds."

"Peste! These priests are scourges sent to torment men in every shape! They inflict hard lessons in childhood, teach asperity in youth, and make us superstitious and silly in age. I do not wonder that my brave compatriots drove them from France; they did nothing but devour like locusts, and deface the beauties of providence.''

"Raoul, thou art speaking of the ministers of God!'' Ghita observed meekly, but in sorrow.

"Pardon me, dearest Ghita; I have no patience when I remember what a trifle, after all, threatens to tear us asunder. Thou pretendest to love me?''

"It is not pretense, Raoul, but a deep, and I fear a painful reality.''

"To think that a girl so frank, with a heart so tender, and a soul so true, will allow any secondary thing to divide her from the man of her choice!''

"It is not secondary, but a primary thing, Raoul; O, that I could make thee think so! The question is between thee and God; were it aught else, thou mightest indeed prevail.''

"Why trouble thyself about my religion at all? Are there not thousands of wives who tell their beads, and repeat their aves, while their husbands think of anything but heaven? Thou and I can overlook this difference; others overlook them and keep but one heart between them still. I never would molest thee, Ghita, in thy gentle worship.''

"It is not thou that I dread, Raoul, but myself,'' answered the girl with streaming eyes, though she succeeded in suppressing the sobs that struggled for utterance. "'A house divided against itself cannot stand,' they say; how could a heart that was filled with thee find a place for the love it ought to bear the author of its being? When the husband lives only for the world, it is hard for the wife to think of heaven as she ought.''

Raoul was deeply touched with the feeling Ghita betrayed while he was ready to adore her for the confiding sincerity with which she confessed his power over her heart. His answer was given with seductive tenderness of manner which proved that he was not altogether unworthy of the strange conflict he had created in so gentle a breast.

"Thy God will never desert thee, Ghita,'' he said; "thou hast nothing to fear as my wife, or that of any other man. None but a brute could ever think of molesting thee in thy worship, or in doing aught that thy opinions render necessary or proper. I would tear the tongue from my mouth before reproach, sneer, or argument should be used to bring thee pain after I once felt that thou leanedest on me for support. All that I have said has come from a wish that thou wouldst not misunderstand me in a matter that I know thou think'st important.''

"Ah, Raoul, little dost thou understand the hearts of women. If thy power is so great over me to-day, almost to incline me from the most solemn of all my duties, what would it become when the love of a girl should turn into the absorbing affection of a wife! I find it hard, even now, to reconcile the love I bear to God with the strong feeling thou hast created in my heart. A year of wedded life would endanger more than I can express to you in words.''

"And then the fear of losing thy salvation is stronger than thy worldly attachments?''

"Nay, Raoul, it is not that. I am not selfish or cowardly, as respects myself, I hope; nor do I think at all of any punishment that might follow from a marriage with an unbeliever; what I most apprehend, is being taught to love my God less than I feel I now do, or than, as the creature of his mercy, I ought.''

"Thou speakest as if man could rival the being whom thou worshipest. I have always understood that the love we bear the Deity, and that we bear each other, are of a very different quality. I can see no necessity for their interfering with each other.''

"Nothing can be less alike, Raoul; yet one may impair, if not destroy, the other. O, if thou wouldst but believe that thy Saviour was thy God—if thou couldst but be dead to his love, and not active against him, I might hope for better things; but I dare not pledge all my earthly duties to one who is openly an enemy of my own great Master and Redeemer.''

"I will not, cannot deceive thee, Ghita; that I leave to the priests. Thou know'st my opinions, and must take me as I am, or wholly reject me. This I say, though I feel that disappointment, if you persist in your cruelty, will drive me to some desperate act, by means of which I shall yet taste of the mercies of these English.''

"Say not so, Raoul; be prudent for the sake of your country—''

"But not for thine, Ghita?''

"Yes, Raoul, and for mine also. I wish not to conceal how much happier I shall be in hearing of your welfare and peace of mind. I fear, though an enemy, it will ever give me pleasure to learn that thou art victorious. But here is the road, yonder the cottage where my uncle waits for me, and we must part. Heaven bless thee, Raoul; my prayers will be full of thee. Do not—do not risk more to see me; but if—'' The heart of the girl was so full, that emotion choked her. Raoul listened intently for the next word, but he listened in vain.

"If what, dear Ghita? Thou wert

about to utter some thing that I feel is encouraging."

"Oh! how I hope it may be so, my poor Raoul! I was going to add, if God ever touches thy heart, and thou wouldst stand before his altar, a believer, with one at thy side who is ready and anxious to devote all to thee but her love of the Being who created her, and her treasures of future happiness, seek Ghita; thou wilt find her thou wouldst have."

Raoul stretched forth his arms to clasp the tender girl to his bosom; but, fearful of herself, she avoided him, and fled along the path like one terrified with the apprehension of pursuit. The young man paused a moment, half inclined to follow; then prudence regained its influence, and he bethought him of the necessity of getting to a place of safety while it was yet night. The future was still before him, in hope, and that hope led him to look forward to other occasions to press his suit.

Little, however, did Raoul Yvard, much as he prized her, know Ghita Caraccioli. Her nature was full of womanly sensibilities, it is true, and her heart replete with tenderness for him in particular; but the adoration she paid to God was of the lasting character which endures to the end. In all she said and felt, she was truth itself; and while no false shame interposed to cause her to conceal her attachment, there was a moral armor thrown about her purposes that rendered them impregnable to the assaults of the world.

Our hero found Ithuel sleeping in the boat in perfect security. The Granite man thoroughly understood his situation, and foreseeing a long row before him, he had quietly lain down in the stern-sheet of the yawl, and was taking his rest as tranquilly as he had ever done in his berth on board *Le Feu-Follet*. He was even aroused with difficulty, and he resumed the oar with reluctance. Before descending the funnel, Raoul had taken a survey of the water from the rocks above. He listened intently, to catch any sound that might arise from the English boats. But nothing was visible in the obscurity, while distance or caution prevented anything from being audible. Satisfied that all was safe outside, he determined to row out into the bay, and, making a circuit to avoid his enemies, push to the westward, in the expectation of finding his lugger in the offing. As there was now a considerable land breeze, and the yawl was lightened of so much of her freight, there was little doubt of his being able to effect his purpose, so far as getting out of sight was concerned, at least, long ere the return of light.

"Pardie, Etooelle!" Raoul exclaimed, after he had given the American jog the third, "you sleep like a friar who is paid for saying masses at midnight. Come, mon ami; now is your time to move; all is clear outside."

"Well, natur' they say is a good workman, Captain Rule," answered Ithuel, gaping and rubbing his eyes; "and never did she turn off a prettier hiding-place than this. One sleeps so quietly in it! Heigho! I suppose the ash must be kept moving, or we may yet miss our passage back to France. Shove her bows round, Captain Rule; here is the hole, which is almost as hard to find as it is to thread a needle with a cable. A good shove, and she will shoot out into the open water."

Raoul did as desired. Ithuel touching the tiller, the yawl glided through the opening, and felt the long ground-swell of the glorious bay. The two adventurers looked about them with some concern, as they issued from their hiding-place, but the obscurity was too deep to bring anything in view on the face of the waters. The flashing that occasionally illuminated the summit of Vesuvius resembled heat-lightning, and would have plainly indicated the position of that celebrated mountain had not its dark outlines been visible, exposing a black mass at the head of the bay. The ragged mountain-tops, behind and above Castel-a-Mare were also to be traced, as was the whole range of the nearer coast, though that opposite was only discoverable by the faint glimmerings of a thousand lights, that were appearing and disappearing, like stars eclipsed, on the other side of the broad sheet of placid water. On the bay itself, little could be discerned; under the near coast, nothing, the shadows of the rocks obscuring its borders with a wide belt of darkness.

After looking around them quite a minute in silence, the men dropped their oars and began to pull from under the point, with the intention of making an offing before they set their little lugs.

As they came out, the heavy flap of canvas, quite near, startled their ears, and both turned instinctively to look ahead. There, indeed, was a vessel, standing directly in, threatening even to cross their very track. She was close on a wind, with her larboard tacks aboard, and had evidently just shaken everything, in the expectation of luffing past the point without tacking. Could she succeed in this, it would be in her power to stand on until compelled to go about beneath the very cliffs of the town of Sorrento. This was, in truth, her aim; for again she shook all her sails.

"Peste!" muttered Raoul; "this is a bold pilot; he hugs the rocks as if they were his mistress! We must lie quiet, Etooelle, and let him pass; else he may trouble us."

"'Twill be the wisest, Captain Rule; though I do not think him an Englishman. Hark! The ripple under his bow is like that of a knife going through a ripe watermelon."

"Mon *Feu-Follet!*" exclaimed Raoul, rising and actually extending his arms as if to embrace the beloved craft. "Etooelle, they seek us, for we are far behind our time!"

The stranger drew near fast; when his outlines became visible, there was no mistaking them. The two enormous lugs, the little jigger, the hull almost awash, and the whole of the fairy form, came mistily into view, as the swift bird assumes color and proportion, while it advances out of the depths of the void. The vessel was but a hundred yards distant; in another minute she would be past.

"*Vive la Republique!*" said Raoul, distinctly, though he feared to trust his voice with a loud hail.

Again the canvas flapped, and the trampling of feet were heard on the lugger's deck; then she came sweeping into the wind, within fifty feet of the yawl. Raoul watched the movement; and by the time her way was nearly lost, he was alongside, and had caught a rope. At the next instant he was on board her.

Raoul trod the deck of his lugger again, with the pride of a monarch as he ascends his throne. Certain of her sailing qualities, and confident of his own skill, this gallant seaman was perfectly indifferent to the circumstance that he was environed by powerful enemies. The wind and the hour were propitious, and no sensation of alarm disturbed the exultation of that happy moment. The explanations that passed between him and his first lieutenant, Pintard, were brief but distinct. *Le Feu-Follet* had kept off the land, with her sails lowered, a trim in which a vessel of her rig and lowness in the water would not be visible more than five or six miles, until sufficient time had elapsed, when she was taken into the Gulf of Salerno, to look for signals from the heights of St. Agata. Finding none, she went to sea again, as has been stated, sweeping along the coast in the hope of falling in with intelligence. Although she could not be seen by her enemies, she saw the three cruisers who were on the lookout, and great uneasiness prevailed on board concerning the fates of the absentees.

On the afternoon of that day, the lugger was carried close in with the northwest side of Ischia, which island she rounded at dusk, seemingly intending to anchor at Baiæ, a harbor seldom without allied cruisers. As the wind came off the land, however, she kept away, and passing between Procida and Misenum, she came out into the Bay of Naples, about three hours before meeting Raoul, with the intention of examining the whole of the opposite coast, in search of the yawl. She had seen the light at the gaff of the *Proserpine*, and, at first, supposed it might be a signal for the missing boat. With a view to make sure of it, the lugger had been kept away until the night-glasses announced a ship; when she was hauled up on a wind, and had made two or three successive half-boards, to weather the point where her captain lay concealed; the Marina Grande of Sorrento being one of the places of rendezvous mentioned by our hero, in his last instructions.

There was a scene of lively congratulation, and of even pleasing emotion, on the deck of the lugger, when Raoul so unexpectedly appeared. He had every quality to make himself beloved by his men. Brave, adventurous, active, generous, and kind-hearted, his character rendered him a favorite to a degree that was not common even among the people of that chivalrous nation. The French mariner will bear familiarity better than his great rival and neighbor, the Englishman; and it was natural with our hero to be frank and free with all, whether above him or below him in condition. The temperaments to be brought into subjection were not as rude and intractable as those of the Anglo-Saxon; and the off-hand, dashing character of Raoul was admirably adapted to win both the admiration and the affection of his people. They now thronged about him, without hesitation or reserve, each man anxious to make his good wishes known, his felicitations heard.

"I have kept you playing about the fire, camarades," said Raoul, affected by the proofs of attachment he had received; "but we will now take our revenge. There are English boats in chase of me, at this moment, under the land; we will try to pick up one or two of them by way of letting them know there is still such a vessel as *Le Feu-Follet.*"

An exclamation of pleasure followed; then an old quartermaster, who had actually taught his commander his first lessons in seamanship, shoved through the crowd, and put his questions with a sort of authority.

"Mon capitaine," he said, "have you been near these English?"

"Ay, Benoit; somewhat nearer than I could wish. To own the truth, the reason you have not sooner seen me, was that I was passing my time on board our old friend, *La Proserpine*. Her officers and crew would not lose my company, when they had once begun to enjoy it."

"Peste!—mon chere capitaine—were you a prisoner?"

"Something of that sort, Benoit. At least they had me on a grating, with a rope round the neck, and were about to make me swing off, as a spy, when a happy gun or two from Nelson, up above there, at the town, ordered them to let me go below. As I had no taste for such amusements, and wanted to see mon cher *Feu-Follet*, Etooelle and I got into the yawl and left them; intending to return to be hanged when we can find nothing better to do."

This account required an explanation, which Raoul gave in a very few words, and then the crew were directed to go to their stations, in order that the lugger might be properly worked. The next minute the sails were filled on the larboard tack, as before, and *Le Feu-Follet* again drew ahead, standing in for the cliffs.

"There is a light in motion near Capri, mon capitaine," observed the first lieutenant: "I suppose it to be on board some enemy. They are plenty as gulls about this bay."

"You are very right, Monsieur. 'Tis *La Proserpine;* she shows the lights for her boats. She is too far to leeward to meddle with us, however, and we are pretty certain there is nothing between her and the ships off the town that can do us any harm. Are all our lights concealed? Let them be well looked to, monsieur."

"All safe, mon capitaine. *Le Feu-Follet* never shows her lantern until she wishes to lead an enemy into the mire!"

Raoul laughed, and pronounced the word "Bon" in the emphatic manner peculiar to a Frenchman. Then, as the lugger was drawing swiftly in toward the rocks, he went on the forecastle himself to keep a proper lookout ahead; Ithuel, as usual, standing at his side.

The piano or plain of Sorrento terminates, on the side of the bay, in perpendicular cliffs of tufa, that vary from one to near two hundred feet in height. Those near the town are among the highest, and are lined with villas, convents, and other dwellings, of which the foundations are frequently placed upon shelves of rock fifty feet below the adjacent streets. Raoul had been often here during the short reign of the Rufo faction, and was familiar with most of the coast. He knew that his little lugger might brush against the very rocks, in most places, and was satisfied that if he fell in with the *Proserpine's* boats at all, it must be quite near the land. As the night wind blew directly down the bay, sighing across the campagna, between Vesuvius and Castel-a-Mare, it became necessary to tack offshore as soon as *Le Feu-Follet* got close to the cliffs, where the obscurity was greatest, and her proportions and rig were not discernible at any distance. While in the very act of going round, and before the head-sheets were drawn, Raoul was startled by a sudden hail.

"Felucca, ahoy!" cried one, in English, from a boat that was close on the lugger's bow.

"Halloo!" answered Ithuel, raising an arm, for all near him to be quiet.

"What craft's that?" resumed he in the boat.

"A felucca sent down by the admiral to look for the *Proserpine;* not finding her at Capri, we are turning up to the anchorage of the fleet again."

"Hold on a moment, sir, if you please; I'll come on board you. Perhaps I can help you out of your difficulty; for I happen to know something of that ship."

"Ay, ay; bear a hand, if you please; for we want to make the most of this wind while it stands."

It is singular how easily we are deceived, when the mind commences by taking a wrong direction. Such was now the fact with him in the boat, for he had imbibed the notion that he could trace the outlines of the felucca, of which so many navigate those waters, and the idea that it was the very lugger he had been seeking never crossed his mind. Acting under the delusion, he was soon alongside and on the deck of his enemy.

"Do you know this gentleman, Etooelle?" demanded Raoul, who had gone to the gangway to receive his visitor.

"It is Mr. Clinch, the master's-mate of the accursed *Proserpine;* he who spoke us in the yawl, off the point yonder."

"How!" exclaimed Clinch, his alarm being sufficiently apparent in his voice; "have I fallen into the hands of Frenchmen?"

"You have, monsieur," answered Raoul, courteously, "but not into the hands of enemies. This is *Le Feu-Follet*, and I am Raoul Yvard."

"Then all hope for Jane is gone for ever! I have passed a happy day, though a busy one, for I did begin to think there was some chance for me. A man cannot see Nelson without pulling up, and wishing to be something like him; but a prison is no place for promotion."

"Let us go into my cabin, monsieur. There we can converse more at our ease; and we shall have a light."

Clinch was in despair; it mattered not to him whither he was taken. In the cabin he sat the picture of a helpless man, and a bottle of brandy happening to stand on the table, he eyed it with something like the ferocity with which the hungry wolf may be supposed to gaze at the lamb ere he leaps into the fold.

"Is this the gentleman you mean, Etooelle?" demanded Raoul, when the cabin lamp shone on the prisoner's face; "he who was so rejoiced to hear that his enemy was not hanged?"

"'Tis the same, Captain Rule; in the main he is a good-natured officer, one that does more harm to himself than to any one else. They said in the ship that he went up to Naples to do you some good turn or other."

"Bon! You have been long in your boat, Mr. Clinch, we will give you a warm supper and a glass of wine; after which you are at liberty to seek your frigate, and to return to your own flag."

Clinch stared as if he did not, or could not, believe what he heard; then the truth flashed on his mind, and he burst into tears. Throughout that day his feelings had been in extremes; hope once more opening a long vista of happiness for the future, through the renewed confidence and advice of his captain. Thus far he had done well, and it was by striving to do still better that he had fallen into the hands of the enemy. For a single moment the beautiful fabric which revived hopes had been industriously weaving throughout the day was torn into tatters. The kindness of Raoul's manner, however, his words, and the explanations of Ithuel, removed a mountain from his breast, and he became quite unmanned. There are none so debased as not to retain glimmerings of the bright spirit that is associated with the grosser particles of their material nature. Clinch had in him the living consciousness that he was capable of better things, and he endured moments of deep anguish as the image of the patient, self-devoting and constant Jane rose before his mind's eye to reproach him with his weaknesses.

It is true that she never made these reproaches in terms; so far from that, she would not even believe the slanders of those she mistook for his enemies; but Clinch could not always quiet the spirit within him, and he often felt degraded as he re-membered with how much more firmness Jane supported the load of hope deferred than he did himself. The recent interview with Cuffe had aroused all that remained of ambition and self-respect, and he had left the ship that morning with a full and manly determination to reform, and to make one continued and persevering effort to obtain a commission, and with it Jane. Then followed capture and the moment of deep despair. But Raoul's generosity removed the load, and again the prospect brightened.

CHAPTER XXVI.

RAOUL soon decided on his course. While he was consoling Clinch, orders had been sent to Pintard to look for the other gig; but a few minutes' search under the cliffs satisfied those on deck that she was not to be found; and the fact was so reported below. Nor could all Ithuel's ingenuity extract from the boat's crew any available information on the subject. There was an *esprit du corps* among the *Proserpine*, as between their own ship and *Le Feu-Follet*, which would have withstood, on an occasion like this, both threats and bribes; and he of the Granite State was compelled to give the matter up as hopeless; though, in so doing, he did not fail to ascribe the refusal to betray their shipmates, on the part of these men, to English obstinacy, rather than to any creditable feeling. The disposition to impute the worst to those he hated, however, was not peculiar to Ithuel or his country; it being pretty certain he would have fared no better on board the English frigate, under circumstances at all analogous.

Satisfied, at length, that the other boat had escaped him, and feeling the necessity of getting out of the bay while it was still dark, Raoul reluctantly gave the order to bear up, and put the lugger dead before the wind, wing-and-wing. By the time this was done, the light craft had turned so far to windward as to be under the noble rocks that separate the piano of Sorrento from the shores of Vico; a bold promontory, that buttresses the sea with a wall of near or quite a thousand feet in perpendicular height. Here she felt the force of the land wind; and when her helm was put up, and her sheets eased off, a bird turning on the wing would not have come round more gracefully, and scarcely with greater velocity. The course now lay from point to point, in order to avoid being becalmed within the indentations of the coast. This carired the lugger athwart the cove of Sorrento, rather than into it, and, of course, left Yelverton, who had landed at the smaller Marina, quite out of the line of her course.

So swift was the progress of the little craft, that within fifteen minutes after bearing up, Raoul and Ithuel, who again occupied their stations on the forecastle, saw the headland where they had so lately been concealed, and ordered the helm a-port, in order to sheer out and give it a berth. Then rock was passed after rock, cove after cove, and village after village, until the entrance between Capri and Campanella was again reached. In sweeping down the shore in this manner, the intention was to pick up any boat that might be in the lugger's track; for, while Raoul was disposed to let his prisoner go, he had a strong desire to seize any other officers of the frigate that might fall in his way. The search was ineffectual, however; and when the lugger came out into the open sea, all expectation of further success, of this nature, was reluctantly abandoned.

As *Le Feu-Follet* was now in dangerous proximity to three cruisers of the enemy, the moment was one that called for decision. Fortunately the positions of the English vessels were known to Raoul, a circumstance that lessened the danger, certainly; but it would not do to continue long within a league of their anchorage, with the risk of the land-breeze failing. As yet the darkness, and the shadows of the land, concealed the privateer, and her commander determined, if not literally to make hay while the sun shone, at least to profit by its absence. With this view, then, he ordered the lugger hove-to, the boat of Clinch hauled to the lee gangway, and the prisoners to be all brought on deck; the common men in the waist, and the master's mate aft.

"Here I must lose the pleasure of your company, Monsieur Clinch," said Raoul, with a courtesy that may almost be termed national. "We are quite as near votre belle *Proserpine* as is safe, and I long for notre belle France. The wind is fair to take us off the coast, and two hours will carry us out of sight, even were it noonday. You will have the complaisance to make my duty to Monsieur Cuffe—oui, pardie! and to ces brave Italiens, who are so much ze amis of Sir Smees! Touchez-la."

Raoul laughed, for his heart was light, and sundry droll conceits danced through his brain. As for Clinch, the whole was Greek to him, with the exception that he understood it was the intention of the French to take their vessel off the coast, a circumstance that he was not sorry to learn, though he would have given so much, a few hours earlier, to have known where to find her. Raoul's generosity had worked a revolution in his feelings, however, and nothing was farther from his wishes, now, than to be employed against the celebrated privateersman. Still, he had a duty to perform to the service of which he was a member, another to Jane, and a last to himself.

"Captain Yvard," said the master's mate, taking the other's offered hand, "I shall never forget this kindness on your part; it comes at a most fortunate moment for me. My happiness in this world, and perhaps in the world to come"—an ejaculation of "Bah!" involuntarily escaped the listener—"depended on my being at liberty. I hold it to be fair, however, to tell you the whole truth. I must do all I can to capture or destroy this very lugger, as well as any other of the king's enemies, as soon as I am my own master again."

"Bon! I like your frankness, Monsieur Clinch, as much as I like your humanity. I always look for a brave enemy when un Anglais comes against me; if you are ever in the number, I shall expect nothing worse."

"It will be my duty, Captain Yvard, to report to Captain Cuffe where I found the *Folly*, where I left her, and where I think she is steering! Even your armament, crew, and all such little particulars, I shall be questioned on; I must answer honestly."

"Mon cher, you are 'honest fellow,' as you Anglais say. I wish it was noonday, that you might better see our deck; *Le Feu-Follet* is not ugly, that she should wish to wear a veil. Tell everything, Clinch, mon brave; if Monsieur Cuffe wish to send another party against our lugger, come in the first boat en personne. We shall always be happy to see Monsieur Clinch. As for where we steer, you see our head is toward la belle France; and there is plenty of room for a long chase. Adieu, mon ami; au revoir."

Clinch now shook hands heartily with all the officers; again expressed his sense of the liberality with which he was treated, and this, too, with emotion; then he followed his people into the boat, and pulled away from the lugger's side, holding his course toward the light which was still burning on board the *Proserpine*. At the same time *Le Feu-Follet* filled, and soon disappeared from his eyes in the darkness, running off wing-and-wing, and steering west, as if really making the best of her way toward the Straits of Bonifacio, on her road to France.

But, in fact, Raoul had no such intention. His cruise was not up, and his present position, surrounded as he was with enemies, was full of attraction to one of his temperament. Only the day before he had appeared in the disguise of a lazzarone, he had captured, manned, and sent to Marseilles a valuable store-ship; and he knew that another was hourly expected in the bay. This was an excuse to his people for remaining where they were. But the excitement of constantly running the gauntlet, the pleasure of demonstrating the superior sailing of his lugger, the opportunities for distinction, and every other professional motive were trifling, as compared with the tie which bound him to, the feeling that unceasingly attracted him toward, Ghita. With his love, also, there began to mingle a sensation approaching to despair.

While Ghita was so gentle, and even tender, with him, he had ever found her consistent and singularly firm in her principles. In their recent dialogues, some that we have foreborne to relate on account of their peculiar character, Ghita had expressed her reluctance to trust her fate with one whose God was not her God, with a distinctness and force that left no doubt of the seriousness of her views, or her ability to sustain them in acts. What rendered her resolution more impressive, was the ingenuous manner with which she never hesitated to admit Raoul's power over her affections, leaving no pretext for the common supposition that the girl was acting. The conversation that night weighed heavily on the heart of the lover, and he could not summon sufficient resolution to part, perhaps for months, with such an apparent breach between him and his hopes.

As soon as it was known, therefore, that the lugger was far enough at sea to be out of sight from the boat of Clinch, she came by the wind on the larboard tack again, heading up toward the celebrated ruins of Pæstum, on the eastern shore of the Bay of Salerno. To one accustomed to the sea, there would not have seemed sufficient wind to urge even that light craft along at the rate with which she glided through the water. But the land breeze was charged with the damps of midnight; the canvas thickened from the same cause; and the propelling power had double its apparent force. In an hour after hauling up, *Le Feu-Follet* tacked, quite eight miles distant from the spot where she altered her direction, and far enough to windward to lay her course in directly

for the cliffs beneath the village of St. Agata, or the present residence of Ghita. In proceeding thus Raoul had a double intention before him. English ships were constantly passing between Sicily, Malta and Naples; and, as those bound north would naturally draw in with the land at this point, his position might enable him to strike a sudden blow, with the return of day, should any suitable vessel be in the offing next morning. Then he hoped for a signal from Ghita at least, and such things were very dear to his heart; or, possibly, anxiety and affection might bring her down to the water-side, when another interview would be possible. This was the weakness of passion; and Raoul submitted to its power, like feebler-minded and less resolute men, the hero becoming little better than the vulgar herd under its influence.

The two or three last days and nights had been hours of extreme anxiety and care to the officers and crew of the lugger, as well as to their commander, and all on board began to feel the necessity of sleep. As for Ithuel, he had been in his hammock an hour; and Raoul now thought seriously of following his example. Giving his instructions to the young lieutenant who was in charge of the deck, our hero went below, and in a few minutes he was also lost to present hopes and fears.

Everything seemed propitious to the lugger and the intentions of her commander. The wind went down gradually, until there was little more than air enough to keep steerage-way on the vessel, while the ripple on the water disappeared, leaving nothing behind it but the long, heavy ground-swell that always stirs the bosom of the ocean, like the heaving respiration of some gigantic animal. The morning grew darker, but the surface of the gulf was glassy and tranquil, leaving no immediate motive for watchfulness or care.

These are the lethargic moments of a seaman's life. Days of toil bring nights of drowsiness; and the repose of nature presents a constant temptation to imitate her example. The reaction of excitement destroys the disposition to indulge in the song, the jest, or the tale; and the mind, like the body, is disposed to rest from its labors. Even the murmuring wash of the water, as it rises and falls against the vessel's sides, sounds like a lullaby, and sleep comes to be the one great blessing of existence. Under such circumstances, therefore, it is not surprising that the watch on the deck of the lugger indulged this necessary want. It is permitted to the common men to doze at such moments, while a few are on the alert; but even duty, in the absence of necessity, feels its task to be irksome and difficult of performance. Lookout after lookout lowered his head; the young man who was seated on the arm-chest aft began to lose his consciousness of present things, in dreamy recollections of Provence, his home, and the girl of his youthful admiration. The seaman at the helm alone kept his eyes open, and all his faculties on the alert. This is a station in which vigilance is ever required; and it sometimes happens in vessels where the rigid discipline of a regular service does not exist, that others rely so much on the circumstance, that they forget their own duties, in depending on the due discharge of his, by the man at the wheel.

Such, to a certain degree, was now the fact on board *Le Feu-Follet.* One of the best seamen in the lugger was at the helm, and each individual felt satisfied that no shift of wind would occur, no change of sails become necessary, that Antoine would not be there to admonish them of the circumstance. One day was so like another, too, in that tranquil season of the year, and in that luxurious sea, that all on board knew the regular mutations that the hour produced. The southerly air in the morning, the zephyr in the afternoon, and the land wind at night were as much matters of course as the rising and setting of the sun. No one felt apprehension, while all submitted to the influence of a want of rest and of the drowsiness of the climate.

Not so with Antoine. His hairs were gray. Sleep was no longer so necessary to him. He had much pride of calling, too; was long experienced, and possessed senses sharpened and rendered critical by practice and many dangers. Time and again did he turn his eyes toward Campanella, to ascertain if any signs of the enemy were in sight; the obscurity prevented anything from being visible but the dark outline of the high and rock-bound coast. Then he glanced his eyes over the deck, and felt how completely everything depended on his own vigilance and faithfulness. The look at the sails and to windward brought no cause for uneasiness, however; and, presuming on his isolation, he began to sing, in suppressed tones, an air of the Troubadours; one that he had learned in childhood in his native *langue du midi.* Thus passed the minutes until Antoine saw the first glimmerings of morning peeping out of the darkness, that came above the mountaintops that lay in the vicinity of Eboli. Antoine felt solitary; he was not sorry to greet these symptoms of a return to the animation and communion of a new day.

"Hist! mon lieutenant!" whispered the old mariner, unwilling to expose the drowsiness of his young superior to the gaze of the common men; "mon lieutenant—'tis I, Antoine."

"Eh! Bah! O, Antoine, est-ce-que toi? Bon! what would you have, mon ami?"

"I hear the surf, I think, mon lieutenant. Listen! is not that the water striking on the rocks of the shore?"

"Jamais! You see the land is a mile from us; this coast has no shoals. The captain told us to stand close in, before we hove-to or called him. Pardie! Antoine, how the little witch has traveled in my watch! Here we are, within a musket's range from the heights, yet there has been no wind."

"Pardon, mon lieutenant—I do not like that sound of the surf; it is too near for the shore. Will you have the kindness to step on the forecastle and look ahead, monsieur? the light is beginning to be of use."

The young man yawned, stretched his arms, and walked forward; the first to indulge himself, the first, also, to relieve the uneasiness of an old shipmate, whose experience he respected. Still his step was not as quick as common, and it was near a minute ere he reached the bows, or before he gained the knightheads. But his form was no sooner visible there, than he waved his arms frantically, and shouted in a voice that reached the recesses of the vessel—

"Hard up—hard up with the helm, Antoine! ease off the sheets, mes enfans!"

Le Feu-Follet rose on a heavy groundswell at that moment; in the next she settled down with a shock resembling that which we experience when we leap and alight sooner than was expected. There she lay cradled in a bed of rocks, as immovable as one of the stones around her—stones that had mocked the billows of the Mediterranean, within the known annals of man, more than three thousand years. In a word, the lugger had struck on one of those celebrated islets under the heights of St. Agata, known as the Islands of the Sirens, and which are believed to have been commemorated by the oldest of all the living profane writers, Homer himself. The blow was hardly given, before Raoul appeared on deck. The vessel gave up all that had life in her, and she was at once a scene of alarm, activity and exertion.

It is at such a moment as this, that the

most useful qualities of a naval captain render themselves apparent. Of all around him, Raoul was the calmest, the most collected, and the best qualified to issue the orders that had become necessary. He made no explanation—uttered not a word of reproach—cast not even a glance of disapprobation on any near him. The mischief was done; the one thing needful was to repair it, if possible, leaving to the future the cares of discipline, and the distribution of rewards and punishment.

"She is as fast anchored as a cathedral, mon lieutenant," he quietly observed to the very officer through whose remissness the accident had occurred; "I see no use in these sails. Take them in at once; they may set her further on the rocks, should she happen to lift."

The young man obeyed, every nerve in his body agitated by the sense of delinquency. Then he walked aft, cast one look around him at the desperate condition of the lugger, and, with the impetuosity of character that belongs to his country, he plunged into the sea, from which his body never reappeared. The melancholy suicide was immediately reported to Raoul. "Bon!" was the answer. "Had he done it an hour earlier, *Le Feu - Follet* would not have been shut up on these rocks, like a vessel in a shipyard; mais, mes enfans, courage! We'll yet see if our beautiful lugger cannot be saved."

If there were stoicism and bitterness in this answer, there was not deliberate cruelty. Raoul loved his lugger, next to Ghita, before all things on earth; and, in his eyes, the fault of wrecking her in a calm was to be classed among the unpardonable sins. Still, it was by no means a rare occurrence. Ships, like men, are often cast away by an excess of confidence; and our own coast, one of the safest in the known world for the prudent mariner to approach, on account of the regularity of its soundings, has many a tale to tell of disasters similar to this, which have occurred simply because no signs of danger were apparent. Our hero would not have excused himself for such negligence, and that which self-love will not induce us to pardon, will hardly be conceded to philanthropy.

The pumps were sounded, and it was ascertained that the lugger had come down so easily into her bed, and lay there with so little straining of her seams, that she continued tight as a bottle. This left all the hope which circumstances would allow, of still saving the vessel. Raoul neglected no useful precaution. By this time the light was strong enough to en-able him to see a felucca coming slowly down from Salerno, before the wind, or all that was still left of the night air, and he dispatched Ithuel with an armed boat to seize her, and bring her alongside of the rocks. He took this course with the double purpose of using the prize, if practicable, in getting his own vessel off, or, in the last resort, of making his own escape, and that of his people, in her to France. He did not condescend to explain his motives, however, nor did any one presume to inquire into them. Raoul was now strictly a commander, acting in a desperate emergency. He even succeeded in suppressing the constitutional volubility of his countrymen, and in substituting for it the deep attentive silence of thorough discipline; one of the great causes of his own unusual success in maritime enterprise. To the want of this very silence and attention may be ascribed so many of those naval disasters which have undeniably befallen a people of singular enterprise and courage. Those who wish them well will be glad to learn that the evil has been, in a great measure, repaired.

As soon as the boat was sent to seize the felucca, the yawl was put into the water, and Raoul himself began to sound around the lugger. The rocks of the Sirens, as the islets are called to this day, are sufficiently elevated above the surface of the sea to be visible at some distance; though, lying in a line with the coast, it would not have been easy for the lookouts of *Le Feu-Follet* to discern them at the hour when she struck, even had they been on the alert. The increasing light, however, enabled the French fully to ascertain their position, and to learn the extent of the evil. The lugger had been lifted into a crevice between two of the rocks, by a ground-swell heavier than common; and though there was deep water all around her, it would be impossible to get her afloat again without lightening. So long as the wind did not blow, and the sea did not rise, she was safe enough; but a swell that should force the hull to rise and fall would inevitably cause her to bilge. These facts were learned in five minutes after the yawl was in the water, and much did Raoul rejoice at having so promptly sent Ithuel in quest of the felucca. The rocks were next reconnoitered, in order to ascertain what facilities they offered to favor the discharging of the vessel's stores. Some of them were high enough to protect articles from the wash of the water, but it is at all times difficult to lie alongside of rocks that are exposed to the open sea; the heaving and setting of the element even in calms causing the elevation of its surface so much to vary. On the present occasion, however, the French found less swell than common, and that it was possible to get their stores ashore at two or three different points.

Raoul now directed the work to commence in earnest. The lugger carried four boats; namely, a launch, a cutter, the yawl, and a jolly-boat. The second had been sent after the felucca, with a strong crew in her; but the three others were employed in discharging stores. Raoul perceived at once that the moment was not one for half-way measures, and that large sacrifices must be made, to save the hull of the vessel. This, and the safety of his crew, were the two great objects he kept before him. All his measures were directed to that end. The water was started in the lugger's hold by staving the casks, and the pumps were set in motion as soon as possible. Provisions of all sorts were cast into the sea, for *Le Feu-Follet* had recently supplied herself from a prize, and was a little deeper than her best trim allowed. In short, everything that could be spared was thrown overboard, barely a sufficiency of food and water being retained to last the people until they could reach Corsica, whither it was their captain's intention to proceed, the moment he got his vessel afloat.

The Mediterranean has no regular tides, though the water rises and falls materially, at irregular intervals; either the effect of gales, or of the influence of the adjacent seas. This circumstance prevented the calamity of having gone ashore at high water, while it also prevented the mariners from profiting by any flood. It left them, as they had been placed by the accident itself, mainly dependent on their own exertions.

Under such circumstances, then, our hero set about the discharge of his responsible duties. An hour of active toil, well directed and perseveringly continued, wrought a material change. The vessel was small, while the number of hands was relatively large. At the end of the time mentioned, the officer charged with the duty reported that the hull moved under the power of the heaving sea, and that it might soon be expected to strike with a force to endanger its planks and ribs. This was the time to cease discharging, and to complete the preparations that had been making for heaving the lugger off, it being unsafe to delay that process after the weight was sufficiently lessened to allow it. The launch had carried out an anchor, and was already returning toward the rocks paying out cable as it came in.

But the depth of the water rendered this an anxious service, since there was the danger of dragging the ground-tackle home, on account of the angle on which it lay.

At this moment, with the exception of the difficulty last mentioned, everything seemed propitious. The wind had gone down entirely, the southerly air having lasted but a short time, and no other succeeded it. The sea was certainly not more disturbed than it had been all the morning, which was at its minimum of motion, while the day promised to be calm and clear. Nothing was in sight but the felucca, and she was not only in Ithuel's possession, but she had drawn within half a mile of the rocks, and was sweeping still nearer at each instant. In ten minutes she must come alongside. Raoul had ascertained that there was water enough, where *Le Feu-Follet* lay, to permit a vessel like his prize to touch her; and many things lay on deck, in readiness to be transferred to this tender, previously to beginning to heave. The rocks, too, were well garnished with casks, cordage, shot, ballast, and such other articles as could be come at, the armament and ammunition excepted. These last our hero always treated with religious care, for in all he did there was a latent determination resolutely to defend himself. But there were no signs of any such necessity's being likely to occur, and the officers began to flatter themselves with their ability to get their lugger afloat, and in sailing trim before the usual afternoon's breeze should set in. In waiting, therefore, for the arrival of the felucca, and in order that the work might meet with no interruption when the men once began to heave, the people were ordered to get their breakfasts.

This pause in the proceedings gave Raoul an opportunity to look about him and to reflect. Twenty times did he turn his eyes anxiously toward the heights of St. Agata, where there existed subjects equally of attraction and apprehension. It is scarcely necessary to say that the first was Ghita; while the last arose from the fear that some curious eye might recognize the lugger, and report her condition to the enemies known to be lying at Capri, only a league or two on the other side of the hills. But all was seemingly tranquil there at that early hour; and the lugger making very little show when her canvas was not spread, there was reason to hope that the accident was as yet unseen. The approach of the felucca would probably betray it; though the precaution had been taken to order Ithuel to show no signals of national character.

Raoul Yvard was a very different man, at this moment of leisure and idleness, from what he had been a few hours earlier. Then he trod the deck of his little cruiser with some such feelings as the man who exults in his strength, and rejoices in his youth. Now he felt, as all are apt to feel who are rebuked by misfortune and disease. Nevertheless, his character had lost none of its high chivalry; and even there, as he sat on the taffrail of the stranded *Feu-Follet*, he meditated carrying some stout Englishman by surprise and boarding, in the event of his not succeeding in getting off the lugger. The felucca would greatly aid such an enterprise; and his crew was strong enough, as well as sufficiently trained to promise success.

On such an expedient, even, was he ruminating, as Ithuel, in obedience to an order given through the trumpet, brought his prize alongside, and secured her to the lugger. The men who had accompanied the American were now dismissed to their morning's meal, while Raoul invited their leader to share his frugal repast where he sat. As the two broke their fasts, questions were put and answered, concerning what had occurred during the hour or two the parties had been separated. Raoul's tale was soon told; and then he learned with concern that the felucca had taken to their boat, and escaped to the landing of the Scaricatojo, on finding that the capture of their vessel was inevitable. This proved that the character of the wreck was known, and left but little hope that their situation would not be reported to the English, in the course of the morning.

CHAPTER XXVII.

THE intelligence communicated by Ithuel essentially altered Raoul's views of his actual situation. An active man might go from the Marinella, at the foot of the Scaricatojo, or the place where the crew of the felucca had landed, to the Marina Grande of Sorrento in an hour. At the latter beach, boats were always to be found, and two hours more would carry the messenger, by water, to the ships off Capri, even in a calm. The first of these important hours had now elapsed some time; and he could not doubt that vigorous arms were already employed in pulling across the few leagues of water that separated the island from the shores of Sorrento. The day was calm, it is true; and it would be impossible to move the ships; but two frigates and a heavy sloop-of-war might send such a force against him in boats, as, in his present situation, would render resistance next to hopeless.

Raoul ceased eating, and, standing on the taffrail, he cast anxious looks around him. His sturdy followers, ignorant of all the dangers by which they were environed, were consuming their morning's meal with the characteristic indifference to danger that marks the ordinary conduct of seamen. Even Ithuel, usually so sensitive on the subject of English power, and who had really so much to apprehend, should he again fall into the hands of the Proserpines, was masticating his food with the keen relish of a man who had been hard at work the whole morning. All appeared unconscious of their critical condition; and to Raoul it seemed as if the entire responsibility rested on his shoulders. Fortunately, he was not a man to shrink from his present duties; and he occupied the only leisure moment that would be likely to offer that day, in deliberating on his resources and in maturing his plans.

The armament still remained in the lugger, but it was doubtful if she would float without removing it; and, admitting this necessity, the question arose of what was to be done with it, in order to render it available, in the event of an attack. Two, or even four of the light guns might be worked on the decks of the felucca; and here he determined they should be immediately placed, with a proper supply of cartridges and shot. Twenty men thrown into that light craft, which Ithuel reported as sailing and sweeping well, might prove of the last importance. Then one of the islets had a ruin on it, of what was believed to be an ancient temple. It is true, these ruins were insignificant, and scarcely visible to any distance; but, on a close examination, and by using some of the displaced stones with judgment, it was possible to entrench a party behind them, and make a stout resistance against light missiles or such as boats would most probably use. Raoul got into the yawl, and sculled himself to this spot, examining the capabilities with care and judgment. After this, his mode of proceeding was matured to his own satisfaction.

The usual time had been consumed, and the hands were "turned to"; each officer receiving the orders necessary to the discharge of the duty confided to his particular superintendence. As Ithuel had captured the felucca, Raoul felt it right to intrust him with the command of the prize. He was directed to take on board the armament and ammunition necessary to a defense, to mount the guns in the best manner he could, and to make all the other fighting preparations; while another gang struck into the felucca's hold such articles from the lugger as it was desirable to save.

Another party, under the first lieutenant, landed the remainder of the light carronades, pieces of twelve pounds only, with the proper stores, and commenced the arrangements to place them in battery among the ruins. A small supply of food and water was also transferred to this islet.

While these dispositions were in progress, Raoul himself, assisted by his sailing-master, prepared to heave the lugger off the rocks. To this, at present the most important duty, our hero gave his personal inspection; for it required skill, judgment, and caution. The physical force of the crew was reserved to aid in the attempt. At length everything was ready, and the instant had arrived when the momentous trial was to be made. The lugger had now been ashore quite four hours, and the sun had been up fully three. By this time, Raoul calculated that the English, at Capri, knew of his misfortune, and little leisure remained in which to do a vast deal of work. The hands were all summoned to the bars, therefore, and the toil of heaving commenced.

As soon as the cable got the strain, Raoul felt satisfied that the anchor would hold. Fortunately a fluke had taken a rock, a circumstance that could be known only by the result; but, so long as the iron held together, there was no danger of that material agent's failing them. The last part of the process of lightening was now performed as rapidly as possible, and then came the trial heave at the bars. Every effort was fruitless, however, inch being gained after inch, until it seemed as if the hemp of the cable were extending its minutest fibers, without the hull's moving any more than the rocks on which it lay. Even the boys were called to the bars; but the united force of all hands, the officers included, produced no change. There was an instant when Raoul fancied his best course would be to set fire to the hulk, get on board the felucca, and sweep off to the southward in season to avoid the expected visit from the English. He even called his officers together, and laid the proposition before them. But the project was too feebly urged, and it met with too little response in the breast of his auditors to be successful. The idea of abandoning that beautiful and faultless little craft was too painful, while the remotest hope of preserving it remained.

Raoul had measured his hours with the accuracy of a prudent general. It was now almost time for the English boats to appear, and he began to hope that the Neapolitans had made the great mistake of sending their information to the fleet off Naples, rather than carrying it to the ships at Capri. Should it prove so, he had still the day before him, and might retire under the cover of night. At all events, the lugger could not be abandoned without an enemy in sight, and the people were again called to the bars for a renewed effort. As water might be obtained at a hundred points on the coast, and the distance to Corsica was so small, the last gallon had been started and pumped out, during the recent pause.

Our hero felt that this was the final effort. The hold of *Feu-Follet* was literally empty, and all her spare spars were floating among the rocks. If she could not be started now, he did not possess the means to get her off. The anchor held; the cable, though stretched to the utmost, stood; and every creature but himself was at the bars. The ground-swell had been lessening all the morning, and little aid was now to be had from the rising of the water. Still, that little must be obtained; without it, the task seemed hopeless.

"Get ready, men," cried Raoul, as he paced the taffrail, "and heave at the word. We will wait for a swell, then strain every nerve till something part. Pas encore, mes enfans — pas encore! Stand by! Yonder comes a fellow who will lift us; heave a strain—heave harder — heave body and soul! heave altogether!"

The men obeyed. First they hove a gentle strain; then the effort was increased; and obedient to the order, just as the ground-swell rolled under the lugger's bottom, they threw out their utmost strength, and the hull started for the first time. This was encouraging, though the movement did not exceed six inches. It was a decided movement, and was made in the right direction. This success nerved the people to an increased effort. It was probable that, at the next strain, they would throw a tenth more impetus into their muscles. Of all this, Raoul was aware, and he determined not to let the feeling flag.

"Encore, mes enfans!" he said. "Heave, and get ready! Be watchful —now's your time! Heave and rip the planks off the lugger's bottom; heave men, heave!"

This time the effort answered to the emergency; the swell rolled in, the men threw out their strength, a surge was felt, it was followed up by a strain, and *Le Feu-Follet* shot off her bed into deep water, rolling, for want of ballast, nearly to her hammock-cloths. She soon lay directly over her anchor.

Here was success! triumphant success: and that at a moment when the most sanguine had begun to despair. The men embraced each other, showing a hundred manifestations of extravagant joy. The tears came to Raoul's eyes; but he had no opportunity of concealing them, every officer he had pressing around him to exchange felicitations. The scene was one of happy disorder. It had lasted two or three minutes when Ithuel, always cold and calculating, edged his way through the throng to his commander's side, and pointed significantly in the direction of Campanella. There, indeed, was visible a division of the expected boats. It was pulling toward them, having that moment doubled the cape!

Ithuel's gesture was too significant to escape attention, and every eye followed its direction. The sight was of a nature not to be mistaken. It at once changed the current of feeling in all who beheld it. There was no longer a doubt concerning the manner in which the news of the accident had traveled, or of its effect on the English at Capri. In point of fact, the padrone of the captured felucca, with a sole eye to the recovery of his vessel, had ascended the Scaricatojo, after landing at the Marinella, at its foot, as fast as his legs could carry him; had rather run, than glided, along the narrow lanes of the piano and the hillside to the beach of Sorrento; had thrown himself into a boat, manned by four lusty Sorrento watermen —and Europe does not contain lustier or bolder; had gone on board the *Terpsichore*, and laid his case before Sir Frederick Dashwood, ignorant of the person of the real commanding officer among the three ships. The young baronet, though neither very wise nor very much experienced in his profession, was exceedingly well disposed to seek distinction. It immediately occurred to his mind that the present was a fitting opportunity to gain laurels.

He was second in rank present, and, in virtue of that claim, he fancied that the first could do no more than send him in command of the expedition, which he rightly foresaw Cuffe would order against the French. But there arose a difficulty. As soon as Sir Frederick reported the nature of the intelligence he had received to his senior captain, and his own wish to be employed on the occasion, the rights of Winchester interposed to raise a question.

Cuffe was prompt enough in issuing an order for each ship to man and arm two boats, making six in all, and in giving the necessary details, but he lost some precious time in deciding who was to command. This was the cause of delay, and had given rise to certain hopes in Raoul, that facts were subsequently to destroy. In the end, Sir Frederick prevailed, his rank giving him a decided advantage; and the division of boats that was now approaching was under his orders.

Raoul saw that he had rather more than an hour to spare. To fight the felucca, unsupported, against so many enemies, and that in a calm, was quite out of the question. That small, low craft might destroy a few of her assailants, but she would inevitably be carried at the first onset. There was not time to get the ballast and other equipments into the lugger, so as to render her capable of proper resistance; nor did even she offer the same advantages for a defense, unless in quick motion, as the ruins. It was determined, therefore, to make the best disposition of the two vessels that circumstances would allow, while the dependence should be placed on the solid defences of stone. With this end, Ithuel was directed to haul his felucca to a proper berth; the first lieutenant was ordered to get as much on board *Le Feu-Follet* as possible, in readiness to profit by events; while Raoul himself, selecting thirty of his best men, commenced preparing the guns on the rocks for active service.

A single half-hour wrought a material change in the state of things. Ithuel had succeeded in hauling the felucca into a berth among the islets where she could not easily be approached by boats, and where her carronades might be rendered exceedingly useful. Much of the ballast was again on board the lugger, and a few of her stores, sufficient to render her tolerably stiff, in the event of a breeze springing up; and Raoul had directed the two inside guns of the felucca to be sent on board her and mounted, that she might assist in the defense with a flanking fire. The great difficulty which exists in managing a force at anchor, is the opportunity that is given the assailant of choosing his point of attack, and by bringing several of the vessels in a line, cause them to intercept each other's fire. In order to prevent this as much as in his power, Raoul placed his two floating batteries out of line, though it was impossible to make such a disposition of them as would not leave each exposed, on one point of attack, in a degree greater than any other. Nevertheless, the arrangement was so made, that either a vessel or the ruins might aid each craft respectively against the assault on her weakest point.

When his own guns were ready, and the two vessels moored, Raoul visited both the lugger and the felucca, to inspect their preparations and to say a cheerful word to their men. He found most things to his mind; where they were not, he ordered changes to be made. With the lieutenant his conversation was brief, for that officer was one who possessed much experience in this very sort of warfare, and could be relied on. With Ithuel he was more communicative; not that he distrusted the citizen of the Granite State, but that he knew him to be a man of unusual resources, could the proper spirit be aroused in him.

"Bien, Etooelle," he said, when the inspection was ended, "much will depend on the use you make of these two guns."

"I know that, as well as you do yourself, Captain Rule," answered the other, biting off at least two inches from half a yard of pig-tail; "and, what's more, I know that I fight with a rope round my neck. The spiteful devils will hardly overlook all that's passed; and though it will be dead agin all law, they'll work out their eends on us both, if we don't work out our eends on them. To my mind, the last will be the most agreeable, as well as the most just."

"Bon! Do not throw away your shot, Etooelle."

"I!—why, Captain Rule, I'm nat'rally economical. That would be wasteful, and waste I set down for a sin. The only place I calculate on throwing shot is into the face and eyes of the English. For myself, I wish Nelson himself was in one of them boats; I wish the man no harm, but I do wish he was in one of them very boats."

"And, Etooelle, I do not. It is bad enough as it is, entre nous; and Nelson is very welcome to stay on board his *Foudroyant*, voilà! The enemy is in council; we shall soon hear from them. Adieu, mon ami; remember our two republiques."

Raoul squeezed Ithuel's hand, and entered his boat. The distance to the ruin was trifling, but it was necessary to make a small circuit in order to reach it. While doing this the young mariner discovered a boat pulling from the direction of the Marinella, at the foot of the Scaricatojo, which had got so near, unseen, as at first to startle him by its proximity. A second look, however, satisfied him that no cause of apprehension existed in that quarter. His eye could not be deceived. The boat contained Ghita and her uncle; the latter rowing and the former seated in the stern, with her head bowed to her knees, apparently in tears. Raoul was alone, sculling the light yawl with a single hand, and he exerted himself to meet these unexpected, and, in the circumstances, unwelcome visitors, as far as possible from the rocks. Presently the two boats lay side by side.

"What means this, Ghita!" the young man exclaimed; "do you not see the English yonder, at this moment making their preparations to attack us? In a few minutes we shall be in the midst of a battle, and thou here!"

"I see it all, Raoul," was the answer, "though we did not on quitting the shore; but we would not turn back, having once come upon the bay. I was the first in St. Agata to discover the evil that had befallen thee; from that moment I have never ceased to entreat my uncle, until he has consented to come hither."

"With what motive, Ghita?" asked Raoul, with sparkling eyes. "At length thou relentest—wilt become my wife! In my adversity thou rememberest thou art a woman!"

"Not exactly that, dear Raoul; but I cannot desert thee altogether in this strait. The same object exists now, I fear, that has ever existed to our union; but that is no reason I should not aid thee. We have many friends along the heights here, who will consent to conceal thee; and I come to carry thee and the American to the shore, until an opportunity offer to get thee to thine own France."

"What! desert ces braves, Ghita, at a moment like this! Not to possess thy hand, dearest girl, could I be guilty of an act so base."

"Thy situation is not theirs. The condemnation to death hangs over thee, Raoul; shouldst thou again fall into English hands there will be no mercy for thee."

"Assez; this is no moment for argument. The English are in motion, and there is barely time for thee to get to a safe distance ere they begin to fire. Heaven bless thee, Ghita! This care of thine draws my heart to thee closer than ever; but we must now separate. Signor Giuntotardi, pull more toward Amalfi. I see that the English mean to attack us from the side of the land; pull more toward Amalfi."

"Thou tellest this in vain, Raoul," Ghita quietly but firmly answered. "We have not come here on an unmeaning errand; if thou refuses to go with us, we will remain with thee. These prayers, that thou so despisest, may not prove useless.''

"Ghita! this can never be. We are without cover, almost without defenses; our vessel is unfit to receive thee, and this affair will be very different from that off Elba. Thou wouldst not willingly distract my mind with care for thee, at such a moment!"

"We will remain, Raoul. There may come a moment when thou wilt be glad to have the prayers of believers. God leadeth us hither, either to take thee away, or to remain, and look to thy eternal welfare, amid the din of war.''

Raoul gazed at the beautiful enthusiast with an intensity of love and admiration that even her truthful simplicity had never before excited. Her mild eyes were kindling with holy ardor, her cheeks were flushed, and something like the radiance of heaven seemed to beam upon her countenance. The young man felt that time pressed; he saw no hope of overcoming her resolution in season to escape the approaching boats; and it might be that the two would be safer in some nook of the ruins than in attempting to return to the shore. Then, that never-dying but latent wish to have Ghita with him aided his hasty reasoning, and he decided to permit the girl and her uncle to come upon the islet that he was to defend in person.

Some signs of impatience had begun to manifest themselves among his people ere Raoul made up his mind to the course he would follow; but when he landed, supporting Ghita, that chivalry of character and homage to the sex, which distinguish the southern Frenchman, changed the current of feeling, and their two acquaintances were received with acclamation. The act of self-devotion seemed heroic, and that is always enough to draw applause among a people so keenly alive to glory. Still, the time to make the necessary dispositions was short. Fortunately, the surgeon had taken his post on this islet, as the probable scene of the warmest conflict; and he had contrived to make his preparations to receive the hurt in a cavity of the rock, behind a portion of the ruin, where a person would be reasonably safe. Raoul saw the advantages of this position, and he led Ghita and her uncle to it, without pausing to deliberate. Here he tenderly embraced the girl, a liberty Ghita could not repel at such a moment; then he tore himself away to attend to duties which had now become urgently pressing.

In point of fact, Sir Frederick Dashwood had made his dispositions, and was advancing to the assault, being already within the range of grape. For the obvious

reason of preventing the French from attempting to escape to the shore, he chose to approach from that side himself—an arrangement that best suited Raoul; who, foreseeing the probability of the course, had made his own preparations with an eye to such an event.

Of boats, there were eight in sight, though only seven were drawing near, and were in line. Six had strong crews, were armed, and were evidently fitted for action. Of these, three had light boat-guns in their bows, while the other three carried small-arms men only. The seventh boat was the *Terpsichore's* gig, with its usual crew, armed; though it was used by the commanding officer himself as a sort of *cheval de bataille*, in the stricter meaning of the term. In other words, Sir Frederick Dashwood pulled through the line in it, to give his orders and encourage his people. The eighth boat, which kept aloof, quite out of the range of grape, was a shore craft, belonging to Capri, in which Andrea Barrofaldi and Vito Viti had come, expressly to witness the capture or destruction of their old enemy. When Raoul was taken in the Bay of Naples, these two worthies fancied that their mission was ended—that they might return with credit to Porto Ferrajo, and again hold up their heads, with dignity and self-complacency, among the functionaries of the island.

But the recent escape, and the manner in which they had been connected with it, entirely altered the state of things. A new load of responsibility rested on their shoulders; fresh opprobrium was to be met and put down; and the last acquisition of ridicule promised to throw the first proofs of their simplicity and dullness entirely into the shade. Had not Griffin and his associates been implicated in the affair, it is probable the vice-governatore and the podesta would have been still more obnoxious to censure; but as things were, the sly looks, open jests, and oblique innuendoes of all they met in the ship, had determined the honest magistrates to retire to their proper pursuits on *terra firma*, at the earliest occasion. In the meantime, to escape persecution, and to obtain a modicum of the glory that was now to be earned, they had hired a boat, and accompanied the expedition, in the character of amateurs. It formed no part of their plan, however, to share in the combat; a view of its incidents being quite as much, as Vito Viti strongly maintained when his friend made a suggestion to the contrary, as was necessary to vindicate their conduct and courage in the judgment of every Elban.

"Cospetto!" he exclaimed, in the warmth of opposition, "Signor Andrea, your propositions are more in the spirit of an unreflecting boy, than in that of a discreet vice-governatore. If we take swords and muskets into the boat, as you appear to wish, the devil may tempt us to use them; and what does either of us know of such things? The pen is a more befitting weapon for a magistrate than a keen-edged sword or a foul-smelling piece of fire-arms. I am amazed that your native sensibilities do not teach you this. There is an indecency in men's mistaking their duties; and of all things on earth, Heaven protect me from falling into such an error! A false position is despicable."

"Thou art warm, friend Vito, and that without occasion. For my part, I think men should be prepared for any emergency that may happen. History is full of examples in which civilians and scholars— ay, even churchmen—have distinguished themselves by feats of arms, on proper occasions; and I confess to a philosophical curiosity to ascertain the sensations with which men seek and expose life."

"That's your besetting weakness, Signor Andrea, and the emergency drives me so far to lose sight of the respect that a podesta owes to a vice-governatore, as to feel constrained to tell you as much. Philosophy plays the very devil with your judgment. With about half of what you possess, the grand duke couldn't boast of a more sensible subject. As for history, I don't believe anything that's in it; more especially since the nations of the north have begun to write it. Italy once had histories, but where are they now? For my part, I never heard of a man's fighting who was not regularly bred to arms, unless it might be some fellow who had reason to wish he had never been born."

"I can name you several men of letters, in particular, whose fame as soldiers is only eclipsed by that earned by their more peaceful labors, honest Vito; Michael Angelo Buonarotti, for instance, to say nothing of various warlike popes, cardinals and bishops. But we can discuss this matter after the battle is over. Thou seest the English already quitting their ships, and we shall be in the rear of the combatants."

"So much the better; Corpo di Bacco! who ever heard of an army that carries its brains in its head, like a human being? No, no, Signor Andrea; I have provided myself with a string of beads, which I intend to count over, with aves and paters, while the firing lasts, like a good Catholic. If you are so hot, and bent on making one in this battle, you may proclaim in a loud voice one of the speeches of the ancient consuls and generals, such as you will find them in any of the old books."

Vito Viti prevailed. The vice-governatore was obliged to leave the arms behind him, and this, too, without making any great difference in the result of the day's fighting, inasmuch as the boatmen employed, in addition to asking a triple price for their time and labor, obstinately refused to go nearer to the French than half a league. Distant as this was, however, Raoul, while reconnoitering the enemy with a glass, detected the presence of the two Elbans. He laughed outright at the discovery, notwithstanding the many serious reflections that naturally pressed upon his mind at such a moment.

But this was not the time to indulge in merriment, and the countenance of our hero almost immediately resumed its look of care. Now that he felt certain of the manner in which the English intended to assail him, he had new orders to give to all his subordinates. As has been said, the principal point was to make the different guns support each other. In order to do this effectually, it became necessary to spring the lugger's broadside round more obliquely toward the felucca; which accomplished, Raoul deemed his arrangements complete.

Then followed the pause which ordinarily prevails between preparation and the battle. This, in a vessel, is always a period of profound and solemn stillness. So important to concert, order, and intelligent obedience, in the narrow compass, and amid the active evolutions of a ship, does silence become at such moments, that one of the first duties of discipline is to inculcate its absolute necessity; and a thousand men shall be seen standing in their batteries, ready to serve the fierce engines of war, without a sound arising among them all of sufficient force to still the washing of the gentlest waves. It is true, the French were not now strictly arrayed for a naval action; but they carried into the present conflict the habits and discipline of the peculiar branch of service to which they belonged.

CHAPTER XXVIII.

OUR battle will be told with greater clearness, if the reader is furnished with an outline of its order. As has been more than once intimated already, Sir Frederick Dashwood had made all his preparations to commence the assault from the side of the land, the object being to prevent a retreat to the shore. Raoul had foreseen the probability of this, and, with a special view to prevent the two vessels from being easily boarded, he had caused both to be placed in such positions as left low barriers of rock between them and that quarter of the bay. These rocks were portions that were not visible at any distance, being just awash, as it is termed, or on a level with the surface of the water; offering the same sort of protection against an attack in boats that ditches afford in cases of assaults on *terra firma.* This was a material advantage to the expected defense, and our hero showed his discrimination in adopting it. On board the felucca, which was named the *Holy Michael,* was Ithuel with fifteen men, and two twelve-pound carronades, with a proper supply of small arms and ammunition. The Granite man was the only officer, though he had with him three or four of the lugger's best men.

Le Feu-Follet was confided to the care of Jules Pintard, her first lieutenant, who had under his immediate orders some five-and-twenty of the crew, to work four more of the carronades. The lugger had a part only of her ballast in, and something like a third of her stores. The remainder of both still lay on the adjacent rocks, in waiting for the result of the day. She was thought, however, to be sufficiently steady for any service that might be expected of her while moored, and might even have carried whole sail, in light winds, with perfect safety. All four of her guns were brought over on one side in readiness to use in battery in the same direction. By this arrangement the French essentially increased their means of defense, bringing all their artillery into use at the same time; an expedient that could not have been adopted had they been fought in broadside.

Raoul had planted among the ruins the remaining four guns. With the aid of a few planks, the breechings, tackles, and other appliances of a vessel, this had been easily effected; and, on reviewing his work, he had great confidence in the permanency of his pieces. The ruins themselves were no great matter; at a little distance they were scarcely perceptible; though aided by the formation of the natural rock, and by removing some of the stones to more favorable positions, they answered the purpose of the seamen sufficiently well. The carronades were placed *en barbette;* but a falling of the surface of the rock enabled the men to cover even their heads, by stepping back a few feet. The danger would be

much the greatest to those whose duty it was to reload.

The surgeon, Carlo Guintotardi, and Ghita, were established in a cavity of the rocks, protected against missiles, so long as the enemy continued on the side next the land, and yet within fifteen feet of the battery. Here the former made the usual bloody-looking, if not bloody-minded, preparations for applying tourniquets and for amputating, all unheeded, however, by his two companions, both of whom were lost to the scene around them in devout prayer.

Just as these several dispositions were completed, Ithuel, who ever kept an eye to windward, called out to Raoul, and inquired if it might not be well to run the yards up to the mast-heads, as they would be more out of the way in their places aloft than littering the decks. There was no possible objection to the measure, it being a dead calm, and both the lugger and the felucca swayed their yards into their places, the sails being bent, and hanging in the brails. This is the ordinary state of craft of the latter rig, though not always that of luggers; and the Granite man, mindful that his own gear was down in consequence of having been lowered by her former owners previously to the capture, bethought him of the expediency of getting everything ready for a run. He wished the lugger to be in an equal state of preparation, it being plain enough that two to be pursued would embarrass the English, in a chase, twice as much as one. This was the reason of his suggestion, and he felt happier for seeing it attended to.

On the other side, all preliminary difficulties had been disposed of. Captain Sir Frederick Dashwood was in command, and Lieutenants Winchester and Griffin, after a few open protestations, certain grimaces, and divers secret curses, were fain to submit. The discussion, however, had produced one result, not altogether unfavorable to the Proserpines. Cuffe sent four of her boats against the enemy, while he restricted the *Terpsichore* to two, including her gig, and the *Ringdove* to two. Each ship sent her launches, as a matter of course, with a twelve-pound boat-gun on its grating. Winchester was in that of the *Proserpine;* Mr. Stothard, the second on the other frigate, was in the *Terpsichore's,* and McBean, as of right, commanded the *Ringdove's.* Griffin was in the first cutter of his own ship, and Clinch had charge of the second. The third was headed by Strand, whose call was to have precedence on the occasion. The other boats had subordinates from their respective ships. All were in good heart; and while all expected a severe struggle for her, knowing the desperate character of their enemy, every man in the boats felt confident that the lugger was finally to fall into British hands. Still a grave consideration of the possible consequences to the actors mingled with the exultation of the more reflecting men among the assailants.

Sir Frederick Dashwood, who ought to have felt the moral responsibility of his command, of all the higher officers present, was the most indifferent to the consequences. Constitutionally brave, personal considerations had little influence on him; habitually confident of English prowess, he expected victory and credit as a matter of course; and, favored by birth, fortune, and parliamentary interest, he gave himself no trouble as to the possibility of a failure, certain (though not avowing that certainty even to himself) that any little mishap would be covered by the broad mantle of the accident that had so early raised him to the rank he held.

In making his dispositions for the fight, however, Sir Frederick had not disdained the counsels of men older and more experienced than himself. Cuffe had given him much good advice, before they parted, and Winchester and Strand had been particularly recommended to him as seamen whose suggestions might turn out to be useful.

"I send a master's-mate named Clinch, in charge of one of our boats, too, Dashwood," added the senior captain, as he concluded his remarks; "who is one of the most experienced seamen in the *Proserpine.* He has seen much boat-service, and has always behaved himself well. A vile practice of drinking has kept the poor fellow under; but he is now determined to make an effort, and I beg you will put him forward to-day, that he may have a chance. Jack Clinch has the right sort of stuff in him, if opportunities offer to bring it out."

"I flatter myself, Cuffe, that all hands will meet with opportunity enough," answered Sir Frederick, in his drawling way; "for I intend to put 'em all in together, like a thorough pack coming in at the death. I've seen Lord Echo's harriers so close, at the end of a long chase, that you might have covered the whole with this ship's main-course; and I intend it shall be so with our boats to-day. By the way, Cuffe, that would be a pretty figure for a dispatch, and would make Bronte smile—ha! wouldn't it?"

"D——n the figure, the harriers, and the dispatch, too, Dashwood first; win the day, before you begin to write poetry about it. Bronte, as you call Nelson, has lightning in him, as well as thunder, and there isn't an admiral in the service who cares less for blood and private rank than himself. The way to make him smile is to do a thing neatly and well. For God's sake, be careful of the men; we are short-handed as it is, and can't afford such another scrape as that off Porto Ferrajo."

"Never fear for us, Cuffe; you'll never miss the men I shall expend."

Every captain had a word to say to his officers; but none other worth recording, with the exception of what passed between Lyon and his first lieutenant.

"Ye'll remember, Airchy, that a ship can have a reputation for economy, as well as a man. There's several of our countrymen about the admiralty just now; and next to courage and enterprise, they view the expenditures with the keenest eyes. I've known an admiral reach a red ribbon just on that one quality, his accounts showing cheaper ships and cheaper squadrons than any in the sairvice. Ye'll all do your duties for the honor o' Scotland; but there's six or seven Leith and Glasgow lads in the boats, that it may be as well not to let murder themselves, out of a' need. I've put the whole of the last draft from the river guard-ship into the boats, and with them there's no great occasion to be tender. They're the sweepings of the Thames and Wapping; and quite half of them would have been at Botany Bay before this had they not been sent here."

"Does the law about being in sight apply to the boats or to the ships, the day, Captain Lyon?"

"To the boats, man; or who the de'il do you think would sairve in them! It is a pitiful affair, altogether, as it has turned out; the honor being little more than the profit, I opine; and yet 'twill never do to let old Scotia lag astairn in a hand-to-hand battle. Ye'll remember, we have a name for coming to the claymore; and so do yer best, every mither's son o' ye."

McBean grunted assent and went about his work as methodically as if it were a sum in algebra. The second lieutenant of the *Terpsichore* was a young Irishman, with a sweet, musical voice; and, as the boats left the ships, he was with difficulty kept in the line, straining to move ahead, with his face on a grin, and his cheers stimulating the men to undue or unreasonable efforts. Such is an outline of the English materials on this occasion; both parties being now ready for the struggle. If we add that it was already past two, and that all hands began to feel some anxiety on the score of the wind, which might soon be expected, the preliminary picture is sufficiently sketched.

Sir Frederick Dashwood had formed his line about a mile within the rocks, with one branch in the center, and one at each extremity. That in the center was commanded by O'Leary, his own lieutenant; that on the left of his force by McBean, and the one on its right by Winchester. O'Leary was flanked by Griffin and Clinch, in the *Proserpine's* cutters, while the intervals were filled by the remaining boats. The captain kept moving about in his own gig, giving his directions, somewhat confusedly, beyond a question; yet with a cheerfulness and indifference of air that aided in keeping alive the general *gaite de cœur*. When all was ready, he gave the signal to advance, pulling, for the first half-mile, chivalrously in advance of the line with his own gig.

Raoul had noted the smallest movement of the enemy with a glass, and with grave attention. Nothing escaped his jealous watchfulness; and he saw that Sir Frederick had made a capital error in the outset. Had he strengthened his center, by putting all his carronades in the same battery, as it might be, the chances for success would have been doubled; but, by dividing them, he so far weakened their effect, as to render it certain no one of the three French batteries could be wholly crippled by their fire. This, of course, left the difficult task to the English of pushing up to their hand-to-hand work under the embarrassment of receiving constant discharges of grape and canister.

The few minutes that intervened between the order to advance, and the moment when the boats got within a quarter of a mile of the rock, were passed in a profound quiet, neither side making any noise, though Raoul had no small difficulty in restraining the constitutional impatience of his own men to begin. A boat presents so small an object, however, to artillerists as little skilled as seamen generally are, who depend more on general calculations than on the direct or scientific aim, the latter being usually defeated by the motion of their vessels, that he was unwilling to throw away even his canister. A Frenchman himself, however, he could refrain no longer, and he pointed a carronade, firing it with his own hand. This was the commencement of the strife. All the other guns in the ruin followed, and the lugger kept time as it might be by note. The English rose, gave three cheers, and each launch discharged her gun. At the same instant the two men who held the matches in the felucca applied them briskly to the vents of their respective pieces. To their surprise, neither exploded, and, on examination, it was discovered that the priming had vanished. To own the truth, he of the Granite State had slyly brushed his hand over the guns, and robbed them of this great essential of their force. He held the priming-horns in his own hands, and resolutely refused to allow them to pass into those of any other person.

It was fortunate Ithuel was known to be such a determined hater of the English, else might his life have been the forfeit of this seeming act of treachery. But he meditated no such dereliction of duty. Perfectly aware of the impossibility of preventing his men from firing, did they possess the means, this deliberate and calculating personage had resorted to this expedient to reserve his own effort, until, in his judgment, it might prove the most available. His men murmured, but, too much excited to deliberate, they poured in a discharge of musketry, as the only means of annoying the enemy then left them. Even Raoul glanced aside, a little wondering at not hearing the felucca's carronades, but perceiving her people busy with their fire-arms, he believed all right.

The first discharge in such an affair is usually the most destructive. On the present occasion, the firing was not without serious effects. The English, much the most exposed, suffered in proportion. Four men were hurt in Winchester's boat, two in Griffin's, six or eight men in the other launches and cutters; and one of Sir Frederick's gig-men was shot through the heart—a circumstance which induced that officer to drop alongside of a cutter, and exchange the dead body for a living man.

On the rocks, but one man was injured. A round shot had hit a stone, shivering it in fragments, and struck down a valuable seaman, just as he was advancing, with a gallant mien, to spunge one of the guns.

"Poor Josef!" said Raoul, as he witnessed the man's fall; "carry him to the surgeon, mes braves."

"Mon capitaine, Josef is dead."

This decided the matter, and the body was laid aside, while another stepped forward and spunged the gun. At that moment Raoul found leisure to walk a yard or two toward the rear, in order to ascertain if the cover of Ghita were sufficient. The girl was on her knees, lost to all around her; could he have read her heart, he would have found it divided between entreaties to the Deity and love for himself.

The lugger sustained no harm. O'Leary had overshot her, in his desire to make his missiles reach. Not even a canister had lodged in her spars, or torn her sails. The usual luck appeared to attend her, and the people on board fought with renewed confidence and zeal. Not so with the felucca, however. Here the fire of the English had been most destructive. The wary and calculating McBean had given his attention to this portion of the French defenses and the consequences partook of the sagacity and discretion of the man. A charge of canister had swept across the felucca's decks, more than decimating Ithuel's small force: for it actually killed one, and wounded three of his party.

But, the din once commenced, there was no leisure for a pause. The fire was kept up with animation on both sides, and men fell rapidly. The boats cheered and pressed ahead, the water becoming covered with a wide sheet of smoke.

In moments like this, the safest course for the assailants is to push on. This the English did, firing and cheering at every fathom they advanced, but suffering also. The constant discharge of the carronades, and the total absence of wind, soon caused a body of smoke to collect in front of the rock, while the English brought on with them another, trailing along the water, the effects of their own fire. The two shrouds soon united, and then there was a minute when the boats could only be seen with indistinctness. This was Ithuel's moment. Perceiving that the ten or twelve men who remained to him were engrossed with their muskets, he pointed the two carronades himself, and primed them from the horns which he had never quitted. For the felucca, he felt no present concern. Winchester and all the boats in the center of the English line were most in advance, the fire of the ruins urging them to the greatest exertion. McBean, besides being more distant, could not cross the rock in front of the felucca without making a circuit, and he must as yet be ignorant of the existence of the impediment. Ithuel was cool and calculating by nature, as well as by habit; but this immunity from present risk probably increased the immediate possession of qualities so important in battle. His carronades were loaded to their muzzles with bags of bullets, and he beckoned to the best seaman of his party to take one of the matches, while he used the other himself, each holding a monkey's-tail in one hand, in readiness to train the light gun as circumstances required. The pieces had been depressed by Ithuel himself, in the midst of the fray, and nothing remained but to wait the moment for using them.

This moment was now near. The object of the English was to land on the principal islet, and to carry the ruin by storm. In order to do this, all the boats of their center converged in their courses to the same point; and the smoke being driven off by each concussion of the guns, a dark cluster of the enemy diverged from the ragged outline of the vapor, within fifty yards of the intended point of landing. Ithuel and his companion were ready. Together they sighted, and together they fired. This unexpected discharge from a quarter that had been so comparatively silent surprised both friends and foes, and it drove a fresh mantle of smoke momentarily athwart the rock and the open space in its front.

A cry arose from the dense shroud of battle, that differed from the shouts of success and courage. Physical agony had extorted shrieks from the stoutest of hearts, and even the French in the ruins paused to look for the next act of the desperate drama. Raoul seized the opportunity to prepare for the expected hand-to-hand struggle; but it was unnecessary. The cessation in the firing was common in both parties, and it gave the vapor a minute in which to lift the curtain from the water.

When the late obstacle was raised high enough to admit of a view, the result became evident. All the English boats but one had scattered, and were pulling swiftly, in different directions, from the scene of slaughter. By taking this course, they diverted and divided the fire of their enemies; an expedient of which it would have been happier had they bethought them earlier. The remaining boat was a cutter of the *Terpsichore*. It had received the weight of canister from Ithuel's own gun, and of sixteen men it had contained when it left the frigate's side, but two escaped. These fellows had thrown themselves into the sea, and were picked up by passing boats. The cutter itself came drifting slowly in toward the rock, announcing the nature of its fearful cargo by the groans and cries that arose from out its bosom. Raoul stopped the fire, equally from humanity and policy, after a few discharges at the retreating boats; and the first act of the battle closed.

The breathing time gave both parties a desirable opportunity for ascertaining in what positions they were left. In the whole, the French had lost the services of eleven men ; all, with the exception of Ithuel's four, in the ruin. The loss of the English amounted to thirty-three, including several officers. The master's-mate, who had commanded the crippled cutter, lay over its stern, flat on his back, with no less than five musket balls through his chest. His passage into another state of existence had been sudden as the flight of the electric spark. Of his late companions, several were dead also ; though most were still enduring the pain of fractured bones and bruised nerves. The boat itself slowly touched the rocks, raising fresh cries among the wounded by the agony they endured from the shocks of rising and falling under the ground-swell.

Raoul was too deliberate, and too much collected, not to feel his advantage. Anxious to keep his means of further defense in the best condition, he directed all the guns to cease, and the damages to be repaired. Then he went with a party toward the boat that had fallen into his hands. To encumber himself with prisoners, of any sort, in his actual situation, would have been a capital mistake, but to do this with wounded men would have been an act of folly. The boat had tourniquets and other similar appliances in it, and he directed some of the French to use them on those that wanted them most. He also supplied the parched lips of the sufferers with water ; when, conceiving that his duty was performed, he gave an order to haul the boat on one side, and to shove it forcibly out of the line of any coming conflict.

"Halloo, Captain Rule !" called out Ithuel, "you are wrong there. Let the boat lie where it is, and it will answer a better turn than another breastwork. The English will scarcely fire through their own wounded."

The look that Raoul cast toward his auxiliary was fierce, even indignant ; but, disregarding the advice, he motioned for his own men to obey the order he had already given them. Then, as if mindful of Ithuel's importance, his late timely succor, and the necessity of not offending him, he walked to the side of the islet nearest to the felucca, and spoke cautiously and cheerfully to him whose advice he had just treated with indifference, if not with disdain. This was not hypocrisy, but a prudent adaptation of his means to his circumstances.

"Bon, brave Etooelle," he said, "your bags of bullets were welcome friends, and they arrived at the right moment."

"Why, Captain Rule, in the Granite country we are never wasteful of our means. You can always wait for the white of Englishmen's eyes in these affairs. They're spiteful devils, on the whull, and seem to be near-sighted to a man. They came so clus' at Bunker Hill, our folks—"

"Bon," repeated Raoul, feeling no wish to hear a thrice-told tale gone through again, Bunker Hill invariably placing Ithuel on a great horse in the way of bragging ; for he not only imagined that great victory a New England triumph, as in fact it was, but he was much disposed to encourage the opinion that it was in a great measure "Granite." "Bon," interrupted Raoul, "Bunkair was good ; mais, les Roches aux Sirens is bettair. If you have more de ces balles, load encore."

"What think you of this, Captain Rule ?" asked the other, pointing up at a little vane that began to flutter at the head of one of his masts. "Here is the west wind, and an opportunity offers to be off. Let us take wit, and run !"

Raoul started, and gazed at the heavens, the vane, and the surface of the sea ; the latter beginning to show a slightly ruffled surface. Then his eye wandered toward Ghita. The girl had risen from her knees, and her eyes followed his every movement. When they met his, with a sweet, imploring smile, she pointed upward, as if beseeching him to pay the debt of gratitude he owed to that dread Being who had as yet borne him unharmed through the fray. He understood her meaning, kissed his hand in affectionate gallantry, and turned toward Ithuel, to pursue the discourse.

"It is too soon," he said. "We are impregnable here, and the wind is still too light. An hour hence and we will all go together."

Ithuel grumbled, but his commander heeded it not. The judgment of the latter had decided right. The boats were rallying within musket-shot, indifferent to the danger, and it was evident the attack was to be renewed. To have attempted to escape at such an instant would have been throwing away the great advantage of the ruins, and might have endangered all, without benefiting any one.

In point of fact, Sir Frederick Dashwood had become keenly alive to a sense of the disgrace he was likely to incur, in the event of the ship's going round, and robbing him of the credit of capturing the lugger. The usually apathetic nature of this young man was thoroughly aroused, and, like all who are difficult to excite, he became respectable when his energies were awakened. The boats were already collected ; all the disabled were put into one of them, and ordered off to the ships ;

and with those that remained arrangements were made to renew the attempt. It was fortunate that Cuffe had sent an expedition so strong-handed; for, notwithstanding the loss, the three launches and the cutters could still muster double the number of the French.

This time, Sir Frederick was willing to listen to counsel. Winchester, McBean, Griffin and Strand united in advising that the boats should separate and make their assaults at different points. This would prevent the possibility of a recurrence of so concentrated a disaster as that which had already befallen them. To the Scotchman was assigned the felucca; the *Terpsichore's* launch was to assail the lugger; while the two cutters, and the heavier boat of the *Proserpine*, were to dash in at the ruins. Sir Frederick still remained in his own gig, to push for the point that might seem to require his presence.

McBean was the first to fire on this occasion. He threw a round-shot from his carronade into the felucca, aimed by himself, and directed with care. It fell upon one of Ithuel's carronades, broke it into a dozen pieces, knocked down no less than three men, besides injuring others less severely, and actually drove the gun it struck off its slide into the felucca's hold. This was a rough commencement, and the result being seen by all hands, it greatly encouraged the assailants. Three hearty English cheers followed, and Ithuel was so far disconcerted as to fire the remaining gun, loaded as before with bullets, at least two minutes too soon.

The sea was thrown into a foam, but not a man in the boats was hurt. Then the fire became general; gun after gun exploding; the rattling of small arms filling up the pauses. The boats came on with steady, strong pulls of the oar, and this too with an impunity that often happens, though difficult to be explained. Several shot fell among the ruins, knocking the stones about, and for a minute or two all the injury was on one side. But Pintard and Ithuel felt the security conferred by the rocks in their front, and each endeavored to give one effective discharge. Ithuel succeeded the best. He repaid McBean in his own coin, sending a grist of bullets into the bows of his launch, which admonished that prudent officer of the necessity of sheering toward the islet of the ruins. Pintard's assailant was brought up by the barrier in front, and turned aside also. Then, in the midst of a cloud of smoke, shouts, curses, cries, shrieks, orders, and the roar of guns, all the English precipitated themselves in a body on the principal post, and became the masters of the battery in the twinkling of an eye.

CHAPTER XXIX.

IN scenes like that just related it is not easy to collect details. All that was ever known beyond the impetuous manner of the assault in which the ruins were carried, was in the dire result. Half the French on the islet were weltering in their blood, and the surface of the rocks was well sprinkled with enemies who had not been more fortunate. It had been a desperate onset, in which mortification increased natural intrepidty, which had been nobly resisted, but in which numbers had necessarily prevailed. Among the English slain was Sir Frederick Dashwood himself; he lay about a yard from his own gig, with a ball directly through his head. Griffin was seriously hurt, but Clinch was untouched, on the low rampart, waving an English Jack, after having hauled down a similar emblem of the French. His boat had first touched the rock, her crew had first reached the ruin, and of all in her he himself had taken the lead. Desperately had he contended for Jane and a commission, and this time Providence appeared to smile on his efforts. As for Raoul, he lay in front of his own rampart, having rushed forward to meet the party of Clinch, and had actually crossed swords with his late prisoner, when a musket-ball, fired by the hands of McBeau, traversed his body.

"Courage, mes braves! en avant!" he was heard to shout, as he leaped the low wall, to repel the invaders; and when he lay on the hard rock, his voice was still strong enough to make itself heard, crying, "Lieutenant—nom de Dieu—sauve mon *Feu-Follet!*"

It is probable that Pintard would not have stirred, even at this order, had not the English ships been seen, at that instant, coming round Campanella, with a leading westerly wind. The flap of canvas was audible near by, too, and turning, he saw the *Michael* falling off under her foresail, and already gathering steerage-way. Not a soul was visible on her decks, Ithuel, who steered, lying so close as to be hid by her waist-cloths. The hawsers of the lugger were cut, and *Le Feu-Follet* started back like an affrighted steed. It was only to let go the brails, and her foresail fell. Light, and feeling the breeze, which now came in strong puffs, she shot out of the little bay and wore short round on her keel. Two or three of the English boats attempted to follow, but it was idle. Winchester, who now commanded, recalled them, saying that it remained for the ships to perform their task. The day had been too bloody, indeed, to think of more than securing the present success, and of attending to the hurt.

Leaving the party on the islets for a moment, we will follow the two vessels in their attempt to escape. Pintard and his companions abandoned Raoul with heavy hearts, but they plainly saw him prostrated on the rocks, and by the hand placed on his side, understood the desperate nature of his wound. Like him, they felt some such interest as one entertains for a beloved mistress in the fate of the lugger, and the words, "Sauve mon *Feu-Follet!*" were ringing in their ears.

As soon as the lugger got round, she set her after-sail, and then she began to glide through the water with the usual knife-like parting of the element under her bows. The course she steered took her directly out of the bay, seeming to lead across the fore-foots of the English ships. Ithuel did not imitate this maneuver. He kept more away in the line for Pæstum, rightly enough believing that in the greedy desire to overtake the lugger his own movement would pass unheeded. The owner of this craft was still on board the *Terpsichore;* but every remonstrance and all the requests he made that his own vessel might be followed and captured were utterly unheeded by the lieutenant now in command. To him, as to all others in authority, there seemed to be but one thing desirable, and that was to secure the lugger. Of course none yet knew of the fatal character of the struggle on the rocks, or of the death of the English leader; though the nature of the result was sufficiently understood by seeing the English Jack flying among the ruins, and the two vessels under way, endeavoring to escape.

The season was now so far advanced as to render the old stability of the breezes a little uncertain. The zephyr had come early, and it had come fresh; but there were symptoms of a sirocco about the barometer and in the atmosphere. This rendered all in the ships eager to secure their prize before a shift of wind should come. Now that there were three fast vessels in chase, none doubted of the final result; and Cuffe paced the quarter-deck of the *Proserpine*, rubbing his hands with delight, as he regarded all the propitious signs of the times.

The *Ringdove* was ordered by signal to haul up south-southwest, or close on a wind, with a view to make such an offing as would prevent the possibility of the lugger's getting outside of the ships and gaining the wind of them, an achievement Cuffe thought she might very well be enabled to accomplish, could she once fairly come by the wind under circumstances that would prevent any of his vessels from bringing her under their guns. The *Terpsichore* was directed to run well into the bay to see that a similar artifice was not practiced in that direction; while the *Proserpine* shaped her own course at the angle that would intercept the chase, should the latter continue to stand on.

It was an easy thing for the French to set all their canvas, the hamper of the lugger being so simple. This was soon done; and Pintard watched the result with intense interest, well knowing that everything now depended on heels, and ignorant what might be the effect of her present trim on the sailing of his beautiful craft. Luckily, some attention had been paid to her lines in striking in the ballast again; and it was soon found that the vessel was likely to behave well. Pintard thought her so light as to be tender; but, not daring to haul up high enough to prove her in that way, it remained a matter of opinion only. It was enough for him that she lay so far to the west of south as to promise to clear the point of Piane, and that she skimmed along the water at a rate that bade fair to distance all three of her pursuers. Anxious to get an offing, however, which would allow him to alter his course at night in more directions than one, he kept luffing, as the wind favored, so as sensibly to edge off the land.

As the two chases commenced their flight quite a mile to the southward of the ships, having that much the start of them on account of the position of the rocks, it rendered them both tolerably free from all danger of shot at the beginning of the race. The course steered by Ithuel soon placed him beyond their reach altogether; and Cuffe knew that little would be gained, while much might be lost, in making an attempt of this sort on the lugger. Consequently not a gun was fired; but the result was thrown fairly on the canvas, and on the sailing of the respective vessels.

Such was the state of things at the beginning of this chase. The wind freshened fast, and soon blew a strong breeze; one that drove the ships ahead under clouds of studding-sails and stay-sails— the latter being much used at that period —at the rate of quite ten knots an hour. But neither gained on *Le Feu-Follet*. The course was by no means favorable to her, the wind being well on her quarter; still, she rather gained than was gained on. All four vessels went off rapidly to the southward, as a matter of course; nor was it long before they were to leeward of the felucca, which had both shortened sail and hauled up to the eastward, as soon as Ithuel felt satisfied he was not to be followed.

After a sufficient time had elapsed, the *Holy Michael* tacked and came out of the bay, crossing the wake of the *Terpsichore* just beyond gun-shot. Of course, this maneuver was seen from the frigate; and the padrone of the felucca tore his hair, threw himself on the quarter-deck, and played many other desperate antics, in the indulgence of his despair, or to excite sympathy: but all in vain; the lieutenant was obstinate, refusing to alter tack or sheet to chase a mere felucca, with so glorious an object in full view before him as the celebrated lugger of Raoul Yvard. As a matter of course, Ithuel passed out to sea unmolested; and it may as well be said here that, in due time, he reached Marseilles in safety, where the felucca was sold, and the Granite seaman disappeared for a season. There will be occasion to speak of him once again in this legend.

The trial of speed must soon have satisfied Pintard that he had little to apprehend from his pursuers, even with the breeze there was. But circumstances favored the lugger. The wind hauled materially to the northward, and before the sun set it enabled the French to run off wing-and-wing, still edging from the land. It now began to blow so heavily as to compel the ships to reduce their light canvas. Some time before the night set in, both frigates and the sloop were under main-top-gallant sails only, with topmast and lower studding-sails on each side. *Le Feu-Follet* made no change. Her jigger had been taken in, as soon as she kept dead away, and then she dashed ahead, under her two enormous lugs, confident in their powers of endurance. The night was not very dark; but it promised to carry her beyond the vision of her pursuers even before eight bells, did the present difference in sailing continue.

A stern chase is proverbially a long chase. For one fast vessel to outsail another a single mile in an hour is a great superiority; and even in such circumstances many hours must elapse ere one loses sight of the other by day. The three English ships held way together surprisingly, the *Proserpine* leading a little; while *Le Feu-Follet* might possibly have found herself, at the end of six hours'

chase, some four miles in advance of her, three of which she had gained since keeping off wing-and-wing. The lightness of the little craft essentially aided her. The canvas had less weight to drag after it; and Pintard observed that the hull seemed to skim the waves, as soon as the sharp stem had divided them, and the water took the bearings of the vessel. Hour after hour did he sit on the bowsprit, watching her progress; a crest of foam scarce appearing ahead, before it was glittering under the lugger's bottom. Occasionally, a pursuing sea cast the stern upward, as if about to throw it in advance of the bows; but *Le Feu-Follet* was too much accustomed to this treatment to be disturbed, and she ever rose on the billow, like a bubble, and then the glancing arrow scarce surpassed the speed with which she hastened forward, as if to recover lost time.

Cuffe did not quit the deck until the bell struck two, in the middle watch. This made it one o'clock. Yelverton and the master kept the watches between them, but the captain was always near with his advice and orders.

"That craft seems faster when she gets her sails wing-and-wing than she is even close-hauled, it seems to me, Yelverton," observed Cuffe, after taking a long look at the chase with the night-glass; "I begin to be afraid we shall lose her. Neither of the other ships does anything to help us. Here we are all three, dead in her wake, following each other like so many old maids going to church of a Sunday morning."

"It would have been better, Captain Cuffe, had the *Ringdove* kept more to the westward, and the frigate further east. Fast as the lugger is with her wings spread, she's faster with them jammed up on a wind. I expect every moment to find her sheering off to the westward, and gradually getting us in her wake on a wind. I fear we should find that worse work than even this, sir."

"I would not lose her now, for a thousand pounds! I do not see what the d—l Dashwood was about, that he did not secure her when he got possession of the rocks. I shall rattle him down a little as soon as we meet."

Cuffe would have been shocked had he known that the body of Sir Frederick Dashwood was, just at that moment, going through the melancholy process of being carried on board a two-decker, up at Naples, the captain of which was his kinsman. But he did not know it, nor did he learn of his death for more than a week; or after the body had been interred.

"Take the glass, Yelverton, and look at her. To me she grows very dim—she must be leaving us fast. Be careful to note if there are any signs of an intention to sheer to the westward."

"That can hardly be done without jibbing her forward lug; hang me, Captain Cuffe, if I can see her at all. Ah! here she is, dead ahead as before, but as dim as a ghost. I can barely make out her canvas; she is still wing-and-wing, d—n her, looking more like the specter of a craft than a real thing. I lost her in that yaw, sir; I wish you would try, Captain Cuffe; do my best I cannot find her again."

Cuffe did try, but without success. Once, indeed, he fancied he saw her, but further examination satisfied him it was a mistake. So long had he been gazing at the same object, that it was easy for the illusion to pass before his mind's eye of imagining a dim outline of the little lugger flying away, like the scud of the heavens, wing-and-wing, ever seeming to elude his observation. That night he dreamed of her, and there were happily five minutes during which his wandering thoughts actually portrayed the process of taking possession, and of manning the prize.

Previously to this, however, signals were made to the other ships, ordering them to alter their courses, with a view to meet anticipated changes in that of *Le Feu-Follet.* Lyon was sent to the westward, the *Terpsichore* a little easterly, while the *Proserpine* ventured so far as to steer southwest, after two o'clock. But a sudden and violent shift of wind came an hour before day. It was the expected, nay, the announced sirocco, and it brought the lugger to windward beyond all dispute. The south breeze came strong from the first puff; and, while it did not amount to a gale until the afternoon of the next day, it blew heavily, in squalls, after the first hour.

When the day dawned, the three ships were out of sight of each other. The *Proserpine,* which we shall accompany, as our old acquaintance, and an actor in what is to succeed, was under double-reefed topsails, with her head up as high as west-southwest, laboring along through the troughs of the seas left by the late Tramontana. The weather was thick, rain and drizzle coming in the squalls, and there were moments when the water could not be seen a cable's length from the ship; at no time was the usual horizon fairly visible. In this manner the frigate struggled ahead, Cuffe unwilling to abandon all hopes of success, and yet seeing little pros-

pect of its accomplishment. The lookouts were aloft, as usual, but it was as much for form as for any great use they were likely to be, since it was seldom a man could see further from the cross-trees than he could from the deck.

The officers, as well as the men, had breakfasted. A species of sullen discontent pervaded the ship, and the recent kind feelings toward Raoul Yvard had nearly vanished in disappointment. Some began to grumble about the chances of the other ships falling in with the lugger, while others swore that "It mattered not who saw her; catch her none could who had not an illicit understanding with the Father of Lies. She was well named Jack-o'-Lantern; for Jack-o'-Lantern she was, and Jack-o'-Lantern would she ever prove to be. As well might a false fire be followed in a meadow, as such a craft at sea. They might think themselves fortunate if the officers and people sent against her in the boats ever got back to their own wholesome ship again."

In the midst of such prognostics and complaints, the captain of the fore-top shouted the words "Sail, ho!" The usual inquiry and answer followed, and the officers got a glimpse of the object. The stranger was distant half-a-league, and he was seen very indistinctly on account of the haze; but seen he was.

"'Tis a xebec," growled the master, who was one of the grumblers of the day, "a fellow with his hold crammed with a wine that would cover the handsomest woman's face in Lunnun with wrinkles."

"By Jupiter Ammon!" Cuffe exclaimed, "'tis *Le Few-Folly* or I do not know an old acquaintance. Quarter-master, hand me the glass — not that, the shorter glass is the best."

"Long or short, you'll never make that out," muttered the master. "The *Folly* has more folly about her than I give her credit for, if we get another look at her this summer."

"What do you make of him, Captain Cuffe?" Yelverton eagerly demanded.

"Just what I told you, sir; 'tis the lugger—and—I cannot be mistaken. Aye, by Jove, she is coming down before it, wing-and-wing, again! That's her play, just now, it would seem, and she does not appear to have got enough of it yet."

An attentive look satisfied Yelverton that his commander was right. Even the master had to confess his error, though he did it ungraciously and with reluctance. It was the lugger, of a certainty, though so dimly seen as to render it difficult at moments to trace her outlines at all. She was running in a line that would carry her astern of the frigate about a mile, and she was rather more than thrice that distance to windward.

"She cannot see us," said Cuffe, thoughtfully. "Beyond a doubt she thinks us to windward, and is endeavoring to get out of our neighborhood. We must get round, gentlemen, and now is a favorable moment. Tack ship at once, Mr. Yelverton; I think she'll do it."

The experiment was made, and it succeeded. The *Proserpine* worked beautifully, and Yelverton knew how to humor her to a nicety. In five minutes the ship was round and everything trimmed on the other tack; close-reefed mizzen, and double-reefed fore and main-topsail—a reefed mainsail, with other sails to suit. As she was kept a rap full, or a little off, indeed, to prevent the lugger from slipping past, she might have gone from five to six knots.

The next five minutes were intensely interesting to the people of the *Proserpine*. The weather became thicker, and all traces of *Le Feu-Follet* were lost. Still, when last seen, she was wing-and-wing, flying rather than sailing down toward their own track. By Cuffe's calculations, the two vessels would nearly meet in less than a quarter of an hour, should neither alter their course. Several guns were got ready, in preparation for such a rencounter.

"Let the weather hold thick a few minutes longer, and we have her!" cried Cuffe. "Mr. Yelverton, you must go down and see to those guns yourself. Plump it right into her, if you're ordered to fire. The fellow has no hamper, and stripping him must be a matter of pure accident. Make it too hot for him on deck, and he'll have to give up. Raoul Yvard or the d—l!"

"There she is, sir!" shouted a midshipman from a cathead, for everybody who dared had crowded forward to get an early look at the chase.

There she was, sure enough, wing-and-wing, as before. The dullness of the lugger's lookouts has never been explained, as a matter of course; but it was supposed, when all the circumstances came to be known, that most of her people were asleep, to recover from the recent extraordinary fatigue, and a night in which all hands had been kept on deck, in readiness to make sail; the vessel having but some thirty souls in her. At length the frigate was seen, the weather lighting, and it was not an instant too soon. The two vessels, at that critical instant, were about half-a-mile apart, *Le Feu-Follet* bearing directly off the *Proserpine's* weather-bow. In the twinkling of an eye, the former jibbed;

then she was seen coming to the wind, losing sufficient ground in doing so, to bring her just in range with the two weather chase-guns. Cuffe instantly gave the order to open a fire.

"What the d—l has got into her?" exclaimed the captain; "she topples like a mock mandarin—she used to be as stiff as a church! What can it mean, sir?"

The master did not know, but we may say that the lugger was flying light, too much so for the canvas she carried; for, in such heavy weather, there was no time to shorten sail. She lurched heavily under the sea that was now getting up, and a squall striking her, her lee guns were completely buried. Just at this moment the *Proserpine* belched forth her flame and smoke. The shot could not be followed, and no one knew where they struck. Four had been fired, when a squall succeeded that shut in the chase, and, of course, the firing was suspended. So severe was this momentary effort of the African gales, hot, drowsy, and deadening as they are, that the *Proserpine* started her mizzen-topsail sheet, and clewed up her main-course, to save the spar. But the tack was instantly boarded again, and the topsail set. A gleam of sunshine succeeded, but the lugger had disappeared!

The sun did not remain visible, and that faintly, more than a minute; still, the eye could range several miles for thrice that period. After this the horizon became more limited, but no squall occurred for a quarter of an hour. When the lugger was missed, the *Proserpine* was heading up within half a point of the spot at which she was supposed to be. In a short time she drove past this point, perhaps a hundred fathoms to leeward of it. Here she tacked, and stretching off a sufficient distance to the southward and westward, came round again, and heading up east-southeast, was thought to sweep along over the empty track. Not a sign of the missing vessel was discovered. The sea had swallowed all, lugger, people, and hamper. It was supposed that, owing to the fact that so many light articles had been left on the rocks, nothing remained to float. All had accompanied *Le Feu-Follet* to the bottom. Of boats there were none, these being at the islet of the ruins, and, if any seaman swam off in the desperate attempt to save his life in the midst of the caldron of waters, he did not succeed, or was overlooked by the English in their search. The latter, indeed, may have miscalculated their distances, and not have passed within a cable's-length of the place where the victims, if any such there were, still struggled for existence.

Cuffe, and all around him, were forcibly struck with so unlooked-for and so dire a calamity. The loss of a vessel, under such circumstances, produces an effect like a sudden death among companions. It is a fate all may meet with, and it induces reflection and sadness. Still, the English did not give up the hope of rescuing some unfortunate wretch, clinging to a spar, or supporting himself by supernatural efforts, for several hours. At noon, however, the ship squared away and ran for Naples before the wind, being drawn aside from her course by another chase, in which she succeeded better, capturing a sloop of war, which she carried in a few days later.

The first act of Cuffe, on anchoring in the fleet, was to go on board the *Foudroyant,* and report himself and his proceedings to the rear-admiral. Nelson had heard nothing of the result, beyond what had occurred at the islets, and the separation of the ships.

"Well, Cuffe," he said, reaching out his remaining hand kindly to his old Agamemnon, as the other entered the cabin, "the fellow has got off, after all! It has been a bad business altogether, but we must make the best of it. Where do you fancy the lugger to be?"

Cuffe explained what had happened, and put into the admiral's hand an official letter, explaining his recent success. With the last Nelson was pleased—at the first surprised. After a long, thoughtful pause, he went into the after-cabin and returned, throwing a small jack-like flag on the floor.

"As Lyon was cruising about," he said, "and his sloop was pitching her cathead under, this thing was washed upon a spare anchor, where it stuck. It's a queer flag. Can it have any connection with the lugger?"

Cuffe looked, and he immediately recognized the little *ala-e-ala* jack, that the Italians had described to him in their conversations. It was the only vestige that was ever found of the *Wing-and-Wing.*

CHAPTER XXX.

WE must return to the rocks, and the melancholy scene they offered. Our purposes will be answered, however, by advancing the time into the evening, omitting many things that the reader can imagine, without our relating them.

It is scarcely necessary to say that Andrea Barrofaldi and Vito Viti took no part in the bloody transactions we have related. When all was over, however, they drew near to the rocks, and, sitting in their boat, contemplating the sad spectacle presented within the narrow compass of the islet of the ruins, the following short dialogue occurred between them:

"Vice-governatore," demanded the podesta, pointing to the place where lay Sir Frederick, a motionless corpse, Raoul bleeding, and others writhing under their wounds, "do you call this reality, or is it a part of that damnable doctrine which is enough to set the whole earth by the ears, and to turn men into tigers and hawks?"

"I fear, neighbor Vito, this will only prove too true. I see the bodies of Sir Dashwood and Sir Smees; and God knows how many more have this day departed for the world of spirits."

"Leaving behind them only a world of shadows," muttered Vito Viti, even that melancholy spectacle failing to draw his thoughts altogether from a discussion that had now lasted near four-and-twenty hours. But the moment was not propitious to argument, and the two Italians landed. This was within half an hour after the struggle had ceased; and our intentions are to advance the time to the moment mentioned in the opening of this chapter.

We must give here, however, a rapid sketch of the proceedings that narrowed down the view to that we intend shortly to lay before the reader. As soon as there was leisure, Winchester made a survey of the field of battle. He found many of his own men slain, and more wounded. Of the French on the islet, quite half were hurt; but the mortal wound received by their leader was the blow that all lamented. The surgeon soon pronounced Raoul's case to be hopeless; and this declaration was heard with regret even by generous enemies. The defense had been desperate; it would have succeeded, had it been within the scope of possibility for so few courageous men to repel double their number of those who were equally brave. Both sides had fought for honor; and, when this is the case, victory generally awaits the strongest.

As soon as it was perceived that all the ships were likely to be led far to the leeward in chase, the English officers felt the necessity of acting for themselves. The medical men had been busy from the first, and in the course of a couple of hours, all had been done for the wounded that present circumstances would allow. The amputations were few, and each vessel having sent a surgeon, these were all made, while the other appliances had been successfully used in such cases as would be benefited by them. The day was drawing to a close, and the distance from the fleet was so great as to call for exertion.

As soon, therefore, as the uninjured men were refreshed and the wounded cared for, the latter were put into launches, in the best manner they might be, and the cutters took them in tow. One had no sooner received its melancholy freight, than it left the islets, on its way to the hospital-ship of the fleet. The others succeeded, in turn; the unhurt French willingly offering to assist in the performance of this pious duty. At length, but three boats remained. One was Sir Frederick's gig, which Winchester had kept for his own particular use; another was the yawl of Andrea Barrofaldi; and the third, the little craft in which Carlo Giuntotardi had come from the shore. Of the French, no one remained but the surgeon of the lugger, Raoul's steward and personal attendant, and Raoul himself. If to these be added the two Italians and their oarsmen, Carlo, and his niece, with Winchester and his boat's crew, we enumerate all who now remained at the rocks.

By this time the sun had sunk below the adjacent hills, and it was necessary to decide on some course. Winchester consulted the surgeon as to the expediency of removing his patient. Could it be done, it had better be done soon.

"Monsieur lieutenant," answered this personage, a little dryly, "mon brave capitaine has but a short time to live. He has entreated to be left here, on the scene of his glory, and in the company of that female whom he so well loved; mais—you are the victors," shrugging his shoulders, "and you will do your own pleasure."

Winchester colored and bit his lips. The idea of torturing Raoul, either in body or mind, was the last intention of one so humane, but he felt indignant at the implied suspicion. Commanding himself, notwithstanding, he bowed courteously, and intimated that he would remain himself, with his prisoner, until all was over. The Frenchman was surprised, and when he read the sympathy of the other in the expression of his countenance, he felt regret for his own distrust, and still more at having expressed it.

"Mais, monsieur," he answered, "night will soon come; you may have to pass it on the rocks."

"And if we do, doctor, it is no more than we seamen are used to. Boat-service is a common duty with us. I have only to wrap myself in my cloak, to enjoy a seaman's comfort."

This settled the matter, and no more was said. The surgeon, a man accustomed to the exercise of such resources, soon managed to make his dispositions for the final scene. In clearing the lugger, a hundred light articles had been thrown on the islet on which she had touched, and among others were several rude mattresses of the seamen. Two or three of these were procured, placed on the smoothest surface of the rock, and a bed formed for Raoul. The medical man and the seamen would have erected a tent with a sail, but this the wounded man forbade.

"Let me breathe the free air," he said; "I shall use but little of it; let that little be free."

It was useless to oppose such a wish; nor was there any motive in it. The air was pure, and little need be apprehended from the night, in behalf of Ghita, surrounded as they were by the pure waters of the ocean. Even when the Tramontana came, although it was cool, its coolness was not unpleasant, the adjacent hill sheltering the islet from its immediate influence.

The English seamen collected some fuel from the spare spars of the lugger, and lighted a fire on the rocks where they had been found. Food of all sorts was abundant, and several casks of water had been struck out whole, as provision against a siege. Here they made coffee, and cooked enough food for the wants of all the party. The distance prevented their disturbing those who remained near Raoul; while the light of the fire, which was kept in a cheerful blaze, cast a picturesque glow upon the group around the dying man as soon as the night had fairly set in. It superseded, too, the necessity of any lamps or torches.

We pass over all the first outpourings of Ghita's anguish, when she learned the wound of Raoul, her many and fervent prayers, and the scenes that took place during the time that the islet was still crowded with the combatants. More quiet hours succeeded when these last were gone; as the night advanced, something like the fixed tranquillity of settled despair followed the first emotions. When ten o'clock arrived, we reach the moment at which we wish to raise the curtain once more, in order to present the principal actors in the scene.

Raoul lay on the summit of the islet, where his eye could range over the mild waters that washed the rock, and his ear listen to the murmurings of his own element. The Tramontana, as usual, had driven all perceptible vapor from the atmosphere, and the vault of heaven, in its cerulean blue, and spangled with thousands of stars, stretched itself above him, a glorious harbinger for the future, to one who died in hope. The care of Ghita and the attendants had collected around the spot so many little comforts, as to give it the air of a room suddenly divested of sides and ceiling, but habitable and useful. Winchester, fatigued with his day's work, and mindful of the wish that Raoul might so naturally feel to be alone with Ghita, had lain down on a mattress, leaving orders to be called should anything occur; while the surgeon, conscious that he could do no more, had imitated his example, making a similar request. As for Carlo Giuntotardi, he seldom slept; he was at his prayers in the ruins. Andrea and the podesta paced the rock to keep themselves warm, slightly regretting the sudden burst of humanity which had induced them to remain.

Raoul and Ghita were alone. The former lay on his back, his head bolstered, and his face upturned toward the vault of heaven. The pain was over, and life was ebbing fast. Still, the mind was unshackled, and thought busy as ever. His heart was still full of Ghita; though his extraordinary situation, and more especially the glorious view before his eyes, blended certain pictures of the future with his feelings, that were as novel as he found them powerful.

With the girl it was different. As a woman, she felt the force of this sudden blow in a manner she found difficult to bear. Still, she blessed God that what had occurred, happened in her presence as it might be; leaving her the means of acting, and the efficacy of prayer. To say that she did not yet feel the liveliest love for Raoul, all that tenderness which constitutes so large a portion of woman's nature, would be untrue; but her mind was made up to the worst, and her thoughts were of another state of being.

A long pause occurred, in which Raoul remained steadfastly gazing at the starry canopy above.

"It is remarkable, Ghita," he said, at length, "that I, Raoul Yvard—the corsair —the man of wars and tempests, fierce combats and hair-breadth escapes—should be dying here, on this rock, with all those stars looking down upon me, as it might be, from your heaven, seeming to smile upon me!"

"Why not your heaven, as well as mine, Raoul?" Ghita answered tremulously. "It is as vast as he who dwells in it — whose throne it is — and can contain all who love Him and seek His mercy."

"Dost thou think one like me would be received into His presence, Ghita?"

"Do not doubt it; free from all error and weakness Himself, his Holy Spirit delights in the penitent and the sorrowful. Oh! dearest, dearest Raoul, if thou wouldst but pray!"

A gleam like that of triumph glowed on the face of the wounded man; and Ghita, in the intensity of her expectation, rose and stood over him, her features filled with a momentary hope.

"Mon *Feu-Follet!*" exclaimed Raoul, letting the tongue reveal the transient thought which brought the gleam of triumph to his countetance. "Thou, at least, hast escaped! These English will not count thee among their victims, and glut their eyes on thy charming proportions!"

Ghita felt a chill at her heart, She fell back on her seat, and continued watching her lover's countenance with a feeling of despair, though inextinguishable tenderness was still crowding around her soul. Raoul heard the movement; and turning his head he gazed at the girl for quite a minute, with a portion of that intense admiration that used to gleam from his eyes in happier moments.

"It is better as it is, Ghita," he said, "than that I should live without thee. Fate has been kind in thus ending my misery."

"O! Raoul! there is no fate but the holy will of God. Deceive not thyself at this awful moment; bow down thy proud spirit in humility, and turn to Him for succor!"

"Poor Ghita! Well, thine is not the only innocent mind by millions that hath been trammeled by priests; and, I suppose, what has commenced with the beginning will last till the end."

"The beginning and the end are both with God, Raoul. Since the commencement of time hath He established laws which have brought about the trials of thy life—the sadness of this very hour."

"And dost thou think He will pardon all thy care of one so unworthy."

Ghita bowed her head to the mattress over which she leaned, and buried her face in her hands. When the minute of prayer that succeeded was over, and her face was again raised with the flush of feeling tempered by innocence on it, Raoul was lying on his back, his eyes riveted again on the vault of heaven. His professional pursuits had led him further into the study of astronomy than comported with his general education; and, addicted to speculation, its facts had often seized upon his fancy, though they had failed to touch his heart. Hitherto, indeed, he had fallen into the common error of limited research, and found a confirmation of his suspicions in the assumed grasp of his own reason. The dread moment that was so near could not fail of its influence, however; and that unknown future over which he hung, as it might be, suspended by a hair, inevitably led his mind into an inquiry after the unknown God.

"Dost thou know, Ghita," he asked, "that the learned of France tell us that all yonder bright stars are worlds, peopled most probably like this of our own, and to which the earth appears but as a star itself, and that, too, of no great magnitude?"

"And what is this, Raoul, to the power and majesty of Him who created the universe? Ah! think not of the things of his hand, but of Him who made them!"

"Hast thou ever heard, my poor Ghita, that the mind of man hath been able to invent instruments to trace the movements of all these worlds, and hath power even to calculate their wanderings with accuracy, for ages to come?"

"And dost thou know, my poor Raoul, what this mind of man is?"

"A part of his nature—the highest quality; that which maketh him the lord of earth."

"His highest quality, and that which maketh him lord of earth, in one sense, truly; but, after all, a mere fragment—a spot on the width of the heavens—of the Spirit of God himself. It is in this sense that he hath been made in the image of his creator."

"Thou think'st then, Ghita, that man is God, after all."

"Raoul!—Raoul! if thou wouldst not see me die with thee, interpret not my words in this manner!"

"Would it, then, be so hard to quit life in my company, Ghita? To me it would seem supreme felicity were our places to be changed."

"To go whither? Hast thou bethought thee of this, my beloved?"

Raoul answered not for some time. His eyes were fastened on a bright star, and a tumult of thoughts began to crowd upon his brain. There are moments in the life of every man when the mental vision obtains clearer views of remote conclusions, equally in connection with the past and the future, as there are days when an atmosphere purer than common more readily gives up its objects to the physical organs—leaving the mind momentarily the master, almost without control. One of these gleams of truth passed over the faculties of the dying man, and it could not be altogether without its fruits.

Raoul's soul was agitated by novel sensations.

"Do thy priest fancy that they who have known and loved each other in this life," he asked, "will know and love each other in that which they fancy is to come."

"The life that is to come, Raoul, is one all love, or one all hatred. That we may know each other I try to hope; nor do I see any reason for disbelieving it. My uncle is of opinion it must be so."

"Thy uncle, Ghita? What, Carlo Giuntotardi—he who seemeth never to think of things around him—doth a mind like his dwell on thoughts as remote and sublime as this?"

"Little dost thou know or understand him, Raoul. His mind seldom ceases to dwell on thoughts like these; this is the reason why earth, and all it contains, seems so indifferent."

Raoul made no answer, but appearing to suffer under the pain of his wound, the feelings of woman so far prevailed over Ghita's tender nature that she had not the heart to press even his salvation on him at such a moment. She offered him soothing drinks and nursed him with unabated care; and when there seemed to be a cessation to his sufferings, she again passed minutes on her knees, her whole soul absorbed in his future welfare. An hour passed in this manner, all on or near the rock sleeping, overcome by fatigue, but Ghita and the dying man.

"That star haunts me, Ghita!" Raoul at length muttered. "If it be really a world, some all-powerful hand must have created it. Chance never made a world, more than chance made a ship. Thought, mind, intelligence must have governed at the formation of one as well as of the other."

For months Ghita had not known an instant as happy as that. It appeared as if the mind of Raoul were about to extricate itself from the shallow philosophy so much in fashion, and which had hitherto deadened a nature so kind, an intellect ordinarily so clear. Could his thoughts but once take the right direction, she had strong confidence in the distinctness of their views, but most of all in the goodness of the Deity.

"Raoul," she whispered, "God is there, as he is with us, on this rock. His spirit is everywhere, bless him! bless him in thy soul, my beloved, and be forever happy!"

Raoul answered not. His face was upturned, and his eye still remained riveted on that particular star. Ghita would not disturb him, but taking his hand in hers, she once more knelt and resumed her prayers. Minute passed after minute, and neither seemed disposed to speak. At length Ghita became a woman again, and bethought her of her patient's bodily wants. It was time to administer the liquids of the surgeon, and she advanced to hold them to his lips. The eye was still astened on the star, but the lips did not meet her with the customary smile of love. They were compressed, as when the body was about to mingle in the strife of a battle, a sort of stern resolution having settled on them. Raoul Yvard was dead.

The discovery of the truth was a fearful moment to Ghita. Not a living being near her had the consciousness of her situation, all being bound in the sleep of the weary. The first feeling was that which belonged to her sex. She threw herself on the body, and embraced it wildly, giving way to those pent-up emotions which her lover, in his moody humors, was wont to accuse her of not possessing. She kissed the forehead, the cheeks, the pallid, stern lips of the dead ; and, for a time, there was the danger that her own spirit might pass away in the paroxysm of her grief. But it was impossible for Ghita to remain long under the influence of despair. Her gentle spirit had communed too long and too closely with her Heavenly Father, not to resort to his support in all the critical moments of life. She prayed for the tenth time that night, and arose from her knees calm, if not absolutely resigned.

The situation of Ghita was now as wildly picturesque as it was moving to her inmost spirit. All around her still slept, and that, to the eye, as profoundly as he who was only to rise again when the sea and the land give up their dead. The excitement and exertions of the past day produced their reaction, and seldom did sleep exercise a more profound influence. The fire was still burning bright on the islet of the gig-men, casting its rays fairly athwart the ruins, the different sleepers in them, and the immovable body of the dead. At moments, gusts of the Tramontana, which was now blowing fresh, descended so low as to fan the flames, when the glare that succeeded seemed to give a startling reality to all that surrounded the place.

Still the girl was too highly sustained to be moved with anything but her loss and her restless inquietude for the departed spirit. She saw that even her uncle slept, leaving her truly alone with Raoul. Once a feeling of desertion came over her, and she was inclined to arouse some of the sleepers. She did approach the spot where the surgeon lay, and her hand was raised to stir him, when a flash of light shot athward the pallid countenance of Raoul, and she perceived that his eyes were still open. Drawing near, she bent over the body, gazing long and wistfully into those windows of the soul that had so often beamed on her in manly tenderness, and she felt like a miser with his hoarded gold, unwilling to share it with any other.

Throughout the livelong night did Ghita watch by the body of her well-beloved, now hanging over it with a tenderness no change could extinguish, now besieging Heaven with her prayers. Not one awoke to interfere with the strange happiness she felt in those pious offices, or to wound her sensibilities by the surprise or the sneers of the vulgar. Ere the day came, she closed the eyes of Raoul with her own hands, covered his body with a French ensign that lay upon the rock, and sat, patient and resigned, awaiting the moment when some of the others might be ready to aid her in performing the last pious offices in behalf of the dead. As a Romanist, she found a holy consolation in that beautiful portion of her Church's creed that admits of unceasing petition for the souls of the departed, even to the latest hour of earthly things.

Winchester was the first to stir. Starting up, he appeared to be astonished at the situation in which he found himself ; but a glance around told the whole truth. Advancing toward Ghita, he was about to inquire after the welfare of Raoul, when, struck by the expression of her seraphic countenance, he turned to the body and read the truth in the appropriate pall. It was no time for self-upbraidings, or for reproaches to others ; but arousing the sleepers, in a subdued and respectful manner, he gave to the place the quiet and seeming sanctity of a chapel.

Carlo Giuntotardi soon after begged the dead body from the conquerors. There was no motive for denying the request, and it was placed in a boat and towed to the shore, accompanied by all who had remained. The heavy sirocco that soon succeeded drove the waves athwart the islet of the ruins, effectually erasing its stains of blood, and sweeping every trace of *Le Feu-Follet*, and of the recent events, into the sea.

At the foot of the Scaricatojo the seamen constructed a rude bier, and thus they bore the dead up that wild and yet lovely precipice, persevering in their good work until they reached the cottage of Carlo Giuntotardi's sister. A little procession accompanied the body from the first, and Ghita being universally known and respected among the simple inhabitants of those heights, when it entered the street of St. Agata it had grown into a line that included a hundred believers.

The convent, the empty buildings of which still crown the summit of one of the adjacent hills, was then in existence as a religious community; and the influence of Carlo Giuntotardi was sufficient to procure its offices in behalf of the dead. For three days and nights did the body of Raoul Yvard, the unbeliever, lie in the chapel of that holy fraternity, his soul receiving the benefit of masses; then it was committed to holy ground, to await the summons of the last trump.

There is a strange disposition in the human breast to withhold praise from a man when living, that is freely accorded to him when dead. Although we believe that envy, and its attendant evil, detraction, are peculiarly democratic vices, meaning thereby that democracy is the most fertile field in which these human failings luxuriate, yet is there much reason to think that our parent nation is preeminent in the exhibition of the peculiarity first mentioned. That which subsequently awaited Napoleon, after his imprisonment and death, was now exhibited in the case of Raoul Yvard, on a scale suited to his condition and renown. From being detested in the English fleet, he got to be honored and extolled. Now that he was dead and harmless, his seamanship could be praised, his chivalry emulated, and his courage glorified. Winchester, McBean, O'Leary, and Clinch, attended his funeral, quite as a matter of course. They had proved themselves worthy to be there; but many others insisted on being of the party. Some came to get a last look of so celebrated an adventurer, even in his coffin; others to say they had been present; and not a few to catch a glimpse of the girl whose romantic but innocent passion had got to be the subject of much discourse in the ships. The result was such a procession, and such funeral honors, as threw the quiet little hamlet of St. Agata into commotion. All noted the particulars, and all were pleased but Ghita. On her, these tardy compliments failed of their effect, her soul being engrossed with the great care of petitioning Heaven in behalf of the deceased.

Andrea Barrofaldi and Vito Viti, too, figured on this occasion; the latter taking care to let all who would listen understand how closely he had been connected with "Sir Smees"; no longer viewed as an impostor, but honored as a hero. He even created a little difficulty in claiming a precedency for the *toga* over arms on the occasion; well knowing that if the vice-governatore got a conspicuous place in the ceremony, the podesta could not fail to be near at hand. The matter was settled entirely to Andrea's satisfaction, if not to that of his friend.

To confess the truth, Nelson was not sorry for what had occurred. When he learned the desperate nature of Raoul's defense, and heard some traits of his liberal conduct on various occasions, he felt a generous regret at his death; but he thought even this preferable to escape. When Cuffe got in, and brought the report of the lugger's fate, though he would have preferred her capture, the common sentiment settled down into a feeling that both lugger and commander had fared as well as a privateer and her people usually merited.

As a matter of course, those concerned in the capture, and who survived the affair, reaped some advantage from their success. England seldom fails in the duty of conferring rewards, more especially in her marine. When Cook returned from his renowned voyages, it was not to meet with persecution and neglect, but credit and justice. Nelson knew how to appreciate that spirit and enterprise which were so often exercised by himself. As for Sir Frederick Dashwood, little could be done besides giving his name an honorable place on the list of those who had fallen in battle. His heir wore mourning, seemed filled with sorrow, and inwardly rejoiced at being a baronet with some thousands a year. Lyon got his ship; and from that moment he ceased to consider the chase and all connected with *Le Feu-Follet* an unprofitable thing. Airchy followed him to the *Terpsichore*, with visions of prize-money before his eyes, which were tolerably realized in the course of the succeeding five years.

Winchester was promoted into the *Ringdove*, and Griffin became first officer of the *Proserpine*. This, of course, made Yelverton second, and left one vacancy. Thus far the orders had been made out, when Cuffe dined with the admiral, by invitation, *tete-à-tete*.

"One of my objects in having you here to-day, Cuffe," observed Nelson, as they sat together over their wine, the cabin cleared, "was to say something about the vacant berth in your gun-room; and the other was to beg a master's-mate of you, in behalf of Berry. You remember some of your people were received on board here before you got in, the other day?"

"I do, my lord; and I meant to make my acknowledgments for the favor. The poor fellows had a warm time of it at the rocks, and deserved comfortable berths after it was over."

"I believe we gave them as much; at least, I know few suffer in this ship. Well, there was a mate among them, who is a little advanced, and who is likely to stick where he is, by what I learn. We want just such a man for the hold, and I have promised my captain to speak to you about him. Don't let him go if there's any reason for wishing to retain him; but we have three seamen ready to exchange against him; good fellows, too, they tell me."

Cuffe picked some nuts, and appeared a little at a loss for a reply. Nelson saw this, and he fancied the other reluctant to give up his mate.

"Well, I see how it is," he said, smiling. "We must do without him, and you will keep your Mr. Clinch. A thorough officer in a ship's hold is an advantage not to be thrown away; and I suppose, if Hotham had asked such a thing of old Agamemnon, he might have whistled for the favor. The deuce is in it, if we do not get as good a mate somewhere?"

"It's not that, my lord—you're welcome to the man, though a better in his station cannot be had. But, I was in hopes his recent good conduct, and his long services, might give him a lift into the vacant gun-room berth."

"It has a hard look, I grant you, Cuffe, to keep a poor devil ten or fifteen years in the same station, and this, too, after he has served long enough for a commission. I was a captain ten years younger than this Mr. Clinch must be to-day, and it does seem hard; and I doubt not it is just. I have rarely known a midshipman or a mate passed over, in this way, that there has not been some great fault at the bottom. We must think of the service, as well as of generosity."

"I confess all this, my lord; and yet I did hope poor Clinch's delinquencies would at length be forgotten."

"If there are any particular reasons for it, I should like to hear them."

Cuffe now related all that had passed between himself and the master's mate, taking care to give Jane a due place in his history. Nelson began to twitch the stump of his arm, and by the time the story was told, Clinch's promotion was settled. As order was sent forthwith, to the secretary, to make out the orders, and Cuffe carried them back with him to the *Proserpine* that night, when he returned to the ship.

All Nelson's promotions were confirmed by the Admiralty, pretty much as a mat-

ter of course. Among others was that of Clinch, who now became the junior lieutenant of the *Proserpine*. This elevation awakened new feelings within him. He dressed better; refrained from the bottle; paid more attention to his mind; improved in manners, by keeping better company; and in the course of the next twelvemonth, had made rapid advances toward respectability. At the end of that time the ship was sent home; and Jane, in her imagination at least, received the reward of all her virtuous constancy, by becoming his wife. Nor did Cuffe cease his friendly offices here. He succeeded in getting Clinch put in command of a cutter; in which he captured a privateer, after a warm action, within a month. This success procured him a gun-brig, and with her he was still more fortunate; actually cutting out, with her boats, a French sloop-of-war, that was not half manned, it is true, but which was still considered a handsome prize. For this affair he got the sloop; thus demonstrating the caprice of fortune, by whose means he found himself a commander in less than three years after he had been a mate. Here he stuck, however, for a long time, until he got another sloop in fair fight, when he was posted. From that moment, we have lost sight of him.

Cuffe being sent to the Gulf of Genoa, shortly after, seized the opportunity to restore the vice-governatore and his friend to their native island. The fame of their deeds had preceded them, exaggerated, as a matter of course, by the tongue of rumor. It was understood that the two Elbans were actually in the fight in which Raoul Yvard fell; and there being no one to deny it, many even believed that Vito Viti, in particular, had killed the corsair with his own hand. A discreet forbearance on the part of the podesta always kept the matter so completely involved in mystery, that we question if any traveler who should visit the island, even at this day, would be able to learn more than we now tell the reader. In a word, the podesta, forever after, passed for a hero, through one of those mysterious processes by which men sometimes reach fame; quite as much, perhaps, to their own astonishment, as to the surprise of everybody else.

As for Ithuel, he did not appear in America for many years. When he did return, he came back with several thousand dollars; how obtained no one knew, nor did he ever choose to enter into particulars. He now married a widow, and settled in life. In due time he "experienced religion," and at this moment is an active abolitionist, a patron of the temperance cause, teetotally, and a general terror to evil-doers, under the appellation of Deacon Bolt.

It was very different with the meek, pious, and single-minded Ghita; though one was e'en a Roman Catholic, and the other a Protestant, and that, too, of the Puritan school. Our heroine had little of this world left to live for. She continued, however, to reside with her uncle, until his days were numbered; and then she retired to a convent, not so much to comply with any religious superstitions, as to be able to pass her time uninterrupted, in repeating prayers for the soul of Raoul. To her latest hour, and she lived until quite recently, did this pure-minded creature devote herself to what she believed to be the eternal welfare of the man who had so interwoven himself with her virgin affections, as to threaten, at one time, to disturb the just ascendency of the dread Being who had created her.

END OF "WING AND WING.."

THE WEPT OF WISH-TON-WISH.

THE REV. J. R. C.,

OF

****** PENNSYLVANIA.

THE kind and disinterested manner in which you have furnished the materials of the following tale, merits a public acknowledgment. As your reluctance to appear before the world, however, imposes a restraint, you must receive such evidence of gratitude as your own prohibition will allow.

Notwithstanding there are so many striking and deeply interesting events in the early history of those from whom you derive your being, yet are there hundreds of other families in this country, whose traditions, though less accurately and minutely preserved than the little narrative you have submitted to my inspection, would supply the materials of many moving tales. You have every reason to exult in your descent, for, surely, if any man may claim to be a citizen and a proprietor in the Union, it is one, that, like yourself, can point to a line of ancestors, whose origin is lost in the obscurity of time. You are truly an American. In your eyes, we of a brief century or two must appear as little more than denizens quite recently admitted to the privilege of a residence. That you may continue to enjoy peace and happiness, in that land where your fathers so long flourished, is the sincere wish of your obliged friend.

PREFACE.

AT this distant period, when Indian traditions are listened to with the interest that we lend to the events of a dark age, it is not easy to convey a vivid image of the dangers and privations that our ancestors encountered, in preparing the land we enjoy for its present state of security and abundance. It is the humble object of the tale that will be found in the succeeding pages, to perpetuate the recollection of some of the practices and events peculiar to the early days of our history.

The general character of the warfare pursued by the natives is too well known to require any preliminary observations; but it may be advisable to direct the attention of the reader, for a few moments, to those leading circumstances in the history of the times, that may have some connection with the principal business of the legend.

The territory which now composes the three states of Massachusetts, Connecticut, and Rhode Island, is said, by the best-informed of our annalists, to have been formerly occupied by four great nations of Indians, who were, as usual, subdivided into numberless dependent tribes. Of these people, the Massachusetts possessed a large portion of the land which now composes the State of that name; the Wampanoags dwelt in what was once the Colony of Plymouth, and in the northern districts of the Providence Plantations; the Narragansetts held the well-known islands of the beautiful bay which receives its name from their nation, and the more southern counties of the Plantations; while the Pequots, or, as it is ordinarily written and pronounced, the Pequods, were masters of a broad region that lay along the western boundaries of the three other districts.

There is great obscurity thrown around the polity of the Indians who usually occupied the country lying near the sea.

The Europeans, accustomed to despotic governments, very naturally supposed that the chiefs, found in possession of power, were monarchs to whom authority had been transmitted in virtue of their birthrights. They consequently gave them the name of kings.

How far this opinion of the governments of the aborigines was true remains a question, though there is certainly reason to think it less erroneous in respect to the tribes of the Atlantic States, than to those who have since been found further west, where it is sufficiently known that institutions exist which approach much nearer to republics than to monarchies. It may, however, have readily happened that the son, profiting by the advantages of his situation, often succeeded to the authority of the father, by the aid of influence, when the established regulations of the tribe acknowledged no hereditary claim. Let the principle of the descent of power be what it would, it is certain the experience of our ancestors proves, that, in very many instances, the child was seen to occupy the station formerly filled by the father; and that in most of those situations of emergency, in which a people so violent were often placed, the authority he exercised was as summary as it was general.

The appellation of Uncas came, like those of the Cæsars and Pharaohs, to be a sort of synonyme for chief with the Mohegans, a tribe of the Pequods, among whom several warriors of this name were known to govern in due succession. The renowned Metacom, or, as he is better known to the whites, King Philip, was certainly the son of Massasoit, the Sachem of the Wampanoags that the emigrants found in authority when they landed on the rock of Plymouth. Miantonimoh, the daring but hapless rival of that Uncas who ruled the whole of the Pequod nation, was succeeded in authority among the Narragansetts, by his not less heroic and enterprising son, Conanchet; and, even at a much later day, we find instances of this transmission of power, which furnish strong reasons for believing that the order of succession was in the direct line of blood.

The early annals of our history are not wanting in touching and noble examples of savage heroism. Virginia has its legend of the powerful Powhatan and his magnanimous daughter, the ill-requited Pocahontas; and the chronicles of New England are filled with the bold designs and daring enterprises of Miantonimoh, of Metacom, and of Conanchet. All the last-named warriors proved themselves worthy of better fates, dying in a cause and in a manner that, had it been their fortune to have lived in a more advanced state of society, would have enrolled their names among the worthies of the age.

The first serious war to which the settlers of New England were exposed, was the struggle with the Pequods. This people were subdued after a fierce conflict; and from being enemies, all who were not either slain or sent into distant slavery, were glad to become the auxiliaries of their conquerors. This contest occurred within less than twenty years after the Puritans had sought refuge in America.

There is reason to believe that Metacom foresaw the fate of his own people, in the humbled fortune of the Pequods. Though his father had been the earliest and constant friend of the whites, it is probable that the Puritans owed some portion of this amity to a dire necessity. We are told that a terrible malady had raged among the Wampanoags but a short time before the arrival of the emigrants, and that their numbers had been fearfully reduced by its ravages. Some authors have hinted at the probability of this disease having been the yellow fever, whose visitations are known to be at uncertain, and, apparently, at very distant intervals. Whatever might have been the cause of this destruction of his people, Massasoit is believed to have been induced, by the consequences, to cultivate the alliance of a nation who could protect him against the attacks of his ancient and less afflicted foes. But the son appears to have viewed the increasing influence of the whites with eyes more jealous than those of the father. He passed the morning of his life in maturing his great plan for the destruction of the strange race, and his later years were spent in abortive attempts to put this bold design in execution. His restless activity in plotting the confederation against the English, his fierce and ruthless manner of waging the war, his defeat, and his death, are too well known to require repetition.

There is also a wild and romantic interest thrown about the obscure history of a Frenchman of that period. This man is said to have been an officer of rank in the service of his king, and to have belonged to the privileged class which then monopolized all the dignities and emoluments of the kingdom of France. The traditions, and even the written annals of the first century of our possession of America, connect the Baron de la Castine with the Jesuits, who were thought to entertain views of converting the savages to Christianity, not unmingled with the desire of establishing a more temporal dominion over their minds. It is, however, difficult to say whether taste, or religion, or policy, or necessity, induced this nobleman to quit the saloons of Paris for the wilds of the Penobscot. It is merely known that he passed the greater part of his life on that river, in a rude fortress that was then called a palace; that he had many wives, a numerous progeny, and that he possessed a great influence over most of the tribes that dwelt in his vicinity. He is also believed to have been the instrument of furnishing the savages who were hostile to the English, with ammunition, and with weapons of a more deadly character than those used in their earlier wars. In whatever degree he may have participated in the plan to exterminate the Puritans, death prevented him from assisting in the final effort of Metacom.

The Narragansetts are often mentioned in these pages. A few years before the period at which the tale commences, Miantonimoh had waged a ruthless war against Uncas, the Pequod or Mohegan chief. Fortune favored the latter, who, probably assisted by his civilized allies, not only overthrew the bands of the other, but succeeded in capturing the person of his enemy. The chief of the Narragansetts lost his life, through the agency of the whites, on the place that is now known by the appellation of "the Sachem's plain."

It remains only to throw a little light on the leading incidents of the war of King Philip. The first blow was struck in June, 1675, rather more than half a century after the English first landed in New England, and just a century before blood was drawn in the contest which separated the colonies from the mother country. The scene was a settlement near the celebrated Mount Hope, in Rhode Island, where Metacom and his father had both long held their councils. From this point, bloodshed and massacre extended along the whole frontier of New England. Bodies of horse and foot were enrolled to meet the foe, and towns were burnt, and lives were taken by both parties, with little, and often with no respect for age, condition or sex.

In no struggle with the native owners of the soil was the growing power of the whites placed in so great jeopardy, as in this celebrated contest with King Philip. The venerable historian of Connecticut estimates the loss of lives at nearly one-tenth of the whole number of the fighting men, and the destruction of houses and other edifices to have been in an equal proportion. One family in every eleven, throughout all New England, was burnt out. As the colonists nearest the sea were exempt from the danger, an idea may be formed, from this calculation, of the risk and sufferings of those who dwelt in more exposed situations. The Indians did not escape without retaliation. The principal nations, already mentioned, were so much reduced as never afterward to offer any serious resistance to the whites, who have since converted the whole of their ancient hunting grounds into the abodes of civilized man. Metacom, Miantonimoh, and Conanchet, with their warriors, have become the heroes of song and legend, while the descendants of those who laid waste their dominions, and destroyed their race, are yielding a tardy tribute to the high daring and savage grandeur of their characters.

CHAPTER I.

"I may disjoin my hand, but not my faith."
—SHAKESPEARE.

THE incidents of this tale must be sought in a remote period of the annals of America. A colony of self-devoted and pious refugees from religious persecution had landed on the rock of Plymouth, less than half a century before the time at which the narrative commences; and they, and their descendants, had already transformed many a broad waste of wilderness into smiling fields and cheerful villages. The labors of the emigrants had been chiefly limited to the country on the coast, which, by its proximity to the waters that rolled between them and Europe, afforded a semblance of a connection with the land of their forefathers and the distant abodes of civilization. But enterprise, and a desire to search for still more fertile domains, together with the temptation offered by the vast and unknown regions that lay along their western and northern borders, had induced many bold adventurers to penetrate more deeply into the forests. The precise spot to which we desire to transport the imagination of the reader, was one of these establishments of what may, not inaptly, be called the forlorn-hope in the march of civilization through the country.

So little was then known of the great

outlines of the American continent, that, when the Lords Say and Seal, and Brooke, connected with a few associates, obtained a grant of the territory which now composes the State of Connecticut, the king of England affixed his name to a patent which constituted them proprietors of a country that should extend from the shores of the Atlantic to those of the South Sea. Notwithstanding the apparent hopelessness of ever subduing, or of even occupying a territory like this, emigrants from the mother colony of Massachusetts were found ready to commence the herculean labor within fifteen years from the day when they had first put foot upon the well-known rock itself. The fort of Say-Brooke, the towns of Windsor, Hartford, and New Haven, soon sprang into existence, and from that period to this, the little community which then had birth has been steadily, calmly, and prosperously advancing in its career, a model of order and reason, and the hive from which swarms of industrious, hardy, and enlightened yeomen have since spread themselves over a surface so vast as to create an impression that they still aspire to the possession of the immense regions included in their original grant.

Among the religionists whom disgust of persecution had early driven into the voluntary exile of the colonies, was more than a usual proportion of men of character and education. The reckless and the gay younger sons, soldiers unemployed, and students from the Inns of Court, early sought advancement and adventure in the more southern provinces, where slaves offered immunity from labor, and where war, with a bolder and more stirring policy, oftener gave rise to scenes of excitement, and, of course, to the exercise of the faculties best suited to their habits and dispositions. The more grave, and the religiously-disposed, found refuge in the colonies of New England. Thither a multitude of private gentlemen transferred their fortunes and their families, imparting a character of intelligence and a moral elevation to the country, which it has nobly sustained to the present hour.

The nature of the civil wars in England had enlisted many men of deep and sincere piety into the profession of arms. Some of them had retired to the colonies before the troubles of the mother country reached their crisis, and others continued to arrive, throughout the whole period of their existence, until the Restoration; when crowds of those who had been disaffected to the house of Stuart sought the security of these distant possessions.

A stern, fanatical soldier, of the name of Heathcote, had been among the first of his class to throw aside the sword for the implements of industry peculiar to the advancement of a newly-established country. How far the influence of a young wife may have affected his decision, it is not germane to our present object to consider; though the records, from which the matter we are about to relate is gleaned, give reason to suspect that he thought his domestic harmony would not be less secure in the wilds of the new world, than among the companions with whom his earlier associations would naturally have brought him in communion.

Like himself, his consort was born of one of those families, which, taking their rise in the franklins of the times of the Edwards and the Henrys, had become possessors of hereditary landed estates, that, by their gradually-increasing value, had elevated them to the station of small country gentlemen. In most other nations of Europe, they would have been rated in the class of the *petite noblesse*. But the domestic happiness of Capt. Heathcote was doomed to receive a fatal blow from a quarter where circumstances had given him but little reason to apprehend danger.

The very day he landed in the long-wished-for asylum, his wife made him the father of a noble boy, a gift that she bestowed at the melancholy price of her own existence. Twenty years the senior of the woman who had followed his fortunes to these distant regions, the retired warrior had always considered it to be perfectly and absolutely within the order of things, that he himself was to be the first to pay the debt of nature. While the visions which Captain Heathcote entertained of a future world were sufficiently vivid and distinct, there is a reason to think they were seen through a tolerable long vista of quiet and comfortable enjoyment in this. Though the calamity cast an additional aspect of seriousness over a character that was already more than chastened by the subtleties of sectarian doctrines, he was not of a nature to be unmanned by any vicissitudes of human fortune. He lived on, useful and unbending in his habits, a pillar of strength in the way of wisdom and courage to the immediate neighborhood among whom he resided, but reluctant from temper, and from a disposition which had been shadowed by withered happiness, to enact that part in the public affairs of the little state, to which his comparative wealth and previous habits might well have entitled him to aspire.

He gave his son such an education as his own resources and those of the infant colony of Massachusetts afforded, and, by a sort of delusive piety, into whose merits we have no desire to look, he thought he had also furnished a commendable evidence of his own desperate resignation to the will of Providence, in causing him to be publicly christened by the name of Content. His own baptismal appellation was Mark; as indeed had been that of most of his ancestors, for two or three centuries. When the world was a little uppermost in his thoughts, as sometimes happens with the most humbled spirits, he had even been heard to speak of a Sir Mark of his family, who had ridden a knight in the train of one of the more warlike kings of of his native land.

There is some ground for believing that the great parent of evil early looked with a malignant eye on the example of peacefulness, and of unbending morality, that the colonists of New England were setting to the rest of Christendom. At any rate, come from what quarter they might, schisms and doctrinal contentions arose among the emigrants themselves; and men, who together had deserted the firesides of their forefathers in quest of religious peace, were ere long seen separating their fortunes, in order that each might enjoy, unmolested, those peculiar shades of faith, which all had the presumption, no less than the folly, to believe were necessary to propitiate the omnipotent and merciful Father of the universe. If our task were one of theology, a wholesome moral on the vanity, no less than the absurdity of the race, might be here introduced to some advantage.

When Mark Heathcote announced to the community, in which he had now sojourned more than twenty years, that he intended for a second time to establish his altars in the wilderness, in the hope that he and his household might worship God as to them seemed most right, the intelligence was received with a feeling allied to awe. Doctrine and zeal were momentarily forgotten, in the respect and attachment which had been unconsciously created by the united influence of the stern severity of his air, and of the undeniable virtues of his practice. The elders of the settlement communed with him freely and in charity; but the voice of conciliation and alliance came too late. He listened to the reasonings of the ministers, who were assembled from all the adjoining parishes, in sullen respect: and he joined in the petitions for light and instruction that were offered up on the occasion, with the deep reverence with which he ever drew near to the footstool of the Almighty; but he did both in a temper, into which too much positiveness of spiritual pride had entered, to open his heart to that sympathy and charity, which, as they are the characteristics of our mild and forbearing doctrines, should be the study of those who profess to follow their precepts. All that was seemly, and all that was usual, were done; but the purpose of the stubborn sectarian remained unchanged. His final decision is worthy of being recorded.

"My youth was wasted in ungodliness and ignorance," he said, "but in my manhood have I known the Lord. Near two-score years have I toiled for the truth, and all that weary time have I passed in trimming my lamps, lest, like the foolish virgins, I should be caught unprepared; and now, when my loins are girded and my race is nearly run, shall I become a backslider and falsifier of the Word? Much have I endured, as you know, in quitting the earthly mansions of my fathers, and in encountering the dangers of sea and land for the faith; and, rather than let go its hold, will I once more cheerfully devote to the howling wilderness, ease, offspring, and, should it be the will of Providence, life itself!"

The day of parting was one of unfeigned and general sorrow. Notwithstanding the austerity of the old man's character, and the nearly unbending severity of his brow, the milk of human kindness had often been seen distilling from his stern nature in acts that did not admit of misinterpretation. There was scarcely a young beginner in the laborious and ill-requited husbandry of the township he inhabited, a district at no time considered either profitable or fertile, who could not recall some secret and kind aid which had flowed from a hand that, to the world, seemed clenched in cautious and reserved frugality; nor did any of the faithful of his vicinity cast their fortunes together in wedlock, without receiving from him evidence of an interest in their worldly happiness, that was far more substantial than words. On the morning when the vehicles, groaning with the household goods of Mark Heathcote, were seen quitting his door, and taking the road which led to the seaside, not a human being of sufficient age, within many miles of his residence, was absent from the interesting spectacle. The leave-taking, as usual on all serious occasions, was preceded by a hymn and prayer, and then the sternly-minded adventurer embraced his neighbors, with a mien, in which a subdued exterior struggled fearfully and strangely with emotions that more than once threatened to break through even the formidable barriers of his acquired manner. The inhabitants of every building on the road were in the open air, to receive and to return the parting benediction. More than once, they who guided his teams were commanded to halt, and all near, possessing human aspirations and human responsibility, were collected to offer petitions in favor of him who departed and of those who remained. The requests for mortal privileges were somewhat light and hasty, but the askings in behalf of intellectual and spiritual light were long, fervent, and oft-repeated. In this characteristic manner did one of the first of the emigrants to the new world make his second removal into scenes of renewed bodily suffering, privation and danger.

Neither person nor property was transferred from place to place, in this country, at the middle of the seventeenth century, with the dispatch and with the facilities of the present time. The roads were necessarily few and short, and communication by water was irregular, tardy, and far from commodious. A wide barrier of forest lying between that portion of Massachusetts Bay from which Mark Heathcote emigrated, and the spot, near the Connecticut River, to which it was his intention to proceed, he was induced to adopt the latter mode of conveyance. But a long delay intervened between the time when he commenced his short journey to the coast, and the hour when he was finally enabled to embark. During this detention he and his household sojourned among the godly-minded of the narrow peninsula, where there already existed the germ of a flourishing town, and where the spires of a noble and picturesque city now elevate themselves above so many thousand roofs.

The son did not leave the colony of his birth and the haunts of his youth, with the same unwavering obedience to the call of duty as the father. There was a fair, a youthful, and a gentle being in the recently-established town of Boston, of an age, station, opinions, fortunes, and, what was of still greater importance, of sympathies suited to his own. Her form had long mingled with those holy images, which his stern instruction taught him to keep most familiarly before the mirror of his thoughts. It is not surprising, then, that the youth hailed the delay as propitious to his wishes, or that he turned it to the account which the promptings of a pure affection so naturally suggested. He was united to the gentle Ruth Harding only a week before the father sailed on his second pilgrimage.

It is not our intention to dwell on the incidents of the voyage. Though the genius of an extraordinary man had discovered the world which was now beginning to fill with civilized men, navigation at that day was not brilliant in accomplishments. A passage among the shoals of Nantucket must have been one of actual danger, no less than of terror; and the ascent of the Connecticut itself was an exploit worthy of being mentioned. In due time the adventurers arrived at the English fort of Hartford, where they tarried for the season, in order to obtain rest and spiritual comfort. But the peculiarity of doctrine, on which Mark Heathcote laid so much stress, was one that rendered it advisable for him to retire still further from the haunts of men. Accompanied by a few followers, he proceeded on an exploring expedition, and the end of the summer found him once more established on an estate that he had acquired by the usual simple forms practiced in the colonies, and at the trifling cost for which extensive districts were then set apart as the property of individuals.

The love of the things of this life, while it certainly existed, was far from being predominant in the affections of the Puritan. He was frugal from habit and principle, more than from an undue longing after worldly wealth. He contented himself, therefore, with acquiring an estate that should be valuable, rather from its quality and beauty, than from its extent. Many such places offered themselves, between the settlements of Weathersfield and Hartford and that imaginary line which separated the possessions of the colony he had quitted, from those of the one he joined. He made his location, as it is termed in the language of the country, near the northern boundary of the latter. This spot, by the aid of an expenditure, that might have been considered lavish for the country and the age; of some lingering of taste, which even the self-denying and subdued habits of his later life had not entirely extinguished; and of great natural beauty in the distribution of land, water, and wood, the emigrant contrived to convert into an abode that was not more desirable for its retirement from the temptations of the world, than for its rural loveliness.

After this memorable act of conscientious self-devotion, years passed away in quiet, amid a species of negative prosperity. Rumors from the old world reached the ears of the tenants of this secluded settlement, months after the events to which they referred were elsewhere forgotten, and tumults and wars in the sister colonies came to their knowledge only at distant and tardy intervals. In the meantime, the limits of the colonial establishments were gradually extending themselves, and valleys were beginning to be cleared nearer and nearer to their own. Old age had now begun to make some visible impression on the iron frame of the captain ; and the fresh color of youth and health, with which his son had entered the forest, was giving way to the brown covering produced by exposure and toil. We say of toil, for, independently of the habits and opinions of the country, which strongly reprobated idleness, even in those most gifted by fortune, the daily difficulties of their situation, the chase, and the long and intricate passages that the veteran himself was compelled to adventure in the surrounding forest, partook largely of the nature of the term we have used.

Ruth continued blooming and youthful, though maternal anxiety was soon added to her other causes of care. Still, for a long season, naught occurred to excite extraordinary regrets for the step they had taken, or to create particular uneasiness in behalf of the future. The borderers, for such by their frontier position they had in truth become, heard the strange and awful tidings of the dethronement of one king, of the interregnum, as a reign of more than usual vigor and prosperity is called, and of the restoration of the son of him who is strangely enough termed a martyr. To all these eventful and unwonted chances in the fortunes of kings, Mark Heathcote listened with deep and reverential submission to the will of him in whose eyes crowns and scepters are merely the more costly baubles of the world. Like most of his contemporaries, who had sought shelter in the western continent, his political opinions, if not absolutely republican, had a leaning to liberty that was strongly in opposition to the doctrine of the divine rights of the monarch, while he had been too far removed from the stirring passions which had gradually excited those nearer to the throne, to lose their respect for its sanctity, and to sully its brightness with blood.

When the transient and straggling visitors that, at long intervals, visited his settlement, spoke of the Protector, who for so many years ruled England with an iron hand, the eyes of the old man would gleam with sudden and singular interest ; and once, when commenting after evening prayer on the vanity and vicissitudes of this life, he acknowledged that the extraordinary individual who was, in substance if not in name, seated on the throne of the Plantagenets, had been the boon companion and ungodly associate of many of his youthful hours. Then would follow a long, wholesome, extemporaneous homily on the idleness of setting the affections on the things of life, and a half-suppressed, but still intelligible commendation of the wiser course which had led him to raise his own tabernacle in the wilderness, instead of weakening the chances of eternal glory by striving too much for the possession of the treacherous vanities of the world.

But even the gentle and ordinarily little observant Ruth might trace the kindling of the eye, the knitting of the brow, and the flushings of his pale and furrowed cheek, as the murdereous conflicts of the civil wars became the themes of the ancient soldier's discourse. There were moments when religious submission, and we had almost said religious precepts, were partially forgotten, as he explained to his attentive son and listening grandchild, the nature of the onset, or the quality and dignity of the retreat. At such times, his still nervous hand would even wield the blade, in order to instruct the latter in its uses, and many a long winter evening was passed in thus indirectly teaching an art that was so much at variance with the mandates of his divine Master. The chastened soldier, however, never forgot to close his instruction with a petition extraordinary, in the customary prayer, that no descendant of his should ever take life from a being unprepared to die, except in justifiable defense of his faith, his person, or his lawful rights. It must be admitted, that a liberal construction of the reserved privileges would leave sufficient matter to exercise the subtlety of one subject to any extraordinary propensity to arms.

Few opportunities were, however, offered, in their remote situation and with their peaceful habits, for the practice of a theory that had been taught in so many lessons. Indian alarms, as they were termed, were not unfrequent, but, as yet, they had never produced more than terror in the bosoms of the gentle Ruth and her young offspring. It is true, they had heard of travelers massacred, and of families separated by captivity, but, either by a happy fortune, or by more than ordinary prudence in the settlers who were established along that immediate frontier, the knife and the tomahawk had as yet been sparingly used in the colony of Connecticut. A threatening and dangerous struggle with the Dutch, in the adjoining province of New-Netherlands, had been averted by the foresight and moderation of the rulers of the new plantations; and though a warlike and powerful native chief kept the neighboring colonies of Massachusetts and Rhode Island in a state of constant watchfulness, from the cause just mentioned the apprehension of danger was greatly weakened in the breasts of those so remote as the individuals who composed the family of our emigrant.

In this quiet manner did years glide by, the surrounding wilderness slowly retreating from the habitations of the Heathcotes, until they found themselves in possession of as many of the comforts of life as their utter seclusion from the rest of the world could give them reason to expect.

With this preliminary explanation we shall refer the reader to the succeeding narrative for a more minute, and we hope for a more interesting account of the incidents of a legend that may prove too homely for the tastes of those whose imaginations seek the excitement of scenes more stirring, or of a condition of life less natural.

CHAPTER II.

"Sir, I do know you;
And dare, upon the warrant of my art,
Commend a dear thing to you."—KING LEAR.

AT the precise time when the action of our piece commences, a fine and fruitful season was drawing to a close. The harvests of hay and of the smaller corns had long been over, and the younger Heathcote, with his laborers, had passed a day in depriving the luxuriant maize of its tops, in order to secure the nutritious blades for fodder, and to admit the sun and air to harden a grain, that is almost considered the staple production of the region he inhabited. The veteran Mark had ridden among the workmen during their light toil, as well to enjoy a sight which promised abundance to his flocks and herds, as to throw in, on occasion, some wholesome spiritual precept, in which doctrinal subtlety was far more prominent than the rules of practice. The hirelings of his son, for he had long since yielded the management of the estate to Content, were, without an exception, young men born in the country, and long use and much training had accustomed them to a blending of religious exercises with most of the employments of life.

They listened, therefore, with respect, nor did an impious smile or an impatient glance escape the lightest-minded of their number during his exhortations, though the homilies of the old man were neither very brief, nor particularly original. But devotion to the one great cause of their existence, austere habits, and unrelaxed industry in keeping alive a flame of zeal that had been kindled in the other hemisphere, to burn longest and brightest in this, had interwoven the practice mentioned with most of the opinions and pleasures of these metaphysical, though simple-minded people. The toil went on none the less cheerily for the extraordinary accompaniment, and Content himself, by a certain glimmering of superstition, which appears to be the concomitant of excessive religious zeal, was fain to think that the sun shone more brightly on their labors, and that the earth gave forth more of its fruits while these holy sentiments were flowing from the lips of a father whom he piously loved and deeply reverenced.

But when the sun, usually at that season, in the climate of Connecticut, a bright unshrouded orb, fell towards the tree-tops which bounded the western horizon, the old man began to grow weary with his own well-doing. He therefore finished his discourse with a wholesome admonition to the youths to complete their tasks before they quitted the field; and, turning the head of his horse, he rode slowly, and with a musing air, toward the dwellings. It is probable that for some time the thoughts of Mark were occupied with the intellectual matter he had just been handling with so much power; but when his little nag stopped of itself on a small eminence, which the crooked cow-path he was following crossed, his mind yielded to the impression of more worldly and more sensible objects. As the scene that drew his contemplations from so many abstract theories to the realities of life was peculiar to the country, and is more or less connected with the subject of our tale, we shall endeavor briefly to describe it.

A small tributary of the Connecticut divided the view into two nearly equal parts. The fertile flats that extended on each of its banks for more than a mile, had been early stripped of their burden of forest, and they now lay in placid meadows, or in fields from which the grain of the season had lately disappeared, and over which the plow had already left the marks of recent tillage. The whole of the plain, which ascended gently from the rivulet toward the forest, was subdivided into inclosures by numberless fences, constructed in the rude but substantial manner of the country. Rails, in which lightness and economy of wood had been but little consulted, lying in zigzag lines, like the approaches which the besieger makes in his cautious advance to the hostile fortress, were piled on each other, until barriers seven or eight feet in height were interposed to the inroads of vicious cattle. In one spot, a large square vacancy had been cut into the forest, and though numberless stumps of trees darkened its surface, as indeed they did many of the fields on the flats themselves, bright, green grain was sprouting forth luxuriantly from the rich and virgin soil.

High against the side of an adjacent hill, that might aspire to be called a low rocky mountain, a similar invasion had been made on the domain of the trees; but caprice or convenience had induced an abandonment of the clearing, after it had ill requited the toil of felling the timber by a single crop. In this spot, straggling, girdled, and consequently dead trees, piles of logs, and black and charred stumps were seen, deforming the beauty of a field that would otherwise have been striking from its deep setting in the woods.

Much of the surface of this opening, too, was now concealed by bushes, of what is termed the second growth, though here and there places appeared in which the luxuriant white clover, natural to the country, had followed the close grazing of the flocks. The eyes of Mark were bent inquiringly on this clearing, which by an air line might have been half a mile from the place where his horse had stopped, for the sounds of a dozen differently toned cow-bells were brought on the still air of the evening to his ears, from among its bushes.

The evidences of civilization were the least equivocal, however, on and around a natural elevation in the land, which arose so suddenly on the very bank of the stream as to give to it the appearance of a work of art. Whether these mounds once existed everywhere on the face of earth, and have disappeared before long tillage and labor, we shall not presume to conjecture; but we have reason to think that they occur much more frequently in certain parts of our own country than in any other familiarly known to ordinary travelers, unless, perhaps, it may be in some of the valleys of Switzerland. The practiced veteran had chosen the summit of this flattened cone for the establishment of that species of military defense which the situation of the country, and the character of the enemy he had to guard against, rendered advisable, as well as customary.

The dwelling was of wood, and constructed of the ordinary frame-work, with its thin covering of boards. It was long, low, and irregular, bearing marks of having been reared at different periods, as the wants of an increasing family had required additional accommodation. It stood near the verge of the natural declivity, and on that side of the hill where its base was washed by the rivulet, a rude piazza stretching along the whole of its front, and overhanging the stream. Several large, irregular, and clumsy chimneys rose out of different parts of the roofs, another proof that comfort rather than taste had been consulted in the disposition of the buildings. There were also two or three detached offices on the summit of the hill, placed near the dwellings, and at points most convenient for their several uses. A stranger might have remarked that they were so disposed as to form, as far as they went, the different sides of a hollow square.

Notwithstanding the great length of the principal building, and the disposition of the more minute and detached parts, this desirable formation would not, however, have been obtained, if it were not that two rows of rude constructions in logs, from which the bark had not even been stripped, served to eke out the parts that had been deficient. These primeval edifices were used to contain various domestic articles, no less than provisions; they also furnished numerous lodging-rooms for the laborers and the inferior dependents of the farm. By the aid of a few strong and high gates of hewn timber those parts of the building which had not been made to unite in the original construction, were sufficiently connected to oppose so many barriers against admission into the inner court.

But the building which was most conspicuous by its position, no less than by the singularity of its construction, stood on a low, artificial mound, in the center of the quadrangle. It was high, hexagonal in shape, and crowned with a roof that came to a point, and from whose peak rose a towering flagstaff. The foundation was of stone; but, at the height of a man above the earth, the sides were made of massive, squared logs, firmly united by an ingenious combination of their ends, as well as by perpendicular supporters pinned closely into their sides. In this citadel, or block-house, as from its materials it was technically called, there were two different tiers of long, narrow loopholes, but no regular windows. The rays of the setting sun, however, glittering on one or two small openings in the roof, in which glass had been set, furnished evidence that the summit of the building was sometimes used for other purposes than those of defense.

About half way up the sides of the eminence on which the building stood was an unbroken line of high palisadoes, made of the bodies of young trees, firmly knitted together by braces and horizontal pieces of timber, and evidently kept in a state of jealous and complete repair. The air of the whole of this frontier fortress was neat and comfortable, and, considering that the use of artillery was unknown to these forests, not unmilitary.

At no great distance from the base of the hill stood the barns and the stables. They were surrounded by a vast range of rude but warm sheds, beneath which sheep and horned cattle were usually sheltered from the storms of the rigorous winters of the climate. The surfaces of the meadows immediately around the out-buildings were of a smoother and richer sward than those in the distance, and the fences were on a far more artificial, and perhaps durable, though scarcely on a more serviceable plan. A large orchard of some ten or fifteen years' growth, too, added greatly to the air of improvement, which put this smiling valley in such strong and pleasing contrast to the endless and nearly untenanted woods by which is was environed.

Of the interminable forest, it is not necessary to speak. With the solitary exception on the mountain-side, and of here and there a windrow, along which the trees had been uprooted by the furious blasts which sometimes sweep off acres of our trees in a minute, the eye could find no other object to study in the vast setting of this quiet rural picture but the seemingly endless maze of wilderness. The broken surface of the land, however, limited the view to a horizon of no great extent, though the art of man could scarcely devise colors so vivid or so gay as those which were afforded by the brilliant hues of the foliage. The keen, biting frosts, known at the close of a New England autumn, had already touched the broad and fringed leaves of the maples, and the sudden and secret process had been wrought upon all the other varieties of the forest, producing that magical effect which can be nowhere seen except in regions in which nature is so bountiful and luxuriant in summer, and so sudden and so stern in the change of the seasons.

Over this picture of prosperity and peace, the eye of old Mark Heathcote wandered with a keen degree of worldly prudence. The melancholy sounds of the various toned bells, ringing hollow and plaintively among the arches of the woods, gave him reason to believe that the herds of the family were returning voluntarily from their unlimited forest pasturage. His grandson, a fine, spirited boy of some fourteen years, was approaching through the fields. The youngster drove before him a small flock, which domestic necessity compelled the family to keep at great occasional loss, and a heavy expense of time and trouble; both of which could alone protect them from the ravages of the beasts of prey. A species of half-witted serving-lad, whom charity had induced the old man to harbor among his dependents, was seen issuing from the woods, nearly in a line with the neglected clearing on the mountain-side. The latter advanced, shouting and urging before him a drove of colts, as shaggy, as wayward, and nearly as untamed as himself.

" How now, weak one," said the Puritan, with a severe eye, as the two lads approached him with their several charges from different directions, and nearly at the same instant ; " how now, sirrah ! dost worry the cattle in this gait when the eyes of the prudent are turned from thee ? Do as thou wouldst be done by, is a just and healthful admonition, that the learned and the simple, the weak and the strong of mind, should alike recall to their thoughts and their practice. I do not not know that an over-driven colt will be at all more apt to make a gentle and useful beast in its prime, than one treated with kindness and care."

" I believe the evil one has got into all the kine, no less than into the foals," sullenly returned the lad ; " I've called to them in anger, and I've spoken to them as if they had been my natural kin, and yet neither fair word nor foul tongue will bring them to hearken to advice. There is something frightful in the woods this very sundown, master ; or colts that I have driven the summer through would not be apt to give this unfair treatment to one they ought to know to be their friend."

" Thy sheep are counted, Mark ? " resumed the grandfather, turning toward his descendant with a less austere, but always an authoritative brow ; " thy mother hath need of every fleece to provide covering for thee and others like thee ; thou knowest, child, that the creatures are few, and our winters weary and cold."

" My mother's loom shall never be idle from carelessness of mine," returned the confident boy ; " but counting and wishing cannot make seven-and-thirty fleeces, where there are only six-and-thirty backs to carry them. I have been an hour among the briers and bushes of the hill logging, looking for the lost wether, and yet neither lock, hoof, hide, nor horn, is there to say what hath befallen the animal."

"Thou hath lost a sheep! this carelessness will cause thy mother to grieve!"

"Grandfather, I have been no idler. Since the last hunt, the flock hath been allowed to browse the woods; for no man, in all that week, saw wolf, panther, or bear, though the country was up, from the great river to the outer settlements of the colony. The biggest four-footed animal that lost its hide in the muster was a thin-ribbed deer; and the stoutest battle given, was between wild Whittal Ring, here, and a woodchuck that kept him at arm's-length for the better part of an afternoon."

"The tale may be true, but it neither finds that which is lost, nor completeth the number of thy mother's flock. Hast thou ridden carefully throughout the clearing? It is not long since I saw the animal grazing in that quarter. What hast thou twisting in thy fingers, in that wasteful and unthankful manner, Whittal?"

"What would make a winter blanket, if there was enough of it! wool! and wool, too, that came from the thigh of old Straight-Horns; else have I forgotten a leg that gives the longest and coarsest hair at the shearing."

"That truly seemeth a lock from the animal that is wanting," exclaimed the other boy. "There is no other creature in the flock with fleece so coarse and shaggy. Where found you the handful, Whittal Ring?"

"Growing on the branch of a thorn. Queer fruit this, masters, to be seen where young plums ought to ripen!"

"Go, go," interrupted the old man; "thou idlest, and misspendest the time in vain talk. Go, fold thy flock, Mark; and do thou, weak one, house thy charge with less uproar than is wont. We should remember that the voice is given to man, firstly, that he may improve the blessing in thanksgivings and petitions; secondly, to communicate such gifts as may be imparted to himself, and which it is his bounden duty to attempt to impart to others; and then, thirdly, to declare his natural wants and inclinations."

With this admonition, which probably proceeded from a secret consciousness in the Puritan that he had permitted a momentary cloud of selfishness to obscure the brightness of his faith, the party separated. The grandson and the hireling took their several ways to the folds, while old Mark himself slowly continued his course toward the dwellings. It was near enough to the hours of darkness to render the preparations we have mentioned prudent; still, no urgency called for particular haste, in the return of the veteran to the shelter and protection of his own comfortable and secure abode. He therefore loitered along the path, occasionally stopping to look into the prospects of the young crops that were beginning to spring up in readiness for the coming year, and at times bending his gaze around the whole of his limited horizon, like one who had the habit of exceeding and unremitted care.

One of these numerous pauses promised to be much longer than usual. Instead of keeping his understanding eye on the grain, the look of the old man appeared fastened, as by a charm, on some distant and obscure object. Doubt and uncertainty, for many minutes, seemed to mingle in his gaze. But all hesitation had apparently disappeared, as his lips severed, and he spoke, perhaps unconsciously to himself, aloud.

"It is no deception," were the low words, "but a living and an accountable creature of the Lord's. Many a day has passed since such a sight hath been witnessed in this vale; but my eye greatly deceives me, or yonder cometh one ready to ask for hospitality, and, peradventure, for Christian and brotherly communion."

The sight of the aged emigrant had not deceived him. One, who appeared a wayworn and weary traveler, had indeed ridden out of the forest at a point where a path, that was easier to be traced by the blazed trees that lay along its route than by any marks on the earth itself, issued into the cleared land. The progress of the stranger had at first been so wary and slow, as to bear the manner of exceeding and mysterious caution. The blind road, along which he must have ridden not only far but hard, or night had certainly overtaken him in the woods, led to one of the distant settlements that lay near to the fertile banks of the Connecticut. Few ever followed its windings but they who had especial affairs, or extraordinary communion in the way of religious friendships, with the proprietors of the Wish-Ton-Wish, as, in commemoration of the first bird that had been seen by the emigrants, the valley of the Heathcotes was called.

Once fairly in view, any doubt or apprehension that the stranger might at first have entertained, disappeared. He rode boldly and steadily forward, until he drew a rein that his impoverished and weary beast gladly obeyed within a few feet of the proprietor of the valley, whose gaze had never ceased to watch his movements, from the instant when the other first came within view. Before speaking, the stranger, a man whose head was getting gray, apparently as much with hardship as with time, and one whose great weight would have proved a grievous burden, in a long ride, to even a better-conditioned beast than the ill-favored provincial hack he had ridden, dismounted, and threw the bridle loose upon the drooping neck of the animal. The latter, without a moment's delay, and with a greediness that denoted long abstinence, profited by its liberty to crop the herbage where it stood.

"I cannot be mistaken, when I suppose that I have at length reached the valley of the Wish-Ton-Wish," the visitor said, touching a soiled and slouched beaver that more than half concealed his features. The question was put in an English that bespoke a descent from those who dwell in the midland counties of the mother country, rather than in that intonation which is still to be traced, equally in the western portions of England and in the eastern States of the Union. Notwithstanding the purity of his accent, there was enough in the form of his speech to denote a severe compliance with the fashion of the religionists of the times. He used that measured and methodical tone, which was, singularly enough, believed to distinguish an entire absence of affectation in language.

"Thou hast reached the dwelling of him thou seekest; one who is a submissive sojourner in the wilderness of the world, and an humble servitor in the outer temple."

"This then is Mark Heathcote!" repeated the stranger in tones of interest, regarding the other with a look of long, and, possibly, of suspicious investigation.

"Such is the name I bear. A fitting confidence in him who knows so well how to change the wilds into the haunts of men, and much suffering, have made me the master of what thou seest. Whether thou comest to tarry a night, a week, a month, or even for a still longer season, as a brother in care, and I doubt not one who striveth for the right, I bid thee welcome."

The stranger thanked his host by a slow inclination of the head; but the gaze, which began to partake a little of the look of recognition, was still too earnest and engrossing to admit of verbal reply. On the other hand, though the old man had scanned the broad and rusty beaver, the coarse and well-worn doublet, the heavy boots, and, in short, the whole attire of his visitor, in which he saw no vain conformity to idle fashions to condemn, it was evident that personal recollection had not the smallest influence in quickening his hospitality.

"Thou has arrived happily," continued the Puritan; "had night overtaken thee in the forest, unless much practiced in the shifts of our young woodsmen, hunger, frost, and a supperless bed of brush, would have given thee motive to think more of the body than is either profitable or seemly."

The stranger might possibly have known the embarrassment of these several hardships; for the quick and unconscious glance he threw over his soiled dress should have betrayed some familiarity, already, with the privations to which his host alluded. As neither of them, however, seemed disposed to waste further time on matters of such light moment, the traveler put an arm through the bridle of his horse, and, in obedience to an invitation from the owner of the dwelling, they took their way toward the fortified edifice on the natural mound.

The task of furnishing litter and provender to the jaded beast was performed by Whittal Ring under the inspection, and at times under the instructions, of its owner and his host, both of whom appeared to take a kind and commendable interest in the comfort of a faithful hack, that had evidently suffered long and much in the service of its master. When this duty was discharged, the old man and his unknown guest entered the house together; the frank and unpretending hospitality of a country like that they were in rendering suspicion or hesitation qualities that were unknown to the reception of a man of white blood; more especially if he spoke the language of the island, which was then first sending out its swarms to subdue and possess so large a portion of a continent that nearly divides the earth in moieties.

CHAPTER III.

"This is most strange; your father's in some passion
That works him strongly."—TEMPEST.

A FEW hours made a great change in the occupations of the different members of our simple and secluded family. The kine had yielded their nightly tribute; the oxen had been released from the yoke, and were now secure beneath their sheds; the sheep were in their folds, safe from the assaults of the prowling wolf;

and care had been taken to see that every-thing possessing life was gathered within the particular defenses that were provided for its security and comfort. But while all this caution was used in behalf of liv-ing things, the utmost indifference pre-vailed on the subject of that species of movable property which elsewhere would have been guarded with at least an equal jealousy. The homely fabrics of the looms of Ruth lay on their bleaching-ground, to drink in the night-dew; and plows, harrows, carts, saddles, and other similar articles, were left in situations so exposed as to prove that the hand of man had oc-cupations so numerous and so urgent as to render it inconvenient to bestow labor where it was not considered absolutely necessary.

Content himself was the last to quit the fields and the out-buildings. When he reached the postern in the palisadoes, he stopped to call to those above him, in or-der to learn if any yet lingered without the wooden barriers. The answer being in the negative, he entered, and drawing to the small but heavy gate, he secured it with bar, bolt and lock, carefully and jealously, with his own hand. As this was no more than a nightly and necessary pre-caution, the affairs of the family received no interruption. The meal of the hour was soon ended; and conversation, with those light toils which are peculiar to the long evenings of the fall and winter in families on the frontier, succeeded as fitting em-ployments to close the business of a labo-rious and well spent day.

Notwithstanding the entire simplicity which marked the opinions and usages of the colonists at that period, and the great equality of condition which even to this hour distinguishes the particular commu-nity of which we write, choice and inclina-tion drew some natural distinctions in the ordinary intercourse of the inmates of the Heathcote family.

A fire so bright and cheerful blazed on an enormous hearth in a sort of upper kitchen, as to render candles or torches unnecessary. Around it were seated six or seven hardy and athletic young men, some drawing coarse tools carefully through the curvatures of ox-bows, others scraping down the helves of axes, or perhaps fashioning sticks of birch into homely but convenient brooms. A de-mure, side-looking young woman kept her great wheel in motion, while one or two others were passing from room to room, with the notable and stirring industry of handmaidens busied in the more familiar cares of the household. A door com-municated with an inner and superior ap-partment. Here was a smaller but an equally cheerful fire, a floor which had recently been swept, while that without had been freshly sprinkled with river sand; candles of tallow, on a table of cherry-wood from the neighboring forest; walls that were wainscoted in tbe black oak of the country, and a few other arti-cles of a fashion so antique, and of orna-ments so ingenious and rich, as to announce that they had been transported from be-yond sea. Above the mantle were sus-pended the armorial bearings of the Heathcotes and the Hardings, elaborately emblazoned in tent-stitch.

The principal personages of the family were seated around the latter hearth, while a straggler from the other room of more than usual curiosity had placed him-self among them, marking the distinction in ranks, or rather in situation, merely by the extraordinary care which he took that none of the scrapings should litter the spotless oaken floor.

Until this period of the evening, the duties of hospitality and the observances of religion had prevented familiar dis-course. But the offices of the housewife were now ended for the night, the hand-maidens had all retired to their wheels, and, as the bustle of a busy and more stirring domestic industry ceased, the cold and self-restrained silence which had hitherto only been broken by distant and brief observations of courtesy, or by some wholesome allusion to the lost and proba-tionary condition of man, seemed to in-vite an intercourse of a more general character.

"You entered my clearing by the southern path," commenced Mark Heath-cote, addressing himself to his guest with sufficient courtesy, "and needs must bring tidings from the towns on the river side. Has aught been done by our coun-cilors at home in the matter that per-taineth so closely to the well-being of this colony?"

"You would have me say whether he that now sitteth on the throne of England hath listened to the petitions of his people in this province, and hath granted them protection against the abuses which might so readily flow out of his own ill-advised will, or out of the violence and injustice of his successors?"

"We will render unto Cæsar the things that are Cæsar's, and speak reverently of men having authority. I would fain know whether the agent sent by our peo-ple hath gained the ears of those who counsel the prince, and obtained that which he sought?"

"He hath done more," returned the

stranger, with singular asperity; "he hath even gained the ear of the Lord's Anointed."

"Then is Charles of better mind and of stronger justice than report hath spoken. We were told that light manners and unprofitable companions had led him to think more of the vanities of the world and less of the wants of those over whom he hath been called by Providence to rule, than is meet for one that sitteth on a high place. I rejoice that the arguments of the man we sent have prevailed over more evil promptings, and that peace and freedom of conscience are likely to be the fruits of the undertaking. In what manner hath he seen fit to order the future government of this people?"

"Much as it hath ever stood—by their own ordinances. Winthrop hath returned, and is the bearer of a royal charter which granteth all the rights long claimed and practiced. None now dwell under the crown of Britain with fewer offensive demands on their consciences, or with lighter calls on their political duties, than the men of Connecticut."

"It is fitting that thanks should be rendered therefor where thanks are most due," said the Puritan, folding his hands on his bosom, and sitting for a moment with closed eyes, like one who communed with an unseen being. "Is it known by what manner of argument the Lord moved the heart of the prince to hearken to our wants; or was it an open and manifest token of his power?"

"I think it must needs have been the latter," rejoined the visitor, with a manner that grew still more caustic and emphatic. "The bauble, that was the visible agent, could not have weighed greatly with one so proudly seated before the eyes of men."

Until this point in the discourse, Content and Ruth, with their offspring, and two or three other individuals who composed the audience, had listened with the demure gravity which characterized the manners of the country. The language, united with the ill-concealed sarcasm conveyed by the countenance, no less than the emphasis of the speaker, caused them now to raise their eyes, as by a common impulse. The word "bauble" was audibly and curiously repeated. But the look of cold irony had already passed from the features of the stranger, and it had given place to a stern and fixed austerity that imparted a character of grimness to his hard and sunburnt visage. Still he betrayed no disposition to shrink from the subject; but, after regarding his auditors with a glance in which pride and suspicion were strongly blended, he resumed the discourse.

"It is known," he added, "that the grandfather of him the good people of these settlements have commissioned to bear their wants over the sea, lived in the favor of the man who last sat upon the throne of England; and a rumor goeth forth, that the Stuart, in a moment of princely condescension, once decked the finger of his subject with a ring wrought in a curious fashion. It was a token of the love which a monarch may bear a man."

"Such gifts are beacons of friendship, but may not be used as gay and sinful ornaments," observed Mark, while the other paused like one who wished none of the bitterness of his allusions to be lost.

"It matters not whether the bauble lay in the coffers of the Winthrops, or has long been glittering before the eyes of the faithful, in the bay, since it hath finally proved to be a jewel of price," continued the stranger. "It is said in secret that this ring hath returned to the finger of a Stuart, and it is openly proclaimed that Connecticut hath a charter!"

Content and his wife regarded each other in melancholy amazement. Such an evidence of wanton levity and of unworthiness of motive, in one who was intrusted with the gift of earthly government, pained their simple and upright minds, while old Mark, of still more decided and exaggerated ideas of spiritual perfection, distinctly groaned aloud. The stranger took a sensible pleasure in this testimony of their abhorrence of so gross and so unworthy a venality, though he saw no occasion to heighten its effect by further speech. When his host stood erect, and in a voice that was accustomed to obedience called on his family to join, in behalf of the reckless ruler of the land of their fathers, in a petition to him who alone could soften the hearts of princes, he also arose from his seat. But even in this act of devotion, the stranger bore the air of one who wished to do pleasure to his entertainers, rather than to obtain that which was asked.

The prayer, though short, was pointed, fervent, and sufficiently personal. The wheels in the outer room ceased their hum, and a general movement denoted that all there had arisen to join in the office; while one or two of their number, impelled by deeper piety or stronger interest, drew near to the open door between the rooms, in order to listen. With this singular but characteristic interruption, that particular branch of the discourse, which had given rise to it, altogether ceased.

"And have we reason to dread a rising of the savages on the borders?" asked Content, when he found that the moved spirit of his father was not yet sufficiently calmed to return to the examination of temporal things; "one who brought wares from the towns below, a few months since, recited reasons to fear a movement among the red men."

The subject had not sufficient interest to open the ears of the stranger. He was deaf, or he chose to affect deafness, to the interrogatory. Laying his two large and weather - worn, though still muscular hands, on a visage that was much darkened by exposure, he appeared to shut out the objects of the world, while he communed deeply, and, as would seem by a slight tremor, that shook even his powerful frame, terribly, with his own thoughts.

"We have many to whom our hearts strongly cling, to heighten the smallest symptom of alarm from that quarter," added the tender and anxious mother, her eye glancing at the uplifted countenances of two little girls, who, busied with their light needle-work, sat on stools at her feet. "But I rejoice to see that one, who hath journeyed from parts where the minds of the savages must be better understood, hath not feared to do it unarmed."

The traveler slowly uncovered his features, and the glance that his eye shot over the face of the last speaker was not without a gentle and interested expression. Instantly recovering his composure, he arose, and, turning to the double leathern sack, which had been borne on the crupper of his nag, and which now lay at no great distance from his seat, he drew a pair of horseman's pistols from two well contrived pockets in its sides, and laid them deliberately on the table.

"Though little disposed to seek an encounter with any bearing the image of man," he said, "I have not neglected the usual precautions of those who enter the wilderness. Here are weapons that, in steady hands, might easily take life, or, at need, preserve it."

The young Mark drew near with boyish curiosity, and while one finger ventured to touch a lock, as he stole a conscious glance of wrong-doing towards his mother, he said, with as much of contempt in his air as the schooling of his manners would allow—

"An Indian arrow would make a surer aim than a bore as short as this! When the trainer from the Hartford town struck the wild-cat on the hill clearing, he sent the bullet from a five-foot barrel; besides, this short-sighted gun would be a dull weapon in a hug against the keen-edged knife that the wicked Wampanoag is known to carry."

"Boy, thy years are few, and thy boldness of speech marvelous," sternly interrupted his parent in the second degree.

The stranger manifested no displeasure at the confident language of the lad. Encouraging him with a look, which plainly proclaimed that martial qualities in no degree lessened the stripling in his favor, he observed that—

"The youth who is not afraid to think of the fight, or to reason on its chances, will lead to a manhood of spirit and independence. A hundred thousand striplings like this might have spared Winthrop his jewel, and the Stuart the shame of yielding to so vain and so trivial a bribe. But thou may'st also see, child, that had we come to the death-hug, the wicked Wampanoag might have found a blade as keen as his own."

The stranger, while speaking, loosened a few strings of his doublet, and thrust a hand into his bosom. The action enabled more than one eye to catch a momentary glimpse of a weapon of the same description, but of a size much smaller than those he had already so freely exhibited. As he immediately withdrew the member, and again closed the garment with studied care, no one presumed to advert to the circumstance, but all turned their attention to the long sharp hunting knife that he deposited by the side of the pistols, as he concluded. Mark ventured to open its blade, but he turned away with sudden consciousness, when he found that a few fibers of coarse, shaggy wool, that were drawn from the loosened joint, adhered to his fingers.

"Straight-Horns has been against a bush sharper than the thorn!" exclaimed Whittal Ring, who had been at hand, and who watched with childish admiration the smallest proceeding of the different individuals. "A steel for the back of the blade, a few dried leaves and broken sticks, with such a carver, would soon make roast and broiled of the old bell-wether himself. I know that the hair of all my colts is sorrel, and I counted five at sundown, which is just as many as went loping through the underbrush when I loosened them from the hopples in the morning; but six-and-thirty backs can never carry seven-and-thirty growing fleeces of unsheared wool. Master knows that, for he is a scholar and can count a hundred!"

The allusion to the fate of the lost sheep was so plain as to admit of no interpretation of the meaning of the witless speaker. Animals of that class were of the last importance to the comforts of the settlers, and there was not probably one within hearing of Whittal Ring that was at all ignorant of the import of his words. Indeed, the loud chuckle and the open and deriding manner with which the lad himself held above his head the hairy fibers that he had snatched from young Mark, allowed of no concealment had it been desirable.

"This feeble-gifted youth would hint that thy knife hath proved its edge on a wether that is missing from our flock, since the animals went on their mountain range in the morning," said the host, calmly; though even he bent his eye to the floor, as he waited for an answer to a remark, direct as the one his sense of justice, and his indomitable love of right, had prompted.

The stranger demanded, in a voice that lost none of its depth or firmness, "Is hunger a crime, that they who dwell so far from the haunts of selfishness visit it with their anger?"

"The foot of Christian man never approached the gates of Wish-Ton-Wish to be turned away in uncharitableness, but that which is freely given should not be taken in licentiousness. From off the hill where my flock is wont to graze it is easy, through many an opening of the forest, to see these roofs; and it would have been better that the body should languish, than that a grievous sin should be placed on that immortal spirit which is already too deeply laden, unless thou art far more happy than others of the fallen race of Adam."

"Mark Heathcote," said the accused, and ever with an unwavering tone, "look further at those weapons, which, if a guilty man, I have weakly placed within thy power. Thou wilt find more there to wonder at than a few straggling hairs that the spinner would cast from her as too coarse for service."

"It is long since I found pleasure in handling the weapons of strife; may it be longer to the time when they shall be needed in this abode of peace. These are instruments of death, resembling those used in my youth, by cavaliers that rode in the levies of the first Charles and of his pusillanimous father. There was worldly pride and great vanity, with much and damning ungodliness in the wars that I have seen, my children; and yet the carnal man found pleasure in the stirrings of those graceless days! Come hither, younker; thou hast often sought to know the manner in which the horsemen are wont to lead into the combat, when the broad-mouthed artillery and pattering leaden hail have cleared a passage for the struggle of horse to horse, and man to man. Much of the justification of these combats must depend on the inward spirit, and on the temper of him that striketh at the life of a fellow-sinner; but righteous Joshua, it is known, contended with the heathen throughout a supernatural day; and, therefore, always humbly confiding that our cause is just, I will open to thy young mind the uses of a weapon that hath never before been seen in these forests."

"I have hefted many a heavier piece than this," said young Mark, frowning equally with the exertion and with the instigations of his aspiring spirit, as he held out the ponderous weapon in a single hand; "we have guns that might tame a wolf with greater certainty than any barrel of a bore less than my own height. Tell me, grand'ther; at what distance do the mounted warriors you so often name take their sight?"

But the power of speech appeared suddenly to have deserted the aged veteran. He had interrupted his own discourse, and now, instead of answering the interrogatory of the boy, his eye wandered slowly and with a look of painful doubt from the weapon, that he still held before him, to the countenance of the stranger. The latter continued erect, like one courting a strict and meaning examination of his person. This dumb-show could not fail to attract the observation of Content. Rising from his seat, with that quiet but authoritative manner which is still seen in the domestic government of the people of the region where he dwelt, he beckoned to all present to quit the apartment. Ruth and her daughters, the hirelings, the ill-gifted Whittal, and even the reluctant Mark, preceded him to the door, which he closed with respectful care; and then the whole of the wondering party mingled with those of the outer room, leaving the one they had quitted to the sole possession of the aged chief of the settlement, and to his still unknown and mysterious guest.

Many anxious, and to those who were excluded, seemingly interminable minutes passed, and the secret interview appeared to draw no nearer its close. That deep reverence which the years, paternity, and character of the grandfather had inspired, prevented all from approaching the quarter of the apartment nearest the room they had left; but a silence, still as the grave, did all that silence could do to enlighten their minds in a matter of so much general interest. The deep, smothered sentences of the speakers were often heard, each dwelling with steadiness and propriety on his particular theme, but no sound that conveyed meaning to the minds of those without passed the envious walls. At length, the voice of old Mark became more than usually audible; and then Content arose, with a gesture to those around him to imitate his example. The young men threw aside the subjects of their light employments, the maidens left the wheels which had not been turned for many minutes, and the whole party disposed themselves in the decent and simple attitude of prayer. For the third time that evening was the voice of the Puritan heard, pouring out his spirit in a communion with that Being on whom it was his practice to repose all his worldly cares.

But though long accustomed to all the peculiar forms of utterance by which their father ordinarily expressed his pious emotions, neither Content nor his attentive partner was enabled to decide on the nature of the feeling that was now uppermost. At times it appeared to be the language of thanksgiving, and at others it assumed more of the imploring sounds of deprecation and petition; in short, it was so varied, and, though tranquil, so equivocal, if such a term may be applied to so serious a subject, as completely to baffle every conjecture.

Long and weary minutes passed after the voice had entirely ceased, and yet no summons was given to the expecting family, nor did any sound proceed from the inner room which the respectful son was emboldened to construe into evidence that he might presume to enter.

At length apprehension began to mingle with conjectures, and then the husband and wife communed apart, in whispers. The misgivings and doubt of the former soon manifested themselves in still more apparent forms. He arose, and was seen pacing the wide apartment, gradually approaching nearer to the partition which separated the two rooms, evidently prepared to retire beyond the limits of hearing, the moment he should detect any proofs that his uneasiness was without a sufficient cause. Still no sound proceeded from the inner room. The breathless silence which had so shortly before reigned where he was, appeared to be suddenly transferred to the spot in which he was vainly endeavoring to detect the smallest proof of human existence. Again he returned to Ruth, and again they consulted in low voices, as to the step that filial duty seemed to require at their hands. "We were not bidden to withdraw," said his gentle companion; "why not re-join our parent, now that time has been given to understand the subject which so evidently disturbed his mind?"

Content, at length, yielded to this opinion. With that cautious discretion which distinguishes his people, he motioned to the family to follow, in order that no unnecessary exclusion should give rise to conjectures or excite suspicions, of which, after all, the circumstances might prove no justification. Notwithstanding the subdued manners of the age and country, curiosity, and perhaps a better feeling, had become so intense, as to cause all present to obey this silent mandate, by moving as swiftly towards the open door as a never-yielding decency of demeanor would permit.

Old Mark Heathcote occupied the chair in which he had been left, with that calm and unbending gravity of eye and features which were then thought indispensable to a fitting sobriety of spirit. But the stranger had disappeared. There were two or three outlets by which the room, and even the house might be quitted, without the knowledge of those who had so long waited for admission; and the first impression led the family to expect the reappearance of the absent man through one of these exterior passages.

Content, however, read in the expression of his father's eye that the moment of confidence, if it were ever to arrive, had not yet come; and so admirable and perfect was the domestic discipline of this family, that the questions which the son did not see fit to propound, no one of inferior condition, or lesser age, might presume to agitate. With the person of the stranger, every evidence of his recent visit had also vanished.

Mark missed the weapon that had excited his admiration; Whittal looked in vain for the hunting-knife, which had betrayed the fate of the wether; Mrs. Heathcote saw by a hasty glance of the eye, that the leathern sacks, which she had borne in mind ought to be transferred to the sleeping apartment of their guest, were gone; and a mild and playful image of herself, who bore her name no less than most of those features which had rendered her own youth more than usually attractive, sought without success, a massive silver spur, of curious and antique workmanship, which she had been permitted to handle until the moment when the family had been commanded to withdraw.

The night had now worn later than the hour at which it was usual for the people of habits so simple to be out of their beds. The grandfather lighted a taper, and, after bestowing the usual blessing on those around him, with an air as calm as if nothing had occurred, he prepared to retire into his own room. And yet, matter of interest seemed to linger on his mind. Even on the threshold of the door, he turned, and, for an instant, all expected some explanation of a circumstance which began to wear no little of the aspect of an exciting and painful mystery. But their hopes were raised only to be disappointed.

"My thoughts have not kept the passage of the time," he said. "In what hour of the night are we, my son?"

He was told that it was already past the usual moment of sleep.

"No matter; that which Providence hath bestowed for our comfort and support should not be lightly and unthankfully disregarded. Take thou the beast I am wont to ride, thyself, Content, and follow the path which leadeth to the mountain clearing; bring away that which shall meet thine eye, near the first turning of the route towards the river towns. We have got into the last quarter of the year, and in order that our industry may not flag, and that all may be stirring with the sun, let the remainder of the household seek their rest."

Content saw, by the manner of his father, that no departure from the strict letter of these instructions was admissible. He closed the door after his retiring form, and then, by a quiet gesture of authority, indicated to his dependents that they were expected to withdraw. The maidens of Ruth led the children to their chambers, and in a few more minutes none remained in the outer apartment, already so often named, but the obedient son, with his anxious and affectionate consort.

"I will be thy companion, husband," Ruth half-whisperingly commenced, so soon as the little domestic preparations for leaving the fires and securing the doors were ended. "I like not that thou should'st go into the forest alone, at so late an hour of the night."

"One will be with me there who never deserteth those who rely on his protection. Besides, my Ruth, what is there to apprehend in a wilderness like this? The beasts have been lately hunted from the hills, and excepting those who dwell under our own roof, there is not one within a long day's ride."

"We know not! Where is the stranger that came within our doors as the sun was setting?"

"As thou sayest, we know not. My father is not minded to open his lips on the subject of this traveler, and surely we

are not now to learn the lessons of obedience and self-denial."

"It would, notwithstanding, be a great easing to the spirit to hear at least the name of him who hath eaten of our bread, and joined in our family worship, though he were immediately to pass away forever from before the sight."

"That may he have done, already!" returned the less curious and more self-restrained husband. "My father wills not that we inquire."

"And yet there can be little sin in knowing the condition of one whose fortunes and movements can excite neither our envy nor our strife. I would that we had tarried for a closer mingling in the prayers; it was not seemly to desert a guest, who, it would appear, had need of an especial up-offering in his behalf."

"Our spirits joined in the asking, though our ears were shut to the matter of his wants. But it will be needful that I should be afoot with the young men, in the morning, and a mile of measurement would not reach to the turning, in the path to the river towns. Go with me to the postern, and look to the fastenings; I will not keep thee long on thy watch."

Content and his wife now quitted the dwelling by the only door that was left unbarred. Lighted by a moon that was full, though clouded, they passed a gateway between two of the outer buildings, and descended to the palisadoes. The bars and bolts of the little postern were removed, and in a few minutes the former, mounted on the back of his father's own horse, was galloping briskly along the path which led into the part of the forest he was directed to seek.

While the husband was thus proceeding, in obedience to orders that he never hesitated to obey, his faithful wife withdrew within the shelter of the wooden defenses. More in compliance with a precaution that was become habitual, than from any present causes of suspicion, she drew a single bolt and remained at the postern, anxiously awaiting the result of a movement that was as unaccountable as it was extraordinary.

CHAPTER IV.

"I' the name of something holy, sir, why stand you
In this strange stare?" —TEMPEST.

As a girl, Ruth Harding had been one of the mildest and gentlest of the human race. Though new impulses had been given to her naturally kind affections by the attachments of a wife and mother, her disposition suffered no change by marriage. Obedient, disinterested, and devoted to those she loved, as her parents had known her, so, by the experience of many years, had she proved to Content. In the midst of the utmost equanimity of temper and of deportment, her watchful solicitude in behalf of the few who formed the limited circle of her existence, never slumbered. It dwelt unpretendingly but active in her gentle bosom, like a great and moving principle of life. Though circumstances had placed her on a remote and exposed frontier, where time had not been given for the several customary divisions of employments, she was unchanged in habits, in feelings, and in character. The affluence of her husband had elevated her above the necessity of burdensome toil; and, while she had encountered the dangers of the wilderness, and neglected none of the duties of her active station, she had escaped most of those injurious consequences which are a little apt to impair the peculiar loveliness of women. Notwithstanding the exposure of a border life, she remained feminine, attractive, and singularly youthful.

The reader will readily imagine the state of mind with which such a being watched the distant form of a husband, engaged in a duty like that we have described. Notwithstanding the influence of long habit, the forest was rarely approached after night-fall by the boldest woodsman, without some secret consciousness that he encountered a positive danger. It was the hour when its roaming and hungry tenants were known to be most in motion; and the rustling of a leaf or the snapping of a dried twig beneath the light tread of the smallest animal, was apt to conjure up images of the voracious and fire-eyed panther, or perhaps of a lurking biped, which, though more artful, was known to be scarcely less savage. It is true, that hundreds experienced the uneasiness of such sensations who were never fated to undergo the realities of the fearful pictures. Still facts were not wanting to supply sufficient motive for a grave and reasonable apprehension.

Histories of combats with beasts of prey, and of massacres by roving and lawless Indians, were the moving legends of the border. Thrones might be subverted and kingdoms lost and won in distant Europe, and less would be said of the events by those who dwelt in these woods, than of one scene of peculiar and striking forest incident that called for the exercise of the stout courage and keen intelligence of a settler. Such a tale passed from mouth to mouth with the eagerness of powerful personal interest, and many were already transmitted from parent to child, in the form of tradition, until, as in more artificial communities graver improbabilities creep into the doubtful pages of history, exaggeration became too closely blended with truth ever again to be separated.

Under the influence of these feelings, and perhaps prompted by his never-failing discretion, Content had thrown a well-tried piece over his shoulder; and when he rose the ascent on which his father had met the stranger, Ruth caught a glimpse of his form, bending on the neck of his horse, and gliding through the misty light of the hour, resembling one of those fancied images of wayward and hard-riding sprites, of which the tales of the eastern continent are so fond of speaking.

Then followed anxious moments, during which neither sight nor hearing could in the least aid the conjectures of the attentive wife. She listened without breathing, and once or twice she thought the blows of hoofs falling on the earth harder and quicker than common, might be distinguished; but it was only as Content mounted the sudden ascent of the hill-side that he was again seen, for a brief instant, while dashing swiftly into the cover of the woods.

Though Ruth had been familiar with the cares of the frontier, perhaps she had never known a moment more intensely painful than that when the form of her husband became blended with the dark trunks of the trees. The time was to her impatience longer than usual, and under the excitement of a feverish inquietude that had no definite object, she removed the single bolt that held the postern closed, and passed entirely without the stockade. To her oppressed senses the palisadoes appeared to place limits to her vision. Still weary minute passed after minute, without bringing relief. During these anxious moments she became more than usually conscious of the insulated situation in which he and all who were dearest to her heart were placed. The feelings of a wife prevailed. Quitting the side of the acclivity, she began to walk slowly along the path her husband had taken, until apprehension insensibly urged her into a quicker movement. She had paused only when she stood nearly in the center of the clearing, on the eminence where her father had halted that evening to contemplate the growing improvement of his estate.

Here her steps were suddenly arrested,

for she thought a form was issuing from the forest, at that interesting spot which her eye had never ceased to watch. It proved to be no more than the passing shadow of a cloud, denser than common, which threw the body of its darkness on the trees and a portion of its outline on the ground near the margin of the wood. Just at this instant the recollection that she had incautiously left the postern open, flashed upon her mind, and, with feelings divided between husband and children, she commenced her return, in order to repair a neglect, to which habit, no less than prudence, imparted a high degree of culpability. The eyes of the mother, for the feelings of that sacred character were now powerfully uppermost, were fastened on the ground, as she eagerly picked her way along the uneven surface; and so engrossed was her mind by the omission of duty, with which she was severely reproaching herself, that they drank in objects without conveying distinct or intelligible images to her brain.

Notwithstanding the one engrossing thought of the moment, something met her eye that caused even the vacant organ to recoil, and every fiber in her frame to tremble with terror. There was a moment in which delirium nearly heightened terror to madness. Reflection came only when Ruth had reached the distance of many feet from the spot where this startling object had half unconsciously crossed her vision. Then for a single and a fearful instant she paused, like one who debated on the course she ought to follow. Maternal love prevailed, and the deer of her own woods scarcely bounds with greater agility than the mother of the sleeping and defenseless family now fled toward the dwellings. Panting and breathless she gained the postern, which was closed with hands that performed their office more by instinct than in obedience to thought, and doubly and trebly barred.

For the first time in some minutes Ruth now breathed distinctly and without pain. She strove to rally her thoughts, in order to deliberate on the course that prudence and her duty to Content, who was still exposed to the danger she had herself escaped, prescribed. Her first impulse was to give the established signal that was to recall the laborers from the field, or to awake the sleepers, in the event of an alarm; but better reflection told her such a step might prove fatal to him who balanced in her affections against the rest of the world. The struggle in her mind only ended as she clearly and unequivocally caught a view of her husband, issuing from the forest at the very point

where he had entered. The return path, unfortunately, led directly past the spot where such sudden terror had seized her mind. She would have given worlds to have known how to apprise him of a danger with which her own imagination was full, without communicating the warning to other and terrible ears. The night was still, and though the distance was considerable, it was not so great as to render the chances of success desperate. Scarcely knowing what she did, and yet preserving, by a sort of instinctive prudence, the caution which constant exposure weaves into all our habits, the trembling woman made the effort.

"Husband! husband!" she cried, commencing plaintively, but her voice rising with the energy of excitement. "Husband, ride swiftly; our little Ruth lieth in the agony. For her life and thine, ride at thy horse's speed. Seek not the stables, but come with all haste to the postern, it shall be open to thee."

This was certainly a fearful summons for a father's ear, and there is little doubt that, had the feeble powers of Ruth succeeded in conveying the words as far as she had wished, they would have produced the desired effect. But in vain did she call; her weak tones, though raised on the notes of keenest apprehension, could not force their way across so wide a space. And yet had she reason to think they were not entirely lost, for once her husband paused and seemed to listen, and once he quickened the pace of his horse; though neither of these proofs of intelligence was followed by any further sign of his having understood the alarm.

Content was now upon the hillock itself. If Ruth breathed at all during its passage, it was more imperceptible than the gentlest respiration of the sleeping infant. But when she saw him trotting with unconscious security along the path on the side next the dwellings, her impatience broke through all restraint, and throwing open the postern, she renewed her cries, in a voice that was no longer useless. The clattering of the unshodded hoof was again rapid, and in another minute her husband galloped unharmed to her side.

"Enter!" said the nearly dizzy wife, seizing the bridle, and leading the horse within the palisadoes. "Enter, husband, for the love of all that is thine; enter, and be thankful."

"What meaneth this terror, Ruth?" demanded Content, in as much pleasure, perhaps, as he could manifest to one so gentle, for a weakness betrayed in his own behalf, "is thy confidence in him whose eye never closeth, and who equally watcheth the life of man and that of the falling sparrow, lost?"

Ruth was deaf. With hurried hands she drew the fastenings, let fall the bars, and turned a key which forced a triple-bolted lock to perform its office. Not till then did she feel either safe herself, or at liberty to render thanks for the safety of him, over whose danger she had so lately watched in agony.

"Why this care? Hast forgotten that the horse will suffer hunger, at this distance from the rack and manger?"

"Better that he starve than hair of thine should come to harm."

"Nay, nay, Ruth; dost not remember that the beast is the favorite of my father, who will ill brook his passing a night within the palisadoes?"

"Husband, you err; there is one in the fields."

"Is there place where One is not?"

"But I have seen creature of mortal birth, and creature, too, that hath no claim on thee or thine, and who trespasseth on our peace, no less than on our natural rights, to be where he lurketh."

"Go to; thou art not used to be so late from thy pillow, my poor Ruth; sleep hath come over thee, whilst standing on thy watch. Some cloud hath left its shadow on the fields, or, truly, it may be that the hunt did not drive the beasts as far from the clearing as we had thought. Come; since thou wilt cling to my side, lay hand on the bridle of the horse, while I ease him of his burden."

As Content coolly proceeded to the task he had mentioned, the thoughts of his wife were momentarily diverted from their other sources of uneasiness, by the object which lay on the crupper of the nag, and which, until now, had entirely escaped her observation.

"Here is, indeed, the animal this day missing from our flock!" she exclaimed, as the carcass of a sheep fell heavily on the ground.

"Ay; and killed with exceeding judgment, if not aptly dressed to our hands. Mutton will not be wanting for the husking-feast, and the stalled creature whose days were counted may live another season."

"And where didst find the slaughtered beast?"

"On the limb of a growing hickory. Eben Dudley, with all his sleight in butchering, and in setting forth the excellence of his meats, could not have left an animal hanging from the branch of a sapling with greater knowledge of his craft. Thou seest, but a single meal is missing from the carcass, and that thy fleece is unharmed."

"This is not the work of a Pequod!" exclaimed Ruth, surprised at her own discovery; "the red men do their mischief with less care."

"Nor has the tooth of wolf opened the veins of poor Straight-Horns. Here has been judgment in the slaughtering, as well as prudence in the consumption of the food. The hand that cut so lightly had intention of a second visit."

"And our father bid thee seek the creature where it was found! Husband, I fear some heavy judgment for the sins of the parents is likely to befall the children."

"The babes are quietly in their slumbers, and, thus far, little wrong hath been done us. I'll cast the halter from the stalled animal ere I sleep, and Straight-Horns shall content us for the husking. We may have mutton less savory for this evil chance, but the number of thy flock will be unaltered."

"And where is he who hath mingled in our prayers, and hath eaten of our bread; he who counseled so long in secret with our father, and who hath now vanished from among us like a vision?"

"That indeed is a question not readily to be answered," returned Content, who had hitherto maintained a cheerful air, in order to appease what he was fain to believe a causeless terror in the bosom of his partner, but who was induced by this question to drop his head like one that sought reasons within the repository of his own thoughts. "It mattereth not, Ruth Heathcote; the ordering of the affair is in the hands of a man of many years and great experience; should his aged wisdom fail, do we not know that one even wiser than he hath us in his keeping? I will return the beast to his rack, and when we shall have jointly asked favor of eyes that never sleep, we will go in confidence to our rest."

"Husband, thou quittest not the palisadoes again this night," said Ruth, arresting the hand that had already drawn a bolt ere she spoke. "I have a warning of evil."

"I would the stranger had found some other shelter in which to pass his short resting season. That he hath made free with my flock, and that he hath administered to his hunger at some cost, when a single asking would have made him welcome to the best that the owner of the Wish-Ton-Wish can command, are truths that may not be denied. Still is he mortal man, as a goodly appetite hath proven, even should our belief in Providence so far waver as to harbor doubts of its unwillingness to suffer beings of injustice to wander in our forms and substance. I tell thee, Ruth, that the nag will be needed for to-morrow's service, and that our father will give but ill thanks should we leave it to make a bed on this cold hillside. Go to thy rest and to thy prayers, trembler; I will close the postern with all care. Fear not; the stranger is of human wants, and his agency to do evil must needs be limited by human power."

"I fear none of white blood, nor of Christian parentage; the murderous heathen is in our fields."

"Thou dreamest, Ruth!"

"'Tis not a dream. I have seen the glowing eyeballs of a savage. Sleep was little like to come over me when set upon a watch like this. I thought me that the errand was of unknowi character, and that our father was exceedingly aged, and that perchance his senses might be duped, and how an obedient son ought not to be exposed. Thou knowest, Heathcote, that I could not look upon the danger of my children's father with indifference, and I followed to the nut-tree hillock."

"To the nut-tree. It was not prudent in thee—but the postern?"

"It was open; for were the key turned, who was there to admit us quickly had haste been needed?" returned Ruth, momentarily averting her face to conceal the flush excited by conscious delinquency. "Though I failed in caution, 'twas for thy safety, Heathcote. But on that hillock, and in the hollow left by a fallen tree, lies concealed a heathen!"

"I passed the nut-wood in going to the shambles of our strange butcher, and I drew the rein to give breath to the nag near it, as we returned with the burden. It cannot be; some creature of the forest hath alarmed thee."

"Ay! creature, formed, fashioned, gifted like ourselves, in all but color of the skin and blessing of the faith."

"This is a strange delusion! If there were enemy at hand, would men subtle as those you fear suffer the master of the dwelling, and truly I may say it without vain-glory, one as likely as another to struggle stoutly for his own, to escape, when an ill-timed visit to the woods had delivered him unresisting into their hands? Go, go, good Ruth; thou may'st have seen a blackened log—perchance the frosts have left a fire-fly untouched, or it may be that some prowling bear has scented out the sweets of thy lately gathered hives."

Ruth again laid her hand firmly on the arm of her husband, who had withdrawn another bolt, and, looking him steadily in the face, she answered by saying solemnly, and with touching pathos—

"Thinkest thou, husband, that a mother's eye could be deceived?"

It might have been that the allusion to the tender beings whose fate depended on his care, or that the deeply serious, though mild and gentle manner of his consort produced some fresher impression on the mind of Content. Instead of undoing the fastenings of the postern as he had intended, he deliberately drew its bolts again and paused to think.

"If it produce no other benefit than to quiet thy fears, good Ruth," he said, after a moment of reflection, "a little caution will be well repaid. Stay you, then, here, where the hillock may be watched, while I go wake a couple of the people. With stout Eben Dudley and experienced Reuben Ring to back me, my father's horse may surely be stabled."

Ruth contentedly assumed a task that she was quite equal to perform with intelligence and zeal. "Hie thee to the laborers' chambers, for I see a light still burning in the room of those you seek," was the answer she gave to a proposal that at least quieted the intenseness of her fears for him in whose behalf they had so lately been excited nearly to agony.

"It shall be quickly done; nay, stand not thus openly between the beams, wife. Thou mayest place thyself here at the doublings of the wood, beneath the loop, where harm would scarcely reach thee, though shot from artillery were to crush the timber."

With this admonition to be wary of a danger that he had so recently affected to despise, Content departed on his errand. The two laborers he had mentioned by name were youths of mold and strength, and they were well inured to toil, no less than to the particular privations and dangers of a border life. Like most men of their years and condition, they were practiced too in the wiles of Indian cunning; and though the Province of Connecticut, compared to other settlements, had suffered but little in this species of murderous warfare, they both had martial feats and perilous experiences of their own to recount during the light labors of the long winter evenings.

Content crossed the court with a quick step; for, notwithstanding his steady unbelief, the image of his gentle wife posted on her outer watch hurried his movements. The rap he gave at the door on reaching the apartment of those he sought was loud as it was sudden.

"Who calls?" demanded a deep-toned

and firm voice from within, at the first blow of the knuckles on the plank.

"Quit thy beds quickly, and come forth with the arms appointed for a sally."

"That is soon done," answered a stout woodsman, throwing open the door and standing before Content in the garments he had worn throughout the day. "We were just dreaming that the night was not to pass without a summons to the loops."

"Hast seen aught?"

"Our eyes were not shut more than those of others; we saw him enter that no man hath seen depart."

"Come, fellow — Whittal Ring would scarce give wiser speech than this cunning reply of thine. My wife is at the postern, and it is fit we go to relieve her watch. Thou wilt not forget the horns of powder, since it would not tell to our credit, were there service for the pieces, and we lacking in wherewithal to give them a second discharge."

The hirelings obeyed, and as little time was necessary to arm those who never slept without weapons and ammunition within reach of their hands, Content was speedily followed by his dependents. Ruth was found at her post; but when urged by her husband to declare what had passed in his absence, she was compelled to admit that, though the moon had come forth brighter and clearer from behind the clouds, she had seen nothing to add to her alarm.

"We will then lead the beast to his stall, and close our duty by setting a single watch for the rest of the night," said the husband. "Reuben shall keep the postern, while Eben and I will have a care for my father's nag, not forgetting the carcass for the husking-feast. Dost hear, deaf Dudley? Cast the mutton upon the crupper of the beast and follow to the stables."

"Here has been no common workman at my office," said the blunt Eben, who, though an ordinary farm laborer, according to a usage still very generally prevalent in the country, was also skillful in the craft of the butcher. "I have brought many a wether to his end, but this is the first sheep, within all my experience, that hath kept the fleece while a portion of the body has been in the pot! Lie there, poor Straight-Horns, if quiet thou canst be, after such strange butchery. Reuben, I paid thee, as the sun rose, a Spanish piece of silver for the trifle of debt that lay between us in behalf of the good turn thou didst the shoes, which were none the better for the last hunt in the hills. Hast ever that pistareen about thee?"

This question, which was put in a lowered tone, and only to the ear of the party concerned, was answered in the affirmative.

"Give it me, lad; in the morning thou shalt be paid with usurer's interest."

Another summons from Content, who had now led the nag loaded with the carcass of the sheep without the postern, cut short the secret conference. Eben Dudley, having received the coin, hastened to follow. But the distance to the outbuildings was sufficient to enable him to effect his mysterious purpose without discovery. Whilst Content endeavored to calm the apprehensions of his wife, who still persisted in sharing his danger, by such reasons as he could on the instant command, the credulous Dudley placed the thin piece of silver between his teeth, and, with a pressure that denoted the prodigious force of his jaws, caused it to assume a beaten and rounded shape. He then slily dropped the battered coin into the muzzle of his gun, taking care to secure its presence until he himself should send it on its disenchanting message, by a wad torn from the lining of part of his vestments. Supported by this redoubtable auxiliary, the superstitious but still courageous borderer followed his companion, whistling a low air that equally denoted his indifference to danger of an ordinary nature, and his sensibility to impressions of a less earthly character.

They who dwell in the older districts of America, where art and labor have united for generations to clear the earth of its inequalities, and to remove the vestiges of a state of nature, can form but little idea of the thousand objects that may exist in a clearing, to startle the imagination of one who has admitted alarm, when seen in the doubtful light of even a cloudless moon. Still less can they who have never quitted the old world, and who having only seen, can only imagine fields smooth as the surface of tranquil water, picture the effect produced by those lingering remnants, which may be likened to so many moldering monuments of the fallen forest scattered at such an hour over a broad surface of open land. Accustomed as they were to the sight, Content and his partner, excited by their fears, fancied each dark and distant stump a savage, and they passed no angle in the high and heavy fences without throwing a jealous glance to see that some enemy did not lie stretched within its shadows.

Still no new motive for apprehension arose during the brief period that the two adventurers were employed in administering to the comfort of the Puritan's steed. The task was ended, the carcass of the slaughtered Straight - Horns had been secured, and Ruth was already urging her husband to return, when their attention was drawn to the attitude and mien of their companion.

"The man hath departed as he came," said Eben Dudley, who stood shaking his head in open doubt before an empty stall; "here is no beast, though with these eyes did I see the half-wit bring hither a well-filled measure of speckled oats to feed the nag. He who favored us with his presence at the supper and the thanksgiving, hath tired of his company before the hour of rest had come."

"The horse is truly wanting," said Content; "the man must needs be in exceeding haste, to have ridden into the forest as the night grew deepest, and when the longest summer day would scarce bring a better hack than that he rode to another Christian dwelling. There is reason for this industry, but it is enough that it concerns us not. We will now seek our rest, in the certainty that One watcheth our slumbers whose vigilance can never fail."

Though man could not trust himself to sleep in that country without the security of bars and bolts, we have already had occasion to say that property was guarded with but little care. The stable-door was merely closed by a wooden latch, and the party returned from this short sortie, with steps that were a little quickened by a sense of an uneasiness that beset them in forms suited to their several characters. But shelter was at hand, and it was speedily regained.

"Thou hast seen nothing?" said Content to Reuben Ring, who had been chosen for his quick eye, and a sagacity that was as remarkable as was his brother's impotency; "thou hast seen nothing at thy watch?"

"Naught unusual; and yet I like not yonder billet of wood, near to the fence against the knoll. If it were not so plainly a half-burnt log, one might fancy there is life in it. But when fancy is at work, the sight is keen. Once or twice I have thought it seemed to be rolling towards the brook; I am not, even now, certain that when first seen it did not lie eight or ten feet higher against the bank."

"It may be a living thing!"

"On the faith of a woodman's eye, it well may be," said Eben Dudley; "but should it be haunted by a legion of wicked spirits, one may bring it to quiet from the loop at the nearest corner. Stand aside, Madame Heathcote," for the character

and wealth of the proprietors of the valley gave Ruth a claim to this term of respect among the laborers; "let me thrust the piece through the—stop, there is an especial charm in the gun, which it might be sinful to waste on such a creature. It may be no more than some sweet-toothed bear. I will answer for the charge at my own cost, if thou wilt lend me thy musket, Reuben Ring."

"It shall not be," said his master; "one known to my father hath this night entered our dwelling and fed at our board; if he hath departed in a way but little wont among those of this Colony, yet hath he done no great wrong. I will go nigh, and examine with less risk of error."

There was in this proposal too much of that spirit of right-doing, which governed all of those simple regions, to meet serious opposition. Content, supported by Eben Dudley, again quitted the postern, and proceeded directly, though still not without sufficient caution, towards the point where the suspicious object lay. A bend in the fence had first brought it into view, for previously to reaching that point, its apparent direction might for some distance have been taken under shelter of the shadows of the rails, which, at the immediate spot where it was seen, were turned suddenly in a line with the eyes of the spectators. It seemed as if the movements of those who approached were watched; for the instant they left the defenses, the dark object was assuredly motionless; even the keen eye of Reuben Ring beginning to doubt whether some deception of vision had not led him, after all, to mistake a billet of wood for a creature of life.

But Content and his companion were not induced to change their determination. Even when within fifty feet of the object, though the moon fell full and brightly upon the surface, its character baffled conjecture. One affirmed it was the end of a charred log, many of which still lay scattered about the fields, and the others believed it to be some cringing animal of the woods. Twice Content raised his piece to fire, and as often did he let it fall, in reluctance to do injury to even a quadruped of whose character he was ignorant. It is more than probable that his less considerate and but half obedient companion would have decided the question soon after leaving the postern, had not the peculiar contents of his musket rendered him delicate of its uses.

"Look to thy weapons," said the former, loosening his own hunting-knife in his sheath. "We will draw near and make certainty of what is doubtful."

They did so, and the gun of Dudley was thrust rudely into the side of the object of their distrust, before it again betrayed life or motion. Then, indeed, as if further disguise was useless, an Indian lad of some fifteen years rose deliberately to his feet, and stood before them in the sullen dignity of a captured warrior. Content hastily seized the stripling by an arm, and followed by Eben, who occasionally quickened the footsteps of the prisoner by an impetus obtained from the breech of his own musket, they hurriedly returned within the defenses.

"My life against that of Straight-Horns, which is now of no great value," said Dudley, as he pushed the last bolt of the fastenings into its socket, "we hear no more of this red-skin's companions to-night. I never knew an Indian raise his whoop when a scout had fallen into the hands of the enemy."

"This may be true," returned the other, "and yet must a sleeping household be guarded. We may be brought to rely on the overlooking favor of Providence, working with the means of our own manhood, ere the sun shall arise."

Content was a man of few words, but one of exceeding steadiness and resolution in moments of need. He was perfectly aware that an Indian youth, like him he had captured, would not have been found in that place, and under the circumstances in which he was actually taken, without a design of sufficient magnitude to justify the hazard. The tender age of the stripling, too, forbade the belief that he was unaccompanied. But he silently agreed with his laboring man, that the capture would probably cause the attack, if any such were meditated, to be deferred. He therefore instructed his wife to withdraw into her chamber, while he took measures to defend the dwelling in the last emergency. Without giving any unnecessary alarm, a measure that would have produced less effect on an enemy without, than the imposing stillness which now reigned within the defenses, he ordered two or three more of the stoutest of his dependents to be summoned to the palisadoes. A keen scrutiny was made into the state of all the different outlets of the place; muskets were carefully examined; charges were given to be watchful, and regular sentinels were stationed within the shadows of the buildings, at points where, unseen themselves, they could look out in safety upon the fields.

Content then took his captive, with whom he had made no attempt to exchange a syllable, and led him to the block-house. The door which communi-cated with the basement of this building was always open, in readiness for refuge in the event of any sudden alarm. He entered; caused the lad to mount by a ladder to the floor above, and then withdrawing the means of retreat, he turned the key without, in perfect confidence that his prisoner was secure.

Notwithstanding all this care, morning had nearly dawned before the prudent father and husband sought his pillow. His steadiness, however, had prevented the apprehensions, which kept his own eyes and those of his general partner so long open, from extending beyond the few whose services were, in such an emergency, deemed indispensable to safety. Toward the last watches of the night, only, did the images of the scenes through which they had just passed, become dim and confused, and then both husband and wife slept soundly and happily without disturbance.

CHAPTER V.

"Are you so brave? I'll have you talked with anon."
—CORIOLANUS.

THE ax and the brand had been early and effectually used, immediately around the dwelling of the Heathcotes. A double object had been gained by removing most of the vestiges of the forest from the vicinity of the buildings; the necessary improvements were executed with greater facility, and, a consideration of no small importance, the cover which the American savage is known to seek in his attacks was thrown to a distance that greatly diminished the danger of a surprise.

Favored by the advantage which had been obtained by this foresight, and by the brilliancy of a night that soon emulated the brightness of day, the duty of Eben Dudley and of his associate on the watch was rendered easy of accomplishment. Indeed, so secure did they become toward morning, chiefly on account of the capture of the Indian lad, that more than once, eyes that should have been differently employed, yielded to the drowsiness of the hour, and to habit, or were only opened at intervals that left their owners in some doubt as to the passage of the intermediate time. But no sooner did the signs of day approach, than, agreeably to their instructions, the watchers sought their beds, and for an hour or two they slept soundly, and without fear.

When his father had closed the prayers of the morning, Content, in the midst of the assembled family, communicated as many of the incidents of the past night, as in his judgment seemed necessary. His discretion limited the narrative to the capture of the native youth, and to the manner in which he had ordered the watch for the security of the family. On the subject of his own excursion to the forest, and all connected therewith, he was guardedly silent.

It is unnecessary to relate the manner in which this startling information was received. The cold and reserved brow of the Puritan became still more thoughtful; the young men looked grave and resolute; the maidens of the household grew pale, shuddered, and whispered hurriedly together; while the little Ruth and a female child of nearly her own age, named Martha, clung close to the side of the mistress of the family, who, having nothing new to learn, had taught herself to assume the appearance of a resolution she was far from feeling.

The first visitation which befell the listeners, after their eager ears had drunk in the intelligence Content so briefly imparted, was a renewal of the spiritual strivings of his father in the form of prayer. A particular petition was put up in quest of light on their future proceedings, for mercy on all men, for a better mind to those who wandered through the wilderness seeking victims of their wrath, for the gifts of grace on the heathen, and finally for victory over all their carnal enemies, let them come whence or in what aspect they might.

Fortified by these additional exercises, old Mark next made himself the master of all the signs and evidences of the approach of danger, by a more rigid and minute inquiry into the visible circumstances of the arrest of the young savage. Content received a merited and grateful reward for his prudence, in the approbation of one whom he still continued to revere with a mental dependence little less than that with which he had leaned on his father's wisdom in the days of his childhood.

"Thou hast done well and wisely," said his father; "but more remains to be performed by thy wisdom and fortitude. We have had tidings that the heathen near the Providence Plantations are unquiet, and that they are lending their minds to wicked counselors. We are not to sleep in too much security, because a forest journey of a few days lies between their villages and our own clearing. Bring forth the captive; I will question him on the matter of this visit."

Until now, so much did the fears of all turn toward the enemies who were believed to be lurking near, that little thought had been bestowed on the prisoner in the block-house. Content, who well knew the invincible resolution, no less than the art of an Indian, had forborne to question him when taken; for he believed the time to be better suited to vigilant action, than to interrogatories that the character of the boy was likely to render perfectly useless. He now proceeded, however, with an interest that began to quicken as circumstances rendered its indulgence less unsuitable, to seek his captive, in order to bring him before the searching ordeal of his father's authority.

The key of the lower door of the block-house hung where it had been deposited; the ladder was replaced, and Content mounted quietly to the apartment where he had placed his captive. The room was the lowest of three that the building contained, all being above that which might be termed its basement. The latter, having no aperture but its door, was a dark, hexagonal space, partly filled with such articles as might be needed in the event of an alarm, and which, at the same time, were frequently required for the purposes of domestic use. In the center of the area was a deep well, so fitted and protected by a wall of stone as to admit of water being drawn into the rooms above. The door itself was of massive hewn timber. The squared logs of the upper stories projected a little beyond the stonework of the basement, the second tier of the timbers containing a few loops, out of which missiles might be discharged downward, on any assailants that approached nearer than should be deemed safe for the security of the basement. As has been stated, the two principal stories were perforated with long narrow slits through the timber, which answered the double purposes of windows and loop-holes.

Though the apartments were so evidently arranged for defense, the plain domestic furniture they contained was suited to the wants of the family, should they be driven to the building for refuge. There was also an apartment in the roof, or attic, as already mentioned; but it scarcely entered into the more important uses of the block-house. Still the advantage which it received from its elevation was not overlooked. A small cannon, of a kind once known and much used under the name of grasshoppers, had been raised to the place, and time had been when it was rightly considered as of the last importance to the safety of the inmates of the dwelling. For some years its muzzle had been seen by all straggling aborigines who visited the valley, frowning through one of these openings which were now converted into glazed windows; and there is reason to think that the reputation which the little piece of ordnance thus silently obtained, had a powerful agency in so long preserving unmolested the peace of the valley.

The word unmolested is perhaps too strong. More than one alarm had in fact occurred, though no positive acts of violence had ever been committed within the limits which the Puritan claimed as his own. On only one occasion, however, did matters proceed so far that the veteran had been induced to take his post in this warlike attic; where, there is little doubt, had occasion further offered for his services, he would have made a suitable display of his knowledge in the science of gunnery. But the simple history of the Wish-Ton-Wish had furnished another evidence of a political truth, which cannot be too often presented to the attention of our countrymen; we mean, that the best preservative of peace is preparation for war. In the case before us, the hostile attitude assumed by old Mark and his dependents had effected all that was desirable, without proceeding to the extremity of shedding blood. Such peaceful triumphs were far more in accordance with the present principles of the Puritans than they would have been with the reckless temper which had governed his youth.

In the quaint and fanatical humor of the times, he had held a family thanksgiving around the instrument of their security, and from that moment the room itself became a favorite resorting-place for the old soldier. Thither he often mounted, even in the hours of deep night, to indulge in those secret spiritual exercises which formed the chiefest solace, and seemingly, indeed, the great employment of his life. In consequence of this habit, the attic of the block-house came in time to be considered sacred to the uses of the master of the valley. The care and thought of Content had gradually supplied it with many conveniences that might contribute to the personal comfort of his father, while the spirit was engaged in these mental conflicts. At length the old man was known to use the mattress, that among other things it now contained, and to pass the time between the setting and the rising of the sun in its solitude. The aperture originally cut for the exhibition of the grasshopper had been glazed; and no article of comfort, which was once caused to mount the difficult ladder that led to the chamber, was ever seen to descend.

There was something in the austere sanctity of old Mark Heathcote, that was favorable to the practices of an anchorite. The youths of the dwelling regarded his unbending brow, and the undisturbed gravity of the eye it shadowed, with a respect akin to awe. Had the genuine benevolence of his character been less tried, or had he mingled in active life at a later period, it might readily have been his fate to have shared in the persecution which his countrymen heaped on those who were believed to deal with influences it is thought impious to exercise. Under actual circumstances, however, the sentiment went no farther than a deep and universal reverence, that left its object, and the neglected little piece of artillery, to the quiet possession of an apartment, to invade which would have been deemed an act bordering on sacrilege.

The business of Content, on the occasion which caused his present visit to the edifice whose history and description we have thought it expedient thus to give at some length, led him no farther than to the lowest of its more military apartments. On raising the trap, for the first time a feeling of doubt came over him, as to the propriety of having left the boy so long unsolaced by words of kindness, or by deed of charity. It was appeased by observing that his concern was awakened in behalf of one whose spirit was quite equal to sustain greater trials.

The young Indian stood before one of the loops, looking out upon that distant forest in which he had so lately roamed at liberty, with a gaze too riveted to turn aside even at the interruption occasioned by the presence of his captor.

"Come from thy prison, child," said Content, in the tones of mildness; "whatever may have been thy motive in lurking around this dwelling, thou art human, and must know human wants; come forth and receive food; none here will harm thee."

The language of commiseration is universal. Though the words of the speaker were evidently unintelligible to him for whose ears they were intended, their import was conveyed in the kindness of the accents. The eyes of the boy turned slowly from the view of the woods, and he looked his captor long and steadily in the face. Content now indeed discovered that he had spoken in a language that was unknown to his captive, and he endeavored by gestures of kindness to invite the lad to follow him. He was silently and quietly obeyed. On reaching the court, however, the prudence of a border proprietor in some degree overcame his feelings of compassion.

"Bring hither yon tether," he said to Whittal Ring, who at the moment was passing toward the stables; "here is one wild as the most untamed of thy colts. Man is of our nature and of our spirit, let him be of what color it may have pleased Providence to stamp his features; but he who would have a young savage in his keeping on the morrow, must look sharply to his limbs to-day."

The lad submitted quietly until a turn of the rope was passed around one of his arms; but when Content was fain to complete the work by bringing the other limb into the same state of subjection, the boy glided from his grasp, and cast the fetters from him in disdain. This act of decided resistance, was, however, followed by no effort to escape. The moment his person was released from a confinement, which he probably considered as implying distrust of his ability to endure pain with the fortitude of a warrior, the lad turned quietly and proudly to his captor, and, with an eye in which scorn and haughtiness were alike glowing, seemed to defy the fullness of his anger.

"Be it so," resumed the equal-minded Content, "if thou likest not the bonds which, notwithstanding the pride of man, are often healthful to the body, keep then the use of thy limbs, and see that they do no mischief. Whittal, look thou to the postern, and remember it is forbidden to go afield until my father hath had this heathen under examination. The cub is seldom found far from the cunning of the aged bear."

He then made a sign to the boy to follow, and proceeded to the apartment where his father, surrounded by most of the family, awaited their coming. Uncompromising domestic discipline was one of the striking characteristics of the sway of the Puritans That austerity of manner which was thought to mark a sense of a fallen and probationary state was early taught; for, among a people who deemed all mirth a sinful levity, the practice of self-command would readily come to be esteemed the basis of virtue. But whatever might have been the peculiar merit of Mark Heathcote and his household in this particular, it was likely to be exceeded by the exhibition of the same quality in the youth who had so strangely become their captive.

We have already said that this child of the woods might have seen some fifteen years. Though he had shot upward like a vigorous and thrifty plant, and with the freedom of a thriving sapling in his native forests, rearing its branches toward the light, his stature had not yet reached that of man. In height, form, and attitudes, he was a model of active, natural, and graceful boyhood. But while his limbs were so fair in their proportions, they were scarcely muscular; still every movement exhibited a freedom and ease which announced the grace of childhood, without the smallest evidence of that restraint which creeps into our air as the factitious feelings of later life begin to assert their influence. The smooth, rounded trunk of the mountain ash is not more upright and free from blemish than was the figure of the boy, who moved into the curious circle that opened for his entrance and closed against his retreat, with a steadiness of one who came to bestow instead of appearing to receive judgment.

"I will question him," said old Mark Heathcote, attentively regarding the keen and settled eye that met his long, stern gaze, as steadily as a less intelligent creature of the woods would return the look of man. "I will question him; and perchance fear will wring from his lips a confession of the evil that he and his have meditated against me and mine."

"I think he is ignorant of our forms of speech," returned Content; "for the words of neither kindness nor anger will force him to a change of feature."

"It is then meet that we commence by asking him who hath the secret to open all hearts to be our assistant." The Puritan then raised his voice in a short and exceedingly particular petition, in which he implored the Ruler of the Universe to interpret his meaning in the forthcoming examination, in a manner that, had his request been granted, would have savored not a little of the miraculous. With this preparation he proceeded directly to his task. But neither questions, signs, nor prayer, produced the slightest visible effect.

The boy gazed at the rigid and austere countenance of his interrogater, while the words were issuing from his lips; but the instant they ceased, his searching and quick eye rolled over the different curious faces by which he was hemmed in, as if he trusted more to the sense of sight than that of hearing, for the information he naturally sought concerning his future lot. It was found impossible to obtain from him gesture or sound that should betray either the purport of his questionable visit, his own personal appellation, or that of his tribe.

"I have been among the red-skins of the Providence Plantations," Eben Dudley at length ventured to observe; "and their language, though but a crooked and irrational jargon, is not unknown to me.

With the leave of all present," he continued, regarding the Puritan in a manner to betray that this general term meant him alone, "with the leave of all present, I will put it to the younker in such a fashion that he will be glad to answer."

Receiving a look of assent, the borderer uttered certain uncouth and guttural sounds, which, notwithstanding they entirely failed of their effect, he stoutly maintained were the ordinary terms of salutation among the people to whom the prisoner was supposed to belong.

"I know him to be a Narragansett," continued Eben, reddening with vexation at his defeat, and throwing a glance of no peculiar amity at the youth who had so palpably refuted his claim to skill in the Indian tongues; "you see he hath the shells of the sea-side worked into the bordering of his moccasins; and besides this sign, which is certain as that night hath its stars, he beareth the look of a chief that was slain by the Pequods, at the wish of us Christians, after an affair in which, whether it was well done or ill done, I did some part of the work myself."

"And how call you that chief?" demanded Mark.

"Why, he had various names, according to the business he was on. To some he was known as the Leaping Panther, for he was a man of an extraordinary jump; and others again used to style him Pepperage, since there was a saying that neither bullet nor sword could enter his body; though that was a mistake, as his death hath fully proven. But his real name, according to the uses and sounds of his own people, was My Anthony Mow."

"My Anthony Mow!"

"Yes; My, meaning that he was their chief; Anthony, being the given name; and Mow, that of the breed of which he came;" rejoined Eben with confidence, satisfied that he had finally produced a sufficiently sonorous appellative and a perfectly lucid etymology. But criticism was diverted from its aim by the action of the prisoner, as these equivocal sounds struck his ear. Ruth recoiled, and clasped her little namesake closer to her side, when she saw the dazzling brightness of his glowing eyes, and the sudden and expressive dilation of his nostrils. For a moment his lips were compressed with more than the usual force of Indian gravity, and then they slightly severed. A low, soft, and, as even the startled matron was obliged to confess, a plaintive sound issued from between them, repeating mournfully—

"Miantonimoh!"

The word was uttered with a distinct, but deeply guttural enunciation.

"The child mourneth for its parent," exclaimed the sensitive mother. "The hand that slew the warrior may have done an evil deed."

"I see the evident and foreordering will of a wise Providence in this," said Mark Heathcote with solemnity. "The youth hath been deprived of one who might have enticed him still deeper into the bonds of the heathen, and hither hath he been led in order to be placed upon the straight and narrow path. He shall become a dweller among mine, and we will strive against the evil of his mind until instruction shall prevail. Let him be fed and nurtured equally with the things of life and the things of the world; for who knoweth that which is designed in his behalf?"

If there were more of faith than of rational conclusion in this opinion of the old Puritan, there was no external evidence to contradict it. While the examination of the boy was going on in the dwelling, a keen scrutiny had taken place in the out-buildings, and in the adjacent fields. Those engaged in this duty soon returned, to say that not the smallest trace of an ambush was visible about the place; and as the captive himself had no weapons of hostility, even Ruth began to hope that the mysterious conceptions of her father on the subject were not entirely delusive. The captive was now fed, and old Mark was on the point of making a proper beginning in the task he had so gladly assumed, by an up-offering of thanks, when Whittal Ring broke rudely into the room, and disturbed the solemnity of his preparations by a sudden and boisterous outcry.

"Away with scythe and sickle," shouted the witling; "it's many a day since the fields of Wish-Ton-Wish have been trodden down by horsemen in buff jerkins, or ambushed by creeping Wampanaogs."

"There is danger at hand!" exclaimed the sensitive Ruth. "Husband, the warning was timely."

"Here are truly some riding from the forest, and drawing nigh to the dwelling; but as they are seemingly men of our kind and faith, we have need rather of rejoicing than of terror. They bear the air of messengers from the river."

Mark Heathcote listened with surprise, and perhaps with a momentary uneasiness; but all emotion passed away on the instant, for one so disciplined in mind rarely permitted any outward exposure of his secret thoughts. The Puritan calmly issued an order to replace the prisoner in the block-house, assigning the upper of the two principal floors for his keeping; and then he prepared himself to receive guests that were little wont to disturb the quiet of his secluded valley. He was still in the act of giving forth the necessary mandates, when the tramp of horses was heard in the court, and he was summoned to the door to greet his unknown visitors.

"We have reached Wish-Ton-Wish, and the dwelling of Captain Mark Heathcote," said one, who appeared, by his air and better attire, to be the principal of four that composed the party.

"By the favor of Providence, I call myself the unworthy owner of this place of refuge."

"Then a subject so loyal, and a man who hath so long proved himself faithful in the wilderness, will not turn from his door the agents of his anointed master."

"There is One greater than any of earth who hath taught us to leave the the latch free. I pray you to alight, and to partake of that we can offer."

With this courteous but quaint explanation the horsemen dismounted; and, giving their steeds into the keeping of the laborers of the farm, they entered the dwelling.

While the maidens of Ruth were preparing a repast suited to the hour and to the quality of the guests, Mark and his son had abundant opportunity to examine the appearance of the strangers. They were men who seemed to wear visages peculiarly adapted to the character of their entertainers, being in truth so singularly demure and grave in aspect, as to excite some suspicion of their being newly converted zealots to the mortifying customs of the Colony.

Notwithstanding their extraordinary gravity, and contrary to the uses of those regions, too, they bore about their persons certain evidence of being used to the fashions of the other hemisphere. The pistols attached to their saddle-bows, and other accouterments of a warlike aspect would perhaps have attracted no observation, had they not been accompanied by a fashion in the doublet, the hat, and the boot, that denoted a greater intercourse with the mother country than was usual among the less sophisticated natives of those regions. None traversed the forest without the means of defense; but, on the other hand, few wore the hostile implements with so much of a worldly air, or with so many minor particularities of some recent caprice in fashion. As they had, however, announced themselves to be officers of the king, they, who of necessity must be chiefly concerned in the object of their visit, patiently awaited the pleasure of the strangers, to learn why duty had called them so far from all the more ordinary haunts of men; for, like the native owners of the soil, the self-restrained religionists appeared to reckon an indiscreet haste in anything among the more unmanly weaknesses.

Nothing for the first half-hour of their visit escaped the guarded lips of men evidently well skilled in their present duty, which might lead to a clew of its purport. The morning meal passed almost without discourse, and one of the party had arisen with the professed object of looking to their steeds, before he, who seemed the chief, led the conversation to a subject, that by its political bearing might, in some degree, be supposed to have a remote connection with the principal object of his journey to that sequestered valley.

"Have the tiding of the gracious boon that hath lately flowed from the favor of the king, reached the distant settlement?" asked the principal personage, one that wore a far less military air than a younger companion, who, by his confident mien, appeared to be the second in authority.

"To what boon hath thy words import?" demanded the Puritan, turning a glance of the eye at his son and daughter, together with the others in hearing, as if to admonish them to be prudent.

"I speak of the Royal Charter by which the people on the banks of the Connecticut, and they of the Colony of New Haven, are henceforth permitted to unite in goverment; granting them liberty of conscience, and great freedom of self-control."

"Such a gift were worthy of a king! Hath Charles done this?"

"That hath he, and much more that is fitting in a kind and royal mind. The realm is finally freed from the abuses of usurpers, and power now resteth in the hands of a race long set apart for its privileges."

"It is to be wished that practice shall render them expert and sage in its uses," rejoined Mark, somewhat dryly.

"It is a merry prince! and one but little given to the study and exercises of his martyred father; but he hath great cunning in discourse, and few around his dread person have keener wit or more ready tongue."

Mark bowed his head in silence, seemingly little disposed to push the discussion of his earthly master's qualities to a conclusion that might prove offensive to so loyal an admirer. One inclining to suspicion would have seen, or thought he saw, certain equivocal glances from the stranger, while he was thus lauding the vivacious qualities of the restored monarch, which should denote a desire to detect how far the eulogiums might be grateful to his host. He acquiesced, however, in the wishes of the Puritan, though whether understandingly, or without design, it would have been difficult to say, and submitted to change the discourse.

"It is likely, by thy presence, that tidings have reached the Colonies from home," said Content, who understood, by the severe and reserved expression of his father's features, that it was a fitting time for him to interpose.

"There is one arrived in the Bay, within the month, by means of a king's frigate; but no trader hath yet passed between the countries, except the ship which maketh the annual voyage from Bristol to Boston."

"And he who hath arrived—doth he come in authority?" demanded Mark; "or is he merely another servant of the Lord, seeking to rear his tabernacle in the wilderness?"

"Thou shalt know the nature of his errand," returned the stranger, casting a glance of malicious intelligence obliquely towards his companions, at the same time that he arose and placed in the hand of his host a commission which evidently bore the seal of state. "It is expected that all aid will be given to one bearing this warranty, by a subject of a loyalty so approved as that of Captain Mark Heathcote."

CHAPTER VI.

"But, by your leave,
I am an officer of state, and come
To speak with—"—CORIOLANUS.

NOTWITHSTANDING the sharp look which the messenger of the crown deliberately and now openly fastened on the master of Wish-Ton-Wish, while the latter was reading the instrument that was placed before his eyes, there was no evidence of uneasiness to be detected in the unmoved features of the latter. Mark Heathcote had too long schooled his passions to suffer an unseemly manifestation of surprise to escape him; and he was by nature a man of far too much nerve to betray alarm at any trifling exhibition of danger. Returning the parchment to the other, he said with unmoved calmness to his son:

"We must open wide the doors of Wish-Ton-Wish. Here is one charged with authority to look into the secrets of all the dwellings of the Colony." Then, turning with dignity to the agent of the crown, he added, "Thou hast better commence thy duty in season, for we are many and occupy much space."

The face of the stranger flushed a little, it might have been with shame for the vocation in which he had come so far, or it might have been in resentment at so direct a hint that the sooner his disagreeable office should be ended, the better it would please his host. Still, he betrayed no intention of shrinking from its performance. On the contrary, discarding somewhat of that subdued manner which he had probably thought it politic to assume, while sounding the opinions of one so rigid, he broke out rather suddenly in the exhibition of a humor somewhat better suited to the tastes of whom he served.

"Come, then," he cried, winking at his companions, "since doors are opened, it would speak ill of our breeding should we refuse to enter. Captain Heathcote has been a soldier, and he knows how to excuse a traveler's freedom. Surely one who has tasted of the pleasures of the camp must weary at times of this sylvan life?"

"The steadfast in faith weary not, though the road be long and the wayfaring grievous."

"Hum—'tis pity that the journeying between merry England and these colonies is not more brisk. I do not presume to instruct a gentleman who is my senior, and peradventure my better; but opportunity is everything in a man's fortunes. It were charity to let you know, worthy sir, that opinions have changed at home: it is full a twelve-month since I have heard a line of the Psalms, or a verse of St. Paul quoted, in discourse; at least by men who are at all esteemed for their discretion."

"This change in the fashion of speech may better suit thy earthly than thy heavenly master," said Mark Heathcote, sternly.

"Well, well, that peace may exist between us, we will not bandy words about a text more or less, if we may escape the sermon," rejoined the stranger, no longer affecting restraint, but laughing with sufficient freedom at his own conceit; a species of enjoyment in which his companions mingled with great good-will, and without much deference to the humor of those under whose roof they found themselves.

A small glowing spot appeared on the pale cheek of the Puritan, and disappeared again like some transient deception produced by the play of light. Even the meek eye of Content kindled at the insult; but, like his father, the practice of self-denial, and a never slumbering consciousness of his own imperfections, smothered the momentary exhibition of displeasure.

"If thou hast authority to look into the secret places of our habitations, do thy office," he said with a peculiarity of tone which served to remind the other that, though he bore the commission of the Stuart, he was in an extremity of his empire, where even the authority of a king lost some of its value.

Affecting to be, and possibly in reality conscious of his indiscretion, the stranger hastily disposed himself to the execution of his duty.

"It would be a great and pain-saving movement," he said, "were we to assemble the household in one apartment. The government at home would be glad to hear something of the quality of its lieges in this distant quarter. Thou hast doubtless a bell to summon the flocks at stated periods."

"Our people are yet near the dwelling," returned Content: "if it be thy pleasure, none shall be absent from the search."

Gathering from the eye of the other that he was serious in this wish, the quiet colonist proceeded to the gate, and, placing a shell to his mouth, blew one of those blasts that are so often heard in the forests summoning families to their homes, and which are alike used as the signals of peaceful recall, or of alarm. The sound soon brought all within hearing to the court, whither the Puritan and his unpleasant guests now repaired as to the spot best suited to the purpose of the latter.

"Hallam," said the principal personage of the four visitors, addressing him who might once have been, if he were not still, some subaltern in the forces of the Crown, for he was attired in a manner that bespoke him but a half-disguised dragoon, "I leave thee to entertain this goodly assemblage. Thou may'st pass the time in discoursing on the vanities of the world, of which I believe few are better qualified to speak understandingly than thyself, or a few words of admonition to hold fast to the faith would come with fitting weight from thy lips. But look to it, that none of thy flock wander; for here must every creature of them remain, stationary as the indiscreet partner of Lot, till I have cast an eye into all the cunning places of their abode. So set wit to work, and show thy breeding as an entertainer."

After this irreverent charge to his subordinate, the speaker signified to Content and his father that he and his remaining attendant would proceed to a more minute examination of the premises.

When Mark Heathcote saw the man who had so rudely broken upon the peaceful habits of his family was ready to proceed, he advanced steadily in his front, like one who boldly invited inquiry, and by a brave gesture desired him to follow. The stranger, perhaps as much from habit as from any settled design, first cast a free glance around at the bevy of fluttered maidens, leered even upon the modest and meek-eyed Ruth herself, and then took the direction indicated by him who had so unhesitatingly assumed the office of a guide.

The object of this examination still remained a secret between those who made it, and the Puritan who had probably found its motive in the written warranty which had been submitted to his inspection. That it proceeded from fitting authority, none might doubt; and that it was in some manner connected with the events that were known to have wrought so sudden and so great a change in the government of the mother country, all believed probable. Nothwithstanding the seeming mystery of the procedure, the search was not the less rigid. Few habitations of any size or pretension were erected in those times which did not contain certain secret places where valuables and even persons might be concealed, at need.

The strangers displayed great familiarity with the nature and ordinary positions of these private recesses. Not a chest, a closet, nor even a drawer of size, escaped their vigilance; nor was there a plank that sounded hollow, but the master of the valley was called on to explain the cause. In one or two instances, boards were wrested violently from their fastenings, and the cavities beneath were explored, with a wariness that increased as the investigation proceeded without success.

The strangers appeared irritated by their failure. An hour passed in the keenest scrutiny, and nothing had transpired which brought them any nearer to their object. That they had commenced the search with more than usually confident anticipations of a favorable result, might have been gathered from the boldness of tone assumed by their chief, and the pointed personal allusions in which, from time to time, he indulged, often too freely, and always at some expense to the loyalty of the Heathcotes. But when he had completed the circuit of the buildings, having entered all parts from their cellars to the garrets, his spleen became so strong as, in some degree, to get the better of a certain parade of discretion, which he had hitherto managed to maintain in the midst of all his levity.

"Hast seen nothing, Mr. Hallam?" he demanded of the individual left on watch, as they crossed the court in retiring from the last of the out-buildings; "or have those traces which led us to this distant settlement proved false? Captain Heathcote, you have seen that we come not without sufficient warranty, and it is in my power to say we come not without sufficient—"

Checking himself, as if about to utter more than was prudent, he suddenly cast an eye on the block-house, and demanded its uses.

"It is, as thou seest, a building erected for the purposes of defense," replied Mark; "one to which, in the event of an inroad of the savages, the family may fly for refuge."

"Ah! these citadels are not unknown to me. I have met with others during my journey, but none so formidable or so military as this. It hath a soldier for its governor, and should hold out for a reasonable siege. Being a place of pretension, we will look closer into its mystery."

He then signified an intention to close the search by an examination of this edifice. Content unhesitatingly threw open its door, and invited him to enter.

"On the word of one who, though now engaged in a more peaceful calling, has been a campaigner in his time, 'twould be no child's play to carry this tower without artillery. Had thy spies given notice of our approach, Captain Heathcote, the entrance might have been more difficult than we now find it. We have a ladder here! Where the means of mounting are found, there must be something to tempt one to ascend. I will taste your forest air from an upper room."

"You will find the apartment above like this below, merely provided for the security of the unoffending dwellers of the habitations," said Content; while he quietly arranged the ladder before the trap, and then led the way himself to the floor above.

"Here have we loops for the musketoons," cried the stranger, looking about him, understandingly, "and reasonable defenses against shot. Thou hast not forgotten thy art, Captain Heathcote, and I consider myself fortunate in having entered thy fortress by surprise, or I should rather say, in amity, since the peace is not yet broken between us. But why have we

so much of household gear in a place so evidently equipped for war?"

"Thou forgettest that women and children may be driven to this block for a residence," replied Content. "It would show little discretion to neglect matters that might be useful to their wants."

"Is there trouble with the savages?" demanded the stranger, a little quickly; "the gossips of the Colony bade us fear nothing on that head."

"One cannot say at what hour creatures trained in their wild natures may choose to rise. The dwellers on the borders therefore never neglect a fitting caution."

"Hist!" interrupted the stranger; "I hear a footstep above. Ha! the scent will prove true at last! Hilloa, Master Hallam!" he cried, from one of the loops; "let thy statues of salt dissolve, and come hither to the tower. Here is work for a regiment, for well do we know the nature of that we are to deal with."

The sentinel in the court shouted to his companion in the stables; and then openly and boisterously exulting in the prospects of a final success to a search which had hitherto given them useless employment throughout many a long day and weary ride, they rushed together to the block-house.

"Now, worthy lieges of a gracious master," said the leader, when he perceived himself backed by all his armed followers, and speaking with the air of a man flushed with success, "now quickly provide the means of mounting to the upper story. I have thrice heard the tread of man, moving across that floor; though it hath been light and wary, the planks are tell-tales, and have not had their schooling."

Content heard the request, which was uttered sufficiently in the manner of an order, perfectly unmoved. Without betraying either hesitation or concern he disposed himself to comply. Drawing the light ladder through the trap below, he placed it against the one above him, and ascending, he raised the door. He then returned to the floor beneath, making a quite gesture to imply that they who chose might mount. But the strangers regarded each other with very visible doubts. Neither of the inferiors seemed disposed to precede his chief, and the latter evidently hesitated as to the order in which it was meet to make the necessary advance.

"Is there no other manner of mounting but by this narrow ascent?" he asked.

"None. Thou wilt find the ladder secure, and of no difficult height. It is intended for the use of women and children."

" Ay," muttered the officer; " but your women and children are not called upon to confront the devil in a human form. Fellows, are thy weapons in serviceable condition ? Here may be need of spirit ere we get our—Hist ! by the divine right of our gracious master ! there is truly one stirring above. Harkee, my friend ; thou knowest the road so well we will choose to follow thy conduct."

Content, who seldom permitted ordinary events to disturb the equanimity of his temper, quietly assented, and led the way up the ladder, like one who saw no ground for apprehension in the undertaking. The agent of the crown sprang after him, taking care to keep as near as possible to the person of his leader, and calling to his inferiors to lose no time in backing him with their support. The whole mounted through the trap with an alacrity nothing short of that with which they would have pressed through a dangerous breach ; nor did either of the four take time to survey the lodgment he had made, until the whole party was standing in array, with hands grasping the handles of their pistols, or seeking as it were instinctively the hilts of their broadswords.

" By the dark visage of the Stuart ! " exclaimed the principal personage, after satisfying himself by a long and disappointed gaze, that what he said was true, " here is naught but an unarmed savage boy ! "

" Didst expect to meet else ? " demanded the still unmoved Content.

" Hum—that which we expected to meet is sufficiently known to the quaint old gentleman below, and to our own good wisdom. If thou doubtest of our right to look into the very hearts, warranty for that we do can be forthcoming. King Charles had little cause to be tender of his mercies to the dwellers of these colonies, who lent but too willing ears to the whinings and hypocrisies of the wolves in sheep's clothing, of whom old England hath now so happily gotten rid. Thy buildings shall again be rummaged from the bricks of the chimney-tops to the corner-stone in thy cellars, unless deceit and rebellious cunning shall be abandoned, and the truth proclaimed with the openness and fairness of bold-speaking Englishmen."

" I know not what is called the fairness of bold-speaking Englishmen, since fairness of speech is not a quality of one people or of one land ; but well I do know that deceit is sinful, and little of it, I humbly trust, is practiced in this settlement. I am ignorant of what is sought, and therefore it cannot be that I meditate treachery."

" Thou hearest, Hallam ; he reasoneth on a matter that toucheth the peace and safety of the king ! " cried the other, his arrogance of manner increasing with the anger of disappointment. " But why is this dark-skinned boy a prisoner ? Dost dare to constitute thyself a sovereign over the natives of this continent, and affect to have shackles and dungeons for such as meet thy displeasure ! "

" The lad is in truth a captive ; but he has been taken in defense of life, and hath little to complain of more than loss of freedom."

" I will inquire deeply into this proceeding. Though commissioned on an errand of different interest, yet, as one trusted in a matter of moment, I take upon me the office of protecting every oppressed subject of the crown. There may grow discoveries out of this practice, Hallam, fit to go before the council itself."

" Thou wilt find but little here, worthy of the time and attention of those burdened with the care of a nation," returned Content. " The youthful heathen was found lurking near our habitations the past night ; and he is kept where thou seest, that he may not carry the tidings of our condition to his people, who are doubtless outlying in the forest, waiting for a fit moment to work their evil."

" How meanest thou ? " hastily exclaimed the other, " at hand in the forest, didst say ? "

" There can be little doubt. One young as this would scarce be found distant from the warriors of his tribe ; and that the more especially, as he was taken in the commission of an ambush."

" I hope thy people are not without good provision of arms, and other sufficient muniments of resistance. I trust the palisadoes are firm, and the posterns ingeniously defended."

" We look with a diligent eye to our safety, for it is well known to us dwellers on the borders that there is little security but in untiring watchfulness. The young men were at the gates until the morning. and we did intend to make a strong scouting into the woods as the day advanced, in order to look for those signs that may lead us to conclusions on the number and purposes of those by whom we are environed, had not thy visit called us to our duties."

" And why so tardy in speaking of this intent ? " demanded the agent of the king, leading the way down the ladder with suspicious haste. " It is a commendable prudence, and must not be delayed. I take upon me the responsibilities of commanding that all proper care be had in defense of the weaker subjects of the crown who are here collected. Are our roadsters well replenished, Hallam? Duty, as thou sayest, is an imperative master; it recalls us more into the heart of the Colony. I would it might shortly point the way to Europe!" he muttered, as he reached the ground. "Go, fellows; see to our beasts, and let them be speedily prepared for departure."

The attendants, though men of sufficient spirit in open war, and when it was to be exercised in a fashion to which they were accustomed, had, like other mortals, a wholesome deference for unknown and terrific-looking danger. It is a well-known truth, and one that has been proved by the experience of two centuries, that while the European soldier has ever been the readiest to have recourse to the assistance of the terrible warrior of the American forest, he has, in nearly every instance, when retaliation or accident has made him the object instead of the spectator of the ruthless nature of his warfare, betrayed the most salutary, and frequently the most ludicrous apprehension of the prowess of his ally. While Content, therefore, looked so steadily, though still seriously, at the peculiar danger in which he was placed, the four strangers seemingly saw all of its horrors without any of the known means of avoiding them. Their chief quickly abandoned the insolence of office, and the tone of disappointment, for a mien of greater courtesy; and, as policy is often seen suddenly to change the sentiments of even more pretending personages, when interests assume a new aspect, so did his language rapidly take a character of conciliation and courtesy.

The handmaidens were no longer leered at; the mistress of the dwelling was treated with marked deference; and the air of deep respect with which even the principal of the party addressed the aged Puritan, bordered on an exhibition of commendable reverence. Something was said in the way of an apology, for the disagreeable obligations of duty, and of a difference between a manner that was assumed to answer secret purposes, and that which nature and a sense of right would dictate; but neither Mark nor his son appeared to have sufficient interest in the motives of their visitors, to put them to the trouble of repeating explanations that were as awkward to those who uttered them as they were unnecessary to those who listened.

So far from offering any further obstacle to the movements of the family, the borderers were seriously urged to pursue their previous intentions of thoroughly examining the woods. The dwelling was accordingly intrusted, under the orders of the Puritan, to the keeping of about half the laborers, assisted by the Enropeans, who clung with instinctive attachment to the possession of the block-house; their leader repeatedly and rightly enough declaring though ready at all times to risk life on a plain, he had an unconquerable distaste to putting it in jeopardy in a thicket. Attended by Eben Dudley, Reuben Ring, and two other stout youths, all well though lightly armed, Content then left the palisadoes, and took his way towards the forest. They entered the woods at the nearest point, always marching with the caution and vigilance that a sense of the true nature of the risk they ran would inspire, and much practice only could properly direct.

The manner of the search was as simple as it was likely to prove effectual. The scouts commenced a circuit round the clearing, extending their line as far as might be done without cutting off their support, and each man lending his senses attentively to the signs of the trail, or of the lairs, of those dangerous enemies, who they had reason to think were outlying in their neighborhood. But, like the recent search in the buildings, the scouting was for a long time attended by no results. Many weary miles were passed slowly over, and more than half their task was ended, and no signs of being having life was met, except the visible trail of their four guests, and the tracks of a single horse along the path leading to the settlements from the quarter by which the visitor of the previous night had been known to approach. No comments were made by any of the party, as each in succession struck and crossed this path, nearly at the same instant; but a low call from Reuben Ring which soon after met their ears, caused them to assemble in a body at the spot whence the summons had proceeded.

"Here are signs of one passing *from* the clearing," said the quick-eyed woodsman, "and one, too, that is not numbered among the family of Wish-Ton-Wish; since his beast hath had a shodden hoof, a mark which belongeth to no animal of ours."

"We will follow," said Content, immediately striking in upon a straggling trail, that by many unequivocal signs had been left by some animal which had passed that way not many hours before. Their search, however, soon drew to a close. Ere they had gone any great distance, they came upon the half-demolished carcass of a dead horse. There was no mistaking the proprietor of this unfortunate animal. Though some beast, or rather beasts of prey, had fed plentifully on the body, which was still fresh, and had scarcely yet done bleeding, it was plain, by the remains of the torn equipments, as well as by the color and size of the animal, that it was no other than the hack ridden by the unknown and mysterious guest, who, after sharing in the worship and in the evening meal of the family of Wish-Ton-Wish, had so strangely and so suddenly disappeared. The leathern sack, the weapons which had so singularly riveted the gaze of old Mark, and indeed all but the carcass and a ruined saddle, were gone ; but what was left sufficiently served to identify the animal.

"Here has been the tooth of wolf," said Eben Dudley, stooping to examine into the nature of a ragged wound in the neck ; "and here, too, has been cut of knife ; but whether by the hand of a redskin, it exceedeth my art to say."

Each individual of the party now bent curiously over the wound ; but the results of their inquiries went no further than to prove that it was undeniably the horse of the stranger that had forfeited its life. To the fate of its master, however, there was not the slightest clew. Abandoning the investigation, after a long and fruitless examination, they proceeded to finish the circuit of the clearing. Night had approached ere the fatiguing task was accomplished. As Ruth stood at the postern waiting anxiously for their return, she saw by the countenance of her husband, that while nothing had transpired to give any grounds of additional alarm, no satisfactory testimony had been obtained to explain the nature of the painful doubts, with which, as a tender and sensitive mother, she had been distressed throughout the day.

CHAPTER VII.

"Is there not milking-time,
When you go to bed, or kiln-hole,
To whistle off these secrets ; but you must be
Tattling before all our guests ?"—WINTER'S TALE.

LONG experience hath shown that the white man, when placed in situations to acquire such knowledge, readily becomes the master of most of that peculiar skill for which the North American Indian is so remarkable, and which enables him, among other things, to detect the signs of a forest trail, with a quickness and an accuracy of intelligence that amount nearly to an instinct. The fears of the family were therefore greatly quieted by the reports of the scouts, all of whom agreed in the opinion that no party of savages, that could be at all dangerous to a force like their own, was lying near the valley ; and some of whom, the loudest of which number being stout Eben Dudley, boldly offered to answer for the security of those who depended on their vigilance, with their own lives.

These assurances had, beyond a doubt, a soothing influence on the apprehensions of Ruth and her hand-maidens ; but they somewhat failed of their effect with those unwelcome visitors who still continued to cumber Wish-Ton-Wish with their presence. Though they had evidently abandoned all ideas connected with the original object of their visit, they spoke not of departure. On the contrary, as night approached, their chief entered into council with old Mark Heathcote, and made certain propositions for the security of his dwelling, which the Puritan saw no reason to oppose.

A regular watch was, in consequence, set, and maintained till morning, at the palisadoes. The different members of the family retired to their usual places of rest, tranquil in appearance, if not in entire confidence of peace ; and the military messengers to post in the lower of the two fighting apartments of the citadel. With this simple, and to the strangers particularly satisfactory arrangement, the hours of darkness passed away in quiet ; morning returning to the secluded valley, as it had so often done before, with its loveliness unimpaired by violence or tumult.

In the same peaceful manner did the sun set successively three several times, and as often did it arise on the abode of the Heathcotes, without further sign of danger, or motive of alarm. With the passage of time, the agents of the Stuart gradually regained their confidence. Still they never neglected to withdraw within the protection of the block-house with the retiring light ; a post which the subordinate named Hallam more than once gravely observed, they were, by their disciplined and military habits, singularly qualified to maintain. Though the Puritan secretly chafed under this protracted visit, habitual self-denial, and a manner so long subdued, enabled him to conceal his disgust. For the first two days after the alarm, the deportment of his guests was unexceptionable. All their faculties appeared to be engrossed with keen and anxious watchings of the forest, out of which it would seem they expected momentarily to see issue a band of ferocious and ruthless savages; but symptoms of returning levity began to be apparent, as confidence and a feeling of security increased, with the quiet passage of the hours.

It was on the evening of the third day from that on which they had made their appearance in the settlement, that the man called Hallam was seen strolling, for the first time, through the postern so often named, and taking a direction which led toward the out-buildings. His air was less distrustful than it had been for many a weary hour, and his step proportionably confident and assuming. Instead of wearing, as he had been wont, a pair of heavy horseman's pistols at his girdle, he had even laid aside his broadsword, and appeared more in the guise of one who sought his personal ease, than in that cumbersome and martial attire which all of his party, until now, had deemed it prudent to maintain. He cast his glance cursorily over the fields of the Heathcotes, as they glowed under the soft light of a setting sun; nor did his eye even refuse to wander vacantly along the outline of that forest, which his imagination had so lately been peopling with beings of a fierce and ruthless nature.

The hour was one when rustic economy brings the labors of the day to a close. Among those who were more than usually active at that busy moment, was a handmaiden of Ruth, whose clear sweet voice was heard, in one of the inclosures, occasionally rising on the notes of a spiritual song, and as often sinking to a nearly inaudible hum, as she extracted from a favorite animal liberal portions of its nightly tribute to the dairy of her mistress. To that inclosure the stranger, as it were by accident, suffered his sauntering footsteps to stroll, seemingly as much in admiration of the sleek herd as of any other of its comely tenants.

"From what thrush hast taken lessons, my pretty maid, that I mistook thy notes for one of the sweetest songsters of thy woods?" he asked, trusting his person to the support of the pen, in an attitude of easy superiority. "One might fancy it a robin, or a wren, trolling out his evening song, instead of human voice, rising and falling in everyday psalmody."

"The birds of our forest rarely speak," returned the girl, "and the one among them which has most to say, does it like those who are called gentlemen, when they set wit to work to please the ear of simple country maidens."

"And in what fashion may that be?"
"Mockery."

"Ah! I have heard of the creature's skill. It is said to be a compound of the harmony of all other forest songsters, and yet I see little resemblance to the honest language of a soldier in its manner of utterance.

"It speaketh without much meaning; and oftener to cheat the ear than in honest reason."

"Thou forgettest that which I told thee in the morning, child. It would seem that they who named thee have no great cause to exult in their judgment of character, since Unbelief would better describe thy disposition than Faith."

"It may be, that they who named me little knew how great must be credulity, to give ear to all I have been required to credit."

"Thou can'st have no difficulty in admitting that thou art comely, since the eye itself will support thy belief; nor can one of so quick speech fail to know that her wit is sharper than common. Thus far I admit the name of Faith will not surely belie thy character."

"If Eben Dudley hear thee use such vanity-stirring discourse," returned the half-pleased girl, "he might give thee less credit for wit than thou seemest willing to yield to others. I hear his heavy foot among the cattle, and ere long we shall be sure to see a face that hath little more of lightness to boast."

"This Eben Dudley is a personage of no mean importance, I find!" muttered the other, continuing his walk, as the borderer named made his appearance at another entrance of the pen. The glances exchanged between them were far from friendly, though the woodsman permitted the stranger to pass without any oral expression of displeasure.

"The skittish heifer is getting gentle at last, Faith Ring," said the borderer, casting the butt of his musket on the ground with a violence that left a deep impression on the faded sward at his feet. "That brindled ox, old Logger, is not more willing to come into his yoke than is the four-year-old to yield her milk."

"The creature has been getting kind since you taught the manner to tame its humor," returned the dairy girl, in a voice that, spite of every effort of maiden pride, betrayed something of a flurry of her spirits, while she plied her light task with violent industry.

"Umph! I hope some other of my teachings may be as well remembered; but thou art quick at the trick of learning, Faith, as is plain by the ready manner in which thou hast so shortly got the habit of discourse with a man as nimble-tongued as yon riding reprobate from over sea."

"I hope that civil listening is no proof of unseemly discourse on the part of one who hath been trained in modesty of speech, Eben Dudley. Thou has often said, it was the bounden duty of her who was spoken to, to give ear, lest some might say she was of scornful mind, and her name for pride be better earned than that for good nature."

"I see that more of my lessons than I had hoped are still in thy keeping. So thou listeneth thus readily, Faith, because it is meet that a maiden should not be scornful?"

"Thou sayest so. Whatever ill name I may deserve, thou hast no right to count scorn among my failings."

"If I do, may I—" Eben Dudley bit his lip, and checked an expression which would have given grievous offense to one whose habits of decency were as severe as those of his companion. "Thou must have heard much that was profitable to-day, Faith Ring," he added, "considering that thy ear is so open, and that thy opportunities have been great."

"I know not what thou would'st say by speaking of my opportunities," returned the girl, bending still lower beneath the object of her industry, in order to conceal the glow which her own quick consciousness told her was burning on her cheek.

"I would say that the tale must be long that needeth four several trials of private speech to finish."

"Four! As I hope to be believed for a girl of truth in speech or deed, this is but the third time that the stranger hath spoken to me apart since the sun hath risen."

"If I know the number of the fingers of my hand, it is the fourth."

"Nay; how can'st thou, Eben Dudley, who hast been a-field since the crowing of the cock, know what hath passed about the dwellings? It is plain that envy, or some other evil passion, causeth thee to speak angrily."

"How is it that I know! perhaps thou thinkest, Faith, thy brother Reuben only hath the gift of sight."

"The labor must have gone on with great profit to the captain, whilst eyes have been roving over other matters! But perhaps they kept the strong of arm for the lookers-out, and have set them of feebler bodies to the toil."

"I have not been so careless of thy life as to forget, at passing moments, to cast an eye abroad, pert one. Whatever thou

mayest think of the need, there would be fine wailings in the butteries and dairies, did the Wampanoags get into the clearing, and there were none to give the alarm in season.

"Truly, Eben, thy terror of the child in the block must be grievous for one of thy manhood, else would'st thou not watch the buildings so narrowly," retorted Faith, laughing; for with the dexterity of her sex, she began to feel the superiority she was gradually obtaining in the discourse. "Thou dost not remember that we have valiant troopers from old England, to keep the younker from doing harm. But here cometh the brave soldier himself; it will be well to ask vigilance at his hands, or this night may bring us to the tomahawk in our sleep!"

"Thou speakest of the weapon of the savages!" said the messenger, who had drawn near again with a visible willingness to share in an interview which, while he had watched its progress at a distance, appeared to be growing interesting. "I trust all fear is over from that quarter."

"As you say, for *this* quarter," said Eben, adjusting his lips to a low whistle, and coolly looking up to examine the heavenly body to which he meant allusion. "But the *next* quarter may bring us a pretty piece of Indian skirmishing."

"And what hath the moon in common with an incursion of the savages? Are there those among them who study the secret of the stars?"

"They study deviltries and other wickedness more than aught else. It is not easy for the mind of man to fancy horrors such as they design, when Providence has given them success in an inroad."

"But thou did'st speak of the moon! In what manner is the moon leagued with their bloody plots?"

"We have her now in the full, and there is little of the night when the eye of a watcher might not see a red-skin in the clearing; but a different tale may be heard, when an hour or two of jet darkness shall again fall among these woods. There will be a change shortly; it behooveth us therefore to be on our guard."

"Thou thinkest then, truly, that there are outlyers waiting for the fitting moment?" said the officer, with an interest so marked as to cause even the but-half-pacified Faith to glance an arch look at her companion, though he still had reason to distrust a willful expression that lurked in the corner of her eyes, which threatened at each moment to contradict his relation of the sinister omens.

"There may be savages lying in the

hills at a day's journey in the forest : but they know the aim of a white man's musket too well to be sleeping within reach of its range. It is the nature of an Indian to eat and sleep while he has time for quiet, and to fast and murder when the killing hour hath come."

"And what call you the distance to the nearest settlement on the Connecticut ?" demanded the other, with an air so studiously indifferent as to furnish an easy clew to the inner workings of his mind.

"Some twenty hours would bring a nimble runner to the outer habitations, granting small time for food and rest. He that is wise, however, will take but little of the latter, until his head be safely housed within some such building as yon block, or until there shall stand between him and the forest at least a goodly row of oaken pickets."

"There is no path ridden by which travelers may avoid the forest during the darkness ?"

"I know of none. He who quits Wish-Ton-Wish for the towns below must make his pillow of the earth, or be fain to ride as long as beast can carry him."

"We have truly had experience of this necessity journeying hither. Thou thinkest, friend, that the savages are in their resting time, and that they wait the coming quarter of the moon ?"

"To my seeming, we shall not have them sooner," returned Eben Dudley; taking care to conceal all qualification of this opinion, if any such he entertained, by closely locking its purport in a mental reservation.

"And what season is it usual to choose for getting into the saddle, when business calls any to the settlements below ?"

"We never fail to take our departure about the time the sun touches the tall pine which stands on yonder height of the mountain. Much experience hath told us it is the safest hour ; hand of timepiece is not more sure than yon tree."

"I like the night," said the other, looking about him with the air of one suddenly struck with the promising appearance of the weather. "The blackness no longer hangs about the forest, and it seems a fitting moment to push the matter on which we are sent nearer to its conclusion."

So saying, and probably believing that he had sufficiently concealed the motives of his decision, the uneasy dragoon walked with an air of soldierly coolness towards the dwellings, signing at the same time to one of his companions, who was regarding him from a distance, to approach.

"Now dost thou believe, witless Dud-ley, that the four fingers of thy clumsy hand have numbered the full amount of all that thou callst my listenings ?" said Faith, when she thought no other ear but his to whom she spoke could catch her words, and at the same time laughing merrily beneath her heifer, though still speaking with a vexation she could not entirely repress.

"Have I spoken aught but truth ? It is not for such as I to give lessons in journeying to one who follows the honest trade of a man-hunter. I have said that which all who dwell in these parts know to be reasonable."

"Surely naught else. But truth is made so powerful in thy hands, that it needs to be taken, like a bitter healing draught, with closed eyes and at many swallows. One who drinketh of it too freely may well-nigh be strangled. I marvel that he who is so vigilant in providing for the cares of others, should take so little heed of those he is sent to guard."

"I know not thy meaning, Faith. When was danger near the valley and my musket wanting ?"

"The good piece is truer to duty than its master. Thou mayest have lawful license to sleep on thy post, for we maidens know nothing of the pleasure of the captain in these matters ; but it would be as seemly, if not as soldierly, to place the arms at the postern and thyself at the chambers, when next thou hast need of watching and sleeping in the same hour."

Dudley looked as confused as one of his mold and unbending temperament might well be, though he stubbornly refused to understand the allusion of his offended companion.

"Thou hast not discussed with the trooper from over sea in vain," he said, "since thou speakest so wisely of watches and arms."

"Truly he hath much schooled me in the matter."

"Umph ! and what may be the amount of his teaching ?"

"That he who sleepeth at a postern should neither talk too boldly of the enemy, nor expect maidens to put too much trust—"

"In what, Faith ?"

"Thou surely knowest I mean in his watchfulness. My life on it, had one happened to pass at a later hour than common near the night-post of that gentle-spoken soldier, he would not have been found like a sentinel of this household, in the second watch of the night that was gone, dreaming of the good things of Madam's buttery."

"Didst truly come then, girl ?" said

Eben, dropping his voice, and equally manifesting his satisfaction and his shame. "But thou knowest, Faith, that the labor had fallen behind in behalf of the scouting party, and that the toil of yesterday exceeded that of our usual burdens. Nevertheless, I keep the postern again to-night, from eight to twelve, and—"

"Will make a goodly rest of it, I doubt not. Now he who hath been so vigilant throughout the day must needs tire of the task as night draws on. Fare thee well, wakeful Dudley; if thine eyes should open on the morrow, be thankful that the maidens have not stitched thy garments to the palisadoes."

Notwithstanding the efforts of the young man to detain her, the light-footed girl eluded his grasp, and bearing her burden towards the dairy, she tripped along the path with a half-averted face, in which triumph and repentance were already struggling for the possession.

In the meantime the leader of the messengers and his military subordinate had a long and interesting conference. When it was ended, the former took his way to the apartment in which Mark Heathcote was wont to pass those portions of his time that were not occupied in his secret strivings for the faith, or in exercise without, while superintending the laborers in the fields. With some little circumlocution, which was intended to mask his real motives, the agent of the king announced his intention to take his final departure that very night.

"I felt it a duty, as one who has gained experience in arms by some practice in the wars of Europe," he said, "to tarry in thy dwelling while danger threatened from the lurking savage. It would ill become soldiers to speak of their intentions; but had the alarm in truth sounded, thou wilt give faith when I say that the block-house would not have been lightly yielded! I shall make report to them that sent me, that in Captain Mark Heathcote, Charles hath a loyal subject, and the constitution a firm supporter. The rumors, of a seemingly mistaken description, which have led us hither, shall be contradicted, and doubtless it will be found that some accident hath given rise to the deception. Should there be occasion to dwell on the particulars of the late alarm, I trust the readiness of my followers to do good service to one of the king's subjects will not be overlooked."

"It is the striving of an humble spirit to speak naught evil of its fellows, and to conceal no good," returned the reserved Puritan. "If thou hast found thy abode in my dwelling to thy liking, thou art welcome, and if duty or pleasure calleth thee to quit it, peace go with thee. It will be useful to unite with us in asking that thy passage through the wilderness may be unharmed; that he who watchest over the meanest of his creatures should take thee in his especial keeping, and that the savage heathen—"

"Dost think the savage out of his village?" demanded the messenger, with an indecorous rapidity that cut short the enumeration of the particular blessings and dangers that his host thought it meet to include in the leave-taking prayer.

"Thou surely hast not tarried with us to aid in the defense, and yet feel it doubtful that thy services might be useful!" observed Mark Heathcote, dryly.

"I would the Prince of Darkness had thee and all the other diabolicals of these woods in his own good gripe!" muttered the messenger between his teeth; and then, as if guided by a spirit that could not long be quelled, he assumed something more of his unbridled and natural air, boldly declining to join in the prayer on the plea of haste, and the necessity of his looking in person to the movements of his followers. "But this need not prevent thee, worthy captain, from pouring out an asking in our behalf while we are in the saddle," he concluded; "for ourselves, there remaineth much of thy previously-bestowed pious aliment to be digested, though we doubt not that should thy voice be raised in our behalf, while journeying along the first few leagues of the forest, the tread of the hacks would not be heavier, and it is certainty that we ourselves should be none the worse for the favor."

Then casting a glance of ill-concealed levity at one of his followers who had come to say that their steeds awaited, he made the parting salutation with an air in which the respect that one like the Puritan could scarce fail to excite struggled with his habitual contempt for things of a serious character.

The family of Mark Heathcote, the lowest dependent included, saw these strangers depart with inward satisfaction. Even the maidens, in whom nature, in moments weaker than common, had awakened some of the lighter vanities, were gladly rid of gallants who could not soothe their ears with the unction of flattery without frequently giving great offense to their severe principles, by light and irreverent allusions to things on which they themselves were accustomed to think with fitting awe. Eben Dudley could scarcely conceal the chuckle with which he saw the party bury themselves in the forest, though neither he nor any of the more instructed in such matters, believed they incurred serious risk from their sudden enterprise.

The opinion of the scouts proved to be founded on accurate premises. That and many a subsequent night passed without alarm. The season continued to advance, and the laborers pursued their toil to its close without another appeal to their courage, or any additional reasons for vigilance. Whittal Ring followed his colts with impunity among the recesses of the neighboring forests, and the herds of the family went and came as long as the weather would permit them to range the woods, in regularity and peace. The period of the alarm and the visit of the agents of the crown came to be food for. tradition, and during the succeeding winter the former often furnished motive of merriment around the blazing fires that were so necessary to the country and the season.

Still there existed in the family a living memorial of the unusual incidents of that night. The captive remained long after the events which had placed him in the power of the Heathcotes were beginning to be forgotten.

A desire to quicken the seeds of spiritual regeneration, which, however dormant they might be, old Mark Heathcote believed to exist in the whole family of man, and consequently in the young heathen as well as in others, had become a sort of ruling passion in the Puritan. The fashions and mode of thinking of the times had a strong leaning toward superstition, and it was far from difficult for a man of his ascetic habits and exaggerated doctrines to believe that a special interposition had cast the boy into his hands for some hidden but mighty purpose, that time in the good season would not fail to reveal.

Notwithstanding the strong coloring of fanaticism which tinged the character of the religionists of those days, they were rarely wanting in worldly discretion. The agents they saw fit to employ in order to aid the more hidden purposes of Providence, were in common useful and rational. Thus, while Mark never forgot to summon the lad from his prison at the hour of prayer, or to include an especial asking in behalf of the ignorant heathen in general and of this chosen youth in particular, he hesitated to believe that a manifest miracle would be exerted in his favor.

That no blame might attach to the portion of duty that was confided to human means, he had recourse to the discreet agency of kindness and unremitted care. But all attempts to lure the lad into the habits of a civilized man were completely unsuccessful. As the severity of the weather increased, the compassionate and thoughtful Ruth endeavored to induce him to adopt the garments that were found so necessary to the comfort of men who were greatly his superiors in hardihood and in strength. Clothes decorated in a fashion suited to the taste of an Indian were considerately provided, and entreaties and threats were both freely used, with a view to make the captive wear them. On one occasion he was even forcibly clad by Eben Dudley; and being brought in the unwonted guise into the presence of old Mark, the latter offered up an especial petition that the youth might be made to feel the merit of this concession to the principles of a chastened and instructed man.

But within an hour the stout woodsman, who had been made on the occasion so active an instrument of civilization, announced to the admiring Faith that the experiment was unsuccessful; or, as Eben somewhat irreverently described the extraordinary effort of the Puritan, "the heathen hath already resumed his skin leggings and painted waist-cloth, notwithstanding the captain hath strove to pin better garments on his back, by virtue of a prayer that might have clothed the nakedness of a whole tribe." In short, the result proved in the case of this lad, as similar experiments have since proved in so many other instances, the difficulty of tempting one trained in the freedom and ease of a savage, to consent to admit of the restraints of a state of being that is commonly thought to be so much superior. In every instance in which the youthful captive had liberty of choice, he disdainfully rejected the customs of the whites, adhering with a singular and almost heroic pertinacity to the usages of his people and his condition.

The boy was not kept in his bondage without extraordinary care. Once, when trusted in the fields, he had openly attempted to escape; nor was the possession of his person recovered without putting the speed of Eben Dudley and Reuben Ring to a more severe trial, as was confessed by the athletic young borderers themselves, than any they had hitherto undergone. From that moment, he was never permitted to pass the palisades. When duty called the laborers afield, the captive was invariably secured in his prison, where, as some compensation for his confinement, he was supposed to enjoy the benefit of long and familiar communication with Mark Heathcote, who had the habit of passing many hours of each day, and not unfrequently long portions of the night too, within the retirement of the block-house. During the time only when the gates were closed, or when some one of strength and activity sufficient to control his movements was present, was the latter permitted to stroll at will among the buildings of the border fortress. This liberty he never failed to exercise, and often in a manner that overcame the affectionate Ruth with a painful excess of sensibility.

Instead of joining in the play of the other children, the young captive would stand aloof, and regard their sports with a vacant eye, or, drawing near to the palisadoes, he often passed hours in gazing wistfully at those endless forests in which he first drew breath, and which probably contained all that was most prized in the estimation of his simple judgment. Ruth, touched to the heart by this silent but expressive exhibition of suffering, endeavored in vain to win his confidence, with a view of enticing him into employments that might serve to relieve his care. The resolute but still quiet boy would not be lured into a forgetfulness of his origin. He appeared to comprehend the kind intentions of his gentle mistress, and frequently he even suffered himself to be led by the mother into the center of her own joyous and merry offspring; but it was only to look upon their amusements with his former cold air, and to return, at the first opportunity, to his beloved site at the pickets.

Still there were singular and even mysterious evidences of a growing consciousness of the nature of the discourse of which he was occasionally an auditor, that would have betrayed greater familiarity with the language and opinions of the inhabitants of the valley, than his known origin and his absolute withdrawal from communication could give reason to expect. This important and inexplicable fact was proved by the frequent and meaning glances of his dark eye, when aught was uttered in his hearing that affected, ever so remotely, his own condition; and, once or twice, by the haughty gleamings of ferocity that escaped him, when Eben Dudley was heard to vaunt the prowess of the white men in their encounters with the original owners of the country. The Puritan did not fail to note these symptoms of a budding intelligence, as the pledges of a fruit that would more than reward his pious toil; and they served to furnish a great relief to certain occasional repugnance, which all his zeal could not entirely subdue, at being the instrument of causing so much suffering to one who, after all, had inflicted no positive wrong on himself.

At the period of which we are writing, the climate of these States differed materially from that which is now known to their inhabitants. A winter in the Province of Connecticut was attended by many successive falls of snow, until the earth was entirely covered with firmly compressed masses of the frozen element. Occasional thaws and passing storms of rain, that were driven away by a return of the clear and cutting cold of the northwestern gales, were wont at times to lay a covering on the ground, that was congealed to the consistency of ice, until men, and not unfrequently beasts, and sometimes sleighs, were seen moving on its surface, as on the bed of a frozen lake. During the extremity of a season like this, the hardy borderers, who could not toil in their customary pursuits, were wont to range the forest in quest of game, which, driven for food to known resorting places in the woods, then fell most easily a prey to the intelligence and skill of such men as Eben Dudley and Reuben Ring.

The youths never left the dwellings on these hunts, without exciting the most touching interest in their movements, on the part of the Indian boy. On all such occasions he would linger at the loops of his prison throughout the day, listening intently to the reports of the distant muskets, as they resounded in the forest; and the only time during a captivity of so many months, that he was ever seen to smile, was when he examined the grim look and muscular claws of a dead panther, that had fallen beneath the aim of Dudley, in one of these excursions to the mountains. The compassion of all the borderers was powerfully awakened in behalf of the patient and dignified young sufferer, and gladly would they have given their captive the pleasure of joining in the chase, had not the task been one that was far from easy of accomplishment. The former of the woodsmen just mentioned had even volunteered to lead him like a hound in a leash; but this was a species of degradation against which it was certain that a young Indian, ambitious of the character and jealous of the dignity of a warrior, would have openly rebelled.

The quick interest of the observant Ruth had, as it has been seen, early detected a growing intelligence in the boy. The means by which one, who never mingled in the employments, and who rarely seemed to listen to the dialogues of the family, could come to comprehend the meaning of a language that is found sufficiently difficult for a scholar, were, however, as much of a mystery to her as to all around her. Still, by the aid of that instinctive tact which so often enlightens the mind of a woman, was she certain of the fact. Profiting by this knowledge, she assumed the task of endeavoring to obtain an honorary pledge from her protégé, that, if permitted to join the hunters, he would return to the valley at the end of the day. But though the language of the woman was gentle as her own kind nature, and her entreaties that he would give some evidence of having comprehended her meaning were zealous and oft repeated, not the smallest symptom of intelligence, on this occasion, could be extracted from her pupil. Disappointed, and not without sorrow, Ruth had abandoned her compassionate design in despair, when, on a sudden, the old Puritan, who had been a silent spectator of her fruitless efforts, announced his faith in the integrity of the lad, and his intention to permit him to make one of the very next party that should leave the habitation.

The cause of this sudden change in the hitherto stern watchfulness of Mark Heathcote was, like so many other of his impulses, a secret in his own bosom. It has just been said that during the time Ruth was engaged in her kind and fruitless experiment to extract some evidence of intelligence from the boy, the Puritan was a close and interested observer of her efforts. He appeared to sympathize in her disappointment, but the weal of those unconverted tribes who were to be led from the darkness of their ways by the instrumentality of this youth, was far too important to admit the thought of rashly losing the vantage-ground he had gained, in the gradually-expanding intellect of the boy, by running the hazard of an escape. To all appearances, the intention of permitting him to quit the defenses had therefore been entirely abandoned, when old Mark so suddenly announced a change of resolution. The conjectures on the causes of this unlooked-for determination were exceedingly various.

Some believed that the Puritan had been favored with a mysterious intimation of the pleasure of Providence in the matter; and others thought that, beginning to despair of success in his undertaking, he was willing to seek for a more visible manifestation of its purposes, by hazarding the experiment of trusting the boy to the direction of his own impulses. All appeared to be of opinion that if the lad returned, the circumstance might be set down to the intervention of a miracle. Still, with his resolution once taken, the purpose of Mark Heathcote remained unchanged. He announced this unexpected intention after one of his long and solitary visits to the block-house, where it is possible he had held a powerful spiritual strife on the occasion; and, as the weather was exceedingly favorable for such an object, he commanded his dependents to prepare to make the sortie on the following morning.

A sudden and an uncontrollable gleam of delight flashed on the dark features of the captive, when Ruth was about to place in his hands the bow of her own son, and, by signs and words, she gave him to understand that he was to be permitted to use it in the free air of the forest. But the exhibition of pleasure disappeared as quickly as it had been betrayed. When the lad received the weapons, it was rather with the manner of a hunter accustomed to their use, than of one to whose hands they had so long been strangers. As he left the gates of Wish-Ton-Wish, the handmaidens of Ruth clustered about him, in wondering interest; for it was strange to see a youth so long guarded with jealous care, again free and unwatched. Notwithstanding their ordinary dependence on the secret lights and great wisdom of the Puritan, there was a very general impression that the lad, around whose presence there was so much that was mysterious and of interest to their own security, was now to be gazed upon for the last time. The boy himself was unmoved to the last. Still he paused, with his foot on the threshold of the dwelling, and appeared to regard Ruth and her young offspring with momentary concern. Then, assuming the calm air of an Indian warrior, he suffered his eye to grow cold and vacant, following with a nimble step the hunters who were already passing without the palisadoes.

CHAPTER VIII.

"Well, I am your theme: you have the start of me. I am dejected; I am not able to answer the Welsh flannel; ignorance itself is a plummet over me: use me as you will."
—MERRY WIVES OF WINDSOR.

POETS, aided by the general longing of human nature, have given a reputation to the spring that it rarely merits. Though this imaginative class of writers have said so much of its balmy airs and odoriferous gales, we find it nearly everywhere the most reluctant, churlish, and fickle of the four seasons. It is the youth of the year, and, like that probationary period of life, most fitted to afford the promise of better things. There is a constant struggle between reality and hope throughout the whole of this slow-moving and treacherous period, which has an unavoidable tendency to deceive.

All that is said of its grateful productions is fallacious, for the earth is as little likely to yield a generous tribute without the quickening influence of the summer heats, as man is wont to bring forth commendable fruits without the agency of a higher moral power than any he possesses in virtue of his innate propensities. On the other hand, the fall of the year possesses a sweetness, a repose, and a consistency, which may be justly likened to the decline of a well spent life. It is, in all countries and in every climate, the period when physical and moral causes unite to furnish the richest sources of enjoyment. If the spring is the time of hope, autumn is the season of fruition. There is just enough of change to give zest to the current of existence, while there is too little of vicissitude to be pregnant of disappointment. Succeeding to the nakedness of winter, the spring is grateful by comparison; while the glories of autumn are enjoyed after the genial powers of summer have been lavishly expended.

In obedience to this great law of the earth, let poets sing and fancy as they may, the spring and autumn of America partake largely of the universally distinctive characters of the rival seasons. What nature has done on this continent has not been done niggardly; and, while we may boast of a decline of the year that certainly rivals, and, with few exceptions, eclipses the glories of most of the climates of the old world, the opening months rarely fail of equalizing the gifts of Providence, by a very decided exhibition of all the disagreeable qualities for which they are remarkable.

More than half a year had elapsed, between the time when the Indian boy had been found lurking in the valley of the Heathcotes, and that day when he was first permitted to go into the forest, fettered by no other restraint than the moral tie which the owner of the valley either knew, or fancied, would not fail to cause him to return to a bondage he had found so irksome. It was April; but it was April as the month was known a century ago in Connecticut, and as it is even now so often found to disappoint all expectations of that capricious season of the year.

The weather had returned suddenly and violently to the vigor of winter. A thaw had been succeeded by a storm of snow and sleet, and the interlude of the springtime of blossoms had terminated with a biting gale from the northwest, which had apparently placed a permanent seal on the lingering presence of a second February.

On the morning that Content led his followers into the forest, they issued from the postern clad in coats of skin. Their lower limbs were protected by the coarse leggings which they had worn in so many previous hunts during the past winter, if that might be called past which had returned, weakened but little of its keenness, and bearing all the outward marks of January. When last seen, Eben Dudley, the heaviest of the band, was moving firmly on the crust of the snow, with a step as sure as if he had trodden on the frozen earth itself. More than one of the maidens declared, that though they had endeavored to trace the footsteps of the hunters from the palisadoes, it would have exceeded even the sagacity of an Indian eye to follow their trail along the icy path they traveled.

Hour after hour passed without bringing tidings from the chase. The reports of fire-arms had indeed been occasionally heard, ringing among the arches of the woods; and broken echoes were, for some hours, rolling from one recess of the hills to another. But even these signs of the hunters gradually receded with the advance of the day; and, long ere the sun had gained the meridian, and its warmth, at that advanced season not without power, was shed into the valley, the whole range of the adjoining forest lay in its ordinary dull and solemn silence.

The incident of the hunt, apart from the absence of the Indian boy, was one of too common occurrence to give birth to any particular motives of excitement. Ruth quietly busied herself among her women, and when the recollection of those who were scouring the neighboring forest came at all to her mind, it was coupled with the care with which she was providing to administer to their comforts, after the fatigue of a day of extraordinary personal efforts. This was a duty never lightly performed. Her situation was one eminently fitted to foster the best affections of woman, since it admitted of few temptations to yield to other than the most natural feeling; she was, in consequence, known on all occasions to exercise them with the devotedness of her sex.

"Thy father and his companions will look on our care with pleasure," said the thoughtful matron to her youthful image, as she directed a more than usual provision of her larder to be got in readiness for the hunters; "home is ever sweetest after toil and exposure."

"I doubt if Mark be not ready to faint with so weary a march," said the child already introduced by the name of Martha; "he is young to go into the woods, with scouters tall as great Dudley."

"And the heathen," added the little Ruth, "he is young, too, as Mark, though more used to the toil. It may be, mother, that he will never come to us more!"

"That would grieve our venerable parent; for thou knowest, Ruth, that he hath hopes of working on the mind of the boy, until his savage nature shall yield to the secret power. But the sun is falling behind the hill, and the evening is coming in cool as winter; go to the postern, and look out upon the fields. I would know if there be any signs of thy father and his party."

Though Ruth gave this mandate to her daughter, she did not the less neglect to exercise her own faculties in the same grateful office. While the children went, as they were ordered, to the outer gate, the matron herself ascended to the lower apartment of the block, and, from its different loops, she took a long and anxious survey of the limited prospect. The shadows of the trees that lined the western side of the view, were already thrown far across the broad sheet of frozen snow, and the sudden chill which succeeded the disappearance of the sun announced the rapid approach of the night that promised to support the severe character of the past day. A freezing wind, which had brought with it the cold airs of the great lakes, and which had even triumphed over the more natural influence of an April sun, had, however, fallen, leaving a temperature not unlike that which dwells in the milder seasons of the year among the glaciers of the upper Alps.

Ruth was too long accustomed to such forest scenes, and to such a "lingering of winter in the lap of May," to feel, on their account, any additional uneasiness. But the hour had now arrived when she had reason to look for the return of the hunters. With the expectation of seeing their forms issuing from the forest, came the anxiety which is an unavoidable attendant of disappointment. The shadows continued to deepen in the valley, until the gloom thickened to the darkness of night, without bringing any tidings from those without.

When a delay, which was unusual in the members of a family circumstanced like that of the Wish-Ton-Wish, came to be coupled with various little observations that had been made during the day, it was thought that reasons for alarm were beginning, at each instant, to grow more plausible. Reports of fire-arms had been heard, at an early hour, from opposite points in the hills, and in a manner too distinct to be mistaken for echoes; a certain proof that the different members of the hunt had separated in the forest. Under such circumstances, it was not difficult for the imagination of a wife and a mother, of a sister, or of her who secretly confessed a still more tender interest in some one of the hunters, to conjure to the imagination the numberless dangers to which those who were engaged in these expeditions were known to be exposed.

"I doubt that the chase hath drawn them further from the valley than is fitting for the hour and the season," observed Ruth to her maidens, who had gathered in a group about her, at a point that overlooked as much of the cleared land around the buildings as the darkness would allow; "the gravest man becomes thoughtless as the unreflecting child, when led by the eagerness of the pursuit. It is the duty of older heads to think for those that want experience—but into what indiscreet complaints are my fears leading! It may be that my husband is even now striving to collect his party, in order to return. Have any heard his conch sounding the recall?"

"The woods are still as the day the first echo of the ax was heard among the trees," returned Faith. "I did hear that which sounded like a strain of brawling Dudley's songs, but it proved to be no more than the lowing of one of his own oxen. Perchance the animal misseth some of his master's care."

"Whittal Ring hath looked to the beasts, and it may not be that he hath neglected to feed, among others, the creatures of Dudley. Thy mind is given to levity, Faith, in the matter of this young man. It is not seemly that one of thy years and sex should manifest so great displeasure at the name of a youth, who is of an honest nature, and of honest habits, too, though he may appear ungainly to the eye, and have so little favor with one of thy disposition."

"I did not fashion the man," said Faith, biting her lip, and tossing her head; "nor is it aught to me whether he be gainly or not. As to my favor, when he asks it, the man shall not wait long to know the answer. But is not yon figure the fellow himself, Madame Heathcote?— here, coming in from the eastern hill, along the orchard path. The form I mean is just here; you may see it, at this moment, turning by the bend in the brook."

"There is one of a certainty, and it should be one of our hunting party, too; and yet he doth not seem to be of a size or of a gait like that of Eben Dudley. Thou should'st have a knowledge of thy kindred, girl; to me it seemeth thy brother."

"Truly, it may be Reuben Ring; still it hath much of the swagger of the other, though their stature be nearly equal; the manner of carrying the musket is much the same with all the borderers too; one cannot easily tell the form of a man from a stump, by this light, and yet do I think it will prove to be the loitering Dudley."

"Loiterer or not, he is the first to return from this long and weary chase," said Ruth, breathing heavily, like one who regretted that the truth were so. "Go thou to the postern, and admit him, girl. I ordered bolts to be drawn, for I like not to leave a fortress defended by a female garrison, at this hour, with open gates. I will hie to the dwelling and see to the comforts of those who are a-hungered, since it will not be long ere we shall have more of them at hand."

Faith complied, with affected indifference and sufficient delay. By the time she had reached the place of admission, a form was seen ascending the acclivity, and taking the direction which led to the same spot. In the next minute a rude effort to enter announced an arrival without.

"Gently, Master Dudley," said the willful girl, who held the bolt with one hand, though she maliciously delayed to remove it. "We know thou are powerful of arm, and yet the palisadoes will scarcely fall at thy touch. Here are no Sampsons to pull down the pillars on our heads. Perhaps we may not be disposed to give entrance to them who stay abroad out of all season."

"Open the postern, girl," said Eben Dudley; "after which, if thou has aught to say, we shall be better convenienced for discourse."

"It may be that thy conversation is most agreeable when heard from without. Render an account of thy backslidings, throughout this day, penitent Dudley, that I may take pity on thy weariness. But lest hunger should have overcome thy memory, I may serve to help thee to the particulars. The first of thy offenses was to consume more than thy portion of the cold meats; the second was to suffer Reuben Ring to kill the deer, and for thee

to claim it; and a third was a trick thou hast of listening so much to thine own voice, that even the beasts fled thee, from dislike of thy noise."

"Thou triflest unseasonably, Faith; I would speak with the captain without delay."

"It may be that he is better employed than to desire such company. Thou art not the only strange animal by many who hath roared at the gate of Wish-Ton-Wish."

"Have any come within the day, Faith?" demanded the borderer, with the interest such an event would be likely to create in the mind of one who habitually lived in so great retirement.

"What sayest thou to a second visit from the gentle-spoken stranger? he who favored us with so much gay discourse, the by-gone fall of the year. That would be a guest fit to receive! I warrant me his knock would not be heard a second time."

"The gallant had better beware the moon!" exclaimed Dudley, striking the butt of his musket against the ice with so much force as to cause his companion to start in alarm. "What fool's errand hath again brought him to prick his nag so deep into the forest?"

"Nay, thy wit is ever like the unbroken colt, a headstrong runaway. I said not, in full meaning, that the man had come; I only invited thee to give an opinion in the event that he should arrive unexpectedly, though I am far from certain that any here ever expect to see his face again."

"This is foolish prating," returned the youth, provoked at the exhibition of jealousy into which he had been incautiously betrayed. "I tell thee to withdraw the bolt, for I have great need to speak with the captain, or with his son."

"Thou may'st open thy mind to the first, if he will listen to what thou hast to say," returned the girl, removing the impediment to his entrance; "but thou wilt sooner get the ear of the other by remaining at the gate, since he has not yet come in from the forest."

Dudley recoiled a pace, and repeated her words in the tone of one who admitted a feeling of alarm to mingle with his surprise.

"Not in from the forest!" he said; "surely there are none abroad, now that I am home!"

"Why dost say it? I have put my jibe upon thee more in payment of ancient transgressions than for any present offense. So far from being last, thou art the first of the hunters we have yet seen.

Go into the madam without delay, and tell her of the danger, if any there be, that we take speedy measures for our safety."

"That would do little good, truly," muttered the borderer, like one musing. "Stay thou here, and watch the postern, Faith; I will back to the woods; for a timely word or a signal blow from my conch might quicken their footsteps."

"What madness hath beset thee, Dudley! Thou wouldst not go into the forest again, at this hour, and alone, if there be reason for fear? Come further within the gate, man, that I may draw the bolt. The madam will wonder that we tarry here so long."

"Ha!—I hear feet moving in the meadow; I know it by the creaking of the snow; the others are not lagging."

Notwithstanding the apparent certainty of the young man, instead of going forth to meet his friends, he withdrew a step, and with his own hand drew the bolt that Faith had just desired might be fastened; taking care at the same time to let fall a swinging bar of wood, which gave additional security to the fastenings of the postern. His apprehensions, if any such had induced this caution, were however unnecessary; for ere he had time to make, or even to reflect on any further movement, admission was demanded in the well-known voice of the son of him who owned the valley. The bustle of the arrival—for with Content entered a group of companions loaded with venison, put an end to the dialogue. Faith seized the opportunity to glide away in the obscurity, in order to announce to her mistress that the hunters had returned—an office that she performed without entering at all into the particulars of her own interview with Eben Dudley.

It is needless to dwell on the satisfaction with which Ruth received her husband and son, after the uneasiness she had just suffered. Though the severe manners of the province admitted of no violent exhibition of passing emotions, secret joy was reigning in the mild eyes, and glowing about the flushed cheeks of the discreet matron, while she personally officiated in the offices of the evening meal.

The party had returned, teeming with no extraordinary incidents; nor did they appear to be disturbed with any of that seriousness of air which so unequivocally characterized the deportment of him who had preceded them. On the contrary, each had his quiet tale to relate, now perhaps at the expense of a luckless companion, and sometimes in order that no part of his own individual skill as a hunter should be unknown. The delay was accounted for, as similar delays are commonly explained, by distance and the temptations of an unusually successful chase. As the appetites of those who had spent the day in the exciting toil were keen, and the viands tempting, the first half-hour passed quickly, as all such half-hours are wont to pass, in garrulous recitals of personal exploits, and of the hairbreadth escapes of deer, which, had fortune not been fickle, should have now been present as trophies of the skill of the hand by which they fell. It was only after personal vanity was sufficiently appeased, and when the hunger even of a border-man could achieve no more, that the hunters began to look about them with a diminished excitement, and to discuss the events of the day with a fitting calmness, and with a discretion more suited to their ordinary self-command.

"We lost the sound of thy conch, wandering Dudley, as we fell into the deep hollow of the mountain," said Content, in a pause of the discourse; "since which time, neither eye nor ear of any has had trace of thy movements, until we met thee at the postern, stationed like a looker-out on his watch."

The individual addressed had mingled in none of the gayety of the hour. While others fed freely, or joined in the quiet joke, which could escape the lips of even men chastened as his companions, Eben Dudley had tasted sparingly of the viands. Nor had the muscles of his hard countenance once relaxed in a smile. A gravity and a silence so extraordinary, in one so little accustomed to exhibit either quality, did not fail to attract attention. It was universally ascribed to the circumstance that he had returned empty-handed from the hunt; and now that one having authority had seen fit to give such a direction to the discourse, the imaginary delinquent was not permitted to escape unscathed.

"The butcher had little to do with this day's killing," said one of the young men; "as a punishment for his absence from the slaughter, he should be made to go on the hill and bring in the two bucks he will find hanging from a maple sapling near to the drinking spring. Our meat should pass through his hands in some fashion or other, else will it lack savor."

"Ever since the death of the straggling wether, the trade of Eben hath been at a stand," added another; "the downhearted youth seems like one ready to give up his calling to the first stranger that shall ask it."

"Creatures which run at large prove

better mutton than the stalled wether," continued a third; "and thereby custom was getting low before this hunt. Beyond a doubt, he has a full supply for all who shall be likely to seek venison in his stall."

Ruth observed the countenance of her husband grew grave, at these allusions to an event he had always seemed to wish forgotten; and she interposed with a view to lead the minds of those who listened back to matter more fitting to be discussed.

"How is this?" she exclaimed in haste; "hath the stout Dudley lost any of his craft? I have never counted with greater certainty on the riches of the table, than when he hath been sent among the hills for the fat deer or the tender turkey. It would much grieve me to learn that he beginneth to lack the hunter's skill."

"The man is getting melancholy with overfeeding," muttered the willful tones of one busied among the vessels in a distant part of the room. "He taketh his exercise alone, in order that none need discover the failing. I think he be much disposed to go over sea, in order to become a trooper."

Until now, the subject of these mirthful attacks had listened like one too confident of his established reputation to feel concern, but at the sound of the last speaker's voice, he grasped the bushy covering of one entire cheek in his hand, and turning a reproachful and irritated glance at the already half-repentant eye of Faith Ring, all his natural spirit returned.

"It may be that my skill hath left me," he said, "and that I love to be alone, rather than to be troubled with the company of some that might readily be named, no reference being had to such gallants as ride up and down the Colony, putting evil opinions into the thoughts of honest men's daughters; but why is Eben Dudley to bear all the small shot of your humors, when there is another who, it might seem, hath strayed even further from your trail than he?"

Eye sought eye, and each youth by hasty glances endeavored to read the countenances of all the rest of the company, in order to learn who the absentee might be. The young borderers shook their heads, as the features of every well-known face were recognized, and a general exclamation of denial was about to break from their lips, when Ruth exclaimed—

"Truly, the Indian is wanting!"

So constant was the apprehension of danger from the savages, in the breasts of those who dwelt on that exposed frontier, that every man arose at the words, by a sudden and common impulse, and each individual gazed about him in a surprise that was a little akin to dismay.

"The boy was with us when we quitted the forest," said Content, after a moment of death-like stillness. "I spoke to him in commendation of his activity, and of the knowledge he had shown in beating up the secret places of the deer; though there is little reason to think my words were understood."

"And were it not sinful to take such solemn evidence in behalf of so light a matter, I could be qualified on the Book itself, that he was at my elbow as we entered the orchard," added Reuben Ring, a man renowned in that little community for the accuracy of his vision.

"And I will make oath or declaration of any sort, lawful or conscientious, that he came not within the postern when it was opened by my own hand," returned Eben Dudley. "I told off the number of the party as you passed, and right sure am I that no red-skin entered."

"Canst thou tell us aught of the lad?" demanded Ruth, quick to take the alarm on a subject that had so long exercised her care, and given food to her imagination.

"Nothing. With me he hath not been seen since the turn of the day. I have not seen the face of living man from that moment, unless in truth, one of mysterious character, whom I met in the forest, may be so called."

The manner in which the woodman spoke was too serious and too natural, not to give birth in his auditors to some of his own gravity. Perhaps the appearance of the Puritan, at that moment, aided in quieting the levity that had been uppermost in the minds of the young men; for it is certain that, when he entered, a deeper and a general curiosity came over the countenances of all present. Content waited a moment in respectful silence till his father had moved slowly through the circle, and then he prepared himself to look further into an affair that began to assume the appearance of matter worthy of investigation.

CHAPTER IX.

"Last night of all,
When yon same star, that's westward from the pole,
Had made its course to illume that part of heaven
Where now it burns, Marcellus, and myself,
The bell then beating one—"
"Peace, break thee off; look where it comes again."
—HAMLET.

IT is our duty as faithful historians of the events recorded in this homely legend, to conceal no circumstance which may throw the necessary degree of light on its incidents, nor any opinion that may serve for the better instruction of the reader in the characters of its actors. In order that this obligation may be discharged with sufficient clearness and precision, it has now become necessary to make a short digression from the immediate action of the tale.

Enough has been already shown to prove that the Heathcotes lived at a time, and in a country, where very quaint and peculiar religious dogmas had the ascendency. At a period when visible manifestations of the goodness of Providence, not only in spiritual but in temporal gifts, were confidently expected and openly proclaimed, it is not at all surprising that more evil agencies should be thought to exercise their power in a manner that is somewhat opposed to the experience of our own age. As we have no wish, however, to make these pages the vehicle of a theological or metaphysical controversy, we shall deal tenderly with certain important events, that most of the writers who were contemporary with the facts, assert took place in the colonies of New England, at and about the period of which we are now writing. It is sufficiently known that the art of witchcraft, and one even still more diabolical and direct in its origin, were then believed to flourish in that quarter of the world, to a degree that was probably in a very just proportion to the neglect with which most of the other arts of life were treated. There is so much grave and respectable authority to prove the existence of these evil influences, that it requires a pen hardier than any we wield, to attack them without a suitable motive. " Flashy people," says the learned and pious Cotton Mather, Doctor of Divinity and Fellow of the Royal Society, " may burlesque these things ; but when hundreds of the most sober people in a country where they have as much mother wit, certainly, as the rest of mankind, *know them to be true*, nothing but the absurd and froward spirit of Sadducism can question them." Against this grave and credited authority, we pretend to raise no question of skepticism. We submit the testimony of such a writer as conclusive, though as credulity is sometimes found to be bounded by geographical limits, and to possess something of a national character, it may be prudent to refer certain readers who dwell in the other hemisphere to the common law of England on this interesting subject, as it is ingeniously expounded by Keeble, and approved of by the twelve judges of that

highly civilized and enlightened island. With this brief reference to so grave authorities in support of what we have now to offer, we shall return to the matter of the narrative, fully trusting that its incidents will throw some additional light on the subject of so deep and so general concern.

Content waited respectfully until his father had taken his seat, and then perceiving that the venerable Puritan had no immediate intention of moving personally in the affair, he commenced the examination of his dependent as follows ; opening the matter with a seriousness that was abundantly warranted by the gravity of the subject itself.

" Thou hast spoken of one met in the forest," he said ; " proceed with the purport of that interview, and tell us of what manner of man it was."

Thus directly interrogated, Eben Dudley disposed himself to give a full and satisfactory answer. First casting a glance around, so as to embrace every curious and eager countenance, and letting his look rest a little longer than common on a half-interested, half-incredulous, and somewhat ironical dark eye, that was riveted on his own from a distant corner of the room, he commenced his statement as follows :

" It is known to you all," said the borderer, " that when we had gained the mountain-top there was a division of our numbers, in such a fashion that each hunter should sweep his own range of the forest, in order that neither moose, deer, nor bear, might have reasonable chance of escape. Being of large frame, and it may be of swifter foot than common, the young captain saw fit to command Reuben Ring to flank one end of the line, and a man, who is nothing short of him in either speed or strength, to do the same duty on the other. There was nothing particularly worthy of mention that took place on the flank I held for the first two hours ; unless indeed the fact, that three several times did I fall upon a maze of well beaten deer-tracks, that as often led to nothing—"

" These are signs common to the woods, and they are no more than so many proofs that the animal has its sports, like any other playful creature, when not pressed by hunger or by danger," quietly observed Content.

" I pretend not to take those deceitful tracks much into the account," resumed Dudley ; " but shortly after losing the sound of the conch, I roused a noble buck from his lair beneath a thicket of hemlocks, and having the game in view, the chase led me wide-off toward the wilderness, it may have been the distance of two leagues."

"And in all that time had you no fitting moment to strike the beast?"

"None whatever; nor, if opportunity had been given, am I bold to say that hand of mine would have been hardy enough to aim at its life."

"Was there aught in the deer that a hunter should seek to spare it?"

"There was that in the deer, that might bring a Christian man to much serious reflection."

"Deal more openly with the nature and appearance of the animal," said Content, a little less tranquil than usual; while the youths and maidens placed themselves in attitudes still more strongly denoting attention.

Dudley pondered an instant, and then he commenced a less equivocal enumeration of what he conceived to be the marvels of his tale.

"Firstly," he said, "there was no trail, neither to nor from the spot where the creature had made its lair; secondly, when roused, it took not the alarm, but leaped sportingly ahead, taking sufficient care to be beyond the range of musket, without ever becoming hid from the eye; and lastly, its manner of disappearance was as worthy of mention as any other of its movements."

"And in what manner didst thou lose the creature?"

"I had gotten it upon the crest of a hillock, where true eye and steady hand might make sure of a buck of much smaller size, when—didst hear aught that might be accounted wonderful, at a season of the year when the snows are still lying on the earth?"

The auditors regarded one another curiously, each endeavoring to recall some unwonted sound which might sustain a narrative that was fast obtaining the seducing interest of the marvelous.

"Wast sure, Charity, that the howl we heard from the forest was the yell of the beaten hound?" demanded a handmaiden of Ruth, of a blue-eyed companion, who seemed equally well disposed to contribute her share of evidence in support of any exciting legend.

"It might have been other," was the answer; "though the hunters do speak of their having beaten the pup for restiveness."

"There was a tumult among the echoes that sounded like the noises which follow the uproar of a falling tree," said Ruth, thoughtfully. "I remember to have asked if it might not be that some fierce beast had caused a general discharge of the musketry, but my father was of opinion that death had undermined some heavy oak."

"At what hour might this have happened?"

"It was past the turn of the day, for it was at the moment I bethought me of the hunger of those who had toiled since light in the hills."

"That then was the sound I mean. It came not from falling tree, but was uttered in the air, far above all forests. Had it been heard by one better skilled in the secrets of nature—"

"He would say it thundered," interrupted Faith Ring, who, unlike most of the other listeners, manifested little of the quality which was expressed by her name. "Truly, Eben Dudley hath done marvels in this hunt; he hath come in with a thunderbolt in his head, instead of a fat buck on his shoulders!"

"Speak reverently, girl, of that thou dost not comprehend," said Mark Heathcote, with stern authority. "Marvels are manifested equally to the ignorant and to the learned; and although vain-minded pretenders to philosophy affirm that the warring of the elements is no more than nature working out its own purifications, yet do we know, from all ancient authorities, that other manifestations are therein exhibited. Satan may have control over the magazines of the air; he can 'let off the ordnance of heaven.' That 'the Prince of the Powers of Darkness' hath as good a share in chemistry as goes to the making of *aurum fulminans*, is asserted by one of the wisest writers of our age."

From this declaration, and more particularly from the learning discovered in the Puritan's speech, there was no one so hardy as to dissent. Faith was glad to shrink back among the bevy of awe-struck maidens, while Content, after a sufficiently respectful pause, invited the woodsman, who was yet teeming with the most important part of his communication, to proceed.

"While my eye was searching for the lightning which should in reason have attended that thunder, had it been uttered in the manner of nature, the buck had vanished; and when I rushed upon the hillock, in order to keep the game in view, a man mounting its opposite side came so suddenly upon me, that our muskets were at each other's breasts before either had time for speech."

"What manner of man was he?"

"So far as human judgment might determine, he seemed a traveler, who was endeavoring to push through the wilderness, from the towns below to the distant settlements of the Bay Province; but I account it exceedingly wonderful that the trail of a leaping buck should have brought us together in so unwonted a manner!"

"And didst thou see aught of the deer, after that encounter?"

"In the first hurry of the surprise, it did certainly appear as if an animal were bounding along the wood into a distant thicket; but it is known how readily one may be led by seeming probabilities into a false conclusion, and so I account that glimpse a delusion. No doubt the animal having done that which it was commissioned to perform, did then and there disappear, in the manner I have named."

"It might have been thus. And the stranger—had you discourse with him before parting?"

"We tarried together a short hour. He related much marvelous matter of the experiences of the people near the sea. According to the testimony of the stranger, the Powers of Darkness have been manifested in the provinces in a hideous fashion. Numberless of the believers have been persecuted by the invisibles, and greatly have they endured suffering, both in soul and body."

"Of all this have I witnessed surprising instances in my day," said Mark Heathcote, breaking the awful stillness that succeeded the annunciation of so heavy a visitation on the peace of the Colony, with his deep-toned and imposing voice. "Did he with whom you conferred, enter into the particulars of the trials?"

"He spoke also of certain other signs that are thought to foretell the coming of trouble. When I named the weary chase that I had made, and the sound which came from the air, he said that these would be accounted trifles in the towns of the Bay, where the thunder and its lightnings had done much evil work the past season, Satan having especially shown his spite by causing them to do injury to the houses of the Lord."

"There has long been reason to think that the pilgrimage of the righteous into these wilds, will be visited by some fierce opposition of those envious natures, which, fostering evil themselves, cannot brook to look upon the toiling of such as strive to keep the narrow path. We will now resort to the only weapon it is permitted us to wield in this controversy, but which, when handled with diligence and zeal, never fails to lead to victory."

So saying, without waiting to hear more of the tale of Eben Dudley, old Mark Heathcote arose, and assuming the upright attitude usual among the people of his sect, he addressed himself to prayer. The grave and awe-struck but deeply confiding congregation imitated his example, and the lips of the Puritan had parted in the act of utterance, when a low, faltering note, like that produced by a wind instrument, rose on the outer air, and penetrated to the place where the family was assembled. A conch was suspended at the postern, in readiness to be used by any of the family whom accident or occupation should detain beyond the usual hour of closing the gates; and both by the direction and nature of this interruption, it would seem that an applicant for admission stood at the portal. The effect on the auditors was general and instantaneous. Notwithstanding the recent dialogue, the young men involuntarily sought their arms, while the startled females huddled together like a flock of trembling and timid deer.

"There is, of a certainty, a signal from without!" Content at length observed, after waiting to suffer the sounds to die away among the angles of the buildings. "Some hunter who hath strayed from his path, claimeth hospitality."

Eben Dudley shook his head like one who dissented; but, having with all the other youths grasped his musket, he stood as undetermined as the rest concerning the course it was proper to pursue. It is uncertain how long this indecision might have continued, had no further summons been given; but he without appeared too impatient of delay to suffer much time to be lost. The conch sounded again, and with far better success than before. The blast was longer, louder, and bolder, than that which had first pierced the walls of the dwelling, rising full and rich on the air, as though one well practised in the use of the instrument had placed lips to the shell.

Content would scarcely have presumed to disobey a mandate coming from his father, had it been little in conformity with his own intentions. But second thoughts had already shown him the necessity of decision, and he was in the act of motioning to Dudley and Reuben Ring to follow, when the Puritan bade him look to the matter. Making a sign for the rest of the family to remain where they were, and arming himself with a musket which had more than once that day been proved to be of certain aim, he led the way to the postern which has already been so often mentioned.

"Who sounds at my gate?" demanded Content, when he and his followers had gained a position, under cover of a low earthen mound erected expressly for the purpose of commanding the entrance; "who summons a peaceful family, at this hour of the night, to their outer defenses?"

"One who hath need of what he asketh, or he would not disturb thy quiet," was the answer. "Open the postern, Master Heathcote, without fear; it is a brother in the faith, and a subject of the same laws, that asketh the boon."

"Here is truly a Christian man without," said Content, hurrying to the postern, which, without a moment's delay, he threw freely open, saying as he did so, "enter of Heaven's mercy, and be welcome to that we have to bestow."

A tall, and by his tread, a heavy man, wrapped in a riding cloak, bowed to the greeting, and immediately passed beneath the low lintel. Every eye was keenly fastened on the stranger, who, after ascending the acclivity a short distance, paused, while the young men, under their master's orders, carefully and scrupulously renewed the fastenings of the gate. When bolts and bars had done their office, Content joined his guest; and after making another fruitless effort, by the feeble light which fell from the stars, to scan his person, he said in his own meek and quiet manner—

"Thou must have great need of warmth and nourishment. The distance from this valley to the nearest habitation is wearisome, and one who hath journeyed it, in a season like this, may well be nigh fainting. Follow, and deal with that we have to bestow as freely as if it were thine own."

Although the stranger manifested none of that impatience which the heir of the Wish-Ton-Wish appeared to think one so situated might in all reason feel, thus invited he did not hesitate to comply. As he followed in the footsteps of his host, his tread, however, was leisurely and dignified; and, once or twice, when the other half delayed in order to make some passing observation of courtesy, he betrayed no indiscreet anxiety to enter on those personal indulgences which might in reality prove so grateful to one who had journeyed far in an inclement season, and along a road where neither dwelling nor security invited repose.

"Here is warmth and a peaceful welcome," pursued Content, ushering his guest into the center of a group of fearfully anxious faces. "In a little time, other matters shall be added to thy comfort."

When the stranger found himself under the glare of a powerful light, and confronted to so many curious and wondering eyes, for a single instant he hesitated. Then stepping calmly forward, he cast the short riding-cloak, which had closely muffled his features, from his shoulders, and discovered the severe eye, the stern lineaments, and the athletic form of him who had once before been known to enter the doors of Wish-Ton-Wish with little warning, and to have quitted them so mysteriously.

The Puritan had arisen, with quiet and grave courtesy, to receive his visitor; but obvious, powerful, and extraordinary interest gleamed about his usually subdued visage, when, as the features of the other were exposed to view, he recognized the person of the man who advanced to meet him.

"Mark Heathcote," said the stranger, "my visit is to thee. It may, or it may not, prove longer than the last, as thou shalt receive my tidings. Affairs of the last moment demand that there should be little delay in hearing that which I have to offer."

Notwithstanding the excess and nature of the surprise which the veteran Mark had certainly betrayed, it endured just long enough to allow those wondering eyes, which were eagerly devouring all that passed, to note its existence. Then, the subdued and characteristic manner which in general marked his air, instantly returned, and with a quiet gesture, like that which friends use in moments of confidence and security, he beckoned to the other to follow to an inner room. The stranger complied, making a slight bow of recognition to Ruth, as he passed her on the way to the apartment chosen for an interview that was evidently intended to be private.

CHAPTER X.

"*Mar.* Shall I strike at it with my partisan?
Hor. Do, if it will not stand.
Mar. 'Tis here!
Hor. 'Tis here!
Mar. 'Tis gone."—HAMLET.

THE time that this unexpected visitor stood uncloaked and exposed to recognition, before the eyes of the curious group in the outer room, did not much exceed a minute. Still it was long enough to allow men who rarely overlooked the smallest peculiarity of dress or air, to note some of the more distinguishing accompaniments of his attire. The heavy horseman's pistols, once before exhibited, were in his girdle, and young Mark got a glimpse of a silver-handled dagger which had pleased his eye before that night. But the passage of his grandfather and the stranger from the room prevented the boy from determining whether it was entirely of the same fashion as that, which, rather as a memorial of by-gone scenes than for any service that it might now be expected to perform, hung above the bed of the former.

"The man hath not yet parted with his arms!" exclaimed the quick-sighted youth, when he found that every other tongue continued silent. "I would he may now leave them with my grand'ther, that I may chase the skulking Wampanoag to his hiding—"

"Hot-headed boy! Thy tongue is too much given to levity," said Ruth, who had not only resumed her seat, but also the light employment that had been interrupted by the blast at the gate, with a calmness of mien that did not fail in some degree to reassure her maidens. "Instead of cherishing the lessons of peace that are taught thee, thy unruly thoughts are ever bent on strife."

"Is there harm in wishing to be armed with a weapon suited to my years, that I may do service in beating down the power of our enemies; and perhaps aid something, too, in affording security to my mother?"

"Thy mother hath no fears," returned the matron, gravely, while grateful affection prompted a kind but furtive glance toward the high-spirited though sometimes froward lad. "Reason hath already taught me the folly of alarm, because one has knocked at our gate in the night-season. Lay aside thy arms, men; you see that my husband no longer clings to the musket. Be certain that his eye will give us warning when there shall be danger at hand."

The unconcern of her husband was even more strikingly true than the simple language of his wife would appear to convey. Content had not only laid aside his weapon, but he had resumed his seat near the fire, with an air as calm, as assured, and it might have seemed to one watchfully observant, as understanding, as her own. Until now, the stout Dudley had remained leaning on his piece, immovable and apparently unconscious as a statue. But, following the injunctions of one he was accustomed to obey, he placed the musket against the wall, with the care of a hunter, and then running a hand through his shaggy locks, as though the action might quicken ideas that were never remarkably active, he bluntly exclaimed—

"An armed hand is well in these forests, but an armed heel is not less wanting to him who would push a roadster from the Connecticut to the Wish-Ton-Wish, between a rising and a setting sun! The stranger no longer journeys in the saddle,

as is plain by the sign that his boot beareth no spur. When he worried, by dint of hard pricking, the miserable hack that proved food for the wolves, through the forest, he had better appointments. I saw the bones of the animal no later than this day. They have been polished by fowls and frost, till the driven snow of the mountains is not whiter!"

Meaning and uneasy, but hasty glances of the eye were exchanged between Content and Ruth, as Eben Dudley thus uttered the thoughts which had been suggested by the unexpected return of the stranger.

"Go you to the lookout at the western palisadoes," said the latter; "and see if perchance the Indian may not be lurking near the dwellings, ashamed of his delay, and perchance fearful of calling us to his admission. I cannot think that the child means to desert us, with no sign of kindness, and without leave-taking."

"I will not take upon me to say how much or how little of ceremony the youngster may fancy to be due to the master of the valley and his kin; but if not gone already, the snow will not melt more quietly in the thaw than the lad will one day disappear. Reuben Ring, thou hast an eye for light or darkness; come forth with me, that no sign escape us. Should thy sister, Faith, make one of our party, it would not be easy for the red-skin to pass the clearing without a hail."

"Go to," hurriedly answered the female; "it is more womanly that I tarry to see to the wants of him who hath journeyed far and hard, since the rising of the sun. If the boy pass thy vigilance, wakeful Dudley, he will have little cause to fear that of others."

Though Faith so decidedly declined to make one of the party, her brother complied without reluctance. The young men were about to quit the place together, when the latch, on which the hand of Dudley was already laid, rose quietly without aid from his finger, the door opened, and the object of their intended search glided past them, and took his customary position in one of the more retired corners of the room. There was so much of the ordinary noiseless manner of the young captive in this entrance, that for a moment they who witnessed the passage of his dark form across the apartment were led to think the movement no more than the visit he was always permitted to make at that hour. But recollection soon came, and with it not only the suspicious circumstance of his disappearance, but the inexplicable manner of his admission within the gates.

"The pickets must be looked to!" exclaimed Dudley, the instant a second look assured him that his eyes in truth beheld him who had been missing. "The place that a stripling can scale might well admit a host."

"Truly," said Content, "this needeth explanation. Hath not the boy entered when the gate was opened for the stranger? Here cometh one that may speak to the fact!"

"It is so," said the individual named, who re-entered from the inner room in season to hear the nature of the remark. "I found this native child near thy gate, and took upon me the office of a Christian man to bid him welcome. Certain am I, that one, kind of heart and gently disposed, like the mistress of this family, will not turn him away in anger."

"He is no stranger at our fire or at our board," said Ruth; "had it been otherwise thou wouldst have done well."

Eben Dudley looked incredulous. His mind had been powerfully exercised that day with visions of the marvelous, and, of a certainty, there was some reason to distrust the manner in which the reappearance of the youth had been made.

"It will be well to look to the fastenings," he muttered, "lest others, less easy to dispose of, should follow. Now that invisible agencies are at work in the Colony one may not sleep too soundly!"

"Then go thou to the lookout, and keep the watch, till the clock shall strike the hour of midnight," said the Puritan, who uttered the command in a manner to show that he was in truth moved by considerations far deeper than the vague apprehensions of his dependent. "Ere sleep overcome thee another shall be ready for the relief."

Mark Heathcote seldom spoke, but respectful silence permitted the lowest of his syllables to be audible. On the present occasion, when his voice was first heard, such a stillness came over all in his presence that he finished the sentence amid the nearly imperceptible breathings of the listeners. In this momentary but death-like quiet there arose a blast from the conch at the gate that might have seemed an echo of that which had so lately startled the already-excited inmates of the dwelling. At the repetition of sounds so unwonted all sprang to their feet, but no one spoke. Content cast a hurried and inquiring glance at his father, who in his turn had anxiously sought the eye of the stranger. The latter stood firm and unmoved. One hand was clenched upon the back of the chair from which he had arisen, and the other grasped, perhaps

unconsciously, the handle of one of those weapons which had arracted the attention of young Mark, and which still continued thrust through the broad leathern belt that girded his doublet.

"The sound is like that which one little used to deal with earthly instruments might' raise!" muttered one of those whose minds had been prepared, by the narrative of Dudley, to believe in anything marvelous.

"Come from what quarter it may, it is a summons that must be answered," returned Content. "Dudley, thy musket; this visit is so unwonted that more than one hand should do the office of porter."

The borderer instantly complied, muttering between his teeth as he shook the priming deeper into the barrel of his piece, "Your over-sea gallants are quick on the trail to-night!" Then throwing the musket into the hollow of his arm, he cast a look of discontent and resentment toward Faith Ring, and was about to open the door for the passage of Content, when another blast arose on the silence without. The second touch of the shell was firmer, longer, louder, and more true, than that by which it had just been preceded.

"One might fancy the conch was speaking in mockery," observed Content, looking with meaning towards their guest. "Never did sound more resemble sound than these we have just heard, and those thou drew from the shell when asking admission."

A sudden light appeared to break in upon the intelligence of the stranger. Advancing more into the circle, rather with the freedom of long familiarity than with the diffidence of a newly-arrived guest, he motioned for silence as he said—

"Let none move but this stout woodsman, the young captain, and myself. We will go forth, and doubt not that the safety of those within shall be regarded."

Notwithstanding the singularity of this proposal, as it appeared to excite neither surprise nor opposition in the Puritan or his son, the rest of the family offered no objection. The stranger had no sooner spoken, than he advanced near to the torch, and looked closely into the condition of his pistols. Then turning to old Mark, he continued in an undertone—

"Peradventure there will be more worldly strife than any which can flow from the agencies that stir up the unquiet spirits of the colonies. In such an extremity, it may be well to observe a soldier's caution."

"I like not this mockery of sound," returned the Puritan; "it argueth a taunting and fiend-like temper. We have, of late, had in this colony tragical instances of what the disappointed malice of Azazel can attempt; and it would be vain to hope that the evil agencies are not vexed with the sight of my Bethel."

Though the stranger listened to the words of his host with respect, it was plain that his thoughts dwelt on dangers of a different character. The member that still rested on the handle of his weapon was clenched with greater firmness; and a grim, though a melancholy expression was seated about a mouth that was compressed in a manner to denote the physical rather than the spiritual resolution of the man. He made a sign to the two companions he had chosen and led the way to the court.

By this time, the shades of night had materially thickened, and, although the hour was still early, a darkness had come over the valley that rendered it difficult to distinguish objects at any distance from the eye. The obscurity made it necessary that they who now issued from the door of the dwelling should advance with caution, lest, ere properly admonished of its presence, their persons should be exposed to some lurking danger. When the three, however, were safely established behind the thick curtain of plank and earth that covered and commanded the entrance, and where their persons, from the shoulders downward, were completely protected alike from shot and arrow, Content demanded to know who applied at his gates for admission at an hour when they were habitually closed for the night. Instead of receiving, as before, a ready answer, the silence was so profound that his own words were very distinctly heard repeated, as was not uncommon at that quiet hour, among the recesses of the neighboring woods.

"Come it from devil, or come it from man, here is treachery!" whispered the stranger after a fitting pause. "Artifice must be met by artifice; but thou art much abler to advise against the wiles of the forest, than one trained, as I have been, in the less cunning deceptions of Christian warfare."

"What think'st, Dudley?" asked Content. "Will it be well to sally, or shall we wait another signal from the conch?"

"Much dependeth on the quality of the guests expected," returned he of whom counsel was asked. "As for the braggart gallants, that are over-valiant among the maidens, and heavy of heart when they think the screech of the jay an Indian whoop, I care not if ye beat the pickets to the earth, and call upon them to enter on the gallop. I know the manner to send them to the upper story of the block, quicker than the cluck of the turkey can muster its young; but—"

"'Tis well to be discreet in language, in a moment of such serious uncertainty!" interrupted the stranger. "We look for no gallants of the kind."

"Then will I give you a conceit that shall know the reason of the music of yon conch. Go ye two back into the house, making much conversation by the way, in order that any without may hear. When ye have entered, it shall be my task to find such a post nigh the gate that none shall knock again, and no porter be at hand to question them in the matter of their errand."

"This soundeth better," said Content; "and that it may be done with all safety, some others of the young men, who are accustomed to this species of artifice, shall issue by the secret door and lie in wait behind the dwellings, in order that support shall not be wanting in case of violence. Whatever else thou dost, Dudley, remember that thou dost not undue the fastenings of the postern."

"Look to the support," returned the woodsman; "should it be keen-eyed Reuben Ring, I shall feel none the less certain that good aid is at my back. The whole of that family are quick of wit and ready of invention, unless it may be the wight who hath got the form without the reason of a man."

"Thou shalt have Reuben, and none other of his kin," said Content. "Be well advised of the fastenings, and so I wish thee all fitting success, in a deception that cannot be sinful, since it aims only at our safety."

With this injunction, Content and the stranger left Dudley to the practice of his own devices, the former observing the precaution to speak aloud while returning, in order that any listeners without might be led to suppose the whole party had retired from the search, satisfied of its fruitlessness.

In the meantime, the youth left nigh the postern set about the accomplishment of the task he had undertaken, in sober earnest. Instead of descending in a direct line to the palisadoes, he also ascended, and made a circuit among the out-buildings on the margin of the acclivity. Then bending so low as to blend his form with objects on the snow, he gained an angle of the palisadoes, at a point remote from the spot he intended to watch, and, as he hoped, aided by the darkness of the hour and the shadows of the hill, completely protected from observation. When beneath the palisadoes, the sentinel crouched to the earth, creeping with extreme caution along the timber which bound their lower ends, until he found himself arrived at a species of sentry-box, that was erected for the very purpose to which he now intended it should be applied. Once within the cover of this little recess, the sturdy woodsman bestowed his large frame with as much attention to comfort and security as the circumstances would permit. Here he prepared to pass many weary minutes, before there should be further need of his services.

The reader will find no difficulty in believing that one of opinions like those of the borderer did not enter on his silent watch without much distrust of the character of the guests that he might be called upon to receive. Enough has been shown to prove that the suspicion uppermost in his mind was, that the unwelcome agents of the government had returned on the heels of the stranger. But, notwithstanding the seeming probability of this opinion, there were secret misgivings of the earthly origin of the two last windings of the shell. All the legends, and all the most credited evidence in cases of prestigious agency, as it had been exhibited in the colonies of New England, went to show the malignant pleasure the evil spirits found, in indulging their wicked mockeries, or in otherwise tormenting those who placed their support on a faith that was believed to be so repugnant to their own ungrateful and abandoned natures.

Under the impressions naturally excited by the communication he had held with the traveler in the mountains, Eben Dudley found his mind equally divided between the expectation of seeing, at each moment, one of the men whom he had induced to quit the valley so unceremoniously, returning to obtain surreptitiously admission within the gate, or of being made an unwilling witness of some wicked manifestation of that power which was temporarily committed to the invisibles. In both of these expectations, however, he was fated to be disappointed. Notwithstanding the strong spiritual bias of the opinions of the credulous sentinel, there was too much of the dross of temporal things in his composition to elevate him altogether above the weakness of humanity. A mind so encumbered began to weary with its own contemplations; and, as it grew feeble with its extraordinary efforts, the dominion of matter gradually resumed its sway. Thought, instead of being clear and active, as the emergency would have seemed to require, began to grow misty.

Once or twice the borderer half arose, and appeared to look about him with observation; and then, as his large frame fell heavily back into its former semi-recumbent attitude, he grew tranquil and stationary. This movement was several times repeated, at intervals of increasing length, till, at the end of an hour, forgetting alike the hunt, the troopers, and the mysterious agents of evil, the young man yielded to the fatigue of the day. The tall oaks of the adjoining forest stood not more immovable in the quiet of the tranquil hour, than his frame now leaned against the side of its narrow habitation.

How much time was thus lost in inactivity, Eben Dudley could never precisely tell. He always stoutly maintained it could not have been long, since his watch was not disturbed by the smallest of those sounds from the woods, which sometimes occur in deep night, and which may be termed the breathing of the forest in its slumbers. His first distinct recollection was that of feeling a hand grasped with the power of a giant. Springing to his feet, the young man eagerly stretched forth an arm, saying, as he did so, in words sufficiently confused—

"If the buck hath fallen by a shot in the head, I grant him to be thine, Reuben Ring; but if struck in limb or body, I claim the venison for a surer hand."

"Truly, a very just division of the spoil," returned one in an undertone, and speaking as if sounds too loud might be dangerous. "Thou givest the head of the deer for a target to Reuben Ring, and keepest the rest of the creature to thine own uses."

"Who hath sent thee, at this hour, to the postern? Dost not know that there are thought to be strangers outlying in the fields."

"I know that there are some, who are not strangers, inlying on their watch!" said Faith Ring. "What shame would come upon thee, Dudley, did the captain, and they who have been so strongly exercised in prayer within, but suspect how little care thou hast had of their safety, the while!"

"Have they come to harm! If the captain hath held them to spiritual movements, I hope that he will allow that nothing earthly hath passed this postern to disturb the exercise. As I hope to be dealt honestly by, in all matters of character, I have not once quitted the gate since the watch was set."

"Else wouldst thou be the famousest sleep-walker in the Connecticut Colony!

Why, drowsy one, conch cannot raise a louder blast than that thou soundest, when eyes are fairly shut in sleep. This may be watching, according to thy meaning of the word ; but infant in its cradle is not half so ignorant of that which passeth around it, as thou hast been.''

"I think, Faith Ring, that thou hast gotten to be much given to backbiting, and evil saying against friends, since the visit of the gallants from over sea.''

"Out upon gallants from over sea, and thee too, man! I am not a girl to be flouted with bold speech from one who doth not know whether he be sleeping or waking. I tell thee, thy good name would be lost in the family, did it come to the ears of the captain, and more particularly to the knowledge of that soldier-stranger, up in the dwelling, of whom even the madam maketh so great ceremony, that thou hast been watching with a tuneful nose, an open mouth, and a sealed eye.''

"If any but thee hadst said this slander of me, girl, it would go nigh to raise hot speech between us ! Thy brother, Reuben Ring, knows better than to stir my temper by such falsity of accusation.''

"Thou dealest so generously by him that he is prone to forget thy misdeeds. Truly he hath the head of the buck, while thou contentest thyself with the offals and all the less worthy parts ! Go to, Dudley ; thou wast in a heavy dream when I caused thee to awake.''

"A pretty time have we fallen upon, when petticoats are used instead of beards and strong-armed men to go the rounds of the sentinels, and to say who sleepeth and who is watchful ! What hath brought thee so far from the exercises and so nigh the gates, Mistress Faith, now that there is no over-sea gallant to soothe thy ears with lying speech and light declarations.''

"If speech not to be credited is that I seek," returned the girl, "truly the errand hath not been without its reward. What brought me hither, sooth ! Why, the madam hath need of articles from the outer buttery—and—ay—and my ears led me to the postern. Thou knowest, musical Dudley, that I have had occasion to hearken to thy watchful notes before this night. But my time is too useful to be wasted in idleness ; thou art now awake, and may thank her who hath done thee a good turn with no wish to boast of it, that one of a black beard is not the laughing-stock of all the youths in the family. If thou keepest thine own counsel, the captain may yet praise thee for a vigilant sentinel ; though Heaven forgive him the wrong he will do the truth !''

"Perhaps a little anger at unjust suspicions may have prompted more than the matter needed, Faith, when I taxed thee with the love of backbiting, and I do now recall that word ; though I will ever deny that aught more than some wandering recollection concerning the hunt of this day hath come over my thoughts, and perhaps made me even forgetful that it was needful to be silent at the postern ; and, therefore, on the truth of a Christian man, I do forgive thee, the—''

But Faith was already out of sight and hearing. Dudley himself, who began to have certain prickings of conscience concerning the ingratitude he had manifested to one who had taken so much interest in his reputation, now bethought him seriously of that which remained to be done. He had much reason to suspect that there was less of the night before him than he had at first believed, and he became in consequence more sensible of the necessity of making some report of the events of his watch. Accordingly, he cast a scrutinizing glance around in order to make sure that the facts should not contradict his testimony, and then, first examining the fastenings of the postern, he mounted the hill and presented himself before the family. The members of the latter, having in truth passed most of the long interval of his absence in spiritual exercises and in religious conversation, were not so sensible of his delay in reporting as they might otherwise have been.

"What tidings dost thou bring us from without ?" said Content, so soon as the self-relieved sentinel appeared. "Hast seen any, or hast heard that which is suspicious ?''

Ere Dudley would answer, his eye did not fail to study the half-malicious expression of the countenance of her who was busy in some domestic toil, directly opposite to the place where he stood. But reading there no more than a glance of playful though smothered irony, he was encouraged to proceed in his report.

"The watch has been quiet," was the answer ; "and there is little cause to keep the sleepers longer from their beds. Some vigilant eyes, like those of Reuben Ring and my own, had better be open until the morning ; further than that, there is no reason to be wakeful.''

Perhaps the borderer would have dwelt more at large on his own readiness to pass the remainder of the hours of rest in attending to the security of those who slept, had not another wicked glance from the dark, laughing eye of her who stood so favorably placed to observe his countenance admonished him of the prudence of being modest in his professions.

"This alarm hath then happily passed away," said the Puritan, rising. "We will now go to our pillows in thankfulness and peace. Thy service shall not be forgotten, Dudley; for thou hast exposed thyself to seeming danger, at least, in our behalf."

"That hath he!" half-whispered Faith; "and sure am I that we maidens will not forget his readiness to lose the sweets of sleep in order that the feeble may not come to harm."

"Speak not of the trifle," hurriedly returned the other. "There has been some deception in the sound, for it is now my opinion, except to summon us to the gate, that this stranger might enter — the couch has not been touched at all to-night."

"Then is it a deception which is repeated!" exclaimed Content, rising from his chair as a faint and broken blast from the shell, like that which had first announced their visitor, again struggled among the buildings until it reached every ear in the dwelling.

"Here is warning as mysterious as it may prove portentous!" said old Mark Heathcote, when the surprise, not to say the consternation of the moment, had subsided. "Hast seen nothing that might justify this?"

Eben Dudley, like most of the auditors, was too much confounded to reply. All seemed to attend anxiously for the second and more powerful blast, which was to complete the imitation of the stranger's summons. It was not necessary to wait long; for in a time as near as might be to that which had intervened between the two first peals of the horn, followed another, and in a note so true again, as to give it the semblance of an echo.

CHAPTER XI.

"I will watch to-night;
Perchance 'twill walk again."—HAMLET.

"MAY not this be a warning given in mercy?" the Puritan, at all times disposed to yield credit to supernatural manifestations of the care of Providence, demanded with a solemnity that did not fail to produce its impression on most of his auditors. "The history of our colonies is full of the evidences of these merciful interpositions."

"We will thus consider it," returned the stranger, to whom the question seemed more particularly addressed. "The first

measure shall be to seek out the danger to which it points. Let the youth they call Dudley give me the aid of his powerful frame and manly courage, then trust the discovery of the meaning of these frequent speakings of the conch to me."

"Surely, Submission, thou wilt not again be first to go forth!" exclaimed Mark, in a surprise that was equally manifested by Content and Ruth, the latter of whom pressed her little image to her side as though the bare proposal presented a powerful picture of supernatural danger. "'Twill be well to think maturely on the step, ere thou runnest the hazard of such an adventure."

"Better it should be I," said Content, "who am accustomed to forest signs, and all the usual testimonials of the presence of those who may wish us harm."

"No," said he, who for the first time had been called "Submission," a name that savored of the religious enthusiasm of the times, and which might have been adopted as an open avowal of his readiness to bow beneath some peculiar dispensation of Providence. "This service shall be mine. Thou art both husband and father; and many are there who look to thy safety as to their rock of earthly support and comfort, while neither kindred, nor—but we will not speak of things foreign to our purpose! Thou knowest, Mark Heathcote, that peril and I are no strangers. There is little need to bid me be prudent. Come, bold woodsman; shoulder thy musket, and be ready to do credit to thy manhood should there be reason to prove it."

"And why not Reuben Ring?" said a hurried female voice, that all knew to proceed from the lips of the sister of the youth just named. "He is quick of eye and ready of hand in trials like these; would it not be well to succor thy party with such aid?"

"Peace, girl," meekly observed Ruth. "This matter is already in the ordering of one used to command; there needeth no counsel from thy short experience."

Faith shrank back, abashed; the flush which had mantled over her brown cheek deepening to a tint like that of blood.

Submission (we use the appellation in the absence of all others) fastened a searching glance for a single moment on the countenance of the girl; and then, as if his intention had not been diverted from the principal subject in hand, he rejoined coolly—

"We go as scouters and observers of that which may hereafter call for the ready assistance of this youth; but numbers would expose us to observation, without adding to our usefulness—and yet,'' he added, arresting his footstep, which was already turned toward the door, and looking earnestly and long at the Indian boy, ''perhaps there standeth one who might much enlighten us, would he but speak!''

This remark drew every eye on the person of the captive. The lad stood the scrutiny with the undismayed and immovable composure of his race. But though his eye met the looks of those around him haughtily and in pride, it was not gleaming with any of that stern defiance which had so often been known to glitter in his glances, when he had reason to think that his fortunes or his person was the subject of the peculiar observation of those with whom he dwelt. On the contrary, the expression of his dark visage was rather that of amity than of hatred, and there was a moment when the look he cast upon Ruth and her offspring was visibly touched with a feeling of concern. A glance charged with such a meaning could not escape the quick-sighted vigilance of a mother.

''The child hath proved himself worthy to be trusted,'' she said; ''and in the name of him who looketh into and knoweth all hearts, let him once more go forth.''

Her lips became sealed, for again the conch announced the seeming impatience of those without to be admitted. The full tones of the shell thrilled on the nerves of the listeners, as though they proclaimed the coming of some great and fearful judgment.

In the midst of these often-repeated and mysterious sounds, Submission alone seemed calm and unmoved. Turning his look from the countenance of the boy, whose head had dropped upon his breast as the last notes of the conch rang among the buildings, he motioned hurriedly to Dudley to follow, and left the place.

There was, in good truth, that in the secluded situation of the valley, the darkness of the hour, and the nature of the several interruptions, which might readily awaken deep concern in the breasts of men as firm even as those who now issued into the open air, in quest of the solution of doubts that were becoming intensely painful. The stranger, or Submission, as we may in future have frequent occasion to call him, led the way in silence to a point of the eminence without the buildings, where the eye might overlook the palisadoes that hedged the sides of the acclivity, and command a view beyond of all that the dusky and imperfect light would reveal.

It was a scene that required familiarity with a border life to be looked on at any moment with indifference. The broad, nearly interminable, and seemingly trackless forest lay about them, bounding the view to the narrow limits of the valley, as though it were some straitened oasis amidst an ocean of wilderness. Within the boundaries of the cleared land objects were less indistinct, though even those nearest and most known were now seen only in the confused and gloomy outlines of night.

Across this dim prospect Submission and his companion gazed long and cautiously.

''There is naught but motionless stumps and fences loaded with snow,'' said the former, when his eye had roamed over the whole circuit of the view which lay on the side of the valley where they stood. ''We must go forth, that we may look nearer to the fields.''

''This way, then, is the postern,'' said Dudley, observing that the other took a direction opposite to that which led to the gate. But a gesture of authority induced him at the next instant to restrain his voice, and to follow whither his companion chose to lead the way.

The stranger made a circuit of half the hill ere he descended to the palisadoes, at a point where lay long and massive piles of wood, which had been collected for the fuel of the family. This spot was one that overlooked the steepest acclivity of the eminence, which was in itself, just there, so difficult of ascent, as to render the provision of the pickets far less necessary than in its more even faces. Still no useful precaution for the security of the family had been neglected, even at this strong point of the works. The piles of wood were laid at such a distance from the pickets as to afford no facilities for scaling them, while, on the other hand, they formed platforms and breast-works that might have greatly added to the safety of those who should be required to defend this portion of the fortress. Taking his way directly amid the parallel piles, the stranger descended rapidly through the whole of their mazes, until he had reached the open space between the outer of the rows and the palisadoes, a space that was warily left too wide to be passed by the leap of man.

'' 'Tis many a day since foot of mine has been in this spot,'' said Eben Dudley, feeling his way along a path that his companion threaded without any apparent hesitation. ''My own hand laid this outer pile some winters since, and certain am I, that, from that hour to this, man hath not touched a billet of the wood. And yet, for one who hath come from over sea, it would appear that thou hast no great difficulty in making way among the narrow lanes!"

"He that hath sight may well choose between air and beechen logs," returned the other, stopping at the palisadoes, and in a place that was concealed from any prying eyes within the works, by triple and quadruple barriers of wood. Feeling in his girdle, he then drew forth something which Dudley was not long in discovering to be a key. While the latter, aided by the little light that fell from the heavens, was endeavoring to make the most of his eyes, Submission applied the instrument to a lock that was artfully sunk in one of the timbers, at the height of a man's breast from the ground, and giving a couple of vigorous turns, a piece of the palisado, some half a fathom long, yielded on a powerful hinge below, and falling, made an opening sufficiently large for the passage of a human body.

"Here is a sally-port ready provided for our sortie," the stranger coolly observed, motioning to the other to precede him. When Dudley had passed, his companion followed, and the opening was then carefully closed and locked.

"Now is all fast again, and we are in the fields without raising alarm to any of mortal birth, at least," continued the guide, thrusting a hand into the folds of his doublet, as if to feel for a weapon, and preparing to descend the difficult declivity which still lay between him and the base of the hill. Eben Dudley hesitated to follow. The interview with the traveler in the mountains occurred to his heated imagination, and the visions of a prestigious agency revived with all their original force. The whole manner and the mysterious character of his companion was little likely to reassure a mind disturbed with such images.

"There is a rumor going in the colony," muttered the borderer, "that the invisibles are permitted for a time to work their evil; and it may well happen that some of their ungodly members shall journey to the Wish-Ton-Wish, in lack of better employment."

"Thou sayest truly," replied the stranger; "but the power that allows of their wicked torments may have seen fit to provide an agent of his own to defeat their subtleties. We will now draw near to the gate, in order that an eye may be kept on their malicious designs."

Submission spoke with gravity, and not without a certain manner of solemnity. Dudley yielded, though with a divided and a disturbed mind, to his suggestion. Still he followed in the footsteps of the stranger, with a caution that might well have eluded the vigilance of any agency short of that which drew its means of information from sources deeper than any of human power.

When the two watchers had found a secret and suitable place, not far from the postern, they disposed themselves in silence to await the result. The outbuildings lay in deep quiet, not a sound of any sort arising from all of the many tenants they were known to contain. The lines of ragged fences; the blackened stumps, capped with little pyramids of snow; the taller and sometimes suspicious-looking stubs; an insulated tree, and finally the broad border of forest—were alike motionless, gloomy, and clothed in the doubtful forms of night. Still, the space around the well-secured and trebly-barred postern was vacant. A sheet of spotless snow served as a background, that would have been sure to betray the presence of any object passing over its surface. Even the conch might be seen suspended from one of the timbers, as mute and inoffensive as the hour when it had been washed by the waves on the sands of the seashore.

"Here will we watch for the coming of the stranger, be he commissioned by the powers of air, or be he one sent on an errand of earth," whispered Submission, preparing his arms for immediate use, and disposing of his person, at the same time, in a manner most convenient to endure the weariness of a patient watch.

"I would my mind were at ease on the question of right-doing in dealing harm to one who disturbs the quiet of a border family," said Dudley, in a tone sufficiently repressed for caution; "it may be found prudent to strike the first blow, should one like an over-sea gallant, after all, be inclined to trouble us at this hour."

"In that strait, thou wilt do well to give little heed to the order of the offenses," gloomily returned the other. "Should another messenger of England appear—"

He paused, for a note of the conch was heard rising gradually on the air, until the whole of the wide valley was filled with its rich and melancholy sound.

"Lip of man is not at the shell!" exclaimed the stranger, who like Dudley had made a forward movement toward the postern, the instant the blast reached his ear, and who like Dudley recoiled in an amazement that even his practiced self-command could not conceal, as he undeniably perceived the truth of that his speech affirmed. "This exceedeth all former instances of marvelous visitations!"

"It is vain to pretend to raise the feeble nature of man to the level of things coming from the invisible world," returned the woodsman at his side. "In such a strait, it is seemly that sinful men should withdraw to the dwellings, where we may sustain our feebleness by the spiritual strivings of the captain."

To this discreet proposal the stranger raised no objection. Without taking the time necessary to effect their retreat with the precaution that had been observed in their advance, the two adventurers quickly found themselves at the secret entrance through which they had so lately issued.

"Enter," said the stranger, lowering the piece of the palisado for the passage of his companion. "Enter of a Heaven's sake! for it is truly meet that we assemble all our spiritual succor."

Dudley was in the act of complying, when a dark line, accompanied by a low rushing sound, cut the air between his head and that of his companion. At the next instant a flint-headed arrow quivered in the timber.

"The heathen!" shouted the borderer, recovering all his manhood as the familiar danger became apparent, and throwing back a stream of fire in the direction from which the treacherous missile had come. "To the palisadoes, men! the bloody heathen is upon us!"

"The heathen!" echoed the stranger, in a deep, steady, commanding voice that had evidently often raised the warning in scenes of even greater emergency, and leveling a pistol, which brought a dark form that was gliding across the snow to one knee, "The heathen! the bloody heathen is upon us!"

As if both assailants and assailed paused, one moment of profound stillness succeeded this fierce interruption of the quiet of the night. Then the cries of the two adventurers were answered by a burst of yells from a wide circle, that nearly environed the hill. At the same moment each dark object in the fields gave up a human form. The shouts were followed by a cloud of arrows, that rendered further delay without the cover of the palisadoes eminently hazardous. Dudley entered; but the passage of the stranger would have been cut off by a leaping, whooping band that pressed fiercely on his rear, had not a broad sheet of flame, glancing from the hill directly in their swarthy and grim countenances, driven the assailants back upon their own footsteps. In another moment, the bolts of the lock were passed,

and the two fugitives were in safety behind the ponderous piles of wood.

CHAPTER XII.

"There need no ghost, my lord, come from the grave
To tell us this." —HAMLET.

ALTHOUGH the minds of most, if not of all the inmates of the Wish-Ton-Wish, had been so powerfully exercised that night with the belief that the powers of the invisible world were about to be let loose upon them, the danger had now presented itself in a shape too palpable to admit of further doubt. The cry of "the heathen" had been raised from every lip; even the daughter and elève of Ruth repeated it, as they fled wailing through the buildings; and, for a moment, terror and surprise appeared to involve the assailed in inextricable confusion. But the promptitude of the young men in rushing to the rescue, with the steadiness of Content, soon restored order. Even the females assumed at least the semblance of composure, the family having been too long trained to meet the exigency of such an emergency to be thrown entirely off its guard, for more than the first and the most appalling moments of the alarm.

The effect of the sudden repulse was such as all experience taught the colonists to expect, in their Indian warfare. The uproar of the onset ceased as abruptly as it had commenced, and a calmness so tranquil, and a stillness so profound succeeded, that one who had for the first time witnessed such a scene, might readily have fancied it the effects of some wild and fearful illusion.

During these moments of general and deep silence, the two adventurers, whose retreat had probably hastened the assault by offering the temptation of an easy passage within the works, left the cover of the piles of wood, and ascended the hill to the place where Dudley knew Content was to be posted in the event of a summons to the defenses.

"Unless much inquiry hath deceived me in the nature of the heathen's craftiness," said the stranger," "we shall have breathing-time ere the onset be renewed. The experience of a soldier bids me say, that prudence now urges us to look into the number and position of our foes, that we may order our resistance with better understanding of their force."

"In what manner of way may this be done? Thou seest naught about us but the quiet and the darkness of night. Speak of the number of our enemies we cannot, and sally forth we may not, without certain destruction to all who quit the palisadoes."

"Thou forgettest that we have a hostage in the boy; he may be turned to some advantage, if our power over his person be used with discretion."

"I doubt that we deceive ourselves with a hope that is vain," returned Content, leading the way as he spoke, however, toward the court which communicated with the principal dwelling. "I have closely studied the eye of that lad, since his unaccountable entrance within the works, and little do I find there that should teach us to expect confidence. It will be happy if some secret understanding with those without has not aided him in passing the palisadoes, and that he prove not a dangerous spy on our force and movements."

"In regard to that he hath entered the dwelling without sound of conch or aid of postern, be not disturbed," returned the stranger with composure. "Were it fitting, this mystery might be of easy explanation; but it may truly need all our sagacity to discover whether he hath connection with our foes! The mind of a native does not give up its secrets like the surface of a vanity-feeding mirror."

The stranger spoke like a man who wrapped a portion of his thoughts in reserve, and his companion listened as one who comprehended more than it might be seemly or discreet to betray. With this secret and yet equivocal understanding of each other's meaning, they entered the dwelling, and soon found themselves in the presence of those they sought.

The constant danger of their situation had compelled the family to bring themselves within the habits of a methodical and severely regulated order of defense. Duties were assigned, in the event of alarm, to the feeblest bodies and the faintest hearts; and during the moments which preceded the visit of her husband, Ruth had been endeavoring to commit to her female subordinates the several necessary charges that usage, and more particularly the emergency of the hour, appeared so imperiously to require.

"Hasten, Charity, to the block," she said; "and look into the condition of the buckets and the ladders, that should the heathen drive us to its shelter, provision of water, and means of retreat, be not wanting in our extremity; and hie thee, Faith, into the upper apartments, to see that no lights may direct their murderous aim at any in the chambers. Thoughts come tardily, when the arrow or the bullet hath already taken its flight! And now

that the first assault is over, Mark, and we may hope to meet the wiles of the enemy by some prudence of our own, thou mayest go forth to thy father. It would have been tempting Providence too rashly, hadst thou rushed, unbidden and uninformed, into the first hurry of the danger. Come hither, child, and receive the blessing and prayers of thy mother; after which thou shalt, with better trust in Providence, place thy young person among the combatants in the hope of victory. Remember that thou art now of an age to do justice to thy name and origin, and yet art thou of years too tender to be foremost in speech, and far less in action on such a night as this."

A momentary flush, that only served to render the succeeding paleness more obvious, passed across the brow of the mother. She stooped and imprinted a kiss on the forehead of the impatient boy, who scarcely waited to receive this act of tenderness, ere he hurried to place himself in the ranks of her defenders.

"And now," said Ruth, slowly turning her eye from the door by which the lad had disappeared, and speaking with a sort of unnatural composure, "and now we will look to the safety of those who can be of little service, except as sentinels to sound the alarm. When thou art certain, Faith, that no neglected light is in the rooms above, take the children to the secret chambers; thence they may look upon the fields without danger from any chance direction of the savages' aim. Thou knowest, Faith, my frequent teaching in this matter; let no sounds of alarm nor frightful whoopings of the people without cause thee to quit the spot; since thou wilt there be safer than in the block, against which many missiles will doubtless be driven on account of its seeming air of strength. Timely notice shall be given of the change, should we seek its security. Thou wilt descend only shouldst thou see enemies scaling the palisadoes on the side which overhangs the stream; since there have we the fewest eyes to watch their movements. Remember on the side of the outbuildings and of the fields, our force is chiefly posted; there can be less reason, therefore, that thou shouldst expose thy lives by endeavoring to look too curiously into that which passeth in the fields. Go, my children, and a heavenly Providence prove thy guardian!"

Ruth stooped to kiss the cheek that her daughter offered to the salute. The embrace was then given to the other child, who was, in truth, scarcely less near her heart, being the orphan daughter of one who had been as a sister in her affections. But, unlike the kiss she had impressed on the forehead of Mark, the present embraces were hasty, and evidently awakened less intense emotion. She had committed the boy to a known and positive danger, but, under the semblance of some usefulness, she sent the others to a place believed to be even less exposed, so long as the enemy could be kept without the works, than the citadel itself. Still, a feeling of deep and maternal tenderness came over her mind, as her daughter retired; and yielding to its sudden impulse, she recalled the girl to her side.

"Thou wilt repeat the prayer for especial protection against the dangers of the wilderness," she solemnly continued. "In thy asking, fail not to remember him to whom thou owest being, and who now exposeth life, that we may be safe. Thou knowest the Christian's rock; place thy faith in its foundation."

"And they who seek to kill us," demanded the well-instructed child; "are they too of the number of those for whom he died?"

"It may not be doubted, though the manner of the dispensation be so mysterious! Barbarians in their habits, and ruthless in their enmities, they are creatures of our nature, and equally objects of his care."

Flaxen locks, that half covered a forehead and face across which ran the most delicate tracery of veins, added luster to a skin as spotlessly fair as if the warm breezes of that latitude had never fanned the countenance of the girl. Through this maze of ringlets, the child turned her full, clear, blue eyes, bending her looks, in wonder and in fear, on the dark visage of the captive Indian youth, who at that moment was to her a subject of secret horror. Unconscious of the interest he excited, the lad stood calm, haughty, and seemingly unobservant, cautious to let no sign of weakness or of concern escape him, in this scene of womanly emotion.

"Mother," whispered the still wondering child; "may we not let him go into the forest? I do not love to—"

"This is no time for speech. Go to thy hiding-place, my child, and remember both thy askings and the cautions I have named. Go, and heavenly care protect thy innocent head!"

Ruth again stooped, and bowing her face until the features were lost in the rich tresses of her daughter, a moment passed during which there was an eloquent silence. When she arose, a tear glistened on the cheek of the child. The latter had received the embrace more in apathy than in concern; and now, when, led toward the upper rooms, she moved from the presence of her mother, it was with an eye that never bent its riveted gaze from the features of the young Indian, until the intervening walls hid him entirely from her sight.

"Thou hast been thoughtful and like thyself, my good Ruth," said Content, who at that moment entered, and who rewarded the self-command of his wife by a look of the kindest approbation. "The youths have not been more prompt in meeting the foe at the stockades, than thy maidens in looking to their less hardy duties. All is again quiet without; and we come, now, rather for consultation, than for any purposes of strife."

"Then must we summon our father from his post at the artillery, in the block."

"It is not needful," interrupted the stranger. "Time presses, for this calm may be too shortly succeeded by a tempest that all our power shall not quell. Bring forth the captive."

Content signed to the boy to approach, and when he was in reach of his hand, he placed him full before the stranger.

"I know not thy name, nor even that of thy people," commenced the other, after a long pause, in which he seemed to study deeply the countenance of the lad; "but certain am I, though a more wicked spirit may still be struggling for the mastery in thy wild mind, that nobleness of feeling is no stranger to thy bosom. Speak; hast thou aught to impart concerning the danger that besets this family? I have learned much this night from thy manner, but to be clearly understood, it is now time that thou shouldst speak in words."

The youth kept his eye fastened on that of the speaker, until the other had ended, and then he bent it slowly, but with searching observation, on the anxious countenance of Ruth. It seemed as if he balanced between his pride and his sympathies. The latter prevailed; for, conquering the deep reluctance of an Indian, he spoke openly, and for the first time since his captivity, in the language of the hated race.

"I hear the whoops of warriors," was his calm answer. "Have the ears of the pale men been shut?"

"Thou hast spoken with the young men of thy tribe in the forest, and thou hadst knowledge of this onset?"

The youth made no reply, though the keen look of his interrogator was met steadily, and without fear. Perceiving that he had demanded more than would be answered, the stranger changed his mode of investigation, masking his inquiries with a little more of artifice.

" It may not be that a great tribe is on the bloody path ! " he said ; " warriors would have walked over the timbers of the palisadoes like bending reeds ! 'Tis a Pequot, who hath broken faith with a Christian, and who is now abroad, prowling as a wolf in the night."

A sudden and wild expression gleamed over the swarthy features of the boy. His lips moved, and the words that issued from between them were uttered in the tones of biting scorn. Still he rather muttered than pronounced aloud—

" The Pequot is a dog ! "

" It is as I had thought : the knaves are out of their villages, that the Yengeese may feed their squaws. But a Narragansett, or a Wampanoag, is a man ; he scorns to lurk in the darkness. When he comes, the sun will light his path. The Pequot steals in silence, for he fears that the warriors will hear his tread."

It was not easy to detect any evidence that the captive listened, either to the commendation or the censure, with answering sympathy ; for marble is not colder than were the muscles of his unmoved countenance.

The stranger studied the expression of his features in vain, and drawing so near as to lay his hand on the naked shoulder of the lad, he added—" Boy, thou hast heard much moving matter concerning the nature of our Christian faith, and thou hast been the subject of many a fervent asking ; it may not be that so much good seed hath been altogether scattered by the way-side ! Speak ; may I again trust thee ? "

" Let my father look on the snow. The print of the moccasin goes and comes."

" It is true. Thus far hast thou proved honest. But when the war-whoop shall be thrilling through thy young blood, the temptation to join the warriors may be too strong. Hast any gage, any pledge, in which we may find warranty for letting thee depart ? "

The boy regarded his interrogator with a look that plainly denoted ignorance of his meaning.

" I would know what thou canst leave with me, to show that our eyes shall again look upon thy face, when we have opened the gate for thy passage into the fields."

Still the gaze of the other was wondering and confused.

" When the white man goes upon the war path, and would put trust in his foe, he takes surety for his faith, by holding the life of one dear as a warranty of its truth. What canst offer, that I may know thou wilt return from the errand on which I would fain send thee ? "

" The path is open."

" Open, but not certain to be used. Fear may cause thee to forget the way it leads."

The captive now understood the meaning of the other's doubts, but, as if disdaining to reply, he bent his eyes aside, and stood in one of those immovable attitudes which so often gave him the air of a piece of dark statuary.

Content and his wife had listened to this short dialogue, in a manner to prove that they possessed some secret knowledge which lessened the wonder they might otherwise have felt, at witnessing so obvious proofs of a secret acquaintance between the speakers. Both, however, manifested unequivocal signs of astonishment, when they first heard English sounds issuing from the lips of the boy. There was, at least, the semblance of hope in the mediation of one who had received, and who had appeared to acknowledge, so much kindness from herself ; and Ruth clung to the cheering expectation with the quickness of maternal care.

" Let the boy depart," she said. " I will be his hostage ; and should he prove false, there can be less to fear in his absence than in his presence."

The obvious truth of the latter assertion probably weighed more with the stranger than the unmeaning pledge of the woman.

" There is reason in this," he resumed. " Go, then, into the fields, and say to thy people that they have mistaken the path ; that they are on hath led them to the dwelling of a friend. Here are no Pequots, nor any of the men of the Manhattoes ; but Christian Yengeese, who have long dealt with the Indian as one just man dealeth with another. Go, and when thy signal shall be heard at the gate, it shall be opened to thee for readmission."

Thus saying, the stranger motioned to the boy to follow, taking care as they left the room together, to instruct him in all such minor matters as might assist in effecting the pacific object of the mission on which he was employed.

A few minutes of doubt and of fearful suspense succeeded this experiment. The stranger, after seeing that egress was permitted to his messenger, had returned to the dwelling and rejoined his companions. He passed the moments in pacing the apartment, with the strides of one in whom powerful concern was strongly at work. At times, the sound of his heavy footstep ceased, and then all listened intently, in order to catch any sound that might instruct them in the nature of the scene that was passing without. In the midst of one of these pauses, a yell like that of savage delight arose in the fields. It was succeeded by the death-like and portentous calm which had rendered the time since the momentary attack even more alarming than when the danger had a positive and known character. But all the attention the most intense anxiety could now lend, furnished no additional clew to the movements of their foes. For many minutes the quiet of midnight reigned both within and without the defenses. In the midst of this suspense the latch of the door was lifted, and their messenger appeared with that noiseless tread and collected mien which distinguished the people of his race.

"Thou hast met the warriors of thy tribe?" hastily demanded the stranger.

"The noise did not cheat the Yengeese. It was not a girl laughing in the woods."

"And thou hast said to thy people, 'we are friends'?"

"The words of my father were spoken."

"And heard—Were they loud enough to enter the ears of the young men?"

The boy was silent.

"Speak," continued the stranger, elevating his form proudly, like one ready to breast a more severe shock. "Thou hast men for thy listeners. Is the pipe of the savage filled? Will he smoke in peace, or holdeth he the tomahawk in a clenched hand?"

The countenance of the boy worked with a feeling that it was not usual for an Indian to betray. He bent his look with concern on the mild eyes of the anxious Ruth; then drawing a hand slowly from beneath the light robe that partly covered his body, he cast at the feet of the stranger a bundle of arrows, wrapped in the glossy and striped skin of the rattlesnake.

"This is a warning we may not misconceive!" said Content, raising the well-known emblem of ruthless hostility to the light, and exhibiting it before the eyes of his less instructed companion. "Boy, what have the people of my race done, that thy warriors should seek their blood to this extremity?"

When the boy had discharged his duty he moved aside, and appeared unwilling to observe the effect which his message might produce on his companions. But thus questioned, all gentle feelings were near being forgotten in the sudden force of passion. A hasty glance at Ruth quelled the emotion, and he continued as calm as ever, and silent.

"Boy," repeated Content, "I ask thee why thy people seek our blood?"

The passage of the electric spark is not more subtle, nor is it scarcely more brilliant than was the gleam that shot into the dark eye of the Indian. The organ seemed to emit rays coruscant as the glance of the serpent. His form appeared to swell with the inward strivings of the spirit, and for a moment there was every appearance of a fierce and uncontrollable burst of ferocious passion. The conquest of feeling was, however, but momentary. He regained his self-command by a surprising effort of will, and advancing so near to him who had asked this bold question, as to lay a finger on his breast, the young savage haughtily said—

"See! this world is very wide. There is room on it for the panther and the deer. Why have the Yengeese and the red men met?"

"We waste the precious moments in probing the stern nature of a heathen," said the stranger. "The object of his people is certain, and, with the aid of the Christian's staff, we will beat back their power. Prudence requireth at our hands that the lad be secured; after which, will we repair to the stockades and prove ourselves men."

Against this proposal no reasonable objection could be raised. Content was about to secure the person of his captive in a cellar, when a suggestion of his wife caused him to change his purpose. Notwithstanding the sudden and fierce mien of the youth, there had been such an intelligence created between them by looks of kindness and interest, that the mother was reluctant to abandon all hope of his aid.

"Miantonimoh!" she said, "though others distrust thy purpose, I will have confidence. Come, then, with me; and while I give thee promise of safety in thine own person, I ask at thy hands the office of a protector for my babes."

The boy made no reply; but as he passively followed his conductress to the chambers, Ruth fancied she read assurance of his faith in the expression of his eloquent eye. At the same moment her husband and Submission left the house to take their stations at the palisadoes.

CHAPTER XIII.

"Thou art my good youth: my page;
I'll be thy master: walk with me; speak freely."
—CYMBELINE.

THE apartment in which Ruth had directed the children to be placed was in the attic, and, as already stated, on the side of the building which faced the stream that ran at the foot of the hill. It had a single projecting window, through which there was a view of the forest and of the fields on that side of the valley. Small openings in its sides admitted also of glimpses of the grounds which lay further in the rear. In addition to the covering of the roofs, and of the massive framework of the building, an interior partition of timber protected the place against the entrance of most missiles then known in the warfare of the country. During the infancy of the children this room had been their sleeping apartment; nor was it abandoned for that purpose until the additional outworks, which increased with time around the dwellings, had emboldened the family to trust themselves at night in situations more convenient, and which were believed to be no less equally secure against surprise.

"I know thee to be one who feeleth the obligations of a warrior," said Ruth, as she ushered her follower into the presence of the children. "Thou wilt not deceive me; the lives of these tender ones are in thy keeping. Look to them, Miantonimoh, and the Christian's God will remember thee in thine own hour of necessity!"

The boy made no reply, but in a gentle expression which was visible in his dark visage, the mother endeavored to find the pledge she sought. Then as the youth, with the delicacy of his race, moved aside in order that they who were bound to each other by ties so near might indulge their feelings without observation, Ruth again drew near her offspring with all the tenderness of a mother beaming in her eyes.

"Once more I bid thee not to look too curiously at the fearful strife that may arise in front of our habitation," she said. "The heathen is truly upon us, with bloody mind. Young as well as old must now show faith in the protection of our master, and such courage as befitteth believers."

"And why is it, mother," demanded her child, "that they seek to do us harm? Have we ever done evil to them?"

"I may not say. He that hath made the earth, hath given it to us for our uses, and reason would seem to teach that if portions of its surface are vacant, he that needeth truly, may occupy."

"The savage!" whispered the child, nestling still nearer to the bosom of her stooping parent. "His eye glittereth like the star which hangs above the trees."

"Peace, daughter; his fierce nature broodeth over some fancied wrong!"

"Surely, we are here rightfully. I have heard my father say that when the Lord made me a present to his arms, our valley was a tangled forest, and that much toil only has made it as it is."

"I hope that what we enjoy, we enjoy rightfully! And yet it seemeth that the savage is ready to deny our claims."

"And where do these bloody enemies dwell? Have they, too, valleys like this, and do the Christians break into them to shed blood in the night?"

"They are of wild and fierce habits, Ruth, and little do they know of our manner of life. Woman is not cherished as among the people of thy father's race; for force of body is more regarded than kinder ties."

The little auditor shuddered, and when she buried her face deeper in the bosom of her parent, it was with a more quickened sense of maternal affection, and with a livelier view than her infant perception had ever yet known of the gentle charities of kindred. When she had spoken, the matron impressed the final kiss on the forehead of each of the children, and asking aloud that God might bless them, she turned to go to the performance of duties that called for the exhibition of very different qualities. Before quitting the room, however, she once more approached the boy, and holding the light before his steady eye, she said solemnly—

"I trust my babes to the keeping of a young warrior!"

The look he returned was like the others, cold but not discouraging. A gaze of many moments elicited no reply; and Ruth prepared to quit the place, troubled by uncertainty concerning the intentions of the guardian she left with the girls, while she still trusted that the many acts of kindness which she had shown him during his captivity, would not go without their reward. Her hand rested on the bolt of the door, in indecision. The moment was favorable to the character of the youth; for she recalled the manner of his return that night, no less than his former acts of faith, and she was about to leave the passage for his egress open, when an uproar arose on the air which filled the valley with all the hideous cries and yells of a savage onset. Drawing the bolt, the startled woman descended, without further thought, and rushed to her post, with the hurry of one who saw only the necessity of exertion in another scene.

"Stand to the timbers, Reuben Ring! Bear back the skulking murderers on their bloody followers! The pikes! Here, Dudley, is opening for thy valor. The Lord have mercy on the souls of the ignorant heathen!" mingled with the reports of musketry, the whoops of the warriors, the whizzing of bullets and arrows, with all the other accompaniments of such a contest, were the fearful sounds that saluted the senses of Ruth as she issued into the court. The valley was occasionally lighted by the explosion of firearms, and then, at times, the horrible din prevailed in the gloom of deep darkness. Happily, in the midst of all this confusion and violence, the young men of the valley were true to their duties. An alarming attempt to scale the stockade had already been repulsed, and the true character of two or three feints having been ascertained, the principal force of the garrison was now actively employed in resisting the main attack.

"In the name of him who is with us in every danger!" exclaimed Ruth, advancing to two figures that were so busily engaged in their own concerns as not to heed her approach, "tell me how goes the struggle? Where are my husband and the boy? Or has it pleased Providence that any of our people should be stricken?"

"It hath pleased the devil," returned Eben Dudley, somewhat irreverently for one of that chastened school, "to send an Indian arrow through jerkin and skin into this arm of mine! Softly, Faith; dost think, girl, that the covering of man is like the coat of a sheep, from which the fleece may be plucked at will. I am no molting fowl, nor is this arrow a feather of my wing. The Lord forgive the rogue for the ill turn he hath done my flesh, say I, and amen like a Christian! He will have occasion too for the mercy, seeing he hath nothing further to hope for in this world. Now, Faith, I acknowledge the debt of thy kindness, and let there be no more cutting speech between us. Thy tongue often pricketh more sorely than the Indian's arrow."

"Whose fault is it that old acquaintance hath sometimes been overlooked in new conversations? Thou knowest that, wooed by proper speech, no maiden in the Colony is wont to render gentler answer. Dost feel uneasiness in thine arm, Dudley?"

"'Tis not tickling with a straw, to drive a flint-headed arrow to the bone! I forgive thee the matter of too much discourse with the trooper, and all the side-cuts of thy overambling tongue, on conditions that—"

"Out with thee, brawler! Wouldst be prating here the night long on pretense of a broken skin and the savage at our gates? A fine character will the madam render of thy deeds when the other youths have beaten back the Indian, and thou loitering among the buildings!"

The discomfited borderer was about to curse in his heart the versatile humor of his mistress, when he saw, by a sideglance, that ears which had no concern in the subject had like to have shared in the matter of their discourse. Seizing the weapon which was leaning against the foundation of the block, he hurried past the mistress of the family, and in another minute his voice and his musket were again heard ringing in the uproar.

"Does he bring tidings from the palisadoes?" repeated Ruth, too anxious that the young man should return to his post to arrest his retreat. "What saith he of the onset?"

"The savage hath suffered for his boldness, and little harm hath yet come to our people. Except that yon block of a man hath managed to put arm before the passage of an arrow, I know not that any of our people have been harmed."

"Hearken! they retire, Ruth. The yells are less near, and our young men will prevail! Go thou to thy charge among the piles of the fuel, and see that no lurker remaineth to do injury. The Lord hath remembered mercy, and it may yet arrive that this evil shall pass away from before us!"

The quick ear of Ruth had not deceived her. The tumult of the assault was gradually receding from the works, and though the flashings of the muskets and the bellowing reports that rang in the surrounding forest were not less frequent than before, it was plain that the critical moment of the onset was already past. In place of the fierce effort to carry the stockade by surprise, the savages had now resorted to means that were more methodical, and which, though not so appalling in appearance, were perhaps quite as certain of final success. Ruth profited by a momentary cessation in the flight of the missiles to seek those in whose welfare she had placed her chief concern.

"Has other then brave Dudley suffered by this assault?" demanded the anxious wife, as she passed swiftly among a group of dusky figures that were collected in consultation on the brow of the declivity; "has any need of such care as a woman's hand may bestow? Heathcote, thy person is unharmed!"

"Truly, one of great mercy hath watched over it, for little opportunity hath been given to look to our own safety. I fear that some of our young men have not regarded the covers with the attention that prudence requires."

" The thougtless Mark hath not forgotten my admonitions ! Boy, thou hast never lost sight of duty so far as to precede thy father ? "

" One sees or thinks little but of the redskins when the whoop is ringing among the timbers of the palisadoes, mother," returned the boy, dashing his hand across his brow, in order that the drops of blood which were trickling from a furrow left by the passage of an arrow might no tbe seen. " I have kept near my father, but whether in his front or in his rear the darkness hath not permitted me to note."

" The lad hath behaved in a bold and seemly manner," said the stranger; "and he hath shown the metal of his grandsire's stock. Ha ! what is't we see gleaming among the sheds ? A sortie may be needed to save the granaries and thy folds from destruction ! "

" To the barns ! to the barns ! " shouted two of the youths, from their several lookouts. "The brand is in the buildings!" exclaimed a maiden, who discharged a similar duty under cover of the dwellings. Then followed a discharge of muskets, all of which were leveled at the glancing light that was glaring in fearful proximity to the combustible materials which filled the most of the outbuildings. A savage yell, and the sudden extinguishment of the blazing knot, announced the fatal accuracy of the aim.

" This may not be neglected ! " exclaimed Content, moved to extraordinary excitement by the extremity of the danger. " Father ! " he called aloud, " 'tis fitting time to show our utmost strength."

A moment of suspense succeeded this summons. The whole valley was then as suddenly lighted as if a torrent of the electric fluid had flashed across its gloomy bed ; a sheet of flame glanced from the attic of the block, and then came the roar of the little piece of artillery, which had so long dwelt there in silence. The rattling of a shot among the sheds, and the rending of timber, followed. Fifty dark forms were seen by the momentary light gliding from among the out-buildings, in an alarm natural to their ignorance, and with an agility proportioned to their alarm. The moment was propitious. Content silently motioned to Reuben Ring; they passed the postern together, and disappeared in the direction of the barns. The period of their absence was one of intense care to Ruth, and it was not without its anxiety even to those whose nerves were better steeled. A few moments, however, served to appease these feelings; for the adventurers returned in safety and as silently as they had quitted the defenses. The trampling of feet on the crust of the snow, the neighing of horses, and the bellowing of frightened cattle, as the terrified beasts scattered about the fields, soon proclaimed the object of the risk which had just been run.

" Enter," whispered Ruth, who held the postern with her own hand. " Enter of Heaven's mercy ! Thou hast given liberty to every hoof, that no living creature perish by the flames?"

" All; and truly not too speedily—for, see—the brand is at work !"

Content had much reason to felicitate himself on his expedition ; for, even while he spoke, half-concealed torches, made as usual of blazing knots of pine, were again seen glancing across the fields, evidently approaching the out-buildings, by such indirect and covered paths as might protect those who bore them from the shot of the garrison. A final and common effort was made to arrest the danger. The muskets of the young men were active, and more than once did the citadel of the stern old Puritan give forth its flood of flame, in order to beat back the dangerous visitants. A few shrieks of savage disappointment and of bodily anguish announced the success of these discharges; but though most of those who approached the barns were either driven back in fear or suffered for their temerity, one among them, more wary or more practiced than his companions, found means to effect his object.

The firing had ceased, and the besieged were congratulating themselves on success, when a sudden light glared across the fields. A sheet of flame soon came curling over the crest of a wheat-stack, and quickly wrapped the inflammable material in its fierce torrent. Against this destruction there remained no remedy. The barns and inclosures, which so lately had been lying in the darkness of the hour, were instantly illuminated, and life would have been the penalty paid by any of either party who should dare to trust his person within the bright glare. The borderers were soon compelled to fall back, even within the shadows of the hill, and to seek such covers as the stockades offered in order to avoid the aim of the arrow or the bullet.

" This is a mournful spectacle to one that has harvested in charity with all men," said Content to the trembler who convulsively grasped his arm, as the flame whirled in the currents of the heated air, and sweeping once or twice across the roof of a shed, left a portion of its torrent creeping insidiously along the wooden covering. " The ingathering of a blessed season is about to melt into ashes before the brand of these accur—"

"Peace, Heathcote! What is wealth, or the fullness of thy granaries, to that which remains. Check these repinings of thy spirit, and bless God that he leaveth us our babes, and the safety of our inner roofs."

"Thou sayest truly," returned the husband, endeavoring to imitate the meek resignation of his companion. "What indeed are the gifts of the world, set in the balance against the peace of mind— ha! that evil blast of wind sealeth the destruction of our harvest! The fierce element is in the heart of the granaries."

Ruth made no reply, for though less moved by worldly cares than her husband, the frightful progress of the conflagration alarmed her with a sense of personal danger. The flames had passed from roof to roof, and meeting everywhere with fuel of the most combustible nature, the whole of the vast range of barns, sheds, granaries, cribs, and out-buildings, was just breaking forth in the brightness of a torrent of fire. Until this moment, suspense, with hope on one side and apprehension on the other, had kept both parties mute spectators of the scene. But yells of triumph soon proclaimed the delight with which the Indians witnessed the completion of their fell design. Their whoops followed this burst of pleasure, and a third onset was made.

The combatants now fought, under a brightness which, though less natural, was scarcely less brilliant than that of noonday. Stimulated by the prospect of success which was offered by the conflagration, the savages rushed upon the stockade with more audacity than it was usual to display in their cautious warfare. A broad shadow was cast, by the hill and its buildings, across the fields on the side opposite to the flames, and through this belt of comparative gloom, the fiercest of the band made their way to the very palisadoes with impunity. Their presence was announced by the yell of delight, for too many curious eyes had been drinking in the fearful beauty of the conflagration to note their approach until the attack had nearly proved successful. The rushes to the defense and to the attack were now alike quick and headlong. Volleys were useless, for the timbers offered equal security to both assailant and assailed. It was a struggle of hand to hand, in which numbers would have prevailed, had it not been the good fortune of the weaker party to act on the defensive. Blows of the knife were passed swiftly between the timbers, and occasionally the discharge of the mus-

ket, or the twanging of the bow, was heard.

"Stand to the timbers, my men!" said the deep tones of the stranger, who spoke in the midst of the fierce struggle with that commanding and stirring cheerfulness that familiarity with danger can alone inspire. "Stand to the defenses, and they are impassable. Ha! 'twas well meant, friend savage," he muttered between his teeth, as he parried, at some jeopardy to one hand, a thrust aimed at his throat, while with the other he seized the warrior who had inflicted the blow, and drawing his naked breast with the power of a giant, full against the opening between the timbers, he buried his own keen blade to its haft in the body. The eyes of the victim rolled wildly, and when the iron hand which bound him to the wood with the power of a vise, loosened its grasp, he fell motionless on the earth. This death was succeeded by the usual yell of disappointment, and the assailants disappeared as swiftly as they had approached.

"God be praised, that we have to rejoice in this advantage!" said Content, enumerating the individuals of his force, with an anxious eye, when all were again assembled at the stand on the hill, where, favored by the glaring light, they could overlook in comparative security the more exposed parts of their defenses. "We count our own, though I fear me many may have suffered."

The silence and the occupations of his listeners, most of whom were stanching their blood, was a sufficient answer.

"Hist, father!" said the quick-eyed and observant Mark; "one remaineth on the palisado nearest the wicket. It is a savage? or do I see a stump in the field beyond?"

All eyes followed the direction of the hand of the speaker, and there was seen, of a certainty, something clinging to the inner side of one of the timbers, that bore a marked resemblance to the human form. The part of the stockades, where the seeming figure clung, lay more in obscurity than the rest of the defenses, and doubts as to its character were not alone confined to the quick-sighted lad who had first detected its presence.

"Who hangs upon our palisadoes?" called Eben Dudley. "Speak, that we do not harm a friend!"

The wood itself was not more immovable than the dark object, until the report of the borderer's musket was heard, and then it came tumbling to the earth like an insensible mass.

"Fallen like a stricken bear from his tree! Life was in it, or no bullet of mine could have loosened the hold ! '' exclaimed Dudley, a little in exultation, as he saw the success of his aim.

"I will go forward and see that he is past—"

The mouth of young Mark was stopped by the hand of the stranger, who calmly observed—

"I will look into the fate of the heathen myself.'' He was about to proceed to the spot, when the supposed dead or wounded man sprang to his feet, with a yell that rang in echoes along the margin of the forest, and bounded toward the cover of the buildings with high and active leaps. Two or three muskets sent their streaks of flame across his path, but seemingly without success. Jumping in a manner to elude the certainty of their fire, the unharmed savage gave forth another yell of triumph, and disappeared among the angles of the dwellings. His cries were understood, for answering whoops were heard in the fields, and the foe without again rallied to the attack.

"This may not be neglected,'' said he who, more by his self-possession and air of authority, than by any known right to command, had insensibly assumed so much control in the important business of that night. "One like this, within our walls, may quickly bring destruction on the garrison. The postern may be opened to an inroad—"

"A triple lock secures it,'' interrupted Content. "The key is hid where none know to seek it, other than such as are of our household.''

"And happily the means of passing the private wicket are in my possession,'' muttered the other, in an undertone. "So far, well ; but the brand ! the brand ! the maidens must look to the fires and lights, while the youths make good the stockade, since this assault admitteth not of further delay.''

So saying, the stranger gave an example of courage by proceeding to his stand at the pickets, where, supported by his companions, he continued to defend the approaches against a discharge of arrows and bullets that was more distant, but scarcely less dangerous to the safety of those who showed themselves on the side of the acclivity, than those which had been previously showered upon the garrison.

In the meantime, Ruth summoned her assistants, and hastened to discharge the duty which had just been prescribed. Water was cast freely on all the fires, and, as the still raging conflagration continued to give far more light than was either necessary or safe, care was taken to extinguish any torch or candle that, in the hurry of alarm, might have been left to molder in its socket, throughout the extensive range of the dwellings and the offices.

CHAPTER XIV.

"Thou mild, sad mother—
　　Quit him not so soon !
Mother, in mercy, stay !
Despair and death are with him, and canst thou,
With that kind, earthward look, go leave him
　　now ?''
　　　　　　　　　　　　—DANA.

WHEN these precautions were taken, the females returned to their several lookouts, and Ruth, whose duty it was in moments of danger to exercise a general superintendence, was left to her meditations and to such watchfulness as her fears might excite. Quitting the inner rooms, she approached the door that communicated with the court, and for a moment lost the recollection of her immediate cares in a view of the imposing scene by which she was surrounded.

By this time, the whole of the vast range of outbuildings which had been constructed—as was usual in the colonies—of the most combustible materials and with no regard to the expenditure of wood, was wrapt in fire. Notwithstanding the position of the intermediate edifices, broad flashes of light were constantly crossing the court itself, on whose surface she was able to distinguish the smallest object, while the heavens before her were glaring with a lurid red. Through the openings between the buildings of the quadrangle the eye could look out upon the fields, where she saw every evidence of a sullen intention on the part of the savages to persevere in their object.

Dark, fierce-looking, and nearly naked human forms were seen flitting from cover to cover, while there was no stump nor log within arrow's flight of the defenses that did not protect the person of a daring and indefatigable enemy. It was plain the Indians were there in hundreds, and as the assaults continued after the failure of a surprise, it was too evident that they were bent on victory, at some hazard to themselves. No usual means of adding to the horrors of the scene were neglected. Whoops and yells were incessantly ringing around the place, while the loud and often-repeated tones of a conch betrayed the artifice by which the savages had so often endeavored, in the earlier part of the night, to lure the garrison out of the palisadoes. A few scattering shot, discharged with deliberation and from every exposed point within the works, proclaimed both the coolness and the vigilance of the defendants. The little gun in the block-house was silent; for the Puritan knew too well its real power to lessen its reputation by a too frequent use. The weapon was therefore reserved for those moments of pressing danger that would be sure to arrive.

On this spectacle Ruth gazed in fearful sadness. The long-sustained and sylvan security of her abode was violently destroyed, and in the place of a quiet which had approached as near as may be on earth to that holy peace for which her spirit strove, she and all she most loved were suddenly confronted to the most frightful exhibition of human horrors. In such a moment, the feelings of a mother were likely to revive; and ere time was given for reflection, aided by the light of the conflagration, the matron was moving swiftly through the intricate passages of the dwelling, in quest of those whom she had placed in the security of the chambers.

"Thou hast remembered to avoid looking on the fields, my children," said the nearly breathless woman as she entered the room. "Be thankful, babes; hitherto the efforts of the savages have been vain, and we still remain masters of our habitations."

"Why is the night so red? Come hither, mother; thou mayest look into the wood as if the sun were shining!"

"The heathens have fired our granaries, and what thou seest is the light of the flames. But happily they cannot put brand into the dwellings, while thy father and the young men stand to their weapons. We must be grateful for this security, frail as it seemeth. Thou hast knelt, my Ruth, and hast remembered to think of thy father and brother in thy prayers."

"I will do so again, mother," whispered the child, bending to her knees, and wrapping her young features in the garments of the matron.

"Why hide thy countenance? One young and innocent as thou may lift thine eyes to Heaven with confidence."

"Mother, I see the Indian unless my face be hid. He looketh at me, I fear, with wish to do us harm."

"Thou art not just to Miantonimoh, child," answered Ruth, as she glanced her eye rapidly round to seek the boy, who had modestly withdrawn into a remote and shaded corner of the room. "I left him with thee for a guardian, and not as one who would wish to injure. Now think of thy God," imprinting a kiss on the cold, marble-like forehead of her daughter, "and have reliance in his goodness. Miantonimoh, I again leave you with a charge to be their protector," she added,

quitting her daughter and advancing toward the youth.

"Mother!" shrieked the child, "come to me, or I die!"

Ruth turned from the listening captive with the quickness of instinct. A glance showed her the jeopardy of her offspring. A naked savage, dark, powerful of frame, and fierce in the frightful masquerade of his war-paint, stood winding the silken hair of the girl in one hand, while he already held the glittering ax above a head that seemed inevitably devoted to destruction.

"Mercy! mercy!" exclaimed Ruth, hoarse with horror, and dropping to her knees, as much from inability to stand as with intent to petition. "Monster, strike me; but spare the child!"

The eyes of the Indian rolled over the person of the speaker, but it was with an expression that seemed rather to enumerate the number of his victims than to announce any change of purpose. With a fiend - like purpose that bespoke much knowledge of the ruthless practice, he again swung the quivering but speechless child in the air, and prepared to direct the weapon with a fell certainty of aim. The tomahawk had made its last circuit, and an instant would have decided the fate of the victim, when the captive boy stood in front of the frightful actor in this revolting scene. By a quick, forward movement of his arm, the blow was arrested. The deep guttural ejaculation, which betrays the surprise of an Indian, broke from the chest of the savage, while his hand fell to his side, and the form of the suspended girl was suffered again to touch the floor. The look and gesture with which the boy had interfered, expressed authority rather than resentment or horror. His air was calm, collected, and, as it appeared by the effect, imposing.

"Go," he said, in the language of the fierce people from whom he had sprung; "the warriors of the pale men are calling thee by name."

"The snow is red with the blood of our young men," the other fiercely answered: "and not a scalp is at the belt of my people."

"These are mine," returned the boy, with dignity, sweeping his arm while speaking, in a manner to show that he extended protection to all present.

The warrior gazed about him grimly, and like one but half-convinced. He had incurred a danger too fearful in entering the stockade to be easily diverted from his purpose.

"Listen!" he continued, after a short

pause, during which the artillery of the Puritan had again bellowed in the uproar without. "The thunder is with the Yengeese! Our young women will look another way, and call us Pequots, should there be no scalps on our pole."

For a single moment the countenance of the boy changed, and his resolution seemed to waver. The other, who watched his eyes with longing eagerness, again seized his victim by the hair, when Ruth shrieked in the accents of despair—

"Boy! boy! if thou art not with us, God hath deserted us!"

"She is mine," burst fiercely from the lips of the lad. "Hear my words, Wompahwisset: the blood of my father is very warm within me."

The other paused, and the blow was once more suspended. The glaring eyeballs of the savage rested intently on the swelling form and stern countenance of the young hero, whose uplifted hand appeared to menace instant punishment, should he dare to disregard the mediation. The lips of the warrior severed, and the word "Miantonimoh" was uttered as softly as if it recalled a feeling of sorrow. Then, as a sudden burst of yells rose above the roar of the conflagration, the fierce Indian turned in his tracks, and abandoning the trembling and nearly insensible child, he bounded away like a hound loosened on a fresh scent of blood.

"Boy! boy!" murmured the mother; "heathen or Christian, there is one that will bless thee—"

A rapid gesture of the hand interrupted the fervent expression of her gratitude. Pointing after the form of the retreating savage, the lad encircled his own head with a finger, in a manner that could not be mistaken, as he uttered steadily, but with the deep emphasis of an Indian—

"The young pale-face has a scalp!"

Ruth heard no more. With instinctive rapidity, every feeling of her soul quickened nearly to agony, she rushed below, in order to warn Mark against the machinations of so fearful an enemy. Her step was heard but for a moment in the vacant chambers, and then the Indian boy, whose steadiness and authority had just been so signally exerted in favor of the children, resumed his attitude of meditation as quietly as if he took no further interest in the frightful events of the night.

The situation of the garrison was now, indeed, to the last degree critical. A torrent of fire had passed from the further extremity of the out-houses to that which stood nearest to the defenses; and as building after building melted beneath its raging power, the palisadoes became heated nearly to the point of ignition. The alarm created by this imminent danger had already been given, and when Ruth issued into the court a female was rushing past her, seemingly on some errand of the last necessity.

"Hast seen him?" demanded the breathless mother, arresting the steps of the quick-moving girl.

"Not since the savage made his last onset; but I warrant me he may be found near the western loops, making good the works against the enemy!"

"Surely he is not foremost in the fray! Of whom speakest thou, Faith? I questioned thee of Mark. There is one, even now, raging within the pickets, seeking a victim."

"Truly, I thought it had been a question of——the boy is with his father and the stranger soldier, who does such deeds of valor in our behalf. I have seen no enemy within the palisadoes, Madam Heathcote, since the entry of the man who escaped by favor of the powers of darkness from the shot of Eben Dudley's musket."

"And is this evil like to pass from us," resumed Ruth, breathing more freely, as she learned the safety of her son, "or does Providence veil its face in anger?"

"We keep our own, though the savage hath pressed the young men to extremity. Oh! it gladdened heart to see how brave a guard Rueben Ring and others near him made in our behalf. I do think me, Madam Heathcote, that after all there is real manhood in the brawler Dudley! Truly, the youth hath done marvels in the way of exposure and resistance. Twenty times this night have I expected to see him slain."

"And he that lieth there?" half-whispered the alarmed Ruth, pointing to a spot near them, where, aside from the movements of those who still acted in the bustle of the combat, one lay stretched on the earth—"who hath fallen?"

The cheek of Faith blanched to a whiteness that nearly equaled that of the linen, which, even in the hurry of such a scene, some friendly hand had found leisure to throw in decent sadness over the form.

"That!" said the faltering girl; "though hurt and bleeding, my brother Reuben surely keepeth the loop at the western angle; nor is Whittal wanting in sufficient sense to take heed of danger. This may not be the stranger, for under the covers of the postern-breastwork he holdeth counsel with the young captain."

"Art certain, girl?"

"I saw them both within the minute.

Would to God we could hear the shout of noisy Dudley, Madam Heathcote; his cry cheereth the heart, in a moment awful as this!"

"Lift the cloth," said Ruth, with calm solemnity, "that we may know which of our friends hath been called to the great account."

Faith hesitated; and when by a powerful effort, in which secret interest had as deep an influence as obedience, she did comply, it was with a sort of desperate resolution. On raising the linen, the eyes of the two women rested on the pallid countenance of one who had been transfixed by an iron-headed arrow. The girl dropped the linen, and in a voice that sounded like a burst of hysterical feeling, she exclaimed—

"'Tis but the youth that came lately among us! We are spared the loss of any ancient friend."

"'Tis one who died for our safety. I would give largely of this world's comforts, that this calamity might not have been, or that greater leisure for the last fearful reckoning had been accorded. But we may not lose the moments in mourning. Hie thee, girl, and sound the alarm that a savage lurketh within our walls, and that he skulketh in quest of a secret blow. Bid all be wary. If the young Mark should cross thy path, speak to him twice of this danger; the child hath a froward spirit, and may not hearken to words uttered in too great hurry."

With this charge Ruth quitted her maiden. While the latter proceeded to give the necessary notice, the other sought the spot where she had just learned there was reason to believe her husband might be found.

Content and the stranger were in fact met in consultation over the danger which threatened destruction to their most important means of defense. The savages themselves appeared to be conscious that the flames were working in their favor; for their efforts sensibly slackened, and having already severely suffered in their attempts to annoy the garrison, they had fallen back to their covers, and awaited the moment when their practiced cunning should tell them they might, with more flattering promises of success, again rally to the onset. A brief explanation served to make Ruth acquainted with the imminent jeopardy of their situation. Under a sense of a more appalling danger she lost the recollection of her former purpose, and with a contracted and sorrowing eye she stood like her companions, in impotent helplessness, an entranced spectator of the progress of the destruction.

"A soldier should not waste words in useless plaints," observed the stranger, folding his arms like one who was conscious that human effort could do no more, "else should I say, 'tis pity that he who drew yon line of stockade hath not remembered the uses of the ditch."

"I will summon the maidens to the wells," said Ruth.

"'Twill not avail us. The arrow would be among them, nor could mortal long endure the heat of yon glowing furnace. Thou seest that the timbers already smoke and blacken under its fierceness."

The stranger was still speaking, when a small quivering flame played on the corners of the palisado nearest the burning pile. The element fluttered like a waving line along the edges of the heated wood, after which it spread over the whole surface of the timber, from its larger base to the pointed summit. As if this had merely been the signal of a general destruction, the flames kindled in fifty places at the same instant, and then the whole line of the stockade, nearest the conflagration, was covered with fire. A yell of triumph arose in the fields, and a flight of arrows, sailing tauntingly into the works, announced the fierce impatience of those who watched the increase of the conflagration.

"We shall be driven to our block," said Content. "Assemble thy maidens, Ruth, and make speedy preparation for the last retreat."

"I go; but hazard not thy life in any vain endeavor to retard the flames. There will yet be time for all that is needful to our security."

"I know not," hurriedly observed the stranger. "Here cometh the assault in a new aspect!"

The feet of Ruth were arrested. On looking upwards she saw the object which had drawn this remark from the last speaker. A small bright ball of fire had arisen out of the fields, and, describing an arc in the air, it sailed above their heads and fell on the shingles of a building which formed part of the quadrangle of the inner court. The movement was that of an arrow thrown from a distant bow, and its way was to be traced by a long trail of light, that followed its course like a blazing meteor. This burning arrow had been sent with a cool and practiced judgment. It lighted upon a portion of the combustibles that were nearly as inflammable as gunpowder, and the eye had scarcely succeeded in tracing it to its fall, ere the bright flames were seen stealing over the heated roof.

"One struggle for our habitations!"

cried Content — but the hand of the stranger was placed firmly on his shoulder. At that instant, a dozen similar meteor-looking balls shot into the air, and fell in as many different places on the already half-kindled pile. Further efforts would have been useless. Relinquishing the hope of saving his property, every thought was now given to personal safety.

Ruth recovered from her short trance, and hastened with hurried steps to perform her well-known office. Then came a few minutes of exertion, during which the females transferred all that was necessary to their subsistence, and which had not been already provided in the block, to their little citadel. The glowing light, which penetrated the darkest passages among the buildings, prevented this movement from being made without discovery. The whoop summoned their enemies to another attack. The arrows thickened in the air, and the important duty was not performed without risk, as all were obliged, in some degree, to expose their persons, while passing to and fro loaded with necessaries. The gathering smoke, however, served in some measure for a screen; and it was not long before Content received the welcome tidings that he might command the retreat of his young men from the palisadoes. The conch sounded the necessary signal, and ere the foe had time to understand its meaning, or profit by the defenseless state of the works, every individual within them had reached the door of the block in safety. Still, there was more of hurry and confusion than altogether comported with their safety. They who were assigned to that duty, however, mounted eagerly to the loops, and stood in readiness to pour out their fire on whoever might dare to come within its reach, while a few still lingered in the court, to see that no necessary provision for resistance, or of safety, was forgotten. Ruth had been foremost in exertion, and she now stood pressing her hands to her temples, like one whose mind was bewildered by her own efforts.

"Our fallen friend!" she said. "Shall we leave his remains to be mangled by the savages?"

"Surely not; Dudley, thy hand. We will bear the body within the lower—ha! death hath struck another of our family."

The alarm with which Content made this discovery passed quickly to all in hearing. It was but too apparent, by the shape of the linen, that two bodies lay beneath its folds. Anxious and rapid looks were cast from face to face in order to learn who was missing; and then, conscious of the hazard of further delay, Content raised the linen in order to remove all doubts by certainty. The form of the young borderer, who was known to have fallen, was first slowly and reverently uncovered: but even the most self-restrained among the spectators started back in horror as his robbed and reeking head showed that a savage hand had worked its ruthless will on the unresisting corpse.

"The other!" Ruth struggled to say, and it was only as her husband had half-removed the linen that she could succeed in uttering the words—"Beware the other!"

The warning was not useless, for the linen waved violently as it rose under the hand of Content, and a grim Indian sprang into the very center of the startled group. Sweeping his armed hand widely about him, the savage broke through the receding circle, and giving forth the appalling whoop of his tribe, he bounded into the open door of the principal dwelling, so swiftly as utterly to defeat any design of pursuit. The arms of Ruth were frantically extended towards the place where he had disappeared, and she was about to rush madly on his footsteps, when the hand of her husband stopped the movement.

"Wouldst hazard life, to save some worthless trifle?"

"Husband, release me!" returned the woman, nearly choked with her agony—"nature hath slept within me."

"Fear blindeth thy reason!"

The form of Ruth ceased to struggle. All the madness which had been glaring wildly about her eyes, disappeared in the settled look of an almost preternatural calm. Collecting the whole of her mental energy in one desperate effort of self-command, she turned to her husband, and, as her bosom swelled with the terror that seemed to stop her breath, she said in a voice that was frightful by its composure—

"If thou hast a father's heart, release me. Our babes have been forgotten!"

The hand of Content relaxed its hold, and, in another instant, the form of his wife was lost to view on the track that had just been taken by the successful savage. This was the luckless moment chosen by the foe to push his advantage. A fierce burst of yells proclaimed the activity of the assailants, and a general discharge from the loops of the block-house sufficiently apprised those in the court that the onset of the enemy was now pushed into the very heart of the defenses. All had mounted, but the few who lingered to discharge the melancholy duty to the dead. They were too few to render resistance prudent, and yet too many to think of deserting the distracted mother and her offspring without an effort.

"Enter," said Content, pointing to the door of the block. "It is my duty to share the fate of those nearest my blood."

The stranger made no answer. Placing his powerful hands on the nearly stupefied husband, he thrust his person, by an irresistible effort, within the basement of the building, and then he signed, by a quick gesture, for all around him to follow. After the last form had entered, he commanded that the fastenings of the door should be secured, remaining himself, as he believed, alone without. But when by a rapid glance he saw there was another gazing in dull awe on the features of the fallen man, it was too late to rectify the mistake. Yells were now rising out of the black smoke that was rolling in volumes from the heated buildings, and it was plain that only a few feet divided them from their pursuers. Beckoning the man who had been excluded from the block to follow, the stern soldier rushed into the principal dwelling, which was still but little injured by the fire. Guided rather by chance than by any knowledge of the windings of the building, he soon found himself in the chambers. He was now at a loss whither to proceed. At that moment, his companion, who was no other than Whittal Ring, took the lead, and in another instant they were at the door of the secret apartment.

"Hist!" said the stranger, raising a hand to command silence as he entered the room. "Our hope is in secrecy."

"And how may we escape without detection?" demanded the mother, pointing about her at objects illuminated by a light so powerful as to penetrate every cranny of the ill-constructed building. "The noonday sun is scarce brighter than this dreadful fire!"

"God is in the elements! His guiding hand shall point the way. But here we may not tarry, for the flames are already on the shingles. Follow, and speak not!"

Ruth pressed the children to her side, and the whole party left the apartment of the attic in a body. Their descent to a lower room was made quickly, and without discovery. But here their leader paused, for the state of things without was one to demand the utmost steadiness of nerve, and great reflection.

The Indians had by this time gained command of the whole of Mark Heathcote's possessions, with the exception of the block-house; and as their first act had been to apply the brand wherever it might be wanting, the roar of the conflagration was now heard in every direction.

The discharge of muskets and the whoops of the combatants, however, while they added to the horrible din of such a scene, proclaimed the unconquered resolution of those who held the citadel. A window of the room they occupied enabled the stranger to take a cautious survey of what was passing without. The court, lighted to the brilliancy of day, was empty; for the increasing heat of the fires, no less than the discharges from the loops, still kept the cautious savages to their covers. There was barely hope that the space between the dwelling and the block-house might yet be passed in safety.

"I would I had asked that the door of the block should be held in hand," muttered Submission; "it would be death to linger an instant in that fierce light; nor have we any manner of—"

A touch was laid upon his arm, and turning, the speaker saw the dark eye of the captive boy looking steadily in his face.

"Wilt do it?" demanded the other, in a manner to show that he doubted, while he hoped.

A speaking gesture of assent was the answer, and then the form of the lad was seen gliding quietly from the room.

Another instant, and Miantonimoh appeared in the court. He walked with the deliberation that one would have shown in moments of the most entire security. A hand was raised toward the loops, as if to betoken amity, and then dropping the limb, he moved with the same slow step into the very center of the area. Here the boy stood in the fullest glare of the conflagration, and turned his face deliberately on every side of him. The action showed that he wished to invite all eyes to examine his person. At this moment the yells ceased in the surrounding covers, proclaiming alike the common feeling that was awakened by his appearance, and the hazard that any other would have incurred by exposing himself in that fearful scene. When this act of exceeding confidence had been performed, the boy drew a pace nearer to the entrance of the block.

"Comest thou in peace, or is this another device of Indian treachery?" demanded a voice, through an opening in the door left expressly for the purpose of parley.

The boy raised the palm of one hand toward the speaker, while he laid the other with a gesture of confidence on his naked breast.

"Hast aught to offer in behalf of my wife and babes? If gold will buy their ransom, name thy price."

Miantonimoh was at no loss to comprehend the other's meaning. With the readiness of one whose faculties had been early schooled in the inventions of emergencies, he made a gesture that said even more than his figurative words, as he answered—

"Can a woman of the pale-faces pass through wood? An Indian arrow is swifter than the foot of my mother."

"Boy, I trust thee," returned the voice from within the loop. "If thou deceivest beings so feeble and so innocent, Heaven will remember the wrong."

Miantonimoh again made a sign to show that caution must be used, and then he retired with a step calm and measured as that used in his advance. Another pause to the shouts betrayed the interest of those whose fierce eyes watched his movements in the distance.

When the young Indian had rejoined the party in the dwelling, he led them, without being observed by the lurking band that still hovered in the smoke of the surrounding buildings, to a spot that commanded a full view of their short but perilous route. At this moment the door of the block-house half opened, and was closed again. Still the stranger hesitated, for he saw how little was the chance that all should cross the court unharmed, and to pass it by repeated trials he knew to be impossible.

"Boy," he said, "thou, who hast done thus much may still do more. Ask mercy for these children, in some manner that may touch the hearts of thy people."

Miantonimoh shook his head, and pointing to the ghastly corpse that lay in the court, he answered coldly—

"The red man has tasted blood."

"Then must the desperate trial be done! Think not of thy children, devoted and daring mother, but look only to thine own safety. This witless youth and I will charge ourselves with the care of the innocents."

Ruth waved him away with her hand, pressing her mute and trembling daughter to her bosom, in a manner to show that her resolution was taken. The stranger yielded, and turning to Whittal, who stood near him, seemingly as much occupied in vacant admiration of the blazing piles as in any apprehension of his own personal danger, he bade him look to the safety of the remaining child. Moving in front himself, he was about to offer Ruth such protection as the case afforded, when a window in the rear of the house was dashed inwards, announcing the entrance of the enemy, and the imminent danger that their flight would be intercepted. There

was no time to lose, for it was now certain that only a single room separated them from their foes. The generous nature of Ruth was aroused, and catching Martha from the arms of Whittal Ring, she endeavored by a desperate effort, in which feeling rather than any reasonable motive predominated, to envelop both the children in her robe.

"I am with ye!" whispered the agitated woman: "hush ye, hush ye, babes! thy mother is nigh!"

The stranger was very differently employed. The instant the crash of glass was heard, he rushed to the rear; and he had already grappled with the savage so often named, and who acted as guide to a dozen fierce and yelling followers.

"To the block!" shouted the steady soldier, while with a powerful arm he held his enemy in the throat of the narrow passage, stopping the approach of those in the rear by the body of his foe. "For the love of life and children, woman, to the block!"

The summons rang frightfully in the ears of Ruth, but in that moment of extreme jeopardy her presence of mind was lost. The cry was repeated, and not till then did the bewildered mother catch her daughter from the floor. With eyes still bent on the fierce struggle in her rear, she clasped the child to her heart and fled, calling on Whittal Ring to follow. The lad obeyed, and ere she had half crossed the court the stranger, still holding his savage shield between him and his enemies, was seen endeavoring to take the same direction. The whoops, the flight of arrows, and the discharges of musketry that succeeded, proclaimed the whole extent of the danger. But fear had lent unnatural vigor to the limbs of Ruth, and the gliding arrows themselves scarce sailed more swiftly through the heated air than she darted into the open door of the block. Whittal Ring was less successful. As he crossed the court, bearing the child intrusted to his care, an arrow pierced his flesh. Stung by the pain, the witless lad turned in anger to chide the hand that had inflcted the injury.

"On, foolish boy!" cried the stranger, as he passed him, still making a target of the body of the savage that was writhing in his grasp. "On, for thy life, and that of the babe!"

The mandate came too late. The hand of an Indian was already on the innocent victim, and in the next instant the child was sweeping the air, while with a short yell the keen axe flourished above his head. A shot from the loops laid the monster dead in his tracks. The girl was instantly seized by another hand, and as the captor with his prize darted unharmed into the dwelling, there arose in the block a common exclamation of the name of "Miantonimoh!" Two more of the savages profited by the pause of horror that followed, to lay hands on the wounded Whittal and to drag him within the blazing building. At the same moment, the stranger cast the unresisting savage back upon the weapons of his companions. The bleeding and half-strangled Indian met the blows which had been aimed at the life of the soldier, and as he staggered and fell his vigorous conqueror disappeared in the block. The door of the little citadel was instantly closed, and the savages, who rushed headlong against the entrance, heard the fitting of the bars which secured it against their attacks. The yell of retreat was raised, and in the next instant the court was left to the possession of the dead.

CHAPTER XV.

"Did Heaven look on,
And would not take their part?—
        Heaven rest them now?"—MACBETH.

"We will be thankful for this blessing," said Content, as he aided the half-unconscious Ruth to mount the ladder, yielding himself to a feeling of nature that said little against his manhood. "If we have lost one that we loved, God hath spared our own child!"

His breathless wife threw herself into a seat, and folding the treasure to her bosom, she whispered rather than said aloud—"From my soul, Heathcote, am I grateful!"

"Thou shieldest the babe from my sight," returned the father, stooping to conceal a tear that was stealing down his brown cheek, under the pretense of embracing the child—but suddenly recoiling, he added in alarm—"Ruth!"

Startled by the tone in which her husband uttered her name, the mother threw aside the folds of her dress which still concealed the girl, and stretching her out to the length of an arm, she saw that, in the hurry of the appalling scene, the children had been exchanged, and that she had saved the life of Martha!

Notwithstanding the generous disposition of Ruth, it was impossible to repress the feeling of disappointment which came over her with the consciousness of the mistake. Nature at first had sway, and to a degree that was fearfully powerful.

"It is not our babe!" shrieked the mother, still holding the child at the length of her arm, and gazing at its innocent and terrified countenance, with an expression that Martha had never yet seen gleaming from eyes that were in common so soft and so indulgent.

"I am thine! I am thine!" murmured the little trembler, struggling in vain to reach the bosom that had so long cherished her infancy. "If not thine, whose am I?"

The gaze of Ruth was still wild—the workings of her features hysterical.

"Madam—Mrs. Heathcote—mother!" came timidly and at intervals, from the lips of the orphan. Then the heart of Ruth relented. She clasped the daughter of her friend to her breast, and nature found a temporary relief in one of those frightful exhibitions of anguish which appear to threaten the dissolution of the link which connects the soul with the body.

"Come, daughter of John Harding," said Content, looking around him with the assumed composure of a chastened man, while natural regret struggled hard at his heart; "this has been God's pleasure. It is meet that we kiss his parental hand. Let us be thankful," he added, with a quivering lip but steady eye, "that even this mercy hath been shown. Our babe is with the Indian, but our hopes are far beyond the reach of savage malignity. We have not 'laid up treasure where moth and rust can corrupt, or where thieves may break in and steal.' It may be that the morning shall bring means of parley, and haply, opportunity of ransom."

There was the glimmering of hope in this suggestion. The idea seemed to give a new direction to the thoughts of Ruth, and the change enabled the long habits of self-restraint to regain something of their former ascendency. The fountains of her tears became dry, and after one short and terrible struggle, she was again enabled to appear composed. But at no time during the continuance of that fearful struggle was Ruth Heathcote again the same ready and useful agent of activity and order that she had been in the earlier events of the night.

It is scarcely necessary to remind the reader that the brief burst of parental agony which has just been related, escaped Content and his wife amid a scene in which the other actors were too much occupied by their exertions to note its exhibition. The fate of those in the block was too evidently approaching its close, to allow of any interest in such an episode to the great tragedy of the moment.

The character of the contest had in some

measure changed. There was no longer any immediate apprehension from the missiles of the assailants, though danger pressed upon the besieged in a new and even in a more horrible aspect. Now and then indeed an arrow quivered in the openings of the loops, and the blunt Dudley had once a narrow escape from the passage of a bullet, which, guided by chance, or aimed by a hand surer than common, glanced through one of the narrow slits, and would have terminated the history of the borderer, had not the head it obliquely encountered been too solid to yield even to such an assault. The attention of the garrison was chiefly called to the imminent danger of the surrounding fire. Though the probability of such an emergency as that in which the family was now placed, had certainly been foreseen, and in some degree guarded against, in the size of the area and in the construction of the block, yet it was found that the danger exceeded all former calculations.

For the basement, there was no reason to feel alarm. It was of stone, and of a thickness and a material to put at defiance any artifice that their enemy might find time to practice. Even the two upper stories were comparatively safe ; for they were composed of blocks so solid as to require time to heat them, and they were consequently as little liable to combustion as wood well could be. But the roof, like all of that, and indeed like most of the present day in America, was composed of short inflammable shingles of pine. The superior height of the tower was some little protection ; but as the flames rose roaring above the buildings of the court, and waved in wide circuits around the heated area, the whole of the fragile covering of the block was often wrapped in folds of fire. The result may be anticipated. Content was first recalled from the bitterness of his parental regret, by a cry which passed among the family, that the roof of their little citadel was in flames. One of the ordinary wells of the habitation was in the basement of the edifice, and it was fortunate that no precaution necessary to render it serviceable in an emergency like that which was now arrived, had been neglected.

A well-secured shaft of stone rose through the lower apartment into the upper floor. Profiting by this happy precaution, the handmaidens of Ruth plied the buckets with diligence, while the young men cast water freely on the roof, from the windows of the attic. The latter duty it may readily be supposed was not performed without hazard. Flights of arrows were constantly directed against the laborers, and more than one of the youths received greater or less injuries while exposed to their annoyance. There were indeed a few minutes during which it remained a question of grave interest how far the risk they ran was likely to be crowned with success. The excessive heat of so many fires, and the occasional contact with the flames, as they swept in eddies over the place, began to render it doubtful whether any human efforts could long arrest the evil. Even the massive and moistened logs of the body of the work began to smoke, and it was found by experiment, that the hand could rest but a moment on their surface.

During this interval of deep suspense, all the men posted at the loops were called to aid in extinguishing the fire. Resistance was forgotten in the discharge of a duty that had become still more pressing. Ruth herself was aroused by the nature of the alarm, and all hands and all minds were arduously occupied in a toil that diverted attention from incidents which had less interest, because they were teeming less with instant destruction. Danger is known to lose its terrors by familiarity. The young borderers became reckless of their persons in the ardor of exertion, and as success began to crown their efforts, something like the levity of happier moments got the better of their concern. Stolen and curious glances were thrown around a place that had so long been kept sacred to the secret uses of the Puritan, when it was found that the flames were subdued, and that the present danger was averted. The light glared powerfully though several openings in the shingles no less than through the windows, and every eye was enabled to scan the contents of an apartment which all had longed, though none had ever before presumed to enter.

"The captain looketh well to the body," whispered Reuben Ring to one of his comrades, as he wiped the effects of the toil from a sunburnt brow. "Thou seest, Hiram, that there is good store of cheer."

"The buttery is not better stored !" returned the other, with the shrewdness and ready observation of a borderman. "It is known that he never toucheth that which the cow yields, except as it comes from the creature, and here we find of the best that the madam's dairy can yield !"

"Surely you buff jerkin is like to those worn by the idle cavaliers at home ! I think it be long since the captain hath ridden forth in such a guise."

"That may be matter of ancient usage, for thou seest he hath relics of the fashion of the English troopers in this bit of steel ;

it is like he holdeth deep exercise over the vanities of his youth, while recalling the times in which they were worn."

This conjecture appeared to satisfy the other, though it is probable that a sight of a fresh store of bodily aliment, which was soon after exposed, in order to gain access to the roof, might have led to some further inferences, had more time been given to conjectures. But at this moment a new wail proceeded from the maidens who plied the buckets beneath.

"To the loops! to the loops, or we are lost!" was a summons that admitted of no delay. Led by the stranger, the young men rushed below, where, in truth, they found a serious demand on all their activity and courage.

The Indians were wanting in none of the sagacity which so remarkably distinguishes the warfare of this cunning race. The time spent by the family in arresting the flames had not been thrown away by the assailants. Profiting by the attention of those within, to efforts that were literally of the last importance, they had found means to convey burning brands to the door of the block, against which they had piled a mass of blazing combustibles, that threatened shortly to open the way into the basement of the citadel itself. In order to mask this design, and to protect their approaches, the savages had succeeded in dragging bundles of straw and other similar materials to the foot of the work, to which the fire soon communicated, and which consequently served both to increase the actual danger of the building and to distract the attention of those by whom it was defended.

Although the water that fell from the roof served to retard the progress of these flames, it contributed to produce the effect of all others that was most desired by the savages. The dense volumes of smoke that arose from the half-smothered fire first apprised the females of the new danger which assailed them. When Content and the stranger reached the principal floor of their citadel, it required some little time and no small degree of coolness to comprehend the situation in which they were now placed. The vapor that rolled upward from the wet straw and hay had already penetrated into the apartment, and it was with no slight difficulty that they who occupied it were enabled to distinguish objects, or even to breathe.

"Here is matter to exercise our utmost fortitude," said the stranger to his constant companion. "We must look to this new device, or we come to the fate of death by fire. Summon the stoutest-hearted of thy youths, and I will lead them to a sortie, ere the evil get past a remedy."

"That were certain victory to the heathen. Thou hearest, by their yells, that 'tis no small band of scouters who beleaguer us; a tribe hath sent forth its chosen warriors to do their wickedness. Better is it that we bestir ourselves to drive them from our door, and to prevent the further annoyance of this cloud, since, to issue from the block, at this moment, would be to offer our heads to the tomahawk; and to ask mercy is as vain as to hope to move the rock with tears.''

"And in what manner may we do this needful service?"

"Our muskets will still command the entrance, by means of these downward loops, and water may be yet applied through the same openings. Thought hath been had of this danger, in the disposition of the place."

"Then, of Heaven's mercy! delay not the effort."

The necessary measures were taken instantly. Eben Dudley applied the muzzle of his piece to a loop, and discharged it downwards, in the direction of the endangered door. But aim was impossible in the obscurity, and his want of success was proclaimed by a taunting shout of triumph. Then followed a flood of water, which, however, was scarcely of more service, since the savages had foreseen its use, and had made a provision against its effects by placing boards and such vessels as they found scattered among the buildings, above the fire, in a manner to prevent most of the fluid from reaching its aim.

"Come hither with thy musket, Reuben Ring," said Content, hurriedly; "the wind stirreth the smoke here; the savages will heap fuel against the wall."

The borderer complied. There were in fact moments when dark human forms were to be seen gliding in silence around the building, though the density of the vapor rendered the forms indistinct, and their movements doubtful. With a cool and practiced eye the youth sought a victim; but as he discharged his musket an object glanced near his own visage, as though the bullet had recoiled on him who had given it a very different mission. Stepping backwards a little hurriedly, he saw the stranger pointing through the smoke at an arrow, which still quivered in the floor above them.

"We cannot long abide these assaults," the soldier muttered; "something must be speedily devised, or we fall."

His words ceased, for a yell that appeared to lift the floor on which he stood, announced the destruction of the door and the presence of the savages in the basement of the tower. Both parties appeared momentarily confounded at this unexpected success; for while the one stood mute with astonishment and dread, the other did little more than triumph. But this inaction soon ended. The conflict was resumed, though the efforts of the assailants began to assume the confidence of victory, while on the part of the besieged they partook fearfully of the aspect of despair.

A few muskets were discharged, both from below and above, at the intermediate floor, but the thickness of the planks prevented the bullets from doing injury. Then commenced a struggle, in which the respective qualities of the combatants were exhibited in a singularly characteristic manner. While the Indians improved their advantages beneath, with all the arts known to savage warfare, the young men resisted with that wonderful aptitude of expedient and readiness of execution which distinguish the American borderer.

The first attempt of the assailants was to burn the floor of the lower apartment. In order to effect this, they threw vast piles of straw into the basement. But ere the brand was applied, water had reduced the inflammable material to a black and murky pile. Still the smoke had nearly effected a conquest which the fire itself had failed to achieve. So suffocating indeed were the clouds of vapor which ascended through the crevices, that the females were compelled to seek a refuge in the attic. Here the openings in the roof, and a swift current of air, relieved them in some degree from its annoyance.

When it was found that the command of the well afforded the besieged the means of protecting the wood-work of the interior, an effort was made to cut off the communication with the water, by forcing a passage into the circular stone shaft, through which it was drawn into the room above. This attempt was defeated by the readiness of the youths, who soon cut holes in the floor, whence they sent down certain death on all beneath. Perhaps no part of the assault was more obstinate than that which accompanied this effort; nor did either assailant or assailed, at any time during its continuance, suffer greater personal injury. After a long and fierce struggle, the resistance was effectual, and the savages had recourse to new schemes in order to effect their ruthless object.

During the first moments of their entrance, and with a view to reap the fruits of the victory when the garrison should be more effectually subdued, most of the furniture of the dwelling had been scattered by the conquerors on the side of the hill. Among other articles, some six or seven beds had been dragged from the dormitories. These were now brought into play as powerful instruments in the assault. They were cast, one by one, on the still burning though smothered flames in the basement of the block, whence they sent up a cloud of their intolerable effluvia. At this trying moment the appalling cry was heard in the block that the well had failed! The buckets ascended as empty as they went down, and they were thrown aside as no longer useful. The savages seemed to comprehend their advanatge, for they profited by the confusion that succeeded among the assailed to feed the slumbering fires. The flames kindled fiercely, and in less than a minute they became too violent to be subdued. They were soon seen playing on the planks of the floor above. The subtle element flashed from point to point, and it was not long ere it was stealing up the outer side of the heated block itself.

The savages now knew that conquest was sure. Yells and whoopings proclaimed the fierce delight with which they witnessed the certainty of their victory. Still there was something portentous in the death-like silence with which the victims within the block awaited their fate. The whole exterior of the building was already wrapped in flames, and yet no show of further resistance, no petition for mercy, issued from its bosom. The unnatural and frightful stillness that reigned within was gradually communicated to those without. The cries and shouts of triumph ceased, and the crackling of the flames, or the falling of timber in the adjoining buildings, alone disturbed the awful calm. At length a solitary voice was heard in the block. Its tones were deep, solemn, and imploring. The fierce beings who surrounded the glowing pile bent forward to listen, for their quick faculties caught the first sounds that were audible. It was Mark Heathcote pouring out his spirit in prayer.

The petition was fervent, but steady, and though uttered in words that were unintelligible to those without, they knew enough of the practices of the colonists to be aware that it was the chief of the pale-faces holding communion with his God. Partly in awe, and partly in doubt of what might be the consequences of so mysterious an asking, the dark crowd withdrew to a little distance, and silently watched the progress of the destruction. They had heard strange sayings of the power of the

"To the block!" shouted the steady soldier, while with a powerful arm he held his enemy in the throat of the narrow passage, stopping the approach of those in the rear by the body of his foe. "For the love of life and children, woman, to the block!"—*The Wept of Wish-Ton-Wish.*

Deity of the invaders, and as their victims appeared suddenly to cease using any of the known means of safety, they appeared to expect, perhaps they did expect, some unequivocal manifestation of the power of the Great Spirit of the stranger.

Still no sign of pity, no relenting from the ruthless barbarity of the warfare, escaped any of the assailants. If they thought at all of the temporal fate of those who might still exist within the fiery pile, it was only to indulge in some passing regret that the obstinacy of the defense had deprived them of the glory of bearing the usual bloody tokens of victory in triumph to their villages. But even these peculiar and deeply-rooted feelings were forgotten, as the progress of the flames placed the hope of its indulgence beyond all possibility.

The roof of the block rekindled, and, by the light that shone through the loops, it was but too evident the interior was in a blaze. Once or twice smothered sounds came out of the place as if suppressed shrieks were escaping the females; but they ceased so suddenly as to leave doubts among the auditors whether it were more than the deception of their own excited fancies.

The savages had witnessed many a similar scene of human suffering, but never one before in which death was met with so unmoved a calmness. The serenity that reigned in the blazing block communicated to them a feeling of awe; and when the pile came a tumbling and blackened mass of ruins to the earth, they avoided the place like men that dreaded the vengeance of a Deity who knew how to infuse so deep a sentiment of resignation into the breasts of his worshipers.

Though the yells of victory were again heard in the valley that night, and though the sun had arisen before the conquerors had deserted the hill, but few of the band found resolution to approach the smoldering pile where they had witnessed so impressive an exhibition of Christian fortitude. The few that did draw near stood around the spot rather in the reverence with which an Indian visits the graves of the just, than in the fierce rejoicings with which he is known to glut his revenge over a fallen enemy.

CHAPTER XVI.

" What are these,
So withered, and so wild in their attire;
That look not like the inhabitants of earth,
And yet are on't ? "—MACBETH.

THAT sternness of the season, which has already been mentioned in these pages, is never of long continuance in the month of April. A change in the wind had been noted by the hunters even before they retired from the range among the hills : and though too seriously occupied to pay close attention to the progress of the thaw, more than one of the young men had found occasion to remark that the final breaking up of the winter had arrived. Long ere the scene of the preceding chapter reached its height, the southern winds had mingled with the heat of the conflagration. Warm airs, that had been following the course of the Gulf Stream, were driven to the land, and, sweeping over the narrow island that at this point forms the advanced work of the continent, but a few short hours had passed before they destroyed every chilling remnant of the dominion of winter. Warm, bland, and rushing in torrents, the subtle currents penetrated the forests. melted the snows from the fields, and as all alike felt the genial influence, it appeared to bestow a renovated existence on man and beast. With morning, therefore, a landscape very different from that last placed before the mind of the reader, presented itself in the valley of the Wish-Ton-Wish.

The winter had entirely disappeared, and as the buds had begun to swell under the occasional warmth of the spring, one ignorant of the past would not have supposed that the advance of the season had been subject to so stern an interruption. But the principal and most melancholy change was in the more artificial parts of the view. Instead of those simple and happy habitations which had crowned the little eminence, there remained only a mass of blackened, and charred ruins. A few abused and half-destroyed articles of household furniture lay scattered on the sides of the hill, and here and there a dozen palisadoes, favored by some accidental cause, had partially escaped the flames. Eight or ten massive and drearylooking stacks of chimneys rose out of the smoking piles. In the center of the desolation was the stone basement of the block-house, on which still stood a few gloomy masses of the timber resembling coal. The naked and unsupported shaft of the well reared its circular pillar from the center, looking like a dark monument of the past.

The wide ruin of the outbuildings blackened one side of the clearing, and, in different places, the fences, like radii diverging from the common center of destruction, had led off the flames into the fields. A few domestic animals ruminated in the background, and even the feathered inhabitants of the barns still kept aloof, as if warned by their instinct that danger lurked around the site of their ancient abodes. In all other respects the view was calm and lovely as ever. The sun shone from a sky in which no cloud was visible. The blandness of the winds, and the brightness of the heavens, lent an air of animation to even the leafless forest ; and the white vapor, that continued to rise from the smoldering piles, floated high over the hills, as the peaceful smoke of the cottage curled above its roof.

The ruthless band which had occasioned this sudden change was already far on the way to its villages, or haply it sought some other scene of blood. A skillful eye might have traced the route these fierce creatures of the woods had taken, by fences hurled from their places, or by the carcass of some animal that had fallen, in the wantonness of victory, beneath a parting blow. Of all these wild beings, one only remained ; and he appeared to linger at the spot in the indulgence of feelings that were foreign to those passions that had so recently stirred the bosoms of his comrades.

It was with a slow, noiseless step, that the solitary loiterer moved about the scene of destruction. He was first seen treading with a thoughtful air, among the ruins of the buildings that had formed the quadrangle, and then, seemingly led by an interest in the fate of those who had so miserably perished, he drew nearer to the pile in its center. The nicest and most attentive ear could not have detected the fall of his foot, as the Indian placed it within the gloomy circle of the ruined wall ; nor is the breathing of the infant less audible than the manner in which he drew breath, while standing in a place so lately consecrated by the agony and martyrdom of a Christian family. It was the boy called Miantonimoh, seeking some melancholy memorial of those with whom he had so long dwelt in amity, if not in confidence.

One skilled in the history of savage passions might have found a clew to the workings of the mind of the youth, in the play of his speaking features. As his dark glittering eye rolled over the smoldering fragments, it seemed to search keenly for some vestige of the human form. The element, however, had done its work too greedily, to have left many visible memorials of its fury. An object resembling that he sought, however, caught his glance, and stepping lightly to the spot where it lay, he raised the bone of a powerful arm from the brands. The

flashing of his eye, as it lighted on this sad object, was wild and exulting, like that of the savage when he first feels the fierce joy of glutted vengeance ; but gentler recollections came with the gaze, and tender feelings evidently usurped the place of the hatred he had been taught to bear a race who were so fast sweeping his people from the earth. The relic fell from his hand, and had Ruth been there to witness the melancholy and relenting shade that clouded his swarthy features, she might have found pleasure in the certainty that all her kindness had not been wasted.

Regret soon gave place to awe. To the imagination of the Indian, it seemed as if a still voice, like that which is believed to issue from the grave, was heard in the place. Bending his body forward, he listened with the intensity and acuteness of a savage. He thought the smothered tones of Mark Heathcote were again audible, holding communion with his God. The chisel of the Grecian would have loved to delineate the attitudes and movements of the wondering boy, as he slowly and reverently withdrew from the spot. His look was riveted on the vacancy where the upper apartments of the block had stood, and where he had last seen the family calling in their extremity on their Deity for aid. Imagination still painted the victims in their burning pile. For a minute longer, during which brief space the young Indian probably expected to see some vision of the pale-faces, did he linger near ; and then, with a musing air and softened mind, he trod lightly along the path which led on the trail of his people. When his active form reached the boundary of the forest, he again paused, and taking a final gaze at the place where fortune had made him a witness to so much domestic peace and to so much sudden misery, his form was quickly swallowed in the gloom of his native woods.

The work of the savages now seemed complete. An effectual check appeared to be placed to the further progress of civilization in the ill-fated valley of the Wish-Ton-Wish. Had nature been left to its own work, a few years would have covered the deserted clearing with its ancient vegetation ; and half a century would have again buried the whole of its quiet glades in the shadows of the forest. But it was otherwise decreed.

The sun had reached the meridian, and the hostile band had been gone some hours, before aught occurred likely to affect this seeming decision of Providence. To one acquainted with the recent horrors, the breathing of the airs over the ruins might have passed for the whisperings of departed spirits. In short, it appeared as if the silence of the wilderness had once more resumed its reign, when it was suddenly though slightly interrupted. A movement was made within the ruins of the block. It sounded as if billets of wood were gradually and cautiously displaced, and then a human head was reared slowly, and with marked suspicion, above the shaft of the well. The wild and unearthly air of this seeming specter was in keeping with the rest of the scene. A face begrimed with smoke and stained with blood, a head bound in some fragment of a soiled dress, and eyes that were glaring in a species of dull horror, were objects in unison with all the other frightful accessories of the place.

"What seest thou?" demanded a deep voice from within the walls of the shaft. "Shall we again come to our weapons, or have the agents of Moloch departed? Speak, entranced youth! what dost behold?"

"A sight to make a wolf weep!" returned Eben Dudley, raising his large frame so as to stand erect on the shaft, where he commanded a bird's-eye view of most of the desolation of the valley. "Evil though it may be, we may not say that forewarning signs have been withheld. But what is the cunningest man, when mortal wisdom is weighed in the scale against the craft of devils? Come forth! Belial hath done his worst, and we have a breathing-time."

The sounds which issued still deeper from the well denoted the satisfaction with which this intelligence was received, no less than the alacrity with which the summons of the borderer was obeyed. Sundry blocks of wood and short pieces of plank were first passed with care up to the hands of Dudley, who cast them like useless lumber among the other ruins of the building. He then descended from his perch, and made room for others to follow.

The stranger next arose. After him came Content, the Puritan, Reuben Ring, and, in short, all the youths, with the exception of those who had unhappily fallen in the contest. After these had mounted, and each in turn had leaped to the ground, a very brief preparation served for the liberation of the more feeble of the body. The readiness of border skill soon sufficed to arrange the necessary means. By the aid of chains and buckets, Ruth and the little Martha, Faith and all the handmaidens, without even one exception, were successfully drawn from the bowels of the earth, and restored to the light of day.

It is scarcely necessary to say to those whom experience has best fitted to judge of such an achievement, that no great time or labor was necessary for its accomplishment.

It is not our intention to harass the feelings of the reader further than is required by a simple narrative of the incidents of the legend. We shall therefore say nothing of the bodily pain, or of the mental alarm, by which this ingenious retreat from the flames and the tomahawk had been effected. The suffering was chiefly confined to apprehension; for as the descent was easy, so had the readiness and ingenuity of the young men found means, by the aid of articles of furniture first cast into the shaft, and by well-secured fragments of the floors properly placed across, both to render the situation of the females and children less painful than might at first be supposed, and effectually to protect them from the tumbling block. But little of the latter, however, was likely to affect their safety, as the form of the building was, in itself, a sufficient security against the fall of its heavier parts.

The meeting of the family amid the desolation of the valley, though relieved by the consciousness of having escaped a more shocking fate, may easily be imagined. The first act was to render brief but solemn thanks for their deliverance, and, then, with the promptitude of people trained in hardship, their attention was given to those measures which prudence told them were yet necessary.

A few of the more active and experienced of the youths were dispatched in order to ascertain the direction taken by the Indians, and to gain what intelligence they might concerning their future movements. The maidens hastened to collect the kine, while others searched with heavy hearts among the ruins, in quest of such articles of food and comfort as could be found, in order to administer to the first wants of nature.

Two hours had effected most of that which could immediately be done in these several pursuits. The young men returned with the assurance that the trails announced the certain and final retreat of the savages. The cows had yielded their tribute, and such provision had been made against hunger as circumstances would allow. The arms had been examined and put, as far as the injuries they had received would admit, in readiness for instant service. A few hasty preparations had been made in order to protect the females against the cold airs of the coming night; and, in short, all was done that the intelligence of a borderman could suggest, or his exceeding readiness in expedients could in so brief a space supply.

The sun began to fall toward the tops of the beeches that crowned the western outline of the view before all these necessary arrangements were ended. It was not till then, however, that Reuben Ring, accompanied by another youth of equal activity and courage, appeared before the Puritan, equipped as well as men in their situation might be for a journey through the forest.

"Go," said the old religionist, when the youths presented themselves before him— "Go; carry forth the tidings of this visitation, that men come to our succor. I ask not vengeance on the deluded and heathenish imitators of the worshipers of Moloch. They have ignorantly done this evil. Let no man arm in behalf of the wrongs of one sinful and erring. Rather let them look into the secret abominations of their own hearts, in order that they crush the living worm, which, by gnawing on the seeds of a healthful hope, may yet destroy the fruits of the promise in their own souls. I would that there be profit in this example of divine displeasure. Go— make the circuit of the settlements for some fifty miles, and bid such of the neighbors as may be spared, come to our aid. They shall be welcome; and may it be long ere any of them send invitation to me or mine to enter their clearings on the like melancholy duty. Depart, and bear in mind that you are messengers of peace; that your errand toucheth not the feelings of vengeance, but that it is succor in all fitting reason, and no arming of the hand to chase the savage to his retreats, that I ask of the brethren."

With this final admonition, the young men took their leaves. Still it was evident by their frowning brows, and compressed lips, that some part of its forgiving principle might be forgotten, should chance in their journey bring them on the trail of any wandering inhabitant of the forest. In a few minutes they were seen passing with swift steps from the fields into the depths of the forest, along that path which led to the towns that lay lower on the Connecticut.

Another task still remained to be performed. In making the temporary arrangements for the shelter of the family, attention had been first paid to the blockhouse. The walls of the basement of this building were still standing and it was found easy by means of half-burnt timbers, with an occasional board that had escaped the conflagration, to cover it in a manner that offered a temporary protection against the weather. This simple and hasty construction, with an extremely inartificial office erected around the stack of a chimney, embraced nearly all that could be done until time and assistance should enable them to commence other dwellings. In clearing the ruins of the little tower of its rubbish, the remains of those who had perished in the fray were piously collected. The body of the youth who had died in the earlier hours of the attack, was found but half consumed in the court, and the bones of two more who fell within the block, were collected from among the ruins. It had now become a melancholy duty to consign them all to the earth with decent solemnity.

The time selected for this sad office was just as the western horizon began to glow with that which one of our own poets has so beautifully termed, "the pomp that brings and shuts the day." The sun was in the tree-tops, and a softer or sweeter light could not have been chosen for such a ceremony. Most of the fields still lay in the soft brightness of the hour, though the forest was rapidly getting the more obscure look of night. A broad and gloomy margin was spreading from the boundary of the woods, and here and there a solitary tree cast its shadow on the meadows without its limits, throwing a dark ragged line in bold relief on the glow of the sun's rays. One—it was the dusky image of a high and waving pine, that reared its dark green pyramid of never-fading foliage nearly a hundred feet above the humbler growth of beeches—cast its shade to the side of the eminence of the block. Here the pointed extremity of the shadow was seen, stealing slowly toward the open grave — an emblem of that oblivion in which its humble tenants were so shortly to be wrapped.

At this spot Mark Heathcote and his remaining companions had assembled. An oaken chair saved from the flames was the seat of the father, and two parallel benches formed of planks placed on stones, held the other members of the family. The grave lay between. The patriarch had taken his station at one of its ends, while the stranger, so often named in these pages, stood with folded arms and a thoughtful brow at the other. The bridle of a horse caparisoned in that imperfect manner which the straitened means of the borderers now rendered necessary, was hanging from one of the half-burnt palisadoes, in the background.

"A just, but a merciful hand hath been laid heavily on my household," commenced the old Puritan, with the calmness of one who had long been accustomed to chasten his regrets by humility. "He that hath given freely, hath taken away, and One that hath long smiled upon my weakness, hath now veiled his face in anger. I have known him in his power to bless. It was meet that I should see him in his displeasure. A heart that was waxing confident, would have hardened in its pride. At that which hath befallen, let no man murmur. Let none imitate the speech of her who spoke foolishly; 'What! shall we receive good at the hand of God, and shall we not receive evil?' I would that the feeble-minded of the world—they that jeopard the soul on vanities, they that look with scorn on the neediness of the flesh—might behold the riches of One steadfast. I would that they might know the consolation of the righteous! Let the voice of thanksgiving be heard in the wilderness. Open thy mouths in praise, that the gratitude of a penitent be not hid!"

As the deep tones of the speaker ceased, his stern eye fell upon the features of the nearest youth, and it seemed to demand an audible response to his own lofty expression of resignation. But the sacrifice exceeded the power of the individual to whom had been made this silent, but intelligible appeal. After regarding the relics that lay at his feet, casting a wandering glance at the desolation which had swept over a place his own hand had helped to decorate, and receiving a renewed consciousness of his own bodily suffering in the shooting pain of his wounds, the young borderer averted his look, and seemed to recoil from so officious a display of submission. Observing his inability to reply, Mark continued—

"Hath no one a voice to praise the Lord? The bands of the heathen have fallen upon my herds; the brand hath been kindled within my dwellings; my people have died by the violence of the unenlightened, and none are here to say that the Lord is just! I would that the shouts of thanksgiving should arise in my fields! I would that the song of praise should grow louder than the whoop of the savage, and that all the land might speak joyfulness!"

A long, deep, and expecting pause succeeded. Then Content rejoined, in his quiet tones, speaking firmly, but with the modest utterance he rarely failed to use—

"The hand that hath held the balance is just," he said, "and we have been found wanting. He that made the wilderness blossom, hath caused the ignorant and the barbarous to be the instruments of his will. He hath arrested the season of our prosperity, that we may know he is the Lord. He hath spoken in the whirl-wind, but his mercy granteth that our ears shall know his voice."

As his son ceased, a gleam of satisfaction shot across the countenance of the Puritan. His eye next turned inquiringly towards Ruth, who sat among her maidens the image of womanly sorrow. Common interest seemed to still the breathing of the little assemblage, and sympathy was quite as active as curiosity, when each one present suffered a glance to steal toward her benignant but pallid face. The eye of the mother was gazing earnestly, but without a tear, on the melancholy spectacle before her. It unconsciously sought among the dried and shriveled remnants of mortality that lay at her feet, some relic of the cherub she had lost. A shudder and struggle followed, after which her gentle voice breathed so low that those nearest her person could scarce distinguish the words—

"The Lord gave, and the Lord hath taken away; blessed be his holy name!"

"Now know I that he who hath smote me, is merciful; for he chasteneth them he loveth," said Mark Heathcote, rising with dignity to address his household. "Our life is a life of pride. The young are wont to wax insolent, while he of many years saith to his own heart, "it is good to be here." There is a fearful mystery in One who sitteth on high. The heavens are his throne, and he hath created the earth for his footstool. Let not the vanity of the weak of mind presume to understand it; for 'who that hath the breath of life, lived before the hills?' The bonds of the evil one, of Satan, and of the sons of Belial, have been loosened, that the faith of the elect may be purified, that the names of those written since the foundation of the earth were laid, may be read in letters of pure gold. The time of man is but a moment in the reckoning of him whose life is eternity—earth the habitation of a season!

"The bones of the bold, of the youthful, and of the strong of yesterday, lie at our feet. None know what an hour may bring forth. In a single night, my children, hath this been done. They whose voices were heard in my halls, are now speechless, and they who so lately rejoiced, are sorrowing. Yet hath this seeming evil been ordered that good may come thereof. We are dwellers in a wild and distant land," he continued, insensibly permitting his thoughts to incline toward the more mournful details of their affliction. "Our earthly home is afar off. Hither have we been led by the flaming pillar of Truth, and yet the malice of the persecutors hath not forgotten to follow. One houseless, and sought like the hunted deer, is again driven to flee. We have the canopy of the stars for a roof. None may tarry longer to worship secretly within our walls. But the path of the faithful, though full of thorns, leadeth to quiet, and the final rest of the just man can never know alarm. He that hath borne hunger and thirst, and the pains of the flesh, for the sake of truth, knoweth how to be satisfied; nor will the hours of bodily suffering be accounted weary to him whose goal is the peace of the righteous." The strong lineaments of the stranger grew even more than usually austere, and as the Puritan continued, the hand which rested on the handle of a pistol, grasped the weapon until the fingers seemed imbedded in the wood. He bowed, however, as if to acknowledge the personal allusion, and remained silent.

"If any mourn the death of those who have rendered up their being, struggling, as it may be permitted, in behalf of life and dwelling," continued Mark Heathcote, regarding a female near him, "let her remember, that from the beginning of the world were his days numbered, and that not a sparrow falleth without answering the ends of wisdom. Rather let the fulfillment of things remind us of the vanity of life, that we may learn how easy it is to become immortal. If the youth hath been cut down, seemingly like unripened grass, he hath fallen by the sickle of one who knoweth best when to begin the in-gathering of the harvest to his eternal garners. Though a spirit bound unto his, as one feeble is wont to lean on the strength of man and mourn over his fall, let her sorrow be mingled with rejoicing." A convulsive sob broke out of the bosom of the handmaiden who was known to have been affianced to one of the dead, and for a moment the address of Mark was interrupted. But when silence again ensued, he continued, the subject leading him, by a transition that was natural, to allude to his own sorrows. "Death hath been no stranger in my habitation," he said. "His shaft fell heaviest when it struck her, who, like those that have here fallen, was in the pride of her youth, and when her soul was glad with the first joy of the birth of a man-child! Thou who sittest on high!" he added, turning a glazed and tearless eye to heaven; "thou knowest how heavy was that blow, and thou hast written down the strivings of an oppressed soul. The burden was not found too heavy for endurance. The sacrifice hath not sufficed; the world was again getting uppermost in my heart.

"Thou didst bestow an image of that innocence and loveliness that dwelleth in the skies, and this hast thou taken away, that we might know thy power. To this judgment we bow. If thou hast called our child to the mansions of bliss, she is wholly thine, and we presume not to complain; but if thou hast still left her to wander further in the pilgrimage of life, we confide in thy goodness. She is of a long-suffering race, and thou wilt not desert her to the blindness of the heathen. She is thine, she is wholly thine, King of Heaven! and yet hast thou permitted our hearts to yearn towards her with the fondness of earthly love. We await some further manifestation of thy will, that we may know whether the fountains of our affection shall be dried in the certainty of her blessedness—" (scalding tears were rolling down the cheeks of the pallid and immovable mother) "or whether hope, nay, whether duty to thee calleth for the interference of those bound to her in the tenderness of the flesh. When the blow was heaviest on the bruised spirit of a lone and solitary wanderer, in a strange and savage land, he held not back the offspring it was thy will to grant him in the place of her called to thyself; and now that the child hath become a man, he too layeth, like Abraham of old, the infant of his love, a willing offering at thy feet. Do with it as to thy never-failing wisdom seemeth best."

The words were interrupted by a heavy groan, that burst from the chest of Content. A deep silence ensued, but when the assembly ventured to throw looks of sympathy and awe at the bereaved father, they saw that he had arisen and stood gazing steadily at the speaker, as if he wondered, equally with the others, whence such a sound of suffering could have come. The Puritan renewed the subject, but his voice faltered, and for an instant, as he proceeded, his hearers were oppressed with the spectacle of an aged and dignified man shaken with grief. Conscious of his weakness, the old man ceased speaking in exhortation, and addressed himself to prayer. While thus engaged, his tones again became clear, firm, and distinct, and the petition was ended in the midst of a deep and holy calm.

With the performance of this preliminary office, the simple ceremony was brought to its close. The remains were lowered, in solemn silence, into the grave, and the earth was soon replaced by the young men. Mark Heathcote then invoked aloud the blessing of God on his household, and bowing in person, as he had before done in spirit, to the will of

Heaven, he motioned to the family to withdraw.

The interview that succeeded was over the resting-place of the dead. The hand of the stranger was firmly clenched in that of the Puritan, and the stern self-command of both appeared to give way, before the regrets of a friendship that had endured through so many trying scenes.

"Thou knowest that I may not tarry," said the former, as if he replied to some expressed wish of his companion. "They would make me a sacrifice to the Moloch of their vanities; and yet would I fain abide until the weight of this heavy blow may be forgotten. I found thee in peace, and I quit thee in the depths of suffering!"

"Thou distrustest me, or thou dost injustice to thine own belief," interrupted the Puritan, with a smile, that shone on his haggard and austere visage, as the rays of the setting sun light a wintry cloud. "Seemed I happier when this hand placed that of a loved bride into mine own, than thou now seest me in this wilderness, houseless, stripped of my wealth, and, God forgive the ingratitude, but I had almost said, childless! No, indeed, thou mayest not tarry, for the blood-hounds of tyranny will be on their scent; here is shelter no longer."

The eyes of both turned, by a common and melancholy feeling, toward the ruin of the block. The stranger then pressed the hand of his friend in both his own, and said in a struggling voice—

"Mark Heathcote, adieu! He that hath a roof for the persecuted wanderer shall not long be houseless; neither shall the resigned forever know sorrow."

His words sounded in the ears of his companion like the revelation of a prophecy. They again pressed their hands together, and, regarding each other with looks in which kindness could not be altogether smothered by the repulsive character of an acquired air, they parted. The Puritan slowly took his way to the dreary shelter which covered his family; while the stranger was shortly after seen urging the beast he had mounted, across the pastures of the valley, toward one of the most retired paths of the wilderness.

CHAPTER XVII.

"Together toward the village then we walked;
And of old friends and places much we talked;
And who had died, who left them, would he tell;
And who still in their father's mansion dwell."
—DANA.

WE leave the imagination of the reader to supply an interval of several years.

Before the thread of the narrative shall be resumed, it will be necessary to take another hasty view of the condition of the country in which the scene of our legend had place.

The exertions of the provincials were no longer limited to the first efforts of a colonial existence. The establishments of New England had passed the ordeal of experiment, and were become permanent. Massachusetts was already populous; and Connecticut, the colony with which we have more immediate connection, was sufficiently peopled to manifest a portion of that enterprise which has since made her active little community so remarkable. The effects of these increased exertions were becoming extensively visible; and we shall endeavor to set one of these changes, as distinctly as our feeble powers will allow, before the eyes of those who read these pages.

When compared with the progress of society in the other hemisphere, the condition of what is called in America a new settlement, becomes anomalous. There, the arts of life have been the fruits of an intelligence that has progressively accumulated with the advancement of civilization; while here, improvement is in a great degree the consequence of experience elsewhere acquired. Necessity, prompted by an understanding of its wants, incited by a commendable spirit of emulation, and encouraged by liberty, early gave birth to those improvements which have converted a wilderness into the abodes of abundance and security, with a rapidity that wears the appearance of magic. Industry has wrought with the confidence of knowledge, and the result has been peculiar.

It is scarcely necessary to say that in a country where the laws favor all commendable enterprise, where unnecessary artificial restrictions are unknown, and where the hand of man has not yet exhausted its efforts, the adventurer is allowed the greatest freedom of choice in selecting the field of his enterprise. The agriculturist passes the heath and the barren, to seat himself on the river-bottom; the trader looks for the site of demand and supply; and the artisan quits his native village to seek employment in situations where labor will meet its fullest reward. It is a consequence of this extraordinary freedom of election, that, while the great picture of American society has been sketched with so much boldness, a large portion of the filling-up still remains to be done. The emigrant has consulted his immediate interests; and, while no very extensive and profitable territory throughout the whole of our immense possessions has been wholly neglected, neither has any particular district yet attained the finish of improvement. The city is even now seen in the wilderness, and the wilderness often continues near the city, while the latter is sending forth its swarms to distant scenes of industry. After thirty years of fostering care on the part of the government, the Capital itself presents its disjointed and sickly villages in the center of the deserted "old fields" of Maryland, while numberless youthful rivals are flourishing on the waters of the West, in spots where the bear has ranged and the wolf howled, long since the former has been termed a city.

Thus it is that high civilization, a state of infant existence, and positive barbarity, are often brought so near each other within the borders of this Republic. The traveler who has passed the night in an inn that would not disgrace the oldest country in Europe, may be compelled to dine in the shantee* of a hunter; the smooth and graveled road sometimes ends in an impassable swamp; the spires of the town are often hid by the branches of a tangled forest, and the canal leads to a seemingly barren and unprofitable mountain. He that does not return to see what another year may bring forth, commonly bears away from these scenes recollections that conduce to error. To see America with the eyes of truth, it is necessary to look often; and in order to understand the actual condition of these States, it should be remembered that it is equally unjust to believe that all the intermediate points partake of the improvements of particular places, as to infer the want of civilization at more remote establishments, from a few unfavorable facts gleaned near the center. By an accidental concurrence of moral and physical causes, much of that equality which distinguishes the institutions of the country is extended to the progress of society over its whole surface.

Although the impetus of improvement was not so great in the time of Mark Heathcote as in our own days, the principle of its power was actively in existence. Of this fact we shall furnish a sufficient evidence, by pursuing our inten-

tion of describing one of those changes to which allusion has already been made.

The reader will remember that the age of which we write had advanced into the last quarter of the seventeenth century. The precise moment at which the action of the tale must re-commence, was that period of the day when the gray of twilight was redeeming objects from the deep darkness with which the night draws to its close. The month was June, and the scene such as it may be necessary to describe with some particularity.

Had there been light, and had one been favorably placed to enjoy a bird's-eye view of the spot, he would have seen a broad and undulating field of leafy forest, in which the various deciduous trees of New England were relieved by the deeper verdure of occasional masses of evergreen. In the center of this swelling and nearly interminable outline of woods, was a valley that spread between three low mountains. Over the bottom land, for the distance of several miles, all the signs of a settlement in a state of rapid and prosperous improvement were visible. The devious course of a deep and swift brook, that in the other hemisphere would have been termed a river, was to be traced through the meadows by its borders of willow and sumach. At a point near the center of the valley the waters had been arrested by a small dam; and a mill, whose wheel at that early hour was without motion, stood on the artificial mound. Near it was the site of a New England hamlet.

The number of dwellings in the village might have been forty. They were, as usual, constructed of a firm frame-work, neatly covered with sidings of boards. There was a surprising air of equality in the general aspect of the houses; and, if there were question of any country but our own, it might be added there was an unusual appearance of comfort and abundance in even the humblest of them all. They were mostly of two lower stories, the superior overhanging the inferior by a foot or two; a mode of construction much in use in the earlier days of the eastern colonies. As paint was but little used at that time, none of the buildings exhibited a color different from that the wood would naturally assume after the exposure of a few years to the weather. Each had its single chimney in the center of the roof, and but two or three showed more than a solitary window on each side of the principal or outer door. In front of every dwelling was a small, neat court, in greensward, separated from the public road by a light fence of deal. Double rows of young and vigorous elms lined

---

* *Shanty*, or *Shantee*, is a word much used in the newer settlements. It strictly means a rude cabin of bark and brush, such as is often erected in the forest for temporary purposes. But the borderers often quaintly apply it to their own habitations. The only derivation which the writer has heard for this American word, is one that supposes it to be a corruption of *Chienté*, a term said to be used among the Canadians to express a dog-kennel.

each side of the wide street, while an enormous sycamore still kept possession of the spot in its center which it had occupied when the white man entered the forest.

Beneath the shade of this tree the inhabitants often collected to gather tidings of each other's welfare, or to listen to some matter of interest that rumor had borne from the towns nearer the sea. A narrow and little-used wheel track ran with a graceful and sinuous route through the center of the wide and grassy street. Reduced in appearance to little more than a bridle-path, it was to be traced without the hamlet, between high fences of wood for a mile or two, to the points where it entered the forest. Here and there roses were pressing through the openings of the fences before the doors of the different habitations, and bushes of fragrant lilacs stood in the angles of most of the courts.

The dwellings were detached. Each occupied its own insulated plot of ground, with a garden in its rear. The out-buildings were thrown to that distance which the cheapness of land and security from fire rendered both easy and expedient.

The church stood in the center of the highway, and near one end of the hamlet. In the exterior and ornaments of the important temple, the taste of the times had been fastidiously consulted, its form and simplicity forming no slight resemblance to the self-denying doctrines and quaint humors of the religionists who worshiped beneath its roof. The building, like all the rest, was of wood, and externally of two stories. It possessed a tower, without a spire—the former alone serving to denote its sacred character. In the construction of this edifice, especial care had been taken to eschew all deviations from direct lines and right angles. Those narrow-arched passages for the admission of light that are elsewhere so common, were then thought by the stern moralists of New England to have some mysterious connection with her of the scarlet mantle. The priest would as soon have thought of appearing before his flock in the vanities of stole and cassock, as the congregation of admitting the repudiated ornaments into the outline of their severe architecture. Had the Genii of the Lamp suddenly exchanged the windows of the sacred edifice with those of the inn that stood nearly opposite, the closest critic of the settlement could never have detected the liberty, since, in the form, dimensions, and style of the two, there was no visible difference.

A little inclosure at no great distance from the church, and on one side of the street, had been set apart for the final resting-place of those who had finished their race on earth. It contained but a solitary grave.

The inn was to be distinguished from the surrounding buildings, by its superior size, an open horse-shed, and a sort of protruding air with which it thrust itself on the line of the street, as if to invite the traveler to enter. A sign swung on a gallows-looking post that, in consequence of frosty nights and warm days, had already deviated from the perpendicular. It bore a conceit that at the first glance might have gladdened the heart of a naturalist with the belief that he had made the discovery of some unknown bird. The artist, however, had sufficiently provided against the consequences of so embarrassing a blunder, by considerately writing beneath the offspring of his pencil, "This is the sign of the Whip-Poor-Will;" a name, that the most unlettered traveler in those regions would be likely to know was vulgarly given to the Wish-Ton-Wish, or the American night-hawk.

But few relics of the forest remained immediately around the hamlet. The trees had long been felled, and sufficient time had elapsed to remove most of the vestiges of their former existence. But as the eye receded from the cluster of buildings, the signs of more recent inroads on the wilderness became apparent, until the view terminated with openings, in which piled logs and mazes of felled trees announced the recent use of the ax.

At that early day, the American husbandman, like the agriculturists of most of Europe, dwelt in his village. The dread of violence from the savages had given rise to a custom similar to that which centuries before had been produced in the other hemisphere by the inroads of more pretending barbarians, and which, with few and distant exceptions, has deprived rural scenery of a charm that, it would seem, time and a better condition of society are slow to repair. Some remains of this ancient practice are still to be traced in the portion of the Union of which we write, where even at this day the farmer often quits the village to seek his scattered fields in his neighborhood. Still, as man has never been the subject of a system here, and as each individual has always had the liberty of consulting his own temper, bolder spirits early began to break through a practice, by which quite as much was lost in convenience as was gained in security. Even in the scene we have been describing, ten or twelve humble habitations were distributed among the recent clearings on the side of the mountains, and in situations too remote to promise much security against any sudden inroad of the common enemy.

For general protection, in cases of the last extremity, however, a stockaded dwelling, not unlike that which we have had occasion to describe in our earlier pages, stood in a convenient spot near the hamlet. Its defenses were stronger and more elaborate than usual, the pickets being furnished with flanking block-houses; and, in other respects, the building bore the aspect of a work equal to any resistance that might be required in the warfare of those regions. The ordinary habitation of the priest was within its gates; and hither most of the sick were timely conveyed, in order to anticipate the necessity of removals at more inconvenient moments.

It is scarcely necessary to tell the American, that heavy wooden fences subdivided the whole of this little landscape into inclosures of some eight or ten acres in extent; that, here and there, cattle and flocks were grazing without herdsmen or shepherds, and that while the fields nearest to the dwellings were beginning to assume the appearance of a careful and improved husbandry, those more remote became gradually wilder and less cultivated, until the half-reclaimed openings, with their blackened stubs and barked trees, were blended with the gloom of the living forest. These are more or less the accompaniments of every rural scene in districts of the country where time has not yet effected more than the first two stages of improvement.

At the distance of a short half-mile from the fortified house, or garrison, as by a singular corruption of terms the stockaded building was called, stood a building of pretensions altogether superior to any in the hamlet. The buildings in question, though simple, were extensive; and though scarcely other than such as might belong to an agriculturist in easy circumstances, still they were remarkable in that settlement, by the comforts which time alone could accumulate, and some of which denoted an advanced condition for a frontier family. In short, there was an air about the establishment, as in the disposition of its out-buildings, in the superior workmanship, and in the materials, and in the numberless other well-known circumstances, which went to show that the whole of the edifices were reconstructions. The fields near this habitation exhibited smoother surfaces than those in the distance. The fences were lighter and less rude; the stumps had absolutely disappeared; and the gardens and homestead were well planted with flourishing fruit-trees. A conical eminence arose at a short distance in the rear of the principal dwelling. It was covered with that beautiful and peculiar ornament of an American farm, a regular, thrifty, and luxuriant apple-orchard. Still, age had not given its full beauty to the plantation, which might have had a growth of some eight or ten years.

A blackened tower of stone, which sustained the charred ruins of a superstructure of wood, though of no great height in itself, rose above the tallest of the trees, and stood a sufficient memorial of some scene of violence in the brief history of the valley. There was also a small blockhouse near the habitation; but, by the air of neglect that reigned around, it was quite apparent the little work had been of a hurried construction, and of but temporary use. A few young plantations of fruit-trees were also to be seen in different parts of the valley, which was beginning to exhibit many other evidences of an improved agriculture.

So far as all these artificial changes went, they were of an English character. But it was England devoid alike of its luxury and its poverty, and with a superfluity of space that gave to the meanest habitation in the view an air of abundance and comfort that is so often wanting about the dwellings of the comparatively rich, in countries where man is found bearing a far greater numerical proportion to the soil than was then, or is even now the case, in the regions of which we write.

CHAPTER XVIII.

"Come hither, neighbor Sea-coal—God hath blessed you with a good name; to be a well-favored man is the gift of fortune; but to write and read comes by Nature."—MUCH ADO ABOUT NOTHING.

IT has already been said, that the hour at which the action of the tale must recommence, was early morning. The usual coolness of night, in a country extensively covered with wood, had passed, and the warmth of a summer morning, in that low latitude, was causing the streaks of light vapor, that floated about the meadows, to rise above the trees. The feathery patches united to form a cloud that sailed away toward the summit of a distant mountain, which appeared to be a common rendezvous for all the mists that had been generated by the past hours of darkness.

Though the burnished sky announced his near approach, the sun was not yet visible. Notwithstanding the earliness of the hour, a man was already mounting a little ascent in the road, at no great distance from the southern entrance of the hamlet, and at a point where he could command a view of all the objects described in the preceding chapter. A musket thrown across his left shoulder, with the horn and pouch at his sides, together with the little wallet at his back, proclaimed him one who had either been engaged in a hunt, or in some short expedition of even a less peaceable character. His dress was of the usual material and fashion of a countryman of the age and colony, though a short broadsword, that was thrust through a wampum belt which girded his body, might have attracted observation. In all other respects, he had the air of an inhabitant of the hamlet, who had found occasion to quit his abode on some affair of pleasure or of duty, that had made no very serious demand on his time.

Whether native or stranger, few ever passed the hillock named without pausing to gaze at the quiet loveliness of the cluster of houses that lay in full view from its summit. The individual mentioned loitered as usual, but, instead of following the line of the path, his eye rather sought some object in the direction of the fields. Moving leisurely to the nearest fence, he threw down the upper rails of a pair of bars, and beckoned to a horseman, who was picking his way across a broken bit of pasture land, to enter the highway by the passage he had opened.

" Put the spur smartly into the pacer's flank," said he who had done this act of civility, observing that the other hesitated to urge his beast across the irregular and somewhat scattered pile ; " my word for it, the jade goes over them all, without touching with more than three of her four feet. Fie, doctor ! there is never a cow in the Wish-Ton-Wish, but it would take the leap to be in the first at the milking."

" Softly, ensign," returned the timid equestrian, laying the emphasis on the final syllable of his companion's title, and pronouncing the first as if it were spelt with the third instead of the second vowel. " Thy courage is meet for one set apart for deeds of valor, but it would be a sorrowful day when the ailing of the valley should knock at my door, and a broken limb be made the apology for want of succor. Thy efforts will not avail thee, man ; for the mare hath had schooling, as well as her master. I have trained the beast to methodical habits, and she hath come to have a rooted dislike to all irregularities of movement. So, cease tugging at the

rein, as if thou wouldst compel her to pass the pile in spite of her teeth, and throw down the upper bar altogether."

" A doctor in these rugged parts should be mounted on one of those ambling birds of which we read," said the other, removing the obstacle to the secure passage of his friend ; " for truly a journey at night, in the paths of these clearings, is not always as safe moving as that which is said to be enjoyed by the settlers nearer sea."

" And where hast found mention of a bird of a size and velocity fit to be the bearer of the weight of a man ? " demanded he who was mounted, with a vivacity that betrayed some jealousy on the subject of a monopoly of learning. " I had thought there was never a book in the valley, out of mine own closet, that dealeth in these abstrusities ! "

" Dost think the Scriptures are strangers to us ? There—thou art now in the public path, and thy journey is without danger. It is matter of marvel to many in this settlement, how thou movest about at midnight, among upturned roots of trees, holes, logs and stumps, without falling—"

" I have told thee, ensign, it is by virtue of much training given to the beast. Certain am I, that neither whip nor spur would compel the animal to pass the bounds of discretion. Often have I traveled this bridle-path, without fear, as in truth without danger, when sight was a sense of as little use as that of smelling."

" I was about to say falling into thine own hands, which would be a tumble of little less jeopardy than even that of the wicked spirits."

The medical man affected to laugh at his companion's joke ; but, remembering the dignity suited to one of his calling, he immediately resumed the discourse with gravity—

" These may be matters of levity with those who know little of the hardships that are endured in the practice of the settlements. Here have I been on yonder mountain, guided by the instinct of my horse—"

" Ha ! hath there been a call at the dwelling of my brother Ring ? " demanded the pedestrian, observing by the direction of the other's eye, the road he had been traveling.

" Truly, there hath ; and at the unseasonable hour that is wont in a very unreasonable proportion of the cases of my practice."

" And Reuben numbereth another boy to the four that he could count yesterday ? "

The medical man held up three of his fingers, in a significant manner, as he nodded assent.

"This putteth Faith something in arrears," returned he who has been called ensign, and who was no other than the reader's old acquaintance Eben Dudley, preferred to that station in the train-band of the valley. "The heart of my brother Reuben will be gladdened by these tidings when he shall return from the scout."

"There will be occasion for thankfulness since he will find seven beneath a roof where he left but four!"

"I will close the bargain with the young captain for the mountain lot this very day!" muttered Dudley, like one suddenly convinced of the prudence of a long-debated measure. "Seven pounds of the colony money is no usurer's price, after all, for a hundred acres of heavily-timbered land; and they in full view of a settlement where boys come three at a time!"

The equestrian strapped his horse, and regarding his companion intently and with a significant air, he answered—

"Thou hast now fallen on the clew of an important mystery, Ensign Dudley. This continent was created with a design. The fact is apparent by it riches, its climate, its magnitude, its facilities of navigation, and chiefly in that it hath been left undiscovered until the advanced condition of society hath given opportunity and encouragement to men of a certain degree of merit to adventure in its behalf. Consider, neighbor, the wonderful progress it hath already made in the arts and in learning, in reputation and in resources, and thou wilt agree with me in the conclusion that all this hath been done with a design."

"'Twould be presuming to doubt it; for he hath indeed a short memory to whom it shall be necessary to recall the time when this very valley was little other than a den for beasts of prey, and this beaten highway a deer-track. Dost think that Reuben will be like to raise the whole of the recent gift?"

"With judgment, and by the blessing of Providence. The mind is active, Ensign Dudley, when the body is journeying among the forests; and much have my thoughts been exercised in this matter, while thou and others have been in your slumbers. Here have we the colonies in their first century, and yet thou knowest to what a pass of improvement they have arrived. They tell me the Hartford settlement is getting to be apportioned like the towns of mother England, that there is reason to think the day may come when the provinces shall have a power, and a convenience of culture and communication, equaling that which belongeth to some parts of the venerable island itself!"

"Nay, nay, Doctor Ergot," returned the other with an incredulous smile, "that is exceeding the bounds of a discretionable expectation."

"Thou wilt remember that I said equaling to *certain* parts. I think we may justly imagine, that ere many centuries shall elapse, there may be millions counted in these regions, and truly that, too, where one seeth naught at present but the savage and the beast."

"I will go with any man, in this question, as far as reason will justify; but doubtless thou hast read in the books uttered by writers over sea, the matters concerning the condition of those countries, wherein it is plain that we may never hope to reach the exalted excellence they enjoy."

"Neighbor Dudley, thou seemest disposed to push an unguarded expression to extremity. I said equaling *certain* parts, meaning always, too, in certain things. Now it is known in philosophy, that the stature of man hath degenerated, and must degenerate in these regions, in obedience to established laws of nature; therefore it is meet that allowance should be made for some deficiency in less material qualities."

"It is like, then, that the better sort of the men over sea are ill-disposed to quit their country," returned the ensign, glancing an eye of some unbelief along the muscular proportions of his own vigorous frame. "We have no less than three from the old countries in our village, here, and yet I do not find them men like to have been sought for at the building of Babel."

"This is settling a knotty and learned point by the evidence of a few shallow exceptions. I presume to tell you, Ensign Dudley, that the science, and wisdom, and philosophy of Europe, have been exceeding active in this matter; and they have proved to their own perfect satisfaction, which is the same thing as disposing of the question without appeal, that man and beast, plant and tree, hill and dale, lake and pond, sun, air, fire and water, are all wanting in some of the perfectness of the older regions. I respect a patriotic sentiment, and can carry the disposition to applaud the bounties received from the hands of a beneficent Creator as far as any man; but that which hath been demonstrated by science, or collected by learning, is placed too far beyond the objections of light-minded cavilers, to be doubted by graver faculties."

"I shall not contend against things that are proven," returned Dudley, who was quite as meek in discussion as he was powerful and active in more physical contests; "since it needs be that the learning of men in the old countries must have an exceeding excellence, in virtue of its great age. It would be a visit to remember, should some of its rare advantages be dispersed in these our own youthful regions!"

"And can it be said that our mental wants have been forgotten — that the nakedness of the mind hath been suffered to go without its comely vestment, neighbor Dudley? To me it seemeth that therein we have unwonted reason to rejoice, and that the equilibrium of nature is in a manner restored by the healing exercises of art. It is unseemly in an unenlightened province to insist on qualities that have been discreetly disproven; but learning is a transferable and communicable gift, and it is meet to affirm that it is to be found here, in quantities adapted to the wants of the colony."

"I'll not gainsay it, for having been more of an adventurer in the forest than one who hath traveled in quest of sights among the settlements along the seashore, it may happen that many things are to be seen there, of which my poor abilities have formed no opinion."

"And are we utterly unenlightened, even in this distant valley, ensign?" returned the leech, leaning over the neck of his horse, and addressing his companion in a mild and persuasive tone, that he had probably acquired in his extensive practice among the females of the settlement. "Are we to be classed with the heathen in knowledge, or to be accounted as the unnurtured men who are known once to have roamed through these forests in quest of their game! Without assuming any infallibility of judgment, or aspiring to any peculiarity of information, it doth not appear to my defective understanding, Master Dudley, that the progress of the settlement hath ever been checked for want of necessary foresight, nor that the growth of reason among us hath ever been stunted from any lack of mental aliment. Our councils are not barren of wisdom, ensign, nor hath it often arrived that abstrusities have been propounded, that some one intellect, to say no more in our own favor, hath not been known to grapple with successfully."

"That there are men, or perhaps I ought to say that there *is a man*, in the valley, who is equal to many marvels in the way of enlightened gifts—"

"I knew we should come to peaceable conclusions, Ensign Dudley," interrupted the other, rising erect in his saddle, with an air of appeased dignity; "for I have ever found you a discreet and consequent reasoner, and one who is never known to resist conviction, when truth is pressed with understanding. That the men from over sea are not often so well gifted as some—we will say, for the sake of a convenient illustration, as thyself, ensign— is placed beyond the reach of debate, since sight teaches us that numberless exceptions may be found to all the more general and distinctive laws of nature. I think we are not likely to carry our disagreement further?"

"It is impossible to make head against one so ready with his knowledge," returned the other, well content to exist in his own person a striking exception to the inferiority of his fellows; "though it appeareth to me that my brother Ring might be chosen as another instance of a reasonable stature; a fact that thou mayest see, doctor, by regarding him as he approaches through yon meadow. He hath been, like myself, on the scout among the mountains."

"There are many instances of physical merit among thy connections, Master Dudley," returned the complaisant physician; "though it would seem that thy brother hath not found his companion among them. He is attended by an ill-grown, and, it may be added, an ill-favored comrade, that I know not."

"Ha! It would seem that Reuben hath fallen on the trail of savages! The man in company is certainly in paint and blanket. It may be well to pause at yonder opening, and await their coming."

As this proposition imposed no particular inconvenience, the doctor readily assented. The two drew nigh to the place where the men, whom they saw crossing the fields in the distance, were expected to enter the highway.

But little time was lost in attendance. Ere many minutes had elapsed, Reuben Ring, accoutered and armed like the borderer already introduced in this chapter, arrived at the opening, followed by the stranger whose appearance had caused so much surprise to those who watched their approach.

"What now, sergeant," exclaimed Dudley, when the other was within ear-shot, speaking a little in the manner of one who had a legal right to propound his questions; "hast fallen on a trail of the savage, and made a captive? or hath some owl permitted one of its brood to fall from the nest across thy footpath?"

"I believe the creature may be accounted a man," returned the successful Reuben, throwing the breech of his gun to the earth, and leaning on its long barrel, while he intently regarded the half-painted, vacant, and extremely equivocal countenance of his captive. "He hath the colors of a Narragansett about the brow and eyes, and yet he faileth greatly in the form and movements."

"There are anomalies in the physicals of an Indian, as in those of other men," interrupted Doctor Ergot, with a meaning glance at Dudley. "The conclusion of our neighbor Ring may be too hasty, since paint is the fruit of art, and may be applied to any of our faces, after an established usage. But the evidences of nature are far less to be distrusted. It hath come within the province of my studies to note the differences in formation, which occur in the different families of man; and nothing is more readily to be known to an eye skilled in these abstrusities than the aboriginal of the tribe Narragansett. Set the man more in a position of examination, neighbors, and it shall shortly be seen to which race he belongs. Thou wilt note in this little facility of investigation, ensign, a clear evidence of most of the matters that have this morning been agitated between us. Doth the patient speak English?"

"Therein have I found some difficulty of inquiry," returned Reuben, or as he should now be, and as he was usually called, Sergeant Ring. "He hath been spoken to in the language of a Christian, no less than in that of a heathen, and as yet no reply hath been made, while he obeys commands uttered in both forms of speech."

"It mattereth not," said Ergot, dismounting and drawing near to his subject, with a look toward Dudley that should seem to court his admiration.

"Happily the examination before me leaneth but little on any subtleties of speech. Let the man be placed in an attitude of ease, one in which nature may not be fettered by restraint. The conformation of the whole head is remarkably aboriginal, but the distinction of tribes is not to be sought in these general delineations. The forehead, as you see, neighbors, is retreating and narrow, the cheek-bones as usual high, and the olfactory member, as in all of the natives, inclining to Roman."

"Now to me it would seem that the nose of the man hath a marked upturning at the end," Dudley ventured to remark,

as the other ran volubly over the general and well-known distinctive points of physical construction in an Indian.

"As an exception! Thou seest, ensign, by this elevation of the bone, and the protuberance of the more fleshy parts, that the peculiarity is an exception. I should rather have said that the nose originally inclined to the Roman. The departure from regularity has been produced by some casualty of their warfare, such as a blow from a tomahawk, or the gash of a knife—aye! here thou seest the scar left by the weapon! It is concealed by the paint; but remove that, and you will find that it hath all the form of a cicatrix of a corresponding shape. These departures from generalities have a tendency to confound pretenders; a happy circumstance in itself for the progress of knowledge on fixed principles. Place the subject more erect, that we may see the natural movement of the muscles. Here is an evidence of great aquatic habits in the dimensions of the foot, which go to confirm original conceptions. It is a happy proof, through which reasonable and prudent conclusions confirm the quick-sighted glances of practice. I pronounce the fellow to be a Narragansett."

"Is it then a Narragansett that hath a foot to confound a trail?" returned Eben Dudley, who had been studying the movements and attitudes of the captive with quite as much keenness, and with something more of understanding than the leech. "Brother Ring, hast ever known an Indian leave such an out-turning foot-print on the leaves?"

"Ensign, I marvel that a man of thy discretion should dwell on a slight variety of movement, when a case exists in which the laws of nature may be traced to their sources. This training for the Indian troubles hath made thee critical in the position of a foot. I have said that the fellow is a Narragansett, and what I have uttered hath not been lightly ventured. Here is the peculiar formation of the foot, which hath been obtained in infancy, a fullness in the muscles of the breast and shoulders, from unusual exercise in an element denser than the air, and a nicer construction in—"

The physician paused, for Dudley had coolly advanced to the captive, and raising the thin rope of deer-skin which was thrown over the whole of his superior members, he exposed the unequivocal skin of a white man. This would have proved an embarrassing refutation to one accustomed to the conflict of wits; but monopoly in certain branches of knowledge had produced in favor of Doctor Ergot an acknowledged superiority, that in its effects might be likened to the predominating influence of any other aristocracy on those faculties that have been benumbed by its operation. His opinion changed, which is more than can be said of his countenance; for with the readiness of invention which is so often practiced in the felicitous institutions we have named, and by which the reasoning, instead of regulating, is adapted to the practice, he exclaimed with uplifted hands and eyes that bespoke the fullness of his admiration—

"Here have we another proof of the wonderful agency by which the changes in nature are gradually wrought! Now do we see in this Narragansett—"

"The man is white!" interrupted Dudley, tapping the naked shoulder, which he still held exposed to view.

"White, but not a tittle the less a Narragansett. Your captive, beyond a doubt, oweth his existence to Christian parentage, but accident hath thrown him early among the aboriginals, and all those parts which were liable to change were fast getting to assume the peculiarities of the tribe. He is one of those beautiful and connecting links in the chain of knowledge, by which science followeth up its deductions to demonstration."

"I should ill brook coming to harm for doing violence to a subject of the king," said Reuben Ring, a steady, open-faced yeoman, who thought far less of the subtleties of his companion than of discharging his social duties in a manner fitting the character of a quiet and well-conditioned citizen. "We have had so much of stirring tidings latterly, concerning the manner the savages conduct their warfare, that it behoveth men in places of trust to be vigilant; for," glancing his eyes toward the ruin of the distant block-house, "thou knowest, brother Dudley, that we have occasion to be watchful in a settlement as deep in the forest as this."

"I will answer for the indemnity, Sergeant Ring," said Dudley, with an air of dignity. "I take upon myself the keeping of this stranger, and will see that he be borne, properly, and in fitting season, before the authorities. In the meantime, duty hath caused us to overlook matters of moment in thy household, which it may be seemly to communicate. Abundance hath not been neglectful of thy interests, during the scout."

"What!" demanded the husband, with rather more of earnestness than was generally exhibited by one of habits as restrained as his own; "hath the woman called upon the neighbors during my absence?"

Dudley nodded an assent.

"And shall I find another boy beneath my roof?"

Doctor Ergot nodded three times, with a gravity that might have suited a communication even more weighty than the one he made.

"Thy woman rarely doth a good turn by halves, Reuben. Thou wilt find that she hath made provision for a successor to our good neighbor Ergot, since a seventh son is born in thy house."

The broad, honest face of the father flushed with joy, and then a feeling less selfish came over him. He asked, with a slight tremor in the voice, that was none the less touching for coming from the lips of one so stout of frame and firm of movement—

"And the woman?—in what manner doth Abundance bear up under the blessing?"

"Bravely," returned the leech; "go to thy dwelling, Sergeant Ring, and praise God that there is one to look to its concerns in thy absence. He who hath received the gift of seven sons in five years, need never be a poor nor a dependent man in a country like this. Seven farms, added to that pretty homestead of mountain-land which thou now tillest, will render thee a patriarch in thine age, and sustain the name of Ring, hundreds of years hence, when these colonies shall become peopled and powerful, and, I say it boldly, caring not who may call me one that vaunteth out of reason, equal to some of your lofty and self-extolled kingdoms of Europe—ay, even peradventure to the mighty sovereignty of Portugal itself! I have enumerated thy future farms at seven, for the allusion of the ensign to the virtues of men born with natural propensities to the healing art must be taken as a pleasant speech, since it is mere delusion of old wives' fancy, and it would be particularly unnecessary here, where every reasonable situation of this nature is already occupied. Go to thy wife, sergeant, and bid her be of good cheer, for she hath done herself, thee, and thy country, a service, and that without dabbling in pursuits foreign to her comprehension."

The sturdy yeoman, on whom this rich gift of Providence had been dispensed, raised his hat, and placing it decently before his face, he offered up a silent thanksgiving for the favor. Then transferring his captive to the keeping of his superior and kinsman, he was soon seen striding over the fields toward his upland dwelling, with a heavy foot, though with a light heart.

In the meantime, Dudley and his companion bestowed a more particular attention on the silent and nearly motionless object of their curiosity. Though the captive appeared to be of middle age, his eye was unmeaning, his air timid and uncertain, and his form cringing and ungainly. In all these particulars, he was seen to differ from the known peculiarities of a native warrior.

Previously to departing, Reuben Ring had explained that while traversing the woods, on that duty of watchfulness to which the state of the colony and some recent signs had given rise, this wandering person had been encountered and secured, as seemed necessary to the safety of the settlement. He had neither sought nor avoided his captor; but when questioned concerning his tribe, his motives for traversing those hills, and his future intentions, no satisfactory reply could be extracted. He had scarcely spoken, and the little that he said was uttered in a jargon between the language of his interrogator and the dialect of some barbarous nation. Though there was much in the actual state of the colonies, and in the circumstances in which this wanderer had been found, to justify his detention, little had in truth been discovered, to supply a clew either to any material facts in his history, or to any of his views in being in the immediate vicinity of the valley.

Guided only by this barren information, Dudley and his companion endeavored, as they moved towards the hamlet, to entrap their prisoner into some confession of his object, by putting their questions with a sagacity not unusual to men in remote and difficult situations, where necessity and danger are apt to keep alive all the native energies of the human mind. The answers were little connected and unintelligible, sometimes seeming to exhibit the finest subtlety of savage cunning, and at others appearing to possess the mental helplessness of the most abject fatuity.

CHAPTER XIX.

" I am not prone to weeping, as our sex
    Commonly are ;—
            But I have
    That honorable grief lodged here, which burns
    Worse than tears drown."—WINTER'S TALE.

IF the pen of a compiler, like that we wield, possessed the mechanical power of the stage, it would be easy to shift the scenes of this legend as rapidly and effectively as is required for its right understanding, and for the proper maintenance of its interest. That which cannot be done with the magical aid of machinery, must be attempted by less ambitious, and we fear by far less efficacious means.

At the same early hour of the day, and at no great distance from the spot where Dudley announced his good fortune to his brother Ring, another morning meeting had taken place between persons of the same blood and connections. From the instant when the pale light that precedes the day was first seen in the heavens, the windows and doors of the considerable dwelling, on the opposite side of the valley, had been unbarred. Ere the glow of the sun had gilded the sky over the outline of the eastern woods, this example of industry and providence was followed by the inmates of every house in the village, or on the surrounding hills; and by the time the golden globe itself was visible above the trees, there was not a human being in all that settlement, of proper age and health, who was not actively afoot.

It is unnecessary to say that the dwelling particularly named was the present habitation of the household of Mark Heathcote. Though age had sapped the foundations of his strength, and had nearly dried the channels of his existence, the venerable religionist still lived. While his physical perfection had been gradually giving way before the ordinary decay of nature, the moral man was but little altered. It is even probable that his visions of futurity were less dimmed by the mists of carnal interests than when last seen, and that the spirit had gained some portion of that energy which had certainly been abstracted from the more corporeal parts of his existence. At the hour already named, the Puritan was seated in the piazza, which stretched along the whole front of a dwelling that, however it might be deficient in architectural proportions, was not wanting in the more substantial comforts of a spacious and commodious frontier residence. In order to obtain a faithful portrait of a man so intimately connected with our tale, the reader will fancy him one who had numbered four-score and ten years, with a visage on which deep and constant mental striving had wrought many and menacing furrows, a form that trembled while it yet exhibited the ruins of powerful limb and flexible muscle, and a countenance on which ascetic reflections had engraved a severity that was but faintly relieved by the gleamings of a natural kindness which no acquired habit nor any traces of metaphysical thought could ever entirely erase.

Across this picture of venerable and self-mortifying age, the first rays of the sun were now softly cast, lighting a dimmed eye and furrowed face with a look of brightness and peace. Perhaps the blandness of the expression belonged as much to the season and the hour, as to the habitual character of the man. This benignancy of feature, unusual rather in its strength than in its existence, might have been heightened by the fact that his spirit had just wrought in prayer, as was usual, in the circle of his children and dependents, ere they left those retired parts of the building where they had found rest and security during the night. Of the former, none known and cherished in the domestic circle had been absent; and the ample provision that was making for the morning meal sufficiently showed that the number of the latter had in no degree diminished since the reader was familiar with the domestic economy of his household.

Time had produced no very striking alteration in the appearance of Content. It is true that the brown hue of his features had deepened, and that his frame was beginning to lose some of its elasticity and ease of action in the more measured movements of middle age. But the governed temperament of the individual had always kept the animal in more than usual subjection. Even his earlier days had rather exhibited the promise than the performance of the ordinary youthful qualities. Mental gravity had long before produced a corresponding physical effect. In reference to his exterior, and using the language of the painter, it would now be said that, without having wrought any change in form and proportions, the colors had been mellowed by time. If a few hairs of gray were sprinkled here and there around his brow, it was as moss gathers on the stones of the edifice, rather furnishing evidence of its increased adhesion and approved stability, than denoting any symptoms of decay.

Not so with his gentle and devoted partner. That softness and sweetness of air which had first touched the heart of Content were still to be seen, though they existed amid the traces of a constant and a corroding grief. The freshness of youth had departed, and in its place was visible the more lasting, and, in her case, the more affecting beauty of expression. The eye of Ruth had lost none of its gentleness, and her smile still continued kind and attractive; but the former was often painfully vacant, seeming to look inward upon those secret and withering sources of sorrow that were deeply and almost mysteriously seated in her heart; while the latter resembled the cold brightness of that planet which illumines objects by re-

pelling the borrowed luster from its own bosom. The matronly form, the feminine beaming of the countenance, and the melodious voice, yet remained; but the first had been shaken till it stood on the very verge of a premature decay; the second had a mingling of anxious care in its most sympathetic movements, and the last was seldom without that fearful thrill which so deeply affects the senses by conveying to the understanding a meaning so foreign from the words.

And yet an uninterested and ordinary observer might not have seen, in the faded comeliness and blighted maturity of the matron, more than the every-day signs that betray the turn in the tide of human existence. As befitted such a subject, the coloring of sorrow had been traced by a hand too delicate to leave the lines visible to every vulgar eye. Like the master-touches of art, her grief, as it was beyond the sympathies, so it lay beyond the ken of those whom excellence may fail to excite, or in whom absence can deaden affections. Still her feelings were true to all who had any claims on her love. The predominance of wasting grief over the more genial springs of her enjoyments, only went to prove how much greater is the influence of the generous than the selfish qualities of our nature in a heart that is truly endowed with tenderness. It is scarce necessary to say that this gentle and constant woman sorrowed for her child.

Had Ruth Heathcote known that the girl ceased to live, it would not have been difficult for one of her faith to have deposited her regrets by the side of hopes that were so justifiable in the grave of the innocent. But the living death to which her offspring might be condemned, was rarely absent from her thoughts. She listened to the maxims of resignation, which were heard flowing from lips she loved, with the fondness of a woman and the meekness of a Christian; and then, even while the holy lessons were still sounding in her attentive organs, the workings of an unconquerable nature led her insidiously back to the sorrow of a mother.

The imagination of this devoted and feminine being had never possessed an undue control over her reason. Her visions of happiness with the man whom her judgment not less than her inclination approved, had been such as experience and religion might justify. But she was now fated to learn there is a fearful poetry in sorrow, which can sketch with a grace and an imaginative power that no feebler efforts of a heated fancy may ever equal. She heard the sweet breathing of her slumbering infant in the whispering of the summer airs; its plaints came to her ears amid the howlings of the gale; while the eager question and fond reply were mixed up with the most ordinary intercourse of her own household.

To her the laugh of childish happiness that often came on the still air of evening from the hamlet, sounded like the voice of mourning; and scarce an infantile sport met her eye that did not bring with it a pang of anguish. Twice since the events of the inroad had she been a mother; and, as if an eternal blight were doomed to destroy her hopes, the little creatures to whom she had given birth, slept side by side near the base of the ruined block. Thither she often went, but it was rather to be the victim of those cruel images of her fancy, than as a mourner. Her visions of the dead were calm and even consolatory, but if ever her thoughts mounted to the abodes of eternal peace, and her feeble fancy essayed to embody the forms of the blessed, her mental eye sought her who was not, rather than those who were believed to be secure in their felicity. Wasting and delusory as were these glimpses of the mind, there were others far more harrowing, because they presented themselves with more of the coarse and certain features of the world. It was the common, and perhaps it was the better, opinion of the inhabitants of the valley, that death had early sealed the fate of those who had fallen into the hands of the savages on the occasion of the inroad.

Such a result was in conformity with the known practices and ruthless passions of the conquerors, who seldom spared life unless to render revenge more cruelly refined, or to bring consolation to some bereaved mother of the tribe by offering a substitute for the dead in the person of a captive. There was relief to picture the face of the laughing cherub in the clouds, or to listen to its light footstep in the empty halls of the dwelling; for in these illusive images of the brain, suffering was confined to her own bosom. But when stern reality usurped the place of fancy, and she saw her living daughter shivering in the wintry blasts or sinking beneath the fierce heats of the climate, cheerless in the desolation of female servitude, and suffering meekly the lot of physical weakness beneath a savage master, she endured that anguish which was gradually exhausting the springs of life.

Though the father was not altogether exempt from similar sorrow, it beset him less ceaselessly. He knew how to struggle with the workings of his mind as best became a man. Though strongly impressed with the belief that the captives had early been put beyond the reach of suffering, he had neglected no duty which tenderness to his sorrowing partner, parental love, or Christian duty, could require at his hands.

The Indians had retired on the crust of the snow, and with the thaw every footprint, or sign by which such wary foes might be traced, had vanished. It remained matter of doubt to what tribe or even to what nation the marauders belonged. The peace of the colony had not yet been openly broken, and the inroad had been rather a violent and fierce symptom of the evils that were contemplated, than the actual commencement of the ruthless hostilities which had since ravaged the frontier. But while policy had kept the colonists quiet, private affection omitted no rational means of effecting the restoration of the sufferers, in the event of their having been spared.

Scouts had passed among the conspiring and but half-peaceable tribes nearest to the settlement, and rewards and menaces had both been liberally used, in order to ascertain the character of the savages who had laid waste the valley, as well as the more interesting fortunes of their hapless victims. Every expedient to detect the truth had failed. The Narragansetts affirmed that their constant enemies, the Mohicans, acting with their customary treachery, had plundered their English friends, while the Mohicans vehemently threw back the imputation on the Narragansetts. At other times, some Indians affected to make dark allusions to the hostile feelings of fierce warriors, who, under the name of the Five Nations, were known to reside within the limits of the Dutch colony of New Netherlands, and to dwell upon the jealousy of the pale-faces who spoke a language different from that of the Yengeese. In short, inquiry had produced no result, and Content, when he did permit his fancy to represent his daughter as still living, was forced to admit to himself the probability that she might be buried far in the ocean of wilderness which then covered most of the surface of this continent.

Once, indeed, a rumor of an exciting nature had reached the family. An itinerant trader bound from the wilds of the interior to a mart on the sea-shore, had entered the valley. He brought with him a report that a child answering in some respects to the appearance which might now be supposed to belong to her who was lost was living among the savages, on the banks of the smaller lakes of the adjoining colony. The distance to this spot was great; the path led through a thousand dangers, and the result was far from certain. Yet it quickened hopes which had long been dormant. Ruth never urged any request that might involve serious hazard to her husband, and for many months the latter had even ceased to speak on the subject. Still, nature was working powerfully within him. His eyes, at all times reflecting and calm, grew more thoughtful; deeper lines of care gathered about his brow, and at length melancholy took possession of a countenance which was usually so placid.

It was at this precise period that Eben Dudley chose to urge the suit he had always pressed after his own desultory fashion on the decision of Faith. One of those well ordered accidents, which, from time to time, had brought the girl and the young borderer in private conversation, enabled him to effect his design with sufficient clearness. Faith heard him without betraying any of her ordinary waywardness, and answered with as little prevarication as the subject seemed to demand.

"This is well, Eben Dudley," she said, "and it is no more than an honest girl hath a right to hear from one who hath taken as many means as thou to get into her favor. But he who would have his life tormented by me, hath a solemn duty to do, ere I listen to his wishes."

"I have been in the lower towns and studied their manner of life, and I have been upon the scouts of the colony, to keep the Indians in their wigwams," returned the suitor, endeavoring to recount the feats of manliness that might reasonably be expected of one inclined to venture on so hazardous an experiment as matrimony. "The bargain with the young captain for the hill lot, and for a village homestead, is drawing near a close, and as the neighbors will not be backward at the stone-bee, or the raising, I see nothing to—"

"Thou deceivest thyself, observant Dudley," interrupted the girl, "if thou believest eye of thine can see that which is to be sought, ere one and the same fortune shall be the property of thee and me. Hast noted, Eben, the manner in which the cheek of the madam hath paled, and how her eye is getting sunken, since the time when the fur trader tarried with us, the week of the storm?"

"I cannot say that there is much change in the wearing of the madam within the bearing of my memory," answered Dudley, who was never remarkable for minute observations of this nature, however keen he might prove in subjects more intimately connected with his daily pursuits. "She is not young

and blooming as thou, Faith; nor is it often that we see—"

"I tell thee, man, that sorrow preyeth upon her form, and that she liveth but in the memory of the lost infant!"

"This is carrying mourning beyond the bounds of reason. The child is at peace, as is thy brother Whittal, beyond all manner of question. That we have not discovered their bones, is owing to the fire, which left but little to tell of—"

"Thy head is a charnel-house, dull Dudley; but this picture of its furniture shall not suffice for me. The man who is to be my husband, must have a feeling for a mother's sorrows!"

"What is now getting uppermost in thy mind, Faith? Is it for me to bring back the dead to life, or to place a child that hath been lost so many years, once more in the arms of its parents?"

"It is. Nay, open not thine eyes, as if light were first breaking into the darkness of a clouded brain! I repeat, it is!"

"I am glad that we have got to these open declarations; for too much of my life hath been already wasted in unsettled gallanting, when sound wisdom and the example of all around me have shown that in order to become the father of a family, and to be esteemed for a substantial settler, I should have both cleared and wived some years ago. I wish to deal justly by all, and having given thee reason to think that the day might come when we should live together, as is fitting to people of our condition, I felt it a duty to ask thee to share my chances; but now that thou dealest in impossibilities, it is needful to seek elsewhere."

"This hath ever been thy way when a good understanding hath been established between us. Thy mind is ever getting into some discontent, and then blame is heaped on one who rarely doth anything that should in reason offend thee. What madness maketh thee dream that I ask impossibilities? Surely, Dudley thou canst not have noticed the manner in which the nature of the madam is giving way before the consuming heat of her grief; thou canst not look into the sorrow of woman, or thou wouldst have listened with more kindness to a plan of traveling the woods for a short season, in order that it might be known whether she of whom the trader spoke is the lost one of our family, or the child of some stranger!"

Though Faith spoke with vexation, she also spoke with feeling. Her dark eye swam in tears, and the color of her brown cheek deepened, until her companion saw new reasons to forget his discontent in sympathies, which, however obtuse they might be, were never entirely dormant.

"If a journey of a few hundred miles be all thou askest, girl, why speak in parables?" he good-naturedly replied. "The kind word was not wanting to put me on such a trial. We will be married on the Sabbath, and, please Heaven, the Wednesday or the Saturday at most, shall see me on the path of the western trader."

"No delay. Thou must depart with the sun. The more active thou provest on the journey, the sooner wilt thou have the power to make me repent a foolish deed."

But Faith had been persuaded to relax a little from this severity. They were married on the Sabbath, and the following day Content and Dudley left the valley in quest of the distant tribe on which the scion of another stock was said to have been so violently engrafted.

It is needless to dwell on the dangers and privations of such an expedition. The Hudson, the Delaware, and the Susquehanna, rivers that were then better know in tales than to the inhabitants of New England, were all crossed; and after a painful and hazardous journey, the adventurers reached the first of that collection of small interior lakes whose banks are now so beautifully decorated with villages and farms. Here, in the bosom of savage tribes, and exposed to every danger of field and flood, supported only by his hopes, and by the presence of a stout companion that hardships or danger could not easily subdue, the father diligently sought his child.

At length a people was found who held a captive that answered the description of the trader. We shall not dwell on the feelings with which Content approached the village that contained this little descendant of a white race. He had not concealed his errand; and the sacred character in which he came, found pity and respect even among those barbarous tenants of the wilderness. A deputation of the chiefs received him in the skirts of their clearing. He was conducted to a wigwam where a council-fire was lighted, and an interpreter opened the subject by placing the amount of the ransom offered, and the professions of peace with which the strangers came, in the fairest light before his auditors. It is not usual for the American savage to loosen his hold easily on one naturalized in his tribe. But the meek air and noble confidence of Content touched the latent qualities of those generous though fierce children of the woods. The girl was sent for, that she might stand in the presence of the elders of the nation.

No language can paint the sensation with which Content first looked upon this adopted daughter of the savages. The years and sex were in accordance with his wishes; but in place of the golden hair and azure eyes of the cherub he had lost, there appeared a girl in whose jet-black tresses and equally dark organs of sight, he might better trace a descendant of the French of the Canadas, than one sprung from his own Saxon lineage. The father was not quick of mind in the ordinary occupations of life, but nature was now big within him. There needed no second glance to say how cruelly his hopes had been deceived. A smothered groan struggled from his chest, and then his self-command returned with the imposing grandeur of Christian resignation. He arose, and thanking the chiefs for their indulgence, he made no secret of the mistake by which he had been led so far on a fruitless errand. While speaking, the signs and gestures of Dudley gave him reason to believe that his companion had something of importance to communicate.

In a private interview, the latter suggested the expediency of concealing the truth, and of rescuing the child they had in fact discovered from the hands of her barbarous masters. It was now too late to practice a deception that might have availed for this object, had the stern principles of Content permitted the artifice. But transferring some portion of the interest which he felt for the fortunes of his own offspring to that of the unknown parent, who like himself most probably mourned the uncertain fate of the girl before him, he tendered the ransom intended for Ruth in behalf of the captive. It was rejected. Disappointed in both their objects, the adventurers were obliged to quit the village with weary feet and still heavier hearts.

If any who read these pages have ever felt the agony of suspense in a matter involving the best of human affections, they will know how to appreciate the sufferings of the mother during the month that her husband was absent on this holy errand. At times hope brightened around her heart, until the glow of pleasure was again mantling on her cheek and playing in her eye. The first week of the adventure was one almost of happiness. The hazards of the journey were nearly forgotten in its anticipated results, and though occasional apprehensions quickened the pulses of one whose system answered so fearfully to the movements of the spirit, there was a predominance of hope in all her anticipations.

She again passed among her maidens with a mien in which joy was struggling with the meekness of subdued habits, and her smiles once more began to beam with renovated happiness. To his dying day old Mark Heathcote never forgot the sudden sensation that was created by the soft laugh that on some unexpected occasion came to his ear from the lips of his son's wife. Though years had elapsed between the moment when that unwonted sound was heard, and the time at which the action of the tale now stands, he never heard it repeated. To heighten the feelings which were now uppermost in the mind of Ruth, when within a day's march of the village to which he was going, Content had found the means to send the tidings of his prospects of success. It was over all these renewed wishes that disappointment was to throw its chill, and it was affections thus riveted that were to be again blighted by the cruelest of all withering influences —that of hope defeated.

It was near the hour of the setting of the sun when Content and Dudley reached the deserted clearing on their return to the valley. Their path led through this opening on the mountain-side, and there was one point among the bushes from which the buildings had already arisen from the ashes of the burning might be distinctly seen. Until now, the husband and father had believed himself equal to any effort that duty might require in the progress of this mournful service. But here he paused, and communicated a wish to his companion that he would go ahead and break the nature of the deception that led them so far on a fruitless mission. Perhaps Content was himself ignorant of all he wished, or to what unskillful hands he had confided a commission of more than ordinary delicacy. He merely felt his own inability, and with a weakness that may find some apology in his feelings, he saw his companion depart without instructions or indeed without any other guide than nature.

Though Faith had betrayed no marked uneasiness during the absence of the travelers, her quick eye was the first to discover the form of her husband, as he came with a tired step across the fields, in the direction of the dwellings. Long ere Dudley reached the house, every one of its inmates had assembled on the piazza. This was no meeting of turbulent delight or of clamorous greetings. The adventurer drew near amid a silence so oppressive, that it utterly disconcerted a studied project, by which he had hoped to announce his tidings in a manner suited to the occasion. His hand was on the gate of the little court, and still none spoke; his foot was on the low step, and yet no voice bade him welcome. The looks of the little group were rather fixed on the features of Ruth than on the person of him who approached. Her face was pallid as death, her eye contracted, but filled with the mental effort that sustained her, and her lip scarce trembled, as in obedience to a feeling still stronger than the one which had so long oppressed her, she exclaimed—

"Eben Dudley, where hast thou left my husband?"

"The young captain was foot-weary, and he tarried in the second growth of the hill; but so brave a walker cannot be far behind. We shall see him soon, at the opening by the dead beech; and it is there that I recommend the madan—"

"It was thoughtful in Heathcote, and like his usual kindness, to devise this well-meant caution," said Ruth, across whose countenance a smile so radiant passed, that it imparted the expression which is believed to characterize the peculiar benignancy of angels. "Still it was unnecessary; for he should have known that we place our strength on the Rock of Ages. Tell me, in what manner hath my precious one borne the exceeding weariness of thy tangled route?"

The wandering glance of the messenger had gone from face to face, until it became fastened on the countenance of his own wife, in a settled, unmeaning gaze.

"Nay, Faith hath demeaned well, both as my assistant and as thy partner, and thou mayest see that her comeliness is in no degree changed. And did the babe falter in this weary passage, or did she retard thy movements by her fretfulness? But I know thy nature, man; she hath been borne over many long miles of mountain-side and treacherous swamp in thine own vigorous arms. Thou answerest not, Dudley!" exclaimed Ruth, taking the alarm, and laying a hand firmly on the shoulder of him she questioned, as forcing his half-averted face to meet her eye, she seemed to read his soul.

The muscles of the sunburnt and strong features of the borderer worked involuntarily, his broad chest swelled to its utmost expansion, big burning drops rolled out upon his brown cheeks, and then taking the arm of Ruth in one of his own powerful hands, he compelled her to release her hold, with a firm but respectful exercise of his strength ; and thrusting the form of his own wife without ceremony aside, he passed through the circle, and entered the dwelling with the tread of a giant.

The head of Ruth dropped upon her bosom, the paleness again came over her cheeks, and it was then that the inward look of the eye might first be seen, which afterward became so constant and so painful an expression in her countenance. From that hour to the time in which the family of the Wish-Ton-Wish is again brought immediately before the reader, no further rumors were ever heard, to lessen or increase the wasting regrets of her bosom.

CHAPTER XX.

"Sir, he hath never fed of the dainties that are bred in a book; he hath not eaten paper, as it were; he hath not drunk ink: his intellect is not replenished; he is only an animal—only sensible in the duller parts."—LOVE'S LABOR'S LOST.

"HERE cometh Faith, to bring us tidings of the hamlet," said the husband of the woman whose character we have so feebly sketched, as he took his seat in the piazza, at the early hour and in the group already mentioned. "The ensign hath been abroad on the hills throughout the night, with a chosen party of our people; and perchance she hath been sent with the substance that they have gathered concerning the unknown trail."

"The heavy-footed Dudley hath scarce mounted to the dividing ridge, where report goeth the prints of moccasins were seen," observed a young man, who in his person bore all the evidences of an active and healthful manhood. "Of what service is the scouting that faileth of the necessary distance by the weariness of its leader?"

"If thou believest, boy, that thy young foot is equal to contend with the sinews of Eben Dudley, there may be occasion to show the magnitude of thy error, ere the danger of this Indian out-breaking shall pass away. Thou art too stubborn of will, Mark, to be yet trusted with the leading of parties that may hold the safety of all who dwell in the Wish-Ton-Wish within their keeping."

The young man looked displeased; but, fearful that his father might observe and misinterpret his humor into a personal disrespect, he turned away, permitting his frowning eye to rest for an instant on the timid and stolen glance of a maiden, whose cheek was glowing like the eastern sky, as she busied herself with the preparations of the table.

"What welcome news dost bring from the sign of the Whip-Poor-Will?" Content asked of the woman who had now come within the little gate of his court.

"Hast seen the ensign since the party took the hill-paths, or is it some traveler who hath charged thee with matter for our ears?"

"Eye of man hath not seen the man since he girded himself with the sword of office," returned Faith, entering the piazza and nodding salutation to those around her; "and as for strangers, when the clock shall strike noon, it will be one month to the day that the last of them was housed within my doors. But I complain not of the want of custom, as the ensign would never quit the bar, and his gossip to go into the mountain lots, so long as there was one to fill his ears with the marvels of the old countries, or even to discourse of the home-stirrings of the colonies themselves."

"Thou speakest lightly, Faith, of one who merits thy respect and thy duty."

The eye of the former studied the meek countenance of her from whom this reproof came, with an intenseness and a melancholy that showed her thoughts were on other matters, and then, as if suddenly recalled to what had passed, she resumed—

"Truly, what with duty to the man as a husband, and respect to him as an officer of the colony, Madam Heathcote, the task is not one of easy bearing. If the king's representative had given the colors to my brother Reuben, and left the Dudley with the halberd in his hand, the preferment would have been ample for one of his qualities, and all the better for the credit of the settlement."

"The governor distributed his favor according to the advice of men competent to distinguish merit," said Content. "Eben was foremost in the bloody affair among the people of the plantations, where his manhood was of good example to all in company. Should he continue as faithful and as valiant, thou mayest yet live to see thyself the consort of a captain!"

"Not for glory gained in this night's marching; for yonder cometh the man with a sound body, and seemingly with the stomach of a Cæsar—ay, and I'll answer for it, of a regiment, too! It is no trifle that will satisfy his appetite, after one of these—ha! Pray Heaven the fellow be not harmed. Truly, he hath our neighbor Ergot in attendance."

"There is other than he too; for one cometh in the rear whose gait and air are unknown to me. The trail hath been struck, and Dudley leadeth a captive! A savage in his paint and cloak of skin is taken."

This assertion caused all to rise—for the excitement of an apprehended inroad was still strong in the minds of those secluded people. Not a syllable more was uttered until the scout and his companion were before them.

The quick glance of Faith had scanned the person of her husband, and, resuming her spirits with the certainty that he was unharmed, she was the first to greet him with words :

"How now, Ensign Dudley ?" said the woman, quite possibly vexed that she had unguardedly betrayed a greater interest in his welfare than she might always deem prudent. "How now, ensign—hath the campaign ended with no better trophy than this ?"

"The fellow is not a chief, nor, by his step and dull look, even a warrior; but he was, nevertheless, a lurker nigh the settlements, and it was thought prudent to bring him in," returned the husband, addressing himself to Content, while he answered the salutation of his wife with a sufficiently brief nod. "My own scouting hath brought nothing to light; but my brother Ring hath fallen on the trail of him that is here present, and it is not a little that we are puzzled in probing, as the good Doctor Ergot calleth it, into the meaning of his errand."

"Of what tribe may the savage be ?"

"There hath been discussion among us on that matter," returned Dudley, with an oblique glance of the eye toward the physician. "Some have said he is a Narragansett, while others think he cometh of a stock still further east."

"In giving that opinion, I spoke merely of his secondary or acquired habits,' interrupted Ergot ; "for, having reference to his original, the man is assuredly a white."

"A white !" repeated all around him.

"Beyond a cavil, as may be seen by divers particulars in his outward conformation, viz., in the shape of the head, the muscles of the arms and of the legs, the air and gait, besides sundry other signs, that are familar to men who have made the physical peculiarities of the two races their study."

"One of which is this !" continued Dudley, throwing up the robe of the captive, and giving his companions the ocular evidence which had so satisfactorily removed all his own doubts. "Though the color of the skin may not be proof positive, like that named by our neighbor Ergot, it is still something in helping a man of little learning to make up an opinion in such a matter."

"Madam !" exclaimed Faith so suddenly as to cause her she addressed to start, "for the sake of Heaven's mercy !

let thy maidens bring soap and water, that the face of this man may be cleansed of its paint."

"What foolishness is thy brain set upon ?" rejoined the ensign, who had latterly affected some of that superior gravity which might be supposed to belong to his official station. "We are not now under the roof of the Whip-Poor-Will, wife of mine, but in the presence of those who need none of thy suggestions to give proper forms to an examination of office."

Faith heeded no reproof. Instead of waiting for others to perform that which she had desired, she applied herself to the task, with a dexterity that had been acquired by long practice, and a zeal that seemed awakened by some extraordinary emotion. In a minute the colors had disappeared from the features of the captive, and, though deeply tanned by exposure to an American sun and to sultry winds, his face was unequivocally that of one who owed his origin to a European ancestry. The movements of the eager woman were watched with curious interest by all present, and when the short task was ended, a murmur of surprise broke simultaneously from every lip.

"There is meaning in this masquerade," observed Content, who had long and intently studied the dull and ungainly countenance that was exposed to his scrutiny by the operation. "I have heard of Christian men who have sold themselves to gain, and who, forgetting religion and the love of their race, have been known to league with the savage in order to pursue rapine in the settlements. This wretch hath the subtlety of one of the French of the Canadas in his eyes."

"Away ! away !" cried Faith, forcing herself in front of the speaker, and, by placing her two hands on the shaven crown of the prisoner, forming a sort of shade to his features. "Away with all folly about the Frenchers and wicked leagues ! This is no plotting miscreant, but a stricken innocent ! Whittal—my brother Whittal, dost know me ?"

The tears rolled down the cheeks of the wayward woman as she gazed into the face of her witless relative, whose eye lighted with one of its occasional gleamings of intelligence, and who indulged in a low, vacant laugh, ere he answered her earnest interrogatory.

"Some speak like men from over sea," he said, "and some speak like men of the woods. Is there such a thing as bear's meat or a mouthful of hominy in the wigwam ?"

Had the voice of one long known to be in the grave, broken on the ears of the family, it would scarcely have produced a deeper sensation, or have quickened the blood more violently about their hearts, than this sudden and utterly unexpected discovery of the character of their captive. Wonder and awe held them mute for a time, and then Ruth was seen standing before the restored wanderer, her hands clasped in the attitude of petition, her eye contracted and imploring, and her whole person expressive of the suspense and excitement which had roused her long latent emotions to agony.

"Tell me," said a thrilling voice that might have quickened the intellect of one even duller than the man addressed, "as thou hast pity in thy heart, tell me if my babe yet live?"

"'Tis a good babe," returned the other, and then laughing again in his own vacant and unmeaning manner, he bent his eyes with a species of stupid wonder on Faith, in whose appearance there was far less change than in the speaking but wasted countenance of her who stood immediately before him.

"Give leave, dearest madam," interposed the sister; "I know the nature of the boy, and could ever do more with him than any other."

But this request was useless. The system of the mother, in its present state of excitement, was unequal to further effort. Sinking into the watchful arms of Content, she was borne away, and, for a minute, the anxious interest of the handmaidens left none but the men on the piazza.

"Whittal—my old playfellow, Whittal Ring," said the son of Content, advancing with a humid eye to take the hand of the prisoner. "Hast forgotten, man, the companion of thy early days? It is young Mark Heathcote that speaks."

The other looked up into his countenance, for a moment, with a reviving recollection; but shaking his head, he drew back in marked displeasure, muttering loud enough to be heard—

"What a fasle liar is a pale-face! Here is one of the tall rogues wishing to pass for a loping boy!"

What more he uttered his auditors never knew, for he instantly changed his language to some dialect of an Indian tribe.

"The mind of the unhappy youth hath even been more blunted by exposure and the usages of a savage life, than by nature," said Content, who with most of the others had been recalled, by his interest in the examination, to the scene they had momentarily quitted. "Let the sister deal tenderly with the lad, and, in Heaven's time, shall we learn the truth."

The deep feeling of the father clothed his words with authority. The eager group gave place, and something like the solemnity of an official examination succeeded to the irregular and hurried interrogatories which had first broken on the dull intellect of the recovered wanderer.

The dependents took their stations in a circle around the chair of the Puritan, by whose side was placed Content, while Faith induced her brother to be seated on the step of the piazza, in a manner that all might hear. The attention of the brother himself was drawn from the formality of the arrangement by placing food in his hands.

"And now, Whittal, I would know," commenced the ready woman, when a deep silence denoted the attention of the auditors, "I would know if thou rememberest the day I clad thee in garments of boughten cloth from over sea; and how fond thou wast of being seen among the kine in colors so gay?"

The young man looked up in her face as if the tones of her voice gave him pleasure; but, instead of making any reply, he preferred to munch the bread with which she had endeavored to lure him back to their ancient confidence.

"Surely, boy, thou canst not so soon have forgotten the gift I bought, with the hard earnings of a wheel that turned at night. The tail of yon peacock is not finer than thou then wast—but I will make thee such another garment, that thou mayest go with the trainers to their weekly musters."

The youth dropped the robe of skin that covered the upper part of his body, and making a forward gesture, with the gravity of an Indian, he answered—

"Whittal is a warrior on his path; he has no time for the talk of the women!"

"Now, brother, thou forgettest the manner in which I was wont to feed thy hunger, as the frost pinched thee, in the cold mornings, and at the hour when the kine needed thy care; else thou wouldst not call me woman."

"Hast ever been on the trail of a Pequot? Knowst how to whoop among the men?"

"What is an Indian whoop to the bleating of the flocks, or the bellowing of cattle in the bushes! Thou rememberest the sound of the bells, as they tinkled among the second growth of an evening?"

The former herdsman turned his head, and seemed to lend his attention, as a dog listens to an approaching footstep. But the gleam of recollection was quickly lost. In the next moment, he yielded to the more positive, and possibly more urgent, demands of his appetite.

"Then hast thou lost the use of ears; else thou wouldst not say that thou forgettest the sound of the bells."

"Didst ever hear a wolf howl?" exclaimed the other. "That's a sound for a hunter! I saw the great chief strike the striped panther, when the boldest warrior of the tribe grew white as a craven pale-face at his leaps!"

"Talk not to me of your ravenous beasts and great chiefs, but rather let us think of the days when we were young, and when thou hadst delight in the sports of a Christian childhood. Hast forgotten, Whittal, how our mother used to give us leave to pass the idle time in games among the snow?"

"Nipset hath a mother in her wigwam, but he asketh no leave to go on the hunt. He is a man; the next snow, he will be a warrior."

"Silly boy! This is some treachery of the savage, by which he has bound thy weakness with the fetters of his craftiness. Thy mother, Whittal, was a woman of Christian belief, and one of a white race; and a kind and mourning mother was she over thy feeble-mindedness! Dost thou remember, unthankful of heart! how she nursed thy sickly hours in boyhood, and how she administered to all thy bodily wants? Who was it that fed thee when a-hungered, or who had compassion on thy waywardness, when others tired of thy idle deeds, or grew impatient at thy weakness?"

The brother looked, for an instant, at the flushed features of the speaker, as if glimmerings of some faintly distinguished scenes crossed the visions of his mind; but the animal still predominated, and he continued to feed his hunger.

"This exceedeth human endurance!" exclaimed the excited Faith. "Look into this eye, weak one, and say if thou knowest her who supplied the place of that mother whom thou refusest to remember —she who hath toiled for thy comfort, and who hath never refused to listen to all thy plaints, and to soften all thy sufferings. Look at this eye, and speak—dost know me?"

"Certain!" returned the other, laughing with a half intelligent expression of recognition; "'tis a woman of the pale-faces, and I warrant me, one that will never be satisfied till she hath all the furs of the Americas on her back, and all the venison of the woods in her kitchen. Didst ever hear the tradition, how that wicked race got into the hunting-grounds and robbed the warriors of the country?"

The disappointment of Faith had made her too impatient to lend a pleased attention to this tale; but, at that moment, a form appeared at her side, and by a quiet gesture directed her to humor the temper of the wanderer.

It was Ruth, in whose pale cheek and anxious eye all the intenseness of a mother's longings might be traced in its most touching aspect. Though so lately helpless and sinking beneath her emotions, the sacred feelings which now sustained her seemed to supply the place of all other aid; and as she glided past the listening circle, even Content himself had not believed it necessary to offer succor or to interpose with remonstrance. Her quiet, meaning gesture seemed to say, "proceed, and show all the indulgence to the weakness of the young man." The rising discontent of Faith was checked by habitual reverence, and she prepared to obey.

"And what say the silly traditions of which you speak?" she added, ere the current of his dull ideas had time to change its direction.

"'Tis spoken by the old men in the villages, and what is there said is gospel-true. You see all around you land that is covered with hill and valley, and which once bore wood, without the fear of the ax, and over which game was spread with a bountiful hand. There are runners and hunters in our tribe, who have been on a straight path toward the setting sun, until their legs were weary and their eyes could not see the clouds that hang over the salt lake, and yet they say, 'tis everywhere beautiful as yonder green mountain. Tall trees and shady woods, rivers and lakes filled with fish, and deer and beaver plentiful as the sands on the sea-shore. All this land and water the Great Spirit gave to men of red-skins; for them he loved, since they spoke truth in their tribes, were true to their friends, hated their enemies, and knew how to take scalps.

"Now, a thousand snows had come and melted, since this gift was made," continued Whittal, who spoke with the air of one charged with the narration of a grave tradition, though he probably did no more than relate what many repetitions had rendered familiar to his inactive mind, "and yet none but redskins were seen to hunt the moose, or to go on the war-path. Then the Great Spirit grew angry; he hid his face from his children, because they quarreled among themselves. Big canoes came out of the rising sun, and brought a hungry and wicked people into the land. At first, the strangers spoke soft and complaining like women. They begged room for a few wigwams, and said if the warriors would give them ground to plant they would ask their God to look upon the red men. But when they grew strong they forgot their words and made liars of themselves. Oh, they are wicked knaves! A pale-face is a panther. When a-hungered, you can hear him whining in the bushes like a strayed infant; but when you come within his leap beware of tooth and claw."

"This evil-minded race, then, robbed the red warriors of their land?"

"Certain! They spoke like sick women till they grew strong, and then they out-deviled the Pequods themselves in wickedness; feeding the warriors with their burning milk, and slaying with blazing inventions, that they made out of the yellow meal."

"And the Pequods! was their great warrior dead before the coming of the men from over sea?"

"You are a woman that has never heard a tradition, or you would know better! A Pequod is a weak and crawling cub."

"And thou—thou art, then, a Narragansett?"

"Don't I look like a man?"

"I had mistaken thee for one of our nearer neighbors, the Mohegan Pequods."

"The Mohicans are basket makers for the Yengeese; but the Narragansett goes leaping through the woods like a wolf on the trail of the deer!"

"All this is quite in reason, and now thou pointest to its justice, I cannot fail but see it. But we have curiosity to know more of the great tribe. Hast ever heard of one of thy people, Whittal, known as Miantonimoh—'tis a chief of some renown?"

The witless youth had continued to eat at intervals, but, on hearing this question, he seemed suddenly to forget his appetite. For a moment he looked down, and then he answered slowly and not without solemnity—

"A man cannot live forever."

"What!" said Faith, motioning to her deeply-interested auditors to restrain their impatience, "has he quitted his people? And thou lived with him, Whittal, ere he came to his end?"

"He never looked on Nipset, or Nipset on him."

"I know naught of this Nipset; tell me of the great Miantonimoh."

"Dost need to hear twice? The sachem is gone to the far land, and Nipset will be a warrior when the next snow comes?"

Disappointment threw a cloud on every countenance, and the beam of hope, which had been kindled in the eye of Ruth, changed to the former painful expression of deep inward suffering. But Faith still managed to repress all speech among those who listened, continuing the examination, after a short delay that her vexation rendered unavoidable.

"I had thought that Miantonimoh was still a warrior in his tribe," she said. "In what battle did he fall?"

"Mohican Uncas did that wicked deed. The pale-men gave him great riches to murder the sachem."

"Thou speakest of the father; but there was another Miantonimoh; he who in boyhood dwelt among the people of white blood."

Whittal listened attentively, and after seeming to rally his thoughts, he shook his head, saying before he again began to eat—

"There never was but one of the name, and there never will be another. Two eagles do not build their nests in the same tree."

"Thou sayest truly," continued Faith; well knowing that to dispute the information of her brother was, in effect, to close his mouth. "Now tell me of Conanchet, the present Narragansett sachem — he who hath leagued with Metacom, and hath of late been driven from his fastness near the sea—doth he yet live?"

The expression of the brother's countenance underwent another change. In place of the childish importance with which he had hitherto replied to the questions of his sister, a look of overreaching cunning gathered about his dull eye. The organ glanced slowly and cautiously around him, as if its owner expected to detect some visible sign of those covert intentions he so evidently distrusted. Instead of answering, the wanderer continued his meal, though less like one who had need of sustenance, than one resolved to make no communications which might prove dangerous. This change was not unobserved by Faith, nor by any of those who so intently watched the means by which she had been endeavoring to thread the confused ideas of one so dull, and yet who at need seemed so practiced in savage artifice. She prudently altered her manner of interrogating by endeavoring to lead his thoughts to other matters.

"I warrant me," continued the sister, "that thou now beginnest to call to mind the times when thou led'st the cattle among the bushes, and how thou wert wont to call on Faith to give thee food, when a-weary with threading the woods in quest of the kine. Hast ever been assailed by the Narragansetts thyself, Whittal, when dwelling in the house of a pale-face?"

The brother ceased eating. Again he appeared to muse, as intently as was possible for one of his circumscribed intellects. But shaking his head in the negative, he silently resumed the grateful office of mastication.

"What! hast come to be a warrior, and never known a scalp taken, or seen a fire lighted in the roof of a wigwam?"

Whittal laid down the food, and turned to his sister. His face was teeming with a wild and fierce meaning, and he indulged in a low but triumphant laugh. When this exhibition of satisfaction was over, he consented to reply.

"Certain," he said. "We went on a path in the night, against the lying Yengeese, and no burning of the woods ever scorched the 'arth as we blackened their fields! All their proud housen were turned into piles of coals."

"And where and when did you this act of brave vengeance?"

"They called the place after the bird of night; as if an Indian name could save them from an Indian massacre!"

"Ha! 'Tis of the Wish-Ton-Wish thou speakest! But thou wast a sufferer, and not an actor, brother, in that heartless burning."

"Thou liest like a wicked woman of the pale-faces, as thou art! Nipset was only a boy on that path, but he went with his people. I tell thee we singed the very 'arth with our brands, and not a head of them all ever rose again from the ashes."

Notwithstanding her great self-command, and the object that was constantly before the mind of Faith, she shuddered at the fierce pleasure with which her brother pronounced the extent of the vengeance that in his imaginary character he believed he had taken on his enemies. Still, cautious not to destroy an illusion which might aid her in the so long-defeated and so anxiously-desired discovery, the woman repressed her horror, and continued—

"True—yet some were spared; surely the warriors carried prisoners back to their village. Thou didst not slay all?"

"All."

"Nay; thou speakest now of the miserables who were wrapped in the blazing block; but—but some without might have fallen into thy hands, ere the assailed sought shelter in the tower. Surely, surely thou didst not kill all?"

The hard breathing of Ruth caught the ear of Whittal, and for a moment he turned to regard her countenance in dull wonder. But again shaking his head, he answered, in a low, positive tone—

"All;—ay, to the screeching women and crying babes!"

"Surely, there is a child,—I would say there is a woman in the tribe of fairer skin and of form different from most of thy people. Was not such a one led a captive from the burning of the Wish-Ton-Wish?"

"Dost think the deer will live with the wolf, or hast ever found the cowardly pigeon in the nest of the hawk?"

"Nay, thou art of different color thyself, Whittal, and it well may be thou art not alone."

The youth regarded his sister a moment with marked displeasure, and then on turning to eat he muttered—

"There is as much fire in snow as truth in a lying Yengeese!"

"This examination must close," said Content, with a heavy sigh; "at another hour we may hope to push the matter to some more fortunate result; but yonder cometh one charged with especial service from the towns below, as would seem by the fact that he disregardeth the holiness of the day, no less than by the earnest manner in which he is journeying."

As the individual named was visible to all who chose to look in the direction of the hamlet, his sudden appearance caused a general interruption to the interest which had been so strongly awakened on a subject that was familiar to every resident in the valley.

The early hour, the gait at which the stranger urged his horse, the manner in which he passed the open and inviting door of the Whip-Poor-Will, proclaimed him a messenger, who probably bore some communication of importance from the government of the colony to the younger Heathcote, who filled the highest station of official authority in that distant settlement. Observations to this purport had passed from mouth to mouth, and curiosity was actively alive by the time the horseman rode into the court. There he dismounted, and covered with the dust of the road he presented himself, with the air of one who had passed the night in the saddle, before the man he sought.

"I have orders for Captain Content Heathcote," said the messenger, saluting all around him with the usual grave but studied courtesy of the people to whom he belonged.

"He is here to receive and to obey," was the answer.

The traveler wore a little of that mysteriousness that is so grateful to certain minds, which, from inability to command respect in any other manner, are fond of making secrets of matters that might as well be revealed. In obedience to this feeling he expressed a desire that his communications might be made apart. Content quietly motioned for him to follow, leading the way into an inner apartment of the house. As a new direction was given by this interruption to the thoughts of the spectators of the foregoing scene, we shall also take the opportunity to digress, in order to lay before the reader some general facts that may be necessary to the connection of the subsequent parts of the legend.

CHAPTER XXI.

" Be careful what you do, sir ; lest your justice
Prove violence."—WINTER'S TALE.

THE designs of the celebrated Metacom had been betrayed to the colonists by the treachery of a subordinate warrior, named Sausaman. The punishment of this treason led to inquiries which terminated in accusations against the great sachem of the Wampanoags. Scorning to vindicate himself before enemies that he hated, and perhaps distrusting their clemency, Metacom no longer endeavored to cloak his proceedings, but throwing aside the emblems of peace, he openly appeared with an armed hand.

The tragedy had commenced about a year before the period at which the tale has now arrived. A scene not unlike that detailed in the foregoing pages took place; the brand, the knife, and the tomahawk doing their work of destruction, without pity and without remorse. But unlike the inroad of the Wish-Ton-Wish, this expedition was immediately followed by others, until the whole of New England was engaged in the celebrated war, to which we have before referred.

The entire white population of the colonies of New England had shortly before been estimated at one hundred and twenty thousand souls. Of this number it was thought that sixteen thousand men were capable of bearing arms. Had time been given for the maturity of the plans of Metacom, he might have readily assembled bands of warriors, who, aided by their familiarity with the woods, and accustomed to the privations of such a warfare, would have threatened serious danger to the growing strength of the whites. But the ordinary and selfish feelings of man were as active among these wild tribes as they are known to be in more artificial communities. The indefatigable Metacom, like that Indian hero of our own times, Tecumthè, had passed years in endeavoring to appease ancient enmities and to lull jealousies, in order that all of red blood might unite in crushing a foe that promised, should he be longer undisturbed in his march to power, soon to be too formidable for their united efforts to subdue.

The premature explosion in some measure averted the danger. It gave the English time to strike several severe blows against the tribe of their great enemy, before his allies had determined to make common cause of his design. The summer and autumn of 1675 had been passed in active hostilities between the English and Wampanoags, without openly drawing any other nation into the contest. Some of the Pequods, with their dependent tribes, even took sides with the whites; and we read of the Mohicans being actively employed in harassing the sachem on his well-known retreat from that neck of land, where he had been hemmed in by the English, with the expectation that he might be starved into submission.

The warfare of the first summer was, as might be expected, attended by various degrees of success, fortune quite as often favoring the red men, in their desultory attempts at annoyance, as their more disciplined enemies. Instead of confining his operations to his own circumscribed and easily environed districts, Metacom had led his warriors to the distant settlements on the Connecticut ; and it was during the operations of this season that several of the towns on that river were first assailed and laid in ashes. Active hostilities had in some measure ceased between the Wampanoags and the English, with the cold weather, most of the troops retiring to their homes, while the Indians apparently paused to take breath for their final effort.

It was, however, previously to this cessation of activity, that the commissioners of the united colonies, as they were called, met to devise the means of a concerted resistance. Unlike their former dangers from the same quarter, it was manifest by the manner in which a hostile feeling was spreading around their whole frontier that a leading spirit had given as much of unity and design to the movements of the foe as could probably ever be created among a people so separated by distance and so divided in communities. Right or wrong, the colonists gravely decided that the war on their part was just. Great preparations were therefore made to carry it on the ensuing summer, in a manner more suited to their means, and to the absolute necessities of their situation. It was in consequence of the arrangements made for bringing a portion of the inhabitants of the Colony of Connecticut into the field that we find the principal characters of our legend in the warlike guise in which they have just been re-introduced to the reader.

Although the Narragansetts had not at first been openly implicated in the attacks on the colonists, facts soon came to the knowledge of the latter, which left no doubt of the state of feeling in that nation. Many of their young men were discovered among the followers of Metacom, and arms taken from whites who had been slain in the different encounters were also seen in their villages. One of the first measures of the commissioners, therefore, was to anticipate more serious opposition, by directing an overwhelming force against this people. The party collected on that occasion was probably the largest military body which the English at that early day had ever assembled in their colonies. It consisted of a thousand men, of whom no inconsiderable number was cavalry—a species of troops that, as all subsequent experience has shown, is admirably adapted to operations against so active and so subtle a foe.

The attack was made in the depth of winter, and it proved fearfully destructive to the assailed. The defense of Conanchet, the young sachem of the Narragansetts, was every way worthy of his high character for courage and mental resources, nor was the victory gained without serious loss to the colonists. The native chief had collected his warriors, and taken post on a small area of firm land that was situated in the center of a densely wooded swamp; and the preparations for resistance betrayed a singular familiarity with the military expedients of a white man. There had been a palisadoed breast-work, a species of redoubt, and a regular block-house to overcome, ere the colonists could penetrate into the fortified village itself. The first attempts were unsuccessful, the Indians having repulsed their enemies with loss. But better arms and greater concert finally prevailed, though not without a struggle that lasted for many hours, and not until the defendants were, in truth, nearly surrounded.

The events of that memorable day made a deep impression on the minds of men who were rarely excited by any incidents of a great and moving character. It was still the subject of earnest, and not unfrequently of melancholy discourse, around the firesides of the colonists; nor was the victory achieved without accompaniments, which, however unavoidable they might have been, had a tendency to raise doubts in the minds of conscientious religionists, concerning the lawfulness of their cause. It is said that a village of six hundred cabins was burnt, and that hundreds of dead and wounded were consumed in the conflagration. A thousand warriors were thought to have lost their lives in this affair, and it was believed that the power of the nation was broken forever. The sufferers among the colonists themselves were numerous, and mourning came into a vast many families, with the tidings of victory.

In this expedition most of the men of the Wish-Ton-Wish had been conspicuous actors, under the orders of Content. They had not escaped with impunity; but it was confidently hoped that their courage was to meet its reward in a long continuance of peace, which was the more desirable on account of their remote and exposed situation.

In the meantime the Narragansetts were far from being subdued. Throughout the whole continuance of the inclement season they had caused alarms on the frontiers; and in one or two instances their renowned sachem had taken signal vengeance for the dire affair in which his people had so heavily suffered. As the spring advanced the inroads became still more frequent, and the appearances of danger so far increased as to require a new call on the colonists to arm. The messenger introduced in the last chapter was charged with matter that had a reference to the events of this war; and it was with an especial communication of great urgency that he had now demanded his secret audience with the leader of the military force of the valley.

"Thou hast affairs of moment to deal with, Captain Heathcote," said the hard-riding traveler, when he found himself alone with Content. "The orders of his honor are to spare neither whip nor spur, until the chief men of the borders shall be warned of the actual situation of the colony."

"Hath aught of moving interest occurred that his honor deemeth there is necessity for unusual watchfulness? We had hoped that the prayers of the pious were not in vain; and that a time of quiet was about to succeed to that violence, of which, bounden by our social covenants, we have unhappily been unwilling spectators. The bloody assault of Pettyquamscott hath exercised our minds severely—nay, it hath even raised doubts of the lawfulness of some of our deeds."

"Thou hast a commendable spirit of forgiveness, Captain Heathcote, or thy memory would extend to other scenes than those which bear relation to the punishment of an enemy so remorseless. It is said on the river, that the valley of Wish-Ton-Wish hath been visited by the savage in its day, and men speak freely of the wrongs suffered by its owners on that pitiless occasion."

"The truth may not be denied, even that good should come thereof. It is certain that much suffering was inflicted on me and on mine, by the inroad of which you speak; nevertheless we have ever striven to consider it as a merciful chastisement inflicted for manifold sins, rather than as a subject that might be remembered, in order to stimulate passions that, in all reason as in all charity, should slumber as much as a weak nature will allow."

"This is well, Captain Heathcote, and in exceeding conformity with the most received doctrines," returned the stranger, slightly gaping, either for want of rest the previous night, or from disinclination to so grave a subject; "but it hath little connection with present duties. My charge beareth especial concern with the further destruction of the Indians, rather than to any inward searchings into the condition of our own mental misgivings, concerning any right it may be thought proper to question, that hath a reference to the duty of self-pretection. There is no unworthy dweller in the Connecticut Colony, sir, that hath endeavored more to cultivate a tender conscience than the wretched sinner who standeth before you; for I have the exceeding happiness to sit under the outpourings of a spirit that hath few mortal superiors in the matter of precious gifts. I now speak of Dr. Calvin Pope; a most worthy and soul-quieting divine; one who spareth not the goad when the conscience needeth pricking, nor hesitateth to dispense consolation to him who seeth his fallen estate; and one that never faileth to deal with charity, and humbleness of spirit, and forbearance with the failings of friends, and forgiveness of enemies, as the chiefest signs of a renovated moral existence; and therefore, there can be but little reason to distrust the spiritual rightfulness of all that listen to the riches of his discourse. But when it cometh to be question of life or death, a matter of dominion and possession of these fair lands, that the Lord hath given—why, sir, then I say that, like the Israelites dealing with the sinful occupants of Canaan, it behooveth us to be true to each other, and to look upon the heathen with a distrustful eye."

"There may be reason in that thou utterest," observed Content, sorrowfully. "Still it is lawful to mourn even the necessity which conduceth to all this strife. I had hoped that they who direct the councils of the colony might have resorted to less violent means of persuasion, to lead the savage back to reason, than that which cometh from the armed hand. Of what nature is thy special errand?"

"Of deep urgency, sir, as will be seen in the narration," returned the other, dropping his voice like one habitually given to the dramatic part of diplomacy, however unskillful he might have been in its more intellectual accomplishments. "Thou wast in the Pettyquamscott scourging, and need not be reminded of the manner in which the Lord dealt with our enemies on that favor-dispensing day; but it may not be known to one so remote from the stirring and daily transactions of Christendom, in what manner the savage hath taken the chastisement. The restless and still unconquered Conanchet hath deserted his towns and taken refuge in the open woods; where it exceedeth the skill and usage of our civilized men of war to discover, at all times, the position and force of their enemies. The consequences may be easily conjectured. The savage hath broken in upon, and laid waste, in whole or in part, firstly—Lancaster, on the tenth," counting on his fingers, "when many were led into captivity; secondly, Marlborough, on the twentieth; on the thirteenth ultimo, Groton; Warwick, on the seventeenth; and Rehoboth, Chelmsford, Andover, Weymouth, and divers other places, have been greatly sufferers, between the latter period and the day when I quitted the abode of his honor. Pierce, of Scituate, a stout warrior, and one practiced in the wiles of this nature of warfare, hath been cut off with a whole company of followers; and Wadsworth and Brockleband, men known and esteemed for courage and skill have left their bones in the woods, sleeping in common among their luckless followers."

"These are truly tidings to cause us to mourn over the abandoned condition of our nature," said Content, in whose meek mind there was no affectation of regrets on such a subject. "It is not easy to see in what manner the evil may be arrested without again going forth to do battle."

"Such is the opinion of his honor, and of all who sit with him in council; for we have sufficient knowledge of the proceedings of the enemy, to be sure that the master-spirit of wickedness, in the person of him called Philip, is raging up and down the whole extent of the borders, awakening the tribes to what he calleth the necessity of resisting further aggression, and stirring up their vengeance by divers subtle expedients of malicious cunning."

"And what manner of proceeding had been ordered in so urgent a strait by the wisdom of our rulers?"

"First, there is a fast ordained, that we come to the duty as men purified by mental struggle and deep self-examination; secondly, it is recommended that the congregations deal with more than wonted severity with all back-sliders and evil-doers, in order that the towns may not fall under the Divine displeasure, as happened to them that dwelt in the devoted cities of Canaan; thirdly, it is determined to lend our feeble aid to the ordering of Providence, by calling forth the alloted number of the trained bands; and fourthly, it is contemplated to counteract the seeds of vengeance, by setting a labor-earning price on the heads of our enemies."

"I accord with the three first of these expedients, as the known and lawful resorts of Christian men," said Content. "But the latter seemeth a measure that needeth to be entertained with great wariness of manner, and some distrust of purpose."

"Fear not, since all suiting and economical discretion is active in the minds of our rulers, who have pondered sagaciously on so grave a policy. It is not intended to offer more than half the reward that is held forth by our more wealthy and elder city of the bay; and there is some acute question about the necessity of bidding at all for any of tender years. And now, Captain Heathcote, with the good leave of so respectable a subject, I will proceed to lay before you the details of the number and the nature of the force that it is hoped you will lead in person in the ensuing campaign."

As the result of that which followed will be seen in the course of the legend, it is not necessary to accompany the messenger any further in his communication. We shall therefore leave him and Content busied with the matter of their conference, and proceed to give some account of the other personages connected with our subject.

When interrupted, as already related, by the arrival of the stranger, Faith had endeavored by a new expedient to elicit some evidences of a more just remembrance from the dull mind of her brother. Accompanied by most of the dependents of the family, she had led him to the summit of that hill which was now crowned with the foliage of a young and thrifty orchard, and placing him at the foot of the ruin, she tried to excite a train of recollections that should lead to deeper impressions, and possibly, by their aid, to a discovery of the important circumstance that all so much longed to have explained.

The experiment proved no happy result. The place, and indeed the whole valley, had undergone so great a change, that one more liberally gifted might have hesitated to believe them those that have been described in our earlier pages. This rapid alteration of objects, which elsewhere know so little change in a long course of ages, is a fact familiar to all who reside in the newer districts of the Union. It is caused by the rapid improvements that are made in the first stages of a settlement. To fell the forest alone, is to give an entirely new aspect to the view; and it is far from easy to see in a village and in cultivated fields, however recent the existence of the one or imperfect the other, any traces of a spot that a short time before was known as the haunt of the wolf or the refuge of the deer.

The features, and more particularly the eye of his sister, had stirred long-dormant recollections in the mind of Whittal Ring; and though these glimpses of the past were detached and indistinct, they had sufficed to quicken that ancient confidence which was partially exhibited in their opening conference. But it exceeded his feeble powers to recall objects that would appeal to no very lively sympathies, and which had themselves undergone so material alterations. Still the witless youth did not look on the ruin entirely without some strivings of his nature. Although the sward around its base was lively in the brightest verdure of early summer, and the delicious odor of the wild clover saluted his senses, still there was that in the blackened and ragged walls, the position of the tower, and the view of the surrounding hills, shorn as so much of them now were, that evidently spoke to his earliest impressions. He looked at the spot as a hound gazes at a master who has been so long lost as even to deaden his instinct; and at times, as his companions endeavored to aid his faint images, it would seem as if memory were likely to triumph, and all those deceptive opinions which habit and Indian wiles had drawn over his dull mind, were about to vanish before the light of reality. But the allurements of a life in which there was so much of the freedom of nature mingled with the fascinating pleasures of the chase and of the woods, were not to be dispossessed so readily.

When Faith artfully led him back to those animal enjoyments of which he had been so fond in boyhood, the fantasy of her brother seemed most to waver; but whenever it became apparent that the dignity of a warrior, and all the more recent and far more alluring delights of his later life were to be abandoned ere his being could return into its former existence, his dull faculties obstinately refused to lend themselves to a change that, in his case, would have been little short of that attributed to the transmigration of souls.

After an hour of anxious, and frequently, on the part of Faith, of angry efforts to extract some evidences of his recollection of the condition of life to which he had once belonged, the attempt for the moment was abandoned. At times, it seemed as if the woman were about to prevail. He often called himself Whittal, but he continued to insist that he was also Nipset, a man of the Narragansetts, who had a mother in his wigwam, and who had reason to believe that he should be numbered among the warriors of his tribe ere the fall of another snow.

In the meantime a very different scene was passing at the place where the first examination had been held, and which had been immediately deserted by most of the spectators, on the sudden arrival of the messenger. But a solitary individual was seated at the spacious board, which had been provided alike for those who owned and presided over the estate, and for their dependents to the very meanest. The individual who remained had thrown himself into a seat, less with the air of him who consults the demands of appetite, than of one whose thoughts were so engrossing as to render him indifferent to the situation or employment of his more corporeal part. His head rested on his arms, the latter effectually concealing the face, as they were spread over the plain but exquisitely neat table of cherry-wood, which, by being placed at the side of one of less costly material, was intended to form the only distinction between the guests, as, in more ancient times and in other countries, the salt was known to mark the difference in rank among those who partook of the same feast.

"Mark," said a timid voice at his elbow, "thou art weary with this night-watching, and with the scouting on the hills. Dost not think of taking food before seeking thy rest?"

"I sleep not," returned the youth, raising his head, and gently pushing aside the basin of simple food that was offered by one whose eye looked feelingly on his flushed features, and whose suffused cheek perhaps betrayed there was a secret consciousness that the glance was kinder than maiden diffidence should allow. "I sleep not, Martha, nor doth it seem to me that I shall ever sleep again."

"Thou frightest me by this wild and unhappy eye. Hast suffered aught in the march on the mountains?"

"Dost think one of my years and strength unable to bear the weariness of a few hours' watching in the forest? The body is well, but the mind endureth grievously."

"And wilt not say what causeth this vexation? Thou knowest, Mark, that there are none in this dwelling—nay, I am certain, I might add in this valley, that do not wish thee happiness."

"'Tis kind to say it, good Martha; but thou never hadst a sister!"

"'Tis true, I am all of my race; and yet to me it seemeth that no tie of blood could have been nearer than the love I bore to her who is lost."

"Nor mother! Thou never knewest what 'tis to reverence a parent."

"And is not thy mother mine?" answered a voice that was deeply melancholy, and yet so soft that it caused the young man to gaze intently at his companion, for a moment, ere he again spoke.

"True, true," he said hurriedly. "Thou must and dost love her who hath nursed thy infancy, and brought thee, with care and tenderness, to so fair and happy a womanhood." The eye of Martha grew brighter, and the color of her healthful cheek deepened, as Mark unconsciously uttered this simple commendation of her appearance; but as she shrank, with female sensitiveness, from his observation, the change was unnoticed, and he continued: "Thou seest that my mother is drooping hourly under this sorrow for our little Ruth; and who can say what may be the end of a grief that endureth so long."

"'Tis true that there hath been reason to fear much in her behalf; but, of late, hope hath gotten the better of apprehension. Thou dost not well, nay, I am not assured thou dost not evil, to permit this discontent with Providence, because thy mother yieldeth to a little more than her usual mourning, on account of the unexpected return of one so nearly connected with her that we have lost."

"'Tis not that, girl—'tis not that!"

"If thou refusest to say what 'tis that giveth thee this pain, I can do little more than pity."

"Listen, and I will say. It is now many years, as thou knowest, since the

"Lord!" said Meek, stretching his meager arms with the palms of the
hands open high above the head of his flock, "at thy bidding we go forth!"
—*The Wept of Wish-Ton-Wish.*

savage Mohawk or Narragansett, Pequod or Wampanoag, broke in upon our settlement, and did his vengeance. We were then children, Martha; and 'tis as a child that I have thought of that merciless burning. Our little Ruth was, like thyself, a blooming infant of some seven or eight years; and I know not how the folly hath beset me, but it hath been ever as one of that innocence and age, that I have continued to think of my sister."

"Surely thou knowest that time cannot stay; the greater therefore is the reason that we should be industrious to improve—"

"'Tis what our duty teacheth. I tell thee, Martha, that at night, when dreams come over me, as they sometimes will, and I see our Ruth wandering in the forest, it is as a playful, laughing child, such as we knew her; and even while waking, do I fancy my sister at my knee, as she was wont to stand when listening to those idle tales with which we lightened our childhood."

"But we had our birth in the same year and month—dost think of me too, Mark, as one of that childish age?"

"Of thee! That cannot well be. Do I not see that thou art grown into the condition of a woman, that thy little tresses of brown have become the jet black and flowing hair that becomes thy years, and that thou hast the stature—and, I say it not in idleness of speech, Martha, for thou knowest my tongue is no vain flatterer— but do I not see that thou hast grown into all the excellence of a most comely maiden? But 'tis not thus, or rather 'twas not thus, with her we mourn; for till this hour have I ever pictured my sister the little innocent we sported with, that gloomy night she was snatched from our arms by the cruelty of the savage."

"And what hath changed this pleasing image of our Ruth?" asked his companion, half covering her face to conceal the still deeper glow of female gratification which had been kindled by the words just heard. "I often think of her as thou hast described, nor do I now see why we may not still believe her, if she yet live, all that we could desire to see."

"That cannot be. The delusion is gone, and in its place a frightful truth has visited me. Here is Whittal Ring, whom we lost a boy; thou seest he is returned a man, and a savage! No, no; my sister is no longer the child I loved to think her, but one grown into the estate of womanhood."

"Thou thinkest of her unkindly, while thou thinkest of others far less endowed by nature with too much indulgence; for

thou rememberest, Mark, she was ever of more pleasing aspect than any that we knew."

"I know not that—I say not that—I think not that. But be she what hardships and exposure may have made her, still must Ruth Heathcote be far too good for an Indian wigwam. Oh! 'tis horrible to believe that she is the bondwoman, the servitor, the wife of a savage!"

Martha recoiled, and an entire minute passed, during which she made no reply. It was evident that the revolting idea for the first time crossed her mind, and all the natural feelings of gratified and maiden pride vanished before the genuine and pure sympathies of a female bosom.

"This cannot be," she at length murmured—"it can never be! Our Ruth must still remember the lessons taught her in her infancy. She knoweth she is born of Christian lineage! of reputable name! of exalted hope! of glorious promise!"

"Thou seest by the manner of Whittal, who is of greater age, how little of that taught can withstand the wily savage."

"But Whittal faileth of Nature's gifts; he hath ever been below the rest of men in understanding."

"And yet to what degree of Indian cunning hath he already attained."

"But Mark," rejoined his companion timidly, as if, while she felt all its force, she only consented to urge the argument in tenderness to the harassed feelings of the brother, "we are of equal years; that which hath happened to me may well have been the fortune of our Ruth."

"Dost mean, that being unespoused thyself, or that having at thy years inclinations that are free, my sister may have escaped the bitter curse of being the wife of a Narragansett, or what is not less frightful, the slave of his humors?"

"Truly, I mean little else than the former."

"And not the latter," continued the young man, with a quickness that showed some sudden revolution in his thoughts. "But though with opinions that are decided, and with kindness awakened in behalf of one favored, thou hesitatest, Martha, it is not like that a girl left in the fetters of savage life would so long pause to think. Even here in the settlements all are not difficult of judgment as thou!"

The long lashes vibrated above the dark eyes of the maiden, and for an instant it seemed as if she had no intention to reply. But looking timidly aside, she answered in a voice so low, that her companion scarcely gathered the meaning of what she uttered.

"I know not how I may have earned

this false character among my friends," she said ; "for to me it ever seemeth that what I feel and think is but too easily known."

"Then is the smart gallant from the Hartford town, who cometh and goeth so often between this distant settlement and his father's house, better assured of his success than I had thought. He will not journey the long road much oftener alone!"

"I have angered thee, Mark, or thou wouldst not speak with so cold an eye to one who hath ever lived with thee in kindness."

"I do not speak in anger, for 'twould be both unreasonable and unmanly to deny all of thy sex right of choice ; but yet it doth seem right that when taste is suited and judgment appeased, there should be little motive for withholding speech."

"And wouldst thou have a maiden of my years in haste to believe that she was sought, when haply it may be that he of whom you speak is in quest of thy society and friendship, rather than of my favor?"

"Then might he spare much labor and some bodily suffering, unless he finds great pleasure in the saddle ; for I know not a youth in the Connecticut Colony for whom I have smaller esteem. Others may see matter of approval in him, but to me, he is of bold speech, ungainly air, and great disagreeableness of discourse."

"I am happy that at last we find ourselves of one mind ; for that thou sayest of the youth, is much as I have long considered him."

"Thou! Thou thinkest of the gallant thus! Then why dost listen to his suit? I had believed thee a girl too honest, Martha, to affect such niceties of deception. With this opinion of his character why not refuse his company?"

"Can a maiden speak too hastily?"

"And if here, and ready to ask thy favor, the answer would be—"

"No!" said the girl, raising her eyes for an instant, and bashfully meeting the eager look of her companion, though she uttered the monosyllable firmly.

Mark seemed bewildered. An entirely new and a novel idea took possession of his brain. The change was apparent by his altering countenance, and a cheek that glowed like flame. What he might have said, most of our readers over fifteen may presume ; but at that moment the voices of those who had accompanied Whittal to the ruin were heard on their return, and Martha glided away so silently as to leave him for a moment ignorant of her absence.

CHAPTER XXII.

"Oh! when amid the throngs of men
The heart grows sick of hollow mirth,
How willingly we turn us, then,
Away from this cold earth ;
And look into thy azure breast,
For seats of innocence and rest!"
—BRYANT'S *Skies.*

THE day was the Sabbath. This religious festival, which is even now observed in most of the States of the Union with a strictness that is little heeded in the rest of Christendom, was then reverenced with a severity suited to the austere habits of the colonists. The circumstance that one should journey on such a day, had attracted the observation of all in the hamlet ; but as the stranger had been seen to ride toward the dwelling of the Heathcotes, and the times were known to teem with more than ordinary interest to the province, it was believed that he found his justification in some apology of necessity. Still none ventured forth to inquire into the motive of this extraordinary visit. At the end of an hour the horseman was seen to depart as he had arrived, seemingly urged on by the calls of some pressing emergency. He had in truth proceeded further with his tidings, though the lawfulness of discharging even this imperious duty on the Sabbath had been gravely considered in the Councils of those who had sent him. Happily they had found, or thought they had found, in some of the narratives of the sacred volume, a sufficient precedent to bid their messenger proceed.

In the meantime the unusual excitement which had been so unexpectedly awakened in the dwelling of the Heathcotes, began to subside in that quiet which is in so beautiful accordance with the sacred character of the day. The sun rose bright and cloudless over the hills, every vapor of the past night melting before his genial warmth into the invisible element. The valley then lay in that species of holy calm which conveys so sweet and so forcible an appeal to the heart. The world presented a picture of the glorious handiwork of Him who seems to invite the gratitude and adoration of his creatures. To the mind yet untainted, there is exquisite loveliness and even godlike repose in such a scene. The universal stillness permits the softest natural sounds to be heard ; and the buzz of the bee or the wing of the humming-bird reaches the ear like the loud notes of a general anthem. This temporary repose is full of meaning. It should teach how much of the beauty of this world's enjoyments, how much of its peace, and even how much of the comeliness of Nature itself is dependent on the spirit by which we are actuated. When man reposes, all around him seems anxious to contribute to his rest ; and when he abandons the contentions of grosser interests to elevate his spirit, all living things appear to unite in worship. Although this apparent sympathy of Nature may be less true than imaginative, its lesson is not destroyed, since it sufficiently shows that what man chooses to consider good in this world is good, and that most of its strife and deformities proceed from its own perversity.

The tenants of the valley of the Wish-Ton-Wish were little wont to disturb the quiet of the Sabbath. Their error lay in the other extreme, since they impaired the charities of life by endeavoring to raise man altogether above the weakness of his nature. They substituted the revolting aspect of a sublimated austerity, for that gracious though regulated exterior, by which all in the body may best illustrate their hopes or exhibit their gratitude. The peculiar air of those of whom we write, was generated by the error of the times and of the country, though something of its singularly rigid character might have been derived from the precepts and example of the individual who had the direction of the spiritual interests of the parish. As this person will have further connection with the matter of the legend, he shall be more familiarly introduced in its pages.

The Reverend Meek Wolfe was, in spirit, a rare combination of the humblest self-abasement and of fierce spiritual denunciation. Like so many others of his sacred calling in the colony he inhabited, he was not only the descendant of a line of priests, but it was his greatest earthly hope that he should also become the progenitor of a race in whom the ministry was to be perpetuated as severely as if the regulated formula of the Mosaic dispensation were still in existence. He had been educated in the infant college of Harvard, an institution that the emigrants from England had the wisdom and enterprise to found within the first five-and-twenty years of their colonial residence. Here this scion of so pious and orthodox a stock had abundantly qualified himself for the intellectual warfare of his future life, by regarding one set of opinions so steadily as to leave little reason to apprehend he would ever abandon the most trifling outworks of his faith. No citadel ever presented a more hopeless curtain to the besieger, than did the mind of this zealot to the efforts of conviction ; for on the side of his opponents, he contrived that every avenue should be closed by a wall blank as indomitable obstinacy could oppose. He appeared to think that all the minor conditions of argument and reason had been disposed of by his ancestors, and that it only remained for him to strengthen the many defenses of his subject, and now and then to scatter by a fierce sortie the doctrinal skirmishers who might occasionally approach his parish.

There was a remarkable singleness of mind in this religionist, which, while it in some measure rendered even his bigotry respectable, greatly aided in clearing the knotty subject with which he dealt of much embarrassing matter. In his eyes, the straight and narrow path would hold but few besides his own flock. He admitted some fortuitous exceptions, in one or two of the nearest parishes, with whose clergymen he was in the habit of exchanging pulpits ; and perhaps, here and there, in a saint of the other hemisphere, or of the more distant towns of the Colonies, the brightness of whose faith was something aided, in his eyes, by distance, as this opaque globe of ours is thought to appear a ball of light to those who inhabit its satellite. In short, there was an admixture of seeming charity with an exclusiveness of hope, an unweariness of exertion with a coolness of exterior, a disregard of self with the most complacent security, and an uncomplaining submission to temporal evils with the loftiest spiritual pretensions, that in some measure rendered him a man as difficult to comprehend as to describe.

At an early hour in the forenoon, a little bell that was suspended in an awkward belfry perched on the roof of the meeting-house, began to summon the congregation to the place of worship. The call was promptly obeyed, and ere the first notes had reached the echoes of the hills, the wide and grassy street was covered with family groups, all taking the same direction. Foremost in each little party walked the austere father, perhaps bearing on his arms a suckled infant, or some child yet too young to sustain its own weight ; while at a decent distance followed the equally grave matron, casting oblique and severe glances at the little troop around her, in whom acquired habits had yet some conquests to obtain over the lighter impulses of vanity. Where there was no child to need support, or where the mother chose to assume the office of bearing her infant in person, the man was seen to carry one of the heavy muskets of the day ; and when his arms were otherwise employed, the stoutest of his boys served in the capacity of armor-bearer. But in no instance was this needful precaution neglected, the state of the province and the character of the enemy requiring that vigilance should mingle even with their devotions. There was no loitering on the path, no light and worldly discourse by the way, nor even any salutations, other than those grave and serious recognitions by hat and eye, which usage tolerated as the utmost limit of courtesy on the weekly festival.

When the bell changed its tone, Meek appeared from the gate of the fortified house where he resided, in quality of castellan, on account of its public character, its additional security and the circumstance that his studious habits permitted him to discharge the trust with less waste of manual labor than it would cost the village were the responsible office confided to one of more active habits. His consort followed, but at even a greater distance than that taken by the wives of other men, as if she felt the awful necessity of averting even the remotest possibility of scandal from one of so sacred a profession. Nine offspring of various ages, and one female assistant, of years too tender to be a wife herself, composed the household of the divine; and it was a proof of the salubrious air of the valley that all were present, since nothing but illness was ever deemed a sufficient excuse for absence from the common worship. As this little flock issued from the palisadoes, a female, in whose pale cheek the effects of recent illness might yet be traced, held open the gate for the entrance of Reuben Ring, and a stout youth, who bore the prolific consort of the former, with her bounteous gift, into the citadel of the village, a place of refuge that nothing but the undaunted resolution of the woman prevented her from occupying before, since more than half of the children of the valley had first seen the light within the security of its defenses.

The family of Meek preceded him into the temple, and when the feet of the minister himself crossed its threshold, there was no human form visible without its walls. The bell ceased its monotonous and mournful note, and the tall, gaunt form of the divine moved through the narrow aisle to its usual post, with the air of one who had already more than half rejected the burden of bodily encumbrance. A searching and stern glance was thrown around, as if he possessed an instinctive power to detect all delinquents, and then seating himself, the deep stillness that always preceded the exercises reigned in the place.

When the divine next showed his austere countenance to his expecting people, its meaning was expressive rather of some matter of worldly import, than of that absence of carnal interest with which he usually strove to draw near to his Creator in prayer.

"Captain Content Heathcote," he said, with grave severity, after permitting a short pause to awaken reverence, "there has one ridden through this valley on the Lord's day, making thy habitation his halting-place. Hath the traveler warranty for this disrespect of the Sabbath, and canst thou find sufficient reason in his motive, for permitting the stranger within thy gates to neglect the solemn ordinance delivered on the Mount?"

"He rideth on especial commission," answered Content, who had respectfully arisen when thus addressed by name; "for matter of grave interest to the well-being of the Colony is contained in the subject of his errand."

"There is naught more deeply connected with the well-being of man, whether resident in this colony or in more lofty empires, than reverence to God's declared will," returned Meek, but half appeased by the apology. "It would have been expedient for one who in common not only setteth so good an example himself, but who is also charged with the mantle of authority, to have looked with distrust into the pretenses of a necessity that may be only seeming."

"The motive shall be declared to the people at a fitting moment; but it hath seemed more wise to retain the substance of the horseman's errand until worship hath been offered, without the alloy of temporal concerns."

"Therein hast thou acted discreetly; for a divided mind giveth but little joy above. I hope there is equal reason why all of thy household are not with thee in the temple?"

Notwithstanding the usual self-command of Content, he did not revert to this subject without emotion. Casting a subdued glance at the empty seat where she whom he so much loved was wont to worship at his side, he said, in a voice that evidently struggled to maintain its customary equanimity—

"There has been powerful interest awakened beneath my roof this day, and it may be that the duty of the Sabbath has been overlooked by minds so exercised. If we have therein sinned, I hope he that looketh kindly on the penitent, will forgive! She of whom thou speakest, hath been shaken by the violence of grief renewed; though willing in spirit, a feeble and sinking frame is not equal to support the fatigue of appearing here, even though it be the house of God."

This extraordinary exercise of pastoral authority was uninterrupted, even by the breathings of the congregation. Any incident of an unusual character had attraction for the inhabitants of a village so remote; but here was deep, domestic interest, connected with breach of usage and indeed of law, and all heightened by that secret influence that leads us to listen with singular satisfaction to those emotions in others which it is believed to be natural to wish to conceal. Not a syllable that fell from the lips of the divine, or of Content—not a deep tone of severity in the former, nor a struggling accent of the latter, escaped the dullest ear in that assembly. Notwithstanding the grave and regulated air that was common to all, it is needless to say there was pleasure in the little interruption of this scene, which, however, was far from being extraordinary in a community where it was not only believed that spiritual authority might extend itself to the most familiar practices, but where few domestic interests were deemed so exclusive, or individual feelings considered so sacred, that a very large proportion of the whole neighborhood might not claim a right to participate largely in both. The Reverend Mr. Wolfe was appeased by the explanation, and after allowing a sufficient time to elapse, in order that the minds of the congregation should recover their tone, he proceeded with the regular services of the morning.

It is needless to recount the well-known manner of the religious exercises of the Puritans. Enough of their forms and of their substance has been transmitted to us to render both manner and doctrine familiar to most of our readers. We shall therefore confine our duty to a relation of such portions of the ceremonies—if that which sedulously avoided every appearance of form, can thus be termed—as have an immediate connection with the incidents.

The divine had gone through the short opening prayer, had read the passage of holy writ, had given out the verses of the psalm, and had joined in the strange nasal melody with which his flock endeavored to render it doubly acceptable, and had ended his long and fervent wrestling of the spirit in a colloquial petition of some forty minutes' duration, in which direct allusion had been made not only to the subject of his recent examination, but to divers other familiar interests of his parishioners, and all without any departure from the usual zeal on his own part, or of the customary

attention and grave decorum on that of his people. But when, for the second time, he arose to read another song of worship and thanksgiving, a form was seen in the center or principal aisle, that as well by its attire and aspect, as by the unusual and irreverent tardiness of its appearance, attracted general observation. Interruptions of this nature were unfrequent, and even the long practiced and abstracted minister paused for an instant, ere he proceeded with the hymn, though there was a suspicion current among the more instructed of his parishioners, that the sonorous version was an effusion of his own muse.

The intruder was Whittal Ring. The witless young man had strayed from the abode of his sister, and found his way into that general receptacle, where most of the village was congregated. During his former residence in the valley, there had been no temple, and the edifice, its interior arrangements, the faces of those it contained, and the business on which they had assembled, appeared alike strangers to him. It was only when the people lifted up their voices in the song of praise, that some glimmerings of his ancient recollections were discoverable in his inactive countenance. Then, indeed, he betrayed a portion of the delight which powerful sounds can quicken, even in beings of his unhappy mental constitution. As he was satisfied, however, to remain in a retired part of the aisle, listening with dull admiration, even the grave Ensign Dudley, whose eye had once or twice seemed ominous of displeasure, saw no necessity for interference.

Meek had chosen for his text, on that day, a passage from the book of Judges; "And the children of Israel did evil in the sight of the Lord; and the Lord delivered them into the hands of Midian seven years." With this text the subtle-minded divine dealt powerfully, entering largely into the mysteries and allegorical allusions then so much in vogue. In whatever manner he viewed the subject, he found reason to liken the suffering, bereaved, and yet chosen dwellers of the colonies, to the race of the Hebrews. If they were not set apart and marked from all others of the earth, in order that one mightier than man should spring from their loins, they were led into that distant wilderness, far from the temptations of licentious luxury, or the worldly-mindedness of those who built their structure of faith on the sands of temporal honors, to preserve the Word in purity. As there appeared no reason on the part of the divine himself to distrust his construction of the words he had quoted, so it was evident that most of his listeners willingly lent their ears to so soothing an argument.

In reference to Midian, the preacher was far less explicit. That the great father of evil was in some way intended by this allusion could not be doubted; but in what manner the chosen inhabitants of those regions were to feel his malign influence was matter of more uncertainty. At times, the greedy ears of those who had long been wrought up into the impression that visible manifestations of the anger or of the love of Providence were daily presented to their eyes, were flattered with the stern joy of believing that the war which then raged around them was intended to put their moral armor to the proof, and that out of the triumph of their victories were to flow honor and security to the Church. Then came ambiguous qualifications, which left it questionable whether a return of the invisible powers, that had been known to be so busy in the provinces, were not the judgment intended. It is not to be supposed that Meek himself had the clearest mental intelligence on a point of this subtlety, for there was something of misty hallucination in the manner in which he treated it, as will be seen by his closing words.

"To imagine that Azazel regardeth the long suffering and steadfastness of a chosen people with a pleasant eye," he said, "is to believe that the marrow of righteousness can exist in the carrion of deceit. We have already seen his envious spirit raging in many tragical instances. If required to raise a warning beacon to your eyes, by which the presence of this treacherous enemy might be known, I should say, in the words of one learned and ingenious in this craftiness, that 'when a person, having full reason, doth knowingly and wittingly seek and obtain of the devil, or any other god besides the true God Jehovah, an ability to do or know strange things, which he cannot by his own human abilities arrive unto,' that then he may distrust his gifts and tremble for his soul. And, oh! my brethren, how many of ye cling at this very moment to those tragical delusions, and worship the things of the world, instead of fattening on the famine of the desert, which is the sustenance of them that would live forever! Lift your eyes upwards, my brethren—"

"Rather turn them to the earth!" interrupted a deep, authoritative voice from the body of the church; "there is present need of all your faculties to save life, and even to guard the tabernacle of the Lord!"

Religious exercises composed the recreation of the dwellers in that distant settlement. When they met in companies to lighten the load of life, prayer and songs of praise were among the usual indulgences of the entertainment. To them a sermon was like a gay scenic exhibition in other and vainer communities, and none listened to the Word with cold and inattentive ears. In literal obedience to the command of the preacher, and sympathizing with his own action, every eye in the congregation had been turned toward the naked rafters of the roof, when the unknown tones of him who spoke broke the momentary delusion. It is needless to say that, by a common movement, they sought an explanation of this extraordinary appeal. The divine became mute, equally with wonder and with indignation.

A first glance was enough to assure all present that new and important interests were likely to be awakened. A stranger of grave aspect, and of a calm but understanding eye, stood at the side of Whittal Ring. His attire was of the simple guise and homely materials of the country. Still he bore about his person enough of the equipments of one familiar with the wars of the eastern hemispere to strike the senses. His hand was armed with a shining broadsword, such as was then used by the cavaliers of England, and at his back was slung the short carbine of one who battled in the saddle. His mien was dignified and even commanding, and there was no second look necessary to show that he was an intruder of a character altogether different from the moping innocent at his side.

"Why is one of an unknown countenance come to disturb the worship of the temple?" demanded Meek, when astonishment permitted utterance. "Thrice hath this holy day been profaned by the foot of the stranger, and well may it be doubted whether we live not under an evil agency."

"Arm, men of the Wish-Ton-Wish! arm, and to your defenses!"

A cry arose without, that seemed to circle the whole valley; and then a thousand whoops rolled out of the arches of the forest, and appeared to meet in one hostile din above the devoted hamlet. These were sounds that had been too often heard, or too often described, not to be generally understood. A scene of wild confusion followed.

Each man, on entering the church, had deposited his arms at the door, and thither most of the stout borderers were now seen hastening, to resume their weapons. Women gathered their children to their sides, and the wails of horror and alarm were beginning to break through the restraints of habit.

"Peace!" exclaimed the pastor, seemingly excited to a degree above human emotion. "Ere we go forth, let there be a voice raised to our heavenly Father. The asking shall be as a thousand men of war battling in our behalf!"

The commotion ceased as suddenly as if a mandate had been issued from that place to which their petition was to be addressed. Even the stranger, who had regarded the preparations with a stern but anxious eye, bowed his head, and seemed to join in the prayer, with a devoted and confiding heart.

"Lord!" said Meek, stretching his meager arms, with the palms of the hands open, high above the heads of his flock, "at thy bidding, we go forth; with thy aid, the gates of hell shall not prevail against us; with thy mercy, there is hope in heaven and on earth. It is for thy tabernacle that we shed blood; it is for thy Word that we contend. Battle in our behalf, Kings of Kings! send thy heavenly legions to our succor, that the song of victory may be incense at thy altars, and a foul hearing to the ears of the enemy—Amen."

There was a depth in the voice of the speaker, a supernatural calmness in the tones, and so great a confidence in the support of the mighty ally implored, that the words went to every heart. It was impossible that nature should not be powerful within, but a high and exciting enthusiasm began to lift the people far above its influence. Thus awakened by an appeal of feelings that had never slumbered, and stimulated by all the moving interests of life, the men of the valley poured out of the temple in defense of person and fireside, and, as they believed, of religion and of God.

There was pressing necessity not only for this zeal, but for all the physical energies of the stoutest of their numbers. The spectacle that met the view on issuing into the open air was one that might have appalled the hearts of warriors more practiced, and have paralyzed the efforts of men less susceptible to the impressions of religious excitement.

Dark forms were leaping through the fields on the hillsides; and all adown the slopes that conducted to the valley armed savages were seen pouring madly forward, on their path of destruction and vengeance. Behind them, the brand and the knife had been already used; for the log tenement, the stacks, and the outbuildings of Reuben Ring, and of several others who dwelt in the skirts of the settlement, were sending forth clouds of murky smoke, in which forked and angry flames were already flashing fiercely. But danger most pressed still nearer. A long line of fierce warriors was even in the meadows; and in no direction could the eye be turned that it did not meet with the appalling proof that the village was completely surrounded by an overwhelming superiority of force.

"To the garrison!" shouted some of the foremost of those who first saw the nature and imminency of the danger, pressing forward themselves in the direction of the fortified house. "To the garrison or we are lost!"

"Hold!" exclaimed that voice which was so strange to the ears of most of those who heard it, but which spoke in a manner that by its compass and firmness commanded obedience. "With this mad disorder we are truly lost. Let Captain Content Heathcote come to my councils."

Notwithstanding the tumult and confusion which had now in truth begun to rage fearfully around him, the quiet and self-restrained individual to whom the legal and perhaps moral right to command belonged, had lost none of his customary composure. It was plain by the look of powerful amazement with which he had at first regarded the stranger on his sudden interruption of the service, and by the glances of secret intelligence and of recognition they exchanged, that they had met before. But this was no time for greetings or explanations, nor was that a scene in which to waste the precious moments in useless contests about opinions.

"I am here," said he who was thus called for; "ready to lead whither thy prudence and experience shall point the way."

"Speak to thy people, and separate the combatants in three bodies of equal strength. One shall press forward to the meadows, and beat back the savage ere he encircle the palisadoed house; the second shall proceed with the feeble and tender in their flight to its covers; and with the third—but thou knowest that which I would do with the third. Hasten, or we lose all by tardiness."

It was perhaps fortunate that orders so necessary and so urgent were given to one little accustomed to superfluity of speech. Without offering either commendation or dissent, Content obeyed. Accustomed to his authority, and conscious of the critical situation of all that was dear, the men of the village yielded an obedience more prompt and effective than it is usual to meet in soldiers who are not familiar with habits of discipline. The fighting men were quickly separated into three bodies, consisting of rather more than a score of combatants in each. One, commanded by Eben Dudley, advanced at quick time toward the meadows in the rear of the fortress, that the whooping body of savages, who were already threatening to cut off the retreat of the women and children, should be checked; while another departed in a nearly opposite direction, taking the street of the hamlet, for the purpose of meeting those who advanced by the southern entrance of the valley. The third and last of these small but devoted bodies remained stationary, in attendance for more definite orders.

At the moment when the first of these little divisions of force was ready to move, the divine appeared in its front, with an air in which spiritual reliance on the purposes of Providence, and some show of temporal determination, were singularly united. In one hand he bore a Bible, which he raised on high as the sacred standard of his followers, and in the other he brandished a short broadsword, in a manner that proved there might be danger in encountering its blade. The volume was open, and at brief intervals the divine read in a high and excited voice such passages as accidentally met his eye, the leaves blowing about in a manner to produce a rather remarkable admixture of doctrine and sentiment. But to these trifling moral incongruities, both the pastor and his parishioners were alike indifferent; their subtle mental exercises having given birth to a tendency of aptly reconciling all seeming discrepancies, as well as of accommodating the most abstruse doctrines to the more familiar interests of life.

"Israel and the Philistines had put their battle in array, army against army," commenced Meek, as the troop he led began its advance. Then reading at short intervals, he continued, "Behold, I will do a thing in Israel, at which both the ears of every one that heareth it shall tingle."—"Oh house of Aaron, trust in the Lord; he is thy help and thy shield."—"Deliver me, O Lord, from the evil man; preserve me from the violent man."—"Let burning coals fall upon them; let them be cast into the fire; into deep pits, that they rise not again."—"Let the wicked fall into their own nets, whilst that I, withal, escape."—"Therefore doth my father love me, because I lay down my life, that I may take it again."—"He that hateth me, hateth my father also."—"Father, forgive them, for they know not what they do."—"They have heard that it hath been said,

an eye for an eye, and a tooth for a tooth."—"For Joshua drew not his hand back, wherewith he stretched out the spear, until he had utterly destroyed all the inhabitants of Ai——" Thus far the words of Meek were intelligible to those who remained, but distance soon confounded the syllables. Then naught was audible but the yells of the enemy, the tramp of the men who pressed in the rear of the priest, with a display of military pomp as formidable as their limited means would allow, and those clear high tones, which sounded in the ears and quickened the blood at the hearts of his followers as though they had been trumpet-blasts. In a few more minutes the little band was scattered behind the covers of the fields, and the rattling of fire-arms succeeded to the quaint and characteristic manner of their march.

While this movement was made in front, the party ordered to cover the village was not idle. Commanded by a sturdy yeoman, who filled the office of lieutenant, it advanced with less of religious display, but with equal activity in the direction of the south; and the sounds of contention were quickly heard, proclaiming both the urgency of the measure and the warmth of the conflict.

In the meantime equal decision, though tempered by some circumstances of deep personal interest, was displayed by those who had been left in front of the church. As soon as the band of Meek had got to such a distance as to promise security to those who followed, the stranger commanded the children to be led toward the fortified house. This duty was performed by the trembling mothers, who had been persuaded with difficulty to defer it until cooler heads should pronounce that the proper moment had come. A few of the women dispersed among the dwellings in quest of the infirm, while all the boys of proper age were actively employed in transporting indispensable articles from the village within the palisadoes. As these several movements were simultaneous, but a very few minutes elapsed between the time when the orders were issued and the moment when they were accomplished.

"I had intended that thou shouldst have had the charge in the meadows," said the stranger to Content, when naught remained to be performed, but that which had been reserved for the last of the three little bands of fighting men. "But as the work proceedeth bravely in that quarter, we will move in company. Why doth this maiden tarry?"

"Trully, I know not, unless it may be of fear. There is an opening for thy passage into the fort, Martha, with others of thy sex."

"I will follow the fighters that are about to march to the rescue of them that remain in our habitation," said the girl, in a low but steady voice.

"And how know'st thou that such is the service intended for those here arrayed?" demanded the stranger, with a little show of displeasure that his military purposes should have been anticipated.

"I see it in the countenances of them that tarry," returned the other, gazing furtively towards Mark, who, posted in the little line, could with difficulty brook a delay which threatened his father's house, and those whom it held, with so much jeopardy.

"Forward!" cried the stranger. "Here is no leisure for dispute. Let the maiden take wisdom and hasten to the fort. Follow, men, stout of heart, or we come too late to the succor."

Martha waited until the party had advanced a few paces, and then, instead of obeying the repeated mandate to consult her personal safety, she took the direction of the armed band.

"I fear me that 'twill exceed our strength," observed the stranger, who marched in front at the side of Content, "to make good the dwelling, at so great distance from further aid."

"And yet the visitation will be heavy that shall drive us for a second time to the fields for a resting-place. In what manner didst get warning of this inroad?"

"The savages believed themselves concealed in the cunning place, where thou know'st that my eye had opportunity to overlook their artifices. There is a Providence in our least seeming calculations: an imprisonment of weary years hath its reward in this warning!"

Content appeared to acquiesce, but the situation of affairs prevented the discourse from becoming more minute.

As they approached the dwelling of the Heathcotes, better opportunity of observing the condition of things in and around the house was of course obtained. The position of the building would have rendered any attempt on the part of those in it to gain the fort, ere the arrival of assistance, desperately hazardous, since the meadows that lay between them were already alive with the ferocious warriors of the enemy. But it was evident that the Puritan, whose infirmities kept him within doors, entertained no such design; for it was shortly apparent that those within were closing and barring the windows of the habitation, and that other provisions

for defense were in the course of active preparation. The feelings of Content, who knew that the house contained only his wife and father, with one female assistant, were excited to agony, as the party he commanded drew near on one side, at a distance about equal to that of a band of the enemy, who were advancing diagonally from the woods on the other. He saw the efforts of those so dear to him, as they had recourse to the means of security provided to repel the very danger which now threatened; and to his eyes it appeared that the trembling hands of Ruth had lost their power, when haste and confusion more than once defeated the object of her exertions.

"We must break and charge, or the savage will be too speedy!" he said, in tones that grew thick from breathing quicker than was wont, for one of his calm temperament. "See! they enter the orchard! In another minute they will be masters of the dwelling!"

But his companion marched with a firmer step, and looked with a cooler eye. There was in his gaze the understanding of a man practiced in scenes of sudden danger, and in his mien the authority of one accustomed to command.

"Fear not," he answered; "the art of old Mark Heathcote hath departed from him, or he still knoweth how to make good his citadel against a first onset. If we quit our order the superiority of concert will be lost, and being few in numbers defeat will be certain; but with this front, and a fitting steadiness, our march may not be repulsed. To thee, Captain Content Heathcote, it need not be told that he who now counsels hath seen the strife of savages ere this hour."

"I know it well—but dost not see my Ruth laboring at the ill-fated shutter of the chamber? The woman will be slain in her heedlessness—for, hark! there beginneth the volley of the enemy!"

"No, 'tis he who led my troop in a far different warfare!" exclaimed the stranger, whose form grew more erect, and whose thoughtful and deeply-furrowed features assumed something like the stern pleasure which kindles in the soldier as the sounds of contention increase. "'Tis old Mark Heathcote, true to his breeding and his name! he hath let off the culverin upon the knaves! behold, they are already disposed to abandon one who speaketh so boldly, and are breaking through the fences to the left, that we may taste something of their quality. Now, bold Englishmen, strong of hand and stout of heart, you have training in your duty, and you shall not be wanting in example.

You have wives and children at hand, looking at your deeds; and there is One above that taketh note of the manner in which you serve in this cause. Here is an opening for your skill; scourge the cannibals with the hand of death! On, on to the onset, and to victory!"

CHAPTER XXIII.

*" Hect.					Is this Achilles?*
Achil. I am Achilles.
Hect. Stand fair, I pray thee: let me look on thee."
—TROILUS AND CRESSIDA.

IT may now be necessary to take a rapid glance at the situation of the whole combat, which had begun to thicken in different parts of the valley. The party led by Dudley and exhorted by Meek, had broken its order on reaching the meadows behind the fort, and seeking the covers of the stumps and fences, it had thrown in its fire with good effect on the irregular band that had pressed into the fields. This decision quickly caused a change in the manner of the advance. The Indians took to covers in their turn, and the struggle assumed that desultory but dangerous character, in which the steadiness and resources of the individual are put to the severest trial. Success appeared to vacillate; the white men at one time widening the distance between them and their friends in the dwelling, and, at another, falling back as if disposed to seek the shelter of the palisadoes. Although numbers were greatly in favor of the Indians, weapons and skill supported the cause of their adversaries. It was the evident wish of the former to break in upon the little band that opposed their progress to the village, in and about which they saw that scene of hurried exertion which has already been described—a spectacle but little likely to cool the furious ardor of an Indian onset. But the wary manner in which Dudley conducted his battle, rendered this an experiment of exceeding hazard.

However heavy of intellect the ensign might appear on other occasions, the present was one every way adapted to draw out his best and most manly qualities. Of large and powerful stature, he felt in moments of strife a degree of confidence in himself, that was commensurate with the amount of physical force he wielded. To this hardy assurance was to be added no trifling portion of the sort of enthusiam that can be awakened in the most sluggish bosoms, and which, like the anger of an even-tempered man, is only the more formidable from the usually quiet habits of the individual. Nor was this the first, by many, of Ensign Dudley's warlike deeds. Besides the desperate affair already related in these pages, he had been engaged in divers hostile expeditions against the aborigines, and on all occasions had he shown a cool head and a resolute mind.

There was pressing necessity for both these essential qualities in the situation in which the ensign now found himself. By properly extending his little force, and yet keeping it at the same time perfectly within supporting distance, by emulating the caution of his foes in consulting the covers, and by reserving a portion of his fire throughout the broken and yet well ordered line, the savages were finally beaten back, from stump to stump, from hillock to hillock, and fence to fence, until they had fairly entered the margin of the forest. Further, the experienced eye of the borderer saw he could not follow. Many of his men were bleeding, and growing weaker as the wounds still flowed. The protection of the trees gave the enemy too great an advantage for their position to be forced, and destruction would have been the inevitable consequence of the close struggle which must have followed a charge. In this stage of the combat Dudley began to cast anxious and inquiring looks behind him. He saw that support was not to be expected, and he also saw with regret that many of the women and children were still busy transporting necessaries from the village into the fort. Falling back to a better line of covers, and to a distance that materially lessened the danger of the arrows, the weapon used by quite two-thirds of his enemies, he awaited in sullen silence the proper moment to effect a further retreat.

It was while the party of Dudley stood thus at bay that a fierce yell rang in the arches of the forest. It was an exclamation of pleasure, uttered in the wild manner of those people; as if the tenants of the woods were animated by some sudden and general impulse of joy. The crouching yeomen regarded each other in uneasiness, but seeing no sign of wavering in the steady mien of their leader, each man kept close, awaiting some further exhibition of the devices of their foes. Ere another minute had passed two warriors appeared at the margin of the wood, where they stood apparently in contemplation of the different scenes that were acting in various parts of the valley. More than one musket was leveled with the intent to injure them, but a sign from Dudley prevented attempts that would most probably have been frustrated by the never-slumbering vigilance of a North American Indian.

There was, however, something in the air and port of these two individuals that had its share in producing the forbearance of Dudley. They were evidently both chiefs, and of far more than usual estimation. As was common with the military leaders of the Indians, they were men also of large and commanding stature. Viewed at the distance from which they were seen, one seemed a warrior who had reached the meridian of his days, while the other had the lighter step and more flexible movement of a much briefer existence. Both were well armed; and, as was usual with the people of their origin on the war-path, they were clad only in the customary scanty covering of waist-cloths and leggings. The former, however, were of scarlet, and the latter were rich in the fringes and bright colors of Indian ornaments. The elder of the two wore a gay belt of wampum around his head in the form of a turban; but the younger appeared with a shaven crown, on which nothing but the customary chivalrous scalp-lock was visible.

The consultation, like most of the incidents that have been just related, occupied but a very few minutes. The eldest of the chiefs issued some orders. The mind of Dudley was anxiously endeavoring to anticipate their nature, when the two disappeared together. The ensign would now have been left entirely to vague conjectures, had not the rapid execution of the mandates that had been issued to the youngest of the Indians soon left him in no doubt of their intentions. Another loud and general shout drew his attention toward the right; and when he had endeavored to strengthen his position by calling three or four of the best marksmen to that end of his little line, the youngest of the chiefs was seen bounding across the meadows, leading a train of whooping followers to the covers that commanded its opposite extremity. In short, the position of Dudley was completely turned; and the stumps and angles of the fences which secreted his men were likely to become of no further use. The emergency demanded decision. Collecting his yeomen ere the enemy had time to profit by his advantage, the ensign ordered a rapid retreat toward the fort. In this movement he was favored by the formation of the ground, a circumstance that had been well considered on the advance; and in a very few minutes the party found itself safely posted under the protection of a scattering fire from the palisadoes, which immediately checked the pursuit of the whooping and exulting foe. The wounded men, after a stern or rather sullen halt, that was intended to exhibit the unconquerable determination of the whites, withdrew into the works for succor, leaving the command of Dudley reduced by nearly one-half of its numbers. With this diminished force, however, he promptly turned his attention toward the assistance of those who combated at the opposite extremity of the village.

Allusion has already been made to the manner in which the houses of a new settlement were clustered near each other, at the commencement of the colonial establishments. In addition to the more obvious and sufficient motive, which has given rise to the same inconvenience and unpicturesque manner of building over nine-tenths of the continent of Europe, there had been found a religious inducement for conforming to the custom. One of the enactments of the Puritans said, that "no man shall set his dwelling-house above the distance of half-a-mile, or a mile at farthest, from the meeting of the congregation where the church doth usually assemble for the worship of God." "The support of the worship of God, in church fellowship," was the reason alleged for this arbitrary provision of the law; but it is quite probable that support against danger of a more temporal character was another motive. There were those within the fort who believed the smoking piles that were to be seen, here and there, in the clearings on the hills, owed their destruction to a disregard of that protection which was thought to be yielded to those who leaned with the greatest confidence, even in the forms of earthly transactions, on the sustaining power of an all-seeing and all-directing Providence. Among this number was Reuben Ring, who submitted to the loss of his habitation, as to a merited punishment for the light-mindedness that had tempted him to erect a dwelling at the utmost limits of the prescribed distance.

As the party of Dudley retreated, that sturdy yeoman stood at a window of the chamber in which his prolific partner with her recent gift were safely lodged, for in that moment of confusion the husband was compelled to discharge the double duty of sentinel and nurse. He had just fired his piece, and he had reason to think with success, on the enemies that pressed too closely on the retiring party, and as he reloaded the gun, he turned a melancholy eye on the pile of smoking embers, that now lay where his humble but comfortable habitation had so lately stood.

"I fear me, Abundance." he said, shaking his head with a sigh, "that there was error in the measurement between the meeting and the clearing. Some misgivings of the lawfulness of stretching the chain across the hollows came over me at the time; but the pleasant knoll, where the dwelling stood, was so healthful and commodious, that, if it were a sin, I hope it is one that is forgiven! There doth not seem so much as the meanest of its logs, that is not now melted into white ashes by the fire!"

"Raise me, husband," returned the wife in the weak voice natural to her feeble situation; "raise me with thine arm, that I may look upon the place where my babes first saw the light."

Her request was granted, and, for a minute, the woman gazed in mute grief at the destruction of her comfortable home. Then, as a fresh yell from the foe rose on the air without, she trembled, and turned with a mother's care toward the unconscious beings that slumbered at her side.

"Thy brother hath been driven by the heathen to the foot of the palisadoes," observed the other, after regarding his companion with manly kindness for a moment, "and he hath lessened his force by many that are wounded."

A short but eloquent pause succeeded. The woman turned her tearful eyes upward, and stretching out a bloodless hand, she answered—

"I know what thou wouldst do—it is not meet that Sergeant Ring should be a woman-tender, when the Indian enemy is in his neighbor's fields! Go to thy duty, and that which is to be done, do manfully! and yet would I have thee remember how many there are who lean upon thy life for a father's care."

The yeoman first cast a cautious look around him, for this the decent and stern usages of the Puritans exacted, and perceiving that the girl who had occasionally entered to tend the sick was not present, he stooped, and impressing his lips on the cheek of his wife, he threw a yearning look at his offspring, shouldered his musket, and descended to the court.

When Reuben Ring joined the party of Dudley, the latter had just issued an order to march to the support of those who still stoutly defended the southern entry of the village. The labor of securing necessaries was not yet ended, and it was on every account an object of the last importance to make good the hamlet against the enemy. The task, however, was not as difficult as the force of the Indians might at first have given reason to believe. The conflict, by this time, had extended to the party which was headed by Content, and, in consequence, the Indians were compelled to contend with a divided force. The buildings themselves, with the fences and out-houses, were so many breast-works, and it was plain that the assailants acted with a caution and concert, that betrayed the direction of some mind more highly gifted than those which ordinarily fall to the lot of uncivilized men.

The task of Dudley was not so difficult as before, since the enemy ceased to press upon his march, preferring to watch the movements of those who held the fortified house, of whose numbers they were ignorant, and of whose attacks they were evidently jealous. As soon as the re-enforcement reached the lieutenant who defended the village, he commanded the charge, and his men advanced with shouts and clamor, some singing spiritual songs, others lifting up their voices in prayer, while a few availed themselves of the downright and perhaps equally effective means of raising sounds as fearful as possible. The whole being backed by spirited and well-directed discharges of musketry, the effort was successful. In a few minutes the enemy fled, leaving that side of the valley momentarily free from danger.

Pursuit would have been folly. After posting a few lookouts in secret and safe positions among the houses, the whole party returned, with an intention of cutting off the enemy who still held the meadows near the garrison. In this design, however, their intentions were frustrated. The instant they were pressed, the Indians gave way, evidently for the purpose of gaining the protection of the woods; and when the whites returned to their works, they were followed in a manner to show that they could make no further movement without the hazard of a serious assault. In this condition, the men in and about the fort were compelled to be inefficient spectators of the scene that was taking place around the "Heath-cote-house," as the dwelling of old Mark was commonly called.

The fortified building had been erected for the protection of the village and its inhabitants, an object that its position rendered feasible; but it could offer no aid to those who dwelt without the range of the musketry. The only piece of artillery belonging to the settlement, was the culverin which had been discharged by the Puritan, and which served for the moment to check the advance of his enemies. But the exclamations of the stranger, and the appeal to his men, with which the last chapter closed, sufficiently proclaimed that the attack was diverted from the house, and that work of a bloody character now offered itself to those he and his companion led.

The ground around the dwelling of the Heathcotes admitted of closer and more deadly conflict than that on which the other portions of the combat had occurred. Time had given size to the orchards, and wealth had multiplied and rendered more secure the inclosures and out-buildings. It was in one of the former that the hostile parties met, and came to that issue which the warlike stranger had foreseen.

Content, like Dudley, caused his men to separate, and they threw their fire with the same guarded reservation that had been practiced by the other party. Success again attended the efforts of discipline; the whites gradually beating back their enemies, until there was a probability of forcing them entirely into the open ground in their rear, a success that would have been tantamount to a victory. But at this flattering moment, yells were heard behind the leaping and whooping band that was still seen gliding through the openings of the smoke, resembling so many dark and malignant specters acting their evil rites. Then, as a chief with a turbaned head, terrific voice, and commanding stature, appeared in their front, the whole of the wavering line received an onward impulse. The yells redoubled; another warrior was seen brandishing a tomahawk on one flank, and the whole of the deep phalanx came rushing in upon the whites, threatening to sweep them away, as the outbreaking torrent carries desolation in its course.

"Men, to your square!" shouted the stranger, disregarding cover and life together, in such a pressing emergency; "to your square, Christians, and be firm."

The command was repeated by Content, and echoed from mouth to mouth. But before those on the flanks could reach the center, the shock had come. All order being lost, the combat was hand to hand, one party fighting fiercely for victory, and the other knowing that they stood at the awful peril of their lives. After the first discharge of the musket and the twang of the bow, the struggle was maintained with knife and ax; the thrust of the former, or the descent of the keen and glittering tomahawk, being answered by sweeping and crushing blows of the musket's butt, or by throttling grasps of hands that were clenched in the death-gripe. Men fell on each other in piles, and when the conqueror rose to shake off the bodies of those who gasped at his feet, his frowning eye rested alike on friend and enemy. The orchard rang with yells of the Indians, but the colonists fought in mute despair. Sullen resolution only gave way with life; and it happened more than once, that fearful day, that the usual reeking token of an Indian triumph was swung before the stern and still conscious eyes of the mangled victim from whose head it had been torn.

In this frightful scene of slaughter and ferocity, the principal personages of our legend were not idle. By a tacit but intelligent understanding, the stranger with Content and his son placed themselves back to back, and struggled manfully against their luckless fortune. The former showed himself no soldier of parade; for, knowing the uselessness of orders when each one fought for life, he dealt out powerful blows in silence. His example was nobly emulated by Content; and young Mark moved limb and muscle with the vigorous activity of his age. A first onset of the enemy was repelled, and for a moment there was a faint prospect of escape. At the suggestion of the stranger, the three moved in their order toward the dwelling, with the intention of trusting to their personal activity when released from the throng. But at this luckless instant, when hope was beginning to assume the air of probability, a chief came stalking through the horrible melee, seeking on each side some victim of his uplifted ax. A crowd of the inferior herd pressed at his heels, and a first glance told the assailed that the decisive moment had come.

At the sight of so many of their hated enemies still living and capable of suffering, a common and triumphant shout burst from the lips of the Indians. Their leader, like one superior to the more vulgar emotions of his followers, alone approached in silence. As the band opened and divided to encircle the victims, chance brought him face to face with Mark. Like his foe the Indian warrior was still in the freshness and vigor of young manhood. In stature, years, and agility, the antagonists seemed equal; and, as the followers of the chief threw themselves on the stranger and Content, like men who knew their leader needed no aid, there was every appearance of a fierce and doubtful struggle. But, while neither of the combatants showed any desire to avoid the contest, neither was in haste to give the commencing blow. A painter, or rather sculptor, would have seized the attitudes of these young combatants for a rich exhibition of the power of his art.

Mark, like most of his friends, had cast aside all superfluous vestments ere he approached the scene of strife. The upper part of his body was naked to the shirt, and even this had been torn asunder by the rude encounters through which he had already passed. The whole of his full and heaving chest was bare, exposing the white skin and blue veins of one whose fathers had come from toward the rising sun. His swelling form rested on a leg that seemed planted in defiance, while the other was thrown in front like a lever to control the expected movements. His arms were extended to the rear, the hands grasping the barrel of a musket which threatened death to all who should come within its sweep. The head, covered with the short, curling, yellow hair of his Saxon lineage, was a little advanced above the left shoulder, and seemed placed in a manner to preserve the equipoise of the whole frame. The brow was flushed, the lips compressed and resolute, the veins of the neck and temples swollen nearly to bursting, and the eyes contracted, but of a gaze that spoke equally the feelings of desperate determination and of entranced surprise.

On the other hand, the Indian warrior was a man still more likely to be remarked. The habits of his people had brought him, as usual, into the field with naked limbs and nearly uncovered body. The position of his frame was that of one prepared to leap; and it would have been a comparison tolerated by the license of poetry to have likened his straight and agile form to the semblance of a crouching panther. The projecting leg sustained the body, bending under its load more with the free play of muscle and sinew than from any weight, while the slightly stooping head was a little advanced beyond the perpendicular. One hand was clenched on the helve of an ax that lay in a line with the right thigh, while the other was placed with a firm gripe on the buck-horn handle of a knife that was still sheathed at his girdle. The expression of the face was earnest, severe, and perhaps a little fierce, and yet the whole was tempered by the immovable and dignified calm of a chief of high qualities. The eye, however, was gazing and riveted; and, like that of the youth whose life he threatened, it appeared singularly contracted with wonder.

The momentary pause that succeeded the movement by which the two antagonists threw themselves into these fine attitudes was full of meaning. Neither spoke, neither permitted play of muscle, neither even seemed to breathe. The delay was not like that of preparation, for each stood ready for his deadly effort, nor would it have been possible to trace in the com-

pressed energy of the countenance of Mark, or in the lofty and more practiced bearing of the front and eye of the Indian, anything like wavering of purpose. An emotion foreign to the scene appeared to possess them both, each active brain unconsciously accommodating itself to the bloody business of the hour, while the inscrutable agency of the mind held them for a brief interval in check.

A yell of death from the mouth of a savage who was beaten to the very feet of his chief by a blow of the stranger, and an encouraging shout from the lips of the latter, broke the short trance. The knees of the chief bent still lower, the head of the tomahawk was a little raised, the blade of the knife was seen glittering from its sheath, and the butt of Mark's musket had receded to the utmost tension of his sinews, when a shriek and a yell, different from any before heard that day, sounded near. At the same moment, the blows of both the combatants were suspended, though by the agency of very different degrees of force. Mark felt the arms of one cast around his limbs with a power sufficient to embarrass, though not to subdue him, while the well known voice of Whittal Ring sounded in his ears—

"Murder the lying and hungry palefaces! They leave us no food but air—no drink but water!"

On the other hand, when the chief turned in anger to strike the daring one who presumed to arrest his arm, he saw at his feet the kneeling figure, the uplifted hands, and agonized features of Martha. Averting the blow that a follower already aimed at the life of the suppliant, he spoke rapidly in his own language, and pointed to the struggling Mark. The nearest Indians cast themselves on the already half-captured youth. A whoop brought a hundred more to the spot, and then a calm as sudden, and almost as fearful, as the previous tumult prevailed in the orchard. It was succeeded by the long-drawn, frightful, and yet meaning yell by which the American warrior proclaims his victory.

With the end of the tumult in the orchard, the sounds of strife ceased in all the valley. Though conscious of the success of their enemies, the men in the fort saw the certainty of destruction, not only to themselves, but to those feeble ones whom they should be compelled to leave without a sufficient defense, were they to attempt a sortie to that distance from their works. They were, therefore, compelled to remain passive and grave spectators of an evil they had not the means to avert.

CHAPTER XXIV.

" Were such things here, as we do speak about ?
  Or have we eaten of the insane root
  That takes the reason prisoner ? "—MACBETH.

AN hour later presented a different scene. Bands of the enemy, that in civilized warfare would be called parties of observation, lingered in the skirts of the forest nearest to the village ; and the settlers still stood to their arms, posted among the buildings, or maintaining their array at the foot of the palisadoes. Though the toil of securing the valuables continued, it was evident that, as the first terrors of alarm had disappeared, the owners of the hamlet began to regain some assurance in their ability to make it good against their enemies. Even the women were now seen moving through its grassy street with greater seeming confidence, and there was a regularity in the air of the armed men, which denoted a determination that was calculated to impose on their wild and undisciplined assailants.

But the dwelling, the out-buildings, and all the implements of domestic comfort, which had so lately contributed to the ease of the Heathcotes, were completely in possession of the Indians. The open shutters and doors, the scattered and half-destroyed furniture, the air of devastation and waste, and the general abandonment of all interest in the protection of property, proclaimed the licentious disorder of a successful assault. Still the work of destruction and plunder did not go on. Although here and there might be seen some warrior, decorated, according to the humors of his savage taste, with the personal effects of the former inmates of the building, every hand had been checked, and the furious tempers of the conquerors had been quieted, seemingly by the agency of some unseen and extraordinary authority. The men, who so lately had been moved by the fiercest passions of our nature, were suddenly restrained, if not appeased ; and, instead of that exulting indulgence of vengeance which commonly accompanies an Indian triumph, the warriors stalked about the buildings and through the adjacent grounds, in a silence which, though gloomy and sullen, was marked by their characteristic submission to events.

The principal leaders of the inroad, and all the surviving sufferers by the defeat, were assembled in the piazza of the dwelling. Ruth, pale, sorrowing, and mourning for others rather than for herself, stood a little apart, attended by Martha and the young assistant whose luckless fortune it was to be found at her post on this eventful day. Content, the stranger, and Mark, were near, subdued and bound, the sole survivors of all that band they had so recently led into the conflict. The gray hairs and bodily infirmities of the Puritan spared him the same degradation. The only other being present, of European origin, was Whittal Ring. The innocent stalked slowly among the prisoners, sometimes permitting ancient recollections and sympathies to come over his dull intellect, but oftener taunting the unfortunate with the injustice of their race, and with the wrongs of his adopted people.

The chiefs of the successful party stood in the center, apparently engaged in some grave deliberation. As they were few in number, it was evident that the council only included men of the highest importance. Chiefs of inferior rank, but of great names in the limited renown of those simple tribes, conversed in knots among the trees, or paced the court at a respectable distance from the consultation of their superiors.

The least practiced eye could not mistake the person of him on whom the greatest weight of authority had fallen. The turbaned warrior, already introduced in these pages, occupied the center of the group, in the calm and dignified attitude of an Indian who hearkens to or who utters advice. His musket was borne by one who stood in waiting, while the knife and ax were returned to his girdle. He had thrown a light blanket, or it might be better termed a robe of scarlet cloth, over his left shoulder, whence it gracefully fell in folds, leaving the whole of the right arm free, and most of his ample chest exposed to view. From beneath this mantle blood fell slowly in drops, dyeing the floor on which he stood. The countenance of this warrior was grave, though there was a quickness in the movements of an ever-restless eye, that denoted great mental activity, no less than the disquiet of suspicion. One skilled in physiognomy might too have thought, that a shade of suppressed discontent was struggling with the self-command of habits that had become part of the nature of the individual.

The two companions nearest this chief were, like himself, men past the middle age, and of mien and expression that were similar, though less strikingly marked ; neither showing those signs of displeasure, which occasionally shot from organs that, in spite of a mind so trained and so despotic, could not always restrain their glittering brightness. One was speaking, and by his glance it was evident that the subject of his discourse was the fourth and last of their number, who had placed himself in a position that prevented his being an auditor of what was said.

In the person of the latter chief, the reader will recognize the youth who had confronted Mark, and whose rapid movement on the flank of Dudley had first driven the colonists from the meadows. The eloquent expression of limb, the tension of sinews, and the compression of muscles, as last exhibited, were now gone. They had given place to the peculiar repose that distinguishes the Indian warrior in his moments of inaction, quite as much as it marks the manner of one schooled in the forms of more polished life. With one hand he leaned lightly on a musket, while from the wrist of the other, which hung loose at his side, depended, by a thong of deer's sinew, a tomahawk from which fell drops of human blood. His person bore no other covering than that in which he had fought, and, unlike his more aged companion in authority, his body had escaped without a wound.

In form and in features, this young warrior might be deemed a model of the excellence of Indian manhood. The limbs were full, round, faultlessly straight, and distinguished by an appearance of extreme activity, without being equally remarkable for muscle. In the latter particular, in the upright attitude, and in the distant and noble gaze which so often elevated his front, there was a close affinity to the statue of the Pythian Apollo; while in the full though slightly effeminate chest, there was an equal resemblance to that look of animal indulgence which is to be traced in the severe representations of Bacchus. This resemblance, however, to a deity that is little apt to awaken lofty sentiments in the spectator, was not displeasing, since it in some measure relieved the sternness of an eye that penetrated like the glance of the eagle, and that might otherwise have left an impression of too little sympathy with the familiar weaknesses of humanity. Still the young chief was less to be remarked by this peculiar fullness of chest, the fruit of intervals of inaction, constant indulgence of the first wants of nature, and a total exemption from toil, than most of those who either counseled in secret near, or paced the grounds about the building. In him, it was rather a point to be admired than a blemish; for it seemed to say, that notwithstanding the evidences of austerity which custom, and perhaps character, as well as rank, had gathered in his air, there was a heart beneath that might be touched by the charities of humanity. On the present occasion, the glances of his roving eye, though searching and full of meaning, were evidently weakened by an expression that betrayed a strange and unwonted confusion of mind.

The conference of the three was ended, and the warrior with a turbaned head advanced toward his captives, with the step of a man whose mind had come to a decision. As the dreaded chief drew near, Whittal retired, stealing to the side of the young warrior, in a manner that denoted greater familiarity, and perhaps greater confidence. A sudden thought lighted the countenance of the latter. He led the innocent to the extremity of the piazza, spoke low and earnestly, pointing to the forest, and when he saw that his messenger was already crossing the fields at the top of his speed, he moved with a calm dignity into the center of the group, taking his station so near his friend that the folds of the scarlet blanket brushed his elbow. Until this movement the silence was not broken. When the great chief felt the passage of the other, he glanced a look of hesitation at his friends, but resuming his former air of composure, he spoke:

"Man of many winters," he commenced, in an English that was quite intelligible, while it betrayed a difficulty of speech we shall not attempt imitating, "why hath the Great Spirit made thy race like hungry wolves?—why hath a pale-face the stomach of a buzzard, the throat of a hound, and the heart of a deer? Thou hast seen many meltings of the snow; thou rememberest the young tree a sapling. Tell me, why is the mind of a Yengeese so big, that it must hold all that lies between the rising and the setting sun? Speak, for we would know the reason why arms so long are found on so little bodies."

The events of that day had been of a nature to awaken all the latent energies of the Puritan. He had lifted up his spirit, with the morning, in the customary warmth with which he ever hailed the Sabbath; the excitement of the assault had found him sustained above most earthly calamities, and while it quickened feelings that can never become extinct in one who has been familiar with martial usages, it left him, stern in his manhood, and exalted in his sentiments of submission and endurance. Under such influences, he answered with an austerity that equaled the gravity of the Indian:

"The Lord hath delivered us into the bonds of the heathen," he said, "and yet his name shall be blessed beneath my roof! Out of evil shall come good; and from this triumph of the ignorant shall proceed an everlasting victory!"

The chief gazed intently at the speaker, whose attenuated frame, venerable face, and long locks, aided by the hectic of enthusiasm that played beneath a glazed and deep-set eye, imparted a character that seemed to rise superior to human weakness. Bending his head in superstitious reverence, he turned gravely to those who, appearing to possess more of the world in their natures, were more fitting subjects for the designs he meditated.

"The mind of my father is strong, but his body is like a branch of the scorched hemlock!" was the pithy declaration with which he prefaced his next remark. "Why is this?" he continued, looking severely at the three who had so lately been opposed to him in deadly contest. "Here are men with skins like the blossom of the dogwood, and yet their hands are so dark that I cannot see them!"

"They have been blackened by toil beneath a burning sun," returned Content, who knew how to discourse in the figurative language of the people in whose power he found himself, "We have labored, that our women and children might eat."

"No — the blood of red men hath changed their color."

"We have taken up the hatchet, that the land which the Great Spirit hath given might still be ours, and that our scalps might not be blown about in the smoke of a wigwam. Would a Narragansett hide his arms, and tie up his hands, with the war-whoop ringing in his ears?"

When allusion was made to the ownership of the valley, the blood rushed into the cheek of the warrior in such a flood that it deepened even the natural swarthy hue; but, clenching the handle of his ax convulsively, he continued to listen, like one accustomed to entire self-command.

"What a red man does may be seen," he answered, pointing with a grim smile toward the orchard; exposing, by the movement of the blanket, as he raised his arm, two of the reeking trophies of victory attached to his belt. "Our ears are open very wide. We listen, to hear in what manner the hunting grounds of the Indian have become the plowed fields of the Yengeese. Now let my wise men hearken, that they may grow more cunning, as the snows settle on their heads. The pale men have a secret to make the black seem white!"

"Narragansett—"

"Wampanoag!" interrupted the chief, with the lofty air with which an Indian identifies himself with the glory of his people; then glancing a milder look at the young warrior at his elbow, he added, hastily, and in the tone of a courtier, "'tis very good—Narragansett or Wampanoag—Wampanoag or Narragansett. The red men are brothers and friends. They have broken down the fences between their hunting grounds, and they have cleared the paths between their villages of briers. What have you to say to the Narragansett?—he has not yet shut his ear."

"Wampanoag, if such be thy tribe," resumed Content, "thou shalt hear that which my conscience teacheth is language to be uttered. The God of an Englishman is the God of men of all ranks, and of all time." His listeners shook their heads doubtingly, with the exception of the youngest chief, whose eye never varied its direction while the other spoke, each word appearing to enter deep within the recesses of his mind. "In defiance of these signs of blasphemy, do I still proclaim the power of him I worship!" Content continued; "my God is thy God; and he now looketh equally on the deeds, and searcheth, with inscrutable knowledge, into the hearts of both. This earth is his footstool; yonder heaven his throne! I pretend not to enter into his sacred mysteries, or to proclaim the reason why one-half of his fair work hath been so long left in that slough of ignorance and heathenish abomination in which my fathers found it; why these hills never before echoed the songs of praise, or why the valleys have been so long mute. These are truths hid in the secret designs of his sacred purpose, and they may not be known until the last fulfillment.

"But a great and righteous spirit hath led hither men filled with the love of truth and pregnant with the designs of a heavily-burdened faith, inasmuch as their longings are for things pure, while the consciousness of their transgressions bends them in deep humility to the dust. Thou bringest against us the charge of coveting thy lands, and of bearing minds filled with the corruption of riches. This cometh of ignorance of that which hath been abandoned, in order that the spirit of the godly might hold fast to the truth. When the Yengeese came into this wilderness, he left behind him all that can delight the eye, please the senses, and feed the longing of the human heart in the country of his fathers; for fair as is the work of the Lord in other lands, there is none that is so excellent as that from which these pilgrims in the wilderness have departed. In that favored isle, the earth groaneth with the abundance of its products; the odors of its sweet savors salute the nostrils, and the eye is never wearied in gazing at its loveliness. No; the men of the pale-faces have deserted home, and all that sweeteneth life, that they might serve God; and not at the instigations of craving minds or of evil vanities!"

Content paused—for as he grew warm with the spirit by which he was animated, he had insensibly strayed from the closer points of his subject. His conquerors maintained the decorous gravity with which an Indian always listens to the speech of another, until he had ended, and then the Great Chief, or Wampanoag, as he had proclaimed himself to be, laid a finger lightly on the shoulder of his prisoner, as he demanded—

"Why have the people of the Yengeese lost themselves on a blind path? If the country they have left is pleasant, cannot their God hear them from the wigwams of their fathers? See—if our trees are but bushes, leave them to the red man; he will find room beneath their branches to lie in the shade. If our rivers are small, it is because the Indians are little. If the hills are low and the valleys narrow, the legs of my poor people are weary with much hunting, and they will journey among them the easier. Now what the Great Spirit hath made for a red man, a red man should keep. They whose skins are like the light of the morning, should go back toward the rising sun, out of which they have come to do us wrong."

The chief spoke calmly; but it was like a man much accustomed to deal in the subtleties of controversy, according to the fashion of the people to whom he belonged.

"God hath otherwise decreed," said Content. "He hath led his servants thither, that the incense of praise may arise from the wilderness."

"Your Spirit is a wicked Spirit. Your ears have been cheated. The counsel that told your young men to come so far, was not spoken in the voice of the Manitou. It came from the tongue of one that loves to see game scarce, and the squaws hungry. Go—you follow the mocker, or your hands would not be so dark."

"I know not what injury may have been done the Wampanoags, by men of wicked minds; for some such there are, even in the dwellings of the well-disposed —but wrong to any hath never come from those that dwell within my doors. For these lands, a price hath been paid, and what is now seen of abundance in the valley, hath been wrought by much labor. Thou art a Wampanoag, and dost know that the hunting grounds of thy tribe have been held sacred by my people. Are not the fences standing which their hands placed, and not even the hoof of colt should trample the corn? and when was it known that the Indian came for justice against the trespassing ox, and did not find it?"

"The moose doth not taste the grass at the root—he liveth on the tree! He doth not stoop to feed on that which he treadeth under foot! Does the hawk look for the mosquito? His eye is too big. He can see a bird. Go—when the deer have been killed, the Wampanoags will break down the fence with their own hands. The arm of a hungry man is strong. A cunning pale-face hath made that fence; it shutteth out the colt, and it shutteth in the Indian. But the mind of a warrior is too big; it will not be kept at grass with the ox."

A low but expressive murmur of satisfaction from the mouths of his grim companions, succeeded this reply of the chief.

"The country of thy tribe is far distant," returned Content, "and I will not lay untruth to my soul, by presuming to say whether justice or injustice hath been done them in the partition of the lands. But in this valley hath wrong never been done to the red man. What Indian hath asked for food, and not got it? If he hath been a-thirst, the cider came at his wish; if he hath been a-cold, there was a seat by the hearth; and yet hath there been reason why the hatchet should be in my hand, and why my foot should be on the war-path! For many seasons we lived on lands which were bought of both red and white man, in peace. But though the sun shone clear so long, the clouds came at last. There was a dark night fell upon this valley. Wampanoag, and death and the brand entered my dwelling together. Our young men were killed, and—our spirits were sorely tried."

Content paused—for his voice became thick, and his eye had caught a glimpse of the pale and drooping countenance of her who leaned on the arm of the still excited and frowning Mark for support. The young chief listened with a charmed ear. As Content had proceeded, his body was inclined a little forward, and his whole attitude was that which men unconsciously assume when intently occupied in listening to the sounds of the deepest interest.

"But the sun rose again!" said the great chief, pointing at the evidences of prosperity which were everywhere apparent in the settlement, casting at the same time an uneasy and suspicious glance at his youngest companion. "The morning was clear, though the night was so dark. The cunning of a pale-face knows how to make corn grow on a rock. The foolish Indian eats roots, when crops fail and grain is scarce."

"God ceased to be angry," returned Content meekly, folding his arms in a manner to show that he wished to speak no more.

The great chief was about to continue, when his younger associate laid a finger on his naked shoulder, and by a sign indicated that he wished to hold communication with him apart. The former met the request with respect, though it might be discovered that he little liked the expression of his companion's features, and that he yielded with reluctance, if not with disgust. But the countenance of the youth was firm, and it would have needed more than usual hardihood to refuse a request seconded by so steady and so meaning an eye. The elder spoke to the warrior nearest his elbow, addressing him by the name of Annawon, and then, by a gesture so natural and so dignified that it might have graced the air of a courtier, he announced his readiness to proceed. Notwithstanding the habitual reverence of the aborigines for age, the others gave way for the passage of the young man in a manner to proclaim that merit or birth, or both, had united to purchase for him a personal distinction which far exceeded that shown in common to men of his years. The two chiefs left the piazza in the noiseless manner of the moccasined foot.

The passage of these dignified warriors toward the grounds in the rear of the dwelling, as it was characteristic of their habits, is worthy of being mentioned. Neither spoke, neither manifested any womanish impatience to pry into the musings of the other's mind, and neither failed in those slight but still sensible courtesies by which the path was rendered commodious and the footing sure. They had reached the summit of the elevation so often named, ere they believed themselves sufficiently retired to indulge in a discourse which might otherwise have enlightened profane ears. When beneath the shade of the fragrant orchard which grew on the hill, the senior of the two stopped, and throwing about him one of those quick, nearly imperceptible, and yet wary glances by which an Indian understands his precise position, as it were by instinct, he commenced the dialogue. The discourse was in the dialect of their race; but as it is not probable that many who read these pages would be much enlightened were we to record it in the precise words in which it has been transmitted to us, a translation into English, as freely as the subject requires and the geniuses of the two languages will admit, shall be attempted.

"What would my brother have?" commenced he with the turbaned head, uttering the guttural sounds in the low, soothing tones of friendship, and even of affection. "What troubles the great sachem of the Narragansetts? His thoughts seem uneasy. I think there is more before his eye than one whose sight is getting dim can see. Doth he behold the spirit of the brave Miantonimoh, who died like a dog, beneath the blows of cowardly Pequods and false-tongued Yengeese? Or does his heart swell with longing to see the scalps of treacherous pale-faces hanging at his belt? Speak, my son; the hatchet hath long been buried in the path between our villages, and thy words will enter the ears of a friend."

"I do not see the spirit of my father," returned the young sachem; "he is afar off in the hunting-grounds of just warriors. My eyes are too weak to look over so many mountains and across so many rivers. He is chasing the moose in grounds where there are no briers; he needeth not the sight of a young man to tell him which way the trail leadeth. Why should I look at the place where the Pequod and the pale-face took his life? The fire which scorched this hill hath blackened the spot, and I can no longer find the marks of blood."

"My son is very wise—cunning beyond his winters! That which hath been once revenged, is forgotten. He looks no further than six moons. He sees the warriors of the Yengeese coming into his village, murdering his old women, and slaying the Narragansett girls; killing his warriors from behind, and lighting their fires with the bones of red men. I will now stop my ears, for the groans of the slaughtered make my soul feel weak."

"Wampanoag," answered the other, with a fierce flashing of his eagle eye, and laying his hand firmly on his breast, "the night the snows were red with the blood of my people, is here! my mind is dark; none of my race have since looked upon the place where the lodges of the Narragansetts stood, and yet it hath never been hid from our sight. Since that time have we traveled in the woods, bearing on our backs all that is left but our sorrow—that we carry in our hearts."

"Why is my brother troubled? There are many scalps among his people, and see, his own tomahawk is very red! Let him quiet his anger till the night cometh, and there will be a deeper stain on the ax. I know he is in a hurry, but our councils say it is better to wait for darkness, since the cunning of the pale-faces is too strong for the hands of our young men."

"When was a Narragansett slow to leap, after the whoop was given, or unwilling to stay when men of gray heads say 'tis better? I like your counsel—it is full of wisdom. Yet an Indian is but a man! Can he fight with the God of the Yengeese? He is too weak. An Indian is but a man, though his skin be red!"

"I look into the clouds, at the trees, among the lodges," said the other, affecting to gaze curiously at the different objects he named, "but I cannot see the white Manitou. The pale men were talking to him when we raised the whoop in their fields, and yet he has not heard them. Go; my son has struck their warriors with a strong hand; has he forgotten to count how many dead lie among the trees, with the sweet-smelling blossoms?"

"Metacom," returned he who has been called the Sachem of the Narragansetts, stepping cautiously nearer to his friend, and speaking lower, as if he feared an invisible auditor; "though hast put hate into the bosoms of the red men, but canst thou make them more cunning than the spirits? Hate is very strong, but cunning hath a longer arm. See," he added, raising the fingers of his two hands before the eyes of his attentive companion, "ten snows have come and melted since there stood a lodge of the pale-faces on this hill. Conanchet was then a boy. His hand had struck nothing but deer. His heart was full of wishes. By day he thought of Pequod scalps, at night he heard the dying words of Miantonimoh. Though slain by cowardly Pequods and lying Yengeese, his father came with the night into his wigwam, to talk to his son. 'Does the child of so many great sachems grow big?' would he say; 'is his arm getting strong, his foot light, his eye quick, his heart valiant? Will Conanchet be like his fathers? when will the young Sachem of the Narragansetts become a man?' Why should I tell my brother of these visits? Metacom hath often seen the long line of Wampanoag chiefs, in his sleep. The brave sachems sometimes enter into the heart of their son!"

The lofty-minded though wily Philip struck his hand heavily upon his naked breast, as he answered—

"They are always here. Metacom has no soul but the spirit of his fathers!"

"When he was tired of silence the murdered Miantonimoh spoke aloud," continued Conanchet, after permitting the customary courteous pause to succeed the emphatic words of his companion. "He bade his son arise, and go among the Yengeese, that he might return with scalps to hang in his wigwam: for the eyes of the dead chief liked not to see the place so empty. The voice of Conanchet was then too feeble for the council-fire; he said nothing—he went alone. An evil spirit gave him into the hands of the pale-faces. He was a captive many moons. They shut him in a cage, like a tamed panther! It was here. The news of his ill-luck passed from the mouths of the young men of the Yengeese to the hunters, and from the hunters it came to the ears of the Narragansetts. My people had lost their sachem, and they came to seek him. Metacom, the boy had felt the power of the God of the Yengeese! His mind began to grow weak; he thought less of revenge; the spirit of his father came no more at night. There was much talking with the unknown God, and the words of his enemies were kind. He hunted with them. When he met the trail of his warriors in the woods his mind was troubled, for he knew their errand. Still he saw his father's spirit and waited.

"The whoop was heard that night; many died, and the Narragansetts took scalps. Thou seest this lodge of stone, over which fire has passed. There was then a cunning place above, and in it the pale men went to fight for their lives. But the fire kindled, and then there was no hope. The soul of Conanchet was moved at that sight, for there was much honesty in them within. Though their skins were so white, they had not slain his father. But the flames would not be spoken to, and the place became like the coals of a deserted council-fire. All within were turned to ashes. If the spirit of Miantonimoh rejoiced, it was well, but the soul of his son was very heavy. The weakness was on him, and he no longer thought of boasting of his deeds at the war-post."

"That fire scorched the stain of blood from the sachem's plain?"

"It did. Since that time I have not seen the marks of my father's blood. Gray heads and boys were in that fire, and when the timbers fell nothing was left but coals. Yet do they, who were in the blazing lodge, stand there!"

The attentive Metacom started, and glanced a hasty look at the ruin.

"Does my son see spirits in the air!" he asked hastily.

"No, they live; they are bound for the torments. In the white head, is he who talked much with his God. The elder chief who struck our young men so hard was then also a captive in this lodge. He who spoke, and she who seems even paler than her race, died that night; and yet are they now here! Even the brave youth that was so hard to conquer looks like a boy that was in the fire! The Yengeese deal with unknown gods; they are too cunning for an Indian!"

Philip heard this strange tale, as a being educated in superstitious legends would be apt to listen; and yet it was with a leaning to incredulity, that was generated by his fierce and indomitable desire for the destruction of the hated race. He had prevailed, in the councils of his nation, over many similar signs of supernatural agency that was exercised in favor of his enemies, but never before had facts so imposing come so directly and from so high a source before his mind. Even the proud resolution and far-sighted wisdom of this sagacious chief was shaken by such testimony, and there was a single moment when the idea of abandoning a league that seemed desperate took possession of his brain. But true to himself and his cause, second thoughts and a firmer purpose restored his resolution, though they could not remove the perplexity of his doubts.

"What does Conanchet wish?" he said. "Twice have his warriors broken into this valley, and twice have the tomahawks of his young men been redder than the head of the woodpecker. The fire was not good fire; the tomahawk will kill surer. Had not the voice of my brother said to his young men, 'let the scalps of the prisoners alone,' he could not now say, 'yet do they now stand here!'"

"My mind is troubled, friend of my father. Let them be questioned artfully, that the truth be known."

Metacom mused an instant; then smiling in a friendly manner on his young and much moved companion he made a sign to a youth who was straying about the fields to approach. This young warrior was made the bearer of an order to lead the captives to the hill, after which the two chiefs stalked to and fro in silence, each brooding over what had passed, in a humor that was suited to his particular character and more familiar feelings.

CHAPTER XXV.

"No withered witch shall here be seen,
    No goblins lead their nightly crew;
The female fays shall haunt the green,
    And dress thy grave with pearly dew."—COLLINS.

IT is rarely indeed that the philosophy of a dignified Indian is so far disturbed as to destroy the appearance of equanimity. When Content and the family of the Heathcotes appeared on the hill, they found the chiefs still pacing the orchard, with the outward composure of men unmoved, and with the gravity that was suited to their rank. Annawon, who had acted as their conductor, caused the captives to be placed in a row, choosing the foot of the ruin for their position, and then he patiently awaited the moment when his superiors might be pleased to renew the examination. In this habitual silence there was nothing of the abject air of Asiatic deference. It proceeded from the habit of self-command which taught the Indian to repress all natural emotions. A very similar effect was produced by the religious abasement of those whom fortune had now thrown into their power.

It would have been a curious study for one interested in the manners of the human species, to note the difference between the calm, physical, and perfect self-possession of the wild tenants of the forest, and the ascetic, spiritually sustained, and yet meek submission to Providence, that was exhibited by most of the prisoners. We say of most, for there was an exception. The brow of young Mark still retained its frown, and the angry character of his eye was only lost when by chance it lighted on the drooping form and pallid features of his mother. There was ample time for these several and peculiar qualities to be thus silently exhibited, many minutes passing before either of the sachems seemed inclined to recommence the conference. At length Philip, or Metacom, as we shall indifferently call him, drew near and spoke.

"This earth is a good earth," he said; "it is of many colors, to please the eyes of Him who made it. In one part it is dark, and as the worm taketh the color of the leaf on which he crawls, there the hunters are black; in another part it is white, and that is the part where pale men are born and where they should die; or they may miss the road which leads to their happy hunting-grounds. Many just warriors who have been killed on distant war-paths still wander in the woods because the trail is hid and their sight dim. It is not good to trust so much to the cunning of——"

"Wretched and blind worshiper of Apollyon!" interrupted the Puritan, "we are not of the idolatrous and foolish-minded! It hath been accorded to us to know the Lord; to his chosen worshipers all regions are alike. The spirit can mount equally through snows and whirlwinds; the tempest and the calm; from the lands of the sun and the lands of frosts; from the depths of the ocean, from fire, from the forest——"

He was interrupted in his turn. At the word fire, the finger of Metacom fell meaningly on his shoulder, and when he had ceased, for until then no Indian would have spoken, the other gravely asked—

"And when a man of a pale skin hath gone up in the fire can he again walk upon earth? Is the river between this clearing and the pleasant fields of a Yengeese so narrow that the just men can step across it when they please?"

"This is the conceit of one wallowing in the slough of heathenish abominations! Child of ignorance! know that the barriers which separate heaven from earth are impassable; for what purified being could endure the wickedness of the flesh?"

"This is a lie of the false pale-faces," said the wily Philip; "it is told that the Indian might not learn their cunning and become stronger than a Yengeese. My father, and those with him, were once burnt in this lodge, and now he standeth here, ready to take the tomahawk!"

"To be angered at this blasphemy, would ill denote the pity that I feel," said Mark, more excited at the charge of necromancy than he was willing to own; "and yet to suffer so fatal an error to spread among these deluded victims of Satan, would be neglect of duty. Thou hast heard some legend of thy wild people, man of the Wampanoags, which may heap double perdition on thy soul lest thou shouldst happily be rescued from the fangs of the deceiver. It is true, that I and mine were in exceeding jeopardy in this tower, and that to the eyes of men without we seemed melted with the heat of the flames; but the Lord put it into our spirits to seek refuge whither fire could not come. The well was made the instrument of our safety, for the fulfillment of his own inscrutable designs."

Notwithstanding the long practiced and exceeding subtlety of the listeners, they heard this simple explanation of that which they had deemed a miracle, with a wonder that could not readily be concealed. Delight at the excellence of the artifice was evidently the first and common emotion of them both; nor would they yield implicit faith until assured beyond a doubt that what they heard was true. The lit-

tle iron door, which had permitted access to the well, for the ordinary domestic purposes of the family, was still there; and it was only after each had cast a look down the deep shaft, that he appeared satisfied of the practicability of the deed. Then a look of triumph gleamed in the swarthy visage of Philip, while the features of his associate expressed equally his satisfaction and his regret. They walked apart, musing on what they had just seen and heard; and when they spoke, it was again in the language of their people.

"My son hath a tongue that cannot lie," observed Metacom, in a soothing, flattering accent. "What he hath seen, he tells; and what he tells, is true. Conanchet is not a boy, but a chief whose wisdom is gray, while his limbs are young. Now why shall not his people take the scalps of these Yengeese, that they may never go any more into holes in the earth, like cunning foxes?"

"The sachem hath a very bloody mind," returned the young chief, quicker than was common for men of his station. "Let the arms of the warriors rest, till they meet the armed bands of the Yengeese, or they will be too tired to strike heavily. My young men have taken scalps since the sun came over the trees, and they are satisfied—Why does Metacom look so hard? What does my father see?"

"A dark spot in the middle of a white plain. The grass is not green; it is red as blood. It is too dark for the blood of a pale-face. It is the rich blood of a great warrior. The rains cannot wash it out; it grows darker every sun. The snows do not whiten it; it hath been there many winters. The birds scream as they fly over it; the wolf howls; the lizards creep another way."

"Thine eyes are getting old; fire hath blackened the place, and what thou seest is coal."

"The fire was kindled in a well; it did not burn bright. What I see is blood."

"Wampanoag," rejoined Conanchet, fiercely, "I have scorched the spot with the lodges of the Yengeese. The grave of my father is covered with scalps taken by the hand of his son—Why does Metacom look again? What does the chief see?"

"An Indian town burning in the midst of the snow; the young men struck from behind; the girls screaming; the children broiling on coals, and the old men dying like dogs! It is the village of the cowardly Pequods—No, I see better; the Yengeese are in the country of the Great

Narragansett, and the brave sachem is there, fighting! I shut my eyes, for smoke blinds them!"

Conanchet heard this allusion to the recent and deplorable fate of the principal establishment of his tribe in sullen silence; for the desire of revenge, which had been so fearfully awakened, seemed now to be slumbering, if it were not entirely quelled by the agency of some mysterious and potent feeling. He rolled his eyes gloomily, from the apparently abstracted countenance of his artful companion, to those of the captives, whose fate only awaited his judgment, since the band which had that morning broken in upon the Wish-Ton-Wish was, with but few exceptions, composed of the surviving warriors of his own powerful nation. But, while his look was displeased, faculties that were schooled so highly could not easily be mistaken in what passed, even in the most cursory manner, before his sight.

"What sees my father next?" he asked, with an interest he could not control, detecting another change in the features of Metacom.

"One who is neither white nor red. A young woman, that boundeth like a skipping fawn; who hath lived in a wigwam, doing nothing; who speaks with two tongues; who holds her hands before the eyes of a great warrior till he is blind as the owl in the sun—I see her—"

Metacom paused, for at that moment a being that singularly resembled this description appeared before him, offering the reality of the imaginary picture he was drawing with so much irony and art.

The movement of the timid hare is scarce more hurried, or more undecided, than that of the creature who now suddenly presented herself to the warriors. It was apparent, by the hesitating and half-retreating step that succeeded the light bound with which she came in view, that she dreaded to advance, while she knew not how far it might be proper to retire. For the first moment, she stood in a suspended and doubting posture, such as one might suppose a creature of mist would assume ere it vanished, and then, meeting the eye of Conanchet, the uplifted foot retouched the earth, and her whole form sank into the modest and shrinking attitude of an Indian girl, who stood in the presence of a sachem of her tribe. As this female is to enact no mean part in that which follows, the reader may be thankful for a more minute description of her person.

The age of the stranger was under twenty. In form she rose above the usual stature of an Indian maid, though the proportions of her person were as light and buoyant as at all comported with the fullness that properly belonged to her years. The limbs, seen below the folds of a short kirtle of bright scarlet cloth, were just and tapering, even to the nicest proportions of classic beauty; and never did foot of higher instep, and softer roundness, grace a feathered moccasin. Though the person, from neck to knees, was hid by a tightly-fitting vest of calico and the short kirtle named, enough of the shape was visible to betray outlines that had never been injured, either by the mistaken devices of art or by the baneful effects of toil. The skin was only visible at the hands, face, and neck. Its luster having been a little dimmed by exposure, a rich, rosy tint had usurped the natural brightness of a complexion that had once been fair even to brilliancy. The eye was full, sweet, and of a blue that emulated the sky of evening; the brows, soft and arched; the nose, straight, delicate, and slightly Grecian; the forehead, fuller than that which properly belonged to a girl of the Narragansetts, but regular, delicate and polished; and the hair, instead of drooping in long straight tresses of jet black, broke out of the restraints of a band of beaded wampum, in ringlets of golden yellow.

The peculiarities that distinguished this female from the others of her tribe were not confined alone to the indelible marks of nature. Her step was more elastic—her gait more erect and graceful—her foot less inwardly inclined, and her whole movements freer and more decided than those of a race doomed from infancy to subjection and labor. Though ornamented by some of the prized inventions of the hated race to which she evidently owed her birth, she had the wild and timid look of those with whom she had grown into womanhood. Her beauty would have been remarkable in any region of the earth, while the play of muscle, the ingenuous beaming of the eye, and the freedom of limb and action were such as seldom pass beyond the years of childhood, among people who, in attempting to improve, so often mar the works of nature.

Although the color of the eye was so very different from that which generally belongs to one of Indian origin, the manner of its quick and searching glance, and of the half-alarmed and yet understanding look with which this extraordinary creature made herself mistress of the more general character of the assemblage before which she had been summoned, was like the half-instinctive knowledge of one accustomed to the constant and keenest exercise of her faculties. Pointing with a finger toward Whittal Ring, who stood a little in the background, a low, sweet voice was heard, asking, in the language of the Indians—

"Why has Conanchet sent for his woman from the woods?"

The young sachem made no reply. An ordinary spectator could not have detected about him even a consciousness of the speaker's presence. On the contrary, he maintained the lofty reserve of a chief engaged in affairs of moment. However deeply his thoughts might have been troubled, it was not easy to trace any evidence of the state of his mind in the calmness of features that appeared habitually immovable. For a single treacherous instant only, was a glance of kindness shot toward the timid and attentive girl, and then throwing the still bloody tomahawk into the hollow of one arm, while the hand of the other firmly grasped its handle, he remained unchanged in feature, as he was rigid in limb. Not so with Philip. When the intruder first appeared, a dark and lowering gleam of discontent gathered at his brow. It quickly changed to a look of sarcastic and biting scorn.

"Does my brother again wish to know what I see?" he demanded, when sufficient time had passed, after the unanswered question of the female, to show that his companion was not disposed to answer.

"What does the sachem of the Wampanoags now behold?" returned Conanchet, proudly, unwilling to show that any circumstance had occurred to interrupt the subject of their conference.

"A sight that his eyes will not believe. He sees a great tribe on the war-path. There are many braves, and a chief whose fathers came from the clouds. Their hands are in the air. They strike heavy blows; the arrow is swift, and the bullet is not seen to enter—but it kills. Blood runs from the wounds that is of the color of water. Now he does not see, but he hears! 'Tis the scalp-whoop, and the warriors are very glad. The chiefs in the happy hunting grounds are coming with joy to meet Indians that are killed; for they know the scalp-whoop of their children."

The expressive countenance of the young sachem involuntarily responded to this description of the scene through which he had just passed; and it was impossible for one so tutored to prevent the blood from rushing faster to a heart that ever beat strongly with the wishes of a warrior.

"What sees my father next?" he

asked, triumph insensibly stealing into the tones of his voice.

"A messenger: and then he hears—the moccasins of squaws!"

"Enough;—Metacom, the women of the Narragansetts have no lodges. Their villages are in coals, and they follow the young men for food."

"I see no deer. The hunter will not find venison in a clearing of the pale-faces. But the corn is full of milk. Conanchet is very hungry; he hath sent for his woman, that he may eat!"

The fingers of that hand which grasped the handle of the tomahawk appeared to bury themselves in the wood. The glittering ax itself was slightly raised; but the fierce gleaming of resentment subsided, as the anger of the young sachem vanished, and a dignified calm again settled on his countenance.

"Go, Wampanoag," he said, waving a hand proudly, as if determined to be no longer harassed by the language of his wily associate. "My young men will raise the whoop when they hear my voice, and they will kill deer for their women. Sachem, my mind is my own."

Philip answered to the look which accompanied these words with one that threatened vengeance; but smothering his anger with his accustomed wisdom, he left the hill, assuming an air that affected more of commiseration than of resentment.

"Why has Conanchet sent for a woman from the woods?" repeated the same soft voice, nearer to the elbow of the young sachem, and which spoke with less of the timidity of the sex, now that the troubled spirit of the Indians of those regions had disappeared.

"Narra-mattah, come near," returned the young chief, changing the deep and proud tones in which he had addressed his restless and bold companion in arms to those which better suited the gentle ear for which his words were intended. "Fear not, daughter of the morning; for those around us are of a race used to see women at the council-fires. Now look, with an open eye. Is there anything among these trees that seemeth like an ancient tradition? Hast ever beheld such a valley in thy dreams? Have yonder pale-faces, whom the tomahawks of my young men spared, been led before thee by the Great Spirit in the dark night?"

The female listened in deep attention. Her gaze was wild and uncertain, and yet it was not absolutely without gleamings of a half-reviving intelligence. Until that moment she had been too much occupied in conjecturing the subject of her visit, to regard the natural objects by which she was surrounded ; but with her attention thus directly turned upon them, her organs of sight embraced each and all, with the discrimination that is so remarkable in those whose faculties are quickened by danger and necessity. Passing from side to side, her swift glances ran over the distant hamlet, with its little fort, the buildings in the near grounds, the soft and verdant fields—the fragrant orchard, beneath whose leafy shades she stood, and the blackened tower that rose in its center like some gloomy memorial, placed there to remind the spectator not to trust too fondly to the signs of peace and loveliness that reigned around. Shaking back the ringlets that had blown about her temples, the wondering female returned thoughtfully and in silence to her place.

"'Tis a village of the Yengeese!" she said, after a long and expressive pause. "A Narragansett woman does not love to look at the lodges of the hated race."

"Listen—Lies have never entered the ears of Narra-mattah. My tongue hath spoken like the tongue of a chief. Thou didst not come of the sumach, but of the snow. This hand of thine is not like the hands of the women of my tribe; it is little, for the Great Spirit did not make it for work ; it is of the color of the sky in the morning, for thy fathers were born near the place where the sun rises. Thy blood is like spring-water. All this thou knowest, for none have spoken falsely in thy ear. Speak—dost thou never see the wigwam of thy father? Does not his voice whisper to thee in the language of his people?"

The female stood in the attitude which a sibyl might be supposed to assume, while listening to the occult mandates of the mysterious oracle, every faculty entranced and attentive.

"Why does Conanchet ask these questions of his wife? He knows what she knows ; he sees what she sees ; his mind is her mind. If the Great Spirit made her skin of a different color, he made her heart the same. Narra-mattah will not listen to the lying language; she shuts her ears, for there is deceit in its sounds. She tries to forget it. One tongue can say all she wishes to speak to Conanchet ; why should she look back in dreams, when a great chief is her husband?"

The eye of the warrior, as he looked upon the ingenuous and confiding face of the speaker, was kind to fondness. The firmness had passed away, and in its place was left the winning softness of affection, which, as it belongs to nature, is seen, at times, in the expression of an Indian's eye, as strongly as it is ever known to sweeten the intercourse of a more polished condition of life.

"Girl," he said with emphasis, after a moment of thought, as if he would recall her and himself to more important duties, "this is a warpath ; all on it are men. Thou wast like the pigeon before its wing opens, when I brought thee from the nest; still the winds of many winters had blown upon thee. Dost never think of the warmth and of the food of the lodge in which thou hast passed so many seasons?"

"The wigwam of Conanchet is warm ; no woman of the tribe hath as many furs as Narra-mattah."

"He is a great hunter! when they hear his moccasin, the beavers lie down to be killed ! But the men of the pale-faces hold the plow. Does not 'the driven snow' think of those who fenced the wigwam of her father from the cold, or of the manner in which the Yengeese live?"

His youthful and attentive wife seemed to reflect ; but raising her face, with an expression of content that could not be counterfeited, she shook her head in the negative.

"Does she never see a fire kindled among the lodges, or hear the whoops of warriors as they break into a settlement?"

"Many fires have been kindled before her eyes. The ashes of the Narragansett town are not yet cold."

"Does not Narra-mattah hear her father speaking to the God of the Yengeese ! Listen—he is asking favor of his child?"

"The Great Spirit of the Narragansett has ears for his people."

"But I hear a softer voice ! 'Tis a woman of the pale-faces among her children ; cannot the daughter hear?"

Narra-mattah, or "the driven snow," laid her hand lightly on the arm of the chief, and she looked wistfully and long into his face, without an answer. The gaze seemed to deprecate the anger that might be awakened by what she was about to reveal.

"Chief of my people," she said, encouraged by his still calm and gentle brow to proceed, "what a girl of the clearings sees in her dreams shall not be hid. It is not the lodges of her race, for the wigwam of her husband is warmer. It is not the food and clothes of a cunning people, for who is richer than the wife of a great chief? It is not her father speaking to their Spirit, for there is none stronger than Manitou. Narra-mattah has forgotten all ; she does not wish to think of things like these. She knows how to hate a hungry and craving race. But she sees one that the wives of the Narragansetts do not see. She sees a woman with a white skin; her eyes look softly on her child in her dreams; it is not an eye, it is a tongue! It says, What does the wife of Conanchet wish?—is she cold? here are furs—is she hungry? here is venison—is she tired? the arms of the pale woman open that an Indian girl may sleep. When there is silence in the lodges, when Conanchet and his young men lie down, then does this pale woman speak. Sachem, she does not talk of the battles of her people, nor of the scalps that her warriors have taken, nor of the manner in which the Pequods and Mohicans fear her tribe. She does not tell how a young Narragansett should obey her husband, nor how the woman must keep food in the lodges for the hunters that are wearied; her tongue useth strange words. It names a mighty and just Spirit, it telleth of peace and not of war; it soundeth as one talking from the clouds; it is like the falling of the water among rocks. Narra-mattah loves to listen, for the words seem to her like the Wish-Ton-Wish, when he whistles in the woods."

Conanchet had fastened a look of deep and affectionate interest on the wild and sweet countenance of the being who stood before him. She had spoken in that attitude of earnest and natural eloquence that no art can equal; and when she ceased, he laid a hand, in kind but melancholy fondness, on the half-inclined and motionless head, as he answered:

"This is the bird of night, singing to its young! The Great Spirit of thy fathers is angry, that thou livest in the lodge of a Narragansett. His sight is too cunning to be cheated. He knows that the moccason, and the wampum, and the robe of furs are liars; he sees the color of the skin beneath."

"Conanchet, no," returned the female, hurriedly, and with a decision her timidity did not give reason to expect. "He seeth further than the skin, and knoweth the color of the mind. He hath forgotten that one of his girls is missing."

"It is not so. The eagle of my people was taken into the lodges of the pale-faces. He was young, and they taught him to sing with another tongue. The colors of his feathers were changed, and they thought to cheat the Manitou. But when the door was open, he spread his wings and flew back to his nest. It is not so. What hath been done is good, and what will be done is better. Come, there is a straight path before us."

Thus saying, Conanchet motioned to his wife to follow toward the group of captives. The foregoing dialogue had occurred in a place where the two parties were partially concealed from each other by the ruin; but as the distance was so trifling, the sachem and his companion were soon confronted by those he sought. Leaving his wife a little without the circle, Conanchet advanced, and taking the unresisting and half-unconscious Ruth by the arm, he led her forward. He placed the two females in attitudes where each might look the other full in the face. Strong emotion struggled in a countenance which, in spite of its fierce mask of war-paint, could not entirely conceal its workings.

"See," he said in English, looking earnestly from one to the other. "The Good Spirit is not ashamed of his work. What he hath done, he hath done; Narragansett nor Yengeese can alter it. This is the white bird that came from the sea," he added, touching the shoulder of Ruth lightly with a finger, "and this the young, that she warmed under her wing."

Then, folding his arms on his naked breast, he appeared to summon his energy, lest, in the scene that he knew must follow, his manhood might be betrayed into some act unworthy of his name.

The captives were necessarily ignorant of the meaning of the scene which they had just witnessed. So many strange and savage-looking forms were constantly passing and repassing before their eyes that the arrival of one more or less was not likely to be noted. Until she heard Conanchet speak in her native tongue, Ruth had lent no attention to the interview between him and his wife. But the figurative language and no less remarkable action of the Narragansett had the effect to arouse her suddenly, and in the most exciting manner, from her melancholy.

No child of tender age ever unexpectedly came before the eyes of Ruth Heathcote, without painfully recalling the image of the cherub she had lost. The playful voice of infancy never surprised her ear, without the sound conveying a pang to the heart; nor could allusion, ever so remote, be made to persons or events that bore resemblance to the sad incidents of her own life, without quickening the never-dying pulses of maternal love. No wonder, then, that when she found herself in the situation and under the circumstances described, nature grew strong within her, and that her mind caught glimpses, however dim and indistinct they might be, of a truth that the reader has already anticipated. Still, a certain and intelligible clew was wanting. Fancy had ever painted her child in the innocence and infancy in which it had been torn from her arms; and here, while there was so much to correspond with reasonable expectation, there was little to answer to the long and fondly cherished picture. The delusion, if so holy and natural a feeling may thus be termed, had been too deeply seated to be dispossessed at a glance. Gazing long, earnestly, and with features that varied with every changing feeling, she held the stranger at the length of her two arms, alike unwilling to release her hold, or to admit her closer to a heart which might rightfully be the property of another.

"Who art thou?" demanded the mother, in a voice that was tremulous with the emotions of that sacred character. "Speak, mysterious and lovely being—who art thou?"

Narra-mattah had turned a terriffed and imploring look at the immovable and calm form of the chief, as if she sought protection from him at whose hands she had been accustomed to receive it. But a different sensation took possession of her mind, when she heard sounds which had too often soothed the ear of infancy ever to be forgotten. Struggling ceased, and her pliant form assumed the attitude of intense and entranced attention. Her head was bent aside, as if the ear were eager to drink in a repetition of the tones, while her bewildered and delighted eye still sought the countenance of her husband.

"Vision of the woods! wilt thou not answer?" continued Ruth. "If there is reverence for the Holy One of Israel in thine heart, answer that I may know thee!"

"Hist! Conanchet!" murmured the wife, over whose features the glow of pleased and wild surprise continued to deepen. "Come near, sachem, the spirit that talketh to Narra-mattah in her dreams is nigh."

"Woman of the Yengeese!" said the husband, advancing with dignity to the spot, "let the clouds blow from thy sight.—Wife of a Narragansett! see clearly. The Manitou of your race speaks strong. He telleth a mother to know her child!"

Ruth could hesitate no longer; neither sound nor exclamation escaped her, but as she strained the yielding frame of her recovered daughter to her heart it appeared as if she strove to incorporate the two bodies into one. A cry of pleasure and astonishment drew all around her. Then came the evidence of the power of nature

when strongly awakened. Age and youth alike acknowledged its potency, and recent alarms were overlooked in the pure joy of such a moment. The spirit of even the lofty-minded Conanchet was shaken. Raising the hand, at whose wrist still hung the bloody tomahawk, he veiled his face, and, turning aside, that none might see the weakness of so great a warrior, he wept.

CHAPTER XXVI.

"One sees more devils than vast hell can hold;
    That is the madman:—"
                    —MIDSUMMER NIGHT'S DREAM.

ON quitting the hill Philip had summoned his Wampanoags, and supported by the obedient and fierce Annawon, a savage that might, under better auspices, have proved a worthy lieutenant to Cæsar, he left the fields of Wish-Ton-Wish. Accustomed to see these sudden outbreakings of temper in their leaders, the followers of Conanchet, who would have preserved their air of composure under far more trying circumstances, saw him depart equally without question and without alarm. But when their own sachem appeared on the ground, which was still red with the blood of the combatants, and made known his intention to abandon a conquest that seemed more than half achieved, he was not heard without murmuring. The authority of an Indian chief is far from despotic, and though there is reason to think it is often aided, if not generated, by the accidental causes of birth and descent, it receives its main support in the personal qualities of him who rules. Happily for the Narragansett leader, even his renowned father, the hapless Miantonimoh, had not purchased a higher name for wisdom or for daring than that which had been fairly won by his still youthful son.

The savage humors and the rankling desire for vengeance in the boldest of his subalterns were made to quail before the menacing glances of an eye that seldom threatened without performance; nor was there one of them all, when challenged to come forth to brave the anger or to oppose the eloquence of his chief, who did not shrink from a contest which habitual respect had taught them to believe would be far too unequal for success. Within less than an hour after Ruth had clasped her child to her bosom the invaders had altogether disappeared. The dead of their party were withdrawn and concealed with all the usual care, in order that no scalp of a warrior might be left in the hands of his enemies.

It was not unusual for the Indians to retire satisfied with the results of their first blow. So much of their military success was dependent on surprise, that it oftener happened the retreat commenced with its failure, than that victory was obtained by perseverance.

So long as the battle raged, their courage was equal to all its dangers; but among people who made so great a merit of artifice, it is not at all surprising that they seldom put more to the hazard than was justified by the most severe discretion. When it was known, therefore, that the foe had disappeared in the forest, the inhabitants of the village were more ready to believe the movement was the result of their own manful resistance, than to seek motives that might not prove so soothing to their self-esteem. The retreat was thought to be quite in rule, and though prudence forbade pursuit, able and well-limbed scouts were sent on their trail, as well to prevent a renewal of the surprise, as to enable the forces of the Colony to know the tribe of their enemies, and the direction which they had taken.

Then came a scene of solemn ceremonies and of deep affliction. Though the parties led by Dudley and the lieutenant had been so fortunate as to escape with a few immaterial wounds, the soldiers headed by Content, with the exception of those already named, had fallen to a man. Death had struck, at a blow, twenty of the most efficient individuals, out of that isolated and simple community. Under circumstances in which victory was so barren and so dearly bought, sorrow was a feeling far stronger than rejoicing. Exultation took the aspect of humility, and while the men were conscious of their well-deserving, they were the more sensible of their dependence on a power they could neither influence nor comprehend. The characteristic opinions of the religionists became still more exalted, and the close of the day was quite as remarkable for an exhibition of the peculiarly exaggerated impressions of the colonists, as its opening had been frightful in violence and blood.

When one of the more active of the runners returned with the news that the Indians had retired through the forest with a broad trail, a sure sign that they meditated no further concealment near the valley, and that they had already been traced many miles on their retreat, the villagers returned to their usual habitations. The dead were then distributed among those who claimed the nearest right to the performance of the last duties of affection; and it might have been truly said, that mourning had taken up its abode in nearly every dwelling. The ties of blood were so general in a society thus limited, and, where they failed, the charities of life were so intimate and so natural, that not an individual of them escaped without feeling that the events of the day had robbed him, forever, of some one on whom he was partially dependent for comfort or happiness.

As the day drew toward its close, the little bell again summoned the congregation to the church. On this solemn occasion, but few of those who still lived to hear its sounds were absent. The moment when Meek arose for prayer was one of general and intense feeling. The places so lately occupied by those who had fallen were now empty, and they resembled so many eloquent blanks in the description of what had passed, expressing far more than any language could impart. The appeal of the divine was in his usual strain of sublimated piety, mysterious insights into the hidden purposes of Providence being strangely blended with the more intelligible wants and passions of man. While he gave Heaven the glory of the victory, he spoke with a lofty and pretending humility of the instruments of its power; and although seemingly willing to acknowledge that his people abundantly deserved the heavy blow which had alighted on them, there was an evident impatience of the agents by which it had been inflicted. The principles of the sectarian were so singularly qualified by the feelings of the borderer, that one subtle in argument would have found little difficulty in detecting flaws in the reasoning of this zealot; but as so much was obscured by metaphysical mists, and so much was left for the generalities of doctrine, his hearers, without an exception, made such an application of what he uttered as apparently rendered every mind satisfied.

The sermon was as extemporaneous as the prayer, if anything can come extempore from a mind so drilled and fortified in opinion. It contained much the same matter, delivered a little less in the form of an apostrophe. The stricken congregation, while they were encouraged with the belief that they were vessels set apart for some great and glorious end of Providence, were plainly told that they merited far heavier affliction than this which had now befallen; and they were reminded that it was their duty to desire even condemnation, that he who framed the heavens and the earth might be glorified! Then they heard comfortable conclusions, which might reasonably teach them to expect, that though in the abstract such were the obligations of the real Christian, there was good reason to think that all who listened to doctrines so pure would be remembered with an especial favor.

So useful a servant of the temple as Meek Wolfe did not forget the practical application of his subject. It is true, that no visible emblem of the cross was shown to excite his hearers, nor were they stimulated to loosen bloodhounds on the trail of their enemies; but the former was kept sufficiently before the mind's eye by constant allusions to its merits, and the Indians were pointed at as the instruments by which the great father of evil hoped to prevent "the wilderness from blossoming like the rose," and "yielding the sweet savors of godliness." Philip and Conanchet were openly denounced by name; some dark insinuations being made, that the person of the former was no more than the favorite tenement of Moloch; while the hearer was left to devise a suitable spirit for the government of the physical powers of the other, from among any of the more evil agencies that were named in the Bible. Any doubts of the lawfulness of the contest, that might assail tender consciences, were brushed away by a bold and decided hand. There was no attempt at justification, however; for all difficulties of this nature were resolved by the imperative obligations of duty.

A few ingenious allusions to the manner in which the Israelites dispossessed the occupants of Judea, were of great service in this particular part of the subject, since it was not difficult to convince men, who so strongly felt the impulses of religious excitement, that they were stimulated rightfully. Fortified by this advantage, Mr. Wolfe manifested no desire to avoid the main question. He affirmed that if the empire of the true faith could be established by no other means, a circumstance which he assumed it was sufficiently apparent to all understandings could not be done, he pronounced it the duty of young and old, the weak and the strong, to unite in assisting to visit the former possessors of the country with what he termed the wrath of an offended Deity. He spoke of the fearful slaughter of the preceding winter, in which neither years nor sex had been spared, as a triumph of the righteous cause, and as an encouragement to persevere. Then, by a transition that was not extraordinary in an age so remarkable for religious subtleties, Meek returned to the more mild and obvious truths which pervade the doctrines of him whose Church he professed to uphold. His hearers were admonished to observe lives of humility and charity, and were piously dismissed, with his benediction, to their several homes.

The congregation quitted the building with the feelings of men who thought themselves favored by peculiar and extraordinary intelligences with the Author of all truth, while the army of Mahomet itself was scarcely less influenced by fanaticism than these blinded zealots. There was something so grateful to human frailty in reconciling their resentments and their temporal interests to their religious duties, that it should excite little wonder when we add that most of them were fully prepared to become ministers of vengeance in the hands of any bold leader. While the inhabitants of the settlement were thus struggling between passions so contradictory, the shades of evening gradually fell upon their village, and then came darkness with the rapid strides with which it follows the setting of the sun in a low latitude.

Some time before the shadows of the trees were getting the grotesque and exaggerated forms which precede the last rays of the luminary, and while the people were still listening to their pastor, a solitary individual was placed on a giddy eyrie, whence he might note the movements of those who dwelt in the hamlet, without being the object of observation himself. A short spur of the mountain projected into the valley, on the side nearest to the dwelling of the Heathcotes. A little tumbling brook, which the melting of the snows and the occasional heavy rains of the climate periodically increased into a torrent, had worn a deep ravine in its rocky bosom. Time and the constant action of the water, aided by the driving storms of winter and autumn, had converted many of the different faces of this ravine into wild-looking pictures of the residences of men. There was, however, one spot in particular, around which a closer inspection than that which the distance of the houses in the settlement offered, might have detected far more plausible signs of the agency of human hands than any that were afforded by the fancied resemblance of fantastic angles and accidental formations.

Precisely at that point where a sweep of the mountain permitted the best view of the valley, did the rocks assume the wildest, the most confused, and consequently the most favorable appearance for the construction of any residence which it was desirable should escape the curious eyes of the settlers, at the same time that it possessed the advantage of overlooking their proceedings. A hermit would have chosen the place as a spot suited to distant and calm observation of the world, while it was every way adapted to solitary reflection and ascetic devotion. All who have journeyed through the narrow and water-worn vineyards and meadows which are washed by the Rhone, ere that river pours its tribute into the Lake of Leman, have seen some such site, occupied by one who has devoted his life to seclusion and the altar, overhanging the village of St. Maurice, in the Canton of le Valais. But there is an air of obtrusiveness in the Swiss hermitage that did not belong to the place of which we write, since the one is perched upon its high and narrow ledge, as if to show the world in what dangerous and circumscribed limits God may be worshiped ; while the other sought exemption for absolute solitude, while it courted secrecy with the most jealous caution. A small hut had been erected against a side of the rock, in a manner that presented an oblique angle. Care had been taken to surround it with such natural objects as left little reason to apprehend that its real character could be known by any who did not absolutely mount to the difficult shelf on which it stood. Light entered into this primitive and humble abode by a window that looked into the ravine, and a low door opened on the side next the valley. The construction was partly of stone and partly of logs, with a roof of bark and a chimney of mud and sticks.

One who, by his severe and gloomy brow, was a fit possessor of so secluded a tenement, was, at the hour named, seated on a stone at the most salient angle of the mountain, and at the place where the eye commanded the widest and least obstructed view of the abodes of man in the distance. Stones had been rolled together in a manner to form a little breastwork in his front, so that had there been any wandering gaze sweeping over the face of the mountain, it was far from probable that it would have detected the presence of a man whose whole form, with the exception of the superior parts, was so effectually concealed.

It would have been difficult to say whether this secluded being had thus placed himself in order to indulge in some habitual and fancied communication with the little world of the valley, or whether he sat at his post in watchfulness. There was an appearance of each of these occupations in his air; for a time his eye was melancholy and softened, as if his spirit found pleasure in the charities natural to the species ; and at others, the brows contracted with sternness, while the lips be-

came more than usually compressed, like those of a man who threw himself on his own innate resolution for support.

The solitude of the place, the air of universal quiet which reigned above, the boundless leafy carpet over which the eye looked from that elevated point, and the breathing stillness of the bosom of the woods, united to give grandeur to the scene. The figure of the tenant of the ravine was as immovable as any other object of the view. It seemed, in all but color and expression, of stone. An elbow was leaning on the little screen in front, and the head was supported by a hand. At the distance of an arrow's flight, the eye might readily have supposed it no more than another of the accidental imitations which have been worn in the rock by the changes of centuries. An hour passed, and scarce a limb had been changed or a muscle relieved. Either contemplation, or the patient awaiting of some looked-for event, appeared to suspend the ordinary functions of life. At length an interruption occurred to this extraordinary inaction. A rustling, not louder than that which would have been made by the leap of a squirrel, was first heard in the bushes above. It was succeeded by a crackling of branches, and then a fragment of rock came bounding down the precipice, until it shot over the head of the still motionless hermit, and fell, with a noise that drew a succession of echoes from the caverns of the place, into the ravine beneath.

Notwithstanding the suddenness of this interruption and the extraordinary fracas with which it was accompanied, he who might be supposed to be most affected by it, manifested none of the usual symptoms of fear or surprise. He listened intently until the last sound had died away, but it was with expectation rather than with alarm. Arising slowly, he looked warily about him, and then walking with a quick step along the ledge which led to his hut, he disappeared through its door. In another minute, however, he was again seen at his former post, a short carbine, such as was then used by mounted warriors, lying across his knee. If doubt or perplexity beset the mind of this individual at so palpable a sign that the solitude he courted was in danger of being interrupted, it was not of a nature sufficiently strong to disturb the equanimity of his aspect. A second time the branches rustled, and the sounds proceeded from a lower part of the precipice, as if the foot that caused the disturbance was in the act of descending. Though no one was visible, the nature of the noise could no longer be mistaken. It was evidently the tread of a human foot; for no beast of a weight sufficient to produce so great an impression would have chosen to rove across a spot where the support of hands was nearly as necessary as that of the other limbs.

"Come forward!" said he who in all but the accessories of dress and hostile preparation might so well be termed a hermit—"I am already here."

The words were not given to the air, for one suddenly appeared on the ledge at the side next the settlement, and within twenty feet of the speaker. When glance met glance, the surprise which evidently took possession of the intruder and of him who appeared to claim a better right to be where they met, seemed mutual. The carbine of the latter, and a musket carried by the former, fell into the dangerous line of aim at the same instant, and in a moment they were thrown upwards again, as if a common impulse controlled them. The resident signed to the other to draw nigher, and then every appearance of hostility disappeared in that sort of familiarity which confidence begets.

"How is it," said the former to his guest, when both were calmly seated behind the little screen of stones, "that thou hast fallen upon the secret place? The foot of stranger hath not often trod these rocks, and no man before thee hath ever descended the precipice."

"A moccasin is sure," returned the other with Indian brevity. "My father hath a good eye. He can see very far from the door of his lodge."

"Thou knowest that the men of my color speak often to their Great Spirit, and they do not love to ask his favor in the highways. This place is sacred to his holy name."

The intruder was the young Sachem of the Narragansetts, and he who, notwithstanding this plausible apology, so palpably sought secrecy rather than solitude, was the man that has so often been introduced into these pages under the shade of mystery. The instant recognition and the mutual confidence require no further explanation, since enough has already been developed in the course of the narrative to show that they were no strangers to each other. Still the meeting had not taken place without uneasiness on the one part, and great though admirably veiled surprise on the other. As became his high station and lofty character, the bearing of Conanchet betrayed none of the littleness of a vulgar curiosity. He met his ancient acquaintance with the calm dignity of his rank, and it would have been difficult for the most inquiring eye to have detected a wandering glance, a single prying look, or any other sign that he deemed the place at all extraordinary for such an interview. He listened to the little explanations of the other with grave courtesy, and suffered a short time to elapse before he made any reply.

"The Manitou of the pale men," he then said, "should be pleased with my father. His words are often in the ears of the Great Spirit! The trees and the rocks know them."

"Like all of a sinful and fallen race," returned the stranger with the severe air of the age, "I have much need of my askings. But why dost thou think that my voice is so often heard in this secret place?"

The finger of Conanchet pointed to the worn rock at his feet, and his eye glanced furtively at the beaten path which led between the spot and the door of the lodge.

"A Yengeese hath a hard heel, but it is softer than stone. The hoof of the deer would pass many times to leave such a trail."

"Thou art quick of eye, Narragansett, and yet thy judgment may be deceived. My tongue is not the only one that speaketh to the God of my people."

The sachem bent his head slightly, in acquiescence, as if unwilling to press the subject. But his companion was not so easily satisfied, for he felt the consciousness of a fruitless attempt at deception goading him to some plausible means of quieting the suspicions of the Indian.

"That I am now alone, may be matter of pleasure or of accident" he added; "thou knowest that this hath been a busy and bloody day among the pale men, and there are dead and dying in their lodges. One who hath no wigwam of his own may have found time to worship by himself."

"The mind is very cunning," returned Conanchet; "it can hear when the ear is deaf—it can see when the eye is shut. My father hath spoken to the Good Spirit with the rest of his tribe."

As the chief concluded, he pointed significantly toward the distant church, out of which the excited congregation we have described was at that moment pouring into the green and little-trodden street of the hamlet. The other appeared to understand his meaning, and, at the same same instant to feel the folly, as well as the uselessness, of attempting any longer to mislead one that already knew so much of his former mode of life.

"Indian, thou sayest true," he rejoined gloomily: "the mind seeth far, and it seeth often in the bitterness of sorrow.

My spirit was communing with the spirits of those thou seest, when thy step was first heard; besides thine own, the feet of man never mounted to this place, except it be of those who minister to my bodily wants. Thou sayest true; the mental sight is keen; and far beyond those distant hills, on which the last rays of the setting sun are now shining so gloriously, doth mine often bear me in spirit. Thou wast once my fellow-lodger, youth, and much pleasure had I in striving to open thy young mind to the truths of our race, and to teach thee to speak with the tongue of a Christian; but years have passed away—hark! There cometh one up the path. Hast thou dread of a Yengeese?"

The calm mien with which Conanchet had been listening changed to a cold smile. His hand had felt for the lock of his musket some time before his companion had betrayed any consciousness of the approaching footstep; but until questioned, no change of countenance was visible.

" Is my father afraid for his friend?" he asked, pointing in the direction of him who approached. " Is it an armed warrior?"

"No; he cometh with the means of sustaining a burden that must be borne, until it pleaseth him who knoweth what is good for all his creatures to ease me of it. It may be the parent of her thou hast this day restored to her friends, or it may be the brother; for, at times, I owe this kindness to different members of that worthy family."

A look of intelligence shot across the swarthy features of the chief. His decision appeared taken. Arising, he left his weapon at the feet of his companion, and moved swiftly along the ledge, as if to meet the intruder. In another instant he returned, bearing a little bundle closely enveloped in belts of richly-beaded wampum. Placing the latter gently by the side of the old man, for time had changed the color of the solitary's hair to gray, he said, in a low, quick voice, pointing with significance at what he had done—

" The messenger will not go back with an empty hand. My father is wise; he will say what is good."

There was little time for further explanation. The door of the hut had scarcely closed on Conanchet, before Mark Heathcote appeared at the point where the path bent around the angle of the precipice.

" Thou knowest what hath passed, and wilt suffer me to depart with brief discourse," said the young man, placing food at the feet of him he had come to seek; " ha! what hast here?—didst gain this in the fray of the morning?"

" It is booty that I freely bestow; take it to the house of thy father. It is left with that object. Now tell me of the manner in which death hath dwelt with our people, for thou knowest that necessity drove me from among them so soon as liberty was granted."

Mark showed no disposition to gratify the other's wish. He gazed on the bundle of Conanchet, as if his eye had never before looked on a similar object, and keenly contending passions were playing about a brow that was seldom as tranquil as suited the self-denying habits of the times and country.

" It shall be done, Narragansett!" he said, speaking between his clenched teeth; " it shall be done!" Then turning on his heel, he stalked along the giddy path with a rapidity of stride that kept the other in fearful suspense for his safety until his active form had disappeared.

The recluse arose and sought the occupant of his humble abode.

" Come forth," he said, opening the narrow door for the passage of the chief. " The youth hath departed with thy burden, and thou art now alone with an ancient associate."

Conanchet reappeared at the summons, but it was with an eye less glowing and a brow less stern than when he entered the little cabin. As he moved slowly to the stone he had before occupied, his step was arrested for a moment, and a look of melancholy regret seemed to be cast at the spot where he had laid the bundle. Conquering his feelings, however, in the habitual self-command of his people, he resumed his seat, with the air of one that was grave by nature, while he appeared to exert no effort in order to preserve the admirable equanimity of his features. A long and thoughtful silence succeeded, and then the solitary spoke.

" We have made a friend of the Narragansett chief," he said, " and this league with Philip is broken!"

" Yengeese," returned the other, " I am full of the blood of sachems."

" Why should the Indian and the white do each other this violence? The earth is large, and there is place for men of all colors and of all nations on its surface."

" My father hath found but little," said the other, bestowing such a cautious glance at the narrow limits of his host, as at once betrayed the sarcastic purport of his words, while it equally bespoke the courtesy of his mind.

" A light-minded and vain prince is seated on the throne of a once godly nation, chief, and darkness has again come over a land which of late shone with a clear and shining light! The just are made to flee from the habitations of their infancy, and the temples of the elect are abandoned to the abominations of idolatry. Oh, England! England! when will thy cup of bitterness be full? When shall this judgment pass from thee? My spirit groaneth over thy fall; yea, my inmost soul is saddened with the spectacle of thy misery!"

Conanchet was too delicate to regard the glazed eye and flushed forehead of the speaker, but he listened in amazement and in ignorance. Such expressions had often met his ear before, and though his tender years had probably prevented their producing much effect, now that he again heard them in his manhood, they conveyed no intelligible meaning to his mind. Suddenly laying a finger on the knee of his companion, he said—

"The arm of my father was raised on the side of the Yengeese to-day; yet they give him no seat at their council-fire!"

"The sinful man, who ruleth in the island whence my people came, hath an arm that is long as his mind is vain. Though debarred from the councils of this valley, chief, time hath been when my voice was heard in councils that struck heavily at the power of his race. These eyes have seen justice done on him who gave existence to the double-tongued instrument of Belial, that now governeth a rich and glorious realm!"

"My father hath taken the scalp of a great chief!"

"I helped to take his head!" returned the solitary, a ray of bitter exultation gleaming through the habitual austerity of his brow.

"Come! The eagle flies above the clouds that he may move his wings freely. The panther leaps longest on the widest plain; the biggest fish swim in the deep water. My father cannot stretch himself between these rocks. He is too big to lie down in a little wigwam. The woods are wide; let him change the color of his skin, and be a gray-head at the council-fire of my nation. The warriors will listen to what he says, for his hand hath done a strong deed!"

"It may not be—it may not be, Narragansett. That which hath been generated in the spirit must abide, and it would be 'easier for the blackamoor to become white, or for the leopard to change his spots,' than for one who hath felt the power of the Lord to cast aside his gifts. But I meet thy proffers of amity in a charitable and forgiving spirit. My mind is ever with my people; yet is there place for other friendships. Break, then, this league with the evil-minded and turbulent Philip, and let the hatchet be forever buried in the path between thy village and the towns of the Yengeese."

"Where is my village? There is a dark place near the islands on the shores of the Great Lake; but I see no lodges."

"We will rebuild thy towns, and people them anew. Let there be peace between us."

"My mind is ever with my people," returned the Indian, repeating the other's words with an emphasis that could not be mistaken.

A long and melancholy pause succeeded; and when the conversation was renewed, it had reference to those events which had taken place in the fortunes of each since the time when they were both tenants of the block-house that stood amid the ancient habitations of the Heathcotes. Each appeared too well to comprehend the character of the other to attempt any further efforts toward producing a change of purpose; and darkness had gathered about the place before they arose to enter the hut of the solitary.

CHAPTER XXVII.

"Sleep, thou hast been a grandsire, and begot
A father to me; and thou hast created
A mother and two brothers."—CYMBELINE.

THE short twilight was already passed when old Mark Heathcote ended the evening prayer. The mixed character of the remarkable events of that day had given birth to a feeling which could find no other relief than that which flowed from the usual zealous, confiding, and exalted outpouring of the spirit. On the present occasion he had even resorted to an extraordinary, and what one less devout might be tempted to think, a supererogatory offering of thanksgiving and praise. After dismissing the attendants of the establishment, supported by the arm of his son, he had withdrawn into an inner apartment, and there, surrounded only by those who had the nearest claims on his affections, the old man again raised his voice to laud the Being who, in the midst of so much general grief, had deigned to look upon his particular race with the eyes of remembrance and of favor. He spoke of his recovered grandchild by name, and he dealt with the whole subject of her captivity among the heathen, and her restoration to the foot of the altar, with the fervor of one who saw the wise decrees of Providence in the event, and with the tenderness of sentiment that age was far from having extinguished. It was at the close of this private and peculiar worship, that we return into the presence of the family.

The spirit of reform had driven those who so violently felt its influence into many usages that, to say the least, were quite as ungracious to the imagination, as the customs they termed idolatrous were obnoxious to the attacks of their own un-accomodating theories. The first Protestants had expelled so much from the service of the altar, that little was left for the Puritan to destroy, without incurring the risk of leaving it naked of its loveliness. By a strange substitution of subtlety for humility, it was thought pharisaical to bend the knee in public, lest the great essential of spiritual worship might be supplanted by the more attainable merit of formula; and while rigid aspects and prescribed deportments of a new character were observed with all the zeal of converts, ancient and even natural practices were condemned—chiefly, we believe, from that necessity of innovation which appears to be an unavoidable attendent of all plans of improvement, whether they are successful or the reverse. But though the Puritans refused to bow their stubborn limbs when the eye of man was on them, even while asking boons suited to their own sublimated opinions, it was permitted to assume in private an attitude which was thought to admit of so gross an abuse, inasmuch as it infers a claim to a religious vitality, while in truth the soul might only be slumbering in the security of mere moral pretension.

On the present occasion, they who worshiped in secret had bent their bodies to the humblest posture of devotion. When Ruth Heathcote arose from her knees, it was with a hand clasped in that of the child whom her recent devotion was well suited to make her think had been rescued from a condition far more gloomy than that of the grave. She had used a gentle violence to force the wondering being at her side to join, so far as externals could go, in the prayer; and now it was ended, she sought the countenance of her daughter, in order to read the impression the scene had produced, with all the solicitude of a Christian, heightened by the tenderest maternal love.

Narra-mattah, as we shall continue to call her, in air, expression, and attitude, resembled one who had a fancied existence in the delusion of some exciting dream. Her ear remembered sounds which had so often been repeated in her infancy, and her memory recalled indistinct recollec-

tions of most of the objects and usages that were so suddenly replaced before her eyes; but the former now conveyed their meaning to a mind that had gained its strength under a very different system of theology, and the latter came too late to supplant usages that were rooted in her affections by the aid of all those wild and seductive habits, that are known to become nearly unconquerable in those who have long been subject to their influence. She stood, therefore, in the center of the grave, self-restrained group of her nearest kin, like an alien to their blood, resembling some timid and but half-tamed tenant of the air, that human art had endeavored to domesticate, by placing it in the society of the more tranquil and confiding inhabitants of the aviary.

Notwithstanding the strength of her affections, and her devotion to all the natural duties of her station, Ruth Heathcote was not now to learn the manner in which she was to subdue any violence in their exhibition. The first indulgence of joy and gratitude was over, and in its place appeared the never-tiring, vigilant, engrossing, but regulated watchfulness, which the events would naturally create. The doubts, misgivings, and even fearful apprehensions that beset her, were smothered in an appearance of satisfaction; and something like gleamings of happiness were again seen playing about a brow that had so long been clouded with an unobtrusive but corroding care.

"And thou recallest thine infancy, my Ruth?" asked the mother, when the respectful period of silence which ever succeeded prayer in that family was passed; "thy thoughts have not been altogether strangers to us, but nature hath had its place in thy heart. Tell us, child, of thy wanderings in the forest, and of the suffering that one so tender must have undergone among a barbarous people. There is pleasure in listening to all thou hast seen and felt, now that we know there is an end to unhappiness."

She spoke to an ear that was deaf to language like this. Narra-mattah evidently understood her words, while their meaning was wrapped in an obscurity that she was neither desirous nor capable of comprehending. Keeping a gaze, in which pleasure and wonder were powerfully blended, on that soft look of affection which beamed from her mother's eye, she felt hurriedly among the folds of her dress, and drawing a belt that was gayly ornamented after the most ingenious fashion of her adopted people, she approached her half-pleased, half-distressed parent, and with hands that trembled equally with timidity and pleasure, she arranged it around her person in a manner to show its richness to the best advantage. Pleased with her performance, the artless being eagerly sought approbation in eyes that bespoke little else than regret. Alarmed at an expression she could not translate, the gaze of Narra-mattah wandered, as if it sought support against some sensation to which she was a stranger. Whittal Ring had stolen into the room, and missing the customary features of her own cherished home, the looks of the startled creature rested on the countenance of the witless wanderer. She pointed eagerly at the work of her hands, appealing by an eloquent and artless gesture to the taste of one who would know whether she had done well.

"Bravely !" returned Whittal, approaching nearer to the subject of his admiration—" 'tis a brave belt, and none but the wife of a sachem could make so rare a gift ? "

The girl folded her arms meekly on her bosom, again appeared satisfied with herself and with the world.

"Here is the hand of him visible who dealeth in all wickedness," said the Puritan. "To corrupt the heart with vanities, and to mislead the affections by luring them to the things of life, is the guile in which he delighteth. A fallen nature lendeth but too ready aid. We must deal with the child in fervor and watchfulness, or better that her bones were lying by the side of those little ones of thy flock, who are already inheritors of the promise."

Respect kept Ruth silent ; but while she sorrowed over the ignorance of her child, natural affection was strong at her heart. With the tact of a woman and the tenderness of a mother, she both saw and felt that severity was not the means to effect the improvement they desired. Taking a seat herself, she drew her child to her person, and first imploring silence by a glance at those around her, she proceeded, in a manner that was dictated by the mysterious influence of nature, to fathom the depth of her daughter's mind.

"Come nearer, Narra-mattah," she said, using the name to which the other would alone answer. "Thou art still in thy youth, my child ; but it hath pleased him whose will is law, to have made thee the witness of many changes in this varying life. Tell me if thou recallest the days of infancy, and if thy thoughts ever returned to thy father's house, during those weary years thou wast kept from our view ? "

Ruth used gentle force to draw her daughter nearer while speaking, and the latter sank into that posture from which she had just arisen, kneeling, as she had often done in infancy, at her mother's side. The attitude was too full of tender recollections not to be grateful, and the half-alarmed being of the forest was suffered to retain it during most of the dialogue that followed. But while she was thus obedient in person, by the vacancy or rather wonder of an eye that was so eloquent to express all the emotions and knowledge of which she was the mistress, Narra-mattah plainly manifested that little more than the endearment of her mother's words and manner was intelligible. Ruth saw the meaning of her hesitation, and smothering the pang it caused, she endeavored to adapt her language to the habits of one so artless.

"Even the gray heads of thy people were once young," she resumed ; "and they remember the lodges of their fathers. Does my daughter ever think of the time when she played among the children of the pale-faces?"

The attentive being at the knee of Ruth listened greedily. Her knowledge of the language of her childhood had been sufficiently implanted before her captivity, and it had been too often exercised by intercourse with the whites, and more particularly with Whittal Ring, to leave her in any doubt of the meaning of what she now heard. Stealing a timid look over a shoulder, she sought the countenance of Martha, and studying her lineaments for near a minute with intense regard, she laughed aloud in the contagious merriment of an Indian girl.

"Thou hast not forgotten us ! That glance at her who was the companion of thy infancy assures me, and we shall soon again possess our Ruth in affection as we now possess her in the body. I will not speak to thee of that fearful night when the violence of the savage robbed us of thy presence, nor of the bitter sorrow which beset us at thy loss ; but there is One who must still be known to thee, my child ; he who sitteth above the clouds, who holdeth the earth in the hollow of his hand, and who looketh in mercy on all that journey on the path to which his own finger pointeth. Hath he yet a place in thy thoughts? Thou rememberest his holy name, and still thinkest of his power ? "

The listener bent her head aside, as if to catch the full meaning of what she heard, the shadows of deep reverence passing over a face that had so lately been smiling. After a pause she audibly murmured the word—

"Manitou."

"Manitou, or Jehovah; God, or King of Kings, and Lord of Lords! it mattereth little which term is used to express his power. Thou knowest him then, and hast never ceased to call upon his name?"

"Narra-mattah is a woman. She is afraid to speak to the Manitou aloud. He knows the voices of the chiefs, and opens his ears when they ask help."

The Puritan groaned, but Ruth succeeded in quelling her own anguish, lest she should disturb the reviving confidence of her daughter.

"This may be the Manitou of an Indian," she said, "but it is not the Christian's God. Thou art of a race which worships differently, and it is proper that thou shouldst call on the name of the Deity of thy fathers. Even the Narragansett teacheth this truth! Thy skin is white, and thy ears should hearken to the traditions of the men of thy blood."

The head of the daughter drooped at this allusion to her color, as if she would fain conceal the mortifying truth from every eye; but she had not time for answer ere Whittal Ring drew near, and pointing to the burning color of her cheeks, that were deepened as much with shame as with the heats of an American sun, he said—

"The wife of the sachem hath begun to change. She will soon be like Nipset—all red," he added, laying a finger on a part of his own arm, where the sun and the winds had not yet destroyed the original color; "the Evil-Spirit poured water into his blood too, but it will come out again. As soon as he is so dark that the Evil Spirit will not know him, he will go on the war-path, and then the lying pale-faces may dig up the bones of their fathers and move toward the sunrise, or his lodge will be lined with hair of the color of a deer!"

"And thou, my daughter! canst thou hear this threat against the people of thy nation—of thy blood—of thy God, without a shudder?"

The eye of Narra-mattah seemed in doubt; still it regarded Whittal with its accustomed look of kindness. The innocent, full of his imaginary glory, raised his hand in exultation, and by gestures that could not easily be misunderstood, he indicated the manner in which he intended to rob his victims of the usual trophy. While the youth was enacting the disgusting but expressive pantomime, Ruth watched the countenance of her child in breathless agony. She would have been relieved by a single glance of disapprobation, by a solitary movement of a rebellious muscle, or by the smallest sign that the tender nature of one so lovely, and otherwise so gentle, revolted at so unequivocal evidence of the barbarous practices of her adopted people.

But no empress of Rome could have witnessed the dying agonies of the hapless gladiator, no consort of a more modern prince could read the bloody list of the victims of her husband's triumph, nor any betrothed fair listen to the murderous deeds of him her imagination had painted as an hero, with less indifference to human suffering than that with which the wife of the Sachem of the Narragansetts looked on the mimic representation of those exploits which had purchased for her husband a renown so highly prized. It was but too apparent that the representation, rude and savage as it was, conveyed to her mind nothing but pictures in which the chosen companion of a warrior should rejoice. The varying features and answering eye too plainly proclaimed the sympathy of one taught to exult in the success of the combatant; and when Whittal, excited by his own exertions, broke out into an exhibition of a violence more ruthless even than common, he was openly rewarded by another laugh. The soft, exquisitely feminine tones of this involuntary burst of pleasure sounded in the ears of Ruth like a knell over the moral beauty of her child. Still subduing her feelings, she passed a hand thoughtfully over her own pallid brow, and appeared to muse long on the desolation of a mind that had once promised to be so pure.

The colonists had not yet severed all those natural ties which bound them to the eastern hemisphere. Their legends, their pride, and in many instances their memories, aided in keeping alive a feeling of amity, and it might be added of faith, in favor of the land of their ancestors. With some of their descendants, even to the present hour, the *beau-ideal* of excellence, in all that pertains to human qualities and human happiness, is connected with the images of the country, from which they sprang. Distance is known to cast a softening mist, equally over the moral and physical vision. The blue outline of mountain which melts into its glowing background of sky, is not more pleasing than the pictures which fancy sometimes draws of less material things; but, as he comes near, the disappointed traveler too often finds nakedness and deformity, where he so fondly imagined beauty only was to be seen. No wonder then that the dwellers of the simple provinces of New England blended recollections of the country they still called home, with most of their poetical pictures of life. They retained the language, the books, and most of the habits, of the English. But different circumstances, divided interests, and peculiar opinions, were gradually beginning to open those breaches which time has since widened, and which promise soon to leave little in common between the two peoples, except the same forms of speech and a common origin; it is to be hoped that some charity may be blended with these ties.

The singularly restrained habits of the religionists, throughout the whole of the British provinces, were in marked opposition to the mere embellishments of life. The arts were permitted only as they served its most useful and obvious purposes. With them, music was confined to the worship of God, and, for a long time after the original sentiment, the song was never known to lead the mind astray from what was conceived to be the one great object of existence. No verse was sung but such as blended holy ideas with the pleasures of harmony; nor were the sounds of revelry ever heard within their borders. Still, words adapted to their peculiar condition had come into use, and though poetry was neither a common nor a brilliant property of the mind, among a people thus disciplined to ascetic practices, it early exhibited its power in quaint versification, that was always intended, though with a success it is almost pardonable to doubt, to redound to the glory of the Deity. It was but a natural enlargement of this pious practice, to adapt some of these spiritual songs to purposes of the nursery.

When Ruth Heathcote passed her hand thoughtfully across her brow, it was with a painful conviction that her dominion over the mind of her child was sadly weakened, if not lost forever. But the efforts of maternal love are not easily repulsed. An idea flashed upon her brain, and she proceeded to try the efficacy of the experiment it suggested. Nature had endowed her with a melodious voice, and an ear that taught her to regulate sounds in a manner that seldom failed to touch the heart. She possessed the genius of music, which is melody, unweakened by those exaggerated affectations with which it is often encumbered by what is pretendingly called science. Drawing her daughter nearer to her knee, she commenced one of the songs then much used by the mothers of the colony, her voice scarcely rising above the whispering of the evening air, in its first notes, but gradually gaining, as she proceeded, the richness and compass that a strain so simple required.

At the first low breathing notes of this nursery song, Narrah-mattah became as motionless as if her rounded and unfettered form had been wrought in marble. Pleasure lighted her eyes, as strain succeeded strain; and ere the second verse was ended, her look, her attitude, and every muscle of her ingenuous features, were eloquent in the expression of delight. Ruth did not hazard the experiment without trembling for its result. Emotion imparted feeling to the music, and when, for the third time in the course of her song, she addressed her child, she saw the soft blue eyes that gazed wistfully on her face swimming in tears. Encouraged by this unequivocal evidence of success, nature grew still more powerful in its efforts, and the closing verse was sung to an ear that nestled near her heart, as it had often done during the early years of Narra-mattah while listening to its melancholy melody.

Content was a quiet but an anxious witness of this touching evidence of a reviving intelligence between his wife and child. He best understood the look that beamed in the eyes of the former, while her arms were, with extreme caution, folded around her who still leaned upon her bosom, as if fearful one so timid might be frightened from her security by any sudden or unaccustomed interruption. A minute passed in the deepest silence. Even Whittal Ring was lulled into quiet, and long and sorrowing years had passed since Ruth enjoyed moments of happiness so pure and unalloyed. The stillness was broken by a heavy step in the outer room; a door was thrown open by a hand more violent than common, and then young Mark appeared, his face flushed with exertion, his brow seemingly retaining the frown of battle, and with a tread that betrayed a spirit goaded by some fierce and unwelcome passion. The burden of Conanchet was on his arm. He laid it upon a table; then pointing, in a manner that appeared to challenge attention, he turned, and left the room as abruptly as he had entered.

A cry of joy burst from the lips of Narra-mattah, the instant the beaded belts caught her eye. The arms of Ruth relaxed their hold in surprise, and before amazement had time to give place to more connected ideas, the wild being at her knee had flown to the table, returned, resumed her former posture, opened the folds of the cloth, and was holding before the bewildered gaze of her mother the patient features of an Indian babe.

It would exceed the powers of the unambitious pen we wield to convey to the reader a just idea of the mixed emotions that struggled for mastery in the countenance of Ruth. The innate and never-dying sentiment of maternal joy was opposed by all those feelings of pride, that prejudice could not fail to implant even in the bosom of one so meek. There was no need to tell the history of the parentage of the little suppliant, who already looked up into her face with that peculiar calm which renders his race so remarkable. Though its glance was weakened by infancy, the dark glittering eye of Conanchet was there; there were also to be seen the receding forehead and the compressed lip of the father; but all these marks of his origin were softened by touches of that beauty which had rendered the infancy of her own child so remarkable.

"See!" said Narra-mattah, raising the infant still nearer to the riveted gaze of Ruth; "'tis a sachem of the red men! The little eagle hath left his nest too soon."

Ruth could not resist the appeal of her beloved. Bending her head low, so as entirely to conceal her own flushed face, she imprinted a kiss on the forehead of the Indian boy. But the jealous eye of the young mother was not to be deceived. Narra-mattah detected the difference between the cold salute and those fervent embraces she had herself received, and disappointment produced a chill about her own heart. Replacing the folds of the cloth with quiet dignity, she arose from her knee and withdrew in sadness to a distant corner of the room. There she took a seat, and with a glance that might almost be termed reproachful, she commenced a low Indian song to her infant.

"The wisdom of Providence is in this as in all its dispensations," whispered Content, over the shoulder of his nearly insensible partner. "Had we received her as she was lost, the favor might have exceeded our deservings. Our daughter is grieved that thou turnest a cold eye on her babe."

The appeal was sufficient for one whose affections had been wounded rather than chilled. It recalled Ruth to recollection, and it served at once to dissipate the shades of regret that had been unconsciously permitted to gather around her brow. The displeasure, or it would be more true to term it sorrow, of the young mother was easily appeased. A smile on her infant brought the blood back to her heart in a swift and tumultuous current; and Ruth herself soon forgot that she had any reason for regret in the innocent delight with which her own daughter now hastened to display the physical excellence of the boy. From this scene of natural feeling, Content was too quickly summoned by the intelligence that some one without awaited his presence on business of the last importance to the welfare of the settlement.

CHAPTER XXVIII.

"It will have blood; they say, blood
Will have blood!"—MACBETH.

THE visitors were Dr. Ergot, the Reverend Meek Wolfe, Ensign Dudley, and Reuben Ring. Content found these four individuals seated in an outer room, in a grave and restrained manner, that would have done no discredit to the self-command of an Indian council. He was saluted with those staid and composed greetings which are still much used in the intercourse of the people of the Eastern States of this Republic, and which have obtained for them a reputation, where they are little known, of a want of the more active charities of our nature. But that was peculiarly the age of sublimated doctrines, of self-mortification, and of severe moral government, and most men believe it a merit to exhibit, on all occasions, the dominion of the mind over the mere animal impulses. The usage, which took its rise in exalted ideas of spiritual perfection, has since grown into a habit, which, though weakened by the influence of the age, still exists to a degree that often leads to an erroneous estimate of character.

At the entrance of the master of the house, there was some such decorous silence as that which is known to precede the communications of the aborigines. At length Ensign Dudley, in whom matter, most probably in consequence of its bulk, bore more than a usual proportion to his less material part, manifested some evidences of impatience that the divine should proceed to business. Thus admonished, or possibly conceiving that a sufficient concession had been made to the dignity of man's nature, Meek opened his mouth to speak.

"Captain Content Heathcote," he commenced, with that mystical involution of his subject which practice had rendered nearly inseparable from all his communications; "Captain Content Heathcote, this hath been a day of awful visitations, and of gracious temporal gifts. The heathen hath been smitten severely by the hand of the believer, and the believer hath been made to pay the penalty of his want of faith, by the infliction of a savage agency. Azazel hath been loosened in our village, the legions of wickedness have been suffered to go at large in our fields, and yet the Lord hath remembered his people, and hath borne them through a trial of blood as perilous as was the passage of his chosen nation through the billows of the Red Sea. There is cause of mourning, and cause of joy, in this manifestation of his will; of sorrow that we have merited his anger, and of rejoicing that enough of redeeming grace hath been found to save the Gomorrah of our hearts. But I speak to one trained in spiritual discipline, and schooled in the vicissitudes of the world, and further discourse is not necessary to quicken his apprehension. We will therefore turn to more instant and temporal exercises. Have all of thy household escaped unharmed throughout the strivings of this bloody day?"

"We praise the Lord that such hath been his pleasure," returned Content. "Other than as sorrow hath assailed us through the mourning of friends, the blow hath fallen lightly on me and mine."

"Thou hast had thy season; the parent ceaseth to chastise, while former punishments are remembered. But here is Sergeant Ring, with matter to communicate, that may still leave business for thy courage and thy wisdom."

Content turned his quiet look upon the yeoman, and seemed to await his speech. Reuben Ring, who was a man of many solid and valuable qualities, would most probably have been exercising the military functions of his brother-in-law at that very moment, had he been equally gifted with a fluent discourse. But his feats lay rather in doing than in speaking, and the tide of popularity had in consequence set less strongly in his favor than might have happened had the reverse been the case. The present, however, was a moment when it was necessary to overcome his natural reluctance to speak, and it was not long before he replied to the inquiring glance of his commander's eye.

"The captain knows the manner in which we scourged the savages at the southern end of the valley," the sturdy yeoman began, "and it is not necessary to deal with the particulars at length. There were six-and-twenty red-skins slain in the meadows, besides as many more that left the ground in the arms of their friends. As for the people, we got a few hurts, but each man came back on his own limbs."

"This is much as the matter hath been reported."

"Then there was a party sent to brush the woods on the trail of the Indians," resumed Reuben, without appearing to regard the interruption. "The scouts broke off in pairs in the duty, and finally men got to searching singly, of which number I was one. The two men of whom there is question—"

"Of what men dost speak?" demanded Content.

"The two men of whom there is question," returned the other, continuing the direct course of his own manner in relating events, without appearing to see the necessity of connecting the threads of his communication; "the men of whom I have spoken to the minister and the ensign—"

"Proceed," said Content, who understood his man.

"After one of these men was brought to his end, I saw no reason for making the day bloodier than it already was, the more especially as the Lord had caused it to begin with a merciful hand, which shed its bounties on my own dwelling. Under such an opinion of right-doing the other was bound and led into the clearings."

"Thou hast made a captive?"

The lips of Reuben scarce severed as he muttered a low assent; but the Ensign Dudley took upon himself the duty of entering into further explanations, which the point where his kinsman left the narrative enabled him to do with sufficient intelligence.

"As the sergeant hath related," he said, "one of the heathen fell, and the other is now without, awaiting a judgment in the matter of his fortune."

"I trust there is no wish to harm him," said Content, glancing an eye uneasily around at his companions. "Strife hath done enough in our settlement this day. The sergeant hath a right to claim the scalp-bounty, for the man that is slain; but for him that liveth, let there be mercy!"

"Mercy is a quality of heavenly origin," replied Meek Wolfe, "and it should not be perverted to defeat the purposes of heavenly wisdom. Azazel must not triumph, though the tribe of the Narragansetts should be swept with the besom of destruction. Truly, we are an erring and a fallible race, Captain Heathcote; and the greater, therefore, the necessity that we submit without rebellion to the inward monitors that are implanted, by grace, to teach us the road of our duty—"

"I cannot consent to shed blood, now that the strife hath ceased," hastily interrupted Content. "Praised be Providence! we are victors; and it is time to lean to counsels of charity."

"Such are the deceptions of a short-sighted wisdom!" returned the divine, his dim, sunken eye shining with the promptings of an exaggerated and subtle spirit. "The end of all is good, and we may not, without mortal danger, presume to doubt the suggestions of heavenly gifts. But there is no question here concerning the execution of the captive, since he proffereth to be of service in far greater things than any that can depend on his life or his death. The heathen rendered up his liberty with little struggle, and hath propositions that may lead us to a profitable conclusion of this day's trials."

"If he can aid in aught that shall shorten the perils and wantonness of this ruthless war, he shall find none better disposed to listen than I."

"He professeth ability to do that service."

"Then of Heaven's mercy! let him be brought forth, that we counsel on his proposals."

Meek made a gesture to Sergeant Ring, who quitted the apartment for a moment, and shortly after, returned followed by his captive. The Indian was one of those dark and malignant-looking savages that possess most of the sinister properties of their condition, with few or none of the redeeming qualities. His eye was lowering and distrustful, bespeaking equally apprehension and revenge; his form of that middling degree of perfection which leaves as little to admire as to condemn, and his attire such as denoted him one who might be ranked among the warriors of a secondary class. Still, in the composure of his mien, the tranquillity of his step, and the self-possession of all his movements, he displayed that high bearing his people rarely fail to exhibit, ere too much intercourse with the whites begins to destroy their distinctive traits.

"Here is the Narragansett," said Reuben Ring, causing his prisoner to appear in the center of the room; "he is no chief, as may be gathered from his uncertain look."

"If he effect that of which there hath been question, his rank mattereth little. We seek to stop the currents of blood that flow like running water in these devoted colonies."

"This will he do," rejoined the divine, "or we shall hold him answerable for breach of promise."

"And in what doth he profess to aid in stopping the work of death?"

"By yielding the fierce Philip, and his savage ally, the roving Conanchet, to the judgment. Those chiefs destroyed, our temple may be entered in peace, and the voice of thanksgiving shall again rise in our Bethel, without the profane interruption of savage shrieks."

Content started, and even recoiled a step, as he listened to the nature of the proposed peace-offering.

"And have we warranty for such a proceeding, should this man prove true?" he asked, in a voice that sufficently denoted his own doubts of the propriety of such a measure.

"There is the law, the necessities of a suffering nature, and God's glory, for our justification," dryly returned the divine.

"This outsteppeth the discreet exercise of a delegated authority. I like not to assume so great power, without written mandates for its execution."

"The objection hath raised a little difficulty in my own mind," observed Ensign Dudley; "and as it hath set thoughts at work, it is possible that what I have to offer will meet the captain's good approbation."

Content knew that his ancient servitor was, though often uncouth in its exhibition, at the bottom a man of humane heart. On the other hand, while he scarce admitted the truth to himself, he had a secret dread of the exaggerated sentiments of his spiritual guide; and he consequently listened to the interruption of Eben with a gratification he scarcely wished to conceal.

"Speak openly," he said; "when men counsel in a matter of this weight, each standeth on the surety of his proper gifts."

"Then may this business be dispatched without the embarrassment the captain seems to dread. We have an Indian, who offers to lead a party through the forests to the haunts of the bloody chiefs, therein bringing affairs to the issue of manhood and discretion."

"And wherein do you propose any departure from the suggestions that have already been made?"

Ensign Dudley had not risen to his present rank without acquiring a suitable portion of the reserve which is so often found to dignify official sentiments. Having ventured the opinion already placed, however vaguely, before his hearers, he was patiently awaiting its effects on the mind of his superior, when the latter, by his earnest and unsuspecting countenance, no less than by the question just given, showed that he was still in the dark as to the expedient the subaltern wished to suggest.

"I think there will be no necessity for making more captives," resumed Eben, "since the one we have appears to create difficulties in our councils. If there be any law in the colony which says that men must strike with a gentle hand in open battle, it is a law but little spoken of in common discourse; and, though no pretender to the wisdom of legislators, I will make bold to add, it is a law that may as well be forgotten until this outbreaking of the savages shall be quelled."

"We deal with an enemy that never stays his hand at the cry of mercy," observed Meek Wolfe, "and though charity be the fruit of Christian qualities, there is a duty greater than any which belongeth to earth. We are no more than weak and feeble instruments in the hands of Providence, and as such our minds should not be hardened to our inward promptings. If evidence of better feeling could be found in the deeds of the heathen, we might raise our hopes to the completion of things; but the powers of darkness still rage in their hearts, and we are taught to believe that the tree is known by its fruits."

Content signed to all to await his return, and left the room. In another minute he was seen leading his daughter into the center of the circle. The half-alarmed young woman clasped her swaddled boy to her bosom, as she gazed timidly at the grave faces of the borderers; and her eye recoiled in fear, when its hurried glance met the sunken, glazed, excited, and yet equivocal-looking organ of the Reverend Mr. Wolfe.

"Thou hast said that the savage never hearkens to the cry of mercy," resumed Content; "here is living evidence that thou hast spoken in error. The misfortune that early befell my family is not unknown to any in this settlement; thou seest in this trembling creature the daughter of our love—her we have so long mourned. The wept of my household is again with us; our hearts have been oppressed, they are now gladdened. God hath returned our child!"

There was deep, rich pathos in the tones of the father that affected most of his auditors, though each manifested his sensibilities in a manner suited to his peculiar habits of mind. The nature of the divine was touched, and all the energies of his severe principles were wanting to sustain him above the manifestation of a weakness that he might have believed derogatory to his spiritual exaltation of character. He therefore sat mute, with hands folded on his knee, betraying the struggles of an awakened sympathy only by a firmer compression of the interlocked fingers, and an occasional and involuntary movement of the stronger muscles of the face. Dudley suffered a smile of pleasure to lighten

his broad, open countenance; and the physician, who had hitherto been merely a listener, uttered a few low syllables of admiration of the physical perfection of the being before him, with which there was mingled some evidence of natural good feeling.

Reuben Ring was the only individual who openly betrayed the whole degree of the interest he took in the restoration of the lost female. The stout yeoman arose, and moving to the entranced Narramattah, he took the infant into his large hands, and for a moment the honest borderer gazed at the boy with a wistful and softened eye. Then raising the diminutive face of the infant to his own expanded and bold features, he touched his cheek with his lips, and returned the babe to its mother, who witnessed the whole proceeding in some such tribulation as the startled wren exhibits when the foot of the urchin is seen to draw too near the nest of its young.

"Thou seest that the hand of the Narragansett hath been stayed," said Content, when a deep silence had succeeded this little movement, and speaking in a tone which betrayed hopes of victory.

"The ways of Providence are mysterious!" returned Meek; "wherein they bring comfort to the heart, it is right that we exhibit gratitude; and wherein they are charged with the present affliction, it is meet to bow with humbled spirits to their orderings. But the visitations on families are merely—"

He paused, for at that moment a door opened, and a party entered bearing a burden, which they deposited with decent and grave respect on the floor in the very center of the room. The unceremonious manner of the entrance, the assured and the common gravity of their air, proclaimed that the villagers felt their errand to be a sufficient apology for this intrusion. Had not the business of the past day naturally led to such a belief, the manner and aspects of those who had borne the burden would have announced it to be a human body.

"I had believed that none fell in this day's strife, but those who met their end near my own door," said Content, after a long, respectful, and sorrowing pause. "Remove the face-cloth that we may know on whom the blow hath fallen."

One of the young men obeyed. It was not easy to recognize through the mutilations of savage barbarity the features of the sufferer. But a second and steadier look showed the gory and still agonized countenance of the individual who had that morning left the Wish-Ton-Wish on the message of the colonial authorities. Even men as practiced as those present in the horrible inventions of Indian cruelty, turned sickening away from a spectacle that was calculated to chill the blood of all who had not become callous to human affliction. Content made a sign to cover the miserable remnants of mortality, and hid his face with a shudder.

It is not necessary to dwell on the scene that followed. Meek Wolfe availed himself of this unexpected event to press his plan on the attention of the commanding officer of the settlement, who was certainly far better disposed to listen to his proposals than before this palpable evidence of the ruthless character of their enemies was presented to his view. Still Content listened with reluctance, nor was it without the intention of exercising an ulterior discretion in the case, that he finally consented to give orders for the departure of a body of men with the approach of the morning light. As much of the discourse was managed with those half-intelligible allusions that distinguished men of their habits, it is probable that every individual present had his own particular views on the subject; though it is certain one and all faithfully believed that he was solely influenced by a justifiable regard to his temporal interest; which was in some degree rendered still more praiseworthy by a reference to the service of his Divine Master.

As the party returned, Dudley lingered a moment alone with his former master. The face of the honest-meaning ensign was charged with more than its usual significance; and he even paused a little after all were beyond hearing, ere he could muster resolution to propose the subject that was so evidently uppermost in his mind.

"Captain Content Heathcote," he at length commenced, "evil or good comes not alone in this life. Thou hast found her that was sought with so much pain and danger, but thou hast found with her more than a Christian gentleman can desire. I am a man of humble station, but I may make bold to know what should be the feelings of a father whose child is restored, replenished by such an over-bountiful gift."

"Speak plainer," said Content firmly.

"Then I would say, that it may not be grateful to one who taketh his place among the best in this colony, to have an offspring with an Indian cross of blood, and over whose birth no rite of Christian marriage hath been said. Here is Abundance, a woman of exceeding usefulness in a newly settled region, hath made Reuben a gift of three noble boys this very morning. The accession is little known, and less discoursed of, in that the good wife is accustomed to such liberality, and that the day hath brought forth still greater events. Now a child more or less to such a woman can neither raise question among the neighbors nor make any extraordinary difference to the household. My brother Ring would be happy to add the boy to his stock; and should there be any remarks concerning the color of the younker, at a future day, it should give no reason of surprise had the whole four been born, on the day of such an inroad, red as Metacom himself?"

Content heard his companion to the end without interruption. His countenance, for a single instant, as the meaning of the ensign became unequivocal, reddened with a worldly feeling to which he had long been a stranger, but the painful expression as quickly disappeared, and in its place reigned the meek submission to Providence that habitually characterized his mien.

"That I have been troubled with this vain thought I shall not deny," he answered; "but the Lord hath given me strength to resist. It is his will that one sprung of heathen lineage shall come beneath my roof, and let his will be done! My child and all that are hers are welcome."

Ensign Dudley pressed the point no further, and they separated.

CHAPTER XXIX.

"Tarry a little;—there is something else."
—Merchant of Venice.

We shift the scene. The reader will transport himself from the valley of the Wish-Ton-Wish to the bosom of a deep and dark wood.

It may be thought that such scenes have been too often described to need any repetition. Still, as it is possible that these pages may fall into the hands of some who have never quitted the older members of the Union, we shall endeavor to give them a faint impression concerning the appearance of the place to which it has become our duty to transfer the action of the tale.

Although it is certain that inanimate, like animate nature, has its period, the existence of the tree has no fixed and common limit. The oak, the elm, and the linden, the quick-growing sycamore and the tall pine, has each its own laws for the government of its growth, its magnitude and its duration. By this provision of nature, the wilderness, in the midst of so many successive changes, is always maintained at the point nearest to perfection, since the accessions are so few and gradual as to preserve its character.

The American forest exhibits in the highest degree the grandeur of repose. As nature never does violence to its own laws, the soil throws out the plant which it is best qualified to support, and the eye is not often disappointed by a sickly vegetation. There ever seems a generous emulation in the trees, which is not to be found among others of different families, when left to pursue their existence in the solitude of the fields. Each struggles toward the light, and an equality in bulk and a similarity in form are thus produced, which scarce belong to their distinctive characters. The effect may be easily imagined. The vaulted arches beneath are filled with thousands of high, unbroken columns, which sustain one vast and trembling canopy of leaves. A pleasing gloom and an imposing silence have their interminable reign below, while an outer and another atmosphere seems to rest on the cloud of foliage.

While the light plays on the varying surface of the tree-tops, one somber and little-varied hue colors the earth. Dead and moss-covered logs; mounds covered with decomposed vegetable substances, the graves of long-past generations of trees; cavities left by the fall of some uprooted trunk; dark fungi, that flourish around the decayed roots of those about to lose their hold, with a few slender and delicate plants of a minor growth, and which best succeed in the shade, form the accompaniments of the lower scene. The whole is tempered, and in summer rendered grateful, by a freshness which equals that of the subterranean vault, without possessing any of its chilling dampness. In the midst of this gloomy solitude the foot of man is rarely heard. An occasional glimpse of the bounding deer or trotting moose is almost the only interruption on the earth itself; while the heavy bear or leaping panther is, at long intervals, met seated on the branches of some venerable tree. There are moments, too, when troops of hungry wolves are found hunting on the trail of the deer; but these are seen rather as exceptions to the stillness of the place, than as accessories that should properly be introduced into the picture. Even the birds are, in common, mute, or when they do break the silence, it is in a discordance that suits the character of their wild abode.

Through such a scene two men were in-dustriously journeying on the day which succeeded the inroad last described. They marched as wont, one after the other, the younger and more active leading the way through the monotony of the woods, as accurately and as unhesitatingly as the mariner directs his course by the aid of the needle over the waste of waters. He in front was light, agile, and seemingly unwearied; while the one who followed was a man of heavy mold, whose step denoted less practice in the exercise of the forest, and possibly some failing of natural vigor.

"Thine eye, Narragansett, is an unerring compass by which to steer, and thy leg a never-wearied steed," said the latter, casting the butt of his musket on the end of a moldering log, while he leaned on the barrel for support. "If thou movest on the war-path with the same diligence as thou usest in our errand of peace, well may the colonist dread thy enmity."

The other turned, and without seeking aid from the gun which rested against his shoulder, he pointed at the several objects he named, and answered—

"My father is this aged sycamore; it leans against the young oak. Conanchet is a straight pine. There is great cunning in gray hairs," added the chief, stepping lightly forward until a finger rested on the arm of Submission; can they tell the time when we shall lie under the moss like a dead hemlock?"

"That exceedeth the wisdom of man. It is enough, sachem, if when we fall, we may say with truth, that the land we shadowed is no poorer for our growth. Thy bones will lie in the earth where thy fathers trod, but mine may whiten in the vault of some gloomy forest."

The quiet of the Indian's face was disturbed. The pupils of his dark eyes contracted, his nostrils dilated, and his full chest heaved, and then all reposed like the sluggish ocean after a vain effort to heave its waters into some swelling wave, during a general calm.

"Fire hath scorched the prints of my father's moccasins from the earth," he said, with a smile that was placid though bitter, "and my eyes cannot find them. I shall die under that shelter," pointing through an opening in the foliage to the blue void; "the falling leaves will cover my bones."

"Then hath the Lord given us a new bond of friendship. There is a yew-tree and a quiet churchyard in the country afar, where generations of my race sleep in their graves. The place is white with stones, that bear the name of—"

Submission suddenly ceased to speak,

and when his eye was raised to that of his companion it was just in time to detect the manner in which the curious interest of the latter changed suddenly to cold reserve, and to note the high courtesy of the air with which the Indian turned the discourse.

"There is water beyond the little hill," he said. "Let my father drink and grow strong, that he may live to lie in the clearings."

The other bowed, and they proceeded to the spot in silence. It would seem by the length of time that was now lost in taking the required refreshment, that the travelers had journeyed long and far. The Narragansett ate more sparingly, however, than his companion; for his mind appeared to sustain a weight that was far more grievous than the fatigue which had been endured by the body. Still his composure was little disturbed outwardly—for during the silent repast he maintained the air of a dignified warrior, rather than that of a man whose air could be much affected by inward sorrow. When nature was appeased, they both arose, and continued their route through the pathless forest.

For an hour after quitting the spring, the progress of our two adventurers was swift, and uninterrupted by any passing observation or momentary pause. At the end of that time, however, the speed of Conanchet began to slacken, and his eye, instead of maintaining its steady and forward direction, was seen to wander with some of the appearance of indecision.

"Thou hast lost those secret signs by which we have so far threaded the woods," observed his companion; "one tree is like another, and I see no difference in this wilderness of nature; but if thou art at fault, we may truly despair of our object."

"Here is the nest of the eagle," returned Conanchet, pointing at the object he named perched on the upper and whitened branches of the dead pine; "and my father may see the council-tree in this oak—but there are no Wampanoags!"

"There are many eagles in this forest—nor is that oak one that may not have its fellow. Thine eye hath been deceived, sachem, and some false sign hath led us astray."

Conanchet looked at his companion attentively. After a moment, he quietly asked—

"Did my father ever mistake his path, in going from his wigwam to the place where he looked upon the house of his Great Spirit?"

"The matter of that often traveled path was different, Narragansett. My foot had worn the rock with many passings, and the distance was a span. But we have journeyed through leagues of forest, and our route hath lain across brook and hill, through brake and morass, where human vision hath not been able to detect the smallest sign of the presence of man."

"My father is old," said the Indian, respectfully. "His eye is not as quick as when he took the scalp of the Great Chief, or he would know the print of a moccasin. See"—making his companion observe the mark of a human foot that was barely discernible by the manner in which the dead leaves had been displaced—"his rock is worn, but it is harder than the ground. He cannot tell by its signs who passed, or when."

"Here is truly that which ingenuity may portray as the print of man's foot; but it is alone, and may be some accident of the wind."

"Let my father look on every side; he will see that a tribe hath passed."

"This may be true, though my vision is unequal to detect that thou wouldst show. But if a tribe hath passed, let us follow."

Conanchet shook his head, and spread the fingers of his two hands in a manner to describe the radii of a circle.

"Hugh!" he said, starting even while he was thus significantly answering by gestures, "a moccasin comes!"

Submission, who had so often and so recently been arrayed against the savages, involuntarily sought the lock of his carbine. His look and action were menacing, though his roving eye could see no object to excite alarm.

Not so Conanchet. His quicker and more practiced vision soon caught a glimpse of the warrior who was approaching, occasionally concealed by the trunks of trees, and whose tread on the dried leaves had first betrayed his proximity. Folding his arms on his naked bosom, the Narragansett chief awaited the coming of the other, in an attitude of calmness and dignity. Neither did he speak nor suffer a muscle to play, until a hand was placed on one of his arms, and he who had drawn near, said, in tones of amity and respect—

"The young sachem hath come to look for his brother?"

"Wampanoag, I have followed the trail, that your ears may listen to the talk of a pale-face."

The third person in this interview was Metacom. He shot a haughty and fierce glance at the stranger, and then turned to his companion in arms, with recovered calmness, to reply.

"Has Conanchet counted his young men since they raised the whoop?" he asked, in the language of the aborigines. "I saw many go into the fields, that never came back. Let the white man die."

"Wampanoag, he is led by the wampum of a sachem. I have not counted my young men; but I know that they are strong enough to say that what their chief hath promised shall be done."

"If the Yengeese is a friend to my brother, he is welcome. The wigwam of Metacom is open; let him enter it."

Philip made a sign for the others to follow, and led the way to the place he had named.

The spot chosen by Philip for his temporary encampment was suited to such a purpose. There was a thicket denser than common on one of its sides—a steep and high rock protected and sheltered its rear; a swift and wide brook dashed over fragments that had fallen, with time, from the precipice in its front, and toward the setting sun a whirlwind had opened a long and melancholy glade through the forest. A few huts of brush leaned against the base of the hill, and the scanty implements of their domestic economy were scattered among the habitations of the savages. The whole party did not number twenty; for, as has been said, the Wampanoag had acted latterly more by the agency of his allies, than with the materials of his own proper force.

The three were soon seated on a rock whose foot was washed by the rapid current of the tumbling water. A few gloomy looking and fierce Indians watched the conference in the background.

"My brother hath followed my trail, that my ears may hear the words of a Yengeese," Philip commenced, after a sufficient period had elapsed to escape the imputation of curiosity. "Let him speak."

"I have come single into the jaws of the lion, restless and remorseless leader of the savages," returned the bold exile, "that you may hear the words of peace. Why hath the son seen the acts of the English so differently from the father? Massasoit was a friend of the persecuted and patient pilgrims who have sought rest and refuge in this Bethel of the faithful; but thou hast hardened thy heart to their prayers, and seekest the blood of those who wish thee no wrong. Doubtless thy nature is one of pride and mistaken vanities, like that of all thy race, and it hath seemed needful to the vain-glory of

thy name and nation to battle against men of a different origin. But know there is One who is master of all here on earth, as he is King of Heaven! It is his pleasure that the sweet savor of his worship should arise from the wilderness. His will is law, and they that would withstand do but kick against the pricks. Listen then to peaceful counsels, that the land may be parceled justly to meet the wants of all, and the country be prepared for the incense of the altar."

This exhortation was uttered in a deep and almost unearthly voice, and with a degree of excitement that was probably increased by the intensity with which the solitary had lately been brooding over his peculiar opinions, and the terrible scenes in which he had so recently been an actor. Philip listened with the high courtesy of an Indian prince. Unintelligible as was the meaning of the speaker, his countenance betrayed no gleaming of impatience, his lip no smile of ridicule. On the contrary, a noble and lofty gravity reigned in every feature; and ignorant as he was of what the other wished to say, his attentive eye and bending head expressed every wish to comprehend.

"My pale friend hath spoken very wisely," he said, when the other ceased to speak. "But he doth not see clearly in these woods; he sits too much in the shade; his eye is better in a clearing. Metacom is not a fierce beast. His claws are worn out; his legs are tired with traveling; he cannot jump far. My pale friend wants to divide the land. Why trouble the Great Spirit to do his work twice? He gave the Wampanoags their hunting grounds, and places on the salt lake to catch their fish and clams, and he did not forget his children, the Narragansetts. He put them in the midst of the water, for that he saw they could swim. Did he forget the Yengeese? or did he put them in a swamp, where they would turn into frogs and lizards?"

"Heathen, my voice shall never deny the bounties of my God! His hand hath placed my fathers in a fertile land, rich in the good things of the world, fortunate in position, sea-girt and impregnable. Happy is he who can find justification in dwelling within its borders!"

An empty gourd lay on the rock, at the side of Metacom. Bending over the stream he filled it to the brim with water, and held the vessel before the eyes of his companions.

"See," he said, pointing to the even surface of the fluid; "so much hath the Great Spirit said it shall hold. Now," he added, filling the hollow of the other hand from the brook, and casting its contents into the gourd, "now my brother knows that some must come away. It is so with his country. There is no longer room in it for my pale friend."

"Did I attempt to deceive thine ears with this tale, I should lay falsehood to my soul. We are many, and sorry am I to say that some among us are like unto them that were called 'Legion.' But to say that there is not still place for all to die where they are born, is to utter damning untruth."

"The land of the Yengeese is then good—very good," returned Philip; "but their young men like one that is better."

"Thy nature, Wampanoag, is not equal to comprehend the motives which have led us hither, and our discourse is getting vain."

"My brother Conanchet is a sachem. The leaves that fall from the trees of his country, in the season of frost, blow into my hunting grounds. We are neighbors and friends," slightly bending his head to the Narragansett. "When a wicked Indian runs from the islands to the wigwams of my people, he is whipped and sent back. We keep the path between us open only for honest red men."

Philip spoke with a sneer that his habitual loftiness of manner did not conceal from his associate chief, though it was so slight as entirely to escape the observation of him who was the subject of his sarcasm. The former took the alarm, and for the first time during the dialogue did he break silence.

"My pale father is a brave warrior," said the young sachem of the Narragansetts. "His hand took the scalp of the Great Sagamore of his people!"

The countenance of Metacom changed instantly. In place of the ironical scorn that was gathering about his lip, its expression became serious and respectful. He gazed steadily at the hard and weather-beaten features of his guest; and it is probable that words of higher courtesy than any he had yet used would have fallen from him, had not at that moment a signal been given by a young Indian, set to watch on the summit of the rock, that one approached. Both Metacom and Conanchet appeared to hear this cry with some uneasiness. Neither, however, arose, nor did either betray such evidence of alarm as denoted a deeper interest in the interruption than the circumstances might very naturally create. A warrior was shortly seen entering the encampment, from the side of the forest which was known to lie in the direction of Wish-Ton-Wish.

The moment Conanchet saw the person of the newly-arrived man, his eye and attitude resumed their former repose, though the look of Metacom still continued gloomy and distrustful. The difference in the manner of the chiefs was not however sufficiently strong to be remarked by Submission, who was about to resume the discourse, when the new-comer moved past the cluster of warriors in the encampment, and took his seat near them, on a stone so low, that the water laved his feet. As usual, there was no greeting between the Indians for some moments, the three appearing to regard the arrival as a mere thing of course. But the uneasiness of Metacom prompted a communication sooner than common.

"Mohtucket," he said, in the language of their tribe, "hath lost the trail of his friends. We thought the crows of the pale men were picking his bones!"

"There was no scalp at his belt, and Mohtucket was ashamed to be seen among the young men with an empty hand."

"He remembered that he had too often come back without striking a dead enemy," returned Metacom, about whose firm mouth lurked an expression of ill-concealed contempt. "Has he now touched a warror?"

The Indian, who was merely a man of the inferior class, held up the trophy which hung at his girdle, to the examination of the chief. Metacom looked at the disgusting object with the calmness and nearly with the interest that a virtuoso would lavish on an antique memorial of some triumph of former ages. His finger was thrust through a hole in the skin, and then, while he resumed his former position, he observed dryly—

"A bullet hath hit the head. The arrow of Mohtucket doth little harm!"

"Metacom hath never looked on his young man like a friend since the brother of Mohtucket was killed."

The glance that Philip cast at his underling, though it was not unmingled with suspicion, was one of princely and savage scorn. The white auditor had not been able to understand the discourse, but the dissatisfaction and uneasiness of the eyes of both were too obvious not to show that the conference was far from being amicable.

"The sachem hath discontent with his young man," he observed, " and from this may he understand the nature of that which leadeth many to quit the land of their fathers, beneath the rising sun, to come to this wilderness in the west. If he will now listen I will touch further on the business of my errand, and deal more at large with the subject we have but so lightly skimmed.''

Philip manifested attention. He smiled on his guest, and even bowed his assent to the proposal; still his keen eye seemed to read the soul of his subordinate, through the veil of his gloomy visage. There was a play of the fingers of his right hand when the arm fell from its position across his bosom to his thigh, as if they itched to grasp the knife, whose buck-horn handle lay within a few inches of their reach. Yet his air to the white man was composed and dignified. The latter was again about to speak, when the arches of the forest suddenly rang with the report of a musket. All in and near the encampment sprang to their feet at the well-known sound, and yet all continued as motionless as if so many dark but breathing statues had been planted there. The rustling of leaves was heard, and then the body of the young Indian who had been posted on the rock rolled to the edge of the precipice, whence it fell like a log on the yielding roof of one of the lodges beneath. A shout issued from the forest behind, a volley roared among the trees, and glancing lead was whistling through the air, and cutting twigs from the undergrowth on every side. Two more of the Wampanoags were seen rolling on the earth in the death agony.

The voice of Annawon was heard in the encampment, and at the next instant the place was deserted.

During the startling and fearful moment the four individuals near the stream were inactive. Conanchet and his Christian friend stood to their arms, but it was rather as men cling to the means of defense in moments of great jeopardy, than with any intention of offensive hostilities. Metacom seemed undecided. Accustomed to receive and inflict surprises, a warrior so experienced could not be disconcerted; still he hesitated as to the course he ought to take. But when Annawon, who was nearer the scene, sounded the signal of retreat, he sprang toward the returned straggler, and with a single blow of his tomahawk brained the traitor. Glances of fierce revenge, and of inextinguishable though disappointed hatred, were exchanged between the victim and his chief, as the former lay on the rock, gasping for breath; and then the latter turned in his tracks, and raised the dripping weapon over the head of the white man.

"Wampanoag, no!" said Conanchet, in a voice of thunder. "Our lives are one."

Philip hesitated. Fierce and dangerous passions were struggling in his breast, but the habitual self-command of the wily politician of those woods prevailed. Even in that scene of blood and alarm he smiled on his powerful and fearless young ally; then pointing to the deepest shades of the forest he bounded toward them with the activity of a deer.

CHAPTER XXX.

"But peace be with him!
That life is better life, past fearing death,
Than that which lives to fear."
—MEASURE FOR MEASURE.

COURAGE is both a comparative and an improvable virtue. If the fear of death be a weakness common to the race, it is one that is capable of being diminished by frequent exposure, and even rendered extinct by reflection. It was, therefore, with sensibilities entirely changed from their natural course, that the two individuals who were left alone by the retreat of Philip, saw the nature and the approach of the danger that now beset them. Their position near the brook had so far protected them from the bullets of the assailants; but it was equally obvious to both, that in a minute or two the colonists would enter an encampment that was already deserted. Each, in consequence, acted according to those opinions which had been fostered by the habits of their respective lives.

As Conanchet had no act of vengeance like that which Metacom had performed, immediately before his eyes, he had, at the first alarm, given all his faculties to the nature of the attack. The first minute was sufficient to understand its character, and the second enabled him to decide.

"Come," he said, hastily, but with perfect self-possession, pointing as he spoke to the swift-running stream at his feet; "we will go with the water, let the marks of our trail run before."

Submission hesitated. There was something like haughty military pride in the stern determination of his eye, which seemed reluctant to incur the disgrace of a flight so unequivocal, and, as he might have believed, so unworthy of his character.

"No, Narragansett," he answered; "flee for thy life, but leave me to reap the harvest of my deeds. They can but leave my bones by the side of those of this traitor at my feet."

The mien of Conanchet was neither excited nor displeased. He quietly drew the corner of his light robe over a shoulder, and was about to resume his seat on the stone from which he had but a minute before arisen, when his companion again urged him to fly.

"The enemies of a chief must not say that he led his friend into a trap, and that when his leg was fast he ran away himself like a lucky fox. If my brother stays to be killed, Conanchet will be found near him."

"Heathen, heathen!" returned the other, moved nearly to tears by the loyalty of his guide; "many a Christian man might take lessons from thy faith. Lead on—I will follow at the utmost of my speed."

The Narragansett sprang into the brook and took its downward course—a direction opposite to that which Philip had chosen. There was wisdom in this expedient; for though their pursuers might see that the water was troubled, there was no certainty as to the direction of the fugitives. Conanchet had foreseen this little advantage, and with the instinctive readiness of his people, he did not fail to make it of service. Metacom had been influenced by the course taken by his warriors, who had retired under shelter of the rocks.

Ere the two fugitives had gone any great distance they heard the shouts of their enemies in the encampment; and soon after, scattering shots announced that Philip had already rallied his people to resistance. There was an assurance of safety in the latter circumstance, which caused them to relax their speed.

"My foot is not as active as in days that are past," said Submission; "we will therefore recover strength while we may, lest we be yet taken at emergency. Narragansett, thou hast ever kept thy faith with me, and come of what race or worship in what manner thou mayst, there is one to remember it."

"My father looked with the eye of a friend on the Indian boy that was kept like a young bear in a cage. He taught him to speak with the tongue of a Yengeese."

"We passed weary months together in our prison, chief; and Apollyon must have been strong in a heart, to resist the opportunity of friendship, in such a situation. But, even there, my confidence and care were repaid, for without thy mysterious hints, gathered from signs thou hadst gleaned thyself during the hunt, it would not have been in my power to warn my friends that thy people contemplated an attack, the unhappy night of the burning. Narragansett, we have done many acts of kindness, each in his own fashion,

and I am ready to confess this last not to be the least of thy favors. Though of white blood and of Christian origin, I can almost say that my heart is Indian."

"Then die an Indian's death!" shouted a voice within twenty feet of the spot where they were wading down the stream.

The menacing words were rather accompanied than seconded by a shot, and Submission fell. Conanchet cast his musket into the water, and turned to raise his companion.

"It was merely age dealing with the slippery stones of the brook," said the latter, as he recovered his footing. "That had well-nigh been a fatal discharge! but God, for his own purpose, hath still averted the blow.

Conanchet did not speak. Seizing his gun, which lay at the bottom of the stream, he drew his friend after him to the shore, and plunged into the thicket that lined its banks. Here they were momentarily protected from missiles. But the shouts that succeeded the discharge of the muskets, were accompanied by yells that he knew to proceed from Pequods and Mohicans, tribes that were in deadly hostility to his own people. The hope of concealing their trail from such pursuers was not to be indulged, and for his companion to escape by flight he knew to be impossible. There was no time to lose. In such emergencies, with an Indian, thought takes the character of instinct. The fugitives stood at the foot of a sapling, whose top was completely concealed by masses of leaves, which belonged to the under-brush that clustered around its trunk. Into this tree he assisted Submission to ascend, and then, without explaining his own views, he instantly left the spot, rendering his own trail as broad and perceptible as possible, by beating down the bushes as he passed.

The expedient of the faithful Narragansett was completely successful. Before he had got a hundred yards from the place, he saw the foremost of the hostile Indians hunting like bloodhounds on his footsteps. His movement was slow, until he saw that, having his person in view, all of the pursuers had passed the tree. Then, the arrow parting from the bow was scarce swifter than his flight.

The pursuit now partook of all the exciting incidents and ingenious expedients of an Indian chase. Conanchet was soon hunted from his cover, and obliged to trust his person in the more open parts of the forest. Miles of hill and ravine, of plain, of rocks, of morass and stream were crossed, and still the trained warrior held on his way unbroken in spirit and scarce wearied in limb. The merit of a savage in such an employment rests more on his bottom than on his speed. The three or four colonists, who had been sent with the party of amicable Indians to intercept those who might attempt to escape down the stream, were early thrown out; and the struggle was now entirely between the fugitive and men equally practiced in limb and ingenious in expedient.

The Pequods had a great advantage in their number. The frequent doublings of the fugitive kept the chase within the circle of a mile, and as each of his enemies tired, there were always fresh pursuers to take his place. In such a contest the result could not be questionable. After more than two hours of powerful exertion, the foot of Conanchet began to fail, and his speed very sensibly to flag. Exhausted by efforts that had been nearly supernatural, the breathless warrior cast his person prostrate on the earth, and lay for several minutes as if he were dead.

During this breathing time his throbbing pulses grew more calm, his heart beat less violently, and the circulation was gradually returning to the tranquil flow of nature in a state of rest. It was at this moment, when his energies were recruited by rest, that the chief heard the tread of the moccasins on his trail. Rising, he looked back on the course over which he had just passed with so much pain. But a single warrior was in view. Hope for an instant regained the ascendency, and he raised his musket to fell his approaching adversary. The aim was cool, long, and it would have been fatal had not the useless tick of the lock reminded him of the condition of the gun. He cast the wet and unserviceable piece away and grasped his tomahawk; but a band of Pequods rushed in to the rescue, rendering resistance madness. Perceiving the hopelessness of his situation, the sachem of the Narragansetts dropped his tomahawk, loosened his belt, and advanced unarmed, with a noble resignation, to meet his foes. In the next instant he was their prisoner.

"Bring me to your chief," said the captive, haughtily, when the common herd into whose hands he had fallen would have questioned him on the subject of his companion's and of his own fate. "My tongue is used to speak with sachems."

He was obeyed, and before an hour had passed the renowned Conanchet stood confronted with his most deadly enemy.

The place of meeting was the deserted encampment of the band of Philip. Here most of the pursuers had already assembled, including all of the colonists who had been engaged in the expedition. The latter consisted of Meek Wolfe, Ensign Dudley, Sergeant Ring, and a dozen private men of the village.

The result of the enterprise was, by this time, generally known. Though Metacom, its principle object, had escaped; yet, when it was understood that the sachem of the Narragansetts had fallen into their hands, there was not an individual of the party who did not think his personal risk more than amply compensated. Though the Mohicans and Pequods restrained their exultation, lest the pride of their captive should be soothed by such an evidence of his importance, the white men drew around the prisoner with an interest and a joy they did not care to conceal. Still, as he had yielded to an Indian, there was an affectation of leaving the chief to the clemency of his conquerors. Perhaps some deeply pondered scheme of policy had its influence in this act of seeming justice.

When Conanchet was placed in the center of the curious circle, he found himself immediately in presence of the principal chief of the tribe of the Mohicans. It was Uncas, son of that Uncas whose fortunes had also prevailed, aided by the whites, in the conflict with his father, the hapless but noble Miantonimoh. Fate had now decreed that the same evil star, which had governed the destinies of the ancestor, should extend its influence to the second generation.

The race of Uncas, though weakened of its power, and shorn of much of its peculiar grandeur by a vicious alliance with the English, still retained most of the fine qualities of savage heroism. He, who now stood forth to receive his captive, was a warrior of middle age, of just proportions, of a grave, though fierce aspect, and of an eye and countenance that expressed all those contradictory traits of character which render the savage warrior almost as admirable as he is appalling. Until this moment the rival chieftains had never met except in the confusion of battle. For a few minutes neither spoke. Each stood regarding the fine outlines, the eagle eye, the proud bearing, and the severe gravity of the other in secret admiration, but with a calmness so immovable as entirely to conceal the workings of his thoughts. At length they began to assume miens suited to the part each was to enact in the coming scene. The countenance of Uncas became ironical and exulting, while that of his captive grew still more cold and unconcerned.

"My young men," said the former, "have taken a fox skulking in the bushes. His legs were very long; but he had no heart to use them."

Conanchet folded his arms on his bosom, and the glance of his quiet eye seemed to tell his enemy that devices so common were unworthy of them both. The other either understood its meaning, or loftier feelings prevailed, for he added, in a better taste—

"Is Conanchet tired of his life that he comes among my young men?"

"Mohican," said the Narragansett chief, " he has been there before; if Uncas will count his warriors he will see that some are wanting."

"There are no traditions among the Indians of the islands!" said the other, with an ironical glance at the chiefs near him. "They have never heard of Miantonimoh; they do not know such a field as the Sachem's Plain!"

The countenance of the prisoner changed. For a single instant it appeared to grow dark, as if a deep shadow were cast athwart it; and then every feature rested, as before, in dignified repose. His conqueror watched the play of his lineaments, and when he thought nature was getting the ascendency, exultation gleamed about his own fierce eye; but when the self-possession of the Narragansett returned, he affected to think no more of an effort that had been fruitless.

"If the men of the islands know little," he continued, "it is not so with the Mohicans. There was once a great sachem among the Narragansetts; he was wiser than the beaver, swifter than the moose, and more cunning than the red fox. But he could not see into to-morrow. Foolish counselors told him to go upon the war-path against the Pequods and Mohicans. He lost his scalp; it hangs in the smoke of my wigwam. We shall see if it will know the hair of his son. Narragansett, here are wise men of the pale-faces; they will speak to you. If they offer a pipe, smoke; for tobacco is not plenty with your tribe."

Uncas then turned away, leaving his prisoner to the interrogatories of his white allies.

"Here is the look of Miantonimoh, Sergeant Ring," observed Ensign Dudley to his wife's brother, after he had contemplated for a reasonable time the features of the prisoner. "I see the eye and the tread of the father in this young sachem. And more, Sergeant Ring; the chief favors the boy we picked up in the fields some dozen years agone, and kept in the block for the matter of many

months, caged like a young panther. Hast forgotten the night, Reuben, and the lad, and the block? A fiery oven is not hotter than that pile was getting before we dove into the earth. I never fail to think of it when the good minister is dealing powerfully with the punishments of the wicked, and the furnaces of Tophet!"

The silent yeoman comprehended the disconnected allusions of his relative, nor was he slow in seeing the palpable resemblance between their prisoner and the Indian boy whose person had once been so familiar to his eye. Admiration and surprise were blended in his honest face, with an expression that appeared to announce deep regret. As neither of these individuals, however, was the principal personage of their party, each was fain to remain an attentive and interested observer of that which followed.

"Worshiper of Baal!" commenced the sepulchral voice of the divine, "it has pleased the King of Heaven and earth to protect his people! The triumph of thy evil nature hath been short, and now cometh the judgment!"

These words were uttered to ears that affected deafness. In the presence of his most deadly foe, and a captive, Conanchet was not a man to suffer his resolution to waver. He looked coldly and vacantly on the speaker, nor could the most suspicious or the most practiced eye have detected in his mien his knowledge of the English language. Deceived by the stoicism of the prisoner, Meek muttered a few words, in which the Narragansett was strangely dealt by, denunciations and petitions in his favor being blended in the quaint and exaggerated fashions of the times; and then he submitted to the interference of those present, who were charged with the duty of deciding on the fate of the Indian.

Although Eben Dudley was the principal and the efficient military man in this little expedition from the valley, he was accompanied by those whose authority was predominant in all matters that did not strictly appertain to the executive portion of the duty. Commissioners, named by the government of the Colony, had come out with the party, clothed with power to dispose of Philip, should that dreaded chief, as was expected, fall into the hands of the English. To these persons the fate of Conanchet was now referred.

We shall not detain the narrative to dwell on the particulars of the council. The question was gravely considered, and it was decided with a deep and conscientious sense of the responsibility of those who acted as judges. Several hours were passed in deliberation, Meek opening and closing the proceedings by solemn prayers. The judgment was then announced to Uncas by the divine himself.

" The wise men of my people have consulted together in the matter of this Narragansett," he said, "and their spirits have wrestled powerfully with the subject. In coming to their conclusion, if it wear the aspect of time-serving, let all remember the providence of Heaven hath so interwoven the interests of man with its own good purposes, that to the carnal eye they may outwardly seem to be inseparable. But that which is here done is done in good faith to our ruling principle, which is good faith to thee and to all others who support the altar in this wilderness. And herein is our decision : We commit the Narragansett to thy justice, since it is evident that while he is at large, neither thou, who art a feeble prop to the Church in these regions, nor we, who are its humble and unworthy servitors, are safe. Take him, then, and deal with him according to thy wisdom. We place limits to thy power in only two things. It is not meet that any born of humanity, and having human sensibilities, should suffer more in the flesh than may be necessary to the ends of duty ; we therefore decree that thy captive shall not die by torture ; and, for the better security of this our charitable decision, two of our number shall accompany thee and him to the place of execution ; it being always supposed it is thy intention to inflict the pains of death. Another condition of this concession to a foreordained necessity is, that a Christian minister may be at hand, in order that the sufferer may depart with the prayers of one accustomed to lift his voice in petitions to the footstool of the Almighty."

The Mohegan chief heard this sentence with deep attention. When he found he was to be denied the satisfaction of proving, or perhaps of overcoming, the resolution of his enemy, a deep cloud passed across his swarthy visage. But the strength of his tribe had long been broken, and to resist would have been as unprofitable as to repine would have been unseemly. The conditions were therefore accepted, and preparations were accordingly made among the Indians to proceed to judgment.

These people had few contradictory principles to appease, and no subtleties to distract their decision. Direct, fearless, and simple in all their practices, they did little more than gather the voices of the chiefs and acquaint their captive with the result. They knew that fortune had thrown an implacable enemy into their hands, and they believed that self-preservation demanded his life. To them it mattered little whether he had arrows in his hands, or yielded himself an unarmed prisoner. He knew the risk he ran in submitting, and he had probably consulted his own character, rather than their benefit, in throwing away his arms. They therefore pronounced the judgment of death against their captive, merely respecting the decree of their white allies, which had commanded them to spare the torture.

So soon as this determination was known, the commissioners of the Colony hastened away from the spot with consciences that required some aid from the sciences of their subtle doctrines, in order to render them quiet. They were, however, ingenious casuists ; and as they hurried along their return path, most of the party were satisfied that they had rather manifested a merciful interposition, than exercised any act of positive cruelty.

During the two or three hours which had passed in these solemn and usual preparations, Conanchet was seated on a rock, a close but apparently an unmoved spectator of all that passed. His eye was mild, and at times melancholy ; but its brightness and its steadiness remained unimpaired. When his sentence was announced, it exhibited no change ; and he saw all the pale men depart, with the calmness he had maintained throughout. It was only as Uncas, attended by the body of his party and the two white superintendents who had been left, approached, that his spirit seemed to awaken.

"My people have said that there shall be no more wolves in the woods," said Uncas ; "and they have commanded our young men to slay the hungriest of them all."

" It is well ! " coldly returned the other.

A gleaming of admiration, and perhaps of humanity, came over the grim countenance of Uncas, as he gazed at the repose which reigned in the firm features of his victim. For an instant, his purpose wavered.

"The Mohicans are a great tribe ! " he added ; "and the race of Uncas is getting few. We will paint our brother so that the lying Narragansetts shall not know him, and he will be a warrior on the mainland."

This relenting of his enemy had a corresponding effect on the generous temper of Conanchet. The lofty pride deserted his eye, and his look became milder and more human. For a minute, intense thought brooded around his brow ; the grim muscles of his mouth played a little, though scarcely enough to be seen, and then he spoke.

"Mohican," he said, "why should your young men be in a hurry? My scalp will be the scalp of a great chief to-morrow. They will not take two, should they strike their prisoner now."

"Hath Conanchet forgotten anything, that he is not ready?"

"Sachem, he is always ready—but—" he paused, and spoke in tones that faltered,—"does a Mohican live alone?"

"How many suns does the Narragansett ask?"

"One; when the shadow of that pine points toward the brook, Conanchet will be ready. He will then stand in the shade, with naked hands."

"Go," said Uncas, with dignity; "I have heard the words of a sagamore."

Conanchet turned, and passing swiftly through the silent crowd, his person was soon lost in the surrounding forest.

CHAPTER XXXI.

"Therefore, lay bare your bosom."
—MERCHANT OF VENICE.

THE night that succeeded was wild and melancholy. The moon was nearly full, but its place in the heavens was only seen, as the masses of vapor which drove through the air occasionally opened, suffering short gleams of fitful light to fall on the scene below. A southwestern wind rather moaned than sighed through the forest, and there were moments when its freshness increased, till every leaf seemed a tongue, and each low plant appeared to be endowed with the gift of speech. With the exception of these imposing and not unpleasing natural sounds, there was a solemn quiet in and about the village of the Wish-Ton-Wish. An hour before the moment when we resume the action of the legend, the sun had settled into the neighboring forest, and most of its simple and laborious inhabitants had already sought their rest.

The lights, however, still shone through many of the windows of the "Heathcote house," as, in the language of the country, the dwelling of the Puritan was termed. There was the usual stirring industry in and about the offices, and the ordinary calm was reigning in the superior parts of the habitation. A solitary man was to be seen on its piazza. It was young Mark Heathcote, who paced the long and narrow gallery, as if impatient of some interruption to his wishes.

The uneasiness of the young man was of short continuance; for, ere he had been many minutes at his post a door opened, and two light and timid forms glided out of the house.

"Thou hast not come alone, Martha," said the youth, half displeased. "I told thee that the matter I had to say was for thine own ear."

"It is our Ruth. Thou knowest, Mark, that she may not be left alone, for we fear her return to the forest. She is like some ill-tamed fawn, that would be apt to leap away at the first well-known sound from the woods. Even now, I fear that we are too much asunder."

"Fear nothing; my sister fondles her infant, and she thinketh not of flight; thou seest I am here to intercept her, were such her intention. Now speak with candor, Martha, and say if thou meanest in sincerity that the visits of the Hartford gallant were less to thy liking than most of thy friends have believed?"

"What I have said cannot be recalled."

"Still it may be repented of."

"I do not number the dislike I may feel for the young man among my failings. I am too happy here, in this family, to wish to quit it. And now that our sister—there is one speaking to her at this moment, Mark!"

"'Tis only the innocent," returned the young man, glancing his eye to the other end of the piazza. "They confer often together. Whittal hath just come in from the woods, where he is much inclined to pass an hour or two, each evening. Thou wast saying that now we have our sister—"

"I feel less desire to change my abode."

"Then why not stay with us forever, Martha?"

"Hist?" interrupted his companion, who, though conscious of what she was about to listen to, shrank, with the waywardness of human nature, from the very declaration she most wished to hear, "hist—there was a movement. Ah! Ruth and Whittal are fled!"

"They seek some amusement for the babe—they are near the out-buildings. Then why not accept a right to remain forever—"

"It may not be, Mark," cried the girl, wresting her hand from his grasp; "they are fled!"

Mark reluctantly released his hold, and followed to the spot where his sister had been sitting. She was, in truth, gone; though some minutes passed before even Martha seriously believed that she had disappeared without an intention of returning. The agitation of both rendered the search ill-directed and uncertain, and there was perhaps a secret satisfaction in prolonging their interview even in this vague manner, that prevented them for some time from giving the alarm. When that moment did come, it was too late. The fields were examined, the orchards and outhouses thoroughly searched, without any traces of the fugitives. It would have been useless to enter the forest in the darkness, and all that could be done in reason, was to set a watch during the night, and to prepare for a more active and intelligent pursuit in the morning.

But, long before the sun arose, the small and melancholy party of the fugitives threaded the woods at such a distance from the valley, as would have rendered the plan of the family entirely nugatory. Conanchet had led the way over a thousand forest knolls, across watercourses, and through dark glens, followed by his silent partner, with an industry that would have baffled the zeal of even those from whom they fled. Whittal Ring, bearing the infant on his back, trudged with unwearied step in the rear. Hours had passed in this manner, and not a syllable had been uttered by either of the three. Once or twice they had stopped at some spot where water, limpid as the air, gushed from the rocks; and, drinking from the hollows of their hands, the march had been resumed with the same speechless industry as before.

At length Conanchet paused. He studied the position of the sun gravely, and took a long and anxious look at the signs of the forest, in order that he might not be deceived in its quarter. To an unpracticed eye, the arches of the trees, the leaf-covered earth, and the moldering logs, would have seemed everywhere the same. But it was not easy to deceive one so trained in the woods. Satisfied equally with the progress he had made, and with the hour, the chief signed to his two companions to place themselves at his side, and took a seat on a low shelf of rock that thrust its naked head out of the side of a hill.

For many minutes after all were seated, no one broke the silence. The eye of Narra-mattah sought the countenance of her husband, as the eye of woman seeks instruction from the expression of features that she has been taught to revere; but still she spoke not. The innocent laid the patient babe at the feet of its mother, and imitated her reserve.

"Is the air of the woods pleasant to the honeysuckle, after living in the wigwam of her people?" asked Conanchet, breaking the long silence. "Can a flower, which blossomed in the sun, like the shade?"

"A woman of the Narragansetts is happiest in the lodge of her husband."

The eye of the chief met her confiding look with affection, then it fell, mild and full of kindness, on the features of the infant that lay at their feet. There was a minute, during which an expression of bitter melancholy gathered about his brow.

"The Spirit that made the earth," he continued, "is very cunning. He has known where to put the hemlock, and where the oak should grow. He has left the moose and the deer to the Indian hunter, and he has given the horse and the ox to a pale-face. Each tribe hath its own hunting-grounds and its game. The Narragansetts know the taste of a clam, while the Mohawks eat the berries of the mountains. Thou hast seen the bright bow which shines in the skies, Narra-mattah, and knowest how one color is mixed with another, like paint on a warrior's face. The leaf of the hemlock is like the leaf of the sumach; the ash, the chestnut; the chestnut, the linden; and the linden, the broad-leaved tree which bears the red fruit in the clearing of the Yengeese; but the tree of the red fruit is little like the hemlock! Conanchet is a tall and straight hemlock, and the father of Narra-mattah is a tree of the clearing that bears the red fruit. The Great Spirit was angry when they grew together."

The sensitive wife understood but too well the current of the chief's thoughts. Suppressing the pain she felt, however, she answered with the readiness of a woman whose imagination was quickened by her affections.

"What Conanchet hath said is true. But the Yengeese have put the apple of their own land on the thorn of our woods, and the fruit is good!"

"It is like that boy," said the chief, pointing to his son; "neither red nor pale. No, Narra-mattah; what the Great Spirit hath commanded, even a sachem must do."

"And doth Conanchet say this fruit is not good?" asked his wife, lifting the smiling boy with a mother's joy before his eyes.

The heart of the warrior was touched. Bending his head, he kissed the babe, with such fondness as parents less stern are wont to exhibit. For a moment, he appeared to have satisfaction in gazing at the promise of the child. But, as he raised his head, his eye caught a glimpse of the sun, and the whole expression of his countenance changed. Motioning to his wife to replace the infant on the earth, he turned to her with solemnity, and continued—

"Let the tongue of Narra-mattah speak without fear. She hath been in the lodges of her father, and hath tasted of their plenty. Is her heart glad?"

The young wife paused. The question brought with it a sudden recollection of all those reviving sensations, of that tender solicitude, and of those soothing sympathies of which she had so lately been the subject. But these feelings soon vanished; for, without daring to lift her eyes to meet the attentive and anxious gaze of the chief, she said firmly, though with a voice that was subdued by diffidence—

"Narra-mattah is a wife."

"Then she will listen to the words of her husband. Conanchet is a chief no longer. He is a prisoner of the Mohicans. Uncas waits for him in the woods!"

Notwithstanding the recent declaration of the young wife, she heard of this calamity with little of the calmness of an Indian woman. At first it seemed as if her senses refused to comprehend the meaning of the words. Wonder, doubt, horror, and fearful certainty, each in its turn prevailed; for she was too well schooled in all the usages and opinions of the people with whom she dwelt, not to understand the jeopardy in which her husband was placed.

"The sachem of the Narragansetts a prisoner of Mohican Uncas!" she repeated in a low tone, as if the sound of her voice were necessary to dispel some horrible illusion. "No! Uncas is not a warrior to strike Conanchet!"

"Hear my words," said the chief, touching the shoulder of his wife, as one arouses a friend from his slumbers. "There is a pale-face in these woods who is a burrowing fox. He hides his head from the Yengeese. When his people were on the trail, barking like hungry wolves, this man trusted to a sagamore. It was a swift chase, and my father is getting very old. He went up a young hickory like a bear, and Conanchet led off the lying tribe. But he is not a moose. His legs cannot go like running water forever!"

"And why did the great Narragansett give his life for a stranger!"

"The man is a brave," returned the sachem, proudly; "he took the scalp of a sagamore!"

Again Narra-mattah was silent. She brooded in nearly stupid amazement on the frightful truth.

"The Great Spirit sees that the man and his wife are of different tribes," she at length ventured to rejoin. "He wishes them to become the same people. Let Conanchet quit the woods, and go into the clearings, with the mother of his boy. Her white father will be glad, and Mohican Uncas will not dare to follow."

"Woman, I am a sachem, and a warrior among my people!"

There was a severe and cold displeasure in the voice of Conanchet that his companion had never before heard. He spoke in the manner of a chief to his woman, rather than with that manly softness with which he had been accustomed to address the scion of the pale-faces. The words came over her heart like a withering chill, and affliction kept her mute. The chief himself sat a moment longer in a stern calmness, and then rising in displeasure he pointed to the sun, and beckoned to his companions to proceed. In a time that appeared to the throbbing heart of her who followed his swift footsteps but a moment, they had turned a little eminence, and in another minute they stood in the presence of a party that evidenty awaited their coming. This grave group consisted only of Uncas, two of his fiercest-looking and most athletic warriors, the divine, and Eben Dudley.

Advancing rapidly to the spot where his enemy stood, Conanchet took his post at the foot of the fatal tree. Pointing to the shadow, which had not yet turned toward the east, he folded his arms on his naked bosom, and assumed an air of haughty unconcern. These movements were made in the midst of a profound stillness.

Disappointment, unwilling admiration, and distrust, all struggled through the mask of practiced composure, in the dark countenance of Uncas. He regarded his long hated and terrible foe with an eye that seemed willing to detect some lurking signs of weakness. It would not have been easy to say whether he most felt respect or regret at the faith of the Narragansett. Accompanied by his two grim warriors, the chief examined the position of the shadow with critical minuteness, and when there no longer existed a pretext for affecting to doubt the punctuality of their captive, a deep ejaculation of assent issued from the chest of each. Like some wary judge, whose justice is fettered by legal precedents, as if satisfied there was no flaw in the proceedings, the Mohican then signed to the white men to draw near.

"Man of a wild and unreclaimed nature!" commenced Meek Wolfe, in his usual admonitory and ascetic tones, "the hour of thy existence draws to its end! Judgment hath had rule; thou hast been weighed in the balances and art found wanting. But Christian charity is never weary. We may not resist the ordinances of Providence, but we may temper the blow to the offender. That thou art here to die is a mandate decreed in equity, and rendered awful by mystery; but further, submission to the will of Heaven doth not exact. Heathen, thou hast a soul, and it is about to leave its earthly tenement for the unknown world—"

Until now, the captive had listened with the courtesy of a savage when unexcited. He had even gazed at the quiet enthusiasm and singularly contradictory passions that shone in the deep lines of the speaker's face, with some such reverence as he might have manifested at an exhibition of one of the pretended revelations of a prophet of his tribe. But when the divine came to touch upon his condition after death, his mind received a clear, and to him an unerring clew to the truth. Laying a finger suddenly on the shoulder of Meek, he interrupted him by saying—

"My father forgets that the skin of his son is red. The path to the happy hunting grounds of just Indians lies before him."

"Heathen, in thy words hath the master spirit of delusion and sin uttered his blasphemies!"

"Hist! Did my father see that which stirred the bush?"

"It was the viewless wind, idolatrous and idle-minded infant in the form of adult man!"

"And yet my father speaks to it," returned the Indian, with the grave but cutting sarcasm of his people. "See," he added, haughtily, and even with ferocity, "the shadow hath passed the root of the tree. Let the cunning man of the pale-faces stand aside; a sachem is ready to die!"

Meek groaned audibly and in real sorrow; for notwithstanding the veil which exalted theories and doctrinal subtleties had drawn before his judgment, the charities of the man were grounded in truth. Bowing to what he believed to be a mysterious dispensation of the will of Heaven, he withdrew to a short distance, and kneeling on a rock, his voice was heard during the remainder of the ceremonies, lifting its tones in fervent prayer for the soul of the condemned.

The divine had no sooner quitted the place, than Uncas motioned to Dudley to approach. Though the nature of the borderer was essentially honest and kind, he was in opinion and prejudice but a creature of the times. If he had assented to the judgment which committed the captive to the mercy of his implacable enemies, he had the merit of having suggested the expedient that was to protect the sufferer from those refinements in cruelty which the savages were known to be too ready to inflict. He had even volunteered to be one of the agents to enforce his own expedient, though in so doing he had committed no little violence to his natural inclinations. The reader will therefore judge of his conduct in this particular, with the degree of lenity that a right consideration of the condition of the country and of the usages of the age may require. There was even a relenting and a yielding of purpose in the countenance of this witness of the scene, that was favorable to the safety of the captive, as he now spoke. His address was first to Uncas.

"A happy fortune, Mohican, something aided by the power of the white men, hath put this Narragansett into thy hands," he said. "It is certain that the commissioners of the colony have consented that thou shouldst exercise thy will on his life; but there is a voice in the breast of every human being, which should be stronger than the voice of revenge, and that is the voice of mercy. It is not yet too late to hearken to it. Take the promise of the Narragansett for his faith—take more: take a hostage in this child, which with its mother shall be guarded among the English, and let the prisoner go."

"My brother asketh with a big mind!" said Uncas, dryly.

"I know not how nor why it is I ask with this earnestness," resumed Dudley, "but there are old recollections and former kindnesses, in the face and manner of this Indian! And here, too, is one, in the woman that I know is tied to some of our settlements, with a bond nearer than that of common charity. Mohican, I will add a goodly gift of powder and of muskets, if thou wilt listen to mercy and take the faith of the Narragansett."

Uncas pointed with ironical coldness to his captive, as he said—

"Let Conanchet speak!"

"Thou hearest, Narragansett. If the man I begin to suspect thee to be, thou knowest something of the usages of the whites. Speak! Wilt swear to keep peace with the Mohicans, and to bury the hatchet in the path between your villages?"

"The fire that burnt the lodges of my people turned the heart of Conanchet to stone," was the steady answer.

"Then can I do no more than see the

treaty respected," returned Dudley, in disappointment. "Thou hast thy nature, and it will have way. The Lord have mercy on thee, Indian, and render thee such judgment as is meet for one of savage opportunities."

He made a gesture to Uncas that he had done, and fell back a few paces from the tree, his honest features expressing all his concern, while his eye did not refuse to do its duty by closly watching each movement of the adverse parties. At the same instant the grim attendants of the Mohican chief, in obedience to a sign, took their stations on each side of the captive. They evidently waited for the last and fatal signal, to complete their unrelenting purpose. At this grave moment there was a pause, as if each of the principal actors pondered serious matter in his inmost mind.

"The Narragansett hath not spoken to his woman," said Uncas, secretly hoping that his enemy might yet betray some unmanly weakness in a moment of so severe trial. "She is near."

"I said my heart was stone," coldly returned the Narragansett.

"See! the girl creepeth like a frightened fowl among the leaves. If my brother Conanchet will look, he will see his beloved."

The countenance of Conanchet grew dark, but it did not waver.

"We will go among the bushes, if the sachem is afraid to speak to his woman with the eyes of a Mohican on him. A warrior is not a curious girl, that he wishes to see the sorrow of a chief!"

Conanchet felt hurriedly for some weapon that might strike his enemy to the earth, and then a low murmuring sound at his elbow stole so softly on his ear as suddenly to divert the tempest of passion.

"Will not a sachem look at his boy?" demanded the suppliant. "It is a son of a great warrior. Why is the face of his father so dark on him?"

Narra-mattah had drawn near enough to her husband to be within reach of his hand. With extended arms she held the pledge of their former happiness toward the chief, as if to beseech a last and kindly look of recognition and love.

"Will not the great Narragansett look at his boy?" she repeated, in a voice that sounded like the lowest notes of some touching melody. "Why is his face so dark on a woman of his tribe?"

Even the stern features of the Mohican sagamore showed that he was touched. Beckoning to his grim attendants to move behind the tree, he turned and walked aside with the noble air of a savage, when influenced by his better feelings. Then light shot into the clouded countenance of Conanchet. His eyes sought the face of his stricken and grieved consort, who mourned less for his danger than she grieved for his displeasure. He received the boy from her hands, and studied his features long and intently. Beckoning to Dudley, who alone gazed on the scene, he placed the infant in his arms.

"See!" he said, pointing to the child. "It is a blossom of the clearings. It will not live in the shade."

He then fastened a look on his trembling partner. There was a husband's love in the gaze. "Flower of the open land!" he said; "the Manitou of thy race will place thee in the fields of thy fathers. The sun will shine upon thee, and the winds from beyond the salt lake will blow the clouds into the woods. A just and great chief cannot shut his ear to the Good Spirit of his people. Mine calls his son to hunt among the braves that have gone on the long path. Thine points another way. Go, hear his voice and obey. Let thy mind be like a wide clearing. Let all its shadows be next the woods; let it forget the dream it dreamt among the trees. 'Tis the will of the Manitou."

"Conanchet asketh much of his wife. Her soul is only the soul of a woman!"

"A woman of the pale-faces; now let her seek her tribe. Narra-mattah, thy people speak strange traditions. They say that one just man died for all colors. I know not. Conanchet is a child among the cunning, and a man with the warriors. If this be true, he will look for his woman and boy in the happy hunting grounds, and they will come to him. There is no hunter of the Yengeese that can kill so many deer. Let Narra-mattah forget her chief till that time, and then, when she calls him by name, let her speak strong; for he will be very glad to hear her voice again. Go! A sagamore is about to start on a long journey. He takes leave of his wife with a heavy spirit. She will put a little flower of two colors before her eyes, and be happy in its growth. Now let her go. A sagamore is about to die."

The attentive woman caught each slow and measured syllable, as one trained in superstitious legends would listen to the words of an oracle. But, accustomed to obedience and bewildered with her grief, she hesitated no longer. The head of Narra-mattah sank on her bosom as she left him, and her face was buried in her robe. The step with which she passed Uncas was so light as to be inaudible; but when he saw her tottering form, turning swiftly, he stretched an arm high in the air. The terrible mutes just showed themselves from behind the tree, and vanished. Conanchet started, and it seemed as if he were about to plunge forward ; but, recovering himself by a desperate effort, his body sank back against the tree, and he fell in the attitude of a chief seated in council. There was a smile of fierce triumph on his face, and his lips evidently moved. Uncas did not breathe as he bent forward to listen :—

"Mohican, I die before my heart is soft !" uttered firmly, but with a struggle, reached his ears. Then came two long and heavy respirations. One was the returning breath of Uncas, and the other the dying sigh of the last sachem of the broken and dispersed tribe of the Narragansetts.

CHAPTER XXXII.

" Each lonely scene shall thee restore ;
  For thee the tear be duly shed ;
  Beloved till life could charm no more,
  And mourned till pity's self be dead."
  —COLLINS.

AN hour later and the principal actors in the foregoing scene had disappeared. There remained only the widowed Narramattah, with Dudley, the divine, and Whittal Ring.

The body of Conanchet still continued, where he had died, seated like a chief in council. The daughter of Content and Ruth had stolen to its side, and she had taken her seat, in that species of dull woe, which so frequently attends the first moments of any unexpected and overwhelming affliction. She neither spoke, sobbed, nor sorrowed in any way that grief is wont to affect the human system. The mind seemed palsied, though a withering sense of the blow was fearfully engraven on every lineament of her eloquent face. The color deserted her cheeks, the lips were bloodless, while at moments they quivered convulsively, like the tremulous movement of the sleeping infant; and at long intervals her bosom heaved, as if the spirit within struggled heavily to escape from its earthly prison. The child lay unheeded at her side, and Whittal Ring had placed himself on the opposite side of the corpse.

The two agents appointed by the Colony to witness the death of Conanchet stood near, gazing mournfully on the piteous spectacle. The instant the spirit of the condemned man fled, the prayers of the divine had ceased, for he believed that then the soul had gone to judgment. But there was more of human charity and less of that exaggerated severity in his aspect, than was ordinarily seated in the deep lines of his austere countenance. Now that the deed was done, and the excitement of his exalted theories had given way to the more positive appearance of the result, he might even have moments of harassing doubts concerning the lawfulness of an act that he had hitherto veiled under the forms of a legal and necessary execution of justice. The mind of Eben Dudley vacillated with none of the subtleties of doctrine or of law. As there had been less exaggeration in his original views of the necessity of the proceeding, so was there more steadiness in his contemplation of its fulfillment. Feelings, they might be termed emotions, of a different nature troubled the breast of this resolute but justly disposed borderer.

"This hath been a melancholy visitation of necessity, and a severe manifestation of the fore-ordering will," said the ensign, as he gazed at the sad spectacle before him. " Father and son have both died, as it were, in my presence, and both have departed for the world of spirits in a manner to prove the inscrutableness of Providence. But dost not see, here, in the face of her who looketh like a form of stone, traces of a countenance that is familiar ?"

"Thou hast allusion to the consort of Captain Content Heathcote ?"

"Truly, to her only. Thou art not, reverend sir, of sufficient residence at the Wish-Ton-Wish, to remember that lady in her youthfulness. But to me, the hour when the captain led his followers into the wilderness seemeth but as a morning of the past season, I was then active in limb, and something idle in reflection and discourse; it was in that journey that the woman who is now the mother of my children and I first made acquaintance. I have seen many comely females in my time, but never did I look on one so pleasant to the eye, as was the consort of the captain until the night of the burning. Thou hast often heard the loss she then met, and from that hour her beauty hath been that of the October leaf, rather than its loveliness in the season of fertility. Now look on the face of this mourner, and say if there be not here such an image as she water reflects from the overhanging bush. In verity, I could believe it was the sorrowing eye and the bereaved look of the mother herself ! "

" Grief hath struck its blows heavily on this unoffending victim," uttered Meek, with great and subdued softness in his manner. " The voice of petition must be raised in her behalf, or—"

"Hist!—there are some in the forest; I hear the rustling of leaves."

"The voice of him who made the earth whispereth in the winds; his breath is the movement of nature!"

"Here are living men!—But, happily, the meeting is friendly, and there will be no further occasion for strife. The heart of a father is sure as ready eye and swift foot."

Dudley suffered his musket to fall at his side, and both he and his companions stood in attitudes of decent composure to await the arrival of those who approached. The party that drew near arrived on the side of the tree opposite to that on which the death of Conanchet had occurred. The enormous trunk and swelling roots of the pine concealed the group at its feet, but the persons of Meek and the ensign were soon observed. The instant they were discovered, he who led the new-comers bent his footsteps in that direction.

"If, as thou hast supposed, the Narragansett hath again led her thou hast so long mourned into the forest," said Submission, who acted as guide to those who followed, "here are we at no great distance from the place of his resort. It was near yon rock that he gave the meeting with the bloody-minded Philip, and the place where I received the boon of a useless and much-afflicted life from his care is within the bosom of that thicket which borders the brook. This minister of the Lord, and our stout friend the ensign, may have further matter to tell us of his movements."

The speaker had stopped within a short distance of the two he named, but still on the side of the tree opposite to that where the body lay. He had addressed his words to Content, who also halted to await the arrival of Ruth, who came in the rear supported by her son, and attended by Faith and the physician, all equipped like persons engaged in a search through the forest. A mother's heart had sustained the feeble woman for many a weary mile, but her steps had begun to drag shortly before they so happily fell upon the signs of human beings near the spot where they now met the two agents of the Colony.

Notwithstanding the deep interest which belonged to the respective pursuits of the individuals who composed these two parties, the interview was opened with no lively signs of feeling on either side. To them a journey in the forest possessed no novelties, and after traversing its mazes for a day, the newly arrived encountered their friends as men meet on more beaten tracks in countries where roads unavoidably lead them to cross each other's paths. Even the appearance of Submission in front of the travelers elicited no marks of surprise in the unmoved features of those who witnessed his approach. Indeed, the mutual composure of one who had so long concealed his person, and of those who had more than once seen him in striking and mysterious situations, might well justify a belief that the secret of his presence near the valley had not been confined to the family of the Heathcotes. This fact is rendered still more probable by the recollection of the honesty of Dudley, and of the professional characters of the two others.

"We are on the trail of one fled, as the truant fawn seeketh again the covers of the woods," said Content. "Our hunt was uncertain, and it might have been vain, so many feet have lately crossed the forest, were it not that Providence hath cast our route on that of our friend here, who hath had reason to know the probable situation of the Indian camp. Hast seen aught of the Sachem of the Narragansetts, Dudley? and where are those thou ledst against the subtle Philip? That thou fell upon his party we have heard; though further than thy general success we have yet to learn. The Wampanoag escaped thee?"

"The wicked agencies that back him in his designs profited the savage in his extremity. Else would his fate have been that which I fear a far worthier spirit hath been doomed to suffer."

"Of whom dost speak?—but it mattereth not. We seek our child; she whom thou hast known, and whom thou hast so lately seen, hath again left us. We seek her in the camp of him who hath been to her—Dudley, hast seen aught of the Narragansett sachem?"

The ensign looked at Ruth as he had once before been seen to gaze on the sorrowing features of the woman; but he spoke not. Meek folded his arms on his breast, and seemed to pray inwardly. There was, however, one who broke the silence, though his tones were low and menacing.

"It was a bloody deed!" muttered the innocent. "The lying Mohican hath struck a great chief from behind. Let him dig the prints of his moccasin from the earth, with his nails, like a burrowing fox; for there'll be one on his trail before he can hide his head. Nipset will be a warrior the next snow!"

"There speaks my witless brother!" exclaimed Faith, rushing ahead—she recoiled, covered her face with her hands, and sank upon the ground, under the violence of the surprise that followed.

Though time moved with his ordinary pace, it appeared to those who witnessed the scene which succeeded, as if the emotions of many days were collected within the brief compass of a few minutes. We shall not dwell on the first harrowing and exciting moments of the appalling discovery.

A short half-hour served to make each person acquainted with all that was necessary to know. We shall therefore transfer the narrative to the end of that period.

The body of Conanchet still rested against the tree. The eyes were open, and though glazed in death, there still remained about the brow, the compressed lips, and the expansive nostrils, much of that lofty firmness which had sustained him in the last trial of life. The arms were passive at its sides, but one hand was clenched in the manner with which it had so often grasped the tomahawk, while the other had lost its power in a vain effort to seek the place in the girdle where the keen knife should have been. These two movements had probably been involuntary, for, in all other respects, the form was expressive of dignity and repose. At its side the imaginary Nipset still held his place, menacing discontent betraying itself through the ordinary dull fatuity of his countenance.

The others present were collected around the mother and her stricken child. It would seem that all other feelings were, for the moment, absorbed in apprehensions for the latter. There was much reason to dread that the recent shock had suddenly deranged some of that fearful machinery which links the soul to the body. This effect, however, was more to be apprehended by a general apathy and failing of the system, than by any violent and intelligible symptom.

The pulses still vibrated, but it was heavily, and like the irregular and faltering evolutions of the mill, which the dying breeze is ceasing to fan. The pallid countenance was fixed in its expression of anguish. Color there was none, even the lips resembling the unnatural character which is given by images of wax. Her limbs, like her features, were immovable; and yet there was, at moments, a working of the latter, which would seem to imply not only consciousness, but vivid and painful recollections of the realities of her situation.

"This surpasseth my art," said Doctor Ergot, raising himself from a long and silent examination of the pulse; "there

is a mystery in the construction of the body, which human knowledge hath not yet unveiled. The currents of existence are sometimes frozen in an incomprehensible manner and this I conceive to be a case that would confound the most learned of our art, even in the oldest countries of the earth. It hath been my fortune to see many arrive but few depart from this busy world, and yet do I presume to foretell that here is one destined to quit its limits ere the natural number of her days has been filled!"

"Let us address ourselves, in behalf of that which shall never die, to him who hath ordered the event from the commencement of time," said Meek, motioning to those around him to join in prayer.

The divine then lifted up his voice, under the arches of the forest, in an ardent, pious, and eloquent petition. When this solemn duty was performed, attention was again bestowed on the sufferer. To the susprise of all, it was found that the blood had revisited her face, and that her radiant eyes were lighted with an expression of brightness and peace. She even motioned to be raised, in order that those near her person might be better seen.

"Dost know us?" asked the trembling Ruth. "Look on thy friends, longmourned and much-suffering daughter? 'Tis she who sorrowed over thy infant afflictions, who rejoiced in thy childish happiness, and who hath so bitterly wept thy loss, that craveth the boon. In this awful moment, recall the lessons of youth. Surely, surely, the God that bestowed thee in mercy, though he hath led thee on a wonderful and inscrutable path, will not desert thee at the end! Think of thy early instruction, child of my love; feeble of spirit as thou art, the seed may yet quicken, though it hath been cast where the glory of the promise hath so long been hid."

"Mother!" said a low struggling voice in reply. The word reached every ear, and it caused a general and breathless attention. The sound was soft and low, perhaps infantile, but it was uttered without accent, and clearly.

"Mother—why are we in the forest?" continued the speaker. "Have any robbed us of our home that we dwell beneath the trees?"

Ruth raised a hand imploringly, for none to interrupt the illusion.

"Nature hath revived the recollections of her youth," she whispered. "Let the spirit depart, if such be his holy will, in the blessedness of infant innocence!"

"Why do Mark and Martha stay?" continued the other. "It is not safe, thou knowest, mother, to wander far in the woods; the heathen may be out of their towns, and one cannot say what evil chance might happen to the indiscreet?"

A groan struggled from the chest of Content, and the muscular hand of Dudley compressed itself on the shoulder of his wife, until the breathlessly attentive woman withdrew, unconsciously, with pain.

"I've said as much to Mark, for he doth not always remember thy warnings, mother; and those children do so love to wander together!—but Mark is, in common, good; do not chide if he stray too far, mother—thou wilt not chide!"

The youth turned his head, for even at that moment the pride of young manhood prompted him to conceal his weakness.

"Hast prayed to-day, my daughter?" said Ruth, struggling to be composed. "Thou shouldst not forget thy duty to his blessed name, even though we are houseless in the woods."

"I will pray now, mother," said the creature of this mysterious hallucination, struggling to bow her face into the lap of Ruth. Her wish was indulged, and for a minute, the same low childish voice was heard distinctly repeating the words of a prayer adapted to the earliest period of life. Feeble as were the sounds, none of their intonations escaped the listeners, until near the close, when a species of holy calm seemed to absorb the utterance. Ruth raised the form of her child, and saw that the features bore the placid look of a sleeping infant. Life played upon them, as the flickering light lingers on the dying torch. Her dove-like eyes looked up into the face of Ruth, and the anguish of the mother was alleviated by a smile of intelligence and love. The full and sweet organs next rolled from face to face, recognition and pleasure accompanying each change. On Whittal they became perplexed and doubtful, but when they met the fixed, frowning, and still commanding eye of the dead chief, their wandering ceased forever. There was a minute, during which fear, doubt, wildness, and early recollections, struggled for the mastery. The hands of Narramattah trembled, and she clung convulsively to the robe of Ruth.

"Mother! mother!" whispered the agitated victim of so many conflicting emotions, "I will pray again—an evil spirit besets me."

Ruth felt the force of her grasp, and heard the breathing of a few words of petition; after which the voice was mute and the hands relaxed their hold. When the face of the nearly insensible parent was withdrawn, to the others the dead appeared to gaze at each other with a mysterious and unearthly intelligence. The look of the Narragansett was still, as in his hour of pride, haughty, unyielding, and filled with defiance; while that of the creature who had so long lived in his kindness was perplexed, timid, but not without a character of hope. A solemn calm succeeded, and when Meek raised his voice again in the forest, it was to ask the Omnipotent Ruler of heaven and earth to sanctify his dispensation to those who survived.

The changes which have been wrought on this continent within a century and a half are very wonderful. Cities have appeared where the wilderness then covered the ground, and there is good reason to believe that a flourishing town now stands on or near the spot where Conanchet met his death. But, notwithstanding so much activity has prevailed in the country, the valley of this legend remains but little altered. The hamlet has increased to a village; the farms possess more of the air of cultivation; the dwellings are enlarged, and are somewhat more commodious; the churches are increased to three; the garrisoned houses, and all other signs of apprehension from violence, have long since disappeared; but still the place is secluded, little known, and strongly impressed with the marks of its original sylvan character.

A descendant of Mark and Martha is, at this hour, the proprietor of the estate on which so many of the moving incidents of our simple tale were enacted. Even the building, which was the second habitation of his ancestors, is in part standing, though additions and improvements have greatly changed its form. The orchards, which in 1675, were young and thrifty, are now old and decaying. The trees have yielded their character for excellence, to those varieties of the fruit which the soil and the climate have since made known to the inhabitants. Still they stand, for it is known that fearful scenes occurred beneath their shades, and there is a deep moral interest attached to their existence.

The ruins of the block-house, though much dilapidated and crumbling, are also visible. At their foot is the last abode of all the Heathcotes who have lived and died in that vicinity, for near two centuries. The graves of those of later times are known by tablets of marble; but nearer to the ruin are many whose monuments, half-concealed in the grass, are cut in the common coarse freestone of the country.

One, who took an interest in the recollection of days long gone, had occasion a few years since to visit the spot. It was easy to trace the births and deaths of generations, by the visible records on the more pretending monuments of those interred within a hundred years. Beyond that period research became difficult and painful. But his zeal was not to be easily defeated.

To every little mound, one only excepted, there was a stone, and on each stone, illegible as it might be, there was an inscription. The undistinguished grave, it was presumed, by its size and its position, was that which contained the bones of those who fell in the night of the burning. There was another, which bore, in deep letters, the name of the Puritan. His death occurred in 1680. At its side there was an humble stone, on which, with great difficulty, was traced the single word "Submission." It was impossible to ascertain whether the date was 1680, or 1690. The same mystery remained about the death of this man as had clouded so much of his life. His real name, parentage, or character, further than they have been revealed in these pages, was never traced. There still remains, however, in the family of the Heathcotes, an orderly-book of a troop of horse, which tradition says had some connection with his fortunes. Affixed to this defaced and imperfect document, is a fragment of some diary or journal, which has reference to the condemnation of Charles I. to the scaffold.

The body of Content lay near his infant children, and it would seem that he still lived in the first quarter of the last century. There was an aged man, lately in existence, who remembers to have seen him, a white-headed patriarch, reverend by his years, and respected for his meekness and justice. He had passed nearly or quite half-a-century unmarried. This melancholy fact was sufficiently shown by the date on the stone of the nearest mound. The inscription denoted it to be the grave of "Ruth, daughter of George Harding of the Colony of Massachusetts Bay, and wife of Captain Content Heathcote." She died in the autumn of 1675, with, as the stone reveals, "a spirit broken for the purposes of earth, by much family affliction, though with hopes justified by the covenant, and her faith in the Lord."

The divine, who lately officiated, if he do not now officiate in the principal church of the village, is called the Reverend Meek Lamb. Though claiming a descent from him who ministered in the temple at the period of our tale, time and intermarriages have produced this change in the name, and happily some others in doctrinal interpretations of duty. When this worthy servant of the Church found the object which had led one born in another State, and claiming descent from a line of religionists who had left the common country of their ancestors to worship in still another manner, to take an interest in the fortunes of those who first inhabited the valley, he found a pleasure in aiding the inquiries. The abodes of the Dudleys and Rings were numerous in the village and its environs. He showed a stone, surrounded by many others that bore these names, on which was rudely carved, "I am Nipset, a Narragansett; the next snow, I shall be a warrior!" There is a rumor, that though the hapless brother of Faith gradually returned to the ways of civilized life, he had frequent glimpses of those seducing pleasures which he had once enjoyed in the freedom of the woods.

Whilst wandering through these melancholy remains of former scenes, a question was put to the divine concerning the place where Conanchet was interred. He readily offered to show it. The grave was on the hill, and distinguished only by a headstone that the grass had concealed from former search. It merely bore the words—"The Narragansett."

"And this at its side?" asked the inquirer. "Here is one also, before unnoted."

The divine bent in the grass, and scraped the moss from the humble monument. He then pointed to a line, carved with more than usual care. The inscription simply said—

"The Wept of Wish-Ton-Wish."

END OF "THE WEPT OF WISH-TON-WISH."

PRECAUTION.

CHAPTER I.

"I WONDER if we are to have a neighbor in the Deanery soon?" inquired Clara Moseley, addressing herself to a small party assembled in her father's drawing-room, while standing at a window which commanded a distant view of the house in question.

"Oh, yes," replied her brother; "the agent has let it to a Mr. Jarvis for a couple of years, and he is to take possession this week."

"And who is the Mr. Jarvis that is about to become so near a neighbor?" asked Sir Edward Moseley.

"Why, sir, I learn he has been a capital merchant; that he has retired from business with a large fortune; that he has, like yourself, sir, an only hope for his declining years in a son, an officer in the army; and, moreover, that he has a couple of fine daughters; so, sir, he is a man of family in one sense at least, you see. But," dropping his voice, "whether he is a man of family in your sense, Jane," looking at his second sister, "is more than I could discover."

"I hope you did not take the trouble, sir, to inquire on my account," retorted Jane, coloring slightly with vexation at his speech.

"Indeed I did, my dear sis, and solely on your account," replied the laughing brother, "for you well know that no gentility, no husband; and it's dull work to you young ladies without at least a possibility of matrimony. As for Clara, she is—"

Here he was stopped by his younger sister Emily placing his hand on his mouth, as she whispered in his ear, "John, you forget the anxiety of a certain gentleman about a fair incognita at Bath, and a list of inquiries concerning her lineage, and a few other indispensables." John, in his turn, colored, and affectionately kissing the hand which kept him silent, addressed himself to Jane, and by his vivacity and good humor soon restored her to complacency.

"I rejoice," said Lady Moseley, "that Sir William has found a tenant, however; for next to occupying it himself, it is a most desirable thing to have a good tenant in it, on account of the circle in which we live."

"And Mr. Jarvis has the great goodness of money, by John's account," caustically observed Mrs. Wilson, who was a sister of Sir Edward's.

"Let me tell you, madam," cried the rector of the parish, looking around him pleasantly, and who was a pretty constant and always a welcome visitor in the family, "that a great deal of money is a very good thing in itself, and that a great many very good things may be done with it."

"Such as paying tithes, ha! doctor," cried Mr. Haughton, a gentleman of landed property in the neighborhood, of plain exterior, but great goodness of heart, and between whom and the rector subsisted the most cordial good-will.

"Ay, tithes, or halves, as the baronet did here, when he forgave old Gregson one-half his rent and his children the other."

"Well, but, my dear," said Sir Edward to his wife, "you must not starve our friends because we are to have a neighbor. William has stood with the dining-room door open these five minutes—"

Lady Moseley gave her hand to the rector, and the company followed them, without any order, to the dinner-table.

The party assembled around the hospitable board of the baronet was composed, beside the before-mentioned persons, of the wife of Mr. Haughton, a woman of much good sense and modesty of deportment; their daughter, a young lady conspicuous for nothing but good nature; and the wife and son of the rector—the latter but lately admitted to holy orders himself.

The remainder of the day passed in an uninterrupted flow of pleasant conversation, the natural consequence of a unison of opinions on all leading questions, the parties having long known and esteemed each other for those qualities which soonest reconcile us to the common frailties of our nature. On parting at the usual hour, it was agreed to meet that day week at the rectory; and the doctor, on making his bow to Lady Moseley, observed that he intended, in virtue of his office, to make an early call on the Jarvis family, and that, if possible, he would persuade them to be of the party.

Sir Edward Moseley was descended from one of the most respectable of the creations of his order by James, and had inherited, with many of the virtues of his ancestor, an estate which placed him among the greatest landed proprietors of the county. But, as it had been an invariable rule never to deduct a single acre from the inheritance of the eldest son, and the extravagance of his mother, who was the daughter of a nobleman, had much embarrassed the affairs of his father, Sir Edward, on coming into possession of his estate, had wisely determined to withdraw from the gay world, by renting his house in town, and retiring altogether to his respectable mansion, about a hundred miles from the metropolis. Here he hoped, by a course of systematic but liberal economy, to release himself from all embarrassments, and to make such a provision for his younger children, the three daughters already mentioned, as he conceived their birth entitled them to expect. Seventeen years enabled him to accomplish this plan; and, for more than eighteen months, Sir Edward had resumed the hospitality and appearance usual in his family, and had even promised his delighted girls to take possession, the ensuing winter, of the house in St. James's Square. Nature had not qualified Sir Edward for great or continued exertions, and the prudent decision he had taken to retrieve his fortunes was perhaps an act of as much forecast and vigor as his talents or energy would afford; it was the step most obviously for his interests, and the one that was safest both in its execution and consequences, and as such it had been adopted: but, had it required a single particle more of enterprise or calculation, it would have been beyond his powers, and the heir might have yet labored under the difficulties which distressed his more brilliant but less prudent parent.

The baronet was warmly attached to his wife, and as she was a woman of many valuable and no obnoxious qualities, civil and attentive by habit to all around her, and perfectly disinterested in her attachments to her own family, nothing in nature could partake more of perfection in the eyes of her husband and children than the con-duct of this beloved relative. Yet Lady Moseley had her failings, however, although few were disposed to view her errors with that severity which truth and a just discrimination of character render necessary. Her union had been one of love, and for a time it had been objected to by the friends of her husband, on the score of fortune; but constancy and perseverance prevailed, and the protracted and inconsequent opposition of his parents had left no other effects than an aversion in the children to the exercise of parental authority, in marrying their own descendants—an aversion which, though common to both the worthy baronet and his wife, was somewhat different in its two subjects. In the husband, it was quiescent; but in the wife, it was slightly shaded with the female *esprit de corps* of having her daughters comfortably established, and that in due season. Lady Moseley was religious, but hardly pious; she was charitable in deeds, but not always in opinion; her intentions were pure, but neither her prejudices nor her reasoning powers suffered her to be at all times consistent. Still, few knew her that did not love her; and none were ever heard to say aught against her breeding, her morals, or her disposition.

The sister of Sir Edward had been married, early in life, to an officer in the army, who, spending much of his time abroad on service, had left her a prey to that solicitude to which she was necessarily subjected by her attachment to her husband. To find relief from this perpetual and life-wearing anxiety, an invaluable friend had pointed out the only true remedy of which her case admitted —a research into her own heart, and the employments of active benevolence. The death of her husband, who lost his life in battle, caused her to withdraw in a great measure from the world, and gave time and inducement for reflections, which led to impressions on religion that were sufficiently correct in themselves, and indispensable as the basis of future happiness, but which became slightly tinctured with the sternness of her vigorous mind, and possibly at times were more unbending than was compatible with the comforts of this world; a fault, however, of manner, more than of matter. Warmly attached to her brother and his children, Mrs. Wilson, who had never been a mother herself, yielded to their earnest entreaties to become one of the family; and, although left by the late General Wilson with a large income, ever since his death she had given up her own establishment and devoted most of her time to the formation of the character of her youngest niece. Lady Moseley had submitted this child entirely to the control of the aunt; and it was commonly thought Emily would inherit the very handsome sum left at the disposal of the general's widow.

Both Sir Edward and Lady Moseley possessed a large share of personal beauty when young, and it had descended in common to all their children, but more particularly to their two youngest daughters. Although a strong family resemblance, both in person and character, existed between these closely-connected relatives, yet it existed with shades of distinction that had very different effects on their conduct, and led to results which stamped their lives with widely-differing degrees of happiness.

Between the families at Moseley Hall and the rectory there had existed for many years an intimacy founded on esteem and on long intercourse. Doctor Ives was a clergyman of deep piety, and of very considerable talents; he possessed, in addition to a moderate benefice, an independent fortune, in right of his wife, who was the only child of a distinguished naval officer. Both were well connected, well bred, and well disposed to their fellow-creatures. They were blessed with but one child, the young divine we have mentioned, who promised to equal his father in all those qualities which had made the doctor the delight of his friends, and almost the idol of his parishioners.

Between Francis Ives and Clara Moseley there had been an attachment, which had grown with their years, from childhood. He had been her companion in their youthful recreations, had espoused her little quarrels, and participated in her innocent pleasures, for so many years, and with such an evident preference for each other in the youthful pair, that, on leaving college to enter on the duties of his sacred calling with his father, Francis rightly judged that none other would make his future life as happy as the mild, the tender, the unassuming Clara. Their passion, if so gentle a feeling deserve the term, received the sanction of their parents, and the two families waited only for the establishment of the young divine, to perfect the union.

The retirement of Sir Edward's family had been uniform, with the exception of an occasional visit to an aged uncle of his wife's, and who, in return, spent much of his time with them at the Hall, and who had openly declared his intention of making the children of Lady Moseley his heirs. The visits of Mr. Benfield were always hailed with joy, and as an event that called for

more than ordinary gayety; for, although rough in manner, and somewhat infirm from years, the old bachelor, who was rather addicted to the customs in which he had indulged in his youth, and was fond of dwelling on the scenes of former days, was universally beloved where he was intimately known, for an unbounded though eccentric philanthropy.

The illness of the mother-in-law of Mrs. Wilson had called her to Bath the winter preceding the spring when our history commences, and she had been accompanied thither by her nephew and favorite niece. John and Emily, during the month of their residence in that city, were in the practice of making daily excursions in its environs. It was in one of these little drives that they were of accidental service to a very young and very beautiful woman, apparently in low health. They had taken her up in their carriage, and conveyed her to a farm-house where she resided, during a faintness which had come over her in a walk; and her beauty, air, and manner, altogether so different from those around her, had interested them both to a painful degree. They had ventured to call the following day to inquire after her welfare, and this visit led to a slight intercourse, which continued for the fortnight they remained there.

John had given himself some trouble to ascertain who she was, but in vain. They could merely learn that her life was blameless, that she saw no one but themselves, and her dialect raised a suspicion that she was not English. It was to this unknown fair Emily alluded in her playful attempt to stop the heedless rattle of her brother, who was not always restrained from uttering what he thought by a proper regard for the feelings of others.

CHAPTER II.

The morning succeeding the day of the dinner at the Hall, Mrs. Wilson, with all her nieces and her nephew, availed herself of the fineness of the weather to walk to the rectory, where they were all in the habit of making informal and friendly visits. They had just got out of the little village of B——, which lay in their route, when a rather handsome traveling-carriage and four passed them, and took the road which led to the Deanery.

"As I live," cried John, "there go our new neighbors the Jarvises; yes, yes, that must be the old merchant muffled up in the corner; I mistook him at first for a pile of bandboxes; then the rosy-cheeked lady, with so many feathers, must be the old lady—Heaven forgive me, Mrs. Jarvis, I mean—ay, and the two others the belles."

"You are in a hurry to pronounce them belles, John," said Jane, pettishly; "it would be well to see more of them before you speak so decidedly."

"Oh!" replied John, "I have seen *enough* of them, and "—he was interrupted by the whirling of a tilbury and tandem, followed by a couple of servants on horseback. All about this vehicle and its masters bore the stamp of decided fashion; and our party had followed it with their eyes for a short distance, when, having reached a fork in the roads, it stopped, and evidently waited the coming up of the pedestrians, as if to make an inquiry. A single glance of the eye was sufficient to apprise the gentleman on the cushion (who held the reins) of the kind of people he had to deal with; and stepping from his carriage, he met them with a graceful bow, and after handsomely apologizing for the trouble he was giving, he desired to know which road led to the Deanery. "The right," replied John, returning the salutation.

"Ask them, colonel," cried the charioteer, "whether the old gentleman went right or not."

The colonel, in the manner of a perfect gentleman, but with a look of compassion for his companion's want of tact, made the desired inquiry; which being satisfactorily answered, he again bowed, and was retiring, as one of several pointers who followed the cavalcade sprang upon Jane and soiled her walking-dress with his dirty feet.

"Come hither, Dido!" cried the colonel, hastening to beat the dog back from the young lady; and again he apologized in the same collected and handsome manner. Then turning to one of the servants, he said, "Call in the dog, sir," and rejoined his companion. The air of this gentleman was peculiarly pleasant; it would not have been difficult to pronounce him a soldier had he not been addressed as such by his younger, and certainly less polished companion. The colonel was apparently about thirty, and of extremely handsome face and figure; while his driving-friend appeared several years younger, and of altogether different material.

"I wonder," said Jane, as they turned a corner which hid them from view, "who they are?"

"Who they are?" cried the brother; "why, the Jarvises, to be sure; didn't you hear them ask the road to the Deanery?"

"Oh! the one that drove, *he* may be a Jarvis, but not the gentleman who spoke to us—surely not, John; besides, he was called colonel, you know."

"Yes, yes," said John, with one of his quizzing expressions, "Colonel Jarvis—that must be the alderman; they are commonly colonels of city volunteers; yes, that must have been the old gem'-mun who spoke to us, and I was right, after all, about the bandboxes."

"You forget," said Clara, smiling, "the polite inquiry concerning the old gem'mun."

"Ah! true; who the deuce can this colonel be, then—for young Jarvis is only a captain, I know. Who do you think he is, Jane?"

"How do you think I can tell you, John? But, whoever he is, he owns the tilbury, although he did not drive it; and he is a gentleman both by birth and manners."

"Why, Jane, if you know so much of him, you should know more; but it is all guess with you."

"No, it is not guess; I am certain of what I say."

The aunt and sisters, who had taken little interest in the dialogue, looked at her with some surprise, which John observing, he exclaimed, "Poh! she knows no more than we all know."

"Indeed, I do."

"Poh, poh! if you know, tell."

"Why, the arms were different."

John laughed as he said, "That *is* a good reason, sure enough, for the tilbury's being the colonel's property; but now for his blood; how did you discover that, sis—by his gait and actions, as we say of horses?"

Jane colored a little, and laughed faintly. "The arms on the tilbury had six quarterings."

Emily now laughed, and Mrs. Wilson and Clara smiled, while John continued his teasing until they reached the rectory.

While chatting with the doctor and his wife, Francis returned from his morning ride, and told them the Jarvis family had arrived. He had witnessed an unpleasant accident to a gig, in which were Captain Jarvis and a friend, a Colonel Egerton; it had been awkwardly driven in turning into the Deanery gate, and upset. The colonel received some injury to his ankle—nothing serious, however, he hoped; but such as to put him under the care of the young ladies, probably, for a few days. After the exclamations which usually follow such details, Jane ventured to inquire who Colonel Egerton was.

"I understood at the time, from one of

the servants, that he is a nephew of Sir Edgar Egerton, and a lieutenant-colonel on half pay, or furlough, or some such thing."

"How did he bear his misfortune, Mr. Francis?" inquired Mrs. Wilson.

"Certainly as a gentleman, madam, if not as a Christian," replied the young clergyman, slyly smiling; "indeed, most men of gallantry would, I believe, rejoice in an accident which drew forth so much sympathy as both the Miss Jarvises manifested."

"How fortunate you should all happen to be near!" said the tender-hearted Clara.

"Are the young ladies pretty?" asked Jane, with something of hesitation in her manner.

"Why, I rather think they are; but I took very little notice of their appearance, as the colonel was really in evident pain."

"This, then," cried the doctor, "affords me an additional excuse for calling on them at an early day; so I'll e'en go to-morrow."

"I trust Doctor Ives wants no apologies for performing his duty," said Mrs. Wilson.

"He is fond of making them, though," said Mrs. Ives, speaking with a benevolent smile, and for the first time in the little conversation.

It was then arranged that the rector should make his official visit, as intended, by himself; and, on his report, the ladies would act. After remaining at the rectory an hour, they returned to the Hall, attended by Francis.

The next day the doctor drove in, and informed them the Jarvis family were happily settled, and the colonel in no danger, excepting from the fascinations of the two young ladies, who took such palpable care of him that he wanted for nothing, and they might drive over whenever they pleased, without fear of intruding unseasonably.

Mr. Jarvis received his guests with the frankness of good feelings, if not with the polish of high life; while his wife, who seldom thought of the former, would have been mortally offended with the person who could have suggested that she omitted any of the elegances of the latter. Her daughters were rather pretty, but wanted, both in appearance and manner, the inexpressible air of *haut ton* which so eminently distinguished the easy but polished deportment of Colonel Egerton, whom they found reclining on a sofa, with his leg on a chair, amply secured in numerous bandages, but unable to rise. Notwithstanding the awkwardness of his situation, he was by far the least discomposed person of the party, and having

pleasantly excused himself, he appeared to think no more of the matter.

The captain, Mrs. Jarvis remarked, had gone out with his dogs to try the grounds around them, "for he seems to live only with his horses and his gun: young men, my lady, nowadays, appear to forget that there are any things in the world but themselves. Now I told Harry that your ladyship and daughters would favor us with a call this morning; but no—there he went, as if Mr. Jarvis was unable to buy us a dinner, and we should all starve but for his quails and pheasants."

"Quails and pheasants!" cried John, in consternation, "does Captain Jarvis shoot quails and pheasants at this time of the year?"

"Mrs. Jarvis, sir," said Colonel Egerton, with a correcting smile, "understands the allegiance due from us gentlemen to the ladies better than the rules of sporting; my friend the captain has taken his fishing-rod, I believe."

"It is all one, fish or birds," continued Mrs. Jarvis; "he is out of the way when he is wanted, and I believe we can buy fish as easily as birds. I wish he would take pattern after yourself, colonel, in these matters."

Colonel Egerton laughed pleasantly, but he did not blush; and Miss Jarvis observed, with a look of something like admiration thrown on his reclining figure, that "when Harry had been in the army as long as his friend, he would know the usages of good society, she hoped, as well."

"Yes," said her mother, "the army is certainly the place to polish a young man;" and turning to Mrs. Wilson, she abruptly added, "Your husband, I believe, was in the army, ma'am?"

"I hope," said Emily, hastily, "that we shall have the pleasure of seeing you soon, Miss Jarvis, at the Hall," preventing by her promptitude the necessity of a reply from her aunt. The young lady promised to make an early visit, and the subject changed to a general and uninteresting discourse on the neighborhood, the country, the weather, and other ordinary topics.

"Now, John," cried Jane in triumph, as they drove from the door, "you must acknowledge my heraldic witchcraft, as you are pleased to call it, is right for once at least."

"Oh! no doubt, Jenny," said John, who was accustomed to use that appellation to her as a provocation, when he wished what he called an enlivening scene; but Mrs. Wilson put a damper on his hopes by a remark to his mother, and the habitual respect of both the combatants kept them silent.

Jane Moseley was endowed by nature with an excellent understanding, one at least equal to that of her brother; but she wanted the more essential requisites of a well-governed mind. Masters had been provided by Sir Edward for all his daughters, and if they were not acquainted with the usual acquirements of young women in their rank of life, it was not his fault; his system of economy had not embraced a denial of opportunity to any of his children, and the baronet was apt to think all *was* done, when they were put where all *might* be done. Feeling herself and parents entitled to enter into all the gayeties and splendors of some of the richer families in their vicinity, Jane, who had grown up during the temporary eclipse of Sir Edward's fortunes, had sought that self-consolation so common to people in her situation, which was to be found in reviewing the former grandeur of her house; and she had thus contracted a degree of family pride. If Clara's weaknesses were less striking than those of Jane, it was because she had less imagination, and because that in loving Francis Ives she had so long admired a character where so little was to be found that could be censured, and she might be said to have contracted a habit of judging correctly, without being able at all times to give a reason for her conduct or her opinions.

CHAPTER III.

THE day fixed for one of the stated visits of Mr. Benfield had now arrived; and John, and Emily, who was the old bachelor's favorite niece, went in the baronet's post-chaise to the town of F——, a distance of twenty miles, to meet him, in order to accompany him in the remainder of his journey to the Hall: it being a settled rule with the old man that his carriage-horses should return to their own stables every night, where he imagined they could alone find that comfort and care to which their age and services gave them a claim. The day was uncommonly pleasant, and the young people were in high spirits with the expectation of meeting their respected relative, whose absence had been prolonged a few days by a severe fit of gout.

"Now, Emily," cried John, as he settled himself comfortably by the side of his sister in the chaise, "let me know honestly how you like the Jarvises, and particularly how you like the handsome colonel."

"Then, John, honestly, I neither like nor dislike the Jarvises or the handsome colonel."

"Well, then, there is no great diversity in our sentiments, as Jane would say."

"John!"

"Emily!"

"I do not like to hear you speak so disrespectfully of our sister, whom I am sure you love as tenderly as I do myself."

"I acknowledge my error," said the brother, taking her hand and affectionately kissing it, "and will endeavor to offend no more; but this Colonel Egerton, sister, is certainly a gentleman, both by blood and in manners, as Jane"—Emily interrupted him with a laugh, which John took very good-naturedly, repeating his remark without alluding to their sister.

"Yes," said Emily, "he is genteel in his deportment, if that be what you mean; I know nothing of his family."

"Oh, I have taken a peep into Jane's 'Baronetage,' where I find him set down as Sir Edgar's heir."

"There is something about him," said Emily, musing, "that I do not much admire; he is too easy—there is no nature. I always feel afraid such people will laugh at me as soon as my back is turned, and for those very things they seem most to admire to my face. If I might be allowed to judge, I should say his manner wants one thing, without which no one can be truly agreeable."

"What's that?"

"Sincerity."

"Ah! that's my great recommendation. But I am afraid I shall have to take the poacher up, with his quails and his pheasants, indeed."

"You know the colonel explained that to be a mistake."

"What they call explaining away; but, unluckily, I saw the gentleman returning with his gun on his shoulder, and followed by a brace of pointers."

"There's a specimen of the colonel's manners, then," said Emily, smiling; "it will do until the truth be known."

"And Jane, when she saw him also, praised his good nature and consideration, in what she was pleased to call relieving the awkwardness of my remark."

Emily, finding her brother disposed to dwell on the foibles of Jane, a thing he was rather addicted to at times, was silent. They rode some distance before John, who was ever as ready to atone as he was to offend, again apologized, again promised reformation, and during the remainder of the ride only forgot himself twice more in the same way.

They reached F—— two hours before

the lumbering coach of their uncle drove into the yard of the inn, and had sufficient time to refresh their own horses for the journey homeward.

Mr. Benfield was a bachelor of eighty, but retained the personal activity of a man of sixty. He was strongly attached to all the fashions and opinions of his youth, during which he had sat one term in Parliament, having been a great beau and courtier in the commencement of the reign. A disappointment in an affair of the heart drove him into retirement; and for the last fifty years he had dwelt exclusively at a seat he owned within forty miles of Moseley Hall, the mistresss of which was the only child of his only brother. In figure, he was tall and spare, very erect for his years; and he faithfully preserved in his attire, servants, carriages, and indeed everything around him, as much of the fashions of his youth as circumstances would allow. Such, then, was a faint outline of the character and appearance of the old man, who, dressed in a cocked hat, bag-wig, and sword, took the offered arm of John Moseley to alight from his coach.

"So," cried the old gentleman, having made good his footing on the ground, as he stopped short and stared John in the face, "you have made out to come twenty miles to meet an old cynic, have you, sir? But I thought I bid thee bring Emmy with thee."

John pointed to the window, where his sister stood anxiously watching her uncle's movements. On catching her eye, he smiled kindly, and pursued his way into the house, talking to himself.

"Ay, there she is, indeed. I remember now, when I was a youngster, of going with my kinsman, old Lord Gosford, to meet his sister, the Lady Juliana, when she first came from school"—this was the lady whose infidelity had driven him from the world—"and a beauty she was indeed, something like Emmy there; only she was taller, and her eyes were black, and her hair too, that was black; and she was not so fair as Emmy, and she was fatter, and she stooped a little — very little. Oh! they are wonderfully alike, though; don't you think they were, nephew?" He stopped at the door of the room; while John, who in his description could not see a resemblance which existed nowhere but in the old man's affections, was fain to say, "Yes; but they were related, you know, uncle, and that explains the likeness."

"True, boy, true," said his uncle, pleased at a reason for a thing he wished and which flattered his propensi-ties. He had once before told Emily she put him in mind of his housekeeper, a woman as old as himself, and without a tooth in her head.

On meeting his niece, Mr. Benfield—who, like many others that feel strongly, wore in common the affectation of indifference and displeasure—yielded to his fondness, and folding her in his arms, kissed her affectionately, while a tear glistened in his eye; and then pushing her gently from him he exclaimed, "Come, come, Emmy, don't strangle me, don't strangle me, girl; let me live in peace the little while I have to remain here—so," seating himself composedly in an armchair his niece had placed for him with a cushion, "so Anne writes me, Sir William Harris has let the Deanery."

"Oh, yes, uncle," cried John.

"I'll thank you, young gentleman," said Mr. Benfield, sternly, "not to interrupt me when I am speaking to a lady; that is, if you please, sir. Then Sir William has let the Deanery to a London merchant, a Mr. Jarvis. Now I knew three people of that name; one was a hackney coachman, when I was a member of the Parliament of this realm, and drove me often to the House; another was a *valet-de-chambre* to my Lord Gosford; and the third, I take it, is the very man who has become your neighbor. If it be the person I mean, Emmy dear, he is like—like—ay, very like old Peter, my steward."

John, unable to contain his mirth at this discovery of a likeness between the prototype of Mr. Benfield himself in leanness of figure, and the jolly rotundity of the merchant, was obliged to leave the room; Emily, though she could not forbear smiling at the comparison, quietly said, "You will meet him to-morrow, dear uncle, and then you will be able to judge for yourself."

"Yes, yes," muttered the old man, "very like old Peter, my steward; as like as two peas." The parallel was by no means as ridiculous as might be supposed; its history being as follows:

Mr. Benfield had placed twenty thousand pounds in the hands of a broker, with positive orders for him to pay it away immediately for government stock, bought by the former on his account; but disregarding this injunction, the broker had managed the transaction in such a way as to postpone the payments, until, on his faiiure, he had given up that and a much larger sum to Mr. Jarvis, to satisfy what he called an honorary debt. In elucidating the transaction Mr. Jarvis paid Benfield Lodge a visit, and honestly restored the bachelor his property. This act and the high opinion he entertained of Mrs. Wilson, with his unbounded love for Emily, were the few things which prevented his believing some dreadful judgment was about to visit this world for its increasing wickedness and follies. As his own steward was one of the honestest fellows living, he had ever after fancied that there was a personal resemblance between him and the conscientious merchant.

The horses being ready, the old bachelor was placed carefully between his nephew and niece, and in that manner they rode on quietly to the Hall, the dread of accident keeping Mr. Benfield silent most of the way. On passing, however, a stately castle, about ten miles from the termination of their ride, he began one of his speeches with,

"Emmy, dear, does Lord Bolton come often to see you?"

"Very seldom, sir; his employment keeps him much of his time at St. James's, and then he has an estate in Ireland."

"I knew his father well—he was distantly connected by marriage with my friend Lord Gosford; you could not remember him, I suspect" (John rolled his eyes at this suggestion of his sister's recollection of a man who had been forty years dead); "he always voted with me in the Parliament of this realm; he was a thoroughly honest man; very much such a man to look at as Peter Johnson, my steward; but I am told his son likes the good things of the ministry; well, well, William Pitt was the only minister to my mind. There was the Scotchman of whom they made a marquis; I never could endure him—always voted against him."

"Right or wrong, uncle," cried John, who loved a little mischief in his heart.

"No, sir—right, but never wrong. Lord Gosford always voted against him too; and do you think, jackanapes, that my friend the Earl of Gosford and—and —myself were ever wrong? No, sir, men in my day were different creatures from what they are now; we were never wrong, sir; we loved our country, and had no motive for being in the wrong."

"How was it with Lord Bute, uncle?"

"Lord Bute, sir," cried the old man, with great warmth, "was the minister, sir—he was the minister; ay, he was the minister, sir, and was paid for what he did."

"But Lord Chatham, was he not the minister too?"

Now nothing vexed the old gentleman more than to hear William Pitt called by his tardy honors; and yet, unwilling to give up what he thought his political opinions, he exclaimed with an unanswerable positiveness of argument.

"Billy Pitt, sir, was the minister, sir; but—but—but, he was *our* minister, sir."

Emily, unable to see her uncle agitated by such useless disputes, threw a reproachful glance on her brother as she observed, timidly,

"That was a glorious administration, sir, I believe."

"Glorious indeed! Emmy dear," said the bachelor, softening with the sound of her voice and the recollections of his younger days; "we beat the French everywhere—in America—in Germany; —we took," counting on his fingers, "we took Quebec—yes, Lord Gosford lost a cousin there; and we took all the Canadas; and we took their fleets: there was a young man killed in the battle between Hawke and Conflans, who was much attached to Lady Juliana—poor soul! how much she regretted him when dead, though she never could abide him when living— ah! she was a tender-hearted creature!"

Mr. Benfield, like many others, continued to love imaginary qualities in his mistress, long after her heartless coquetry had disgusted him with her person: a kind of feeling which springs from self-love, which finds it necessary to seek consolation in creating beauties that may justify our follies to ourselves, and which often keeps alive the semblance of the passion when even hope, or real admiration, is extinct.

On reaching the Hall every one was rejoiced to see their really affectionate and worthy relative, and the evening passed in the tranquil enjoyment of the blessings which Providence had profusely scattered around the family of the baronet, but which are too often hazarded by a neglect of duty that springs from too great security, or an indolence which renders us averse to the precaution necessary to insure their continuance.

CHAPTER IV.

"You are welcome, Sir Edward," said the venerable rector, as he took the baronet by the hand; "I was fearful a return of your rheumatism would deprive us of this pleasure, and prevent my making you acquainted with the new occupants of the Deanery, who have consented to dine with us to-day, and to whom I have promised, in particular, an introduction to Sir Edward Moseley."

"I thank you, my dear doctor," rejoined

the baronet; "I have not only come myself, but have persuaded Mr. Benfield to make one of the party; there he comes, leaning on Emiiy's arm, and finding fault with Mrs. Wilson's new-fashioned barouche, which he says has given him cold."

The rector received the unexpected guest with the kindness of his nature, and an inward smile at the incongruous assemblage he was likely to have around him by the arrival of the Jarvises, who at that moment drove to his door. The introductions between the baronet and the new comers had passed, and Miss Jarvis had made a prettily worded apology on behalf of the colonel, who was not yet well enough to come out, but whose politeness had insisted on their not remaining at home on his account, as Mr. Benfield, having composedly put on his spectacles, walked deliberately up to the place where the merchant had seated himself, and having examined him through his glasses to his satisfaction, took them off, and carefully wiping them, he began to talk to himself as he put them into his pocket— "No, no; it's not Jack, the hackney coachman, nor my Lord Gosford's gentleman, but"—cordially holding out both hands—"it's the man who saved my twenty thousand pounds."

Mr. Jarvis, whom shame and embarrassment had kept silent during this examination, exchanged greetings sincerely with his old acquaintance, who now took a seat in silence by his side; while his wife, whose face had begun to kindle with indignation at the commencement of the old gentleman's soliloquy, observing that somehow or other it had not only terminated without degradation to her spouse, but with something like credit, turned complacently to Mrs. Ives, with an apology for the absence of her son.

"I cannot divine, ma'am, where he has got to; he is ever keeping us waiting for him." And, addressing Jane, "These military men become so unsettled in their habits, that I often tell Harry he should never quit the camp."

"In Hyde Park, you should add, my dear, for he has never been in any other," bluntly observed her husband.

To this speech no reply was made, but it was evidently little relished by the ladies of the family, who were a good deal jealous of the laurels of the only hero their race had ever produced. The arrival and introduction of the captain himself changed the discourse, which turned on the comforts of their present residence.

"Pray, my lady," cried the captain, who had taken a chair familiarly by the side of the baronet's wife, "why is the house called the Deanery? I am afraid I shall be taken for a son of the Church, when I invite my friends to visit my father at the Deanery."

"But you may add at the same time, sir, if you please," dryly remarked Mr. Jarvis, "that it is occupied by an old man who has been preaching and lecturing all his life; and, like others of the trade, I believe, in vain."

"You must except our good friend the doctor here, at least, sir," said Mrs. Wilson, who, observing that her sister shrank from a familiarity she was unused to, took upon herself the office of replying to the captain's question. "The father of the present Sir William held that station in the Church; and, although the house was his private property, it took its name from the circumstance, which has been continued ever since."

"Is it not a droll life Sir William leads," cried Miss Jarvis, looking at John Moseley, "riding about all summer from one watering-place to another, and letting his house year after year in the manner he does?"

"Sir William," said Doctor Ives gravely, "is devoted to his daughter's wishes; and, since his accession to his title, has come into possession of another residence in an adjoining county, which, I believe, he retains in his own hands."

"Are you acquainted with Miss Harris?" continued the lady, addressing herself to Clara; though, without waiting for an answer, she added, "she is a great belle— all the gentlemen are dying for her."

"Or her fortune," said her sister, with a pretty toss of the head; "for my part I never could see anything so captivating in her, although so much is said about her at Bath and Brighton."

"You know her, then," mildly observed Clara.

"Why, I cannot say—we are exactly acquainted," the young lady hesitatingly answered, coloring violently.

"What do you mean by exactly acquainted, Sally?" put in the father, with a laugh; "did you ever speak to, or were you ever in a room with her, in your life, unless it might be at a concert or a ball?"

The mortification of Miss Sarah was too evident for concealment, and it happily was relieved by a summons to dinner.

"Never, my dear child," said Mrs. Wilson to Emily—the aunt being fond of introducing a moral from the occasional incidents of every-day life—"never subject yourself to a similar mortification, by commenting on the characters of those you don't know: ignorance makes you liable to great errors; and if they should happen to be above you in life, it will only excite their contempt, should it reach their ears, while those to whom your remarks are made will think it envy."

"Truth is sometimes blundered on," whispered John, who held his sister's arm, waiting for his aunt to precede them to the dining-room.

The merchant paid too great a compliment to the rector's dinner to think of renewing the disagreeable conversation; and as John Moseley and the young clergyman were seated next the two ladies, they soon forgot what, among themselves, they would call their father's rudeness, in receiving the attentions of a couple of remarkably agreeable young men.

"Pray, Mr. Francis, when do you preach for us?" asked Mr. Haughton; "I'm very anxious to hear you hold forth from the pulpit, where I have so often heard your father with pleasure. I doubt not you will prove orthodox, or you will be the only man, I believe, in the congregation, the rector has left in ignorance of the theory of our religion, at least."

The doctor bowed to the compliment, as he replied to the question for his son, that on the next Sunday they were to have the pleasure of hearing Frank, who had promised to assist him on that day.

"Any prospects of a living soon?" continued Mr. Haughton, helping himself bountifully to a piece of plum-pudding as he spoke. John Moseley laughed aloud, and Clara blushed to the eyes; while the doctor, turning to Sir Edward, observed, with an air of interest, "Sir Edward, the living of Bolton is vacant, and I should like exceedingly to obtain it for my son. The advowson belongs to the earl, who will dispose of it only to great interest, I am afraid."

Clara was certainly too busily occupied in picking raisins from her pudding to hear this remark, but accidentally stole, from under her long eyelashes, a timid glance at her father, as he replied—

"I am sorry, my friend, I have not sufficient interest with his lordship to apply on my own account; but he is so seldom here, we are barely acquainted"—and the good baronet looked really concerned.

"Clara," said Francis Ives, in a low and affectionate tone, "have you read the books I sent you?"

Clara answered him with a smile in the negative, but promised amendment as soon as she had leisure.

"Do you ride much on horseback, Mr. Moseley?" abruptly asked Miss Sarah, turning her back on the young divine, and facing the gentleman she addressed.

John, who was now hemmed in between the sisters, replied with a rueful expression that brought a smile into the face of Emily, who was placed opposite him—

"Yes, ma'am, and sometimes I am ridden."

"Ridden, sir! what do you mean by that!"

"Oh! only my aunt there occasionally gives me a lecture."

"I understand." said the lady, pointing slyly with her finger at her own father.

"Does it feel good?" John inquired, with a look of great sympathy. But the lady, who now felt awkwardly, without knowing exactly why, shook her head in silence, and forced a faint laugh.

"Whom have we here?" cried Captain Jarvis, who was looking out at a window which commanded a view of the approach to the house—"the apothecary and his attendant, judging from the equipage."

The rector threw an inquiring look on a servant, who told his master they were strangers to him.

"Have them shown up, doctor," cried the benevolent baronet, who loved to see every one as happy as himself, "and give them some of your excellent pasty, for the sake of hospitality and the credit of your cook, I beg of you."

As this request was politely seconded by others of the party, the rector ordered his servants to show in the strangers.

On opening the parlor door, a gentleman, apparently sixty years of age, appeared, leaning on the arm of a youth of five-and-twenty. There was sufficient resemblance between the two for the most indifferent observer to pronounce them father and son; but the helpless debility and emaciated figure of the former were finely contrasted by the vigorous health and manly beauty of the latter, who supported his venerable parent into the room with a grace and tenderness that struck most of the beholders with a sensation of pleasure. The doctor and Mrs. Ives rose from their seats involuntarily, and each stood for a moment lost in an astonishment that was mingled with grief. Recollecting himself, the rector grasped the extended hand of the senior in both his own, and endeavored to utter something, but in vain. The tears followed each other down his cheeks, as he looked on the faded and careworn figure which stood before him; while his wife, unable to control her feelings, sank back into a chair, and wept aloud.

Throwing open the door of an adjoining room, and retaining the hand of the invalid, the doctor gently led the way, followed by his wife and son. The former, having recovered from the first burst of her sorrow, and regardless of everything else, now anxiously watched the enfeebled step of the stranger. On reaching the door, they both turned and bowed to the company in a manner of so much dignity, mingled with sweetness, that all, not excepting Mr. Benfield, rose from their seats to return the salutation. On passing from the dining-parlor, the door was closed, leaving the company standing round the table in mute astonishment and commiseration. Not a word had been spoken, and the rector's family had left them without apology or explanation. Francis, however, soon returned, and was followed in a few minutes by his mother, who, slightly apologizing for her absence, turned the discourse on the approaching Sunday, and the intention of Francis to preach on that day. The Moseleys were too well-bred to make any inquiries, and the Deanery family was afraid. Sir Edward retired at a very early hour, and was followed by the remainder of the party.

"Well," cried Mrs. Jarvis, as they drove from the door, "this may be good breeding; but, for my part, I think both the doctor and Mrs. Ives behaved very rudely, with the crying and sobbing."

"They are nobody of much consequence," cried her eldest daughter, casting a contemptuous glance on a plain traveling-chaise which stood before the rector's stables.

"'Twas sickening," said Miss Sarah, with a shrug; while her father, turning his eyes on each speaker in succession, very deliberately helped himself to a pinch of snuff, his ordinary recourse against a family quarrel. The curiosity of the ladies was, however, more lively than they chose to avow; and Mrs. Jarvis bade her maid go over to the rectory that evening, with her compliments to Mrs. Ives; she had lost a lace veil, which her maid knew, and she thought it might have been left at the rectory.

"And, Jones, when you are there, you can inquire of the servants—I would not distress Mrs. Ives for the world—how Mr. —Mr.—what's his name?—oh! I have forgotten his name! just bring me his name too, Jones; and, as it may make some difference in our party, just find out how long they stay; and—and—any other little thing, Jones, which can be of use, you know."

Off went Jones, and within an hour she had returned. With an important look, she commenced her narrative, the daughters being accidentally present, and it might be on purpose.

"Why, ma'am, I went across the fields, and William was good enough to go with me; so when we got there, I rang, and they showed us into the servants' room, and I gave my message, and the veil was not there. Why, ma'am, there's the veil now, on the back o' that chair."

"Very well, very well, Jones, never mind the veil," cried the impatient mistress.

"So, ma'am, while they were looking for the veil, I just asked one of the maids what company had arrived, but "—here Jones looked very suspicious, and shook her head ominously—"would you think it, ma'am, not a soul of them knew! But, ma'am, there was the doctor and his son, praying and reading with the old gentleman the whole time—and—"

"And what, Jones?"

"Why, ma'am, I expect he has been a great sinner, or he wouldn't want so much praying just as he is about to die."

"Die!" cried all three at once; "will he die?"

"O yes," continued Jones, "they all agree he must die; but this praying so much is just like the criminals. I'm sure no honest persons needs so much praying, ma'am."

"No, indeed," said the mother. "No, indeed," responded the daughters, as they retired to their several rooms for the night.

CHAPTER V.

THERE is something in the season of spring which peculiarly excites the feelings of devotion. The dreariness of winter has passed, and with it the deadened affections of our nature. New life, new vigor, arises within us, as we walk abroad and feel the genial gales of April breathe upon us; and our hopes, our wishes, awaken with the revival of the vegetable world. It is then that the heart, which has been impressed with the goodness of the Creator, feels that goodness brought, as it were, into very contact with the senses. The eye loves to wander over the bountiful provisions nature is throwing forth in every direction for our comfort, and fixes its gaze on the clouds, which, having lost the chilling thinness of winter, roll in rich volumes, amid the clear and softened fields of azure so peculiar to the season, leading the mind insensibly to dwell on the things of another and a better world. It was on such a day that the inhabitants of B—— thronged toward the village church, for the double purpose of pouring out their thanksgivings and of hearing the first efforts of their rector's son in the duties of his sacred calling.

Among the crowd whom curiosity, or a better feeling, had drawn forth were to be seen the flaring equipage of the Jarvises, and the handsome carriages of Sir Edward Moseley and his sister. All the members of the latter family felt a lively anxiety for the success of the young divine. But knowing, as they well did, the strength of his native talents, the excellence of his education, and the fervor of his piety, it was an anxiety that partook more of hope than of fear. There was one heart however, among them that palpitated with an emotion that hardly admitted of control, as they approached the sacred edifice, for it had identified itself completely with the welfare of the rector's son. There never was a softer, truer heart than that which now almost audibly beat within the bosom of Clara Moseley; and she had given it to the young divine with all its purity and truth.

The entrance of a congregation into the sanctuary will at all times furnish, to an attentive observer, food for much useful speculation, if it be chastened with a proper charity for the weaknesses of others; and most people are ignorant of the insight they are giving into their characters and dispositions, by such an apparently trivial circumstance as their weekly approach to the tabernacles of the Lord. Christianity, while it chastens and amends the heart, leaves the natural powers unaltered; and it cannot be doubted that its operation is, or ought to be, proportionate to the abilities and opportunities of the subject of its holy impression— "Unto whomsoever much is given, much will be required." While we acknowledge that the thoughts might be better employed in preparing for those humiliations of the spirit and thanksgivings of the heart which are required of all, and are so necessary to all, we must be indulged in a hasty view of some of the personages of our history, as they entered the church of B——.

On the countenance of the baronet was the dignity and composure of a mind at peace with itself and mankind. His step was rather more deliberate than common; his eye rested on the pavement, and on turning into his pew, as he prepared to kneel, in the first humble petition of our beautiful service, he raised it toward the altar with an expression of benevolence and reverence that spoke contentment not unmixed with faith.

In the demeanor of Lady Moseley, all was graceful and decent, while nothing could be properly said to be studied. She followed her husband with a step of equal deliberation, though it was slightly varied by a manner which, while it appeared natural to herself, might have been artificial in another; a cambric handkerchief concealed her face as she sank composedly by the side of Sir Edward, in a style which showed, that while she remembered her Maker, she had not entirely forgotten herself.

The walk of Mrs. Wilson was quicker than that of her sister. Her eye, directed before her, was fixed, as if in settled gaze, on that eternity which she was approaching. The lines of her contemplative face were unaltered, unless there might be traced a deeper shade of humility than was ordinarily seen on her pale, but expressive countenance: her petition was long; and on rising from her humble posture, the person was indeed to be seen, but the soul appeared absorbed in contemplations beyond the limits of this sphere.

There was a restlessness and varying of color, in the ordinarily placid Clara, which prevented a display of her usual manner; while Jane walked gracefully, and with a tincture of her mother's manner, by her side. She stole one hastily withdrawn glance to the Deanery pew ere she kneeled, and then, on rising handed her smelling-bottle affectionately to her elder sister.

Emily glided behind her companions with a face beaming with a look of innocence and love. As she sank in the act of supplication, the rich glow of her healthful cheek lost some of its brilliancy; but, on rising, it beamed with a renewed luster, that plainly indicated a heart touched with the sanctity of its situation.

In the composed and sedate manner of Mr. Jarvis, as he steadily pursued his way to the pew of Sir William Harris, you might have been justified in expecting the entrance of another Sir Edward Moseley in substance, if not in externals. But the deliberate separation of the flaps of his coat, as he comfortably seated himself, when you thought him about to kneel, followed by a pinch of snuff as he threw his eye around the building, led you at once to conjecture, that what at first had been mistaken for reverence, was the abstraction of some earthly calculation; and that his attendance was in compliance with custom, and not a little depended upon the thickness of his cushions, and the room he found for the disposition of two rather unwieldy legs.

The ladies of the family followed, in garments carefully selected for the advantageous display of their persons. As they sailed into their seats, where it would seem the improvidence of Sir William's steward had neglected some important accommodation (some time being spent in preparation to be seated), the old lady, whose size and flesh really put kneeling out of the question, bent forward for a moment at an angle of eighty with the horizon, while her daughters prettily bowed their heads, with all proper precaution for the safety of their superb millinery.

At length the rector, accompanied by his son, appeared from the vestry. There was a dignity and solemnity in the manner in which this pious divine entered on the duties of his profession, which disposed the heart to listen with reverence and humility to precepts that were accompanied with so impressive an exterior. The stillness of expectation pervaded the church, when the pew opener led the way to the same interesting father and son whose entrance had interrupted the guests the preceding day at the rectory. Every eye was turned on the emaciated parent, bending into the grave, and, as it were, kept from it by the supporting tenderness of his child. Hastily throwing open the door of her own pew, Mrs. Ives buried her face in her handkerchief; and her husband had proceeded far in the morning service before she raised it again to the view of the congregation. In the voice of the rector, there was an unusual softness and tremor that his people attributed to the feelings of a father about to witness the first efforts of an only child, but which in reality were owing to another and a deeper cause.

Prayers were ended, and the younger Ives ascended the pulpit. For a moment he paused; when, casting an anxious glance at the pew of the baronet, he commenced his sermon. He had chosen for his discourse the necessity of placing our dependence on divine grace. After having learnedly, but in the most unaffected manner displayed the necessity of this dependence, as derived from revelation, he proceeded to paint the hope, the resignation, the felicity of a Christian's death-bed. Warmed by the subject, his animation soon lent a heightened interest to his language; and at a moment when all around him were entranced by the eloquence of the youthful divine, a sudden and deep-drawn sigh drew every eye to the rector's pew. The younger stranger sat motionless as a statue, holding in his arms the lifeless body of his parent, who had fallen that moment a corpse by his side. All was now confusion; the almost insensible young man was relieved from his burden; and, led by the rector, they left the church. The congregation dispersed in silence, or assembled in little groups to converse on the awful event they had witnessed. None knew the deceased; he was the rector's friend, and to his residence the body was removed. The young man was evidently his child; but here all information ended. They had arrived in a private chaise, but with post-horses, and without attendants.

Their arrival at the parsonage was detailed by the Jarvis ladies with a few exaggerations that gave additional interest to the whole event, and which, by creating an impression with some whom gentler feelings would not have restrained, that there was something of mystery about them, prevented many distressing questions to the Ives's, that the baronet's family forebore putting on the score of delicacy. The body left B—— at the close of the week, accompanied by Francis Ives and the unweariedly attentive and interesting son. The doctor and his wife went into deep mourning, and Clara received a short note from her lover, on the morning of their departure, acquainting her with his intended absence for a month, but throwing no light upon the affair. The London papers, however, contained the following obituary notice, and which, as it could refer to no other person, as a matter of course, was supposed to allude to the rector's friend.

"Died, suddenly, at B——, on the 20th instant, George Denbigh, Esq., aged 63."

CHAPTER VI.

DURING the week of mourning, the intercourse between Moseley Hall and the rectory was confined to messages and notes of inquiry after each other's welfare; but the visits of the Moseleys to the Deanery had been returned; and the day after the appearance of the obituary paragraph, the family of the latter dined by invitation at the Hall. Colonel Egerton had recovered the use of his leg, and was included in the party. Between this gentleman and Mr. Benfield there appeared, from the first moment of their introduction, a repugnance which was rather increased by time, and which the old gentleman manifested by a demeanor loaded with the overstrained ceremony of the day, and which in the colonel only showed itself by avoiding, when possible, all intercourse with the object of his aversion. Both Sir Edward and Lady Moseley, on the contrary, were not slow in manifesting their favorable impressions in behalf of the gentleman.

The latter, in particular, having ascertained to her satisfaction that he was the undoubted heir to the title, and most probably to the estates of his uncle, Sir Edgar Egerton, felt herself strongly disposed to encourage an acquaintance she found so agreeable, and to which she could see no reasonable objection. Captain Jarvis, who was extremely offensive to her, from his vulgar familiarity, she barely tolerated, from the necessity of being civil, and keeping up sociability in the neighborhood. It is true, she could not help being surprised that a gentleman as polished as the colonel could find any pleasure in an associate like his friend, or even in the hardly more softened females of his family; then again, the flattering suggestion would present itself, that possibly he might have seen Emily at Bath, or Jane elsewhere, and availed himself of the acquaintance of young Jarvis to get into their neighborhood. Lady Moseley had never been vain, or much interested about the disposal of her own person, previously to her attachment to her husband; but her daughters called forth not a little of her natural pride—we had almost said of her selfishness.

The attentions of the colonel were of the most delicate and insinuating kind; and Mrs. Wilson several times turned away in displeasure at herself, for listening with too much satisfaction to nothings, uttered in an agreeable manner, or, what was worse, false sentiments supported with the gloss of language and a fascinating deportment. The anxiety of this lady on behalf of Emily kept her ever on the alert, when chance, or any chain of circumstances, threw her in the way of forming new connections of any kind; and of late, as her charge approached the period of life her sex were apt to make that choice from which there is no retreat, her solicitude to examine the characters of the men who approached her was really painful. As to Lady Moseley, her wishes disposed her to be easily satisfied, and her mind naturally shrank from an investigation to which she felt herself unequal; while Mrs. Wilson was governed by the convictions of a sound discretion, matured by long and deep reasoning, all acting on a temper at all times ardent, and a watchfulness calculated to endure to the end.

"Pray, my lady," said Mrs. Jarvis, with a look of something like importance, "have you made any discovery about this Mr. Denbigh, who died in the church lately?"

"I did not know, ma'am," replied Lady Moseley, "there was any discovery to be made."

"You know, Lady Moseley," said Colonel Egerton, "that in town, all the little accompaniments of such a melancholy death would have found their way into the prints! and I suppose this is what Mrs. Jarvis alludes to."

"Oh, yes," cried Mrs. Jarvis, "the colonel is right." But the colonel was always right with that lady.

Lady Moseley bowed her head with dignity, and the colonel had too much tact to pursue the conversation; but the captain, whom nothing had ever yet abashed, exclaimed—

"These Denbighs could not be people of much importance—I have never heard the name before."

"It is the family name of the Duke of Derwent, I believe," dryly remarked Sir Edward.

"Oh, I am sure neither the old man nor his son looked much like a duke, or so much as an officer either," exclaimed Mrs. Jarvis, who thought the latter rank the dignity in degree next below nobility.

"There sat, in the Parliament of this realm, when I was a member, a General Denbigh," said Mr. Benfield, with his usual deliberation; "he was always on the same side with Lord Gosford and myself. He and his friend, Sir Peter Howell, who was the admiral that took the French squadron, in the glorious administration of Billy Pitt, and afterward took an island with this same General Denbigh; ay, the old admiral was a hearty blade—a good deal such a looking man as my Hector would make." Hector was Mr. Benfield's bull-dog.

"Mercy!" whispered John to Clara, "that's your grandfather that is to be, Uncle Benfield is speaking of."

Clara smiled, as she ventured to say, "Sir Peter was Mrs. Ives's father, sir."

"Indeed!" said the old gentleman, with a look of surprise; "I never knew that before. I cannot say they resemble each other much."

"Pray, uncle, does Frank look much like the family?" asked John with an air of unconquerable gravity.

"But, sir, interrupted Emily, "were General Denbigh and Admiral Howell related?"

"Not that I ever knew, Emmy dear. Sir Frederick Denbigh did not look much like the admiral; he rather resembled " (gathering himself up into an air of formality, and bowing stiffly to Colonel Egerton) "this gentleman, here."

"I have not the honor of the connection," observed the colonel, withdrawing behind the chair of Jane.

Mrs. Wilson changed the conversation to one more general; but the little that had fallen from Mr. Benfield gave reason for believing a connection, in some way of which they were ignorant, existed between the descendants of the two veterans, and which explained the interest they felt in each other.

During dinner, Colonel Egerton placed himself next to Emily, and Miss Jarvis took the chair on the other side. He spoke of the gay world, of watering-places, novels, plays; and, still finding his companion reserved, and either unwilling or unable to talk freely, he tried his favorite sentiment. He had read poetry, and a remark of his lighted up a spark of intelligence in the beautiful face of his companion that for a moment deceived him; but as he went on to point out his favorite beauties, it gave place to a settled composure, which at last led him to imagine the casket contained no gem equal to the promise of its brilliant exterior. After resting from one of his most labored displays of feeling and imagery, he accidentally caught the eyes of Jane fastened on him with an expression of no dubious import, and the soldier changed his battery. In Jane he found a more willing auditor; poetry was the food she lived on, and in works of the imagination she found her greatest delight. An animated discussion of the merits of their favorite authors now took place—to renew which, the colonel early left the dining-room, for the society of the ladies; John, who disliked drinking excessively, being happy of an excuse to attend him.

The younger ladies had clustered together round a window; and even Emily in her heart rejoiced that the gentlemen had come to relieve herself and sisters from the arduous task of entertaining women who appeared not to possess a single taste or opinion in common with themselves.

"You were saying, Miss Moseley," observed the colonel, in his most agreeable manner, as he approached them, "you thought Campbell the most musical poet we have. I hope you will unite with me in excepting Moore."

Jane colored, as with some awkwardness she replied, "Moore was certainly poetical."

"Has Moore written much?" innocently asked Emily.

"Not half as much as he ought," cried Miss Jarvis. "Oh! I could live on his beautiful lines."

Jane turned away in disgust; and that evening, while alone with Clara, she took a volume of Moore's songs, and very coolly consigned them to the flames. Her sister naturally asked an explanation of so extraordinary a procedure.

"Oh!" cried Jane, "I can't abide the book, since that vulgar Miss Jarvis speaks of it with so much interest. I really believe Aunt Wilson is right in not suffering Emily to read such things." And Jane, who had often devoured the treacherous lines with ardor, shrank with fastidious delicacy from the indulgence of a perverted taste, when it became exposed, coupled with the vulgarity of unblushing audacity.

Colonel Egerton immediately changed the subject to one less objectionable, and spoke of a campaign he had made in Spain. He possessed the happy faculty of giving an interest to all he advanced, whether true or not; and, as he never contradicted, or even opposed unless to yield gracefully, when a lady was his opponent, his conversation insensibly attracted, by putting the sex in good humor with themselves. Such a man, aided by the powerful assistants of person and manners, and no inconsiderable colloquial talents, Mrs. Wilson knew to be extremely dangerous as a companion to a youthful female heart; and as his visit was to extend to a couple of months, she resolved to reconnoiter the state of her pupil's opinion forthwith in reference to his merits.

She had taken too much pains in forming the mind of Emily to apprehend she would fall a victim to the eye; but she also knew that personal grace sweetened a benevolent expression, and added force even to the oracles of wisdom. She labored a little herself under the disadvantage of what John called a didactic manner, and which, although she had not the ability, or rather taste, to amend, she had yet the sense to discern. It was the great error of Mrs. Wilson to attempt to convince, where she might have influenced; but her ardor of temperament, and great love of truth, kept her as it were tilting with the vices of mankind, and consequently sometimes in unprofitable combat. With her charge, however, this could never be said to be the case. Emily knew her heart, felt her love, and revered her principles too deeply, to throw away an admonition, or disregard a precept, that fell from lips she knew never spoke idly or without consideration.

John had felt tempted to push the conversation with Miss Jarvis, and he was about to utter something rapturous respecting the melodious poison of Little's poems, as the blue eye of Emily rested on him in the fullness of sisterly affection, and, checking his love of the ridiculous, he quietly yielded to his respect for the innocence of his sisters ; and, as if eager to draw the attention of all from the hateful subject, he put question after question to Egerton concerning the Spaniards and their customs.

"Did you ever meet Lord Pendennyss in Spain, Colonel Egerton?" inquired Mrs. Wilson, with interest.

"Never, madam," he replied. "I have much reason to regret that our service lay in different parts of the country ; his lordship was much with the duke, and I made the campaign under Marshal Beresford."

Emily left the group at the window, and, taking a seat on the sofa by the side of her aunt, insensibly led her to forget the gloomy thoughts which had begun to steal over her ; which the colonel, approaching where they sat, continued, by asking—

"Are you acquainted with the earl, madam?"

"Not in person, but by character," said Mrs. Wilson, in a melancholy manner.

"His character as a soldier was very high. He had no superior of his years in Spain, I am told."

No reply was made to this remark, and Emily endeavored anxiously to draw the mind of her aunt to reflections of a more agreeable nature. The colonel, whose vigilance to please was ever on the alert, kindly aided her, and they soon succeeded.

The merchant withdrew, with his family and guest, in proper season ; and Mrs. Wilson, heedful of her duty, took the opportunity of a quarter of an hour's privacy in her own dressing-room, in the evening, to touch gently on the subject of the gentlemen they had seen that day.

"How are you pleased, Emily, with your new acquaintances?" familiarly commenced Mrs. Wilson.

"Oh! aunt, don't ask me. As John says, they are *new*, indeed."

"I am not sorry," continued the aunt, "to have you observe more closely than you have been used to the manners of such women as the Jarvises. They are too abrupt and unpleasant to create a dread of any imitation ; but the gentlemen are heroes in very different styles."

"Different from each other, indeed."

"To which do you give the preference, my dear?"

"Preference, aunt!" said her niece, with a look of astonishment ; "preference is a strong word for either ; but I rather think the captain the most eligible companion of the two. I do believe you see the worst of him ; and although I acknowl-

edge it to be bad enough, he might amend; but the colonel "—

"Go on," said Mrs. Wilson.

"Why, everything about the colonel seems so seated, so ingrafted in his nature, so—so very self-satisfied, that I am afraid it would be a difficult task to take the first step in amendment—to convince him of its necessity."

"And is it then so necessary?"

Emily looked up from arranging some laces with an expression of surprise, as she replied :

"Did you not hear him talk of those poems, and attempt to point out the beauties of several works? I thought everything he uttered was referred to taste, and that not a very natural one ; at least," she added with a laugh, "it differed greatly from mine. He seemed to forget altogether there was such a thing as principle : and then he spoke of some woman to Jane, who had left her father for her lover, with so much admiration of her feelings, to take up with poverty and love, as he called it, in place of condemning her want of filial piety—I am sure, aunt, if you had heard that, you would not admire him so much."

"I do not admire him at all, child ; I only want to know your sentiments, and I am happy to find them so correct. It is as you think : Colonel Egerton appears to refer nothing to principle ; even the more generous feelings, I am afraid are corrupted in him from too low intercourse with the surface of society. There is by far too much pliability about him for principle of any kind, unless indeed it be a principle to please, no matter how. No one who has deeply-seated opinions of right and wrong will ever abandon them, even in the courtesies of polite intercourse; they may be silent, but never acquiescent. In short, my dear, the dread of offending our Maker ought to be so superior to that of offending our fellow-creatures, that we should endeavor, I believe, to be even more unbending to the follies of the world than we are."

"And yet the colonel is what they call a good companion—I mean a pleasant one."

"In the ordinary meaning of the words, he is certainly, my dear ; yet you soon tire of sentiments which will not stand the test of examination, and of a manner you cannot but see is artificial—he may do very well for a companion, but very ill for a friend. In short, Colonel Egerton has neither been satisfied to yield to his natural impressions, nor to obtain new ones from a proper source ; he has copied from bad models, and his work must necessarily be imperfect."

Kissing her niece, Mrs. Wilson then retired into her own room with the happy assurance that she had not labored in vain; but that, with divine aid, she had implanted a guide in the bosom of her charge that could not fail, with ordinary care, to lead her straight through the devious path of females duties.

CHAPTER VII.

A MONTH now passed in the ordinary occupations and amusements of a country life, during which both Lady Moseley and Jane manifested a desire to keep up the Deanery acquaintance that surprised Emily a little, who had ever seen her mother shrink from communication with those whose breeding subjected her own delicacy to the little shocks she could but ill conceal. In Jane this desire was still more inexplicable; for Jane had, in a decided way very common to her, avowed her disgust of the manners of their new associates at the commencement of the acquaintance; and yet Jane would now even quit her own society for that of Miss Jarvis, especially if Colonel Egerton happened to be of the party. The innocence of Emily prevented her scanning the motives for the conduct of her sister, and she set seriously about an examination into her own deportment to find the latent cause, in order, wherever an opportunity should offer, to evince her regret, had it been her misfortune to have erred, by the tenderness of her own manner.

For a short time the colonel seemed at a loss where to make his choice; but a few days determined him, and Jane was evidently the favorite. It is true, that in the presence of the Jarvis ladies he was more guarded and general in his attentions; but as John, from a motive of charity, had taken the direction of the sports into his own hands, and as they were in the frequent habit of meeting at the hall preparatory to their morning excursions, the colonel suddenly became a sportsman. The ladies would often accompany them in their morning excursions; and as John would certainly be a baronet, and the colonel might not if his uncle married, he had the comfort of being sometimes ridden, as well as of riding.

One morning, having all prepared for an excursion on horseback, as they stood at the door ready to mount, Francis Ives drove up in his father's gig, and for a moment arrested the party. Francis was a favorite with the whole Moseley family, and their greetings were warm

and sincere. He found they meant to take the rectory in their ride, and insisted that they should proceed. "Clara would take a seat with him." As he spoke, the cast of his countenance brought the color into the cheeks of his intended; she suffered herself, however, to be handed into the vacant seat in the gig, and they moved on. John, who was at the bottom good-natured, and loved both Francis and Clara very sincerely, soon set Captain Jarvis and his sister what he called "scrub racing," and necessity, in some measure, compelled the rest of the equestrians to hard riding, in order to keep up with the sports.

"That will do, that will do," cried John, casting his eye back and perceiving they had lost sight of the gig, and nearly so of Colonel Egerton and Jane; "why, you carry it off like a jockey, captain—better than any amateur I have ever seen, unless indeed it be your sister."

The lady, encouraged by his commendations, whipped on, followed by her brother and sister at half speed.

"There, Emily," said John, quietly dropping by her side, "I see no reason you and I should break our necks to show the blood of our horses. Now do you know I think we are going to have a wedding in the family soon?"

Emily looked at him in amazement.

"Frank has got a living; I saw it the moment he drove up. He came in like somebody. Yes, I daresay he has calculated the tithes already a dozen times."

John was right. The Earl of Bolton had, unsolicited, given him the desired living of his own parish; and Francis was at the moment pressing the blushing Clara to fix the day that was to put a period to his long probation. Clara, who had not a particle of coquetry about her, promised to be his as soon as he was inducted, an event that was to take place the following week; and then followed those delightful little arrangements and plans with which youthful hope is so fond of filling up the void of life.

"Doctor," said John, as he came out of the rectory to assist Clara from the gig, "the parson here is a careful driver; see, he has not turned a hair."

He kissed the burning cheek of his sister as she touched the ground, and whispered significantly—

"You need tell me nothing, my dear—I know all—I consent."

Mrs. Ives folded her future daughter to her bosom; and the benevolent smile of the good rector, together with the kind and affectionate manner of her sisters, assured Clara the approaching nuptials were anticipated, as a matter of course. Colonel Egerton offered his compliments to Francis on his perferment to the living, with the polish of high breeding, and not without an appearance of interest ; and Emily thought him, for the first time, as handsome as he was generally reputed to be. The ladies undertook to say something civil in their turn ; and John put the captain, by a hint, on the same track.

"You are quite lucky, sir," said the captain, "in getting so good a living with so little trouble ; I wish you joy of it with all my heart ; Mr. Moseley tells me it is a capital thing now for a gentleman of your profession. For my part, I prefer a scarlet coat to a black one ; but there must be parsons, you know, or how should we get married or say grace ?"

Frances thanked him for his good wishes, and Egerton paid a handsome compliment to the liberality of the earl : "he doubted not he found that gratification which always attends a disinterested act ;" and Jane applauded the sentiment with a smile.

The baronet, when he was made acquainted with the situation of affairs, promised Francis that no unnecessary delay should intervene, and the marriage was happily arranged for the following week. Lady Moseley, when she retired to the drawing-room after dinner, commenced a recital of the ceremony, and the company to be invited on the occasion. Etiquette and the decencies of life were not only the forte but the fault of this lady ; and she had gone on to the enumeration of about the fortieth personage in the ceremonials, before Clara found courage to say that "Mr. Ives and myself both wish to be married at the altar, and to proceed to Bolton Rectory immediately after the ceremony." To this her mother warmly objected ; and argument and respectful remonstrance had followed each other for some time, before Clara submitted in silence, with difficulty restraining her tears. This appeal to the better feelings of the mother triumphed ; and the love of parade yielded to love of her offspring. Clara, with a lightened heart, kissed and thanked her, and accompanied by Emily left the room. Jane had risen to follow them, but catching a glimpse of the tilbury of Colonel Egerton, she reseated herself.

He had merely driven over at the earnest entreaties of the ladies to beg Miss Jane would accept a seat back with him ; "they had some little project on foot, and could not proceed without her assistance."

Mrs. Wilson looked gravely at her sister, as she smiled acquiescence to his wishes ; and the daughter, who but the minute before had forgotten there was any other person in the world but Clara, flew for her hat and shawl, in order, as she said to herself, that the politeness of Colonel Egerton might not keep him waiting. Lady Moseley resumed her seat by the side of her sister with an air of great complacency, as she returned from the window, after having seen her daughter off. For some time each was occupied quietly with her needle, when Mrs. Wilson suddenly broke the silence by saying—

"Who is Colonel Egerton ?"

Lady Moseley looked up for a moment in amazement ; but, recollecting herself, answered—

"The nephew and heir of Sir Edgar Egerton, sister."

This was spoken in a rather positive way, as if it were unanswerable ; yet, as there was nothing harsh in the reply, Mrs. Wilson continued—

"Do you not think him attentive to Jane ?"

Pleasure sparkled in the still brilliant eyes of Lady Moseley, as she exclaimed—

"Do you think so ?"

"I do ; and you will pardon me if I say improperly so. I think you were wrong in suffering Jane to go with him this afternoon."

"Why improperly, Charlotte ? If Colonel Egerton is polite enough to show Jane such attentions, should I not be wrong in rudely rejecting them ?"

"The rudeness of refusing a request that is improper to grant is a very venial offense. I confess I think it improper to allow any attentions to be forced on us that may subject us to disagreeable consequences. But the attentions of Colonel Egerton are becoming marked, Anne."

"Do you for a moment doubt their being honorable, or that he dares to trifle with a daughter of Sir Edward Moseley ?"

"I should hope not, certainly, although it may be well to guard even against such a misfortune. But I am of opinion it is quite as important to know whether he is *worthy* to be her husband as it is to know that he is in a situation to become so."

"On what points, Charlotte, would you wish to be more assured ? You know his birth, and probable fortune ; you see his manners and disposition. But these latter are things for Jane to decide on ; *she* is to live with him, and it is proper she should be suited in these respects."

"I do not deny his fortune or his disposition, but I complain that we give him credit for the last, and for still more important requisites, without evidence of his possessing any of them. His principles, his habits, his very character, what do we know of them? I say we, for you know, Anne, your children are as dear to me, as my own would have been."

"I believe you sincerely, but the things you mention are points for Jane to decide on. If she be pleased, I have no right to complain. I am determined never to control the affections of my children."

"Had you said never to *force* the affections of your children, you would have said enough; but to control, or rather to guide the affections of a child, especially a daughter, is, in some cases, a duty as imperative as it would be to avert any other impending calamity. Surely the proper time to do this is before the affections of the child are likely to endanger her peace of mind."

"I have seldom seen much good result from the interference of parents," said Lady Moseley, a little pertinaciously.

"True; for, to be of use, unless in extraordinary cases, it should not be seen. You will pardon me, Anne, but I have often thought parents are too frequently in extremes—determined to make the election for their children, or leaving them entirely to their own vanity and inexperience, to govern, not only their own lives, but, I may say, to leave an impression on future generations. And, after all, what is this love? In nineteen cases in twenty of what we call affairs of the heart, it would be better to term them affairs of the *imagination*."

"And is there not a great deal of imagination in all love?" inquired Lady Moseley, smiling.

"Undoubtedly, there is some; but there is one important difference; in affairs of the imagination, the admired object is gifted with all those qualities we esteem, as a matter of course; and there is a certain set of females who are ever ready to bestow this admiration on any applicant for their favors who may not be strikingly objectionable. The necessity of being courted makes our sex rather too much disposed to admire improper suitors."

"But how do you distinguish affairs of the heart, Charlotte, from those of the fancy?"

"When the heart takes the lead, it is not difficult to detect it. Such sentiments generally follow long intercourse, and opportunities of judging the real character. They are the only attachments that are likely to stand the test of worldly trials."

"Suppose Emily to be the object of Colonel Egerton's pursuit, then, sister, in what manner would you proceed to destroy the influence I acknowledge he is gaining over Jane?"

"I cannot suppose such a case," said Mrs. Wilson, gravely; and then, observing that her sister looked as if she required an explanation, she continued—

"My attention has been directed to the forming of such principles, and such a taste, if I may use the expression, under those principles, that I feel no apprehension Emily will ever allow her affections to be ensnared by a man of the opinions and views of Colonel Egerton. I am impressed with a twofold duty in watching the feelings of my charge. She has so much singleness of heart, such real strength of native feeling, that, should an improper man gain possession of her affections, the struggle between her duty and her love would be weighty indeed; and should it proceed so far as to make it her duty to love an unworthy object, I am sure she would sink under it. Emily would die in the same circumstances under which Jane would only awake from a dream, and be wretched."

"I thought you entertained a better opinion of Jane, sister," said Lady Moseley, reproachfully.

"I think her admirably calculated to make an invaluable wife and mother; but she is so much under the influence of her fancy, that she seldom gives her heart an opportunity of displaying its excellences; and again she dwells so much upon imaginary perfections, that adulation has become necessary to her. The man who flatters her delicately, will be sure to win her esteem; and every woman might love the being possessed of the qualities she will not fail to endow him with."

"I do not know that I rightly understand how you would avert all these sad consequences of improvident affections," said Lady Moseley.

"Prevention is better than cure. I would first implant such opinions as would lessen the danger of intercourse; and as for particular attentions from improper objects, it should be my care to prevent them, by prohibiting, or rather impeding, the intimacy which might give rise to them. And least of all," said Mrs. Wilson, with a friendly smile, as she rose to leave the room, "would I suffer a fear of being impolite to endanger the happiness of a young woman intrusted to my care."

CHAPTER VIII.

FRANCIS, who labored with the ardor of a lover, soon completed the necessary arrangements and alterations in his new parsonage. The living was a good one; and, as the rector was enabled to make a very considerable annual allowance from the private fortune his wife had brought him, and as Sir Edward had twenty thousand pounds in the funds for each of his daughters, one portion of which was immediately settled on Clara, the youthful couple had not only a sufficient but an abundant provision for their station in life; and they entered on their matrimonial duties with as good a prospect of happiness as the ills of this world can give to health, affection, and competency. Their union had been deferred by Doctor Ives until his son was established, with a view to keep him under his own direction during the critical period of his first impressions in the priesthood; and as no objection now remained, or rather, the only one he ever felt was removed by the proximity of Bolton to his own parish, he now joyfully united the lovers at the altar of the village church, in the presence of his wife and Clara's immediate relatives. On leaving the church, Francis handed his bride into his own carriage, which conveyed them to their new residence, amid the good wishes of his parishioners and the prayer of their relatives and friends.

Doctor and Mrs. Ives retired to the rectory, to the sober enjoyment of the felicity of their only child; while the baronet and his lady felt a gloom that belied all the wishes of the latter for the establishment of her daughters. Jane and Emily acted as bridesmaids to their sister; and as both the former and her mother had insisted there should be two groomsmen as a counterpoise, John was empowered with a *carte-blanche* to make a provision accordingly. At first, he intimated his intention of calling on Mr. Benfield; but he finally settled down, to the no small mortification of the before-mentioned ladies, into writing a note to his kinsman, Lord Chatterton, whose residence was then in London, and who in reply, after expressing his sincere regret that an accident would prevent his having the pleasure of attending, stated the intention of his mother and two sisters to pay them an early visit of congratulation, as soon as his own health would allow of his traveling. This answer arrived only the day preceding that fixed for the wedding, and at the very moment they were expecting his lordship in proper person.

"There," cried Jane, in triumph, "I told you it was silly to send so far on so sudden an occasion; now, after all, what is to be done?—it will be so awkward when Clara's friends call to see her—oh! John, John, you are a Marplot."

"Jenny, Jenny, you are a make-plot," said John, coolly taking up his hat to leave the room.

"Which way, my son?" said the baronet, who met him at the door.

"To the Deanery, sir, to try to get Captain Jarvis to act as bridesmaid—I beg his pardon, groomsman, to-morrow—Chatterton has been thrown from his horse and can't come."

"John!"

"Jenny!"

"I am sure," said Jane, indignation glowing in her pretty face, "that if Captain Jarvis is to be an attendant, Clara must excuse my acting. I do not choose to be associated with Captain Jarvis."

"John," said his mother, with dignity, "your trifling is unseasonable; certainly Colonel Egerton is a more fitting person on every account, and I desire, under present circumstances, that you ask the colonel."

"Your ladyship's wishes are orders to to me," said John, gayly kissing his hand as he left the room.

The colonel was but too happy in having it in his power to be of service in any manner to a gentleman he respected as much as Mr. Francis Ives. He accepted the duty, and was the only person present at the ceremony who did not stand within the bonds of consanguinity to the parties. He was invited by the baronet to dine at the Hall, as a matter of course, and notwithstanding the repeated injunctions of Mrs. Jarvis and her daughters, to return immediately with an account of the dress of the bride, and with other important items of a similar nature, the invitation was accepted. On reaching the Hall, Emily retired immediately to her own room, and at her appearance when the dinner-bell rang, the paleness of her cheeks and the redness of her eyes afforded sufficient proof that the translation of a companion from her own to another family was an event, however happy in itself, not unmingled with grief. The day, however, passed off tolerably well for people who are expected to be premeditatedly happy, and when, in their hearts, they are really more disposed to weep than to laugh. Jane and the colonel had more of the conversation to themselves during dinner: even the joyous and thoughtless John wearing his gayety in a less graceful manner than usual. He was actually detected by his aunt in looking with moistened eyes at the vacant chair a servant had, from habit, placed at the table, in a spot where Clara had been accustomed to sit.

"This beef is not done, Saunders," said the baronet to his butler, "or my appetite is not as good as usual to-day. Colonel Egerton, will you allow me the pleasure of a glass of sherry?"

The wine was drunk, and the game succeeded the beef; but still Sir Edward could not eat.

"How glad Clara will be to see us all the day after to-morrow!" said Mrs. Wilson; "your new housekeepers delight in their first efforts in entertaining their friends."

Lady Moseley smiled through her tears, and, turning to her husband, said, "We will go early, my dear, that we may see the improvements Francis has been making, before we dine." The baronet nodded assent, but his heart was too full to speak; and apologizing to the colonel for his absence, on the plea of some business with his people, he left the room.

All this time, the attentions of Colonel Egerton to both mother and daughter were of the most delicate kind. He spoke of Clara as if his office of groomsman entitled him to an interest in her welfare; with John he was kind and sociable; and even Mrs. Wilson acknowledged, after he had taken his leave, that he possessed a wonderful faculty of making himself agreeable; and she began to think that, under all circumstances, he might possibly prove as advantageous a connection as Jane could expect to form. Had any one, however, proposed him as a husband for Emily, affection would have quickened her judgment in a way that would have urged her to a very different decision.

Soon after the baronet left the room, a traveling-carriage, with suitable attendants, drove to the door. The sound of the wheels drew most of the company to a window. "A baronet's coronet!" cried Jane, catching a glimpse of the ornaments of the harness.

"The Chattertons," echoed her brother, running out of the room to meet them.

The mother of Sir Edward was a daughter of this family, and a sister of the grandfather of the present lord. The connection had always been kept up with a show of cordiality between Sir Edward and his cousin, although their manner of living and habits were very different. The baron was a courtier and a placeman. His estates, which he could not alienate, produced about ten thousand a year, but the income he could and did spend; and the high perquisites of his situation under government, amounting to as much more, were melted away year after year, without making the provision for his daughters that his duty and the observance of his promise to his wife's father required at his hands. He had been dead about two years, and his son found himself saddled with the support of an unjointured mother and unportioned sisters. Money was not the idol the young lord worshiped, nor even pleasure. He was affectionate to his surviving parent, and his first act was to settle, during his own life, two thousand a year on her; while he commenced setting aside as much more for each of his sisters, annually. This abridged him greatly in his own expenditures; yet, as they made but one family, and the dowager was really a *managing* woman in more senses than one, they made a very tolerable figure. The son was anxious to follow the example of Sir Edward Moseley, and give up his town-house, for at least a time; but his mother had exclaimed, with something like horror, at the proposal—

"Chatterton, would you give it up at the moment it can be of the most use to us?" and she threw a glance at her daughters that would have discovered her motive to Mrs. Wilson, which was lost on her son; he, poor soul, thinking she found it convenient to support the interest he had been making for the place held by his father—one of more emolument than service, or even honor. The contending parties were so equally matched, that this situation was kept, as it were, in abeyance, waiting the arrival of some acquisition of interest to one or other of the claimants. The interest of the peer, however, had begun to lose ground at the period of which we speak, and his careful mother saw new motives for activity in providing for her children. Mrs. Wilson herself could not be more vigilant in examining the candidates for Emily's favors than was the dowager Lady Chatterton in behalf of her daughter. It is true, the task of the former lady was by far the most arduous, for it involved a study of character and development of principle; while that of the latter would have ended with the footing of a rent-roll, provided it contained five figures. Sir Edward's was well known to contain that number, and two of them were not ciphers. Mr. Benfield was rich, and John Moseley was a very agreeable young man. "Weddings are the season of love," thought the prudent dowager, "and Grace is extremely pretty." Chatterton, who never refused his mother anything in his power to grant, and who was particularly dutiful when a visit to Moseley Hall was in question, suffered himself to be persuaded his shoulder was well; and they had left town the day before the wedding, thinking to be in time for all the gayeties, if not for the ceremony itself.

There existed but little similarity between the persons and manners of this young nobleman and the baronet's heir. The beauty of Chatterton was almost feminine. His skin, his color, his eyes, his teeth, were such as many a belle had sighed after; and his manners were bashful and retiring. Yet an intimacy had commenced between the boys at school, which ripened into friendship between the young men at college, and had been maintained ever since, probably as much from the contrarities of character as from any other cause. With the baron, John was more sedate than ordinary; with John, Chatterton found unusual animation. But a secret charm which John held over the young peer was his profound respect and unvarying affection for his youngest sister, Emily. This was common ground; and no dreams of future happiness, no visions of dawning wealth, crossed the imagination of Chatterton, in which Emily was not the fairy to give birth to the one, or the benevolent dispenser of the hoards of the other.

The arrival of this family was a happy relief from the oppression which hung on the spirits of the Moseleys, and their reception marked with the mild benevolence which belonged to the nature of the baronet, and that *empressement* which so eminently distinguished the manners of his wife.

The Honorable Misses Chatterton were both handsome; but the younger was, if possible, a softened picture of her brother. There was the same retiring bashfulness and the same sweetness of temper as distinguished the baron, and Grace was the peculiar favorite of Emily Moseley. Nothing of the strained or sentimental nature which so often characterizes what are called female friendships, however, had crept into the communications between these young women. Emily loved her sisters too well to go out of her own family for a repository of her griefs or a partaker in her joys. Had her life been checkered with such passions, her own sisters were too near her own age to suffer her to think of a confidence in which the holy ties of natural affection did not give a claim to a participation. Mrs. Wilson had found it necessary to give her charge very different views on many subjects from those which Jane and Clara had been suffered to imbibe of themselves; but in no degree had she impaired the obligations of filial piety or family concord. Emily was, if anything, more respectful to her parents, more affectionate to her friends, than any of her connec-

tions; for in her the warmth of natural feeling was heightened by an unvarying sense of duty.

In Grace Chatterton she found, in many respects, a temper and taste resembling her own. She therefore loved her better than others who had equally general claims on her partiality, and as such a friend she now received her with cordial and sincere affection.

Jane, who had not felt satisfied with the ordering of Providence for the disposal of her sympathies, and had long felt a restlessness that prompted her to look abroad for a confiding spirit to whom to communicate her—secrets she had none that delicacy would suffer her to reveal, but to communicate her—crude opinions and reflections, had early selected Catherine for this person. Catherine, however, had not stood the test of trial. For a short time the love of heraldry kept them together; but Jane, finding her companion's gusto limited to the charms of the coronet and supporters chiefly, abandoned the attempt in despair, and was actually on the lookout for a new candidate for the vacant station as Colonel Egerton came into the neighborhood. A really delicate female mind shrinks from the exposure of its love to the other sex; and Jane began to be less anxious to form a connection which would either violate the sensibility of her nature, or lead to treachery to her friend.

"I regret extremely, Lady Moseley," said the dowager, as they entered the drawing-room, "that the accident which befell Chatterton should have kept us until it was too late for the ceremony; we made it a point to hasten with our congratulations, however, as soon as Astley Cooper thought it safe for him to travel."

"I feel indebted for your kindness," replied the smiling hostess; "we are always happy to have our friends around us, and none more than yourself and family. We were fortunate in finding a friend to supply your son's place, in order that the young people might go to the altar in a proper manner. Lady Chatterton, allow me to present our friend, Colonel Egerton"—adding, in a low tone, and with a little emphasis, "heir to Sir Edgar."

The colonel bowed gracefully, and the dowager dropped a hasty courtesy at the commencement of the speech; but a lower bend followed the closing remark, and a glance of the eye was thrown in quest of her daughters, as if she instinctively wished to bring them into what the sailors term "the line of battle."

————

CHAPTER IX.

The following morning, Emily and Grace, declining the invitation to join the colonel and John in their usual rides, walked to the rectory, accompanied by Mrs. Wilson and Chatterton. The ladies felt a desire to witness the happiness that they so well knew reigned in the rectory, for Francis had promised his father to drive Clara over in the course of the day. Emily longed to see Clara, from whom it appeared that she had been already separated a month. Her impatience as they approached the house hurried her ahead of her companions, who waited the more sober gait of Mrs. Wilson. She entered the parlor at the rectory without meeting any one, glowing with exercise, her hair falling over her shoulders, released from the confinement of the hat she had thrown down hastily as she reached the door. In the room there stood a gentleman in deep black, with his back toward the entrance, intent on a book, and she naturally concluded it was Francis.

"Where is dear Clara, Frank?" cried the beautiful girl, laying her hand affectionately on his shoulder.

The gentlemen turned suddenly, and presented to her astonished gaze the well-remembered countenance of the young man whose parent's death was not likely to be forgotten at B——.

"I thought, sir," said Emily, almost sinking with confusion, "that Mr. Frances Ives"—

"Your brother has not yet arrived, Miss Moseley," simply replied the stranger, who felt for her embarrassment. "But I will immediately acquaint Mrs. Ives with your visit." Bowing, he delicately left the room.

Emily, who felt greatly relieved by his manner, immediately confined her hair in its proper bounds, and had recovered her composure by the time her aunt and friends joined her. She had no time to mention the incident, and laugh at her own precipitation, when the rector's wife came into the room.

Chatterton and his sister were both known to Mrs. Ives, and both were favorites. She was pleased to see them; and, after reproaching the brother with compelling her son to ask a favor of a comparative stranger, she turned to Emily, and smilingly said—

"You found the parlor occupied, I believe?"

"Yes," said Emily, laughing and blushing; "I suppose Mr. Denbigh told you of my heedlessness."

"He told me of your attention in calling so soon to inquire after Clara, but said nothing more." A servant just then telling her Francis wished to see her, she excused herself and withdrew. In the door she met Mr. Denbigh, who made way for her, saying, "Your son has arrived, ma'am;" and in an easy but respectful manner he took his place among the guests, no introduction passing, and none seeming necessary. His misfortunes appeared to have made him acquainted with Mrs. Wilson, and his strikingly ingenuous manner won insensibly on the confidence of those who heard him. Everything was natural, yet everything was softened by education; and the little party in the rector's parlor in fifteen minutes felt as if they had known him for years. The doctor and his son now joined them. Clara had not come, but she was looking forward in delightful expectation of to-morrow, and wished greatly for Emily as a guest at the new abode. This pleasure Mrs. Wilson promised she should have as soon as they had got over the hurry of their visit. "Our friends," she added, turning to Grace, "will overlook the nicer punctilios of ceremony, where sisterly regards calls for the discharge of more important duties. Clara needs the society of Emily just now."

"Certainly," said Grace, mildly; "I hope no useless ceremony on the part of Emily would prevent her manifesting natural attachment to her sister—I should feel hurt at her not entertaining a better opinion of us than to suppose so for a moment."

"This, young ladies, is the real feeling to keep alive esteem," cried the doctor, gayly. "Go on, and say and do nothing of which either can disapprove, when tried by the standard of duty, and you need never be afraid of losing a friend that is worth keeping."

It was three o'clock before the carriage of Mrs. Wilson arrived at the rectory; and the time stole away insensibly in free and friendly communications. Denbigh had joined modestly, and with the degree of interest a stranger might be supposed to feel in the occurrences of a circle to which he was nearly a stranger. There was at times a slight display of awkwardness, however, about both him and Mrs. Ives, for which Mrs. Wilson easily accounted by recollections of his recent loss, and the scene they had all witnessed in that very room. This embarrassment escaped the notice of the rest of the party. On the arrival of the carriage, Mrs. Wilson took her leave.

"I like this Mr. Denbigh greatly," said Lord Chatterton, as they drove from the door; "there is something strikingly natural and winning in his manner."

"In his matter, too, judging of the little we have seen of him," replied Mrs. Wilson.

"Who is he, ma'am?"

"I rather suspect he is some way related to Mrs. Ives. Her staying from Bolton to-day must be owing to Mr. Denbigh; and, as the doctor has just gone, he must be near enough to them to be neither wholly neglected nor yet a tax upon their politeness. I rather wonder he did not go with them."

"I heard him tell Francis," remarked Emily, "that he could not think of intruding, and he insisted on Mrs. Ives's going, but she had employments to keep her at home."

The carriage soon reached an angle in the road where the highways between Bolton Castle and Moseley Hall intersected each other at a point on the estate of the former. Mrs. Wilson stopped a moment to inquire after an aged pensioner, who had lately met with a loss in business, which she was fearful must have greatly distressed him. In crossing a ford in the little river between his cottage and the market-town, the stream, which had been swollen unexpectedly higher than usual by heavy rains, had swept away his horse and cart loaded with the entire produce of his small field, and with much difficulty he had saved even his own life. Mrs. Wilson had not had it in her power until this moment to inquire particularly into the affair, or to offer the relief she was ever ready to bestow on proper objects. Contrary to her expectations, she found Humphreys in high spirits, showing his delighted grandchildren a new cart and horse which stood at the door, and exultingly pointing out the excellent qualities of both. He ceased talking on the approach of the party, and at the request of his ancient benefactress he gave a particular account of the affair.

"And where did you get this new cart and horse, Humphreys?" inquired Mrs. Wilson, when he had ended.

"Oh, madam, I went up to the castle to see the steward, and Mr. Martin just mentioned my loss to Lord Pendennyss, ma'am, and my lord ordered me this cart, ma'am, and this noble horse, and twenty golden guineas into the bargain, to put me on my legs again. God bless him for it, forever."

"It was very kind of his lordship, indeed," said Mrs. Wilson, thoughtfully. "I did not know he was at the castle."

"He's gone already, madam. The servants told me that he just called to see the earl, on his way to Lon'on; but, finding he'd went a few days agone to Ireland, my lord went for Lon'on, without stopping the night even. Ah! madam," continued the old man, who stood leaning on a stick, with his hat in his hand, "he's a great blessing to the poor; his servants say he gives thousands every year to the poor who are in want: he is main rich, too—some people say much richer and more great like than the earl himself. I'm sure I have need to bless him every day of my life."

Mrs. Wilson smiled mournfully as she wished Humphreys good day, and put up her purse, finding the old man so well provided for; a display of competition in charity never entering into her system of benevolence.

"His lordship is munificent in his bounty," said Emily, as they drove from the door.

"Does it not savor of thoughtlessness to bestow so much where he can know so little?" Lord Chatterton ventured to inquire.

"He is," replied Mrs. Wilson, "as old Humphreys says, main rich; but the son of the old man, and the father of these children, is a soldier in the ——th dragoons, of which the earl is colonel, and that accounts to me for his liberality"—recollecting, with a sigh, the feelings which had drawn her out of the usual circle of her charities in the case of this same man.

"Did you ever see Lord Pendennyss, aunt?"

"Never, my dear. He has been much abroad, but my letters were filled with his praises, and I confess my disappointment is great in not seeing him on this visit to Lord Bolton, who is his relation; but," fixing her eyes thoughtfully on her niece, "we shall meet in London this winter, I trust."

As she spoke, a cloud passed over her features, and she continued much absorbed in thought for the remainder of their drive.

General Wilson had been a cavalry officer, and he commanded the very regiment now held by Lord Pendennyss. In an excursion near the British camp he had been rescued from captivity, if not from death, by a gallant and timely interference of this young nobleman, then in command of a troop in the same corps. He had mentioned the occurrence to his wife in his letters, and from that day his correspondence was filled with the praises of the bravery and goodness to the soldiery of his young comrade. When he fell, he had been supported from the field near by, and he actually died in the arms of, the young peer. A letter announcing his death had been received by his widow from the earl himself, and the tender and affectionate manner in which he spoke of her husband had taken a deep hold on her affections. All the circumstances together threw an interest around him that had made Mrs. Wilson almost entertain the romantic wish he might be found worthy and disposed to solicit the hand of Emily. Her anxious inquiries into his character had been attended with such answers as flattered her wishes: but the military duties of the earl, or his private affairs, had never allowed a meeting : and she was now compelled to look forward to what John laughingly termed their winter campaign, as the only probable place where she could be gratified with the sight of a young man to whom she owed so much, and whose name was connected with some of the most tender though most melancholy recollections of her.life.

Colonel Egerton, who now appeared to be almost domesticated in the family, was again of the party at dinner, to the no small satisfaction of the dowager, who from proper inquiries in the course of the day had learned that Sir Edgar's heir was likely to have the necessary number of figures in the sum total of his rental. While sitting in the drawing-room that afternoon, she made an attempt to bring her eldest daughter and the elegant soldier together over a chess-board—a game the young lady had been required to learn because it was one at which a gentleman could be kept longer than any other without having his attention drawn away by any of those straggling charms which might be traveling a drawing-room "seeking whom they may devour." It was also a game admirably suited to the display of a beautiful hand and arm. But the mother had for a long time been puzzled to discover a way of bringing in the foot also, the young lady being particularly remarkable for the beauty of that portion of the frame. In vain her daughter hinted at dancing, an amusement of which she was passionately fond. The wary mother knew too well the effects of concentrated force to listen to the suggestion : dancing might do for every manager, but she prided herself in acting *en masse*, like Napoleon, whose tactics consisted in overwhelming by uniting his forces on a given point. After many experiments in her own person, she endeavored to improve Catharine's manner of sitting, and by dint of twisting and turning she contrived that her pretty foot and ankle should be

thrown forward in a way that the eye, dropping from the move, should unavoidably rest on this beauteous object ; giving, as it were, a Scylla and Charybdis to her daughter's charms.

John Moseley was the first person on whom she undertook to try the effect of her invention ; and, after comfortably seating the parties, she withdrew to a little distance, to watch the effect.

"Check to your king, Miss Chatterton," cried John, early in the game—and the young lady thrust out her foot. "Check to *your* king, Mr. Moseley," echoed the damsel, and John's eyes wandered from hand to foot and foot to hand. "Check king and queen, sir."—"Checkmate."—"Did you speak?" said John. Looking up, he caught the eye of the dowager fixed on him in triumph. "Oh, ho !" said the young man, internally, "Mother Chatterton, are you playing too?" and, coolly taking up his hat, he walked off, nor could they ever get him seated at the game again.

"You beat me too easily, Miss Chatterton," he would say when pressed to play ; "before I have time to look up, it's ' Check-mate '—excuse me."

The dowager next settled down into a more covert attack through Grace ; but here she had two to contend with ; her own forces rebelled, and the war had been protracted to the present hour with varied success, and at least without any material captures, on one side.

Colonel Egerton entered on the duties of his dangerous undertaking with the indifference of foolhardiness. The game was played with tolerable ability by both parties ; but no emotions, no absence of mind, could be discovered on the part of the gentleman. Feet and hands were in motion ; still the colonel played as well as usual ; he had answers for all Jane's questions, and smiles for his partner ; but no checkmate could she obtain until, willfully throwing away an advantage, he suffered the lady to win the game. The dowager was satisfied nothing could be done with the colonel.

CHAPTER X.

THE first carriages that rolled over the lawn to Bolton parsonage, on the succeeding day, were those of the baronet and his sister ; the latter in advance.

"There, Francis," cried Emily, who was impatiently waiting for him to remove some slight obstruction to her alighting—"thank you, thank you ; that will do."

In the next moment she was in the extended arms of Clara. After pressing each other to their bosoms for a few moments in silence, Emily looked up, with a tear glistening in her eye, and first noticed the form of Denbigh, who was modestly withdrawing, as if unwilling to intrude on such pure and domestic feelings as the sisters were betraying, unconscious of the presence of a witness. Mrs. Wilson and Jane, followed by Mrs. Chatterton, now entered, and cordial salutes and greetings flowed upon Clara from her various friends.

The baronet's coach reached the door; it contained himself and wife, Mr. Benfield, and Lady Chatterton. Clara stood on the portico of the building, ready to receive them; her face all smiles, and tears, and blushes, and her arm locked in that of Emily.

"I wish you joy of your new abode, Mrs. Francis." Lady Moseley forgot her form, and bursting into tears, she pressed her daughter with ardor to her bosom.

"Clara, my love!" said the baronet, hastily wiping his eyes, and succeeding his wife in the embrace of their child. He kissed her, and, pressing Francis by the hand, walked into the house in silence.

"Well, well," cried the dowager, as she saluted her cousin, "all looks comfortable and genteel here, upon my word, Mrs. Ives: grapery—hot-houses—everything in good style, too; and Sir Edward tells me the living is worth a good five hundred a year."

"So, girl, I suppose you expect a kiss," said Mr. Benfield, who ascended the steps slowly and with difficulty. "Kissing has gone much out of fashion lately. I remember, on the marriage of my friend, Lord Gosford, in the year fifty-eight, that all the maids and attendants were properly saluted in order. The lady Juliana was quite young then—not more than fifteen; it was there I got my first salute from her — but — so — kiss me." After which he continued, as they went into the house: "Marrying in that day was a serious business. You might visit a lady a dozen times before you could get a sight of her naked hand. Who's that?" stopping short, and looking earnestly at Denbigh, who now approached them.

"Mr. Denbigh, sir," said Clara; "my uncle, Mr. Benfield."

"Did you ever know, sir, a gentleman of your name, who sat in the Parliament of this realm in the year sixty?" Mr. Benfield abruptly asked, as soon as the civilities of the introduction were exchanged. "You don't look much like him."

"That was rather before my day, sir," said Denbigh, with a smile, respectfully offering to relieve Clara, who supported him on one side, while Emily held his arm on the other.

The old gentleman was particularly averse to strangers, and Emily was in terror lest he should say something rude; but, after examining Denbigh again from head to foot, he took the offered arm, and coolly replied—

"True, very true; that was sixty years ago; you can hardly recollect as long. Ah! Mr. Denbigh, times are sadly altered since my youth. People who were then glad to ride on a pillion now drive their coaches; men who thought ale a luxury, drink their port; ay! and those who went barefoot must have their shoes and stockings, too. Luxury, sir, and the love of ease, will ruin this mighty empire. Corruption has taken hold of everything; the ministry buy the members, the members buy the ministry; everything is bought and sold. Now, sir, in the Parliament in which I had the honor of a seat, there was a knot of us, as upright as posts, sir. My Lord Gosford was one, and General Denbigh was another, although I can't say he was much a favorite with me. You do not look in the least like him. How was he related to you, sir?"

"He was my grandfather," replied Denbigh, looking pleasantly at Emily, as if to tell her he understood the character of her uncle.

Had the old man continued his speech an hour longer, Denbigh would not have complained. They had stopped while talking, and he thus became confronted with the beautiful figure that supported the other arm. Denbigh contemplated in admiration the varying countenance which now blushed with apprehension, and now smiled in affection, or even with an archer expression, as her uncle proceeded in his harangue on the times. But all felicity in this world has an end, as well as misery. Denbigh retained the recollection of that speech long after Mr. Benfield was comfortably seated in the parlor, though for his life he could not recollect a word he had said.

The Haughtons, and Jarvises, and a few more of their intimate acquaintances, arrived, and the parsonage had a busy air; but John, who had undertaken to drive Grace Chatterton in his own phaeton, was yet absent. Some little anxiety had begun to be manifested, when he appeared dashing through the gates at a great rate, and with the skill of a member of the four-in-hand.

Lady Chatterton had begun to be seriously uneasy, and she was about to speak to her son to go in quest of them, as they came in sight; but now her fears vanished, and she could only suppose that a desire to have Grace alone could keep one who had the reputation of a Jehu so much behind the rest of the party. She met them in great spirits, crying:

"Upon my word, Mr. Moseley, I began to think you had taken the road to Scotland, you staid so long."

"Your daughter, my Lady Chatterton," said John, pithily, "would go to Scotland neither with me nor any other man, or I am greatly deceived in her character. Clara, my sister, how do you do?" He saluted the bride with great warmth and affection.

"But what detained you, Moseley?" inquired the mother.

"One of the horses was restive, and he broke the harness. We merely stopped in the village while it was mended."

"And how did Grace behave?" asked Emily, laughing.

"Oh, a thousand times better than you would, sister; as she always does, and like an angel."

The only point in dispute between Emily and her brother was her want of faith in his driving; while poor Grace, naturally timid, and unwilling to oppose any one, particularly the gentleman who then held the reins, had governed herself sufficiently to be silent and motionless. Indeed, she could hardly do otherwise had she wished it, so great was his impetuosity of character; and John felt flattered to a degree of which he was himself unconscious. Self-complacency, aided by the merit, the beauty, and the delicacy of the young lady herself, might have led to the very results her mother so anxiously wished to produce, had that mother been satisfied with letting things take their course. But managers very generally overdo their work.

"Grace is a good girl," said her gratified mother; "and you found her very valiant, Mr. Moseley?"

"Oh, as brave as Cæsar," answered John, carelessly, in a way that was not quite free from irony.

Grace, whose burning cheek showed but too plainly that praise from John Moseley was an incense too powerful for her resistance, now sank back behind some of the company endeavoring to conceal the tears that almost gushed from her eyes. Denbigh was a silent spectator of the whole scene, and he now considerately observed, that he had lately seen an improvement which would obviate the difficulty Mr. Moseley had experienced.

John turned to the speaker, and they were soon engaged in the discussion of curbs and buckles, when the tilbury of Colonel Egerton drove to the door, containing himself and his friend, the captain.

The bride undoubtedly received congratulations that day more sincere than those which were now offered, but none were delivered in a more graceful and insinuating manner than the compliments which fell from Colonel Egerton. He passed round the room, speaking to his acquaintances, until he arrived at the chair of Jane, who was seated next her aunt. Here he stopped, and, glancing his eye round, and saluting with bows and smiles the remainder of the party, he appeared fixed at the center of all attraction.

"There is a gentleman I think I have never seen before," he observed to Mrs. Wilson, casting his eyes on Denbigh, whose back was toward him, in discourse with Mr. Benfield.

"It is Mr. Denbigh, of whom you heard us speak," replied Mrs. Wilson. While she spoke, Denbigh faced them. Egerton started as he caught a view of his face, and seemed to gaze on the countenance which was open to his inspection with an earnestness that showed an interest of some kind, but of a nature that was inexplicable to Mrs. Wilson, who was the only observer of this singular recognition; for such it evidently was. All was now natural in the colonel for the moment; his color sensibly changed, and there was an expression of doubt in his face. It might be fear, it might be horror, it might be a strong aversion; it clearly was not love. Emily sat by her aunt, and Denbigh approached them, making a cheerful remark. It was impossible for the colonel to avoid him had he wished it, and he kept his ground. Mrs. Wilson thought she would try the experiment of an introduction.

"Colonel Egerton—Mr. Denbigh."

Both gentlemen bowed, but nothing striking was seen in the deportment of either. The colonel, who was not exactly at ease, said hastily—

"Mr. Denbigh is or has been in the army, I believe."

Denbigh was now taken by surprise in his turn. He cast a look on Egerton of fixed and settled meaning; then carelessly observed, but still as if requiring an answer—

"I am yet; but I do not recollect having had the pleasure of meeting with Colonel Egerton on service."

"Your countenance is familiar, sir,"

replied the colonel, coldly; "but at this moment I cannot tax my memory with the place of our meeting, though one sees so many strange faces in a campaign, that they come and go like shadows."

He then changed the conversation. It was some time, however, before either gentleman entirely recovered his ease, and many days elapsed ere anything like intercourse passed between them. The colonel attached himself during this visit to Jane, with occasional notices of the Misses Jarvis, who began to manifest symptoms of uneasiness at the decided preference he showed to a lady they now chose to look upon, in some measure, as a rival.

Mrs. Wilson and her charge, on the other hand, were entertained by the conversation of Chatterton and Denbigh, relieved by occasional sallies from the lively John. There was something in the person and manners of Denbigh that insensibly attracted those whom chance threw in his way. His face was not strikingly handsome, but it was noble; and when he smiled, or was much animated, it invariably communicated a spark of his own enthusiasm to the beholder. His figure was faultless; his air and manner, if less easy than those of Colonel Egerton, were more sincere and ingenuous; his breeding was clearly higher; his respect for others rather bordering on the old school. But in his voice there existed a charm which would make him, when he spoke, to a female ear, almost resistless: it was soft, deep, melodious, and winning.

"Baronet," said the rector, looking with a smile toward his son and daughter, "I love to see my children happy, and Mrs. Ives threatens a divorce if I go on in the manner I have commenced. She says I desert her for Bolton."

"Why, doctor, if our wives conspire against us, and prevent our enjoying a comfortable dish of tea with Clara, or a glass of wine with Frank, we must call in the higher authorities as umpires. What say you, sister? Is a parent to desert his child in any case?"

"My opinion is," said Mrs. Wilson with a smile, yet speaking with emphasis, "that a parent is *not* to desert a child, in any case or manner."

"Do you hear that, my Lady Moseley?" cried the good-humored baronet.

"Do you hear that, my Lady Chatterton?" echoed John, who had just taken a seat by Grace, when her mother approached them.

"I hear it, but do not see the application, Mr. Moseley."

"No, my lady! Why, there is the honorable Miss Chatterton almost dying to play a game of her favorite chess with Mr. Denbigh. She has beaten us all but him, and her triumph will not be complete until she has him, too, at her feet."

And as Denbigh politely offered to meet the challenge, the board was produced, and the parties were seated. Lady Chatterton stood leaning over her daughter's chair—with a view, however, to prevent any of those consequences she was generally fond of seeing result from this amusement; every measure taken by this prudent mother being literally governed by judicious calculation.

"Umph!" thought John, as he viewed the players, while listening with pleasure to the opinions of Grace, who had recovered her composure and spirits—"Kate, after all, has played one game without using her feet."

CHAPTER XI.

TEN days or a fortnight flew swiftly by, during which Mrs. Wilson suffered Emily to give Clara a week, having first ascertained that Denbigh was a settled resident at the rectory, and thereby not likely to be oftener at the house of Francis than at the Hall, where he was a frequent and welcome guest, both on his own account and as a friend of Doctor Ives. Emily had returned, and she brought the bride and groom with her; when one evening as they were pleasantly seated at their various amusements, with the ease of old acquaintances, Mr. Haughton entered. It was at an hour rather unusual for his visits; and throwing down his hat, after making the usual inquiries, he began without preface:

"I know, good people, you are all wondering what has brought me out this time of night; but the truth is, Lucy has coaxed her mother to persuade me into a ball in honor of the times. So, my lady, I have consented; and my wife and daughter have been buying up all the finery in B——, by the way, I suppose, of anticipating their friends. There is a regiment of foot come into barracks within fifteen miles of us, and to-morrow I must beat up for recruits among the officers—girls are never wanting on such occasions."

"Why," cried the baronet, "you are growing young again, my friend."

"No, Sir Edward, but my daughter is young, and life has so many cares, that I am willing she should get rid of as many as she can at my expense."

"Surely you would not wish her to dance them away," said Mrs. Wilson. "Such relief, I am afraid, will prove temporary."

"Do you disapprove of dancing, ma'am?" said Mr. Haughton, who held her opinions in great respect, as well as a little dread.

"I neither approve nor disapprove of it. Jumping up and down is innocent enough in itself, and, if it must be done, it is well it were done gracefully. As for the accompaniments of dancing, I say nothing —what do you say, Doctor Ives?"

"To what, my dear madam?"

"To dancing."

"Oh, let the girls dance, if they enjoy it."

"I am glad you think so, doctor," cried the delighted Mr. Haughton. "I was afraid I recollected your advising your son never to dance nor to play at games of chance."

"You thought right, my friend," said the doctor, laying down his newspaper; "I did give that advice to Frank, whom you will please to remember is now rector of Bolton. I do not object to dancing as not innocent in itself, or as an elegant exercise; but it is, like drinking, generally carried to excess. Now, as a Christian, I am opposed to all excesses; the music and company lead to intemperance in the recreation, and they often induce neglect of duties—but so may anything else."

"I like a game of whist, doctor, greatly," said Mr. Haughton; "but observing that you never play, and recollecting your advice to Mr. Francis, I have forbidden cards when you are my guest."

"I thank you for the compliment, good sir," replied the doctor, with a smile; "still I would much rather see you play cards than hear you talk scandal, as you sometimes do."

"Scandal!" echoed Mr. Haughton.

"Ay, scandal," said the doctor, coolly, "such as the remark you made the last time, which was only yesterday, I called to see you. You accused Sir Edward of being wrong in letting that poacher off so easily; the baronet, you said, did not shoot himself, and did not know how to prize game as he ought."

"Scandal, doctor—do you call that scandal? Why, I told Sir Edward so himself, two or three times."

"I know you did, and that was rude."

"Rude! I hope sincerely Sir Edward has put no such construction on it?"

The baronet smiled kindly, and shook his head.

"Because the baronet chooses to forgive your offenses, it does not alter their nature," said the doctor, gravely; "no, you must repent and amend; you impeached his motives for doing a benevolent act, and that I call scandal."

"Why, doctor, I was angry the fellow should be let loose; he is a pest to all the game in the county, and every sportsman will tell you so. Here, Mr. Moseley, you know Jackson, the poacher?"

"Oh! a poacher is an intolerable wretch!" cried Captain Jarvis.

"Oh! a poacher," echoed John, looking drolly at Emily—"hang all poachers!"

"Poacher or no poacher, does not alter the scandal," said the doctor. "Now let me tell you, good sir, I would rather play at fifty games of whist than make one such speech, unless indeed it interfered with my duties. Now, sir, with your leave, I'll explain myself as to my son. There is an artifical levity about dancing that adds to the dignity of no man; from some it may detract. A clergyman, for instance, is supposed to have other things to do; and it might hurt him in the opinions of those with whom his influence is necessary, and impair his usefulness: therefore a clergyman should never dance. In the same way with cards: they are the common instruments of gambling, and an odium is attached to them on that account. Women and clergymen must respect the prejudices of mankind in some cases, or lose their influence in society."

"I did hope to have the pleasure of your company, doctor," said Mr. Haughton, hesitatingly.

"And if it will give you pleasure," cried the rector, "you shall have it with all my heart, good sir; it would be a greater evil to wound the feelings of such a neighbor as Mr. Haughton, than to show my face once at a ball." And, rising, he laid his hand on the shoulder of the other kindly. "Both your scandal and rudeness are easily forgiven; but I wish to show you the common error of the world, which has attached odium to certain things, while it charitably overlooks others of a more heinous nature."

Mr. Haughton, who had at first been a little staggered with the attack of the doctor, recovered himself, and, laying a handful of notes on the table, hoped he should have the pleasure of seeing everybody. The invitation was generally accepted, and the worthy man departed, happy if his friends did but come, and were pleased.

"Do you dance, Miss Moseley?" inquired Denbigh of Emily, as he sat watching her graceful movements in netting a purse for her father.

"Oh, yes! the doctor said nothing of

us girls, you know. I suppose he thinks we have no dignity to lose."

"Admonitions are generally thrown away on young ladies when pleasure is in the question," said the doctor, with a look of almost paternal affection.

"I hope you do not seriously disapprove of it in moderation," said Mrs. Wilson.

"That depends, madam, upon circumstances. If it is to be made subsidiary to envy, malice, coquetry, vanity, or any other such little lady-like accomplishment, it certainly had better be let alone. But in moderation, and with the feelings of my little pet here, I should be cynical, indeed, to object."

Denbigh appeared lost in his own ruminations during this dialogue; and as the doctor ended, he turned to the captain, who was overlooking a game of chess between the colonel and Jane (of which the latter had become remarkably fond of late, playing with her hands and eyes instead of her feet), and inquired the name of the corps in barracks at F——.

"The ——th foot, sir," replied the captain, haughtily, who neither respected him, owing to his want of consequence, nor loved him, from the manner in which Emily listened to his conversation.

"Will Miss Moseley forgive a bold request?" said Denbigh, with some hesitation.

Emily looked up from her work in silence, but with some little flutterings at the heart.

"The honor of her hand for the first dance," continued Denbigh, observing she was in expectation that he would proceed.

Emily laughingly said, "Certainly, Mr. Denbigh, if you can submit to the degradation."

The London papers now came in, and most of the gentlemen sat down to their perusal. The colonel, however, replaced the men for a second game, and Denbigh still kept his place beside Mrs. Wilson and her niece. The manners, the sentiments, the whole exterior of this gentleman were such as both the taste and judgment of the aunt approved of; his qualities were those which insensibly gained on the heart; and yet Mrs. Wilson noticed, with a slight uneasiness, the very evident satisfaction her niece took in his society. In Doctor Ives she had great confidence, yet Doctor Ives was a friend, and probably judged him favorably; and again, Doctor Ives was not to suppose he was introducing a candidate for the hand of Emily in every gentleman he brought to the Hall. Mrs. Wilson had seen too often the ill consequences of trusting to impressions received from inferences of companionship, not to know the only safe way was to judge for ourselves.

The opinions of others might be partial —might be prejudiced; and many an improper connection had been formed by listening to the sentiments of those who spoke without interest, and consequently without examination. Not a few matches are made by this idle commendation of others, uttered by those who are respected, and which are probably suggested more by a desire to please than by reflection or even knowledge. In short, Mrs. Wilson knew that, as our happiness chiefly interests ourselves, so it was to ourselves, or to those few whose interest was equal to our own, we could only trust those important inquiries necessary to establish a permanent opinion of character. With Doctor Ives her communications on subjects of duty were frequent and confiding; and, although she sometimes thought his benevolence disposed him to be rather too lenient to the faults of mankind, she entertained a profound respect for his judgment. It had great influence with her, if it were not always conclusive. She determined, therefore, to have an early conversation with him on the subject so near her heart, and be in a great measure regulated by his answers in the steps to be immediately taken. Every day gave her what she thought melancholy proof of the ill consequences of neglecting a duty, in the increasing intimacy of Colonel Egerton and Jane.

"Here, aunt," cried John, as he ran over a paper, "is a paragraph relating to your favorite youth, our trusty and well-beloved cousin, the Earl of Pendennyss."

"Read it," said Mrs. Wilson, with an interest his name never failed to excite.

"'We noticed to-day the equipage of the gallant Lord Pendennyss before the gates of Annandale house, and understand the noble earl is last from Bolton Castle, Northamptonshire.'"

"A very important fact," said Captain Jarvis, sarcastically. "Colonel Egerton and myself got as far as the village, to pay our respects to him, when he had gone on to town."

"The earl's character, both as a man and a soldier," observed the colonel, "gives him a claim to our attentions that his rank would not; on that account we would have called."

"Brother," said Mrs. Wilson, "you would oblige me greatly by asking his lordship to waive ceremony. His visits to Bolton castle will probably be frequent, now we have peace; and the owner is so much from home, that we may never see him without some such invitation."

" Do you want him as a husband for Emily ? " cried John, as he gayly seated himself by the side of his sister.

Mrs. Wilson smiled at an observation which reminded her of one of her romantic wishes; and, as she raised her head to reply in the same tone, met the eye of Denbigh fixed on her with an expression that kept her silent. " This is really an incomprehensible young man in some respects," thought the cautious widow, his startling looks on the introduction to the colonel crossing her mind at the same time ; and, observing the doctor opening the door that led to the baronet's library, Mrs. Wilson, who generally acted as soon as she decided, followed him. As their conversations were known often to relate to the little offices of charity in which they both delighted, the movement excited no surprise, and she entered the library with the doctor uninterrupted.

" Doctor," said Mrs. Wilson, impatient to proceed to the point, " you know my maxim, ' Prevention is better than cure.' This young friend of yours is very interesting."

" Do you feel yourself in danger ? " said the young doctor smiling.

" Not very imminent," replied the lady, laughing good-naturedly. Seating herself, she continued, " Who is he, and who was his father, if I may ask ? "

" George Denbigh, madam, both father and son," said the doctor, gravely.

" Ah, doctor, I am almost tempted to wish Frank had been a girl. You know what I wish to learn."

" Put your questions in order, dear madam," said the doctor, in a kind manner, " and they shall be answered."

" His principles ? "

" So far as I can learn, they are good. His acts, as they have come to my notice, are highly meritorious, and I hope they originated in proper motives. I have seen but little of him of late years, however, and on this head you are nearly as good a judge as myself. His filial piety," said the doctor, dashing a tear from his eye, and speaking with fervor, " was lovely."

" His temper—his disposition ? "

" His temper is under great command, although naturally ardent ; his disposition eminently benevolent toward his fellow-creatures."

" His connections ? "

" Suitable, said the doctor, gravely.

His fortune was of but little moment. Emily would be amply provided for all the customary necessaries of her station ; and, thanking the divine, Mrs. Wilson returned to the parlor, easy in mind, and determined to let things take their own course for a time, but in no degree to relax the vigilance of her observation.

On her return to the room, Mrs. Wilson observed Denbigh approached Egerton, and enter into conversation of a general nature. It was the first time anything more than unavoidable courtesies had passed between them. The colonel appeared slightly uneasy under his novel situation ; while, on the other hand, his companion showed an anxiety to be on a more friendly footing than heretofore. There was something mysterious in the feelings manifested by both these gentlemen that greatly puzzled the good lady ; and, from its complexion, she feared one or the other was not entirely free from censure. It could not have been a quarrel, or their names would have been familiar to each other. They had both served in Spain, she knew, and excesses were often committed by gentlemen at a distance from home their pride would have prevented where they were anxious to maintain a character. Gambling, and a few other prominent vices, floated through her imagination, until, wearied of conjectures where she had no data, and supposing, after all, it might be only her imagination, she turned to more pleasant reflections.

CHAPTER XII.

THE bright eyes of Emily Moseley unconsciously wandered round the brilliant assemblage at Mr. Haughton's, as she took her seat, in search of her partner. The rooms were filled with scarlet coats and belles from the little town of F—— ; and if the company were not the most select imaginable, it was disposed to enjoy the passing moment cheerfully and in lightness of heart. Ere, however, she could make out to scan the countenances of the men, young Jarvis, decked in the full robes of his dignity, as captain in the ——th foot, approached and solicited the honor of her hand. The colonel had already secured her sister, and it was by the instigation of his friend that Jarvis had been thus early in his application. Emily thanked him, and pleaded her engagement. The mortified youth, who had thought dancing with the ladies a favor conferred on them, from the anxiety his sister always manifested to get partners, stood for a few moments in sullen silence ; and then, as if to be revenged on the sex, he determined not to dance the whole evening. Accordingly, he withdrew to a room appropriated to the gentlemen, where he found a few of the military beaux, keeping alive the stimulus they had brought with them from the mess-table.

Clara had prudently decided to comport herself as became a clergyman's wife, and she declined dancing altogether. Catherine Chatterton was entitled to open the ball, as superior in years and rank to any who were disposed to enjoy the amusement. The dowager, who in her heart loved to show her airs upon such occasions, had chosen to be later than the rest of the family; and Lucy had to entreat her father to have patience more than once during the interregnum in their sports created by Lady Chatterton's fashion. This lady at length appeared, attended by her son, and followed by her daughters, ornamented in all the taste of the reigning fashions. Dr. Ives and his wife, who came late from choice, soon appeared, accompanied by their guests, and the dancing commenced. Denbigh had thrown aside his black for the evening, and as he approached to claim her promised hand, Emily thought him, if not as handsome, much more interesting than Colonel Egerton, who just then passed them while leading her sister to the set. Emily danced beautifully, but perfectly like a lady, as did Jane; but Denbigh, although graceful in his movements and in time, knew but little of the art; and but for the assistance of his partner, he would have more than once gone wrong in the figure.

He very gravely asked her opinion of his performance as he handed her to a chair, and she laughingly told him his movements were but a better sort of march. He was about to reply, when Jarvis approached. By the aid of a pint of wine and his own reflections, the youth wrought himself into something of a passion, especially as he saw Denbigh enter, after Emily had declined dancing with himself. There was a gentleman in the corps who unfortunately was addicted to the bottle, and he had fastened on Jarvis, as a man at leisure, to keep him company. Wine openeth the heart; and the captain, having taken a peep at the dancers, and seen the disposition of affairs, returned to his bottle companion bursting with the indignity offered to his person. He dropped a hint, and a question or two brought the whole grievance forth.

There is a certain set of men in every service who imbibe extravagant notions that are revolting to humanity, and which too often prove to be fatal in their results. Their morals are never correct, and the little they have set loosely about them. In their own cases, their appeals to arms are not always so prompt; but in that of their friends, their perceptions of honor are intuitively keen, and their inflexibility in preserving it from reproach unbending; and such is the weakness of mankind — their tenderness on points where the nicer feelings of a soldier are involved—that these machines of custom, these thermometers graduated to the scale of false honor, usurp the place of reason and benevolence, and become too often the arbiters of life and death to a whole corps. Such, then, was the confidant to whom Jarvis communicated the cause of his disgust, and the consequences may easily be imagined. As he passed Emily and Denbigh, he threw a look of fierceness at the latter, which he meant as an indication of his hostile intentions. It was lost on his rival, who at that moment was filled with passions of a very different kind from those which Captain Jarvis thought agitated his own bosom; for had his new friend left him alone, the captain would have gone quietly home, and gone to sleep.

"Have you ever fought?" said Captain Digby, coolly, to his companion, as they seated themselves in his father's parlor, whither they had retired to make their arrangements for the following morning.

"Yes," said Jarvis, with a stupid look, "I fought once with Tom Halliday, at school."

"At school! My dear friend, you commenced young, indeed," said Digby, helping himself to another glass. "And how did it end?"

"Oh! Tom got the better, so I cried, enough," said Jarvis, surlily.

"Enough! I hope you did not flinch," eyeing him keenly. "Where were you hit?"

"He hit me all over."

"All over! The d——l! Did you use small shot? How did you fight?"

"With fists," said Jarvis, yawning.

His companion, seeing how matters were, rang for his servant to put him to bed, remaining himself an hour longer to finish the bottle.

Soon after Jarvis had given Denbigh the look big with his intended vengeance, Colonel Egerton approached Emily, asking permission to present Sir Herbert Nicholson, the lieutenant-colonel of the regiment, and a gentleman who was ambitious of the honor of her acquaintance; a particular friend of his own. Emily gracefully bowed her assent. Soon after, turning her eyes on Denbigh, who had been speaking to her at the moment, she saw him looking intently on the two soldiers, who were making their way through the crowd to the place where she sat. He stammered, said something she could not understand, and precipitately withdrew; and although both she and her aunt sought his figure in the gay throng that flitted around them, he was seen no more that evening.

"Are you acquainted with Mr. Denbigh?" said Emily to her parther, after looking in vain to find his person in the crowd.

"Denbigh! Denbigh! I have known one or two of that name," replied the gentleman. "In the army there are several."

"Yes," said Emily, musing, "he is in the army;" and, looking up, she saw her companion reading her countenance with an expression that brought the color to her cheeks with a glow that was painful. Sir Herbert smiled, and observed that the room was warm. Emily acquiesced in the remark, for the first time in her life conscious of a feeling she was ashamed to have scrutinized, and glad of any excuse to hide her confusion.

"Grace Chatterton is really beautiful to-night," whispered John Moseley to his sister Clara. "I have a mind to ask her to dance."

"Do, John," replied his sister, looking with pleasure on her beautiful cousin, who, observing the movements of John as he drew near where she sat, moved her face on each side rapidly, in search of some one who was apparently not to be found. Her breathing became sensibly quicker, and John was on the point of speaking to her as the dowager stepped in between them. There is nothing so flattering to the vanity of a man as the discovery of emotions in a young woman excited by himself, and which the party evidently wishes to conceal; there is nothing so touching, so sure to captivate; or, if it seem to be affected, so sure to disgust.

"Now, Mr. Moseley," cried the mother, "you shall not ask Grace to dance! She can refuse you nothing, and she has been up the last two figures."

"Your wishes are irresistible, Lady Chatterton," said John, coolly turning on his heel. On gaining the other side of the room, he turned to reconnoiter the scene. The dowager was fanning herself as violently as if *she* had been up the last two figures, instead of her daughter; while Grace sat with her eyes fastened on the floor, paler than usual. "Grace," thought the young man, "would be very handsome—very sweet—very—very everything that is agreeable, if—if it were not for Mother Chatterton." He then led out one of the prettiest girls in the room.

Colonel Egerton was peculiarly fitted to shine in a ballroom. He danced gracefully and with spirit; was perfectly at home with all the usages of the best society, and was never neglectful of any of those little courtesies which have their charm for the moment: and Jane Moseley, who saw all those she loved around her, apparently as happy as herself, found in her judgment or the convictions of her principles no counterpoise against the weight of such attractions, all centered as it were in one effort to please herself. His flattery was deep, for it was respectful; his tastes were her tastes—his opinions her opinions. On the formation of their acquaintance they differed on some trifling point of poetical criticism, and for nearly a month the colonel had maintained his opinion with a show of firmness; but opportunities not wanting for the discussion, he had felt constrained to yield to her better judgment, her purer taste.

The conquest of Colonel Egerton was complete; and Jane, who saw in his attentions the submission of a devoted heart, began to look forward to the moment with trembling that was to remove the thin barrier that existed between the adulation of the eyes and the most delicate assiduity to please, and the open confidence of declared love. Jane Moseley had a heart to love, and to love strongly; her danger existed in her imagination: it was brilliant, unchastened by her judgment—we had almost said unfettered by her principles. Principles such as are found in every-day maxims and rules of conduct sufficient to restrain her within the bounds of perfect decorum she was furnished with in abundance; but to that principle which was to teach her submission in opposition to her wishes—to that principle that could alone afford her security against the treachery of her own passions—she was an utter stranger.

The family of Sir Edward were among the first to retire; and as the Chattertons had their own carriage, Mrs. Wilson and her charge returned alone in the coach of the former. Emily, who had been rather out of spirits the latter part of the evening, broke the silence by suddenly observing—

"Colonel Egerton is, or soon will be, a perfect hero!"

Her aunt, somewhat surprised, both with the abruptness and with the strength of the remark, inquired her meaning.

"Oh, Jane will make him one, whether or not."

This was spoken with an air of vexation which she was unused to, and Mrs. Wilson gravely corrected her for speaking in a disrespectful manner of her sister—one whom neither her years nor situation entitled her in any measure to advise or control. There was an impropriety in judging so near and dear a relation harshly, even in thought. Emily pressed the hand of her aunt, and tremulously acknowledged her error; but she added that she felt a momentary irritation at the idea of a man of Colonel Egerton's character gaining the command over feelings such as her sister possessed. Mrs. Wilson kissed the cheek of her niece, while she inwardly acknowledged the probable truth of the very remark she had thought it her duty to censure. That the imagination of Jane would supply her lover with those qualities she most honored herself, she believed was taken as a matter of course; and that when the veil she had helped to throw before her own eyes was removed, she would cease to respect, and of course cease to love him, when too late to remedy the evil, she greatly feared. But in the approaching fate of Jane she saw new cause to call forth her own activity.

Emily Moseley had just completed her eighteenth year, and was gifted by nature with a vivacity and ardency of feeling that gave a heightened zest to the enjoyments of that happy age. She was artless, but intelligent; cheerful, with a deep conviction of the necessity of piety; and uniform in her practice of all the important duties. The unwearied exertions of her aunt, aided by her own quickness of perception, had made her familiar with the attainments suitable to her sex and years. For music she had no taste; and the time which would have been thrown away in endeavoring to cultivate a talent she did not possess, was dedicated, under the discreet guidance of her aunt, to works which had a tendency both to qualify her for the duties of this life, and fit her for that which comes hereafter. It might be said Emily Moseley had never read a book that contained a sentiment or inculcated an opinion improper for her sex or dangerous to her morals; and it was not difficult for those who knew the fact, to fancy they could perceive the consequences in her guileless countenance and innocent deportment. Her looks, her actions, her thoughts, wore as much of nature as the discipline of her well-regulated mind and softened manners could admit. In person she was of the middle size, exquisitely formed, graceful and elastic in her step—without, however, the least departure from her natural movements; her eye was a dark blue, with an expression of joy and intelligence: at times it seemed all soul, and again all heart; her color was rather high, but it varied with every emotion of her bosom; her feelings were strong, ardent, and devoted to those she loved. Her preceptress had never found it necessary to repeat an admonition of any kind, since her arrival at years to discriminate between the right and the wrong.

"I wish," said Doctor Ives to his wife, the evening his son had asked their permission to address Clara, "Francis had chosen my little Emily."

"Clara is a good girl," replied his wife. "She is so mild, so affectionate, that I doubt not she will make him happy. Frank might have done worse at the Hall."

"For himself he has done well, I hope," said the father; "a young woman of Clara's heart may make any man happy; but a union with purity, sense, principles, like those of Emily, would be more—it would be blissful."

Mrs. Ives smiled at her husband's animation. "You remind me more of the romantic youth I once knew than of the grave divine. There is but one man I know that I could wish to give Emily to: it is Lumley. If Lumley sees her, he will woo her; and if he woos, he will win her."

"And Lumley I believe to be worthy of her," cried the rector, now taking up a candle to retire for the night.

CHAPTER XIII.

THE following day brought a large party of the military *élégants* to the Hall, in acceptance of the baronet's hospitable invitation to dinner. Lady Moseley was delighted; so long as her husband's or her children's interest had demanded a sacrifice of her love of society it had been made without a sigh, almost without a thought. The ties of affinity in her were sacred; and to the happiness, the comfort of those in which she felt an interest, there were few sacrifices of her own propensities she would not cheerfully have made: it was this very love of her offspring that made her anxious to dispose of her daughters in wedlock. Her own marriage had been so happy that she naturally concluded it the state most likely to insure the happiness of her children; and with Lady Moseley, as with thousands of others, who, averse or unequal to the labors of investigation, jump to conclusions over the long line of connecting reasons, marriage was marriage, a husband was a husband. It is true there were certain indispensables, without which the formation of a connection was a thing she considered not within the bounds of Nature. There must be fitness in fortune, in condition, in education and manners; there must be no glaring evil, although she did not ask for positive good.

A professor of religion herself, had any one told her it was a duty of her calling to guard against a connection with any but a Christian for her girls, she would have wondered at the ignorance that would embarrass the marriage state with feelings exclusively belonging to the individual. Had any one told her it were possible to give her child to any but a gentleman, she would have wondered at the want of feeling that could devote the softness of Jane or Emily to the association with rudeness or vulgarity. It was the misfortune of Lady Moseley to limit her views of marriage to the scene of this life, forgetful that every union gives existence to a long line of immortal beings, whose future welfare depends greatly on the force of early examples, or the strength of early impressions.

The necessity for restriction in their expenditures had ceased, and the baronet and his wife greatly enjoyed the first opportunity their secluded situation had given them, to draw around their board their fellow-creatures of their own stamp. In the former, it was pure philanthropy; the same feeling urged him to seek out and relieve distress in humble life; while in the latter it was love of station and seemliness. It was becoming the owner of Moseley Hall, and it was what the daughters of the Benfield family had done since the Conquest.

"I am extremely sorry," said the good baronet at dinner, "Mr. Denbigh declined our invitation to-day; I hope he will yet ride over in the evening."

Looks of a singular import were exchanged between Colonel Egerton and Sir Herbert Nicholson, at the mention of Denbigh's name; which, as the latter had just asked the favor of taking wine with Mrs. Wilson, did not escape her notice. Emily had innocently mentioned his precipitate retreat the night before; and he had, when reminded of his engagement to dine with them that very day, and promised an introduction to Sir Herbert Nicholson by John, in her presence, suddenly excused himself and withdrew. With an indefinite suspicion of something wrong, she ventured, therefore, to address Sir Herbert Nicholson.

"Did you know Mr. Denbigh in Spain?"

"I told Miss Emily Moseley, I believe, last evening, that I knew some of the name," replied the gentleman evasively; then pausing a moment he added with great emphasis, "there is a circumstance connected with one of that name, I shall ever remember."

"It was creditable, no doubt, Sir Herbert," cried young Jarvis, sarcastically. The soldier affected not to hear the question, and asked Jane to take wine with him. Lord Chatterton, however, putting his knife and fork down gravely, and with a glow of animation, observed with unusual spirit—

"I have no doubt it was, sir."

Jarvis, in his turn, affected not to hear this speech, and nothing further was said, as Sir Edward saw that the name of Mr. Denbigh excited a sensation among his guests for which he was unable to account, and which he soon forgot himself.

After the company had retired, Lord Chatterton, however, related to the astonished and indignant family of the baronet, the substance of the following scene, of which he had been a witness that morning, while on a visit to Denbigh at the rectory. They had been sitting in the parlor by themselves, over their breakfast, when a Captain Digby was announced.

"I have the honor of waiting upon you, Mr. Denbigh," said the soldier, with the stiff formality of a professed duellist, "on behalf of Captain Jarvis, but will postpone my business until you are at leisure," glancing his eye on Chatterton.

"I know of no business with Captain Jarvis," said Denbigh, politely handing the stranger a chair, "to which Lord Chatterton cannot be privy; if he will excuse the interruption." The nobleman bowed, and Captain Digby, a little awed by the rank of Denbigh's friend, proceeded in a more measured manner.

"Captain Jarvis has empowered me, sir, to make any arrangement with yourself or friend, previously to your meeting, which he hopes may be as soon as possible, if convenient to yourself," replied the soldier, coolly.

Denbigh viewed him for a moment with astonishment, in silence; when recollecting himself, he said mildly, and without the least agitation, "I cannot effect, sir, not to understand your meaning, but am at a loss to imagine what act of mine can have made Mr. Jarvis wish to make such an appeal."

"Surely Mr. Denbigh cannot think a man of Captain Jarvis's spirit can quietly submit to the indignity put upon him last evening, by your dancing with Miss Moseley, after she had declined the honor to himself," said the captain, affecting an incredulous smile. " My Lord Chatterton and myself can easily settle the preliminaries, as Captain Jarvis is much disposed to consult your wishes, sir, in this affair."

" If he consults my wishes," said Denbigh, smiling, " he will think no more about it."

" At what time, sir, will it be convenient to give him the meeting ? " Then, speaking with a kind of bravado gentlemen of his cast are fond of assuming, " my friend would not hurry any settlement of your affairs."

" I can never meet Captain Jarvis with hostile intentions," replied Denbigh, calmly.

" Sir ! "

" I decline the combat, sir," said Denbigh, with more firmness.

" Your reasons, sir, if you please ? " asked Captain Digby, compressing his lips, and drawing up with an air of personal interest.

" Surely," cried Chatterton, who had with difficulty restrained his feelings, " surely Mr. Denbigh could never so far forget himself as cruelly to expose Miss Moseley by accepting this invitation."

" Your reason, my lord," said Denbigh, with interest, " would at all times have its weight ; but I wish not to qualify an act of what I conceive to be principle by any lesser consideration. I cannot meet Captain Jarvis, or any other man, in private combat. There can exist no necessity for an appeal to arms in any society where the laws rule, and I am averse to bloodshed."

" Very extraordinary," muttered Captain Digby, somewhat at a loss how to act ; but the calm and collected manner of Denbigh prevented a reply ; and after declining a cup of tea, a liquor he never drank, he withdrew, saying he would acquaint his friend with Mr. Denbigh's singular notions.

Captain Digby had left Jarvis at an inn, about half a mile from the rectory, for the convenience of receiving early information of the result of his conference. The young man had walked up and down the room during Digby's absence, in a train of reflections entirely new to him. He was the only son of his aged father and mother, the protector of his sisters, and, he might say, the sole hope of a rising family ; and then, possibly, Denbigh might not have meant to offend him—he might even have been engaged before they came to the house ; or if not, it might have been inadvertence on the part of Miss Moseley.

That Denbigh would offer some explanation he believed, and he had fully made up his mind to accept it, let it be what it might, as his fighting friend entered.

" Well," said Jarvis, in a tone that denoted anything but a consciousness that all *was* well.

" He says he will not meet you," dryly exclaimed his friend, throwing himself into a chair, and ordering a glass of brandy and water.

" Not meet me ! " exclaimed Jarvis, in surprise. " Engaged, perhaps ? "

" Engaged to his d—d conscience."

" To his conscience ! I do not know whether I rightly understand you, Captain Digby," said Jarvis, catching his breath, and raising his voice a very little.

" Then, Captain Jarvis," said his friend, tossing off his brandy, and speaking with great deliberation, " he says that nothing—understand me—*nothing* will ever make him fight a duel."

" He will not ? " cried Jarvis, in a loud voice.

" No, he will not," said Digby, handing his glass to the waiter for a fresh supply.

" He shall by——! "

" I don't know how you will make him."

" Make him ! I'll—I'll post him."

" Never do that," said the captain, turning to him as he leaned his elbows on the table. " It only makes both parties ridiculous. But I'll tell you what you may do. There's a Lord Chatterton who takes the matter up with warmth. If I were not afraid of his interests hurting my promotion, I should have resented something that fell from him myself. He will fight, I dare say, and I'll just return and require an explanation of his words on your behalf."

" No, no," said Jarvis, rather hastily ; " he—*he* is related to the Moseleys, and I have views there it might injure."

" Did you think to forward your views by making the young lady the subject of a duel ? " asked Captain Digby, sarcastically, and eying his companion with contempt.

" Yes, yes," said Jarvis ; " it would certainly hurt my views."

" Here's to the health of his Majesty's gallant —— regiment of foot ! " cried Captain Digby, in a tone of irony, when three-quarters drunk, at the mess-table, that evening, " and to its champion, Captain Henry Jarvis ! "

One of the corps was present accidentally as a guest ; and the following week the inhabitants of F—— saw the regiment in their barracks marching to slow time after the body of Horace Digby.

Lord Chatterton, in relating the part of

the foregoing circumstances which fell under his observation, did ample justice to the conduct of Denbigh; a degree of liberality which did him no little credit, as he plainly saw in that gentleman he had, or soon would have, a rival in the dearest wish of his heart; and the smiling approbation with which his cousin Emily rewarded him for his candor almost sickened him with apprehension. The ladies were not slow in expressing their disgust at the conduct of Jarvis, or backward in their approval of Denbigh's forbearance.

Lady Moseley turned with horror from a picture in which she could see nothing but murder and bloodshed; but both Mrs. Wilson and her niece secretly applauded a sacrifice of worldly feelings on the altar of duty; the former admiring the consistent refusal of admitting any collateral inducements in explanation of his decision; the latter, while she saw the act in its true colors, could hardly help believing that a regard for *her* feelings had, in a trifling degree, its influence in inducing him to decline the meeting. Mrs. Wilson saw at once what a hold such unusual conduct would take on the feelings of her niece, and inwardly determined to increase, if possible, the watchfulness she had invariably observed on all he said or did, as likely to elucidate his real character; well knowing that the requisites to bring or to keep happiness in the married state were numerous and indispensable; and that the display of a particular excellence, however good in itself, was by no means conclusive as to character; in short, that we perhaps as often meet with a favorite principle as with a besetting sin.

CHAPTER XIV.

Sir Edward Moseley had some difficulty in restraining the impetuosity of his son, who was disposed to resent this impertinent interference of young Jarvis with the conduct of his favorite sister; indeed, the young man only yielded to his profound respect to his father's commands, aided by a strong representation on the part of his sister, of the disagreeable consequences of connecting her name with such a quarrel. It was seldom the good baronet felt himself called on to act as decidedly as on the present occasion. He spoke to the merchant in warm, but gentlemanlike terms, of the consequences which might have resulted to his own child from the intemperate act of his son; exculpated Emily entirely from censure, by explaining her engagement to dance with Denbigh, previously to Captain Jarvis's application; and hinted the necessity, if the affair was not amicably terminated, of protecting the peace of mind of his daughters against any similar exposure, by declining the acquaintance of a neighbor he respected as much as Mr. Jarvis.

The merchant was a man of few words, but of great promptitude. He had made his fortune, and more than once saved it, by his decision; and assuring the baronet he should hear no more of it, he took his hat and hurried home from the village where the conversation passed. On arriving at his own house, he found the family collected in the parlor for a morning ride, and throwing himself into a chair, he broke out on the whole party with great violence.

"So, Mrs. Jarvis," he cried, "you *would* spoil a very tolerable book-keeper, by wishing to have a soldier in your family; and there stands the puppy who would have blown out the brains of a deserving young man, if the good sense of Mr. Denbigh had not denied him the opportunity."

"Mercy!" cried the alarmed matron, on whom Newgate (for her early life had been passed near its walls), with all its horrors, floated, and a contemplation of its punishments had been her juvenile lessons of morality—"Harry! Harry! would you commit murder?"

"Murder!" echoed her son, looking askance, as if dodging the bailiffs. "No, mother; I wanted nothing but what was fair. Mr. Denbigh would have had an equal chance to blow out my brains; I am sure everything would have been fair."

"Equal chance!" muttered his father, who had cooled himself, in some measure, by an extra pinch of snuff; "no, sir; you have no brains to lose. But I have promised Sir Edward that you shall make proper apologies to himself, to his daughter, and to Mr. Denbigh." This was rather exceeding the truth, but the alderman prided himself on performing rather more than he promised.

"Apology!" exclaimed the captain. "Why, sir, the apology is due to me. Ask Colonel Egerton if he ever heard of apologies being made by the challenger."

"No, sure," said the mother, who, having made out the truth of the matter, thought it was likely enough to be creditable to her child. "Colonel Egerton never heard of such a thing. Did you, colonel?"

"Why, madam," said the colonel, hesitatingly, and politely handing the merchant his snuff-box, which, in his agitation, had fallen on the floor, " circumstances sometimes justify a departure from ordinary measures. You are certainly right, as a rule; but not knowing the particulars in the present case, it is difficult for me to decide. Miss Jarvis, the tilbury is ready."

The colonel bowed respectfully to the merchant, kissed his hand to his wife, and led their daughter to his carriage.

" Do you make the apologies? " asked Mr. Jarvis, as the door closed.

" No, sir," replied the captain, sullenly.

" Then you must make your pay answer for the next six months," cried the father, taking a signed draft on his banker from his pocket, coolly tearing it in two pieces, carefully putting the name in his mouth, and chewing it into a ball.

" Why, alderman," said his wife (a name she never used unless she had something to gain from her spouse, who loved to hear the apellation after he had relinquished the office), " it appears to me that Harry has shown nothing but a proper spirit. You are unkind—indeed you are."

" A proper spirit? In what way? Do you know anything of the matter? "

" It is a proper spirit for a soldier to fight, I suppose," said the wife, a little at a loss to explain.

" Spirit or no spirit — apology, or ten and sixpence."

" Harry," said his mother, holding up her finger in a menacing attitude, as soon as her husband had left the room (for he had last spoken with the door in his hand), " if you *do* beg his pardon, you are no son of mine."

" No," cried Miss Sarah, " nor any brother of mine. It would be insufferably mean."

" Who will pay my debts? " asked the son, looking up at the ceiling.

" Why, I would, my child, if—if—I had not spent my own allowance."

" I would," echoed the sister; " but if we go to Bath, you know, I shall want all my money."

" Who will pay my debts? " repeated the son.

" Apology, indeed! Who is he, that you, a son of Alderman—of—Mr. Jarvis, of the Deanery, B——, Northamptonshire, should beg his pardon—a vagrant that nobody knows? "

" Who will pay my debts? " again inquired the captain, drumming with his foot.

" Harry," exclaimed the mother, " do you love money better than honor—a soldier's honor? "

" No, mother; but I like good eating and drinking. Think, mother—it's a cool five hundred; and that's a famous deal of money."

" Harry," cried the mother, in a rage, " you are not fit for a soldier! I wish I were in your place."

" I wish, with all my heart, you had been for an hour this morning," thought the son. After arguing for some time longer, they compromised, by agreeing to leave it to the decision of Colonel Egerton, who, the mother did not doubt, would applaud her maintaining the Jarvis dignity, a family in which he took quite as much interest as he felt for his own—so he had told her fifty times. The captain, however, determined within himself to touch the five hundred, let the colonel decide as he might; but the colonel's decision obviated all difficulties. The question was put to him by Mrs. Jarvis, on his return from the airing, with no doubt the decision would be favorable to her opinion. The colonel and herself, she said, never disagreed; and the lady was right—for wherever his interest made it desirable to convert Mrs. Jarvis to his side of the question, Egerton had a manner of doing it that never failed to succeed.

" Why, madam," said he, with one of his most agreeable smiles, " apologies are different things at different times. You are certainly right in your sentiments, as relates to a proper spirit in a soldier; but no one can doubt the spirit of the captain, after the stand he took in this affair. If Mr. Denbigh would not meet him (a very extraordinary measure, indeed, I confess), what can your son do more? He cannot *make* a man fight against his will, you know."

" True, true," cried the matron, impatiently, " I do not want him to fight; Heaven forbid! But why should he, the challenger, beg pardon? I am sure, to have the thing regular, Mr. Denbigh is the one to ask forgiveness."

The colonel felt at a little loss how to reply, when Jarvis, in whom the thoughts of the five hundred pounds had worked a revolution, exclaimed—

" You know, mother, I accused him—that is, I suspected him of dancing with Miss Moseley against my right to her. Now you find that it was all a mistake, and so I had better act with dignity, and confess my error."

" Oh, by all means," cried the colonel, who saw the danger of an embarrassing rupture between the families otherwise; " delicacy to *your* sex particularly requires that, ma'am, from your son; " and he accidentally dropped a letter as he spoke.

"From Sir Edgar, colonel?" asked Mrs. Jarvis, as he stooped to pick it up.

"From Sir Edgar, ma'am, and he begs to be remembered to yourself and all of your amiable family."

Mrs. Jarvis inclined her body, in what she intended for a graceful bend, and sighed—a casual observer might have thought, with maternal anxiety for the reputation of her child—but it was conjugal regret that the political obstinacy of the alderman had prevented his carrying up an address, and thus becoming Sir Timothy. Sir Edgar's heir prevailed, and the captain received permission to do what he had done several hours before.

On leaving the room, after the first discussion, and before the appeal, the captain had hastened to his father with his concessions. The old gentleman knew too well the influence of five hundred pounds to doubt the effect in the present instance, and he had ordered his carriage for the excursion. It came, and to the Hall they proceeded. The captain found his intended antagonist, and in a rather uncouth manner he made the required concession. He was restored to his former favor—no great distinction—and his visits to the Hall were suffered, but with a dislike Emily could never conquer, nor at all times conceal.

Denbigh was occupied with a book, when Jarvis commenced his speech to the baronet and his daughter, and was apparently too much engaged with its contents to understand what was going on, as the captain blundered through. It was necessary, the captain saw, by a glance of his father's eyes, to say something to that gentleman, who had delicately withdrawn to a distant window. His speech was consequently made here too, and Mrs Wilson could not avoid stealing a look at them. Denbigh smiled, and bowed in silence. It is enough, thought the widow; the offense was not against him, it was against his Maker; he should not arrogate to himself, in any manner, the right to forgive, or to require apologies—the whole is consistent. The subject was never afterward alluded to; Denbigh appeared to have forgotten it; and Jane sighed gently, as she devoutly hoped the colonel was not a duelist.

Several days passed before the Deanery ladies could sufficiently forgive the indignity their family had sustained, to resume the customary intercourse. Like all other grievances, where the passions are chiefly interested, it was forgotten in time, however, and things were put in some measure on their former footing. The death of Digby served to increase the horror of the Moseleys, and Jarvis himself felt rather uncomfortable, on more accounts than one, at the fatal termination of the unpleasant business.

Chatterton, who to his friends had not hesitated to avow his attachment to his cousin, but who had never proposed for her, as his present views and fortune were not, in his estimation, sufficient for her proper support, had pushed every interest he possessed, and left no steps unattempted an honorable man could resort to, to effect his object. The desire to provide for his sisters had been backed by the ardor of a passion that had reached its crisis; and the young peer who could not, in the present state of things, abandon the field to a rival so formidable as Denbigh, even to further his views to preferment, was waiting in anxious suspense the decision on his application. A letter from his friend informed him his opponent was likely to succeed; that, in short, all hopes of success had left him. Chatterton was in despair. On the following day, however, he received a second letter from the same friend, unexpectedly announcing his appointment. After mentioning the fact, he went on to say—"The cause of this sudden revolution in your favor is unknown to me, and unless your lordship has obtained interest I am ignorant of, it is one of the most singular instances of ministerial caprice I have ever known." Chatterton was as much at a loss as his friend to understand the affair; but it mattered not; he could now offer to Emily—it was a patent office of great value, and a few years would amply portion his sisters. That very day, therefore, he proposed, and was refused.

Emily had a difficult task to avoid self-reproach, in regulating her deportment on this occasion. She was fond of Chatterton as a relation—as her brother's friend—as the brother of Grace, and even on his own account; but it was the fondness of a sister. His manner—his words, although never addressed to herself, were sometimes overheard unintentionally, and sometimes reached her through her sisters, had left her in no doubt of his attachment; she was excessively grieved at the discovery, and had innocently appealed to her aunt for directions how to proceed. Of his intentions she had no doubt, but at the same time he had not put her in a situation to dispel his hopes; as to encouragement, in the usual meaning of the term, she gave none to him, nor to any one else. There are no little attentions that lovers are fond of showing to their mistresses, and which mistresses are fond of receiving, that Emily ever permitted to any gentleman—no rides, no walks, no *tete-a-tetes.* Always natural and unaffected, there was a simple dignity about her that forbade the request, almost the thought, in the gentlemen of her acquaintance; she had no amusements, no pleasures of any kind in which her sisters were not her companions; and if anything was on the carpet that required an attendant, John was ever ready. He was devoted to her; the decided preference she gave him over every other man upon such occasions flattered his affections; and he would, at any time, leave even Grace Chatterton to attend his sister. All this too was without affectation, and was generally without notice. Emily so looked the delicacy and reserve she acted with so little ostentation that not even her own sex had affixed to her conduct the epithet of squeamish; it was difficult, therefore, for her to do anything which would show Lord Chatterton her disinclination to his suit, without assuming a dislike she did not feel, or giving him slights that neither good-breeding nor good-nature could justify. At one time, indeed, she had expressed a wish to return to Clara; but this Mrs. Wilson thought would only protract the evil, and she was compelled to wait his own time. The peer himself did not rejoice more in his ability to make the offer, therefore, than Emily did to have it in her power to decline it. Her rejection was firm and unqualified, but uttered with a grace and a tenderness to his feelings, that bound her lover tighter than ever in her chains, and he resolved on immediate flight as his only recourse.

"I hope nothing unpleasant has occurred to Lord Chatterton," said Denbigh, with great interest, as he reached the spot where the young peer stood leaning his head against a tree, on his way from the rectory to the hall.

Chatterton raised his face as he spoke; there were evident traces of tears on it, and Denbigh, greatly shocked, was about to proceed as the other caught his arm.

"Mr. Denbigh," said the young man, in a voice almost choked with emotion, "may you never know the pain I have felt this morning. Emily—Emily Moseley—is lost to me—forever."

For a moment the blood rushed to the face of Denbigh, and his eyes flashed with a look that Chatterton could not stand. He turned, as the voice of Denbigh, in those remarkable tones which distinguished it from every other voice he had ever heard, uttered—

"Chatterton, my lord, we are friends, I hope—I wish it, from my heart."

"Go, Mr. Denbigh, go. You were going to Miss Moseley—do not let me detain you."

"I am going with *you*, Lord Chatterton, unless you forbid it," said Denbigh, with emphasis, slipping his arm through that of the peer.

For two hours they walked together in the park; and when they appeared at dinner, Emily wondered why Mr. Denbigh had taken a seat next to her mother, instead of his usual place between herself and her aunt. In the evening he announced his intention of leaving B—— for a short time with Lord Chatterton. They were going to London together; but he hoped to return within ten days. This sudden determination caused some surprise; but as the dowager supposed it was to secure the new situation, and the remainder of their friends thought it might be business, it was soon forgotten, though much regretted for the time. The gentlemen left the Hall that night to proceed to an inn, from which they could obtain a chaise and horses; and the following morning, when the baronet's family assembled around their social breakfast, they were many miles on the road to the metropolis.

CHAPTER XV.

LADY CHATTERTON, finding that little was to be expected in her present situation, excepting what she looked forward to from the varying admiration of John Moseley to her youngest daughter, determined to accept an invitation of some standing to a nobleman's seat about fifty miles from the Hall, and, in order to keep things in their proper places, to leave Grace with her friends, who had expressed a wish to that effect. Accordingly, the day succeeding the departure of her son, she proceeded on her expedition, accompanied by her willing assistant in the matrimonial speculations.

Grace Chatterton was by nature retiring and delicate; but her feelings were acute, and on the subject of female propriety sensitive to a degree that the great want of it in a relation she loved as much as her mother had possibly in some measure increased. Her affections were too single in their objects to have left her long in doubt as to their nature with respect to the baronet's son; and it was one of the most painful orders she had ever received, that which compelled her to accept her cousin's invitation. Her mother was peremptory, however, and Grace was obliged to comply. Every delicate feeling she possessed revolted at the step;

the visit itself was unwished for on her part; but there did exist a reason which had reconciled her to that—the wedding of Clara. But now to remain, after all her family had gone, in the house where resided the man who had as yet never solicited those affections she had been unable to withhold, it was humiliating—it was degrading her in her own esteem, and she could scarcely endure it.

It is said that women are fertile in inventions to further their schemes of personal gratification, vanity, or even mischief. It may be it is true; but the writer of these pages is a man—one who has seen much of the other sex, and he is happy to have an opportunity of paying a tribute to female purity and female truth. That there are hearts so disinterested as to lose the considerations of self, in advancing the happiness of those they love; that there are minds so pure as to recoil with disgust from the admission of deception, indelicacy, or management, he knows; for he has seen it from long and close examination. He regrets that the very artlessness of those who are most pure in the one sex, subjects them to the suspicions of the grosser materials which compose the other. He believes that innocency, singleness of heart, ardency of feeling, and unalloyed, shrinking delicacy, sometimes exist in the female bosom, to an extent that but few men are happy enough to discover, and that most men believe incompatible with the frailties of human nature.

Grace Chatterton possessed no little of what may almost be called this ethereal spirit, and a visit to Bolton parsonage was immediately proposed by her to Emily. The latter, too innocent herself to suspect the motives of her cousin, was happy to be allowed to devote a fortnight to Clara, uninterrupted by the noisy round of visiting and congratulations which had attended her first week; and Mrs. Wilson and the two girls left the Hall the same day with the dowager Lady Chatterton. Francis and Clara were happy to receive them, and they were immediately domesticated in their new abode. Doctor Ives and his wife had postponed an annual visit to a relation of the former on account of the marriage of their son; and they now availed themselves of this visit to perform their own engagement. B—— appeared in some measure deserted, and Egerton had the field almost to himself. Summer had arrived, and the country bloomed in all its luxuriance of vegetation; everything was propitious to the indulgence of the softer passions; and Lady Moseley, ever a strict adherent to

forms and decorum, admitted the intercourse between Jane and her admirer to be carried to as great lengths as those forms would justify. Still the colonel was not explicit; and Jane, whose delicacy dreaded the exposure of feelings that was involved in his declaration, gave or sought no marked opportunities for the avowal of his passion. Yet they were seldom separate, and both Sir Edward and his wife looked forward to their future union as a thing not to be doubted. Lady Moseley had given up her youngest child so absolutely to the government of her aunt, that she seldom thought of her future establishment. She had that kind of reposing confidence in Mrs. Wilson's proceedings that feeble minds ever bestow on those who are much superior to them: and she even approved of a system in many respects which she could not endeavor to imitate. Her affection for Emily was not, however, less than what she felt for her other children; she was, in fact, her favorite, and, had the discipline of Mrs. Wilson admitted of so weak an interference, might have been injured as such.

John Moseley had been able to find out exactly the hour they breakfasted at the Deanery, the length of time it took Egerton's horses to go the distance between that house and the Hall; and on the sixth morning after the departure of his aunt, John's bays were in his phaeton, and, allowing ten minutes for the mile and a half to the park-gates, John had got happily off his own territories before he met the tilbury traveling eastward. "I am not to know which road the colonel may turn," thought John; and after a few friendly but rather hasty greetings, the bays were again in full trot to the parsonage.

"John," said Emily, holding out her hand affectionately, and smiling a little archly, as he approached the window where she stood, "you should take a lesson in driving from Frank; you have turned more than one hair, I believe."

"How is Clara?" cried John, hastily taking the offered hand, with a kiss, "ay, and aunt Wilson?"

"Both well, brother, and out walking this fine morning."

"How happens it you are not with them?" inquired the brother, throwing his eyes round the room. "Have they left you alone?"

"No, Grace has this moment left me."

"Well, Emily," said John, taking his seat very composedly, but keeping his eyes on the door, "I have come to dine with you. I thought I owed Clara a visit, and have managed nicely to give the colonel the go-by."

" Clara will be happy to see you, dear John, and so will aunt, and so am I "— as she drew aside his fine hair with her fingers to cool his forehead.

" And why not Grace, too ? " asked John, with a look of a little alarm.

" And Grace, too, I fancy—but here she is, to answer for herself." Grace said little on her entrance, but her eyes were brighter than usual, and she looked so contented and happy, that Emily observed to her, in an affectionate manner—

" I knew the eau-de-Cologne would do your head good."

" Is Miss Chatterton unwell ? " asked John with a look of interest.

" A slight headache," said Grace, faintly, " but I feel much better."

" Want of air and exercise ; my horses are at the door; the phaeton will hold three easily ; run, sister, for your hat," almost pushing Emily out of the room as he spoke. In a few minutes the horses might have been suffering for air, but surely not for exercise.

" I wish," cried John, with impatience, when at the distance of a couple of miles from the parsonage, " that gentleman had driven his gig out of the road."

There was a small group on one side of the road, consisting of a man, a woman, and several children. The owner of the gig had alighted, and was in the act of speaking to them, as the phaeton approached at a great rate.

" John," cried Emily, in terror, " you never can pass—you will upset us."

" There is no danger, dear Grace," said the brother, endeavoring to check his horses ; he succeeded in part, but not so as to prevent his passing at a spot where the road was very narrow ; a wheel hit violently against a stone, and some of its works gave way. The gentleman immediately hastened to his assistance—it was Denbigh.

" Miss Moseley ! " cried he, in a voice of the tenderest interest, " you are not hurt in the least, I hope ? "

" No," said Emily, recovering her breath, " only frightened ; " and taking his hand, she sprang from the carriage.

Miss Chatterton found courage to wait quietly for the care of John. His " dear Grace " had thrilled on every nerve, and she afterward often laughed at Emily for her terror when there was so little danger. The horses were not in the least frightened, and, after a little mending, John declared all was safe. To ask Emily to enter the carriage again was to exact no little sacrifice of her feelings to her

reason; and she stood in a suspense that too plainly showed that the terror she had been in had not left her.

" If," said Denbigh, modestly, " if Mr. Moseley will take the ladies in my gig, I will drive the phaeton to the Hall, as it is rather unsafe for so heavy a load."

" No, no, Denbigh," said John, coolly, " you are not used to such mettled nags as mine—it would be indiscreet for you to drive them ; if, however, you will be good enough to take Emily into your gig— Grace Chatterton, I am sure, is not afraid to trust my driving, and we might all get back as well as ever."

Grace gave her hand almost unconsciously to John, and he handed her into the phaeton, as Denbigh stood willing to execute his part of the arrangement, but too diffident to speak. It was not a moment for affectation, if Emily had been capable of it, and blushing with the novelty of her situation, she took her place in the gig. Denbigh stopped and turned his eyes on the little group with which he had been talking, and at that moment they caught the attention of John also. The latter inquired after their situation. The tale was a piteous one, the distress evidently real. The husband had been gardener to a gentleman in a neighboring county, and he had been lately discharged to make way, in the difficulty of the times, for a relation of the steward, who was in want of the place. Suddenly thrown on the world, with a wife and four children, with but the wages of a week for his and their support, they had traveled thus far on the way to a neighboring parish where he said he had a right to and must seek public assistance. The children were crying for hunger, and the mother, who was a nurse, had been unable to walk further than where she sat, but had sunk on the ground overcome with fatigue and weak from the want of nourishment.

Neither Emily nor Grace could refrain from tears at the recital of these heavy woes ; the want of sustenance was something so shocking in itself, and brought, as it were, immediately before their eyes, the appeal was irresistible. John forgot his bays—forgot even Grace, as he listened to the affecting story related by the woman, who was much revived by some nutriment Denbigh had obtained from a cottage near them, and to which they were about to proceed by his directions as Moseley interrupted them. His hand shook, his eyes glistened as he took his purse from his pocket, and gave several guineas from it to the mendicant. Grace thought John had never appeared so handsome as the moment he handed the money to the gardener; his face glowed with unusual excitement, and his symmetry had lost the only charm he wanted in common, softness. Denbigh, after waiting patiently until Moseley had bestowed his alms, gravely repeated his directions for their proceeding to the cottage, when the carriages moved on.

Emily revolved in her mind, during their short ride, the horrid distress she had witnessed. It had taken a strong hold on her feelings. Like her brother, she was warm-hearted and compassionate, if we may use the term, to excess; and had she been prepared with the means, the gardener would have reaped a double harvest of donations. It struck her, at the moment, unpleasantly, that Denbigh had been so backward in his liberality. The man had rather sullenly displayed half a crown as his gift, in contrast with the golden shower of John's generosity. It had been even somewhat offensive in its exhibition, and urged her brother to a more hasty departure than, under other circumstances, he would just at the moment have felt disposed to make. Denbigh, however, had taken no notice of the indignity, and continued his directions in the same mild and benevolent manner he had used during the whole interview. "Half a crown was but little," thought Emily, "for a family that was starving;" and, unwilling to judge harshly of one she had begun to value so highly, she came to the painful conclusion that her companion was not as rich as he deserved to be. Emily had not yet to learn that charity was in proportion to the means of the donor, and a gentle wish insensibly stole over her that Denbigh might in some way become more richly endowed with the good things of this world.

Until this moment her thoughts had never turned to his temporal condition. She knew he was an officer in the army, but of what rank, or even of what regiment, she was ignorant. He had frequently touched in his conversations on the customs of the different countries he had seen. He had served in Italy, in the north of Europe, in the West Indies, in Spain. Of the manners of the people, of their characters, he not unfrequently spoke, and with a degree of intelligence, a liberality, a justness of discrimination, that had charmed his auditors; but on the point of personal service he had maintained a silence that was inflexible, and not a little surprising—more particularly of that part of his history which related to the latter country; from all which she was rather inclined to think his military

rank was not as high as she thought he merited, and that possibly he felt an awkwardness of putting it in contrast with the more elevated station of Colonel Egerton. The same idea had struck the whole family, and prevented any inquiries which might be painful. He was so connected with the mournful event of his father's death that no questions could be put with propriety to the doctor's family; and if Francis had been more communicative to Clara, she was too good a wife to mention it, and her own family was possessed of too just a sense of propriety to touch upon points that might bring her conjugal fidelity in question.

Though Denbigh appeared a little abstracted during the ride, his questions concerning Sir Edward and her friends were kind and affectionate. As they approached the house, he suffered his horse to walk, and, after some hesitation, he took a letter from his pocket, and handing it to her, said—

"I hope Miss Moseley will not think me impertinent in becoming the bearer of a letter from her cousin, Lord Chatterton. He requested it so earnestly that I could not refuse taking what I am sensible is a great liberty; for it would be deception did I affect to be ignorant of his admiration, or of his generous treatment of a passion she cannot return. Chatterton"—and he smiled mournfully—"is yet too true to cease his commendations."

Emily blushed painfully, but she took the letter in silence; and as Denbigh pursued the topic no further, the little distance they had to go was ridden in silence. On entering the gates, however, he said, inquiringly, and with much interest—

"I sincerely hope I have not given offense to your delicacy, Miss Moseley. Lord Chatterton has made me an unwilling confidant. I need not say the secret is sacred, on more accounts than one."

"Surely not, Mr. Denbigh," replied Emily, in a low tone; and the gig stopping, she hastened to accept the assistance of her brother to alight.

"Well, sister," cried John, laughing, "Denbigh is a disciple to Frank's system of horseflesh. Hairs smooth enough here, I see. Grace and I thought you would never get home." Now John fibbed a little, for neither Grace nor he had thought in the least about them, or anything else but each other, from the moment they separated until the gig arrived.

Emily made no reply to this speech; and, as the gentlemen were engaged in giving directions concerning their horses, she seized an opportunity to read Chatterton's letter:

"I avail myself of the return of my friend Mr. Denbigh to that happy family from which reason requires my self-banishment, to assure my amiable cousin of my continued respect for her character, and to convince her of my gratitude for the tenderness she has manifested to feelings she cannot return. I may even venture to tell her—what few women would be pleased to hear, but what I know Emily Moseley too well to doubt, for a moment, will give her unalloyed pleasure—that owing to the kind, the benevolent, the brotherly attentions of my true friend, Mr. Denbigh, I have already gained a peace of mind and resignation I once thought were lost to me forever. Ah! Emily, my beloved cousin, in Denbigh you will find, I doubt not, a mind, principles, congenial to your own. It is impossible that he could see you without wishing to possess such a treasure; and, if I have a wish that is now uppermost in my heart, it is, that you may learn to esteem each other as you ought—when, I doubt not, you will become as happy as you both deserve to be. What greater earthly blessings can I implore upon you?

"CHATTERTON."

Emily, while reading this epistle, felt a confusion but little inferior to that which would have oppressed her had Denbigh himself been at her feet, soliciting that love Chatterton thought him so worthy of possessing; and when they met, she could hardly look in the face a man who, it would seem, had been so openly selected by another as the fittest to be her partner for life. The unaltered manner of Denbigh himself, however, soon convinced her that he was entirely ignorant of the contents of the note, and it greatly relieved her from the awkwardness his presence at first occasioned.

Francis soon returned, accompanied by his wife and aunt, and was overjoyed to find the guest who had so unexpectedly arrived. His parents had not yet returned from their visit, and Denbigh, of course, would remain at his present quarters. John promised to continue with them for a couple of days; and everything was soon settled to the perfect satisfaction of the whole party. Mrs. Wilson knew the great danger of suffering young people to be inmates of the same house too well, wantonly to incur the penalties, but her visit had nearly expired, and it might give her a better opportunity of judging Denbigh's character; and Grace Chatterton, though too delicate to follow herself, was well contented to be followed, especially when John Moseley was the pursuer.

CHAPTER XVI.

"I AM sorry, aunt, Mr. Denbigh is not rich," said Emily to Mrs. Wilson, after they had retired in the evening, almost unconscious of what she uttered. The latter looked at her niece in surprise, at a remark so abrupt, and one so very different from the ordinary train of Emily's reflections, as she required an explanation. Emily, slightly coloring at the channel her thoughts had insensibly strayed into, gave her aunt an account of their adventure in the course of the morning's drive, and touched lightly on the difference in the amount of the alms of her brother and those of Mr. Denbigh.

"The bestowal of money is not always an act of charity," observed Mrs. Wilson, gravely, and the subject was dropped; though neither ceased to dwell on it in her thoughts, until sleep closed the eyes of both.

The following day Mrs. Wilson invited Grace and Emily to accompany her in a walk, the gentlemen having preceded them in pursuit of their different avocations. Francis had his regular visits of spiritual consolation; John had gone to the Hall for his pointers and fowling-piece, the season for woodcock having arrived; and Denbigh had proceeded no one knew whither. On gaining the highroad, Mrs. Wilson desired her companions to lead the way to the cottage, where the family of the mendicant gardener had been lodged, and thither they soon arrived. On knocking at the door, they were immediately admitted to an outer room, in which they found the wife of the laborer who inhabited the building, engaged in her customary morning employments. They explained the motives of the visit, and were told that the family they sought were in an adjoining room, but she rather thought at that moment engaged with a clergyman who had called a quarter of an hour before. "I expect, my lady, it's the new rector, who everybody says is so good to the poor and needy; but I have not found time yet to go to church to hear his reverence preach, ma'am," courtesying and handing the freshly-dusted chairs to her unexpected visitors. The ladies seated themselves, too delicate to interrupt Francis in his sacred duties, and were silently waiting his appearance, when a voice was distinctly heard through the thin partition—the first note of which undeceived them as to the character of the gardener's visitor, "It appears, then, Davis, by your own confession," said Denbigh, mildly, but in a tone of reproof, "that your frequent acts of intemperance have at least given ground for the steward's procuring your discharge, if they have not justified him in doing that which his duty to your common employment required."

"It is hard, sir," replied the man sullenly, "to be thrown on the world with a family like mine, to make way for a younger man with but one child."

"It may be unfortunate for your wife and children," said Denbigh, "but just, as respects yourself. I have already convinced you that my interference or reproof is not an empty one; carry the letter to the person to whom it is directed, and I pledge you, you shall have a new trial, and should you conduct yourself soberly and with propriety, continued and ample support; the second letter will gain your children immediate admission to the school I mentioned; and I now leave you, with an earnest injunction to remember that habits of intemperance not only disqualify you to support those who have such great claims on your protection, but inevitably lead to a loss of those powers which are necessary to insure your own eternal welfare."

"May Heaven bless your honor," cried the woman, with fervor, and evidently in tears, "both for what you have said, and what you have done. Thomas only wants to be taken from temptation to become a sober man again—an honest one he has ever been, I am sure."

"I have selected a place for him," replied Denbigh, "where there is no exposure through improper companions, and everything now depends on himself, under Providence."

Mrs. Wilson had risen from her chair on the first intimation given by Denbigh of his intention to go, but had paused at the door to listen to this last speech; when, beckoning her companions, she hastily withdrew, having first made a small present to the woman of the cottage, and requested her not to mention their having called.

"What becomes now of the comparative charity of your brother and Mr. Denbigh, Emily?" asked Mrs. Wilson, as they gained the road on their return homewards. Emily was not accustomed to hear any act of John lightly spoken of without at least manifesting some emotion which betrayed her sisterly regard; but on the present occasion she chose to be silent; while Grace, after waiting in expectation that her cousin would speak, ventured to say timidly—

"I am sure, dear madam, Mr. Moseley was very liberal, and the tears were in his eyes while he gave the money. I was looking directly at them the whole time."

"John is compassionate by nature, continued Mrs. Wilson, with an almost imperceptible smile. "I have no doubt his sympathies were warmly enlisted in behalf of this family; and possessing much, he gave liberally. I have no doubt he would have undergone personal privation to have relieved their distress, and endured both pain and labor with such an excitement before him. But what is all that to the charity of Mr. Denbigh?"

Grace was unused to contend, and, least of all, with Mrs. Wilson; but, unwilling to abandon John to such censure, with increased animation, she said—

"If bestowing freely, and feeling for the distress you relieve, be not commendable, madam, I am sure I am ignorant what is."

"That compassion for the woes of others is beautiful in itself, and the want of it an invariable evidence of corruption from too much, and an ill-governed intercourse with the world, I am willing to acknowledge, my dear Grace," said Mrs. Wilson, kindly; "but the relief of misery, where the heart has not undergone this hardening ordeal, is only a relief to our own feelings; this is compassion; but Christian charity is a higher order of duty; it enters into every sensation of the heart; disposes us to judge as well as to act favorably to our fellow-creatures; is deeply seated in the sense of our own unworthiness; keeps a single eye, in its dispensations of temporal benefits, to the everlasting happiness of the objects of its bounty; is consistent, well-regulated; in short," and Mrs. Wilson's pale cheek glowed with an unusual richness of color —"it is an humble attempt to copy after the heavenly example of our Redeemer, in sacrificing ourselves to the welfare of others, and does and must proceed from a love of his person, and an obedience to his mandates."

"And Mr. Denbigh, aunt," exclaimed Emily, the blood mantling to her cheek with a sympathetic glow, while she lost all consideration for John in the strength of her feelings, "his charity you think to be of this discription?"

"So far, my child, as we can understand motives from the nature of the conduct, such appears to have been the charity of Mr. Denbigh."

Grace was silenced, if not convinced; and the ladies continued their walk, lost in their own reflections, until they reached a bend in the road which hid the cottage from view. Emily involuntarily turned her head as they arrived at the spot, and saw that Denbigh had approached within a few paces of them. On joining them, he commenced his complimentary address in such a way as convinced them the cottager had been true to the injunction given by Mrs. Wilson. No mention was made of the gardener, and Denbigh began a lively description of some foreign scenery, of which their present situation reminded him. The discourse was maintained with great interest, by himself and Mrs. Wilson, for the remainder of their walk.

It was yet early when they reached the parsonage, where they found John, who had driven to the Hall to breakfast, and who, instead of pursuing his favorite amusement of shooting, laid down his gun as they entered, observing : " It is rather soon yet for the woodcocks, and I believe I will listen to your entertaining conversation, ladies, for the rest of the morning." He threw himself upon a sofa at no great distance from Grace, and in such a position as enabled him, without rudeness, to study the features of her lovely face, while Denbigh read aloud to the ladies Campbell's beautiful description of wedded love, in Gertrude of Wyoming.

There was a chastened correctness in the ordinary manner of Denbigh which wore the appearance of the influence of his reason, and a subjection of the passions, that, if anything, gave him less interest with Emily than had it been marked by an evidence of stronger feeling. But on the present occasion this objection was removed ; his reading was impressive ; he dwelt on those passages which most pleased him with a warmth of eulogium fully equal to her own undisguised sensations. In the hour occupied in the reading this exquisite little poem, and in commenting on its merits and sentiments, Denbigh gained more on her imagination than in all their former intercourse.

His ideas were as pure, as chastened, and almost as vivid as those of the poet ; and Emily listened to his periods with intense attention, as they flowed from him in language as glowing as his ideas. The poem had been first read to her by her brother, and she was surprised to discover how she had overlooked its beauties on that occasion. Even John acknowledged that it certainly appeared a different thing now from what he had then thought it ; but Emily had taxed his declamatory power in the height of the pleasant season, and, somehow or other, John now imagined that Gertrude was just such a delicate, feminine, warm-hearted, domestic girl as Grace Chatterton. As Denbigh closed the book, and entered into a general conversation with Clara and her sister, John followed Grace to a window,

and speaking in a tone of unusual softness for him, he said—

" Do you know, Miss Chatterton, I have accepted your brother's invitation to go into Suffolk this summer, and that you are to be plagued with me and my pointers again ? "

" Plagued, Mr. Moseley ! " said Grace, in a voice even softer than his own. " I am sure—I am sure, we none of us think you or your dogs in the least a plague."

" Ah ! Grace," and John was about to become what he had never been before— sentimental—when he saw the carriage of Chatterton, containing the dowager and Catherine, entering the parsonage gates. " Pshaw ! " *thought* John, " there comes Mother Chatterton." " Ah ! Grace," said John, " there are your mother and sister returned already."

" Already ! " said the young lady, and, for the first time in her life, she felt rather unlike a dutiful child. Five minutes could have made no great difference to her mother, and she would greatly have liked to hear what John Moseley meant to have said ; for the alteration in his manner convinced her that his first "ah ! Grace" was to have been continued in a somewhat different language from that in which the second "ah ! Grace !" was ended.

Young Moseley and her daughter, standing together at the open window, caught the attention of Lady Chatterton the moment she got a view of the house, and she entered with a good humor she had not felt since the disappointment in her late expedition in behalf of Catherine ; for the gentleman she had had in view in this excursion had been taken up by another rover, acting on her own account, and backed by a little more wit and a good deal more money than what Kate could be fairly thought to possess. Nothing further in that quarter offering in the way of her occupation, she turned her horses' heads toward London, that great theater on which there never was a loss for actors. The salutations had hardly passed before, turning to John, she exclaimed, with what she intended for a most motherly smile. " What ! not shooting this fine day, Mr. Moseley ? I thought you never missed a day in the season."

" It is rather early yet, my lady," said John, coolly, a little alarmed by the expression of her countenance.

" Oh ! " continued the dowager, in the same strain, " I see how it is ; the ladies have too many attractions for so gallant a young man as yourself." Now as Grace, her own daughter, was the only lady of the party who could, reasonably be supposed to have much influence over John's movements—a young gentleman seldom caring as much for his own as for other people's sisters, this may be fairly set down as a pretty broad hint of the opinion the dowager entertained of the real state of things ; and John saw it and Grace saw it. The former coolly replied, " Why, upon the whole, if you will excuse the neglect, I will try a shot this fine day." In five minutes, Carlo and Rover were both delighted. Grace kept her place at the window, from a feeling she could not define, and of which perhaps she was unconscious, until the gate closed, and the shrubbery hid the sportsman from her sight, and then she withdrew to her room to weep.

Had Grace Chatterton been a particle less delicate—less retiring—blessed with a managing mother, as she was, John Moseley would not have thought another moment about her. But, on every occasion when the dowager made any of her open attacks, Grace discovered so much distress, so much unwillingness to second them, that a suspicion of a confederacy never entered his brain. It is not to be supposed that Lady Chatterton's maneuvers were limited to the direct and palpable schemes we have mentioned ; no—these were the effervescence, the exuberance of her zeal ; but as is generally the case, they sufficiently proved the groundwork of all her other machinations ; none of the little artifices of such as placing—of leaving alone—of showing similarity of tastes— of compliments to the gentlemen, were neglected. This latter business she had contrived to get Catherine to take off her hands ; but Grace could never pay a compliment in her life, unless changing of color, trembling, undulations of the bosom, and such natural movements can be so called ; but she loved dearly to receive them from John Moseley.

" Well, my child," said the mother as she seated herself by the side of her daughter, who hastily endeavored to conceal her tears, "when are we to have a wedding ? I trust everything is settled between you and Mr. Moseley, by this time."

" Mother ! mother ! " said Grace, nearly gasping for breath, " mother, you will break my heart, indeed you will." She hid her face in the clothes of the bed by which she sat, and wept with a feeling of despair.

" Tut, my dear," replied the dowager, not noticing her anguish, or mistaking it for a girlish shame, " you young people are fools in these matters, but Sir Ed-

ward and myself will arrange everything as it should be."

The daughter now not only looked up, but sprang from her seat, her hands clasped together, her eyes fixed in horror, her cheek pale as death ; but the mother had retired, and Grace sank back into her chair with a sensation of disgrace, of despair, which could not have been surpassed, had she really merited the obloquy and shame which she thought were about to be heaped upon her.

CHAPTER XVII.

THE succeeding morning, the whole party, with the exception of Denbigh, returned to the Hall. Nothing had occurred out of the ordinary course of the colonel's assiduities ; and Jane, whose sense of propriety forbade the indulgence of premeditated *tete-à-tetes*, and such little accompaniments of every-day attachments, was rejoiced to see a sister she loved, and an aunt she respected, once more in the bosom of her family.

The dowager impatiently waited an opportunity to effect what she intended for a master-stroke of policy in the disposal of Grace. Like all other managers, she thought no one equal to herself in devising ways and means, and was unwilling to leave anything to nature. Grace had invariably thwarted all her schemes by her obstinacy ; and as she thought young Moseley really attached to her, she determined by a bold stroke to remove the impediments of false shame, and the dread of repulse, which she believed alone kept the youth from an avowal of his wishes, and get rid at once of a plague that had annoyed her not a litte—her daughter's delicacy.

Sir Edward spent an hour every morning in his library, overlooking his accounts and in other necessary employments of a similar nature, and it was here she determined to have the conference.

" My Lady Chatterton, you do me honor," said the baronet, handing her a chair on her entrance.

" Upon my word, cousin," cried the dowager, " you have a very convenient apartment here," looking around her in affected admiration of all she saw.

The baronet replied, and a short discourse on the arrangements of the whole house insensibly led to some remarks on the taste of his mother, the honorable Lady Moseley (a Chatterton), until, having warmed the feelings of the old gentleman by some well-timed compliments of that nature, she ventured on the principal object of her visit.

"I am happy to find, Sir Edward, you are so well pleased with the family as to wish to make another selection from it. I sincerely hope it may prove as judicious as the former one."

Sir Edward was a little at a loss to understand her meaning, although he thought it might allude to his son, who he had some time suspected had views on Grace Chatterton; and willing to know the truth, and rather pleased to find John had selected a young woman he loved in his heart, he observed—

"I am not sure I rightly understand your ladyship, though I hope I do."

"No!" cried the dowager, in a well-counterfeited affectation of surprise. Perhaps, after all, maternal anxiety has deceived me, then. Mr. Moseley could hardly have ventured to proceed without your approbation."

"I have ever declined influencing any of my children, Lady Chatterton," said the baronet, "and John is not ignorant of my sentiments. I sincerely hope, however, you allude to an attachment to Grace?"

"I did, certainly, Sir Edward," said the lady, hesitatingly. "I may be deceived; but you must understand the feelings of a mother, and a young woman ought not to be trifled with."

"My son is incapable of trifling, I hope," cried Sir Edward, with animation, "and least of all, with Grace Chatterton. No; you are quite right. If he has made his choice, he should not be ashamed to avow it."

"I would not wish, on any account, to hurry matters," said the dowager; "but the report which is abroad will prevent other young men from putting in their claims, Sir Edward" (sighing). "I have a mother's feelings; if I have been hasty, your goodness will overlook it." And Lady Chatterton placed her handkerchief to her eyes, to conceal the tears that did not flow.

Sir Edward thought all this very natural, and as it should be, and he sought an early conference with his son.

"John," said the father, taking his hand kindly, "you have no reason to doubt my affection or my compliance to your wishes. Fortune is a thing out of the question with a young man of your expectations." And Sir Edward, in his eagerness to smooth the way, went on: "You can live here, or occupy my small seat at Wiltshire. I can allow you five thousand a year, with much ease to myself. Indeed, your mother and myself

would both straiten ourselves, to add to your comforts; but it is unnecessary— we have enough, and you have enough."

Sir Edward, in a few moments, would have settled everything to the dowager's perfect satisfaction, had not John interrupted him by the exclamation of—

"To what do you allude, father?"

"Allude?" said Sir Edward, simply. "Why, Grace Chatterton, my son."

"Grace Chatterton! Sir Edward. What have I to do with Grace Chatterton?"

"Her mother has made me acquainted with your proposals, and—"

"Proposals!"

"Attentions, I ought to have said; and you have no reason to apprehend anything from me, my child."

"Attentions!" said John, haughtily. "I hope Lady Chatterton does not accuse me of improper attentions to her daughter?"

"No, not improper, my son," said his father: "on the contrary, she is much pleased with them."

"She is, is she? But I am displeased that she should undertake to put constructions on my acts that no attention or words of mine will justify."

It was now Sir Edward's turn to be surprised. He had thought he was doing his son a kindness, when he had only been forwarding the dowager's schemes; but averse from contention, and wondering at his cousin's mistake, which he at once attributed to her anxiety in behalf of a favorite daughter, he told John he was sorry there had been any misapprehension, and left him.

"No, no," said Moseley, internally, as he paced up and down his father's library, "my lady dowager, you are not going to force a wife down my throat. If you do, I am mistaken; and Grace, if Grace"— John softened and began to feel unhappy a little, but anger prevailed.

From the moment Grace Chatterton conceived a dread of her mother's saying anything to Sir Edward, her whole conduct was altered. She could hardly look any of the family in the face, and it was her most ardent wish that they might depart. John she avoided as she would an adder, though it nearly broke her heart to do so.

Mr. Benfield had staid longer than usual, and he now wished to return. John Moseley eagerly profited by this opportunity, and the very day after the conversation in the library he went to Benfield Lodge as a dutiful nephew, to see his venerable uncle safely restored once more to the abode of his ancestors.

Lady Chatterton now perceived, when too late, that she had overshot her mark, while at the same time she wondered at the reason of a result so strange from such well-digested and well-conducted plans. She determined, however, never again to interfere between her daughter and the baronet's heir; concluding with a nearer approach to the truth than always accompanied her deductions, that they resembled ordinary lovers in neither their temperaments nor opinions.

Perceiving no further use in remaining any longer at the Hall, she took her leave, and accompanied by both her daughters, proceeded to the capital, where she expected to meet her son.

Dr. Ives and his wife returned to the rectory on the same day, and Denbigh immediately resumed his abode under their roof. The intercourse between the rector's family and Sir Edward's was renewed with all its former friendly confidence.

Colonel Egerton began to speak of his departure also, but hinted at intentions of visiting L—— at the period of the baronet's visit to his uncle, before he proceeded to town in the winter.

L—— was a small village on the coast, within a mile of Benfield Lodge; and from its natural convenience, it had long been resorted to by the neighboring gentry for the benefit of sea-bathing. The baronet had promised Mr. Benfield his visit should be made at an earlier day than usual, in order to gratify Jane with a visit to Bath, before they went to London, at which town they were promised by Mrs. Jarvis the pleasure of her society, and that of her son and daughters.

PRECAUTION is a word of simple meaning in itself, but various are the ways adopted by different individuals in this life to enforce its import; and not a few are the evils which it is thought necessary to guard against. To provide in season against the dangers of want, personal injury, loss of character, and a great many other such acknowledged misfortunes, has become a kind of instinctive process of our natures. The few exceptions which exist only go to prove the rule: in addition to these, almost every man has some ruling propensity to gratify, to advance which his ingenuity is ever on the alert, or some apprehended evil to avert, which calls all his prudence into activity. Yet how seldom is it exerted, in order to give a rational ground to expect permanent happiness in wedlock.

Marriage is called a lottery, and it is thought, like all other lotteries, there are more blanks than prizes; yet is it not made more precarious than it ought to be, by our neglect of that degree of precaution which we would be ridiculed for omitting in conducting our every-day concerns? Is not the standard of matrimonial felicity placed too low? Ought we not to look more to the possession of principles than to the possession of wealth? Or is it at all justifiable in the Christian to commit a child, a daughter, to the keeping of a man who wants the very essential they acknowledge most necessary to constitute a perfect character? Most men revolt at infidelity in a woman, and most men, however licentious themselves, look for at least the exterior of religion in their wives. The education of their children is a serious responsibility; and although seldom conducted on such rules as will stand the test of reason, it is not to be entirely shaken off: they choose their early impressions should be correct, their infant conduct at least blameless. And are not one-half mankind of the male sex? Are precepts in religion, in morals, only for females? Are we to reverse the theory of the Mohammedans, and though we do not believe it, act as if *men* had no souls? Is not the example of the father as important to the son as that of the mother to the daughter? In short, is there any security against the commission of enormities, but an humble and devout dependence on the assistance of that Almighty Power, which alone is able to hold us up against temptation?

Uniformity of taste is no doubt necessary to what we call love, but is not taste acquired? Would our daughters admire a handsome deist, if properly impressed with a horror of his doctrines, sooner than they now would admire a handsome Mohammedan? We would refuse our children to a pious dissenter, to give them to impious members of the establishment: we make the substance less than the shadow.

Our principal characters are possessed of these diversified views of the evils to be averted. Mrs. Wilson considers Christianity an indispensable requisite in the husband to be *permitted* to her charge, and watches against the *possibility* of any other than a Christian's gaining the affections of Emily. Lady Chatterton considers the want of an establishment as the unpardonable sin, and directs her energies to prevent this evil; while John Moseley looks upon a free will as a birthright of an Englishman, and is, at the present moment, anxiously alive to prevent the dowager's making him the husband of Grace, the thing of all others he most strenuously desires.

———

CHAPTER XVIII.

JOHN MOSELEY returned from L—— within a week, and appeared as if his whole delight consisted in knocking over the inoffensive birds. His restlessness induced him to make Jarvis his companion; for although he abhorred the captain's style of pursuing the sport, being in his opinion both out of rule and without taste, yet he was a constitutional fidget, and suited his own moving propensities at the moment. Egerton and Denbigh were both frequently at the Hall, but generally gave their time to the ladies, neither being much inclined to the favorite amusement of John.

There was a little arbor within the walls of the park, which for years had been a retreat from the summer heats to the ladies of the Moseley family; even so long ago as the youth of Mrs. Wilson, it had been in vogue, and she loved it with a kind of melancholy pleasure, as the spot where she had first listened to the language of love from the lips of her late husband. Into this arbor the ladies had one day retired, during the warmth of a noonday sun, with the exception of Lady Moseley, who had her own engagement in the house. Between Egerton and Denbigh there was maintained a kind of courtly intercourse, which prevented any disagreeable collision from their evident dislike. Mrs. Wilson thought, on the part of Denbigh, it was the forbearance of a principled indulgence to another's weakness; while the colonel's otherwise uniform good breeding was hardly able to conceal something amounting to very near repugnance. Egerton had taken his seat on the ground, near the feet of Jane; and Denbigh was stationed on a bench placed without the arbor, but so near as to have the full benefit of the shade of the noble oak, branches of which had been trained so as to compose its principal covering.

It might have been accident that gave each his particular situation; but it is certain that they were so placed as not to be in sight of each other, and so placed that the colonel was ready to hand Jane her scissors, or any other little implement that she occasionally dropped, and that Denbigh could read every lineament of the animated countenance of Emily as she listened to his description of the curiosities of Egypt, a country in which he had spent a few months while attached to the army in Sicily. In this situation we will leave them for an hour, happy in the society of each other, while we trace the route of John Moseley and his companion, in their pursuit of woodcock, the same day.

"Do you know, Moseley," said Jarvis, who began to think he was a favorite with John, now that he was admitted to his *menus plaisirs*, "that I have taken it into my head this Mr. Denbigh was very happy to plead his morals for not meeting me. He is a soldier, but I cannot find out what battles he has been in."

"Captain Jarvis," said John, coolly, "the less you say about that business the better. Call in Rover."

Now, another of Jarvis's recommendations was a set of lungs that might have been heard half a mile with great ease on a still morning.

"Why," said Jarvis, rather humbly, "I am sensible, Mr. Moseley, I was very wrong as regards your sister; but don't you think it a little odd in a soldier not to fight when properly called upon?"

"I suppose Mr. Denbigh did not think himself properly called upon, or perhaps he had heard what a great shot you were."

Six months before his appearance in B——, Captain Jarvis had been a clerk in the counting-room of Jarvis, Baxter & Co., and had never held fire-arms of any kind in his hand, with the exception of an old blunderbuss, which had been a kind of sentinel over the iron chest for years. On mounting the cockade, he had taken up shooting as a martial exercise, inasmuch as the burning of gunpowder was an attendant of the recreation. He had never killed but one bird in his life, and that was an owl, of which he took the advantage of daylight and his stocking feet to knock off a tree in the Deanery grounds, very early after his arrival. In his trials with John, he sometimes pulled trigger at the same moment with his companion; and as the bird generally fell, he thought he had an equal claim to the honor. He was fond of warring with crows and birds of the larger sort, and invariably went provided with small balls fitted to the bore of his fowling-piece for such accidental rencontres. He had another habit, which was not a little annoying to John, who had several times tried in vain to break him of it—that of shooting at marks. If birds were not plenty, he would throw up a chip, and sometimes his hat, by way of shooting on the wing.

As the day was excessively hot, and the game kept close, John felt willing to return from such unprofitable labor. The captain now commenced his chip firing, which in a few minutes was succeeded by his hat.

"See, Moseley, see; I have hit the band," cried the captain delighted to find that he had at last wounded his old antagonist. "I don't think you can beat that, yourself."

"I am not sure I can," said John, slipping a handful of gravel in the muzzle of his piece slyly, "but I can do as you did—try."

"Do," cried the captain, pleased to get his companion down to his own level of amusements. "Are you ready?"

"Yes; throw."

Jarvis threw, and John fired: the hat fairly bounced.

"Have I hit it?" asked John, while reloading the barrel he had discharged.

"Hit it!" said the captain, looking ruefully at his hat. "It looks like a cullender; but Moseley, your gun don't scatter well; a dozen shot have gone through in the same place."

"It does look rather like a cullender," said John, as he overlooked his companion's beaver, "and, by the *size* of some of the holes, one that has been a good deal used."

The reports of the fowling-pieces announced to the party in the arbor the return of the sportsmen, it being an invariable practice with John Moseley to discharge his gun before he came in; and Jarvis had imitated him, from a wish to be what he called in rule."

"Mr. Denbigh," said John, as he put down his gun, "Captain Jarvis has got the better of his hat at last."

Denbigh smiled without speaking; and the captain, unwilling to have anything to say to a gentleman to whom he had been obliged to apologize, went into the arbor to show the mangled condition of his head-piece to the colonel, on whose sympathies he felt a kind of claim, being of the same corps. John complained of thirst, and went to a little run of water but a short distance from them, in order to satisfy it. The interruption of Jarvis was particularly unseasonable. Jane was relating, in a manner peculiar to herself, in which was mingled that indefinable exchange of looks lovers are so fond of, some incident of her early life to the colonel that greatly interested him. Knowing the captain's foibles, he pointed, therefore, with his finger, as he said:

"There is one of your old enemies, a hawk."

Jarvis threw down his hat, and ran with a boyish eagerness to drive away the intruder. In his haste, he caught up the gun of John Moseley, and loading it rapidly, threw in a ball from his usual stock; but whether the hawk saw and knew him, or whether it saw something else it liked better, it made a dart for the baronet's poultry-yard at no great distance, and was out of sight in a minute. Seeing that his foe had vanished, the captain laid the piece where he had found it, and, recovering his old train of ideas, picked up his hat again.

"John," said Emily, as she approached him affectionately, "you were too warm to drink."

"Stand off, sis," cried John, playfully, taking up the gun from against the body of the tree, and dropping it toward her.

Jarvis had endeavored to make an appeal to the commiseration of Emily in favor of the neglected beaver, and was within a few feet of them. At this moment, recoiling from the muzzle of the gun, he exclaimed, "It is loaded!" "Hold!" cried Denbigh, in a voice of horror, as he sprang between John and his sister. Both were too late; the piece was discharged. Denbigh, turning to Emily, and smiling mournfully, gazed for a moment at her with an expression of tenderness, of pleasure, of sorrow, so blended that she retained the recollection of it for life, and fell at her feet.

The gun dropped from the nerveless grasp of young Moseley. Emily sank in insensibility by the side of her preserver. Mrs. Wilson and Jane stood speechless and aghast. The colonel alone retained the presence of mind necessary to devise the steps to be immediately taken. He sprang to the examination of Denbigh; the eyes of the wounded man were open, and his recollection perfect; the first were fixed in intense observation on the inanimate body which lay at his side.

"Leave me, Colonel Egerton," he said, speaking with difficulty, and pointing in the direction of the little run of water; "assist Miss Moseley—your hat—your hat will answer."

Accustomed to scenes of blood, and not ignorant that time and care were the remedies to be applied to the wounded man, Egerton flew to the stream, and returning immediately, by the help of her sister and Mrs. Wilson, soon restored Emily to life. The ladies and John had now begun to act. The tenderest assiduities of Jane were devoted to her sister; while Mrs. Wilson, observing her niece to be uninjured by anything but the shock, assisted John in supporting the wounded man.

Denbigh spoke, requesting to be carried to the house; and Jarvis was dispatched for help. Within half an hour, Denbigh was placed on a couch in the house of Sir Edward, and was quietly waiting for that professional aid which could only decide on his probable fate. The group assembled in the room were in fearful expectation of the arrival of the surgeons, in pursuit of whom messengers had been sent both to the barracks in F—— and to the town itself. Sir Edward sat by the side of the sufferer, holding one of his hands in his own, now turning his tearful eyes on that daughter who had so lately been rescued as it were from the certainty of death, in mute gratitude and thanksgiving, and now dwelling on the countenance of him who, by bravely interposing his bosom to the blow, had incurred in his own person the imminent danger of a similar fate, with a painful sense of his perilous situation, and devout and earnest prayers for his safety.

Emily was with her father, as with the rest of his family, a decided favorite ; and no reward would have been sufficient, no gratitude lively enough, in the estimation of the baronet, to compensate the protector of such a child. She sat between her mother and Jane, with a hand held by each, pale and oppressed with a load of gratitude, of thanksgiving, of woe, that almost bowed her to the earth. Lady Moseley and Jane were both sensibly touched with the deliverance of Emily, and manifested the interest they took in her by the tenderest caresses, while Mrs. Wilson sat calmly collected within herself, occasionally giving those few directions which were necessary under the circumstances, and offering up her silent petitions in behalf of the sufferer. John had taken horse immediately for F——, and Jarvis had volunteered to go to the rectory and Bolton. Denbigh inquired frequently and with much anxiety for Dr. Ives ; but the rector was absent from home on a visit to a sick parishioner, and it was late in the evening before he arrived. Within three hours of the accident, however, Dr. Black, the surgeon of the ——th, reached the Hall, and immediately proceeded to examine the wound. The ball had penetrated the right breast, and gone directly through the body ; it was extracted with very little difficulty, and his attendant acquainted the anxious friends of Denbigh that the heart certainly, and he hoped the lungs, had escaped uninjured. The ball was a very small one, and the principal danger to be apprehended was from fever ; he had taken the usual precautions against that, and, should it not set in with a violence greater than he apprehended at present, the patient might be abroad within the month.

"But," continued the surgeon, with the hardened indifference of his profession, "the gentleman has had a narrow chance in the passage of the ball itself ; half an inch would have settled his accounts with this world."

This information greatly relieved the family, and orders were given to preserve a silence in the house that would favor the patient's disposition to quiet, or, if possible, sleep.

Dr. Ives now reached the hall. Mrs. Wilson had never seen the rector in the agitation, or with the want of self-command he was in, as she met him at the entrance of the house.

"Is he alive ?—is there hope ?—where is George ? " cried the doctor, as he caught the extended hand of Mrs. Wilson. She briefly acquainted him with the surgeon's report, and the reasonable ground there was to expect Denbigh would survive the injury."

"May God be praised," said the rector, in a suppressed voice, as he hastily withdrew into another room. Mrs. Wilson followed him slowly and in silence ; but was checked on opening the door with the sight of the rector on his knees, the tears stealing down his venerable cheeks in quick succession. "Surely," thought the widow, as she drew back unnoticed, " a youth capable of exciting such affection in a man like Dr. Ives, cannot be unworthy."

Denbigh, hearing of the arrival of his friend, desired to see him alone. Their conference was short, and the rector returned from it with increased hopes of the termination of this dreadful accident. He immediately left the Hall for his own house, with a promise of returning early on the following morning.

During the night, however, the symptoms became unfavorable ; and before the return of Dr. Ives, Denbigh was in a state of delirium from the height of his fever, and the apprehensions of his friends were renewed with additional force.

"What, what, my good sir, do you think of him ? " said the baronet to the family physician, with an emotion that the danger of his dearest child would not have exceeded, and within hearing of most of his children, who were collected in the antechamber of the room in which Denbigh was placed.

"It is impossible to say, Sir Edward," replied the physician ; "he refuses all medicines, and unless this fever abates, there is but little hope of recovery."

Emily stood during this question and answer, motionless, pale as death, and with her hands clasped together, betraying, by the workings of her fingers in a kind of convulsive motion, the intensity of her interest. She had seen the draught prepared which it was so desirable that Denbigh should take, and it now stood rejected on a table, where it could be seen through the open door of his room. Almost breathless, she glided in, and taking the draught in her hand, she approached the bed, by which sat John alone, listening with a feeling of despair to the wanderings of the sick man. Emily hesitated once or twice, as she drew near Denbigh; her face had lost the paleness of anxiety, and glowed with another emotion.

"Mr. Denbigh—dear Denbigh," said Emily, with energy, unconsciously dropping her voice into the softest notes of persuasion, "will you refuse *me?—me,* Emily Moseley, whose life you have saved?"

"Emily Moseley!" repeated Denbigh, and in those tones so remarkable to his natural voice. "Is she safe? I thought she was killed—dead." Then, as if recollecting himself, he gazed intently on her countenance—his eye became less fiery—his muscles relaxed—he smiled, and took, with the docility of a well-trained child, the prescribed medicines from her hand. His ideas still wandered, but his physician, profiting by the command Emily possessed over his patient, increased his care, and by night the fever had abated, and before morning the wounded man was in a profound sleep. During the whole day it was thought necessary to keep Emily by the side of his bed; but at times it was no trifling tax on her feelings to remain there. He spoke of her by name in the tenderest manner, although incoherently, and in terms that restored to the blanched cheeks of the distressed girl more than the richness of their native color.

His thoughts were not confined to Emily, however; he talked of his father, of his mother, and freqently spoke of his poor deserted Marian. The latter name he dwelt on in the language of the warmest affection, condemned his own desertion of her, and, taking Emily for her, would beg her forgiveness, tell her her sufferings had been enough, and that he would return, and never leave her again. At such moments his nurse would sometimes show, by the paleness of her cheeks, her anxiety for his health; and then, as he addressed her by her proper appellation, all her emotions appeared absorbed in the sense of shame at the praises with which he overwhelmed her. Mrs. Wilson succeeded her in the charge of the patient, and she retired to seek that repose she so greatly needed.

On the second morning after receiving the wound, Denbigh dropped into a deep sleep, from which he awoke refreshed and perfectly collected in mind. The fever had left him, and his attendants pronounced, with the usual cautions, to prevent a relapse, his recovery certain. It were impossible to have communicated any intelligence more grateful to all the members of the Moseley family; for Jane had even lost sight of her own lover, in sympathy for the fate of a man who had sacrificed himself to save her beloved sister.

CHAPTER XIX.

THE recovery of Denbigh was as rapid as the most sanguine expectation of his friends could hope for, and in ten days he left his bed, and would sit an hour or two at a time in his dressing-room, where Mrs. Wilson, accompanied by Jane or Emily, came and read to him; and it was a remark of Sir Edward's gamekeeper, that the woodcocks had become so tame during the time Mr. Moseley was shut up in attendance on his friend, that Captain Jarvis was at last actually seen to bag one honestly.

As Jarvis felt something like a consciousness that but for his folly the accident would not have happened, and also something very like shame for the manner he had shrunk from the danger Denbigh had so nobly met, he pretended a recall to his regiment, then on duty near London, and left the Deanery. He went off as he came in—in the colonel's tilbury, and accompanied by his friend and his pointers. John, who saw them pass from the windows of Denbigh's dressing-room, fervently prayed he might never come back again—the chip-shooting poacher!

Colonel Egerton had taken leave of Jane the evening preceding, with many assurances of the anxiety with which he should look forward to the moment of their meeting at L——, whither he intended repairing as soon as his corps had gone through its annual review. Jane had followed the bent of her natural feelings too much, during the period of Denbigh's uncertain fate, to think much of her lover, or anything else but her rescued sister and her preserver; but now the former was pronounced in safety and the latter, by the very reaction of her grief, was, if possible, happier than ever, Jane dwelt in melancholy sadness on the perfections of the man who had taken with him the best affections (as she thought) of her heart. With him all was perfect: his morals were unexceptionable; his manners showed it; his tenderness of disposition manifest, for they had wept together over the distresses of more than one fictitious heroine; his temper, how amiable! he was never angry—she had never seen it; his opinions, his tastes, how correct! they were her own; his form, his face, how agreeable!—her eyes had seen it, and her heart acknowledged it; besides, his eyes confessed the power of her own charms; he was brave, for he was a soldier;—in short, as Emily had predicted, he was a hero—for he was Colonel Egerton.

Had Jane been possessed of less exuberance of fancy, she might have been a little at a loss to identify all these good properties with her hero; or had she possessed a matured or well-regulated judgment to control that fancy, they might possibly have assumed a different appearance. No explanation had taken place between them, however. Jane knew, both by her own feelings and by all the legends of love from its earliest days, that the moment of parting was generally a crisis in affairs of the heart, and, with a backwardness occasioned by her modesty, had rather avoided than sought an opportunity to favor the colonel's wishes. Egerton had not been over-anxious to come to the point, and everything was left as here tofore: neither, however, appeared to doubt in the least the state of the other's affections; and there might be said to exist between them one of those not unusual engagements by implication which it would have been, in their own estimation, a breach of faith to recede from, but which, like all other bargains that are loosely made, are sometimes violated when convenient. Man is a creature that, as experience has sufficiently proved, it is necessary to keep in his proper place in society by wholesome restrictions; and we have often thought it a matter of regret that some well-understood regulations did not exist by which it became not only customary, but incumbent on him, to proceed in his road to the temple of Hymen.

We know that it is ungenerous, ignoble, almost unprecedented, to doubt the faith, the constancy, of a male paragon; yet, somehow, as the papers occasionally give us a sample of such infidelity; as we have sometimes seen a solitary female brooding over her woes in silence, and, with the seemliness of feminine decorum, shrinking from the discovery of its cause, or which the grave has revealed for the first time, we cannot but wish that either the watchfulness of the parent, or a sense of self-preservation in the daughter, would, for the want of a better, cause them to adhere to those old conventional forms of courtship which require a man to speak to be understood, and a woman to answer to be committed.

There was a little parlor in the house of Sir Edward Moseley, that was the privileged retreat of none but the members of his own family. Here the ladies were accustomed to withdraw into the bosom of their domestic quietude, when occasional visitors had disturbed their ordinary intercourse; and many were the hasty and unreserved communications it had witnessed between the sisters, in their stolen flights from the graver scenes of the principal apartments. It might be said to be sacred to the pious feelings of the domestic affections.

Sir Edward would retire to it when fatigued with his occupations, certain of finding some one of those he loved to draw his thoughts off from the cares of life to the little incidents of his children's happiness; and Lady Moseley, even in the proudest hours of her reviving splendor, seldom passed the door without looking in, with a smile, on the faces she might find there. It was, in fact, the room in the large mansion of the baronet, expressly devoted, by long usage and common consent, to the purest feelings of human nature. Into this apartment Denbigh had gained admission, as the one nearest to his own room, and requiring the least effort of his returning strength to reach; and, perhaps, by an undefinable feeling of the Moseleys which had begun to connect him with themselves, partly from his winning manners, and partly by the sense of the obligation he had laid them under.

One warm day, John and his friend had sought this retreat, in expectation of meeting his sisters, who they found, however, on inquiry, had walked to the arbor. After remaining conversing for an hour by themselves, John was called away to attend to a pointer that had been taken ill, and Denbigh, throwing a handkerchief over his head to guard against the danger of cold, quietly composed himself on one of the comfortable sofas of the room, with a disposition to sleep. Before he had entirely lost his consciousness, a light step moving near him, caught his ear; believing it to be a servant unwilling to disturb him, he endeavored to continue in his present mood, until the quick but stifled breathing of some one nearer than before roused his curiosity. He commanded himself, however, sufficiently, to remain quiet; a blind of a window near him was carefully closed; a screen drawn from a corner and placed so as sensibly to destroy the slight draught of air in which he had laid himself; and other arrangements were making, but with a care to avoid disturbing him that rendered them hardly audible. Presently the step approached him again, the breathing was quicker, though gentle, the handkerchief was moved, but the hand was withdrawn hastily, as if afraid of itself.

Another effort was successful, and Denbigh stole a glance through his dark lashes, on the figure of Emily as she stood over him in the fullness of her charms, and with a face in which glowed an interest he had never witnessed in it before. It undoubtedly was *gratitude.* For a moment she gazed on him, as her color increased in richness. His hand was carelessly thrown over an arm of the sofa; she stooped toward it with her face gently, but with an air of modesty that shone in her very figure. Denbigh felt the warmth of her breath, but her lips did not touch it. Had he been inclined to judge the actions of Emily Moseley harshly, it were impossible to mistake the movement for anything but the impulse of natural feeling. There was a pledge of innocence, of modesty, in her countenance, that would have prevented any misconstruction; and he continued quietly awaiting what the preparations on her little mahogany secretary were intended for.

Mrs. Wilson entertained a great · abhorrence of what are commonly called accomplishments in a woman; she knew that too much of that precious time which could never be recalled, was thrown away in endeavoring to acquire a smattering in what, if known, could never be of use to the party, and what can never be well known but to a few, whom nature and long practice have enabled to conquer. Yet as her niece had early manifested a taste for painting, and a vivid perception of the beauties of nature, her inclination had been indulged, and Emily Moseley sketched with neatness and accuracy, and with great readiness. It would have been no subject of surprise, had admiration, or some more powerful feeling, betrayed to the artist, on this occasion, the deception the young man was practicing. She had entered the room from her walk, warm and careless; her hair, than which none was more beautiful, had strayed on her shoulders, freed from the confinement of the comb, and a lock was finely contrasted to the rich color of a cheek that almost burnt with the exercise and the excitement. Her dress, white as the first snow of the winter; her looks, as she now turned them on the face of the sleeper, and betrayed by their animation the success of her art, formed a picture in itself, that Denbigh would have been content to gaze on forever. Her back was to a window, that threw its strong light on the paper—the figures of which were reflected, as she occasionally held it up to study its effect, in a large mirror so placed that Denbigh caught a view of her subject.

He knew it at a glance—the arbor—the gun—himself, all were there; it appeared to have been drawn before—it must have been, from its perfect state, and Emily had seized a favorable moment to complete his own resemblance. Her touches were light and finishing, and as the picture was frequently held up for consideration, he had some time allowed for studying it. His own resemblance was strong; his eyes were turned on herself, to whom Denbigh thought she had not done ample justice, but the man who held the gun bore no likeness to John Moseley, except in dress. A slight movement of the muscles of the sleeper's mouth might have betrayed his consciousness, had not Emily been too intent on the picture, as she turned it in such a way that a strong light fell on the recoiling figure of Captain Jarvis. The resemblance was wonderful. Denbigh thought he would have known it, had he seen it in the Academy itself. The noise of some one approaching closed the portfolio; it was only a servant, yet Emily did not resume her pencil. Denbigh watched her motions, as she put the picture carefully in a private drawer of the secretary, reopened the blind, replaced the screen, and laid the handkerchief, the last thing, on his face, with a movement almost imperceptible to himself.

"It is later than I thought," said Denbigh, looking at his watch; "I owe an apology, Miss Moseley, for making so free with your parlor; but I was too lazy to move."

"Apology! Mr. Denbigh," cried Emily, with a color varying with every word she spoke, and trembling at what she thought the nearness of detection, "you have no apology to make for your present debility; and, surely, surely, least of all to me!"

"I understand from Mr. Moseley," continued Denbigh, with a smile, "that our obligation is at least mutual; to your perseverance and care, Miss Moseley, after the physicians had given me up, I believe I am, under Providence, indebted for my recovery."

Emily was not vain, and least of all addicted to a display of any of her acquirements; very few even of her friends knew she ever held a pencil in her hand; yet did she now unaccountably throw open her portfolio, and offer its contents to the examination of her companion. It was done almost instantaneously, and with great freedom, though not without certain flushings of the face and heavings of the bosom, that would have eclipsed Grace Chatterton in her happiest moments of natural flattery. Whatever might have been the wishes of Mr. Denbigh to pursue a subject which had begun to grow extremely interesting, both from its import and the feelings of the parties, it would have been rude to decline viewing the contents of a lady's portfolio. The drawings were, many of them, interesting, and the exhibitor of them now appeared as anxious to remove them in haste, as she had but the moment before been to direct his attention to her performances. Denbigh would have given much to dare to ask for the paper so carefully secreted in the private drawer; but neither the principal agency he had himself in the scene, nor delicacy to his companion's wish for concealment, would allow of the request.

"Doctor Ives! how happy I am to see you," said Emily, hastily closing her portfolio, and before Denbigh had gone half through its contents; "you have become almost a stranger to us since Clara left us."

"No, no, my little friend, never a stranger, I hope, at Moseley Hall," cried the doctor, pleasantly; "George, I am happy to see you look so well—you have even a color—there is a letter for you, from Marian."

Denbigh took the letter eagerly, and retired to a window to peruse it. His hand shook as he broke the seal, and his interest in the writer, or its contents, could not have escaped the notice of any observer, however indifferent.

"Now, Miss Emily, if you will have the goodness to order me a glass of wine and water after my ride, believe me, you will do a very charitable act," cried the doctor, as he took his seat on the sofa.

Emily was standing by the little table, deeply musing on the contents of her portfolio; for her eyes were intently fixed on the outside, as if she expected to see through the leather covering their merits and faults.

"Miss Emily Moseley," continued the doctor, gravely, "am I to die of thirst or not, this warm day?"

"Do you wish anything, Doctor Ives?"

"A servant to get me a glass of wine and water."

"Why did you not ask me, my dear sir?" said Emily, as she threw open a cellaret, and handed him what he wanted.

"There, my dear, there is a great plenty," said the doctor, with an arch expression; "I really thought I had asked you thrice—but I believe you were studying something in that portfolio."

Emily blushed, and endeavored to laugh at her own absence of mind; but she would have given the world to know who Marian was.

CHAPTER XX.

As a month had elapsed since ne received his wound, Denbigh took an opportunity, one morning at breakfast, where he was well enough now to meet his friends, to announce his intention of trespassing no longer on their kindness, but of returning that day to the rectory. The communication distressed the whole family, and the baronet turned to him in the most cordial manner, as he took one of his hands, and said with an air of solemnity—

"Mr. Denbigh, I could wish you to make this house your home; Dr. Ives may have known you longer, and may have the claim of relationship on you, but I am certain he cannot love you better; and are not the ties of gratitude as binding as those of blood?"

Denbigh was affected by the kindness of Sir Edward's manner.

"The regiment I belong to, Sir Edward, will be reviewed next week, and it has become my duty to leave here; there is one it is proper I should visit, a near connection, who is acquainted with the escape I have met with, and wishes naturally to see me; besides, my dear Sir Edward, she has many causes of sorrow, and it is a debt I owe her affection to endeavor to relieve them."

It was the first time he had ever spoken of his family, or hardly of himself, and the silence which prevailed plainly showed the interest his listeners took in the little he uttered.

That connection, thought Emily—I wonder if her name be Marian? But nothing further passed, excepting the affectionate regrets of her father, and the promises of Denbigh to visit them again before he left B——, and of joining them at L—— immediately after the review of which he had spoken. As soon as he had breakfasted, John drove him in his phaeton to the rectory.

Mrs. Wilson, like the rest of the baronet's family, had been too deeply impressed with the debt they owed this young man to interfere with her favorite system of caution against too great an intimacy between her niece and her preserver. Close observation and the opinion of Dr. Ives had prepared her to give him her esteem;

but the gallantry, the self-devotion he had displayed to Emily was an act calculated to remove heavier objections than she could imagine as likely to exist to his becoming her husband. That he meant it, was evident from his whole deportment of late. Since the morning the portfolio was produced, Denbigh had given a more decided preference to her niece. The nice discrimination of Mrs. Wilson would not have said his feelings had become stronger, but that he labored less to conceal them.

That he loved her niece she suspected from the first fortnight of their acquaintance, and it had given additional stimulus to her investigation into his character; but to doubt it, after stepping between her and death, would have been to have mistaken human nature. There was one qualification she would have wished to have been certain he possessed: before this accident, she would have made it an indispensable one; but the gratitude, the affections of Emily, she believed now to be too deeply engaged to make the strict inquiry she otherwise would have done; and she had the best of reasons for believing that if Denbigh were not a true Christian, he was at least a strictly moral man, and assuredly one who well understood the beauties of a religion she almost conceived it impossible for any impartial and intelligent man long to resist. Perhaps Mrs. Wilson, having in some measure interfered with her system, like others, had, on finding it impossible to conduct so that reason would justify all she did, began to find reasons for what she thought best to be done under the circumstances. Denbigh, however, both by his acts and his opinions, had created such an estimate of his worth in the breast of Mrs. Wilson, that there would have been but little danger of a repulse had no fortuitous accident helped him in his way to her favor.

"Who have we here?" said lady Moseley. "A landaulet and four—the Earl of Bolton, I declare!"

Lady Moseley turned from the window with that collected grace she so well loved, and so well knew how to assume, to receive her noble visitor. Lord Bolton was a bachelor of sixty-five, who had long been attached to the court, and retained much of the manners of the old school. His principal estate was in Ireland, and most of that time which his duty at Windsor did not require he gave to the improvement of his Irish property. Thus, although on perfectly good terms with the baronet's family, they seldom met. With General Wilson he had been at college, and to his widow he always showed much

of that regard he had invariably professed for her husband. The obligation he had conferred, unasked, on Francis Ives, was one conferred on all his friends, and his reception was now warmer than usual.

"My Lady Moseley," said the earl, bowing formally on her hand, "your looks do ample justice to the air of Northamptonshire. I hope you enjoy your usual health."

Then, waiting her equally courteous answer, he paid his compliments, in succession, to all the members of the family; a mode undoubtedly well adapted to discover ther several conditions, but not a little tedious in its operations, and somewhat tiresome to the legs.

"We are under a debt of gratitude to your lordship," said Sir Edward, in his simple and warm-hearted way, "that I am sorry it is not in our power to repay more amply than by our thanks."

The earl was, or affected to be, surprised, as he required an explanation.

"The living at Bolton," said Lady Moseley, with dignity.

"Yes," continued her husband; "in giving the living to Frank you did me a favor, equal to what you would have done had he been my own child; and unsolicited, too, my lord, it was an additional compliment."

The earl sat rather uneasy during this speech, but the love of truth prevailed; for he had been too much round the person of our beloved sovereign not to retain all the impressions of his youth; and after a little struggle with his self-love, he answered—

"Not unsolicited, Sir Edward. I have no doubt, had my better fortune allowed me the acquaintance of my present rector, his own merit would have obtained what a sense of justice requires I should say was granted to an applicant to whom the ear of royalty itself would not have been deaf."

It was the turn of the Moseleys now to look surprised, and Sir Edward ventured to ask an explanation.

"It was my cousin, the Earl of Pendennyss, who applied for it, as a favor done to himself; and Pendennyss is a man not to be refused anything."

"Lord Pendennyss!" exclaimed Mrs. Wilson, with animation; "and in what way came we to be under this obligation to Lord Pendennyss?"

"He did me the honor of a call during my visit to Ireland, madam," replied the earl; "and on inquiring of my steward after his old friend, Doctor Stevens, learned his death, and the claims of Mr. Ives; but the reason he gave *me* was his interest in the widow of General Wilson," bowing with much solemnity to the lady as he spoke.

"I am gratified to find the earl yet remembers us," said Mrs. Wilson, struggling to restrain her tears. "Are we to have the pleasure of seeing him soon?"

"I received a letter from him yesterday, saying he should be here in all next week, madam." And turning pleasantly to Jane and her sister, he continued, "Sir Edward, you have here rewards fit for heavier services, and the earl is a great admirer of female charms."

"Is he not married, my lord?" asked the baronet, with great simplicity.

"No, baronet, nor engaged; but how long he will remain so after his hardihood in venturing into this neighborhood, will, I trust, depend on one of these young ladies."

Jane looked grave—for trifling on love was heresy, in her estimation; but Emily laughed, with an expression in which a skillful physiognomist might have read— if he means me, he is mistaken.

"Your cousin, Lord Chatterton, has found interest, Sir Edward," continued the peer, "to obtain his father's situation; and if reports speak truth, he wishes to become more nearly related to you, baronet."

"I do not well see how that can happen," said Sir Edward with a smile, and who had not art enough to conceal his thoughts, "unless he takes my sister here."

The cheeks of both the young ladies now vied with the rose; and the peer, observing he had touched on forbidden ground, added, "Chatterton was fortunate to find friends able to bear up against the powerful interest of Lord Haverford."

"To whom was he indebted for the place, my lord?" asked Mrs. Wilson.

"It was whispered at court, madam," said the earl, sensibly lowering his voice, and speaking with an air of mystery— "and a lord of the bed-chamber is fonder of discoveries than a lord of the council— that His Grace of Derwent threw the whole of his parliamentary interest into the scale on the baron's side, but you are not to suppose," raising his hand gracefully, with a wave of rejection, "that I speak from authority; only a surmise, Sir Edward; only a surmise, my lady."

"Is not the name of the Duke of Derwent, Denbigh?" inquired Mrs. Wilson, with a thoughtful manner.

"Certainly, madam, Denbigh," replied the earl, with a gravity with which he always spoke of dignities; one of our most ancient names, and descended on the female side from the Plantagenets and Tudors."

He now rose to take his leave, and on bowing to the younger ladies laughingly repeated his intention of bringing his cousin (an epithet he never omitted) Pendennyss to their feet.

"Do you think, sister," said Lady Moseley, after the earl had retired, "that Mr. Denbigh is of the house of Derwent?"

"I cannot say," replied Mrs. Wilson, musing, "yet it is odd, Chatterton told me of his acquaintance with Lady Harriet Denbigh, but not with the Duke."

As this was spoken in the manner of a soliloquy, it received no answer, and was in fact but little attended to by any of the party, excepting Emily, who glanced her eye once or twice at her aunt as she was speaking, with an interest the name of Denbigh never failed to excite. Harriet was, she thought, a pretty name, but Marian was a prettier; if, thought Emily, I could know a Marian Denbigh, I am sure I could love her, and her name, too.

The Moseleys now began to make their preparations for their departure to L——, and the end of the succeeding week was fixed for the period at which they were to go. Mrs. Wilson urged a delay of two or three days, in order to give her an opportunity of meeting with the Earl of Pendennyss, a young man in whom, although she had relinquished her former romantic wish of uniting him to Emily, in favor of Denbigh, she yet felt a deep interest, growing out of his connection with the last moments of her husband, and his uniformly high character.

Sir Edward accordingly acquainted his uncle, that on the following Saturday he might expect to receive himself and family, intending to leave the Hall in the afternoon of the preceding day, and reach Benfield Lodge to dinner. This arrangement once made, and Mr. Benfield notified of it, was unalterable, the old man holding a variation from an engagement a deadly sin. The week succeeding the accident which had nearly proved so fatal to Denbigh, the inhabitants of the Hall were surprised with the approach of a being, as singular in his manners and dress as the equipage which conveyed him to the door of the house. The latter consisted of a high-backed, old-fashioned sulky, loaded with leather and large-headed brass nails; wheels at least a quarter larger in circumference than those of the present day, and wings on each side large enough to have supported a full grown roc in the highest regions of the upper air. It was drawn by a horse, once white, but whose milky hue was tarnished through age with large and numerous red spots, and whose mane and tail did not appear to have suffered by the shears during the present reign.

The being who alighted from this antiquated vehicle was tall and excessively thin, wore his own hair drawn over his almost naked head into a long, thin queue, which reached half-way down his back, closely cased in numerous windings of leather, or the skin of some fish. His drab coat was in shape between a frock and a close-body—close-body, indeed, it was; for the buttons, which were in size about equal to an old-fashioned china saucer, were buttoned to the very throat, thereby setting off his shape to peculiar advantage; his breeches were buckskin, and much soiled; his stockings blue yarn, although it was midsummer; and his shoes were provided with buckles of dimensions proportionate to the aforesaid buttons; his age might have been seventy, but his walk was quick, and the movements of his whole system showed great activity both of mind and body. He was ushered into the room where the gentlemen were sitting, and having made a low and extremely modest bow, he deliberately put on his spectacles, thrust his hand into an outside pocket of his coat, and produced from under its huge flaps a black leathern pocket-book about as large as a good-sized octavo volume; after examining the multitude of papers it contained carefully, he selected a letter, and having returned the pocket-book to its ample apartment, read aloud:

"For Sir Edward Moseley, bart., of Moseley Hall, B——, Northamptonshire— with care and speed, by the hands of Mr. Peter Johnson, steward of Benfield Lodge, Norfolk;" and dropping his sharp voice, he stalked up to the baronet and presented the epistle, with another reverence.

"Ah, my good friend, Johnson," said Sir Edward, as soon as he delivered his errand (for until he saw the contents of the letter, he had thought some accident had occurred to his uncle), "this is the first visit you have ever honored me with; come, take a glass of wine before you go to your dinner; let us drink that it may not be the last."

"Sir Edward Moseley, and you, honorable gentlemen, will pardon me," replied the steward, in his own solemn key, "this is the first time I was ever out of his majesty's county of Norfolk, and I devoutly wish it may prove the last—gentlemen, I drink your honorable healths."

This was the only real speech the old man made during his visit, unless an occasional monosyllabic reply to a question could be thought so. He remained, by Sir Edward's positive order, until the following day; for, having delivered his message, and receiving its answer, he was about to take his departure that evening, thinking he might get a good piece on his road homeward, as it wanted half an hour to sunset. On the following morning, with the sun, he was on his way to the house in which he had been born, and which he had never left for twenty-four hours at a time in his life. In the evening as he was ushered in by John (who had known him from his own childhood, and loved to show him attention) to the room in which he was to sleep, he broke what the young man called his inveterate silence, with, "Young Mr. Moseley — young gentleman—might I presume—to ask—to see the gentleman?"

"What gentleman?" cried John, astonished at the request, and at his speaking so much.

"That saved Miss Emmy's life, sir."

John now fully comprehended him, and led the way to Denbigh's room; he was asleep, but they were admitted to his bedside. The steward stood for ten minutes gazing on the sleeper in silence; and John observed, as he blew his nose on regaining his own apartment, that his little gray eyes twinkled with a luster which could not be taken for anything but a tear.

As the letter was as characteristic of the writer as its bearer was of his vocation, we may be excused giving it at length.

"Dear Sir Edward and Nephew :—

"Your letter reached the lodge too late to be answered that evening, as I was about to step into my bed; but I hasten to write my congratulations, remembering the often repeated maxim of my kinsman, Lord Gosford, that letters should be answered immediately; indeed, a neglect of it had very nigh brought about an affair of honor between the earl and Sir Stephens Hallet. Sir Stephens was always opposed to us in the House of Commons of this realm; and I have often thought something might have passed in the debate itself, which commenced the correspondence, as the earl certainly told him as much as if he were a traitor to his king and country.

"But it seems that your daughter Emily has been rescued from death by the grandson of General Denbigh, who sat with us in the house. Now I always had a good opinion of this young Denbigh, who reminds me, every time I look at him, of my late brother, your father-in-law that was;

and I send my steward, Peter Johnson, express to the Hall, in order that he may see the sick man, and bring me back a true account how he fares; for, should he be wanting for anything within the gift of Roderic Benfield, he has only to speak to have it; not that I suppose, nephew, you will willingly allow him to suffer for anything, but Peter is a man of close observation although he is of few words, and may suggest some thing beneficial that might escape younger heads. I pray for —that is, I hope, the young man will recover, as your letter gives great hopes; and if he should want any little matter to help him along in the army, as I take it he is not over wealthy, you have now a good opportunity to offer your assistance handsomely; and, that it may not interfere with your arrangements for this winter, your draft on me for five thousand pounds will be paid at sight; for fear he may be proud, and not choose to accept your assistance, I have this morning detained Peter, while he has put a codicil in my will, leaving him ten thousand pounds. You may tell Emily she is a naughty child, or she would have written me the whole story; but, poor dear, I suppose she has other things on her mind just now. God bless Mr. —— that is, God bless you all, and try if you cannot get a lieutenant-colonelcy at once—the brother of Lady Juliana's friend was made a lieutenant-colonel at the first step.

"RODERIC BENFIELD."

The result of Peter's reconnoitering expedition has never reached our knowledge, unless the arrival of a servant, some days after he took his leave, with a pair of enormous goggles, and which the old gentleman assured his nephew in a note, both Peter and himself had found useful to weak eyes in their occasional sickness, might have been owing to the prudent forecast of the sagacious steward.

CHAPTER XXI.

THE morning on which Denbigh left B—— was a melancholy one to all the members of the little circle, in which he had been so distinguished for his modesty, his intelligence, and his disinterested intrepidity. Sir Edward took an opportunity solemnly to express his gratitude for the services he had rendered him, and, having retired to his library, delicately and earnestly pressed his availing himself of the liberal offer of Mr. Benfield to advance his interests in the army.

"Look upon me, my dear Mr. Denbigh," said the good baronet, pressing him by the hand, while the tears stood in his eyes, "as a father, to supply the place of the one you have so recently lost. You *are* my child; I feel as a parent to you, and must be suffered to act as one."

To this affectionate offer of Sir Edward, Denbigh replied with an emotion equal to that of the baronet, though he declined with respectful language, his offered assistance as unnecessary. He had friends powerful enough to advance his interests, without resorting to the use of money; and, on taking Sir Edward's hand, as he left the apartment, he added, with great warmth, "yet, my dear sir, the day will come, I hope, when I shall ask a boon from your hands, that no act of mine or a life of service could entitle me to receive."

The baronet smiled his assent to a request he already understood, and Denbigh withdrew.

John Moseley insisted on putting the bays in requisition to carry Denbigh for the first stage, and they now stood caparisoned for the jaunt, with their master in a less joyous mood than common, waiting the appearance of his companion.

Emily delighted in their annual excursion to Benfield Lodge. She was beloved so warmly, and returned the affection of its owner so sincerely, that the arrival of the day never failed to excite that flow of spirits which generally accompanies anticipated pleasures, ere experience has proved how trifling are the greatest enjoyments the scenes of this life bestow. Yet, as the day of their departure drew near, her spirits sunk in proportion; and, on the morning of Denbigh's leave-taking, Emily seemed anything but excessively happy. There was a tremor in her voice and a redness in her eyes that alarmed Lady Moseley; but, as the paleness of her cheeks was immediately succeeded by as fine a color as the heart could wish, the anxious mother allowed herself to be persuaded by Mrs. Wilson there was no danger, and she accompanied her sister to her own room for some purpose of domestic economy. It was at this moment Denbigh entered; he had paid his adieus to the matrons at the door, and been directed by them to the little parlor in quest of Emily.

"I have come to make my parting compliments, Miss Moseley," he said, in a tremulous voice, as he ventured to hold forth his hand. "May heaven preserve you," he continued, holding it in fervor to his bosom; then dropping it he hastily retired, as if unwilling to trust himself any longer to utter all he felt. Emily stood a few moments, pale and almost inanimate, as the tears flowed rapidly from her eyes; and then she sought a shelter in a seat of the window. Lady Moseley, on returning, was alarmed lest the draught would increase her indisposition; but her sister, observing that the window commanded a view of the road, thought the air too mild to do her injury.

The personages who composed the society at B—— had now, in a great measure, separated, in pursuit of their duties or their pleasures. The merchant and his family left the Deanery for a watering-place. Francis and Clara had gone on a little tour of pleasure in the northern counties, to take L—— in their return homeward; and the morning arrived for the commencement of the baronet's journey to the same place. The carriages had been ordered, and servants were running in various ways, busily employed in their several occupations, when Mrs. Wilson, accompanied by John and his sisters, returned from a walk they had taken to avoid the bustle of the house. A short distance from the park gates, an equipage was observed approaching, creating by its numerous horses and attendants a dust which drove the pedestrians to one side of the road. An uncommonly elegant and admirably fitted traveling barouche and six rolled by, with the graceful steadiness of an English equipage; several servants on horseback were in attendance; our little party were struck with the beauty of the whole *establishment*.

"Can it be possible Lord Bolton drives such elegant horses?" cried John, with the ardor of a connoisseur in that noble animal. "They are the finest set in the kingdom."

Jane's eyes had seen, through the clouds of dust, the armorial bearings, which seemed to float in the dark, glossy panels of the carriage, and she observed, "It is an earl's coronet, but they are not the Bolton arms." Mrs. Wilson and Emily had noticed a gentleman reclining at his ease, as the owner of the gallant show; but its passage was too rapid to enable them to distinguish the features of the courteous old earl; indeed, Mrs. Wilson remarked, she thought him a younger man than her friend.

"Pray, sir," said John to a tardy groom, as he civilly walked his horse by the ladies, "who has passed in the barouche?"

"My Lord Pendennyss, sir."

"Pendennyss?" exclaimed Mrs. Wilson, with a tone of regret, "how unfortunate!"

She had seen the day named for his visit pass without his arrival, and now, as it was too late to profit by the opportunity, he had come for the second time into her neighborhood. Emily had learnt, by the solicitude of her aunt, to take an interest in the young peer's movements, and desired John to ask a question or two of the groom.

"Where does your lord stop to-night?"

"At Bolton Castle, sir; and I heard my lord tell his valet that he intended staying one day hereabouts, and the day after to-morrow he goes to Wales, your honor."

"I thank you, friend," said John; when the man spurred his horse after the cavalcade. The carriages were at the door, and Sir Edward had been hurrying Jane to enter, as a servant in a rich livery and well mounted galloped up and delivered a letter for Mrs. Wilson, who, on opening it, read the following:

"The Earl of Pendennyss begs leave to present his most respectful compliments to Mrs. Wilson and the family of Sir Edward Moseley. Lord Pendennyss will have the honor of paying his respects in person at any moment that the widow of his late invaluable friend, Lieutenant-General Wilson, will please to appoint.

"Bolton Castle, Friday evening."

To this note Mrs. Wilson, bitterly regretting the necessity which compelled her to forego the pleasure of meeting her paragon, wrote in reply a short letter, disliking the formality of a note.

"My Lord—" I sincerely regret that an engagement which cannot be postponed compels us to leave Moseley Hall within the hour, and must, in consequence, deprive us of the pleasure of your intended visit. But as circumstances have connected your lordship with some of the dearest, although the most melancholy events of my life, I earnestly beg you will no longer consider us as strangers to your person, as we have long ceased to be to your character. It will afford me the greatest pleasure to hear that there will be a prospect of our meeting in town next winter, where I may find a more fitting opportunity of expressing those grateful feelings so long due to your lordship from your sincere friend,

"Charlotte Wilson.

"Moseley Hall, Friday morning."

With this answer the servant was dispatched, and the carriages moved on. John had induced Emily to trust herself once more to the bays and his skill; but, on perceiving the melancholy of her aunt, she insisted on exchanging seats with Jane, who had accepted a place in the carriage of Mrs. Wilson. No objection being made, Mrs. Wilson and her niece rode the first afternoon together in her traveling chaise. The road runs within a quarter of a mile of Bolton Castle, and the ladies endeavored in vain to get a glimpse of the person of the young nobleman. Emily was willing to gratify her aunt's propensity to dwell on the character and history of her favorite; and hoping to withdraw her attention gradually from more unpleasant recollections, asked several trifling questions relating to those points.

"The earl must be very rich, aunt, from the style he maintains."

"Very, my dear; his family I am unacquainted with, but I understand his title is an extremely ancient one; and some one, I believe Lord Bolton, mentioned that his estates in Wales alone exceeded fifty thousand a year."

"Much good might be done," said Emily, thoughtfully, "with such a fortune."

"Much good *is* done," cried her aunt, with fervor. "I am told by every one who knows him, his donations are large and frequent. Sir Herbert Nicholson said he was extremely simple in his habits, and it leaves large sums at his disposal every year."

"The bestowal of money is not always charity," said Emily, with an arch smile and a slight color.

Mrs. Wilson smiled in her turn as she answered, "Not always, but it is charity to hope for the best."

"Sir Herbert knew him, then?" said Emily.

"Perfectly well; they were associated together in the service for several years, and he spoke of him with a fervor equal to my warmest expectations."

The Moseley Arms in F—— was kept by an old butler of the family, and Sir Edward every year, in going to or coming from L——, spent a night under its roof. He was received by its master with a respect that none who ever knew the baronet well, could withhold from his goodness of heart and many virtues.

"Well, Jackson," said the baronet, kindly, as he was seated at the supper-table, "how does custom increase with you —I hope you and the master of the Dun Cow are more amicable than formerly?"

"Why, Sir Edward," replied the host, who had lost a little of the deference of the servant in the landlord, but none of his real respect, "Mr. Daniels and I are more upon a footing of

late than we was, when your goodness enabled me to take the house; then he got all the great travelers, and for more than a twelvemonth I had not a title in my house but yourself and a great London doctor that was called here to see a sick person in the town. He had the impudence to call me the knight barrow-knight, your honor, and we had a quarrel upon that account."

"I am glad, however, to find you are gaining in the rank of your customers, and trust, as the occasion has ceased, you will be more inclined to be good-natured to each other."

"Why, as to good nature, Sir Edward, I lived with your honor ten years, and you must know somewhat of my temper," said Jackson, with the self-satisfaction of an approving conscience; "but Sam Daniels is a man who is never easy unless he is left quietly at the top of the ladder; however," continued the host, with a chuckle, "I have given him a dose lately."

"How so, Jackson?" inquired the baronet, willing to gratify the man's wish to relate his triumphs.

"Your honor must have heard mention made of a great lord, the Duke of Derwent; well, Sir Edward, about six weeks agone, he passed through with my Lord Chatterton."

"Chatterton! exclaimed John, interrupting him, "has he been so near us again, and so lately?"

"Yes, Mr. Moseley," replied Jackson, with a look of importance; "they dashed into my yard with their chaise and four, with five servants, and would you think it, Sir Edward, they hadn't been in the house ten minutes, before Daniel's son was fishing from the servants who they were; I told him, Sir Edward—dukes don't come every day."

"How came you to get his grace away from the Dun Cow—chance?"

"No, your honor," said the host, pointing to his sign, and bowing reverently to his old master, "the Moseley Arms did it. Mr. Daniels used to taunt me with having worn a livery, and has said more than once he could milk his cow, but that your honor's arms would never lift me into a comfortable seat for life; so I just sent him a message by the way of letting him know my good fortune, your honor."

"And what was it?"

"Only that your honor's arms had shoved a duke and a baron into my house —that's all."

"And I suppose Daniel's legs shoved your messenger out of his," said John, laughing.

"No, Mr. Moseley; Daniels would hardly dare do that: but yesterday, your honor, yesterday evening, beat everything. Daniels was seated before his door, and I was taking a pipe at mine, Sir Edward, as a coach and six, with servants upon servants, drove down the street; it got near us, and the boys were reining the horses into the yard of the Dun Cow, as the gentleman in the coach saw my sign; he sent a groom to inquire who kept the house; I got up, your honor, and told him my name, sir. 'Mr. Jackson,' said his lordship, 'my respect for the family of Sir Edward Moseley is too great not to give my custom to an old servant of his family.'"

"Indeed," said the baronet; "pray, who was my lord?"

"The Earl of Pendennyss, your honor. Oh, he is a sweet gentleman, and he asked all about my living with your honor, and about Madam Wilson."

"Did his lordship stay the night?" inquired Mrs. Wilson, excessively gratified at a discovery of the disposition manifested by the earl toward her.

"Yes, madam, he left here after breakfast."

"What message did you send the Dun Cow this time, Jackson?" cried John.

Jackson looked a little foolish, but the question being repeated, he answered— "Why, sir, I was a little crowded for room, and so, your honor, so I just sent Tom across the street to know if Mr. Daniels couldn't keep a couple of the grooms."

"And Tom got his head broke?"

"No, Mr. John, the tankard missed him; but if—"

"Very well," said the baronet, willing to change the conversation, "you have been so fortunate of late, you can afford to be generous; and I advise you to cultivate harmony with your neighbor, or I may take my arms down, and you may lose your noble visitors—see my room prepared."

"Yes, your honor," said the host, and bowing respectfully he withdrew.

"At least, aunt," cried John, pleasantly, "we have the pleasure of supping in the same room with the puissant earl, albeit there be twenty-four hours' difference in the time."

"I sincerely wish there had not been that difference," observed his father, taking his sister kindly by the hand.

"Such an equipage must have been a harvest indeed to Jackson," remarked the mother, as they broke up for the evening.

The whole establishment at Benfield Lodge were drawn up to receive them on the following day in the great hall, and in the center was fixed the upright and lank figure of its master, with his companion in leanness, honest Peter Johnson, on his right.

"I have made out, Sir Edward and my Lady Moseley, to get as far as my entrance, to receive the favor you are conferring upon me. It was a rule in my day, and one invariably practiced by all the great nobility, such as Lord Gosford—and—and—his sister, the Lady Juliana Dayton, always to receive and quit their guests in the country at the great entrance; and in conformity—ah, Emmy, dear," cried the old gentleman, folding her in his arms, as the tears rolled down his cheeks, forgetting his speech in the warmth of his feeling, "You are saved to us again; God be praised—there, that will do, let me breathe, let me breathe;" and then by way of getting rid of his softer feelings, he turned upon John; "So, youngster, you would be playing with edge tools, and put the life of your sister in danger. No gentleman held a gun in my day; that is no gentleman about the court. My Lord Gosford had never killed a bird in his life, or drove his horse; no, sir, gentlemen then were not coachmen. Peter, how old was I before I took the reins of the chaise, in driving round the estate—the time you broke your arm? it was—"

Peter, who stood a little behind his master, in modest retirement, and who had only thought his elegant form brought thither to embellish the show, when called upon, advanced a step, made a low bow, and answered in his sharp key:

"In the year 1798, your honor, and the 38th of his present majesty, and the 64th year of your life, sir, June the 12th, about meridian."

Peter dropped back as he finished; but recollecting himself, regained his place with a bow, as he added, "new style."

"How are you, old style?" cried John, with a slap on the back that made the steward jump again.

"Mr. John Moseley—young gentleman"—a term Peter had left off using to the baronet within the last ten years, "did you think—to bring home—the goggles?"

"Oh, yes," said John, gravely, producing them from his pocket. Most of the party having entered the parlor, he put them carefully on the bald head of the steward—"There, Mr. Peter Johnson, you have your property again, safe and sound."

"And Mr. Denbigh said he felt much indebted to your consideration in sending them," said Emily, soothingly, as she took them off with her beautiful hands.

"Ah, Miss Emmy," said the steward, with one of his best bows, "that was—a noble act; God bless him!" then holding up his finger significantly, "the fourteenth codicil—to master's will," and Peter laid his finger alongside his nose, as he nodded his head in silence.

"I hope the thirteenth contains the name of honest Peter Johnson," said the young lady who felt herself uncommonly well pleased with the steward's conversation.

"As witness, Miss Emmy—witness to all—but God forbid," said the steward with solemnity, "I shall ever live to see the proving of them; no, Miss Emmy, master has done for me what he intended, while I had youth to enjoy it. I am rich, Miss Emmy—good three hundred a year."

Emily, who had seldom heard so long a speech as the old man's gratitude drew from him, expressed her pleasure at hearing it, and shaking him kindly by the hand, left him for the parlor.

"Niece," said Mr. Benfield, having scanned the party closely with his eyes, "where is Colonel Denbigh?"

"Colonel Egerton, you mean, sir," interrupted Lady Moseley.

"No, my Lady Moseley," replied her uncle, with great formality, "I mean Colonel Denbigh. I take it he is a colonel by this time," looking expressively at the baronet; "and who is fitter to be a colonel or a general than a man who is not afraid of gunpowder."

"Colonels must have been scarce in your youth, sir," cried John, who had rather a mischievous propensity to start the old man on his hobby.

"No, jackanapes, gentlemen killed one another then, although they did not torment the innocent birds: honor was as dear to a gentleman of George the Second's court as to those of his grandson's, and honesty too, sirrah—ay, honesty. I remember when we were in, there was not a man of doubtful integrity in the ministry, or on our side even; and then again, when we went out, the opposition benches were filled with sterling characters, making a parliament that was correct throughout. Can you show me such a thing at this day?"

CHAPTER XXII.

A FEW days after the arrival of the Moseleys at the lodge, John drove his sisters to the little village of L——, which, at that time was thronged with an un-usual number of visitors. It had, among other fashionable arrangements for the accommodation of its guests, one of those circulators of good and evil, a public library. Books are, in a great measure, the instruments of controlling the opinions of a nation like ours. They are an engine, alike powerful to save or to destroy. It cannot be denied that our libraries contain as many volumes of the latter as the former description; for we rank among the latter that long catalogue of idle productions, which, if they produce no other evil, lead to the misspending of time, *our own* perhaps included. But we cannot refrain expressing our regret, that such formidable weapons in the cause of morality, should be suffered to be wielded by any indifferent or mercenary dealer, who undoubtedly will consult rather the public tastes than the private good: the evil may be remediless, yet we love to express our sentiments, though we should suggest nothing new or even profitable.

Into one of these 'haunts of the idle, then, John Moseley entered, with a lovely sister leaning on either arm. Books were the entertainers of Jane, and instructors of Emily. Sir Edward was fond of reading of a certain sort—that which required no great depth of thought, or labor of research; and, like most others who are averse to contention, and disposed to be easily satisfied, the baronet sometimes found he had harbored opinions on things not exactly reconcilable with the truth, or even with each other. It is quite as dangerous to give up your faculties to the guidance of the author you are perusing, as it is unprofitable to be captiously scrutinizing every syllable he may happen to advance; and Sir Edward was, if anything, a little inclined to the dangerous propensity. Unpleasant Sir Edward Moseley never was. Lady Moseley very seldom took a book in her hand: her opinions were established to her own satisfaction on all important points, and on the minor ones she made it a rule to coincide with the popular feeling.

Jane had a mind more active than her father, and more brilliant than her mother; and if she had not imbibed injurious impressions from the unlicensed and indiscriminate reading she practiced, it was more owing to the fortunate circumstance that the baronet's library contained nothing extremely offensive to a pure taste, nor dangerous to good morals, than to any precaution of her parents against the deadly, the irretrievable injury to be sustained from ungoverned liberty in this respect to a female mind. On the other hand, Mrs. Wilson had inculcated the necessity of restraint, in selecting the books for her perusal, so strenuously on her niece, that what at first had been the effects of obedience and submission, had now settled into taste and habit; and Emily seldom opened a book, unless in search of information; or if it were the indulgence of a less commendable spirit, it was an indulgence chastened by a taste and judgment that lessened the danger, if it did not entirely remove it.

The room was filled with gentlemen and ladies; and, while John was exchanging his greetings with several of the neighboring gentry of his acquaintance, his sisters were running hastily over a catalogue of the books kept for circulation, as an elderly lady, of foreign accent and dress, entered; and, depositing a couple of religious works on the counter, she inquired for the remainder of the set. The peculiarity of her idiom and her proximity to the sisters caused them both to look up at the moment, and, to the surprise of Jane, her sister uttered a slight exclamation of pleasure. The foreigner was attracted by the sound, and, after a moment's hesitation, she respectfully courtesied. Emily, advancing, kindly offered her hand, and the usual inquiries after each other's welfare succeeded. To the questions asked after the friend of the matron, Emily learned, with some surprise, and no less satisfaction, that she resided in a retired cottage, about five miles from L——, where they had been for the last six months, and where they expected to remain for some time, "until she could prevail on Mrs. Fitzgerald to return to Spain; a thing, now there was peace, of which she did not despair." After asking leave to call on them in their retreat, and exchanging good wishes, the Spanish lady withdrew, and, as Jane had made her selection, was followed immediately by John Moseley and his sisters. Emily, in their walk home, acquainted her brother that the companion of their Bath incognita had been at the library, and that for the first time she had learned that their young acquaintance was or had been, married, and her name.

John listened to his sister with the interest which the beautiful Spaniard had excited at the time they first met, and laughingly told her he could not believe their unknown friend had ever been a wife. To satisfy this doubt, and to gratify a wish they both had to renew their acquaintance with the foreigner, they agreed to drive to the cottage the following morning, accompanied by Mrs. Wilson and Jane, if she would go; but the next day was the one appointed by Egerton for his arrival at L——, and Jane, under a pretense of writing letters, declined the excursion. She had carefully examined the papers since his departure; had seen his name included in the arrivals at London; and, at a later day, had read an account of the review by the commander-in-chief of the regiment to which he belonged. He had never written to any of her friends; but, judging from her own feelings, she did not in the least doubt he would be as punctual as love could make him. Mrs. Wilson listened to her niece's account of the unexpected interview in the library with pleasure, and cheerfully promised to accompany them in their morning's excursion, as she had both a wish to alleviate sorrow, and a desire to better understand the character of this accidental acquaintance of Emily's.

Mr. Benfield and the baronet had a long conversation in relation to Denbigh's fortune the morning after their arrival; and the old man was loud in his expression of dissatisfaction at the youngster's pride. As the baronet, however, in the fullness of his affection and simplicity, betrayed to his uncle his expectation of a union between Denbigh and his daughter, Mr. Benfield became contented with his reward; one fit, he thought, for any services. On the whole "it was best, as he was to marry Emmy, he should sell out of the army; and, as there would be an election soon, he would bring him into parliament—yes—yes—it did a man so much good to sit one term in the parliament of this realm—to study human nature. All his own knowledge in that way was raised on the foundations laid in the House." To this Sir Edward cordially assented, and the gentlemen separated, happy in their arrangements to advance the welfare of two beings they so sincerely loved.

Although the care and wisdom of Mrs. Wilson had prohibited the admission of any romantic or enthusiastic expectations of happiness into the day-dreams of her charge, yet the buoyancy of health, of hope, of youth, of innocence, had elevated Emily to a height of enjoyment hitherto unknown to her usually placid and disciplined pleasures. Denbigh certainly mingled in most of her thoughts, both of the past and the future, and she stood on the threshold of that fantastic edifice in which Jane ordinarily resided. Emily was in the situation perhaps the most dangerous to a young female Christian: her heart, her affections, were given to a man, to appearance, every way worthy of possessing them, it is true; but she had admitted a rival in her love to her Maker; and to keep those feelings distinct, to bend the passions in due submission to the more powerful considerations of endless duty of unbounded gratitude, is one of the most trying struggles of Christian fortitude. We are much more apt to forget our God in prosperity than adversity. The weakness of human nature drives us to seek assistance in distress; but vanity and worldly-mindedness often induce us to imagine we control the happiness we only enjoy.

Sir Edward and Lady Moseley could see nothing in the prospect of the future but lives of peace and contentment for their children. Clara was happily settled, and her sisters were on the eve of making connections with men of family, condition, and certain character. What more could be done for them? They must, like other people, take their chances in the lottery of life; they could only hope and pray for their prosperity, and this they did with great sincerity. Not so Mrs. Wilson; she had guarded the invaluable charge intrusted to her keeping with too much assiduity, too keen an interest, too just a sense of the awful responsibility she had undertaken, to desert her post at the moment watchfulness was most required. By a temperate, but firm and well-chosen conversation she kept alive the sense of her real condition in her niece, and labored hard to prevent the blandishments of life from supplanting the lively hope of enjoying another existence. She endeavored, by her pious example, her prayers, and her judicious allusions, to keep the passion of love in the breast of Emily secondary to the more important object of her creation; and by the aid of a kind and Almighty Providence, her labors, though arduous, were crowned with success.

As the family were seated round the table after dinner, on the day of their walk to the library, John Moseley, awakening from a reverie, exclaimed suddenly.

"Which do you think the handsomest, Emily—Grace Chatterton or Miss Fitzgerald?"

Emily laughed, as she answered, "Grace, certainly; do you not think so, brother?"

"Yes, on the whole; but don't you think Grace looks like her mother at times?"

"Oh no, she is the image of Chatterton."

"She is like yourself, Emmy dear," said Mr. Benfield, who was listening to their conversation.

"Me, dear uncle? I have never heard it remarked before."

"Yes, yes, she is as much like you as she can stare. I never saw as great a resemblance, excepting between you and Lady Juliana—Lady Juliana, Emmy, was a beauty in her day; very like her uncle, old Admiral Griffin—you can't remember the admiral—he lost an eye in a battle with the Dutch, and part of his cheek in a frigate, when a young man fighting the Dons. Oh, he was a pleasant old gentleman; many a guinea has he given me when I was a boy at school."

"And he looked like Grace Chatterton, uncle, did he?" asked John, innocently.

"No, sir, he did not; who said he looked like Grace Chatterton, jackanapes?"

"Why, I thought you made it out, sir: but perhaps it was the description that deceived me—his eye and cheek, uncle."

"Did Lord Gosford leave children, uncle?" inquired Emily, throwing a look of reproach at John.

"No, Emmy dear; his only child, a son, died at school. I shall never forget the grief of poor Lady Juliana. She postponed a visit to Bath three weeks on account of it. A gentleman who was paying his addresses to her at the time, offered then, and was refused—indeed, her self-denial raised such an admiration of her in the men, that immediately after the death of young Lord Dayton, no less than seven gentlemen offered, and were refused in one week. I heard Lady Juliana say, that what between lawyers and suitors, she had not a moment's peace."

"Lawyers?" cried Sir Edward: "what had she to do with lawyers?"

"Why, Sir Edward, six thousand a year fell to her by the death of her nephew; and there were trustees and deeds to be made out—poor young woman, she was so affected, Emmy, I don't think she went out for a week—all the time at home reading papers, and attending to her important concerns. Oh! she was a woman of taste; her mourning, and liveries, and new carriage, were more admired than those of any one about the court. Yes, yes, the title is extinct; I know of none of the name now. The earl did not survive his loss but six years, and the countess died broken-hearted, about a twelvemonth before him."

"And Lady Juliana, uncle," inquired Jonn, "what became of her; did she marry?"

The old man helped himself to a glass of wine. and looked over his shoulder to see if Peter was at hand. Peter, who had been originally butler, and had made it a condition of his preferment, that whenever there was company, he should be allowed to preside at the sideboard, was now at his station. Mr. Benfield, seeing his old friend near him, ventured to talk on a subject he seldom trusted himself with in company.

"Why, yes—yes—she *did* marry, it's true, although she did tell me she intended to die a maid ; but—hem—I suppose—hem—it was compassion for the old viscount, who often said he could not live without her ; and then it gave her the power of doing so much good, a jointure of five thousand a year added to her own income : yet—hem—I do confess I did not think she would have chosen such an old and infirm man—but, Peter, give me a glass of claret." Peter handed the claret, and the old man proceeded : "They say he was very cross to her, and that, no doubt, must have made her unhappy, she was so very tender-hearted."

How much longer the old gentleman would have continued in this strain, it is impossible to say ; but he was interrupted by the opening of the parlor door, and the sudden appearance on its threshold of Denbigh. Every countenance glowed with pleasure at this unexpected return of their favorite ; and but for the prudent caution of Mrs. Wilson, in handing a glass of water to her niece, the surprise might have proved too much for her. The salutations of Denbigh were returned by the different members of the family with a cordiality that must have told him how much he was valued by all its branches ; and after briefly informing them that his interview was over, and that he had thrown himself into a chaise and traveled post until he had rejoined them, he took his seat by Mr. Benfield, who received him with a marked preference, exceeding that which he had shown to any man who had ever entered his doors, Lord Gosford himself not excepted.

Peter removed from his station behind his master's chair to one where he could face the new comers ; and after wiping his eyes until they filled so rapidly with water that at last he was noticed by the delighted John to put on the identical goggles which his care had provided for Denbigh in his illness, his laugh drew the attention of the rest to the honest steward, and when Denbigh was told this was Mr. Benfield's ambassador to the hall, he rose from his chair, and taking the old man by the hand, kindly thanked him for his thoughtful consideration for his weak eyes.

Peter took the offered hand in both his own, and after making one or two unsuccessful efforts to speak, he uttered, "Thank you, thank you ! may Heaven bless you," and burst into tears. This stopped the laugh, and John followed the steward from the room, while his master exclaimed, wiping his eyes, "Kind and condescending ; just such another as my old friend, the Earl of Gosford."

CHAPTER XXIII.

At the appointed hour the carriage of Mrs. Wilson was ready to convey herself and niece to the cottage of Mrs. Fitzgerald. John was left behind under the pretense of keeping Denbigh company in his morning avocations, but really because Mrs. Wilson doubted the propriety of his becoming a visiting acquaintance at the house, tenanted as the cottage was represented to be. John was too fond of his friend to make any serious objections, and was satisfied for the present by sending his compliments, and requesting his sister to ask permission for him to call in one of his morning excursions in order to pay his personal respects.

They found the cottage a beautiful and genteel, though a very small and retired dwelling, almost hid by the trees and shrubs which surrounded it, and its mistress in its little veranda, expecting the arrival of Emily. Mrs. Fitzgerald was a Spaniard, under twenty, of a melancholy, yet highly interesting countenance ; her manners were soft and retiring, but evidently bore the impression of good company, if not of high life. She was extremely pleased with this renewal of attention on the part of Emily, and expressed her gratitude to both ladies for their kindness in seeking her out in her solitude. She presented her more matronly companion to them, by the name of Donna Lorenza ; and as nothing but good feeling prevailed, and useless ceremony was banished, the little party were soon ou terms of friendly intercourse. The young widow (for such her dress indicated her to be) did the honors of her house with graceful ease, and conducted her visitors into her little grounds, which, together with the cottage, gave evident proofs of the taste and elegance of its occupant. The establishment she supported she represented as very small ; two women and an aged man servant, with occasionally a laborer for the garden and shrubbery.

They never visited ; it was a resolution she had made on fixing her residence here, but if Mrs. Wilson and Miss Moseley would forgive the rudeness of not returning their call, nothing would give her more satisfaction than a frequent renewal of their visits. Mrs. Wilson took so deep an interest in the misfortunes of this young female, and was so much pleased with the modest resignation of her manner, that it required little persuasion on the part of the recluse to obtain a promise of soon repeating her visit. Emily mentioned the request of John, and Mrs. Fitzgerald received it with a mournful smile, as she replied that Mr. Moseley had laid her under such an obligation in their first interview, she could not deny herself the pleasure of again thanking him for it; but she must be excused if she desired they would limit their attendants to him, as there was but one gentleman in England whose visits she admitted, and it was seldom indeed he called; he had seen her but once since she had resided in Norfolk.

After giving a promise not to suffer any one else to accompany them, and promising an early call again, our ladies returned to Benfield Lodge in season to dress for dinner. On entering the drawing-room they found the elegant person of Colonel Egerton leaning on the back of Jane's chair. He had arrived during their absence, and immediately sought the baronet's family. His reception, if not as warm as that given to Denbigh, was cordial from all but the master of the house; and even he was in such spirits by the company around him, and the prospects of Emily's marriage (which he considered as settled), that he forced himself to an appearance of good-will he did not feel. Colonel Egerton was either deceived by his manner, or too much a man of the world to discover his suspicion, and everything in consequence was very harmoniously, if not sincerely, conducted between them.

Lady Moseley was completely happy. If she had the least doubts before, as to the intentions of Egerton, they were now removed. His journey to that unfashionable watering-place was owing to his passion; and however she might at times have doubted as to Sir Edgar's heir, Denbigh she thought a man of too little consequence in the world, to make it possible he would neglect to profit by his situation in the family of Sir Edward Moseley. She was satisfied with both connections. Mr. Benfield had told her General Sir Frederick Denbigh was nearly allied to the Duke of Derwent, and Denbigh had said the general was his grandfather. Wealth she knew Emily would possess from both her uncle and aunt; and the services of the gentleman had their due weight upon the feelings of the affection-

ate mother. The greatest of her maternal anxieties was removed, and she looked forward to the peaceful enjoyment of the remnant of her days in the bosom of her descendents. John, the heir of a baronetcy and 15,000 pounds a year, might suit himself; and Grace Chatterton, she thought, would be likely to prove the future Lady Moseley.

Sir Edward, without entering so deeply into anticipations of the future as his wife, experienced an equal degree of contentment; and it would have been a difficult task to discover in the island a roof, under which there resided at the moment more happy countenances than at Benfield Lodge; for as its master had insisted on Denbigh becoming an inmate, he was obliged to extend his hospitality in an equal degree to Colonel Egerton; indeed, the subject had been fully canvassed between him and Peter the morning of his arrival, and was near being decided against his admission, when the steward, who had picked up all the incidents of the arbor scene from the servants) and of course with many exaggerations), mentioned to his master that the colonel was very active, and that he even contrived to bring water to revive Miss Emmy a great distance, in the hat of Captain Jarvis, which was full of holes, Mr. John having blown it off the head of the captain without hurting a hair, in firing at a woodcock. This mollified the master a little, and he agreed to suspend his decision for further observation. At dinner, the colonel happening to admire the really handsome face of Lord Gosford, as delineated by Sir Joshua Reynolds, which graced the dining-room of Benfield Lodge, its master, in a moment of unusual kindness, gave the invitation; it was politely accepted, and the colonel at once domesticated.

The face of John Moseley alone, at times, exhibited evidences of care and thought, and at such moments it might be a subject of doubt whether he thought the most of Grace Chatterton or her mother; if the latter, the former was sure to lose ground in his estimation; a serious misfortune to John, not to be able to love Grace without alloy. His letters from her brother mentioned his being still at Denbigh Castle, in Westmoreland, the seat of his friend the Duke of Derwent; and John thought one or two of his encomiums on Lady Harriet Denbigh, the sister of his grace, augured that the unkindness of Emily might in time be forgotten. The dowager and her daughters were at the seat of a maiden aunt in Yorkshire, where, as John knew no male animal was allowed admittance, he was tolerably easy at the disposition of things. Nothing but legacy-hunting he knew would induce the dowager to submit to such a banishment from the other sex; but that was so preferable to husband-hunting he was satisfied. "I wish," said John, mentally, as he finished the perusal of his letter, "mother Chatterton would get married herself, and she might let Kate and Grace manage for themselves. Kate would do very well, I daresay, and how would Grace make out!" John sighed, and whistled for Dido and Rover.

In the manners of Colonel Egerton there was the same general disposition to please, and the same unremitted attention to the wishes and amusements of Jane. They had renewed their poetical investigations, and Jane eagerly encouraged a taste which afforded her delicacy some little coloring for the indulgence of an association different from the real truth, and which, in her estimation, was necessary to her happiness. Mrs. Wilson thought the distance between the two suitors for the favor of her nieces was, if anything, increased by their short separation, and particularly noticed on the part of the colonel an aversion to Denbigh that at times painfully alarmed, by exciting apprehensions for the future happiness of the precious treasure she had prepared herself to yield to his solicitations, whenever properly proffered. In the intercourse between Emily and her preserver, as there was nothing to condemn, so there was much to admire. The attentions of Denbigh were pointed, although less exclusive than those of the colonel: and the aunt was pleased to observe that if the manners of Egerton had more of the gloss of life, those of Denbigh were certainly distinguished by a more finished delicacy and propriety.

The one appeared the influence of custom and association, with a tincture of artifice; the other, benevolence, with a just perception of what was due to others, and with an air of sincerity, when speaking of sentiments and principles, that was particularly pleasing to the watchful widow. At times, however, she could not but observe an air of restraint, if not of awkwardness, about him that was a little surprising. It was most observable in mixed society, and once or twice her imagination pictured his sensations into something like alarm. These unpleasant interruptions to her admiration were soon forgotten in her just appreciation of the more solid parts of his character, which appeared literally to be unexceptionable; and when momentary uneasiness would steal over her, the remembrance of the opinion of Dr. Ives, his behavior with Jar-

vis, his charity, and chiefly his devotion to her niece, would not fail to drive the disagreeable thoughts from her mind. Emily herself moved about, the image of joy and innocence. If Denbigh were near her, she was happy; if absent, she suffered no uneasiness. Her feelings were so ardent, and yet so pure, that jealousy had no admission.

Perhaps no circumstances existed to excite this usual attendant of the passion; but as the heart of Emily was more enchained than her imagination, her affections were not of the restless nature of ordinary attachments, though more dangerous to her peace of mind in the event of an unfortunate issue. With Denbigh she never walked or rode alone. He had never made the request, and her delicacy would have shrunk from such an open manifestation of her preference; but he read to her and her aunt; he accompanied them in their little excursions; and once or twice John noticed that she took the offered hand of Denbigh to assist her over any little impediment in their course, instead of her usual unobtrusive custom of taking his arm on such occasions. "Well, Miss Emily," thought John, "you appear to have chosen another favorite," on her doing this three times in succession in one of their walks. "How strange it is women will quit their natural friends for a face they have hardly seen." John forgot his own—"There is no danger, dear Grace," when his sister was almost dead with apprehension.

But John loved Emily too well to witness her preference of another with satisfaction, even though Denbigh was the favorite; a feeling which soon wore away, however, by dint of custom and reflection. Mr. Benfield had taken it into his head that if the wedding of Emily could be solemnized while the family was at the lodge, it would render him the happiest of men; and how to compass this object, was the occupation of a whole morning's contemplation. Happily for Emily's blushes, the old gentleman harbored the most fastidious notions of female delicacy, and never in conversation made the most distant allusion to the expected connection. He, therefore, in conformity with these feelings, could do nothing openly; all must be the effect of management; and as he thought Peter one of the best contrivers in the world, to his ingenuity he determined to refer the arrangement. The bell rang—"Send Johnson to me, David."

In a few minutes the drab coat and blue yarn stockings entered his dressing-room with the body of Mr. Peter Johnson snugly cased within them.

"Peter," commenced Mr. Benfield, pointing kindly to a chair, which the steward respectfully declined, "I suppose you know that Mr. Denbigh, the grandson of General Denbigh, who was in Parliament with me, is about to marry my little Emmy?"

Peter smiled, as he bowed an assent.

"Now, Peter, a wedding would, of all things, make me most happy; that is, to have it here in the lodge. It would remind me so much of the marriage of Lord Gosford, and the bridesmaids. I wish your opinion how to bring it about before they leave us. Sir Edward and Anne decline interfering, and Mrs. Wilson I am afraid to speak to on the subject."

Peter was not a little alarmed by this sudden requisition on his inventive faculties, especially as a lady was in the case; but, as he prided himself on serving his master, and loved the hilarity of a wedding in his heart, he cogitated for some time in silence, when, having thought a preliminary question or two necessary, he broke it with saying—

"Everything, I suppose, master, is settled between the young people?"

"Everything, I take it, Peter."

"And Sir Edward and my lady?"

"Willing; perfectly willing."

"And Madam Wilson, sir?"

"Willing, Peter, willing."

"And Mr. John and Miss Jane?"

"All willing; the whole family is willing, to the best of my belief."

"There is the Rev. Mr. Ives and Mrs. Ives, master?"

"They wish it, I know. Don't you think they wish others as happy as themselves, Peter?"

"No doubt they do, master. Well, then, as everybody is willing, and the young people agreeable, the only thing to be done, sir, is—"

"Is what, Peter?" exclaimed his impatient master, observing him to hesitate.

"Why, sir, to send for the priest, I take it."

"Pshaw! Peter Johnson, I know that myself," replied the dissatisfied old man. "Cannot you help me to a better plan?"

"Why, master." said Peter, "I would have done as well for Miss Emmy and your honor as I would have done for myself. Now, sir, when I courted Patty Steele, your honor, in the year of our Lord one thousand seven hundred and sixty-five, I should have been married but for one difficulty, which your honor says is removed in the case of Miss Emmy."

"What was that, Peter?" asked his master, in a tender tone.

"She wasn't willing, sir."

"Very well, poor Peter," replied Mr. Benfield, mildly, "you may go." And the steward, bowing low, withdrew.

The similarity of their fortunes in love was a strong link in the sympathies which bound the master and man together, and the former never failed to be softened by an allusion to Patty. The want of tact in the man, on the present occasion, after much reflection, was attributed by his master to the fact that Peter had never sat in Parliament.

CHAPTER XXIV.

MRS. WILSON and Emily, in the fortnight they had been at Benfield Lodge, paid frequent and long visits to the cottage; and each succeeding interview left a more favorable impression of the character of its mistress, and a greater certainty that she was unfortunate. The latter, however, alluded very slightly to her situation or former life; she was a Protestant, to the great surprise of Mrs. Wilson; and one that misery had made nearly acquainted with the religion she professed. Their conversations chiefly turned on the customs of her own, as contrasted with those of her adopted country, or in a pleasant exchange of opinions, which the ladies possessed in complete unison. One morning John had accompanied them and been admitted; Mrs. Fitzgerald receiving him with the frankness of an old acquaintance, though with the reserve of a Spanish lady. His visits were permitted under the direction of his aunt, but no others of the gentlemen were included among her guests. Mrs. Wilson had casually mentioned, in the absence of her niece, the interposition of Denbigh between her and death; and Mrs. Fitzgerald was so much pleased at the noble conduct of the gentleman as to express a desire to see him; but the impressions of the moment appeared to have died away, as nothing more was said by either lady on the subject, and was apparently forgotten.

Mrs. Fitzgerald was found one morning weeping over a letter she held in her hand, and the Donna Lorenzo was endeavoring to console her. The situation of this latter lady was somewhat doubtful; she appeared neither wholly a friend nor a menial. In the manners of the two there was a striking difference; although the Donna was not vulgar, she was far from possessing the polish of her more juvenile friend, and Mrs. Wilson considered her to be in a station between that of a housekeeper and that of a companion. After hoping that no unpleasant intelligence occasioned the distress they witnessed, the ladies were delicately about to take their leave, when Mrs. Fitzgerald entreated them to remain.

"Your kind attention to me, dear madam, and the goodness of Miss Moseley, give you a claim to know more of the unfortunate being your sympathy has so greatly assisted to attain her peace of mind. This letter is from the gentleman of whom you have heard me speak, as once visiting me, and though it has struck me with unusual force, it contains no more than I expected to hear, perhaps no more than I deserve to hear."

"I hope your friend has not been unnecessarily harsh : severity is not the best way, always, of effecting repentence, and I feel certain that you, my young friend, can have been guilty of no offense that does not rather require gentle than stern reproof," said Mrs. Wilson.

"I thank you, dear madam, for your indulgent opinion of me, but although I have suffered much, I am willing to confess it is a merited punishment; you are, however, mistaken as to the source of my present sorrow. Lord Pendennyss is the cause of grief, I believe, to no one, much less to me."

"Lord Pendennyss!" exclaimed Emily, in surprise, unconsciously looking at her aunt.

"Pendennyss!" reiterated Mrs. Wilson, with animation; "and he is your friend, too?"

"Yes, madam; to his lordship I owe everything — honor — comfort—religion— and even life itself."

Mrs. Wilson's cheek glowed with an unusual color at this discovery of another act of benevolence and virtue, in a young nobleman whose character she had so long admired, and whose person she had in vain wished to meet.

"You know the earl, then?" inquired Mrs. Fitzgerald.

"By reputation, only, my dear," said Mrs. Wilson; "but that is enough to convince me a friend of his must be a worthy character, if anything were wanting to make us your friends."

The conversation was continued for some time, Mrs. Fitzgerald saying she did not feel equal just then to the undertaking, but the next day, if they would honor her with another call, she would make them acquainted with the incidents of her life, and the reasons she had for speaking in such terms of Lord Pendennyss. The promise to see her was cheer-

fully made by Mrs. Wilson, and her confidence accepted; not from a desire to gratify an idle curiosity, but a belief that it was necessary to probe a wound to cure it ; and a correct opinion, that she would be a better adviser for a young and lovely woman than even Pendennyss; for the Donna Lorenza she could hardly consider in a capacity to offer advice, much less dictation. They then took their leave, and Emily, during their ride, broke the silence with exclaiming—

"Wherever we hear of Lord Pendennyss, aunt, we hear of him favorably."

"A certain sign, my dear, he is deserving of it. There is hardly any man who has not his enemies, and those are seldom just ; but we have met with none of the earl's yet."

"Fifty thousand a year will make many friends," observed Emily, shaking her head.

"Doubtless, my love, or as many enemies; but honor, life, and religion, my child, are debts not owing to money—in this country, at least."

To this remark Emily assented ; and after expressing her own admiration of the character of the young nobleman she dropped into a reverie. How many of his virtues she identified with the person of Mr. Denbigh it is not, just now, our task to enumerate ; but judges of human nature may easily determine, and that too without having sat in the Parliament of this realm.

The morning this conversation occurred at the cottage, Mr. and Mrs. Jarvis, with their daughters, made their unexpected appearance at L——. The arrival of a post-chaise and four, with a gig, was an event soon circulated through the little village, and the names of its owners reached the lodge just as Jane had allowed herself to be persuaded by the colonel to take her first walk with him unaccompanied by a third person. Walking is much more propitious to declarations than riding; and whether it was premeditated on the part of the colonel or not, or whether he was afraid that Mrs. Jarvis or some one else would interfere, he availed himself of this opportunity, and had hardly got out of hearing of her brother and Denbigh before he made Jane an explicit offer of his hand. The surprise was so great that some time elapsed before the distressed girl could reply. This she, however, at length did, but incoherently , she referred him to her parents, as the arbiters of her fate, well knowing that her wishes had long been those of her father and mother.

With this the colonel was obliged to be

satisfied for the present. But their walk had not ended, before he gradually drew from the confiding girl an acknowledgment that, should her parents decline his offer, she would be very little less miserable than himself; indeed, the most tenacious lover might have been content with the proofs of regard that Jane, unused to control her feelings, allowed herself to manifest on this occasion. Egerton was in raptures; a life devoted to her would never half repay her condescension; and as their confidence increased with their walk, Jane re-entered the lodge with a degree of happiness in her heart she had never before experienced. The much dreaded declaration—her own distressing acknowledgments, were made, and nothing further remained but to live and be happy. She flew into the arms of her mother, and, hiding her blushes in her bosom, acquainted her with the colonel's offer and her own wishes. Lady Moseley, who was prepared for such a communication, and had rather wondered at its tardiness, kissed her daughter affectionately, as she promised to speak to her father, and to obtain his approbation.

"But," she added, with a degree of formality and caution which had better preceded than have followed the courtship, "we must make the usual inquiries, my child, into the fitness of Colonel Egerton as a husband for our daughter. Once assured of that, you have nothing to fear."

The baronet was requested to grant an audience to Colonel Egerton, who now appeared as determined to expedite things, as he had been dilatory before. On meeting Sir Edward, he made known his pretensions and hopes. The father, who had been previously notified by his wife of what was forthcoming, gave a general answer, similar to the speech of the mother, and the colonel bowed in acquiescence.

In the evening, the Jarvis family favored the inhabitants of the lodge with a visit, and Mrs. Wilson was struck with the singularity of their reception of the colonel. Miss Jarvis, especially, was rude to both him and Jane, and it struck all who witnessed it as a burst of jealous feeling for disappointed hopes; but to no one, excepting Mrs. Wilson, did it occur that the conduct of the gentleman could be at all implicated in the transaction. Mr. Benfield was happy to see under his roof again the best of the trio of Jarvises he had known, and something like sociability prevailed. There was to be a ball, Miss Jarvis remarked, at L——, the following day, which would help to enliven the scene a little, especially as there were a couple

of frigates at anchor, a few miles off, and the officers were expected to join the party. This intelligence had but little effect on the ladies of the Moseley family; yet, as their uncle desired that, out of respect to his neighbors, if invited, they would go, they cheerfully assented. During the evening, Mrs. Wilson observed Egerton in familiar conversation with Miss Jarvis; and as she had been notified of his situation with respect to Jane, she determined to watch narrowly into the causes of so singular a change of deportment in the young lady. Mrs. Jarvis retained her respect for the colonel in full force, and called out to him across the room, a few minutes before she departed—

"Well, colonel, I am happy to tell you I have heard very lately from your uncle, Sir Edgar."

"Indeed, madam!" replied the colonel, starting. "He was well, I hope?"

"Very well, the day before yesterday. His neighbor, old Mr. Holt, is a lodger in the same house with us at L——; and as I thought you would like to hear, I made particular inquiries about the baronet." The word baronet was pronounced with emphasis and a look of triumph, as if it would say, you see *we* have baronets as well as you. As no answer was made by Egerton, excepting an acknowledging bow, the merchant and his family departed.

"Well, John," cried Emily, with a smile, "we have heard more good to-day of our trusty and well-beloved cousin, the Earl of Pendennyss."

"Indeed!" exclaimed her brother. "You must keep Emily for his lordship, positively, aunt: she is almost as great an admirer of him as yourself."

"I apprehended it is necessary she should be quite as much so, to become his wife," said Mrs. Wilson.

"Really," said Emily, more gravely, "if all one hears of him be true, or even half, it would be no difficult task to admire him."

Denbigh was standing leaning on the back of a chair, in a situation where he could view the animated countenance of Emily as she spoke, and Mrs. Wilson noticed an uneasiness and a changing of color in him that appeared uncommon from so trifling a cause. Is it possible, she thought, Denbigh can harbor so mean a passion as envy? He walked away, as if unwilling to hear more, and appeared much engrossed with his own reflections for the remainder of the evening. There were moments of doubting which crossed the mind of Mrs. Wilson with a keenness of apprehension proportionate to her deep interest in Emily, with respect to certain traits in the character of Denbigh; and this, what she thought a display of unworthy feeling, was one of them. In the course of the evening, the cards for the expected ball arrived, and were accepted. As this new arrangement for the morrow interfered with the intended visit of Mrs. Fitzgerald, a servant was sent with a note of explanation in the morning, and a request that on the following day the promised communication might be made. To this arrangement the recluse assented, and Emily prepared for the ball with a melancholy recollection of the consequences which grew out of the last she had attended—melancholy at the fate of Digby, and pleasure at the principles manifested by Denbigh, on the occasion. The latter, however, with a smile, excused himself from being of the party, telling Emily he was so awkward that he feared some unpleasant consequences to himself or his friends would arise from his inadvertencies, did he venture again with her into such an assemby.

Emily sighed gently, as she entered the carriage of her aunt early in the afternoon, leaving Denbigh in the door of the lodge, and Egerton absent on the execution of some business; the former to amuse himself as he could until the following morning, and the latter to join them in the dance in the evening.

The arrangement included an excursion on the water, attended by the bands from the frigates, a collation, and in the evening a ball. One of the vessels was commanded by a Lord Henry Stapleton, a fine young man, who, struck with the beauty and appearance of the sisters, sought an introduction to the baronet's family, and engaged the hand of Emily for the first dance. His frank and gentlemanlike deportment was pleasing to his new acquaintances; the more so, as it was peculiarly suited to their situation, at the moment. Mrs. Wilson was in unusual spirits, and maintained an animated conversation with the young sailor, in the course of which he spoke of his cruising on the coast of Spain, and by accident he mentioned his having carried out to that country, upon one occasion, Lord Pendennyss. This was common ground between them, and Lord Henry was as enthusiastic in his praises of the earl as Mrs. Wilson's partiality could desire. He also knew Colonel Egerton slightly, and expressed his pleasure, in polite terms, when they met in the evening in the ball-room, at being able to renew his acquaintance.

The evening passed off as such evenings generally do — in gayety, listlessness, dancing, gaping, and heart-burnings, according to the dispositions and good or evil fortune of the several individuals who compose the assembly. Mrs. Wilson, while her nieces were dancing, moved her seat to be near a window, and found herself in the vicinity of two elderly gentlemen, who were commenting on the company. After making several commonplace remarks, one of them inquired of the other, " Who is that military gentleman among the naval beaux, Holt ? "

" That is the hopeful nephew of my friend and neighbor, Sir Edgar Egerton; he is here dancing and misspending his time and money, when I know Sir Edgar gave him a thousand pounds six months ago, on express condition he should not leave the regiment or take a card in his hand for a twelvemonth."

" He plays, then ? "

" Sadly ; he is, on the whole, a very bad young man."

As they changed their topics, Mrs. Wilson joined her sister, dreadfully shocked at this intimation of the vices of a man so near an alliance with her brother's child. She was thankful it was not too late to avert part of the evil, and determined to acquaint Sir Edward, at once, with what she had heard, in order that an investigation might establish the colonel's innocence or guilt.

CHAPTER XXV.

THEY returned to the lodge at an early hour, and Mrs. Wilson, after meditating upon the course she ought to take, resolved to have a conversation with her brother that evening after supper. Accordingly, as they were among the last to retire, she mentioned her wish to detain him, and when left by themselves, the baronet taking his seat by her on a sofa, she commenced as follows, willing to avoid her unpleasant information until the last moment.

" I wished to say something to you, brother, relating to my charge ; you have, no doubt, observed the attentions of Mr. Denbigh to Emily ? "

" Certainly, sister, and with great pleasure ; you must not suppose I wish to interfere with the authority I have so freely relinquished to you, Charlotte, when I inquire if Emily favors his views or not ? "

" Neither Emily nor I, my dear brother, wish ever to question your right, not only to inquire into, but to control the conduct of your child ;—she is yours, Edward, by a tie nothing can break, and we both love you too much to wish it. There is nothing you may be more certain of, than that, without the approbation of her parents, Emily would accept of no offer, however splendid or agreeable to her own wishes."

"Nay, sister, I would not wish unduly to influence my child in an affair of so much importance to herself; but my interest in Denbigh is little short of that I feel for my daughter."

"I trust," continued Mrs. Wilson, "Emily is too deeply impressed with her duty to forget the impressive mandate, 'to honor her father and mother': yes, Sir Edward, I am mistaken if she would not relinquish the dearest object of her affections, at your request; and at the same time, I am persuaded she would, under no circumstances, approach the altar with a man she did not both love and esteem."

The baronet did not appear exactly to understand his sister's distinction, as he observed, "I am not sure I rightly comprehend the difference you make, Charlotte."

"Only, brother, that she would feel a promise made at the altar to love a man she felt averse to, or honor one she could not esteem, as a breach of a duty paramount to all earthly considerations," replied his sister: "but to answer your question—Denbigh has never offered, and when he does, I do not think he will be refused."

"Refused!" cried the baronet, "I sincerely hope not; I wish, with all my heart, they were married already."

"Emily is very young," said Mrs. Wilson, "and need not hurry; I was in hopes she would remain single a few years longer."

"Well," said the baronet, "you and Lady Moseley, sister, have different notions on the subject of marrying the girls."

Mrs. Wilson replied, with a good humored smile, "You have made Anne so good a husband, Ned, that she forgets there are any bad ones in the world; *my* greatest anxiety is that the husband of my niece may be a Christian; indeed, I know not how I can reconcile it to my conscience, as a Christian myself, to omit this important qualification."

"I am sure, Charlotte, both Denbigh and Egerton appear to have a great respect for religion; they are punctual at church, and very attentive to the service;" Mrs. Wilson smiled as he proceeded, "but religion may come after marriage."

"Yes, brother, and I know it may not come at all; no really pious woman can be happy without her husband is in what she deems the road to future happiness himself; and it is idle—it is worse—it is almost impious to marry with a view to reform a husband; indeed, she greatly endangers her own safety thereby; for few of us, I believe, but find the temptation to err as much as we can contend with, without calling in the aid of example against us, in an object we love; indeed, it appears to me the life of such a woman must be a struggle between conflicting duties."

"Why," said the baronet, "if your plan were generally adopted, I am afraid it would give a deadly blow to matrimony."

"I have nothing to do with generals, brother; I am acting for individual happiness, and discharging individual duties; at the same time, I cannot agree with you in its effects on the community. I think no man who dispassionately examines the subject, will be other than a Christian; and, rather than remain bachelors, they would take even that trouble; if the strife of our sex were less for a husband, wives would increase in value."

"But how is it, Charlotte," said the baronet, pleasantly, "your sex do not use your power, and reform the age?"

"The work of reformation, Sir Edward," replied his sister, gravely, "is an arduous one, indeed, and I despair of seeing it general in my day; but, much, very much, might be done toward it, if those who have the guidance of youth would take that trouble with their pupils that good faith requires of them, to discharge the minor duties of life."

"Women ought to marry," observed the baronet, musing.

"Marriage is certainly the natural and most desirable state for a woman, but how few are they who, having entered it, know how to discharge its duties; more particularly those of a mother! On the subject of marrying our daughters, for instance, instead of qualifying them to make a proper choice, they are generally left to pick up such principles and opinions as they may come at, as it were, by chance. It is true, if the parent be a Christian in name, certain of the externals of religion are observed; but what are these, if not enforced by a consistent example in the instructor."

"Useful precepts are seldom lost, I believe, sister," said Sir Edward, with confidence.

"Always useful, my dear brother; but young people are more observant than we are apt to imagine, and are wonderfully ingenious in devising excuses to themselves for their conduct. I have often heard it offered as an apology, that father and mother knew it, or perhaps did it, and therefore it could not be wrong: association is all important to a child."

"I believe no family of consequence admits of improper associates within my knowledge," said the baronet.

Mrs. Wilson smiled as she answered, "I am sure I hope not, Edward; but are the qualifications we require in companions for our daughters, always such as are most reconcilable with our good sense or our consciences? A single communication with an objectionable character is a precedent, if known and unobserved, which will be offered to excuse acquaintances with worse persons: with the other sex, especially, their acquaintance should be very guarded and select."

"You would make many old maids, sister."

"I doubt it greatly, brother; it would rather bring female society in demand. I often regret that selfishness, cupidity, and the kind of strife which prevails in our sex, on the road to matrimony, have brought celibacy into disrepute. For my part, I never see an old maid, but I am willing to think she is so from choice or principle, and, although not in her proper place, yet serviceable, by keeping alive feelings necessary to exist, that marriages may not become curses instead of blessings."

"A kind of Eddystone, to prevent matrimonial shipwrecks," said the brother, gayly.

"Their lot may be solitary, baronet, and in some measure cheerless, but infinitely preferable to a marriage that may lead them astray from their duties, or give birth to a family which are to be turned on the world—without any religion but form—without any morals but truisms—or without even a conscience which has not been seared by indulgence. I hope that Anne in the performance of her system, will have no cause to regret its failure."

"Clara chose for herself, and has done well, Charlotte; and so, I doubt not, will Jane and Emily; and I confess I think their mother is right."

"It is true," said Mrs. Wilson, "Clara has done well, though under circumstances of but little risk; she might have jumped into your fish-pond, and escaped with life, but the chances are she would drown; nor do I dispute the right of the girls to choose for themselves; but I say the rights extend to requiring us to qualify them to make their choice. I am sorry, Edward, to be the instigator of doubts in your breast of the worth of any one, especially as it may give you pain."

Here Mrs. Wilson took her brother affectionately by the hand, and communicated what she had overheard that evening. Although the impressions of the baronet were not as vivid or as deep as those of his sister, his parental love was too great not to make him extremely uneasy under the intelligence; and after thanking her for her attention to his children's welfare, he kissed her and withdrew. In passing to his own room, he met Egerton, that moment returned from escorting the Jarvis ladies to their lodgings; a task he had undertaken at the request of Jane, as they were without any male attendant. Sir Edward's heart was too full not to seek immediate relief, and as he had strong hopes of the innocence of the colonel, though he could give no reason for his expectation, he returned with him to the parlor, and in a few words acquainted him with the slanders which had been circulated at his expense; begging him by all means to disprove them as soon as possible. The colonel was struck with the circumstance at first, but assured Sir Edward it was entirely untrue. He never played, as he might have noticed, and that Mr. Holt was an ancient enemy of his. He would in the morning take measures to convince Sir Edward that he stood higher in the estimation of his uncle than Mr. Holt had thought proper to state. Much relieved by this explanation, the baronet, forgetting that this heavy charge removed, he only stood where he did before he took time for his inquiries, assured him, that if he could convince him, or rather his sister, he did not gamble, he would receive him as a son-in-law with pleasure. The gentlemen shook hands and parted.

Denbigh had retired to his room early, telling Mr. Benfield he did not feel well, and thus missed the party at supper; and by twelve, silence prevailed in the house.

As usual after a previous day of pleasure, the party were late in assembling on the following, yet Denbigh was the last who made his appearance. Mrs. Wilson thought he threw a look round the room as he entered, which prevented his making his salutations in his usual easy and polished manner. In a few minutes, however, his awkwardness was removed, and they took their seats at the table. At that moment the door of the room was thrown hastily open, and Mr. Jarvis entered abruptly, and with a look bordering on wildness in his eye—"Is she not here?" exclaimed the merchant, scanning the company closely.

"Who?" inquired all in a breath.

"Polly—my daughter—my child," said the merchant, endeavoring to control his feelings; "did she not come here this morning with Colonel Egerton?"

He was answered in the negative, and he briefly explained the cause of his anxiety. The colonel had called very early, and sent her maid up to his daughter who rose immediately. They had quitted the house together, leaving word the Miss Moseleys had sent for the young lady to breakfast, for some particular reason. Such was the latitude allowed by his wife, that nothing was suspected until one of the servants of the house said he had seen Colonel Egerton and a lady drive out of the village that morning in a post-chaise and four.

Then the old gentleman first took the alarm, and he proceeded instantly to the lodge in quest of his daughter. Of the elopement there now remained no doubt, and an examination into the state of the colonel's room, who, it had been thought, was not yet risen, gave assurance of it. Here was at once sad confirmation that the opinion of Mr. Holt was a just one. Although every heart felt for Jane during this dreadful explanation, no eye was turned on her excepting the stolen and anxious glances of her sister; but when all was confirmed, and nothing remained but to reflect or act upon the circumstances, she naturally engrossed the whole attention of her fond parents. Jane had listened in indignation to the commencement of the narrative of Mr. Jarvis, and so firmly was Egerton enshrined in purity within her imagination, that not until it was ascertained that both his servant and his clothes were missing, would she admit a thought injurious to his truth. Then indeed the feelings of Mr. Jarvis, his plain statement corroborated by this testimony, struck her at once as true; and as she rose to leave the room, she fell senseless into the arms of Emily, who, observing her movement and loss of color, had flown to her assistance. Denbigh had drawn the merchant out in vain efforts to appease him, and happily no one witnessed this effect of Jane's passion but her nearest relatives.

She was immediately removed to her own room, and in a short time was in bed with a burning fever. The bursts of her grief were uncontrolled and violent. At times she reproached herself—her friends —Egerton; in short, she was guilty of all the inconsistent sensations that disappointed hopes, accompanied by the consciousness of weakness on our part, seldom fail to give rise to; the presence of her friends was irksome to her, and it was only to the soft and insinuating blandishments of Emily's love that she would at all yield. Perseverance and affection at length prevailed, and as Emily took the opportunity of some refreshments to infuse a strong soporific, Jane lost her consciousness of misery in a temporary repose. In the meantime a more searching inquiry had been able to trace out the manner and direction of the journey of the fugitives.

It appeared the colonel left the lodge immediately after his conversation with Sir Edward; he slept at a tavern, and caused his servant to remove his baggage at daylight; here he had ordered a chaise and horses, and then proceeded, as mentioned, to the lodgings of Mr. Jarvis. What arguments he used with Miss Jarvis to urge her to a sudden flight, remained a secret; but from the remarks of Mrs. Jarvis and Miss Sarah, there was reason to believe that he had induced them to think, from the commencement, that his intentions were single, and Mary Jarvis their object. How he contrived to gloss over his attentions to Jane in such a manner as to deceive those ladies, caused no little surprise; but it was obvious it had been done, and the Moseleys were not without hopes, his situation with Jane would not make the noise in the world such occurrences seldom fail to excite.

In the afternoon a letter was handed to Mr. Jarvis, and by him immediately communicated to the baronet and Denbigh, both of whom he considered as among his best friends. It was from Egerton, and written in a respectful manner; he apologized for his elopement, and excused it on the ground of a wish to avoid the delay of a license or the publishing of bans, as he was in hourly expectation of a summons to his regiment, and contained many promises of making an attentive husband, and an affectionate son. The fugitives were on the road to Scotland, whence they intended immediately to return to London and to wait the commands of their parents. The baronet, in a voice trembling with emotion at the sufferings of his own child, congratulated the merchant that things were no worse; while Denbigh curled his lips as he read the epistle, and thought settlements were a greater inconvenience than the bans—for it was a well-known fact, that a maiden aunt had left the Jarvises twenty thousand pounds between them.

CHAPTER XXVI.

ALTHOUGH the affections of Jane had sustained a heavy blow, her pride had received a greater, and no persuasions of her mother or sister could induce her to leave her room. She talked little, but once or twice she yielded to the affectionate attentions of Emily, and poured out her sorrows into the bosom of her sister. At such moments she would declare her intention of never appearing in the world again. One of these paroxysms of sorrow was witnessed by her mother, and, for the first time, self-reproach mingled in the grief of the matron. Had she trusted less to appearances and to the opinions of indifferent and ill-judging acquaintances, her daughter might have been apprised in season of the character of the man who had stolen her affections. To a direct exhibition of misery Lady Moseley was always sensible, and, for the moment, she became alive to its causes and consequences ; but a timely and judicious safeguard against future moral evils was a forecast neither her inactivity of mind nor abilities were equal to.

We shall leave Jane to brood over her lover's misconduct, while we regret she is without the consolation alone able to bear her up against the misfortunes of life, and return to the other personages of our history.

The visit of Mrs. Fitzgerald had been postponed in consequence of Jane's indisposition ; but a week after the colonel's departure, Mrs. Wilson thought, as Jane had consented to leave her room, and Emily really began to look pale from her confinement by the side of a sick bed, she would redeem the pledge she had given the recluse on the following morning. They found the ladies at the cottage happy to see them, and anxious to hear of the health of Jane, of whose illness they had been informed by note. After offering her guests some refreshments, Mrs. Fitzgerald, who appeared laboring under a greater melancholy than usual, proceeded to make them acquainted with the incidents of her life.

The daughter of an English merchant at Lisbon had fled from the house of her father to the protection of an Irish officer in the service of his Catholic Majesty ; they were united, and the colonel immediately took his bride to Madrid. The offspring of this union were a son and daughter. The former, at an early age, had entered into the service of his king, and had, as usual, been bred in the faith of his ancestors ; but the Señora McCarthy had been educated and yet remained a Protestant, and, contrary to her faith to her husband, secretly instructed her daughter in the same belief. At the age of seventeen, a principal grandee of the court of Charles sought the hand of the general's child. The Conde d'Alzada was a match not to be refused, and they were united in the heartless and formal manner in which marriages are too often entered into, in countries where the customs of society prevent an intercourse between the sexes. The conde never possessed the affections of his wife. Of a stern and unyielding disposition, his harshness repelled her love ; and as she naturally turned her eyes to the home of her childhood, she cherished all those peculiar sentiments she had imbibed from her mother.

Thus, although she appeared to the world a Catholic, she lived in secret a Protestant. Her parents had always used the English language in their family, and she spoke it as fluently as the Spanish. To encourage her recollections of this strong feature, which distinguished the house of her father from the others she entered, she perused closely and constantly those books which the death of her mother placed at her disposal. These were principally Protestant works on religious subjects, and the countess became a strong sectarian, without becoming a Christian. As she was compelled to use the same books in teaching her only child, the Donna Julia, English, the consequences of the original false step of her grandmother were perpetuated in the person of this young lady. In learning English, she also learned to secede from the faith of her father, and entailed upon herself a life of either persecution or hypocrisy. The countess was guilty of the unpardonable error of complaining to their child of the treatment she received from her husband ; and as these conversations were held in English, and were consecrated by the tears of the mother, they made an indelible impression on the youthful mind of Julia, who grew up with the conviction that next to being a Catholic herself, the greatest evil of life was to be the wife of one.

On her attaining her fifteenth year, she had the misfortune (if it could be termed one) to lose her mother, and within the year her father presented to her a nobleman of the vicinity as her future husband. How long the religious faith of Julia would have endured, unsupported by example in others, and assailed by the passions soliciting in behalf of a young and handsome cavalier, it might be difficult to pronounce ; but as her suitor was neither very young, and the reverse of very handsome, it is certain the more he wooed, the more confirmed she became in her heresy, until, in a moment of desperation, and as an only refuge against his solicitations, she candidly avowed her creed. The anger of her father was violent and lasting; she was doomed to a convent, as both a penance for her sins and a means of reformation. Physical resistance was not in her power, but mentally she determined never to yield. Her body was immured, but her mind continued unshaken and rather more settled in her belief, by the aid of those passions which had been excited by injudicious harshness. For two years she continued in her novitiate, obstinately refusing to take the vows of the order, and at the end of that period the situation of her country had called her father and uncle to the field as defenders of the rights of their lawful prince. Perhaps to this it was owing that harsher measures were not adopted in her case.

The war now raged around them in its greatest horrors, until at length a general battle was fought in the neighborhood, and the dormitories of the peaceful nuns were crowded with wounded British officers. Among others of his nation was a Major Fitzgerald, a young man of strikingly handsome countenance and pleasant manners. Chance threw him under the more immediate charge of Julia; his recovery was slow, and for a time doubtful, and as much owing to good nursing as science. The major was grateful, and Julia unhappy as she was beautiful. That love should be the offspring of this association, will excite no surprise. A brigade of British encamping in the vicinity of the convent, the young couple sought its protection from Spanish vengeance and Romish cruelty. They were married by the chaplain of the brigade, and for a month they were happy.

As Napoleon was daily expected in person at the seat of war, his generals were alive to their own interests, if not to that of their master. The body of troops in which Fitzgerald had sought a refuge, being an advanced party of the main army, were surprised and defeated with loss. After doing his duty as a soldier at his post, the major, in endeavoring to secure the retreat of Julia, was intercepted, and they both fell into the hands of the enemy. They were kindly treated, and allowed every indulgence their situation admitted, until a small escort of prisoners was sent to the frontiers; in this they were included, and had proceeded to the neighborhood of the Pyrenees, when, in their turn, the French

were assailed suddenly and entirely routed; and the captive Spaniards, of which the party, with the exception of our young couple, consisted, released. As the French guard made a resistance until overpowered by numbers, an unfortunate ball struck Major Fitzgerald to the earth—he survived but an hour, and died where he fell, on the open field. An English officer, the last of his retiring countrymen, was attracted by the sight of a woman weeping over the body of a fallen man, and approached them. In a few words Fitzgerald explained his situation to this gentleman, and exacted a pledge from him to guard his Julia, in safety, to his mother in England.

The stranger promised everything the dying husband required, and by the time death had closed the eyes of Fitzgerald, he had procured from some peasants a rude conveyance, into which the body, with its almost equally lifeless widow, was placed. The party which intercepted the convoy of prisoners had been out from the British camp on other duty, but its commander hearing of the escort, had pushed rapidly into a country covered by the enemy to effect their rescue; and his service done, he was compelled to make a hasty retreat to insure his own security. To this was owing the indifference which left the major to the care of the Spanish peasantry who had gathered to the spot, and the retreating troops had got several miles on their return, before the widow and her protector commenced their journey. It was impossible to overtake them, and the inhabitants acquainting the gentleman that a body of French dragoons were already harassing their rear, he was compelled to seek another route to the camp. This, with some trouble and no little danger, he at last effected; and the day following the skirmish, Julia found herself lodged in a retired Spanish dwelling, several miles within the advanced posts of the British army. The body of her husband was respectfully interred, and Julia was left to mourn her irretrievable loss, uninterrupted by anything but by the hasty visits of the officer in whose care she had been left—visits which he stole from his more important duties as a soldier.

A month glided by in this melancholy manner, leaving to Mrs. Fitzgerald the only consolation she would receive—her incessant visits to the grave of her husband. The calls of her protector, however, became more frequent; and at length he announced his intended departure for Lisbon, on his way to England. A small covered vehicle, drawn by one horse, was to convey them to the city, at which place he promised to procure her a female attendant, and necessaries for the voyage home. It was no time or place for delicate punctilio; and Julia quietly, but with a heart nearly broken, prepared to submit to the wishes of her late husband. After leaving the dwelling, the manners of her guide sensibly altered; he became complimentary and assiduous to please, but in a way rather to offend than conciliate; until his attentions became so irksome that Julia actually meditated stopping at some of the villages through which they passed, and abandoning the attempt of visiting England entirely. But the desire to comply with Fitzgerald's wish, that she would console his mother for the loss of an only child, and the dread of the anger of her relatives, determined her to persevere until they reached Lisbon, where she was resolved to separate forever from the disagreeable and unknown guardian into whose keeping she had been thrown by chance.

The last day of their weary ride, while passing a wood, the officer so far forgot his own character and Julia's misfortunes as to offer personal indignities. Grown desperate from her situation, Mrs. Fitzgerald sprang from the vehicle, and by her cries attracted the notice of an officer who was riding express on the same road with themselves. He advanced to her assistance at speed, but as he arrived near them, a pistol fired from the carriage brought his horse down, and the treacherous friend was enabled to escape undetected. Julia endeavored to explain her situation to her rescuer; and by her distress and appearance satisfied him at once of its truth. Within a short time, a strong escort of light dragoons came up, and the officer dispatched some for a conveyance, and others in pursuit of that disgrace to the army, the villainous guide: the former was soon obtained, but no tidings could be had of the latter. The carriage was found at a short distance, without the horse and with the baggage of Julia, but with no vestige of its owner. She never knew his name, and either accident or art had so completely enveloped him in mystery, that all efforts to unfold it then were fruitless, and had continued so ever since.

On their arrival in Lisbon, every attention was shown to the disconsolate widow the most refined delicacy could dictate, and every comfort and respect were procured for her which the princely fortune, high rank, and higher character of the Earl of Pendennyss could command. It was this nobleman who, on his way from headquarters with dispatches for England, had been the means of preserving Julia from a fate worse than death. A packet was in waiting for the earl, and they proceeded in her for home. The Donna Lorenza was the widow of a subaltern Spanish officer, who had fallen under the orders and near Pendennyss, and the interest he took in her brave husband had induced him to offer her, on the destruction of her little fortune by the enemy, his protection: for near two years he had maintained her at Lisbon, and now judging her a proper person, had persuaded her to accompany Mrs. Fitzgerald to England.

On the passage, which was very tedious, the earl became more intimately acquainted with the history and character of his young friend, and by a course of gentle yet powerful expedients had drawn her mind gradually from its gloomy contemplation of futurity, to a juster sense of good and evil. The peculiarity of her religious persuasion afforded an introduction to frequent discussions of the real opinions of that church to which Julia had hitherto belonged, although ignorant of all its essential and vital truths. These conversations, which were renewed repeatedly in their intercourse while under the protection of his sister in London, laid the foundations of a faith which left her nothing to hope for but the happy termination of her earthly probation.

The mother of Fitzgerald was dead, and as he had no near relative left, Julia found herself alone in the world. Her husband had taken the precaution to make a will in season; it was properly authenticated, and his widow, by the powerful assistance of Pendennyss, was put in quiet possession of a little independency. It was while waiting the decision of this affair that Mrs. Fitzgerald resided for a short time near Bath. As soon as it was terminated, the earl and his sister had seen her settled in her present abode, and once more since had they visited her; but delicacy had kept him away from the cottage, although his attempts to serve her had been constant, though not always successful. He had, on his return to Spain, seen her father, and interceded with him on her behalf, but in vain. The anger of the Spaniard remained unappeased, and for a season he did not renew his efforts; but having heard that her father was indisposed, Julia had employed the earl once more to make her peace with him, without prevailing. The letter the ladies had found her weeping over was from Pendennyss, informing her of his want of success on that occasion.

The substance of the foregoing narrative was related by Mrs. Fitzgerald to Mrs. Wilson, who repeated it to Emily in their ride home. The compassion of both ladies was strongly moved in behalf of the young widow; yet Mrs. Wilson did not fail to point out to her niece the consequences of deception, and chiefly the misery which had followed from an abandonment of some of the primary duties of life—obedience and respect to her parent. Emily, though keenly alive to all the principles inculcated by her aunt, found so much to be pitied in the fate of her friend, that her failings lost their proper appearance in her eyes, and for a while she could think of nothing but Julia and her misfortunes. Previously to their leaving the cottage, Mrs. Fitzgerald, with glowing cheeks and some hesitation, informed Mrs. Wilson she had yet another important communication to make, but would postpone it until her next visit, which Mrs. Wilson promised should be on the succeeding day.

CHAPTER XXVII.

EMILY threw a look of pleasure on Denbigh as he handed her from the carriage, which would have said, if looks could talk, " In the principles, you have displayed on more than one occasion, I have a pledge of your worth." As he led her into the house, he laughingly informed her that he had that morning received a letter which would make his absence from L—— necessary for a short time, and that he must remonstrate against these long and repeated visits to a cottage where all attendants of the male sex were excluded, as they encroached greatly on his pleasures and improvements, bowing, as he spoke, to Mrs. Wilson. To this Emily replied, gayly, that possibly, if he conducted himself to their satisfaction, they would intercede for his admission. Expressing his pleasure at this promise, as Mrs. Wilson thought, rather awkwardly, Denbigh changed the conversation. At dinner he repeated to the family what he had mentioned to Emily of his departure, and also his expectation of meeting with Lord Chatterton during his journey.

"Have you heard from Chatterton lately, John?" inquired Sir Edward Moseley.

"Yes, sir, to-day; he had left Denbigh Castle a fortnight since, and writes he is to meet his friend, the duke, at Bath."

"Are you connected with his grace, Mr. Denbigh?" asked Lady Moseley.

A smile of indefinite meaning played on the expressive face of Denbigh, as he answered slightly—

"On the side of my father, madam?"

"He has a sister," continued Lady Moseley, willing to know more of Chatterton's friends and Denbigh's relatives.

"He has," was the brief reply.

"Her name is Harriet," observed Mrs. Wilson. Denbigh bowed his assent in silence, and Emily timidly added—

"Lady Harriet Denbigh?"

"Lady Harriet Denbigh—will you do me the favor to take wine?"

The manner of the gentleman during this dialogue had not been in the least unpleasant, but it was peculiar; it prohibited anything further on the subject; and Emily was obliged to be content without knowing who Marian was, or whether her name was to be found in the Denbigh family or not. Emily was not in the least jealous, but she wished to know all to whom her lover was dear.

" Do the dowager and the young ladies accompany Chatterton?" asked Sir Edward as he turned to John, who was eating his fruit in silence.

" Yes, sir—I hope—that is, I believe she will," was the answer.

"She! Who is she, my son?"

" Grace Chatterton," said John, starting from his meditations. "Did you not ask me about Grace, Sir Edward?"

"Not particularly, I believe," said the baronet dryly.

Denbigh again smiled: it was a smile different from any Mrs. Wilson had ever seen on his countenance, and gave an entirely novel expression to his face; it was full of meaning, it was knowing—spoke more of the man of the world than anything she had before noticed in him, and left on her mind one of those vague impressions she was often troubled with, that there was something about Denbigh in character or condition, or both, that was mysterious.

The spirit of Jane was too great to leave her a pining or pensive maiden; yet her feelings had sustained a shock that time alone could cure. She appeared again among her friends; but the consciousness of her expectations with respect to the colonel being known to them, threw around her a hauteur and distance foreign to her natural manner. Emily alone, whose every movement sprang from the spontaneous feelings of her heart, and whose words and actions were influenced by the finest and most affectionate delicacy, such as she was not conscious of possessing herself, won upon the better feelings of her sister so far as to restore between them the usual exchange of kindness and sympathy. But Jane admitted no confidence; she found nothing consoling, nothing solid, to justify her attachment to Egerton; nothing, indeed, excepting such external advantages as she was now ashamed to admit had ever the power over her they in reality had possessed. The marriage of the fugitives in Scotland had been announced; and as the impression that Egerton was to be connected with the Moseleys was destroyed, of course their every-day acquaintances, feeling the restraints removed that such an opinion had once imposed, were free in their comments on his character.

Sir Edward and Lady Moseley were astonished to find how many things to his disadvantage were generally known; that he gambled, intrigued, and was in debt, were no secrets, apparently to anybody but to those who were most interested in knowing the truth; while Mrs. Wilson saw in these facts additional reasons for examining and judging for ourselves; the world uniformly concealing from the party and his friends their honest opinions of his character. Some of these insinuations reached the ears of Jane; her aunt having rightly judged, that the surest way to destroy Egerton's power over the imagination of her niece was to strip him of his fictitious qualities, suggested this expedient to Lady Moseley; and some of their visitors had thought, as the colonel had certainly been attentive to Miss Moseley, it would give her pleasure to know that her rival had not made the most eligible match in the kingdom. The project of Mrs. Wilson succeeded in a great measure; but although Egerton fell, Jane did not find she rose in her own estimation; and her friends wisely concluded that time was the only remedy that could restore her former serenity.

In the morning, Mrs. Wilson, unwilling to have Emily present at a conversation she intended to hold with Denbigh, with a view to satisfy her annoying doubts as to some minor points in his character, after excusing herself to her niece, invited that gentleman to a morning drive. He accepted her invitation cheerfully; and Mrs. Wilson saw, it was only as they drove from the door without Emily, that he betrayed the faintest reluctance to the jaunt. When they had got a short distance from the lodge she acquainted him with her intention of presenting him to Mrs. Fitzgerald, whither she had ordered the coachman to proceed. Denbigh started as she mentioned the name, and after a few moment's silence, desired Mrs. Wilson

to allow him to stop the carriage; he was not very well—was sorry to be so rude—but with her permission, he would alight and return to the house. As he requested in an earnest manner that she would proceed without him, and by no means disappoint her friend, Mrs. Wilson complied; yet, somewhat at a loss to account for his sudden illness, she turned her head to see how the sick man fared, a short time after he had left her, and was not a little surprised to see him talking very composedly with John, who had met him on his way to the fields with his gun. Lovesick, thought Mrs. Wilson, with a smile; and as she rode on she came to the conclusion that, as Denbigh was to leave them soon, Emily would have an important communication to make on her return.

"Well," thought Mrs. Wilson, with a sigh, "if it is to happen, it may as well be done at once."

Mrs. Fitzgerald was expecting her, and appeared rather pleased than otherwise that she had come alone. After some introductory conversation, the ladies withdrew by themselves, and Julia acquainted Mrs. Wilson with a new source of uneasiness. To-day the ladies had promised to visit her, but had been prevented by the arrangements for the ball, the Donna Lorenza had driven to the village to make some purchases, attended as usual by their only man-servant, and Mrs. Fitzgerald was sitting in the little parlor, in momentary expectation of her friends, by herself. The sound of footsteps drew her to the door, which she opened for the admission of the wretch whose treachery to her dying husband's requests had given her so much uneasiness. Horror—fear—surprise—altogether, prevented her from making any alarm at the moment, and she sank into a chair. He stood between her and the door, as he endeavored to draw her into a conversation; he assured her she had nothing to fear; that he loved her, and her alone; that he was about to be married to a daughter of Sir Edward Moseley, but would give her up, fortune, everything, if she would consent to become his wife—that the views of her protector, he doubted not, were dishonorable—that he himself was willing to atone for his former excess of passion, by a life devoted to her.

How much longer he would have gone on, and what further he would have offered, is unknown; for Mrs. Fitzgerald, having recovered herself a little, darted to the bell on the other side of the room. He tried to prevent her ringing it, but was too late; a short struggle followed, when the sound of the footsteps of the maid compelled him to retreat precipitately. Mrs. Fitzgerald added, that his assertion concerning Miss Moseley had given her incredible uneasiness, and prevented her making the communication yesterday; but she understood this morning through her maid, that a Colonel Egerton, who had been supposed to be engaged to one of Sir Edward's daughters, had eloped with another lady. That Egerton was her persecutor, she did not now entertain a doubt; but that it was in the power of Mrs. Wilson probably to make the discovery, as in the struggle between them for the bell, a pocket-book had fallen from the breast-pocket of his coat, and his retreat was too sudden to recover it.

As she put the book into the hands of Mrs. Wilson, she desired she would take means to return it to its owner; its contents might be of value, though she had not thought it correct to examine it. Mrs. Wilson took the book, and as she dropped it into her work-bag, smiled at the Spanish punctilio of her friend in not looking into her prize under the peculiar circumstances.

A few questions as to the place and year of his first attempts, soon convinced her it was Egerton whose unlicensed passions had given so much trouble to Mrs. Fitzgerald. He had served but one campaign in Spain, and in that year, and that division of the army; and surely *his principles* were no restraint upon his conduct. Mrs. Fitzgerald begged the advice of her more experienced friend as to the steps she ought to take; to which the former asked if she had made Lord Pendennyss acquainted with the occurrence. The young widow's cheek glowed as she answered, that, at the same time she felt assured the base insinuation of Egerton was unfounded, it had created a repugnance in her to troubling the earl any more than was necessary in her affairs; and as she kissed the hand of Mrs. Wilson, she added—" besides, your goodness, my dear madam, renders any other adviser unnecessary now." Mrs. Wilson pressed her hand affectionately, and assured her of her good wishes and unaltered esteem. She commended her delicacy, and plainly told the young widow, that however unexceptionable the character of Pendennyss might be, a female friend was the only one a woman in her situation could repose confidence in, without justly incurring the sarcasms of the world.

As Egerton was now married, and would not probably offer, for the present at least, any further molestation to Mrs. Fitzgerald, it was concluded to be unnecessary to take any immediate measures of precaution; and Mrs. Wilson thought the purse of Mr. Jarvis might be made the means of keeping him within proper bounds in future. The merchant was prompt, and not easily intimidated; and the slightest intimation of the truth would, she knew, be sufficient to engage him on their side, heart and hand.

The ladies parted, with a promise of meeting soon again, and an additional interest in each other by the communications of that and the preceding day.

Mrs. Wilson had ridden half the distance between the cottage and the lodge, before it occurred to her they had not absolutely ascertained, by the best means in their possession, the identity of Colonel Egerton with Julia's persecutor. She accordingly took the pocket-book from her bag, and opened it for examination; a couple of letters fell from it into her lap, and conceiving their direction would establish all she wished to know, as they had been read, she turned to the superscription of one of them, and saw—" George Denbigh, Esq.," in the well-known handwriting of Dr. Ives. Mrs. Wilson felt herself overcome to a degree that compelled her to lower a glass of the carriage for air. She sat gazing on the letters until the characters swam before her eyes in undistinguished confusion; and with difficulty she rallied her thoughts to the point necessary for investigation.

As soon as she found herself equal to the task, she examined the letters with the closest scrutiny, and opened them both to be sure there was no mistake. She saw the dates, the " dear George " at the commencements, and the doctor's name subscribed, before she would believe they were real; it was then the truth appeared to break upon her in a flood of light. The aversion of Denbigh to speak of Spain, or of his services in that country —his avoiding Sir Herbert Nicholson, and that gentleman's observations respecting him—Colonel Egerton's and his own manners—his absence from the ball, and startling looks on the following morning, and at different times before and since—his displeasure at the name of Pendennyss on various occasions—and his cheerful acceptance of her invitation to ride until he knew her destination, and singular manner of leaving her—were all accounted for by this dreadful discovery, and Mrs. Wilson found the solution of her doubts rushing on her mind with a force and rapidity that sickened her.

The misfortunes of Mrs. Fitzgerald, the unfortunate issue of the passion of Jane, were trifles in the estimation of Mrs. Wilson compared to the discovery of Denbigh's unworthiness. She revolved in her mind his conduct on various occasions, and wondered how one who could behave so well in common could thus yield to temptation on a particular occasion. His recent attempts, his hypocrisy, however, proved that his villainy was systematic, and she was not weak enough to hide from herself the evidence of his guilt or of its enormity. His interposition between Emily and death she attributed now to natural courage, and perhaps in some measure to chance; but his profound and unvarying reverence for holy things, his consistent charity, his refusing to fight, to what were they owing? And Mrs. Wilson mourned the weakness of human nature, while she acknowledged to herself there might be men, qualified by nature, and even disposed by reason and grace, to prove ornaments to religion and the world, who fell beneath the maddening influence of their besetting sins. The superficial and interested vices of Egerton vanished before these awful and deeply seated offenses of Denbigh, and the correct widow saw at a glance that he was the last man to be intrusted with the happiness of her niece; but how to break this heart-rending discovery to Emily was a new source of uneasiness to her, and the carriage stopped at the door of the lodge ere she had determined on the first step required of her by duty.

Her brother handed her out, and, filled with the dread that Denbigh had availed himself of the opportunity of her absence to press his suit with Emily, she eagerly inquired after him. She was rejoiced to hear he had returned with John for a fowling-piece, and together they had gone in pursuit of game, although she saw in it a convincing proof that a desire to avoid Mrs. Fitzgerald, and not indisposition, had induced him to leave her. As a last alternative, she resolved to have the pocket-book returned to him in her presence, in order to see if he acknowledged it to be his property; and, accordingly, she instructed her own man to hand it to him while at dinner, simply saying he had lost it.

The open and unsuspecting air with which her niece met Denbigh on his return, gave Mrs. Wilson an additional shock, and she could hardly command herself sufficiently to extend the common courtesies of good breeding to Mr. Benfield's guest.

While sitting at the dessert, her servant handed the pocket-book as directed by his mistress, to its owner, saying, "Your pocket-book, I believe, Mr. Denbigh."

Denbigh took the book, and held it in his hand for a moment in surprise, and then fixed his eye keenly on the man, as he inquired where he found it, and how he knew it was his. These interrogatories Francis was not prepared to answer, and in his confusion he naturally turned his eyes on his mistress. Denbigh followed their direction with his own, and in encountering the looks of the lady, he asked in a stammering manner, and with a face of scarlet—

"Am I indebted to you, madam, for my property?"

"No, sir; it was given to me by one who found it, to restore it to you," said Mrs. Wilson, gravely, and the subject was dropped, both appearing willing to say no more. Yet Denbigh was abstracted and absent during the remainder of the repast, and Emily spoke to him once or twice without obtaining an answer. Mrs. Wilson caught his eye several times fixed on her with an inquiring and doubtful expression, that convinced her he was alarmed. If any confirmation of his guilt had been wanting, the consciousness he betrayed during this scene afforded it; and she set seriously about considering the shortest and best method of interrupting his intercourse with Emily, before he had drawn from her an acknowledgment of her love.

CHAPTER XXVIII.

ON withdrawing to her dressing-room after dinner, Mrs. Wilson commenced the disagreeable duty of removing the veil from the eyes of her niece, by recounting to her the substance of Mrs. Fitzgerald's last communication. To the innocence of Emily such persecution could excite no other sensations than surprise and horror; and as her aunt omitted the part concerning the daughter of Sir Edward Moseley, she naturally expressed her wonder as to who the wretch could be.

"Possibly, aunt," she said, with an involuntary shudder, "some of the many gentlemen we have lately seen, and one who has had art enough to conceal his real character from the world."

"Concealment, my love," replied Mrs. Wilson, "would be hardly necessary. Such is the fashionable laxity of morals, that I doubt not many of his associates would laugh at his misconduct, and that he would still continue to pass with the world as an honorable man."

"And ready," cried her niece, "to sacrifice human life, in the defense of any ridiculous punctilio."

"Or," added Mrs. Wilson, striving to draw nearer to the subject, "with a closer veil of hypocrisy, wear even an affectation of principle and moral feeling that would seem to forbid such a departure from duty in favor of custom."

"Oh! no, dear aunt," exclaimed Emily, with glowing cheeks and eyes dancing with pleasure, "he would hardly dare to be so very base. It would be profanity."

Mrs. Wilson sighed heavily as she witnessed that confiding esteem which would not permit her niece even to suspect that an act which in Denbigh had been so warmly applauded, could, even in another, proceed from unworthy motives; and she found it would be necessary to speak in the plainest terms, to awaken her suspicions. Willing, however, to come gradually to the distressing truth, she replied—

"And yet, my dear, men who pride themselves greatly on their morals, nay, even some who wear the mask of religion, and perhaps deceive themselves, admit and practice this very appeal to arms. Such inconsistencies are by no means uncommon. And why then might there not, with equal probability, be others who would revolt at murder, and yet not hesitate being guilty of lesser enormities? This is, in some measure, the case of every man; and it is only to consider killing in unlawful encounters as murder, to make it one in point."

"Hypocrisy is so mean a vice, I should not think a brave man could stoop to it," said Emily, "and Julia admits he was brave."

"And would not a brave man revolt at the cowardice of insulting an unprotected woman? And your hero did that too," replied Mrs. Wilson, bitterly, losing her self-command in indignation.

"Oh! do not call him my hero, I beg of you, dear aunt," said Emily, starting, excited by so extraordinary an allusion, but instantly losing the unpleasant sensation in the delightful consciousness of the superiority of the man on whom she had bestowed her own admiration.

"In fact, my child," continued her aunt, "our natures are guilty of the grossest inconsistencies. The vilest wretch has generally some property on which he values himself, and the most perfect are too often frail on some tender point. Long and tried friendships are those only which can be trusted, and these oftentimes fail."

Emily looked at her aunt in surprise at hearing her utter such unusual sentiments; for Mrs. Wilson, at the same time

she had, by divine assistance, deeply impressed her niece with the frailty of her nature, had withheld the disgusting representation of human vices from her view, as unnecessary to her situation and dangerous to her humility.

After a short pause, Mrs. Wilson continued, "Marriage is a fearful step in a woman, and one she is compelled, in some measure, to adventure her happiness on, without fitting opportunities of judging of the merit of the man she confides in. Jane is an instance in point, but I devoutly hope you are not to be another."

While speaking, Mrs. Wilson had taken the hand of Emily, and by her looks and solemn manner she had succeeded in alarming her niece, although Denbigh was yet furthest from the thoughts of Emily. The aunt reached her a glass of water, and willing to get rid of the hateful subject, she continued, hurriedly, "Did you not notice the pocket-book Francis gave to Mr. Denbigh?" Emily fixed her inquiring eyes on her aunt, as the other added, "It was the one Mrs. Fitzgerald gave me to-day." Something like an indefinite glimpse of the facts crossed the mind of Emily; and as it most obviously involved a separation from Denbigh, she sank lifeless into the extended arms of her aunt. This had been anticipated by Mrs. Wilson, and a timely application of restoratives soon brought her back to a consciousness of misery. Mrs. Wilson, unwilling any one but herself should witness this first burst of grief, succeeded in getting her niece to her own room and in bed. Emily made no lamentations—shed no tears—asked no questions—her eye was fixed, and every faculty appeared oppressed with the load on her heart. Mrs. Wilson knew her situation too well to intrude with unseasonable consolation or useless reflections, but sat patiently by her side, waiting anxiously for the moment she could be of service.

At length the uplifted eyes and clasped hands of Emily assured her she had not forgotten herself or her duty, and she was rewarded for her labor and forbearance by a flood of tears. Emily was now able to listen to a more full statement of the reasons her aunt had for believing in the guilt of Denbigh, and she felt as if her heart was frozen up forever, as the proofs followed each other until they amounted to demonstration. As there was some indication of fever from her agitated state of mind, her aunt required she should remain in her room until morning; and Emily, feeling every way unequal to a meeting with Denbigh, gladly assented. After ringing for her maid to sit in the adjoining room, Mrs. Wilson went below, and announced to the family the indisposition of her charge and her desire to obtain a little sleep. Denbigh looked anxious to inquire after the health of Emily, but there was a restraint on all his actions since the return of his book that persuaded Mrs. Wilson he apprehended that a detection of his conduct had taken place. He did venture to ask when they were to have the pleasure of seeing Miss Moseley again, hoping it would be that evening, as he had fixed the morning for his departure ; and when he learned that Emily had retired for the night, his anxiety was sensibly increased, and he instantly withdrew. Mrs. Wilson was alone in the drawing-room, and about to join her niece, as Denbigh entered it with a letter in his hand ; he approached her with a diffident and constrained manner, and commenced the following dialogue :

"My anxiety and situation will plead my apology for troubling Miss Moseley at this time—may I ask you, madam, to deliver this letter—I hardly dare ask you for your good offices."

Mrs. Wilson took the letter, and coldly replied,

"Certainly, sir ; and I sincerely wish I could be of any real service to you."

"I perceive, madam," said Denbigh, like one that was choking, "I have forfeited your good opinion — that pocket-book—"

"Has made a dreadful discovery," said Mrs. Wilson, shuddering.

"Will not one offense be pardoned, dear madam ?" cried Denbigh, with warmth ; "if you knew my circumstances—the cruel reasons—why—why did I neglect the paternal advice of Dr. Ives?"

"It is not yet too late, sir," said Mrs. Wilson, more mildly, "for your own good ; as for us, your deception—"

"Is unpardonable—I see it—I feel it," cried he, in the accent of despair; "yet Emily—Emily may relent—you will at least give her my letter—anything is better than this suspense."

"You shall have an answer from Emily this evening, and one entirely unbiased by me," said Mrs. Wilson. As she closed the door, she observed Denbigh gazing on her retiring figure with a countenance of despair, that caused a feeling of pity to mingle with her detestation of his vices. On opening the door of Emily's room, Mrs. Wilson found her niece in tears, and her anxiety for her health was alleviated. She knew or hoped, that if she could once call in the assistance of her judgment and piety to lessen her sorrows, Emily, however she might mourn, would become resigned to her situation ; and the first step to attain this was the exercise of those faculties which had been, as it were, momentarily annihilated. Mrs. Wilson kissed her niece with tenderness, as she placed the letter in her hand, and told her she would call for her answer within an hour. Employment, and the necessity of acting, would, she thought, be the surest means of reviving her energies; nor was she disappointed. When the aunt returned for the expected answer, she was informed by the maid in the ante-chamber, that Miss Moseley was up, and had been writing. On entering, Mrs. Wilson stood a moment in admiration of the picture before her. Emily was on her knees, and, by her side, on the carpet, lay the letter and its answer ; her face was hid by her hair, and her hands were closed in the fervent grasp of petition. In a minute she rose, and approaching her aunt with an air of profound resignation, but great steadiness, she handed her the letters, her own unsealed :

"Read them, madam, and if you approve of mine, I will thank you to deliver it."

Her aunt folded her in her arms, until Emily, finding herself yielding under the effects of sympathy, begged to be left alone. On withdrawing to her own room, Mrs. Wilson read the contents of the two letters.

"I rely greatly on the goodness of Miss Moseley to pardon the liberty I am taking, at a moment she is so unfit for such a subject ; but my departure—my feelings—must plead my apology. From the moment of my first acquaintance with you, I have been a cheerful subject to your loveliness and innocence. I feel—I know—I am not deserving of such a blessing ; but since knowing you, as I do, it is impossible not to strive to win you. You have often thanked me as the preserver of your life, but you little knew the deep interest I had in its safety. Without it, my own would be valueless. By accepting my offered hand, you will place me among the happiest, or, by rejecting it, the most wretched of men."

To this note which was unsigned, and evidently written under great agitation of mind, Emily had penned the following reply :

"Sir—It is with much regret that I find myself reduced to the possibility of giving uneasiness to one to whom I am under such heavy obligations. It will never be in my power to accept the honor you have offered me : and I beg you to receive my thanks for the compliment

conveyed in your request, as well as my good wishes for your happiness in future, and fervent prayers that you may be ever found worthy of it. Your humble servant,
"EMILY MOSELEY."

Perfectly satisfied with this answer, Mrs. Wilson went below in order to deliver it at once. She thought it probable, as Denbigh had already sent his baggage to a tavern, preparatory to his intended journey, they would not meet again; and as she felt a strong wish, both on account of Dr. Ives, and out of respect to the services of the young man himself, to conceal his conduct from the world entirely, she was in hopes that his absence might make any disclosure unnecessary. He took the letter from her with a trembling hand, and casting one of his very expressive looks at her, as if to read her thoughts, he withdrew.

Emily had fallen asleep free from fever, and Mrs. Wilson had descended to the supper room, when Mr. Benfield was first struck with the absence of his favorite. An inquiry after Denbigh was instituted, and, while they were waiting his appearance, a servant handed the old man a note.

"From whom?" cried Mr. Benfield, in surprise.

"Mr. Denbigh, sir," said the servant.

"Mr. Denbigh?" exclaimed Mr. Benfield; "no accident, I hope—I remember when Lord Gosford—here, Peter, your eyes are young; read it for me, read it aloud."

As all but Mrs. Wilson were anxiously waiting to know the meaning of this message, and Peter had many preparations to go through before his youthful eyes could make out the contents, John hastily caught the letter out of his hand, saying he would save him the trouble, and, in obedience to his uncle's wishes, he read aloud:

"Mr. Denbigh, being under the necessity of leaving L—— immediately, and, unable to endure the pain of taking leave, avails himself of this means of tendering his warmest thanks to Mr. Benfield, for his hospitality, and to his amiable guests for their many kindnesses. As he contemplates leaving England, he desires to wish them all a long and an affectionate farewell."

"Farewell!" cried Mr. Benfield; "farewell—does he say farewell, John? Here Peter, run—no, you are too old—John, run—bring my hat; I'll go myself to the village—some love quarrel—Emily sick—and Denbigh going away—yes—yes, I did so myself—Lady Juliana, poor dear soul,

she was a long time before she could forget it—but Peter"—Peter had disappeared the instant the letter was finished, and he was quickly followed by John. Sir Edward and Lady Moseley were lost in amazement at this sudden movement of Denbigh, and the breast of each of the affectionate parents were filled with a vague apprehension that the peace of mind of another child was at stake.

Jane felt a renewal of her woes, in the anticipation of something similar for her sister—for the fancy of Jane was yet active, and she did not cease to consider the defection of Egerton a kind of unmerited misfortune and fatality, instead of a probable consequence of want of principle. Like Mr. Benfield, she was in danger of raising an ideal idol, and of spending the remainder of her days in devotion to qualities, rarely if ever found identified with a person that never had existed. The old gentleman was entirely engrossed by a different object; and, having in his own opinion decided there must have been one of those misunderstandings which sometimes had occurred to himself and Lady Juliana, he quietly composed himself to eat his salad at the supper-table; on turning his head, however, in quest of his first glass of wine, he observed Peter standing quietly by the sideboard with the favorite goggles over his eyes. Now Peter was troubled with two kinds of debility about his organs of vision; one was age and natural weakness, while the other proceeded more directly from the heart. His master knew of these facts, and he took the alarm. Again the wine-glass dropped from his nerveless hand, as he said in a trembling tone:

"Peter, I thought you went—"

"Yes, master," said Peter laconically.

"You saw him, Peter—will he return?"

Peter was busily occupied at his glasses, although no one was dry.

"Peter," repeated Mr. Benfield, rising from his seat, "is he coming in time for supper?"

Peter was obliged to reply, and deliberately uncasing his eyes and blowing his nose, he was on the point of opening his mouth as John came into the room, and threw himself into a chair with an air of great vexation, Peter pointed to the young gentleman in silence, and retired.

"John," cried Sir Edward, "where is Denbigh?"

"Gone, sir."

"Gone?"

"Yes, my dear father," said John, "gone without saying good-by to one of us—without telling us whither, or when to return. It was cruel in him—unkind—

I'll never forgive him "—and John, whose feelings were strong, and unusually excited, hid his face between his hands on the table. As he raised his head to reply to a question of Mr. Benfield—of " how he knew he had gone, for the coach did not go until daylight?" Mrs. Wilson saw evident marks of tears. Such proofs of emotion in one like John Moseley gave her the satisfaction of knowing that if she had been deceived, it was by a concurrence of circumstances and a depth of hypocrisy almost exceeding belief; self-reproach added less than common, therefore, to the uneasiness of the moment.

"I saw the innkeeper, uncle," said John, "who told me that Denbigh left there at eight o'clock in a post-chaise and four; but I will go to London in the morning myself." This was no sooner said than it was corroborated by acts, for the young man immediately commenced his preparations for the journey. The family separated that evening with melancholy hearts; and the host and his privy counselor were closeted for half an hour ere they retired to their night's repose. John took his leave of them, and left the lodge for the inn, with his man, in order to be ready for the mail. Mrs. Wilson looked in upon Emily before she withdrew herself, and found her awake, but perfectly calm and composed: she said but little, appearing desirous of avoiding all allusions to Denbigh; and after her aunt had simply acquainted her with his departure, and her resolution to conceal the cause, the subject was dropped.

Mrs. Wilson, on entering her own room, thought deeply on the discoveries of the day; they had interfered with her favorite system of morals, baffled her ablest calculations upon causes and effects, but in no degree had impaired her faith or reliance on Providence. She knew one exception did not destroy a rule: she was certain without principles there was no security for good conduct, and the case of Denbigh proved it. To discover these principles, might be difficult; but was a task imperiously required at her hands, as she believed, ere she yielded the present and future happiness of her pupil to the power of any man.

CHAPTER XXIX.

THE day had not yet dawned, when John Moseley was summoned to take his seat in the mail for London. Three of the places were already occupied, and John was compelled to get a seat for his man on the outside. An intercourse with strangers is particularly irksome to an Englishman, and none appeared disposed, for a long time, to break the silence. The coach had left the little village of L—— far behind it, before any of the rational beings it contained thought it prudent or becoming to bend in the least to the charities of our nature, in a communication with a fellow-creature of whose name or condition he happened to be ignorant. This reserve is unquestionably characteristic of the nation; to what is it owing—modesty? Did not national and deep personal vanity appear at once to refute the assertion, we might enter into an investigation of it. The good opinion of himself in an Englishman is more deeply seated, though less buoyant, than that of his neighbors; in them it is more of manner, in us more of feeling; and the wound inflicted on the self-love of the two is very different.

The Frenchman wonders at its rudeness, but soon forgets the charge; while an Englishman broods over it in silence and mortification. It is said this distinction in character is owing to the different estimation of principles and morals in the two nations. The solidity and purity of our ethics and religious creeds may have given a superior tone to our moral feeling; but has that man a tenable ground to value himself on either, whose respect to sacred things grows out of a respect to himself: on the other hand, is not humility the very foundation of the real Christian? For our part, we should be glad to see this national reserve lessened, if not done entirely away; we believe it is founded in pride and uncharitableness, and could wish to see men thrown accidentally together on the roads of the country, mindful that they are also traveling in company the highway of life, and that the goal of their destination is equally attainable by all.

John Moseley was occupied with thoughts very different from those of any of his fellow-travelers, as they proceeded rapidly on their route; and it was only when roused from his meditations by accidentally coming in contact with the hilt of a sword, that he looked up, and in the glimmerings of the morning's light recognized the person of Lord Henry Stapleton; their eyes met, and—" My Lord,"—"Mr. Moseley,"—were repeated in mutual surprise. John was eminently a social being, and he was happy to find recourse against his gloomy thoughts in the conversation of the dashing young sailor. The frigate of the other had entered the bay the night before, and he was going to town to the wedding of his sister; the coach of his brother the marquis was to meet him about twenty miles from town, and the ship was ordered round to Yarmouth, where he was to rejoin her.

"But how are your lovely sisters, Moseley?" cried the young sailor, in a frank and careless manner. "I should have been half in love with one of them if I had time—and money; both are necessary to marriage nowadays, you know."

"As to time," said John, with a laugh, "I believe that may be dispensed with, though money is certainly a different thing."

"Oh, time, too," replied his lordship. "I have never time enough to do anything as it ought to be done—always hurried—I wish you could recommend to me a lady who would take the trouble off my hands."

"It might be done," said John with a smile, and the image of Kate Chatterton crossed his brain, but it was soon succeeded by that of her more lovely sister. "But how do you manage on board your ship—hurried there, too?"

"Oh! never there," replied the captain, gravely; "that's duty, you know, and everything must be regular, of course; on shore it is a different thing—there I am only a passenger. L—— has a charming society, Mr. Moseley—a week or ten days ago I was shooting, and came to a beautiful cottage about five miles from the village, that was the abode of a much more beautiful woman, a Spaniard, a Mrs. Fitzgerald—I am positively in love with her; so soft, so polished, so modest—"

"How came you acquainted with her?" inquired Moseley, interrupting him in a little surprise.

"Chance, my dear fellow, chance. I was thirsty and approached for a drink of water; she was sitting in the veranda, and being hurried for time, you know, it saved the trouble of introduction. I fancy she is troubled with the same complaint, for she managed to get rid of me in no time, and with a great deal of politeness. I found out her name, however, at the next house."

During this rattling talk, John had fixed his eyes on the face of one of the passengers who sat opposite to him. The stranger appeared to be about fifty years of age, strongly pock-marked, with a stiff military air, and had the dress and exterior of a gentleman. His face was much sunburnt, though naturally very fair; and his dark keen eye was intently fixed on the sailor as he continued his remarks.

"Do you know such a lady, Moseley?"

"Yes," said John, "though very slightly; she is visited by one of my sisters, and—"

"Yourself," cried Lord Henry, with a laugh.

"Myself, once or twice, my lord, certainly," answered John, gravely; "but a lady visited by Emily Moseley and Mrs. Wilson is a proper companion for any one. Mrs. Fitzgerald is very retired in her manner of living, and chance made us acquainted; but not being, like your lordship, in want of time, we have endeavored to cultivate her society, as we found it very agreeable."

The countenance of the stranger underwent several changes during this speech of John's, and at its close his eyes rested on him with a softer expression than generally marked its rigid and compressed muscles. Willing to change a discourse that was growing too particular for a mail coach, John addressed himself to the opposite passengers, while his eye yet dwelt on the face of the military stranger.

"We are likely to have a fine day, gentlemen." The soldier bowed stiffly as he smiled his assent, and the other passenger humbly answered, "Very, Mr. John," in the well-known tones of honest Peter Johnson. Moseley started, as he turned his face for the first time on the lank figure which was modestly compressed into the smallest possible compass in the corner of the coach, in a way not to come in contact with any of his neighbors.

"Johnson," exclaimed John, in astonishment, "you here! Where are you going—to London?"

"To London, Mr. John," replied Peter, with a look of much importance; and then, by way of silencing further interrogatories, he added, "On my master's business, sir."

Both Moseley and Lord Henry examined him closely; the former wondering what could take the steward, at the age of seventy, for the first time in his life, into the vortex of the capital; and the latter in admiration at the figure and equipments of the old man. Peter was in full costume, with the exception of the goggles, and was in reality a subject to be gazed at; but nothing relaxed the muscles or attracted the particular notice of the soldier, who, having regained his set form of countenance, appeared drawn up in himself, waiting patiently for the moment he was expected to act. Nor did he utter more than as many words in the course of the first fifty miles of their journey. His dialect was singular, and such as put his hearers at a loss to determine his country. Lord Henry stared at him every time he spoke, as if to say, what countrymen are you? until at length he suggested to John he was some officer whom the downfall of Bonaparte had driven into retirement.

"Indeed, Moseley," he added, as they were about to resume their carriage after a change of horses, "we must draw him out and see what he thinks of his master now—delicately, you know." The soldier was however, impervious to his lordship's attacks, until the project was finally abandoned in despair. As Peter was much too modest to talk in the presence of Mr. John Moseley and a lord, the young men had most of the discourse to themselves. At a village fifteen miles from London, a fashionable carriage and four, with the coronet of a marquis, was in waiting for Lord Henry. John refused his invitation to take a seat with him to town; for he had traced Denbigh from stage to stage, and was fearful of losing sight of him, unless he persevered in the manner he had commenced. Peter and he accordingly were put down safely at an inn in the Strand, and Moseley hastened to make his inquiries after the object of his pursuit. Such a chaise had arrived an hour before, and the gentleman had ordered his trunk to a neighboring hotel. After obtaining the address and ordering a hackney coach, he hastened to the house; but inquiring for Mr. Denbigh, to his great mortification was told they knew of no such gentleman. John turned away from the person he was speaking to in visible disappointment, when a servant respectfully inquired if the gentleman had not come from L——, in Norfolk, that day. "He had," was the reply. "Then follow me, sir, if you please." They knocked at a door of one of the parlors, and the servant entered: he returned, and John was shown into a room, where Denbigh was sitting with his head resting on his hand, and apparently musing. On seeing who required admittance, he sprang from his seat and exclaimed—

"Mr. Moseley! Do I see aright?"

"Denbigh," cried John, stretching out his hand to him, "was this kind—was it like yourself—to leave us so unexpectedly, and for so long a time, too, as your note mentioned?"

Denbigh waved his hand to the servant to retire, and handed a chair to his friend.

"Mr. Moseley," said he, struggling with his feelings, "you appear ignorant of my proposals to your sister."

"Perfectly," answered the amazed John.

"And her rejection of them."

"Is it possible?" cried the brother,

pacing up and down the room. "I acknowledge I did expect you to offer, but not to be refused."

Denbigh placed in the other's hand the letter of Emily, which, having read, John returned with a sigh. "This, then, is the reason you left us," he continued. "Emily is not capricious—it cannot be a sudden pique—she means as she says."

"Yes, Mr. Moseley," said Denbigh, mournfully; "your sister is faultless—but I am not worthy of her—my deception"—here the door again opened to the admission of Peter Johnson. Both the gentlemen rose at this sudden interruption, and the steward advancing to the table, once more produced the formidable pocket-book, the spectacles, and a letter. He ran over its direction—"For George Denbigh, Esquire, London, by the hands of Peter Johnson, with care and speed." After the observance of these preliminaries, he delivered the missive to its lawful owner, who opened it, and rapidly perused its contents. Denbigh was much affected with whatever the latter might be, and kindly took the steward by the hand, as he thanked him for this renewed instance of the interest he took in him. If he would tell him where a letter would find him in the morning, he would send a reply to the one he had received. Peter gave his address, but appeared unwilling to go, until assured again and again that the answer would be infallibly sent. Taking a small account-book out of his pocket, and referring to its contents, the steward said, "Master has with Coutts & Co. £7,000; in the bank £5,000. It can be easily done, sir, and never felt by us."

Denbigh smiled in reply, as he assured the steward he would take proper notice of his master's offers in his own answer. The door again opened, and the military stranger was admitted to their presence. He bowed, appeared not a little surprised to find two of his mail-coach companions there, and handed Denbigh a letter, in quite as formal although in a more silent manner than the steward. The soldier was invited to be seated, and the letter was perused with an evident curiosity on the part of Denbigh. As soon as the latter ended it, he addressed the stranger in a language which John rightly judged to be Spanish, and Peter took it to be Greek. For a few minutes the conversation was maintained between them with great earnestness, his fellow-travelers marveling much at the garrulity of the soldier; however, the stranger soon rose to retire, when the door was thrown open for the fourth time, and a voice cried out,

"Here I am, George, safe and sound—

ready to kiss the bridesmaids, if they will let me—and I can find time—bless me, Moseley!—old marlin-spike!—general!—whew, where is the coachman and guard?" It was Lord Henry Stapleton. The Spaniard bowed again in silence, and withdrew, while Denbigh threw open the door of an adjoining room and excused himself, as he desired Lord Henry to walk in there for a few minutes.

"Upon my word," cried the heedless sailor, as he complied, "we might as well have stuck together, Moseley; we were bound to one port it seems."

"You know Lord Henry?" said John, as he withdrew.

"Yes," said Denbigh, and he again required his address of Peter, which having been given, the steward departed. The conversation between the two friends did not return to the course it was taking when they were interrupted, as Moseley felt a delicacy in making any allusion to the probable cause of his sister's refusal. He had, however, begun to hope it was not irremovable, and with the determination of renewing his visit in the morning, he took his leave, to allow Denbigh to attend to his other guest, Lord Henry Stapleton.

About twelve o'clock on the following morning, John and the steward met at the door of the hotel where Denbigh lodged, in quest of the same person. The latter held in his hand the answer to his master's letter, but wished particularly to see its writer. On inquiring, to their mutual surprise they were told that the gentleman had left there early in the morning, having discharged his lodgings, and that they were unable to say whither he had gone. To hunt for a man without a clew, in the city of London, is usually time misspent. Of this Moseley was perfectly sensible, and disregarding a proposition of Peter's, he returned to his own lodgings.

The proposal of the steward, if it did not do much credit to his sagacity, was much in favor of his perseverance and enterprise. It was no other than that John should take one side of the street and he the other, in order to inquire at every house in the place, until the fugitive was discovered. "Sir," said Peter, with great simplicity, "when our neighbor White lost his little girl, this was the way we found her, although we went nearly through L—— before we succeeded, Mr. John." Peter was obliged to abandon this expedient for want of an associate, and as no message was left at the lodgings of Moseley, he started with a heavy heart on his return to Benfield Lodge. But Moseley's zeal was too warm in the cause of his friend, notwithstanding his unmerited desertion, to discontinue the search for him. He sought out the town residence of the Marquis of Eltringham, the brother of Lord Henry, and was told that both the marquis and his brother had left town early that morning for his seat in Devonshire, to attend the wedding of their sister.

"Did they go alone?" asked John, musing.

"There were two chaises, the marquis's and his grace's."

"Who was his grace?" inquired John.

"Why, the Duke of Derwent, to be sure."

"And the duke—was he alone?"

"There was a gentleman with his grace, but they did not know his name."

As nothing further could be learned, John withdrew. A good deal of irritation mixed with the vexation of Moseley at his disappointment; for Denbigh, he thought, too evidently wished to avoid him. That he was the companion of his kinsman, the Duke of Derwent, he had now no doubt, and he entirely relinquished all expectations of finding him in London or its environs. While retracing his steps, in no enviable state of mind, to his lodgings, with a resolution of returning immediately to L——, his arm was suddenly taken by his friend Chatterton. If any man could have consoled John at that moment, it was the baron. Questions and answers were rapidly exchanged between them; and with increased satisfaction, John learned that in the next square he could have the pleasure of paying his respects to his kinswoman, the Dowager Lady Chatterton, and her two daughters. Chatterton inquired warmly after Emily, and in a particularly kind manner concerning Mr. Denbigh, hearing with undisguised astonishment the absence of the latter from the Moseley family.

Lady Chatterton had disciplined her feelings upon the subject of Grace and John into such a state of subordination, that the fastidious jealousy of the young man now found no ground of alarm in anything she said or did. It cannot be denied the dowager was delighted to see him again; and if it were fair to draw any conclusions from colorings, palpitations, and other such little accompaniments of female feeling, Grace was not excessively sorry. It is true, it was the best possible opportunity to ascertain all about her friend Emily and the rest of the family; and Grace was extremely happy to have intelligence of their general welfare so direct as was afforded by this visit of Mr. Moseley. Grace looked all she expressed, and possibly a little more; and John thought she looked very beautiful.

There was present an elderly gentleman, of apparently indifferent health, although his manners were extremely lively, and his dress particularly studied. A few minutes' observation convinced Moseley this gentleman was a candidate for the favor of Kate; and a game of chess being soon introduced, he also saw he was one thought worthy of peculiar care and attention. He had been introduced to him as Lord Herriefield, and soon discovered by his conversation that he was a peer who promised little toward rendering the house of incurables more convalescent than it was before his admission. Chatterton mentioned him as a distant connection of his mother; a gentleman who had lately returned from filling an official situation in the East Indies, to take his seat among the lords by the death of his brother.

He was a bachelor, and reputed rich, much of his wealth being personal property, acquired by himself abroad. The dutiful son might have added, if respect and feeling had not kept him silent, that his offers of settling a large jointure upon his elder sister had been accepted, and that the following week was to make her the bride of the emaciated debauchee who now sat by her side. He might also have said that when the proposition was made to himself and Grace, both had shrunk from the alliance with disgust; and that both had united in humble though vain remonstrances to their mother against the sacrifice, and in petitions to their sister that she would not be accessory to her own misery. There was no pecuniary sacrifice they would not make to her, to avert such a connection; but all was fruitless—Kate was resolved to be a viscountess, and her mother was equally determined that she should be rich.

CHAPTER XXX.

A DAY elapsed between the departure of Denbigh and the reappearance of Emily among her friends. An indifferent observer would have thought her much graver and less animated than usual. A loss of the rich color which ordinarily glowed on her healthful cheek, might be noticed; but the placid sweetness and graceful composure which regulated her former conduct pervaded all she did or uttered. Not so with Jane; her pride had suffered more than her feelings—her im-

agination had been more deceived than her judgment—and although too well bred and soft by nature to become rude or captious, she was changed from a communicative to a reserved, from a confiding to a suspicious companion. Her parents noticed this alteration with an uneasiness that was somewhat embittered by the consciousness of a neglect of some of those duties that experience now seemed to indicate, could never be forgotten with impunity.

Francis and Clara had arrived from their northern tour, so happy in each other, and so contented with their lot, that it required some little exercise of fortitude in both Lady Moseley and her daughters to expel unpleasant recollections while they contemplated it. Their relation of the little incidents of their tour had, however, an effect to withdraw the attention of their friends in some degree from late occurrences; and a melancholy and sympathizing kind of association had taken place of the unbounded confidence and gayety, which so lately prevailed at Benfield Lodge. Mr. Benfield mingled with his solemnity an air of mystery, and he was frequently noticed by his relatives looking over old papers, and was apparently employed in preparations that indicated movements of more than usual importance.

The family were collected in one of the parlors on an extremely unpleasant day, the fourth after the departure of John, when the thin person of Johnson stalked in among them. All eyes were fixed on him in expectation of what he had to communicate, and all apparently dreading to break the silence, from an apprehension that his communication would be unpleasant. In the meantime Peter, who had respectfully left his hat at the door, proceeded to uncase his body from the multiplied defenses he had taken against the inclemency of the weather. His master stood erect with an outstretched hand, ready to receive the reply to his epistle; and Johnson having liberated his body from thraldom, produced the black leathern pocket-book, and from its contents a letter, when he read aloud—Roderic Benfield, Esq., Benfield Lodge, Norfolk; favored by Mr. ——. Here Peter's modesty got the better of his method. He had never been called Mr. Johnson by anybody, old or young; all knew him in that neighborhood as Peter Johnson—and he had very nearly been guilty of the temerity of arrogating to himself another title, in the presence of those he most respected; a degree of self-elevation from which he escaped with the loss of a small piece of his tongue. Mr. Benfield took the letter with an eagerness that plainly indicated the deep interest he took in its contents, while Emily, with a tremulous voice and flushed cheek, approached the steward with a glass of wine.

"Peter," she said, "take this; it will do you good."

"Thank you, Miss Emma," said Peter, casting his eyes from her to his master, as the latter, having finished his letter, exclaimed, with a strange mixture of consideration and disappointment—

"Johnson, you must change your clothes immediately, or you will take cold; you look now like old Moses, the Jew beggar."

Peter sighed heavily at this comparison, and saw in it a confirmation of his fears; for he well knew, that to his being the bearer of unpleasant tidings was he indebted for a resemblance to anything unpleasant to his master, and Moses was the old gentleman's aversion.

The baronet now followed his uncle from the room to his library, entering it at the same moment with the steward, who had been summoned by his master to an audience.

Pointing to a chair for his nephew, Mr. Benfield commenced the discourse with saying.

"Peter, you saw Mr. Denbigh; how did he look?"

"As usual, master," said Peter, laconically, still piqued at being likened to old Moses.

"And what did he say to the offer? Did he not make any comments on it? He was not offended at it, I hope?" demanded Mr. Benfield.

"He said nothing but what he has written to your honor," replied the steward, losing a little of his constrained manner in real good feeling to his master.

"May I ask what the offer was?" inquired Sir Edward.

Mr. Benfield, regarding him a moment in silence, said, "Certainly, you are nearly concerned in his welfare; your daughter"—the old man stopped, turned to his letter-book, and handed the baronet a copy of the epistle he sent to Denbigh. It read as follows:

"DEAR FRIEND, MR. DENBIGH—I have thought a great deal on the reason of your sudden departure from a house I had begun to hope you thought your own; and by calling to mind my own feelings when Lady Juliana became the heiress to her nephew's estate, take it for granted you have been governed by the same sentiments; which I know both by my own experience and that of the bearer, Peter Johnson, is a never-failing accompaniment of pure affection. Yes, my dear Denbigh, I honor your delicacy in not wishing to become indebted to a stranger, as it were, for the money on which you subsist, and that stranger your wife—who ought in reason to look up to you, instead of you looking up to her; which was the true cause Lord Gosford would not marry the countess—on account of her great wealth, as he assured me himself; notwithstanding envious people said it was because her ladyship loved Mr. Chaworth better: so in order to remove these impediments of delicacy, I have to make three propositions, namely, that I bring you into Parliament the next election for my own borough—that you take possession of the lodge the day you marry Emmy, while I will live, for the little time I have to stay here, in the large cottage built by my uncle—and that I give you your legacy of ten thousand pounds down, to prevent trouble hereafter.

"As I know nothing but delicacy has driven you away from us, I make no doubt you will now find all objections removed, and that Peter will bring back the joyful intelligence of your return to us, as soon as the business you left us on is completed.

"Your uncle, that is to be,
        "RODERIC BENFIELD."

"N. B. As Johnson is a stranger to the ways of the town, I wish you to advise his inexperience, particularly against the arts of designing women, Peter being a man of considerable estate, and great modesty."

"There, nephew," cried Mr. Benfield, as the baronet finished reading the letter aloud, "is it not unreasonable to refuse my offers? Now read his answer."

"Words are wanting to express the sensations which have been excited by Mr. Benfield's letter; but it would be impossible for any man to be so base as to avail himself of such liberality: the recollection of it, together with that of his many virtues, will long continue deeply impressed on the heart of him whom Mr. Benfield would, if within the power of man, render the happiest among human beings."

The steward listened eagerly to this answer, but after it was done he was as much at a loss to know its contents as before its perusal. He knew it was unfavorable to their wishes, but could not comprehend its meaning or expressions, and immmediately attributed their ambiguity to the strange conference he had witnessed between Denbigh and the military stranger.

"Master," exclaimed Peter, with something of the elation of a discoverer, "I know the cause, it shows itself in the letter: there was a man talking Greek to him while he was reading your letter."

"Greek!" exclaimed Sir Edward in astonishment.

"Greek!" said the uncle. "Lord Gosford read Greek; but I believe never conversed in that language."

"Yes, Sir Edward—yes, your honor—pure wild Greek; it must have been something of that kind," added Peter, with positiveness, "that would make a man refuse such offers—Miss Emily—the lodge—£10,000!"—and the steward shook his head with much satisfaction at having discovered the cause.

Sir Edward smiled at the simplicity of Johnson, but disliking the idea attached to the refusal of his daughter, said,

"Perhaps, after all, uncle, there has been some misunderstanding between Emily and Denbigh, which may have driven him from us so suddenly."

Mr. Benfield and his steward exchanged looks, and a new idea broke upon them at the instant. They had both suffered in that way; and after all it might prove that Emily was the one whose taste or feelings had subverted their schemes. The impression, once made, soon became strong, and the party separated; the master thinking alternately on Lady Juliana and his niece, while the man, after heaving one heavy sigh to the memory of Patty Steele, proceeded to the usual occupations of his office.

Mrs. Wilson, thinking a ride would be of service to Emily, and having the fullest confidence in her self-command and resignation, availed herself of a fine day to pay a visit to their friend in the cottage. Mrs. Fitzgerald received them in her usual manner, but a single glance of her eye sufficed to show the aunt that she noticed the altered appearance of Emily and her manners, although without knowing its true reason, which she did not deem it prudent to explain. Julia handed her friend a note which she said she had received the day before, and desired their counsel how to proceed in the present emergency. As Emily was to be made acquainted with its contents, her aunt read it aloud as follows:

"MY DEAR NIECE—Your father and myself had been induced to think you were leading a disgraceful life, with the officer your husband had consigned you to the care of; for hearing of your captivity, I had arrived with a band of guerillas, on the spot where you were rescued, early the next morning, and there learned of the peasants your misfortunes and retreat. The enemy pressed us too much to allow us to deviate from our route at the time; but natural affection and the wishes of your father have led me to make a journey to England, in order to satisfy our doubts as regards your conduct. I have seen you, heard your character in the neighborhood, and after much and long search have found out the officer, and am satisfied, that so far as concerns your deportment, you are an injured woman. I have therefore to propose to you, on my own behalf, and that of the conde, that you adopt the faith of your country, and return with me to the arms of your parent, whose heiress you will be, and whose life you may be the means of prolonging. Direct your answer to me, to the care of our ambassador; and as you decide, I am your mother's brother.

"LOUIS M'CARTHY Y HARRISON."

"On what point do you wish my advice," said Mrs. Wilson, kindly, after she had finished reading the letter, "and when do you expect to see your uncle?"

"Would you have me accept the offer of my father, dear madam, or am I to remain separated from him for the short residue of his life?"

Mrs. Fitzgerald was affected to tears, as she asked this question, and waited her answer, in silent dread of its nature.

"Is the condition of a change of religion an immovable one?" inquired Mrs. Wilson, in a thoughtful manner.

"O! doubtless," replied Julia, shuddering; "but I am deservedly punished for my early disobedience, and bow in submission to the will of Providence. I feel now all that horror of a change of my religion, I once only affected; I must live and die a Protestant, madam."

"Certainly, I hope so, my dear," said Mrs. Wilson; "I am not a bigot, and think it unfortunate you were not, in your circumstances, bred a pious Catholic. It would have saved you much misery, and might have rendered the close of your father's life more happy; but as your present creed embraces doctrines too much at variance with the Romish Church to renounce the one or to adopt the other, with your views, it will be impossible to change your Church without committing a heavy offense against the opinions and practices of every denomination of Christians. I should hope a proper representation of this to your uncle would have its weight, or they might be satisfied with your being a Christian, without becoming a Catholic."

"Ah! my dear madam," answered Mrs. Fitzgerald, despairingly, "you little know the opinions of my countrymen on this subject."

"Surely, surely," cried Mrs. Wilson, "parental affection is a stronger feeling than bigotry."

Mrs. Fitzgerald shook her head in a manner which bespoke both her apprehensions and her filial regard.

"Julia ought not, must not desert her father, dear aunt," said Emily, her face glowing with the ardency of her feelings.

"And ought she to desert her heavenly Father, my child?" asked the aunt, mildly.

"Are the duties conflicting, dearest aunt?"

"The conde makes them so. Julia is, I trust, in sincerity a Christian, and with what face can she offer up her daily petitions to her Creator, while she wears a mask to her earthly father; or how can she profess to honor doctrines that she herself believes to be false, or practice customs she thinks improper?"

"Never, never," exclaimed Julia, with fervor; "the struggle is dreadful, but I submit to the greater duty."

"And you decide rightly, my friend," said Mrs. Wilson, soothingly; "but you need relax no efforts to convince the conde of your wishes: truth and nature will finally conquer."

"Ah!" cried Mrs. Fitzgerald, "the sad consequences of one false step in early life!"

"Rather," added Mrs. Wilson, "the sad consequences, of one false step in generations gone by. Had your grandmother listened to the voice of prudence and duty, she never would have deserted her parents for a comparative stranger, and entailed upon her descendants a train of evils which yet exist in your person."

"It will be a sad blow to my poor uncle, too," said Mrs. Fitzgerald "he who once loved me so much."

"When do you expect to see him?" inquired Emily.

Julia informed them she expected him hourly; as fearful a written statement of her views would drive him from the country without paying her a visit before he departed, she had earnestly entreated him to see her without delay.

On taking their leave, the ladies promised to obey her her summons whenever called to meet the general, as Mrs. Wil-

son thought she might be better able to give advice to a friend, by knowing more of the character of her relatives, than she could do with her present information.

One day intervened, and it was spent in the united society of Lady Moseley and her daughters, while Sir Edward and Francis rode to a neighboring town on business; and on the succeeding, Mrs. Fitzgerald apprised them of the arrival of General M'Carthy.

Immediately after breakfast Mrs. Wilson and Emily drove to the cottage, the aunt both wishing the latter as a companion in her ride, and believing the excitement would have a tendency to prevent her niece from indulging in reflections, alike dangerous to her peace of mind and at variance with her duties.

Our readers have probably anticipated, that the stage companion of John Moseley was the Spanish general, who had just been making those inquiries into the manner of his niece's living which terminated so happily in her acquittal. With that part of his history which relates to the injurious attempts on her before she arrived at Lisbon, he appears to have been ignorant, or his interview with Denbigh might have terminated very differently from the manner already related.

A description of the appearance of the gentleman presented to Mrs. Wilson is unnecessary, as it has been given already; and the discerning matron thought she read through the rigid and set features of the soldier a shade of kinder feelings which might be wrought into an advantageous intercession on behalf of Julia. The general was evidently endeavoring to keep his feelings within due bounds, before the decision of his niece might render it proper for him to indulge in that affection for her, which his eye plainly showed existed under the cover of his assumed manner.

It was an effort of great fortitude on the part of Julia to acquaint her uncle with her resolution; but as it must be done, she seized a moment after Mrs. Wilson had at some length defended her adhering to her present faith, until religiously impressed with its errors, to inform him such was her unalterable resolution. He heard her patiently, and without anger, but in visible surprise. He had construed her summons to her house into a measure preparatory to accepting his conditions; yet he betrayed no emotion, after the first expression of his wonder; he told her distinctly a renunciation of her heresy was the only condition on which her father would own her either as his heiress or his child. Julia deeply regretted the decision, but was firm; and her friends left her to enjoy uninterruptedly, for one day, the society of so near a relative. During this day every doubt as to the propriety of her conduct, if any yet remained, was removed by a relation of her little story to her uncle; and after it was completed he expressed great uneasiness to get to London again, in order to meet a gentleman he had seen there, under a different impression as to his merits than what now appeared to be just. Who the gentleman was, or what these impressions were, Julia was left to conjecture, taciturnity being a favorite property in the general.

CHAPTER XXXI.

THE sun had just risen on one of the loveliest vales of Caernarvonshire, as a traveling chaise and six swept up to the door of a princely mansion, so situated as to command a prospect of the fertile and extensive domains, the rental of which filled the coffers of its rich owner, having a beautiful view of the Irish Channel in the distance.

Everything around this stately edifice bespoke the magnificence of its ancient possessors and the taste of its present master. It was irregular, but built of the best materials, and in the tastes of the different ages in which its various parts had been erected; and now in the nineteenth century it preserved the baronial grandeur of the thirteenth, mingled with the comforts of this later period.

The lofty turrets of its towers were tipped with the golden light of the sun, and the neighboring peasantry had commenced their daily labors, as the different attendants of the equipage we have mentioned collected around it at the great entrance to the building. The beautiful black horses, with coats as shining as the polished leather with which they were caparisoned, the elegant and fashionable finish of the vehicle, with its numerous grooms, postilions, and footmen, all wearing the livery of one master, gave evidence of wealth and rank.

In attendance there were four outriders, walking leisurely about, awaiting the appearance of those for whose comforts and pleasures they were kept to contribute; while a fifth, who, like the others, was equipped with a horse, appeared to bear a doubtful station. The form of the latter was athletic, and apparently drilled into a severer submission than could be seen in the movements of the liveried attendants: his dress was peculiar, being neither quite menial nor quite military, but partaking

of both characters. His horse was heavier and better managed than those of the others, and by its side was a charger, that was prepared for the use of no common equestrian. Both were coal-black, as were all the others of the cavalcade; but the pistols of the two latter, and housings of their saddles, bore the aspect of use and elegance united.

The postilions were mounted, listlessly waiting the pleasure of their superiors; when the laughs and jokes of the menials were instantly succeeded by a respectful and profound silence, as a gentleman and lady appeared on the portico of the building. The former was a young man of commanding stature and genteel appearance; and his air, although that of one used to command, was softened by a character of benevolence and gentleness, that might be rightly supposed to give birth to the willing alacrity with which all his requests or orders were attended to.

The lady was also young, and resembled her companion both in features and expression, for both were noble, both were handsome. The former was attired for the road; the latter had thrown a shawl around her elegant form, and by her morning dress showed that a separation of the two was about to happen. Taking the hand of the gentleman with both of her own, as she pressed it with fingers interlocked, the lady said, in a voice of music, and with great affection.

"Then, my dear brother, I shall certainly hear from you within the week, and see you next?"

"Certainly," replied the gentleman, as he tenderly paid his adieus; then throwing himself into the chaise, it dashed from the door, like the passage of a meteor. The horsemen followed; the unridden charger, obedient to the orders of his keeper, wheeled gracefully into his station; and in an instant they were all lost amidst the wood, through which the road to the park gates conducted.

After lingering without until the last of her brother's followers had receded from her sight, the lady retired through ranks of liveried footmen and maids, whom curiosity or respect had collected.

The young traveler wore a gloom on his expressive features, amidst the pageantry that surrounded him, which showed the insufficiency of wealth and honors to fill the sum of human happiness. As his carriage rolled proudly up an eminence ere he had reached the confines of his extensive park, his eyes rested, for a moment, on a scene in which meadows, forests, fields waving with golden corn, comfortable farm-houses surrounded with innumerable cottages, were seen in almost endless variety. All these owned him for their lord, and one quiet smile of satisfaction beamed on his face as he gazed on the unlimited view. Could the heart of that youth have been read, it would at that moment have told a story very different from the feelings such a scene is apt to excite; it would have spoken the consciousness of well-applied wealth, the gratification of contemplating meritorious deeds, and a heartfelt gratitude to the Being which had enabled him to become the dispenser of happiness to so many of his fellow creatures.

"Which way, my lord, so early?" cried a gentleman in a phaeton, as he drew up on his way to a watering-place, to pay his own parting compliments.

"To Eltringham, Sir Owen, to attend the marriage of my kinsman, Mr. Denbigh, to one of the sisters of the marquis."

A few more questions and answers, and the gentlemen, exchanging friendly adieus, pursued each his own course; Sir Owen Ap Rice pushing forward for Cheltenham, and the Earl of Pendennyss proceeding to act as groomsman to his cousin.

The gates of Eltringham were open to the admission of many an equipage on the following day, and the heart of the Lady Laura beat quick, as the sound of wheels, at different times, reached her ears. At last an unusual movement in the house drew her to a window of her dressing-room, and the blood rushed to her heart as she beheld the equipages which were rapidly approaching, and through the mist which stole over her eyes she saw alight from the first, the Duke of Derwent and the bridegroom. The next contained Lord Pendennyss, and the last the Bishop of ——. Lady Laura waited to see no more, but with a heart filled with terror, hope, joy, and uneasiness, she threw herself into the arms of one of her sisters.

"Ah!" exclaimed Lord Henry Stapleton, about a week after the wedding of his sister, seizing John suddenly by the arm, while the latter was taking his morning walk to the residence of the Dowager Lady Chatterton, "Moseley, you dissipated youth, in town yet! you told me you should stay but a day, and here I find you at the end of a fortnight."

John blushed a little at the consciousness of his reason for sending a written, instead of carrying a verbal report, of the result of his journey, but replied,

"Yes, my friend Chatterton unexpectedly arrived, and so—and so—"

"And so you did not go, I presume you mean," cried Lord Henry, with a laugh.

"Yes," said John, "and so I staid—but where is Denbigh?"

"Where?—why with his wife, where every well-behaved man should be, especially for the first month," rejoined the sailor, gayly.

"Wife!" echoed John, as soon as he felt able to give utterance to his words —"wife! is he married?"

"Married," cried Lord Henry, imitating his manner, "are you yet to learn that? Why did you ask for him?"

"Ask for him?" said Moseley, yet lost in astonishment; "but when—how—where did he marry—my lord?"

Lord Henry looked at him for a moment with a surprise little short of his own, as he answered more gravely:

"When?—last Tuesday; how?—by special license, and the Bishop of ——; where?—at Eltringham. Yes, my dear fellow," continued he, with his former gayety, "George is my brother now—and a fine fellow he is."

"I really wish your lordship much joy," said John, struggling to command his feelings.

"Thank you—thank you," replied the sailor; "a jolly time we had of it, Moseley. I wish, with all my heart, you had been there; no bolting or running away as soon as spliced, but a regularly-constructed, old-fashioned wedding; all my doings. I wrote Laura that time was scarce, and I had none to throw away on fooleries; so, dear, good soul, she consented to let me have everything my own way. We had Derwent and Pendennyss, the marquis, Lord William and myself, for groomsmen, and my three sisters—ah, that was bad, but there was no helping it —Lady Harriet Denbigh, and an old maid, a cousin of ours, for bridesmaids; could not help the old maid, either, upon my honor, or be quite certain I would."

How much of what he said Moseley heard, we cannot say; for had he talked an hour longer he would have been uninterrupted. Lord Henry was too much engaged with his description to notice his companion's taciturnity or surprise, and after walking a square or two together they parted; the sailor being on the wing for his frigate at Yarmouth.

John continued his course, musing on the intelligence he had just heard. That Denbigh could forget Emily so soon, he would not believe, and he greatly feared he had been driven into a step, from despair, that he might hereafter repent of. The avoiding of himself was now fully explained; but would Lady Laura Stapleton accept a man for a husband at so short a notice? and for the first time a suspicion that something in the character of Denbigh was wrong, mingled in his reflections on his sister's refusal of his offers.

Lord and Lady Herriefield were on the eve of their departure for the continent (for Catherine had been led to the altar the preceding week), a southern climate having been described as necessary to the bridegroom's constitution; and the dowager and Grace were about to proceed to the seat of the baron's within a couple of miles of Bath. Chatterton himself had his own engagements, but he promised to be there in company with his friend Derwent within a fortnight; the former visit having been postponed by the marriages in their respective families.

John had been assiduous in his attentions during the season of forced gayety which followed the nuptials of Kate; and as the dowager's time was monopolized with the ceremonials of that event, Grace had risen greatly in his estimation. If Grace Chatterton was not more miserable than usual, at what she thought was the destruction of her sister's happiness, it was owing to the presence and unconcealed affection of John Moseley.

The carriage of Lord Herriefield was in waiting when John rang for admittance. On opening the door and entering the drawing-room, he saw the bride and bridegroom, with their mother and sister, accoutered for an excursion among the shops of Bond Street; for Kate was dying to find a vent for some of her surplus pin-money—her husband to show his handsome wife in the face of the world—the mother to display the triumph of her matrimonial schemes. And Grace was forced to obey her mother's commands, in accompanying her sister as an attendant, not to be dispensed with at all in her circumstances.

The entrance of John at that instant, though nothing more than what occurred every day at that hour, deranged the whole plan; the dowager, for a moment, forgot her resolution, and forgot the necessity of Grace's appearance, exclaiming with evident satisfaction.

"Here is Mr. Moseley come to keep you company, Grace; so, after all, you must consult your headache and stay at home. Indeed, my love, I never can consent you should go out. I not only wish, but insist you remain within this morning."

Lord Herriefield looked at his mother-in-law in some surprise, and threw a suspicious glance on his own rib at the moment, which spoke as plainly as looks can speak,

"Is it possible I have been taken in, after all?"

Grace was unused to resist her mother's commands, and throwing off her hat and shawl, reseated herself with more composure than she would probably have done, had not the attention of Moseley been more delicate and pointed of late than formerly.

As they passed the porter, Lady Chatterton observed to him significantly—"Nobody at home, Willis." "Yes, my lady," was the laconic reply, and Lord Herriefield, as he took his seat by the side of his wife in the carriage, thought she was not as handsome as usual.

Lady Chatterton that morning unguardedly laid the foundation of years of misery for her eldest daughter; or rather the foundations were already laid in the ill-assorted and heartless, unprincipled union she had labored with success to effect. But she had that morning stripped the mask from her own character prematurely, and excited suspicions in the breast of her son-in-law, which time only served to confirm, and memory to brood over.

Lord Herriefield had been too long in the world not to understand all the ordinary arts of match-makers and match-hunters. Like most of his own sex who have associated freely with the worst part of the other, his opinions of female excellences were by no means extravagant or romantic. Kate had pleased his eye; she was of a noble family; young, and at that moment interestingly quiet, having nothing particularly in view. She had a taste of her own, and Lord Herriefield was by no means in conformity with it; consequently, she expended none of those pretty little arts upon him which she occasionally practiced, and which his experience would immediately have detected. Her disgust he had attributed to disinterestedness; and as Kate had fixed her eye on a young officer lately returned from France, and her mother on a duke who was mourning the death of a third wife, devising means to console him with a fourth—the viscount had got a good deal enamored with the lady, before either she or her mother took any particular notice that there was such a being in existence. His title was not the most elevated, but it was ancient. His paternal acres were not numerous, but his East India shares were. He was not very young, but he was not very old; and as the duke died of a fit of the gout in his stomach, and the officer ran away with a girl in her teens from a boarding school, the dowager and her daughter, after thoroughly scanning the fashionable world, determined, for want of a better, that *he* would do.

It is not to be supposed that the mother and child held any open communication with each other to this effect. The delicacy and pride of both would have been greatly injured by such a suspicion; yet they arrived simultaneously at the same conclusion, as well as at another of equal importance to the completion of their schemes on the viscount. It was simply to adhere to the same conduct which had made him a captive, as most likely to insure the victory.

There was such a general understanding between the two it can excite no surprise that they co-operated harmoniously as it were by signal.

For two people, correctly impressed with their duties and responsibilities, to arrive at the same conclusion in the government of their conduct, would be merely a matter of course; and so with those who are more or less under the dominion of the world. They will pursue their plans with a degree of concurrence amounting nearly to sympathy; and thus had Kate and her mother, until this morning, kept up the masquerade so well that the viscount was as confiding as a country Corydon. When he first witnessed the dowager's management with Grace and John, however, and his wife's careless disregard of a thing which appeared too much a matter of course to be quite agreeable, his newly awakened distrust approached conviction.

Grace Chatterton both sang and played exquisitely; it was, however, seldom she could sufficiently overcome her desire, when John was an auditor, to appear to advantage.

As the party went down stairs, and Moseley had gone with them part of the way, she threw herself unconsciously on a seat, and began a beautiful song that was fashionable at the time. Her feelings were in consonance with the words, and Grace was very happy both in execution and voice.

John had reached the back of her seat before she was at all sensible of his return, and Grace lost her self-command immediately. She rose and took a seat on a sofa, and the young man was immediately at her side.

"Ah, Grace," said John, the lady's heart beating high, "you certainly do sing as you do everything, admirably."

"I am happy you think so, Mr. Moseley," returned Grace, looking everywhere but in his face.

John's eyes ran over her beauties, as with palpitating bosom and varying color she sat confused at the unusual warmth of his language and manner.

Fortunately a remarkable striking likeness of the dowager hung directly over their heads, and John taking her unresisting hand, continued,

"Dear Grace, you resemble your mother very much in features, and what is better still, in character."

"I could wish," said Grace, venturing to look up, "to resemble your sister Emily in the latter."

"And why not to be her sister, dear Grace?" said he with ardor. "You are worthy to become her sister. Tell me, Grace, dear Miss Chatterton—can you—will you make me the happiest of men? May I present another inestimable daughter to my parents?"

As John paused for an answer Grace looked up, and he waited her reply in evident anxiety; but she continued silent, now pale as death, and now of the color of the rose, and he added:

"I hope I have not offended you, dearest Grace; you are all that is desirable to me; my hopes, my happiness, are centered in you. Unless you consent to become my wife, I must be very wretched."

Grace burst into a flood of tears as her lover, interested deeply in their cause, gently drew her toward him. Her head sank on his shoulder, as she fairly whispered something that was inaudible, but which he did not fail to interpret into everything he most wished to hear. John was in ecstasies. Every unpleasant feeling of suspicion had left him. Of Grace's innocence of maneuvering he never doubted, but John did not relish the idea of being entrapped into anything, even a step which he desired. An uninterrupted communication followed; it was as confiding as their affections; and the return of the dowager and her children first recalled them to the recollection of other people.

One glance at the eye was enough for Lady Chatterton. She saw the traces of tears on the cheeks and in the eyes of Grace, and the dowager was satisfied; she knew his friends would not object; and as Grace attended her to her dressing-room, she cried on entering it, "Well, child, when is the wedding to be? You will wear me out with so much gayety."

Grace was shocked, but did not, as formerly, weep over her mother's interference in agony and dread. John had opened his whole soul to her, observing the greatest delicacy toward her mother, and she now felt her happiness placed in the keeping of a man whose honor she believed much exceeded that of any other human being.

CHAPTER XXXII.

THE seniors of the party at Benfield Lodge were all assembled one morning in a parlor, when its master and the baronet were occupied in the perusal of the London papers. Clara had persuaded her sisters to accompany her and Francis in an excursion as far as the village.

Jane yet continued reserved and distant to most of her friends; while Emily's conduct would have escaped unnoticed, did not her blanched cheek and wandering looks at times speak a language not to be misunderstood. With all her relatives she maintained the affectionate intercourse she had always supported; though not even to her aunt did the name of Denbigh pass her lips. But in her most private and humble petitions to God she never forgot to mingle with her requests for spiritual blessings on herself fervent prayers for the conversion of the preserver of her life.

Mrs. Wilson, as she sat by the side of her sister at their needles, first discovered an unusual uneasiness in their venerable host, while he turned his paper over and over as if unwilling or unable to comprehend some part of its contents, until he rang the bell violently, and bid the servant to send Johnson to him without a moment's delay.

"Peter," said Mr. Benfield, doubtingly, "read that—your eyes are young, Peter; read that."

Peter took the paper, and after having adjusted his spectacles to his satisfaction, he proceeded to obey his master's injunctions; but the same defect of vision as suddenly seized the steward as it had affected his master. He turned the paper sideways, and appeared to be spelling the matter of the paragraph to himself. Peter would have given his three hundred a year to have had the impatient John Moseley at hand, to relieve him from his task; but the anxiety of Mr. Benfield overcoming his fear of the worst, he inquired in a tremulous tone—

"Peter? hem! Peter, what do you think?"

"Why, your honor," replied the steward, stealing a look at his master, "it does seem so, indeed."

"I remember," said the master, "when Lord Gosford saw the marriage of the countess announced he——"

Here the old gentleman was obliged to stop, and rising with dignity, and leaning on the arm of his faithful servant, he left the room.

Mrs. Wilson immediately took up the paper, and her eye catching the paragraph at a glance, she read aloud as follows to her expecting friends:

"Married, by special license, at the seat of the Most Noble the Marquis of Eltringham, in Devonshire, by the Right Rev. Lord Bishop of——, George Denbigh, Esq., Lieutenant Colonel of his Majesty's —— regiment of dragoons, to the Right Honorable Lady Laura Stapleton, eldest sister of the Marquis. Eltringham was honored on the present happy occasion with the presence of his grace of Derwent, and the gallant Lord Pendennyss, kinsman of the bridegroom, and Captain Lord Henry Stapleton, of the Royal Navy. We understand that the happy couple proceed to Denbigh Castle immediately after the honeymoon."

Although Mrs. Wilson had given up the expectation of ever seeing her niece the wife of Denbigh, she felt an indescribable shock as she read this paragraph. The strongest feeling was horror at the danger Emily had been in of contracting an alliance with such a man. His avoiding the ball, at which he knew Lord Henry was expected, was explained to her by this marriage; for with John, she could not believe a woman like Lady Laura Stapleton was to be won in the short space of one fortnight, or indeed less. There was too evidently a mystery yet to be developed, and, she felt certain, one that would not elevate his character in her opinion.

Neither Sir Edward nor Lady Moseley had given up the expectation of seeing Denbigh again, as a suitor for Emily's hand, and to both of them this certainty of his loss was a heavy blow. The baronet took up the paper, and after perusing the article, he muttered in a low tone, as he wiped the tears from his eyes, "Heaven bless him; I sincerely hope she is worthy of him." Worthy of him, thought Mrs. Wilson, with a feeling of indignation, as, taking up the paper, she retired to her own room, whither Emily, at that moment returned from her walk, had proceeded. As her niece must hear this news, she thought the sooner the better. The exercise, and the unreserved conversation of Francis and Clara, had restored in some degree the bloom to the cheek of Emily; and Mrs. Wilson felt it necessary to struggle with herself before she could summon sufficient resolution to invade the returning peace of her charge. However, having already decided on her course, she proceeded to the discharge of what she thought to be a duty.

"Emily, my child," she whispered, pressing her affectionately to her bosom, "you have been all I could wish and more than I expected, under your arduous struggles. But one more pang, and I trust your recollections on this painful subject will be done away."

Emily looked at her aunt in anxious expectation of what was coming, and quietly taking the paper, followed the direction of Mrs. Wilson's finger to the article on the marriage of Denbigh.

There was a momentary struggle in Emily for self-command. She was obliged to find support in a chair. The returning richness of color, excited by her walk, vanished; but, recovering herself, she pressed the hand of her anxious guardian, and, gently waving her back, proceeded to her own room.

On her return to the company the same control of her feelings which had distinguished her conduct of late was again visible; and, although her aunt most narrowly watched her movements, looks and speeches, she could discern no visible alteration by this confirmation of misconduct. The truth was, that in Emily Moseley the obligations of duty were so imperative, her sense of her dependence on Providence so humbling and yet so confiding, that, as soon as she was taught to believe her lover unworthy of her esteem, that moment an insuperable barrier separated them. His marriage could add nothing to the distance between them. It was impossible they could be united; and although a secret lingering of the affections over his fallen character might and did exist, it existed without any romantic expectations of miracles in his favor, or vain wishes of reformation, in which self was the prominent feeling.

She might be said to be keenly alive to all that concerned his welfare or movements, if she did not harbor the passion of love; but it showed itself in prayers for his amendment of life, and the most ardent petitions for his future and eternal happiness. She had set about, seriously and with much energy, the task of erasing from her heart sentiments which, however delightful she had found it to entertain in times past, were now in direct variance with her duty. She knew that a weak indulgence of such passions would tend to draw her mind from, and disqualify her to discharge, those various calls on her time and her exertions which could alone enable her to assist others, or effect in her own person the great purposes of her creation. It was never lost sight of by Emily Moseley that her existence here was preparatory to an immensely more important state hereafter. She was consequently in charity with all mankind; and if grown a little more distrustful of the intentions of her fellow-creatures, it was a mistrust bottomed in a clear view of the frailties of our nature; and self-examination was among the not unfrequent speculations she made on this hasty marriage of her former lover.

Mrs. Wilson saw all this, and was soon made acquainted by her niece in terms with her views of her own condition; and although she had to, and did deeply regret, that all her caution had not been able to guard against deception, where it was most important for her to guide aright, yet she was cheered with the reflection that her previous care, with the blessings of Providence, had admirably fitted her charge to combat and overcome the consequences of their mistaken confidence.

The gloom which this little paragraph excited extended to every individual in the family, for all had placed Denbigh by the side of John in their affections, ever since his weighty services to Emily.

A letter from John announcing his intention of meeting them at Bath, as well as his new relation with Grace, relieved in some measure this general depression of spirits. Mr. Benfield alone found no consolation in the approaching nuptials. John he regarded as his nephew, and Grace he thought a very good sort of young woman; but neither of them were beings of the same genus with Emily and Denbigh.

"Peter," said he one day, after they had both been expending their ingenuity in vain efforts to discover the cause of this so-much-desired marriage being so unexpectedly frustrated, "have I not often told you that fate governed these things, in order that men might be humbled in this life? Now, Peter, had the Lady Juliana wedded with a mind congenial to her own, she might have been mistress of Benfield Lodge to this very hour."

"Yes, your honor—but there's Miss Emmy's legacy."

And Peter withdrew, thinking what would have been the consequences had Patty Steele been more willing, when he wished to make her Mrs. Peter Johnson— an association by no means uncommon in the mind of the steward; for if Patty had ever a rival in his affections it was in the person of Emily Moseley, though, indeed, with very different degrees and coloring of esteem.

The excursions to the cottage had been continued by Mrs. Wilson and Emily, and, as no gentleman was now in the family to interfere with their communications, a general visit to the young widow had been made by the Moseleys, including Sir Edward and Mr. Ives.

The Jarvises had gone to London to receive their children, now penitent in more senses than one; and Sir Edward learned with pleasure that Egerton and his wife had been admitted into the family of the merchant.

Sir Edgar had died suddenly, and the entailed estates had fallen to his successor, the colonel, now Sir Harry; but the bulk of his wealth, being in convertible property, he had given by will to his other nephew, a young clergyman, and a son of a younger brother. Mary, as well as her mother, was greatly disappointed by this deprivation of what they considered their lawful splendor; but they found great consolation in the new dignity of Lady Egerton, whose greatest wish now was to meet the Moseleys, in order that she might precede them in or out of some place where such ceremonials are observed. The sound of "Lady Egerton's carriage stops the way," was delightful, and it never failed to be used on all occasions, although her ladyship was mistress of only a hired vehicle.

A slight insight into the situation of things among them may be found in the following narrative of their views, as revealed in a discussion which took place about a fortnight after the reunion of the family under one roof.

Mrs. Jarvis was mistress of a very handsome coach, the gift of her husband for her own private use. After having satisfied herself the baronet (a dignity he had enjoyed just twenty-four hours) did not possess the ability to furnish his lady, as she termed her daughter, with such a luxury, she magnanimously determined to relinquish her own, in support of the new-found elevation of her daughter. Accordingly, a consultation on the alterations which were necessary took place between the ladies—"The arms must be altered, of course," Lady Egerton observed, "and Sir Harry's, with the bloody hand and six quarterings, put in their place; then the liveries, they must be changed."

"Oh, mercy! my lady, if the arms are altered, Mr. Jarvis will be sure to notice it, and he would never forgive me; and perhaps——"

"Perhaps what?" exclaimed the new-made lady, with a disdainful toss of her head.

"Why," replied the mother, warmly, "not give me the hundred pounds he promised, to have it new lined and painted!"

"Fiddlesticks with the painting, Mrs. Jarvis," cried the *lady*, with dignity: "no carriage shall be called mine that does not bear my arms and the bloody hand."

"Why, your ladyship is unreasonable —indeed you are," said Mrs. Jarvis, coaxingly; and then, after a moment's thought, she continued, "is it the arms or the baronetcy you want, my dear?"

"Oh, I care nothing for the arms, but I am determined, now I am a baronet's lady, Mrs. Jarvis, to have the proper emblem of my rank."

"Certainly, my lady, that's true dignity. Well, then, we will put the bloody hand on your father's arms, and he will never notice it, for he never sees such things."

The arrangement was happily completed, and for a few days the coach of Mr. Jarvis bore about the titled dame, until one unlucky day the merchant, who still went on 'Change when any great bargain in the stocks was to be made, arrived at his own door suddenly, to procure a calculation he had made on the leaf of his prayer-book the last Sunday during sermon. This he obtained after some search. In his haste, he drove to his broker's in the carriage of his wife, to save time, it happening to be in waiting at the moment, and the distance not great. Mr. Jarvis forgot to order the man to return, and for an hour the vehicle stood in one of the most public places in the city. The consequence was, that when Mr Jarvis undertook to examine into his gains, with the account rendered of the transaction by his broker, he was astonished to read, "Sir Timothy Jarvis, Bart., in account with John Smith, Dr." Sir Timothy examined the account in as many different ways as Mr. Benfield had examined the marriage of Denbigh, before he would believe his eyes; and, when assured of the fact, he immediately caught up his hat and went to find the man who had dared to insult him, as it were, in defiance of the formality of business. He had not proceeded one square in the city before he met a friend, who spoke to him by the title; an explanation of the mistake followed, and the quasi-baronet proceeded to his stables. Here by actual examination he detected the fraud. An explanation with his consort followed; and the painter's brush soon effaced the emblem of dignity from the panels of the coach. All this was easy, but with his waggish companions on 'Change and in the city (where, notwithstanding his wife's fashionable propensities, he loved to resort), he was Sir Timothy still.

Mr. Jarvis, though a man of much modesty, was one of great decision, and he determined to have the laugh on his side. A newly purchased borough of his sent up an address flaming with patriotism, and it was presented by his own hands. The merchant seldom kneeled to his Creator, but on this occasion he humbled himself dutifully before his prince, and left the presence with a legal right to the appellation which his old companions had affixed to him sarcastically.

The rapture of Lady Jarvis may be more easily imagined than faithfully described, the Christian name of her husband alone throwing any alloy into the enjoyment of her elevation; but by a license of speech she ordered, and addressed in her own practice, the softer and more familiar appellation of Sir Timo. Two servants were discharged the first week, because, unused to titles, they had addressed her as mistress; and her son, the captain, then at a watering-place, was made acquainted by express with the joyful intelligence.

All this time Sir Henry Egerton was but little seen among his new relatives. He had his own engagements and haunts, and spent most of his time at a fashionable gaming house in the West End. As, however, the town was deserted, Lady Jarvis, with her daughters, having condescended to pay a round of city visits, to show off her airs and dignity to her old friends, persuaded Sir Timo that the hour for their visit to Bath had arrived, and they were soon comfortably settled in that city.

Lady Chatterton and her youngest daughter had arrived at the seat of her son, and John Moseley, as happy as the certainty of love returned, and the approbation of his friends, could make him, was in lodgings in the town. Sir Edward notified his son of his approaching visit to Bath, and John took proper accommodations for the family, which he occupied for a few days by himself as *locum tenens.*

Lord and Lady Herriefield had departed for the south of France; and Kate, removed from the scences of her earliest enjoyments and the bosom of her own family, and under the protection of a man she neither loved nor respected, began to feel the insufficiency of a name or of a fortune to constitute felicity. Lord Herriefield was of a suspicious and harsh temper, the first propensity being greatly increased by his former associations, and the latter not being removed by the humility of his eastern dependents. But the situation of her child gave no uneasiness to the managing mother, who thought her in the high-road to happiness, and was gratified at the result of her labors. Once or twice, indeed, her habits had overcome her caution so much as to endeavor to promote, a day or two sooner than had been arranged, the wedding of Grace; but her imprudence was checked instantly by the recoiling of Moseley from her insinuations in disgust; and the absence of the young man for twenty-four hours gave her timely warning of the danger of such an interference with one of such fastidious feelings. John punished himself as much as the dowager on these occasions; but the smiling face of Grace, with her hand frankly placed in his own at his return, never failed to do away the unpleasant sensations created by her mother's care.

The Chatterton and Jarvis families met in the rooms, soon after the arrival of the latter, when the lady of the knight, followed by both her daughters, approached the dowager with a most friendly salute of recognition. Lady Chatterton, really forgetful of the persons of her B—— acquaintance, and disliking the vulgarity of her air, drew up into an appearance of great dignity, as she hoped the lady was well. The merchant's wife felt the consciousness of rank too much to be repulsed in this manner, and believing that the dowager had merely forgotten her face, she added, with a simpering smile, in imitation of what she had seen better bred people practice with success:

"Lady Jarvis—my lady—your ladyship don't remember me—Lady Jarvis of the Deanery, B——, Northamptonshire, and my daughters, Lady Egerton and Miss Jarvis." Lady Egerton bowed stiffly to the recognizing smile the dowager now condescended to bestow; but Sarah, remembering a certain handsome lord in the family, was more urbane, determining at the moment to make the promotion of her mother and sister stepping-stones to greater elevation for herself.

"I hope my lord is well," continued the city lady. "I regret that Sir Timo, and Sir Harry, and Captain Jarvis, are not here this morning to pay their respects to your ladyship; but as we shall see naturally a good deal of each other, it must be deferred to a more fitting opportunity."

"Certainly, madam," replied the dowager, as, passing her compliments with those of Grace, she drew back from so open a conversation with creatures of such doubtful standing in the fashionable world.

CHAPTER XXXIII.

ON taking leave of Mrs. Fitzgerald, Emily and her aunt settled a plan of correspondence; the deserted situation of this young woman having created great interest in the breasts of her new friends. General M'Carthy had returned to Spain without receding from his orginal proposal, and his niece was left to mourn her early departure from one of the most solemn duties of life.

Mr. Benfield, thwarted in one of his most favorite schemes of happiness for the residue of his life, obstinately refused to make one of the party at Bath; and Ives and Clara having returned to Bolton, the remainder of the Moseleys arrived at the lodgings of John a very few days after the interview of the preceding chapter, with hearts ill qualified to enter into the gayeties of the place, though, in obedience to the wishes of Lady Moseley, to see and to be seen once more on that great theater of fashionable amusement.

The friends of the family who had known them iu times past were numerous, and were glad to renew their acquaintance with those they had always esteemed; so that they found themselves immediately surrounded by a circle of smiling faces and dashing equipages.

Sir William Harris, the proprietor of the deanery and a former neighbor, with his showy daughter, were among the first te visit them. Sir William was a man of handsome estate and exceptionable character, but entirely governed by the whims and desires of his only child. Caroline Harris wanted neither sense nor beauty, but, expecting a fortune, she had placed her views too high. She at first aimed at the peerage, and, while she felt herself entitled to suit her tastes as well as her ambition, had failed of her object by ill-concealed efforts to attain it. She had justly acquired the reputation of the reverse of a coquette, or yet of a prude; still she had never yet received an offer, and at the age of twenty-six had now begun to lower her thoughts to the commonalty. Her fortune would have easily obtained her a husband here, but she was determined to pick among the lower supporters of the aristocracy of the nation. With the Moseleys she had been early acquainted, though some years their senior; a circumstance, however, to which she took care never to allude unnecessarily.

The meeting between Grace and the Moseleys was tender and sincere. John's countenance glowed with delight, as he saw his future wife folded successively in the arms of those he loved, and Grace's tears and blushes added twofold charms to her native beauty. Jane relaxed from her reserve to receive her future sister, and determined with herself to appear in the world, in order to show Sir Henry Egerton that she did not feel the blow he had inflicted as severely as the truth might have proved.

The dowager found some little occupation, for a few days, in settling with Lady Moseley the preliminaries of the wedding; but the latter had suffered too much through her youngest daughters to enter into these formalities with her ancient spirit. All things were, however, happily settled; and Ives making a journey for the express purpose, John and Grace were united privately at the altar of one of the principal churches at Bath. Chatterton had been summoned on the occasion; and the same paper which announced the nuptials, contained amongst the fashionable arrivals, the names of the Duke of Derwent and his sister, the Marquis of Eltringham and sisters, among whom was to be found Lady Laura Denbigh. Lady Chatterton carelessly remarked, in presence of her friends, the husband of the latter was summoned to the death-bed of a relative, from whom he had great expectations. Emily's color did certairly change as she listened to this news, but not allowing her thoughts to dwell on the subject, she was soon enabled to recall her serenity of appearance.

But Jane and Emily were delicately placed. The lover of the former, and the wives of the lovers of both, were in the way of daily, if not hourly rencounters; and it required all the energies of the young women to appear with composure before them. The elder was supported by pride, the younger by principle. The first was restless, haughty, distant, and repulsive. The last mild, humble, reserved, but eminently attractive. The one was suspected by all around her; the other was unnoticed by any but her nearest and dearest friends.

The first rencounter with these dreaded guests occurred at the rooms one evening, where the elder ladies had insisted on the bride's making her appearance. The Jarvises were there before them, and at their entrance caught the eyes of the group. Lady Jarvis approached immediately, filled with exultation—her husband with respect. The latter was received with cordiality—the former politely, but with distance. The young ladies and Sir Henry bowed distantly, and the gentlemen soon drew off into another part of the room: his absence alone kept Jane from fainting. The handsome figure of Egerton standing by the side of Mary Jarvis, as her acknowledged husband, was near proving too much for her pride, notwithstanding all her efforts; and he looked so much like the imaginary being she had set up as the object of her worship, that her heart was also in danger of rebellings.

"Positively, Sir Edward and my lady, both Sir Timo and myself, and, I dare say, Sir Harry and Lady Egerton too, are delighted to see you comfortably at Bath among us. Mrs. Moseley, I wish you much happiness; Lady Chatterton too. I suppose your ladyship recollects me now; I am Lady Jarvis. Mr. Moseley, I regret, for your sake, that my son, Captain Jarvis, is not here; you were so fond of each other, and both so loved your guns."

"Positively, my Lady Jarvis," said Moseley, dryly, "my feelings on the occasion are as strong as your own; but I presume the captain is much too good a shot for me by this time."

"Why, yes; he improves greatly in most things he undertakes," rejoined the smiling dame, "and I hope he will soon learn, like you, to shoot, with the *harrows* of Cupid. I hope the honorable Mrs. Moseley is well?"

Grace bowed mildly, as she answered to the interrogatory, and smiled at the thought of Jarvis put in competition with her husband in this species of archery, when a voice immediately behind where they sat caught the ears of the whole party; all it said was:

"Harriet, you forgot to show me Marian's letter."

"Yes, but I will to-morrow," was the reply.

It was the tone of Denbigh. Emily almost fell from her seat as it first reached her, and the eyes of all but herself were immediately turned in quest of the speaker. He had approached within a few feet of them, supporting a lady on each arm. A second look convinced the Moseleys that they were mistaken. It was not Denbigh, but a young man whose figure, face, and air resembled him strongly, and whose voice possessed the same soft, melodious tones which had distinguished that of Denbigh. This party seated themselves within a very short distance of the Moseleys, and they continued their conversation.

"You heard from the colonel to-day, too, I believe," continued the gentleman, turning to the lady who sat next to Emily.

"Yes, he is a very punctual correspondent; I hear every other day."

"How is his uncle, Laura?" inquired her female companion.

"Rather better; but I will thank your grace to find the marquis and Miss Howard."

"Bring them to us," rejoined the other.

"Yes," said the former lady, with a laugh, "and Eltringham will thank you too, I daresay."

In an instant the duke returned, accompanied by a gentleman of thirty and an elderly lady, who might have been safely taken for fifty without offense to anybody but herself.

During these speeches their auditors had listened with almost breathless interest. Emily had stolen a glance which satisfied her it was not Denbigh himself, and it greatly relieved her; but was startled at discovering that she was actually seated by the side of his young and lovely wife. When an opportunity offered she dwelt on the amiable, frank countenance of her rival with melancholy satisfaction; at least, she thought, he may yet be happy, and I hope penitent.

It was a mixture of love and gratitude which prompted this wish, both sentiments not easily got rid of when once ingrafted into our better feelings. John eyed the strangers with a displeasure for which he could not account at once, and saw, in the ancient lady, the bridesmaid Lord Henry had so unwillingly admitted to that distinction.

Lady Jarvis was astounded with her vicinity to so much nobility, and she drew back to her family to study its movements to advantage; while Lady Chatterton sighed heavily as she contemplated the fine figures of an unmarried duke and marquis, and she without a single child to dispose of. The remainder of the party continued to view them with curiosity, and listened with interest to what they said.

Two or three young ladies had now joined the strangers, attended by a couple of gentlemen, and the conversation became general. The ladies declined dancing entirely, but appeared willing to throw away an hour in comments on their neighbors.

"William," said one of the young ladies, "there is your old messmate, Colonel Egerton."

"Yes, I observe him," replied her brother. "I see him;" but, smiling significantly, he continued, "we are messmates no longer."

"He is a sad character," said the marquis with a shrug.

"William, I would advise you to be cautious of his acquaintance."

"I thank you," replied Lord William, "but I believe I understand him thoroughly."

Jane manifested strong emotion during these remarks, while Sir Edward and his wife averted their faces from a simultaneous feeling of self-reproach. Their eyes met, and mutual concessions were contained in the glance; yet their feelings were unnoticed by their companions, for over the fulfillment of her often-repeated forewarnings of neglect and duty to our children, Mrs. Wilson had mourned in sincerity, but she had forgotten to triumph.

"When are we to see Pendennyss?" inquired the marquis; "I hope he will be here with George—I have a mind to beat up his quarters in Wales this season —what say you, Derwent?"

"I intend it, if I can persuade Lady Harriet to quit the gayeties of Bath so soon—what say *you*, sister—will you be in readiness to attend me so early?"

This question was asked in an arch tone, and drew the eyes of her friends on the person to whom it was addressed.

"I am ready now, Frederick, if you wish it," answered the sister hastily, and coloring excessively as she spoke.

"But where is Chatterton? I thought he was here—he had a sister married here last week," inquired Lord William Stapleton, addressing no one in particular.

A slight movement in their neighbors attracted the attention of the party.

"What a lovely young woman," whispered the duke to Lady Laura, "your neighbor is!"

The lady smiled her assent, and as Emily overheard it, she rose with glowing cheeks, and proposed a walk round the room.

Chatterton soon after entered. The young peer had acknowledged to Emily, that, deprived of hope as he had been by her firm refusal of his hand, his efforts had been directed to the suppression of a passion which could never be successful; but his esteem, his respect, remained in full force. He did not touch at all on the subject of Denbigh, and she supposed that he thought his marriage was a step that required justification.

The Moseleys had commenced their promenade round the room as Chatterton came in. He paid his compliments to them as soon as he entered, and walked with their party. The noble visitors followed their example, and the two parties met. Chatterton was delighted to see them, the duke was particularly fond of him; and, had one been present of sufficient observation, the agitation of his sister, Lady Harriet Denbigh, would have accounted for the doubts of her brother as respects her willingness to leave Bath.

A few words of explanation passed; the duke and his friends appeared to urge something on Chatterton, who acted as their ambassador, and the consequence was an introduction of the two parties to each other. This was conducted with the ease of the present fashion—it was general, and occurred, as it were, incidentally, in the course of the evening.

Both Lady Harriet and Lady Laura Denbigh were particularly attentive to Emily. They took their seats by her, and manifested a preference for her conversation that struck Mrs. Wilson as remarkable. Could it be that the really attractive manners and beauty of her niece had caught the fancy of these ladies, or was there a deeper seated cause for the desire to draw Emily out, that both of them evinced? Mrs. Wilson had heard a rumor that Chatterton was thought attentive to Lady Harriet, and the other was the wife of Denbigh; was it possible the quondam suitors of her niece had related to their present favorites the situation they had stood in as regarded Emily? It was odd, to say no more; and the widow dwelt on the innocent countenance of the bride with pity and admiration. Emily herself was not a little abashed at the notice of her new acquaintances, especially Lady Laura's; but as their admiration appeared sincere, as well as their desire to be on terms of intimacy with the Moseleys, they parted, on the whole, mutually pleased.

The conversation several times was embarrassing to the baronet's family, and at moments distressingly so to their daughters.

At the close of the evening they all formed one group at a little distance from the rest of the company, and in a situation to command a view of it.

"Who is that vulgar-looking woman," said Lady Sarah Stapleton, "seated next to Sir Henry Egerton, brother?"

"No less a personage than my Lady Jarvis," replied the marquis, gravely, "and the mother-in-law of Sir Harry, and the wife of Sir Timo— "; this was said with a look of drollery that showed the marquis was a bit of a quiz.

"Married!" cried Lord William, "mercy on the woman who is Egerton's wife. He is the greatest latitudinarian among the ladies of any man in England — nothing — no, nothing would tempt me to let such a man marry a sister of mine!"

Ah, thought Mrs. Wilson, how we may be deceived in character, with the best intentions, after all! In what are the open vices of Egerton worse than the more hidden ones of Denbigh?"

These freely expressed opinions on the character of Sir Henry were excessively awkward to some of the listeners, to whom they were connected with unpleasant recollections of duties neglected and affections thrown away.

Sir Edward Moseley was not disposed to judge his fellow-creatures harshly; and it was as much owing to his philanthropy as to his indolence, that he had been so remiss in his attention to the associates of his daughters. But the veil once removed, and the consequences brought home to him through his child, no man was more alive to the necessity of caution on this important particular; and Sir Edward formed many salutary resolutions for the goverment of his future conduct, in relation to those whom an experience nearly fatal in its results had now greatly qualified to take care of themselves. But to resume our narrative—Lady Laura had maintained with Emily a conversation, which was enlivened by occasional remarks from the rest of the party, in the course of which the nerves as well as the principles of Emily were put to a severe trial.

"My brother Henry," said Lady Laura, "who is a captain in the navy, once had the pleasure of seeing you, Miss Moseley, and in some measure made me acquainted with you before we met."

"I dined with Lord Henry at L——, and was much indebted to his polite attentions in an excursion on the water," replied Emily, simply.

"Oh, I am sure his attentions were exclusive," cried the sister; "indeed, he told us that nothing but want of time prevented his being deeply in love—he had even the audacity to tell Denbigh it was fortunate for me he had never seen you, or I should have been left to lead apes."

"And I suppose you believe him now," cried Lord William, laughing, as he bowed to Emily.

His sister laughed in her turn, but shook her head, in the confidence of conjugal affection.

"It is all conjecture, for the colonel said he had never enjoyed the pleasure of meeting Miss Moseley, so I will not boast of what my powers might have done; Miss Moseley," continued Lady Laura, blushing slightly at her inclination to talk of an absent husband, so lately her lover, "I hope to have the pleasure of presenting Colonel Denbigh to you soon."

"I think," said Emily, with a strong horror of deception, and a mighty struggle to suppress her feelings, "Colonel Denbigh was mistaken in saying that we had never met; he was of material service to me once, and I owe him a debt of gratitude that I only wish I could properly repay."

Lady Laura listened in surprise; but as Emily paused she could not delicately, as his wife, remind her further of the obligation by asking what the service was, and hesitating a moment, continued—

"Henry quite made you the subject of conversation among us. Lord Chatterton too, who visited us for a day, was equally warm in his eulogiums. I really thought they created a curiosity in the duke and Pendennyss to behold their idol."

"A curiosity that would be ill rewarded in its indulgence," said Emily, abashed by the personality of the discourse.

"So says the modesty of Miss Moseley," said the Duke of Derwent, in the peculiar tone which distinguished the softer keys of Denbigh's voice.

Emily's heart beat quick as she heard them, and she was afterward vexed to remember with how much pleasure she had listened to this opinion of the duke. Was it the sentiment, or was it the voice? She, however, gathered strength to answer, with a dignity that repressed further praises:—

"Your grace is willing to divest me of what little I possess."

"Pendennyss is a man of a thousand," continued Lady Laura, with the privilege of a married woman. "I do wish he would join us at Bath—is there no hope, duke?"

"I am afraid not," replied his grace: "he keeps himself immured in Wales with his sister, who is as much of a hermit as he is himself."

"There was a story of an inamorata in private somewhere," cried the marquis; "why, at one time it was even said he was privately married to her."

"Scandal, my lord," said the duke, gravely: "Pendennyss is of unexceptionable morals, and the lady you mean is the widow of Major Fitzgerald, whom you knew. Pendennyss never sees her, though by accident he was once of very great service to her."

Mrs. Wilson breathed freely again, as she heard this explanation, and thought if the marquis knew all how differently would he judge Pendennyss, as well as others.

"Oh! I have the highest opinion of Lord Pendennyss," cried the marquis.

The Moseleys were not sorry that the usual hour of returning put an end to the conversation and their embarrassment.

CHAPTER XXXIV.

DURING the succeeding fortnight, the intercourse between the Moseleys and their new acquaintances increased daily. It was rather awkward at first on the part of Emily, and her beating pulse and changing color too often showed the alarm of feelings not yet overcome, when any allusions were made to the absent husband of one of the ladies. Still, as her parents encouraged the acquaintance, and her aunt thought the best way to get rid of the remaining weakness with respect to Denbigh was not to shrink from even an interview with the gentleman himself, Emily succeeded in conquering her reluctance; and as the high opinion entertained by Lady Laura of her husband was expressed in a thousand artless ways, an interest was created in her that promised in time to weaken if not destroy the impression that had been made by Denbigh himself.

On the other hand, Egerton carefully avoided all collision with the Moseleys. Once, indeed, he endeavored to renew his acquaintance with John, but a haughty repulse almost produced a quarrel.

What representations Egerton had thought proper to make to his wife, we are unable to say, but she appeared to resent something, as she never approached the dwelling or persons of her quondam associates, although in her heart she was dying to be on terms of intimacy with their titled friends. Her incorrigible mother was restrained by no such or any other consideration, and contrived to fasten on the dowager and Lady Harriet a kind of bowing acquaintance, which she made great use of at the rooms.

The duke sought out the society of Emily wherever he could obtain it; and Mrs. Wilson thought her niece admitted his approaches with less reluctance than that of any other of the gentlemen around her. At first she was surprised, but a closer observation betrayed to her the latent cause.

Derwent resembled Denbigh greatly in person and voice, although there were distinctions easily to be made on an acquaintance. The duke had an air of command and hauteur that was never to be seen in his cousin. But his admiration of Emily he did not attempt to conceal; and, as he ever addressed her in the respectful language and identical voice of Denbigh, the observant widow easily perceived that it was the remains of her attachment to the one that induced her niece to listen with such evident pleasure to the conversation of the other.

The Duke of Derwent wanted many of the indispensable requisites of a husband, in the eyes of Mrs. Wilson; yet, as she thought Emily out of all danger at the present of any new attachment, she admitted the association under no other restraint than the uniform propriety of all that Emily said or did.

"Your niece will one day be a duchess, Mrs. Wilson," whispered Lady Laura, as Derwent and Emily were running over a new poem one morning, in the lodgings of Sir Edward; the former reading a fine extract aloud so strikingly in the air and voice of Denbigh, as to call all the animation of the unconscious Emily into her expressive face.

Mrs. Wilson sighed as she reflected on the strength of those feelings which even principles and testimony had not been able wholly to subdue, as she answered—

"Not of Derwent, I believe. But how wonderfully the duke resembles your husband at times," she added, entirely thrown off her guard.

Lady Laura was evidently surprised.

"Yes, at times he does; they are brothers' children, you know: the voice in all that connection is remarkable. Pendennyss, though a degree further off in blood, possesses it; and Lady Harriet, you perceive, has the same characteristic. There has been some siren in the family, in days past."

Sir Edward and Lady Moseley saw the attention of the duke with the greatest pleasure. Though not slaves to the ambition of wealth and rank, they were certainly no objection in their eyes; and a proper suitor Lady Moseley thought the most probable means of driving the recollection of Denbigh from the mind of her daughter. The latter consideration had great weight in inducing her to cultivate an acquaintance so embarrassing on many accounts.

The colonel, however, wrote to his wife the impossibility of his quitting his uncle while he continued so unwell, and it was settled that the bride should join him, under the escort of Lord William.

The same tenderness distinguished Denbigh on this occasion that had appeared so lovely when exercised to his dying father. Yet, thought Mrs. Wilson, how insufficient are good feelings to effect what can only be the result of good principles.

Caroline Harris was frequently of the parties of pleasure, walks, rides, and dinners, which the Moseleys were compelled to join in; and as the Marquis of Eltringham had given her one day some little encouragement, she determined to make an expiring effort at the peerage before she condescended to enter into an examination of the qualities of Captain Jarvis, who, his mother had persuaded her, was an Apollo, that had great hopes of being one day a lord, as both the captain and herself had commenced laying up a certain sum quarterly for the purpose of buying a title hereafter—an ingenious expedient of Jarvis's to get into his hands a portion of the allowance of his mother.

Eltringham was strongly addicted to the ridiculous, and without committing himself in the least, drew the lady out on divers occasions, for the amusement of himself and the duke—who enjoyed, without practicing, that species of joke.

The collisions between ill-concealed art and as ill-concealed irony had been practiced with impunity by the marquis for a fortnight, and the lady's imagination began to revel in the delights of a triumph, when a really respectable offer was made to Miss Harris by a neighbor of her father's in the country—one she would rejoice to have received a few days before, but which, in consequence of hopes created by the following occurrence, she haughtily rejected.

It was at the lodgings of the baronet that Lady Laura exclaimed one day.

"Marriage is a lottery, certainly, and neither Sir Henry nor Lady Egerton appears to have drawn a prize."

Here Jane stole from the room.

"Never, sister," cried the marquis. "I will deny that. Any man can select a prize from your sex, if he only knows his own taste."

"Taste is a poor criterion, I am afraid," said Mrs. Wilson, gravely, "on which to found matrimonial felicity."

"To what would you refer the decision, my dear madam?" inquired the Lady Laura.

"Judgment."

Lady Laura shook her head doubtingly. "You remind me so much of Lord Pendennyss! Everything he wishes to bring under the subject of judgment and principles."

"And is he wrong, Lady Laura?" asked Mrs. Wilson, pleased to find such correct views existed in one of whom she thought so highly.

"Not wrong, my dear madam, only impracticable. What do you think, marquis, of choosing a wife in conformity to your principles, and without consulting your tastes?"

Mrs. Wilson shook her head with a laugh, and disclaimed any such statement of the case : but the marquis, who disliked one of John's didactic conversations very much, gayly interrupted her by saying—

"Oh! taste is everything with me. The woman of my heart against the world, if she suits my fancy, and satisfies my judgment."

"And what may this fancy of your lordship be?" said Mrs. Wilson, willing to gratify the trifling. "What kind of a woman do you mean to choose? How tall, for instance?"

"Why, madam," cried the marquis, rather unprepared for such a cathechism, and looking around him until the outstretched neck and eager attention of Coroline Harris caught his eye, when he added with an air of great simplicity—"about the height of Miss Harris."

"How old?" asked Mrs. Wilson, with a smile.

"Not too young, madam, certainly. I am thirty-two—my wife must be five or six-and-twenty. Am I old enough, do you think, Derwent?" he added in a whisper to the duke.

"Within ten years," was the reply.

Mrs. Wilson continued—

"She must read and write, I suppose?"

"Why, faith," said the marquis, "I am not fond of a bookish sort of woman, and least of all a scholar."

"You had better take Miss Howard," whispered his brother. "She is old enough—never reads—and is just the height."

"No, no, Will," rejoined the brother; "rather too old that. Now I admire a woman who has confidence in herself. One that understands the proprieties of life, and has, if possible, been at the head of an establishment before she is to take charge of mine."

The delighted Caroline wriggled about in her chair, and, unable to contain herself longer, inquired :

"Noble blood, of course, you would require my lord?"

"Why, no! I rather think the best wives are to be found in a medium. I would wish to elevate my wife myself. A baronet's daughter, for instance."

Here Lady Jarvis, who had entered during the dialogue and caught a clew to the topic they were engaged in, drew near, and ventured to ask if he thought a simple knight too low.

The marquis, who did not expect such an attack, was a little at a loss for an answer; but recovering himself, answered gravely, under the apprehension of another design on his person, that "he did think that would be forgetting his duty to his descendants."

Lady Jarvis sighed, and fell back in

disappointment; while Miss Harris turning to the nobleman, in a soft voice desired him to ring for her carriage. As he handed her down she ventured to inquire if his lordship had ever met with such a woman as he described.

"Oh, Miss Harris," he whispered, as he handed her into the coach, "how can you ask me such a question? You are very cruel. Drive on, coachman."

"How, cruel, my lord?" said Miss Harris, eagerly. "Stop, John. How, cruel, my lord?" and she stretched her neck out of the window as the marquis, kissing his hand to her, ordered the man to proceed.

"Don't you hear your lady, sir?"

Lady Jarvis had followed them down, also with a view to catch anything which might be said, having apologized for her hasty visit; and as the marquis handed her politely into her carriage, she also begged "he would favor Sir Timo and Sir Henry with a call;" which being promised, Eltringham returned to the room.

"When am I to salute a marchioness of Eltringham?" cried Lady Laura to her brother; "one on the new standard set up by your lordship?"

"Whenever Miss Harris can make up her mind to the sacrifice," replied the brother very gravely. "Ah me! how very considerate some of your sex are, for the modesty of ours."

"I wish you joy with all my heart, my lord marquis," exclaimed John Moseley. "I was once favored with the notice of that same lady for a week or two, but a viscount saved me from capture."

"I really think, Moseley," said the duke, innocently, but speaking with animation, "an intriguing daughter worse than a managing mother."

John's gravity for a moment vanished, as he replied in a lowered key.

"Oh, much worse."

Grace's heart was in her throat until, by stealing a glance at her husband, she saw the cloud passing over his fine brow; and happening to catch her affectionate smile, his face was at once lighted into a look of pleasantry.

"I would advise caution, my lord. Caroline Harris has the advantage of experience in her trade, and was expert from the first."

"John—John," said Sir Edward with warmth, "Sir William is my friend, and his daughter must be respected."

"Then, baronet," cried the marquis, "she has one recommendation I was ignorant of, and as such I am silent; but ought not Sir William to teach his daughter to respect herself? I view these hus-band-hunting ladies as pirates on the ocean of love, and lawful objects for any roving cruiser like myself to fire at. At one time I was simple enough to retire as they advanced, but you know, madam," turning to Mrs. Wilson with a droll look, "flight only encourages pursuit, so I now give battle in self-defense."

"And I hope successfully, my lord," observed the lady. "Miss Harris, brother, does appear to have grown desperate in her attacks, which were formerly much more masked than at present. I believe it is generally the case, when a young woman throws aside the delicacy and feelings which ought to be the characteristics of her sex, and which teach her studiously to conceal her admiration, that she either becomes in time cynical and disagreeable to all around her from disappointment, or persevering in her efforts, as it were, runs amuck for her husband. Now in justice to the gentleman I must say, baronet, there are strong symptoms of the Malay about Caroline Harris."

"Amuck, amuck," cried the marquis, as, in obedience to the signal of his sister, he rose to withdraw.

Jane had retired to her own room in a mortification of spirit she could ill conceal during this conversation, and she felt a degree of humiliation which almost drove her to the desperate resolution of hiding herself forever from the world. The man she had so fondly enshrined in her heart proving to be so notoriously unworthy as to be the subject of unreserved censure in general company, was a reproach to her delicacy, her observation, her judgment, that was the more severe from being true; and she wept in bitterness over her fallen happiness.

Emily had noticed the movement of Jane, and waited anxiously for the departure of the visitors to hasten to her room. She knocked two or three times before her sister replied to her request for admittance.

"Jane, my dear Jane," said Emily, soothingly, "will you not admit me?"

Jane could not resist any longer the affection of her sister, and the door was opened; but as Emily endeavored to take her hand she drew back coldly, and cried—

"I wonder you, who are so happy, will leave the gay scene below for the society of an humbled wretch like me;" and overcome with the violence of her emotion, she burst into tears.

"Happy!" repeated Emily, in a tone of anguish, "happy, did you say, Jane? Oh, little do you know my sufferings, or you would never speak so cruelly!"

Jane, in her turn, surprised at the strength of Emily's language, considered her weeping sister with commiseration; and then, her thoughts recurring to her own case, she continued with energy—

"Yes, Emily, happy; for whatever may have been the reason of Denbigh's conduct, he is respected; and if you do or did love him, he was worthy of it. But I," said Jane, wildly, "threw away my affections on a wretch—*a mere impostor*—and I am miserable forever."

"No, dear Jane," rejoined Emily, having recovered her self-possession, "not miserable—nor forever. You have many, very many sources of happiness yet within your reach, even in this world. I—I do think, even our strongest attachments may be overcome by energy and a sense of duty. And oh! how I wish I could see you make the effort."

For a moment the voice of the youthful moralist had failed her; but anxiety in behalf of her sister overcame her feelings, and she ended the sentence with earnestness.

"Emily," said Jane, with obstinacy, and yet in tears, "you don't know what blighted affections are. To endure the scorn of the world, and see the man you once thought near being your husband married to another, who is showing herself in triumph before you wherever you go!"

"Hear me, Jane, before you reproach me further, and then judge between us." Emily paused a moment to acquire nerve to proceed, and then related to her astonished sister the little history of her own disappointments. She did not affect to conceal her attachment for Denbigh. With glowing cheeks she acknowledged that she found a necessity for all her efforts to keep her rebellious feelings yet in subjection; and as she recounted generally his conduct to Mrs. Fitzgerald, she concluded by saying, "But, Jane, I can see enough to call forth my gratitude; and altogether with yourself, I feel at this moment as if my affections were sealed forever, I wish to make no hasty resolutions, nor act in any manner as if I were unworthy of the lot Providence has assigned me."

"Unworthy? no!—you have no reasons for self-reproach. If Mr. Denbigh has had the art to conceal his crimes from you, he did it to the rest of the world also, and has married a woman of rank and character. But how differently are we situated! Emily—I—I have no such consolation."

"You have the consolation, my sister, of knowing there is an interest made for you where we all require it most, and it is there I endeavor to seek my support," said Emily, in a low and humble tone. "A review of our own errors takes away the keenness of our perception of the wrongs done us, and by placing us in charity with the rest of the world, disposes us to enjoy calmly the blessings within our reach. Besides, Jane, we have parents whose happiness is locked up in that of their children, and we should—we must overcome the feelings which disqualify us for our common duties, on their account."

"Ah!" cried Jane, "how can I move about in the world, while I know the eyes of all are on me, in curiosity to discover how I bear my disappointments. But you, Emily, are unsuspected. It is easy for you to affect a gayety you do not feel."

"I neither affect nor feel any gayety," said her sister, mildly. "But are there not the eyes of One on us, of infinitely more power to punish or reward than what may be found in the opinions of the world? Have we no duties? For what is our wealth, our knowledge, our time given us, but to improve for our own and for the eternal welfare of those around us? Come then, my sister, we have both been deceived—let us endeavor not to be culpable."

"I wish from my soul, we could leave Bath," cried Jane. "The place, the people are hateful to me!"

"Jane," said Emily, "rather say you hate their vices, and wish for their amendment; but do not indiscriminately condemn a whole community for the wrongs you have sustained from one of its members."

Jane allowed herself to be consoled, though by no means convinced, by this effort of her sister; and they both found a relief by thus unburdening their hearts to each other, that in future brought them more nearly together, and was of mutual assistance in supporting them in the promiscuous circles in which they were obliged to mix.

With all her fortitude and principle, one of the last things Emily would have desired was an interview with Denbigh; and she was happily relieved from the present danger of it by the departure of Lady Laura and her brother, to go to the residence of the colonel's sick uncle.

Both Mrs. Wilson and Emily suspected that a dread of meeting them had detained him from his intented journey to Bath; and neither was sorry to perceive what they considered as latent signs of grace—

a grace which Egerton appeared entirely to be without.

"He may yet see his errors, and make a kind and affectionate husband," thought Emily : and then, as the image of Denbigh rose in her imagination, surrounded with the domestic virtues, she roused herself from the dangerous reflection to the exercise of the duties in which she found a refuge from unpardonable wishes.

CHAPTER XXXV.

Nothing material occurred for a fortnight after the departure of Lady Laura, the Moseleys entering soberly into the amusements of the place, and Derwent and Chatterton becoming more pointed every day in their attentions—the one to Emily, and the other to Lady Harriet ; when the dowager received a pressing entreaty from Catherine to hasten to her at Lisbon, where her husband had taken up his abode for a time, after much doubt and indecision as to his place of residence. Lady Herriefield stated generally in her letter, that she was miserable, and that without the support of her mother she could not exist under the present grievances : but what was the cause of those grievances, or what grounds she had for her misery, she left unexplained.

Lady Chatterton was not wanting in maternal regard, and she promptly determined to proceed to Portugal in the next packet. John felt inclined for a little excursion with his bride ; and out of compassion to the baron, who was in a dilemma between his duty and his love (for Lady Harriet about that time was particularly attractive), he offered his services.

Chatterton allowed himself to be persuaded by the good-natured John, that his mother could safely cross the ocean under the protection of the latter. Accordingly, at the end of the before mentioned fortnight, the dowager, John, Grace, and Jane, commenced their journey to Falmouth.

Jane had offered to accompany Grace, as a companion in her return (it being expected Lady Chatterton would remain in the country with her daughter), and her parents appreciating her motives, permitted the excursion, with a hope it would draw her thoughts from past events.

Although Grace shed a few tears at parting with Emily and her friends, it was impossible for Mrs. Moseley to be long unhappy, with the face of John smiling by her side ; and they pursued their route

uninterruptedly. In due season they reached the port of embarkation.

The following morning the packet got under weigh, and a favorable breeze soon wafted them out of sight of their native shores. The ladies were too much indisposed the first day to appear on the deck ; but the weather becoming calm and the sea smooth, Grace and Jane ventured out of the confinement of their staterooms, to respire the fresh air above.

There were but few passengers, and those chiefly ladies—the wives of officers on foreign stations, on their way to join their husbands. As these had been accustomed to moving in the world, their disposition to accommodate soon removed the awkwardness of a first meeting, and our travelers began to be at home in their novel situation.

While Grace stood leaning on the arm of her husband, and clinging to his support, both from affection and a dread of the motion of the vessel, Jane ventured with one of the ladies to attempt to walk round the deck of the ship. Unaccustomed to such an uncertain foothold, the walkers were prevented falling by the kind interposition of a gentleman, who for the first time had shown himself among them at that moment. The accident, and their situation led to a conversation which was renewed at different times during their passage, and in some measure created an intimacy between our party and the stranger. He was addressed by the commander of the vessel as Mr. Harland ; and Lady Chatterton exercised her ingenuity in the investigation of his history, by which she made the following discovery :

The Rev. and Hon. Mr. Harland was the younger son of an Irish earl, who had early embraced the sacred profession in that Church, in which he held a valuable living in the gift of his father's family. His father was yet alive, and then at Lisbon with his mother and sister, in attendance on his elder brother who had been sent there in a deep decline a couple of months before. It had been the wish of his parents to have taken all their children with them ; but a sense of duty had kept the young clergyman in the exercise of his holy office, until a request of his dying brother, and the directions of his father, caused him to hasten abroad to witness the decease of the one, and to afford all the solace within his power to the others.

It may be easily imagined that the discovery of the rank of their accidental acquaintance, with the almost certainty that existed of his being the heir of his father's honors, in no degree impaired his consequence in the eyes of the dowager ;

and it is certain, his visible anxiety and depressed spirits, his unaffected piety, and disinterested hopes for his brother's recovery, no less elevated him in the opinions of her companions.

There was at the moment, a kind of sympathy between Harland and Jane, notwithstanding the melancholy which gave rise to it proceeding from such very different causes; and as the lady, although with diminished bloom, retained all her personal charms rather heightened than otherwise by the softness of low spirits, the young clergyman sometimes relieved his apprehensions of his brother's death by admitting the image of Jane among his more melancholy reflections.

The voyage was tedious, and some time before it was ended the dowager had given Grace an intimation of the probability there was of Jane's becoming, at some future day, a countess. Grace sincerely hoped that whatever she became she would be as happy as she thought all allied to John deserved to be.

They entered the bay of Lisbon early in the morning; and as the ship had been expected for some days, a boat came alongside with a note for Mr. Harland, before they had anchored. It apprised him of the death of his brother. The young man threw himself precipitately into it, and was soon employed in one of the loveliest offices of his vocation, that of healing the wounds of the afflicted.

Lady Herriefield received her mother in a sort of sullen satisfaction, and her companions with an awkwardness she could ill conceal. It required no great observation in the travelers to discover that their arrival was entirely unexpected by the viscount, if it were not equally disagreeable indeed, one day's residence under his roof assured them all that no great degree of domestic felicity was an inmate of the dwelling.

From the moment Lord Herriefield became suspicious that he had been the dupe of the management of Kate and her mother, he viewed every act of his wife with a prejudiced eye. It was easy, with his knowledge of human nature, to detect her selfishness and worldly-mindedness; for as these were faults she was unconscious of possessing, so she was unguarded in her exposure of them. But her designs, in a matrimonial point of view, having ended with her marriage, had the viscount treated her with any of the courtesies due her sex and station, she might, with her disposition, have been contented in the enjoyment of rank and in the possession of wealth; but their more private hours were invariably rendered unpleasant by the overflowings of her husband's resentment at having been deceived in his judgment of the female sex.

There is no point upon which men are more tender than their privilege of suiting themselves in a partner for life, although many of both sexes are influenced in this important selection more by the wishes and whims of others than is usually suspected; yet, as all imagine what is the result of contrivance and management is the election of free will and taste, so long as they are ignorant, they are contented. Lord Herriefield wanted this bliss of ignorance; and, with contempt for his wife, was mingled anger at his own want of foresight.

Very few people can tamely submit to self-reproach; and as the cause of this irritated state of mind was both not only constantly present, but completely within his power, the viscount determined to give her as little reason to exult in the success of her plans as possible. Jealous he was, from temperament, from bad associations, and the want of confidence in the principles of his wife, the freedom of foreign manners having an additional tendency to excite his baneful passion to an unusual degree. Abridged in her pleasures, reproached with motives she was incapable of harboring, and disappointed in all those enjoyments her mother had ever led her to believe the invariable accompaniments of married life, where proper attention had been paid to the necessary qualifications of riches and rank, Kate had written to the dowager with the hope her presence might restrain, or her advice teach her, successfully to oppose the unfeeling conduct of the viscount.

Lady Chatterton never having implanted any of her favorite systems in her daughter, so much by precept as by the force of example in her own person, as well as by indirect eulogiums on certain people who were endowed with those qualities and blessings she most admired, on the present occasion Catherine did not burden herself in terms to her mother; but by a regular gradation of complaints, aimed more at the world than at her husband, she soon let the knowing dowager see their application, and in the end completely removed the veil from her domestic grievances.

The example of John and Grace for a short time awed the peer into dissembling his disgust for his spouse; but the ice once broken, their presence soon ceased to affect either the frequency or the severity of his remarks, when under its influence.

From such exhibitions of matrimonial

discord, Grace shrank timidly into the retirement of her room, and Jane, with dignity, would follow her example; while John at times became a listener with a spirit barely curbed within the bounds of prudence, and at others he sought in the company of his wife and sister relief from the violence of his feelings.

John never admired nor respected Catherine, for she wanted those very qualities he chiefly loved in her sister; yet, as she was a woman, and one nearly connected with him, he found it impossible to remain a quiet spectator of the unmanly treatment she often received from her husband; he therefore made preparations for his return to England by the first packet, abridging his intended residence in Lisbon more than a month.

Lady Chatterton endeavored all within her power to heal the breach between Kate and her husband, but it greatly exceeded her abilities. It was too late to implant such principles in her daughter as, by a long course of self-denial and submission, might have won the love of the viscount, had the mother been acquainted with them herself; so that, having induced her child to marry with a view to obtaining precedence and a jointure, she once more set to work to undo part of her former labors, by bringing about a decent separation between the husband and wife, in such a manner as to secure to her child the possession of her wealth and the esteem of the world. The latter, though certainly a somewhat difficult undertaking, was greatly lessened by the assistance of the former.

John and his wife determined to seize the opportunity to examine the environs of the city. In one of these daily rides they met their fellow-traveler, Mr., now Lord Harland. He was rejoiced to see them again, and hearing of their intended departure, informed them of his being about to return to England in the same vessel—his parents and sister contemplating ending the winter in Portugal.

The intercourse between the two families was kept up with a show of civilities between the noblemen, and much real good-will on the part of the juniors of the circle, until the day arrived for the sailing of the packet.

Lady Chatterton was left behind with Catherine, as yet unable to circumvent her schemes with prudence; it being deemed by the world a worse offense to separate, than to join together one's children in the bands of wedlock.

The confinement of a vessel is very propitious to those intimacies which lead to attachments. The necessity of being agreeable is a check upon the captious, and the desire to lessen the dullness of the scene a stimulus to the lively; and though the noble divine and Jane could not possibly be ranked in either class the effect was the same. The nobleman was much enamored, and Jane unconsciously gratified. It is true, love had never entered her thoughts in its direct and unequivocal form; but admiration is so consoling to those laboring under self-condemnation, and flattery of a certain kind so very soothing to all, it is not to be wondered that she listened with increasing pleasure to the interesting conversation of Harland on all occasions, and more particularly, as often happened, when exclusively addressed to herself.

Grace had of late reflected more seriously on the subject of her eternal welfare than she had been accustomed to do in the house of her mother; and the example of Emily, with the precepts of Mrs. Wilson, had not been thrown away upon her. It is a singular fact that more women feel a disposition to religion soon after marriage, than at any other period of life; and whether it is that, having attained the most important station this life affords the sex, they are more willing to turn their thoughts to a provision for the next, or whether it be owing to any other cause, Mrs. Moseley was included in the number. She became sensibly touched with her situation, and as Harland was both devout and able as well as anxious to instruct, one of the party, at least, had cause to rejoice in the journey for the remainder of her days. But precisely as Grace increased in her own faith, so did her anxiety after the welfare of her husband receive new excitement; and John, for the first time, became the cause of sorrow to his affectionate companion.

The deep interest Harland took in the opening conviction of Mrs. Moseley, did not so entirely engross his thoughts as to prevent the too frequent contemplation of the charms of her friend for his own peace of mind; and by the time the vessel reached Falmouth, he had determined to make a tender of his hand and title to the acceptance of Miss Moseley. Jane did not love Egerton; on the contrary, she despised him; but the time had been when all her romantic feelings, every thought of her brilliant imagination, had been filled with his image, and Jane felt it a species of indelicacy to admit the impression of another so soon, or even at all. These objections would, in time, have been overcome, as her affections became more and more enlisted on behalf of Harland, had she admitted his addresses; but there was an impediment that Jane considered insurmountable to a union with any man.

She had once communicated her passion to its object. There had been the confidence of approved love; and she had now no heart for Harland, but one that had avowedly been a slave to another. To conceal this from him would be unjust and not reconcilable to good faith; to confess it, humiliating, and without the pale of probability. It was the misfortune of Jane to keep the world too constantly before her, and to lose sight too much of her really depraved nature, to relish the idea of humbling herself so low in the opinion of a fellow-creature. The refusal of Harland's offer was the consequence, although she had begun to feel an esteem for him that would, no doubt, have given rise to an attachment in time, far stronger and more deeply seated than her passing fancy for Colonel Egerton had been.

If the horror of imposing on the credulity of Harland a wounded heart was creditable to Jane, and showed an elevation of character, that under proper guidance, would have placed her in the first ranks of her sex, the pride which condemned her to a station nature did not design her for, was irreconcilable with the humility a just view of her condition could not fail to produce; and the second sad consequence of the indulgent weakness of her parents, was confirming their child in passions directly at variance with the first duties of a Christian.

We have so little right to value ourselves on anything, that pride is a sentiment of very doubtful service, and one certainly that is unable to effect any useful results, which will not equally flow from good principles.

Harland was disappointed and grieved, but prudently judging that occupation and absence would remove recollections which could not be very deep, they parted at Falmouth, and our travelers proceeded on their journey for B——, whither, during their absence, Sir Edward's family had returned to spend a month, before they removed to town for the residue of the winter.

The meeting of the two parties was warm and tender, and as Jane had many things to recount, and John as many to laugh at, their arrival threw a gayety around Moseley Hall, to which it had for months been a stranger.

One of the first acts of Grace, after her return, was to enter strictly into the exercise of all those duties and ordinances required by her Church and the present state of her mind, and from the hands of Dr. Ives she received her first communion at the altar.

As the season had now become far advanced, and the fashionable world had been some time assembled in the metropolis, the baronet commenced his arrangements to take possession of his town house, after an interval of nineteen years. John proceeded to the capital first; and the necessary domestics procured, furniture supplied, and other arrangements usual to the appearance of a wealthy family in the world having been completed, he returned with the information that all was ready for their triumphal entrance.

Sir Edward, feeling that a separation for so long a time, and at such an unusual distance, in the very advanced age of Mr. Benfield, would be improper, paid him a visit with the intention of persuading him to make one of his family for the next four months. Emily was his companion, and their solicitations were happily crowned with a success they had not anticipated. Averse to being deprived of Peter's society, the honest steward was included in the party.

"Nephew," said Mr. Benfield, beginning to waver in his objections to the undertaking, as the arguments pro and con were produced, " there are instances of gentlemen not in parliament going to town in the winter, I know. You are one yourself; and old Sir John Cowel, who never could get in, although he ran for every city in the kingdom, never missed his winter in Soho. Yes, yes—the thing is admissible—but had I known your wishes before, I would certainly have kept my borough if it were only for the appearance of the thing—besides," continued the old man, shaking his head, "his Majesty's ministers require the aid of some more experienced members in these critical times; for what should an old man like me do in Westminster, unless it were to aid his country with his advice?"

"Make his friends happy with his company, dear uncle," said Emily, taking his hand between both her own, and smiling affectionately on the old gentleman as she spoke.

"Ah! Emmy dear!" cried Mr. Benfield, looking on her with melancholy pleasure, "you are not to be resisted—just such another as the sister of my old friend, Lord Gosford; she could always coax me out of anything. I remember now, I heard the earl tell her once he could not afford to buy a pair of diamond ear-rings; and she looked—only looked, did not speak! Emmy!—that I bought them with intent to present them to her myself."

" And did she take them, uncle ? " asked his niece, in a little surprise.

" Oh, yes ! When I told her if she did not I would throw them into the river, as no one else should wear what had been intended for her ; poor soul ! how delicate and unwilling she was. I had to convince her they cost three hundred pounds, before she would listen to it ; and then she thought it such a pity to throw away a thing of so much value. It would have been wicked, you know, Emmy dear ; and she was much opposed to wickedness and sin in any shape."

" She must have been a very unexceptionable character, indeed," cried the baronet, with a smile, as he proceeded to make the necessary orders for their journey.

But we must return to the party left at Bath.

CHAPTER XXXVI.

THE letters of Lady Laura informed her friends that she and Colonel Denbigh had decided to remain with his uncle until the recovery of the latter was complete, and then to proceed to Denbigh Castle, to meet the duke and his sister during the approaching holidays.

Emily was much relieved by this postponement of an interview which she would gladly have avoided forever ; and her aunt sincerely rejoiced that her niece was allowed more time to eradicate impressions which, she saw with pain, her charge had yet a struggle to overcome.

There were so many points to admire in the character of Denbigh—his friends spoke of him with such decided partiality, Dr. Ives, in his frequent letters, alluded to him with so much affection—that Emily frequently detected herself in weighing the testimony of his guilt, and indulging the expectation that circumstances had deceived them all in their judgment of his conduct. Then his marriage would cross her mind ; and with the conviction of the impropriety of admitting him to her thoughts at all, would come the mass of circumstantial testimony which had accumulated against him.

Derwent served greatly to keep alive the recollections of his person, however ; and as Lady Harriet seemed to live only in the society of the Moseleys, not a day passed without giving the duke some opportunity of indirectly preferring his suit.

Emily not only appeared, but in fact was, unconscious of his admiration, and entered into their amusements with a satisfaction that was increased by the belief that the unfortunate attachment her cousin Chatterton had once professed for herself, was forgotten in the more certain enjoyments of a successful love.

Lady Harriet was a woman of manners and character very different from Emily Moseley, yet had she, in a great measure, erased the impressions made by the beauty of his kinswoman from the bosom of the baron.

Chatterton, under the depression of his first disappointment, it will be remembered, had left B—— in company with Mr. Denbigh. The interest of the duke had been unaccountably exerted to procure him the place he had so long solicited in vain, and gratitude required his early acknowledgments for the favor. His manner, so very different from a successful applicant for a valuable office, had struck both Derwent and his sister as singular. Before, however, a week's intercourse had passed between them, his own frankness had made them acquainted with the cause ; and a double wish prevailed in the bosom of Lady Harriet, to know the woman who could resist the beauty of Chatterton, and to relieve him from the weight imposed on his spirits by disappointed affection.

The manners of Lady Harriet Denbigh were not in the least forward or masculine ; but they had the freedom of high rank, mingled with a good deal of the ease of fashionable life. Mrs. Wilson noticed, moreover, in her conduct to Chatterton, a something exceeding the interest of ordinary communications in their situation, which might possibly have been attributed more to feeling than to manner. It is certain one of the surest methods to drive Emily from his thoughts, was to dwell on the perfections of some other lady ; and Lady Harriet was so constantly before him in his visit into Westmoreland, so soothing, so evidently pleased with his presence, that the baron made rapid advances in attaining his object.

He had alluded, in his letter to Emily, to the obligation he was under to the services of Denbigh in erasing his unfortunate partiality for her ; but what those services were we are unable to say, unless they were the usual arguments of the plainest good sense, enforced in the singularly insinuating and kind manner which distinguished that gentleman. In fact, Lord Chatterton was not formed by nature to love long, deprived of hope, or to resist long the flattery of a preference from such a woman as Harriet Denbigh.

On the other hand, Derwent was warm in his encomiums on Emily to all but herself; and Mrs. Wilson again thought it prudent to examine into the state of her feelings, in order to discover if there was any danger of his unremitted efforts drawing Emily into a connection that neither her religion nor prudence could wholly approve.

Derwent was a man of the world—a Christian only in name; and the cautious widow determined to withdraw in season, should she find grounds for her apprehension.

About ten days after the departure of the dowager and her companions, Lady Harriet exclaimed, in one of her morning visits—

"Lady Moseley! I have now hopes of presenting to you soon the most polished man in the United Kingdom!"

"As a husband! Lady Harriet!" inquired the other, with a smile.

"Oh, no! only as a cousin, a second cousin! madam!" replied Lady Harriet, blushing a little, and looking in the opposite direction to the one in which Chatterton was placed.

"But his name? You forget our curiosity! What is his name?" cried Mrs. Wilson, entering into the trifling for the moment.

"Pendennyss, to be sure, my dear madam: whom else can I mean?"

"And you expect the earl at Bath?" Mrs. Wilson eagerly inquired.

"He has given us such hopes, and Derwent has written him to-day, pressing the journey."

"You will be disappointed, I am afraid, sister," said the duke. "Pendennyss has become so fond of Wales of late, that it is difficult to get him out of it."

"But," said Mrs. Wilson, "he will take his seat in parliament during the winter, my lord?"

"I hope he will, madam; though Lord Eltringham holds his proxies, in my absence, in all important questions before the house."

"Your grace will attend, I trust," said Sir Edward. "The pleasure of your company is among my expected enjoyments in the town."

"You are very good, Sir Edward," replied the duke, looking at Emily. "It will somewhat depend on circumstances, I believe."

Lady Harriet smiled, and the speech seemed understood by all but the lady most concerned in it.

"Lord Pendennyss is a universal favorite, and deservedly so," cried the duke. "He has set an example to the nobility, which few are equal to imitate. An only son, with an immense estate, he has de-

voted himself to the profession of a soldier, and gained great reputation by it in the world; nor has he neglected any of his private duties as a man—"

"Or a Christian, I hope," said Mrs. Wilson, delighted with the praises of the earl.

"Nor of a Christian, I believe," continued the duke; "he appears consistent, humble, and sincere—three requisites, I believe, for that character."

"Does not your grace know?" said Emily, with a benevolent smile.

Derwent colored slightly as he answered—

"Not as well as I ought; but"—lowering his voice for her alone, he added, "under proper instruction I think I might learn."

"Then I would recommend that book to you, my lord," rejoined Emily, with a blush, pointing to a pocket Bible which lay near her, though still ignorant of the allusion he meant to convey.

"May I ask the honor of an audience of Miss Moseley," said Derwent, in the same low tone, "whenever her leisure will admit her of granting the favor?"

Emily was surprised; but from the previous conversation and the current of her thoughts at the moment, supposing his communication had some reference to the subject before them, she rose from the chair, and unobtrusively, but certainly with an air of perfect innocence and composure, she went into the adjoining room, the door of which was open very near them.

Caroline Harris had abandoned all ideas of a coronet with the departure of the Marquis of Eltringham and his sisters for their own seat; and as a final effort of her fading charms, had begun to calculate the capabilities of Captain Jarvis, who had at this time honored Bath with his company.

It is true, the lady would have greatly preferred her father's neighbor, but that was an irretrievable step. He had retired, disgusted with her haughty dismissal of his hopes, and was a man who, although he greatly admired her fortune, was not to be recalled by any beck or smile which might grow out of caprice.

Lady Jarvis had, indeed, rather magnified the personal qualifications of her son; but the disposition they had manifested to devote some of their surplus wealth to purchasing a title, had great weight, for Miss Harris would cheerfully, at any time, have sacrificed one-half her own fortune to be called my lady. Jarvis would make but a shabby-looking lord, 'tis true; but then what a lord's wife would she not make herself! His father was a merchant, to be sure, but then merchants were always immensely rich, and a few thousand pounds, properly applied, might make the merchant's son a baron. She therefore resolved to inquire, the first opportunity, into the condition of the sinking fund of his plebeianism, and had serious thoughts of contributing her mite toward the advancement of the desired object, did she find it within the bounds of probable success.

An occasion soon offered, by the invitation of the captain to accompany him in an excursion in the tilbury of his brother-in-law.

In this ride they passed the equipages of Lady Harriet and Mrs. Wilson, with their respective mistresses, taking an airing. In passing the latter, Jarvis bowed (for he had renewed his acquaintance at the rooms without daring to visit at the lodgings of Sir Edward), and Miss Harris saw both parties as they dashed by them.

"You know the Moseleys, Caroline?" said Jarvis, with the freedom her manners had established between them.

"Yes," replied the lady, drawing her head back from a view of the carriages; "what fine arms those of the duke's are—and the coronet, it is so noble—so rich—I am sure if I were a man," laying great emphasis on the word—"I would be a lord."

"If you could, you mean," cried the captain.

"Could—why money will buy a title, you know—only most people are fonder of their cash than of honor."

"That's right," said the unreflecting captain; "money is the thing after all. Now what do you suppose our last mess-bill came to?"

"Oh, don't talk of eating and drinking," cried Miss Harris, in affected aversion; "it is beneath the consideration of nobility."

"Then any one may be a lord for me," said Jarvis, dryly, "if they are not to eat and drink; why, what do they live for, but such sort of things!"

"A soldier lives to fight and gain honor and distinction"—for his wife—Miss Harris would have added, had she spoken all she thought.

"A poor way that of spending a man's time," said the captain. "Now there is Captain Jones in our regiment; they say he loves fighting as much as eating: if he do, he is a bloodthirsty fellow."

"You know how intimate I am with your dear mother," continued the lady, bent on the principal object; "she has made me acquainted with her greatest wish."

"Her greatest wish!" cried the captain in astonishment; "why, what can that be?—a new coach and horses?"

"No, I mean one much dearer to us—I should say to her, than any such trifles; she has told me of the _plan._"

"Plan!" said Jarvis, still in wonder; "what plan?"

"About the fund for the peerage, you know. Of course, the thing is sacred with me, as, indeed, I am equally interested with you all in its success."

Jarvis eyed her with a knowing look, and as she concluded, rolling his eyes in an expression of significance, he said—

"What, serve Sir William some such way, eh?"

"I will assist a little, if it be necessary, Henry," said the lady, tenderly, "although my mite cannot amount to a great deal."

During this speech, the captain was wondering what she could mean; but, having had a suspicion, from something that had fallen from his mother, that the lady was intended for him as a wife, and that she might be as great a dupe as Lady Jarvis herself, he was resolved to know the whole, and to act accordingly.

"I think it might be made to do," he replied, evasively, in order to discover the extent of his companion's information.

"Do!" cried Miss Harris, with fervor, "it cannot fail! How much do you suppose will be wanting to buy a barony, for instance?"

"Hem!" said Jarvis; "you mean more than we have already?"

"Certainly."

"Why, about a thousand pounds, I think, will do it, with what we have," said Jarvis, affecting to calculate.

"Is that all?" cried the delighted Caroline; and the captain grew in an instant, in her estimation, three inches higher;—quite noble in his air, and, in short, very tolerably handsome.

From that moment, Miss Harris, in her own mind, had fixed the fate of Captain Jarvis, and had determined to be his wife, whenever she could persuade him to offer himself; a thing she had no doubt of accomplishing with comparative ease. Not so the captain. Like all weak men, there was nothing of which he stood more in terror than of ridicule. He had heard the maneuvers of Miss Harris laughed at by many of the young men in Bath, and was by no means disposed to add himself to the food for mirth of these wags; and, indeed, had cultivated her acquaintance with a kind of bravado to some of his bottle companions, in order to show his ability to oppose all her arts, when most exposed to them; for it is one of the greatest difficulties to the success of this description of ladies, that their characters soon become suspected, and do them infinitely more injury than all their skill in their vocation.

With these views in the respective champions the campaign opened, and the lady, on her return, acquainted his mother with the situation of the privy purse, that was to promote her darling child to the enviable distinction of the peerage. Lady Jarvis was for purchasing a baronetcy on the spot, with what they had, under the impression that when ready for another promotion they would only have to pay the difference, as they did in the army when he received his captaincy. As, however, the son was opposed to any arrangement that might make the producing the few hundred pounds he had obtained from his mother's folly necessary, she was obliged to postpone the wished-for day until their united efforts could compass the means of effecting the main point. As an earnest, however, of her spirit in the cause, she gave him a fifty pound note, that morning obtained from her husband, and which the captain lost at one throw of the dice to his brother-in-law the same evening.

During the preceding events Egerton had either studiously avoided all collision with the Moseleys, or his engagements had confined him to such very different scenes that they never met.

The baronet had felt his presence a reproach, and Lady Moseley rejoiced that Egerton yet possessed sufficient shame to keep him from insulting her with his company.

It was a month after the departure of Lady Chatterton that Sir Edward returned to B——, as related in the preceding chapter, and that the arrangements for the London winter were commenced.

The day preceding their leaving Bath, the engagement of Chatterton with Lady Harriet was made public among their mutual friends, and an intimation was given that their nuptials would be celebrated before the family of the duke left his seat for the capital.

Something of the pleasure that she had for a long time been a stranger to, was felt by Emily Moseley as the well remembered tower of the village church of B—— struck her sight on their return from their protracted excursion. More than four months had elapsed since they had commenced their travels, and in that period what changes of sentiments had she not witnessed in others; of opinions of mankind in general, and of one individual in particular, had she not experienced in her own person. The benevolent smiles, the respectful salutations they received, in passing the little group of houses which, clustered round the church, had obtained the name of " the village," conveyed a sensation of delight that can only be felt by the deserving and virtuous; and the smiling faces, in several instances glistening with tears, which met them at the hall, gave ample testimony to the worth of both the master and his servants.

Francis and Clara were in waiting to receive them, and a very few minutes elapsed before the rector and Mrs. Ives, having heard they had passed, drove in also. In saluting the different members of the family, Mrs. Wilson noticed the startled look of the doctor, as the change in Emily's appearance first met his eyes. Her bloom, if not gone, was greatly diminished; and it was only when under the excitement of strong emotions that her face possessed that radiance which had so eminently distinguished it before her late journey.

"Where did you last see my friend George?" said the doctor to Mrs. Wilson, in the course of the first afternoon, as he took a seat by her side, apart from the rest of the family.

"At L——," said Mrs. Wilson, gravely.

"L——!" cried the doctor, in evident amazement. "Was he not at Bath then during your stay there?"

"No; I understood he was in attendance on some sick relative, which detained him from his friends," said Mrs. Wilson, wondering why the doctor chose to introduce so delicate a topic. Of his guilt in relation to Mrs. Fitzgerald he was doubtless ignorant, but surely not of his marriage.

"It is now sometime since I heard from him," continued the doctor, regarding Mrs. Wilson expressively, but to which the lady only replied with a gentle inclination of the body; and the rector, after pausing a moment, continued:

"You will not think me impertinent if I am bold enough to ask, has George ever expressed a wish to become connected with your niece by other ties than those of friendship?"

"He did," answered the widow, after a little hesitation.

"He did, and—"

"Was refused," continued Mrs. Wilson, with a slight feeling for the dignity of her sex, which for a moment caused her to lose sight of justice to Denbigh.

Dr. Ives was silent; but manifested by his dejected countenance the interest he had taken in this anticipated connection, and as Mrs. Wilson had spoken with ill-concealed reluctance on the subject at all, the rector did not attempt a renewal of the disagreeable topic; though she saw, for sometime afterward, whenever the baronet or his wife mentioned the name of Denbigh, that the eyes of the rector were turned on them in intense interest.

CHAPTER XXXVII.

"STEVENSON has returned, and I certainly must hear from Harriet," exclaimed the sister of Pendennyss, as she stood at a window watching the return of a servant from the neighboring post-office.

"I am afraid," rejoined the earl, who was seated by the breakfast-table, waiting the leisure of the lady to give him his cup of tea—"you find Wales very dull, sister. I sincerely hope both Derwent and Harriet will not forget their promise of visiting us this month."

The lady slowly took her seat at the table, engrossed in her own reflections, when the man entered with his budget of news; and having deposited sundry papers and letters he respectfully withdrew. The earl glanced his eyes over the directions of the epistles, and turning to his servants said, "Answer the bell when called." Three or four liveried footmen deposited their silver salvers and different implements of servitude, and the peer and his sister were left to themselves.

"Here is one from the duke to me, and one for you from his sister," said the brother; "I propose they be read aloud for our mutual advantage." To this proposal the lady, whose curiosity to hear the contents of Derwent's letter greatly exceeded her interest in that of his sister, cheerfully acquiesced, and her brother first broke the seal of his own epistle, and read its contents as follows:

"Notwithstanding my promise of seeing you this month in Caernarvonshire, I remain here yet, my dear Pendennyss, unable to tear myself from the attractions I have found in this city, although the pleasure of their comtemplation has been purchased at the expense of mortified feelings and unrequited affections. It is a truth (though possibly difficult to be believed), that this mercenary age has produced a female disengaged, young, and by

no means very rich, who has refused a jointure of six thousand a year, with the privilege of walking at a coronation within a dozen of royalty itself."

Here the accidental falling of a cup from the hands of the fair listener caused some little interruption to the reading of the brother; but as the lady, with a good deal of trepidation and many blushes, apologized hastily for the confusion her awkwardness had made, the earl continued to read.

"I could almost worship her independence: for I know the wishes of both her parents were for my success. I confess to you freely, that my vanity has been a good deal hurt, as I really thought myself agreeable to her. She certainly listened to my conversation and admitted my approaches, with more satisfaction than those of any other of the men around her; and when I ventured to hint to her this circumstance, as some justification for my presumption, she frankly acknowledged the truth of my impression, and without explaining the reasons for her conduct, deeply regretted the construction I had been led to place upon the circumstance. Yes, my lord, I felt it necessary to apologize to Emily Moseley for presuming to aspire to the honor of possessing so much loveliness and virtue. The accidental advantages of rank and wealth lose all their importance, when opposed to her delicacy, ingenuousness, and unaffected principles.

"I have heard it intimated lately, that George Denbigh was in some way or other instrumental in saving her life once; and that to her gratitude, and to my resemblance to the colonel, am I indebted to a consideration with Miss Moseley, which, although it has been the means of buoying me up with false hopes, I can never regret, from the pleasure her society has afforded me. I have remarked, on my mentioning his name to her, that she showed unusual emotion; and as Denbigh is already a husband, and myself rejected, the field is now fairly open to you. You will enter on your enterprise with great advantage, as you have the same flattering resemblance, and, if anything, the voice, which, I am told, is our greatest recommendation with the ladies, in higher perfection than either George or your humble servant."

Here the reader stopped of his own accord, and was so intently absorbed in his meditations, that the almost breathless curiosity of his sister was obliged to find relief by desiring him to proceed. Roused by the sound of her voice, the earl changed color sensibly, and continued:

"But to be serious on a subject of great

importance to my future life (for I some-times think her negative will make Den-bigh a duke), the lovely girl did not appear happy at the time of our interview, nor do I think she enjoys at any time the spirits nature has evidently given her. Harriet is nearly as great an admirer of Miss Moseley, and takes her refusal to heart as much as myself; she even at-tempted to intercede with her in my be-half. But the charming girl, though mild, grateful, and delicate, was firm and un-equivocal, and left no grounds for the remotest expectation of success from per-severance on my part.

"As Harriet had received an intimation that both Miss Moseley and her aunt en-tertained extremely rigid notions on the score of religion, she took occasion to introduce the subject in her conference with the former, and was told in reply, 'that other considerations would have determined her to decline the honor I intended her; but that, under any cir-cumstances, a more intimate knowledge of my principles would be necessary before she could entertain a thought of accept-ing my hand, or, indeed, that of any other man.' Think of that, Pendennyss! The principles of a duke!—now a dukedom and forty thousand a year would furnish a character, with most people, for a Nero.

"I trust the important object I have had in view here is a sufficient excuse for my breach of promise to you; and I am serious when I wish you (unless the pretty Spaniard has, as I sometimes suspect, made you a captive) to see, and endeavor to bring me in some degree connected with, the charming family of Sir Edward Moseley.

"The aunt, Mrs. Wilson, often speaks of you with the greatest interest, and, from some cause or other, is strongly en-listed in your favor, and Miss Moseley hears your name mentioned with evident pleasure. *Your* religion or principles cannot be doubted. You can offer larger settlements, as honorable if not as ele-vated a title, a far more illustrious name, purchased by your own services and per-sonal merit greatly exceeding the preten-sions of your assured friend and relative,
"DERWENT."

Both brother and sister were occupied with their own reflections for several min-utes after the letter was ended, and the silence was broken first by the latter saying with a low tone to her brother—

"You must endeavor to become ac-quainted with Mrs. Wilson; she is, I know, very anxious to see you, and your friendship for the general requires it of you."

"I owe General Wilson much," replied the brother, in a melancholy voice; "and when we go to Annerdale House, I wish you to make the acquaintance of the ladies of the Moseley family, should they be in town this winter;—but you have yet the letter of Harriet to read."

After first hastily running over its con-tents, the lady commenced the fulfillment of her part of the engagement.

"Frederick has been so much engrossed of late with his own affairs, that he has forgotten there is such a creature in ex-istence as his sister, or, indeed, any one else but a Miss Emily Moseley, and conse-quently I have been unable to fulfill my promise of making you a visit, for want of proper escort, and—and—perhaps some other considerations, not worth mention-ing in a letter I know you will read to the earl.

"Yes, my dear cousin, Frederick Den-bigh has supplicated the daughter of a country baronet to become a duchess; and, hear it, ye marriage-seeking nymphs and marriage-making dames! has suppli-cated in vain!

"I confess to you, when the thing was first in agitation, my aristocratic blood roused itself at the anticipated connection: but finding on examination that Sir Ed-ward was of no doubtful lineage, and that the blood of the Chattertons runs in his veins, and finding the young lady every-thing I could wish in a sister, my scruples soon disappeared, with the folly that en-gendered them.

"There was no necessity for any alarm, for the lady very decidedly refused the honor offered her by Derwent, and what makes the matter worse, refused the solicitations of his sister also.

"I have fifty times been surprised by my own condescension, and to this mo-ment am at a loss to know whether it was to the lady's worth, my brother's happi-ness, or the Chatterton blood, that I finally yielded. Heigho! this Chatter-ton is certainly much too handsome for a man; but I forget you have never seen him."

(Here an arch smile stole over the feat-ures of the listener, as his sister contin-ued)—"To return to my narration, I had half a mind to send for a Miss Harris there is here, to learn the most approved fashion of a lady preferring a suit, but as fame said she was just now practicing on a certain hero yclept Captain Jarvis, heir to Sir Timo of that name, it struck me her system might be rather too abrupt, so I was fain to adopt the best plan— that of trusting to nature and my own feelings for words.

"Nobility is certainly a very pretty thing (for those who have it), but I would defy the old Margravine of —— to keep up the semblance of superiority with Emily Moseley. She is so very natural, so very beautiful, and withal at times a little arch, that one is afraid to set up any other distinctions than such as can be fairly supported.

"I commenced with hoping her determination to reject the hand of Frederick was not an unalterable one. (Yes, I called him Frederick, what I never did out of my own family before in my life.) There was a considerable tremor in the voice of Miss Moseley, as she replied, 'I now perceive, when too late, that my indiscretion has given reason to my friends to think that I have entertained intentions toward his grace, of which I entreat you to believe me, Lady Harriet, I am innocent. Indeed—indeed, as anything more than an agreeable acquaintance I have never allowed myself to think of your brother;' and from my soul I believe her. We continued our conversation for half an hour longer, and such was the ingenuousness, delicacy, and high religious feeling displayed by the charming girl, that if I entered the room with a spark of regret that I was compelled to solicit another to favor my brother's love, I left it with a feeling that my efforts had been unsuccessful! Yes! thou peerless sister of the more peerless Pendennyss! I once thought of your ladyship as a wife for Derwent—"

A glass of water was necessary to enable the reader to clear her voice, which grew husky from speaking so long.

"But I now openly avow, neither your birth, your hundred thousand pounds, nor your merit, would put you on a footing, in my estimation, with my Emily. You may form some idea of her power to captivate, and of her indifference to her conquests, when I mention that she once refused— but I forget, you don't know him, and therefore cannot be a judge. The thing is finally decided, and we shortly go into Westmoreland, and next week, the Moseleys return to Northamptonshire. I don't know when I shall be able to visit you, and think I may *now* safely invite you to Denbigh Castle, although a month ago I might have hesitated. Love to the earl, and kind assurance to yourself of unalterable regard. HARRIET DENBIGH."

"P. S. I believe I forgot to mention that Mrs. Moseley, a sister of Lord Chatterton, has gone to Portugal, and that the peer himself is to go into the country with us; there is, I suppose, a fellow-feeling between *them* just now, though I do not think Chatterton looks so very miserable as he might. Adieu."

On ending this second epistle the same silence which had succeeded the reading of the first prevailed, until the lady, with an arch expression, interrupted it by saying.

"Harriet will, I think, soon grace the peerage."

"And happily, I trust," replied the brother.

"Do you know Lord Chatterton?"

"I do; he is very amiable, and admirably calculated to contrast with the lively gayety of Harriet Denbigh."

"You believe in loving our opposites, I see," rejoined the lady; and then affectionately stretching out her hand to him, she added, "but, Pendennyss, you must give me for a sister one as nearly like yourself as possible."

"That might please your affections," answered the earl, with a smile, "but how would it comport with my tastes? Will you suffer me to describe the kind of man *you* are to select for your future lord, unless, indeed, you have decided the point already?"

The lady colored violently, and appearing anxious to change the subject, she tumbled over two or three unopened letters, as she cried eagerly—

"Here is one from the Donna Julia." The earl instantly broke the seal and read aloud; no secrets existing between them in relation to their mutual friend.

"MY LORD,—I hasten to write to you what I know it will give you pleasure to hear, concerning my future prospects in life. My uncle, General M'Carthy, has written me the cheerful tidings, that my father has consented to receive his only child without any other sacrifice than a condition of attending the service of the Catholic Church without any professions on my side, or even an understanding that I am conforming to its peculiar tenets. This may be, in some measure, irksome at times, and possibly distressing; but the worship of God, with a proper humiliation of spirit, I have learnt to consider as a privilege to us here, and I owe a duty to my earthly father of penitence and care in his later years that will justify the measure in the eyes of my heavenly One. I have, therefore, acquainted my uncle in reply, that I am willing to attend the conde's summons at any moment he will choose to make them; and I thought it a debt due your care and friendship to apprise your lordship of my approaching departure from this country; indeed, I have great reason for believing that your kind and unremitted efforts to attain this object have already prepared you to expect this result.

"I feel it will be impossible to quit England without seeing you and your sister, to thank you for the many, very many favors, of both a temporal and eternal nature, you have been the agents of conferring on me. The cruel suggestions which I dreaded, and which it appears had reached the ears of my friends in Spain, have prevented my troubling your lordship of late unnecessarily with my concerns. The consideration of a friend to your character (Mrs. Wilson) has removed the necessity of applying for your advice; she and her charming niece, Miss Emily Moseley, have been, next to yourselves, the greatest solace I have had in my exile, and united you will be remembered in my prayers. I will merely mention here, deferring the explanation until I see you in London, that I have been visited by the wretch from whom you delivered me in Portugal, and that the means of ascertaining his name have fallen into my hands. You will be the best judge of the proper steps to be taken; but I wish, by all means, something may be done to prevent his attempting to see me in Spain. Should it be discovered to my relations there that he has any such intentions it would certainly terminate in his death, and possibly in my disgrace. Wishing you and your kind sister all possible happiness, I remain,

"Your lordship's obliged friend,
"JULIA FITZGERALD."

"Oh!" cried the sister, as she concluded the letter, "we must certainly see her before she goes. What a wretch that persecutor of hers must be! how persevering in his villany!"

"He does exceed my ideas of effrontery," said the earl, in great warmth— "but he may offend too far; the laws shall interpose their power to defeat his schemes, should he ever repeat them."

"He attempted to take your life, brother," said the lady, shuddering, "if I remember the tale aright."

"Why, I have endeavored to free him from that imputation," rejoined the brother, musing: "he certainly fired a pistol, but the latter hit my horse at such a distance from myself, that I believe his object was to disable me and not murder. His escape has astonished me; he must have fled by himself into the woods, as Harmer was but a short distance behind

me, admirably mounted, and the escort was up and in full pursuit within ten minutes. After all, it may be for the best he was not taken; for I am persuaded the dragoons would have sabered him on the spot, and he may have parents of respectability, or a wife to kill by the knowledge of his misconduct."

"This Emily Moseley must be a faultless being," cried the sister, as she ran over the contents of Julia's letter. "Three different letters, and each containing her praises!"

The earl made no reply, but opening the duke's letter again, he appeared to be studying its contents. His color slightly changed as he dwelt on its passages, and turning to his sister he inquired if she had a mind to try the air of Westmoreland for a couple of weeks or a month.

"As you say, my lord," replied the lady with cheeks of scarlet.

"Then I say we will go. I wish much to see Derwent, and I think there will be a wedding during our visit."

He rang the bell, and the almost untasted breakfast was removed in a few minutes. A servant announced that his horse was in readiness. The earl wished his sister a friendly good morning, and proceeded to the door, where was standing one of the noble black horses before mentioned, held by a groom, and the military-looking attendant ready mounted on another.

Throwing himself into the saddle, the young peer rode gracefully from the door, followed by his attendant horseman. During this ride, the master suffered his steed to take whatever course most pleased himself, and his follower looked up in surprise more than once, to see the careless manner in which the Earl of Pendennyss, confessedly one of the best horsemen in England, managed his noble animal. Having, however, got without the gates of his own park, and into the vicinity of numberless cottages and farm-houses, the master recovered his recollection, and the man ceased to wonder.

For three hours the equestrians pursued their course through the beautiful vale which opened gracefully opposite one of the fronts of the castle; and if faces of smiling welcome, inquiries after his own and his sister's welfare, which evidently sprang from the heart, or the most familiar but respectful representations of their own prosperity or misfortunes, gave any testimony of the feelings entertained by the tenantry of this noble estate for their landlord, the situation of the young nobleman might be justly considered envied.

As the hour for dinner approached, they turned the heads of their horses toward home; and on entering the park, removed from the scene of industry and activity without, the earl relapsed into his fit of musing. A short distance from the house he suddenly called, "Harmer." The man drove his spurs into the loins of his horse, and in an instant was by the side of his master, which he signified by raising his hand to his cap with the palm opening outward.

"You must prepare to go to Spain when required, in attendance on Mrs. Fitzgerald."

The man received his order with the indifference of one used to adventures and movements, and having laconically signified his assent, he drew his horse back again into his station in the rear.

CHAPTER XXXVIII.

THE day succeeding the arrival of the Moseleys at the seat of their ancestors, Mrs. Wilson observed Emily silently putting on her pelisse, and walking out unattended by either of the domesties or any of the family. There was a peculiar melancholy in her air and manner, which inclined the cautious aunt to suspect that her charge was bent on the indulgence of some ill-judged weakness; more particularly as the direction she took led to the arbor, a theater in which Denbigh had been so conspicuous an actor. Hastily throwing a cloak over her own shoulders, Mrs. Wilson followed Emily, with the double purpose of ascertaining her views, and, if necessary, of interposing her own authority against the repetition of similar excursions.

As Emily approached the arbor, whither in truth she had directed her steps, its faded vegetation and chilling aspect, so different from its verdure and luxuriance when she last saw it, came over her heart as a symbol of her own blighted prospects and deadened affections. The recollection of Denbigh's conduct on that spot, of his general benevolence and assiduity to please, being forcibly recalled to her mind at the instant, forgetful of her object in visiting the arbor, Emily yielded to her sensibilities, and sank on the seat weeping as if her heart would break.

She had not time to dry her eyes and to collect her scattered thoughts, before Mrs. Wilson entered the arbor. Eying her niece for a moment with a sternness unusual for the one to adopt or the other to receive, she said—

"It is a solemn obligation we owe our religion and ourselves, to endeavor to suppress such passions as are incompatible with our duties; and there is no weakness greater than blindly adhering to the wrong, when we are convinced of our error. It is as fatal to good morals as it is unjust to ourselves to persevere, from selfish motives, in believing those innocent whom evidence has convicted as guilty. Many a weak woman has sealed her own misery by such willful obstinacy, aided by the unpardonable vanity of believing herself able to control a man that the laws of God could not restrain."

"Oh, dear madam, speak not so unkindly to me," sobbed the weeping girl; "I—I am guilty of no such weakness, I assure you;" and looking up with an air of profound resignation and piety, she continued: "Here on this spot, where he saved my life, I was about to offer up my prayers for his conviction of the error of his ways, and for the pardon of his too—too heavy transgressions."

Mrs. Wilson, softened almost to tears herself, viewed her for a moment with a mixture of delight, and continued in a milder tone:

"I believe you, my dear. I am certain, although you may have loved Denbigh much, that you love your Maker and his ordinances more; and I have no apprehensions that, were he a disengaged man, and you alone in the world—unsupported by anything but your sense of duty—you would ever so far forget yourself as to become his wife. But does not your religion, does not your own usefulness in society, require you wholly to free your heart from the power of a man who has so unworthily usurped a dominion over it?"

To this Emily replied, in a hardly audible voice, "Certainly—and I pray constantly for it."

"It is well, my love," said the aunt, soothingly; "you cannot fail with such means, and your own exertions, finally to prevail over your own worst enemies, your passions. The task our sex has to sustain is, at the best, an arduous one; but so much the greater is our credit if we do it well."

"Oh! how is an unguided girl ever to judge aright, if—" cried Emily, clasping her hands and speaking with great energy, and she would have said, "one like Denbigh in appearance be so vile!" Shame, however, kept her silent.

"Few men can support such a veil of hypocrisy as that with which I sometimes think Denbigh must deceive even himself. His case is an extraordinary exception to a very sacred rule—'that the tree is known by its fruits,'" replied her aunt. "There is no safer way of judging of character that one's opportunities will not admit of more closely investigating, than by examining into and duly appreciating early impressions. The man or woman who has constantly seen the practice of piety before them, from infancy to the noon of life, will seldom so far abandon the recollection of virtue as to be guilty of great enormities. Even divine truth has promised that his blessings or his curses shall extend to many generations. It is true, that with our most guarded prudence we may be deceived." Mrs. Wilson paused and sighed heavily, as her own case, connected with the loves of Denbigh and her niece, occurred strongly to her mind.

"Yet," she continued, "we may lessen the danger much by guarding against it; and it seems to me no more than what self-preservation requires in a young woman. But for a religious parent to neglect it, is a willful abandonment of a most solemn duty."

As Mrs. Wilson concluded, her niece, who had recovered the command of her feelings, pressed her hand in silence to her lips, and showed a disposition to retire from a spot which she found recalled too many recollections of a man whose image it was her imperious duty to banish, on every consideration of propriety and religion.

Their walk into the house was silent, and their thoughts were drawn from the unpleasant topic by finding a letter from Julia, announcing her intended departure from this country, and her wish to take leave of them in London before she sailed. As she had mentioned the probable day for that event, both the ladies were delighted to find it was posterior to the time fixed by Sir Edward for their own visit to the capital.

Had Jane, instead of Emily, been the one that suffered through the agency of Mrs. Fitzgerald, however innocently on the part of the lady, her violent and uncontrolled passions would have either blindly united the innocent with the guilty in her resentments; or, if a sense of justice had vindicated the lady in her judgment, yet her pride and ill-guided delicacy would have felt her name a reproach, that would have forbidden any intercourse with her or any belonging to her.

Not so with her sister. The sufferings of Mrs. Fitzgerald had taken a strong hold on her youthful feelings, and a similarity of opinions and practices on the great object of their lives, had brought them together in a manner no misconduct in a third person could weaken. It is true, the recollection of Denbigh was intimately blended with the fate of Mrs. Fitzgerald. But Emily sought support against her feelings from a quarter that rather required an investigation of them than a desire to *drown* care with thought.

She never indulged in romantic reflections in which the image of Denbigh was associated. This she had hardly done in her happiest moments; and his marriage, if nothing else had interfered, now absolutely put it out of the question. But, although a Christian, and an humble and devout one, Emily Moseley was a woman, and had loved ardently, confidingly, and gratefully. Marriage is the business of life with her sex—with all, next to a preparation for a better world—and it cannot be supposed that a first passion in a bosom like that of our heroine was to be suddenly erased, and to leave no vestiges of its existence.

Her partiality for the society of Derwent, her meditations in which she sometimes detected herself drawing a picture of what Denbigh might have been, if early care had been taken to impress him with his situation in this world, and from which she generally retired to her closet and her knees, were the remains of feelings too strong and too pure to be torn from her in a moment.

The arrival of John, with Grace and Jane, enlivened not only the family but the neighborhood. Mr. Haughton and his numerous friends poured in on the young couple with their congratulations, and a few weeks stole by insensibly, previously to the commencement of the journeys of Sir Edward and his son, the one to Benfield Lodge and the other to St. James's Square.

On the return of the travelers, a few days before they commenced their journey to the capital, John laughingly told his uncle that, although he himself greatly admired the taste of Mr. Peter Johnson in dress, yet he doubted whether the present style of fashions in the metropolis would not be scandalized by the appearance of the honest steward.

John had in fact noticed, in their former visit to London, a mob of mischievous boys eying Peter with indications of rebellious movements which threatened the old man, and from which he had retreated by taking a coach, and he now made the suggestion from pure good-nature, to save him any future trouble from a similar cause.

They were at dinner when Moseley made the remark, and the steward was in his place at the sideboard—for his master was at home. Drawing near at the mention of his name first, and casting an eye over his figure to see if all was decent, Peter respectfully broke silence, determined to defend his own cause.

" Why! Mr. John—Mr. John Moseley! if I might judge, for an elderly man, and a serving man," said the steward, bowing humbly, " I am no disparagement to my friends, or even to my honored master."

Johnson's vindication of his wardrobe drew the eyes of the family upon him, and an involuntary smile passed from one to the other, as they admired his starched figure and drab frock, or rather doublet with sleeves and skirts. Sir Edward being of the same opinion with his son, observed—

" I do think, Uncle Benfield, there might be an improvement in the dress of your steward without much trouble to the ingenuity of his tailor."

" Sir Edward Moseley—honorable sir," said the steward, beginning to grow alarmed, " if I may be so bold, you young gentlemen may like gay clothes ; but as for me and his honor, we are used to such as we wear, and what we are used to we love."

The old man spoke with earnestness, and drew the particular attention of his master to a review of his attire. After reflecting that no gentleman in the house had been attended by any servitor in such a gard, Mr. Benfield thought it time to give his sentiments on the subject.

" Why, I remember that my Lord Gosford's gentleman never wore a livery, nor can I say that he dressed exactly after the manner of Johnson. Every member had his body servant, and they were not unfrequently taken for their masters. Lady Juliana, too, after the death of her nephew, had one or two attendants out of livery, and in a different fashion from your attire. Peter, I think with John Moseley there, we must alter you a little for the sake of appearance."

" Your honor ! " stammered out Peter, in increased terror ; " for Mr. John Moseley and Sir Edward, and youngerly gentlemen like, dress may do. Now, your honor, if—" and Peter, turning to Grace, bowed nearly to the floor—" I had such a sweet, most beautiful young lady to smile on me, I might wish to change ; but, sir, my day has gone by." Peter sighed as the recollection of Patty Steele and his youthful love floated across his brain. Grace blushed and thanked him for the compliment, and gave her opinion that his gallantry merited a better costume.

" Peter," said his master decidedly, " I think Mrs Moseley is right. If I should

call on the viscountess (the Lady Juliana, who yet survived, an ancient dowager of seventy), I shall want your attendance, and in your present garb you cannot fail to shock her delicate feelings. You remind me now I think, every time I look at you, of old Harry, the earl's gamekeeper, one of the most cruel men I ever knew."

This decided the matter. Peter well knew that his master's antipathy to old Harry arose from his having pursued a poacher one day, in place of helping the Lady Juliana over a stile, in her flight from a bull that was playing his gambols in the same field ; and not for the world would the faithful steward retain even a feature, if it brought unpleasant recollections to his kind master. He at one time thought of closing his innovations on his wardrobe, however, with a change of his nether garment ; as, with a great deal of study, he could only make out the resemblance between himself and the obnoxious gamekeeper to consist in the leathern breeches. But fearful of some points escaping his memory in forty years, he tamely acquiesced in all John's alterations, and appeared at his station three days afterward newly decked from head to foot in a more modern suit of snuff-color.

The change once made, Peter greatly admired himself in a glass, and thought, could he have had the taste of Mr. John Moseley in his youth to direct his toilet, that the hard heart of Patty Steele would not always have continued so obdurate.

Sir Edward wished to collect his neighbors round him once more before he left them for another four months ; and accordingly the rector and his wife, Francis and Clara, the Haughtons, with a few others, dined at the Hall by invitation, the last day of their stay in Northhamptonshire. The company had left the table to join the ladies, when Grace came into the drawing-room with a face covered with smiles and beaming with pleasure.

" You look like the bearer of good news, Mrs. Moseley," cried the rector, catching a glimpse of her countenance as she passed.

" Good ! I sincerely hope and believe," replied Grace. " My letters from my brother announce that his marriage took place last week, and give us hopes of seeing them all in town within the month."

" Married ! " exclaimed Mr. Haughton, casting his eyes unconsciously on Emily, " my Lord Chatterton married ! May I ask the name of the bride, my dear Mrs. Moseley ? "

" To Lady Harriet Denbigh—and at

Denbigh Castle in Westmoreland; but very privately, as you may suppose from seeing Moseley and myself here," answered Grace, her cheeks yet glowing with surprise and pleasure at the intelligence.

"Lady Harriet Denbigh?" echoed Mr. Haughton; "what! a kinswoman of our old friend? *your* friend, Miss Emily?" the recollection of the service he had performed at the arbor still fresh in his memory.

Emily commanded herself sufficiently to reply, "Brothers' children, I believe, sir."

"But a *lady*—how came she my lady?" continued the good man, anxious to know the whole, and ignorant of any reasons for delicacy where so great a favorite as Denbigh was in the question.

"She is the daughter of the Duke of Derwent," said Mrs. Moseley, as willing as himself to talk of her new sister.

"How happens it that the death of old Mr. Denbigh was announced as plain George Denbigh, Esq., if he was the brother of a duke?" said Jane, forgetting, for a moment, the presence of Dr. and Mrs. Ives, in her surviving passion for genealogy; "should he not have been called Lord George, or honorable?"

This was the first time any allusion had been made to the sudden death in the church by any of the Moseleys in the hearing of the rector's family; and the speaker sat in breathless terror at her own inadvertency. But Dr. Ives, observing that a profound silence prevailed as soon as Jane ended, answered mildly, though in a way to prevent any further comment—

"The late duke's succeeding a cousin-german in the title, was the reason, I presume. Emily, I am to hear from you by letter, I hope, after you enter into the gayeties of the metropolis?"

This Emily cheerfully promised, and the conversation took another turn.

Mrs. Wilson had carefully avoided all communications with the rector concerning his youthful friend, and the doctor appeared unwilling to commence anything which might lead to his name being mentioned. "He is disappointed in him as well as ourselves," thought the widow, "and it must be unpleasant to have his image recalled. He saw his attentions to Emily, and he knows of his marriage to Lady Laura, of course, and he loves us all, and Emily in particular, too well not to feel hurt by his conduct."

"Sir Edward!" cried Mr. Haughton, with a laugh, "baronets are likely to be plenty. Have you heard how near we were to have another in the neighborhood lately?"

Sir Edward answered in the negative, and his neighbor continued—

"Why, no less a man than Captain Jarvis, promoted to the bloody hand."

"Captain Jarvis!" exclaimed five or six at once; "explain yourself, Mr. Haughton."

"My near neighbor, young Walker, has been to Bath on an unusual business—his health—and for the benefit of the country he has brought back a pretty piece of scandal. It seems that Lady Jarvis, as I am told she is since she left here, wished to have her hopeful heir made a lord, and that the two united for some six months in forming a kind of savings bank between themselves, to enable them at some future day to bribe the minister to honor the peerage with such a prodigy. After a while the daughter of our late acquaintance, Sir William Harris, became an accessory to the plot, and a contributor, too, to the tune of a couple of hundred pounds. Some circumstances, however, at length made this latter lady suspicious, and she wished to audit the books. The captain prevaricated—the lady remonstrated, until the gentleman, with more truth than manners, told her that she was a fool—the money he had expended or lost at dice; and that he did not think the ministers quite so silly as to make him a lord, or that he himself was such a fool as to make her his wife: so the whole thing exploded."

John listened with a delight but little short of what he had felt when Grace owned her love, and anxious to know all, eagerly inquired—

"But is it true? How was it found out?"

"Oh, the lady complained of part, and the captain tells all to get the laugh on his side; so that Walker says the former is the derision, and the latter the contempt of all Bath."

"Poor Sir William," said the baronet, with feeling; "he is much to be pitied."

"I am afraid he has nothing to blame but his own indulgence," remarked the rector.

"You don't know the worst of it," replied Mr. Haughton. "*We* poor people are made to suffer—Lady Jarvis wept and fretted Sir Timo out of his lease, which has been given up, and a new house is to be taken in another part of the kingdom, where neither Miss Harris nor the story is known."

"Then Sir William has to procure a new tenant," said Lady Moseley, not in the least regretting the loss of the old one.

"No! my lady!" continued Mr. Haughton, with a smile. "Walker is, you know, an attorney, and does some business occasionally for Sir William. When Jarvis gave up the lease, the baronet, who finds himself a little short of money, offered the deanery for sale, it being a useless place to him; and the very next day, while Walker was with Sir William, a gentleman called, and without higgling agreed to pay down at once his thirty thousand pounds for it."

"And who is the purchaser?" inquired Lady Moseley, eagerly.

"The Earl of Pendennyss."

"Lord Pendennyss!" exclaimed Mrs. Wilson, in rapture.

"Pendennyss!" cried the rector, eying the aunt and Emily with a smile.

"Pendennyss!" echoed all in the room in amazement.

"Yes," said Mr. Haughton, "it is now the property of the earl, who says he has bought it for his sister."

CHAPTER XXXIX.

MRS. WILSON found time the ensuing day to ascertain, before they left the hall, the truth of the tale related by Mr. Haughton. The deanery had certainly changed its master, and a new steward had already arrived to take possession in the name of his lord. What induced Pendennyss to make this purchase she was at loss to conceive—most probably some arrangement between himself and Lord Bolton. But whatever might be his motive, it in some measure insured his becoming for a season their neighbor; and Mrs. Wilson felt a degree of pleasure at the circumstance that she had been a stranger to for a long time—a pleasure which was greatly heightened as she dwelt on the lovely face of the companion who occupied the other seat in her traveling chaise.

The road to London led by the gates of the deanery, and near them they passed a servant in the livery of those they had once seen following the equipage of the earl. Anxious to know anything which might hasten her acquaintance with this admired nobleman, Mrs. Wilson stopped her carriage to inquire.

"Pray, sir, whom do you serve?"

"My Lord Pendennyss, ma'am," replied the man, respectfully taking off his hat.

"The earl is not here?" asked Mrs. Wilson, with interest.

"Oh no, madam; I am here in waiting on his steward. My lord is in Westmoreland, with his grace and Colonel Denbigh, and the ladies."

"Does he remain there long?" continued the anxious widow, desirous of knowing all she could learn.

"I believe not, madam; most of our people have gone to Annerdale House, and my lord is expected in town with the duke and the colonel."

As the servant was an elderly man, and appeared to understand the movements of his master so well, Mrs. Wilson was put in unusual spirits by this prospect of a speedy termination to her anxiety to meet Pendennyss.

"Annerdale House is the earl's town residence?" quietly inquired Emily.

"Yes; he got the fortune of the last duke of that title, but how I do not exactly know. I believe, however, through his mother. General Wilson did not know his family; indeed, Pendennyss bore a second title during his lifetime. But did you observe how very civil his servant was, as well as the one John spoke to before—a sure sign their master is a gentleman!"

Emily smiled at the strong partialities of her aunt, and replied, "Your handsome chaise and attendants will draw respect from most men in his situation, dear aunt, be their masters who they may."

The expected pleasure of meeting the earl was a topic frequently touched upon between her aunt and Emily during their journey; the former beginning to entertain hopes she would have laughed at herself for, could they have been fairly laid before her; and the latter entertaining a profound respect for his character, but chiefly governed by a wish to gratify her companion.

The third day they reached the baronet's handsome house in St. James's Square, and found that the forethought of John had provided everything in the best and most comfortable manner.

It was the first visit of both Jane and Emily to the metropolis; and under the protection of their almost equally curious mother, and escorted by John, they wisely determined to visit the curiosities, while their leisure yet admitted of the opportunity. For the first two weeks their time was chiefly employed in the indulgence of this unfashionable and vulgar propensity, which if it had no other tendency, served greatly to draw the thoughts of both the young women from the recollections of the last few months.

While her sister and nieces were thus employed, Mrs. Wilson, assisted by Grace, was occupied in getting things in preparation to do credit to the baronet's hospitality.

The second week after their arrival, Mrs. Moseley was delighted by seeing advance upon her unexpectedly, through the door of the breakfast parlor, her brother, with his bride leaning on his arm. After the most sincere greetings and congratulations, Lady Chatterton cried out gayly:

"You see, my dear Lady Moseley, I am determined to banish ceremony between us, and so, instead of sending you my card, have come myself to notify you of my arrival. Chatterton would not suffer me even to swallow my breakfast, he was so impatient to show me off."

"You are placing things exactly on the footing I wish to see ourselves with all our connections," replied Lady Moseley, kindly; "but what have you done with the duke? is he not in your train?"   •

"Oh! he has gone to Canterbury with George Denbigh, madam," cried the lady, shaking her head reproachfully though affectionately at Emily; "his grace dislikes London just now excessively, he says, and the colonel being obliged to leave his wife on regimental business, Derwent was good enough to keep him company during his exile."

"And Lady Laura, do we see her?" inquired Lady Moseley.

"She came with us. Pendennyss and his sister follow immediately; so, my dear madam, the dramatis personæ will all be on the stage soon."

Cards and visits now began to accumulate on the Moseleys, and their time no longer admitted of that unfettered leisure which they had enjoyed at their entrance on the scene. Mrs. Wilson, for herself and charge, adopted a rule for the government of her manner of living which was consistent with her duties. They mixed in general society sparingly; and, above all, they rigidly adhered to the obedience to the injunction which commanded them to keep the Sabbath day holy; a duty of no trifling difficulty to perform in fashionable society in the city of London, or, indeed, in any other place where the influence of fashion has supplanted the laws of God.

Mrs. Wilson was not a bigot; but she knew and performed her duty rigidly. It was a pleasure to her to do so. It would have been misery to do otherwise. In the singleness of heart and deep piety of her niece, she had a willing pupil to her system of morals and a rigid follower of her religious practices. As they both knew that the temptations to go astray were greater in town than in country, they kept a strict guard over the tendency to err, and in watchfulness found their greatest security.

John Moseley, next to his friends, loved his bays: indeed, if the aggregate of his affections for these and Lady Herriefield had been put in opposite scales, we strongly suspect the side of the horses would predominate.

One Sunday, soon after being domesticated, John, who had soberly attended morning service with the ladies, came into a little room where the more reflecting part of the family were assembled, in search of his wife.

Grace, we have before mentioned, had become a real member of that church in which she had been educated, and had entered, under the direction of Dr. Ives and Mrs. Wilson, into an observance of its wholesome ordinances. Grace was certainly piously inclined, if not devout. Her feelings on the subject of religion had been sensibly awakened during their voyage to Lisbon; and at the period of which we write, Mrs. Moseley was as sincerely disposed to perform her duty as her powers admitted. To the request of her husband, that she would take a seat in his phaeton while he drove her round the park once or twice, Grace gave a mild refusal, by saying,

"It is Sunday, my dear Moseley."

"Do you think I don't know that?" cried John, gayly. "There will be everybody there, and the better day, the better deed."

Now, Moseley, if he had been asked to apply this speech to the case before them, would have frankly owned his inability; but his wife did not make the trial: she was contented with saying, as she laid down her book to look on a face she so tenderly loved,

"Ah! Moseley, you should have set a better example to those below you in life."

"I wish to set an example," returned her husband, with an affectionate smile, "to all above as well as below me, in order that they may find out the path to happiness, by exhibiting to the world a model of a wife in yourself, dear Grace."

As this was uttered with a sincerity which distinguished the manner of Moseley, his wife was more pleased with the compliment than she would have been willing to make known; and John spoke no more than he thought; for a desire to show his handsome wife was the ruling passion for a moment.

The husband was too pressing and the wife too fond not to yield the point; and Grace took her seat in the carriage with a kind of half-formed resolution to improve the opportunity by a discourse on serious subjects—a resolution which terminated as all others do, that postpone one duty to discharge another of less magnitude; it was forgotten.

Mrs. Wilson had listened with interest to the efforts of John to prevail on his wife to take the ride, and on her leaving the room to comply she observed to Emily, with whom she now remained alone—

"Here is a consequence of a difference in religious views between man and wife, my child: John, in place of supporting Grace in the discharge of her duties, has been the actual cause of her going astray."

Emily felt the force of her aunt's remark, and saw its justice; yet her love for the offender induced her to say—

"John will not lead her openly astray, for he has a sincere respect for religion, and this offense is not unpardonable, dear aunt."

"The offense is assuredly not unpardonable," replied Mrs. Wilson, "and to infinite mercy it is hard to say what is; but it is an offense, and directly in the face of an express ordinance of the Lord; it is even throwing off the *appearance* of keeping the Sabbath day holy, much less observing the substance of the commandment; and as to John's respect for holy things in this instance, it was injurious to his wife. Had he been an open deist she would have shrunk from the act in suspicion of its sinfulness. Either John must become a Christian, or I am afraid Grace will fall from her undertaking."

Mrs. Wilson shook her head mournfully, while Emily offered up a silent petition that the first might speedily be the case.

Lady Laura had been early in her visit to the Moseleys; and as Denbigh had both a town residence and a seat in parliament, it appeared next to impossible to avoid meeting him or to requite the pressing civilities of his wife by harsh refusals, that might prove in the end injurious to themselves by creating a suspicion that resentment at his not choosing a partner from among them governed the conduct of the Moseleys toward a man to whom they were under such a heavy obligation.

Had Sir Edward known as much as his sister and daughters, he would probably have discountenanced the acquaintance altogether; but owing to the ignorance of the rest of her friends of what had passed, Mrs. Wilson and Emily had not only the assiduities of Lady Laura, but the wishes of their own family to contend with, and consequently she submitted to the association with a reluctance that was, in some measure, counteracted by their

regard for Lady Laura, and by compassion for her abused confidence.

A distant connection of Lady Moseley's had managed to collect in her house a few hundred of her nominal friends, and as she had been particularly attentive in calling in person on her venerable relative, Mr. Benfield, soon after his arrival in town, out of respect to her father's cousin, or perhaps mindful of his approaching end, and remembering there were such things as codicils to wills, the old man, flattered by her notice, and yet too gallant to reject the favor of a lady, consented to accompany the remainder of the family on the occasion.

Most of their acquaintances were there, and Lady Moseley soon found herself engaged in a party at quadrille, while the young people were occupied by the usual amusements of their age in such scenes. Emily alone, feeling but little desire to enter into the gayety of general conversation with a host of gentlemen who had collected round her aunt and sisters, offered her arm to Mr. Benfield, on seeing him manifest a disposition to take a closer view of the company, and walked away with him.

They wandered from room to room, unconscious of the observation attracted by the sight of a man in the costume of Mr. Benfield, leaning on the arm of so young and lovely a woman as his niece; and many an exclamation of surprise, ridicule, admiration and wonder had been made, unnoticed by the pair, until finding the crowd rather inconvenient to her companion, Emily gently drew him into one of the apartments where the card-tables and the general absence of beauty made room less difficult to be found.

"Ah! Emmy dear," said the old gentleman, wiping his face, "times are much changed, I see, since my youth. Then you would see no such throngs assembled in so small a space; gentlemen shoving ladies, and yes, Emmy," continued her uncle in a lower tone, as if afraid of uttering something dangerous, "the ladies themselves shouldering the men. I remember at a drum given by Lady Gosford, that although I may, without vanity, say I was one of the gallantest men in the room, I came in contact with but one of the ladies during the whole evening, with the exception of handing the Lady Juliana to a chair, and that," said her uncle, stopping short and lowering his voice to a whisper, "was occasioned by a mischance in the old duchess in rising from her seat when she had taken too much strong waters, as she was at times a little troubled with a pain in the chest."

Emily smiled at the casualty of her grace, and they proceeded slowly through the tables until their passage was stopped by a party at the game of whist, which, by its incongruous mixture of ages and character, forcibly drew her attention.

The party was composed of a young man of five or six and twenty, who threw down his cards in careless indifference, and heedlessly played with the guineas which were laid on the side of the table as markers, or the fruits of a former victory; or by stealing hasty and repeated glances through the vista of the tables into the gayer scenes of the adjoining rooms, proved he was in duresse, and waited for an opportunity to make his escape from the tedium of cards and ugliness to the life of conversation and beauty.

His partner was a woman of doubtful age, and one whose countenance rather indicated that the uncertainty was likely to continue until the record of the tombstone divulged the so often contested circumstance to the world. Her eyes also wandered to the gayer scenes, but with an expression of censoriousness mingled with longings; nor did she neglect the progress of the game as frequently as her more heedless partner. A glance thrown on the golden pair which was placed between her and her neighbor on the right, marked the importance of the *corner*, and she shuffled the cards with a nervousness which plainly denoted her apprehension of the consequences of her partner's abstraction.

Her neighbor on the right was a man of sixty, and his vestments announced him a servant of the sanctuary. His intentness on the game proceeded, no doubt, from his habits of reflection; his smile at success quite possibly from charity to his neighbors; his frown in adversity from displeasure at the triumphs of the wicked, for such in his heart he had set down Miss Wigram to be; and his unconquerable gravity in the employment from a profound regard to the dignity of his holy office.

The fourth performer in this trial of memories was an ancient lady, gayly dressed, and intently eager on the game. Between her and the young man was a large pile of guineas, which appeared to be her exclusive property, from which she repeatedly, during the play, tendered one to his acceptance on the event of a hand or a trick, and to which she seldom failed from inadvertence to add his mite, contributing to accumulate the pile.

"Two double and the rub, my dear doctor," exclaimed the senior lady, in triumph. "Sir William, you owe me ten."

The money was paid as easily as it had been won, and the dowager proceeded to settle some bets with her female antagonist.

"Two more, I fancy, ma'am," said she, closely scanning the contributions of the maiden.

"I believe it is right, my lady," was the answer, with a look that said pretty plainly, that or nothing.

"I beg pardon, my dear, here are but four; and you remember two on the corner, and four on the points. Doctor, I will trouble you for a couple of guineas from Miss Wigram's store; I am in haste to get to the countess's route."

The doctor was coolly helping himself from the said store, under the watchful eyes of its owner, and secretly exulting in his own judgment in requiring the stakes, when the maiden replied in great warmth:

"Your ladyship forgets the two you lost to me at Mrs. Howard's."

"It must be a mistake, my dear, I always pay as I lose," cried the dowager, with great spirit, stretching over the table and helping herself to the disputed money.

Mr. Benfield and Emily had stood silent spectators of the whole scene, the latter in astonishment to meet such manners in such society, and the former under feelings it would have been difficult to describe; for in the face of the dowager, which was inflamed partly from passion and more from high living, he recognized the remains of his Lady Juliana, now the Dowager Viscountess Haverford.

"Emmy, dear," said the old man, with a heavy-drawn sigh, as if awaking from a long and troubled dream, "we will go."

The phantom of forty years had vanished before the truth; and the fancies of retirement, simplicity, and a diseased imagination yielded to the influence of life and common sense.

CHAPTER XL.

WITH Harriet, now closely connected with them by marriage as well as attachment, the baronet's family maintained a most friendly intercourse; and Mrs. Wilson and Emily, a prodigious favorite with her new cousin, consented to pass a day soberly with her during an excursion of her husband to Windsor on business connected with his station. They had, accordingly, driven round to an early breakfast; and Chatterton, after politely regretting his loss, and thanking them for their consideration for his wife, made his bow.

Lady Harriet Denbigh had brought the baron a very substantial addition to his fortune; and as his sisters were both provided for by ample settlements, the pecuniary distresses which had existed a twelvemonth before had been entirely removed. Chatterton's income was now large, his demands upon it small, and he kept up an establishment in proportion to the rank of both husband and wife.

"Mrs. Wilson," cried the hostess, twirling her cup as she followed with her eyes the retreating figure of her husband at the door, "I am about to take up the trade of Miss Harris, and become a match-maker."

"Not on your own behalf so soon, surely," rejoined the widow.

"Oh, no, my fortune is made for life, or not at all," continued the other, gayly; "but in behalf of our little friend Emily, here."

"Me!" cried Emily, starting from a reverie, in which the prospect of happiness to Lady Laura was the subject; "you are very good, Harriet; for whom do you intend me?"

"Whom! Who is good enough for you, but my cousin Pendennyss? Ah!" she cried, laughing, as she caught Emily by the hand, "Derwent and myself both settled the matter long since, and I know you will yield when you come to know him."

"The duke!" cried the other, with a surprise and innocence that immediately brought a blush of the brightest vermilion into her face.

"Yes, the duke," said Lady Chatterton. "You may think it odd for a discarded lover to dispose of his mistress so soon, but both our hearts are set upon it. The earl arrived last night, and this day he and his sister dine with us in a sober way: now, my dear madam," turning to Mrs. Wilson, "have I not prepared an agreeable surprise for you?"

"Surprise, indeed," said the widow, excessively gratified at the probable termination to her anxieties for this meeting; "but where are they from?"

"From Northamptonshire, where the earl has already purchased a residence, I understand, and in your neighborhood, too; so, you perceive, *he* at least begins to think of the thing."

"A certain evidence, truly," cried Emily, "his having purchased the house. But was he without a residence that he bought the deanery?"

"Oh, no! he has a palace in town, and three seats in the country; but none in Northamptonshire but this," said the lady, with a laugh. "To own the truth, he did offer to let George Denbigh have it for the next summer, but the colonel chose to be nearer Eltringham; and I take it, it was only a ruse in the earl to cloak his own designs. You may depend upon it, we trumpeted your praises to him incessantly in Westmoreland."

"And is Colonel Denbigh in town?" said Mrs. Wilson, stealing an anxious glance toward her niece, who, in spite of all her efforts, sensibly changed color.

"Oh, yes! and Laura is as happy—as happy—as myself," said Lady Chatterton, with a glow on her cheeks, as she attended to the request of her housekeeper, and left the room.

Her guests sat in silence, occupied with their own reflections, while they heard a summons at the door of the house. It was opened, and footsteps approached the door of their own room. It was pushed partly open, as a voice on the other side said, speaking to a servant without—

"Very well. Do not disturb your lady; I am in no haste."

At the sound of its well-known tones, both the ladies almost sprang from their seats. Here could be no resemblance, and a moment removed their doubts. The speaker entered—it was Denbigh.

He stood for a moment fixed as a statue. It was evident the surprise was mutual. His face was pale as death, and then instantly was succeeded by a glow of fire. Approaching them, he paid his compliments with great earnestness, and in a voice in which his softest tones preponderated.

"I am happy, very happy, to be so fortunate in again meeting with such friends, and so unexpectedly."

Mrs. Wilson bowed in silence to his compliment, and Emily, pale as himself, sat with her eyes fastened on the carpet, without daring to trust her voice with an attempt to speak.

After struggling with his mortified feelings for a moment, Denbigh rose from the chair he had taken, and drawing near the sofa on which the ladies were placed, exclaimed with fervor—

"Tell me, dear madam, lovely, too lovely Miss Moseley, has one act of folly, of wickedness, if you please, lost me your good opinion forever? Derwent had given me hopes that you yet retained some esteem for my character, lowered, as I acknowledge it to be, in my own estimation?"

"The Duke of Derwent? Mr. Denbigh!"

"Do not, do not use a name, dear madam, almost hateful to me," cried he, in a tone of despair.

"If," said Mrs. Wilson, gravely, "you have made your own name disreputable, I can only regret it, but——"

"Call me by my title—oh! do not remind me of my folly; I cannot bear it, and from you."

"Your title!" exclaimed Mrs. Wilson, with a cry of wonder, and Emily turned on him a face in which the flashes of color and succeeding paleness were as quick, and almost as vivid, as the glow of lightning. He caught their astonishment in equal surprise.

"How is this? some dreadful mistake, of which I am yet in ignorance," he cried, taking the unresisting hand of Mrs. Wilson, and pressing it with warmth between both his own, as he added, "do not leave me in suspense."

"For the sake of truth, for my sake, for the sake of this suffering innocent, say, in sincerity, who and what you are," said Mrs. Wilson in a solemn voice, gazing on him in dread of his reply.

Still retaining her hand, he dropped on his knees before her, as he answered—

"I am the pupil, the child of your late husband, the companion of his dangers, the sharer of his joys and griefs, and would I could add, the friend of his widow. I am the Earl of Pendennyss."

Mrs. Wilson's head dropped on the shoulders of the kneeling youth, her arms were thrown in fervor around his neck, and she burst into a flood of tears. For a moment, both were absorbed in their own feelings; but a cry from Pendennyss aroused the aunt to the situation of her niece.

Emily had fallen senseless on the sofa.

An hour elapsed before her engagements admitted of the return of Lady Chatterton to the breakfast parlor, where she was surprised to find the breakfast equipage yet standing, and her cousin, the earl. Looking from one to the other in surprise, she exclaimed—

"Very sociable, upon my word; how long has your lordship honored my house with your presence, and have you taken the liberty to introduce yourself to Mrs. Wilson and Miss Moseley?"

"Sociability and ease are the fashion of the day. I have been here an hour, my dear coz, and *have* taken the liberty of *introducing myself* to Mrs. Wilson and Miss Moseley," replied the earl, gravely, although a smile of meaning lighted his handsome features as he uttered the latter part of the sentence, which was returned by Emily with a look of archness and pleasure that would have graced her happiest moments of juvenile joy.

There was such an interchange of looks, and such a visible alteration in the appearance of her guests, that it could not but attract the notice of Lady Chatterton. After listening to the conversation between them for some time in silence, and wondering what could have wrought so sudden a change below stairs, she broke forth with saying—

"Upon my word, you are an incomprehensible party to me. I left you ladies alone, and find a gentleman with you. I left you grave, if not melancholy, and find you all life and gayety. I find you with a stranger, and you talk with him about walks, and rides, and scenes, and acquaintances. Will *you*, madam, or *you*, my lord, be so kind as to explain these seeming inconsistencies?"

"No," cried the earl, "to punish your curiosity, I will keep you in ignorance; but Marian is in waiting for me at your neighbor's, Mrs. Wilmot, and I must hasten to her—you will see us both by five." Rising from his seat he took the offered hand of Mrs. Wilson and pressed it to his lips. To Emily he also extended his hand, and received hers in return, though with a face suffused with the color of the rose. Pendennyss held it to his heart for a moment with fervor, and kissing it, precipitately left the room. Emily concealed her face with her hands, and, dissolving in tears, sought the retirement of an adjoining apartment.

All these unaccountable movements filled Lady Chatterton with amazement, that would have been too painful for further endurance; and Mrs. Wilson, knowing that further concealment with so near a connection would be impossible, if not unnecessary, entered into a brief explanation of the earl's masquerade (although ignorant herself of its cause, or of the means of supporting it), and his present relation with her niece.

"I declare it is provoking," cried Lady Chatterton, with a tear in her eye, "to have such ingenious plans as Derwent and I had made lost from the want of necessity in putting them in force. Your demure niece has deceived us all handsomely; and my rigid cousin, too—I will rate him soundly for his deception."

"I believe he already repents sincerely of his having practiced it," said Mrs. Wilson, "and is sufficiently punished for his error by its consequence. A life of misery for four months is a serious penalty to a lover."

"Yes," said the other; "I am afraid his punishment was not confined to himself alone; he has made others suffer from his misconduct. I will rate him famously, depend upon it, I will."

If anything, the interest felt by Lady Chatterton for her friend was increased by the discovery of the affections of Pendennyss, and a few hours were passed by the three, in we will not say sober delight, for transport would be a better word. Lady Chatterton frankly declared that she would rather see Emily the wife of the earl than of her brother, for *he* alone was good enough for her; and Mrs. Wilson felt an exhilaration of spirits, in the completion of her most sanguine wishes, that neither her years, her philosophy, nor even her religion, could entirely restrain. The face of Emily was a continued blush, her eye sparkled with the luster of renewed hope, and her bosom was heaving with the purest emotions of happiness.

At the appointed hour the rattling of wheels announced the approach of the earl and his sister.

Pendennyss came into the room with a young woman of great personal beauty and extremely feminine manners leaning on his arm. He first announced her to Mrs. Wilson as his sister, Lady Marian Denbigh, who received her with a frank cordiality that made them instantly acquainted. Emily, although confiding in the fullest manner in the truth and worth of her lover, had felt an inexplicable sensation of pleasure, as she heard the ear; speak of his sister by the name of Marian 1 love is such an unquiet, and generally such an engrossing passion, that few avoid unnecessary uneasiness while under its influence, unless so situated as to enjoy a mutual confidence.

As this once so formidable Marian approached to salute her with an extended hand, Emily rose, with a face illumined with pleasure, to receive her. Marian viewed her for a moment intently, and folding her arms around her, whispered softly, as she pressed her to her heart, "My sister, my only sister."

Our heroine was affected to tears, and Pendennyss gently separating the two he loved best in the world, they soon became calm.

Lady Marian was extremely like her brother, and had a family resemblance to her cousin Harriet; but her manners were softer and more retiring, and she had a slight tinge of a settled melancholy. When her brother spoke she was generally silent, not in fear, but in love. She evidently regarded him among the first of human beings, and all her love was amply returned.

Both the aunt and niece studied the manners of the earl closely, and found several shades of distinction between what he was and what he had been. He was now the perfect man of the world, without having lost the frank sincerity which caused you to believe all he said. Had Pendennyss once told Mrs. Wilson, with his natural air and manner, "I am innocent," she would have believed him, and an earlier investigation would have saved them months of misery; but the consciousness of his deception had oppressed him with the curse of the wicked.

Pendennyss had lost that air of embarrassment and alarm which had so often startled the aunt, even in her hours of greatest confidence, and which had their original in the awkwardness of disguise. But he retained his softness, his respect, his modest diffidence of his opinions, although somewhat corrected now by his acknowledged experience and acquaintance with man.

Mrs. Wilson thought these decided trifling alterations in manner were improvements; but it required some days and a few tender speeches to reconcile Emily to any change in the appearance of Denbigh.

Lady Marian had ordered her carriage early, as she had not anticipated the pleasure she found, and was engaged to accompany her cousin, Lady Laura, to a fashionable rout that evening. Unwilling to be torn from his newly-found friends, the earl proposed that the three ladies should accompany his sister to Annerdale House, and then accept himself as an escort to their own residence. To this Harriet assented, and, leaving a message for Chatterton, they entered the coach of Marian, and Pendennyss, mounting the dicky, drove off.

Annerdale House was among the best edifices of London. It had been erected in the preceding century, and Emily for a moment felt, as she went through its splendid apartments, that it threw a chill around her domestic affections; but the figure of Pendennyss by her side reconciled her to a magnificence she had been unused to, which looked the lord, indeed; but with so much modesty and softness, and so much attention to herself, that, before she left the house, Emily began to think it very possible to enjoy happiness even in the lap of splendor.

The names of Colonel Denbigh and Lady Laura were soon announced, and this formidable gentleman made his appearance. He resembled Pendennyss more than even the duke, and appeared about the same age.

Mrs. Wilson soon saw that she had no grounds for pitying Lady Laura. The colonel was a polished, elegant man, of evident good sense and knowledge of the world, and apparently devoted to his wife. He was called George frequently by all his relatives, and he, not unfrequently, used the same term himself in speaking to the earl. Something was said of a much admired bust, and the doors of a large library were opened to view it. Emily was running over the backs of a case of books, until her eye rested on one ; and half smiling and blushing she turned to Pendennyss, who watched every movement, as she said, playfully,

" Pity me, my lord, and lend me this volume."

" What is it you read ? " he asked, as he bowed his cheerful assent.

But Emily hid the book in her handkerchief. Pendennyss noticing an unwillingness, though an extremely playful one, to let him into the secret, examined the case, and perceiving her motive, smiled, as he took down another volume and said—

" I am not an Irish, but an English peer, Emily. You had the wrong volume."

Emily laughed, with deeper blushes, when she found her wishes detected, while the earl, opening the volume he held—the first of Debrett's Peerage—pointed with his finger to the article concerning his own family, and said to Mrs. Wilson, who had joined them at the instant—

" To-morrow, dear madam, I shall beg your attention to a melancholy tale, and which may, in some slight degree, extenuate the offense I was guilty of in assuming, or rather in maintaining, an accidental disguise."

As he ended, he went to the others, to draw off their attention, while Emily and her aunt examined the paragraph. It was as follows :

" George Denbigh—Earl of Pendennyss —and Baron Lumley, of Lumley Castle— Baron Pendennyss—Beaumaris, and Fitzwalter, born ——, of ——, in the year of ——; a bachelor." The list of earls and nobles occupied several pages, but the closing article was as follows :

" George, the 21st earl, succeeded his mother Marian, late Countess of Pendennyss, in her own right, being born of her marriage with George Denbigh, Esq., a cousin-german to Frederick, the 9th Duke of Derwent."

" Heir apparent. The titles being to heirs general, will descend to his lordship's sister, Lady Marian Denbigh, should the present earl die without lawful issue."

As much of the explanation of the mystery of our tale is involved in the foregoing paragraphs, may we be allowed to relate in our own language what Pendennyss made his friends acquainted with at different times, and in a manner suitable to the subject and his situation.

CHAPTER XLI.

IT was at the close of that war which lost this country the wealthiest and most populous of her American colonies, that a fleet of ships were returning from their service among the islands of the New World, to seek for their worn out and battered hulks, and equally weakened crews, the repairs and comforts of England and home.

The latter word, to the mariner the most endearing of all sounds, had, as it were, drawn together by instinct a group of sailors on the forecastle of the proudest ship of the squadron, who gazed with varied emotions on the land which gave them birth, but with one common feeling of joy that the day of attaining it was at length arrived.

The water curled from the bows of this castle of the ocean in increasing waves and growing murmurs, that at times drew the attention of the veteran tar to their quickening progress, and having cheered his heart with the sight, he cast his experienced eye in silence on the swelling sails, to see if nothing more could be done to shorten the distance between him and his country.

Hundreds of eyes were fixed on the land of their birth, and hundreds of hearts were beating in that one vessel with the awakening delights of domestic love and renewed affections ; but no tongue broke the disciplined silence of the ship into sounds that overcame the propitious ripple of the water.

On the highest summit of their towering mast floated a small blue flag, the symbol of authority, and beneath it paced a man to and fro the deck, which was abandoned by his inferiors to his more elevated rank. His square-built form and care-worn features, which had lost the brilliancy of an English complexion, and hair whitened prematurely, spoke of bodily vigor and arduous services which had put that vigor to the severest trials.

At each turn of his walk, as he faced the land of his nativity, a lurking smile stole over his sunburnt features, and then a glance of his eye would scan the progress of the far-stretched squadron which obeyed his orders, and which he was now returning to his superiors, undiminished in numbers, and proud with victory.

By himself stood an officer in a uniform differing from all around him. His figure was small, his eye restless, quick, and piercing, and bent on those shores to which he was unwillingly advancing, with a look of anxiety and mortification, that showed him the late commander of those vessels around them, which, by displaying their double flags, manifested to the eye of the seaman a recent change of masters.

Occasionally the conqueror would stop, and by some effort of well meant, but rather uncouth civility, endeavor to soften the hours of captivity; efforts which were received with the courtesy of the most punctilious etiquette, but a restraint which showed that they were unwelcome.

It was, perhaps, the most unlucky moment that had occurred within the two months of their association, for an exchange of their better feelings. The honest heart of the English tar dilated with ill-concealed delight at his approach to the termination of labors performed with credit and honor, and his smiles and good-humor, which partly proceeded from the feelings of a father and a friend, were daggers to the heart of his discomfited rival.

A third personage now appeared from the cabin of the vessel, and approached the spot where the adverse admirals at the moment were engaged in one of these constrained conferences.

The appearance and dress of this gentleman differed widely from the two just described. He was tall, graceful, and dignified; he was a soldier, and clearly of high rank. His carefully dressed hair concealed the ravages of time; and on the quarter-deck of a first-rate his attire and manners were suited to a field-day in the park.

"I really insist, monsieur," cried the admiral, good-naturedly, "that you shall take part of my chaise to London. You are a stranger, and it will help to keep up your spirits by the way."

"You are very good, Monsieur Howell," replied the Frenchman with a polite bow and forced smile, misconstruing ill-judged benevolence into a wish for his person to grace a triumph—"but I have accepted the offer Monsieur le General Denbigh was so good as to make me."

"Then comte is engaged to me, Howell," said the general, with a courtly smile, "and, indeed, you must leave the ship to-night, or as soon as we anchor. But I shall take daylight and to-morrow."

"Well—well—Denbigh," exclaimed the other, rubbing his hands with pleasure as he viewed the increasing power of the wind, "only make yourselves happy, and I am contented."

A few hours intervened before they reached the Bay of Plymouth, and round the table, after their dinner, were seated the general and English admiral. The comte, under the pretense of preparing his things for a removal, had retired to his apartment to conceal his feelings; and the captain of the ship was above, superintending the approach of the vessel to her anchorage. Two or three well-emptied bottles of wine yet remained; but as the healths of all the branches of the House of Brunswick had been propitiated from their contents, with a polite remembrance of Louis XVI. and Marie Antoinette from General Denbigh, neither of the superiors was much inclined for action.

"Is the *Thunderer* in her station?" said the admiral to the signal lieutenant, who at that moment came below with a report.

"Yes, sir, and has answered."

"Very well—make the signal to prepare to anchor."

"Ay, ay, sir."

"And here, Bennet," to the retiring lieutenant, "call the transports all in shore of us."

"Three hundred and eighty-four, sir," said the officer, looking at his signal-book.

The admiral cast his eye at the book, and nodded an assent.

"And let the *Mermaid—Flora—Weasel —Bruiser*, and all the sloops, lie well off, until we have landed the soldiers; the pilot says the channel is full of luggers, and Jonathan has grown very saucy."

The lieutenant made a complying bow, and was retiring to execute these orders, as Admiral Howell, taking up a bottle not yet entirely deserted by its former tenant, cried stoutly—"Here, Bennet— I forgot—take a glass of wine; drink success to ourselves, and defeat to the French all over the world."

The general pointed significantly to the adjoining cabin of the French admiral, as he pressed his hand on his lips for silence.

"Oh!" cried Admiral Howell, recollecting himself, continuing in a whisper, "you can drink it in your heart, notwithstanding."

The signal officer nodded, and drank the liquor. As he smacked his lips while going on deck, he thought to himself, these nabobs drink famous good wine.

Although the feelings of General Denbigh were under much more command and disciplined obedience than those of his friends, yet was he too unusually elated with his return to home and expected honors. If the admiral had captured a fleet, *he* had taken an island; and hand in hand they had co-operated in unusual harmony through the difficulties of an arduous campaign. This rather singular circumstance was owing to their personal friendship. From their youth they had been companions, and although of very different characters and habits, chance had cemented their intimacy in more advanced life. While in subordinate stations, they had been associated together in service; and the general and admiral, in command of an army and fleet, had once before returned to England with less renown, as a colonel and a captain of a frigate. The great family influence of the soldier, with the known circumstance of their harmony, had procured them this later command, and home, with its comforts and rewards, was close before them. Pouring out a glass of Madeira, the general, who always calculated what he said, exclaimed—

"Peter—we have been friends from boys."

"To be sure we have," said the admiral, looking up in a little surprise at this unexpected commencement—"and it will not be my fault if we do not die such, Frederick."

Dying was a subject the general did not much delight in, although of conspicuous courage in the field; and he proceeded to his more important purpose—

"I could never find, although I have looked over our family tree so often, that we are in any manner related, Howell."

"I believe it is too late to mend that matter now," said the admiral, musing.

"Why no—hem—I think not, Howell; take a glass of this Burgundy."

The admiral shook his head with a stubborn resolution to taste nothing French, but he helped himself to a bountiful stock of Madeira, as he replied—

"I should like to know how you can bring it about this time of day, Denbigh?"

"How much money will you be able to give that girl of yours, Peter?" said his friend, evading the point.

"Forty thousand down, my good fellow, and as much more when I die," cried the open-hearted sailor, with a nod of exultation.

"George, my youngest son, will not be rich—but Francis will be a duke, and have a noble estate; yet," said the general, meditating, "he is so unhappy in his disposition and uncouth in his man-

ners, I cannot think of offering him to your daughter as a husband."

"Isabel shall marry a good-natured man, like myself, or not at all," said the admiral, positively, but not in the least suspecting the drift of his friend, who was influenced by anything but a regard for the lady's happiness.

Francis, his first born, was, in truth, as he had described; but his governing wish was to provide for his favorite George. Dukes could never want wives, but unportioned captains in the guards might.

"George is one of the best tempers in the world," said his father, with strong feeling, "and the delight of us all. I could wish he had been the heir to the family honors."

"*That* it is certainly too late to help," cried the admiral, wondering if the ingenuity of his friend could devise a remedy for this evil too.

"Too late, indeed," said the other, with a heavy sigh, "but Howell, what say you to matching Isabel with my favorite George?"

"Denbigh," cried the sailor, eying him keenly, "Isabel is my only child, and a dutiful, good girl; one that will obey orders if she breaks owners, as we sailors say. Now I did think of marrying her to a seaman, when a proper man came athwart my course; yet your son is a soldier, and that is next to being in the navy; if so be you had made him come aboard me, when I wanted you to, there would have been no objection at all; however, when occasion offers, I will overhaul the lad, and if I find him stanch he may turn in with Bell, and welcome."

This was uttered in perfect simplicity, and with no intention of giving offense, partaking partly of the nature of a soliloquy; so the general, greatly encouraged, was about to push the point, when a gun was fired from their own ship.

"There's some of them lubberly transports won't mind our signals; they have had these soldiers so long on board they get as clumsy as the red coats themselves," muttered the admiral, hastening on deck to enforce his commands.

A shot or two, sent significantly in the direction of the wanderers, but so as not to hit them, restored order; and within an hour forty line-of-battle ships and a hundred transports were disposed in the best manner for convenience and safety.

On their presentation to their sovereign, both veterans were embellished with the ribbon of the Bath; and as their exploits filled the mouths of the newsmongers, and the columns of the public prints of the day, the new knights began to think more seriously of building a monument to their victories, in a union between their children. The admiral, however, determined to do nothing with his eyes shut, and he demanded a scrutiny.

"Where is the boy who is to be a duke?" exclaimed he, one day, when his friend had introduced the point with a view to a final arrangement. "Bell has good blood in her veins—is a tight-built little vessel—clean heel'd and trim, and would make as good a duchess as the best of them; so, Denbigh, I will begin by taking a survey of the senior."

To this the general had no objection, as he well knew that Francis would be wide of pleasing the tastes of an open-hearted, simple man, like the sailor. They met accordingly for what the general facetiously called the review, and what the admiral innocently termed his survey, at the house of the former, when the young gentlemen were submitted to his inspection.

Francis Denbigh was about four and twenty, of a feeble body, and with a face marked with the small-pox, to approaching deformity; his eye was brilliant and piercing, but unsettled, and at times wild—his manner awkward, constrained, and timid. There would be seen, it is true, an intelligence and animation, which occasionally lighted his countenance into gleams of sunshine, that caused you to overlook the lesser accompaniments of complexion and features in the expression; but they were transient, and inevitably vanished whenever his father spoke or in any manner mingled in his pursuits.

An observer close as Mrs. Wilson would have said that the feelings of the father and son were not such as ought to exist between parent and child.

But the admiral, who regarded model and rigging a good deal, satisfied himself with muttering, as he turned his eyes on the junior—

"He may do for a duke—but I would not have him for a cockswain."

George was a year younger than Francis; in form, stature, and personal grace, the counterpart of his father; his eye was less keen but more attractive than that of his brother; his air open, polished, and manly.

"Ah!" thought the sailor, as he ended a satisfactory survey of the youth, "what a thousand pities Denbigh did not send him to sea!"

The thing was soon settled, and George was to be the happy man. Sir Peter concluded to dine with his friend, in order to settle preliminaries over the bottle by themselves; the young men and their mother being engaged to their uncle the duke.

"Well, Denbigh," cried the admiral, as the last servant withdrew, "when do you mean to have the young couple spliced?"

"Why," replied the wary soldier, who knew he could not calculate on obedience to his mandate with as great a certainty as his friend—"the better way is to bring the young people together, in order that they may become acquainted, you know."

"Acquainted — together"— cried his companion, in a little surprise, "what better way is there to bring them together, than to have them up before a priest, or to make them acquainted by letting them swing in the same hammock?"

"It might answer the end, indeed," said the general, with a smile, "but somehow or other, it is always the best method to bring young folks together, to let them have their own way in the affair for a time."

"Own way!" rejoined Sir Peter, bluntly, "did you ever find it answer to let a woman have her own way, Sir Frederick?"

"Not common women certainly, my good friend," said the general, "but such a girl as my intended daughter is an exception."

"I don't know that," cried the sailor; "Bell is a good girl, but she has her quirks and whims like all the sex."

"You have had no trouble with her as yet, I believe, Howell," said Sir Frederick, cavalierly, throwing an inquiring glance on his friend at the same time.

"No, not yet—nor do I think she will ever dare to mutiny; but there has been one wishing to take her in tow already since we got in."

"How!" said the other in alarm, "who—what is he? Some officer in the navy, I suppose."

"No, he was a kind of chaplain, one Parson Ives, a good sort of a youth enough, and a prodigious favorite with my sister, Lady Hawker."

"Well, what did you answer, Peter?" said his companion, in increasing uneasiness; "did you put him off?"

"Off! to be sure I did—do you think I wanted a barber's clerk for a son-in-law? No, no, Denbigh; a soldier is bad enough, without having a preacher."

The general compressed his lips at this direct attack on a profession that he thought the most honorable of any in the world, in some resentment; but remembering the eighty thousand pounds, and accustomed to the ways of the other, he curbed his temper, and inquired—

"But Miss Howell—your daughter—

how did she stand affected to this priest?"

"How — why — how?—why, I never asked her."

"Never asked her?"

"No, never asked her: she is my daughter, you know, and bound to obey my orders, and I did not choose she should marry a parson. But, once for all, when is the wedding to take place?"

General Denbigh had indulged his younger son too blindly and too fondly to expect that implicit obedience the admiral calculated to a certainty on, and with every prospect of not being disappointed, from his daughter. Isabel Howell was pretty, mild, and timid, and unused to oppose any of her father's commands; but George Denbigh was haughty, positive, and self-willed, and unless the affair could be so managed as to make him a willing assistant in the courtship, his father knew it might be abandoned at once. He thought his son might be led, but not driven; and, relying on his own powers for managing, the general saw his only safety in executing the scheme was in postponing his advances for a regular siege to the lady's heart.

Sir Peter chafed and swore at this circumlocution. The thing could be done as well in a week as in a year; and the veterans, who, for a miracle, had agreed in their rival stations, and in doubtful moments of success, were near splitting on the point of marrying a girl of nineteen.

As Sir Peter both loved his friend, and had taken a prodigious fancy to the youth, he, however, was fain to submit to a short probation.

"You are always for going a roundabout way to do a thing," said the admiral, as he yielded the point. "Now when you took that battery, had you gone up in front as I advised you, you would have taken it in ten minutes instead of five hours."

"Yes," said the other, with a friendly shake of the hand at parting, "and lost fifty men in place of one by the step."

CHAPTER XLII.

THE Honorable General Denbigh was the youngest of three sons. His seniors, Francis and George, were yet bachelors. The death of a cousin had made Francis a duke while yet a child, and both he and his favorite brother, George, had decided on lives of inactivity and sluggishness.

"When I die, brother," the oldest would say, "you will succeed me, and Frederick can provide heirs for the name hereafter."

This arrangement had been closely adhered to, and the two elder brothers reached the ages of fifty-five and fifty-six without altering their condition. In the meantime Frederick married a young woman of rank and fortune; the fruits of their union being the two young candidates for the hand of Isabel Howell.

Francis Denbigh, the eldest son of the general, was naturally diffident, and in addition it was his misfortune to be the reverse of captivating in external appearance. The small-pox sealed his doom; ignorance, and the violence of the attack, left him indelibly impressed with the ravages of that dreadful disorder. On the other hand his brother escaped without any vestiges of the complaint; and his spotless skin and fine open countenance met the gaze of his mother, after the recovery of the two, in striking contrast to the deformed lineaments of his elder brother. Such an occurrence is sure to excite one of two feelings in the breast of every beholder—pity or disgust; and, unhappily for Francis, maternal tenderness in his case was unable to counteract the latter sensation. George became a favorite and Francis a neutral. The effect was easy to be seen, and it was rapid as it was indelible.

The feelings of Francis were sensitive to an extreme. He had more quickness, more sensibility, more real talent than George; which enabled him to perceive, and caused him to feel more acutely, the partiality of his mother.

As yet, the engagements and duties of the general had kept his children and their improvements out of his sight; but at the ages of eleven and twelve, the feelings of a father began to take pride in the possession of his sons.

On his return from a foreign station, after an absence of two years, his children were ordered from school to meet him. Francis had improved in stature, but not in beauty; George had flourished in both.

The natural diffidence of the former was increased, by perceiving that he was no favorite, and the effect began to show itself on manners at no time engaging. He met his father with doubt, and he saw with anguish that the embrace received by his brother much exceeded in warmth that which had been bestowed on himself.

"Lady Margaret," said the general to his wife, as he followed the boys as they retired from the dinner table, with his eyes, "it is a thousand pities George had not been the elder. *He* would have graced a dukedom or a throne. Frank is only fit for a parson."

This ill-judged speech was uttered sufficiently loud to be overheard by both the sons; on the younger, it made a pleasurable sensation for the moment. His father—his dear father, had thought him fit to be a king; and his father must be a judge, whispered his native vanity; but all this time the connection between the speech and his brother's rights did not present themselves to his mind. George loved his brother too well, too sincerely, to have injured him even in thought; and so far as Francis was concerned, his vanity was as blameless as it was natural.

The effect produced on the mind of Francis was different both in substance and in degree. It mortified his pride, alarmed his delicacy, and wounded his already morbid sensibility to such an extent, as to make him entertain the romantic notion of withdrawing from the world, and of yielding a birthright to one so every way more deserving of it than himself.

From this period might be dated an opinion of Francis's, which never afterward left him; he fancied he was doing injustice to another, and that other, a brother whom he ardently loved, by continuing to exist. Had he met with fondness in his parents, or sociability in his playfellows, these fancies would have left him as he grew into life. But the affections of his parents were settled on his more promising brother; and his manners daily increasing in their repulsive traits, drove his companions to the society of others, more agreeable to their own buoyancy and joy.

Had Francis Denbigh, at this age, met with a guardian clear-sighted enough to fathom his real character, and competent to direct his onward course, he would yet have become an ornament to his name and country, and a useful member of society. But no such guide existed. His natural guardians, in his particular case, were his worst enemies; and the boys left school for college four years afterward, each advanced in his respective properties of attraction and repulsion.

Irreligion is hardly a worse evil in a family than favoritism. When once allowed to exist, in the breast of the parent, though hid apparently from all other eyes, its sad consequences begin to show themselves. Effects are produced, and we look in vain for the cause. The awakened sympathies of reciprocal caresses and fondness are mistaken for uncommon feelings, and the forbidding aspect of deadened affections is miscalled native sensibility.

In this manner the evil increases itself, until manners are formed, and characters created, that must descend with their possessor to the tomb.

In the peculiar formation of the mind of Francis Denbigh, the evil was doubly injurious. His feelings required sympathy and softness, and they met only with coldness and disgust. George alone was an exception to the rule. *He* did love his brother; but even his gayety and spirits finally tired of the dull uniformity of the diseased habits of his senior.

The only refuge Francis found in his solitude, amid the hundreds of the university, was in his muse and in the powers of melody. The voice of his family has been frequently mentioned in these pages: and if, as Lady Laura has intimated, there had ever been a siren in the race, it was a male one. He wrote prettily, and would sing these efforts of his muse to music of his own, drawing crowds around his windows, in the stillness of the night, to listen to sounds as melodious as they were mournful. His poetical efforts partook of the distinctive character of the man, being melancholy, wild, and sometimes pious.

George was always among the most admiring of his brother's auditors, and would feel a yearning of his heart toward him, at such moments, that was painful. But George was too young and too heedless to supply the place of a monitor, or to draw his thoughts into a more salutary train. This was the *duty* of his parents, and should have been their *task*. But the world, his rising honors, and his professional engagements, occupied the time of the father; and fashion, parties, and pleasure killed the time of his mother. When they did think of their children, it was of George; the painful image of Francis being seldom admitted to disturb their serenity.

George Denbigh was open-hearted, without suspicion, and a favorite. The first quality taxed his generosity, the second subjected him to fraud, and the third supplied him with the means. But these means sometimes failed. The fortune of the general, though handsome, was not more than competent to support his style of living. He expected to be a duke himself one day, and was anxious to maintain an appearance now that would not disgrace his future elevation. A system of strict but liberal economy had been adopted in the case of his sons. They had, for the sake of appearances, a stated and equal allowance.

The duke had offered to educate the heir himself, and under his own eye. But to this Lady Margaret had found some ingenious excuse, and one that seemed to herself and the world honorable to her natural feeling; but had the offer been made to George, these reasons would have vanished in the desire to advance his interests, or to gratify his propensities. Such decisions are by no means uncommon; parents having once decided on the merits and abilities of their children, frequently decline the interference of third persons, since the improvement of their denounced offspring might bring their own judgment into question, if it did not convey an indirect censure on their justice.

The heedlessness of George brought his purse to a state of emptiness. His last guinea was gone, and two months were wanting to the end of the quarter. George had played and been cheated. He had ventured to apply to his mother for small sums, when his dress or some trifling indulgence required an advance: and always with success. But here were sixty guineas gone at a blow, and pride, candor, forbade his concealing the manner of his loss, if he made the application. This was dreadful; his own conscience reproached him, and he had so often witnessed the violence of his mother's resentments against Francis, for faults which appeared to him very trivial, not to stand in the utmost dread of her more just displeasure in the present case.

Entering the apartment of his brother, in this disturbed condition, George threw himself into a chair, and with his face concealed between his hands, sat brooding over his forlorn situation.

"George!" said his brother, soothingly, "you are in distress; can I relieve you in any way?"

"Oh no—no—no—Frank; it is entirely out of your power."

"Perhaps not, my dear brother," continued the other, endeavoring to draw his hand into his own.

"Entirely! entirely!" said George, Then springing up in despair, he exclaimed. "But I must live—I cannot die."

"Live! die!" cried Francis, recoiling in horror. "What do you mean by such language? Tell me, George, am I not your brother? Your only brother and best friend?"

Francis felt he had no friend if George was not that friend, and his face grew pale while the tears flowed rapidly down his cheeks.

George could not resist such an appeal. He caught the hand of his brother and made him acquainted with his losses and his wants.

Francis mused some little time over his narration, ere he broke silence.

"It was all you had?"

"The last shilling," cried George, beating his head with his hand.

"How much will you require to make out the quarter?"

"Oh I must have at least fifty guineas, or how can I live at all?"

The ideas of life in George were connected a good deal with the manner it was to be enjoyed. His brother appeared struggling with himself, and then turning to the other, continued—

"But surely, under present circumstances, you could make less do."

"Less, never—hardly that"—interrupted George, vehemently. "If Lady Margaret did not inclose me a note now and then, how could we get along at all? don't you find it so yourself brother?"

"I don't know," said Francis, turning pale—

"Don't know," cried George, catching a view of his altered countenance—"you get the money, though?"

"I do not remember it," said the other, sighing heavily.

"Francis," cried George, comprehending the truth, "you shall share every shilling I receive in future—you shall—indeed you shall."

"Well, then," rejoined Francis with a smile, "it is a bargain; and you will receive from me a supply in your necessities."

Without waiting for an answer, Francis withdrew into an inner apartment, and brought out the required sum for his brother's subsistence for two months. George remonstrated, but Francis was positive; he had been saving, and his stock was ample for his simple habits without it.

"Besides, you forget we are partners, and in the end I shall be a gainer."

George yielded to his wants and his brother's entreaties, and gave him great credit for the disinterestedness of the act. Several weeks passed without any further allusion to this disagreeable subject, which had at least the favorable result of making George more guarded and a better student.

The brothers, from this period, advanced gradually in those distinctive qualities which were to mark the future men; George daily improving in grace and attraction, Francis, in an equal ratio, receding from those very attainments, which it was his too great desire to possess. In the education of his sons, General

Denbigh had preserved the appearance of impartiality; his allowance to each was the same; they were at the same college, they had been at the same school; and if Frank did not improve as much as his younger brother, it was unquestionably his own obstinacy and stupidity, and surely not want of opportunity or faver.

Such, then, were the artificial and accidental causes, which kept a noble, a proud, an acute but a diseased mind, in acquirements much below another every way its inferior, excepting in the happy circumstance of wanting those very excellences, the excess and indiscreet management of which proved the ruin instead of the blessing of their possessor.

The duke would occasionally rouse himself from his lethargy, and complain to the father, that the heir of his honors was far inferior to his younger brother in acquirements, and remonstrate against the course which produced such an unfortunate inequality. On these occasions a superficial statement of his system from the general met the objection; they cost the same money, and he was sure he not only wished but did everything an indulgent parent could, to render Francis worthy of his future honors. Another evil of the admission of feelings of partiality, in the favor of one child to the prejudice of another, is that the malady is contagious as well as lasting; it exists without our own knowledge, and it seldom fails to affect those around us. The uncle soon learnt to distinguish George as the hope of the family, yet Francis must be the heir of its honors, and consequently of its wealth.

The duke and his brother were not much addicted to action, hardly to reflection; but if anything could arouse them to either, it was the reputation of the house of Denbigh. Their ideas of reputation, it is true, were of their own forming.

The hour at length drew near when George expected a supply from the ill-judged generosity of his mother; it came, and with a heart beating with pleasure, the youth flew to the room of Francis with a determination to force the whole of his twenty pounds on his acceptance. On throwing open the door, he saw his brother evidently striving to conceal something behind his books. It was at the hour of breakfast, and George had intended for a novelty to share his brother's morning repast. They always met at dinner, but the other meals were made in their own rooms. George looked in vain for the usual equipage of the table; suspicion flashed upon him; he threw aside the books, and a crust of bread and a glass of water met his eye; the truth now flashed upon him in all its force.

"Francis, my brother, to what has my extravagance reduced you!" exclaimed the contrite George with a heart nearly ready to burst. Francis endeavored to explain, but a sacred regard to the truth held him tongue-tied, until dropping his head on the shoulder of George, he sobbed out—

"It is a trifle: nothing to what I would do for you, my brother."

George felt all the horrors of remorse, and was much too generous to conceal his error any longer; he wrote a circumstantial account of the whole transaction to Lady Margaret.

Francis for a few days was a new being. He had acted nobly, his conscience approved of his motives, and of his delicate concealment of them; he in fact began to think there were in himself the seeds of usefulness, as his brother, who from this moment began to understand his character better, attached himself more closely to him.

The eye of Francis met that of George with the look of acknowledged affection, his mind became less moody, and his face was sometimes embellished with a smile.

The reply of their mother to the communication of George threw a damp on the revived hopes of the senior, and drove him back into himself with tenfold humility.

"I am shocked, my child, to find that you have lowered yourself, and forgot the family you belong to, so much as to frequent those gambling houses, which ought not to be suffered in the neighborhood of the universities: when at a proper age and in proper company, your occasional indulgence at cards I could not object to, as both your father and myself sometimes resort to it as an amusement, but never in low company. The consequence of mingling in such society is, that you were cheated, and such will always be your lot unless you confine yourself to associates more becoming your rank and illustrious name.

"As to Francis, I see every reason to condemn the course he has taken. Being the senior by a year, he should have taken the means to prevent your falling into such company; and he should have acquainted me immediately with your loss, in place of wounding your pride by subjecting you to the mortification of receiving a pecuniary obligation from one so little older than yourself, and exposing his own health by a diet on bread and water, as you wrote me, for a whole month. Both the general and myself are seriously displeased with him, and think of separating you, as you thus connive at each other's follies."

George was too indignant to conceal this letter, and the reflections of Francis were dreadful.

For a short time he actually meditated suicide, as the only method of removing himself from before the advancement of George. Had not George been more attentive and affectionate than formerly, the awful expedient might have been resorted to.

From college the young men went, one into the army and the other to the mansion of his uncle. George became an elegant, gay, open-hearted, admired captain in the guards; and Francis stalked through the hails of his ancestors, their acknowledged future lord, but a misanthrope; hateful to himself and disagreeable to all around him.

This picture may be highly wrought, but the effects, in the case of Francis, were increased by the peculiar tone of his diseased state of mind. The indulgence of favoritism, nevertheless, always brings its own sad consequences, in a greater or less degree, while it seldom fails to give sorrow and penitence to the bosom of the parents.

CHAPTER XLIII.

No little art and management had been necessary to make the admiral auxiliary to the indirect plan proposed by his friend to bring George and Isabel together. This, however, effected, the general turned his whole strategy to the impression to be made on the heart of the young gentleman.

Sir Frederick Denbigh had the same idea of the virtue of management as the Dowager Lady Chatterton, but he understood human nature better. Like a prudent officer, his attacks were all masked; and, like a great officer, they seldom failed of success.

The young couple were thrown in each other's way, and as Isabel was extremely attractive, somewhat the opposite to himself in ardor of temperament and vivacity, modest and sensible, it cannot be expected that the association was maintained by the youth with perfect impunity. Within a couple of months he fancied himself desperately in love with Isabel Howell; and in truth he had some reason for the supposition.

The general watched every movement of his son with a wary and vigilant eye— occasionally adding fuel to the flame by drawing his attention to projects of matrimony in other quarters, until George began to think he was soon to undergo a trial of his constancy, and in consequence he armed himself with a double portion of admiration for his Isabel, in order to enable himself to endure the persecution; while the admiral several times endangered the success of the whole enterprise by volunteer contributions to the hopes of the young man, which only escaped producing an opposite effect to that which was intended by being mistaken for the overflowings of good nature and friendship.

After suffering his son to get, as he thought, sufficiently entangled in the snares of Cupid, Sir Frederick determined to fire a volley from one of his masked batteries, which he rightly judged would bring on a general engagement. They were sitting at the table after dinner alone, when the general took the advantage of the name of Miss Howell being accidentally mentioned, to say—

"By the by, George, my friend the admiral said something yesterday on the subject of your being so much with his daughter. I wish you to be cautious, and not to give the old sailor offense in any way, for he is my particular friend."

"He need be under no violent apprehensions," cried George, coloring highly with shame and pride; "I am sure a Denbigh is no unworthy match for a daughter of Sir Peter Howell."

"Oh! to be sure not, boy; we are as old a house as there is in the kingdom, and as noble, too; but the admiral has queer notions, and perhaps he has some cub of a sailor in his eye for a son-in-law. Be prudent, my boy, be prudent; that is all I ask of you."

The general, satisfied with the effect he had produced, carelessly arose from his seat and joined Lady Margaret in her drawing-room.

George remained for several minutes musing on his father's singular request, as well as the admiral's caution, when he sprang from his seat, caught up his hat and sword, and in ten minutes rang at Sir Peter's door in Grosvenor Square. He was admitted, and ascending to the drawing-room, he met the admiral on his way out. Nothing was further from the thoughts of the veteran than a finesse like the general's; and, delighted to see George on the battle-ground, he pointed significantly over his shoulder toward the door of the room Isabel was in, and exclaimed, with a good-natured smile,

"There she is, my hearty; lay her aside, and hang me if she don't strike. I say, George, faint heart never won fair lady ; remember that, my boy ; no, nor a French ship."

George would have been at some loss to have reconciled this speech to his father's caution, if time had been allowed him to think at all; but the door being open he entered, and found Isabel endeavoring to hide her tears.

The admiral, dissatisfied from the beginning with the tardy method of dispatching things, thought he might be of use in breaking the ice for George, by trumpeting his praises on divers occasions to his daughter. Under all circumstances, he thought she might be learning to love the man, as he was to be her husband ; and speeches like the following had been frequent of late from the parent to the child :

"There's that youngster, George Denbigh; now, Bell, is he not a fine-looking lad ? Then I know he is brave. His father before him was good stuff and a true Englishman. What a proper husband he would make for a young woman, he loves his king and country so; none of your new-fangled notions about religion and government, but a sober, religious churchman ; that is, as much so, girl, as you can expect in the guards. No Methodist, to be sure ; it's a great pity he wasn't sent to sea, don't you think so ? But cheer up, girl, one of these days he may be taking a liking to you yet."

Isabel, whose fears taught her the meaning of these eloquent praises of Captain Denbigh, listened to these harangues in silence, and often meditated on their import by herself in tears.

George approached the sofa on which the lady was seated before she had time to conceal the traces of her sorrow, and in a voice softened by emotion, he took her hand gently as he said—

"What can have occasioned this distress to Miss Howell ? If anything in my power to remove, or which a life devoted to her service can mitigate, she has only to command me to find a cheerful obedience."

"The trifling causes of sorrow in a young woman," replied Isabel, endeavoring to smile, " will hardly require such serious services to remove them."

But the lady was extremely interesting at the moment. George was goaded by his father's caution, and urged on by his own feelings, with great sincerity, and certainly much eloquence, he therefore proffered his love and hand to the acceptance of his mistress.

Isabel heard him in painful silence. She respected him and dreaded his power over her father; but, unwilling to abandon hopes to which she yet clung as to her spring of existence, with a violent effort she determined to throw herself on the generosity of her lover.

During her father's late absence, Isabel had, as usual since the death of her mother, been left with his sister, and had formed an attachment for a young clergyman, a younger son of a baronet, and the present Dr. Ives. The inclination had been mutual ; and as Lady Hawker knew her brother to be perfectly indifferent to money, she could see no possible objection to its indulgence.

On his return, Ives made his proposals, as related ; and although warmly backed by the recommendation of the aunt, he was refused. Out of delicacy, the wishes of Isabel had not been mentioned by her clerical lover, and the admiral supposed he had only complied with his agreement with the general, without in any manner affecting the happiness of his daughter by his answer. But the feelings which prompted the request still remained in full vigor in the lovers ; and Isabel now, with many blushes and some hesitation of utterance, made George fully acquainted with the state of her heart, giving him at the same time to understand that he was the only obstacle to her happiness.

It cannot be supposed that George heard her without pain or mortification. The struggle with self-love was a severe one, but his better feelings prevailed, and he assured the anxious Isabel that from his importunities she had nothing to apprehend in future. The grateful girl overwhelmed him with thanks, and George had to fly ere he repented of his own generosity.

Miss Howell intimated, in the course of her narrative, that a better understanding existed between their parents than the caution of the general had discovered to his unsuspecting child, and George was determined to know the worst at once.

At supper he mentioned, as if in remembrance of his father's injunction, that he had been to take his leave of Miss Howell, since he found his visits gave uneasiness to her friends. " On the whole," he added, endeavoring to yawn carelessly, " I believe I shall visit there no more."

"Nay, nay,"returned Sir Frederick, a little displeased at his son's obedience, " I meant no such thing. Neither the admiral nor myself has the least objection to your visiting in moderation ; indeed, you may marry the girl with all our hearts, if you can agree."

"But we can't agree, I take it," said George, looking up at the wall.

" Why not ?—what hinders ? " cried his father, unguardedly.

" Only—only I don't like her," said the son, tossing off a glass of wine, which nearly strangled him.

" You don't ! " cried the general with great warmth, thrown entirely off his guard by this unexpected declaration ; " and may I presume to ask the reason why you do not like Miss Howell, sir ? "

" Oh, you know one never pretends to give a reason for this sort of feeling, my dear sir."

" Then," cried his father, with increasing heat, " you must allow me to say, my dear sir, that the sooner you get rid of these sort of feelings the better. I choose you shall not only like, but love Miss Howell ; and this I have promised her father."

" I thought that the admiral was displeased with my coming to his house so much—or did I not understand you this morning ? "

" I know nothing of his displeasure, and care less. He has agreed that Isabel shall be your wife, and I have passed my word to the engagement ; and if, sir, you wish to be considered as my son, you will prepare to comply."

George was expecting to discover some management on the part of his father, but by no means so settled an arrangement, and his anger was in proportion to the deception.

To annoy Isabel any further was out of the question ; to betray her, base ; and the next morning he sought an audience with the duke. To him he mentioned his wish for actual service, but hinted that the maternal fondness of Lady Margaret was averse to his seeking it. This was true, and George now pressed his uncle to assist him in effecting an exchange.

The boroughs of the Duke of Derwent were represented by royal members of Parliament, his true brothers being contemporary with Mr. Benfield in that honor ; and a request from a man who sent six members to the Commons, besides having a seat in the Lords in his own person, must be listened to.

Within the week George ceased to be a captain in the guards, and became lieutenant-colonel of a regiment under orders for America.

Sir Frederick soon became sensible of the error his warmth had led him into, and endeavored, by soothing and indulgence, to gain the ground he had so unguardedly lost. But terrible was his anger, and bitter his denunciations, when his son acquainted him with his approaching embarkation with his new regiment for America. They quarreled ; and as the favorite child had never, until now, been thwarted or spoken harshly to, they parted in mutual disgust. With his mother George was more tender ; and as Lady Margaret never thought the match such as the descendant of two lines of dukes was entitled to form, she almost pardoned the offense in the cause.

" What's this here ? " cried Sir Peter Howell, as he ran over a morning paper at the breakfast table : 'Captain Denbigh, late of the guards, has been promoted to the lieutenant-colonelcy of the —— Foot, and sails to-morrow to join that regiment, now on its way to America.' "

" It's a lie, Bell !—it's all a lie ! not but what he ought to be there, too, serving his king and country ; but he never would serve you so."

" Me ? " said Isabel, with a heart throbbing with the contending feelings of admiration for George's generosity, and delight at her own deliverance. " What have I to do with the movements of Mr. Denbigh ? "

" What ! " cried her father in astonishment ; " a'n't you to be his wife, a'n't it all agreed upon—that is, between Sir Frederick and me, which is the same thing, you know— "

Here he was interrupted by the sudden appearance of the general himself, who had just learnt the departure of his son, and hastened, with the double purpose of breaking the intelligence to his friend, and of making his own peace.

" See here, Denbigh," exclaimed the admiral, pointing to the paragraph, " what do you say to that ? "

" Too true—too true, my dear friend," replied the general, shaking his head mournfully.

" Hark ye, Sir Frederick Denbigh, cried the admiral fiercely ; " did you not say that your son George was to marry my daughter ? "

" I certainly did, Sir Peter, and am sorry to say that, in defiance of my entreaties and commands, he has deserted his home, and, in consequence, I have discarded him for ever."

" Now, Denbigh," said the admiral, a good deal mollified by this declaration, " have I not always told you, that in the army you know nothing of discipline ? Why, sir, if he was a son of mine, he should marry blindfolded if I chose to order it. I wish, now, Bell had an offer, and dared to refuse it."

" There is the barber's clerk, you know," said the general, a good deal irritated by the contemptuous manner of his friend.

" And what of that, Sir Frederick ? "

said the sailor sternly; "if I choose her to marry a quill-driver, she shall comply."

"Ah! my good friend," said the general, willing to drop the disagreeable subject, "I am afraid we shall both find it more difficult to control the affections of our children than we at first imagined."

"You do, General Denbigh?" said the admiral, with a curl of contempt on his lip; and ringing the bell violently, he bid the servant send his young lady to him.

On the appearance of Isabel, her father inquired with an air of settled meaning where young Mr. Ives resided. It was only in the next street, and a messenger was sent to him, Sir Peter Howell's compliments, and a request to see him without a moment's delay.

"We'll see, we'll see, my old friend, who keeps the best discipline," muttered the admiral as he paced up and down the room, in eager expectation of the return of his messenger.

The wondering general gazed on his friend, to ascertain if he was out of his senses. He knew he was quick to decide, and excessively obstinate, but he did not think him so crazy as to throw away his daughter in a fit of spleen. It never occurred to Sir Frederick, however, that the engagement with himself was an act of equal injustice and folly, because it was done with more form and deliberation, which, to the eye of sober reason, would rather make the matter worse. Isabel sat in trembling suspense for the issue of the scene, and Ives in a few minutes made his appearance in no little alarm.

On entering, the admiral addressed him abruptly, by inquiring if he still wished to marry that girl, pointing to his dauhgter. The reply was an eager affirmative. Sir Peter beckoned to Isabel, who approached, covered with blushes; and her father having placed her hand in that of her lover, with an air of great solemnity he gave them his blessing. The young people withdrew to another room at Sir Peters's request, when he turned to his friend, delighted with his own decision and authority, and exclaimed,

"There, Fred Denbigh, that is what I call being minded."

The general had penetration enough to see that the result was agreeable to both the young people, a thing he had long apprehended; and being glad to get rid of the affair in any way that did not involve him in a quarrel with his old comrade, he gravely congratulated the admiral on his good fortune and retired.

"Yes, yes," said Sir Peter to himself, as he paced up and down his room, "Denbigh is mortified enough, with his joy, and felicity, and grandchildren. I never had any opinion of their manner of discipline at all; too much bowing and scraping. I'm sorry, though, he is a priest; not but what a priest may be as good a man as another, but let him behave ever so well, he can only get to be a bishop at the most. Heaven forbid he should ever get to be a Pope! After all, his boys may be admirals if they behave themselves;" and he went to seek his daughter, having in imagination manned her nursery with vice and rear-admirals in embryo by the half-dozen.

Sir Peter Howell survived the marriage of his daughter but eighteen months; yet that was sufficient time to become attached to his invaluable son-in-law. Mr. Ives insensibly led the admiral, during his long indisposition, to a more correct view of sacred things than he had been wont to entertain; and the old man breathed his last, blessing both his children for their kindness, and with an humble hope of future happiness. Some time before his death Isabel, whose conscience had always reproached her with the deception practiced on her father, and with the banishment of George from his country and home, threw herself at the feet of Sir Peter, and acknowledged her transgression.

The admiral heard her in astonishment, but not in anger. His opinions of life had sensibly changed, and his great cause of satisfaction with his new son removed all motives for regret for anything but for the fate of poor George. With the noble forbearance and tenderness of the young man to his daughter the hardy veteran was sensibly touched; and his entreaties with Sir Frederick made his peace with a father already longing for the return of his only hope.

The admiral left Colonel Denbigh his blessing, and his favorite pistols, as a remembrance of his esteem; but he did not live to see the reunion with his family.

George had soon learnt, deprived of hope, and in the midst of novelty, to forget a passion which could no longer be prosperous; and two years from his departure returned to England, glowing in health, and improved in person and manners by a more extensive knowledge of the world and mankind.

CHAPTER XLIV.

DURING the time occupied by the foregoing events, Francis continued a gloomy inmate of his uncle's house. The duke and his brother George were too indolent and inactive in their minds to pierce the cloud that mortification and deadened affections had drawn around the real character of their nephew; and although he was tolerated as the heir, he was but little loved as a man.

In losing his brother, Francis lost the only human being with whom he possessed any sympathies in common; and he daily drew more and more into himself, in gloomy meditation on his forlorn situation in the midst of wealth and expected honors. The attentions he received were paid to his rank, and Francis had penetration enough to perceive it. His visits to his parents were visits of ceremony, and in time all parties came to look to their termination with pleasure as to the discontinuance of heartless and forced civilities.

Affection, even in the young man, could not endure, repulsed as his feelings were, forever; and in the course of three years, if his attachments were not alienated from his parents, his ardor had become much abated.

It is a dreadful truth, that the bonds of natural affection can be broken by injustice and contumely; and it is yet more to be deplored, that when from such causes we loosen the ties habit and education have drawn around us, a reaction in our feelings commences; we seldom cease to love, but we begin to hate. Against such awful consequences it is one of the most solemn duties of the parent to provide in season; and what surer safeguard is there, than to inculcate those feelings which teach the mind to love God, and in so doing induce love to the whole human family?

Sir Frederick and Lady Margaret attended the church regularly, repeated the responses with much decency, toasted the Church next to the king, even appeared at the altars of their God, and continued sinners. From such sowings, no good fruit could be expected to flourish; yet Francis was not without his hours of devotion; but his religion was, like himself, reserved, superstitious, ascetic, and gloomy. He never entered into social worship: if he prayed, it was with an ill-concealed wish to end this life of care. If he returned thanks, it was with a bitterness that mocked the throne before which he was prostrate. Such pictures are revolting; but their originals have and do exist; for what enormity is there of which human frality, unchecked by divine assistance, may not be guilty?

Francis received an invitation to visit a brother of his mother's at his seat in the country, about the time of the expected return of George from America; and in compliance with the wishes of his uncles he accepted it. The house was thronged with visitors, and many of them were ladies. To these, the arrival of the unmarried heir of the house of Derwent was a subject of no little interest. His character had, however, preceded him, and a few days of his awkward and, as they conceived, sullen deportment, drove them back to their former beaux, with the exception of one; and she was not only among the fairest of the throng, but decidedly of the highest pretensions on the score of birth and fortune.

Marian Lumley was the only surviving child of the last Duke of Annerdale, with whom had expired the higher honors of his house. But the Earldom of Pendennyss, with numerous ancient baronies, were titles in fee; and together with his princely estates had descended to his daughter as heir-general of the family. A peeress in her own right, with an income far exceeding her utmost means of expenditure, the lovely Countess of Pendennyss was a prize aimed at by all the young nobles of the empire.

Educated in the midst of flatterers and dependents she had become haughty, vain, and supercilious; still she was lovely, and no one knew better how to practice the most winning arts of her sex, when whim or interest prompted her to the trial.

Her host was her guardian and relative; and through his agency she had rejected, at the age of twenty, numerous suitors for her hand. Her eyes were fixed on the ducal coronet; and unfortunately for Francis Denbigh, he was, at the time, the only man of the proper age who could elevate her to that enviable distinction in the kingdom; and an indirect measure of her own had been the means of his invitation to the country.

Like the rest of her young companions, Marian was greatly disappointed on the view of her intended captive, and for a day or two she abandoned him to his melancholy and himself. But ambition was her idol; and to its powerful rival, love, she was yet a stranger. After a few struggles with her inclinations the consideration that their united fortunes and family alliances would make one of the wealthiest and most powerful houses in the kingdom, prevailed. Such early sacrifices of the inclinations in a woman of her beauty, youth and accomplishments, may excite surprise; but where the mind is left uncultivated by the hand of care, the soul untouched by the love of goodness, the human heart seldom fails to set up an idol of its own to worship. In the Countess of Pendennyss this idol was pride.

The remainder of the ladies, from ceasing to wonder at the manners of Francis, had made them the subject of their mirth; and nettled at his apparent indifference to their society, which they erroneously attributed to his sense of importance, they overstepped the bounds of good-breeding in manifesting their displeasure.

"Mr. Denbigh," cried one of the most thoughtless and pretty of the gay tribe to him one day, as Francis sat in a corner abstracted from the scene around him, "when do you mean to favor the world with your brilliant ideas in the shape of a book?"

"Oh! no doubt soon," said a second; "and I expect they will be homilies, or another volume to the 'Whole Duty of Man.'"

"Rather," cried a third, with irony, "another canto to the 'Rape of the Lock,' his ideas are so vivid and full of imagery."

"Or, what do you think," said a fourth, speaking in a voice of harmony and tones of the most soothing tenderness, "of pity and compassion for the follies of those inferior minds who cannot enjoy the reflections of a good sense and modesty peculiarly his own?"

This also might be irony, and Francis thought it so; but the tones were so soft and conciliating, that with a face pale with his emotions he ventured to look up, and met the eye of Marian fixed on him, in an expression that changed his death-like hue into the color of vermilion.

He thought of this speech; he reasoned on it; he dreamt on it. But for the looks which accompanied it, like the rest of the party, he would have thought it the cruelest cut of them all. But that look, those eyes, that voice—what a commentary on her language did they not afford!

Francis was not long in suspense; the next morning an excursion was proposed, which included all but himself in its arrangements. He was either too reserved or too proud to offer services which were not required.

Several gentlemen had contended for the honor of driving the countess in a beautiful phaeton of her own. They grew earnest in their claims: one had been promised by its mistress with an opportunity of trying the ease of the carriage; another was delighted with the excellent training of her horses; in short, all had some particular claim to the distinction, which was urged with a warmth and pertinacity proportionate to the value of the prize to be obtained. Marian heard the several claimants with an ease and indifference natural to her situation, and ended the dispute by saying—

"Gentlemen, as I have made so many promises from the dread of giving offense, I must throw myself on the mercy of Mr. Denbigh, who alone, with the best claims, does not urge them. To you, then," continued she, approaching him with the whip which was to be given the victor, "I adjudge the prize, if you will condescend to accept it."

This was uttered with one of her most attractive smiles, and Francis received the whip with an emotion that he with difficulty could control.

The gentlemen were glad to have the contest decided by adjudging the prize to one so little dangerous, and the ladies sneered at her choice as they left the house.

There was something so soothing in the manners of Lady Pendennyss, she listened to the little he said with such a respectful attention, was so anxious to have him give his opinions, that the unction of flattery, thus sweetly applied and for the first time, could not fail of its wonted effects.

The communications thus commenced continued. It was so easy to be attentive by being simply polite to one unused to notice of any kind, that Marian found the fate of the young man in her hands almost as soon as she attempted to control it.

A new existence opened upon Francis, as day after day she insensibly led him to a display of powers he was unconscious until now of possessing himself. His self-respect began to increase, his limited pleasures to multiply, and he could now look around him with a sense of participation in the delights of life, as he perceived himself of consequence to this much admired woman.

Trifling incidents, managed on her part with consummate art, had led him to the daring inference that he was not entirely indifferent to her; and Francis returned the incipient affection of his mistress with a feeling but little removed from adoration. Week flew by after week, and still he lingered at the residence of his kinsman, unable to tear himself from the society of one so worshiped, and yet afraid to take a step by making a distinct declaration which might involve him in disgrace or ridicule.

The condescension of the countess increased, and she had indirectly given him the most flattering assurances of his success, when George, just arrived from America, having first paid his greetings to his reconciled parents and the happy couple of his generosity, flew to the arms of his brother in Suffolk.

Francis was overjoyed to see George, and George delighted in the visible improvement of his brother. Still Francis was far, very far behind his junior in graces of mind and body; indeed, few men in England were more adapted by nature and education for female society than was Colonel Denbigh, at the period of which we write.

Marian witnessed all his attractions and deeply felt their influence. For the first time she felt the emotions of the gentle passion; and after having sported in the gay world, and trifled with the feelings of others for years, the countess in her turn became an unwilling victim to its power. George met her flame with a corresponding ardor, and the struggle between ambition and love became severe. The brothers, unconsciously, were rivals.

Had George for a moment suspected the situation of the feelings of Francis, his very superiority in the contest would have induced him to retreat from the unnatural rivalry. Had the elder dreamt of the views of his junior, he would have abandoned his dearest hopes in utter despair. Francis had so long been accustomed to consider George as his superior in everything, that a competition with him would have appeared desperate. Marian contrived to keep both in hopes, undecided herself which to choose, and perhaps ready to yield to the first applicant. A sudden event, however, removed all doubts, and decided the fate of the three.

The Duke of Derwent and his bachelor brother became so dissatisfied with the character of their future heir, that they as coolly set about providing themselves with wives as they had performed any other ordinary transaction of life. They married cousins, and on the same day the choice of the ladies was assigned between them by lots; and if his grace got the prettier, his brother certainly got the richest—under the circumstances a very tolerable distribution of fortune's favors.

These double marriages dissolved the charm of Francis, and Lady Pendennyss determined to consult her wishes; a little pointed encouragement brought out the declaration of George, and he was accepted.

Francis, who had never communicated his feelings to any one but the lady, and that only indirectly, was crushed by the blow. He continued in public until the day of their union, was present, composed and silent; but it was the silence of a mountain whose volcanic contents had not reached the surface. The same day he disappeared, and every inquiry after him proved fruitless; search was baffled, and for seven years it was not known what had become of the general's eldest son.

George on marrying resigned his commission, at the entreaties of his wife, and retired to one of her seats, to the enjoyment of ease and domestic love. The countess was enthusiastically attached to him; and as motives for the indulgence of coquetry were wanting, her character became gradually improved by the contemplation of the excellent qualities of her generous husband.

A lurking suspicion of the cause of Francis's sudden disappearance rendered her uneasy at times; but Marian was too much beloved, too happy, in the enjoyment of too many honors, and of too great wealth, to be open to the convictions of conscience. It is in our hours of pain and privation that we begin to feel its sting; if we are prosperous, we fancy we reap the fruits of our own merit; but if we are unfortunate, the voice of truth seldom fails to remind us that we are deserving of our fate:—a blessed provision of Providence that often makes the saddest hours of our earthly career the morn of a day that is to endure forever.

General Denbigh and Lady Margaret both died within five years of the marriage of their favorite child, although both lived to see their descendant, in the person of the infant Lord Lumley.

The duke and his brother George were each blessed with offspring, and in these several descendants of the different branches of the family of Denbigh may be seen the different personages of our history. On the birth of her youngest child, the Lady Marian, the Countess of Pendennyss sustained a shock in her health from which she never wholly recovered; she became nervous, and lost most of her energy both of mind and body. Her husband was her solace; his tenderness remaining unextinguished, while his attentions increased.

As the fortune of Ives and Isabel put the necessity of a living out of the question, and no cure offering for the acceptance of the first, he was happy to avail himself of an offer to become domestic chaplain to his now intimate friend, Mr. Denbigh. For the first six years they were inmates of Pendennyss Castle. The rector of the parish was infirm, and averse to a regular assistant; but the unobtrusive services of Mr. Ives were not less welcome to the pastor than to his parishioners.

Employed in the duties which of right

fell to the incumbent, and intrusted with the spiritual guardianship of the dependents of the castle, our young clergyman had ample occupation for all his time, if not a sufficient theater for his usefulness. Isabel and himself remained the year round in Wales, and the first dawnings of education received by Lord Lumley were those he acquired conjointly with Francis from the care of the latter's father. They formed, with the interval of the time spent by Mr. Denbigh and Lady Pendennyss in town in winter, but one family. To the gentleman, the attachment of the grateful Ives was as strong as it was lasting. Mrs. Ives never ceased to consider him as a self-devoted victim to her happiness; and although a far more brilliant lot had awaited him by the change, yet her own husband could not think it a more happy one.

The birth of Lady Marian had already, in its consequences, begun to throw a gloom round the domestic comforts of Denbigh, when he was to sustain another misfortune in a separation from his friends.

Mr., now Dr. Ives, had early announced his firm intention, whenever an opportunity was afforded him, to enter into the fullest functions of his ministry, as a matter of duty. Such an opportunity now offered at B——, and the doctor became its rector about the period Sir Edward became possessor of his paternal estate.

Denbigh, tried every inducement within his power to keep the doctor in his own society. If as many thousands as his living would give him hundreds could effect it, they would have been at his service; but Denbigh understood the character of the divine too well to offer such an inducement; he however urged the claims of friendship to the utmost, but without success.

The doctor acknowledged the hold both himself and family had gained upon his affections, but he added—

"Consider, my dear Mr. Denbigh, what we would have thought of one of the earlier followers of our Saviour, who from motives of convenience or worldly-mindedness could have deserted his sacred calling. Although the changes in the times may have rendered the modes of conducting them different, necessarily the duties remain the same. The minister of our holy religion, who has once submitted to the call of his divine Master, must allow nothing but ungovernable necessity to turn him from the path he has entered on; and should he so far forget himself, I greatly fear he would plead, when too late to remedy the evil, his worldly duties, his cares, or even his misfortunes, in vain.

Solemn and arduous are his obligations to labor, but when faithfully he has discharged these duties, oh! how glorious must be his reward."

Before such opinions every barrier must fall, and the doctor entered into the cure of his parish without further opposition, though not without unceasing regret on the part of his friend. Their intercourse was, however, maintained by letter, and they also frequently met at Lumley Castle, a seat of the countess's within two days' ride of the doctor's parish, until her increasing indisposition rendered journeying impossible; then, indeed, the doctor extended his rides into Wales, but with longer intervals between his visits, though with the happiest effects to the objects of his journey.

Mr. Denbigh, worn down with watching and blasted hopes, under the direction of the spiritual watchfulness of the rector of B——, became an humble, sincere and pious Christian.

CHAPTER XLV.

It has been already mentioned that the health of Lady Pendennyss suffered a severe shock in giving birth to a daughter. Change of scene was prescribed as a remedy for her disorder, and Denbigh and his wife were on their return from a fruitless excursion among the northern lakes, in pursuit of amusement and relief for the latter, when they were compelled to seek shelter from the fury of a sudden gust in the first building that offered. It was a farm-house of the better sort; and the attendants, carriages, and appearance of their guests, caused no little confusion to its simple inmates. A fire was lighted in the best parlor, and every effort was made by the inhabitants to contribute to the comforts of the travelers.

The countess and her husband were sitting in that kind of listless melancholy which had been too much the companion of their later hours, when, in the interval of the storm, a male voice in an adjoining room commenced singing the following ballad; the notes being low, monotonous, but unusually sweet, and the enunciation so distinct as to render every syllable intelligible:

Oh! I have lived in endless pain,
And I have lived, alas! in vain,
  For none regard my woe—
No father's care conveyed the truth,
No mother's fondness blessed my youth,
Ah! joys too great to know—

And Marian's love and Marian's pride,
Have crushed the heart that would have died
  To save my Marian's tears—
A brother's hand has struck the blow,
Oh! may that brother never know
  Such madly sorrowing years!

But hush my griefs—and hush my song.
I've mourned in vain—I've mourned too long,
  When none have come to soothe—
And dark's the path that lies before,
And dark have been the days of yore,
  And all was dark in youth.

The maids employed around the person of their comfortless mistress, the valet of Denbigh engaged in arranging a dry coat for his master—all suspended their employments to listen in breathless silence to the mournful melody of the song.

But Denbigh himself had started from his seat at the first notes, and he continued until the voice ceased, gazing in vacant horror in the direction of the sounds. A door opened from the parlor to the room of the musician; he rushed through it, and there, in a kind of shed to the building, which hardly sheltered him from the fury of the tempest, clad in the garments of the extremest poverty, with an eye roving in madness, and a body rocking to and fro from mental inquietude, he beheld, seated on a stone, the remains of his long lost brother Francis.

The language of the song was too plain to be misunderstood. The truth glared around George with a violence that dazzled his brain; but he saw it all, he felt it all, and rushing to the feet of his brother, he exclaimed in horror, pressing his hands between his own—

"Francis, my own brother—do you not know me?"

The maniac regarded him with a vacant gaze, but the voice and the person recalled the compositions of his more reasonable moments to his recollection; pushing back the hair of George, so as to expose his fine forehead to view, he contemplated him for a few moments, and then continued to sing, in a voice rendered still sweeter than before by his faint impressions:

His raven locks, that richly curled,
His eye, that proud defiance hurled,
  Have stol'n my Marian's love!
Had I been blest by nature's grace,
With such a form, with such a face,
  Could I so treacherous prove?

And what is man—and what is care—
That he should let such passions tear
  The bases of the soul?
Oh! you should do as I have done—
And having pleasure's summit won,
  Each bursting sob control!

On ending the last stanza, the maniac released his brother, and broke into the wildest laugh of madness.

"Francis!—Oh! Francis, my brother!" cried George in bitterness. A piercing shriek drew his eye to the door he had passed through—on its threshold lay the senseless body of his wife. The distracted husband forgot everything in the situation of his Marian, and raising her in his arms he exclaimed—

"Marian—my Marian, revive—look up—know me."

Francis had followed him and now stood by his side, gazing intently on the lifeless body; his looks became more soft—his eye glanced less wildly—he, too, cried—

"Marian—*my* Marian."

There was a mighty effort; nature could endure no more, he broke a blood-vessel and fell at the feet of George. They flew to his assistance, giving the countess to her women: but he was dead.

For seventeen years Lady Pendennyss survived this shock; but, having reached her own abode, during that long period she never left her room.

In the confidence of his surviving hopes, Dr. Ives and his wife were made acquainted with the real cause of the grief of their friend, but the truth went no further. Denbigh was the guardian of his three young cousins, the duke, his sister, and young George Denbigh; these, with his son, Lord Lumley, and daughter, Lady Marian, were removed from the melancholy of the castle to scenes better adapted to their opening prospects in life. Yet Lumley was fond of the society of his father, and finding him a youth endowed beyond his years, the care of his parent was early turned to the most important of his duties in that sacred office; and when he yielded to his wishes to go into the army, he knew he went a youth of sixteen, possessed of principles and self-denial that would become a man of five-and-twenty.

General Wilson completed the work which the father had begun; and Lord Lumley formed a singular exception to the character of most of his companions.

At the close of the Spanish war he returned home, and was just in time to receive the parting breath of his mother.

A few days before her death the countess requested that her children might be made acquainted with her history and misconduct; and she placed in the hands of her son a letter, with directions for him to open it after her decease. It was addressed to both children, and after recapitulating generally the principal events of her life, continued:

"Thus, my children, you perceive the consequence of indulgence and hardness of heart, which made me insensible to the sufferings of others and regardless of the plainest dictates of justice. Self was my idol. The love of admiration, which was natural to me, was increased by the flatterers who surrounded me; and had the customs of our country suffered royalty to descend in their unions to a grade in life below their own, your uncle would have escaped the fangs of my baneful coquetry.

"Oh! Marian, my child, never descend so low as to practice those arts which have degraded your unhappy mother. I would impress on you, as a memorial of my parting affection, these simple truths—that coquetry stands next to the want of chastity in the scale of female vices; it is in fact a kind of mental prostitution; it is ruinous to all that delicacy of feeling which gives added luster to female charms; it is almost destructive to modesty itself. A woman who has been addicted to its practice, may strive long and in vain to regain that singleness of heart, which can bind her up so closely in her husband and children as to make her a good wife or a mother; and if it should have degenerated into habit, it may lead to the awful result of infidelity to her marriage vows.

"It is vain for a coquette to pretend to religion; its practice involves hypocrisy, falsehood, and deception—everything that is mean—everything that is debasing. In short, as it is bottomed on selfishness and pride, where it has once possessed the mind, it will only yield to the truth-displaying banners of the cross. This, and this only, can remove the evil; for without it she, whom the charms of youth and beauty have enabled to act the coquette, will descend into the vale of life, altered, it is true, but not amended. She will find the world, with its allurements, clinging around her parting years, in vain regrets for days that are flown, and in mercenary views for her descendants. Heaven bless you, my children, console and esteem your inestimable father while he yet remains with you; and place your reliance on that Heavenly Parent who will never desert those who seek him in sincerity and love. Your dying mother, M. PENDENNYSS."

This letter, evidently written under the excitement of deep remorse, made a great impression on both her children. In Lady Marian it was pity, regret, and abhorrence of the fault which had been the principal cause of the wreck of her mother's peace of mind; but in her brother, now Earl of Pendennyss, these feelings were united with a jealous dread of his own probable lot in the chances of matrimony.

His uncle had been the supposed heir to a more elevated title than his own, but he was now the actual possessor of as honorable a name, and of much larger revenues. The great wealth of his maternal grandfather, and the considerable estate of his own father, were, or would soon be, centered in himself; and if a woman as amiable, as faultless, as affection had taught him to believe his mother to be, could yield in her situation to the lure of worldly honors, had he not great reason to dread, that a hand might be bestowed at some day upon himself, when the heart would point out some other destination, if the real wishes of its owner were consulted?

Pendennyss was modest by nature, and humble from principle, though by no means distrustful; yet the shock of discovering his mother's fault, the gloom occasioned by her death and his father's declining health, sometimes led him into a train of reflections which, at others, he would have fervently deprecated.

A short time after the decease of the countess, Mr. Denbigh, finding his constitution fast giving way, under the wasting of a decline he had been in for a year, resolved to finish his days in the abode of his Christian friend, Doctor Ives. For several years they had not met; increasing duties and infirmities on both sides having interrupted their visits.

By easy stages he left the residence of his son in Wales, and accompanied by both his children he reached Lumley Castle much exhausted; here he took a solemn and final leave of Marian, unwilling that she should so soon witness again the death of another parent, and dismissing the earl's equipage and attendants a short day's ride from B——, they proceeded alone to the rectory.

A letter had been forwarded acquainting the doctor of his approaching visit, wishing it to be perfectly private, but not alluding to its object, and naming a day, a week later than the one on which he arrived. This plan was altered on perceiving the torch of life more rapidly approaching the socket than he had at first supposed. His unexpected appearance and reception are known. Denbigh's death and the departure of his son followed; Francis having been Pendennyss's companion to the tomb of his ancestors in Westmoreland.

The earl had a shrinking delicacy, under the knowledge of his family history, that made him anxious to draw all eyes from the contemplation of his mother's conduct; how far the knowledge of it had extended in society he could not know, but he wished it buried with her in the tomb. The peculiar manner of his father's death would attract notice, and might recall attention to the prime cause of his disorder; as yet all was veiled, and he wished the doctor's family to let it remain so. It was, however, impossible that the death of a man of Mr. Denbigh's rank should be unnoticed in the prints, and the care of Francis dictated the simple truth without comments, as it appeared. As regarded the Moseleys, what was more natural than that the son of *Mr. Denbigh* should also be *Mr. Denbigh?*

In the presence of the rector's family no allusions were made to their friends, and the villagers and the neighborhood spoke of them as old and young Mr. Denbigh.

The name of Lord Lumley, now earl of Pendennyss, was known to the whole British nation; but the long retirement of his father and mother had driven them almost from the recollection of their friends. Even Mrs. Wilson supposed her favorite hero a Lumley. Pendennyss Castle had been for centuries the proud residence of that family; and the change of name in its possessor was forgotten with the circumstances that had led to it.

When, therefore, Emily met the earl so unexpectedly the second time at the rectory, she, of course, with all her companions, spoke of him as Mr. Denbigh. On that occasion Pendennyss had called in person, in expectation of meeting his kinsman, Lord Bolton; but finding him absent, he could not resist his desire to visit the rectory. Accordingly, he sent his carriage and servants on to London, leaving them at a convenient spot, and arrived on foot at the house of Doctor Ives. From the same motives that had influenced him before—a wish to indulge, undisturbed by useless ceremony, his melancholy reflections, he desired that his name might not be mentioned.

This was an easy task. Both Dr. and Mrs. Ives had called him, when a child, George or Lumley, and were unused to his new appellation of Pendennyss; indeed, it rather recalled painful recollections to them all.

It may be remembered that circumstances removed the necessity of any introduction to Mrs Wilson and her party; and the difficulty in that instance was happily got rid of.

The earl had often heard Emily Moseley spoken of by his friends, and in their letters they frequently mentioned her name as connected with their pleasures and employments, and always with an affection, Pendennyss thought, exceeding that which they manifested for their son's

wife; and Mrs. Ives, the evening before, to remove unpleasant thoughts, had given him a lively description of her person and character. The earl's curiosity had been a little excited to see this paragon of female beauty and virtue; and, unlike most curiosity on such subjects, he was agreeably disappointed by the examination. He wished to know more, and made interest with the doctor to assist him to continue the incognito with which accident had favored him.

The doctor objected on the ground of principle, and the earl desisted; but the beauty of Emily, aided by her character, had made an impression not to be easily shaken off, and Pendennyss returned to the charge.

His former jealousies were awakened in proportion to his admiration; and, after some time, he threw himself on the mercy of the divine, by declaring his new motive, but without mentioning his parents. The doctor pitied him, for he scanned his feelings thoroughly, and consented to keep silent, but laughingly declared it was bad enough for a divine to be an accessory to, much less aiding in a deception; and that he knew if Emily and Mrs. Wilson learnt his imposition, he would lose ground in their favor by the discovery.

"Surely, George," said the doctor, with a laugh, "you don't mean to marry the young lady as Mr. Denbigh?"

"Oh, no! it is too soon to think of marrying her at all," replied the earl, with a smile; "but, somehow, I should like to see how my reception in the world will be as plain Mr. Denbigh, unprovided for and unknown."

"No doubt, my lord," said the rector, archly, "in proportion to your merits, very unfavorably indeed; but then your humility will be finally elevated by the occasional praises I have heard Mrs. Wilson lavish on your proper character of late."

"I am much indebted to her partiality," continued the earl mournfully; then throwing off his gloomy thoughts he added, "I wonder, my dear doctor, your goodness did not set her right in the latter particular."

"Why, she has hardly given me an opportunity; delicacy and my own feelings have kept me very silent on the subject of your family to any of that connection. They think, I believe, I was a rector in Wales, instead of your father's chaplain; and somehow," continued the doctor, smiling on his wife, "the association with your late parents was so connected in my mind with my most romantic feelings, that although I have delighted in it, I have seldom alluded to it in conversation at all. Mrs. Wilson has spoken of you but twice in my hearing, and that since she has expected to meet you; your name has doubtless recalled the remembrance of her husband."

"I have many, many reasons to remember the general with gratitude," cried the earl with fervor; "but doctor, do not forget my incognito: only call me George; I ask no more."

The plan of Pendennyss was put in execution. Day after day he lingered in Northamptonshire, until his principles and character had grown upon the esteem of the Moseleys in the manner we have mentioned.

His frequent embarrassments were from the dread and shame of a detection. With Sir Herbert Nicholson he had a narrow escape, and Mrs. Fitzgerald and Lord Henry Stapleton he of course avoided: for having gone so far, he was determined to persevere to the end. Egerton he thought knew him, and he disliked his character and manners.

When Chatterton appeared most attentive to Emily, the candor and good opinion of that young nobleman made the earl acquainted with his wishes and his situation. Pendennyss was too generous not to meet his rival on fair grounds. His cousin and the duke were requested to use their united influence secretly to obtain the desired station for the baron. The result is known, and Pendennyss trusted his secret to Chatterton; he took him to London, gave him in charge to Derwent, and returned to prosecute his own suit. His note from Bolton Castle was a *ruse* to conceal his character, as he knew the departure of the baronet's family to an hour, and had so timed his visit to the earl as not to come in collision with the Moseleys.

"Indeed, my lord," cried the doctor to him one day, "your scheme goes on swimmingly, and I am only afraid when your mistress discovers the imposition, you will find your rank producing a different effect from what you have apprehended."

CHAPTER XLVI.

BUT Dr. Ives was mistaken. Had he seen the sparkling eyes and glowing cheeks of Miss Moseley, the smile of satisfaction and happiness which played on the usually thoughtful face of Mrs. Wilson, when the earl handed them into his own carriage, as they left his house on the evening of the discovery, the doctor would have gladly acknowledged the failure of his prognostics. In truth, there was no possible event that, under the circumstances, could have given both aunt and niece such heartfelt pleasure, as the knowledge that Denbigh and the earl were the same person.

Pendennyss stood holding the door of the carriage in his hand, irresolute how to act, when Mrs. Wilson said—

"Surely, my lord, you sup with us."

"A thousand thanks, my dear madam, for the privilege," cried the earl, as he sprang into the coach: the door was closed, and they drove off.

"After the explanations of this morning, my lord," said Mrs. Wilson, willing to remove all doubts between him and Emily, and perhaps anxious to satisfy her own curiosity, "it will be fastidious to conceal our desire to know more of your movements. How came your pocket-book in the possession of Mrs. Fitzgerald?"

"Mrs. Fitzgerald!" cried Pendennyss, in astonishment; "I lost the book in one of the rooms of the Lodge, and supposed it had fallen into your hands, and betrayed my disguise by Emily's rejection of me, and your own altered eye. Was I mistaken then in both?"

Mrs. Wilson now, for the first time, explained their real grounds for refusing his offers, which, in the morning, she had loosely mentioned as owing to a misapprehension of his just character, and recounted the manner of the book falling into the hands of Mrs. Fitzgerald.

The earl listened in amazement, and, after musing with himself, exclaimed—

"I remember taking it from my pocket to show Colonel Egerton some singular plants I had gathered, and think I first missed it when returning to the place where I had then laid it. In some of the side-pockets were letters from Marian, addressed to me, properly; and I naturally thought they had met your eye."

Mrs. Wilson and Emily immediately thought Egerton the real villain, who had caused both themselves and Mrs. Fitzgerald so much uneasiness, and the former mentioned her suspicions to the earl.

"Nothing more probable, dear madam," cried he, "and this explains to me his startled looks when we first met, and his evident dislike to my society, for he must have seen my person, though the carriage hid *him* from my sight."

That Egerton was the wretch, and that through his agency the pocket-book had been carried to the cottage, they all now agreed, and turned to more pleasant subjects.

"Master!—here—master!" said Peter Johnson, as he stood at the window of Mr. Benfield's room, stirring a gruel for the old gentleman's supper, and stretching his neck and straining his eyes to distinguish objects by the light of the lamps —"I do think there is Mr. Denbigh, handing Miss Emmy from a coach covered with gold, and two footmen all dizzened with pride like."

The spoon fell from the hand of Mr. Benfield. He rose briskly from his seat, and adjusting his dress, took the arm of the steward and proceeded to the drawing-room. While these several movements were in operation, which consumed some time, the old bachelor relieved the tedium of Peter's impatience by the following speech:

"Mr. Denbigh!—what, back? I thought he never could let that rascal John shoot him and forsake Emmy after all"—here the old gentleman suddenly recollected Denbigh's marriage, "but now, Peter, it can do no good either. I remember that when my friend, the earl of Gosford"—and again he was checked by the image of the card-table and the viscountess; "but Peter," he said with great warmth, "we can go down and see him, notwithstanding."

"Mr. Denbigh!" exclaimed Sir Edward, in astonishment, when he saw the companion of his sister and child enter the drawing-room, "you are welcome once more to your old friends; your sudden retreat from us gave us much pain, but we suppose Lady Laura had too many attractions to allow us to keep you any longer in Norfolk."

The good baronet sighed as he held out his hand to the man whom he had once hoped to receive as a son.

"Neither Lady Laura, nor any other lady, my dear Sir Edward," cried the earl, as he took the baronet's hand, "drove me from you but the frowns of your own fair daughter; and here she is, ready to acknowledge her offense, and, I hope, to atone for it."

John, who knew of the refusal of his sister, and was not a little displeased with the cavalier treatment he had received at Denbigh's hands, felt indignant at such improper levity in a married man, and approached with—

"Your servant, Mr. Denbigh—I hope my Lady Laura is well."

"Pendennyss understood his look, and replied, very gravely—

"Your servant, Mr. John Moseley—my Lady Laura is, or certainly ought to be, very well, as she has this moment gone to a rout, accompanied by her husband."

The quick eye of John glanced from the earl to his aunt, to Emily; a lurking smile was on all their features. The heightened color of his sister, the flashing eyes of the young nobleman, the face of his aunt, all told him that something uncommon was about to be explained; and, yielding to his feelings, he caught the hand which Pendennyss extended to him, and cried—

"Denbigh, I see—I feel—there is some unaccountable mistake—we are—"

"Brothers!" said the earl emphatically. "Sir Edward—dear Lady Moseley, I throw myself on your mercy. I am an impostor. When your hospitality received me into your house, it is true you admitted George Denbigh; but he is better known as the Earl of Pendennyss."

"The Earl of Pendennyss!" exclaimed Lady Moseley, in a glow of delight, as she saw at once through some juvenile folly a deception which promised both happiness and rank to one of her children. "Is it possible, my dear Charlotte, that this is your unknown friend?"

"The very same, Anne," replied the smiling widow, "and guilty of a folly that, at all events, removes the distance between us a little, by showing that he is subject to the failings of mortality. But the masquerade is ended, and I hope you and Edward will not only treat him as an earl, but receive him as a son."

"Most willingly—most willingly," cried the baronet, with great energy; "be he prince, peer, or beggar, he is the preserver of my child, and as such he is always welcome."

The door now slowly opened, and the venerable bachelor appeared on its threshold.

Pendennyss, who had never forgotten the good will manifested to him by Mr. Benfield, met him with a look of pleasure, as he expressed his happiness at seeing him again in London.

"I never have forgotten your goodness in sending honest Peter such a distance from home, on the object of his visit. I now regret that a feeling of shame occasioned my answering your kindness so laconically." Turning to Mrs. Wilson, he added, "for a time I knew not how to write a letter even, being afraid to sign my proper appellation, and ashamed to use my adopted."

"Mr. Denbigh, I am happy to see you. I did send Peter, it is true, to London, on a message to you—but it is all over now," the old man sighed—"Peter, however, escaped the snares of this wicked place; and if you are happy, I am content. I remember when the Earl of—"

"Pendennyss!" exclaimed the other, "imposed on the hospitality of a worthy man under an assumed appellation, in order to pry into the character of a lovely female, who was only too good for him, and who is now willing to forget his follies, and make him not only the happiest of men, but the nephew of Mr. Benfield."

During this speech the countenance of Mr. Benfield had manifested evident emotion. He looked from one to another, until he saw Mrs. Wilson smiling near him. Pointing to the earl with his finger, he stood unable to speak, as she answered simply—

"Lord Pendennyss."

"And Emmy dear—will you—will you marry him?" cried Mr. Benfield, suppressing his feelings to give utterance to his question.

Emily felt for her uncle, and, blushing deeply, with great frankness she put her hand in that of the earl, who pressed it with rapture again and again to his lips.

Mr. Benfield sank into a chair, and with a heart softened by emotion, burst into tears.

"Peter," he cried, struggling with his feelings. "I am now ready to depart in peace—I shall see my darling Emmy happy, and to her care I shall commit you."

Emily, deeply affected with his love, threw herself into his arms in a torrent of tears, and was removed from them by Pendennyss, in consideration for the feelings of both.

Jane felt no emotions of envy for her sister's happiness; on the contrary, she rejoiced in common with the rest of their friends in her brightening prospects, and they all took their seats at the supper-table, as happy a group as was contained in the wide circle of the metropolis. A few more particulars served to explain the mystery sufficiently, until a more fitting opportunity made them acquainted with the whole of the earl's proceedings.

"My Lord Pendennyss," said Sir Edward, pouring out a glass of wine, and passing the bottle to his neighbor; "I drink your health—and happiness to yourself and my darling child."

The toast was drunk by all the family, and the earl replied to the compliments with his thanks and smiles, while Emily could only notice them with her blushes and tears.

But this was an opportunity not to be lost by the honest steward, who, from affection and long services, had been indulging in familiarities exceeding any other of his master's establishment. He very deliberately helped himself to a glass of wine, and drawing near the seat of the bride-elect, with an humble reverence, commenced his speech as follows:

"My dear Miss Emmy :—Here's hoping you'll live to be a comfort to your honored father, and your honored mother, and my dear honored master, and yourself, and Madam Wilson." The steward paused to clear his voice, and profited by the delay to cast his eye round the table to collect the names : "and Mr. John Moseley, and sweet Mrs. Moseley, and pretty Miss Jane " (Peter had lived too long in the world to compliment one handsome woman in the presence of another, without the qualifying his speech a little) ; "and Mr. Lord Denbigh—earl-like, as they say he now is, and "—Peter stopped a moment to deliberate, and then making another reverence, he put the glass to his lips ; but before he had got half through its contents recollected himself, and replenishing it to the brim, with a smile acknowledging his forgetfulness, continued, "and the Rev. Mr. Francis Ives, and the Rev. Mrs. Francis Ives."

Here the unrestrained laugh of John interrupted him ; and considering with himself that he had included the whole family, he finished his bumper. Whether it was pleasure at his own eloquence, or the unusual allowance, that affected the steward, he was evidently much satisfied with himself, and stepped back behind his master's chair, in great good humor.

Emily, as she thanked him, noticed a tear in the eye of the old man, as he concluded his oration, that would have excused a thousand breaches of fastidious ceremony. But Pendennyss rose from his seat, and took him kindly by the hand, and returned his own thanks for his good wishes.

"I owe you much good will, Mr. Johnson, for your two journeys in my behalf, and trust I never shall forget the manner in which you executed your last mission in particular. We are friends, I trust, for life."

"Thank you—thank your honor's lordship," said the steward, almost unable to utter; "I hope you may live long, to make dear little Miss Emmy as happy—as I know she ought to be."

"But really, my lord," cried John, observing that the steward's affection for his sister had affected her to tears, "it was a singular circumstance, the meeting of the four passengers of the stage so soon at your hotel."

Moseley explained his meaning to the rest of the company.

"Not so much so as you imagine," said

the earl in reply; "yourself and Johnson were in quest of me. Lord Henry Stapleton was under an agreement to meet me that evening at the hotel, as we were both going to his sister's wedding—I having arranged the thing with him by letter previously; and General M'Carthy was also in search of me, on business relating to his niece, the Donna Julia. He had been to Annerdale House, and, through my servants, heard I was at a hotel. It was the first interview between us, and not quite as amicable a one as has since been had in Wales. During my service in Spain, I saw the conde, but not the general. The letter he gave me was from the Spanish ambassador, claiming a right to require Mrs. Fitzgerald from our government, and deprecating my using an influence to counteract his exertions—"

"Which you refused," said Emily, eagerly.

"Not refused," answered the earl, smiling at her warmth, while he admired her friendly zeal, "for it was unnecessary; there is no such power vested in the ministry. But I explicitly told the general, I would oppose any violent measures to restore her to her country and a convent. From the courts, I apprehended nothing for my fair friend."

"Your honor—my lord," said Peter, who had been listening with great attention, "if I may presume just to ask two questions, without offense."

"Say on, my good friend," said Pendennyss, with an encouraging smile.

"Only," continued the steward—hemming, to give proper utterance to his thoughts— "I wish to know, whether you stayed in that same street after you left the hotel—for Mr. John Moseley and I had a slight difference in opinion about it."

The earl smiled, having caught the arch expression of John, and replied—

"I believe I owe you an apology, Moseley, for my cavalier treatment; but guilt makes us all cowards. I found you were ignorant of my incognito, and I was equally ashamed to continue it, or to become the relator of my own folly. Indeed," he continued, smiling on Emily as he spoke, "I thought your sister had pronounced the opinion of all reflecting people on my conduct. I went out of town, Johnson, at day-break. What is the other query?"

"Why, my lord," said Peter, a little disappointed at finding his first surmise untrue, "that outlandish tongue your honor used"—

"Was Spanish," cried the earl.

"And not Greek, Peter," said his master, gravely. "I thought, from the words you endeavored to repeat to me, that you had made a mistake. You need not be disconcerted, however, for I know several members of the Parliament of this realm who could not talk the Greek language, that is, fluently. So it can be no disgrace to a serving-man to be ignorant of it."

Somewhat consoled to find himself as well off as the representatives of his country, Peter resumed his station in silence, when the carriages began to announce the return from the opera. The earl took his leave, and the party retired to rest.

The thanksgivings of Emily that night, ere she laid her head on her pillow, were the purest offering of mortal innocence. The prospect before her was unsullied by a cloud, and she poured out her heart in the fullest confidence of pious love and heartfelt gratitude.

As early on the succeeding morning as good-breeding would allow, and much earlier than the hour sanctioned by fashion, the earl and Lady Marian stopped in the carriage of the latter at the door of Sir Edward Moseley. Their reception was the most flattering that could be offered to people of their stamp; sincere, cordial, and, with a trifling exception in Lady Moseley, unfettered with any useless ceremonies.

Emily felt herself drawn to her new acquaintance with a fondness which doubtless grew out of her situation with her brother: which soon found reasons enough in the soft, ladylike, and sincere manners of Lady Marian, to justify her attachment on her own account.

There was a very handsome suite of drawing-rooms in Sir Edward's house, and the communicating doors were carelessly open. Curiosity to view the furniture, or some such trifling reasons, induced the earl to find his way into the one adjoining that in which the family were seated. It was unquestionably a dread of being lost in a strange house, that induced him to whisper a request to the blushing Emily to be his companion; and lastly, it must have been nothing but a knowledge that a vacant room was easier viewed than one filled with company, that prevented any one from following them. John smiled archly at Grace, doubtless in approbation of the comfortable time his friend was likely to enjoy, in his musings on the taste of their mother. How the door became shut we have ever been at a loss to imagine.

The company without were too good-natured and well satisfied with each other to miss the absentees, until the figure of the earl appeared at the reopened door, beckoning, with a face of rapture, to Lady Moseley and Mrs. Wilson. Sir Edward next disappeared, then Jane, then Grace—then Marian: until John began to think a *tete-à-tete* with Mr. Benfield was to be his morning's amusement.

The lovely countenance of his wife, however, soon relieved his ennui, and John's curiosity was gratified by an order to prepare for his sister's wedding the following week.

Emily might have blushed more than common during this interview, but it is certain she did not smile less; and the earl, Lady Marian assured Sir Edward, was so very different a creature from what he had recently been, that she could hardly think it was the same somber gentleman with whom she had passed the last few months in Wales and Westmoreland.

A messenger was dispatched for Dr. Ives and their friends at B——, to be witnesses to the approaching nuptials; and Lady Moseley at length found an opportunity of indulging her taste for splendor on this joyful occasion.

Money was no consideration; and Mr. Benfield absolutely pined at the thought that the great wealth of the earl put it out of his power to contribute in any manner to the comfort of his Emmy. However, a fifteenth codicil was framed by the ingenuity of Peter and his master, and if it did not contain the name of George Denbigh, it did that of his expected second son, Roderick Benfield Denbigh, to the qualifying circumstance of twenty thousand pounds as a bribe for the name.

"And a very pretty child, I daresay, it will be," said the steward, as he placed the paper in its repository. "I don't know that I ever saw, your honor, a couple that I thought would make a handsomer pair like, except"—Peter's mind dwelt on his own youthful form, coupled with the smiling graces of Patty Steele.

"Yes! they are as handsome as they are good!" replied his master. "I remember now when our speaker took his third wife, the world said that they were as pretty a couple as there was at court. But my Emmy and the earl will be a much finer pair. Oh! Peter Johnson; they are young, and rich, and beloved; but, after all, it avails but little if they be not good."

"Good!" cried the steward in astonishment; "they are as good as angels."

The master's ideas of human excellence had suffered a heavy blow in the view of his viscountess, but he answered mildly.

"As good as mankind can well be."

CHAPTER XLVII.

THE warm weather had now commenced, and Sir Edward, unwilling to be shut up in London at a time the appearance of vegetation gave the country a new interest, and accustomed for many years of his life to devote an hour in his garden each morn, had taken a little ready-furnished cottage a short ride from his residence, with the intention of frequenting it until after the birthday. Thither then Pendennyss took his bride from the altar, and a few days were passed by the newly married pair in this little asylum.

Doctor Ives, with Francis, Clara, and their mother, had obeyed the summons with an alacrity in proportion to the joy they felt on receiving it, and the former had the happiness of officiating on the occasion. It would have been easy for the wealth of the earl to procure a license to enable them to marry in the drawing-room; the permission was obtained, but neither Emily nor himself felt a wish to utter their vows in any other spot than at the altar, and in the house of their Maker.

If there was a single heart that felt the least emotion of regret or uneasiness, it was Lady Moseley, who little relished the retirement of the cottage on so joyful an occasion; but Penndennys silenced her objections by good-humoredly replying—

"The fates have been so kind to me, in giving me castles and seats, you ought to allow me, my dear Lady Moseley, the only opportunity I shall probably ever have of enjoying love in a cottage."

A few days, however, removed the uneasiness of the good matron, who had the felicity within the week of seeing her daughter initiated mistress of Annerdale House.

The morning of their return to this noble mansion the earl presented himself in St. James's Square, with the intelligence of their arrival, and smiling as he bowed to Mrs. Wilson, he continued—

"And to escort you, dear madam, to your new abode."

Mrs. Wilson started with surprise, and with a heart beating quick with emotion, she required an explanation of his words.

"Surely, dearest Mrs. Wilson—more than aunt—my mother—you cannot mean, after having trained my Emily through infancy to maturity in the paths of duty, to desert her in the moment of her greatest trial. I am the pupil of your husband," he continued, taking her hands in his own with reverence and affection; "we are the children of your joint care, and one home, as there is but one heart, must in future contain us."

Mrs. Wilson had wished for, but hardly dared to expect this invitation. It was now urged from the right quarter, and in a manner that was as sincere as it was gratifying. Unable to conceal her tears, the good widow pressed the hand of Pendennyss to her lips as she murmured out her thanks. Sir Edward was prepared also to lose his sister; but unwilling to relinquish the pleasure of her society, he urged her making a common residence between the two families.

"Pendennyss has spoken the truth, my dear brother," cried she, recovering her voice; "Emily is the child of my care and my love—the two beings I love best in this world are now united—but," she added, pressing Lady Moseley to her bosom, "my heart is large enough for you all; you are of my blood, and my gratitude for your affection is boundless. There shall be but one large family of us; and although our duties may separate us for a time, we will, I trust, ever meet in tenderness and love, though with George and Emily I will take up my abode."

"I hope your house in Northampton-shire is not to be vacant always," said Lady Moseley to the earl, anxiously.

"I have no house there, my dear madam," he replied; "when I thought myself about to succeed in my suit before, I directed a lawyer at Bath, where Sir William Harris resided most of his time, to endeavor to purchase the deanery, whenever a good opportunity offered; in my discomfiture," he added, smiling, "I forgot to countermand the order, and he purchased it immediately on its being advertised. For a short time it was an encumbrance to me, but it is now applied to its original purpose. It is the sole property of the countess of Pendennyss, and I doubt not you will see it often and agreeably tenanted."

This intelligence gave great satisfaction to his friends, and the expected summer restored to even Jane a gleam of her former pleasure.

If there be bliss in this life, approaching in any degree to the happiness of the blessed, it is the fruition of long and ardent love, where youth, innocence, piety, and family concord, smile upon the union. And all these were united in the case of the newly married pair; but happiness in this world cannot, or does not, in any situation, exist without alloy.

The peace of mind and fortitude of Emily were fated to receive a blow, as unlooked for to herself as it was unexpected to the world. Bonaparte appeared in France, and Europe became in motion.

From the moment the earl heard the intelligence, his own course was decided. His regiment was the pride of the army, and that it would be ordered to join the duke he did not entertain a doubt.

Emily was, therefore, in some little measure prepared for the blow. It is at such moments as our own acts, or events affecting us, get to be without our control, that faith in the justice and benevolence of God is the most serviceable to the Christian. When others spend their time in useless regrets, he is piously resigned; it even so happens, that when others mourn he can rejoice.

The sound of the bugle, wildly winding its notes, broke on the stillness of the morning in the little village in which was situated the cottage tenanted by Sir Edward Moseley. Almost concealed by the shrubbery which surrounded its piazza, stood the forms of the countess of Pendennyss and her sister Lady Marian, watching eagerly the appearance of those whose approach was thus announced.

The carriage of the ladies, with its idle attendants, was in waiting at a short distance; and the pale face but composed resignation of its mistress, indicated a struggle between conflicting duties.

File after file of heavy horse passed them in military pomp, and the wistful gaze of the two females had scanned them in vain for the well-known, much-beloved countenance of the leader. At length a single horseman approached them, riding deliberately and musing; their forms met his eye, and in an instant Emily was pressed to the bosom of her husband.

"It is the doom of a soldier," said the earl, dashing a tear from his eye; "I had hoped that the peace of the world would not again be assailed for years, and that ambition and jealousy would yield a respite to our bloody profession; but cheer up, my love — hope for the best—your trust is not in the things of this life, and your happiness is without the power of man."

"Ah! Pendennyss — my husband," sobbed Emily, sinking on his bosom, "take with you my prayers — my love — everything that can console you — everything that may profit you. I will not tell you to be careful of your life; your duty teaches you that. As a soldier, expose it; as a husband, guard it; and return to me as you leave me, a lover, the dearest of men, and a Christian."

Unwilling to prolong the pain of parting, the earl gave his wife a last embrace, held Marian affectionately to his bosom, and mounting his horse, was out of sight in an instant.

Within a few days of the departure of Pendennyss, Chatterton was surprised with the entrance of his mother and Catherine. His reception of them was that of a respectful child, and his wife exerted herself to be kind to connections she could not love, in order to give pleasure to a husband she adored. Their tale was soon told. Lord and Lady Herriefield were separated; and the dowager, alive to the dangers of a young woman in Catherine's situation, and without a single principle on which to rest the assurance of her blameless conduct in future, had brought her to England in order to keep off disgrace, by residing with her child herself.

There was nothing in his wife to answer the expectations with which Lord Herriefield married. She had beauty, but with that he was already sated; her simplicity, which, by having her attention drawn elsewhere, had at first charmed him, was succeeded by the knowing conduct of a determined follower of the fashions, and a decided woman of the world.

It had never struck the viscount as impossible that an artless and innocent girl would fall in love with his faded and bilious face, but the moment Catherine betrayed the arts of a manager, he saw at once the artifice that had been practiced; of course he ceased to love her.

Men are flattered for a season with notice that has been unsought, but it never fails to injure the woman who practices it, in the opinion of the other sex, in time. Without a single feeling in common, without a regard to anything but self, in either husband or wife, it could not but happen that a separation must follow, or their days be spent in wrangling and misery. Catherine willingly left her husband; her husband more willingly got rid of her.

During all these movements the dowager had a difficult game to play. It was unbecoming her to encourage the strife, and it was against her wishes to suppress it; she therefore moralized with the peer and frowned upon her daughter.

The viscount listened to her truisms with the attention of a boy who is told by a drunken father how wicked it is to love liquor, and heeded them about as much; while Kate, mistress at all events of two thousand a year, minded her mother's frowns as little as she regarded her smiles; both were indifferent to her.

A few days after the ladies left Lisbon the viscount proceeded to Italy in company with the repudiated wife of a British naval officer; and if Kate was not guilty of an offense of equal magnitude, it was more owing to her mother's present vigilance than to her previous care.

The presence of Mrs. Wilson was a great source of consolation to Emily in the absence of her husband; and as their longer abode in town was useless, the countess declining to be presented without the earl, the whole family decided upon a return into Northamptonshire.

The deanery had been furnished by order of Pendennyss immediately on his marriage; and its mistress hastened to take possession of her new dwelling. The amusement and occupation of this movement, the planning of little improvements, her various duties under her increased responsibilities, kept Emily from dwelling unduly upon the danger of her husband. She sought out among the first objects of her bounty the venerable peasant whose loss had been formerly supplied by Pendennyss on his first visit to B——, after the death of his father. There might not have been the usual discrimination and temporal usefulness in this instance which generally accompanied her benevolent acts; but it was associated with the image of her husband, and it could excite no surprise in Mrs. Wilson, although it did in Marian, to see her sister driving two or three times a week to relieve the necessities of a man who appeared actually to be in want of nothing.

Sir Edward was again among those he loved, and his hospitable board was once more surrounded with the faces of his friends and neighbors. The good-natured Mr. Haughton was always a welcome guest at the hall, and met, soon after their return, the collected family of the baronet, at a dinner given by the latter to his children and one or two of his most intimate neighbors.

"My Lady Pendennyss," cried Mr. Haughton, in the course of the afternoon, "I have news from the earl, which I know it will do your heart good to hear."

Emily smiled at the prospect of hearing in any manner of her husband, although she internally questioned the probability of Mr. Haughton's knowing anything of his movements, of which her daily letters did not apprise her.

"Will you favor me with the particulars of your intelligence, sir?" said the countess.

"He has arrived safe with his regiment near Brussels; I heard it from a neighbor's son who saw him enter the house occupied by Wellington, while he was standing in the crowd without, waiting to get a peep at the duke."

"Oh!" said Mrs. Wilson with a laugh, "Emily knew that ten days ago. Could your friend tell us anything of Bonaparte? We are much interested in his movements just now."

Mr. Haughton, a good deal mortified to find his news stale, mused a moment, as if in doubt to proceed or not; but liking of all things to act the part of a newspaper, he continued—

"Nothing more than you see in the prints. But I suppose your ladyship has heard about Captain Jarvis, too?"

"Why, no," said Emily, laughing; "the movements of Captain Jarvis are not quite as interesting to me as those of Lord Pendennyss—has the duke made him an aide-de-camp?"

"Oh! no," cried the other, exulting at his having something new; "as soon as he heard of the return of Boney, he threw up his commission and got married."

"Married!" cried John; "not to Miss Harris, surely."

"No; to a silly girl he met in Cornwall, who was fool enough to be caught with his gold lace. He married one day, and the next told his disconsolate wife and panic-stricken mother that the honor of the Jarvises must sleep until the supporters of the name became sufficiently numerous to risk them in the field of battle."

"And how did Mrs. Jarvis and Sir Timo's lady relish the news?" inquired John, expecting something ridiculous.

"Not at all," rejoined Mr. Haughton; "the former sobbed, and said she had only married him for his bravery and red coat, and the *lady* exclaimed against the destruction of his budding honors."

"How did it terminate?" asked Mrs. Wilson.

"Why, it seems while they were quarreling about it, the war-office cut the matter short by accepting his resignation. I suppose the commander-in-chief had learned his character; but the matter was warmly contested—they even drove the captain to a declaration of his principles."

"And what kind of ones might they have been, Haughton?" said Sir Edward, dryly.

"Republican."

"Republican!" exclaimed two or three, in surprise.

"Yes, liberty and equality, he contended, were his idols, and he could not find it in his heart to fight against Bonaparte."

"A somewhat singular conclusion," said Mr. Benfield, musing. "I remember when I sat in the House, there was a party who were fond of the cry of this said liberty; but when they got the power they did not seem to me to suffer people

to go more at large than they went before; but I suppose they were diffident of telling the world their minds after they were put in such responsible stations, for fear of the effect of example."

"Most people like liberty as servants but not as masters, uncle," cried John, with a sneer.

"Captain Jarvis, it seems, liked it as a preservative against danger," continued Mr. Haughton. "To avoid ridicule in his new neighborhood, he has consented to his father's wishes, and turned merchant in the city again."

"Where I sincerely hope he will remain," cried John, who, since the accident of the arbor, could not tolerate the unfortunate youth.

"Amen!" said Emily, in an undertone, heard only by her brother.

"But Sir Timo—what has become of Sir Timo—the good, honest merchant?" asked John.

"He has dropt the title, insists on being called plain Mr. Jarvis, and lives entirely in Cornwall. His hopeful son-in-law has gone with his regiment to Flanders; and Lady Egerton, being unable to live without her father's assistance, is obliged to hide her consequence in the west also."

The subject became now disagreeable to Lady Moseley, and it was changed. Such conversations made Jane more reserved and dissatisfied than ever. She had no one respectable excuse to offer for her partiality to her former lover, and when her conscience told her the mortifying fact, was apt to think that others remembered it too.

The letters from the continent now teemed with preparations for the approaching contest; and the apprehensions of our heroine and her friends increased, in proportion to the nearness of the struggle, on which hung not only the fates of thousands of individuals, but of adverse princes and mighty empires. In this confusion of interests, and of jarring of passions, there were offered prayers almost hourly for the safety of Pendennyss, which were as pure and ardent as the love which prompted them.

CHAPTER XLVIII.

NAPOLEON had commenced those daring and rapid movements, which for a time threw the peace of the world into the scale of fortune, and which nothing but the interposition of a ruling Providence could avert from their threatened success. As the ——th dragoons wheeled into a field already deluged with English blood, on the heights of Quatre Bras, the eye of its gallant colonel saw a friendly battalion falling beneath the sabers of the enemy's cuirassiers. The word was passed, the column opens, the sounds of the quivering bugle were heard for a moment above the roar of the cannon and the shouts of the combatants; the charge, sweeping like a whirlwind, fell heavily on those treacherous Frenchmen, who to-day had sworn fidelity to Louis, and to-morrow intended lifting their hands in allegiance to his rival.

"Spare our life in mercy," cried an officer, already dreadfully wounded, who stood shrinking from the impending blow of an enraged Frenchman. An English dragoon dashed at the cuirassier, and with one blow severed his arm from his body.

"Thank God," sighed the wounded officer, sinking beneath the horse's feet.

His rescuer threw himself from the saddle, and raising the fallen man inquired into his wounds. It was Pendennyss, and it was Egerton. The wounded man groaned aloud, as he saw the face of him who had averted the fatal blow; but it was not the hour for explanations or confessions, other than those with which the dying soldiers endeavored to make their tardy peace with their God.

Sir Henry was given in charge to two slightly wounded British soldiers, and the earl remounted: the scattered troops were rallied at the sound of the trumpet, and again and again, led by their dauntless colonel, were seen in the thickest of the fray, with sabers drenched in blood, and voices hoarse with the shouts of victory.

The period between the battles of Quatre Bras and Waterloo was a trying one to the discipline and courage of the British army. The discomfited Prussians on their flank had been routed and compelled to retire, and in their front was an enemy, brave, skillful, and victorious, led by the greatest captain of the age. The prudent commander of the English forces fell back with dignity and reluctance to the field of Waterloo; here the mighty struggle was to terminate, and the eye of every experienced soldier looked on those eminences as on the future graves for thousands.

During this solemn interval of comparative inactivity the mind of Pendennyss dwelt on the affection, the innocence, the beauty and worth of his Emily, until the curdling blood, as he thought on her lot should his life be the purchase of the coming victory, warned him to quit the gloomy subject, for the consolations of

that religion which only could yield him the solace his wounded feelings required. In his former campaigns the earl had been sensible of the mighty changes of death, and had ever kept in view the preparations necessary to meet it with hope and joy; but the world clung around him now, in the best affections of his nature, and it was only as he could picture the happy reunion with his Emily in a future life, that he could look on a separation in this without despair.

The vicinity of the enemy admitted of no relaxation in the strictest watchfulness in the British lines: and the comfortless night of the seventeenth was passed by the earl, and his lieutenant-colonel, George Denbigh, on the same cloak, and under the open canopy of heaven.

As the opening cannon of the enemy gave the signal for the commencing conflict, Pendennyss mounted his charger with a last thought on his distant wife With a mighty struggle he tore her as it were from his bosom, and gave the remainder of the day to duty.

Who has not heard of the events of that fearful hour, on which the fate of Europe hung as it were suspended in the scale? On one side supported by the efforts of desperate resolution, guided by the most consummate art; and on the other defended by a discipline by a discipline and enduring courage almost without a parallel.

The indefatigable Blucher arrived, and the star of Napoleon sank.

Pendennyss threw himself from his horse, on the night of the eighteenth of June, as he gave way by orders, in the pursuit, to the fresher battalions of the Prussians, with the languor that follows unusual excitement, and mental thanksgivings that this bloody work was at length ended. The image of his Emily again broke over the sterner feelings of the battle, like the first glimmerings of light which succeed the awful darkness of the eclipse of the sun: and he again breathed freely, in the consciousness of the happiness which would await his speedy return.

"I am sent for the colonel of the ——th dragoons," said a courier in broken English to a soldier, near where the earl lay on the ground, waiting the preparations of his attendants; "have I found the right regiment, my friend?

"To be sure you have," answered the man, without looking up from his toil on his favorite animal, "you might have tracked us by the dead Frenchman, I should think. So you want my lord, my lad, do you? do we move again to-night?"

suspending his labor for a moment in expectation of a reply.

"Not to my knowledge," rejoined the courier; "my message is to your colonel, from a dying man. Will you point out his station?"

The soldier complied, the message was soon delivered, and Pendennyss prepared to obey its summons immediately. Preceded by the messenger as a guide, and followed by Harmer, the earl retraced his steps over that ground on which he had but a few hours before been engaged in the deadly strife of man to man, hand to hand.

How different is the contemplation of a field of battle during and after the conflict! The excitement, suspended success, shouts, uproar, and confusion of the former, prevent any contemplation of the nicer parts of this confused mass of movements, charges, and retreats; or if a brilliant advance is made, a masterly retreat effected, the imagination is chained by the splendor and glory of the act, without resting for a moment on the sacrifice of individual happiness with which it is purchased. A battle-ground from which the whirlwind of the combat has passed, presents a different sight; it offers the very consummation of human misery.

There may occasionally be an individual, who from station, distempered mind, or the encouragement of chimerical ideas of glory, quits the theater of life with at least the appearance of pleasure in his triumphs. If such there be in reality, if this rapture of departing glory be anything more than the deception of a distempered excitement, the subject of its exhibition is to be greatly pitied. To the Christian, dying in peace with both God and man, can it alone be ceded in the eye of reason, to pour out his existence with a smile on his quivering lip.

And the warrior, who falls in the very arms of victory, after passing a life devoted to the world; even if he sees kingdoms hang suspended on his success, may smile indeed, may utter sentiments full of loyalty and zeal, may be the admiration of the world, and what is his reward! a deathless name, and an existence of misery which knows no termination.

Christianity alone can make us good soldiers in any cause, for he who knows how to live, is always the least afraid to die.

Pendennyss and his companions pushed their way over the ground occupied before the battle by the enemy; descended into and through that little valley in which yet lay, in undistinguished confusion, masses of the dead and dying of either side; and again over the ridge, on which could be marked the situation of those gallant squares which had so long resisted the efforts of the horse and artillery, by the groups of bodies, fallen where they had bravely stood, until even the callous Harmer sickened with the sight of a waste of life that he had but a few hours before exultingly contributed to increase.

Appeals to their feelings as they rode through the field had been frequent, and their progress was much retarded by attempts to contribute to the ease of a wounded or a dying man; but as the courier constantly urged speed, as the only means of securing the object of their ride, these halts were reluctantly abandoned.

It was ten o'clock before they reached the farm-house, where, in the midst of hundreds of his countrymen, lay the former lover of Jane.

As the subject of his confession must be anticipated by the reader, we will give a short relation of his life, and of those acts which more materially affect our history.

Henry Egerton had been turned early on the world, like hundreds of his countrymen, without any principle to counteract the arts of infidelity, or resist the temptations of life. His father held a situation under government, and was devoted to his rise in the diplomatic line. His mother was a woman of fashion, who lived for effect and idle competition with her sisters in weakness and folly. All he learned in his father's house was selfishness, from the example of one, and a love of high life and its extravagance from the other.

He entered the army young, and from choice. The splendor and reputation of the service caught his fancy; and, by pride and constitution, he was indifferent to personal danger. Yet he loved London and its amusements better than glory; and the money of his uncle, Sir Edgar, whose heir he was reputed to be, raised him to the rank of lieutenant-colonel, without his spending an hour in the field.

Egerton had some abilities, and a good deal of ardor of temperament, by nature. The former, from indulgence and example, degenerated into acquiring the art to please in mixed society; and the latter, from want of employment, expended itself at the card table.

The association between the vices is intimate. There really appears to be a kind of modesty in sin that makes it ashamed of good company. If we are unable to reconcile a favorite propensity to our principles, we are apt to abandon the unpleasant restraint on our actions, rather than admit the incongruous mixture. Freed entirely from the fetters of our morals, what is there that our vices will not prompt us to commit? Egerton, like thousands of others, went on from step to step, until he found himself in the world, free to follow all his inclinations, so he violated none of the decencies of life.

When in Spain, in his only campaign, he was accidentally, as has been mentioned, thrown in the way of the Donna Julia, and brought her off the ground under the influence of natural sympathy and national feeling; a kind of merit that makes vice only more dangerous, by making it sometimes amiable. He had not seen his dependent long before her beauty, situation, and his passions decided him to effect her ruin.

This was an occupation that his figure, manners, and propensities had made him an adept in, and nothing was further from his thoughts than the commission of any other than the crime that, according to his code, a gentleman might be guilty of with impunity.

It is, however, the misfortune of sin, that from being our slave it becomes a tyrant; and Egerton attempted what in other countries, and where the laws ruled, might have cost him his life.

The conjecture of Pendennyss was true. He saw the face of the officer who interposed between him and his villainous attempt, but was hid himself from view. He aimed not at his life, but at his own escape. Happily his first shot succeeded, for the earl would have been sacrificed to preserve the character of a man of honor; though no one was more regardless of the estimation he was held in by the virtuous than Colonel Egerton.

In pursuance of his plans on Mrs. Fitzgerald, the colonel had sedulously avoided admitting any of his companions into the secret of his having a female in his care.

When he left the army to return home, he remained until a movement of the troops to a distant part of the country enabled him to effect his own purposes, without incurring their ridicule; and when he found himself obliged to abandon his vehicle for a refuge in the woods, the fear of detection made him alter his course; and under the pretense of wishing to be in a battle about to be fought, he secretly rejoined the army, and the gallantry of Colonel Egerton was mentioned in the next dispatches.

Sir Herbert Nicholson commanded the advanced guard, at which the earl arrived with the Donna Julia; and like every other brave man (unless guilty himself), was indignant at the villainy of the fugitive. The confusion and enormities daily practiced in the theater of the war prevented any close inquiries into the subject, and circumstances had so enveloped Egerton in mystery, that nothing but an interview with the lady herself was likely to expose him.

With Sir Herbert Nicholson he had been in habits of intimacy, and on that gentleman's alluding in a conversation in the barracks at F—— to the lady brought into his quarters before Lisbon, he accidentally omitted mentioning the name of her rescuer. Egerton had never before heard the transaction spoken of, and as he had of course never mentioned the subject himself, was ignorant who had interfered between him and his views; also of the fate of Donna Julia; indeed, he thought it probable that it had not much improved by a change of guardians.

In coming into Northamptonshire he had several views; he wanted a temporary retreat from his creditors. Jarvis had an infant fondness for play, without an adequate skill, and the money of the young ladies, in his necessities, was becoming of importance; but the daughters of Sir Edward Moseley were of a description more suited to his taste, and their portions were as ample as the others. He had become in some degree attached to Jane; and as her imprudent parents, satisfied with his possessing the exterior and requisite recommendations of a gentleman, admitted his visits freely, he determined to make her his wife.

When he met Denbigh the first time, he saw that chance had thrown him in the way of a man who might hold his character in his power. He had never seen him as Pendennyss, and, it will be remembered, was ignorant of the name of Julia's friend; he now learned for the first time that it was Denbigh. Uneasy at he knew not what, fearful of some exposure he knew not how, when Sir Herbert alluded to the occurrence, with a view to rebut the charge, if Denbigh should choose to make one, and with the nearsightedness of guilt, he pretended to know the occurrence, and under the promise of secrecy, mentioned that the name of the officer was Denbigh. He had noticed Denbigh avoiding Sir Herbert at the ball; and judging others from himself, thought it was a wish to avoid any allusions to the lady he had brought into the other's quarters that induced the measure; for he was in hopes that if Denbigh was not as guilty as himself, he was sufficiently so to wish to keep the transaction from the eyes of Emily. He was, however, prepared for an explosion or an alliance with him, when the sudden departure of Sir Herbert removed the danger of a collision. Believing at last that they were to be brothers-in-law, and mistaking the earl for his cousin, whose name he bore, Egerton became reconciled to the association; while Pendennyss, having in his absence heard, on inquiring, some of the vices of the colonel, was debating with himself whether he should expose them to Sir Edward or not.

It was in their occasional interchange of civilities that Pendennyss placed his pocket-book upon a table, while he exhibited the plants to the colonel; the figure of Emily passing the window drew him from the room, and Egerton, having ended his examination, observing the book, put it in his own pocket, to return it to its owner when they next met.

The situation, name, and history of Mrs. Fitzgerald were never mentioned by the Moseleys in public; but Jane, in the confidence of her affections, had told her lover who the inmate of the cottage was. The idea of her being kept there by Denbigh immediately occurred to him, and although he was surprised at the audacity of the thing, he was determined to profit by the occasion.

To pay this visit, he stayed away from the excursion on the water, as Pendennyss had done to avoid his friend, Lord Henry Stapleton. An excuse of business, which served for his apology, kept the colonel from seeing Denbigh to return the book, until after his visit to the cottage. His rhapsody of love, and offers to desert his intended wife, were nothing but the commonplace talk of his purposes; and his presumption in alluding to his situation with Miss Moseley, proceeded from his impressions as to Julia's real character. In the struggle for the bell, the pocket-book of Denbigh accidentally fell from his coat, and the retreat of the colonel was too precipitate to enable him to recover it. Mrs. Fitzgerald was too much alarmed to distinguish nicely, and Egerton proceeded to the ball-room with the indifference of a hardened offender. When the arrival of Miss Jarvis, to whom he had committed himself, prompted him to a speedy declaration, and the unlucky conversation of Mr. Holt brought about a probable detection of his gaming propensities, the colonel determined to get rid of his awkward situation and his debts by a coup-de-main. He accordingly eloped with Miss Jarvis.

What portion of the foregoing narrative made the dying confession of Egerton to the man he had so lately discovered to be the earl of Pendenyss, the reader can easily imagine.

CHAPTER XLIX.

THE harvest had been gathered, and the beautiful vales of Pendennyss were shooting forth a second crop of verdure. The husbandman was turning his prudent forethought to the promises of the coming year, while the castle itself exhibited to the gaze of the wondering peasant a sight of cheerfulness and animation which had not been seen in it since the days of the good duke. Its numerous windows were opened to the light of the sun—its halls teemed with the faces of its happy inmates. Servants in various liveries were seen gliding through its magnificent apartments and multiplied passages. Horses, grooms, and carriages, with varied costumes and different armorial bearings, crowded its spacious stables and offices. Everything spoke society, splendor, and activity without; everything denoted order, propriety, and happiness within.

In a long range of spacious apartments were grouped in the pursuit of their morning employments, or in arranging their duties and pleasures of the day, the guests and owners of the princely abode.

In one room was John Moseley, carefully examining the properties of some flints which were submitted to his examination by his attending servant; while Grace, sitting at his side, playfully snatches the stones from his hand, as she cries half reproachfully, half tenderly:

"You must not devote yourself to your gun so incessantly, Moseley; it is cruel to kill inoffensive birds for your amusement only."

"Ask Emily's cook, and Mr. Haughton's appetite," said John, coolly extending his hand toward her for the flint, " whether no one is gratified but myself. I tell you, Grace, I seldom fire in vain."

"That only makes the matter worse; the slaughter you commit is dreadful."

"Oh!" cried John, with a laugh, "the ci-devant Captain Jarvis is a sportsman to your mind. He would shoot a month without moving a feather; he was a great friend to," throwing an arch look to his solitary sister, who sat on a sofa at a distance, perusing a book, "Jane's feathered songsters."

"But now, Moseley," said Grace, yielding the flints, but gently retaining the hand that took them, "Pendennyss and Chatterton intend driving their wives, like good husbands, to see the beautiful water-fall in the mountains; and what am I to do this long, tedious morning?"

John stole an inquiring glance, to see if his wife was very anxious to join the party, cast one look of regret on a beautiful agate that he had selected, and inquired—

"Do you wish to go very much, Mrs. Moseley?"

"Indeed—indeed I do," said the other, eagerly, "if—"

"If what?"

"You will drive me!" continued she, with a cheek slightly tinged with color.

"Well, then," answered John, with deliberation, and regarding his wife with affection, "I will go on one condition."

"Name it," cried Grace, with still increasing color.

"That you will not expose your health again in going to the church on a Sunday, if it rains."

"The carriage is so close, Moseley," answered Grace, with a paler cheek than before, and eyes fixed on the carpet, "it is impossible I can take cold: you see the earl and countess, and aunt Wilson never miss public worship, when possibly within their power."

"The earl goes with his wife; but what becomes of poor me at such times?" said John, taking her hand and pressing it kindly. "I like to hear a good sermon, but not in bad weather. You must consent to oblige me, who only live in your presence."

Grace smiled faintly, as John, pursuing the point, said:

"What do you say to my condition?"

"Well, then, if you wish," replied Grace, without the look of gayety her hopes had first inspired, "I will not go if it rain."

John ordered his phaeton, and his wife went to her room to prepare for the trip, and to regret her own resolution.

In the recess of a window, in which bloomed a profusion of exotics, stood the figure of Lady Marian Denbigh, playing with a half-blown rose of the richest colors; and before her, leaning against the angle of the wall, stood her kinsman, the Duke of Derwent.

"You heard the plan at the breakfast-table," said his grace, "to visit the little falls in the hill. But I suppose you have seen them too often to undergo the fatigue?"

"Oh no! I love that ride dearly, and should wish to accompany the countess in her first visit to it. I had half a mind to ask George to take me in his phaeton."

"My curricle would be honored with the presence of Lady Marian Denbigh," cried the duke with animation, "if she would accept me for her knight on the occasion."

Marian bowed an assent, in evident satisfaction, as the duke proceeded:

"But if you take me as your knight I should wear your ladyship's colors;" and he held out his hand toward the budding rose.

Lady Marian hesitated a moment—looked out at the prospect—up at the wall—turned, and wondered where her brother was; and still finding the hand of the duke extended, while his eye rested on her in admiration, she gave him the boon with a cheek that vied with the richest tints of the flower. They separated to prepare, and it was on their return from the falls that the duke seemed uncommonly gay and amusing, and the lady silent with her tongue, though her eyes danced in every direction but toward her cousin.

"Really, my dear Lady Moseley," said the dowager, as, seated by the side of her companion, her eyes roved over the magnificence within, and widely extended domains without, "Emily is well established, indeed—better even than my Grace."

"Grace has an affectionate husband," replied the other, gravely, "and one that I hope will make her happy."

"Oh! no doubt happy!" said Lady Chatterton, hastily; "but they say Emily has a jointure of twelve thousand a year—by-the-by," she added, in a low tone, though no one was near enough to hear what she said, "could not the earl have settled Lumley Castle on her instead of the deanery?"

"Upon my word, I never think of such gloomy subjects as provisions for widowhood," cried Lady Moseley. "You have been in Annerdale House—is it not a princely mansion?"

"Princely indeed," rejoined the dowager, sighing; "don't the earl intend increasing the rents of this estate as the leases fall in? I am told they are very low now!"

"I believe not," said the other. "He has enough, and is willing others should prosper. But there is Clara, with her little boy—is he not a lovely child?" cried the grandmother, rising to take the infant in her arms.

"Oh! excessively beautiful!" said the dowager, looking the other way; and, observing Catherine making a movement toward Lord Henry Stapleton, she called to her: "Lady Herriefield, come this way, my dear—I wish to speak to you."

Kate obeyed, with a sullen pout of her pretty lip, and entered into some idle discussion about a cap, though her eyes wandered round the rooms in listless vacancy.

The dowager had the curse of bad impressions in youth to contend with, and labored infinitely harder now to make her daughter act right, than formerly she had ever done to make her act wrong.

"Here! uncle Benfield," cried Emily, with a face glowing with health and animation, as she approached his seat with a glass in her hands. "Here is the negus you wished: I have made it myself, and you will praise it of course."

"Oh! my dear lady Pendennyss," said the old gentleman, rising politely from his seat to receive the beverage; "you are putting yourself to a great deal of trouble for an old bachelor like me; too much, indeed, too much."

"Old bachelors are sometimes more esteemed than young ones," cried the earl, gayly, joining them in time to hear this speech. "Here is my friend, Mr. Peter Johnson; who knows when we may dance at his wedding?"

"My lord, and my lady, and my honored master," said Peter, gravely, in reply, bowing respectfully where he stood waiting to take his master's glass, "I am past the age to think of taking a wife: I am seventy-three coming next 'lammas, counting by the old style."

"What do you intend to do with your three hundred a year," said Emily, with a smile, "unless you bestow it on some good woman, for making the evening of your life comfortable?"

"My lady—hem—my lady," said the steward, blushing; "I had a little thought, with your kind ladyship's consent, as I have no relations, chick or child in the world, what to do with it."

"I should be happy to hear your plan," said the countess, observing that the steward was anxious to communicate something.

"Why, my lady, if my lord and my honored master's agreeable, I did think of making another codicil to master's will in order to dispose of it."

"Your master's will," said the earl, laughing; "why not to your own, good Peter?"

"My honored lord," said the steward, with great humility, "it don't become a poor serving-man like me to make a will."

"But how will you prove it?" said the earl, kindly, willing to convince him of his error; "you must be both dead to prove it."

"Our wills," said Peter, gulping his words, "will be proved on the same day."

His master looked round at him with great affection, and both the earl and Emily were too much struck to say anything. Peter had, however, the subject too much at heart to abandon it just as he had broken the ice. He anxiously wished for the countess's consent to the scheme, for he would not affront her, even after he was dead.

"My lady—Miss Emmy," said Johnson, eagerly, "my plan is, if my honored master's agreeable—to make a codicil, and give my mite to a little—Lady Emily Denbigh."

"Oh! Peter, you and Uncle Benfield are both too good," cried Emily, laughing and blushing, as she hastened to Clara and her mother.

"Thank you, thank you," cried the delighted earl, following his wife with his eyes, and shaking the steward cordially by the hand; "and if no better expedient be adopted by us, you have full permission to do as you please with your money."

"Peter," said his master to him in a low tone, "you should never speak of such things prematurely; now I remember when the Earl of Pendennyss, my nephew, was first presented to me, I was struck with the delicacy and propriety of his demeanor, and the Lady Pendennyss, my niece, too; you never see anything forward, or—Ah! Emmy dear," said the old man, tenderly interrupting himself, "you are too good, to remember your old uncle," taking one of the fine peaches she handed him from a plate.

"My lord," said Mr. Haughton to the earl, "Mrs. Ives and myself have had a contest about the comforts of matrimony; she insists she may be quite as happy at Bolton Parsonage as in this noble castle, and with this rich prospect in view."

"I hope," said Francis, "you are not teaching my wife to be discontented with her humble lot—if so, both your visit and hers will be an unhappy one."

"It would be no easy task, if our good friend intended any such thing by his jests," said Clara, smiling. "I know my true interests, I trust, too well to wish to change my fortune."

"You are right," said Pendennyss; "it is wonderful how little our happiness depends on a temporal condition. When here, or at Lumley Castle, surrounded by my tenantry there are, I confess, moments of weakness, in which the loss of my wealth and rank would be missed greatly; but when on service, subjected to great privations, and surrounded by men superior to me in military rank, who say unto me—go, and I go—come, and I come—I find my enjoyments intrinsically the same."

"That," said Francis, "may be owing to your lordship's tempered feelings, which have taught you to look beyond this world for pleasures and consolation."

"It has, doubtless, an effect," said the earl, "but there is no truth of which I am more fully persuaded, than that our happiness here does not depend upon our lot in life, so we are not suffering for necessaries —even changes bring less real misery than they are supposed to do."

"Doubtless," cried Mr. Haughton, "under the circumstances, I would not wish to change even with your lordship —unless, indeed," he continued, with a smile and bow to the countess, "it were the temptation of your lovely wife."

"You are quite polite," said Emily, laughing, "but I have no desire to deprive Mrs. Haughton of a companion she has made out so well with these twenty years past."

"*Thirty*, my lady, if you please."

"And thirty more, I hope," continued Emily, as a servant announced the several carriages at the door. The younger part of the company now hastened to their different engagements, and Chatterton handed Harriet; John, Grace; and Pendennyss, Emily, into their respective carriages; the duke and Lady Marian following, but at some little distance from the rest of the party.

As the earl drove from the door, the countess looked up to a window at which were standing her aunt and Doctor Ives. She kissed her hand to them, with a face in which glowed the mingled expression of innocence, love, and joy.

Before leaving the park, the party passed Sir Edward, with his wife leaning on one arm and Jane on the other, pursuing their daily walk. The baronet followed the carriages with his eyes, and exchanged looks of the fondest love with his children, as they drove slowly and respectfully by him; and if the glance which followed on Jane did not speak equal pleasure, it surely noted its proper proportion of paternal love.

"You have much reason to congratulate yourself on the happy termination of your labors," said the doctor, with a smile, to the widow; "Emily is placed, so far as human foresight can judge, in the happiest of all stations a female can be in; she is the pious wife of a pious husband, beloved, and deserving of it."

"Yes," said Mrs. Wilson, drawing back from following the phaeton with her eyes, "they are as happy as this world will admit, and, what is better, they are well prepared to meet any reverse of fortune, which may occur, as well as to discharge the duties on which they have entered. I do not think," continued she,

musing, "that Pendennyss can ever doubt the affections of such a woman as Emily."

"I should think not," said the doctor; "but what can excite such a thought in your breast, and one so much to the prejudice of George?"

"The only unpleasant thing I ever observed in him," said Mrs. Wilson, gravely, "is the suspicion which induced him to adopt the disguise in which he entered our family."

"He did not adopt it, Madam; chance and circumstances drew it around him accidentally; and when you consider the peculiar state of his mind from the discovery of his mother's misconduct—his own great wealth and rank—it is not so surprising that he should yield to a deception rather harmless than injurious."

"Dr. Ives," said Mrs. Wilson, "is not wont to defend deceit."

"Nor do I now, madam," replied the doctor, with a smile. "I acknowledge the offense of George, myself, wife, and son. I remonstrated at the time upon principle; I said the end would not justify the means; that a departure from ordinary rules of propriety was at all times dangerous, and seldom practiced with impunity."

"And you failed to convince your hearers," cried Mrs. Wilson, gayly: "a novelty in your case, my good rector."

"I thank you for the compliment," said the doctor. "I did convince them as to the truth of the principle, but the earl contended that his case might make an innocent exception. He had the vanity to think, I believe, that by concealing his real name he injured himself more than any one else, and got rid of the charge in some such way. He is, however, thoroughly convinced of the truth of the position by practice; his sufferings growing out of the mistake of his real character, and which could not have happened had he appeared in proper person, having been greater than he is ready to acknowledge."

"If they study the fate of the Donna Julia, and his own weakness," said the widow, "they will have a salutary moral always at hand, to teach them the importance of two cardinal virtues at least— obedience and truth."

"Julia has suffered much," replied the doctor; "and although she has returned to her father, the consequences of her imprudence are likely to continue. When once the bonds of mutual confidence and respect are broken, they may be partially restored, it is true, but never with a warmth and reliance such as existed previously. To return, however, to yourself, do you not feel a sensation of delight at the prosperous end of your exertions in behalf of Emily?"

"It is certainly pleasant to think we have discharged our duties, and the task is much easier than we are apt to suppose," said Mrs. Wilson; "it is only to commence the foundation, so that it will be able to support the superstructure. I have endeavored to make Emily a Christian. I have endeavored to form such a taste and principles in her, that she would not be apt to admire an improper suitor, and I have labored to prepare her to discharge her continued duties through life, in such a manner and with such a faith, as under the providence of God will result in happiness far exceeding anything she now enjoys. In all these, by the blessing of Heaven, I have succeeded, and had occasion offered, I would have assisted her inexperience through the more delicate decisions of her sex, though in no instance would I attempt to control them."

"You are right, my dear madam," said the doctor, taking her kindly by the hand, "and had I a daughter, I would follow a similar course. Give her delicacy, religion, and a proper taste, aided by the unseen influence of a prudent parent's care, and the chances of a woman for happiness would be much greater than they are; and I am entirely of your opinion, 'That prevention is at all times better than cure.'"

END OF VOLUME NINE.